DON QUIXOTE

DON QUIXOTE

With an Introduction and
Contemporary Criticism

The John Ormsby Translation, Revised

Edited by TIMOTHY McCALLISTER

Ignatius Critical Editions Editor

JOSEPH PEARCE

IGNATIUS PRESS SAN FRANCISCO

Cover image: *Don Quixote and Sancho Panza* by Honoré Daumier.
Collection of the Staatliche Kunsthalle, Karlsruhe, Germany.
Public domain image.

Cover design by John Herreid

ISBN 978-1-62164-763-8 (PB)
ISBN 978-1-64229-336-4 (eBook)
Library of Congress Control Number 2025949178
Printed in India ♾

Tradition is the extension of Democracy through time; it is the proxy of the dead and the enfranchisement of the unborn.

Tradition may be defined as the extension of the franchise. Tradition means giving votes to the most obscure of all classes, our ancestors. It is the democracy of the dead. Tradition refuses to submit to the small and arrogant oligarchy of those who merely happen to be walking about. All democrats object to men being disqualified by the accident of birth; tradition objects to their being disqualified by the accident of death. Democracy tells us not to neglect a good man's opinion, even if he is our groom; tradition asks us not to neglect a good man's opinion, even if he is our father. I, at any rate, cannot separate the two ideas of democracy and tradition.

—G.K. Chesterton

Ignatius Critical Editions—Tradition-Oriented Criticism for a new generation

CONTENTS

INTRODUCTION

Timothy McCallister

The Imagination on New Terms

When a story begins with the words "once upon a time", the last thing on our minds is to wonder *when* the tale we are about to read took place. The phrase calls up a set of assumptions about a certain kind of story. We open ourselves to the possibility that the world held up to us will bear little resemblance to our daily lives—or, for that matter, to any time or place in history. Enchanted beings may roam about; problems may be caused and resolved by powers not available in the natural course of things. We allow for, and even expect, extraordinary coincidences, a polarized moral grid, and a tidy ending.

There is another well-known opening to a story that goes this way: "In a village of La Mancha, the name of which I have no desire to call to mind, there lived not long ago one of those gentlemen that keep a lance in the lance rack, an old buckler, a lean hack, and a greyhound for hunting."[1] Unlike the beginning of a fairy tale, this story points to a historical time and a place we could find on a map. Particulars dominate the lines that follow—fabrics, food, hobbies, household routines—which would have rendered this world familiar to the novel's first audience. Perhaps a reader in 1605, like the protagonist, owned a pair of velvet breeches. He might chuckle to learn that this gentleman ate bacon and eggs on Saturdays, for that was his accustomed meal as well. If the reader was not a member of the nobility, he undoubtedly knew someone who was. At some point early on, the reader would figure out that the history of this small-town hidalgo was imagined. Even though the early modern world lacked the signposts that now direct our expectations—from sections in a bookstore to genre labels on streaming programs—people have always been people, with a divinely endowed, albeit imperfect, ability to evaluate truth claims.

Today we accept that there is a kind of story that, though it did not actually take place, remains meaningful when judged against the real world. In its own way, we can say that the story *is* real. There is an integrity in its design and execution that projects a lifelike presence. Even if the story is set in a distant galaxy and populated with fantastic creatures, if the storytellers do their job well, when they beckon us to enter their imagination, we accept the invitation.

[1] Miguel de Cervantes, *Don Quixote*, ed. Timothy McCallister, Ignatius Critical Editions, ed. Joseph Pearce (San Francisco: Ignatius Press, 2026), p. 25. All subsequent quotations are from this edition and will be cited in the text.

Don Quixote deserves pride of place in the Western canon if for no other reason than that it establishes the terms for the kind of storytelling we call fiction. At its heart, fiction is an act of illusion—a work of the imagination that does not seem to be imagined. To create that illusion, it is necessary for the author and reader to come to an agreement. Each party has something to contribute. Readers promise to suspend their disbelief. As long as they are reading the story, they will pretend that it is relating something that really happened. In turn, the author promises to make the job of pretending as easy as possible. The most straightforward strategy the author can adopt is to create a world that looks like ours. This involves connecting causes and effects with natural processes and filling it with places and objects that match a recognized setting. The key ingredients are the characters. They need to be people with whom the reader can relate.

We can think of the preface to Part I of *Don Quixote* as a contract setting out the terms for the bargain of fiction. With tongue in cheek, Cervantes summons the "idle reader" (see p. 7) and asks each of us to indulge him with our calculated credulity. Unlike a traditional preface, where a disembodied voice discourses about the text to follow, this preface is a full-blown story—with plot, setting, and characters. Cervantes would have us believe that he is struggling to write a respectable preface for his new novel, that a friend comes to his house to advise him, and that after consulting with his friend, he decides to make a preface out of the account of its creation.

We are in no position to accept Cervantes' offer until we see the preface for what it is. What appears to be an innocent vignette about writer's block is really a fanciful piece of entertainment. If we fail to see through the ruse, we are fools; if we see through the ruse and shrug, we are cynics. But if we laugh at the joke, if we wink back at the author and plead for more, fiction has done its magic. The Cervantes critic E. C. Riley refers to irony as the "binding agent" of *Don Quixote*.[2] I would extend Riley's insight to any work of fiction. As a creative enterprise, fiction relies on the ever-present incongruity between what *is* and what *seems to be*. Even before we arrive at the celebrated opening lines of chapter 1, Cervantes has already delivered a fiction masterclass.

The successful reader will reenact page by page the same strategy learned in the preface—to inhabit the reality of what *seems to be* without ever losing touch with the underlying reality of what *is*. The novel will offer itself up as history. Cervantes will insist that he is sharing with us the fruits of his research in the annals of La Mancha, that we are reading the final draft of a text mediated by other texts, translated, assimilated, and polished. The preface has trained us to read with irony, and if we carry that lesson into the main text, we will have no difficulty playing Cervantes' game of pretend.

Unlike his protagonist, Cervantes is willing to stare reality in the face, which strengthens his story's hold on our imaginations. True-to-life detail is essential to perpetuate the illusion of fiction. From clothes and foods to money and musical instruments, *Don Quixote* gives us a fully furnished material world. There are

[2] E. C. Riley, *Cervantes's Theory of the Novel* (Juan de la Cuesta, 1992), p. 31.

stretches of time in Don Quixote and Sancho's travels where nothing much happens, and the narrator is dutiful in bringing this to our attention. Sometimes what is important is not a physical action but a mental process. *Don Quixote* is set in motion by something that happens inside a man's mind while he is sitting in his study. In Part II it becomes more frequent for the narrator to tell us that the protagonist is spending his time reflecting on past encounters. The realism of the novel is perhaps most vivid where it is least enticing. At close quarters, Don Quixote gets a whiff of what results when Sancho bids adieu to a well-digested meal. For those wondering, Sancho has a lice problem, and Don Quixote (if we are to believe his lice-ridden squire) has a hairy mole somewhere on his back. These are not characters we have bargained for but people; we should not be surprised that they have bodies.

Cervantes has a keen sense for knowing when to feed the reader information and when to withhold it. He will go to great lengths to reassure us that his fictional creation is intelligible. An effect does not spring up without a cause. Who is this Knight of the Forest who has entered Don Quixote's delusion of knight-errantry? How is a bronze bust—or a monkey on the shoulder of a patch-eyed puppeteer—able to answer questions about the private lives of strangers? Cervantes devotes pages to explain after the fact what would otherwise remain a mystery. At the same time, our author is happy to leave us with ambiguity if doing so will perpetuate the charade that *Don Quixote* is a work of history. When Don Quixote sings a madrigal, does he prop himself up against a beech or cork tree? How many laces hold up Sancho's breeches? The sources, we are told, do not specify. These are surgical imprecisions that prime us to think of the story as an object to be uncovered rather than the subject of a single man's mind.

Epistemology, the study of knowledge, was the preoccupation of early modern philosophy. Whereas Descartes, Spinoza, and Bacon expressed their thoughts in formal discourses, Cervantes meditates on the nature of knowing in a work of the imagination. Reality and knowledge are not synonyms. Knowing rightly is a challenging process, and we must accept that there are questions we simply cannot answer. Furthermore, people perceive the world differently. Don Quixote sees a castle when everyone else sees an inn. When Don Quixote takes his first roadside meal, the narrator points out that there is more than one word in Spanish for the same kind of fish. In addition, sensory data comes wrapped in a bundle of emotions. A fierce banging sound that whets Don Quixote's curiosity fills Sancho's heart with terror. None of this negates the reality of inns, cod, or fulling mills. But it does re-create a basic aspect of being human—that we are subjects of experience.

I have sketched the argument that *Don Quixote* is a model of fiction-writing in that Cervantes makes it easy for us to inhabit his story. But even the most accommodating author needs the support of a reader whose expectations are calibrated to play along. How does a reader fail to pretend? There are two ways. First, when readers spend their time criticizing instead of imagining, they maroon themselves outside the work of fiction. We catch glimpses of such critics in the characters of the Canon of Toledo (see Part I, chap. 47) and the duke's private chaplain (see Part II, chap. 32). The converse failure of the imagination is rarer and far more entertaining. This is the problem of the reader who forgets to disbelieve. Everything is history; nothing is imagined. You are about to spend a few hundred pages with a man who suffers from this delusion.

The Adventures of Miguel de Cervantes

It is unclear whether Miguel de Cervantes had any inkling that *Don Quixote* would usher in a new way to conceive of imaginative writing. He was not an academic theorist. He did not even attend college. What he did possess was native genius and a lifetime of rich experiences.

Miguel de Cervantes was born in the town of Alcalá de Henares in 1547 and died a few miles away in Madrid in 1616. The adventures he lived in the intervening years more than matched those of his most famous protagonist. The son of an itinerant medical practitioner, his early life was marked by frequent moves and instability, as his father tried to stay one step ahead of his creditors. His formal schooling may have been limited to a stint under the tutelage of Juan López de Hoyos, a respected Madrid humanist. By then, Cervantes was around age twenty.

Today we hold up Miguel de Cervantes as the literary genius who gave us *Don Quixote*. While he certainly swelled with pride as *Don Quixote*'s "stepfather", Cervantes was apt to wax proudest of his service in the Spanish military. The climax of his soldiering came in 1571, when the twenty-four-year-old wielded a matchlock musket in the Battle of Lepanto. There in the Gulf of Corinth, a combined force of Spaniards and Italians proved to the world that the mighty Ottoman navy was not invincible. Despite having fallen ill the day of battle, Cervantes insisted on joining ranks above deck as his galley came alongside an enemy ship. In the ensuing firefight, he received three bullet wounds—two to the chest and one to the arm. He would never again be able to use his left hand. Yet as an old man, he boasted that his crippling injury was "beautiful ... for it was earned in the most memorable and exalted occasion that past ages have seen or ages to come could ever hope to witness."[3]

After a recovery in Italy and further missions around the Mediterranean, Cervantes took passage on a ship bound for Spain in 1575. He carried two letters with him. One was from the Duke of Sessa recommending him for a promotion to captain. The other, which granted him a leave of absence to complete his journey, was signed by John of Austria, half-brother of King Philip II and the commander of the Christian forces at Lepanto. Cervantes was within sight of the coast of Catalonia when Algerian corsairs overtook his ship, ransacking the valuables and enslaving the passengers and crew. Algiers, one of the regencies in the Ottoman Empire's orbit, harbored a human trafficking operation that was the terror of Christendom. The following five years would be the darkest of

[3] Miguel de Cervantes Saavedra, *Novelas Ejemplares*, 27th ed., ed. Harry Sieber (Cátedra, 2010), 1:51.

Cervantes' life. Kept in a public prison, or *bagnio*, he spent his time performing menial tasks, writing to his family to send ransom money, and scheming ways to regain his liberty. Cervantes would make a total of four escape attempts—none of which was successful. For his most elaborate plots (one of which involved sixty fellow captives), he was subject to isolated confinement and torture. Strangely, though, he was not impaled, the gruesome execution normally meted out to slaves who attempted escape.

The two letters Cervantes was carrying at the time of his initial capture added to his misery. Rather than rightly concluding that the man they had taken was a low-ranking soldier of extraordinary mettle, his captors mistakenly concluded that Cervantes was a high-ranking soldier of means. The ransom price they set was impossibly high for his family to pay. In September 1580, Cervantes was chained to an oar on a galley bound for Istanbul, where his master was returning after having finished his term as governor of Algiers. Had the ship left port, it is likely that Miguel de Cervantes would have never been heard from again. As it turned out, a Trinitarian friar on a mission to disburse ransom funds gathered in Spain made the last-minute decision to apply an unexpected surplus to Cervantes. The grateful captive was recalled from the galley and his ransom paid in full.

With his return to Spain, we have the first indication that Cervantes would attempt to make a career of writing. Settling in Madrid, he tried his hand at theater but was unable to turn the venture into a living. Of the two dozen plays he wrote and had staged during this time, only three survive. In 1584, at age thirty-seven, he married the nineteen-year-old Catalina de Salazar, whom he met in the village of Esquivias while attending to a late friend's estate. A settled life in the country apparently did not suit Cervantes. In the next fifteen years, he would spend little time at home. Instead, he accepted a series of royal commissions that sent him traveling throughout the southern region of Andalusia in the orbit of Seville, Spain's largest city and the launching point to its New World empire. In the months leading up to Philip II's disastrous attempted invasion of England (the Spanish Armada of 1588), Cervantes served the Crown as a commissary officer, collecting foodstuffs for the royal galleons. He continued in this role until 1594, when he took up the post of tax collector, charged with recovering delinquent funds owed to the Crown. The jobs did little to endear him with the king's subjects he was pursuing with orders to confiscate their property. For his good-faith efforts to carry out his royal commissions, Cervantes would be jailed and excommunicated in more than one Andalusian village. But with his travels came encounters with people from all walks, a storehouse of anecdotes and personal narratives, and the time to reflect on the momentous years he had lived abroad. No doubt, there was time to read and write, as well.

In 1597, Cervantes found himself jailed in Seville, falsely accused of mishandling Crown monies. He would eventually be cleared of wrongdoing, but his career as a public functionary was over. Thankfully for posterity, his career as a writer was just beginning. If the prison he refers to in the preface to Part I—"where every misery takes lodging and every pitiable sound makes its dwelling" (see

p. 7)—is the Seville prison where he was confined until the spring of 1598, it is in this unlikely place that he conceived the idea to write *Don Quixote*. From this time until the summer of 1604, when the manuscript about a mad hidalgo was handed over to the publisher Francisco de Robles, Cervantes probably dedicated the bulk of his time to writing the novel. He followed the court to Valladolid and then to Madrid, where both he and it would remain.

When *The Ingenious Gentleman Don Quixote of La Mancha* appeared in print in early 1605, there was little indication that it would be successful. Cervantes was fifty-eight years old, without much to show in the way of worldly trophies. His plays had been forgotten. He had published one book, the pastoral romance *La Galatea* (1585), but that had been twenty years before, and the rage for all things bucolic had been supplanted by the gritty picaresque novel. We do not know if Cervantes was surprised by his novel's success, but we do know that within two years of its publication, Don Quixote costumes were appearing in public festivities as far away as Peru.

Perhaps in his last decade, Cervantes was able to live the life he had long dreamed of. Though he was not celebrated as Spain's foremost writer, he became a fixture of Madrid's literary gatherings, alongside Spain's leading men of letters. A good part of his time would have been dedicated to writing the Second Part of *Don Quixote*. But what is most remarkable is that the 1615 sequel to his smash hit was only one of a number of publications that Cervantes gave to the world in his final years. These works—which he had probably begun much earlier—include a collection of novellas, a set of plays and comic interludes, and a sprawling byzantine novel, *The Labors of Persiles and Sigismunda*, which he finished two weeks before his death.

In sum, Miguel de Cervantes was a man of arms and letters—a soldier who fought bravely for his country and a writer who finished his life in a blaze of productivity. He was a modest public functionary who suffered indignities for simply doing his job. He was an incessant reader, a storyteller who could spin extravagant tales just as readily as he could find enchantment in the everyday. Miguel de Cervantes was also a sinner. The only child he fathered was the fruit of an affair with the wife of a Madrid tavernkeeper. While Cervantes' literature vindicates the ideal of marriage, his footloose ways betray that in practice he fell short.

Cervantes was unafraid to poke fun at the received pieties of his day. *Don Quixote*, in particular, does not shrink back from subjecting the trappings of Church and State to comic imitation (parody), which sometimes dissolves into comic ridicule (satire). Yet we would be unfaithful to his life and work if we did not acknowledge a basic orientation toward the Roman Catholic faith. However pointed the critiques his literature lobs at the Church, they come not from a scoffer standing outside but from a worshiper seated in the pews. When Cervantes was put to rest in the Convent of the Discalced Trinitarians in Madrid, it was in the Franciscan habit he had received a few weeks prior upon completing his profession as a tertiary of Saint Francis. As far back as 1580, one of Cervantes' fellow slaves in Algiers recalled him writing poetry "in praise of Our Lord and His Blessed Mother, and the Most Holy Sacrament, and on other holy and pious matters".[4] It should not surprise us, then, to find poems of Marian devotion scattered across his literature. Some of Cervantes' most heroic characters are those who remain faithful to the Catholic faith when pressed to renounce it. Indeed, Cervantes' second last name of Saavedra, which he adopted while he was a slave—under the constant temptation to renounce his faith in exchange for freedom—may hearken to the hero of a Reconquista ballad who chose to die as a Christian rather than live as a Muslim convert.

The imaginary of *Don Quixote*—no less than the fictional worlds created in the rest of Cervantes' stories—would not hold together without the conviction that there is a God in heaven working out all things for the good of his people. The safest assumption is that this conviction was shared by the author.

Two Novels and a Spurious Sequel

Most people who pick up a copy of *Don Quixote* are surprised to find out that they hold two novels in their hands, *The Ingenious Gentleman Don Quixote of La Mancha* (1605) and *Second Part of the Ingenious Knight Don Quixote of La Mancha* (1615). I always enjoy hearing my students' responses when I ask them which volume they prefer. Some like the first for the slapstick, for the iconic episodes of windmills and converging flocks of sheep, or for the wide-ranging interpolated tales. Others prefer the psychological complexities of the sequel or its breathtaking feats of metafiction. The First Part can be chaotic—in more than one sense of the term. With little provocation, Don Quixote sets about breaking things, and in turn, gets broken. By all appearances, the trajectory of the novel may suddenly careen off course. When we thought Don Quixote was in the driver's seat, we find him asleep in the back, while strangers have taken over the wheel. Perhaps, as many scholars have suggested, Cervantes pieced together stories here and there that he had written, not sure whether they would otherwise find a home in print.

At the same time, it will not take much effort on the reader's part to note common themes among disparate literary textures. We hear the stories speaking to each other. Themes of providence and grace saturate the Captive's Tale and the stories of Cardenio and his companions in the Sierra Morena, while *The Impertinent Meddler*, placed in the middle of the two, conjures a world where God's merciful intervention is absent and man is left as sovereign—to catastrophic effect. The dialogues on literature in chapters 47 and 48 invite us to slow down and evaluate the dizzying array of stories that come before. Cervantes, from his sojourn in Italy as a young soldier and later participation in Madrid's literary circle, was conversant in the neo-Aristotelian theory that had emerged in Italian universities during the middle of the sixteenth century. The movement, called in Spain *preceptismo* or *tratadismo*, was built mainly on Aristotle's *Poetics* (along with ideas from Horace and Cicero) to create a comprehensive toolbox

[4] Miguel de Cervantes Saavedra, *Información de Argel*, ed. Adrián J. Sáez (Cátedra, 2019), p. 212.

for evaluating literature. Approaches varied widely, but there was a consensus that the best literature found the happy medium along three axes. The ideal literary work balanced unity and variety, instruction and pleasure. As for the third axis, at one end was verisimilitude, a story's ability to pass itself off as believable. At the other end was *admiratio*, the power of literature to provoke a response of wonder and stir the soul to deep contemplation. The *preceptistas* knew that supernatural interventions and stunning coincidences could awe the reader, but they came at the expense of believability. As the literary theorists of Cervantes' day were trying to work out the details in the abstract, Cervantes, not surprisingly, was busy tackling these problems directly in his fiction.

In writing Part II, Cervantes took a creative approach to the challenge of maintaining unity and variety in proper tension. Gone are the interpolated tales stretching over multiple chapters. Instead, a smaller cast of characters takes a larger role in shaping the story. Whereas in Part I, Don Quixote goes out sallying in search of adventures, we find in the Second Part that the adventures increasingly find him. Cervantes relies on amateur dramatists—the priest and Samson Carrasco, Don Antonio Moreno, and the arch-pranksters, the Aragonese duke and duchess—to generate plots. A theatrical air pervades the novel. Characters consciously take on roles, stepping into parts for a time then stepping out of them. This is most true of our two heroes. Beginning with the episode of the Parliament of Death (see chap. 11), we can never shake the suspicion that, no matter where they go, Don Quixote and Sancho are on stage.

Part II is a feast for anyone fascinated by celebrity culture. Centuries before the advent of cameras and social media, Don Quixote and Sancho can boast that they are famous for being famous, the heroes of the bestselling 1605 history. When they travel about, they are known—but known in the categories that Cide Hamete Benengeli, their unwitting publicist, has marked out for them. Fame feeds on fame, which cramps, rather than extends, the fullness of being human. Don Quixote and Sancho are lifted up and celebrated as objects, but we sense them longing to be set down to earth and returned to the simple joys of subjectivity. It is a glorious moment in Barcelona when Don Quixote, having been paraded through the town with a placard on his back, dismounts from his horse and slips into a printing shop to explore something new (see chap. 62). For a moment, a celebrity can be an anonymous tourist without anyone to gawk at him.

The reader will become familiar with the name Alonso Fernández de Avellaneda, a pseudonymous author who, a year before the publication of Cervantes' 1615 sequel, beat him to the press with his own continuation. Without legal protections for derivative works, unauthorized sequels were common in early modern Spain. Cervantes refused to make peace with this convention. In the preface to Part II, he directs a fusillade of invective against Avellaneda, the more potent because it is charged with his trademark irony. It is important to remember that a novel's prefatory texts are typically the last sections written. We cannot be certain about the timeline, but it is likely that Cervantes wrote chapter 1 to around chapter 58 of his continuation without any knowledge that someone else was at work on the same task.

Avellaneda did Cervantes the unwitting favor of sharpening the focus of Part II. Once the spurious sequel becomes known, the novel takes on a special urgency as its mission becomes to vindicate truth over falsehood. From the beginning, *Don Quixote* has explored the problem of true and false appearances. In the final chapters, Cervantes deftly brings this theme to bear on the truth of how we see ourselves.

Literary characters look most like us when they are alive to the world around and within them. We know that fiction has succeeded when we have entered the story and find ourselves standing alongside characters as they struggle through problems that—though the particulars may be at some remove—are fundamentally human concerns. We keep them company as wide-eyed observers, sometimes laughing at them, sometimes cheering their triumphs, occasionally growing frustrated with them, but always present.

How much greater the triumph of fiction when those struggling characters have something to offer us in return. *Don Quixote* shows us how the lenses we use to evaluate the world may bring us closer to or further from the truth. The "once upon a time" worldview of chivalric literature satisfies a longing to transcend the mundane. The problem is that it's unable to bear the burden of reality. Is there any worldview that sees the mire of earth but can still lift its gaze heavenward? Not directly, but by hidden turns of narrative, this is the question that Cervantes puts to Don Quixote. It is worth reading to the end for his answer.

TEXTUAL NOTE

John Ormsby (1829–1895) was a man not easily daunted. An early member of London's Alpine Club, he was among the first mountain climbers to attempt to summit the peaks of the Grivola and Weisshorn. He traveled widely and published accounts of his adventures abroad. The fruits of his sojourn in Spain, however, are found in his translations of the two cornerstones of Spanish literature, *The Cid* and *Don Quixote*.

Ormsby's four-volume translation of *Don Quixote* (1885) still stands out for its charm, breadth, and its command of the intricacies of Miguel de Cervantes' Spanish. Ormsby excels in re-creating Don Quixote's mock-heroic voice. Open randomly to one of Don Quixote's discourses, and you will hear a man fully immersed in the imaginary world of the chivalric romances, each phrase resonant with a nobility mismatched to its surroundings.

Other aspects of Ormsby's translation present challenges for the modern reader. Cervantes' humor—especially in the mouth of Sancho—is often blunted by the use of Victorian colloquialisms, which are more likely to perplex than entertain. Ormsby's unrelenting fidelity to Spanish grammar, where every pronoun finds an English equivalent, can distract the reader with unnecessary clutter.

My revisions to Ormsby's translation seek to preserve the grandeur of his English style while accommodating Cervantes' masterpiece to a new generation of readers. A greater attention to the novels' humor, a desire for more natural English prose, and the benefit of another century and a half of textual scholarship account for most of my departures from Ormsby's original. In editing the text, I have also sought to bring the translation into line with the standard Spanish edition, a collaborative project among leading Cervantes scholars under the sponsorship of the Royal Spanish Academy.[1] Ormsby, though zealous in reproducing Spanish word order, was not averse to cleaning up what he saw as textual discrepancies. As far as is reasonable, I follow the original novels in all their glorious eccentricity.

[1] Miguel de Cervantes Saavedra, *Don Quijote de la Mancha*, 2nd ed., ed. Francisco Rico (Alfaguara; Real Academia Española, 2015).

The Text of

DON QUIXOTE

THE INGENIOUS GENTLEMAN DON QUIXOTE DE LA MANCHA 1605

DEDICATION

TO THE DUKE OF BÉJAR,[1] MARQUIS OF GIBRALEÓN, COUNT OF BENALCÁZAR AND BAÑARES, VISCOUNT OF PUEBLA DE ALCOCER, MASTER OF THE TOWNS OF CAPILLA, CURIEL AND BURGUILLOS

Confident of the favorable reception and honors that Your Excellency bestows on all varieties of books, as a prince so inclined to favor the fine arts, chiefly those that, by their nobility, do not submit to the slander and bribery of the vulgar, I have determined to bring to light *The Ingenious Gentleman Don Quixote of La Mancha* under the shelter of Your Excellency's illustrious name. With due homage to such grandeur, I pray he will receive it agreeably under his protection. In this shadow, though deprived of that precious ornament of elegance and erudition that clothe the works composed in the houses of men more knowledgeable, may it have the boldness to stand before the judgment of those who, trespassing the bounds of their own ignorance, are quick to condemn with more severity and less justice the writings of others. It is my earnest hope that Your Excellency's good counsel in regard to my honorable purpose will not disdain the smallness of so humble a service.

Miguel de Cervantes

[1] *Duke of Béjar:* Don Alonso López de Zúñiga y Sotomayor (1578–1619). Cervantes perpetually fell short in his hopes of receiving financial support from a noble patron. The dedication is cobbled together from two other books by other authors and is likely the work of the editor, Francisco de Robles. Aside from evidence of the haste in which *Don Quixote* was published, the recycled dedication suggests that Cervantes' relationship with the Duke of Béjar was paper thin.

THE AUTHOR'S PREFACE

Idle reader: You may believe me without any oath that I wish for this book (as it is the offspring of my intellect) to be the most handsome, charming, and clever one that could be imagined. Yet I have been unable to defy Nature's law that like gives birth to like. What, then, could this sterile, untilled imagination of mine give birth to but the story of a dry, shriveled, erratic offspring, full of thoughts of all sorts and such as never came into any other imagination—just as what might be conceived in a prison,[1] where every misery takes lodging and every pitiable sound makes its dwelling? Tranquility, a cheerful retreat, pleasant fields, bright skies, murmuring brooks, peace of mind—these are the things that go far to make even the most barren muses fertile and bring into the world births that fill it with wonder and delight. Sometimes when a father has an ugly, loutish son, the love he bears him so blindfolds his eyes that he does not see his defects, or, rather, takes them for gifts and charms of mind and body, and speaks of them to his friends as wit and grace. I, however—for though I pass for the father, I am but the stepfather to *Don Quixote*—have no desire to follow the current custom of imploring you, dearest reader, almost with tears in my eyes (as others do), to pardon or excuse the defects you will find in this child of mine. You are neither its kinsman nor its friend; your soul is your own and your will as free as the best among us. You are in your own house and master of it as much as the king of his taxes, and you know the common saying, "Under my cloak I kill the king."[2] All of which exempts you from every obligation; you can say what you will of the story without fear of being abused for any ill or rewarded for any good you may say of it.

My wish would be simply to present it to you in its natural and pristine state, without the adornment of a preface or the unending catalogue of obligatory sonnets, epigrams, and eulogies, such as are commonly put at the beginning of books. For I can tell you, though composing it cost me some labor, I found none greater than writing this preface you are now reading. Many a time did I take up my pen to write it, and many a time did I lay it down again, not knowing what to write. One of these times, as I was pondering with the paper before me, a pen

[1] *just as what might be conceived in a prison:* We cannot be certain that Cervantes conceived the idea of *Don Quixote* while he was imprisoned. But if he did, it was most likely when he was jailed in Seville in 1597 having been falsely accused of embezzlement.

[2] *Under my cloak I kill the king:* Literally, "Everyone is free to think as he likes." Spanish culture has a rich stock of sayings (*refranes*), many of which are still in common use. When their sense can be inferred from context or easily glossed, this edition translates them literally.

in my ear, my elbow on the desk, and my cheek in my hand, thinking of what I should say, there came in unexpectedly a certain lively and clever friend of mine, who, seeing me so deep in thought, asked the reason; to which I, making no mystery of it, answered that I was thinking of the preface I had to write for the story of *Don Quixote*, which so troubled me that I had a mind not to include any at all, nor even publish the achievements of so noble a knight.

"For how could you expect me not to feel uneasy about what that ancient lawgiver they call the Public will say when it sees me—after slumbering so long in the silence of oblivion and with a load of so many years upon my back[3]—coming out now with a book as dry as straw, devoid of originality, meager in style, poor in thoughts, wholly lacking in learning and wisdom, without quotations in the margin or annotations at the end, after the fashion of other books I see, which, though all fables and vulgarities, are so full of maxims from Aristotle, Plato, and the whole host of philosophers, that they fill readers with amazement and convince them that the authors are men of learning, erudition, and eloquence. And what shall we say when they quote the Holy Scriptures? One would think they are Saint Thomases or other doctors of the Church,[4] observing as they do a decorum so artful that in one sentence they describe a distracted lover and in the next deliver a devout little sermon that it is a delight to hear and read. There will be none of this in my book, for I have nothing to quote in the margin or to note at the end, and still less do I know what authors I should cite in it, to place them at the beginning, as all do, under the letters A, B, C, beginning with Aristotle and ending with Xenophon, Zoilus, or Zeuxis, though one was a slanderer and the other a painter.[5] Moreover, my book must do without sonnets at the beginning, at least sonnets whose authors are dukes, marquises, counts, bishops, noble ladies, or famous poets. Though if I were to ask two or three obliging friends, I know they would give them to me, and such as from the pens of those who have an unmatched reputation in our Spain.

"In short, my friend," I continued, "I am determined that Señor Don Quixote shall remain buried in the archives of his La Mancha until Heaven provide someone to adorn him with all those things he stands in need of; because I find myself, through my shallowness and want of learning, unequal to supplying them, and because I am a layabout by nature and not inclined to hunt for authors to say

[3] *with a load of so many years upon my back:* Cervantes was fifty-seven when the first part of *Don Quixote* was published, well past the life expectancy of his day. His only prior book-length publication, the pastoral novel *La Galatea*, had been released twenty years before in 1585.

[4] *Saint Thomases or other doctors of the Church:* reference to Saint Thomas Aquinas (1225–1274), Dominican theologian and philosopher honored as a Doctor of the Church in 1567 with the title *Doctor Angelicus* (Angelic Doctor).

[5] *Xenophon, Zoilus, or Zeuxis . . . the other a painter:* Xenophon was a fourth-century B.C. philosopher; Zoilus, fourth-century B.C. grammarian critical of Homer; Zeuxis, fifth-century B.C. painter. The poet and dramatist Lope de Vega (1562–1635) prefaced some of his writings with such an index of ancient luminaries. The shadow of Lope, Cervantes' friend and rival, falls on several passages in the novel.

what I myself can say without them. For all these reasons, you found me deep in thought—motives more than sufficient to account for my reverie."

Hearing this, my friend, giving himself a slap on the forehead and breaking into a hearty laugh, exclaimed, "Before God, brother, at last I am disabused of an error in which I have been labored all this long time I have known you, in which I have taken you to be shrewd and sensible in all you do; but now I see you are as far from that as the heavens are from the earth. Is it possible that things of so little moment and so easy to set right can occupy and perplex a seasoned intellect like yours, fit to break through and crush far greater obstacles? By my faith, this comes not of any want of ability, but of too much indolence and too little knowledge of life. Do you want to know if I am telling the truth? Well, then, attend to me, and you will see in the blink of an eye how I sweep away all your difficulties and supply all those deficiencies which you say check and discourage you from bringing before the world the story of your famous Don Quixote, the light and mirror of all knight-errantry."

"Say on," said I, listening to him talk. "How do you propose to fill the void of my insecurity and bring clarity to the chaos of my confusion?"

To which he answered, "Your first difficulty about the sonnets, epigrams, or complimentary verses which you lack for the beginning, and which ought to be by persons of importance and rank, can be removed if you yourself take a little trouble to write them. You can afterwards baptize them and put any name you like to them, fathering them on Prester John of the Indies or the emperor of Trebizond, who, to my knowledge, were said to have been famous poets.[6] Even if they were not (and should any pedant or university student attack you and question the fact), never care two maravedis[7] for that, for even if they prove a lie against you, they cannot cut off the hand you wrote it with.

"As to references in the margin to the books and authors from whom you take the aphorisms[8] and sayings you put into your story, you need do no more than fit in any sentences or scraps of Latin you may happen to know by heart, or at any rate that will not give you much trouble to look up; so as, when you speak of freedom and captivity, simply follow with

Non bene pro toto libertas venditur auro;[9]

and then refer in the margin to Horace, or whoever said it; or, if you allude to the power of death, to come in with

[6] *Prester John of the Indies or the emperor of Trebizond . . . famous poets:* The fabled medieval king Prester John of the Indies was believed to rule a Christian enclave in Africa or the Indian subcontinent. He and the emperor of the Trebizond, the ruler of one of the successor states to the Eastern Roman Empire, were familiar reference points in the chivalric romances.

[7] *maravedis:* The maravedi is a unit of account and low denomination coin minted in copper pieces of two, four, and eight.

[8] *aphorisms:* proverbs.

[9] Non bene pro toto libertas venditur auro: "Not for all the gold in the world should one's liberty be sold" (from a medieval collection of fables).

Pallida mors æquo pulsat pede pauperum tabernas,
Regumque turres.[10]

"If it be friendship and the love that God commands we show toward our enemy, go at once to the Holy Scriptures, which you can do with a very small amount of research, and quote no less than the words of God himself: *Ego autem dico vobis: diligite inimicos vestros.*[11] If you speak of evil thoughts, turn to the Gospel: *De corde exeunt cogitationes malæ.*[12] If of the fickleness of friends, there is Cato, who will give you his distich:[13]

Donec eris felix multos numerabis amicos,
Tempora si fuerint nubila, solus eris.[14]

"With these and such like bits of Latin they will take you at the least for a grammarian, and that nowadays is no small honor and benefit.

"With regard to adding annotations at the end of the book, you may safely do it in this way. If you mention any giant in your book have it be the giant Goliath, and with this alone (which will cost you almost nothing), you have a grand note, for you can put—*The giant Golias or Goliath was a Philistine whom the shepherd David slew by a mighty blow from a stone in the Terebinth valley, as is related in the Book of Kings*[15]—in the chapter where you find it written.

"Next, to prove yourself a man of erudition in polite literature and cosmography, have the river Tagus named in your story, and there you are at once with another famous annotation, setting forth—*The river Tagus*[16] *was so called after a king of Spain: it has its source in such and such a place and empties into the ocean, kissing the walls of the famous city of Lisbon, and it is a common belief that it has golden sands*, etc. If you should have anything to do with robbers, I will give you the story of Cacus,[17] for I know it by heart; if with loose women, there is the Bishop of Mondoñedo, who will lend you Lamia, Laida, and Flora,[18] any reference to

[10] Pallida mors ... Regumque turres: "Pale death visits alike the pauper in his hut and the king in his tower" (Horace).

[11] Ego autem dico vobis: diligite inimicos vestros: "But I say to you, Love your enemies" (Matthew 5:44).

[12] De corde exeunt cogitationes malæ: "For out of the heart come evil intentions" (Matthew 15:19).

[13] *distich:* couplet.

[14] Donec eris ... solus eris: "In happy times, you will have many friends, but when the skies darken, you will be alone" (Ovid).

[15] Book of Kings: 1 Kings 17 in the Latin Vulgate; 1 Samuel 17 in modern Bibles.

[16] The river Tagus: The Tagus (*Tajo*) River, the longest river in the Iberian Peninsula, runs east to west—from Aragon, through the heart of Castile, to the coast of Portugal.

[17] *Cacus:* Vulcan's cave-dwelling son, who robbed Hercules of his cattle while the hero slept.

[18] *Bishop of Mondoñedo ... Lamia, Laida, and Flora:* The Bishop of Mondoñedo is in reference to Fray Antonio de Guevara (c. 1480–1545), Spanish prelate and best-selling writer notorious for his invented histories. Lamia, Laida, and Flora are three prostitutes who appear in the *Familiar Letters* (1539).

whom will bring you great credit; if with the hard-hearted, Ovid will furnish you with Medea;[19] if with witches or enchantresses, Homer has Calypso,[20] and Virgil Circe;[21] if with valiant captains, Julius Cæsar himself will lend you himself in his own *Commentaries*,[22] and Plutarch will give you a thousand Alexanders.[23] If you should deal with love and happen to know a smidge of Tuscan,[24] you can go to Leo the Hebrew,[25] who will supply you to your heart's content; or if you should not care to go to foreign countries, you have at home Fonseca's *Of the Love of God*,[26] in which is condensed all that you or the most imaginative mind can desire on the subject. In short, all you have to do is to manage to quote these names, or refer to these stories I have mentioned, and leave it to me to insert the annotations and quotations, and I swear by all that's good to fill your margins and use up four sheets at the end of the book.

"Now let us come to those references to authors which other books have and that you need for yours. The remedy for this is very simple: You have only to look out for some book that quotes them all, from A to Z as you say yourself, and then insert the very same alphabet in your book. Though the ruse may be plain to see (because you have so little need to borrow from them), that is no matter; there will probably be some simple enough to believe that you have made use of them all in this plain, artless story of yours. At any rate, if it answers no other purpose, this long catalogue of authors will serve to give a surprising look of authority to your book. Besides, no one will trouble himself to verify whether you have followed them or whether you have not, being no way concerned about it; especially as, if I am not mistaken, this book of yours has no need of any one of those things you say it lacks, for it is, from beginning to end, an attack upon the books of chivalry, of which Aristotle never dreamt, nor Saint Basil said a word, nor Cicero[27] had any knowledge; nor do the niceties of truth nor the observations of astrology come within the range of its fanciful nonsense; nor have geometrical measurements or refutations of the arguments used in rhetoric anything to do with it; nor does it mean to preach to anybody, mixing up things

[19] *Ovid . . . Medea:* In Ovid's *Metamorphoses*, when Medea learned that her husband Jason had taken a new wife, she murdered the children she had borne him.

[20] *Homer has Calypso:* Calypso is the nymph in Homer's *Odyssey*, who charmed Odysseus as she held him captive on her island for seven years.

[21] *Virgil Circe:* Circe is the enchantress who turned Odysseus' crew into swine. In Virgil's *Aeneid*, Aeneas hears the groans and animal cries and sails clear of her island.

[22] *Julius Cæsar . . .* Commentaries: *Commentaries on the Gallic War* (58–49 B.C.) and *Commentaries on the Civil War* (46 B.C.), Julius Caesar's firsthand accounts of his military campaigns.

[23] *Plutarch will give you a thousand Alexanders:* Plutarch's *Parallel Lives* presents the character biographies of ancient figures, including Alexander the Great.

[24] *Tuscan:* Italian.

[25] *Leo the Hebrew:* Judah Leon Abravanel (c. 1460–c. 1530), Portuguese-Jewish philosopher and physician who furthered the revival of Neoplatonism in his *Dialogues of Love*.

[26] *Fonseca's* Of the Love of God: 1592 religious treatise by Fray Cristóbal de Fonseca.

[27] *Aristotle . . . Saint Basil . . . Cicero:* an ABC of writers prized for their teachings on literature and rhetoric.

human and divine, a sort of motley in which no Christian understanding should dress itself. It has only to avail itself of truth to nature in its composition, and the more perfect the imitation the better the work will be. And as this piece of yours aims at nothing more than to destroy the authority and influence which books of chivalry have in the world and with the public, there is no need for you to go begging for aphorisms from philosophers, precepts from Holy Scripture, fables from poets, speeches from orators, or miracles from saints; but merely to take care that your style and diction run musically, pleasantly, and plainly, with clear, proper, and well-placed words, setting forth your purpose to the best of your power, and stating your ideas intelligibly, without confusion or obscurity. Strive, too, that in reading your story the melancholy may be moved to laughter, and the merry made merrier still; that the simple shall not be wearied, that the scrupulous shall marvel at its invention, that the somber shall not despise it, nor the wise fail to praise it. Finally, keep your aim fixed on the destruction of that ill-founded edifice of the books of chivalry, hated by some and praised by many more; for if you succeed in this you will have achieved no small feat."

In profound silence I listened to what my friend said, and his observations made such an impression on me that, without attempting to question them, I admitted their soundness, and out of them I determined to make this preface; wherein, gentle reader, you will perceive my friend's good sense, my good fortune in finding such an adviser in such a time of need, and what you have gained in receiving, without addition or alteration, the story of the famous Don Quixote of La Mancha, who is held by all the inhabitants of the district of Campo de Montiel[28] to have been the consummate chaste lover and the bravest knight that has for many years been seen in that region. I have no desire to magnify the service I render you in making you acquainted with so renowned and honored a knight, but I do desire your thanks for the acquaintance you will make with the famous Sancho Panza, his squire, in whom, to my thinking, I have given you condensed all the squirely humor that is scattered through the host of vain books of chivalry. And so—may God give you health, and may he not forget me. *Vale*.[29]

[28] *Campo de Montiel:* See footnote 6, page 31.

[29] Vale: Latin for "Farewell".

SOME COMMENDATORY VERSES[1]

URGANDA THE UNKNOWN[2]

To the book of Don Quixote of La Mancha

If to be welcomed by the good,
O Book, thou make thy steady aim,
No empty chatterer will dare
To question or dispute thy claim.
But if perchance thou hast a mind
To win of idiots approbation,
Lost labor will be thy reward,
Though they'll pretend appreciation.

They say a goodly shade he finds
Who shelters 'neath a goodly tree;
And such a one thy kindly star
In Béjar[3] bath provided thee:
A royal tree whose spreading boughs
A show of princely fruit display;
A tree that bears a noble Duke,
The Alexander of his day.

Of a Manchegan gentleman
Thy purpose is to tell the story,
Relating how he lost his wits
O'er idle tales of love and glory,
Of "ladies, arms, and cavaliers:"
A new Orlando Furioso—

[1] *Some Commendatory Verses:* Cervantes takes the advice of his friend from the preface and baptizes his own poetic compositions with the names of others. The wrinkle, however, is that the conversation between poets and dedicatees takes place entirely on the plane of fiction. One product of the imagination calls to another, even fictional horse to fictional horse.

[2] *Urganda the Unknown:* enchantress and protector of the title character in *The Four Books of the Virtuous Knight Amadís of Gaul* (1508), the master text of the chivalric romance genre. Garci Rodríguez de Montalvo wrote the fourth volume and edited the first three, the origin of which are subject to debate.

[3] *Béjar:* town near Salamanca and name given to a dukedom created by the king of Castile in 1485, whose titleholder in 1605 is the novel's dedicatee. The family was related to the royal family of Navarre.

Innamorato,[4] rather—who
Won Dulcinea del Toboso.

Put no vain emblems on thy shield;
All figures—that is bragging play.
A modest dedication make,
And give no scoffer room to say,
"What! Álvaro de Luna[5] here?
Or is it Hannibal[6] again?
Or does King Francis[7] at Madrid
Once more of destiny complain?"

Since Heaven it hath not pleased on thee
Deep erudition to bestow,
Or black Latino's gift of tongues,[8]
No Latin let thy pages show.
Ape not philosophy or wit,
Lest one who cannot comprehend,
Make a wry face at thee and ask,
"Why offer flowers to me, my friend?"

Be not a meddler; no affair
Of thine the life thy neighbors lead:
Be prudent; oft the random jest
Recoils upon the jester's head.
Thy constant labor let it be
To earn thyself an honest name,
For fooleries preserved in print
Are perpetuity of shame.

A further counsel bear in mind:
If that thy roof be made of glass,

[4] *Orlando Furioso— / Innamorato:* Orlando Furioso is the title hero of Ludovico Ariosto's 1532 epic poem and chivalric romance, which continues *Orlando Innamorato* (*Orlando in Love*), a text that Matteo Boiardo left unfinished at his death in 1494.

[5] *Álvaro de Luna:* Favorite of King John II of Castile, Álvaro de Luna (c. 1390–1453) wielded near supreme authority until his downfall. He, along with Hannibal and King Francis (see below), were great figures who fell into misfortune.

[6] *Hannibal:* North African general who led the forces of Carthage against the Republic of Rome during the Second Punic War. In exile and facing extradition to Rome, he killed himself by drinking poison.

[7] *King Francis:* King Francis I of France (1494–1547), who was captured in battle and held prisoner by the Spanish in Madrid during the winter of 1525–1526.

[8] *black Latino's gift of tongues:* reference to Juan de Sessa (c. 1518–c. 1597), African slave who rose to be a Latin professor at the University of Granada.

It shows small wit to pick up stones
   To pelt the people as they pass.
Win the attention of the wise,
   And give the thinker food for thought;
Whoso indites[9] frivolities,
   Will but by simpletons be sought.

[9] *indites:* composes.

MADÍS OF GAUL

To Don Quixote of La Mancha

SONNET

Thou that didst imitate that life of mine
When I in lonely sadness on the great
Rock Peña Pobre sat disconsolate,
In self-imposed penance there to pine;[10]
Thou, whose sole beverage was the bitter brine
Of thine own tears, and who withouten[11] plate
Of silver, copper, tin, in lowly state
Off the bare earth and on earth's fruits didst dine;
Live thou, of thine eternal glory sure.
So long as on the round of the fourth sphere
The bright Apollo shall his coursers steer,[12]
In thy renown thou shalt remain secure,
Thy country's name in story shall endure,
And thy sage author stand without a peer.

[10] *Thou that didst . . . penance there to pine:* Don Quixote imitates Amadís' penance in chapter 26.

[11] *withouten:* without.

[12] *fourth sphere . . . Apollo shall his coursers steer:* As the sun god, Phoebus Apollo steers the chariot of the sun across the sky. In the Ptolemaic cosmos, the sun moves through the fourth of the concentric spheres encasing the earth, after the moon, Mercury, and Venus.

DON BELIANÍS OF GREECE[13]

To Don Quixote of La Mancha

SONNET

In slashing, hewing, cleaving, word and deed,
I was the foremost knight of chivalry,
Stout, bold, expert, as e'er the world did see;
Thousands from the oppressor's wrong I freed;
Great were my feats, eternal fame their meed;[14]
In love I proved my truth and loyalty;
The hugest giant was a dwarf for me;
Ever to knighthood's laws gave I good heed.
My mastery the Fickle Goddess[15] owned,
And even Chance, submitting to control,
Grasped by the forelock,[16] yielded to my will.
Yet—though above yon horned moon enthroned
My fortune seems to sit—great Quixote, still
Envy of thy achievements fills my soul.

[13] *Don Belianís of Greece:* hero of Jerónimo Fernández's 1545 chivalric romance of the same name.

[14] *meed:* reward.

[15] *Fickle Goddess:* Fortuna, Roman goddess of chance.

[16] *forelock:* Early modern emblem books portrayed Opportunity (*Occasio*) as a female nude shaved of all her hair except a long forelock held out to the viewer—to be seized before she turned her head.

LADY ORIANA[17]

To Dulcinea del Toboso

SONNET

Oh, fairest Dulcinea, could it be!
It were a pleasant fancy to suppose so—
Could Miraflores change to El Toboso,
And London's town to that which shelters thee!
Oh, could mine but acquire that livery
Of countless charms thy mind and body show so!
Or him, now famous grown—thou mad'st him grow so—
Thy knight, in some dread combat could I see!
Oh, could I be released from Amadís
By exercise of such coy chastity
As led thee gentle Quixote to dismiss!
Then would my heavy sorrow turn to joy;
None would I envy, all would envy me,
And happiness be mine without alloy.

[17] *Lady Oriana:* Amadís' beloved, who lived in the castle of Miraflores, outside London.

GANDALÍN, SQUIRE OF AMADÍS OF GAUL

To Sancho Panza, squire of Don Quixote

SONNET

All hail, illustrious man! Fortune, when she
Bound thee apprentice to the esquire trade,
Her care and tenderness of thee displayed,
Shaping thy course from misadventure free.
No longer now doth proud knight-errantry
Regard with scorn the sickle and the spade;
Of towering arrogance less count is made
Than of plain esquire-like simplicity.
I envy thee thy Dapple,[18] and thy name,
And those alforjas[19] thou wast wont to stuff
With comforts that thy providence proclaim.
Excellent Sancho, hail to thee again!
To thee alone the Ovid of our Spain
Does homage with the rustic kiss and cuff.

[18] *Dapple*: Sancho's donkey.
[19] *alforjas*: Spanish for "saddlebags".

FROM EL DONOSO, THE MOTLEY POET[20]

On Sancho Panza and Rocinante

ON SANCHO

I am the esquire Sancho Pan—[21]
Who served Don Quixote of La Man—;
But from his service I retreat—,
Resolved to pass my life discreet—;
For Villadiego, called the Si—,[22]
Maintained that only in reti—
Was found the secret of well-be—,
According to the *Celesti*—:[23]
A book divine, except for sin—
By speech too plain, in my opin—

ON ROCINANTE

I am that Rocinante fa—,
Great-grandson of great Babie—,[24]
Who, all for being lean and bon—,
Had one Don Quixote for an own—;
But if I matched him well in weak—,
I never took short commons meek—,
But kept myself in corn by steal—,
A trick I learned from Lazaril—,[25]
When with a piece of straw so neat—
The blind man of his wine he cheat—.

[20] *Donoso, the Motley Poet:* a possible reference to Gabriel Lobo Lasso de la Vega (1555–1615), who may have collaborated with Cervantes on the commendatory verses.

[21] *I am the esquire Sancho Pan—:* Cervantes adopts a humorous verse form called *versos de cabo roto* (literally, "verses with broken ends"), in which the poet omits the last unstressed syllable of each line. (The first poem in this section, Urganda's sonnet to the novel, also uses this form in the original.) Far from the "idle reader" of the preface, the reader Cervantes envisions is an active interpreter, partnered with him at every turn in the act of imagination.

[22] *Villadiego, called the Si—:* Villadiego the Silent. "To take Villadiego's stockings" was an early modern Spanish expression for beating a hasty retreat.

[23] *Celesti—: The Celestina* (1494), novel in dialogue about a tragic romance facilitated by a procuress. Cervantes criticizes the novel's graphic nature.

[24] *Babie—:* Babieca, horse of the Spanish epic hero, El Cid. He and Rocinante have a poetic dialogue a few poems below.

[25] *A trick I learned from Lazaril—:* In *Lazarillo de Tormes* (1554), the young beggar steals wine from his blind master by drinking from a straw that he slips into their shared wine cask.

ORLANDO FURIOSO

To Don Quixote of La Mancha

SONNET

If thou art not a Peer, peer thou hast none;
Among a thousand Peers thou art a peer;
Nor is there room for one when thou art near,
Unvanquished victor, great unconquered one!
Orlando, by Angelica undone,[26]
Am I; o'er distant seas condemned to steer,
And to Fame's altars as an offering bear
Valor respected by Oblivion.
I cannot be thy rival, for thy fame
And prowess rise above all rivalry,
Albeit both bereft of wits we go.
But, though the Scythian or the Moor to tame
Was not thy lot, still thou dost rival me:
Love binds us in a fellowship of woe.

[26] *Orlando, by Angelica undone:* Orlando goes mad over his unrequited love for the pagan princess.

THE KNIGHT OF PHŒBUS[27]

To Don Quixote of La Mancha

SONNET

My sword was not to be compared with thine
Phœbus of Spain, marvel of courtesy,
Nor with thy famous arm this hand of mine
That smote from east to west as lightnings fly.
I scorned all empire, and that monarchy
The rosy east held out did I resign
For one glance of Claridiana's eye,
The bright Aurora for whose love I pine.[28]
A miracle of constancy my love;
And banished by her ruthless cruelty,
This arm had might the rage of Hell to tame.
But, Gothic Quixote,[29] happier thou dost prove,
For thou dost live in Dulcinea's name,
And famous, honored, wise, she lives in thee.

[27] *The Knight of Phœbus:* protagonist of *Mirror of Princes and Knights* (Diego Ortúñez de Calahorra, 1555), a cycle of chivalric romances.

[28] *I scorned all empire . . . I pine:* The Knight of Phoebus renounces his claim to the Empire of Tartaria over his love for Claridiana.

[29] *Gothic Quixote:* Spanish nobles of the day boasted of their Germanic lineage.

FROM SOLISDÁN[30]

To Don Quixote of La Mancha

SONNET

Your fantasies, Sir Quixote, it is true,
That crazy brain of yours have quite upset,
But aught[31] of base or mean hath never yet
Been charged by any in reproach to you.
Your deeds are open proof in all men's view;
For you went forth injustice to abate,
And for your pains sore drubbings did you get
From many a rascally and ruffian crew.
If the fair Dulcinea, your heart's queen,
Be unrelenting in her cruelty,
If still your woe be powerless to move her,
In such hard case your comfort let it be
That Sancho was a sorry go-between:
A booby he, hard-hearted she, and you no lover.

[30] *Solisdán:* The identity of this figure is unknown.
[31] *aught:* anything.

DIALOGUE

Between Babieca and Rocinante

SONNET

B. How comes it, Rocinante, you're so lean?
R. I'm underfed, with overwork I'm worn.
B. But what becomes of all the hay and corn?
R. My master gives me none; he's much too mean.
B. Come, come, you show ill-breeding, sir, I ween;
'Tis like an ass your master thus to scorn.
R. He is an ass, will die an ass, an ass was born;
Why, he's in love; what's plainer to be seen?
B. To be in love is folly?
R. No great sense.
B. You're metaphysical.
R. From want of food.
B. Rail at the squire, then.
R. Why, what's the good?
I might indeed complain of him, I grant ye,
But, squire or master, where's the difference?
They're both as sorry hacks as Rocinante.

CHAPTER I

WHICH TREATS OF THE CHARACTER AND PURSUITS OF THE FAMOUS GENTLEMAN DON QUIXOTE OF LA MANCHA

In a village of La Mancha, the name of which I have no desire to call to mind, there lived not long ago one of those gentlemen[1] that keep a lance in the lance rack, an old buckler,[2] a lean hack, and a greyhound for hunting. A stew of rather more beef than lamb, a hash on most nights, bacon and eggs on Saturdays, lentils on Fridays, and a pigeon or so extra on Sundays made away with three-quarters of his income. The rest of it went toward a broadcloth tunic,[3] velvet breeches,[4] and matching overshoes for holidays, while on weekdays he made a fine figure in his best homespun.[5]

He had in his house a housekeeper past forty, a niece under twenty, and a lad for the field and market, who could saddle the hack as well as handle the pruning hook. The age of this gentleman of ours was bordering on fifty; he was of a hardy habit, spare, gaunt-featured, a very early riser and a great sportsman. They will have it his surname was Quixada or Quesada (for here there is some difference of opinion among the authors who write on the subject), although from reasonable conjectures it seems plain that he was called Quexana.[6] This, however, is of but little importance to our tale; it will be enough not to stray a hair's breadth from the truth in the telling of it.

Now you should know that the above-named gentleman whenever he was at leisure (which was mostly all the year round) gave himself up to reading books of chivalry with such ardor and eagerness that he almost entirely neglected his pursuit of hunting and even the management of his property. To such a pitch did his infatuation go that he sold many an acre of farmland to buy books of

[1] *one of those gentlemen:* a hidalgo, a member of the lowest order of Spanish nobility; as with the protagonist, hidalgos were often men of modest income.

[2] *buckler:* small, round leather shield.

[3] *broadcloth tunic: sayo de velarte.* The skirted *sayo de velarte* was made from a black or blue broadcloth of good quality. It had fallen out of fashion by the beginning of the seventeenth century.

[4] *breeches: calzas.* The baggy *calzas* covered the hips down to the thighs.

[5] *homespun: vellorí,* a medium-quality cloth with a taupe color. Don Quixote's wardrobe matches the expectations for a gentleman of his rank.

[6] *surname was Quixada or Quesada . . . he was called Quexana:* Despite the narrator's confidence, the question of Don Quixote's former name will not be settled here.

chivalry to read and brought home as many of them as he could get. Of all these books, there were none he liked so well as those from the pen of the famous Feliciano de Silva, for the clarity of their prose and the subtlety of their ideas were as pearls in his sight, particularly when in his reading he came to a lover's praise or a rival's challenge, where he often found passages like "the reason of the unreason with which my reason is afflicted so weakens my reason that with reason I murmur at your beauty"; or again, "the high heavens, which with your divinity divinely fortify you with the stars, render you deserving of the desert your greatness deserves."[7]

Over phrases of this sort, the poor gentleman's mind fell to pieces as he lay awake trying to understand them and untangle their meaning—what Aristotle himself could not have made out had he come to life again for that sole purpose. He was not at all easy about the wounds that Don Belianís gave and took, because it seemed to him that, great as were the surgeons who had cured him, he must have had his face and body covered all over with seams and scars.[8] He commended, however, the author's way of ending his book with the promise of that interminable adventure.[9] Quite often he was tempted to take up his pen and finish it properly as is there proposed, which no doubt he would have done, and made a successful piece of work of it too, had not greater and more absorbing thoughts prevented him.

He had frequent arguments with the priest of his village (a learned man, and a graduate of Siguenza[10]) as to which had been the better knight, Palmerín of England[11] or Amadís of Gaul. Master Nicholas, the village barber,[12] however, used to say that neither of them came up to the Knight of Phœbus,[13] and that if there was any that could compare with him it was Don Galaor, the brother of Amadís of Gaul, because he had a spirit that was equal to every occasion, and was no dainty knight (nor a crybaby like his brother), while in the matter of valor he was not a whit behind him.

In short, he became so absorbed in his books that he spent his nights from sunset to sunrise and his days from dawn to dark poring over them; and with so little sleep and so much reading his brains dried up and he lost his

[7] *Feliciano de Silva . . . "your greatness deserves"*: quotes taken freely from Feliciano de Silva (d. 1554), whose writings span the chivalric, picaresque, and pastoral genres.

[8] *wounds . . . covered all over with seams and scars:* However many wounds a chivalric hero receives in battle, he is in fine form when it comes time to subdue his next enemy.

[9] *ending his book with the promise of that interminable adventure:* The book ends when the enchanter Fristón sends a chariot pulled by fiery dragons and kidnaps all the main female characters.

[10] *Siguenza:* minor university in northern Castile.

[11] *Palmerín of England:* hero of a Portuguese chivalric romance of the same title, published in Spanish in 1547.

[12] *Master . . . barber:* Aside from cutting hair and shaving faces, the early modern barber was trained to let blood, pull teeth, and, in emergencies, amputate limbs. The title "Master" (*Maese*) was a common form of address for men in this profession.

[13] *Knight of Phœbus:* See footnote 27, page 22.

wits. His imagination grew full of what he used to read about in his books—enchantments, quarrels, battles, challenges, wounds, wooings, romances, torments, and all sorts of impossible nonsense; and it so possessed his mind that the whole fabric of invention and fancy he read of was true, that to him no history in the world was more certain. He used to say that El Cid Ruy Diaz[14] was a very good knight, but that he was not to be compared with the Knight of the Burning Sword[15] who with one backstroke cut in half two fierce and monstrous giants. He thought more highly of Bernardo del Carpio because at Roncesvalles he slew Roland[16] in spite of enchantments, adopting the stratagem Hercules used when he strangled Antæus[17] the son of Terra in his arms. He approved highly of the giant Morgante,[18] because, although he was of the giant breed, which is always insolent and sullen, he alone was affable and well-bred. But above all he admired Reinaldos of Montalban,[19] especially when he saw him sallying forth from his castle and robbing everyone he met, and when beyond the seas he stole that image of Muhammad which, as his history says, was entirely of gold. To have a bout of kicking at that traitor of a Ganelon[20] he would have given his housekeeper, and his niece into the bargain.

With his wits now being quite gone, he hit upon the strangest notion that ever madman in this world hit upon. He decided that it was right and proper, both for the increase of his own honor and for the service of his country, that he should make a knight-errant of himself, roaming the world over in full armor and on horseback in quest of adventures, and putting in practice all that he had read of as being the usual practices of knights-errant—righting every kind of wrong and exposing himself to peril and danger—from which he would reap eternal renown and fame. Already the poor man saw himself crowned by the might of his arm no less than

[14] *El Cid Ruy Diaz:* Rodrigo Díaz de Vivar, eleventh-century historical figure famed for capturing Valencia from the Moors in 1094 and the subject of popular ballads that fictionalized episodes in his life.

[15] *Knight of the Burning Sword:* In the 1530 chivalric romance *Amadís of Greece*, the title character wears the emblem of a burning sword on his chest.

[16] *Bernardo del Carpio . . . at Roncesvalles he slew Roland:* Bernardo del Carpio is the legendary Spanish warrior who is said to have defeated Charlemagne's commander Roland in single combat at the Battle of Roncesvalles (Roncevaux Pass, 778), a historical ambush by Basque forces retaliating for the Frankish destruction of Pamplona's city walls.

[17] *Hercules. . . strangled Antæus:* Antæus, the giant king of Libya, was invincible as long as he touched the ground (his mother was the earth goddess Gaia). Hercules lifted him in the air and strangled him in a bear hug.

[18] *the giant Morgante:* Unlike the stereotypical giant of the chivalric romances (vulgar and malignant), the giant of *Morgante* (Luigi Pulci, 1483) serves faithfully under Orlando (Roland).

[19] *Reinaldos of Montalban:* one of the fabled Twelve Peers of France in the court of Charlemagne who first appears in medieval French ballads. The knight later becomes a familiar figure in Spanish literature and as Rinaldo in *Orlando Furioso*. The robbery of the idol of Muhammad is an episode from *Mirror of Princes and Knights*.

[20] *Ganelon:* In the Roland cycle, Ganelon betrays the French to the Saracens, which leads to their defeat in battle.

the Emperor of Trebizond.[21] And so, carried away by the uncommon pleasure he found in these idle fancies, he set about to put his scheme into execution.

The first thing he did was to clean up some armor that had belonged to his great-grandfather and had been for ages lying forgotten in a corner, eaten with rust and covered with mildew. He scoured and polished it as best he could, but he found one great defect in it, that was not an enclosed helmet but a simple morion.[22] This deficiency, however, his ingenuity supplied, for he put together a kind of half-helmet of pasteboard which, fitted on to the morion, looked like a whole one. It is true that, in order to see if it was strong and fit to stand a cut, he drew his sword and gave it a couple of slashes, the first of which undid in an instant what had taken him a week to do. The ease with which he knocked it to pieces troubled him, and so to guard against that danger he set to work again, attaching iron bars on the inside until he was satisfied with its strength. Not caring to try any more experiments with it, he passed and adopted it as a helmet of the most perfect construction.

He next proceeded to inspect his hack.[23] Though it had more quartos than a real[24] and more blemishes than Gonela's horse[25] (which "*tantum pellis et ossa fuit*")[26] it nonetheless surpassed in his eyes Alexander's Bucephalus[27] and the Cid's Babieca. Four days were spent in thinking what name to give him, because (as he said to himself) it was not right that a horse belonging to a knight so famous, and one with such merits of his own, should be without some distinctive name. He aimed to give him a name that would indicate what he had been before belonging to a knight-errant as well as what he had now become; for it was only reasonable that, his master taking a new character, his horse should take a new name, and that it should be a distinguished and imposing one, befitting the new order and calling he was about to follow. And so, after having composed, crossed out, rejected, added to, unmade, and remade a multitude of names out of his memory and imagination, he decided upon calling him Rocinante[28]—a name, to his thinking, lofty, sonorous, and significant of his condition as a hack before he became what he now was, the first and foremost of all the hacks in the world.

Having come up with a name for his horse so much to his taste, he was anxious to get one for himself. He spent a week more pondering this point, till at last he made up his mind to call himself "Don Quixote,"[29] from which, as has

[21] *Emperor of Trebizond:* See footnote 6, page 9.

[22] *morion:* high-crested helmet without a visor.

[23] *hack: rocín*, a worn-out horse.

[24] *more quartos than a real:* a play on "quartos"—cracks in the hoof of a horse, or a coin valued at four maravedis (compared to a real, valued at thirty-four maravedis).

[25] *Gonela's horse:* Pietro Gonnella, fifteenth-century jester at the court of Ferrara, was known for his haggard horse.

[26] tantum pellis et ossa fuit: Latin for "was nothing but skin and bones".

[27] *Alexander's Bucephalus:* Bucephalus was Alexander the Great's horse.

[28] *Rocinante:* fitting compound of *rocín* (hack) + *antes* (before).

[29] *Don Quixote:* A hidalgo was prohibited from styling himself "Don", roughly equivalent to the English "Sir". Only a knight (*caballero*) could be called "Don". The surname

been already said, the authors of this true history have inferred that his name must have been beyond a doubt Quixada, and not Quesada as others would have it. Recollecting, however, that the valiant Amadís was not content to call himself simply Amadís but added the name of his kingdom and country to make it famous, calling himself Amadís of Gaul, he, like a good knight, resolved to add his own country to his name and style himself Don Quixote of La Mancha, whereby, he considered, he described accurately his origin and country and did it honor in taking from it his surname.

His armor, then, being furbished, his morion turned into a helmet, his hack christened, and he himself confirmed, he came to the conclusion that nothing more was needed now but to find a lady to be in love with; for a knight-errant without love was like a tree without leaves or fruit or a body without a soul. As he said to himself, "If, for my sins, or by my good fortune, I come across some giant hereabouts—a common occurrence with knights-errant—and overthrow him in one onslaught, or cleave him asunder to the waist, or, in short, vanquish and subdue him, will it not be well to have someone I may send him to as a present, that he may come in and fall on his knees before my sweet lady, and in a humble, submissive voice say, 'I am the giant Caraculiambro,[30] lord of the Isle of Malindrania,[31] vanquished in single combat by the never sufficiently extolled knight Don Quixote of La Mancha, who has commanded me to present myself before Your Grace, that Your Highness may dispose of me at your pleasure'?"

Oh, how our worthy knight enjoyed the delivery of this speech, especially when he had thought of someone to call his lady! There was, so the story goes, in a village near his own a very attractive farm girl with whom at one time he had been in love, though, so far as is known, she never learned of or gave a thought to the matter. Her name was Aldonza Lorenzo, and upon her he thought fit to confer the title of Lady of his Thoughts. After some search for a name that would not be out of harmony with her own and would suggest that of a princess and great lady, he decided upon calling her Dulcinea del Toboso[32] (she being of El Toboso) a name, to his mind, musical, original, and significant, like all those he had already bestowed upon himself and the things belonging to him.

"Quixote" (*quixote*, "thigh armor") is an amalgam of the high and low, a preview of much of the novel's humor. At its loftiest, the name is resonant of "Lanzarote" (Lancelot) from the Arthurian cycle. On the other hand, attaching the suffix "-ote" to a word adds emphasis to the point of making light of it.

[30] *Caraculiambro:* The earthy name evokes *cara* (face) and *culo* (butt).

[31] *Malindrania:* not far from *malandrín* (scoundrel).

[32] *Her name was Aldonza Lorenzo . . . Dulcinea del Toboso:* Aldonza Lorenzo is a name typical of a peasant girl. The root of "Dulcinea" is *dulce* (sweet, gentle).

CHAPTER II

WHICH TREATS OF THE FIRST SALLY THE INGENIOUS DON QUIXOTE MADE FROM HOME

These preliminaries settled, he did not care to put off any longer the execution of his plan, urged on by the thought that his delay was the world's loss—considering the wrongs he intended to right, grievances to redress, injustices to repair, abuses to remedy, and duties to discharge. So without giving notice of his intention to anyone and without anybody seeing him, one morning before daybreak (on one of the hottest days of the month of July) he donned his suit of armor and patched-up helmet, mounted Rocinante, braced his buckler, took hold of his lance, and by the back gate of the yard[1] sallied forth upon the plain in the highest of contentment and delight at seeing with what ease he had made a beginning of his grand purpose.

But scarcely did he find himself upon the open plain when a terrible thought struck him, one all but enough to make him abandon the enterprise at the very outset. It occurred to him that he had not been dubbed a knight, and that according to the law of chivalry he neither could nor ought to bear arms against any knight; and that even if he had been dubbed, still he ought to wear the white armor of a novice knight (without a device upon the shield[2]) until he had earned a device by his prowess. These reflections made him waver in his purpose; but with his madness being stronger than any reasoning, he made up his mind to have himself dubbed a knight by the first one he came across, following the example of others in the same situation, as he had read in the books that brought him to this condition. As for white armor, he resolved on the first opportunity to scour his until it was whiter than an ermine. Thus comforting himself he pursued his way, taking the path his horse chose, for in this he believed lay the essence of adventures.

As our newly fledged adventurer paced along he said to himself, "Who knows but that in times to come, when the true history of my famous deeds is made known, the sage who writes it,[3] when he has to set forth my first sally in the early morning, will do it after this fashion: 'Scarce had the rubicund[4] Apollo spread

[1] *yard: corral,* walled enclosure behind the main house divided into areas for farm animals and a vegetable patch.

[2] *white armor . . . device upon the shield:* The armor is white because it has nothing painted on it. The device on the shield is a heraldic emblem.

[3] *sage who writes it:* It is a convention of the chivalric romance that a wizard chronicles the deeds of the knight.

[4] *rubicund:* ruddy, appropriate for Apollo, the god of sun and light.

o'er the face of the broad spacious earth the golden threads of his bright hair, scarce had the little birds of painted plumage attuned their notes to hail with dulcet and mellifluous harmony the coming of the rosy Dawn,[5] which, deserting the soft couch of her jealous spouse, was appearing to mortals at the gates and balconies of the Manchegan horizon, when the renowned knight Don Quixote of La Mancha, quitting the lazy down, mounted his celebrated steed Rocinante and began to traverse the ancient and famous Campo de Montiel,'"[6] which in fact he was actually traversing. "Happy the age, happy the time," he continued, "in which shall be made known my famous deeds, worthy to be cast in bronze, carved in marble, styled in paintings, for a memorial for ever. And you, O sage enchanter, whoever you are, to whom it shall fall to be the chronicler of this wondrous history, forget not, I entreat you, my good Rocinante, the constant companion of my ways and wanderings."

Presently he broke out again, as if he were love-stricken in earnest, "O Princess Dulcinea, lady of this captive heart, a grievous wrong have you done me to drive me forth with scorn and with inexorable obduracy banish me from the presence of your beauty. O lady, deign to hold in remembrance this heart, your vassal, that thus in anguish pines for love of you."

So he went on stringing together these and other absurdities, all in the style of what his books had taught him, imitating their language as well as he could. All the while, he rode so slowly and the sun mounted so rapidly and with such fervor that it was enough to melt his brains if he had any. Nearly all day he traveled without anything remarkable happening to him, at which he was in despair, for he was anxious to encounter someone at once upon whom to try the might of his strong arm.

Some writers say that the first adventure he met with was that of Puerto Lápice; others say it was that of the windmills. What I have ascertained on this point, and what I have found written in the annals of La Mancha, is that he was on the road all day, and toward nightfall his hack and he found themselves dead tired and hungry, when, looking all around to see if he could discover any castle or shepherd's shanty where he might refresh himself and tend to his needs, he saw not far from the road an inn, which was as welcome as a star guiding him to the portals, if not the palaces, of his redemption. Quickening his pace, he reached it just as night was setting in.

At the door were standing two young women, "traveling girls"[7] as they call them, on their way to Seville with some mule drivers[8] who had chanced to stop that night at the inn; and as everything our adventurer saw or imagined seemed

[5] *Dawn:* Aurora, Roman goddess and wife of the mortal Tithonus, who was granted immortality but not eternal youth.

[6] *Campo de Montiel:* Region of southern La Mancha roughly coterminous with the modern province of Ciudad Real. Marked by gently rolling plains, it is bounded on the south by the Sierra Morena, which Don Quixote and Sancho reach in chapter 23.

[7] *traveling girls:* prostitutes.

[8] *mule drivers: arrieros*, who transported goods around the peninsula on pack mules.

to him to take the shape of what he had read, the moment he saw the inn he pictured it to himself as a castle with its four turrets and pinnacles of shining silver, not forgetting the drawbridge and moat and all the trappings usually ascribed to castles of the sort. To this inn, which to him seemed a castle, he advanced, and at a short distance from it he checked Rocinante, hoping that some dwarf would show himself upon the battlements and by trumpet blast give notice that a knight was approaching the castle. But seeing that they were slow about it, and that Rocinante was in a hurry to reach the stable, he made for the inn door and noticed the two young women there, who seemed to him to be two fair maidens or lovely ladies taking their ease at the castle gate.

At this moment it so happened that a swineherd who was going through a harvested field with a drove of pigs (for without any apology, that is what they are called) gave a blast of his horn to herd them together, and suddenly it seemed to Don Quixote to be what he was expecting, the signal of some dwarf announcing his arrival; and so with prodigious satisfaction he rode up to the inn and to the ladies, who, upon seeing a man of this sort approaching in full armor and with lance and buckler, were retreating into the inn in fear. Don Quixote, guessing their fear by their flight, raised his pasteboard visor to reveal his dry dusty visage, and with courteous bearing and gentle voice addressed them, "Flee not, your ladyships, nor fear any affront! For the order of knighthood which I profess brings ill to none, much less to highborn maidens as your appearance proclaims you to be."

The girls stared at him and strained their eyes to make out the features that the clumsy visor obscured. But when they heard themselves called maidens, a thing so outside their profession, they could not restrain their laughter, which made Don Quixote grow indignant and say, "Modesty becomes the fair, and moreover laughter that has little cause is great silliness. This, however, I say not to pain or anger you, for my desire is none other than to serve you."

The incomprehensible language and unpromising looks of our knight only increased the ladies' laughter, which increased his irritation. Matters might have gone farther if at that moment the innkeeper had not come out, who, being a very fat man, was a very peaceful one.[9] He, seeing this grotesque figure armed with a mismatched bridle, lance, buckler, and corselet,[10] was not at all indisposed to join the damsels in their show of amusement; but, in truth, a little fearful of such formidable armament, he thought it best to speak to him graciously. And so he said, "Señor Caballero, if your worship seeks lodging, excepting a bed (for there is not one in the inn), there is plenty of everything else here."

Don Quixote, observing the respectful bearing of the governor of the fortress[11] (for so innkeeper and inn seemed in his eyes), answered, "Sir Castellan,[12] for me anything will suffice, for

[9] *being a very fat man, was a very peaceful one:* According to humoral theory, people with a high proportion of the humor phlegm in their bodies tend to be obese and are inclined to have a peaceful nature.

[10] *corselet:* armor protecting the torso.

[11] *governor of the fortress: alcaide*, official responsible for the administration of a fortress.

[12] *Castellan: castellano*, synonymous with *alcaide*.

'My armor is my only wear,
My only rest the fray.'"[13]

The host supposed he called him Castellan because he took him for a worthy of Castile, though he was in fact an Andalusian, and one from the coast at San Lúcar,[14] as crafty a thief as Cacus[15] and as full of tricks as a well-schooled page.[16] "In that case," said he,

"'Your bed is on the flinty rock,
Your sleep to watch alway';

and if so, you may dismount and safely find a remedy for insomnia under this roof for a year, not just for a single night."

So saying, he advanced to hold the stirrup for Don Quixote, who got down with great difficulty and exertion (for he had not eaten all day), and then charged the host to take great care of his horse, as he was the best creature that ever ate bread in this world. The innkeeper looked him over but did not find him as good as Don Quixote said, nor even half as good. Putting him up in the stable, he returned to see what might be wanted by his guest, whom the girls, who had by this time made their peace with him, were now relieving of his armor. They had taken off his breastplate and backpiece, but they neither knew nor saw how to open his gorget[17] or remove his makeshift helmet, for he had fastened it with green ribbons, which, as there was no untying the knots, would have to be cut. This, however, he would not by any means consent to; and so he remained all evening with his helmet on, the oddest and most amusing figure that can be imagined.

While the oft-handled women were removing his armor, Don Quixote, who took them for ladies of high degree belonging to the castle, recited to them with great grace:

"Oh, never, surely, was there knight
So served by hand of dame,
As served was he, Don Quixote hight,[18]
When from his town he came;
With maidens waiting on himself,
Princesses on his hack—

[13] *My armor . . . the fray*: Don Quixote quotes a ballad, which the innkeeper takes up in his reply.

[14] *Castile, though he was in fact an Andalusian . . . at San Lúcar*: Castile is the central kingdom of Spain that includes La Mancha. Andalusia is the region to the south bordered by the Mediterranean. Sanlúcar, near Cádiz, was frequented by those living on the margins of the law.

[15] *Cacus*: See footnote 17, page 10.

[16] *well-schooled page*: Pages had a reputation for thievery.

[17] *gorget*: piece of armor protecting the throat, which, along with the breastplate and backplate, made up the corselet.

[18] *hight*: named.

—or Rocinante, for that, my ladies, is my horse's name, and Don Quixote of La Mancha is my own. For though I had no intention of declaring myself until my achievements in your service and honor had made me known, the necessity of adapting that old ballad of Lancelot to the present occasion has given you the knowledge of my name altogether prematurely. A time, however, will come for your ladyships to command and me to obey, and then the might of my arm will show my desire to serve you."

The girls, who were not used to hearing language of this sort, had nothing to say in reply; they only asked him if he wanted anything to eat.

"I would gladly eat a bit of something," said Don Quixote, "for I feel it would come very seasonably." The day happened to be a Friday, and in the whole inn there was nothing but some pieces of the fish they call in Castile *abadejo*, in Andalusia *bacallao*, in some places *curadillo*, and in others *troutlet*;[19] so they asked him if he thought he could eat troutlet, for there was no other fish to give him. "If there be troutlets enough," said Don Quixote, "they will be the same thing as a trout; for it is all one to me whether I am given eight reals in small change or a piece of eight. Moreover, it may be that these troutlets are like veal, which is better than beef, or kid, which is better than goat. Whatever it be, let it come quickly, for the burden and pressure of arms cannot be borne without support to the inside."

They laid a table for him at the door of the inn for the sake of fresh air, and the host brought him a portion of ill-soaked and worse cooked cod and a piece of bread as black and moldy as his own armor. It was a laughable sight to see him eating, for having his helmet on and the beaver[20] up, he could not with his own hands put anything into his mouth unless someone else placed it there. This service one of the ladies rendered him. To give him anything to drink was impossible—or would have been so had not the innkeeper hollowed a reed and, putting one end in his mouth, poured the wine into him through the other; all of which he bore with patience rather than cut the ribbons of his helmet.

While this was going on there came up to the inn a sowgelder,[21] who, as he approached, sounded his reed pipe four or five times, and thereby completely convinced Don Quixote that he was in some famous castle and that they were regaling him with music, that the cod was trout, the bread the whitest, the wenches ladies, and the innkeeper the castellan of the castle. Consequently, he held that his enterprise and sally had been to some purpose. But still it distressed him to think he had not been dubbed a knight, for it was plain to him he could not lawfully engage in any adventure without receiving the order of knighthood.

[19] troutlet: Whatever its name, the fish would have been salt-cured, appropriate for a Friday fast from meat.

[20] *beaver:* piece of armor protecting the mouth.

[21] *sowgelder:* one whose job is to spay sows.

CHAPTER III

WHEREIN IS RELATED THE AMUSING WAY IN WHICH DON QUIXOTE HAD HIMSELF DUBBED A KNIGHT

Troubled by this thought, he made haste with his scanty tavern supper. Once he finished, he called the innkeeper and shut himself up in the stable with him. There, he fell on his knees before him and said, "From this spot I rise not, valiant knight, until your courtesy grants me the boon I seek, one that will redound to your praise and the benefit of the human race."

The innkeeper, seeing his guest at his feet and hearing a speech of this kind, stood staring at him in bewilderment, not knowing what to do or say. He entreated him to rise, but it was to no purpose until he had agreed to grant the boon demanded of him.

"I hoped for no less, my lord, from your High Magnificence," replied Don Quixote. "I must tell you that the boon I have asked and your liberality has granted is that you shall dub me knight tomorrow morning, and that tonight I shall keep watch over my arms in the chapel of this your castle. Thus tomorrow, as I have said, will be accomplished what I so much desire, enabling me lawfully to roam through all the four quarters of the world seeking adventures on behalf of those in distress, as is the duty of chivalry and of knights-errant like myself, whose ambition is directed to such deeds."

The innkeeper, who, as has been mentioned, was something of a jokester and already had a suspicion of his guest's lack of wits, was quite convinced of it on hearing talk of this kind. To give himself some entertainment that night, he determined to lead him on, so he told him that he was quite right in pursuing the object he had in view, and that such a motive was natural and becoming in a knight as distinguished as he seemed and his gallant bearing showed him to be; and that he himself in his younger days had followed the same honorable calling, roaming in quest of adventures in various parts of the world, among others the Curing Grounds of Málaga, the Isles of Riarán, the Precinct of Seville, the Little Market of Segovia, the Olivera of Valencia, the Rondilla of Granada, the Strand of San Lúcar, the Colt of Córdoba, the Taverns of Toledo,[1] and various other quarters, where he had proved the nimbleness of his feet and the lightness of his fingers, doing many wrongs, cheating many widows, spoiling maids

[1] *Curing Grounds of Málaga ... Taverns of Toledo:* a catalogue of Spain's seedy neighborhoods.

and swindling minors, and, in short, bringing himself under the notice of almost every tribunal and court of justice in Spain; until at last he had retired to this castle of his, where he was living upon his property and upon that of others and where he received all knights-errant of whatever rank or condition they might be—all for the great love he bore them and that they might share their wealth with him in return for his benevolence.

He told him, moreover, that in this castle of his there was no chapel in which he could keep watch over his armor, as it had been torn down in order to be rebuilt, but that in a case of necessity it might, he knew, be watched anywhere, and he might watch it that night in a courtyard of the castle. In the morning, God willing, the requisite ceremonies could be performed to have him dubbed a knight, and so thoroughly dubbed that nobody could be more so. He asked if he had any money with him, to which Don Quixote replied that he had not a cent, as in the histories of knights-errant he had never read of any of them carrying any. On this point the innkeeper told him he was mistaken; for though not recorded in the histories, because in the author's opinion there was no need to mention anything so obvious and necessary as money and clean shirts, it was not to be supposed therefore that they did not carry them. He should regard it as certain and established that all knights-errant (about whom there were so many full and unimpeachable books) carried well-furnished purses in case of emergency and likewise carried shirts and a little box of ointment to cure the wounds they received. For in those plains and deserts where they engaged in combat and were wounded, there was not always someone to cure them, unless indeed they had for a friend some sage enchanter to aid them at once by fetching through the air upon a cloud some damsel or dwarf with a vial of water of such potency that by tasting one drop of it they were cured of their wounds in an instant and left as sound as if they had not received any damage whatever. But in case this should not occur, the knights of old took care to see that their squires were provided with money and other necessaries, such as bandages and ointments for healing purposes. When it happened that knights had no squires (which was seldom the case) they themselves carried everything in cunning saddlebags that were barely visible on the horse's haunches, as if it were something else of more importance, for carrying saddlebags was not otherwise regarded very favorably among knights-errant. The innkeeper therefore advised him (and, as his godson so soon to be,[2] he might even command him) never from that time forth to travel without money and the usual requirements. He would find the advantage of them when he least expected it.

Don Quixote promised to follow his advice scrupulously. It was arranged at once that he should hold vigil over his armor in a large yard at one side of the inn. Collecting it all together, Don Quixote placed it on a trough that stood by the side of a well, and bracing his buckler on his arm he grasped his lance and began with a stately air to march up and down in front of the trough. As he began his march, night began to fall.

[2] *godson so soon to be:* The novice knight became godson of the knight who dubbed him.

The innkeeper told all the people who were in the inn about the madness of his guest, the vigil over the armor, and the dubbing ceremony he contemplated. Full of wonder at so strange a form of insanity, they flocked to see it from a distance, and observed with what composure he sometimes paced up and down, or sometimes, leaning on his lance, gazed on his armor without taking his eyes off it for very long. As night closed in, with a light from the moon so brilliant that it might vie with his that lent it, everything the novice knight did was plainly seen by all.

Meanwhile, one of the mule drivers lodged in the inn thought fit to water his team, and it was necessary to remove Don Quixote's armor as it lay on the trough. Don Quixote, seeing the other approach, hailed him in a loud voice, "O rash knight, or whoever you are, that comes to lay hands on the armor of the most valorous errant that ever girt on sword, be careful what you do. Touch it not unless you would lay down your life as the penalty of your rashness." The mule driver gave no heed to these words (he would have done better to heed them if he had been heedful of his health); instead, seizing the armor by the straps, he flung it some distance from him.

Seeing this, Don Quixote raised his eyes to heaven, and fixing his thoughts, it seemed, upon his lady Dulcinea, exclaimed, "Aid me, my lady, in this the first affront that presents itself to the breast which you hold in subjection. Let not your favor and protection fail me in this first test." With these words and others to the same purpose, dropping his buckler he lifted his lance with both hands and with it struck such a blow on the mule driver's head that he stretched him on the ground so stunned that, had he followed it up with a second, there would have been no need of a surgeon to cure him. This done, he picked up his armor and returned to his watch with the same serenity as before.

Shortly after this, another, not knowing what had happened (for the mule driver still lay senseless), came with the same object of giving water to his mules and was proceeding to remove the armor in order to clear the trough when Don Quixote, without uttering a word or imploring aid from anyone, once more dropped his buckler and once more lifted his lance and, without breaking his lance to pieces, made more than three of the second mule driver's head, for he laid it open in four.

At the noise, everyone in the inn ran to the spot, among them the innkeeper. Seeing this, Don Quixote braced his buckler on his arm, and with his hand on his sword exclaimed, "O Lady of Beauty, strength and support of my faint heart, it is time for you to turn the eyes of your greatness on this your captive knight on the brink of so mighty an adventure." So inspired did he feel that he would not have flinched if all the mule drivers in the world had assailed him. The companions of the wounded mule driver, realizing the plight they were in, began from a distance to shower stones on Don Quixote, who screened himself as best he could with his buckler, not daring to abandon the trough and leave his armor unprotected. The innkeeper shouted to them to leave him alone, for he had already told them that he was mad, and as a madman he would be set free even if he killed them all.

Don Quixote shouted still louder, calling them knaves and traitors, and the lord of the castle, who allowed knights-errant to be treated in this fashion, a villain and a lowborn knight whom, if he had received the order of knighthood, would be called to account for his treachery. "But of you," he cried, "base and vile rabble, I take no heed. Fling, strike, charge, do all you can against me, you shall see what the reward of your folly and insolence will be." This he uttered with so much spirit and boldness that he filled his assailants with a terrible fear, and as much for this reason as at the persuasion of the innkeeper they left off stoning him. He allowed them to carry off the wounded, and with the same calmness and composure as before resumed the watch over his armor.

The buffoonery of his guest was not much to the innkeeper's liking. He therefore determined to cut matters short and confer upon him at once the accursed order of knighthood before any further misadventure could occur. Approaching him, he apologized for the rudeness that, without his knowledge, had been shown him by these low people who had been well punished for their insolence. As he had already told him, he said, there was no chapel in the castle, nor was it needed for what remained to be done, for as he understood the order's ceremonial rite, the gist of being dubbed a knight lay in the accolade[3] and in the slap on the shoulder, and that could be administered in the middle of a field. Don Quixote, moreover, had now done all that was necessary in keeping watch over his armor, for the requirements were satisfied by a vigil of two hours only, and he had been about it more than four. Don Quixote believed everything and told the innkeeper he stood ready to obey him and to make an end of it with as much haste as possible; for if he were again attacked after having been dubbed a knight, he would not, he thought, leave a soul alive in the castle, except such as out of respect he might choose to spare.

Thus forewarned (and terrified), the castellan brought out at once a book he used to tally the straw and barley he served out to the mule drivers, and with a lad carrying a candle-end and the two damsels already mentioned, he returned to where Don Quixote stood and bade him kneel down. While reading from his account book as if he were repeating some devout recitation, he raised his hand in the middle of his delivery and gave him a sturdy blow on the neck, and then, with his own sword, a smart slap on the shoulder, all the while muttering to himself as if he were saying his prayers.

Having done this, he directed one of the ladies to gird his sword, which she did with great self-possession and gravity, and not a little was required to prevent a burst of laughter at each stage of the ceremony; but what they had already seen of the novice knight's feats kept their laughter within bounds. On girding him with the sword the worthy lady said to him, "May God make your worship a very fortunate knight, and grant you success in battle." Don Quixote asked her name in order that he might from that time forward know to whom he was beholden for the favor he had received, as he meant to confer upon her some portion of

[3] *accolade:* touch of the open hand or sword tip to the neck or shoulders of the kneeling candidate.

the honor he acquired by the might of his arm. She answered with great humility that she was called La Tolosa, and that she was the daughter of a clothes mender of Toledo who lived near the market of Sancho Bienaya, and that wherever she might be she would serve and esteem him as her lord. Don Quixote said in reply that she would do him a favor if thenceforward she assumed the title *Don* and called herself "Doña Tolosa." She promised she would.

The other woman then buckled on his spur, and with her followed almost the same conversation as with the lady of the sword. He asked her name, and she said it was La Molinera, and that she was the daughter of a respectable miller of Antequera. Of her likewise Don Quixote requested that she adopt the title *Don* and call herself "Doña Molinera," making offers to her further services and favors.

Having thus, with hot haste and speed, completed these never-till-now-seen ceremonies, Don Quixote could wait no longer to be on horseback sallying forth in quest of adventures. Saddling Rocinante at once he mounted, and embracing his host, as he returned thanks for his kindness in knighting him, he addressed him in language so extraordinary that it is impossible to convey it. To get him out of the inn, the innkeeper replied with no less rhetoric (though with fewer words), and without calling upon him to settle his bill let him go with a Godspeed.

CHAPTER IV

OF WHAT HAPPENED TO OUR KNIGHT WHEN HE LEFT THE INN

It was near dawn when Don Quixote departed the inn, so delighted, so exuberant at finding himself now dubbed a knight, that joy was bursting through his saddle straps. Recalling, however, the advice of his host as to the necessities he ought to carry with him, especially regarding money and shirts, he determined to go home and provide himself with all, and also with a squire, for he was of a mind to secure a farm laborer, a neighbor of his who was poor and with a family but very well qualified for the office of squire to a knight. With this object he turned his horse's head toward his village, and Rocinante, thus reminded of his old home, stepped out so briskly that he hardly seemed to tread the earth.

He had not gone far, when out of a wooded area on his right there seemed to come feeble cries as of someone in distress. The instant he heard them he exclaimed, "Thanks be to Heaven for the favor it accords me, that it so soon offers an opportunity for me to fulfill the obligation I have undertaken and gather the fruit of my ambition. These cries, no doubt, come from some man or woman in want of help and needing my aid and protection."

Turning round, he led Rocinante in the direction from which the cries seemed to proceed. He had gone but a few paces into the woods when he saw a mare tied to an oak, and tied to another, stripped from the waist upwards, a youth of about fifteen years of age, from whom the cries came. Nor were they without cause, for a farmer of robust frame was flogging him with a belt and following up every blow with scoldings and commands, repeating, "Keep your mouth shut and your eyes open!" while the youth answered, "I won't do it again, my master; by God's passion, I won't do it again! I'll take more care of the flock next time!"

Seeing what was going on, Don Quixote said in an angry voice, "Discourteous knight, it ill becomes you to assail one who cannot defend himself. Mount your steed and take your lance"—for there was a lance leaning against the oak to which the mare was tied—"and I will make you recognize that you are behaving as a coward."

The farmer, seeing before him this figure in full armor brandishing a lance over his head, gave himself up for dead. He answered meekly, "Sir knight, this youth I am disciplining is my servant, employed by me to watch a flock of sheep that I have nearby, and he is so careless that I lose one every day. When I reprove him for being inattentive and wicked he says I do it because I'm stingy, to escape paying him the wages I owe him. Before God, and on my soul, he lies."

"Would he lie in my presence, you vile bumpkin?" said Don Quixote. "By the sun that shines on us, I have a mind to run you through with this lance. Pay him at once without another word. If not, by the God that rules us I will make an end of you and annihilate you on the spot. Release him instantly."

The farmer hung his head, and without a word untied his servant, of whom Don Quixote asked how much his master owed him. He replied, nine months at seven reals a month. Don Quixote added it up, found that it came to seventy-three reals,[1] and told the farmer to pay it immediately, if he did not want to die for it. The trembling rustic replied that as he lived and by the oath he had sworn (though he had not sworn any) it was not so much; for there were to be taken into account and deducted three pairs of shoes he had given him, and a real for two blood lettings when he was sick.[2]

"All that is very well," said Don Quixote; "but let the shoes and the blood lettings be deducted from the blows you have given him without any cause; for if he spoiled the leather of the shoes you paid for, you have damaged that of his body, and if the barber took blood from him when he was sick, you have drawn it when he was sound. On that score, he owes you nothing."

"The problem is, sir knight, that I have no money here. Let Andrés come home with me, and I will pay him all, real by real."

"Me, go with him?" cried the youth. "God forbid it! No, señor, not for the world; for once he is alone with me, he will flay me like a Saint Bartholomew."[3]

"He will do nothing of the kind," said Don Quixote. "I have only to command, and he will obey me. As he has sworn to me by the order of knighthood which he has received, I leave him free, and I guarantee the payment."

"Consider what you are saying, señor," said the youth. "This master of mine is not a knight, and he has not received any order of knighthood. He is Juan Haldudo the Rich of Quintanar."[4]

"That matters little," replied Don Quixote; "there may be Haldudo knights; moreover, everyone is the son of his works."

"That's true," said Andrés. "But this master of mine—what works is he the son of, when he refuses me the wages of my sweat and labor?"

"I do not refuse, brother Andrés," said the farmer. "Be good enough to come along with me, and I swear by all the orders of knighthood there are in the world to pay you as I have agreed, real by real—and perfumed to boot."[5]

"I exempt you from the perfume," said Don Quixote. "Give it to him in reals, and I shall be satisfied. See that you do as you have sworn. If not, by the same

[1] *nine months at seven reals a month . . . seventy-three reals:* The total reals should be sixty-three. It is an open question whether the multiplication error belongs to Don Quixote, Cervantes, or the printer.

[2] *two blood lettings when he was sick:* According to humoral theory, sickness was the result of an imbalance of one or more of the body's four humors. A common remedy was to make an incision in the skin and draw blood, sometimes expedited by attaching leeches to the wound. The release of blood was supposed to take with it the harmful fluids.

[3] *flay me like a Saint Bartholomew:* Saint Bartholomew is reputed to have been martyred by being skinned alive.

[4] *Quintanar:* The village of Quintanar de la Orden is in the vicinity of El Toboso.

[5] *and perfumed to boot:* with an additional benefit, probably "with interest".

oath I swear to come back and hunt you out and punish you. Though you should hide yourself better than a lizard, I shall find you. And if you desire to know who it is who lays this command upon you, that you be more firmly bound to obey it, know that I am the valorous Don Quixote of La Mancha, the undoer of wrongs and injustices. And so, God be with you, and keep in mind what you have promised and sworn under those penalties that have been already declared to you."

So saying, he gave Rocinante the spur and was soon out of reach. The farmer followed him with his eyes, and when he saw that he had left the woods and was no longer in sight, he turned to his boy Andrés and said, "Come here, my son. I want to pay you what I owe you, as that undoer of wrongs has commanded me."

"My oath on it," said Andrés, "your worship will be well advised to obey the command of that good knight—may he live a thousand years—for as he is a valiant and just judge, by Roque,[6] if you don't pay me, he'll come back and do as he said."

"My oath on it, too," said the farmer; "but as I have a strong affection for you, I want to add to the debt in order to add to the payment." And seizing him by the arm, he tied him up again and gave him such a flogging that he left him for dead.

"Now, Master Andrés," said the farmer, "call on the undoer of wrongs. You will find he won't undo that, though I am not sure that I have quite done with you, for I have a good mind to flay you alive." But at last he untied him and gave him leave to go look for his judge in order to put the sentence pronounced into execution.

Andrés went off gloomily, swearing he would go look for the valiant Don Quixote of La Mancha and tell him exactly what had happened, and that everything would have to be repaid to him sevenfold. But for all that, he walked away in tears, while his master stood laughing.

Thus did the valiant Don Quixote right the wrong.

Thoroughly satisfied with what had taken place, as he considered he had made a very happy and noble beginning of his knighthood, Don Quixote took the road toward his village perfectly content with himself, saying in a low voice, "Well may you this day call yourself fortunate above all on earth, O Dulcinea del Toboso, fairest of the fair! For it has fallen to your lot to hold subject and submissive to your full will and pleasure a knight so renowned as is and will be Don Quixote of La Mancha, who, as all the world knows, yesterday received the order of knighthood, and has today righted the greatest wrong and grievance that ever injustice conceived and cruelty perpetrated; who has today plucked the rod from the hand of yonder ruthless oppressor so wantonly lashing that tender child."

He now came to a road branching in four directions, and immediately he was reminded of those crossroads where knights-errant used to stop to consider which road they should take. In imitation of them he halted for a while, and after having deeply considered it, he loosened Rocinante's reins, submitting his own will to that of his hack, who followed his first intention, which was to make straight for his own stable.

[6] *by Roque:* euphemism for "by God".

After he had gone about two miles, Don Quixote observed a large group of people, who, as afterwards became clear, were Toledan merchants on their way to buy silk at Murcia.[7] There were six of them coming along under their sunshades, with four servants mounted, and three muleteers on foot. Scarcely had Don Quixote caught sight of them when it came into his imagination that this must be some new adventure readymade to his purpose of imitating as far as possible the confrontations he had read about in his books.[8] With a lofty bearing and determination he fixed himself firmly in his stirrups, readied his lance, and brought his buckler before his breast. Planting himself in the middle of the road, he stood waiting the approach of these knights-errant, for such he now judged them to be. When they had come near enough to see and hear, he exclaimed with a haughty gesture, "Let everyone hold his place, that each may confess that in all the world there is no maiden fairer than the empress of La Mancha, the peerless Dulcinea del Toboso."

The merchants halted at the sound of these words and the sight of the strange figure that uttered them, and from both figure and words at once guessed the madness of their owner. They wished, however, to find out where this confession demanded of them was leading. One of them, rather fond of a joke and quite sharp-witted, said to him, "Sir knight, we do not know who this good lady is that you speak of. Show her to us, for if she is of such beauty as you suggest, with all our hearts and without any pressure we will confess the truth that is on your part required of us."

"If I were to show her to you," replied Don Quixote, "what merit would you have in confessing a truth so obvious? The essential point is that without seeing her you must believe, confess, affirm, swear, and defend it; else you have to do with me in battle, ill-conditioned, arrogant rabble that you are. Come forward, one by one as the order of knighthood requires, or all together as is the custom and vile usage of your breed. Here do I bide and await you relying on the justice of the cause I maintain."

"Sir knight," replied the merchant, "I entreat your worship in the name of this present company of princes, that, to save us from charging our consciences with the confession of a thing we have never seen or heard of, and one moreover so much to the prejudice of the empresses and queens of La Alcarria and Extremadura,[9] your worship will be pleased to show us some portrait of this lady, though it be no bigger than a grain of wheat;[10] for 'by the thread one gets at

[7] *Murcia:* city on the southeast coast of Spain that was the peninsula's principal producer of silk.

[8] *confrontations he had read about in his books:* In the *paso de armas*, the knight-errant would block a path and challenge to combat anyone who wished to pass.

[9] *La Alcarria and Extremadura:* Both of these are regions of Spain, the former a small plateau on the east side of Madrid and the latter a historic province in the southwest. Neither place has claimed any empress or queen.

[10] *though it be no bigger than a grain of wheat:* Cf. Matthew 17:20: "For truly, I say to you, if you have faith as a grain of mustard seed, you will say to this mountain, 'Move from here to there,' and it will move." The merchant plays on *grano de mostaza* (mustard seed) and *grano de trigo* (grain of wheat).

the ball.' In this way we shall be satisfied and assured, and you will be content and pleased. Indeed, I believe we are already so far agreed with you that even though her portrait should show her blind in one eye and seeping vermilion and sulphur[11] from the other, we would nevertheless, to gratify your worship, say all in her favor that you desire."

"She seeps nothing of the kind, vile rabble," said Don Quixote, burning with rage, "nothing of the kind, I say, only ambergris and civet in cotton.[12] Nor is she one-eyed or humpbacked, but straighter than a Guadarrama spindle.[13] Now you must pay for the blasphemy you have uttered against beauty like that of my lady."

So saying, he charged with leveled lance so furiously against the one who had spoken that if luck had not contrived that Rocinante should stumble midway and fall, it would have gone badly for the saucy merchant. Down went Rocinante, and over went his master, rolling along the ground for some distance. When he tried to rise, he was unable, so encumbered was he with lance, buckler, spurs, helmet, and the weight of his old armor. While he struggled to get up, he kept shouting, "Fly not, cowards! Captives, mark that it is not my fault but my horse's that I am stretched out here!"

One of the muleteers in attendance, who must not have been very good-natured, hearing the poor prostrate man bluster in this way, was unable to refrain from giving him an answer on his ribs. Coming up to him he seized his lance, and having broken it in pieces, with one of them he began to rain so many blows on our Don Quixote that, notwithstanding his armor, he milled him like a measure of wheat. His masters called out not to lay on so hard and to leave him alone, but the muleteer's dander was up, and he did not care to leave off until he had vented the rest of his wrath. Gathering up the remaining fragments of the lance, he finished with a discharge upon the unhappy victim, who all through the storm of sticks that rained on him never ceased threatening heaven, earth, and the brigands (for such they seemed to him). At last the muleteer was tired, and the merchants continued their journey, taking with them matter for talk about the poor fellow who had been thrashed.

The poor fellow, when he found himself alone, made another effort to rise; but if he was unable when whole and sound, how was he to rise after having been beaten and well-nigh knocked to pieces? He counted himself fortunate, nonetheless, as it seemed to him that this was a regular knight-errant's mishap, and in his judgment, entirely the fault of his horse. Still, it was not possible for him to get up, as his whole body was battered with bruises.

[11] *vermilion and sulphur*: poisons of red and yellow color, respectively.

[12] *ambergris and civet in cotton*: The musk of the whale (ambergris) and civet, a small mammal native to tropical Africa and Asia, was stored in glass containers filled with cotton. As the Spanish Empire strengthened its hold across the globe, ports like Seville welcomed an astonishing array of exotic goods.

[13] *Guadarrama spindle*: Wood from the forests north of Madrid was prized for its straightness and used for spindles and kitchen utensils.

CHAPTER V

IN WHICH THE NARRATIVE OF OUR KNIGHT'S MISHAP IS CONTINUED

Finding, then, that, he could not in fact move, he resorted to his usual remedy, which was to think of some passage in his books. His madness brought to his mind the story of Valdovinos and the Marquis of Mantua, when Carloto left him wounded on the mountainside, a tale known by heart by children,[1] not forgotten by young men, and lauded and even believed by the old—and for all that not a whit truer than the miracles of Muhammad. This seemed to him to fit exactly the case in which he found himself, and so making a show of severe suffering, he began to roll on the ground and with feeble breath repeat the very words the wounded knight of the forest is said to have uttered:

> Where art thou, lady mine, that thou
> My sorrow dost not rue?
> Thou canst not know it, lady mine,
> Or else thou art untrue.

On he went with the ballad as far as the lines:

> O noble Marquis of Mantua,
> My uncle and liege lord!

As chance would have it, when he reached this line there happened to come by a peasant from his own village, a neighbor of his, who had been with a load of wheat to the mill. He, seeing the man stretched there, came up to him and asked him who he was and what was the matter with him that he complained so woefully.

Don Quixote was firmly persuaded that this was the Marquis of Mantua, his uncle, so the only answer he gave was to go on with his ballad, in which he told the tale of his misfortune and of the loves of the emperor's son and his wife—all exactly as is sung in the ballad.

The peasant stood amazed at hearing such nonsense. Removing the man's visor, already battered to pieces by blows, he wiped his face, which was covered with dust. As soon as he had done so he recognized him. "Señor Quixana!"—for so he

[1] *story of Valdovinos and the Marquis of Mantua . . . tale known by heart by children:* ballad that tells of the defeat of Valdovinos, nephew of the Marquis of Mantua, at the hands of Carloto, Charlemagne's son. Schools included the ballad in early-grade readers.

appears to have been called when he was in his senses and had not yet changed from a quiet country gentleman into a knight-errant—"Who has brought your worship to this state?" But to all questions the other only went on with his ballad.

Seeing this, the good man removed as well as he could Don Quixote's breastplate and backpiece to see if he had any wound, but he saw no blood nor any mark whatever. He then managed to raise him from the ground, and with no little difficulty hoisted him upon his donkey, which seemed to be the easiest mount for him. He gathered his weapons—down to the splinters of his lance—and tied them on Rocinante. Then leading the hack by the bridle and the donkey by the halter, he took the road for the village, lost in thought over Don Quixote and his absurd chatter.

No less lost in thought was Don Quixote, for with all the blows and bruises he could not sit upright on the donkey and from time to time sent up sighs to heaven, so that once more he drove the peasant to ask what ailed him. It could have been only the devil himself that put into his head tales to match his own adventures, for now, forgetting Valdovinos, he was taken with the thought of the Moor Abindarráez, when the governor of Antequera, Rodrigo de Narváez, took him prisoner and carried him away to his castle.[2] And so when the peasant again asked him how he was and what ailed him, he replied with the same words and phrases that the captive Abindarráez gave to Rodrigo de Narváez, just as he had read the story in the *Diana* of Jorge de Montemayor where it is written, applying it to his own case so aptly that the peasant went along cursing his fate that he had to listen to such nonsense. From all this, he came to the conclusion that his neighbor was crazy and so made all haste to reach the village to be free from Don Quixote's tiresome harangue.

Don Quixote, coming to the end of the matter, said, "Señor Don Rodrigo de Narváez, your worship must know that this fair Jarifa I have mentioned is now the lovely Dulcinea del Toboso, for whom I have done, am doing, and will do the most famous deeds of chivalry that in this world have been seen, are to be seen, or ever shall be seen."

To this the peasant answered, "Señor—sinner that I am!—can't your worship see that I am not Don Rodrigo de Narváez or the Marquis of Mantua, but Pedro Alonso your neighbor, and that your worship is not Valdovinos or Abindarráez, but the worthy gentleman Señor Quixana?"

"I know who I am," replied Don Quixote, "and I know that I can be not only those I have named but all the Twelve Peers of France and even all the Nine

[2] *Moor Abindarráez . . . to his castle*: Don Quixote has shifted from the court of Charlemagne to the final decades of the Reconquista, the centuries-long campaign to end the presence of Muslim rule in the Iberian Peninsula. *The History of the Abencerraje and the Lovely Jarifa* tells of the Moor Abindarráez, of the noble Abencerraje family, who is taken captive in single combat by Rodrigo de Narváez, castellan of the Spanish fortress on the frontier at Antequera. When the Christian knight learns that the captive had been on his way to marry his beloved, Jarifa, he consents to let Abindarráez attend the wedding, with the promise that he will return to his captor in three days. Beginning in 1561, the story was included as an appendix to the pastoral romance *La Diana*.

Worthies,[3] since my achievements surpass all that they have done combined and each separately on his own account."

With this talk and more of the same kind they reached the village just as night was beginning to fall, though the peasant held back until it was a little darker so that the bedraggled hidalgo might not be seen as such a badly mounted knight. When it was what seemed to him the proper time, he entered the village and went to Don Quixote's house, which he found all in confusion. There were the priest and the village barber, who were great friends of Don Quixote, and his housekeeper, who was saying to them in a loud voice, "What does your worship think can have befallen my master, Señor Licentiate Pero Pérez?"[4] for so the priest was called. "It is three days now since anything has been seen of him, or the hack, the buckler, lance, or armor. Miserable me! I am certain of it, as sure as I was born to die, that these accursed books of chivalry he incessantly reads have upset his reason. For I now remember having heard him say to himself often that he would become a knight-errant and go all over the world in quest of adventures. To the devil and Barabbas with such books, which have brought to ruin the finest mind there was in all La Mancha!"

The niece said the same and more: "You must know, Master Nicholas"—for that was the name of the barber—"it was often my uncle's way to stay two days and nights together poring over these unholy books of misadventures, after which he would fling the book away and snatch up his sword and fall to slashing the walls. When he was exhausted he would say he had killed four giants like four towers, and the sweat that flowed from him when he was weary he said was the blood of the wounds he had received in battle. Then he would drink a great jug of cold water and become calm and quiet,[5] saying that this water was a most precious potion which the sage Esquife,[6] a great magician and friend of his, had brought him. But I take all the blame on myself for never having told your worships of my uncle's ravings, that you might have put a stop to them before things had come to this state and burn all these accursed books—for he has a great number—that richly deserve to be burned like heretics."

"So say I too," said the priest, "and by my faith tomorrow shall not pass without public judgment upon them. May they be condemned to the flames, lest they lead those that read to behave as my good friend seems to have behaved."

[3] *Twelve Peers of France and even all the Nine Worthies:* The Twelve Peers of France were the exemplary knights of the court of Charlemagne. The Nine Worthies were legendary warriors of renown: three from the Bible, three from classical antiquity, and three from the Middle Ages.

[4] *Licentiate Pero Pérez:* A licentiate holds a *licenciado*, a college diploma. "Pero" was a common variant of "Pedro".

[5] *drink a great jug . . . and quiet:* The four bodily humors were mapped onto coordinates of hot/cold and dry/wet. Introducing a cold, wet substance into the body was thought to counteract the hot, dry state produced by an excess of the humor choler, which manifested itself in erratic outbursts and restlessness.

[6] *Esquife:* literally "Skiff". The niece means "Alquife", the husband of Urganda the Unknown in *Amadís of Gaul*.

All this the peasant heard, and from it he understood at last what was the matter with his neighbor, so he began calling aloud, "Open, your worships, to Señor Valdovinos and to Señor the Marquis of Mantua, who comes badly wounded, and to Señor Abindarráez, the Moor, whom the valiant Rodrigo de Narváez, the castellan of Antequera, brings captive."

At these words they all hurried out, and when they recognized their friend, master, and uncle, who had not yet dismounted from the donkey because he could not, they ran to embrace him.

"Hold!" cried he. "For I am badly wounded through the fault of my horse. Carry me to bed, and if possible send for the wise Urganda to cure and look after my wounds."

"See there? Plague on it!" exclaimed the housekeeper at this. "Didn't my heart tell the truth as to which of my master's feet was making him limp?[7] To bed with your worship at once, and we will try to cure you here without fetching that Hurgada.[8] A curse I say once more, and a hundred times more, on those books of chivalry that have brought your worship to such a state."

They carried him to bed at once, and after searching for his wounds could find none, though he said he was bruised all over from having had a severe fall with his horse Rocinante when engaged in combat with ten giants, the biggest and the boldest to be found on earth.

"Is that so?" said the priest. "Are there giants in the dance? By the sign of the cross, I will burn them tomorrow before the day is over."

They asked Don Quixote a thousand questions, but he answered every one the same: that they give him something to eat and let him sleep, for that was what he needed most. They did so, and the priest questioned the peasant at great length as to how he had found Don Quixote. He told him everything, especially about the nonsense he had talked when he had been found and on the way home. All of this made the licentiate more determined to do what he did the next day, which was to summon his friend the barber, Master Nicholas, and go with him to Don Quixote's house.

[7] *which of my master's feet was making him limp:* "what was the source of his trouble".
[8] *Hurgada:* literally, "picked at or rummaged through".

CHAPTER VI

OF THE GRAND AND ENTERTAINING INQUIRY THAT THE PRIEST AND BARBER MADE IN THE LIBRARY OF OUR INGENIOUS GENTLEMAN

Who was still sleeping.[1] The priest asked the niece for the keys to the room where the books (the perpetrators of all this mischief) were kept, which she gladly gave him. They all went in, the housekeeper with them, and found more than a hundred volumes of large books very well bound[2] along with other small ones.

The moment the housekeeper saw them she turned around and ran out of the room and came back immediately with a saucer of holy water and a sprinkler,[3] saying, "Here, your worship, señor licentiate, sprinkle this room. Don't leave a single enchanter behind of the many to be found in these books, lest they put a spell on us in revenge for banishing them from this world."

The simplicity of the housekeeper made the licentiate laugh, and he directed the barber to give him the books one by one to see what they contained, as there might be some to be found among them that did not deserve the penalty of fire.

"No," said the niece, "there is no reason for pardoning any at all. Every one of them has done mischief. Better to fling them out the window into the court and make a pile to set them ablaze. Or else carry them to the yard, where a bonfire can be made without the smoke to trouble us." The housekeeper said the same, so eager were they both for the slaughter of those innocents; but the priest would not agree to it without first reading the titles.

The first that Master Nicholas put into his hand was *The Four Books of Amadís of Gaul*.[4] "This seems a mysterious thing," said the priest, "for as I have heard it said, this was the first book of chivalry printed in Spain, and from this all the others derive their birth and origin; so it seems to me that we ought inexorably to condemn it to the flames as the founder of so vile a sect."[5]

[1] *who was still sleeping:* Cervantes pokes fun at the artifice of chapter divisions and their titles.

[2] *very well bound:* Books at the time were generally sold unbound. The fact that Alonso Quixano has paid for expensive binding is a sign of how much he values them.

[3] *sprinkler:* implement for sprinkling holy water, often branches bundled together.

[4] The Four Books of Amadís of Gaul: See footnote 2, page 13.

[5] *condemn it to the flames . . . so vile a sect:* Beginning with the niece's wish in the previous chapter that her uncle's books "be burned like heretics", the language of a religious trial has not been far from the surface. The Tribunal of the Holy Office of the Inquisition, known popularly as the Spanish Inquisition, was founded in 1478 by King Ferdinand II of

"No, sir," said the barber. "I too, have heard it said that this is the best of all the books of this kind that have been written, and so, as something unmatched in its category, it ought to be pardoned."

"True enough," said the priest. "For that reason we will spare its life for the present. Let us see the other one next to it."

"It is," said the barber, "*The Deeds of Esplandián*,[6] the lawful son of Amadís of Gaul."

"Well in truth," said the priest, "the merit of the father must not be put down to the account of the son. Take it, mistress housekeeper. Open the window and fling it into the yard and lay the foundation of the pile for the bonfire we are to make."

The housekeeper obeyed with great satisfaction, and the worthy *Esplandián* went flying into the yard to await with all patience the fire that was in store for him.

"Proceed," said the priest.

"This next one," said the barber, "is *Amadís of Greece*.[7] Indeed, I believe all those on this side are of the same Amadís lineage."

"Then to the yard with the lot of them," said the priest. "To see the burning of Queen Pintiquiniestra, and the shepherd Darinel with his eclogues,[8] and the bedeviled and mixed-up discourses of his author, I would burn with them the father who begot me if he were going about dressed as a knight-errant."

"I am of the same mind," said the barber.

"And so am I," added the niece.

"In that case," said the housekeeper, "here, into the yard with them!"

They were handed to her, and as there were many of them, she spared herself the staircase and flung them down out of the window.

"Who is the portly one there?" asked the priest.

"This," said the barber, "is *Don Olivante of Laura*."[9]

Aragon and Queen Isabel I of Castile to ensure the Catholic orthodoxy of Jewish converts to Christianity. By 1605, it had expanded its purview to investigate all religious nonconformity, including of suspected mystics, witches, crypto-Muslims, and Protestants (who prompted the tribunal to begin publishing an index of banned books in 1551). Though officially an organ of the state, the Inquisition was staffed by Catholic prelates, who investigated charges of heresy and determined what measures were needed to reconcile the offender to the Church. The unrepentant were subject to punishments ranging from fines and public humiliation to death by being burned at the stake. Cervantes' parody of the Holy Office is a striking example of literature's power to level substantive critiques in the guise of entertainment.

[6] The Deeds of Esplandián: 1510 sequel to *Amadís of Gaul*, also by Garci Rodríguez de Montalvo. Alonso Quixano's library is methodically organized.

[7] Amadís of Greece: ninth installment in the *Amadís* cycle, this one written by another author, Feliciano de Silva (1530).

[8] *eclogues:* pastoral poems in a classical style.

[9] Don Olivante of Laura: The full title is *The History of the Invincible Knight Don Olivante of Laura, Prince of Macedonia, Who, for His Amazing Deeds Rose to Be Emperor*

"The author of that book," said the priest, "was the same that wrote *The Garden of Curious Flowers*. Truly there is no deciding which of the two books is the more truthful, or, to put it better, the less deceitful. All I can say is, send this one into the yard for a swaggering fool."

"The one after it is *Florismarte of Hircania*,"[10] said the barber.

"Señor Florismarte here?" said the priest. "Then by my faith he must take up his quarters in the yard, in spite of his marvelous birth and visionary adventures, for the stiffness and dryness of his style deserve nothing else. Into the yard with him and the other, mistress housekeeper."

"With all my heart, señor," said she, and executed the order with great delight.

"This," said the barber, "is *The Knight Platir*."[11]

"An old book that one," said the priest, "but I find no reason for clemency in it. Send it after the others without appeal," which was done.

Another book was opened, and they saw it was entitled *The Knight of the Cross*.[12]

"For the sake of the holy name this book has," said the priest, "its ignorance might be excused; but then, they say, 'behind the cross there's the devil.' To the fire with it."

Taking down another book, the barber said, "This is *The Mirror of Chivalry*."[13]

"Well I know his worship," said the priest. "This is the book where Señor Reinaldos of Montalban goes about with his friends and comrades (greater thieves than Cacus) and the Twelve Peers of France, along with the veracious historian Turpin.[14] To be honest, I am not for condemning them to more than perpetual banishment. For at least they share some of the creativity of the famous Matteo Boiardo, from which the Christian poet Ludovico Ariosto also wove his web. If I find Ariosto here speaking a language different than his own, I shall show no respect whatever; but if he speaks his own tongue, I will give him his due respect."[15]

---

of Constantinople (Antonio de Torquemada, 1564), a large format book that runs over five hundred pages in the first edition. Torquemada's other publication mentioned, *The Garden of Curious Flowers* (1570), is a miscellany on natural history and marvels.

[10] Florismarte of Hircania: The title character's name is slightly different: *First Part of the Grand History of the Most Spirited and Valiant Prince Felixmarte of Hircania and of His Rare Birth* (Melchor Ortega, 1556).

[11] The Knight Platir: *Chronicle of the Most Fierce and Valiant Knight Platir, Son of the Emperor Primaleón* (1533), book in the Palmerín cycle.

[12] The Knight of the Cross: The title could refer to more than one chivalric romance.

[13] The Mirror of Chivalry: Spanish prose adaptation of Matteo Boiardo's *Orlando Innamorato* published in three parts, the first two by Pero López de Santamaría (1525, 1527) and the last by Pedro de Reinosa (1547). These early modern works, including Ariosto's *Orlando Furioso*, develop storylines from the medieval *chansons* about the court of Charlemagne.

[14] *Turpin:* Charlemagne's chaplain and Archbishop of Rheims. In medieval *chansons*, he is portrayed as a paladin and the chronicler of the Twelve Peers' exploits.

[15] *give him his due respect:* The priest criticizes the Spanish translation of Ariosto's *Orlando Furioso*, probably that of Jerónimo Jiménez de Urrea (1549), the captain he subsequently mentions.

"Well, I have him in Italian," said the barber, "but I don't understand him."

"It is just as well you don't,"[16] said the priest. "And on that score we might have excused the captain if he had not brought him into Spain and turned him into Castilian. He robbed him of a great deal of his natural force, and so do all those who try to turn books written in verse into another language, for with all the pains they take and all the cleverness they show, they never can reach the level of the originals as they were first produced. In short, I say that this book, and all that may be found treating of the Matter of France,[17] should be thrown into or deposited in some dry well until after more consideration it is settled what is to be done with them—with the exception of a *Bernardo del Carpio* that is going about and another called *Roncesvalles*.[18] These, if they come into my hands, shall pass at once into those of the housekeeper, and from hers into the fire without any reprieve."

To all this the barber gave his assent and looked upon it as right and proper, being persuaded that the priest was a good Christian and so loyal to the truth that he would not for the world say anything otherwise. Opening another book he saw it was *Palmerín of Oliva*[19] and beside it was another called *Palmerin of England*,"[20] seeing which the licentiate said, "Let the Olive be made into firewood at once and burned until no ashes even are left; and let that Palm of England be kept and preserved as a thing that stands alone, and let another case be made for it like the one Alexander found among the spoils of Darius and set aside for the safe keeping of the works of the poet Homer.[21] This book, my friend, is significant for two reasons, first because it is very good, and secondly because it is said to have been written by a wise and discerning king of Portugal.[22] All the adventures at the Castle of Miraguarda are excellent and of admirable creativity, and the language is polished and clear, faithfully observing the style befitting each speaker with propriety and good judgment. Provided it seems good to you then, Master Nicholas, I say let this and *Amadís of Gaul* be exempt from the penalty of fire. As for all the rest, let them perish without further question or inquiry."

"No, my friend," said the barber, "for the book that I have here is the famous *Don Belianís*."[23]

[16] *It is just as well you don't:* The priest may be alluding to the fact that later Spanish translations of *Orlando Furioso*, which were reviewed by the Inquisition, censored passages deemed anticlerical or licentious.

[17] *Matter of France:* Body of medieval literature associated with the court of Charlemagne.

[18] Bernardo del Carpio *that is going about and another called* Roncesvalles: The first is probably the poem *History of the Feats and Deeds of the Invincible Knight Bernardo del Carpio* (Agustín Alonso, 1585).

[19] Palmerín of Oliva: first in the Palmerín cycle (Francisco Vázquez, 1511).

[20] Palmerín of England: See footnote 11, page 26.

[21] *Alexander . . . Homer:* Plutarch writes that when Alexander the Great defeated the Persian monarch Darius III, he found among the spoils an exquisite coffer that he used to store his most valuable possession: a copy of the *Iliad* that had belonged to his teacher, Aristotle.

[22] *wise and discerning king of Portugal:* It was erroneously believed that Palmerín of England was written by King John II of Portugal.

[23] Don Belianís: See footnote 13, page 17.

"Well, the first part," said the priest, "along with the second, third, and fourth, stand in need of a little rhubarb to purge their excess of bile,[24] and they must be cleared of all that stuff about the Castle of Fame[25] and other more severe blunders. Therefore, let them be allowed an overseas term,[26] and, consistent with their reform, so shall mercy or justice be meted out to them. In the meantime, my friend, keep them in your house and let no one read them."

"With all my heart," said the barber; and not caring to tire himself with reading more books of chivalry, he told the housekeeper to take all the big ones and throw them into the yard. This was not said to one dull or deaf, but to one who enjoyed burning them more than spinning a web.[27] Seizing about eight at a time, she flung them out of the window.

In carrying so many together she let one fall at the feet of the barber, who took it up, curious to know whose it was. He found that it was entitled *History of the Famous Knight Tirante el Blanco*.[28]

"God bless me!" said the priest with a shout, "*Tirante el Blanco* here! Hand it over, my good sir, for I declare that it contains a treasury of enjoyment and a mine of recreation. Here is Don Kyrieleison of Montalban, a valiant knight, and his brother Tomás of Montalban, and the knight Fonseca, along with the battle the bold Tirante fought with the mastiff, the witticisms of the damsel Placerdemivida,[29] the loves and wiles of the widow Reposada, and the empress in love with the squire Hipólito. In truth, my friend, by right of its style it is the best book in the world. Here knights eat and sleep, and die in their beds, and make their wills before dying, and a great deal more of which there is nothing in all the other books. Nevertheless, I say he who wrote it—since he did not produce all this claptrap intentionally—deserves to be sent to the galleys for life.[30] Take it home with you and read it, and you will see that what I have said is true."

[24] *rhubarb to purge their excess of bile:* Rhubarb was used as a purgative to vent choleric humors. The priest may be alluding to Don Belianís' irascible nature.

[25] *Castle of Fame:* magic traveling castle in *Don Belianís*.

[26] *overseas term:* a long period of time.

[27] *spinning a web:* In the criminal underworld, "spinning a web" (*echar una tela*) was a euphemism for "making love".

[28] Tirante el Blanco: *Tirante lo Blanch* (1490, Joanot Martorell), Valencian chivalric romance translated into Castilian in 1511.

[29] *Kyrieleison ... Placerdemivida:* The humor, as evidenced in character names like "Kyrieleison" (Lord, Have Mercy) and "Placerdemivida" (Pleasure of My Life) and the juxtaposition of lofty and mundane, anticipates some of the comedic strategies Cervantes would use in *Don Quixote*.

[30] *deserves to be sent to the galleys for life:* The priest's assessment about *Tirante el Blanco* may be taken in opposite directions, depending on where the reader places the accent in the speaker's irony. In one reading, the priest minimizes the genius of the author and figuratively condemns him to row in the galleys. Another reading takes "sent to the galleys" (*echar a las galeras*) as "sent to the printer", where galleys are typeset proofs used in publishing. Understood this way, the priest praises the writer for accidentally stumbling on something brilliant and wishes for his work to be widely published.

"As you wish," said the barber. "And what are we to do with these little books that are left?"[31]

"These must not be chivalry but poetry," said the priest. Opening one he saw it was the *Diana*[32] of Jorge de Montemayor, and supposing all the others to be of the same kind, he said, "These do not deserve to be burned like the others, for they neither do nor can do the mischief the books of chivalry have done, being books of entertainment that can hurt no one."

"Ah, señor!" said the niece. "Your worship had better order these to be burned as well as the others. For it would be no wonder if, after being cured of his chivalry disorder, my uncle, by reading these, took a fancy to become a shepherd and range the woods and fields singing and piping; or, what would be still worse, to become a poet, which they say is an incurable and infectious malady."

"The damsel is right," said the priest. "We will do well to put this stumbling block and temptation out of our friend's way. To begin then with the *Diana* of Montemayor, I am of the opinion it should not be burned but that it should be expunged of everything having to do with the sage Felicia and the magic water[33] and of almost all the longer pieces of verse. Let it happily keep its prose and the honor of being the first of books of its kind."

"This next one," said the barber, "is the *Diana* entitled *The Second Part*, by the Salamancan, and this other has the same title, and its author is Gil Polo."[34]

"As for the one by the Salamancan," replied the priest, "let it go to swell the number of the condemned in the yard, but let Gil Polo's be preserved as if it came from Apollo himself. Get on, my good sir, and make haste, for it is growing late."

"This book," said the barber, opening another, "is *The Ten Books of the Fortune of Love*,[35] written by Antonio de Lofraso, a Sardinian poet."

"By the orders I have received," said the priest, "since Apollo has been Apollo, the Muses have been Muses, and poets have been poets, so humorous and outlandish a book as this has never been written, and in its way it is the best and the most singular of all of this species that have as yet appeared. He who has not read it may be sure he has never read what is delightful. Give it here, my friend, for I relish having found it more than if they had given me a cassock of Florentine wool."

[31] *these little books that are left:* Sometimes the size of a book gave a hint about its contents. Pastoral romances, whose audience was mostly female, were smaller in size than the large, cumbersome chivalric romances.

[32] Diana: The pastoral romance, which tells in alternating prose and poetry the fortunes of pining shepherds who live in an idyllic countryside, became a literary craze in Spain with the publication of *The Seven Books of La Diana* (1559). In this sense, *La Diana* played an analogous role to *Amadís of Gaul* in spawning a generation of continuations and imitations.

[33] *the sage Felicia and the magic water:* At a crucial juncture in the book, an enchantress dispenses magic water to the love-crossed shepherds, which instantly resolves their conflicts.

[34] Second Part . . . *Gil Polo:* The two sequels are *The Second Part of La Diana* (Alonso Pérez, 1563) and *Diana in Love* (Gil Polo, 1564).

[35] The Ten Books of the Fortune of Love: pastoral romance of 1573.

He put it aside with extreme satisfaction, and the barber went on, "These that come next are *The Shepherd of Iberia*, *Nymphs of Henares*, and *Jealousy's Disenchantment*."[36]

"Then all we have to do," said the priest, "is to hand them over to the secular arm[37] of the housekeeper. Ask me not why, or we shall never be finished."

"This next is *The Shepherd of Fílida*."[38]

"That one's no shepherd," said the priest, "but a highly polished courtier. Let it be preserved as a precious jewel."

"This large one here," said the barber, "is called *The Treasury of Various Poems*."[39]

"If there were not so many of them," said the priest, "they would be more appreciated. This book must be weeded and cleansed of certain vulgarities alongside its excellences. Let it be preserved because the author is a friend of mine, and out of respect for other more heroic and loftier works that he has written."

"This," continued the barber, "is the *Cancionero* of López Maldonado."[40]

"The author of that book, too," said the priest, "is a great friend of mine, and his verses from his own mouth are the admiration of all who hear them. Such is the sweetness of his voice that he enchants when he chants them. The eclogues are quite long, but 'what is good is never excessive.' Let it be kept with those that have been set apart. What book is that next to it?"

"The *Galatea* of Miguel de Cervantes,"[41] said the barber.

"That Cervantes has been for many years a great friend of mine, and to my knowledge he has had more experience in reverses than in verses. His book has its inventive moments; it presents us with something but brings nothing to a conclusion. We must wait for the Second Part it promises. Perhaps with this addition it may succeed in winning the full measure of mercy that is now denied it. In the meantime, my good sir, keep it shut up in your own quarters."

"Very good," said the barber. "Here come three together: The *Araucana* of Don Alonso de Ercilla, the *Austríada* of Juan Rufo, magistrate of Córdoba, and the *Montserrato* of the Valencian poet Cristóbal de Virués."[42]

[36] The Shepherd of Iberia, Nymphs of Henares, *and* Jealousy's Disenchantment: Pastoral romances by Bernardo de la Vega (1591), Bernardo González de Bobadilla (1587), and Bartolomé López de Enciso (1586), respectively.

[37] *secular arm:* If an Inquisition tribunal sentenced an offender to death, it handed over (literally, "relaxed") the offender to the civil authorities to carry out the punishment. In this way, the Holy Office sought to maintain the purity of its professed role as an investigative and disciplining body and not an instrument of punishment.

[38] The Shepherd of Fílida: by Luis Gálvez de Montalvo, 1582.

[39] The Treasury of Various Poems: edited by Pedro de Padilla, 1580.

[40] Cancionero *of López Maldonado:* Anthology of courtly poetry published in 1586. It includes two early poems of Cervantes.

[41] *The* Galatea *of Miguel de Cervantes:* Cervantes' first published book (1585). Few of the love stories are resolved by the end. Cervantes would continue to promise an imminent sequel until the end of his life.

[42] *Here come three . . . de Virués:* These are narrative poems in the epic register. *The Araucana* (1569–1589) tells of the Spanish conquest of Chile and *The Austríada* (1584) of

"These three books," said the priest, "are the best that have been written in Castilian in heroic verse,[43] and they may compare with the most famous of Italy. Let them be preserved as the richest treasures of poetry that Spain possesses."

The priest was too tired to look at any more books, and so he decided that all the rest should be burned without inspection. But just then the barber held open one called *The Tears of Angelica*.[44]

"I should have shed tears myself," said the priest when he heard the title, "had I ordered that book to be burned, for its author was one of the famous poets of the world, not just of Spain, and was very successful in the translation of some of Ovid's fables."

---

the 1571 Spanish naval victory against the Ottomans at Lepanto. *The Montserrato* (1587) narrates the legend of the founding of the monastery at Montserrat.

[43] *heroic verse*: verses of eleven syllables.

[44] The Tears of Angelica: *The First Part of Angelica* (Luis Barahona de Soto, 1586), a spinoff of *Orlando Furioso*.

CHAPTER VII

OF THE SECOND SALLY OF OUR WORTHY KNIGHT DON QUIXOTE OF LA MANCHA

At that moment Don Quixote began to shout out, "Here, here, valiant knights! Here is need for you to put forth the might of your strong arms, for knights of the court[1] are carrying the day in the tournament!"

Called away by this noise and outcry, they proceeded no farther with the scrutiny of the remaining books, and so it is thought that *The Carolea*, *The Lion of Spain*, and *The Deeds of the Emperor*, written by Don Luis de Ávila,[2] went to the fire unseen and unheard; for no doubt they were among those that remained. Perhaps if the priest had seen them they would not have undergone so severe a sentence.

When they reached Don Quixote, he was already out of bed and was still shouting and raving, slashing and cutting all round, as wide awake as if he had never slept. They took hold of him and by force got him back to bed, and when Don Quixote had calmed down a little, addressing the priest, he said to him, "In truth, Señor Archbishop Turpin, it is a great disgrace for us who call ourselves the Twelve Peers so carelessly to allow the knights of the court to gain the victory in this tournament, we the adventurers having carried off the honor on the three former days."

"Hush, my good fellow," said the priest. "If it please God, your luck may turn, and what is lost today may be won tomorrow. For the present let your worship take care of your health, for it seems to me that you are over-fatigued, if not badly wounded."

"Wounded no," said Don Quixote, "but bruised and battered no doubt, for that bastard Don Roland has beaten me with the trunk of an oak tree, and all for envy, because he sees that I alone rival him in his achievements. But I should not call myself Reinaldos[3] of Montalban if he did not pay me for it as soon as I rise from this bed, in spite of all his enchantments. For the present let them bring

[1] *knights of the court: cortesanos*, the competing knights from the hosting castle (what we would call "the home team"), as opposed to the adventurers (*aventureros*) visiting from other courts (see below).

[2] The Carolea ... *Don Luis de Ávila:* three additional narrative poems that recount great historical deeds.

[3] *for that bastard Don Roland . . . Reinaldos:* Don Quixote is reliving a scene at the beginning of *Orlando Furioso* where Orlando (Roland) and Rinaldo (Reinaldos) fight over Angelica.

me something to eat, for that, I feel, is what will be more to my purpose. Leave it to me to avenge myself."

They did as he wished. They gave him something to eat, and once more he fell asleep, leaving them marveling at his madness.

That night the housekeeper burned to ashes all the books that were in the yard and in the whole house. No doubt some of those consumed deserved to be preserved in everlasting archives, but their fate (and the laziness of the examiner) did not permit it, and so in them was verified the proverb, 'The innocent suffer for the guilty.'

One of the remedies the priest and the barber immediately applied to their friend's disorder was to wall up and plaster the room where the books were, so that when he got up he wouldn't find them—perhaps with the cause being removed, the effect would cease. They would say that a sorcerer had carried them off, room and all. This was done with all dispatch.

Two days later Don Quixote got up, and the first thing he did was to go see his books. Not finding the room where he had left it, he wandered about looking for it. He came to the place where the door used to be, tried it with his hands, and turned and twisted his eyes in every direction without saying a word. After a good while, he asked his housekeeper the whereabouts of the room that held his books.

The housekeeper, who had been already well instructed in what she was to answer, said, "What room or what nothing is your worship looking for? There are neither room nor books in this house now, for the devil himself has carried everything away."

"It was not the devil," said the niece, "but a sorcerer who came on a cloud one night after the day your worship first set out. Dismounting from astride a serpent, he entered the room. What he did there I don't know, but after a little while he took off, flying through the roof, and left the house full of smoke. When we went to see what he had done, we saw neither book nor room; but we remember very well, the housekeeper and I, that when he left the old villain said in a loud voice that, because of a private grudge he held against the owner of the books and the room, he had done mischief in that house that would soon be discovered. He said too that his name was the Sage Muñatón."

"He must have said Frestón,"[4] said Don Quixote.

"I don't know whether he called himself Frestón or Fritón,"[5] said the housekeeper, "I only know that his name ended with '-tón.'"

"So it does," said Don Quixote, "and he is a sage enchanter, a great enemy of mine, who has a spite against me because he knows by his arts and lore that in time I am to engage in single combat with a knight whom he befriends and that I am to conquer, and he will be unable to prevent it. For this reason, he endeavors to do to me all the ill he can; but I promise him it will be hard for him to oppose or avoid what is decreed by Heaven."

[4] *Frestón:* The sorcerer *Fristón* is the fictitious chronicler of *Don Belianís of Greece*.
[5] *Fritón: Frito* (Fried).

"Who doubts that?" said the niece. "But, uncle, who involves you in all these quarrels? Would it not be better to remain at peace in your own house instead of roaming the world 'looking for better bread than ever came of wheat,' never reflecting that 'many seek wool and come back shorn'?"

"My dear niece," replied Don Quixote, "how mistaken you are! Before they shear me, I shall have plucked away and stripped off the beards of all who dare to touch even the tip of a single hair of mine."

The two were unwilling to say anything more, as they saw that his anger was kindling.

As it turned out, Don Quixote remained at home two weeks very quietly without showing any signs of a desire to take up his former delusions. During this time, he held lively discussions with his two comrades, the priest and the barber, on the point he maintained, that knights-errant were what the world stood most in need of and that in him was to be accomplished the revival of knight-errantry. The priest sometimes contradicted him, sometimes agreed with him, for if he had not followed this ruse, living with him would have been impossible.

Meanwhile Don Quixote sought a farm laborer, a neighbor of his, an upstanding man (if indeed that title can be given to someone poor), but with very little in the way of brains.[6] In a word, he so talked him over, and with such arguments and promises, that the poor peasant made up his mind to sally forth with him as his squire. Don Quixote told him, among other things, that he ought to be thrilled to accompany him because in the twinkling of an eye one of their adventures would win them an island, which he would get to govern. On these and similar promises Sancho Panza (for so the laborer was called) left wife and children and engaged himself as squire to his neighbor.

Don Quixote next set about getting some money. Selling one thing and pawning another (and making a bad bargain at every turn), he got together a decent sum. He provided himself with a buckler, which he borrowed from a friend, and restoring his battered helmet as best he could, he notified his squire Sancho of the day and hour he meant to set out, that he might provide himself with what he thought most needful. Above all, he charged him to take a saddlebag with him. Sancho said he would, and that he also meant to take a very good donkey he had, as he was not used to going on foot.

About the donkey, Don Quixote hesitated a little, trying to remember whether any knight-errant took with him a donkey-mounted squire, but no example came to his memory. For all that, however, he determined to take him, intending to furnish him with a more honorable mount when the chance presented itself by appropriating the horse of the first discourteous knight he encountered. Himself he provided with shirts and such other things as he could, according to the advice the innkeeper had given him. All of this being done—without Sancho Panza taking leave of his wife and children or Don Quixote taking leave of his

[6] *very little in the way of brains:* literally, "very little salt in his skull", a reference to the practice during baptism of sprinkling salt on the baby's tongue to symbolize the wisdom leading to eternal life.

housekeeper and niece—they sallied forth one night from the village unseen by anyone. They made such good progress that by daylight they were safe from discovery, even should search be made for them.

Sancho rode on his donkey like a patriarch, with his saddlebag and wineskin, eager to see himself made governor of the island his master had promised him. Don Quixote decided upon taking the same route and road he had taken on his first journey, that over the Campo de Montiel, which he traveled with less discomfort than on the last occasion, for as it was early morning and the rays of the sun fell on them at an angle, the heat did not bother them.

And now said Sancho Panza to his master, "Your worship will take care, sir knight-errant, not to forget about the island you've promised me, for no matter how big it might be, I'll have what it takes to govern it."

To which Don Quixote replied, "You must know, friend Sancho Panza, that it was the common practice of the knights-errant of old to make their squires governors of the islands or kingdoms they won, and I am determined that there shall be no failure on my part in so liberal a custom. On the contrary, I mean to improve upon it, for they sometimes, and perhaps most frequently, waited until their squires were old, and then when they had had enough of service and hard days and worse nights, they gave them the title of count, or at the most marquis, of some trifling valley or province. But if you live and I live, it may well be that before six days are over, I will have won some kingdom that has others dependent upon it, which will be just the thing to allow you to be crowned king of one of them. Nor think this difficult, for life and lot fall to such knights in ways never before seen or imagined, so that I might easily give even more than I've promised you."

"In that case," said Sancho Panza, "if I should become a king by one of those miracles your worship speaks of, even Juana Gutiérrez, my old woman, would come to be queen and my children princes."

"Well, who doubts it?" said Don Quixote.

"I doubt it," replied Sancho Panza, "because for my part I'm convinced that though God should shower down kingdoms on earth, not one of them would fit the head of Mari Gutiérrez. Let me tell you, señor, she is not worth two maravedis for a queen. Countess will fit her better, and that only with God's help."

"Leave it to God, Sancho," returned Don Quixote, "for he will give her what suits her best; but do not undervalue yourself so much as to come to be content with anything less than being governor of a province."

"I won't, señor," answered Sancho, "especially since I have such a fine master as your worship, who will know how to give me everything that suits me and that I can handle."

CHAPTER VIII

OF THE SUCCESS THAT THE VALIANT DON QUIXOTE HAD IN THE TERRIBLE AND UNDREAMT-OF ADVENTURE OF THE WINDMILLS, WITH OTHER EVENTS WORTHY TO BE FITLY RECORDED

They presently came in sight of thirty or forty windmills that may be found on that plain, and as soon as Don Quixote saw them he said to his squire, "Fortune is arranging our affairs better than we could have hoped for. Look there, friend Sancho Panza, where thirty or more monstrous giants present themselves, all of whom I mean to engage in battle and slay, and with whose spoils we shall begin to make our fortunes; for this is righteous warfare, and it is a great service to God to sweep so evil a breed from off the face of the earth."

"What giants?" asked Sancho Panza.

"Those you see there," answered his master, "with the long arms, some of them nearly two leagues[1] long."

"Look, your worship," said Sancho, "what we see there are not giants but windmills, and what seem to be their arms are the sails that the wind turns to make the millstone move."

"It is easy to see," replied Don Quixote, "that you are not used to this business of adventures. Those are giants. If you are afraid, away with you from this place and betake yourself to prayer while I engage them in fierce and unequal combat."

With these words, he gave the spur to his steed Rocinante, heedless of the cries of his squire Sancho, who was warning him that without a doubt they were windmills and not giants he was going to attack. So certain was he that they were giants that he neither heard Sancho's cries nor noticed what they were as he approached, but made at them shouting, "Fly not, cowards and vile beings, for a single knight attacks you."

A slight breeze at this moment sprang up, and the great sails began to move, seeing which Don Quixote exclaimed, "Though you flourish more arms than the giant Briareus,[2] you will have to reckon with me!"

[1] *leagues:* A league is roughly three miles or five kilometers. These giants are big, even for a chivalric romance.

[2] *Briareus:* giant with a hundred arms and fifty heads, the offspring of Uranus and Gaia.

Having spoken thus, commending himself with all his heart to his lady Dulcinea, imploring her to support him in such a peril, with lance in rest[3] and buckler raised, he charged at Rocinante's fullest gallop and fell upon the first mill that stood in front of him. As he drove his lance point into the sail, the wind whirled it round with such force that it shattered the lance to pieces, sweeping with it horse and rider, who went rolling over on the plain, both in a sorry condition. Sancho hurried to his aid as fast as his donkey could go. When he drew near, he found his master unable to move, so great was the blow that brought Rocinante down on him.

"God bless me!" said Sancho. "Didn't I tell your worship to think twice about what you were going to do, for they were only windmills? No one could have made any mistake about it unless he had windmills turning in his head."

"Hush, friend Sancho," replied Don Quixote. "The fortunes of war, more than any other endeavor, are subject to constant change. Moreover, I think (and it is the truth) that the same sage Frestón who carried off my study and books has turned these giants into windmills in order to rob me of the glory of vanquishing them. Such is the enmity he bears me. But in the end, his wicked arts will avail but little against my worthy sword."

"God order it as he may," said Sancho Panza, and helping him to rise he got him up again on Rocinante, whose shoulder was half out of joint.

As they discussed the recent adventure, they continued down the road to Puerto Lápice, for there, said Don Quixote, they could not fail to find adventures in abundance and variety, as it was a great thoroughfare. For all that, he was much grieved at the loss of his lance, and saying so to his squire, he added, "I remember having read how a Spanish knight, Diego Pérez de Vargas by name, having broken his sword in battle, tore from an oak a heavy bough or branch, and with it did such things that day, and pounded so many Moors, that he got the surname of "Machuca,"[4] and he and his descendants from that day forth were called "Vargas y Machuca." I mention this because from the first oak I see I mean to tear such another branch, large and stout like that, with which I am resolved to do such deeds that you should consider yourself very fortunate in being found worthy to come and see them and be an eyewitness of things that will with difficulty be believed."

"As God wills," said Sancho, "I believe it all as your worship says it. But straighten yourself a little, for you look slouched on one side, which must be from the great might of your fall."

"That is the truth," said Don Quixote, "and if I make no complaint of the pain, it is because knights-errant are not permitted to complain of any wound, though their very bowels be coming out through it."

[3] *lance in rest:* When the knight was ready to charge, he would set his lance in the lance rest, a metal cradle extending from the side of his breastplate. Because the lance shaft was wider than its handle, the lance rest would secure the weapon against the momentum of the assault.

[4] *Machuca:* derived from the verb *machucar*, "to pound" or "to crush". The incident occurred during the siege of Jérez in 1223.

"If so," said Sancho, "I have nothing to say; but God knows I would rather your worship complained when anything ailed you. For my part, I confess I must complain however small the ache may be—unless this rule about not complaining extends to the squires of knights-errant also."

Don Quixote could not help laughing at his squire's simplicity. He assured him he might complain whenever and however he chose, just as he liked; for thus far, he had never read of anything to the contrary in the order of knighthood.

Sancho pointed out to him that it was dinnertime, to which his master answered that he wanted nothing himself just then, but that his squire might eat when he had a mind. With this permission, Sancho settled himself as comfortably as he could on his beast, and taking out of the saddlebag what he had stowed away in it, he ambled along behind his master munching leisurely, and from time to time taking a pull at the wineskin with a relish that a well-stocked Málaga tavern keeper might have envied.[5] While he went on in this way, one swig after the next, he never gave a thought to any of the promises his master had made him, nor did he count it as hardship but as recreation this going in quest of adventures, however dangerous they might be.

Afterwards, they spent the night among some trees, from one of which Don Quixote plucked a dry branch that would serve well enough as a lance and fixed on it the head he had removed from the broken one. All that night Don Quixote lay awake thinking of his lady Dulcinea in order to conform to what he had read in his books, how many a night in the forests and deserts knights would lie sleepless, lost in the memories of their mistresses. Not so did Sancho Panza spend it, for having his stomach full of something stronger than chicory water[6] he slept the night through; and if his master had not called him, neither the rays of the sun beating on his face nor all the cheery notes of the birds welcoming the approach of day would have had power to waken him. When he got up, he tried the wineskin and found it somewhat less full than the night before, which grieved his heart because they did not seem to be on the way to remedy the deficiency any time soon. Don Quixote did not care to eat breakfast, for as has been already said, he confined himself to savory recollections for nourishment.

They returned to the road they had set out on, leading to Puerto Lápice, and at three in the afternoon they came in sight of it. "Here, brother Sancho Panza," said Don Quixote when he saw it, "we may plunge our hands up to the elbows in what they call adventures; but take heed, even if you see me in the greatest danger in the world, you must not put a hand to your sword in my defense, unless indeed you determine that those who assail me are rabble or base folk. For in that case you may very properly aid me; but if they be knights, it is on no account permitted to you by the laws of knighthood to help me until you yourself have been dubbed a knight."

"Most certainly, señor," replied Sancho, "your worship shall be fully obeyed in this matter—all the more since, for my part, I am peaceful and no friend to

[5] *well-stocked Málaga . . . have envied:* Wines from the region around Málaga had a high reputation in seventeenth-century Spain.

[6] *chicory water:* a sleep aid.

mixing in strife and quarrels. It's true that when it comes to defending my own person, I won't give much heed to those laws; for laws human and divine allow anyone to defend himself against whoever attacks him."

"That I grant," said Don Quixote, "but in this matter of aiding me against knights you must put a restraint upon your natural impetuosity."

"I will do so, I promise," answered Sancho. "I'll keep this precept as carefully as Sunday."

While they were thus talking, there appeared on the road two friars of the Order of Saint Benedict[7] mounted on two dromedaries, for not less tall were the two mules they rode on. They wore traveling spectacles and carried sunshades. Behind them came a coach attended by four or five persons on horseback and two muleteers on foot. In the coach there was, as afterwards was discovered, a Biscayan[8] lady on her way to Seville, where her husband was about to take passage for the Indies with an appointment of great prestige. The friars, though traveling the same road, were not in her company.

Barely had Don Quixote seen them than he said to his squire, "Either I am mistaken, or this is going to be the most famous adventure that has ever been seen, for those black bodies we see there must be, and doubtless are, sorcerers who are carrying off some stolen princess in that coach. With all my might I must undo this wrong."

"This will be worse than the windmills," said Sancho. "Look, señor: those are friars of Saint Benedict, and the coach plainly belongs to some travelers. I tell you to be careful what you do and don't let the devil mislead you."

"I have told you already, Sancho," replied Don Quixote, "that on the subject of adventures you know little. What I say is the truth, as you shall see presently."

So saying, he advanced and posted himself in the middle of the road along which the friars were traveling. As soon as he thought they had come near enough to hear what he said, he cried aloud, "Devilish and unnatural beings, release instantly the highborn princesses whom you are carrying off by force in this coach, else prepare to meet a speedy death as the just punishment of your evil deeds."

The friars drew rein and stood wondering at the appearance of Don Quixote as well as at his words, to which they replied, "Señor Caballero, we are not devilish or unnatural, but two brothers of Saint Benedict following our road. Nor do we know whether or not there are any captive princesses coming in this coach."

"No soft words with me, for I know who you are, lying rabble," said Don Quixote. And without waiting for a reply, he spurred Rocinante and with leveled lance charged the first friar with such fury and determination, that, if the friar had not flung himself off the mule, he would have brought him to the ground against his will and left him wounded badly, if not killed outright. The second brother, seeing how his comrade was treated, drove his heels into his castle of a mule and made off across the country faster than the wind.

[7] *Order of Saint Benedict:* The Benedictines, founded by Benedict of Nursia in 529, are the oldest monastic order in the Catholic Church. Their habits were usually black.

[8] *Biscayan:* from the Basque region in northern Spain.

Sancho Panza, when he saw the friar on the ground, dismounting briskly from his donkey, rushed toward him and began to strip off his habit. At that instant, the friars' muleteers came up and asked what he was stripping him for. Sancho answered that this fell to him lawfully as spoils of the battle that his lord Don Quixote had won. The muleteers, who were not ones to joke and did not understand all this about battles and spoils, seeing that Don Quixote was some distance off talking to the travelers in the coach, fell upon Sancho. Knocking him down, they battered him with kicks and plucked his beard, leaving him stretched breathless and senseless on the ground, then without delay helped the friar to mount. He, trembling, terrified, and pale, as soon as he found himself in the saddle, spurred after his companion, who was standing at a distance looking on, watching the result of the onslaught. Not caring to wait for the end of the affair just begun, the two pursued their journey, making more crosses than if they had the devil after them.

Don Quixote, as has been said, was speaking to the lady in the coach. "Your beauty, my lady," said he, "may now dispose of your person as may be most in accordance with your pleasure, for the pride of your ravishers lies prostrate on the ground through this strong arm of mine. And lest you should be pining to know the name of your deliverer, know that I am called Don Quixote of La Mancha, knight-errant and adventurer, and captive to the peerless and beautiful lady Dulcinea del Toboso. In return for the service you have received of me, I ask no more than that you should return to El Toboso, and on my behalf present yourself before that lady and tell her what I have done to set you free."

One of the squires in attendance upon the coach, a Biscayan, was listening to all Don Quixote was saying. When he heard that Don Quixote would not allow the coach to go on but was insisting that it return at once to El Toboso, he lunged at him, and seizing his lance addressed him in bad Castilian and worse Biscayan after this fashion:[9] "Begone, caballero, and ill go you. By the God made me, unless you leave coach, slay you as here a Biscayan is."

Don Quixote understood him quite well and answered him very calmly, "If you were a knight, which you are not, I should have already chastised your folly and rashness, miserable creature."

To which the Biscayan returned, "I no gentleman? I swear to God you lie so much as I am Christian! If you drop lance and draw sword, soon shall you see you are carrying water to the cat.[10] Biscayan on land, hidalgo at sea, hidalgo at the devil, and look, if you say otherwise, you lie!"

"'*You will see presently,' said Agrajes*,"[11] replied Don Quixote; and throwing his lance on the ground, he drew his sword, braced his buckler on his arm, and attacked the Biscayan bent upon taking his life.

[9] *bad Castilian . . . after this fashion:* The Basque language has nothing in common with Castilian Spanish, which is derived from Latin.

[10] *carrying water to the cat:* The Biscayan means to say "soon you shall see me carrying the cat to water", by which is understood "soon you shall see me get my way."

[11] 'You will see presently,' said Agrajes: Don Quixote quotes a proverbial taunt that Amadís of Gaul uses against an enemy.

The Biscayan saw him coming on, and though he wished to dismount from his mule—for he had no confidence in it, being one of those sorry ones let out for hire—he was forced to draw his sword. Luckily for him, however, he was near the coach, and he was able to snatch from it a cushion that served him for a shield. Thus they went at each other as if they had been two mortal enemies.

The others tried to make peace between them but could not, for the Biscayan declared in his disjointed speech that if they did not let him finish his battle, he would kill his mistress and everyone that tried to prevent him. The lady in the coach, amazed and terrified at what she saw, ordered the coachman to draw aside a little, and set herself to watch this fierce struggle, in the course of which the Biscayan struck Don Quixote a mighty blow on the shoulder over the top of his buckler, which, given to one without armor, would have cleft him to the waist.

Don Quixote, feeling the weight of this prodigious blow, cried aloud saying, "O lady of my soul, Dulcinea, flower of beauty, come to the aid of this your knight, who, in fulfilling his obligations to your beauty, finds himself in this extreme peril." To say this, to lift his sword, to shield himself well behind his buckler, and to assail the Biscayan—all this was the work of an instant, determined as he was to risk all upon a single blow.

The Biscayan, seeing him come on in this way, was convinced of his courage by his spirited bearing and resolved to follow his example. And so he waited for him, keeping well under the cover of his cushion, unable to turn his mule this way or that; for it, dead tired and never meant for this kind of game, could not stir a step.

On then, to repeat, came Don Quixote against the wary Biscayan, with uplifted sword and a firm intention of splitting him in half, while on his side, the Biscayan waited for him sword in hand, under the protection of his cushion. Everyone present stood trembling, waiting in suspense for what would come of the blows that threatened to fall. The lady in the coach and her attendant maids were making a thousand vows and offerings to all the images and shrines of Spain, that God might deliver her squire and all of them from this great peril in which they found themselves.

But to spoil everything, the author of this history leaves the battle here hanging in the air, giving as his excuse that he could find nothing more written about Don Quixote's achievements than what has been already set forth. It is quite true that the second author of this work was unwilling to believe that a history so curious could have been sentenced to oblivion, or that the great lights of La Mancha could have been so undiscerning as not to preserve in their archives or registries some documents referring to this famous knight. Thus persuaded, he did not despair of finding the conclusion of this pleasant history, which, with Heaven's favor, he did find in a way that shall be related in the Second Part.[12]

[12] *the author of this history . . . in the Second Part:* The artifice of multiple authors will become clearer in the next chapter. The text now distinguishes a historian who has recorded the deeds of Don Quixote, described as the author of this history from a writer who has compiled and edited those deeds for publication, the second author. The second author, as narrator, switches to the first person in the next chapter.

SECOND PART OF
THE INGENIOUS GENTLEMAN
DON QUIXOTE DE LA MANCHA

CHAPTER IX

IN WHICH IS BROUGHT TO AN END THE STUPENDOUS BATTLE BETWEEN THE GALLANT BISCAYAN AND THE VALIANT MANCHEGAN

In the First Part of this history, we left the valiant Biscayan and the renowned Don Quixote with drawn swords uplifted, ready to deliver two such slashing blows that if they had fallen at full fury, they would have easily split them asunder from top to toe and laid them open like a pomegranate. And at this critical point, the delightful history came to a stop and was cut short without any intimation from the author where what was missing was to be found.

This distressed me greatly, because the pleasure of having read such a small part turned to vexation at the thought that no clear path presented itself of finding the large part that in my judgment was left of such an interesting tale. It seemed to me to be a thing impossible and contrary to all precedent that so good a knight should have been without some sage to undertake the task of writing his marvelous achievements. Such a thing was never wanting to any of those knights-errant—

> those, of whom they say,
> went out to seek adventure;[1]

for every one of them had, as if by design, one or two sages, who not only recorded their deeds but described their most trivial thoughts and follies, however secret they might be. A good knight of this sort could not have been so unfortunate as not to have what Platir[2] and others like him had in abundance. And so I could not bring myself to believe that such a gallant tale had been left maimed and mutilated. I laid the blame on the evils of Time, the devourer and destroyer of all things, that had either concealed or consumed it.

On the other hand, it struck me that, inasmuch as among his books there had been found such modern ones as *Jealousy's Disenchantment* and *Nymphs and Shepherds of Henares*,[3] his story must likewise be modern, and that though it may not be written down, it might exist in the memory of the people of his village and

[1] *those . . . to seek adventure:* faintly quoted from Petrarch's *Trionfi.*

[2] *Platir:* See footnote 11, page 51.

[3] Jealousy's Disenchantment *and* Nymphs and Shepherds of Henares: Books published, respectively, in 1586 and 1587. The newest book in Alonso Quixano's library, *The Shepherd of Iberia,* was published in 1591.

of villages nearby. This reflection kept me perplexed and longing to know really and truly the whole life and wondrous deeds of our famous Spaniard, Don Quixote of La Mancha, light and mirror of Manchegan chivalry, and the first that in our age and in these calamitous days devoted himself to the labor and exercise of the arms of knight-errantry—righting wrongs, aiding widows, and protecting damsels of that sort that used to ride about on their palfreys, whip in hand, with all their virginity about them, from mountain to mountain and valley to valley; and if it were not for some ruffian or boor with a hood and hatchet or monstrous giant that ravaged them, there were in days of yore damsels that at the end of eighty years (in all which time they had never slept a day under a roof) went to their graves as intact as the mothers that bore them.

I say, then, that in these and other respects our gallant Don Quixote is worthy of everlasting praise, nor should it be withheld even by me for the effort spent in searching for the conclusion of this delightful history; though I know well that if Heaven, chance, and good fortune had not helped me, the world would have remained deprived of an entertainment and pleasure that for a couple of hours or so may well occupy him who shall read it attentively.

The discovery of it occurred in this way:

One day when I was in the Alcaná of Toledo,[4] a boy came by to sell some notebooks and old papers to a silk merchant, and as I am fond of reading even the scraps of paper in the streets, led by this natural bent of mine, I took up one of the notebooks the boy had for sale. I saw that it was in characters I recognized as Arabic, and as I was unable to read them (though I could recognize them), I looked around to see if there were any Spanish-speaking Morisco at hand to read them for me.[5] Nor was there any great difficulty in finding such an interpreter, for even had I sought one for an older and better language[6] I should have found him. In short, chance provided me with one, who, when I told him what I wanted and put the book into his hands, opened it in the middle and after reading a little began to laugh.

I asked him what he was laughing at, and he replied that it was at a note written in the margin of the book. I asked him to tell me what it said; and he, still laughing replied, "In the margin, as I told you, this is written: 'They say that the Dulcinea del Toboso so often mentioned in this history had the best hand of any woman in La Mancha for salting pigs.'"

[4] *Alcaná of Toledo:* commercial district in central Toledo near the cathedral.

[5] *Morisco . . . read them for me:* Eight years after the fall of the last Moorish stronghold of Granada in 1492, the Spanish Crown effectively banned the practice of Islam from the newly acquired territory and in the following decades would outlaw Islam in the rest of Spain. The descendants of the Arabs and Berbers in the Iberian Peninsula, now nominally Christian, came to be called Moriscos. Since 1526 it had been illegal in Castile to speak or write Arabic, though Moorish culture persisted in the face of state repression. The text is either written in the Arabic language or *aljamía,* Castilian Spanish transcribed in Arabic characters.

[6] *older and better language:* i.e., Hebrew. Toledo was notable for its population of *conversos,* descendants of Jews who converted to Christianity prior to the 1492 edict forbidding the practice of Judaism.

When I heard Dulcinea del Toboso named, I was struck with surprise and amazement, for it occurred to me at once that these notebooks contained the history of Don Quixote. With this idea I pressed him to read the beginning. He did so, rendering on the spot the Arabic into Castilian, and told me it meant, "*History of Don Quixote of La Mancha*, written by Cide Hamete Benengeli, Arabic historian."

It required great composure to hide the joy I felt when the title of the book reached my ears. Snatching it from the silk merchant, I bought all the papers and notebooks from the boy for half a real. (Had he any sense, and had he known how eager I was to have them, he might have safely calculated on making more than six reals from the sale.) I withdrew at once with the Morisco into the cloister of the cathedral and begged him to translate all the notebooks that related to Don Quixote into the Castilian tongue without omitting or adding anything to them, offering him whatever payment he pleased. He was satisfied with two arrobas of raisins and two fanegas of wheat[7] and promised to translate them faithfully and with all dispatch. But to make the matter easier, and not to let such a precious find out of my hands, I took him to my house, where in little more than a month and a half he translated everything just as it is set down here.

In the first notebook, the battle between Don Quixote and the Biscayan was drawn in lifelike detail—the two of them holding the same poses that the history describes, their swords raised, the one protected by his buckler, the other by his cushion, and the Biscayan's mule so true to nature that you could tell it was a hired one a bowshot off. The Biscayan had an inscription under his feet which read, DON SANCHO DE AZPETIA,[8] which no doubt must have been his name; and at the feet of Rocinante was another that read, DON QUIXOTE. Rocinante was marvelously portrayed, so long and thin, so lank and lean, with so much backbone and so far gone in consumption, that he showed plainly with what good sense and propriety the name of Rocinante had been bestowed upon him. Near him was Sancho Panza holding the halter of his donkey, at whose feet was another label that read, SANCHO ZANCAS, and according to the picture, he must have had a big belly, a short body, and long shanks, for which reason, no doubt, the names of Panza and Zancas were given him,[9] for by these two surnames the history several times calls him. Some other minor particulars might be mentioned, but they are all of slight importance and have nothing to do with the true relation of the history. And no history can be bad so long as it is true.

If any objection is to be raised about the truth of the present history, it can only be that its author was an Arab, as lying is a very common propensity with

[7] *two arrobas of raisins and two fanegas of wheat:* Two arrobas of raisins would be roughly equivalent to fifty pounds, which along with the nearly two hundred pounds (two fanegas) of wheat, would make a generous supply of couscous, a staple of the Moorish diet.

[8] *Azpetia:* Azpeitia is a village in the present-day province of Guipúzcoa in the Basque Country; also, birthplace of Ignatius of Loyola.

[9] *the names of Panza and Zancas were given him:* "*Panza*" is a colloquial term for "belly". *Zancas* are shanks, the part of the leg between the knee and ankle.

those of that nation; though, as they are such enemies of ours,[10] it is conceivable that there were omissions rather than additions made in the course of it. So it appears to me, for where he could and should give freedom to his pen in praise of so worthy a knight, he seems to me deliberately to pass it over in silence, something ill done and worse conceived, it being the business and duty of historians to be exact, truthful, and wholly free from passion. Neither interest nor fear, hatred nor love, should make them swerve from the path of truth, whose mother is history—rival of time, storehouse of deeds, witness of the past, example and counsel for the present, and warning for the future. In this history, I know will be found all that can be desired in its most agreeable form, and if it be wanting in any good quality, I maintain it is the fault of its hound[11] of an author and not the fault of the subject.

Now then, the Second Part, according to the translation, began in this way:

With trenchant swords poised on high, it seemed as though the two valiant and wrathful combatants stood threatening heaven, earth, and hell—with such daring and resolve did they bear themselves. The fiery Biscayan was the first to strike a blow, which was delivered with such force and fury that had not the sword turned in its course, that single stroke would have sufficed to put an end to the bitter struggle and to all the adventures of our knight. But good fortune, which reserved him for greater things, turned aside the sword of his adversary, so that although it smote him upon the left shoulder, it did him no more harm than to strip that entire side of its armor, carrying away a great part of his helmet with half of his ear, all of which with fearful ruin fell to the ground, leaving him in a sorry plight.

Good God! Who among us could properly describe the rage that filled the heart of our Manchegan when he saw himself treated this way? Let no more be said than that his rage was so great that he raised himself at once in his stirrups, then grasping his sword more firmly with both hands, came down on the Biscayan with such fury, smiting him full over the cushion and over the head (so good a shield proving useless), that he began to bleed from nose, mouth, and ears as if a mountain had fallen on him, reeling and nearly falling backwards from his mule, as no doubt he would have done had he not flung his arms about its neck. He nevertheless slipped his feet out of the stirrups and unclasped his arms, and

[10] *as they are such enemies of ours:* When these words were first published, Spain's Morisco population, concentrated in the south and east of the Iberian Peninsula, numbered in the hundreds of thousands. Rebellions periodically broke out in protest of the Spanish government's campaign of forced assimilation. There is evidence that Morisco insurgents received helped from the Ottoman Turks, the leading Muslim power in the early modern world. When the narrator refers to the enemies of his nation, he probably has the Ottoman Empire in mind, even though Turkish is not an Arabic language. For the previous half century, the Ottomans had been vying with Spain for control of the Mediterranean Sea and a network of city-states on the coast of North Africa. It is worth recalling that Cervantes wielded a harquebus in the Battle of Lepanto (1571), the sea battle that marked the turning point in the Ottoman Empire's quest for Mediterranean dominance.

[11] *hound: galgo*, an epithet used against Muslims.

the mule, frightened by the terrible blow, took off across the plain, and with a few bucks flung its master to the ground.

Don Quixote stood looking on very calmly. When he saw the Biscayan fall, he leapt from his horse and swiftly approached him. Presenting the point of his sword to his eyes, he ordered him to surrender or else he would cut off his head. The Biscayan was so dazed that he was unable to answer a word. It would have ended badly for him (so blind with rage was Don Quixote) had not the ladies in the coach, who had hitherto been watching the combat in great terror, hastened to where Don Quixote stood and implored him with earnest entreaties to grant them the great grace and favor of sparing their squire's life. Don Quixote replied with much gravity and dignity, "In truth, fair ladies, I am well content to do what you ask of me; but it must be on one condition and understanding, which is that this knight promise me to go to the village of El Toboso, and on my behalf present himself before the peerless lady Dulcinea, that she may deal with him as shall be most pleasing to her."

The terrified and disconsolate ladies, without discussing Don Quixote's demand or asking who Dulcinea might be, promised that their squire should do all that had been commanded.

"Then, on the faith of that promise," said Don Quixote, "I shall do him no further harm, though he well deserves it."

CHAPTER X

OF WHAT FURTHER BEFELL DON QUIXOTE WITH THE BISCAYAN AND OF THE DANGER IN WHICH HE FOUND HIMSELF AMONG A PARTY OF YANGUESANS*

By this time Sancho had gotten up (rather the worse for the handling of the friars' muleteers) and stood watching the battle of his master Don Quixote and praying to God in his heart that it might be his will to grant him the victory, that he might thereby win some island to make him governor of, as he had promised. Seeing that the struggle was now over and that his master was returning to mount Rocinante, he approached to hold the stirrup for him. Before he could mount, Sancho went on his knees before him, and taking his hand, kissed it saying, "May it please your worship, Señor Don Quixote, to give me the government of that island which has been won in this hard fight, for be it ever so great, I feel myself as capable to govern it as much and as well as anyone in the world who has ever governed islands."

To which Don Quixote replied, "You must take notice, brother Sancho, that this adventure and those like it are not adventures of islands but of crossroads, in which nothing is won except a broken head or a missing ear. Have patience, for adventures will present themselves from which I may make you not only a governor, but even more."

Sancho gave him many thanks, and again kissing his hand and the skirt of his hauberk,[1] helped him to mount Rocinante. Mounting his donkey himself, Sancho proceeded to follow his master, who at a brisk pace, without taking leave or saying anything further to the ladies belonging to the coach, turned into some woods that were close by. Sancho followed him at his donkey's fastest trot, but Rocinante stepped so quickly that, seeing himself left behind, he was forced to call to his master to wait for him. Don Quixote did so, reining in Rocinante until his weary squire came up, who on reaching him said, "It seems to me, señor, it would be prudent for us to go and take refuge in some church, for seeing how battered the fellow you fought with has been left, it will be no wonder if they

* The reader should note whether the chapter title lives up to its promise. Among the theories for the discrepancy is that the pastoral turn the novel takes in the next few chapters was a late addition to the manuscript. The Yanguesans are discussed in chapter 15.

[1] *hauberk:* tunic of chain mail.

report the affair to the Holy Brotherhood[2] and arrest us. And, faith, if they do, before we come out of jail, we'll have to sweat for it."

"Nonsense," said Don Quixote. "Where have you ever seen or heard that a knight-errant has been arraigned before a court of justice, however many homicides he may have committed?"

"I don't know anything about omecillos,"[3] answered Sancho, "nor in my life have had anything to do with one. I only know that the Holy Brotherhood looks after those who fight in the fields. In that other matter, I don't meddle."

"Then you need not worry, my friend," said Don Quixote, "for I will deliver you out of the hands of the Chaldeans,[4] much more out of those of the Brotherhood. But tell me, as you live, have you seen a more valiant knight than I in all the known world? Have you read in history of any who has or had more vigor in attacking, more spirit in persevering, more dexterity in wounding or skill in overthrowing?"

"The truth is," answered Sancho, "that I have never read any history, for I can neither read nor write. But what I will venture to bet is that a more daring master than your worship I have never served in all the days of my life, and God grant that this daring isn't paid for where I've said. What I beg of your worship is that you get well, for a great deal of blood is flowing from that ear. I have some strips of cloth and a little white ointment in the saddlebag."

"All that might be well dispensed with," said Don Quixote, "if I had remembered to make a vial of the elixir of Fierabras,[5] for a single drop of it spares time and medicine."

"What vial and what elixir is that?" said Sancho Panza.

"It is an elixir," answered Don Quixote, "the recipe of which I have in my memory. With it one need not fear death, nor dread dying of any wound; and so when I make it and give it to you, you need do no more in some battle when you see they have cut me in half through the middle of the body—as is known to happen often—than neatly and with great care, before the blood congeals, to place that part of the body that has fallen to the ground upon the other half that remains in the saddle, taking care to line up each half perfectly with the other. Then you shall give me to drink but two drops of the elixir I have mentioned, and you will see me become sounder than an apple."

"If that's true," said Panza, "from this moment I renounce the government of the promised island, and ask for nothing more in payment of my many and faithful services than that your worship give me the recipe of this superb liquid.

[2] *Holy Brotherhood: Santa Hermandad*, rural police force founded in the fifteenth century to combat lawlessness beyond the confines of urban areas.

[3] *omecillos:* Sancho mistakes *homicidios* for *omecillos* (squabbles).

[4] *Chaldeans:* Babylonians, who oppressed ancient Israel.

[5] *elixir of Fierabras:* miraculous healing potion. According to medieval French literature, when the Saracen giant Fierabras conquered Rome, he discovered some of the ointment used to embalm the body of Jesus. After his conversion to Christianity, Fierabras shared the ointment with the emperor Charlemagne, who returned it to Rome.

For I'm persuaded it will be worth more than two reals an ounce anywhere, and I don't need any more to spend the rest of my life in ease and honor. But it remains to be told if it costs much to make it."

"With less than three reals, six quarts of it may be made," said Don Quixote.

"Sinner that I am!" cried Sancho. "Then why does your worship put off making it and teaching me?"

"Peace, friend," answered Don Quixote. "Greater secrets I mean to teach you and greater favors to bestow upon you. For the present, let us see to dressing my wound, for my ear pains me more than I could wish."

Sancho took out some strips of cloth and ointment from the saddlebag; but when Don Quixote came to see his helmet shattered, he nearly lost his senses. Clapping his hand upon his sword and raising his eyes to heaven, he said, "I swear by the Creator of all things and the four Gospels in their fullest extent, to do as the great Marquis of Mantua did when he swore to avenge the death of his nephew Valdovinos:[6] not to eat bread from a tablecloth, nor make merry with his wife—and other points which, although I don't remember them, I here grant as expressed—until I take complete vengeance upon him who has committed such an offense against me."

Hearing this, Sancho said to him, "Your worship should bear in mind, Señor Don Quixote, that if the knight has done what was commanded of him in going to present himself before my lady Dulcinea del Toboso, he will have done all he was bound to do and doesn't deserve further punishment unless he commits some new offense."

"You have said well and made a valid point," answered Don Quixote. "And so I recall the oath insofar as relates to taking fresh vengeance on him, but I make and confirm it anew to lead the life I have said until such time as I take by force from some knight another helmet such as this one and as good. And think not, Sancho, that I am making smoke with straw in doing so, for I have one to imitate in the matter, since the very same thing to the letter happened in the case of Mambrino's helmet, which cost Sacripante so dear."[7]

"To the devil with all such oaths, señor!" replied Sancho. "They are a danger to salvation and harmful to the conscience. Just tell me now, if after many days we don't come across any man armed with a helmet, what are we to do? Must the oath be observed in spite of all the inconvenience and discomfort it will be to sleep fully dressed and not to sleep in a house, and a thousand other penances contained in the oath of that old fool the Marquis of Mantua, which your worship is now wanting to revive? Look carefully, your worship: there are no men in armor traveling on any of these roads, nothing but letter carriers and mule

[6] *as the great Marquis of Mantua . . . his nephew Valdovinos:* Don Quixote returns to the ballad that captured his imagination in chapter 5.

[7] *Mambrino's helmet, which cost Sacripante so dear:* In *Orlando Innamorato*, the knight Rinaldo defeats the Moorish king Mambrino and takes his helmet as spoils. The helmet appears again in *Orlando Furioso*, where it protects Rinaldo in a battle against the pagan Dardinel (not Sacripante).

drivers, who not only do not wear helmets, but perhaps never heard tell of them in all their lives."

"You are wrong there," said Don Quixote. "We shall not have been above two hours among these crossroads before we see more men in armor than came to Albraca to win the fair Angelica."[8]

"Enough then," said Sancho. "Let it be so. May God grant us success, and may the time for winning that island which is costing me so dear come soon. And then I can die."

"I have already told you, Sancho," said Don Quixote, "not to be uneasy on that score. For if an island should fail, there is the kingdom of Denmark or of Sobradisa,[9] which will fit you as a ring fits the finger—and all the more since, being on *terra firma*, you will like it better. But let us leave that to its own time. See if you have anything for us to eat in that saddlebag, because we must presently go in quest of some castle where we may lodge tonight and make the elixir I told you of, for I swear to you by God, this ear is giving me great pain."

"I have here an onion and a little cheese and a few scraps of bread," said Sancho, "but they are not delicacies fit for a valiant knight like your worship."

"How little you understand!" answered Don Quixote. "I would have you know, Sancho, that it is the glory of knights-errant to go without eating for a month, and even when they do eat, that it should be of what comes first to hand. This would have been clear to you had you read as many histories as I have. For though they are very many, among them all I have found no mention made of knights-errant eating, unless by chance or at sumptuous banquets prepared for them. The rest of the time they lived off trifles. And though it is plain they could not do without eating and performing all the other natural functions—because, in fact, they were men like ourselves—it is plain too that, wandering as they did the most part of their lives through woods and wilds and without a cook, their most usual fare would be rustic provisions such as those you now offer me. Therefore, friend Sancho, do not be distressed by something that gives me pleasure, and do not seek to make a new world or turn knight-errantry on its head."

"Pardon me, your worship," said Sancho, "for seeing as I can't read or write, as I said just now, I don't know about all the rules of the chivalry profession. From now on, I'll stock the saddlebag with every kind of dry fruit for your worship, since you're a knight. For myself, since I'm not one, I will supply it with poultry and other things more substantial."

"I do not say, Sancho," replied Don Quixote, "that it is imperative for knights-errant not to eat anything else but the fruits you speak of, only that their more usual diet must be those—and certain herbs they found in the fields which they knew and I know too."

[8] *Albraca to win the fair Angelica:* In an episode of *Orlando Innamorato*, Angelica is imprisoned in the walled city of Albraca. Knights numbering in the millions lay siege to the fortress to rescue her.

[9] *Sobradisa:* fictional kingdom ruled by Galaor, the brother of Amadís.

"A good thing it is," answered Sancho, "to know those herbs, for to my thinking it will be needful someday to put that knowledge into practice."

Sancho took out what he said he had packed, and the two ate in peace and good company. Anxious to find quarters for the night, they made an end of their poor dry fare with all dispatch, mounted at once, and hurried to reach some habitation before night set in; but daylight and the hope of succeeding in their object failed them as they drew alongside the huts of some goatherds, so they determined to pass the night there. It was as much to Sancho's discontent not to have reached a house as it was to his master's satisfaction to sleep under the open heaven, for he fancied that each time this happened to him, he performed an act of ownership that further proved his claim of knighthood.[10]

[10] *performed an act of ownership . . . his claim of knighthood:* The concept comes from property law.

CHAPTER XI

WHAT BEFELL DON QUIXOTE WITH CERTAIN GOATHERDS

Don Quixote was cordially welcomed by the goatherds, and Sancho, having put up Rocinante and the donkey as best he could, followed the fragrance that came from some pieces of salted goat simmering in a pot on the fire. Although he would have liked in that moment to test whether they were ready to be transferred from the pot to the stomach, he refrained from doing so; for he saw the goatherds remove the pieces of meat from the fire, lay sheepskins on the ground, and quickly spread their rustic table, which they accompanied by signs of hearty goodwill and an invitation for both of them to share what they had. Six of the men belonging to the fold seated themselves around the skins, having first with unaffected courtesy pressed Don Quixote to take a seat upon a trough they placed for him upside down. Don Quixote seated himself, while Sancho remained standing to serve him a cup made of horn.

Seeing him standing, his master said to him, "That you may see, Sancho, the good at the heart of knight-errantry, and how those who fill any office in it are on the high road to be speedily honored and esteemed by the world, I desire that you seat yourself here at my side and in the company of these worthy people, that you be one with me who am your master and natural lord, and that you eat from my plate and drink from whatever I drink from. For the same may be said of knight-errantry as of love, that it makes all equal."

"A great honor!" declared Sancho. "But I may tell your worship that provided I have enough to eat, I can eat it as well or better standing and by myself, than seated alongside an emperor. Actually, if truth be told, what I eat in my corner without form or fuss tastes better to me, even if it's bread and onions, than the turkeys of those other tables where I'm forced to chew slowly, drink little, wipe my mouth every minute, and not sneeze or cough when I feel like it or do other things that are the privileges of liberty and solitude. So, señor, as for these honors your worship would like to give me as a servant and follower of knight-errantry, replace them with something more useful and beneficial to me. Although I fully acknowledge them, I renounce them from this moment to the end of the world."[1]

[1] *Although I fully acknowledge them . . . to the end of the world:* legal formula used to renounce a right or gift.

"For all that," said Don Quixote, "you need to seat yourself, for 'he who humbles himself God exalts.'"[2] And seizing him by the arm, he forced him to take a seat at his side.

The goatherds did not understand this gibberish of squires and knights-errant. All they did was to eat in silence and stare at their guests, who with great dexterity and zeal were stowing away pieces as big as one's fist. The course of meat finished, they spread upon the sheepskins a great heap of dry acorns, and with them they put down half of a cheese harder than if it had been made of mortar. All the while the horn was not idle. It went round so constantly—now full, now empty, like the bucket of a waterwheel—that it soon drained one of the two wineskins that were in sight.

When Don Quixote had quite satisfied his appetite, he took up a handful of the acorns and, contemplating them attentively, held forth in this fashion:

"Happy the age, happy the time, to which the ancients gave the name of golden, not because in that fortunate age the gold so coveted in this our iron one was gained without toil, but because they that lived in it knew not the two words *mine* and *thine*! In that blessed age all things were in common. To win the daily food no labor was required of any save to stretch forth his hand and gather it from the sturdy oaks that stood generously inviting him with their sweet ripe fruit. The clear streams and running brooks yielded their refreshing, limpid waters in noble abundance. The busy and sagacious bees fixed their republic in the clefts of the rocks and hollows of the trees, offering freely the plenteous produce of their fragrant toil to every hand. The mighty cork trees, with no other pretense than their own courtesy, shed the broad, light bark that served at first to roof the houses supported by rude stakes, a protection against the inclemency of heaven alone. Then all was peace, all friendship, all concord. As yet the heavy and crooked plowshare had not dared to rend and pierce the tender bowels of our first mother, who without compulsion yielded from every portion of her broad and fertile bosom all that could satisfy, sustain, and delight the children that then possessed her.

"Then was it that the innocent and fair young shepherdess roamed from vale to vale and hill to hill with flowing locks and no more garments than were needful to cover modestly what modesty desires and has ever sought to cover. Nor were their ornaments like those in use today, set off by Tyrian purple[3] and silk tortured in endless fashions, but the wreathed leaves of the green burdock[4] and ivy, wherewith they went as bravely and becomingly decked as our court ladies with all the strange and exotic fancies that their idle curiosity has taught them. Then the love-thoughts of the heart clothed themselves simply and naturally as the heart conceived them, nor sought to commend themselves by forced and rambling verbiage. Fraud, deceit, and malice had then not yet mingled with truth

[2] *he who humbles himself God exalts:* Matthew 23:12; Luke 14:11.

[3] *Tyrian purple:* The ancient city of Tyre, in modern-day Lebanon, was famous for its trade in a purple dye extracted from sea snails.

[4] *burdock:* shrub with large, woolly leaves native to Europe and Asia.

and sincerity. Justice held her ground, undisturbed and unassailed by the efforts of favor and self-interest, which now so much impair, pervert, and beset her. Arbitrary law had not yet established itself in the mind of the judge, for then there was no cause to judge and no one to be judged. Maidens and modesty, as I have said, wandered at will alone and unattended, without fear of insult from lawlessness or libertine assault, and if they were undone it was of their own will and pleasure.

"But now in this detestable age of ours, not one is safe, though some new labyrinth like that of Crete[5] conceal and surround her. Even there the amorous pestilence will make its way to them through chinks or through the air by the zeal of its accursed insistence and, despite their seclusion, will lead them to ruin. In defense of these, as time advanced and wickedness increased, the order of knights-errant was instituted, to defend maidens, to protect widows, and to aid the orphans and the needy. To this order I belong, brother goatherds, to whom I return thanks for the hospitality and kindly welcome you offer me and my squire. For though by natural law all living are bound to show favor to knights-errant, yet, seeing that without knowing this obligation you have welcomed and feasted me, it is right that with all the goodwill in my power I should thank you for yours."

The entirety of this long harangue (which might very well have been spared) our knight delivered because the acorns they gave him reminded him of the golden age, and the whim seized him to address this unnecessary argument to the goatherds, who listened to him gaping in amazement without saying a word in reply. Sancho likewise held his peace and ate acorns and paid repeated visits to the second wineskin, which they had hung up on a cork tree to keep the wine cool.

Don Quixote was longer in talking than the supper in finishing, at the end of which one of the goatherds said, "So that your worship, sir knight-errant, can say with more truth that we're quick to show you hospitality and goodwill, we would like to entertain you by having one of our fellow goatherds, who will be here shortly, sing for you. He's a very bright lad and deep in love. He can also read and write and play the rebec.[6] What more could you ask for?"

The goatherd had hardly done speaking, when the notes of the rebec reached their ears. Soon after, the player appeared, a very good-looking young man of about twenty-two. His companions asked him if he had eaten, and on his replying that he had, the goatherd who had made the offer said to him, "In that case, Antonio, you would give us great pleasure if you would sing a little so that the gentleman, our guest, can see that even in the mountains and woods there are musicians. We've told him about your abilities, and we would like you to show them off and prove what we say is true. As you live, sit down and sing that ballad about your love that your uncle the prebendary[7] wrote for you, the one so much liked in town."

[5] *labyrinth like that of Crete:* In Greek mythology, King Minos of Crete had the inventor Daedalus construct an elaborate maze to hold the Minotaur, a creature half man and half bull.

[6] *rebec:* small pear-shaped stringed instrument played with a bow.

[7] *prebendary:* clergyman entitled to a special stipend.

"With all my heart," said the young man, and without waiting for more pressing, he seated himself on the trunk of a felled oak, and tuning his rebec, presently began to sing to these words.

ANTONIO'S BALLAD

Thou dost love me well, Olalla;
Well I know it, even though
Love's mute tongues, thine eyes, have never
By their glances told me so.

For I know my love thou knowest,
Therefore, thine to claim I dare:
Once it ceases to be secret,
Love need never feel despair.

True it is, Olalla, sometimes
Thou hast all too plainly shown
That thy heart is brass in hardness,
And thy snowy bosom stone.

Yet for all that, in thy coyness,
And thy fickle fits between,
Hope is there—at least the border
Of her garment may be seen.

Lures to faith are they, those glimpses,
And to faith in thee I hold;
Kindness cannot make it stronger,
Coldness cannot make it cold.

If it be that love is gentle,
In thy gentleness I see
Something holding out assurance
To the hope of winning thee.

If it be that in devotion
Lies a power hearts to move,
That which every day I show thee,
Helpful to my suit should prove.

Many a time thou must have noticed—
If to notice thou dost care—
How I go about on Monday
Dressed in all my Sunday wear.

Love's eyes love to look on brightness;
Love loves what is gaily dressed;
Sunday, Monday, all I care is
Thou shouldst see me in my best.

No account I make of dances,
Or of strains that pleased thee so,
Keeping thee awake from midnight
Till the cocks began to crow;

Or of how I roundly swore it
That there's none so fair as thou;
True it is, but as I said it,
By the girls I'm hated now.

For Teresa of the hillside
At my praise of thee was sore;
Said, "You think you love an angel;
It's a monkey you adore;

"Caught by all her glittering trinkets,
And her borrowed braids of hair,
And a host of made-up beauties
That would Love himself ensnare."

'Twas a lie, and so I told her,
And her cousin at the word
Gave me his defiance for it;
And what followed thou hast heard.

Mine is no high-flown affection,
Mine no passion *par amours*—
As they call it—what I offer
Is an honest love, and pure.

Cunning cords the holy Church has,
Cords of softest silk they be;
Put thy neck beneath the yoke, dear;
Mine will follow, thou wilt see.

Else—and once for all I swear it
By the saint of most renown—
If I ever leave the mountains,
'Twill be in a friar's gown.

Here the goatherd brought his song to an end, and though Don Quixote entreated him to sing more, Sancho was of a different opinion, being more inclined to sleep than to listen to songs. And so he said to his master, "Your worship would do well to find a comfortable place to rest for the night, for the work these good men are at all day doesn't allow them to spend the whole night singing."

"I understand you, Sancho," replied Don Quixote. "It is very clear to me that those visits to the wineskin demand compensation in sleep rather than in music."

"It tasted good to us all, blessed be God," said Sancho.

"I do not deny it," replied Don Quixote. "Settle yourself where you will. Those of my calling are more becomingly employed in watching than in sleeping. Still, it would be as well if you were to dress this ear for me again, for it is giving me more pain than I would like."

Sancho did as he asked him, but one of the goatherds, seeing the wound, told him not to be uneasy, as he would apply a remedy with which it would be soon healed. Gathering some rosemary leaves, of which there was a great quantity there, he chewed them and mixed them with a little salt, and applying them to the ear he secured them firmly with a bandage, assuring him that no other treatment would be required. And so it proved.

CHAPTER XII

OF WHAT A GOATHERD RELATED TO THOSE WITH DON QUIXOTE

Just then another young man, one of those who fetched their provisions from the village, came up and said, "Do you know what's going on in the village, friends?"

"How could we know?" replied one of them.

"Well, then, let me tell you," continued the young man. "This morning that famous student-shepherd called Grisóstomo died, and it is rumored that he died of love for that devil of a village girl Marcela, the daughter of Guillermo the Rich, the one who wanders about these parts dressed like a shepherdess."

"You mean Marcela?" said one.

"Her I mean," answered the goatherd. "The best of it is, he has directed in his will that he is to be buried in the fields like a Moor,[1] and at the foot of the rock where the cork tree spring is, because, as the story goes—and they say he himself said so—that was the place where he first saw her. He's also left other directions which the clergy of the village say should not and must not be obeyed because they smack of paganism. To all this, his great friend Ambrosio the student, who, like him, also went dressed as a shepherd, replies that everything must be done without any omission according to the directions left by Grisóstomo. The village is all in a commotion about this. It's reported, however, that what Ambrosio and all his friends the shepherds desire will be done after all. Tomorrow they are coming to bury him with great ceremony where I said. I'm sure it will be something worth seeing. I, at least, don't want to miss seeing it, even if I knew I wouldn't return to the village tomorrow."

"We will do the same," answered the goatherds, "and cast lots to see who must stay and watch over our goats."

"You say well, Pedro," said one, "but there will be no need of taking that trouble, for I will stay behind for all. Don't suppose it's virtue or lack of curiosity in me; it's that the splinter that ran into my foot the other day will not let me walk."

"For all that, we thank you," answered Pedro.

Don Quixote asked Pedro to tell him who the dead man was and who the shepherdess, to which Pedro replied that all he knew was that the dead man was a wealthy gentleman belonging to a village in those mountains, who had been

[1] *buried in the fields like a Moor:* that is, as opposed to being buried in the parish cemetery.

a student at Salamanca[2] for many years, at the end of which he returned to his village with the reputation of being very learned and deeply read. "Above all, they said, he was learned in the science of the stars and of what went on yonder in the heavens and the sun and the moon, for he told us of the cris of the sun and moon to exact time."

"*Eclipse* it is called, friend, not *cris*, the darkening of those two luminaries," said Don Quixote.

Pedro, not troubling himself with niceties, went on with his story, saying, "Also, he foretold when the year was going to be one of abundance or estility."

"*Sterility*, you mean," said Don Quixote.

"*Sterility* or *estility*," answered Pedro, "it's all the same in the end. And I can tell you that by this his father and friends who believed him grew very rich because they did as he advised them, telling them 'sow barley this year, not wheat; this year you should sow garbanzos and not barley; the next there will be a full crop of olives, and the three following not a drop of oil will be got.'"

"That science is called astrology,"[3] said Don Quixote.

"I don't know what it's called," replied Pedro, "but I know that he knew all this and more besides. To make an end, not many months had passed after he returned from Salamanca, when one day he appeared dressed like a shepherd with his crook and sheepskin, having put off the long gown he wore as a scholar. At the same time his great friend, Ambrosio by name, who had been his companion in his studies, took to the shepherd's dress with him. I forgot to say that Grisóstomo, the deceased, was a great man for writing poetry, so much so that he wrote carols for Christmas Eve and plays for Corpus Christi,[4] which the young men of our village acted, and everyone said they were excellent. When the villagers saw the two scholars so unexpectedly appearing in shepherd's dress, they were lost in wonder and could not guess what had led them to make so extraordinary a change.

"About this time, the father of our Grisóstomo died, and he was left heir to a large amount of property in goods as well as in land, no small number of cattle and sheep, and a large sum of money. To all of this the young man was left owner, free and clear. He certainly deserved it all, for he was a very fine fellow, kind-hearted, a friend to all good people, and with a face like a blessing. It soon came to be known that he had changed his dress with no other purpose than to wander about the countryside after that shepherdess Marcela our lad mentioned

[2] *Salamanca:* Founded in 1218, the University of Salamanca was the largest and most prestigious university in Golden Age Spain. Enrollment at the turn of the seventeenth century averaged between five thousand and seven thousand students. Don Quixote will encounter other Salamanca students down the road.

[3] *astrology:* Today we separate the study of heavenly bodies into astronomy and astrology, but in Cervantes' time, that distinction was not yet clear. There was still a widespread belief, even among the learned, that the stars and planets were a higher order of creation endowed with the power to influence earthly activity, including human affairs.

[4] *Corpus Christi:* Feast day celebrating the Real Presence of Christ in the Eucharist. In addition to the procession of the Eucharistic host through the streets, the festival traditionally included outdoor performances of short religious plays.

a while ago, who the deceased Grisóstomo had fallen in love with. I must tell you now about this girl, for it is well you should know. Perhaps—and even without the perhaps—you will not have heard anything like it all the days of your life, though you should live more years than sarna."

"Say *Sarah*,"[5] said Don Quixote, unable to endure the goatherd's confusion of words.

"The *sarna* lives long enough," answered Pedro, "but if you must go finding fault with my words at every step, señor, we won't get to the end in a year."

"Pardon me, friend," said Don Quixote, "but as there is such a difference between *sarna* and *Sarah*, I spoke up. Yet you have answered very rightly, for *sarna* lives longer than *Sarah*. Continue your story, and I will make no more objections."

"I say then, my dear sir," said the goatherd, "that in our village there was a farmer even richer than Grisóstomo's father who was named Guillermo, upon whom God bestowed, over and above great wealth, a daughter at whose birth her mother died, the most respected woman there was in these parts. I fancy I can see her now with that face that had the sun on one side and the moon on the other; and diligent and kind to the poor besides, for which I trust that at the present moment her soul is in bliss with God in the other world. Her husband Guillermo died of grief at the death of so good a wife, leaving his daughter Marcela, a child and rich, to the care of an uncle of hers, a priest and prebendary in our village. The girl grew up with such beauty that it reminded us of her mother's, which was very great, and yet it was thought that the daughter's would exceed it.

"And so when she reached the age of fourteen or fifteen years, nobody beheld her but blessed God, who had made her so beautiful, and most everyone was smitten with her and completely captivated. Her uncle kept her with great care in tight seclusion, but for all that the fame of her immense beauty spread so that, both for it and for her great wealth, her uncle was asked, solicited, and begged to give her in marriage not only by those of our town but of those many leagues round, and by the persons of highest quality in them. He, being a good Christian man, though he wished to give her then in marriage, seeing her to be old enough, was unwilling to do so without her consent—not that he had any eye to the gain and profit which the custody of the girl's property brought him while he put off her marriage. And, faith, this was said in praise of the good priest in more than one corner of the town. For I would have you know, Sir Errant, that in these little villages everything is picked apart and gossiped about, and rest assured, as I do, that the priest must be over and above good who obliges his parishioners to speak well of him, especially in villages."

"That is the truth," said Don Quixote. "But go on, for the story is very good, and you, good Pedro, tell it with great grace."

"May that of the Lord not be wanting to me," said Pedro. "That's the one to have. To proceed, you must know that though the uncle put before his niece

[5] *live more years than sarna . . . Sarah:* The wife of the patriarch Abraham, Sarah, lived to be 127 years old (Genesis 23:1). Pedro confuses her with *sarna*, the skin disease called mange.

and described to her the qualities of every single one of the many who asked her in marriage, begging her to marry and make a choice according to her own taste, she never gave any other answer than that she had no desire to marry just yet and that being so young she didn't think herself fit to bear the burden of matrimony. These excuses seemed reasonable to her uncle, and so he ceased to press her and waited till she was somewhat more advanced in age and could choose a partner of her liking. For, said he—and he said quite right—parents are not to settle children in life against their will.[6] But lo and behold, when it was least expected, one day the lovely Marcela made her appearance as a shepherdess. And in spite of her uncle and all those of the town who tried to advise her against it, she took to going into the countryside with the other shepherd-lasses of the village and tending her own flock. And so, since she appeared in public, and her beauty came to be seen openly, I could not well tell you how many rich youths, gentlemen, and peasants, have adopted the dress of Grisóstomo and go about these fields courting her. One of these, as has been already said, was our deceased friend, who they say did not merely love but adored her.

"Now you must not suppose that just because Marcela chose a life of such liberty and independence and of so little—or rather no—seclusion she has given any occasion, or even the hint of one, to speak ill of her purity and modesty. On the contrary, so great is the vigilance with which she watches over her honor, that of all those that serve and court her, not one has boasted—or can with truth boast—that she has given him any hope, however small, of obtaining his desire. For although she doesn't shun the company and conversation of the shepherds, and is courteous and even friendly toward them, should one of them come to declare his intention to her, though it be as proper and holy an intention as matrimony, she flings him from her as if he were on a catapult. With this kind of attitude she does more harm in this country than if the plague had gotten into it, for her friendliness and her beauty pull on the heartstrings of those that associate with her to love her and to court her, but her scorn and blunt words bring them to the brink of despair. For this reason, they don't know what to say except to proclaim her aloud cruel and hard-hearted, and other names of the same sort which well describe the nature of her character.

"If you should remain here any time, señor, you would hear these hills and valleys resounding with the laments of the poor rejected fellows who pursue her. Not far from here is a spot where there are a couple of dozen tall beeches, and there is not one of them but has carved into its smooth bark the name of Marcela, and above some a crown carved on it, as though her lover would say more plainly that Marcela wore and deserved it above all human beauty. Here one shepherd sighs;

[6] *settle children in life against their will:* The expression *dar estado* includes marriage as well as a life in the Church, a common calling for men and women of the day. Children tended to have the final word in their choice of spouse or religious vocation, although parents and financial circumstances could exert a strong influence in one direction. Those most constrained were the very poor and the very noble. A prince might be promised in marriage to further a political interest long before he came of age.

there another laments. Over there love songs are heard; here despairing elegies. One of them will pass all the hours of the night seated at the foot of some oak or rock, and there, without having closed his weeping eyes, the sun finds him in the morning lost in his lovelorn thoughts. Another, without relief or rest from his sighs, stretched on the burning sand in the full heat of the sweltering noonday, makes his appeal to the compassionate heavens. Over one and the other, over these and all, the beautiful Marcela triumphs free and careless. All of us that know her are waiting to see what her pride will come to and who is to be the happy man that will succeed in taming a nature so fierce and gaining possession of a beauty so supreme. All that I have told you being such well-established truth, I'm persuaded that what they say of the cause of Grisóstomo's death, as our lad told us, is the same. And so I advise you, señor, do not fail to be present tomorrow at his burial, which will be well worth seeing, for Grisóstomo had many friends, and it is not half a league from this place where he directed he should be buried."

"I will make a point of it," said Don Quixote. "I thank you for the pleasure you have given me by relating so interesting a tale."

"Oh," said the goatherd, "I don't know even the half of what has happened to Marcela's lovers, but perhaps tomorrow we may fall in with some shepherd on the road who can tell us. For now, it will be well for you to go and sleep under cover, for the night air may hurt your wound, though with the remedy I've applied to you, there is no fear of an unpleasant result."

Sancho Panza, who was wishing the goatherd's loquacity to the devil, on his part begged his master to go into Pedro's hut to sleep. He did so and spent all the rest of the night thinking of his lady Dulcinea, in imitation of the lovers of Marcela. Sancho Panza settled himself between Rocinante and his donkey and slept, not like a lover who had been discarded, but like a man who had been soundly kicked.

CHAPTER XIII

IN WHICH IS CONCLUDED THE STORY OF THE SHEPHERDESS MARCELA, WITH OTHER INCIDENTS

Scarcely had day begun to show itself through the balconies of the east, when five of the six goatherds came to rouse Don Quixote and tell him that if he was still of a mind to go and see the much-anticipated burial of Grisóstomo, they would keep him company. Don Quixote, who desired nothing better, rose and ordered Sancho to make ready pack and saddle at once, which he did with all dispatch. And with the same dispatch, the group set out.

They had not gone a quarter of a league when at the meeting of two paths they saw coming toward them some six shepherds dressed in black sheepskins and with their heads crowned with garlands of cypress and bitter oleander.[1] Each of them carried a stout holly staff in his hand, and along with them there came two gentlemen on horseback in handsome traveling dress, with three servants on foot accompanying them. Courteous salutations were exchanged on meeting, and inquiring one of the other which way each party was going, they learned that all were bound for the scene of the burial, so they went on all together.

One of those on horseback addressing his companion said to him, "It seems to me, Señor Vivaldo, that we may count as well spent the delay we shall incur in seeing this remarkable funeral, for remarkable it cannot but be judging by the strange things these shepherds have told us, of both the dead shepherd and the murdering shepherdess."

"So I think, too," replied Vivaldo. "I would delay not only one day but four for the sake of seeing it."

Don Quixote asked them what they had heard of Marcela and Grisóstomo. The traveler answered that the same morning they had met these shepherds, and seeing them dressed in this mournful fashion, they had asked them the reason of their appearing in such a guise; which one of them gave, describing the strange behavior and beauty of a shepherdess called Marcela, and the loves of many who courted her, together with the death of that Grisóstomo to whose burial they were going. In short, he repeated all that Pedro had related to Don Quixote.

This conversation was dropped, and another was begun by him who was called Vivaldo, asking Don Quixote what was the reason that led him to go armed in that fashion in a country so peaceful. To which Don Quixote replied, "The

[1] *cypress and bitter oleander:* plants associated with death.

pursuit of my calling does not permit me to go in any other fashion. Easy life, enjoyment, and repose were invented for soft courtiers, but toil, unrest, and arms were fashioned for those alone whom the world calls knights-errant, of whom I, though unworthy, am the least of all."

The instant they heard this, everyone set him down as a madman. The better to settle the point and discover what kind of madness his was, Vivaldo proceeded to ask him what he meant by "knights-errant."

"Have not your worships," replied Don Quixote, "read the annals and histories of England, in which are recorded the famous deeds of King Arthur, whom we in our popular Castilian invariably call King Artus, with regard to whom it is an ancient tradition, and commonly received all over that kingdom of Great Britain, that this king did not die, but was changed by magic art into a raven, and that in due time he is to return to reign and recover his kingdom and scepter; for which reason it cannot be proved that from that time to this any Englishman ever killed a raven? Well, then, in the time of this good king that famous order of chivalry of the Knights of the Round Table was instituted, and the love affair of Sir Lancelot of the Lake with Queen Guinevere took place, precisely as is there related, the go-between and confidante therein being the highly honorable Lady Quintañona,[2] whence came that ballad so well-known and widely spread in our Spain—

O never surely was there knight
So served by hand of dame,
As served was he Sir Lancelot hight[3]
When he from Britain came—

with all the sweet and delectable course of his achievements in love and war. Handed down from that time, then, this order of chivalry went on extending itself over many and various parts of the world. In it, famous and renowned for their deeds, were the mighty Amadís of Gaul with all his sons and descendants to the fifth generation, and the valiant Felixmarte of Hircania, and the never sufficiently praised Tirante el Blanco—down to our own days, where we have well-nigh seen and heard and talked with the invincible knight Don Belianís of Greece. This, then, sirs, is to be a knight-errant, and what I have spoken of is the order of its chivalry, of which, as I have already said, I, though a sinner, have made profession. What the aforesaid knights professed that same do I profess, and so I go through these solitudes and wilds seeking adventures, resolved in soul

[2] *highly honorable Lady Quintañona:* The legends of Arthur and his knights that began circulating in England and Wales during the early Middle Ages were picked up by Breton minstrels, who adapted them to the tastes of the French aristocracy. Their ballads traveled beyond the Pyrenees, where Spanish poets translated them and added their own touches. Quintañona, the go-between who facilitated the affair between Lancelot and Guinevere, is a uniquely Spanish contribution to the Arthurian tradition. For Don Quixote to call a conspirator in adultery highly honorable is evidence either of his madness or sense of irony.

[3] *hight:* named.

to offer my arm and my person to the greatest peril that fortune may present me in aid of the weak and needy."

By these words, the travelers were able to satisfy themselves of Don Quixote's being out of his senses and of the form of madness that overmastered him, at which they felt the same astonishment that all felt on first becoming acquainted with it. Vivaldo, who was a person of great shrewdness and of a playful temperament, in order to enliven the short journey that they said was required to reach the mountain, the scene of the burial, sought to give him an opportunity of going on with his absurdities. So he said to him, "It seems to me, sir knight-errant, that your worship has chosen one of the most austere professions in the world. I imagine even that of the Carthusian monks[4] is not so austere."

"Austere it may perhaps be," replied our Don Quixote, "but without a shadow of a doubt necessary for the world. For truth be told, the soldier who carries out what his captain orders does no less than the captain himself who gives the order. My meaning is that churchmen in peace and quiet pray to Heaven for the welfare of the world, but we soldiers and knights carry into effect what they pray for, defending it with the might of our arms and the edge of our swords, not under shelter but in the open air, a target for the intolerable rays of the sun in summer and the piercing frosts of winter. Thus are we God's ministers on earth and the arms by which his justice is done therein. And as the business of war and all that relates and belongs to it cannot be conducted without exceedingly great sweat, toil, and exertion, it follows that those who make it their profession have undoubtedly more labor than those who in tranquil peace and quiet are engaged in praying to God to help the weak. I do not mean to say, nor does it enter into my thoughts, that the knight-errant's calling is as good as that of the monk in his cell; I would merely infer from what I endure myself that it is beyond a doubt a more laborious and a more afflicted one, hungrier and thirstier, more wretched, ragged, and flea-bitten. There is no reason to doubt that the knights-errant of yore endured much hardship in the course of their lives. If some of them by the might of their arms did rise to be emperors, in faith it cost them dear in the matter of blood and sweat; and if those who attained to that rank had not had sorcerers and sages to help them, they would have been completely frustrated in their ambitions and disappointed in their hopes."

"I am of the same opinion," replied the traveler; "but one thing among many others seems to me very wrong in knights-errant, and that is that when they find themselves about to engage in some mighty and perilous adventure in which there is manifest danger of losing their lives, they never at the moment of engaging in it think of commending themselves to God, as is the duty of every good Christian in like peril. Instead, they commend themselves to their ladies with as much devotion as if these were their gods, a thing which seems to me to smack somewhat of heathenism."

"Sir," answered Don Quixote, "that cannot be on any account omitted, and the knight-errant would be disgraced who acted otherwise. For it is usual and customary

[4] *Carthusian monks:* The Carthusian Order is a monastic order founded in 1084 devoted to contemplation through solitude and silence.

in knight-errantry that the knight-errant—who on engaging in any great feat of arms has his lady before him—should turn his eyes toward her softly and lovingly, as though with them entreating her to favor and protect him in the hazardous venture he is about to undertake; and even if no one hears him, he is bound to say certain words under his breath, commending himself to her with all his heart. Of this we have innumerable instances in the histories. Nor is it to be supposed from this that they are to omit commending themselves to God, for there will be time and opportunity for doing so while they are engaged in their task."

"For all that," answered the traveler, "I feel some doubt still, because often I have read how words will arise between two knights-errant, and from one thing to another it comes about that their anger is kindled and they wheel their horses round and take a good stretch of field, and then without any more ado, at the top of their speed they come to the charge, and midway there they are accustomed to commend themselves to their ladies. What commonly comes of the encounter is that one falls over the haunches of his horse pierced through and through by his opponent's lance, and as for the other, it is only by holding on to the mane of his horse that he can help falling to the ground. I know not how the dead man had time to commend himself to God in the course of such rapid work as this. It would have been better if those words which he spent in commending himself to his lady in the midst of his charge had been devoted to his duty and obligation as a Christian. Moreover, it is my belief that not all knights-errant have ladies to commend themselves to, for they are not all in love."

"That is impossible," said Don Quixote. "I say it is impossible that there could be a knight-errant without a lady, because to such it is as natural and proper to be in love as to the heavens to have stars. Most certainly no history has been seen in which there is to be found a knight-errant without a beloved, and for the simple reason that without one he would be held no legitimate knight but a bastard, and one who had gained entrance into the stronghold of said knighthood not by the door, but over the wall like a thief and a robber."[5]

"Nevertheless," said the traveler, "if I remember rightly, I think I have read that Don Galaor, the brother of the valiant Amadís of Gaul, never had any special lady to whom he might commend himself, and yet he was not the less esteemed, and was a very valiant and famous knight."

To which our Don Quixote answered, "Sir, 'a single swallow does not make summer.' Moreover, I know that knight was in secret very deeply in love; besides which, that way of falling in love with all that took his fancy was a natural propensity which he could not control. But, in short, it is very manifest that he had one alone whom he made mistress of his will, to whom he commended himself very frequently and very secretly, for he prided himself on being a reticent knight."

"Then if it is essential that every knight-errant should be in love," said the traveler, "it may be fairly supposed that your worship is so, as you are of the order.

[5] *not by the door, but over the wall like a thief and a robber:* See John 10:7–8, where Jesus said, "I am the door of the sheep. All who before me are thieves and robbers." To counter Don Vivaldo's concern that knight-errantry substitutes Christian worship with idolatry, Don Quixote takes Jesus' words about himself and applies them to knight-errantry.

If you do not pride yourself on being as reticent as Don Galaor, I entreat you as earnestly as I can, in the name of all this company and in my own, to inform us of the name, country, rank, and beauty of your lady, for she will esteem herself fortunate if all the world knows that she is loved and served by such a knight as your worship seems to be."

At this Don Quixote heaved a deep sigh and said, "I cannot say positively whether my sweet enemy[6] is pleased or not that the world should know I serve her; I can only say in answer to what has been so courteously asked of me that her name is Dulcinea, her country El Toboso (a village of La Mancha), her rank must be at least that of a princess, since she is my queen and lady; her beauty superhuman, since all the impossible and fanciful attributes of beauty which the poets apply to their ladies are verified in her; her hairs golden, her forehead Elysian fields, her eyebrows rainbows, her eyes suns, her cheeks roses, her lips coral, her teeth pearls, her neck alabaster, her bosom marble, her hands ivory, her fairness snow, and what modesty conceals from sight such, I firmly hold, as rational reflection can only extol, not compare."

"We would like to know her lineage, family, and ancestry," said Vivaldo.

To which Don Quixote replied, "She is not of the ancient Roman Curtii, Caii, or Scipios, nor of the modern Colonnas or Orsini, nor of the Moncadas or Requesenes of Catalonia, nor yet of the Rebellas or Villanovas of Valencia; Palafoxes, Nuzas, Rocabertis, Corellas, Lunas, Alagones, Urreas, Foces, or Gurreas of Aragon; Cerdas, Manriques, Mendozas, or Guzmanes of Castile; Alencastros, Pallas, or Meneses of Portugal.[7] She is of those of El Toboso of La Mancha, a lineage that though modern, may furnish a source of noble blood for the most illustrious families of the ages that are to come. This let none dispute with me save on the condition that Cervino placed at the foot of the trophy of Orlando's arms, saying,

> These let none move
> Who dareth not his might with Roland prove."[8]

"Although mine is of the Cachopines of Laredo,"[9] said the traveler, "I will not venture to compare it with that of El Toboso of La Mancha, though, to tell the truth, no such surname has ever reached my ears until now."

"What?" exclaimed Don Quixote. "It has never reached them?"

The rest of the party went along listening with great attention to the conversation of the pair, and even the goatherds and shepherds recognized how exceedingly out of his wits our Don Quixote was. Sancho Panza alone thought that what his master said was the truth, knowing who he was and having known him

[6] *enemy:* epithet characteristic of the courtly love tradition, in which the knight's love is unrequited.

[7] *Roman Curtii . . . Meneses of Portugal:* illustrious families of their respective cities or kingdoms.

[8] *These let none . . . with Roland prove:* In *Orlando Furioso*, after the hero rescues Cervino of Scotland, the grateful prince etches these lines on a tree bearing Orlando's arms.

[9] *Cachopines of Laredo:* Don Vivaldo hails from Cantabria, in northern Spain.

from his birth. All that he felt any difficulty in believing was the part about the fair Dulcinea del Toboso, because neither any such name nor any such princess had ever come to his knowledge, though he lived very close to El Toboso.

They were going along conversing in this way, when they saw descending a gap between two high mountains some twenty shepherds, all clad in sheepskins of black wool and crowned with garlands, some of which, as became clear later, were of yew and others of cypress.[10] Six of the number were carrying a bier covered with a great variety of flowers and branches, on seeing which one of the goatherds said, "Those who come there are the bearers of Grisóstomo's body, and the foot of that mountain is the place where he ordered them to bury him." They therefore hurried to reach the spot and did so by the time those who came had laid the bier upon the ground, where four of them with sharp pickaxes were digging a grave by the side of a hard rock.

They greeted each other courteously, and then Don Quixote and those who accompanied him turned to examine the bier. On it, covered with flowers, they saw a dead body in the dress of a shepherd, to all appearance about thirty years of age, and showing even in death that in life he had been of handsome features and gallant bearing. Around him on the bier itself were laid some books, and several papers open and folded. Those who were looking on as well as those who were opening the grave and all the others who were there kept a strange silence, until one of those who had borne the body said to another, "Observe carefully, Ambrosio, if this is the place Grisóstomo spoke of, since you are anxious that what he directed in his will should be so strictly complied with."

"This is the place," answered Ambrosio, "for in it many a time did my poor friend tell me the story of his hard fortune. Here it was, he told me, that he saw for the first time that mortal enemy of the human race; and here, too, for the first time he declared to her his passion, as honorable as it was devoted; and here it was that at last Marcela ended by scorning and rejecting him, thus bringing the tragedy of his wretched life to a close. Here, in memory of misfortunes so great, he desired to be laid in the bowels of eternal oblivion."

Then turning to Don Quixote and the travelers he went on to say, "This body, sirs, on which you are looking with compassionate eyes was the abode of a soul on which Heaven bestowed a vast share of its riches. This is the body of Grisóstomo, who was unrivaled in genius, unequaled in courtesy, unapproached in gentle bearing, a phœnix[11] in friendship, generous without limit, stern without arrogance, merry without vulgarity, in short, first in all that constitutes goodness and second to none in all that makes up misfortune. He loved deeply; he was hated. He adored; he was scorned. He wooed a wild beast, he pleaded with marble, he pursued the wind, he cried to the wilderness, he served ingratitude, and for reward was made the prey of death in the mid-course of life, cut short by a shepherdess whom he sought to immortalize in the memory of man, as these

[10] *yew and others of cypress:* The evergreen yew, like the cypress, was associated with death.

[11] *phœnix:* The mythical bird that rises from the ashes of its predecessor is unique among creatures, as Grisóstomo was unique among friends.

papers which you see could fully prove, had he not commanded me to consign them to the fire after having consigned his body to the earth."

"You would deal with them more harshly and cruelly than their owner himself," said Vivaldo, "for it is neither right nor proper to do the will of one who enjoins what is wholly unreasonable. It would not have been reasonable in Augustus Cæsar had he permitted the directions left by the divine Mantuan in his will to be carried into effect.[12] So that, Señor Ambrosio, while you consign your friend's body to the earth, you should not consign his writings to oblivion, for if he gave the order in bitterness of heart, it is not right that you should irrationally obey it. On the contrary, by granting life to those papers, let the cruelty of Marcela live forever, to serve as a warning to the living in ages to come, that they might shun similar dangers and avoid falling into them. I, and all of us who have come here, know already the story of this your love-stricken and heart-broken friend, and we know, too, your friendship, the cause of his death, and the directions he gave at the close of his life. From this sad story may be gathered how great was the cruelty of Marcela, the love of Grisóstomo, and the loyalty of your friendship, together with the end awaiting those who pursue rashly the path that insane passion opens to their eyes. Last night we learned of the death of Grisóstomo and that he was to be buried in this place, and out of curiosity and pity we left our direct road and resolved to come and see with our eyes that which when heard of had so moved our compassion. In consideration of that compassion and our desire to prove it if we might by condolence, we beg of you, excellent Ambrosio—or at least I on my own account entreat you—that instead of burning those papers, you allow me to carry away some of them."

Without waiting for the shepherd's answer, he stretched out his hand and took up some of those papers that were nearest to him; seeing which Ambrosio said, "Out of courtesy, señor, I will grant your request as to those you have taken, but it is futile to expect me not to burn the remainder."

Vivaldo, who was eager to see what the papers contained, opened one of them at once, and saw that its title was "Song of Despair."[13]

Ambrosio hearing it said, "That is the last paper the unhappy man wrote. That you may see, señor, to what an end his misfortunes brought him, read it so that you may be heard, for you will have time enough while we are waiting for the grave to be dug."

"I will do so very willingly," said Vivaldo; and as all the bystanders were equally eager, they gathered round him. He, reading in a loud voice, found that it ran as follows.

[12] *the directions left by the divine Mantuan . . . carried into effect:* According to legend, Virgil (the divine Mantuan) dissatisfied with the state of his unfinished *Aeneid*, ordered that the manuscript be burned with him at this death. Instead, his patron, the emperor Augustus Caesar, intervened and had the text preserved and published.

[13] *Song of Despair: Canción desesperada.* In early modern Spanish, *desesperación* was a euphemism for suicide.

CHAPTER XIV

WHEREIN ARE INSERTED THE DESPAIRING VERSES OF THE DEAD SHEPHERD, TOGETHER WITH OTHER UNEXPECTED EVENTS

GRISÓSTOMO'S SONG

Since thou dost in thy cruelty desire
The ruthless rigor of thy tyranny
From tongue to tongue, from land to land proclaimed,
The very hell will I constrain to lend
This stricken breast of mine deep notes of woe
To serve my need of fitting utterance.
And as I strive to body forth the tale
Of all I suffer, all that thou hast done,
Forth shall the dread voice roll, and bear along
Shreds from my vitals torn for greater pain.
Then listen, not to dulcet harmony,
But to a discord wrung by mad despair
Out of this bosom's depths of bitterness,
To ease my heart and plant a sting in thine.

The lion's roar, the fierce wolf's savage howl,
The horrid hissing of the scaly snake,
The awesome cries of monsters yet unnamed,
The crow's ill-boding croak, the hollow moan
Of wild winds wrestling with the restless sea,
The wrathful bellow of the vanquished bull,
The plaintive sobbing of the widowed dove,
The envied owl's sad note, the wail of woe
That rises from the dreary choir of hell,
Commingled in one sound, confusing sense,
Let all these come to aid my soul's complaint,
For pain like mine demands new modes of song.

No echoes of that discord shall be heard
Where Father Tagus[1] rolls, or on the banks

[1] *Tagus:* See footnote 16, page 10.

Of olive-bordered Betis;[2] to the rocks
Or in deep caverns shall my plaint be told,
And by a lifeless tongue in living words;
Or in dark valleys or on lonely shores,
Where neither foot of man nor sunbeam falls;
Or in among the poison-breathing swarms
Of monsters[3] nourished by the sluggish Nile.
For though it be to solitudes remote
The hoarse, vague echoes of my sorrows sound
Thy matchless cruelty, my dismal fate
Shall carry them to all the spacious world.

Disdain hath power to kill, and patience dies
Slain by suspicion, be it false or true;
And deadly is the force of jealousy;
Long absence makes of life a dreary void;
No hope of happiness can give repose
To him that ever fears to be forgot;
And death, inevitable, waits in hall.
But I, by some strange miracle, live on
A prey to absence, jealousy, disdain;
Racked by suspicion as by certainty;
Forgotten, left to feed my flame alone.
And while I suffer thus, there comes no ray
Of hope to gladden me athwart the gloom;
Nor do I look for it in my despair;
But rather clinging to a cureless woe,
All hope do I abjure for evermore.

Can there be hope where fear is? Were it well,
When far more certain are the grounds of fear?
Ought I to shut mine eyes to jealousy,
If through a thousand heart-wounds it appears?
Who would not give free access to distrust,
Seeing disdain unveiled, and—bitter change!—
All his suspicions turned to certainties,
And the fair truth transformed into a lie?
Oh, thou fierce tyrant of the realms of love,
Oh, Jealousy! Put chains upon these hands,
And bind me with thy strongest cord, Disdain.
But woe is me! Triumphant over all,
My sufferings drown the memory of you.

[2] *Betis:* The Guadalquivir River, known to the Romans as Betis, is Andalusia's main waterway, passing through Córdoba and Seville.

[3] *monsters:* cobras and crocodiles.

And now I die, and since there is no hope
Of happiness for me in life or death,
Still to my fantasy I'll fondly cling.
I'll say that he is wise who loveth well,
And that the soul most free is that most bound
In thraldom[4] to the ancient tyrant Love.
I'll say that she who is mine enemy
In that fair body hath as fair a mind,
And that her coldness is but my desert,
And that by virtue of the pain he sends
Love rules his kingdom with a gentle sway.
Thus, self-deluding, and in bondage sore,
And wearing out the wretched shred of life
To which I am reduced by her disdain,
I'll give this soul and body to the winds,
All hopeless of a crown of bliss in store.

Thou whose injustice hath supplied the cause
That makes me quit the weary life I loathe,
As by this wounded bosom thou canst see
How willingly thy victim I become,
Let not my death, if haply[5] worth a tear,
Cloud the clear heaven that dwells in thy bright
eyes;
I would not have thee expiate in aught[6]
The crime of having made my heart thy prey;
But rather let thy laughter gaily ring
And prove my death to be thy festival.
Fool that I am to bid thee! Well I know
Thy glory gains by my untimely end.

And now it is the time; from hell's abyss
Come thirsting Tantalus,[7] come Sisyphus[8]

[4] *thraldom:* slavery.

[5] *haply:* by chance.

[6] *in aught:* for anything, in any way.

[7] *Tantalus:* For his faithlessness to the gods, Tantalus was punished in the afterlife with a pool of water at his feet and the low-hanging bough of a fruit tree above him. Whenever he reached for food or drink, they receded from his grasp. The image Grisóstomo conjures in the following lines is of Tartarus, the abyss beneath Hades where evildoers are punished. In his dark final days, Grisóstomo inhabits a thought world that mixes elements of classical paganism and a fatalistic Christianity. According to Church teaching, suicide is a mortal sin, for which the offender is condemned to hell.

[8] *Sisyphus:* vicious king condemned to roll or carry a boulder up a steep hill only to have it fall back on him whenever he neared the top.

Heaving the cruel stone, come Tityus[9]
With vulture, and with wheel Ixion[10] come,
And come the sisters of the ceaseless toil;[11]
And all into this breast transfer their pains,
And (if such tribute to despair be due)
Chant in their deepest tones a doleful dirge
Over a corpse unworthy of a shroud.
Let the three-headed guardian of the gate,[12]
And all the monstrous progeny of hell,
The doleful concert join: a lover dead
Methinks can have no fitter obsequies.[13]

Song of despair, grieve not when thou art gone
Forth from this sorrowing heart: my misery
Brings fortune to the cause that gave thee birth;
Then banish sadness even in the tomb.

Grisóstomo's song met with the approval of the listeners, though the reader said it did not seem to him to agree with what he had heard of Marcela's reserve and propriety, for Grisóstomo complained in it of jealousy, suspicion, and absence, all to the prejudice of Marcela's good name.

Ambrosio replied as one who knew well his friend's most secret thoughts, "Señor, to remove that doubt I should tell you that when the unhappy man wrote this song he was away from Marcela, from whom he had voluntarily separated himself, to see if absence would act with him as is its custom. And as everything distresses and every fear haunts the banished lover, so imaginary jealousies and suspicions, dreaded as if they were true, tormented Grisóstomo. Thus, the truth of what the report declares of Marcela's virtue remains unshaken, and with her envy itself should not and cannot find any fault save that of being cruel, somewhat haughty, and very scornful."

"That is true," said Vivaldo.

He was about to read another paper of those he had preserved from the fire when he was stopped by a marvelous vision (for such it seemed) that suddenly presented itself to their eyes. On the summit of the rock where they were digging

[9] *Tityus:* giant who attempted to rape the goddess Leto. As punishment, he was bound in the underworld, where two vultures fed eternally on his liver, which grew back every night.

[10] *Ixion:* After Ixion attempted to seduce Hera, Zeus had him bound to a fiery wheel forever turning.

[11] *sisters of the ceaseless toil:* The Danaïdes, or Belides (the fifty daughters of Danaus, king of Libya), were betrothed against their wills to the fifty sons of their father's twin brother. On their wedding night, forty-nine of them killed their husbands. As punishment for their crimes, the sisters were sentenced to carry leaky jugs of water to fill a bottomless basin.

[12] *three-headed guardian of the gate:* Cerberus, hound of Hades, who stands watch at the gates of the underworld.

[13] *obsequies:* burial rites.

the grave there appeared the shepherdess Marcela, so beautiful that her beauty exceeded its reputation. Those who had never till then beheld her gazed upon her in wonder and silence, and those who were accustomed to see her were not less amazed than those who had never seen her before.

The instant Ambrosio saw her he addressed her with manifest indignation: "Have you come, by chance, cruel basilisk[14] of these mountains, to see if in your presence blood will flow from the wounds of this wretched being your cruelty has robbed of life.[15] Or is it to exult over the cruel work of your nature that you have come; or like another pitiless Nero[16] to look down from that height upon the ruin of his Rome in embers; or in your arrogance to trample on this ill-fated corpse, as the ungrateful daughter trampled on her father Tarquin's?[17] Tell us at once why you have come or what it is you desire. For as I know the thoughts of Grisóstomo never failed to obey you in life, I will make all these who call themselves his friends obey you, though he be dead."

"I come not, Ambrosio for any of the purposes you have named," replied Marcela, "but to defend myself and to prove how unreasonable are all those who blame me for their sorrow and for Grisóstomo's death. Therefore I ask all of you that are here to give me your attention, for it will not take much time or many words to bring the truth home to persons of sense.

"Heaven has made me, so you say, beautiful, and so much so that in spite of yourselves my beauty leads you to love me; and for the love you show me you say, and even insist, that I am bound to love you. By that natural understanding which God has given me I know that everything beautiful attracts love. But I cannot see how, by reason of being loved, that which is loved for its beauty is bound to love that which loves it. Besides, it may happen that the lover of that which is beautiful may be ugly, and ugliness being detestable, it is very absurd to say, 'I love you because you are beautiful; you must love me even if I am ugly.' But supposing the beauty equal on both sides, it does not follow that the inclinations must be therefore alike, for not every beauty excites love. Some beauties may please the eye yet not move the heart. And if every sort of beauty excited love and won the heart, the will would wander vaguely to and fro unable to make choice of any. For as there is an infinity of beautiful objects there must be an infinity of inclinations, and true love, I have heard it said, is indivisible, and must be voluntary and not compelled.

[14] *basilisk:* mythical reptile with a fatal gaze. To call a woman a basilisk in Golden Age Spanish literature was to malign her as cruel for not returning a man's love.

[15] *if in your presence . . . has robbed of life:* It was a popular belief that the murder victim bled in the presence of his killer.

[16] *Nero:* According to a contemporary Spanish ballad, the Roman emperor (A.D. 54–68) started a fire that set the capital ablaze and then watched indifferently from the heights of the Capitoline Hill.

[17] *as the ungrateful daughter trampled on her father Tarquin's:* Tullia, the daughter of Rome's sixth king, conspired with her husband (the future king known as Tarquin the Proud) to overthrow her father. After the king had been murdered and was thrown into the street, she drove her chariot over his body. In a Spanish ballad, Tullia is recast as Tarquin's daughter.

"If this is so, as I believe it to be, why do you desire me to bend my will by force, for no other reason but that you say you love me? Nay—tell me—had Heaven made me ugly, as it has made me beautiful, could I with justice complain of you for not loving me? Moreover, you must remember that the beauty I possess was no choice of mine, for be it what it may, Heaven of its bounty gave it to me without my asking or choosing it; and as the viper, though it kills with its poison, does not deserve to be blamed for the poison it carries—since it is a gift of nature—neither do I deserve reproach for being beautiful. Beauty in a modest woman is like fire at a distance or a sharp sword: the one does not burn, nor does the other cut those who do not come too near. Honor and virtue are the ornaments of the soul, without which the body, even if it is beautiful, has no right to pass for beautiful; but if modesty is one of the virtues that specially lend a grace and charm to soul and body, why should she who is loved for her beauty part with it to gratify one who for his pleasure alone strives with all his might and energy to rob her of it?

"I was born free, and that I might live in freedom I chose the solitude of the fields. In the trees of the mountains I find company, the clear waters of the brooks are my mirrors, and to the trees and waters I make known my thoughts and charms. I am a fire afar off, a sword laid aside. Those whom I have inspired with love by letting them see me, I have by words undeceived, and if their longings live on hope—and I have given none to Grisóstomo or to any other—it cannot justly be said that the death of any is my doing, for it was rather his own obstinacy than my cruelty that killed him. If it be made a charge against me that his wishes were honorable, and that therefore I was bound to yield to them, I answer that when on this very spot where now his grave is made he declared to me his purity of purpose, I told him that mine was to live in perpetual solitude, and that the earth alone should enjoy the fruits of my retirement and the spoils of my beauty. And if, after this open avowal, he chose to persist against hope and steer against the wind, what wonder is it that he should sink in the depths of his infatuation? If I had encouraged him, I should be false; if I had gratified him, I should have acted against my own better resolution and purpose. He was persistent in spite of warning; he despaired without being hated. Consider now if it is reasonable that his suffering should be laid to my charge. Let him who has been deceived complain, let him give way to despair whose encouraged hopes have proved vain, let him flatter himself whom I shall entice, let him boast whom I shall receive; but let not him call me cruel or a murderer to whom I make no promise, upon whom I practice no deception, whom I neither entice nor receive.

"It has not been so far the will of Heaven that I should love by fate, and to expect me to love by choice is in vain. Let this general declaration serve for each of my suitors on his own account, and let it be understood from this time forth that if anyone dies for me it is not of jealousy or misery he dies, for she who loves no one can give no cause for jealousy to any, and candor is not to be confused with scorn. Let him who calls me wild beast and basilisk leave me alone as something dangerous and evil; let him who calls me ungrateful withhold his service. He who calls me wayward, seek not my acquaintance. He who calls me cruel, pursue me not. For this wild beast, this basilisk, this ungrateful, cruel, wayward being will neither seek, serve, welcome, nor follow you. If Grisóstomo's impatience and violent passion killed him, why should my modesty and integrity be blamed? If I preserve my purity in the society of the trees, why should he who would have me preserve it among men, seek to rob me of it? I have, as you know, wealth of my own, and I covet not that of others. My taste is for freedom, and I have no relish for constraint. I neither love nor hate anyone; I do not deceive this one or court that one, or toy with one or play with another. Wholesome conversation with the shepherd girls of these hamlets and the care of my goats are my recreations. My desires are bounded by these mountains, and if they ever wander beyond them it is to contemplate the beauty of the heavens, steps by which the soul travels to its ancient home."

With these words, and not waiting to hear a reply, she turned and passed into the thickest part of a forest that was nearby, leaving all who were there lost in admiration as much of her intelligence[18] as of her beauty. Some—those wounded by the irresistible shafts launched from her bright eyes—made as though they would follow her, heedless of the frank declaration they had heard. Seeing this, and deeming it a fitting occasion for the exercise of his chivalry in aid of distressed damsels, Don Quixote laid his hand on the hilt of his sword and exclaimed in a loud and distinct voice:

"Let no one, whatever his rank or condition, dare to follow the beautiful Marcela under pain of incurring my fierce indignation. She has shown by clear and satisfactory arguments that little or no fault is to be found with her for the death of Grisóstomo, and also how far she is from yielding to the wishes of any of her lovers. For this reason, instead of being followed and persecuted, she should in justice be honored and esteemed by all the good people of the world, for she shows that she is the only woman in it who holds to such a virtuous resolution."

Whether it was because of Don Quixote's threats or because Ambrosio told them to fulfil their duty to their good friend, none of the shepherds stirred from the spot until, having finished the grave and burned Grisóstomo's papers, they laid his body in it, not without many tears from those who stood by. They closed the grave with a heavy stone until a slab was ready that Ambrosio said he meant to have prepared, with an epitaph which was to be to this effect:

Beneath the stone before your eyes
The body of a lover lies;
In life he was a shepherd swain,
In death a victim to disdain.
Ungrateful, cruel, coy, and fair,
Was she that drove him to despair,
And Love hath made her his ally
For spreading wide his tyranny.

[18] *intelligence: discreción*, keen judgment matched with an apt phrase—a prized trait in Baroque Spain.

They then strewed upon the grave a profusion of flowers and branches and, after all had expressed their condolence with his friend Ambrosio, took their leave. Vivaldo and his companion did the same; and Don Quixote bade farewell to his hosts and to the travelers, who pressed him to come with them to Seville, as being such a convenient place for finding adventures, for they presented themselves in every street and round every corner oftener than anywhere else.[19] Don Quixote thanked them for their advice and for their eagerness to do him a favor, and said that for the present he would not and must not go to Seville until he had cleared all these mountains of highwaymen and robbers, of whom reports said they were full. Seeing his firm resolve, the travelers were unwilling to press him further. Once more bidding him farewell, they left him and pursued their journey, in the course of which they did not fail to discuss the story of Marcela and Grisóstomo as well as the madness of Don Quixote. He, on his part, resolved to go in quest of the shepherdess Marcela and offer to her all the service he could render her. But things did not turn out as he expected, as is related in the course of this true history, of which the Second Part ends here.

[19] *Seville . . . oftener than anywhere else:* As the entry point for the empire's New World commerce, Seville had grown to be the largest city in Spain over the course of the previous century. From its opulent merchant class to its seething criminal underworld, the city offered ample material for adventures, which Cervantes (without Don Quixote) pursues in other stories.

THIRD PART OF THE INGENIOUS GENTLEMAN DON QUIXOTE DE LA MANCHA

CHAPTER XV

IN WHICH IS RELATED THE UNFORTUNATE ADVENTURE THAT DON QUIXOTE FELL IN WITH WHEN HE FELL OUT WITH CERTAIN HEARTLESS YANGUESANS[1]

The sage Cide Hamete Benengeli[2] relates that as soon as Don Quixote took leave of his hosts and all who had been present at the burial of Grisóstomo, he and his squire passed into the same forest they had seen the shepherdess Marcela enter. After having wandered for more than two hours in all directions in search of her without finding her, they came to a halt in a glade covered with tender grass, beside which ran a pleasant cool stream that invited and compelled them to pass there the hours of the noontide heat, which by this time was beginning to come on oppressively.

Don Quixote and Sancho dismounted, and turning Rocinante and the donkey loose to feed on the grass that was there in abundance, they ransacked the saddlebag. Without any ceremony, master and man dined on what they found there in peace and good company.

Sancho had not thought it worthwhile to tie up Rocinante, confident that he would be so true to his reputation for being gentle and unexcitable that all the mares in the Córdoba pastures[3] would not lead him into an impropriety. Chance, however, and the devil (who is not always asleep) so ordained that feeding in this valley was a drove of Galician[4] ponies belonging to certain Yanguesan carriers, whose habit it is to take their siesta with their teams in places where grass and water abound. The spot where Don Quixote chanced to be suited the Yanguesans' purpose very well.

It so happened that Rocinante took a fancy to frolic with their ladyships the ponies, and abandoning his usual gait and demeanor as he scented them, he,

[1] *Yanguesans:* natives of the village of Yanguas. There is a Yanguas near Segovia and another near Soria, not far from the border with La Rioja.

[2] *Cide Hamete Benengeli:* See page 71. Until the end of the novel, the narrator will present the story of Don Quixote as a history that he has compiled from the translated chronicles of an Arabic historian.

[3] *mares in the Córdoba pastures:* Horses raised on the banks of the Guadalquivir River, which runs through Córdoba, were highly valued.

[4] *Galician:* from Galicia, the temperate region on Spain's northwest coast.

without asking leave of his master, got up a briskish little trot and headed off to make known to them his desire. They, however, must have been more interested in grazing than anything else, for they received him with their heels and teeth to such effect that they soon broke his girths[5] and left him naked without a saddle to cover him. But what must have been worse to him was that the carriers, seeing the violence that was being done to their mares, came running up armed with stakes[6] and so thrashed him that they brought him sorely battered to the ground.

By this time Don Quixote and Sancho, who had witnessed the drubbing of Rocinante, came up panting.

Don Quixote said to Sancho, "So far as I can see, friend Sancho, these are not knights but base folk of low birth. I mention it because you can lawfully aid me in taking due vengeance for the affront done to Rocinante before our eyes."

"What the devil vengeance can we take," answered Sancho, "if they are more than twenty, and we no more than two—perhaps not even more than one and a half?"

"I count for a hundred," replied Don Quixote.

And cutting short the discussion, he drew his sword and charged at the Yanguesans, while Sancho did the same, excited and impelled by the example of his master. Without any warning, Don Quixote delivered a slash at one of them that laid open the leather jerkin[7] he wore, together with a great portion of his shoulder. The Yanguesans, seeing themselves assaulted by only two men while they were so many, made for their stakes, and driving the two into the middle they began to lay into them with great zeal and energy. By the second blow they had brought Sancho to the ground; Don Quixote fared the same way, all his skill and high spirits availing him nothing. Fate willed that he should fall at the feet of Rocinante, who had not yet risen—from which it may be seen how furiously stakes can pound in angry, boorish hands.

After surveying the mischief they had done, the Yanguesans hastily loaded their team and pursued their journey, leaving the two adventurers a sorry sight and in a sorrier mood.

Sancho was the first to recover his senses. Finding himself close to his master, he called to him in a weak, anguished voice, "Señor Don Quixote! Oh, Señor Don Quixote!"

"What do you want, brother Sancho?" returned Don Quixote in the same feeble suffering tone as Sancho.

"I would like, if it's possible," answered Sancho Panza, "for your worship to give me a couple swigs of that potion of the fiery Blas, if you happen to have it at hand. Perhaps it will be good for broken bones as well as for wounds."

"If only I had it here, wretch that I am, what more should we want?" said Don Quixote. "I swear to you, Sancho Panza, on the faith of a knight-errant, before

[5] *girths:* saddle straps.

[6] *stakes:* Carriers drive stakes into the ground on one side of the pack animal to prop up the pack while they adjust the balance from the other side.

[7] *jerkin:* close-fitting, waist-length jacket, usually without sleeves.

two days are over, unless fortune orders otherwise, I mean to have it in my possession, or my hand will have lost its cunning."

"And how many days do you think it will take before we can get back on our feet?" answered Sancho Panza.

"For myself, I must say I cannot guess how many," said the battered knight Don Quixote. "But I take all the blame upon myself, for I had no business to put hand to sword against men who were not dubbed knights like myself, and so I believe that in punishment for having transgressed the laws of chivalry, the god of battles has permitted this chastisement to be administered to me. For this reason, brother Sancho, it is well you should be made aware of what I am now about to relate to you, for it is of much importance to the welfare of both of us. It is that when you see rabble of this sort affronting our honor, do not wait till I draw sword against them, for I shall not do so at all. Rather, draw your sword and punish them to your heart's content. If any knights come to their aid and defense, I will take care to defend you and assail them with all my might. You have already seen by a thousand signs and proofs what the might of this strong arm of mine is equal to"—such was the self-assurance of the poor gentleman after his victory over the brave Biscayan.

But Sancho did not so fully approve of his master's admonition as to let it pass without saying in reply, "Señor, I am a man of peace, meek and quiet, and I can put up with any affront because I have a wife and children to support and bring up. So let me likewise make your worship aware—as I cannot make it a command—that on no account will I draw sword either against peasant or against knight, and that here before God I forgive the affronts that have been done to me, whether they have been, are, or shall be offered me by high or low, rich or poor, noble or commoner, with no exception whatsoever for rank or condition."

To this his master said in reply, "I wish I had breath enough to speak more easily, and that the pain I feel on this side would abate so as to let me explain to you, Panza, the mistake you are making. Come now, sinner, suppose the wind of fortune, hitherto so adverse, should turn in our favor, filling the sails of our desires so that safely and without impediment we put into port in one of those islands I have promised you. How would it be with you if upon winning it, I made you its lord? Why, you would make it well-nigh impossible through not being a knight nor having any desire to be one, nor possessing the courage nor the will to avenge insults or defend your domain. For you must know that in newly conquered kingdoms and provinces, the minds of the inhabitants are never so quiet nor so well disposed to the new lord that there is no fear of their making some move to change matters once more, and try, as they say, what chance may do for them. Thus, it is essential that the new possessor should have good sense to enable him to govern and valor to attack and defend himself, whatever may befall him."

"In what has just now befallen us," answered Sancho, "I'd have been well pleased to have that good sense and that valor your worship speaks of, but I swear on the faith of a poor man, I'm more fit for plasters[8] than for arguments. See if

[8] *plasters*: poultices, medicated pads applied to a wound.

your worship can get up, and let us help Rocinante, though he doesn't deserve it, for he was the main cause of all these blows. I never knew Rocinante had it in him, for I took him to be a virtuous person and as quiet as myself. In truth, they say right that it takes a long time to get to know people, and that there is nothing sure in this life. Who would have said that, after such mighty slashes as your worship gave that unlucky knight-errant, there was coming, traveling post[9] and at the very heels of them, such a great storm of sticks as has fallen upon our backs?"

"Your back, Sancho," replied Don Quixote, "ought to be used to such squalls, but mine—reared in soft cloth and fine linen—must surely feel more keenly the pain of this mishap. And if it were not that I imagine—why do I say imagine?—know of a certainty that all these discomforts are very necessary to the calling of arms, I would let myself die here from pure frustration."

To this the squire replied, "Señor, as these mishaps are what a fellow reaps from chivalry, tell me if they happen very often, or if they have their own fixed times for coming to pass; because it seems to me that after two harvests, we'll be no good for the third, unless God in his infinite mercy helps us."

"Know, friend Sancho," answered Don Quixote, "that the life of knights-errant is subject to a thousand dangers and reverses, and it is neither more nor less within immediate possibility for knights-errant to become kings and emperors, as experience has shown in the case of many different knights with whose histories I am thoroughly acquainted. I could tell you now—if the pain would let me—of some who simply by might of arm have risen to the high stations I have mentioned; and those same, both before and after, experienced several misfortunes and miseries. The valiant Amadís of Gaul found himself in the power of his mortal enemy Arcaláus the sorcerer, who—it is a known fact—holding him captive, gave him more than two hundred lashes with the reins of his horse while he was tied to one of the pillars of a courtyard. Moreover, there is a certain learned author of no small authority who says that the Knight of Phœbus, being caught in a certain pitfall, which opened under his feet in a certain castle, on falling found himself bound hand and foot in a deep pit underground, where they administered to him one of those things they call clysters,[10] of sand and snow-water, that almost finished him off; and if he had not been aided in that sore extremity by a sage, a great friend of his, it would have gone very hard with the poor knight. So I may well suffer in company with such worthy people, for greater were the affronts which they had to suffer than those which we suffer. For I would have you know, Sancho, that wounds caused by any instruments which happen by chance to be in hand inflict no indignity, and this is laid down in the law of the duel[11] in express

[9] *post:* rapidly.

[10] *clysters:* enemas.

[11] *indignity . . . law of the duel:* Though dueling had been illegal for some time, it was still practiced and continued to thrive in the popular imagination, thanks in large part to the honor play, a genre of theater that peaked in the first half of the seventeenth century. Don Quixote alludes to the complex customs that governed when a mere offense (*agravio*) rose to the level of a dishonor (*afrenta*), which permitted a challenge. The text translates *afrenta* as "indignity".

words. If, for instance, the cobbler strikes another with the last[12] which he has in his hand, though it be in fact a piece of wood, it cannot be said for that reason that he whom he struck with it has been clubbed. I say this lest you should imagine that because we have been drubbed in this skirmish we have therefore suffered any indignity; for the arms those men carried, with which they pounded us, were nothing more than their stakes, and not one of them, so far as I remember, carried rapier, sword, or dagger."

"They didn't give me time to see," answered Sancho, "for hardly had I laid hand on my Tizona[13] when they signed the cross on my back with their sticks in such style that they took the sight from my eyes and the strength from my feet, stretching me where I now lie. It gives me no pain to think whether being hit with those stakes was an indignity or not—nothing like the pain the blows of those stakes gives me, for they will remain as deeply impressed on my memory as on my back."

"For all that let me tell you, brother Panza," said Don Quixote, "that there is no memory which time does not put an end to, and no pain which death does not remove."

"What greater misfortune can there be," replied Panza, "than the one that waits for time to put an end to it and death to remove it? If our mishap were one of those that are cured with a couple of plasters, it wouldn't be so bad; but I'm beginning to think that all the plasters in a hospital won't be enough to put us right."

"No more of that. Pluck strength out of weakness, Sancho, as I mean to do," returned Don Quixote, "and let us see how Rocinante is, for it seems to me that not the least share of this mishap has fallen to the lot of the poor beast."

"No need to wonder about that," replied Sancho, "since he is a knight-errant, too. What I marvel at is that my beast should have come off scot-free where we come out scotched."

"Fortune always leaves a door open in adversity in order to bring relief to it," said Don Quixote. "I say so because this little beast may now supply the lack of Rocinante, carrying me hence to some castle where I may be cured of my wounds. Moreover, I shall not hold it any dishonor to be so mounted, for I remember having read how the good old Silenus, the tutor and instructor of the jolly god of laughter, when he entered the city of the hundred gates, went very contentedly mounted on a handsome donkey."[14]

"It may be true that he went mounted as your worship says," answered Sancho, "but there is a great difference between going mounted and going slung like a sack of manure."

[12] *last:* metal or wooden form a cobbler uses to shape or repair a shoe.

[13] *Tizona:* famed sword of El Cid. Sancho, with no sword to call his own, is speaking sarcastically.

[14] *the good old Silenus . . . mounted on a handsome donkey:* Silenus was the teacher of Bacchus, the god of laughter. He entered Boeotian Thebes in central Greece, where Bacchus resided, on the back of a donkey. Don Quixote confuses this Thebes, known as Thebes of the Seven Gates, with Thebes of the Hundred Gates, which is in Egypt.

To which Don Quixote replied, "Wounds received in battle confer honor instead of taking it away. And so, friend Panza, say no more, but, as I told you before, get up as well as you can and put me on top of your beast in whatever fashion pleases you best, and let us go hence before night comes on and surprises us in these wilds."

"I have heard your worship say," observed Panza, "that it is customary for knights-errant to sleep in wastes and deserts, and that they count it very good fortune."

"That is," said Don Quixote, "when they cannot help it, or when they are in love; and so true is this that there have been knights who have remained two years on rocks, in sunshine and shade and all the inclemencies of heaven, without their ladies knowing anything of it. One of these was Amadís, when, under the name of Beltenebros, he took up his abode on the Peña Pobre—I know not whether it was eight years or eight months, for I am not very sure of the reckoning. At any rate, he stayed there doing penance for I know not what slight he had committed against the Princess Oriana.[15] But no more of this now, Sancho, and make haste before a mishap like Rocinante's befalls the donkey."

"That would be an ever hotter hell!" cried Sancho. And letting off thirty groans and sixty sighs, and a hundred and twenty oaths and curses on whoever it was who had brought him there, he raised himself, stopping halfway bent like a Turkish bow[16] without power to bring himself upright. With all his pains, he saddled his donkey, who had also gone a little astray, yielding to the excessive liberties of the day. He next raised up Rocinante, who, had he possessed a tongue to complain with, would most assuredly have outdone both Sancho and his master.

To be brief, Sancho set Don Quixote on the donkey and secured Rocinante with a leading rein. Taking the donkey by the halter, he proceeded more or less in the direction in which it seemed to him the king's highway[17] might be. As chance was conducting their affairs from good to better, he had not gone a short league when the road came in sight, and on it he spied an inn, which to his annoyance and to the delight of Don Quixote was no less than a castle. Sancho insisted that it was an inn, and his master that it was not an inn but a castle. The dispute lasted so long that before the point was settled, they had time to reach it. Into it Sancho entered with all his train and without further incident.

[15] *slight he had committed against the Princess Oriana:* A hermit gives Amadís the name Beltenebros (the Gloomy Handsome One) when the hero retires to the desolate Peña Pobre (Poor Rock). His beloved, Oriana, has become offended after being misled to believe that Amadís has been favoring another lady. Ignorant of the reason for her anger, Amadís withdraws there to do penance in solitude. The incident from *Amadís of Gaul*, which comes up casually in this conversation, is a seed planted in Don Quixote's mind that will come to fruition later on.

[16] *Turkish bow:* A Turkish bow curves up before it curves out, faintly resembling a person hunched over.

[17] *king's highway:* A road constructed by the crown bore the designation king's highway (*camino real*). Wider and better maintained than other roads, a king's highway facilitated commerce, military transport, and communication between major cities.

CHAPTER XVI

OF WHAT HAPPENED TO THE INGENIOUS GENTLEMAN IN THE INN WHICH HE TOOK TO BE A CASTLE

The innkeeper, seeing Don Quixote slung across the donkey, asked Sancho what was wrong with him. Sancho answered that it was nothing, only that he had fallen down from a rock and had his ribs a little bruised. The innkeeper had a wife whose disposition was not such as those of her calling commonly have, for she was by nature kind-hearted and felt for the sufferings of her neighbors. She at once set about tending Don Quixote and made her daughter, a very attractive girl, help her in taking care of her guest. There was also in the inn as servant an Asturian[1] lass with a broad face, thick neck, and snub nose, blind in one eye and not very sound in the other. The elegance of her shape, to be sure, made up for all her defects. She did not measure seven palms[2] from head to foot, and her shoulders, which overburdened her somewhat, made her contemplate the ground more than she liked.

This graceful lass, to continue, helped the young girl, and the two made up a very bad bed for Don Quixote in a garret that showed evident signs of having formerly served for many years as a hayloft. In this garret, there was also quartered a mule driver whose bed was placed a little beyond our Don Quixote's, and, though only made of the packsaddles and blankets of his mules, had much the advantage of it. For Don Quixote's bed consisted simply of four rough boards on two not very even trestles; a mattress, which, for thinness might have passed for a quilt full of pellets, and were they not seen through the holes to be wool, would to the touch have seemed pebbles in hardness; two sheets made of buckler leather; and a coverlet, the threads of which anyone that chose might have counted without being off by one.

On this accursed bed Don Quixote stretched himself, and the innkeeper's wife and daughter soon covered him with bandages from top to toe, while Maritornes—for that was the name of the Asturian—held the light for them. While bandaging him, the innkeeper's wife, observing how bruised Don Quixote was in some places, remarked that this had more the look of blows than of a fall.

[1] *Asturian:* The region of Asturias is on the northern coast of Spain.

[2] *palms:* handsbreadth, unit used to measure the height of horses.

"They weren't blows," Sancho said. "The rock had many points and projections, and each of them left a bruise." He added, "Señora, see to it some tow[3] is set aside because someone is definitely going to need it. My ribs are quite sore as well."

"Then you, too, must have fallen," said the innkeeper's wife.

"I didn't fall," said Sancho Panza, "but from the shock I got at seeing my master fall, my body aches—just like someone's given me a thousand thwacks."

"That may well be," said the young girl, "for it has many a time happened to me to dream that I was falling down from a tower and never coming to the ground, and when I awoke from the dream I found myself as weak and shaken as if I had really fallen."

"That's it exactly," replied Sancho Panza. "I—without any dreaming, but being more awake than I am now—am hardly less bruised than my master Don Quixote."

"What's the gentleman's name?" asked Maritornes the Asturian.

"Don Quixote of La Mancha," answered Sancho Panza. "He is a knight-adventurer, and one of the best and bravest that have been seen in the world this long time past."

"What is a knight-adventurer?" asked the lass.

"Are you so new in the world that you don't know?" returned Sancho Panza. "Well, then, you must know, sister, that a knight-adventurer is a thing that in two shakes sees himself thrashed and emperor. Today he is the most miserable and needy being in the world, and tomorrow he will have two or three crowns of kingdoms to give his squire."

"Then how is it," asked the innkeeper's wife, "that belonging to so good a master as this, you have not, to judge by appearances, even so much as a county?"

"It's too soon yet," answered Sancho, "for we've been going only a month in quest of adventures, and so far we've met with nothing that can be called one. For it will happen that when one thing is looked for, another thing is found; however, if my master Don Quixote gets well from this wound—or fall—and I am left none the worse for it, I wouldn't trade my hopes for the best title in Spain."

To all this conversation Don Quixote was listening very attentively. Sitting up in bed as well as he could, and taking the innkeeper's wife by the hand he said to her, "Believe me, fair lady, you may call yourself fortunate in having in this castle of yours sheltered my person, which is such that if I do not myself praise it, it is because of what is commonly said, that self-praise debases; but my squire will inform you who I am. I only tell you that I shall preserve forever inscribed on my memory the service you have rendered me in order to tender you my gratitude while life shall last me. Would to Heaven love held me not so enthralled and subject to its laws and to the eyes of that fair ingrate whom I name under my breath, but that those of this lovely damsel might be the masters of my liberty."

[3] *tow:* short or broken fibers left over from combing flax. They were soaked in medicine and used as a wound dressing.

The hostess, her daughter, and the worthy Maritornes listened in bewilderment to the words of the knight-errant; for they understood about as much of them as if he had been talking Greek, though they could gather they were all meant for expressions of goodwill and flattery. Not being accustomed to this kind of language, they stared at him and wondered to themselves, for he seemed to them a man of a different sort from those they were used to. Thanking him in tavernly phrases[4] for his civility, they left him, while the Asturian gave her attention to Sancho, who needed it no less than his master.

The mule driver had arranged with Maritornes for recreation[5] that night, and she had given him her word that when the guests were quiet and the family asleep, she would come in search of him and meet his wishes unreservedly. And it is said of this good lass that she never made promises of the kind without fulfilling them, though she were to make them in a forest and with no witness present. She prided herself greatly on being a lady and held it no disgrace to be in such an employment as servant in an inn, because, she said, misfortunes and ill-luck had brought her to that position.

Don Quixote's hard, narrow, wretched, rickety bed stood first in the middle of this star-lit stable, and close beside it Sancho made his, which merely consisted of a wicker mat and a blanket that looked as if it was of threadbare canvas rather than of wool. Next to these two beds was that of the mule driver, made up, as has been said, of the packsaddles and all the trappings of the two best mules he had, and there were twelve of them—sleek, plump, and in prime condition. For he was one of the rich mule drivers of Arévalo,[6] according to the author of this history, who makes particular mention of this mule driver because he knew him very well, and they even say was in some degree a relation of his. Besides which, Cide Hamete Benengeli was a historian of great research and accuracy in all things, as is very evident since he would not pass over in silence those details already mentioned, however trifling and insignificant they might be, an example that might be followed by those somber historians who relate transactions so curtly and briefly that we hardly get a taste of them, all the substance of the work being left in the inkwell from carelessness, malice, or ignorance. A thousand blessings on the author of *Tablante of Ricamonte*[7] and the author of the other book in which the deeds of Count Tomillas are recounted.[8] With what minuteness they describe everything!

To proceed, then: after having paid a visit to his team and given them their second feed, the mule driver stretched himself on his packsaddles and lay waiting

[4] *tavernly phrases:* To contrast Don Quixote's chivalric register with the speech of his hosts, the narrator invents the fanciful phrase *venteriles razones* (innkeeper-speak).

[5] *recreation:* The uncommon Spanish verb *refocilarse* is used also in the previous chapter to describe Rocinante's desire to frolic with the Galician mares.

[6] *Arévalo:* town in northwest Castile.

[7] Tablante of Ricamonte: French chivalric romance published in Spanish translation in 1513.

[8] *the other book . . . recounted:* Count Tomillas is a character in the *History of Enrique, Son of Oliva* (1498).

for his ever so punctual Maritornes. Sancho was by this time bandaged and had lain down, and though he tried to sleep, the pain of his ribs would not let him, while Don Quixote, with the pain of his, had his eyes as wide open as a rabbit's.

The inn was all in silence, and in the whole of it there was no light except that given by a lantern that hung burning in the middle of the gateway. This strange stillness, and the thoughts always present to our knight's mind of the incidents described at every turn in the books that were the cause of his misfortune, conjured up in his imagination as extraordinary a delusion as can possibly be conceived. He fancied himself to have reached a famous castle (for as has been said, all the inns he lodged in were castles to his eyes), and that the daughter of the innkeeper was daughter of the lord of the castle. She, won by his high-bred bearing, had fallen in love with him and promised to come to his bed for a while that night without the knowledge of her parents. Taking all this fantasy he had constructed for solid fact, he began to feel uneasy and to consider the perilous risk that his virtue was about to encounter. He resolved in his heart to commit no treason to his lady Dulcinea del Toboso, even though Queen Guinevere herself and her lady Quintañona[9] should present themselves before him.

While he was taken up with this nonsense, the time and the hour—an unlucky one for him—arrived for the Asturian to come. She, in her nightshirt, with bare feet and her hair gathered into a fustian coif,[10] with noiseless and cautious steps entered the room where the three were quartered in quest of the mule driver. But scarcely had she come to the door when Don Quixote sensed her presence, and sitting up in his bed in spite of his bandages and the pain of his ribs, he stretched out his arms to receive his beauteous damsel. The Asturian, who came in crouched and in silence, with her hands before her feeling for her lover, encountered the arms of Don Quixote, who grasped her tightly by the wrist. Maritornes did not dare to utter a word as Don Quixote drew her toward him and made her sit down on the bed. He then felt her nightshirt, and although it was of sackcloth, it appeared to him to be of the finest and softest silk. On her wrists she wore some glass beads, but to him they had the sheen of precious Orient pearls. Her hair, which in some measure resembled a horse's mane, he rated as threads of the brightest Arabian gold, whose refulgence dimmed the sun itself. Her breath, which no doubt smelt of yesterday's stale salad,[11] seemed to him to diffuse a sweet aromatic fragrance from her mouth. In short, he drew her portrait in his imagination with the same features and in the same style as what he had seen in his books of the other princesses who, smitten by love, came with all the adornments here described to see their badly wounded knight.[12] So great was the poor gentleman's blindness that neither touch, nor smell, nor anything

[9] *Quintañona:* See footnote 2, page 91.

[10] *fustian coif:* close-fitting cap of coarse cotton.

[11] *yesterday's stale salad:* Whatever else the salad contained, onion was one of its ingredients.

[12] *to see their badly wounded knight:* The lady's surreptitious nocturnal visit to her wounded knight is a set piece in chivalric literature.

else about the good lass that would have made anyone but a mule driver vomit were enough to undeceive him. On the contrary, he was persuaded he had the goddess of beauty in his arms. Holding her firmly in his grasp, he began to speak in a soft, tender voice:

"Would that I found myself, lovely and exalted lady, in a position to repay such a favor as that which you, by the sight of your great beauty, have granted me; but fortune, which is never weary of persecuting the good, has chosen to place me upon this bed, where I lie so bruised and broken that though my inclination would gladly comply with yours, it is impossible. What is more, to this impossibility another yet greater is to be added, which is the faith that I have pledged to the peerless Dulcinea del Toboso, sole lady of my most secret thoughts. Were it not that this stood in the way, I should not be so insensible a knight as to miss the happy opportunity which your great goodness has offered me."

Maritornes was fretting and sweating at finding herself held so closely by Don Quixote, and not understanding or heeding the words he addressed to her, she tried without speaking to free herself. The worthy mule driver, whose unholy thoughts kept him awake, was aware of his wench the moment she entered the door and was listening attentively to all Don Quixote said. Jealous that the Asturian should have broken her word with him for another, he drew nearer to Don Quixote's bed and stood still to see what would come of this talk he could not understand. But when he perceived that the girl was struggling to get free and Don Quixote was trying to hold her, not relishing the joke, he raised his fist and delivered such a terrible blow to the lank jaw of the amorous knight that he bathed his whole mouth in blood. Not content with this, he climbed on top of Don Quixote's chest and, with his feet pacing faster than a trot, trampled his ribs from one end to the other. The bed, which was somewhat flimsy and not very firm on its feet, unable to support the additional weight of the mule driver, came to the ground. At the sound of its mighty crash, the innkeeper awoke and at once concluded that it must be some brawl of Maritornes', since after calling loudly to her, he received no answer. With this suspicion he got up, and lighting a lamp hastened to the place where he had heard the disturbance. Seeing that her master was coming and knowing that his temper was terrible, the girl, frightened and panic-stricken, took refuge in the bed of Sancho Panza, who still slept. There she curled herself up into a ball.

The innkeeper came in yelling, "Where are you, you hussy? No doubt this is your doing."

At this Sancho awoke. Feeling this mass almost on top of him, he thought he was having a nightmare and began to throw fisticuffs all round, of which a certain share fell upon Maritornes. She, irritated by the pain and flinging modesty aside, paid back so many in return to Sancho that she woke him up in spite of himself. Finding himself so handled (by whom he knew not), Sancho raised himself up as well as he could and took hold of Maritornes. And so the two of them commenced the fiercest and most comical battle in the world.

When the mule driver saw by the light of the innkeeper's candle how it fared with his ladylove, he left Don Quixote and ran to bring her the help she needed.

The innkeeper did the same but with a different intention, for his was to punish the lass, as he believed that beyond a doubt she alone was the source of this free-for-all. And so, as the saying goes, cat to rat, rat to rope, rope to stick:[13] the mule driver pounded Sancho, Sancho the lass, she him, and the innkeeper her, and all worked away so briskly that they did not give themselves a moment's rest. The best of it was that the innkeeper's lamp went out, and as they were left in the dark, they pummeled each other in a mass so unmercifully that there was not a sound spot left to lay a hand.

It so happened that there was lodging that night in the inn an officer of what they call the Old Holy Brotherhood of Toledo,[14] who, hearing the extraordinary noise of the conflict, seized his staff and the tin case with his warrants[15] and made his way in the dark into the room crying, "Cease in the name of justice! Cease in the name of the Holy Brotherhood!"

The first person he came upon was the battered Don Quixote, who lay stretched senseless on his back upon his broken-down bed. His hand fell on Don Quixote's beard as he felt about, while he continued to cry, "Make way in the name of justice!" When he realized that the man he had laid hold of did not stir, he concluded that he was dead and that those in the room were his murderers. With this suspicion, he raised his voice still higher, calling out, "Shut the inn gate! See that no one goes out. They have killed a man here!"

His cry startled them all, and each in turn abandoned the fight as the voice reached him. The innkeeper retreated to his room, the mule driver to his pack-saddles, the lass to her quarters. The unlucky Don Quixote and Sancho alone were unable to move from where they were. The officer finally let go of Don Quixote's beard and went out to look for a light to search for and apprehend the culprits. But not finding one (as the innkeeper had purposely extinguished the lantern on retreating to his room), he was compelled to resort to the hearth, where after much time and trouble, he lit another lamp.

[13] *cat to rat . . . rope to stick:* allusion to a traditional children's story.

[14] *what they call the Old Holy Brotherhood of Toledo:* Toledo chapter of the rural police force, called "Old" because it was founded two centuries before the Holy Brotherhood. See footnote 2, page 75.

[15] *warrants:* documents that accredited the officer's authority to execute justice.

CHAPTER XVII

IN WHICH ARE CONTAINED THE INNUMERABLE TROUBLES THAT THE BRAVE DON QUIXOTE AND HIS GOOD SQUIRE SANCHO PANZA ENDURED IN THE INN, WHICH TO HIS MISFORTUNE HE TOOK TO BE A CASTLE

By this time Don Quixote had recovered from his stupor; and in the same tone of voice in which he had called to his squire the day before when he lay stretched "in the valley of the stakes,"[1] he began calling to him now, "Sancho, my friend, are you asleep? Do you sleep, friend Sancho?"

"How can I sleep, curses on it!" returned Sancho bitterly and with great discontent, "when every devil in hell has been coming at me tonight?"

"You are right to believe that," answered Don Quixote, "for either I am ignorant or this castle is enchanted. You must know—but what I am now about to tell you, you must swear to keep secret until after my death."

"I swear it," answered Sancho.

"I say so," continued Don Quixote, "because I hate taking away anyone's good name."

"I say," replied Sancho, "that I swear to keep your secret till the end of your worship's days, and God grant I may be able to reveal it tomorrow."

"Do I do you such injuries, Sancho," said Don Quixote, "that you would see me dead so soon?"

"It's not for that," replied Sancho, "but because I hate keeping secrets very long, and I don't want them to grow rotten in me from over-keeping."

"Be that as it may," said Don Quixote, "I have greater confidence in your love and good nature. And so I would have you know that this night there befell me one of the strangest adventures that I could describe, and to relate it to you briefly you must know that a little while ago the daughter of the lord of this castle came to me, and that she is the most elegant and beautiful damsel that could be found in the wide world. What I could tell you of the charms of her person! What I could say of her lively wit! What of other secret matters which, to preserve the fealty I owe to my lady Dulcinea del Toboso, I shall pass over unnoticed and in silence! I will only tell you that, either Heaven was envious of

[1] *valley of the stakes:* opening line from a ballad: "Through the Valley of the Stakes/the worthy Cid rode forth."

so great a boon placed in my hands by good fortune, or perhaps (and this is more probable) this castle is enchanted, as I have already said. For at the time when I was engaged in the sweetest and most amorous discourse with her, there came, without my seeing or knowing whence it came, a hand attached to some arm of some huge giant, which planted such a fist on my jaws that I have them all bathed in blood, and then pummeled me in such a way that I am in a worse plight than yesterday when the carriers, on account of Rocinante's misbehavior, inflicted on us the injury you know of. From this I conjecture that there must be some enchanted Moor guarding the treasure of this damsel's beauty, and that it is not for me."

"Not for me either," said Sancho, "for more than four hundred Moors have so thrashed me that the drubbing with the stakes was cakes and fancy bread compared to it. Tell me, señor, what do you call this excellent and rare adventure that has left us as we're left now? At least your worship was not so badly off, having in your arms that incomparable beauty you spoke of. But I, what did I have, except the heaviest whacks I think I had in all my life? Unlucky me and the mother that bore me! For I am not a knight-errant and never expect to be one, and of all the mishaps, most of them fall to me."

"Then you have been thrashed, too?" said Don Quixote.

"A pox on my house! Didn't I say so?" said Sancho.

"Be not distressed, friend," said Don Quixote, "for I will now make the precious elixir with which we shall cure ourselves in the twinkling of an eye."

By this time the officer had succeeded in lighting the lamp and came in to see the man that he thought had been killed. Sancho caught sight of him at the door, and seeing him coming in his shirt, with a nightcap on his head, a lamp in his hand, and a very forbidding countenance, he said to his master, "Señor, can it be that this is the enchanted Moor coming back to punish us—if it's possible that anything is left in the inkwell?"

"It cannot be the Moor," answered Don Quixote, "for those under enchantment do not let themselves be seen by anyone."

"If they don't let themselves be seen, they let themselves be felt," said Sancho. "If not, my back could speak volumes."

"Mine could speak, too," said Don Quixote. "But that is not a sufficient reason for believing that what we see is the enchanted Moor."

The officer came up, and finding them engaged in such a peaceful conversation, stood amazed; though Don Quixote, to be sure, still lay on his back—unable to move from the beating and bandages. The officer turned to him and said, "Well, how goes it, good man?"

"I would speak more politely if I were you," replied Don Quixote. "Is it the custom of this country to address knights-errant in that way, you knave?"

The officer, finding himself so disrespectfully treated by such a sorry-looking individual, lost his temper, and raising the lamp full of oil, gave Don Quixote a smashing blow to the head. With everything now turned to darkness, he left.

Sancho Panza said, "That is certainly the enchanted Moor, señor, and he keeps the treasure for others. For us it's only fist blows and lamp whacks."

"So it is," returned Don Quixote. "There is no use in troubling oneself about these matters of enchantment or being angry or vexed at them. For as they are invisible and unearthly, we shall find no one on whom to avenge ourselves, do what we may. Rise, Sancho, if you can, and call the castellan of this fortress. Have him get me a little oil, wine, salt, and rosemary to make the health-restoring elixir, for indeed I believe I have great need of it now, as I am losing much blood from the wound that phantom gave me."

With sharp pain in his bones, Sancho got up and went after the innkeeper in the dark. Meeting the officer, who was looking to see what had become of his enemy, he said to him, "Señor, whoever you are, do us the favor and kindness of giving us a little rosemary, oil, salt, and wine, for it is needed to cure one of the best knights-errant on earth. He is lying on a bed over there, wounded by the hands of the enchanted Moor that haunts this inn."

When the officer heard him talk this way, he took him for a man out of his senses. As day was now beginning to break, he opened the inn gate and, calling the innkeeper, told him what this good man wanted. The innkeeper furnished him with what he required, and Sancho brought it to Don Quixote, who, with his hand to his head, was bewailing the pain of the blow from the lamp. It had done him no more harm than raising a couple of rather large lumps, and what he fancied blood was only the sweat that flowed from him in his sufferings during the recent storm.

To be brief, Don Quixote took the ingredients, from which he made a compound—mixing them all and boiling them a good while until it seemed to him they had come to perfection. He then asked for a vial to pour it into, and as there was not one in the inn, he decided on putting it into a tin oil bottle or flask, which the innkeeper gave him without cost. Over the flask, he repeated more than eighty Pater Nosters and as many more Ave Marias, Salves, and Credos,[2] accompanying each word with the sign of the cross by way of benediction. During all this time, there were present Sancho, the innkeeper, and the officer, for the mule driver was now peacefully engaged in attending to the comfort of his mules.

With this accomplished, Don Quixote was eager to waste no time in experiencing the virtue of this precious elixir (as he considered it), and so he drank nearly a quart of what could not be poured into the flask and was left in the pot in which it had been boiled. Scarcely had he done drinking, when he began to vomit in such a way that nothing was left in his stomach. With the pangs and spasms of vomiting, he broke into a profuse sweat, on account of which he ordered that they cover him up and leave him alone. They did so, and he lay sleeping more than three hours, at the end of which he awoke and felt very great bodily relief and so much ease from his bruises that he thought himself quite cured. He truly believed he had hit upon the elixir of Fierabras and that with this

[2] *eighty Pater Nosters and as many more Ave Marias, Salves, and Credos:* foundational prayers of the Catholic faith: the Lord's Prayer (Pater Noster), Hail Mary (Ave Maria), Hail, Holy Queen (Salve Regina), and Apostles' Creed (Credo).

remedy he might thenceforward, without any fear, face any kind of destruction, battle, or combat, however perilous it might be.

Sancho Panza, who also regarded his master's recovery as miraculous, begged him to give him what was left in the pot, which was no small quantity. Don Quixote consented, and Sancho, taking it with both hands—in good faith and with a better will—gulped down and finished off very little less than his master. It must be said, however, that the stomach of poor Sancho was apparently less delicate than that of his master;[3] for before he vomited, he was seized with such gripings and retchings, such sweats and faintness, that verily and truly he believed his last hour had come. Finding himself so racked and tormented, he cursed the elixir and the scoundrel who had given it to him.

Seeing him in this state, Don Quixote said, "It is my belief, Sancho, that this mischief comes of your not being dubbed a knight, for I am persuaded this liquor cannot be good for those who are not so."

Sancho responded, "If your worship knew that—curses on me and all my kindred!—why did you let me taste it?"

At this moment the concoction took effect, and the poor squire began to discharge from both ends at such a rate that the wicker mat on which he had thrown himself and the canvas blanket he had covering him were fit for nothing afterwards. He sweated and convulsed with such a fury that not only he himself but everyone present thought his end had come. His tribulation lasted about two hours, at the end of which (unlike his master) he was left so weak and exhausted he could not stand.

Don Quixote, who, as has been said, felt himself relieved and well, was eager to take his departure at once in quest of adventures, as it seemed to him that all the time that he lingered there was a disservice to the world and those in it who stood in need of his help and protection—all the more when he had the security and confidence his elixir provided him. Urged by this impulse, he saddled Rocinante himself and put the packsaddle on his squire's beast, then helped Sancho to dress and mount the donkey. After this he mounted his horse, and going over to a corner of the inn, he took hold of a spear[4] he spotted that could serve him as a lance. All those who were present at the inn (of whom there were more than twenty) stood watching him. The innkeeper's daughter was also staring at Don Quixote, just as he never took his eyes off her. From time to time he let out a sigh that he seemed to pluck up from the depths of his bowels; but everyone thought it must be from the pain he felt in his ribs—at least those who had seen him bandaged the night before thought so.

As soon as they were both mounted, Don Quixote called to the host from the gate of the inn and said in a very somber and measured voice, "Señor Castellan, many and great are the favors that I have received in this castle of yours, and I remain under the deepest obligation to be grateful to you for them

[3] *less delicate than that of his master:* i.e., slower to expel a noxious substance.

[4] *spear: lanzón*, short, steel-tipped shaft that a farmer would use to guard a vineyard or melon patch.

all the days of my life. If I can repay them in avenging you of any arrogant foe who may have wronged you, know that my calling is no other than to aid the weak, to avenge those who suffer wrong, and to punish treachery. Search your memory, and if you find anything of this kind you need, only tell me. I promise you by the order of knighthood I have received to obey your every wish to find redress and satisfaction."

The innkeeper replied to him with equal calmness, "Sir knight, I do not want your worship to avenge me of any wrong, because when any is done me I can take what vengeance seems good to me. All I want is for you to pay me the bill you ran up in the inn last night: both for the straw and barley for your two beasts, as well as for supper and beds."

"Then this is an inn?" said Don Quixote.

"And a very respectable one," said the innkeeper.

"I have been under a mistake all this time," said Don Quixote, "for in truth I thought it was a castle, and not a bad one. But since it appears that it is not a castle but an inn, all that can be done now is that you should excuse the payment, since I cannot contravene the rule of knights-errant, of whom I know as a fact—and up to the present I have read nothing to the contrary—that they never paid for lodging or anything else in the inn where they happened to stay. For any hospitality that might be offered them is their rightful due by law in return for the insufferable toil they endure in seeking adventures by night and by day, in summer and in winter, on foot and on horseback, in hunger and thirst, cold and heat, exposed to all the inclemencies of heaven and all the hardships of earth."

"I have little to do with that," replied the innkeeper. "Pay me what you owe me, and let us have no more talk of chivalry, for all I care about is to get my money."

"You are a stupid, scurvy innkeeper," said Don Quixote, and with spurs to Rocinante and a tilt to his spear, he rode out of the inn before anyone could stop him, and pushed on some distance without looking to see if his squire was following behind.

When the innkeeper saw him go without paying, he determined to get payment from Sancho. Sancho, however, said that as his master would not pay neither would he, since, being as he was squire to a knight-errant, the same rule and reason held good for him as for his master with regard to not paying anything in inns and hostels. At this the innkeeper became quite angry and threatened that if he did not pay, he would be compelled to do so in a way he would not like. Sancho answered that by the law of chivalry his master had received, he would not pay a cent, though it cost him his life; for the excellent and ancient usage of knights-errant was not going to be violated by him, nor should the squires of those who were yet to come into the world ever complain or reproach him for having broken so just a privilege.

It was the ill luck of the unfortunate Sancho that among the guests in the inn were four wool carders[5] from Segovia, three needle makers from the Colt of

[5] *wool carders:* tradesmen who produced woolen cloth.

Córdoba, and two lodgers from the Seville Fair,[6] lively and good-natured fellows, though mischievous and fond of joking. Almost as if instigated by a common impulse, they approached Sancho and dismounted him from his donkey, while one of them went in for the blanket on the innkeeper's bed. Into it they flung Sancho, though when they looked up and saw that the ceiling was somewhat lower than what they required for their work, they decided to go out into the yard, which was bounded by the sky. There, setting Sancho in the middle of the blanket, they began to toss him in the air, making sport with him as they would with a dog during carnival.[7]

The cries of the poor blanketed wretch were so loud that they reached the ears of his master, who, halting to listen attentively, was persuaded that some new adventure was coming, until he realized that it was his squire who uttered them. Turning the reins, he came up to the inn with a laborious gallop, and finding it shut went round it to see if there was some way of getting in. As soon as he came to the wall of the yard, which was not very high, he discovered the game being played with his squire. He saw him rising and falling in the air with such grace and nimbleness that, had his rage allowed him, it is my belief he would have laughed. He tried to climb from his horse on to the top of the wall, but he was so bruised and battered that he could not even dismount. And so from atop his horse he began to utter such curses and insults against those who were blanketing Sancho that it would be impossible to write them down accurately.

This wasn't enough, however, to put an end to their laughter or their work. Nor did the flying Sancho cease his lamentations, mingled sometimes with threats, sometimes with entreaties—all to little purpose, or rather, none at all—until from pure exhaustion they left off. They then brought him his donkey and mounted him on top of it with his cloak draped over him. The compassionate Maritornes, seeing him so exhausted, thought fit to refresh him with a jug of water, and that it might be all the cooler she fetched it from the well.[8] Sancho took it, and as he was raising it to his mouth he was stopped by the cries of his master exclaiming, "Sancho, my son, do not drink the water; drink it not, my son, for it will kill you. See, I have here the blessed elixir!" Here, he held up the flask of liquor. "Only drink two drops of it, and you will certainly be restored!"

At these words, Sancho rolled his eyes and, in a still louder voice, said, "Can it be your worship has forgotten that I am not a knight? Or do you want me to vomit up what bowels I have left after last night? Keep your liquor in the name of all the devils, and leave me to myself!"

[6] *Colt of Córdoba . . . Seville Fair*: The Seville Fair neighborhood hosted a weekly market. Both places had a reputation for attracting ruffians.

[7] *blanket, they began to toss . . . during carnival*: Blanketing (*manteo* or *manteamiento*, from *manta*, "blanket") is a Spanish carnival tradition still practiced with dolls made of rags or straw. It typifies the revelry that leads up to the somber season of Lent.

[8] *thought fit to refresh him with a jug of water . . . from the well*: Perhaps an echo of Matthew 10:42: "And whoever gives to one of these little ones even a cup of cold water because he is a disciple, truly, I say to you, he shall not lose his reward."

At one and the same instant, he left off talking and began drinking. But upon tasting at the first sip that it was water, he did not care to have any more but instead begged Maritornes to fetch him some wine. She did this with great goodwill and paid for it with her own money; for indeed they say of her that, though she was in a certain line of work, there was some faint resemblance to a Christian about her. When Sancho had finished drinking, he dug his heels into his donkey, and the gate of the inn being thrown open, he passed out very well pleased at having paid nothing and made his point, though it had been at the expense of his usual guarantor, that is, his backside. It is true that the innkeeper kept his saddlebag in payment of what was owed him, but Sancho departed in such a flurry that he never missed it. The innkeeper, as soon as he saw him off, wanted to bar the gate shut, but the blanketers would not agree to it. For they were fellows who would not have cared two cents about Don Quixote, even had he really been one of the knights-errant of the Round Table.

CHAPTER XVIII

IN WHICH IS RELATED THE DISCOURSE SANCHO PANZA HELD WITH HIS MASTER, DON QUIXOTE, AND OTHER ADVENTURES WORTH RELATING

Sancho reached his master so limp and faint that he was unable to urge on his donkey. When Don Quixote saw the state he was in he said, "I have now come to the conclusion, good Sancho, that this castle or inn is beyond a doubt enchanted, because those who have so atrociously amused themselves with you, what can they be but ghosts or beings of another world? I hold this confirmed by having noticed that when I was by the wall of the yard witnessing the acts of your sad tragedy, it was out of my power to scale it, nor could I even dismount from Rocinante, because they no doubt had me enchanted. For I swear to you by the faith of what I am that if I had been able to climb up or dismount, I would have avenged you in such a way that those vile miscreants would have remembered their fool's game forever, even though in so doing I knew I would be contravening the laws of chivalry, which, as I have often told you, do not permit a knight to lay hands on him who is not one, save in case of urgent and great necessity in defense of his own life and person."

"I would have avenged myself too if I could," said Sancho, "whether I had been a dubbed knight or not, but I wasn't able. Though for my part I'm persuaded those who amused themselves with me were not ghosts or enchanted men, as your worship says, but men of flesh and bone like ourselves. They all had their names, for I heard them name them when they were tossing me. One was called Pedro Martínez, and another Tenorio Hernández, and the innkeeper, I heard, was called Juan Palomeque the Left-handed. So your not being able to leap over the wall of the yard or dismount from your horse, señor, came from something else besides enchantments. What I make out clearly from all this is that these adventures we go seeking will in the end lead us into such misadventures that we won't know which is our right foot. The best and wisest thing, according to my small wits, would be for us to return home and attend to our farms, now that it is harvest time, and give up 'wandering from Zeca to Mecca and from pail to bucket,' as the saying goes."

"How little you know about chivalry, Sancho," replied Don Quixote. "Hold your peace and have patience. The day will come when you will see with your own eyes what an honorable thing it is to wander in the pursuit of this calling.

Nay, tell me, what greater pleasure can there be in the world, or what delight can equal that of winning a battle and triumphing over one's enemy? None, beyond all doubt."

"Very likely," answered Sancho, "though I don't know what that is like. All I know is that since we have been knights-errant, or since your worship has been one—for I have no right to count myself among so honorable a number—we have never won any battle except the one with the Biscayan, and even with that one your worship came out missing half an ear and half a helmet. From that moment till now it has been nothing but thrashings and more thrashings, beatings and more beatings. What's more, I'm the one who gets the blanketing, and I'm the one who stumbles upon enchanted people who I can't avenge myself on so as to know what the delight, as your worship calls it, of conquering an enemy is like."

"That is what vexes me, and what ought to vex you, Sancho," replied Don Quixote. "Henceforward, I will endeavor to have at hand some sword made by such craft that no kind of enchantments can take effect upon him who carries it, and it is even possible that fortune may procure for me that which belonged to Amadís when he was called 'The Knight of the Burning Sword,'[1] which was one of the best swords that ever knight in the world possessed, for besides having the said virtue, it cut like a razor, and there was no armor, however strong and enchanted it might be, that could resist it."

"With my luck," said Sancho, "even if it happened that your worship found some such sword, it would, like the elixir, turn out useful and worthwhile for dubbed knights only, and as for the squires, they might as well feast on tears."

"Fear not, Sancho," said Don Quixote. "Heaven will deal better with you."

Thus talking, Don Quixote and his squire went along when, on the road they were following, Don Quixote observed a large and thick cloud of dust approaching them. On seeing it, he turned to Sancho and said:

"This is the day, Sancho, on which will be seen the blessing my fortune is reserving for me. This, I say, is the day on which as much as on any other shall be displayed the might of my arm, and on which I shall do deeds that shall remain written in the book of fame for all ages to come. Do you see that cloud of dust which rises yonder? Well, all that is being churned up by a vast army made up of diverse and countless nations that comes marching there."

"That being the case, there must be two," said Sancho, "for on the opposite side another cloud of dust just like it is also rising."

Don Quixote turned to look and found that it was true, and rejoicing exceedingly, he concluded that they were two armies about to meet and face off in the midst of that broad plain. For at all times and seasons his fancy was full of the battles, enchantments, adventures, crazy feats, loves, and duels that are recorded in the books of chivalry, and everything he said, thought, or did had reference to such things. Now the cloud of dust he had seen was raised by two great droves of sheep

[1] *Amadís . . . 'The Knight of the Burning Sword'*: The Knight of the Burning Sword is Amadís of Greece, the great-grandson of Amadís of Gaul.

coming along the same road in opposite directions, which, because of the dust, did not become visible until they drew near. But Don Quixote was so insistent that they were armies that Sancho was led to believe it and say, "Well, and what are we to do, señor?"

"What?" said Don Quixote. "Give aid and assistance to the weak and those who need it. You must know, Sancho, that the army which comes opposite to us is conducted and led by the mighty emperor Alifanfarón,[2] lord of the great isle of Trapobana.[3] This other that marches behind me is that of his enemy the king of the Garamantas,[4] Pentapolín of the Rolled-up Sleeve, for he always goes into battle with his right arm bare."

"But why are these two lords such enemies?"

"They are at enmity," replied Don Quixote, "because this Alifanfarón is a wild pagan and is in love with the daughter of Pentapolín, who is very beautiful, and, moreover, a gracious lady and a Christian; and her father is unwilling to bestow her upon the pagan king unless he first abandons the religion of his false prophet Muhammad and adopts his own."

"By my whiskers," said Sancho, "that Pentapolín does quite right, and I'll help him as much as I can."

"In that you will do what is your duty, Sancho," said Don Quixote; "for to engage in battles of this sort does not require one to have been dubbed a knight."

"That I can well understand," answered Sancho. "But where should we put this donkey so that we can be sure to find him when the fight is over? For I believe it has not been the custom so far to go into battle on a beast of this kind."

"That is true," said Don Quixote. "What you had best do with him is to leave him to his own devices, for the horses we shall have when we come out victors will be so many that even Rocinante will run a risk of being swapped for another. But attend to me and observe, for I wish to give you some account of the chief knights who accompany these two armies; and that you may the better see and take note, let us withdraw to that hillock which rises yonder, whence both armies may be seen."

They did so and placed themselves on a knoll from which the two droves that Don Quixote made out to be mighty armies might have been plainly seen had the clouds of dust they raised not obscured them and blinded their view. Nevertheless, seeing in his imagination what could not be seen and did not exist, he began in a loud voice:

"That knight whom you see yonder in yellow armor, who bears upon his shield a lion crowned crouching at the feet of a damsel, is the valiant Laurcalco, lord

[2] *Alifanfarón:* Among Don Quixote's finest talents is his ability to dream up whimsical names. As a rule, they have the lofty sound of a character from a chivalric romance, but there is something in the substance that brings them back to earth. *Alifanfarón* combines the Arabic men's name *Ali* and *fanfarrón* (braggart). To hear the music, the names in the pages that follow are best read aloud.

[3] *Trapobana:* ancient name for the island of Ceylon, now Sri Lanka.

[4] *Garamantas:* ancient people of southern Libya known for their four-horse chariots.

of the Silver Bridge.[5] That one in armor with flowers of gold, who bears on his shield three crowns argent[6] on an azure field, is the dreaded Micocolembo,[7] grand duke of Quirocia. That other hulking figure, on his right hand, is the ever dauntless Brandabarbarán of Boliche,[8] lord of the three Arabias,[9] who for armor wears that serpent skin, and has for a shield a gate which, according to tradition, is one of those of the temple that Samson brought to the ground when by his death he revenged himself upon his enemies.[10]

"Turn your eyes to the other side, and you will see leading the vanguard of this other army the ever victorious and never vanquished Timonel of Carcajona, prince of New Biscay,[11] who comes in armor with arms quartered azure, green, white, and yellow. He bears on his shield a golden cat on a tawny field with a motto that says MEOW, which is the beginning of the name of his lady, who is said to be the peerless Meowlina, daughter of the duke Alfeñiquén of the Algarve.[12] The other, who burdens and presses the loins of that powerful charger and bears arms white as snow and a white shield without any device,[13] is a novice knight. He is a Frenchman by birth, Pierres Papin by name, lord of the baronies of Utrique.[14] That other, who with iron-shod heels strikes the flanks of that nimble parti-colored[15] zebra, and for arms bears an azure vair,[16] is the mighty duke of Nerbia, Espartafilardo of the Forest,[17] who bears for a device on his shield an asparagus plant with a motto in Castilian that says, FOLLOW MY LUCK."

And so he went on naming many knights of one squadron and the other as he imagined them. To all he assigned on the spot their arms, colors, devices, and mottoes, carried away by the illusions of his unheard-of madness. He continued without pause:

[5] *Silver Bridge:* recalls the saying "If your enemy is fleeing, build him a silver bridge."

[6] *argent:* silver or white.

[7] *Micocolembo: mico* (small monkey) + *cola* (tail).

[8] *Boliche:* In urban slang, a *boliche* was a gambling den connected to a brothel.

[9] *three Arabias:* Roman division of the Arabian Peninsula into three districts. Don Quixote mentions one of these, Arabia Felix (present-day Yemen) below.

[10] *has for a shield a gate . . . upon his enemies:* conflation of two incidents from the life of Samson, one in which Samson removes the gates to the city of Gaza, and his final feat, where he dislodges two pillars in the temple of Dagon, causing the building to collapse (Judges 16).

[11] *Timonel of Carcajona, prince of New Biscay: carcajada,* hearty laugh; New Biscay (*Nueva Vizcaya*) was the province of the Spanish Viceroyalty of New Spain, present-day Mexico.

[12] *Alfeñiquén of the Algarve: alfeñique,* confection of sugar paste, honey, and almond oil used to make figurines (by analogy, a person of brittle and delicate nature); the Algarve is the southernmost region of Portugal.

[13] *device:* See footnote 2, page 30.

[14] *Pierres Papin . . . of Utrique:* Pierres Papin may have a been a French hunchback who sold playing cards in Seville. Utrique is the modern city of Utrecht in the Netherlands.

[15] *parti-colored:* with many colors.

[16] *azure vair:* alternating blue and white pattern.

[17] *Espartafilardo of the Forest: esparto,* grass native to Spain woven into cords and baskets.

"People of diverse nations compose this squadron in front.[18] Here are those that drink of the sweet waters of the famous Xanthus;[19] the rustics who tread the Massilian plains;[20] those that sift the pure, fine gold of Arabia Felix; those that enjoy the renowned cool banks of the crystalline Thermodon;[21] those that in many and various ways divert the streams of the golden Pactolus;[22] the Numidians, faithless in their promises; the Persians, renowned in archery; the Parthians and the Medes, who fight as they fly; the Arabs, who ever shift their dwellings; the Scythians,[23] as cruel as they are fair; the Ethiopians, with pierced lips; and countless other nations whose features I recognize and descry, though I cannot recall their names. In this other squadron[24] there come those that drink of the crystal streams of the olive-bearing Betis;[25] those that make smooth their countenances with the water of the ever rich and golden Tagus;[26] those that rejoice in the nourishing flow of the divine Genil;[27] those that roam the Tartesian plains[28] abounding in pasture; those that take their pleasure in the Elysian meadows of Jérez;[29] the rich Manchegans crowned with ruddy ears of corn; the wearers of iron, old relics of the Gothic race; those that bathe in the Pisuerga,[30] renowned for its gentle current; those that feed their herds along the spreading pastures of the winding Guadiana,[31] famed for its hidden course; those that tremble with the cold of the pineclad Pyrenees or the dazzling snows of the lofty Apennine—in a word, as many as all Europe contains."

My gracious heavens! How many provinces, how many nations he named! He gave to each its proper attributes with astonishing speed, so engrossed and steeped was he in what he had read in his lying books.

Sancho Panza hung upon his every word without saying any himself. But from time to time, he turned to try if he could see the knights and giants his master

[18] *squadron in front:* Don Quixote begins by naming squadrons from North Africa and Europe's Asian frontier. In imitation of Homer, Virgil, and some chivalric texts, he associates many of the peoples with their principal river or a prominent land formation.

[19] *Xanthus:* river of Troy.

[20] *rustics who tread the Massilian plains:* Massylii, Berber confederation in ancient North Africa.

[21] *Thermodon:* river of northern Anatolia, present-day Turkey, where the Amazons were said to inhabit.

[22] *Pactolus:* river of Lydia, in western Anatolia, known for its gold-bearing sands.

[23] *Scythians:* nomadic people of the Eurasian Steppe noted for mounted warfare.

[24] *this other squadron:* Don Quixote turns to squadrons hailing from the Iberian Peninsula.

[25] *Betis:* See footnote 2, page 98.

[26] *Tagus:* See footnote 16, page 10.

[27] *Genil:* river of Granada.

[28] *Tartesian plains:* fertile land surrounding Tarifa and present-day Gibraltar.

[29] *Elysian meadows of Jérez:* According to one tradition, the Elysian Fields, the eternal dwelling of the blessed in Greek mythology, were located on the western frontier of what was then the known world, the Atlantic Coast near Jérez de la Frontera.

[30] *Pisuerga:* river of Valladolid.

[31] *Guadiana:* river of central Spain that flows into the Gulf of Cádiz; the erroneous belief that early stretches of the river's course are subterranean dates to antiquity.

was naming. As he could not make out a single one of them, he said, "Señor, if there's any man, knight, or giant around here of the kind you describe, may the devil take him. Maybe it's all enchantment, like the ghosts last night."

"How can you say that?" returned Don Quixote. "Do you not hear the neighing of the steeds, the braying of the trumpets, the roll of the drums?"

"I hear nothing but a great bleating of ewes and sheep," said Sancho—which was true, for by this time the two flocks had come close.

"Your fear, Sancho," said Don Quixote, "prevents you from seeing or hearing correctly. For one of the effects of fear is to trouble the senses and make things appear different from what they are. If you are so afraid, withdraw to one side and leave me to myself, for I alone am enough to bring victory to that side to which I shall give my aid."

And so saying, he gave Rocinante the spur and, putting the lance in rest, shot down the slope like a thunderbolt. Sancho shouted after him crying, "Come back, Señor Don Quixote! I vow to God they are sheep and ewes you are charging. Come back! Unlucky the father who begot me! This is madness! Look, there is no giant, no knight, no cats, no arms, no shields quartered or whole, no azure or devilish vair. What are you doing? Sinner that I am before God!"

But not for all these entreaties did Don Quixote turn back. On the contrary, he went on shouting out, "Hail, knights, you who follow and fight under the banners of the valiant emperor Pentapolín of the Rolled-up Sleeve, follow me all. You shall see how easily I shall give him his revenge over his enemy Alifanfarón of the Trapobana."

So saying, he dashed into the midst of the squadron of sheep and began spearing them with as much zeal and boldness as if he were transfixing mortal enemies in earnest. The shepherds and drovers[32] accompanying the flock shouted to him to stop. Seeing it was no use, they took out their slings and began to greet his ears with stones as big as one's fist. Don Quixote gave no heed to the stones, but lashing out in all directions kept saying, "Where are you, proud Alifanfarón? Come before me. I am a single knight who would gladly prove your prowess hand to hand and make you yield your life as penalty for the wrong you do to the valiant Pentapolín Garamanta."

Here a river pebble came at him that landed in his side and buried a couple ribs in his body. Feeling himself so smitten, he concluded that he was slain or badly wounded for certain. Recollecting his liquor, he drew out his flask and putting it to his mouth began to pour the contents into his stomach. But before he had succeeded in swallowing what seemed to him enough, there came another stone the size of an almond, which struck him on the hand and on the flask so smartly that it smashed it to pieces, knocking three or four teeth and molars out of his mouth in its course and sorely crushing two fingers of his hand. Such was the force of the first blow and of the second that the poor knight in spite of himself came down backwards off his horse. The shepherds approached and felt sure they had killed him, so in all haste they collected their flock together, took

[32] *drovers:* A drover is one who drives cattle or sheep.

up the dead beasts, of which there were more than seven, and made off without waiting to discover anything else.

All this time Sancho stood on the hill watching the crazy feats his master was performing, tearing his beard and cursing the hour when fortune brought them together. When he saw his master knocked to the ground and the shepherds disperse, Sancho ran to him and found him in a very bad state, though not unconscious. He said to him, "Did I not tell you to come back, Señor Don Quixote, and that what you were going to attack were not armies but droves of sheep?"

"Just like that, my enemy—that scoundrel of a sage—can alter things and make them vanish," answered Don Quixote. "You must know, Sancho, that it is a very easy matter for those of his kind to make us believe what they choose. This malignant being who persecutes me, envious of the glory he knew I was to win in this battle, has turned the squadrons of the enemy into droves of sheep. If you do nothing else, I beg of you, Sancho, do this much to undeceive yourself and see that what I say is true: Mount your donkey and follow them quietly, and you shall see that when they have gone some little distance from this, they will return to their original shape and, ceasing to be sheep, will become men in all respects as I described them to you at first. But go not just yet, for I want your assistance. Come close, and see how many of my teeth and molars are missing, for I feel as if there was not one left in my mouth."

Sancho came so close that he almost put his eyes into his mouth. Now just at that moment, the elixir acted on Don Quixote's stomach, so at the very instant when Sancho came to examine his mouth, he discharged all its contents with more force than a musket, and full into the beard of the compassionate squire.

"Holy Mary!" cried Sancho. "What has happened me? No doubt this sinner is mortally wounded, since he vomits blood from his mouth."

But considering the matter a little more closely, he gathered by the color, taste, and smell, that it was not blood but the elixir from the flask he had seen him drink from. He was taken with such a loathing that his stomach turned, and he vomited up his insides over his very master. The two of them made quite a sight.

Sancho ran to his donkey to get something to wipe himself off with and to attend to his master. Not finding his saddlebag, he nearly took leave of his senses. He cursed himself anew, and in his heart he resolved to leave his master and return home, even though he would be forfeiting the wages of his service and all hopes of the promised island.

Don Quixote rose with his left hand to his mouth to keep his teeth from falling out altogether, while with the other hand, he laid hold of Rocinante's bridle (the animal had never stirred from his master's side, so loyal and well-behaved was he). He approached his squire, who stood leaning over his donkey with his hand to his cheek, like one in deep dejection.

Seeing him in this mood, looking so sad, Don Quixote said to him, "Bear in mind, Sancho, that one man is no more than another, unless he does more than another. All these tempests that fall upon us are signs that fair weather is coming shortly and that things will go well with us, for it is impossible for good or evil to last forever. Hence it follows that the evil having lasted long, the good must be now near at hand. So you must not distress yourself at the misfortunes which befall me, since you have no share in them."

"I haven't?" replied Sancho. "By any chance, was the one they blanketed yesterday someone other than my father's son? And the saddlebag that is missing today with all my supplies, did it belong to anyone else but myself?"

"What! Is the saddlebag missing, Sancho?" said Don Quixote.

"Yes, it's missing," answered Sancho.

"In that case we have nothing to eat today," replied Don Quixote.

"That would be the case," answered Sancho, "if there were none of the herbs your worship says you know of in these meadows. They can make up for what knights-errant as unlucky as your worship are in need of."

"For all that," answered Don Quixote, "I would rather have just now a quarter of bread, or a loaf and two herring heads, than all the herbs described by Dioscorides, even with Doctor Laguna's notes.[33] Nevertheless, Sancho the Good, mount your beast and come along with me, for God, who provides for all things, will not fail us, more especially when we are so active in his service as we are. He fails not the mosquitos of the air, nor the grubs of the earth, nor the tadpoles of the water, and is so merciful that he makes his sun to rise on the good and on the evil and sends rain on the unjust and on the just."[34]

"Your worship would make a better preacher than knight-errant," said Sancho.

"Knights-errant knew and ought to know everything, Sancho," said Don Quixote. "For there were knights-errant in former times as well qualified to deliver a sermon or discourse in the middle of an encampment, as if they had graduated from the University of Paris. From this we may see that the lance has never blunted the pen, nor the pen the lance."

"Well, may it be as your worship says," replied Sancho. "Let's be off from here and find some place of shelter for the night, and God grant it may be somewhere where there are no blankets, blanketeers, ghosts, or enchanted Moors. For if there are, I'll give the devil the what for."

"Ask that of God, my son," said Don Quixote. "And lead on where you will, for this time I leave our lodging to your choice. But extend me here your hand, and feel with your finger, and find out how many of my teeth and molars are missing from this right side of my upper jaw, for it is there I feel the pain."

Sancho put in his fingers, and feeling about asked him, "How many molars did your worship used to have on this side?"

"Four," replied Don Quixote, "besides the wisdom tooth, all whole and quite sound."

[33] *Dioscorides, even with Doctor Laguna's notes:* Pedanius Dioscorides' *On Medical Material*, a five-volume encyclopedia of pharmacology, was translated to Spanish from ancient Greek with commentary and illustrations by Dr. Andrés Laguna and published in 1555.

[34] *his sun to rise . . . on the just:* Matthew 5:45.

"Be sure of what you're saying, señor."

"I say four, if not five," answered Don Quixote, "for never in my life have I had tooth or molar extracted, nor has any fallen out or been destroyed by decay or infection."

"Well, then," said Sancho, "in this lower side your worship has no more than two molars and a half, and in the upper neither a half nor any at all, for it is all as smooth as the palm of my hand."

"Unfortunate wretch that I am!" exclaimed Don Quixote, hearing the sad news his squire gave him. "I had rather they despoiled me of an arm, so long as it was not the sword arm. For I tell you, Sancho, a mouth without teeth is like a mill without a millstone, and a tooth is much more to be prized than a diamond. But we who profess the austere order of chivalry are liable to all this. Mount, friend, and lead the way, and I will follow you at whatever pace you choose."

Sancho did as he asked him and proceeded in the direction in which he thought he might find refuge without leaving the king's highway, which was there very much frequented. As they went along, then, at a slow pace—for the pain in Don Quixote's jaws kept him uneasy and ill-disposed for speed—Sancho thought it well to amuse and distract him by talk of some kind, and among the things he said to him was that which will be told in the following chapter.

CHAPTER XIX

OF THE CLEVER DISCOURSE WHICH SANCHO HELD WITH HIS MASTER, AND OF THE ADVENTURE THAT BEFELL HIM WITH A DEAD BODY, TOGETHER WITH OTHER NOTABLE OCCURRENCES

"It seems to me, señor, that all these mishaps that have happened to us lately have been without any doubt a punishment for the offense committed by your worship against the order of chivalry in not keeping the oath you made not to eat bread off a tablecloth or make merry with the queen—and all the rest of it your worship swore to observe—until you had taken that helmet of Malandrino's, or whatever the Moor is called, for I do not very well remember."

"You are very right, Sancho," said Don Quixote. "But to tell the truth, it had escaped my memory. Likewise, you may rely upon it that the blanket incident happened to you because of your fault in not reminding me of it in time. But I will make amends, for there are ways to remedy everything in the order of chivalry."

"Why, have I taken an oath of some sort, then?" asked Sancho.

"It makes no matter that you have not taken an oath," said Don Quixote. "Suffice it that, according to my understanding, you are not quite clear of complicity. And whether you are or not, there will be no harm done in providing ourselves with a remedy."

"In that case," said Sancho, "mind that your worship does not forget this as you did the oath. The ghosts just might take it into their heads to amuse themselves once more with me—or even with your worship if they see you so obstinate."

While engaged in this and other talk, night overtook them on the road before they had reached or discovered any place of shelter. To make matters worse, they were dying of hunger, for with the loss of the saddlebag they had lost their entire pantry and storehouse. To complete the misfortune, they met with an adventure that, without intending to, really had the appearance of one. It so happened that the night closed in somewhat darkly, but for all that they pushed on, Sancho feeling sure that as the road was the king's highway, they might reasonably expect to find some inn within a league or two.

Going along then in this way, the night dark, the squire hungry, the master eager to eat, they saw coming toward them on the road they were traveling a great number of lights that looked just like stars in motion. Sancho was taken aback at the sight of them, nor did Don Quixote altogether relish them. The one pulled up his donkey by the halter, the other his hack by the bridle. They stood still, watching anxiously to see what all this would turn out to be. They found that the lights were approaching them, and the nearer they came the greater they seemed. At this sight, Sancho began to shake like a man dosed with mercury,[1] and Don Quixote's hair stood on end.

The latter, however, plucking up spirit a little, said, "This, no doubt, Sancho, will be a most mighty and perilous adventure, in which it will be necessary for me to put forth all my valor and resolve."

"Unlucky me!" answered Sancho. "If this adventure happens to involve ghosts, as I am beginning to think it does, where will I find the ribs to bear it?"

"Be they ghosts ever so much," said Don Quixote, "I will not permit them to touch a thread of your garments; for if they played tricks with you the time before, it was because I was unable to leap the walls of the yard. But now we are on a wide plain, where I shall be able to wield my sword as I please."

"And if they enchant you and make you numb like they did the last time," said Sancho, "what difference will it make being in the open field or not?"

"For all that," replied Don Quixote, "I entreat you, Sancho, to keep a stout heart, for experience will prove to you what mine is made of."

"I will, please God," answered Sancho, and the two withdrawing to one side of the road set themselves to observe closely what all those moving lights might be. Very soon afterwards, they made out a large group of encamisados,[2] all on horseback, with lighted torches in their hands. The fearful vision completely extinguished the courage of Sancho, who began to chatter with his teeth like one in the cold fit of a four-day fever. His heart sank and his teeth chattered still more when they saw distinctly that behind them there came a funeral litter[3] followed by six more mounted figures in mourning down to the very feet of their mules—for they could tell plainly they were not horses by the easy pace at which they went. As the encamisados came along, they muttered to themselves in a low, plaintive tone. This strange spectacle at such an hour and in such a solitary place was quite enough to strike terror into Sancho's heart, and should have done the same to his master, too. Would that it had! For while Sancho, despite his resolution, had broken down, just the opposite happened to his master. In Don Quixote's imagination, the scene came instantly to life as one of the adventures in his books.

He took it into his head that the litter was a bier on which was borne some sorely wounded or slain knight, to avenge whom was a task reserved for him alone. Without any further deliberation, he set his lance in rest, fixed himself

[1] *mercury:* Loss of motor function is one of the symptoms of mercury poisoning. In the early modern world, the metal was used in silver mining, mirror making, haberdashery, and medicines.

[2] *encamisados:* For night raids, soldiers wore white shirts over their armor to distinguish themselves from the enemy. As we learn, these *encamisados* (literally, "shirt-wearers") have a different purpose.

[3] *funeral litter:* chair or bed covered with black cloth that was carried in procession on shafts.

firmly in his saddle, and with gallant spirit and bearing took up his position in the middle of the road where the encamisados must of necessity pass. As soon as he saw them near at hand, he raised his voice and said:

"Halt, knights, or whosoever you may be, and render me account of who you are, whence you come, where you go, what it is you carry upon that bier. For to judge by appearances, either you have done some wrong or some wrong has been done to you, and it is fitting and necessary that I should know, either that I may chastise you for the evil you have done, or else that I may avenge you for the injury that has been inflicted upon you."

"We are in a hurry," answered one of the encamisados. "The inn is far off, and we cannot stop to give you such an account as you demand." And spurring his mule he moved on.

Don Quixote was mightily provoked by this answer. Seizing the mule by the bridle he said, "Halt, and be more mannerly, and render an account of what I have asked of you; else, prepare for battle, all of you."

The mule was skittish and was so frightened at her bridle being seized that rearing up she flung her rider to the ground over her haunches. An attendant who was on foot, seeing the encamisado fall, began to heap curses on Don Quixote. He, moved to anger, and without any more ado, set his lance in rest and charged at one of the men in mourning, bringing him badly wounded to the ground. As he wheeled round upon the others, the agility with which he attacked and routed them was a sight to see, for it seemed as if wings had that instant grown upon Rocinante, so lightly and proudly did he bear himself. The encamisados were timid people and unarmed, so they speedily made their escape from the fray and set off at a run across the plain with their lighted torches, looking exactly like masked revelers running in some nighttime gala or festival. The mourners, too, curtained and draped in their tunics and gowns, were unable to move themselves, and so with complete safety Don Quixote thrashed them all and drove them off against their will, for they all thought he was no man but a devil from hell come to carry away the dead body they had in the litter.

Sancho beheld all of this, filled with wonder at the audacity of his lord, and said to himself, "Without a doubt this master of mine is as mighty and brave as he says he is."

A burning torch lay on the ground near the first man whom the mule had thrown, by the light of which Don Quixote could see him. Coming up to him, he presented the point of his lance to the man's face, calling on him to give himself up as prisoner, or else he would kill him. To this the prostrate man replied, "I am prisoner enough as it is. I cannot move, for one of my legs is broken. I entreat you, if you are a Christian gentleman, not to kill me, which will be committing grave sacrilege, for I am a licentiate and I hold first orders."[4]

"Then what the devil brought you here, being a churchman?" said Don Quixote.

"What, señor?" said the other. "My bad luck."

[4] *I am a licentiate and I hold first orders:* The vanquished man claims to hold the equivalent of a four-year university degree and has taken minor religious orders.

"Then still worse awaits you," said Don Quixote, "if you do not satisfy me as to all I asked you at first."

"You shall be soon satisfied," said the licentiate. "You must know, then, that though just now I said I was a licentiate, I am only a bachelor.[5] My name is Alonso López. I am a native of Alcobendas. I come from the city of Baeza[6] with eleven others, priests, the ones who fled with the torches, and we are going to the city of Segovia accompanying a dead body which is in that litter, that of a gentleman who died in Baeza, where he was interred. Now, as I said, we are taking his bones to their burial place, which is in Segovia, where he was born."

"And who killed him?" asked Don Quixote.

"God, by means of a malignant fever that took him," answered the bachelor.

"In that case," said Don Quixote, "our Lord has relieved me of the task of avenging his death had any other slain him. Considering who slew him, there is nothing to do but to be silent and shrug one's shoulders. Were he to slew me, I would do the same. And I would have your reverence know that I am a knight of La Mancha, Don Quixote by name, and it is my business and calling to roam the world righting wrongs and redressing injuries."

"I don't know how that part about righting wrongs can be so," said the bachelor, "for from straight you have made me crooked, leaving me with a broken leg that will never see itself straight again all the days of its life. And the injury you have redressed in my case has been to leave me injured in such a way that I will remain injured forever. The height of misadventure it was to cross paths with you who go in search of adventures."

"Things do not all happen in the same way," answered Don Quixote. "The problem was, Señor Bachelor Alonso López, in your coming as you did, by night, dressed in those surplices,[7] with lighted torches, praying, and outfitted for mourning—so that naturally you looked like something evil and of the other world. I could not avoid doing my duty in attacking you. Indeed, I would have attacked you even had I known positively that you were the very devils of hell, for such I certainly took you to be."

"Since my fate has so willed it," said the bachelor, "I entreat you, señor knight-errant, whose errand has been such an evil one for me, to help me out from under this mule, which holds one of my legs caught between the stirrup and the saddle."

"I would have talked on till tomorrow!" said Don Quixote. "How long were you going to wait before telling me of your distress?"

At once he called to Sancho, but his squire had no mind to come, as he was engaged just then in unloading a pack mule well laden with provisions, which these worthy gentlemen had brought with them. Sancho made a bag of his coat, and getting together as much as he could (and as the bag would hold), he loaded his beast. He then attended to his master's call and helped him remove the bachelor from under the mule. Putting him on the beast's back, Sancho gave him the

[5] *bachelor:* roughly equivalent to an associate's degree in the American system.

[6] *Baeza:* in central Andalusia.

[7] *surplices:* loose-fitting white religious vestments.

torch, while Don Quixote bade him follow the track of his companions, of whom he begged pardon on his part for the wrong he could not help doing them.

Sancho added, "If by any chance these gentlemen want to know who the hero was that did this to them, your worship may tell them that he is the famous Don Quixote of La Mancha, otherwise called the Knight of the Woeful Countenance."[8] The bachelor then took his departure.

I forgot to mention that before he did so he said to Don Quixote, "Remember that you stand excommunicated for having laid violent hands on a holy thing: *Juxta illud, 'si quis suadente diabolo,' etc.*"[9]

"I do not understand that Latin," answered Don Quixote, "but I know well I did not lay hands, only this spear. Besides, I did not think I was committing an assault upon priests or things of the Church—which, faithful Christian and Catholic that I am, I respect and revere—but upon phantoms and specters of the other world. But even so, I remember how it fared with El Cid Ruy Díaz when he broke the chair of the ambassador of that king before his Holiness the Pope, for which he was excommunicated; and yet the good Rodrigo de Vivar bore himself that day like a very noble and valiant knight."[10]

On hearing this the bachelor took his departure, as has been said, without making any reply. Don Quixote asked Sancho what had induced him to call him the "Knight of the Woeful Countenance" just then and not before.

"I will tell you," answered Sancho. "It was because I've been looking at you for some time by the light of the torch that unfortunate fellow was carrying, and your worship truly does have of late the sorriest face I ever saw. It must be either owing to the fatigue of this combat, or else to the missing teeth and molars."

"It is not that," replied Don Quixote, "but because the sage whose duty it will be to write the history of my achievements must have thought it proper that I should take some distinctive name as all knights of yore did: one being 'He of the Burning Sword,' another 'He of the Unicorn,' this one 'He of the Damsels,' that 'He of the Phœnix,' another 'The Knight of the Griffin,' and another 'The Knight of Death.'[11] By these names and designations they were known all the world round. And so I say that the aforesaid sage must have put it into your mouth and mind just now to call me 'The Knight of the Woeful Countenance,'

[8] *Knight of the Woeful Countenance:* The honorific *Caballero de la Triste Figura* appears in the third book of the chivalric romance cycle *Clarián de Landanís* (1524). *Triste Figura* is fitting for a knight with a sad face as well as a knight who makes for a sorry sight.

[9] Juxta illud, 'si quis, suadente diabolo,' etc.: Latin, "After that, 'if anyone having been induced by the devil,' etc.", from the *Decretum Gratiani*, twelfth-century compilation of canon law, which states that anyone who lays violent hands on a clergyman is punishable by excommunication.

[10] *El Cid Ruy Díaz . . . valiant knight:* A ballad tells of a visit El Cid makes to the papal court, where he becomes enraged when he sees that the chair for the French king has been set on the same level as the pope's, while the chair for the ambassador of the Spanish king is placed lower.

[11] *'He of the Burning Sword,' . . . 'The Knight of Death':* Each of these titles belongs to the protagonist of a chivalric romance or epic poem.

as I intend to call myself from this day forward; and that such name may fit me better, I mean, when the opportunity offers, to have a very woeful countenance painted on my shield."

"There is no reason, señor, to waste time or money making that countenance," said Sancho. "All that needs to be done is for your worship to come face to face with those who look at you, and without anything more, either image or shield, they will call you 'Him of the Woeful Countenance.' Believe me, I am telling you the truth, for I assure you, señor (and I mean this in good fun), hunger and the loss of your molars have given you such a pitiful face that, as I say, the woeful painting is completely unnecessary."

Don Quixote laughed at Sancho's pleasantry. Nevertheless, he resolved to call himself by that name and have his shield or buckler painted as he envisioned. He would have liked to see whether the body in the litter was nothing but bones, but Sancho would not have it, saying, "Señor, you have ended this perilous adventure more safely for yourself than any of those I've seen. Perhaps it will dawn on these people, though beaten and routed, that it is a single man that has beaten them; and feeling ashamed of themselves, they may take heart and come in search of us looking for trouble. The donkey is in fine form, the mountains close by, our hunger fierce —we have nothing more to do but make good our retreat, and, as the saying goes, 'The dead to the grave and the living to the loaf.'"

Driving his donkey before him, he begged his master to follow. It seemed to Don Quixote that Sancho was right, so he fell in behind without replying.

After proceeding some little distance between two hills, they found themselves in a broad, secluded valley, where they dismounted and Sancho unloaded his beast. Stretched upon the green grass, with hunger for sauce, they ate breakfast, lunch, and dinner all at once, satisfying their appetites with more than one meal that the dead man's clerical friends (who seldom deprive themselves) had brought with them on their pack mule. But another piece of ill-luck befell them, which Sancho held the worst of all, and that was that they had no wine to drink, nor even water to moisten their lips. With thirst tormenting them, Sancho, observing that the meadow where they were was full of green and tender grass, said what will be related in the following chapter.

CHAPTER XX

OF THE NEVER BEFORE SEEN NOR HEARD OF ADVENTURE CARRIED OFF BY THE VALIANT DON QUIXOTE OF LA MANCHA WITH LESS PERIL THAN ANY EVER ACHIEVED BY ANY FAMOUS KNIGHT IN THE WORLD

"Surely it's the case, señor, that this grass is proof of there being nearby some spring or brook to give it moisture. It would be well, then, to move a little farther on, so we can find a place where we can quench this terrible thirst that plagues us, which without a doubt is more distressing than hunger."

The advice seemed good to Don Quixote. With him leading Rocinante by the bridle and Sancho leading his donkey by the halter (after having loaded onto the beast the leftovers from supper), they advanced through the meadow feeling their way, for the darkness of the night made it impossible to see anything. They had not gone two hundred paces when a loud noise of water, as if falling from great rocks, struck their ears. The sound cheered them greatly; but when they stopped to make out where it was coming from, they heard another noise all of a sudden that spoiled the satisfaction the sound of the water gave them—especially for Sancho, who was by nature timid and faint-hearted.

They heard, I say, strokes falling with a measured beat, and a certain rattling of iron and chains that, together with the furious din of the water, would have struck terror into any heart but Don Quixote's. The night was, as has been said, dark, and they had managed to reach a spot among tall trees, whose leaves, stirred by a gentle breeze, made a low ominous sound. Thus it was that the solitude, the environs, the darkness, the noise of the water, and the rustling of the leaves—everything inspired fear and dread; all the more when they realized that the strokes were not ceasing, nor the wind dying down, nor the morning approaching. And to all of this might be added that they were ignorant of where they were.

But Don Quixote, supported by his intrepid heart, leaped on Rocinante; and bracing his buckler on his arm and lowering his spear, he said, "Friend Sancho, know that by Heaven's will I have been born in this our iron age to restore to it the age of gold, or Golden Age, as it is called. I am he for whom perils, mighty achievements, and valiant deeds are reserved. I am, I say again, he who is to revive the Knights of the Round Table, the Twelve of France and the Nine Worthies; and he who is to consign to oblivion the Platirs, the Tablantes, the Olivantes and Tirantes, the Phœbuses and Belianises, with the whole throng of famous knights-errant of days gone by, performing in these in which I live such exploits, marvels, and feats of arms as shall obscure their brightest deeds. You are right, faithful and trusty squire, to mark the gloom of this night, its strange silence, the dull confused murmur of those trees, the awful sound of that water in quest of which we came—water that seems as though it were tumbling and crashing down from the lofty mountains of the moon, and that incessant hammering that wounds and pains our ears. These things, taken together and each by itself, are enough to instill fear, dread, and dismay into the breast of Mars himself, much more into one unaccustomed to affairs and adventures of the kind. All this that I put before you is but an incentive and stimulant to my spirit, making my heart burst in my chest through eagerness to engage in this adventure, arduous as it promises to be. Therefore, tighten Rocinante's girths a little, and God be with you. Wait for me here three days and no more, and if in that time I do not come back, you can return to our village. From there, you would do me a favor and a service if you would go to El Toboso, where you shall say to my incomparable lady Dulcinea that her captive knight has died in attempting things that might make him worthy of being called hers."

When Sancho heard his master's words he began to shed the world's most pitiful tears, saying, "Señor, I don't know why your worship wants to attempt such a fearful adventure. It's night now; no one sees us here. We can easily turn back and take ourselves out of danger, even if we don't drink for three days to come. And as there is no one to see us, all the less will there be anyone to set us down as cowards. Besides, I have many a time heard the priest of our village, who your worship knows well, preach that he who seeks danger perishes in it.[1] So it is not right to tempt God by trying so tremendous a feat which there can be no escape from except by a miracle; and Heaven has performed enough of them for your worship in delivering you from being blanketed, as I was, and bringing you out victorious and unhurt from among all those enemies that were with the dead man.

"And if all this doesn't move or soften your hard heart, let this thought move it: that you will hardly be gone from this spot when from pure fear I will offer my soul to anyone who will take it. I left home and wife and children to come and serve your worship, trusting to do better and not worse. But as 'greed bursts the bag,' it has rent my hopes asunder. For just as I had them highest about getting that accursed island your worship has so often promised me, I see that instead you mean to reward me by deserting me now in a place far from human reach. For God's sake, my master, do not deal so unjustly by me. If your worship will not entirely give up attempting this feat, at least put it off till morning, for from what I learned when I was a shepherd, it cannot be three hours till dawn now, because the end of the horn is overhead and makes midnight in the line of the left arm."[2]

"How can you see, Sancho, where it makes that line," asked Don Quixote, "or where this end or head is that you talk of, when the night is so dark that there is not a star to be seen in the whole heaven?"

[1] *he who seeks danger perishes in it:* Sirach 3:26.

[2] *the end of the horn . . . the left arm:* In the Little Dipper, Polaris (the end of the horn) is the last in the line of stars (the left arm, or handle) that leads down to the bowl.

"That's true," said Sancho, "but fear has sharp eyes and sees things underground, much more above in the sky. Anyway, there is good reason to think that day is about to come upon us."

"Let come what may come," replied Don Quixote. "It shall not be said of me now or at any time that tears or entreaties turned me aside from doing what was in accordance with knightly usage. And so I beg of you, Sancho, hold your peace, for God, who has put it into my heart now to undertake this unparalleled and fearful adventure, will take care to watch over my safety and console your sorrow. What you must do is tighten Rocinante's girths well, and wait here. I shall come back shortly, either alive or dead."

Sancho, seeing it was his master's final decision and how little his tears, counsels, and entreaties mattered to him, determined to have recourse to his own ingenuity to compel him, if he could, to wait till daylight. And so while he tightened the horse's saddle straps, quietly and without being felt, he also tied both Rocinante's legs with his donkey's halter, so that when Don Quixote tried to go he was unable, as the horse could only move by jumps.

Seeing the success of his trick, Sancho Panza said, "See there, señor! Heaven, moved by my tears and prayers, has so ordered it that Rocinante cannot budge. And if you will be obstinate and spur and strike him, you will only provoke fortune, and kick, as they say, against the goads."[3]

At this, Don Quixote grew desperate, but the more he drove his heels into the horse, the less he stirred him. Unsuspecting that Rocinante's legs had been tied, he determined it would be best to settle in and wait till daybreak or until his horse could move, firmly persuaded that all this came of something other than Sancho's ingenuity. And so he said to him, "As it is thus, Sancho, that Rocinante cannot move, I am content to wait till dawn smiles upon us, even though I weep while it delays its coming."

"There is no need to weep," answered Sancho, "for I will entertain your worship by telling stories from now till daybreak, unless indeed you would like to dismount and lie down to sleep a little on the green grass after the fashion of knights-errant, so as to be fresher when day comes and the moment arrives for attempting this extraordinary adventure you are looking forward to."

"What are you talking about dismounting or sleeping for?" said Don Quixote. "Do you think I am one of those knights who takes his rest in the presence of danger? Sleep, as you were born to do, or do what you will; I will act as I think most consistent with my ambitions."

"Don't be angry, my master," replied Sancho, "I didn't mean to say that." Coming close to him, Sancho laid one hand on the pommel of the saddle and the other on the cantle[4] so that he held his master's left thigh in his embrace, not daring to separate a finger's width from him—so afraid was he of the strokes that still resounded with a regular beat. Don Quixote asked him to tell some story to entertain him as he had proposed, to which Sancho replied that he would if his

[3] *kick, as they say, against the goads:* See Acts 26:14, where Jesus tells Saul on his way to Damascus, "Saul, Saul, why do you persecute me? It hurts you to kick against the goads."

[4] *cantle:* raised rear part of a saddle.

dread of what he heard would let him. "All the same," said he, "I will try hard to tell a story which, if I can manage to relate it, and nobody interferes with the telling, is the best of stories. Let your worship give me your attention, for here I begin: 'What was, was; and let the good yet to come be for all, and the evil to him who goes looking for it....' Your worship must know that the way the old folk used to begin their tales was not just as each one pleased, because it was a maxim of Cato Zonzorino the Roman[5] that says 'evil to him who goes looking for it.' This fits like a ring to the finger—which is to say that your worship should keep quiet and not go looking anywhere for evil, and that we should go back by some other road, since nobody is forcing us to follow this one, which afflicts us with so many terrors."

"Go on with your story, Sancho," said Don Quixote, "and leave the choice of our road to my care."

"I say then," continued Sancho, "that in a village of Extremadura[6] there was a goat shepherd—that is to say, one who tended goats. This shepherd or goatherd, as my story goes, was named Lope Ruíz, and this Lope Ruíz was in love with a shepherdess named Torralba; and this shepherdess named Torralba was the daughter of a wealthy rancher, and this wealthy rancher—"

"If that is how you intend to tell your tale, Sancho," said Don Quixote, "repeating twice everything you have to say, you will not be done in two days. Go straight on with it, and tell it like a reasonable man, or else say nothing."

"Where I come from, tales are always told in the very way I'm telling this one," answered Sancho. "I cannot tell it in any other, and it isn't right of your worship to ask me to make new customs."

"Tell it as you will," replied Don Quixote. "Since fate has ordained that I cannot help but listen to you, go on."

"And so, my dear señor," continued Sancho, "as I have said, this shepherd was in love with Torralba the shepherdess. She was a wild, strapping lass with something of a manly look about her, for she had little whiskers. I can almost see her now...."

"Then you knew her?" said Don Quixote.

"I didn't know her," said Sancho, "but the one who told me the story said it was so true and certain that when I told it to another, I could declare and safely swear that I had seen it all myself. So then, in the course of time, the devil, who never sleeps and puts everything in confusion, arranged it that the love the shepherd had for the shepherdess turned into hatred and ill-will. The reason, according to evil tongues, was some little jealousy she caused him that crossed the line and trespassed on forbidden ground. So much did the shepherd hate her from that time forward that, in order to escape from her, he decided to leave the country and go where he would never set eyes on her again. Torralba, when

[5] *Cato Zonzorino the Roman:* Sancho means *Cato Censorino*, reputed author of the *Disticha Catonis*, a collection of maxims used to teach reading in Latin and, in translation, Spanish. *Zonzorino* suggests *zonzo* (foolish).

[6] *Extremadura:* southwest region of Spain bordering Portugal.

she found herself rejected by Lope, was immediately smitten with love for him, though she had never loved him before."

"That is the natural way of women," said Don Quixote, "to scorn the one who loves them, and love the one who hates them. Go on, Sancho."

"It came to pass," said Sancho, "that the shepherd carried out his intention, and driving his goats before him made his way across the plains of Extremadura to pass over into the Kingdom of Portugal. Torralba learned of it and went after him on foot. She followed him at a distance in her bare feet, with a pilgrim's staff in her hand and a pouch around her neck. In this pouch, it is said that she carried a bit of looking-glass and a piece of a comb and some kind of little bottle of paint for her face. Whatever she was carrying, I don't want to trouble myself right now to find out. All I say is that the shepherd, so they say, came with his flock to cross over the river Guadiana, which was at that time swollen and almost overflowing its banks. At the spot he came to, there was neither ferry nor boat nor anyone to take him or his flock to the other side. He was very upset by this, for he saw that Torralba was approaching and would be a great annoyance to him with her tears and entreaties; however, he made a thorough search of the area and discovered a fisherman who had alongside of him a boat so small that it could only hold one person and one goat. Nevertheless, he spoke with him, and the two of them arranged for the fisherman to carry him and his three hundred goats across. The fisherman got into the boat and carried one goat over. He came back and carried another over. He came back again, and then brought over another. Let your worship keep count of the goats the fisherman is taking across, because if I forget about one, the story will be over, and it will be impossible to tell another word of it. To proceed, I must tell you the landing place on the other side was full of mud and slippery, and the fisherman lost a great deal of time in going and coming. Still, he returned for another goat, and another, and another."

"Assume that he brought them all across," said Don Quixote, "and don't keep going and coming in this way, or you will not make an end of bringing them over in a year."

"How many have gone across so far?" asked Sancho.

"How the devil do I know?" replied Don Quixote.

"I told you," said Sancho, "that you were to keep count of them. Well then, by God, that's the end of the story. There's no going any farther."

"How can that be?" said Don Quixote. "Is it so essential to the story to know about every goat that has crossed over, that if there is a mistake about one in the account, you cannot go on with it?"

"No, señor, not a chance," replied Sancho. "When I asked your worship to tell me how many goats had crossed, and you answered you didn't know, at that very instant all I had to say slipped out of my memory. What a shame, for there was much virtue in the story and entertainment, too."

"So, then," said Don Quixote, "the story has come to an end?"

"As much as my mother has," said Sancho.

"In truth," said Don Quixote, "you have told one of the strangest tales or histories that anyone in the world could have imagined, and such a way of telling it and bringing it to an end as was never seen nor will be in a lifetime. But I expected no less from your ready tongue, nor am I surprised, for perhaps those ceaseless beatings have addled your wits."

"All that may be," replied Sancho, "but I know that as to my story, all that can be said is that it ends there where the mistake in counting the crossing of the goats begins."

"Let it end where it will, well and good," said Don Quixote, "and let us see if Rocinante can be moved." Again he spurred him, and again Rocinante leaped in place and remained where he was, so well tied was he.

It so happened that, whether because of the cold of the approaching morning, or because he had eaten something at supper that softened his stomach, or because it was only natural (as is most likely), Sancho felt the urge to do what no one could do for him; but so great was the fear filling his heart that he dared not separate himself from his master by as much as a fingernail. To think that he could avoid doing what he needed to do, however, was also impossible. So to keep the peace, he decided to remove his right hand from the back of the saddle, and with it to untie—gently and noiselessly—the single piece of string holding up his breeches, so that on loosening it they at once fell down around his feet like fetters. He then raised his shirt as well as he could and bared his hind quarters (which were by no means slim ones). He thought this was all he would have to do to end the anguish of this terrible predicament. But with this accomplished, another still greater difficulty presented itself, which was that it seemed to him impossible to relieve himself without making some noise. He ground his teeth and squeezed his shoulders together and held his breath the best he could. Yet for all these precautions, he nonetheless had the misfortune to make a little noise—very different from the one that was causing him so much fear.

On hearing it, Don Quixote asked, "What noise is that, Sancho?"

"I don't know, señor," said he. "It must be something new, for adventures and misadventures never have a small beginning." Once more he tried his luck and succeeded so well that without any further noise or disturbance he found himself relieved of the burden that had given him so much discomfort.

But as Don Quixote's sense of smell was as acute as his hearing, and as Sancho was well-nigh sewn to his master's side, the fumes rose almost in a straight line, so that some of these vapors could not help but reach his master's nose. As soon as they did, Don Quixote came to his nostrils' relief by squeezing them between his fingers. And with a rather nasal tone in his voice, he said, "It seems to me, Sancho, that you are in great fear."

"I am," answered Sancho; "but what has led your worship to notice it now more than before?"

"Because you smell stronger now more than before, and not of ambergris,"[7] answered Don Quixote.

"Very likely," said Sancho, "but that's not my fault; it's your worship's, for leading me about at unseasonable hours and at such an unaccustomed pace."

[7] *ambergris:* waxy, aromatic substance derived from sperm whales, used to make perfume.

"Go back three or four, my friend," said Don Quixote, all the time with his fingers to his nose. "And in the future, pay more attention to your person and to what you owe to mine, for it is my great familiarity with you that has bred this contempt."

Sancho replied, "I bet your worship thinks that I've done something I ought not to with my person."

"'It's only worse if you stir it,' friend Sancho," returned Don Quixote.

With this and similar talk, master and man passed the night, till Sancho, seeing that daybreak was coming on apace, very cautiously untied Rocinante and tied up his breeches. As soon as Rocinante found himself free, though by nature he was not at all spirited, he seemed to come to life and began pawing—for as to prancing, begging his pardon, he knew not what it meant. Don Quixote, observing that Rocinante could move, took it as a good sign and a signal that he should attempt the dread adventure.

By this time, day had fully broken and everything could be made out clearly. Don Quixote saw that he was among some tall chestnut trees, which cast a very deep shade. He perceived likewise that the sound of the strokes did not cease, but he could not discover what caused it. And so without any further delay, he spurred Rocinante, and once more taking leave of Sancho, he told him to wait for him there three days at most, as he had said before. If he should not have returned by that time, he might feel sure it had been God's will that he should end his days in that perilous adventure. He again repeated the message and commission with which he was to go on his behalf to his lady Dulcinea, and told Sancho he was not to be troubled about the payment of his services, for before leaving home he had made his will, in which he would find himself fully recompensed in the matter of wages in due proportion to the time he had served. But if God delivered him safe, sound, and unhurt out of that danger, it was more than certain that he would look upon the promised island. Sancho began to weep afresh on again hearing the moving words of his good master and resolved to stay with him in this endeavor until the very end. From these tears and his honorable resolve, the author of this history infers that Sancho Panza must have been of good birth and at least an Old Christian.[8] The feeling he displayed touched his master—but not so much as to make him show any weakness. On the contrary, hiding what he felt as well as he could, he began to move toward the place from which the sound of the water and the strokes seemed to arise.

Sancho followed on foot, as was his habit, leading by the halter his donkey, a constant comrade in prosperity or adversity. Advancing some distance through the shady chestnut trees, they came upon a little meadow at the foot of some high rocks down which a mighty rush of water flung itself. At the foot of the

[8] *Old Christian:* After pogroms across Castile and Aragon in 1391 led to an influx of Jewish converts to Christianity, Spaniards began to distinguish the New Christians (*cristianos nuevos*) from those without Jewish—and later, Moorish—ancestry (Old Christians, *cristianos viejos*). The distinction perpetuated a sense of social and moral superiority among the Old Christians, often when both qualities were lacking.

rocks were some rudely constructed houses looking more like ruins than houses, from among which came, they surmised, the din and clatter of blows, which still continued without intermission.

Rocinante took fright at the noise of the water and the blows, but quieting him, Don Quixote advanced step by step toward the houses, commending himself with all his heart to his lady, imploring her support in this dreadful hour and enterprise, and on the way commending himself also to God not to forget him. Sancho, who never left his side, stretched his neck as far as he could and peered between Rocinante's legs to see if he could now discover what it was that caused him such fear and apprehension.

They went perhaps a hundred paces farther when they rounded a bend. There, plain and obvious, the true cause appeared to them beyond the possibility of any mistake—the cause of the awful, dread-sounding noise that had kept them all the night in such fear and vexation. It was (dear reader, please do not be annoyed or disappointed): six fulling hammers making a racket by their alternate strokes.[9]

When Don Quixote realized what it was, he was struck dumb and rigid from head to foot. Sancho glanced at him and saw him with his head bent down upon his breast in apparent embarrassment. Don Quixote also glanced at Sancho and saw him with his cheeks puffed out and his mouth full of laughter, evidently ready to explode with it. In spite of his vexation, Don Quixote could not help laughing at the sight of him. When Sancho saw his master begin to laugh, he let go so heartily that he had to hold his sides with both hands to keep himself from bursting. Four times he stopped, and as many times his laughter broke out afresh with the same energy as at first. At this Don Quixote grew furious, above all when he heard him say mockingly, "'Know, friend Sancho, that by Heaven's will I was born in this our iron age to restore to it the age of gold, or Golden Age; I am he for whom perils, mighty achievements, and valiant deeds are reserved ...'"[10] He went on repeating the words that Don Quixote uttered the first time they heard the awful strokes.

When Don Quixote realized that Sancho was making fun of him, so embarrassed and angry was he that he lifted up his spear and landed two blows on him, with such force that if instead of receiving them on his shoulders he had received them on his head, there would have been no wages to pay, unless it were to his heirs. Sancho, seeing that he was getting such an unpleasant return for his joke, and fearing his master might carry it still further, said to him very humbly, "Calm yourself, sir. Honest to God, I'm only joking."

"Well if you are joking, I am not," replied Don Quixote.[11] "Look here, señor jester, if instead of fulling hammers, this had been some perilous adventure, do

[9] *six fulling hammers making a racket by their alternate strokes:* Fulling removes oils and dirt from woolen cloth and shrinks it to a felt fabric. In one method, a water wheel powers leather-covered mallets that beat pieces of wool set in a trough.

[10] *Know, friend Sancho ... valiant deeds are reserved:* The speaker is Sancho, who is impersonating Don Quixote.

[11] *"Well if you are joking, I am not," replied Don Quixote:* In this paragraph of dialogue, Don Quixote reverts to a form of the second-person singular ("you") that he rarely uses

you not think I would have shown the courage required to commit to it and see it to the end? Considering I am a knight, am I, perchance, supposed to know how to distinguish sounds and tell whether or not they come from fulling mills? If that is the case, I have never seen a fulling mill in my life—unlike you, ignorant boor that you are, who was born and bred among them. But turn these six hammers into six giants, and bring them face to face with me, one by one or all together, and if I do not knock them head over heels, then you are free to mock me as much as you like."

"No more of that, señor," returned Sancho. "I admit I went a little too far with the joke. But tell me, your worship, now that there's peace between us (and may God bring you out of all the adventures that may befall you as safe and sound as he has brought you out of this one), wasn't it funny, and doesn't it make for a good story, the great fear we were in? At least the fear I was in; for as to your worship, I see now that you have no idea what it means to be in utter terror."

"I do not deny," said Don Quixote, "that what happened to us may be worth laughing at, but it is not worth making a story about, for not everyone is clever enough to understand the point."

"At any rate," said Sancho, "your worship understood the point of your spear—what would happen when you aimed at my head and hit me on the shoulders with it. Thanks be to God and my diligence for dodging it. But it's no matter, since 'everything will come out in the wash.' I've heard it said 'he loves you well that makes you weep' and also that it is the way with great lords after they speak a hard word to a servant to give him a pair of breeches; though I don't know what they give after blows, unless it's the case that knights-errant after blows give islands, or kingdoms on the mainland."

"That may be how the dice are cast," said Don Quixote, "and all you say will come true. But forgive what has just passed, for you are wise enough to know that our first movements are out of our control. In the future, take care that you curb and restrain your idle tongue in my presence. For in all the books of chivalry I have read (and they are innumerable), I never met with a squire who talked so much to his lord as you do to yours. In fact, I feel it to be a great fault of yours and of mine: of yours, that you have so little respect for me; of mine, that I do not make myself more respected. There was Gandalín, the squire of Amadís of Gaul, who was Count of the Ínsula Firme,[12] and we read of him that he always addressed his lord with his cap in his hand, his head bowed down and his body bent double, *more turquesco*.[13] And then, what shall we say of Gasabal, the squire of Don Galaor, who was so quiet that in order to indicate to us the greatness of

with Sancho. Generally, Don Quixote uses the *tú* form, appropriate for a social superior on intimate terms with an inferior. In this paragraph, he switches to *vos*. The effect is to distance Sancho from him, as if his squire were suddenly nothing more than a servant.

[12] *Gandalín . . . of the Ínsula Firme:* Gandalín's achievements are recorded in *Amadís of Gaul* and *The Deeds of Esplandián*.

[13] more turquesco: "in the Turkish fashion". The phrase likely comes from Mediterranean Lingua Franca (Sabir), a pidgin used to facilitate Mediterranean commerce among speakers of Romance, Turkic, and Arabic languages.

his marvelous taciturnity his name is mentioned only once in the whole of that history, as long as it is truthful? From all I have said, you will gather, Sancho, that there must be a difference between master and man, between lord and lackey, between knight and squire. From this day forward in our conversation we must observe more respect and take fewer liberties, for in whatever way I may be provoked with you it will be bad for the pitcher.[14] The rewards and benefits I have promised you will come in due time, and if they do not, your wages at least will not be lost, as I have already told you."

"Everything your worship says is very good," said Sancho, "but I should like to know—in case the time of rewards should not come, and it might be necessary to fall back on a salary—how much did the squire of a knight-errant get in those days, and were they hired by the month or by the day, like bricklayers?"

"I do not believe," replied Don Quixote, "that such squires were ever on salary but were dependent on rewards.[15] And if I have now mentioned yours in the sealed will I have left at home, it was with a view to what may happen. I know not as yet how chivalry will turn out in these wretched times of ours, and I do not wish my soul to suffer for trifles in the next world; for I would have you know, Sancho, that in this world, there is no condition more hazardous than that of the adventurer."

"That's true," said Sancho, "since the mere noise of the hammers of a fulling mill can disturb and disquiet the heart of such a valiant errant adventurer as your worship. But you may be sure from this moment on that I will not open my lips to make light of anything of your worship's, but only to honor you as my master and natural lord."

"By so doing," replied Don Quixote, "you will live long on the face of the earth; for next to parents, masters are to be respected as though they were parents."[16]

[14] *bad for the pitcher:* "Whether you hit a rock with a pitcher or a pitcher with a rock, it's bad for the pitcher" (Spanish proverb).

[15] *on rewards: a mercedes*, gifts that the master would give his servant. The medieval world that the chivalric romances aspire to re-create was far more dependent on gift transactions than on labor markets where workers received a stipulated income in cash.

[16] *you will live long . . . they were parents:* adapted loosely from Ephesians 6:2–3, where children are told, "Honor your father and mother . . . that you may live long."

CHAPTER XXI

WHICH TREATS OF THE HIGH ADVENTURE AND RICH PRIZE OF MAMBRINO'S HELMET, TOGETHER WITH OTHER THINGS THAT HAPPENED TO OUR INVINCIBLE KNIGHT

It now began to rain a little. Sancho wanted to seek shelter in the fulling mills, but Don Quixote had taken such an abhorrence to them on account of Sancho's joking that he flatly refused to go inside. So turning aside to right, they came upon another road, different from the one they had taken the night before. Shortly afterwards, Don Quixote spotted a man on horseback who wore on his head something that shone like gold. The moment he saw him he turned to Sancho and said:

"I think, Sancho, there is no proverb that is not true, all being maxims drawn from experience itself, the mother of all the sciences—especially that one that says, 'Where one door is shut, another opens.' I say so because if last night fortune shut the door of the adventure we were looking for, cheating us with the fulling mills, it now opens wide another to a better and more certain adventure. If I do not succeed in entering it, it will be my own fault; I cannot lay it to my ignorance of fulling mills, or the darkness of the night. I say this because, if I mistake not, there comes toward us one who wears on his head the helmet of Mambrino, concerning which I took the oath you remember."

"Mind what you say, your worship, and still more what you do," said Sancho, "for I don't want any more fulling mills to finish off fulling and knocking our senses out."

"The devil take you, man!" cried Don Quixote. "What has a helmet to do with fulling mills?"

"What do I know?" replied Sancho. "But, in faith, if I might speak as I used to, I could give you such reasons that your worship would see you were mistaken in what you say."

"How can I be mistaken in what I say, unbelieving traitor?" returned Don Quixote. "Tell me, do you not see yonder knight coming toward us on a dappled gray steed, who has upon his head a helmet of gold?"

"What I see and make out," answered Sancho, "is only a man on a gray donkey like my own, who has something that shines on his head."

"Well, that is the helmet of Mambrino," said Don Quixote. "Stand to one side and leave me alone with him. You will see how without saying a word, to save time, I shall carry off this adventure and possess myself of the helmet I have so longed for."

"I will take care to stand aside," said Sancho "But God grant, I say once more, that it may be oregano and not fulling mills."[1]

"I have told you, brother, that under no condition are you to mention those fulling mills to me again," said Don Quixote, "or I vow—and I say no more—I'll full the soul out of you."[2]

Sancho held his peace in dread lest his master should carry out the vow he had hurled like a bowl at him.

Regarding the helmet, steed, and knight that Don Quixote saw, the truth of the matter was this: There were two villages in the vicinity. One of them was so small that it had neither apothecary's shop nor barber,[3] which the other village close by had; so the barber of the larger served the smaller. In the smaller village, there was a sick man who needed to be bled[4] and another man who wanted to be shaved, for which purposes the barber was headed to their village with a brass basin.[5] But as chance would have it, it began to rain as he was on the way. So as not to spoil his hat, which was probably a new one, he put the basin on his head, which, being clean, glittered at half a league's distance. He rode upon a gray donkey, as Sancho said, and this was what made it seem to Don Quixote to be a dapple-gray steed and a knight and a golden helmet; for everything he saw he made to conform to his crazy chivalry and ill-errant notions. When he saw the poor knight draw near, without entering into any parley with him, he bore down upon him with spear pointed low and at Rocinante's top speed, fully determined to run him through and through.

As he reached him, without slowing the fury of his charge, he cried to him, "Defend yourself, miserable being, or yield me of your own accord that which is rightly my due."

The barber, with no time to think or be afraid, saw this apparition coming down upon him and had no other way of saving himself from the stroke of the lance but to let himself fall off his donkey. No sooner had he touched the ground than he sprang up more nimbly than a deer and sped away across the plain faster than the wind.

He left the basin on the ground, with which Don Quixote contented himself, saying that the pagan had shown his discretion and imitated the beaver, which, finding itself cornered by the hunters, bites and cuts off with its teeth that for which, by its natural instinct, it knows it is pursued.[6]

[1] *oregano and not fulling mills:* "May God grant that it be oregano and not caraway" (Spanish saying). Oregano was the more valued spice.

[2] *I have told you . . . I'll full the soul out of you:* The mere mention of the fulling mills causes Don Quixote in this sentence to slip back into the lordly *vos* form.

[3] *barber:* On the early modern profession of *barber*, see footnote 12, page 26.

[4] *needed to be bled:* See footnote 2, page 41.

[5] *brass basin:* shallow washbasin with a semicircular notch cut out of the wide rim to support the neck. For a haircut or shave, the basin would be filled with soapy water. For a bleeding, the basin would be used to collect the offending humors.

[6] *that for which . . . it knows it is pursued:* It was popularly believed that male beavers castrated themselves to avoid being killed for their castoreum, a yellowish secretion used in perfumes. In fact, both male and female beavers have castor sacs.

He told Sancho to pick up the helmet, who, taking it in his hands, said, "By God, the basin is a good one, and worth a real of eight if it's worth a maravedi."[7]

Sancho handed it to his master, who immediately put it on his head, turning it round, now this way, now that, in search of the visor. Not finding it he said, "Clearly the pagan to whose measure this famous headpiece was first forged must have had a very large head; but the worst part is that half of it is missing."

When Sancho heard him call the basin a headpiece, he was unable to restrain his laughter. But remembering his master's wrath, he checked himself in the midst of it.

"What are you laughing at, Sancho?" asked Don Quixote.

"I'm laughing," he replied, "to think of the huge head the pagan must have had who owned this helmet, for it looks exactly like a barber's basin."

"Do you know what I suspect, Sancho?" said Don Quixote. "I suspect that by some strange accident this enchanted helmet, this renowned piece of armor, fell into the hands of someone who was unable to recognize its inestimable value. Ignorant of what he was doing, only seeing it to be of the purest gold, he melted down one half for the sake of what it might be worth, and of the other made what looks like a barber's basin, as you say. But be that as it may, I recognize the helmet for what it is, and its transformation makes no difference to me. I will have it set right at the first village where there is a blacksmith, and in such style that the helmet the smith god forged for the god of battles[8] shall not surpass it—nor even come close. In the meantime, I will wear it as well as I can, for something is better than nothing, and it will be all the more useful to protect me from any chance stone's blow.

"That is," said Sancho, "if it's not shot with a sling as they were in the battle of the two armies, when they signed the cross on your worship's molars and smashed the flask with that blessed concoction that made me vomit up my innards."

"It does not grieve me much to have lost it," said Don Quixote, "for you know, Sancho, that I have the recipe memorized."

"So have I," answered Sancho, "but if I ever make it again or take a taste of it as long as I live, may this be my last hour. What's more, I have no intention of putting myself in a place where I have need of it. With all my five senses, I mean to keep myself from being wounded or from wounding anyone. As to being blanketed again, I say nothing; for it is hard to prevent mishaps of that sort. If they come, there is nothing for us to do but squeeze our shoulders together, hold our breath, shut our eyes, and let ourselves go where luck and the blanket may send us."

"You are a bad Christian, Sancho," said Don Quixote on hearing this. "Once an injury has been done to you, you never forget it. But know that it is the part of noble and generous hearts not to attach importance to trifles. What lame leg do you have from it, what broken rib, what cracked head, that you cannot

[7] *worth a real of eight if it's worth a maravedi:* A real of eight, or piece of eight (silver coin worth eight reals), was equivalent to 272 maravedis.

[8] *helmet the smith god forged for the god of battles:* Vulcan forged a helmet for Mars.

forgive the jest? For jest and sport it was, properly regarded, and had I not seen it in that light I would have returned and done more mischief in revenging you than the Greeks did for the abduction of Helen[9]—who, if she were alive now, or if my Dulcinea had lived then, you may depend upon it that she would not be so famous for her beauty as she is." Here, he heaved a sigh and sent it aloft.

Sancho said, "I'll take it in jest since I can't take my earnest revenge, but I know what was in jest and what was in earnest, and I know it will never be rubbed out of my memory any more than off my shoulders. But putting that aside, will your worship tell me what are we to do with this dapple-gray steed that looks like a dapple-gray donkey, which that Martino that your worship overthrew has left deserted here? From the way he took to his heels and bolted, he is not likely ever to come back for it. And by my whiskers, that dapple-gray is a good one."

"I have never been in the habit," said Don Quixote, "of taking spoil of those whom I vanquish, nor is it the practice of chivalry to take away their horses and leave them to go on foot, unless indeed it be that the victor has lost his horse in combat, in which case it is lawful to take that of the vanquished as a thing won fairly in war. Therefore, Sancho, leave this horse, or donkey, or whatever you will have it be; for when its owner sees us gone from here, he will come back for it."

"God knows how much I would like to take it," returned Sancho, "or at least to swap it for my own, which does not seem to me as good. The laws of chivalry are awfully strict if they can't be stretched to let one donkey be swapped for another. I'd like to know if I could at least swap our animals' gear."

"On that point, I am not quite certain," answered Don Quixote, "and the matter being doubtful, pending better information, I say you may swap their gear, provided that you have urgent need to do so."

"So urgent is it," answered Sancho, "that if they were for my own person I could not want them more."

Thus authorized, he effected the *mutatio capparum*,[10] rigging out his beast to the nines and then some. This done, they breakfasted on the remains of the spoils of war plundered from the pack mule and drank from the brook that flowed from the fulling mills (without casting a look in that direction, such was their loathing for the fright the mills had caused). All anger and gloom removed, they mounted and, without taking any fixed road (not to fix upon any being the proper thing for true knights-errant), they set out. Their only guide was Rocinante's will, which carried along with it the will of his master—not to mention the donkey's, for he always followed Rocinante's lead with a cheerful and amiable heart. They ended up once again on the king's highway and followed it along without any other aim.

As they went along in this way, Sancho said to his master, "Señor, would your worship give me leave to speak a little to you? For since you laid that hard

[9] *Greeks did for the abduction of Helen:* The abduction of Helen by Paris of Troy was the cause of the Trojan War.

[10] mutatio capparum: Latin, "change of capes", seasonal or ceremonial change in clerical vestments among high-ranking clergy.

command of silence on me several things have gone to rot in my stomach, and I have now just one on the tip of my tongue that I don't want to be spoiled."

"Speak on, Sancho," said Don Quixote, "but be brief in your discourse, for there is no pleasure in one that is long."

"Well then, señor," returned Sancho, "I say that for some days past I have been considering how little is gained by going in search of these adventures that your worship seeks in these wilds and crossroads. Even if we come out victorious from the greatest danger, there is no one to see or know of it, and so the victory must be left untold forever, to the loss of your worship's object and the credit it deserves. It seems to me that it would be better—excepting your worship's better judgment—if we were to go and serve some emperor or other great prince who may have some war on hand. In his service your worship may prove the worth of your person, your great might, and greater understanding—so that when the lord we serve takes note of this, he will have no choice but to reward us, each according to his merits. In that way, you will not be at a loss for someone to set down your achievements in writing so as to preserve their memory for ever. As for my own achievements, I say nothing, since it's unlikely they'll go beyond squirely limits—though I will say that if it's the custom in chivalry to write down the achievements of squires, I don't see why mine should be left out."

"What you say is not without merit, Sancho," answered Don Quixote, "but before that point is reached, it is necessary to roam the world, as it were on probation, seeking adventures, so that with a few victories achieved, name and fame may be acquired. Thus, when the knight betakes himself to the court of some great monarch, he may be already known by his deeds. The instant he enters the city gate and the boys see him, they will all come up and surround him, crying, 'This is the Knight of the Sun'—or the Serpent,[11] or any other title under which he may have achieved great deeds. 'This,' they will say, 'is he who vanquished in single combat the gigantic Brocabruno the Mighty; he who delivered the great Mameluke of Persia out of the long enchantment under which he had been for almost nine hundred years.' From one to another they will go proclaiming his achievements; and presently at the tumult of the boys and the others, the king of that kingdom will appear at the windows of his royal palace, and as soon as he beholds the knight, recognizing him by his arms and the device on his shield, he will as a matter of course say, 'Arise! Forth all ye, knights of my court, to receive the flower of chivalry who cometh hither!' At which command all will come forth, and he himself, advancing halfway down the stairs, will embrace him warmly and salute him, kissing him on the cheek, and will then lead him to the queen's chamber, where the knight will find her with the princess her daughter, who will be one of the most beautiful and accomplished damsels that could with the utmost pains be found anywhere in the known world. Straightway it will come to pass that she will fix her eyes upon the knight and he his upon her, and each will seem to the other something more divine than human, and, without knowing how or why they will be taken and entangled in the inextricable toils

[11] *'Knight of the Sun'—or the Serpent:* epithets from the *Palmerín* cycle.

of love, and sorely distressed in their hearts not to see any way of making their pains and sufferings known by speech. From there, no doubt, his hosts will lead him to some richly adorned chamber of the palace, where, having removed his armor, they will bring him a rich mantle of scarlet for him to robe himself, and if he looked noble in his armor he will look still more so in a quilted doublet.[12]

"When night comes, he will dine with the king, queen, and princess. And all the time he will never take his eyes off her, stealing stealthy glances, unnoticed by those present, and she will do the same, and with equal cautiousness, being, as I have said, a damsel of great discretion. The tables being cleared, suddenly through the door of the hall there will enter a hideous little dwarf followed—between two giants—by a fair dame. The dwarf comes to announce a certain quest, the scheme of an ancient sage; and he who shall achieve it shall be deemed the best knight in the world. The king will then command all those present to undertake it, and none will bring it to a proper conclusion save the visiting knight, to the great enhancement of his fame, at which the princess will be overjoyed and will esteem herself happy and richly rewarded in having fixed and placed her thoughts so high. And the best of it is that this king, or prince, or whatever he is, is engaged in a very bitter war with another as powerful as himself, and the visiting knight, after having been some days at his court, requests leave from him to go and serve him in this war. The king will grant it very readily, and the knight will courteously kiss his hands for the favor done him.

"That night he will take leave of his lady the princess at the window of the chamber where she sleeps, which looks upon a garden, and at which he has already many times conversed with her, the go-between and confidante in the matter being a damsel much trusted by the princess. He will sigh; she will swoon. The damsel will fetch water, much distressed because morning approaches, and for the honor of her lady she would not have them be discovered. At last the princess will come to herself and will present her white hands through the grating to the knight, who will kiss them a thousand and a thousand times, bathing them with his tears. It will be arranged between them how they are to inform each other of what good or ill may befall them, and the princess will entreat him to make his absence as short as possible, which he will promise to do with many oaths. Once more, he kisses her hands and takes his leave in such grief that he is well-nigh ready to die. He betakes him thence to his chamber, flings himself on his bed, cannot sleep for sorrow at parting, rises early in the morning, goes to take leave of the king, queen, and princess, and, as he takes his leave of the pair, it is told him that the princess is indisposed and cannot receive a visit. The knight thinks it is from grief at his departure, his heart is pierced, and he is hardly able to keep from showing his pain. The confidante is present, observes all, goes to tell her mistress, who listens with tears and says that one of her greatest distresses is not knowing who this knight is, and whether he is of kingly lineage or not. The damsel assures her that so much courtesy, gentleness, and gallantry of bearing as her knight possesses could not exist in any save

[12] *quilted doublet: farsetto* (Italian), close-fitting jacket, often with decorative stitching.

one who was royal and illustrious. Her anxiety is thus relieved, and she strives to be of good cheer lest she should excite suspicion in her parents. At the end of two days, she appears in public.

"Meanwhile, the knight has taken his departure. He fights in the war, conquers the king's enemy, wins many cities, triumphs in many battles, returns to the court, sees his lady where he was accustomed to see her, and it is agreed that he shall ask her hand in marriage of her parents as the reward of his services. The king is unwilling to give her away, as he knows not who he is. But nevertheless, whether carried off or however it may be, the princess comes to be his bride, and her father comes to regard it as very good fortune; for it so happens that this knight is proved to be the son of a valiant king of some kingdom, I know not what, for I fancy it is not likely to be on the map. The father dies, the princess inherits, and in two words the knight becomes king. And here at once follows the bestowal of rewards upon his squire and all who have aided him in rising to so exalted a rank. He marries his squire to a damsel of the princess', who will be, no doubt, the one who was confidante in their secret love and is daughter of a very great duke."[13]

"That's what I want, and no mistake about it!" said Sancho. "That's what I'm waiting for. All this, word for word, is in store for your worship under the title of the Knight of the Woeful Countenance."

"You need not doubt it, Sancho," replied Don Quixote, "for in the same manner, and by the same steps as I have described here, knights-errant rise and have risen to be kings and emperors. All we lack now is to find out what king, Christian or pagan, is at war and has a beautiful daughter; but there will be time enough to think of that, for as I have told you, fame must be won in other quarters before repairing to the court. There is another thing, too, that is lacking; for supposing we find a king who is at war and has a beautiful daughter, and that I have won incredible fame throughout the universe, I know not how it can be made out that I am of royal lineage, or even second cousin to an emperor. For the king will not be willing to give me his daughter in marriage unless he is first thoroughly satisfied on this point, however much my famous deeds may deserve it; so that by this deficiency I fear I shall lose what my arm has fairly won. True it is I am a gentleman of known house, of estate and property, and entitled to five hundred salaries in damages.[14] It may be that the sage who shall write my history will so clear up my ancestry and pedigree that I may find myself fifth or sixth in descent from a king. For I would have you know, Sancho, that there are two kinds of lineages in the world. Some trace and derive their descent from kings and princes, whom time has reduced little by little until they end in a point like a pyramid upside down; others spring from the common herd and go on rising step by step until they come to be great lords; so that the difference is that some were

[13] *marries his squire to a damsel . . . daughter of a very great duke:* In the preceding passage, Don Quixote outlines a script that any chivalric romance might have used as a template.

[14] *five hundred salaries in damages:* The expression may refer, with some license, to a hidalgo's right of recovery under medieval law for an offense to his honor.

what they no longer are, and the others are what they formerly were not. I may be of such that after investigation my origin may prove great and famous, with which the king (my father-in-law to be) ought to be satisfied. Should he not be, the princess will so love me that even though she well knew me to be the son of a water carrier, she will take me for her lord and husband in spite of her father. If not, then it is a matter of seizing her and carrying her off where I please. For time or death will put an end to the wrath of her parents."

"It's worth adding," said Sancho, "what some of the wags say, 'Never ask as a favor what you can take by force'; though it would fit better to say, 'A hasty retreat is better than a good man's prayers.' I say so because if my lord the king, your worship's father-in-law, will not give in and hand over my lady the princess, there is nothing to do but, as your worship says, to seize her and truck her away. But the problem is that until you make peace and you get to enjoy your kingdom without trouble, the poor squire is starving as far as rewards go, unless it happens that the go-between damsel who is to be his wife comes along with the princess, and he suffers through his bad luck with her until Heaven orders things differently; for his master, I suppose, may as well give her to him at once for a lawful wife."

"Nobody can object to that," said Don Quixote.

"Then since that may be," said Sancho, "there is nothing to do but to commend ourselves to God, and let fortune take what course it will."

"God guide it according to my wishes and your desires," said Don Quixote, "and villainous be he who thinks himself villainous."

"In God's name let him be so," said Sancho: "I'm an Old Christian, and it's enough for me to be a count."

"More than enough for you," said Don Quixote; "and even if you were not an Old Christian, it would make no difference, because I being the king can easily give you nobility without purchase or service rendered by you. For when I make you a count, you will be at once a gentleman; and they may say what they will, but by my faith they will have to call you 'your lordship,' whether they like it or not."

"Just you wait and see if I'm not a perfect fit for that tittle," said Sancho.

"*Title* you should say, not *tittle*," said his master.

"So be it," answered Sancho. "I'll add that I will know how to behave, for I was once the beadle of a brotherhood, and the beadle's gown sat so well on me that everyone said I looked like I was the chief steward.[15] What will it be, then, when I put a duke's robe on my back, or dress myself in gold and pearls like a count? I believe they'll come a hundred leagues to see me."

"You will look good," said Don Quixote, "but you will need to shave your beard often and not let it get so thick and rough and unkempt, for if you do not

[15] *beadle of a brotherhood . . . chief steward:* Lay confraternities (*cofradías*) were a major part of the civic and religious life of medieval and early modern Spain. These charitable institutions worked with the Church to maintain religious rites, care for the downtrodden, and provide a constructive social outlet for members of the community. Sancho has served as beadle (*muñidor*) for one of these confraternities, responsible for summoning members to meetings and events. The chief steward (*prioste*) presided over the organization.

shave it every second day at least, they will see what kind of person you really are from the distance of a musket shot."

"What more will I need," said Sancho, "than to have a barber and keep him on salary in the house? And if the situation calls, I'll make him go behind me like a noble's footman."

"Why, how do you know that nobles have footmen behind them?" asked Don Quixote.

"I will tell you," answered Sancho. "Years ago, I spent a month in the capital[16] and there I saw taking a walk a very small gentleman who they said was a very great man, and a man following him on horseback at every turn he took, just like he was his tail. I asked why this man didn't join the other man, instead of always going behind him. They answered me that he was his footman, and that it was the custom with nobles to have such people behind them, and ever since then I've know it, for I've never forgotten."

"You are right," said Don Quixote, "and in the same way you may take your barber with you, for customs did not come into use all together, nor were they all invented at once, and you may be the first count to have a barber to follow him. Indeed, shaving one's beard is a greater trust than saddling one's horse."

"I'll see to the barber business," said Sancho; "let your worship take care of becoming a king and making me a count."

"So it shall be," answered Don Quixote, and raising his eyes he saw what will be told in the following chapter.

[16] *in the capital:* literally, "at court". Madrid was established as the capital of Spain in 1561, though it was temporarily moved to Valladolid from 1601 to 1606.

CHAPTER XXII

OF THE FREEDOM DON QUIXOTE CONFERRED ON SEVERAL UNFORTUNATES WHO AGAINST THEIR WILL WERE BEING CARRIED WHERE THEY HAD NO WISH TO GO

Cide Hamete Benengeli, the Arabic and Manchegan author, relates in this most serious, high-sounding, minute, delightful, and original history that after the discussion between the famous Don Quixote of La Mancha and his squire Sancho Panza set down at the end of chapter twenty-one, Don Quixote raised his eyes and saw coming along the road he was following some dozen men on foot strung together by the neck like beads on a great iron chain, and all with shackles on their hands. With them there came also two men on horseback and two on foot—those on horseback with wheel-lock muskets,[1] those on foot with small lances and swords.

As soon as Sancho saw them he said, "That is a chain of galley slaves. On the king's orders, they go by force to the galleys."[2]

"How 'by force'?" asked Don Quixote. "Is it possible that the king uses force against anyone?"

"I don't say that," answered Sancho. "I mean that these people are condemned for their crimes to serve by force in the king's galleys."

"However it may be," replied Don Quixote, "you mean to say that these people are going where they are taking them by force and not of their own will."

"Just so," said Sancho.

"Then in that case," said Don Quixote, "here is a cause for the exercise of my office, to put down force and to aid and defend the wretched."

[1] *wheel-lock muskets:* Pulling the trigger of a wheel-lock musket causes a spring-loaded steel wheel to spin against a piece of pyrite. The sparks created by the friction ignite gunpowder in a pan, which fires the bullet out of the barrel. Developed in the early 1500s, the wheel-lock musket was the first self-igniting mechanism, ideal for situations where there was little time to load. On the more common matchlock firearm, see footnote 9, page 304.

[2] *That is a chain . . . to the galleys:* One of the harshest criminal punishments in early modern Spain was to be sentenced to row in the royal galleys. Galley slaves powered warships that defended against seaborne invasion and kept shipping lanes in the Mediterranean and Atlantic clear of corsairs. If the convicts didn't die from exhaustion, disease, or suicide, they could be killed in battle, drowned in a storm, or captured and enslaved elsewhere.

"Take note, your worship," said Sancho, "Justice, which is the king himself, does no violence or wrong to such people, but punishes them for their crimes."

The chain of galley slaves had by this time approached, and Don Quixote in very courteous language asked those who were in custody of them to be good enough to tell him the reason or reasons for which they were conducting these people in this manner. One of the guards on horseback answered that they were galley slaves belonging to his majesty, that they were going to the galleys, and that was all that was to be said and all he had any business to know.

"Nevertheless," replied Don Quixote, "I should like to know from each of them separately the reason of his misfortune."

To this he added more to the same effect to induce them to tell him what he wanted so civilly that the other mounted guard said to him, "We have here the register and certificate of the sentence for every one of them, but this is no time to take them out and read them. Come and ask the wretches yourself. They can tell if they choose—and they will, for these fellows take as much pleasure in talking about their vile deeds as in doing them."

With this permission, which Don Quixote would have taken even had they not granted it, he approached the chain and asked the first for what sins he was now in such a sorry state.

He answered that it was for being a lover.

"For that only?" replied Don Quixote. "Why, if for being lovers they send people to the galleys, I might have been rowing in them long ago."

"The love is not the sort your worship is thinking of," said the galley slave. "Mine was that I loved a washerwoman's basket of clean linen so well, and held it so close in my embrace, that if the arm of the law had not forced it from me, I should never have let it go of my own will to this moment. I was caught in the act, there was no need for torture,[3] the case was settled, they treated me to a hundred lashes on the back, and three years of gurapas besides. And that's the end of it."

"What are *gurapas*?" asked Don Quixote.

"*Gurapas* are galleys,"[4] answered the galley slave, a young man of about twenty-four and a native, he said, of Piedrahita.[5]

Don Quixote asked the same question of the second, who made no reply, so downcast and melancholy was he; but the first answered for him and said, "He, sir, goes as a canary, I mean as a musician and a singer."

"What!" cried Don Quixote. "For being musicians and singers are people sent to the galleys, too?"

"Yes, sir," answered the galley slave, "for there is nothing worse than singing when under pressure."

[3] *there was no need for torture:* Torture (*tormento*) was used as a means of inducing a confession.

[4] Gurapas *are galleys:* Already during the novel, characters have made passing uses of urban slang, the speech of the criminal underworld. In this episode, *germanía*, as it is called, moves to the foreground.

[5] *Piedrahita:* village near Ávila, in a region still known for cattle farming.

"On the contrary, I have heard say," said Don Quixote, "that he who sings scares away his woes."

"Here, it is the reverse," said the galley slave. "For he who sings once weeps all his life."

"I do not understand it," said Don Quixote.

One of the guards said to him, "Sir, 'to sing under pressure' means with the *non sancta*[6] fraternity 'to confess under torture.'[7] They tortured this sinner and he confessed his crime, which was being a *cuatrero*, that is, a cattle thief, and on his confession they sentenced him to six years in the galleys, besides the two hundred lashes that he carries on his back. He's always dejected and downcast because the other thieves that were left behind and that march here mistreat, snub, jeer, and despise him for confessing and not having enough fortitude to keep up his denial. For they say *no* has no more letters than *sí*, and a criminal will be well off when his life or death depends on his own tongue and not on that of witnesses or evidence. To my thinking, they are not far off the mark."

"And I think so too," answered Don Quixote.

Passing on to the third, he asked him what he had asked the others, and the man answered very readily and unconcernedly, "I am going for five years to their ladyships the gurapas for the lack of ten ducats."[8]

"I will give twenty with pleasure to get you out of that trouble," said Don Quixote.

"That," said the galley slave, "is like a man having money at sea when he is dying of hunger and has no way of buying what he wants. I say so because if at the right time I had had those twenty ducats that your worship now offers me, I would have greased the notary's pen and freshened up the attorney's skill with them, so that today I should be in the middle of the plaza of the Zocodover at Toledo[9] and not on this road tied up like a greyhound. But God is great; patience—that's all."

Don Quixote passed on to the fourth, a man of venerable appearance with a white beard falling below his breast. On hearing himself asked the reason of his being there, he began to weep without answering a word. The fifth acted as his tongue and said, "This worthy man is going to the galleys for four years, after having been treated to the accustomed ceremonies, paraded in his finery and on horseback."[10]

[6] non sancta: Latin, "unholy".

[7] *confess under torture:* There were a variety of tortures used, but the default was waterboarding (*tormento del agua*).

[8] *ducats: ducados.* The *ducado* is a gold coin worth 375 maravedis. It was gradually replaced by the higher-value escudo during the sixteenth and seventeenth centuries.

[9] *Zocodover at Toledo:* the city's principal plaza. It abuts the Alcaná, the commercial district where Cervantes discovers the manuscript of the novel in chapter 9.

[10] *having been treated . . . on horseback:* As the town crier announced his crime, the criminal would be led through the streets on the back of a mule from the prison to the *picota*, a post where he was tied and left exposed to public humiliation.

"That means, as I take it," said Sancho Panza, "to have been put to shame in public."

"Just so," replied the galley slave, "and the offense he received that punishment for was having been an ear-broker,[11] or better, a body-broker. In other words, this gentleman goes as a pimp, not to mention having a bit of the sorcerer about him."

"If that bit had not been thrown in," said Don Quixote, "he would not deserve, for mere pimping, to row in the galleys, but rather to command and be admiral of them. For the office of pimp is no ordinary one, being the office of persons of discretion, one very necessary in a well-ordered state and only to be exercised by persons of good birth. Indeed, there ought to be an inspector and overseer of them, as in other offices, and recognized number, as with the exchange brokers. In this way, many of the evils would be avoided which are caused by this office and calling being in the hands of stupid and ignorant people, the silly women and pages and smooth talkers of little standing and experience, who on the most urgent occasions, and when an immediate decision is needed, let the crumbs freeze on the way to their mouths,[12] and know not which is their right hand. I should like to go farther, and give reasons to show that it is advisable to choose those who are to hold so necessary an office in the state, but this is not the fit place for it. Someday I will expound the matter to someone able to see to and rectify it.[13] All I say now is, that the additional fact of his being a sorcerer has removed the sorrow it gave me to see these white hairs and this venerable countenance in so painful a position on account of his being a pimp; though I know well there are no sorceries in the world that can move or compel the will as some simple folk fancy, for our will is free, nor is there herb or charm that can force it. All that certain silly women and quacks do is to turn men mad with potions and poisons, pretending that they have power to cause love, for as I say, it is an impossibility to compel the will."[14]

[11] *ear-broker:* a commercial intermediary; in *germanía*, a pimp.

[12] *let the crumbs freeze on the way to their mouths:* "don't know what to do".

[13] *Someday I will expound the matter . . . and rectify it:* Don Quixote's praise of a convicted pimp would have likely struck the novel's first audience as excessive, but the acceptance of prostitution that lies behind it was a matter of lively public debate. Those who defended prostitution argued that it was a necessary evil to preserve the social order. Men who visited brothels were less likely to pursue married women or their maiden daughters or to engage in sexual violence. As long as regulators ensured that the prostitutes were housed and fed adequately and that the brothels were not rife with disease, the state would tolerate the vice. Moralists condemned prostitution as incompatible with the Christian ethic. They argued that the abuse- and disease-ridden conditions of prostitutes could not be regulated away and that the men who visited them were corrupted beyond any value to society. The moralists would eventually have the upper hand. The brothels of Castile were closed by royal decree in 1623.

[14] *it is an impossibility to compel the will:* On the cusp of the scientific revolution, belief persisted in the power of planetary movements and herbal concoctions to influence human behavior. Don Quixote directs his ire not at those who believe that these external forces can exert pressure but at those who grant them power to override the will.

"It is true," said the good old man, "and indeed, sir, as far as the charge of sorcery goes, I was not guilty. As to that of being a pimp, I cannot deny it; but I never thought I was doing any harm by it, for my only object was that all the world should enjoy itself and live in peace and quiet without quarrels or troubles. My good intentions were unavailing to save me from going where I never expect to come back from, with this weight of years upon me and a urinary ailment that never gives me a moment's ease."

Again he fell to weeping as before, and such compassion did Sancho feel for him that he took out a real of four[15] from his breast and gave it to him in alms.

Don Quixote went on and asked the next what his crime was, and the man answered with no less but rather much more bravado than the last one.

"I'm here because I carried a joke too far with a couple first cousins of mine, and with a couple other cousins who were not mine. I ended up carrying the joke so far with them all that no devil in hell could sort out the mess of my growing family. Everything was proved against me, I was shown no favor, I had no money, I was near having my neck stretched, they sentenced me to the galleys for six years, and I accepted my fate. I'm punished for my wrong—I, a young man. Let life only last, and with it everything will turn out all right. If you, sir, have anything for the aid of the poor, God will repay you in heaven, and we on earth will take care in our petitions to pray for the life and health of your worship, that they may be as long and as good as your worthy appearance deserves."

This one was in the dress of a student, and one of the guards said he was a great talker and a very elegant Latin scholar.

Behind all these there came a man of thirty, a handsome fellow, except that when he looked, his eyes turned in a little one toward the other. He was bound differently from the rest, for he had to his leg a chain so long that it was wound all round his body, and two rings on his neck. One of the rings was attached to the chain, the other to what they call a "keep-friend" or "friend's foot,"[16] from which hung two irons reaching to his waist with two shackles fixed to them in which his hands were secured by a large padlock. In this way, he could neither raise his hands to his mouth nor lower his head to his hands. Don Quixote asked why this man carried so many more chains than the others. The guard replied that it was because he had committed more crimes than all the rest put together and was so daring and such a villain that, though they marched him in that fashion, they did not feel sure of him but were in dread of his making his escape.

"What crimes can he have committed," said Don Quixote, "if they have not deserved a heavier punishment than being sent to the galleys?"

"He goes for ten years," replied the guard, "which is the same thing as civil death,[17] and all that needs to be said is that this good fellow is the famous Ginés de Pasamonte, otherwise called Ginesillo de Parapilla."

[15] *real of four:* silver coin worth four reals (136 maravedis).

[16] *"keep-friend" or "friend's foot":* forked piece of iron extending from beneath the chin.

[17] *civil death:* life sentence, in which all the criminal's rights as a citizen are extinguished.

"Easy there, señor commissary," said the galley slave at this. "Let's have no fixing of names or surnames. My name is Ginés, not Ginesillo, and my family name is Pasamonte, not Parapilla as you say. Let each one mind his own business, and he will be doing enough."

"Speak with less impertinence, you master thief," replied the commissary, "if you don't want me to make you hold your tongue in spite of your teeth."

"It's easy to see," returned the galley slave, "that man goes as God pleases, but one day it will be clear whether I'm called Ginesillo de Parapilla or not."

"Don't they call you so, you liar?" said the guard.

"They do," returned Ginés, "but I will make them stop calling me so, or they can go to ... I'll say it under my breath. If you, sir, have anything to give us, give it to us at once, and God speed you, for you are becoming tiresome with all this poking into the lives of others. If you want to know about mine, let me tell you I am Ginés de Pasamonte, whose life is written by these fingers."

"He says true," said the commissary, "for he himself has written his story as grand as can be and has left the book in the prison in hock for two hundred reals."

"And I mean to take it out of hock," said Ginés, "even if it were in for two hundred ducats."

"Is it so good?" said Don Quixote.

"So good is it," replied Ginés, "that a fig for *Lazarillo de Tormes*, and every other book of that kind that has been written, or will be written, compared with it.[18] All I'll say about it is that it deals with facts, and facts so beautiful and entertaining that no lies could match them."

"And what is the book's title?" asked Don Quixote.

"The *Life of Ginés de Pasamonte*," replied the subject of it.

"And is it finished?" asked Don Quixote.

"How can it be finished," said the other, "when my life is not yet finished? What I've written is from my birth down to the point when they sent me to the galleys this last time."

"Then you have been there before?" said Don Quixote.

"In the service of God and the king I have been there for four years before now, and I know by this time what the biscuit and kurbash[19] are like," replied Ginés. "It is no great grievance to me to go back to them, for there I shall have time to finish my book. I still have many things left to say, and in the galleys of Spain there is more than enough leisure; though I don't need much for what I have to write, for I know it by heart."

[18] Lazarillo de Tormes ... *compared with it:* The anonymous *Life of Lazarillo de Tormes* (1554) inaugurated the picaresque novel, genre in which a low-born antihero comes of age in the urban underworld, surviving by his wits and trusting no one. The *pícaro* lives on the margin of legality and consorts with fraudsters, prostitutes, pimps, and hypocrites. In *Guzmán de Alfarache*, published just prior to *Don Quixote*, the protagonist (like Ginés) is condemned to the galleys for his crimes. The best of these novels explore the theme of self-knowledge, as Don Quixote's dialogue with Ginés de Pasamonte suggests.

[19] *kurbash:* lash made from animal hide.

"You seem a clever fellow," said Don Quixote.

"And an unfortunate one," replied Ginés, "for misfortune always persecutes great minds."

"It persecutes rogues," said the commissary.

"I told you already to go easy, master commissary," said Pasamonte. "Their lordships yonder didn't give you that staff to mistreat us wretches here but to take us where his majesty orders you. If not, by the life of ... never mind. It is enough that someday the stains made in the inn may come out in the wash. Let everyone hold his tongue and behave well and speak better. And now let us march on, for we have had quite enough of this entertainment."

The commissary lifted his staff to strike Pasamonte in return for his threats, but Don Quixote came between them and begged the officer not to mistreat him, as it was not too much to allow one who had his hands tied to have his tongue a little free.

Turning to the whole chain of them, he said:

"From all you have told me, dear brethren, I make out clearly that though they have punished you for your faults, the punishments you are about to endure do not give you much pleasure, and that you go to them very much against the grain and against your will. Perhaps this one's lack of courage under torture, that one's lack of money, the other's lack of advocacy, and lastly the perverted judgment of the judge may have been the cause of your ruin and of your failure to obtain the justice you had on your side. All of which presents itself now to my mind, urging, persuading, and even compelling me to demonstrate in your case the purpose for which Heaven sent me into the world and caused me to make profession of the order of chivalry to which I belong, and the vow I took therein to give aid to those in need and under the oppression of the strong. But as I know that it is a mark of prudence not to do by foul means what may be done by fair, I will ask these gentlemen, the guards and commissary, to be so good as to release you and let you go in peace, as there will be no lack of others to serve the king under more favorable circumstances. For it seems to me a hard case to make slaves of those whom God and nature have made free. Moreover, sirs of the guard," added Don Quixote, "these poor fellows have done nothing to you. Let each answer for his own sins yonder; there is a God in heaven who will not forget to punish the wicked or reward the good. It is not fitting that honest men should be the instruments of punishment to others, they being therein no way concerned. This request I make thus calmly and gently, that, if you comply with it, I may have reason for thanking you. If you will not voluntarily, this lance and sword together with the might of my arm shall compel you to comply with it by force."

"Precious nonsense!" exclaimed the commissary. "A fine piece of pleasantry he has come out with at last! He wants us to let the king's prisoners go, as if we had any authority to release them, or he to order us to do so! Go your way, sir, and good luck to you. Put that basin straight that you've got on your head, and don't go looking for three feet on a cat."[20]

[20] *don't go looking for three feet on a cat:* "don't go looking for trouble".

"You are the cat, rat, and rascal!" returned Don Quixote, and acting as he spoke, he fell upon him so suddenly that without giving him time to defend himself he brought him to the ground severely wounded with a lance-thrust. How lucky it was for Don Quixote that it was the one that had the musket. The other guards stood thunderstruck and amazed at this unexpected event, but recovering presence of mind, those on horseback seized their swords, and those on foot their pikes, and attacked Don Quixote, who awaited them with great calmness. No doubt it would have gone badly with him if the galley slaves, seeing the chance before them of liberating themselves, had not effected it by managing to break the chain on which they were strung. Such was the confusion that the guards, now rushing at the galley slaves who were breaking loose, now to attack Don Quixote who was waiting for them, did nothing at all that was of any use.

Sancho, on his part, gave a helping hand to release Ginés de Pasamonte, who was the first to leap forth upon the plain free and unfettered, and who, attacking the prostrate commissary, took from him his sword and the musket. With the musket, aiming at one, leveling at another and never discharging it, Ginés drove every one of the guards off the field. They took to flight, not only to escape Pasamonte's musket, but to avoid the showers of stones the now-released galley slaves were raining upon them. Sancho was greatly grieved at the affair, because he anticipated that those who had fled would report the matter to the Holy Brotherhood, who at the summons of the alarm bell would at once sally forth in quest of the offenders. He said so to his master and entreated him to leave the place at once and go into hiding in the mountains that were close by.

"That is all very well," said Don Quixote, "but I know what must be done now." Calling together all the galley slaves, who were now running riot and had stripped the commissary to the skin, he collected them round him to hear what he had to say.

He addressed them as follows: "To be grateful for benefits received is becoming of persons of good birth, and one of the sins most offensive to God is ingratitude. I say so because, sirs, you have already seen by manifest proof the benefit you have received of me. In return for this, it is my wish and good pleasure that, laden with that chain which I have taken off your necks, you at once set out and proceed to the city of El Toboso. There present yourselves before Lady Dulcinea del Toboso and say to her that her knight, he of the Woeful Countenance, sends to commend himself to her; and there recount to her in full detail all the particulars of this notable adventure, up to the recovery of your longed-for liberty. This done, you may go where you will, and good fortune attend you."

Ginés de Pasamonte answered for all, saying, "Sir, the demand that you, our deliverer, makes of us is of all impossibilities the most impossible to comply with, because we cannot go together along the roads but only singly and separate, and each one his own way, attempting to hide ourselves in the belly of the earth to escape the Holy Brotherhood, which, no doubt, will come out in search of us. What your worship may do, and fairly do, is to substitute this service and tribute as regards Lady Dulcinea del Toboso for a certain quantity of Ave Marias and Credos which we will say on your worship's behalf. This is a condition that can be complied with by night as well as by day, running or resting, in peace or in war; but to imagine that we are going now to return to the fleshpots of Egypt[21]—I mean, to take up our chain and set out for El Toboso—is to imagine that it is now night, though it is not yet ten in the morning, and to ask this of us is like 'asking pears of the elm tree'."[22]

"Then by all that's good," said Don Quixote, now stirred to wrath, "Don Son of a Bitch, Don Ginesillo de Paropillo, or whatever your name is, you will have to go alone, with your tail between your legs and that whole chain on your back."

Pasamonte, who was anything but meek, had already become thoroughly convinced that Don Quixote was not quite right in his head, since he had been so foolish as to set them free. Finding himself abused in this fashion, he winked to his companions, and falling back they began to shower stones on Don Quixote at such a rate that he was quite unable to protect himself with his buckler, while poor Rocinante no more heeded the spur than if he had been made of bronze. Sancho planted himself behind his donkey and with him sheltered himself from the hailstorm that poured on both of them. Don Quixote was unable to shield himself so well but that more pebbles than could be counted struck him full on the body with such force that they brought him to the ground. The instant he fell, the student pounced upon him, snatched the basin from his head, and with it struck three or four blows on his shoulders and as many more on the ground, knocking it almost to pieces. They then stripped him of a coat he wore over his armor,[23] and they would have stripped off his stockings if his greaves[24] had not prevented them. From Sancho they took his coat, leaving him in his shirt sleeves; and dividing among themselves the remaining spoils of the battle, they went each one his own way, more concerned about keeping clear of the Holy Brotherhood they dreaded than about burdening themselves with the chain or going to present themselves before Lady Dulcinea del Toboso.

All that were left were the donkey and Rocinante, Sancho and Don Quixote: the donkey with head drooped in reflection, shaking his ears from time to time, as if he thought the storm of stones that assailed them was not yet over; Rocinante stretched beside his master, for he too had been brought to the ground by a stone; Sancho stripped, and trembling with fear of the Holy Brotherhood; and Don Quixote fuming to find himself so mistreated by the very people for whom he had done so much.

[21] *return to the fleshpots of Egypt:* See Exodus 16:2–3, where the Israelites "murmured against Moses and Aaron in the wilderness, and said to them, 'Would that we had died by the hand of the LORD in the land of Egypt, when we sat by the fleshpots and ate bread to the full.'"

[22] *asking pears of the elm tree:* The analogous English expression would be "trying to draw blood from a turnip".

[23] *coat he wore over his armor: ropilla,* short jacket with loose-fitting sleeves, which were slashed to reveal the garment (or armor) underneath.

[24] *greaves:* armor that protects the leg from the knee to the ankle.

CHAPTER XXIII

OF WHAT BEFELL DON QUIXOTE IN THE SIERRA MORENA, WHICH IS ONE OF THE STRANGEST ADVENTURES RELATED IN THIS TRUE HISTORY

Seeing himself mistreated this way, Don Quixote said to his squire, "I have always heard it said, Sancho, that 'to do good to boors is to throw water into the sea.' If I had believed your words, I should have avoided this trouble; but it is done now. Let us be patient and take warning for the future."

"Your worship will take a warning as much as I'm a Turk," returned Sancho. "But since you say that this mischief might have been avoided if you had believed me, believe me now and an even greater one will be avoided. For I tell you, chivalry doesn't matter a thing to the Holy Brotherhood, and they don't care two maravedis for all the knights-errant in the world. I think I can almost hear their arrows whistling past my ears this minute."

"You are a coward by nature, Sancho," said Don Quixote, "but lest you should say I am obstinate, and that I never do as you advise, this once I will take your advice and withdraw out of reach of that fury you so fear. But it must be on one condition: that never, in life or in death, are you to say to anyone that I retreated or drew back from this danger out of fear but only to comply with your entreaties. If you say otherwise, you will be lying, and from this time to that, and from that time to this, I will call out your lie and say that you lie and will lie every time you think it or say it. Answer me no more, for at the mere thought that I am withdrawing or retreating from any danger—above all from this, which does seem to carry some little shadow of fear with it—I am ready to take my stand here and await alone, not only that Holy Brotherhood you talk of and dread, but the brothers of the twelve tribes of Israel, and the Seven Maccabees, and Castor and Pollux, and all the brothers and brotherhoods in the world."[1]

"Señor," replied Sancho, "to retreat is not to flee, and there is no wisdom in waiting when danger outweighs hope. It's the mark of a wise man to preserve himself today for tomorrow, and not risk everything at once. I may be an ignorant peasant, but you should know that I have my share of common sense. So don't repent of having taken my advice, but mount Rocinante if you can; if not

[1] *the Seven Maccabees . . . in the world:* The Seven Maccabees are probably the *five* Maccabean brothers who led the Jewish people in a revolt against Seleucid occupiers; Castor and Pollux were twin sons of Jupiter and Leda famed for their horsemanship in battle.

I'll help you. Follow after me, for I've got a hunch that we need our legs more than we need our hands right now."

Don Quixote mounted without replying, and with Sancho leading the way on his donkey, they entered on one side of the Sierra Morena, which was nearby.[2] It was Sancho's plan to cross it entirely and come out again at El Viso or Almodóvar del Campo and hide for some days among its crags in order to escape the search of the Brotherhood should they come to look for them. He was encouraged in this when he discovered that the stock of provisions carried by the donkey had come safe out of the scuffle with the galley slaves, a circumstance that he regarded as a miracle, seeing how they pillaged and ransacked.

For his part, Don Quixote was thrilled to the heart on entering the mountains, as they seemed to him to be just the place for the adventures he was in quest of. They brought back to his memory the marvelous events that had befallen knights-errant in like solitudes and wilds, and he went along reflecting on these things, so absorbed and carried away by them that he had no thought for anything else.

Nor had Sancho any other care (now that he imagined he was traveling in a safe quarter) than to satisfy his appetite with such remains as were left of the clerical spoils; and so he rode behind his master seated sidesaddle on his donkey, emptying the sack and packing his paunch. As long as he could continue that way, he would not have given a cent to meet with another adventure.

While so engaged, he raised his eyes and saw that his master had halted and was trying with the point of his spear to lift some bulky object that lay upon the ground. He hurried to join him and help him if necessary, and reached him just as with the point of the spear he was raising a saddle pad with a valise attached to it, half or rather wholly rotten and torn. So heavy were they that Sancho had to help to pick them up. His master directed him to see what the valise contained, which Sancho did right away. Though the valise was secured by a chain and padlock, from its torn and rotten condition he was able to see its contents, which were four shirts of fine holland[3] and other articles of linen no less curious than clean. In a handkerchief he found a good quantity of gold escudos.[4]

As soon as he saw them, he exclaimed, "Blessed be all Heaven for sending us an adventure that is good for something!"

Searching further, he found a little memorandum book richly bound. This Don Quixote asked of him, telling him to take the money and keep it for himself. Sancho kissed his hands for the favor and emptied the valise of its linen, which he stowed away in the provision sack.

[2] *the Sierra Morena, which was nearby:* mountain range that runs along the southern border of Castile and Extremadura and the northern border of Andalusia. Don Quixote and Sancho have traveled south to the edge of the Meseta Central, the plateau that occupies the center of the Iberian Peninsula.

[3] *holland:* closely woven cotton or linen fabric.

[4] *escudos:* The *escudo* (shield) was a gold coin introduced in 1566, worth sixteen reals (544 maravedis).

Considering the whole matter, Don Quixote observed, "It seems to me, Sancho—and it is impossible it can be otherwise—that some lost traveler must have crossed this sierra and been attacked and slain by highwaymen, who brought him to this remote spot to bury him."

"That can't be," answered Sancho, "because if they had been robbers, they would not have left this money."

"You are right," said Don Quixote, "and I cannot guess or explain what this may mean. But stay; let us see if in this memorandum book there is anything written by which we may be able to trace out or discover what we want to know."

He opened it, and the first thing he found, written roughly but in a very good hand, was a sonnet. Reading it aloud that Sancho might hear it, he found that it ran as follows:

> Or Love is lacking in intelligence,
> Or to the height of cruelty attains,
> Or else it is my doom to suffer pains
> Beyond the measure due to my offense.
> But if Love be a God, it follows thence
> That he knows all, and certain it remains
> No God loves cruelty; then who ordains
> This penance that enthralls while it torments?
> It were a falsehood, Chloe, you to name;
> Such evil with such goodness cannot live;
> And against Heaven I dare not charge the blame,
> I only know it is my fate to die.
> To him who knows not whence his malady
> A miracle alone a cure can give.

"There's nothing to be learned from that little ditty," said Sancho, "unless by the clue in it, we can solve the whole mystery."

"What clue is there?" said Don Quixote.

"I thought your worship spoke of a clue in it," said Sancho.

"I only said *Chloe*," replied Don Quixote, "and that no doubt, is the name of the lady of whom the author of the sonnet complains. In faith, he must be a tolerable poet, or I know little of the craft."

"Then your worship understands rhyming too?"

"And better than you think," replied Don Quixote, "as you shall see when you carry a letter written in verse from beginning to end to my lady Dulcinea del Toboso. For I would have you know, Sancho, that all or most of the knights-errant in days of yore were great troubadours and great musicians. Both of these accomplishments, or more properly speaking gifts, are the peculiar property of lovers-errant. True it is that the poems of the knights of old have more spirit than style in them."

"Read more, your worship," said Sancho, "and I bet you'll find something else to enlighten us."

Don Quixote turned the page and said, "This is prose and seems to be a letter."

"A correspondence letter, señor?"

"Judging by the beginning, it seems to be a love letter," replied Don Quixote.

"Then let your worship read it aloud," said Sancho, "for I am very fond of matters of love."

"With all my heart," said Don Quixote, and reading it aloud as Sancho had requested him, he found it ran thus:

> Your false promise and my sure misfortune carry me to a place where the news of my death will reach your ears before the words of my complaint. Ungrateful one, you have rejected me for one wealthier but not worthier. If virtue were valued as wealth, I should neither have cause to envy the happiness of others nor weep for misfortunes of my own. What your beauty has raised up your deeds have laid low. By your beauty I believed you to be an angel; by your deeds I know you to be a woman. Peace be with you, bringer of war, and may Heaven grant that the deceit of your husband be ever hidden from you, lest you be left to repent of what you have done and I be obliged to take revenge where I have no desire.

When he had finished the letter, Don Quixote said, "There is less to be gathered from this than from the poem, except that he who wrote it is some rejected lover."

Turning over nearly all the pages of the book, he found more poems and letters, some of which he could read, while others he could not. They were all made up of complaints, laments, misgivings, desires and disgusts, favors and rejections, some rapturous, some melancholy. While Don Quixote examined the book, Sancho examined the valise, not leaving a corner in the whole of it or in the saddle pad that he did not search, peer into, and explore, or seam that he did not rip, or tuft of wool that he did not pick to pieces, lest anything should escape from haste or carelessness—so keen was the covetousness excited in him by the discovery of the escudos, which amounted to near a hundred. Though he found no more booty, he considered that the blanket flights, balsam vomits, stake benedictions, carriers' fisticuffs, missing saddlebag, stolen coat, and all the hunger, thirst, and weariness he had endured in the service of his good master, cheap at the price, as he counted himself more than fully indemnified for all by the payment he received in the gift of the treasure trove.

The Knight of the Woeful Countenance was still very anxious to find out who the owner of the valise could be, conjecturing from the sonnet and letter, from the money in gold, and from the fineness of the shirts, that he must be some wellborn lover whom the scorn and cruelty of his lady had driven to some desperate course; but as in that uninhabited and rugged spot there was no one to be seen of whom he could inquire, he saw nothing else to do but to push on, taking whatever road Rocinante chose—which was where the animal was able to walk—firmly persuaded that among these wilds he could not fail to meet some rare adventure.

As he went along occupied with these thoughts, he noticed on the summit of a height that rose before their eyes a man who went springing from rock to rock and from bramble to bramble with incredible agility. As well as he could make out, he was shoeless, with a thick black beard, long tangled hair, and bare legs and feet.

His thighs were covered by breeches apparently of tawny velvet but so ragged that they showed his skin in several places. He was bareheaded, and notwithstanding the swiftness with which he passed as has been described, the Knight of the Woeful Countenance observed and noted all these details. Though he made the attempt, he was unable to follow him, for it was not granted to the feebleness of Rocinante to make way over such rough ground, he being, moreover, slow-paced and sluggish by nature. Don Quixote at once came to the conclusion that this was the owner of the saddle pad and of the valise and made up his mind to go in search of him, even though he should have to wander a year in those mountains before he found him. And so he directed Sancho to take a short cut over one side of the mountain, while he himself went by the other, and perhaps by this means they might light upon this man who had passed so quickly out of their sight.

"I can't do that," said Sancho, "for when I separate from your worship fear at once takes hold of me and attacks me with all kinds of panics and visions. Let what I now say be a notice that from this time forth I'm not going to stir a finger's width from your presence."

"It shall be so," said he of the Woeful Countenance. "I am very glad that you are willing to rely on my courage, which will never fail you, even though the soul in your body fail you. Come now behind me slowly as well as you can, and make lanterns of your eyes. Let us make the circuit of this ridge; perhaps we shall light upon this man that we saw, who no doubt is no other than the owner of what we found."

To which Sancho answered, "It would be far better not to look for him, for if we find him, and he happens to be the owner of the money, there's no doubt I'm going to have to restore it. It would be better, then, that without taking this needless trouble, I hold onto it until in some other less meddlesome and straightforward way the real owner can be discovered. By then I might have spent it, and then the king will hold me harmless."[5]

"You are wrong there, Sancho," said Don Quixote, "for now that we have a suspicion who the owner is, and have him almost before us, we are bound to seek him and make restitution. If we do not see him, the strong suspicion we have as to his being the owner makes us as guilty as if he were so. And so, friend Sancho, let not our search for him give you any uneasiness, for if we find him it will relieve mine."

So saying he gave Rocinante the spur, and Sancho followed him on his faithful donkey. After having partly made the circuit of the mountain, they found lying in a ravine, dead and half devoured by dogs and pecked by crows, a mule saddled and bridled, all of which still further strengthened their suspicion that he who had fled was the owner of the mule and the saddle pad.

As they stood looking at it, they heard a whistle like that of a shepherd watching his flock. Suddenly on their left there appeared a great number of goats and behind them on the summit of the mountain the goatherd in charge of them, a man advanced in years. Don Quixote called aloud to him and begged him to come down to where they stood. He shouted in return, asking what had brought

[5] *the king will hold me harmless:* that is, he will be declared bankrupt.

them to that spot, seldom or never trodden except by the feet of goats, or of the wolves and other wild beasts that roamed around. Sancho in return asked him to come down, and they would explain all to him.

The goatherd descended, and reaching the place where Don Quixote stood, he said, "I will wager you are looking at that hack mule[6] that lies dead in the hollow there. Faith, it has been lying there now these six months. Tell me, have you come upon its owner around here?"

"We have come upon nobody," answered Don Quixote, "nor on anything except a saddle pad and a little valise that we found not far from this place."

"I found it too," said the goatherd, "but I won't lift it or go near it for fear of bad luck or being charged with theft. The devil is crafty, and things creep up under a fellow's feet to make him fall without knowing why or wherefore."

"That's exactly what I say," said Sancho. "I found it too, and I wouldn't go within a stone's throw of it. I left it there, and there it stays, just as it was. I don't want a dog with a bell."[7]

"Tell me, good man," said Don Quixote, "do you know who is the owner of this property?"

"All I can tell you," said the goatherd, "is that about six months ago, more or less, there arrived at a shepherd's hut about three leagues from here, a youth of well-bred appearance and manners, mounted on that same mule that lies dead here, and with the same saddle pad and valise that you say you found and didn't touch. He asked us what part of this sierra was the most rugged and remote. We told him that it was where we now are; and so in truth it is, for if you push on half a league farther, you might not be able to find your way out. I'm wondering how you have managed to come here, since there is no road or path that leads to this spot. Anyway, I say that when he heard our answer, the youth turned about and made for the place we pointed out to him, leaving us all charmed with his good looks and wondering at his question and the haste we saw him depart with in the direction of the sierra.

"After that we saw him no more, until some days afterwards he crossed the path of one of our shepherds, and without saying a word to him, came up to him and gave him several cuffs and kicks and then turned to the donkey with our provisions and took all the bread and cheese it carried, and having done this made off back again into the sierra with amazing speed. When some of us goatherds learned this, we went in search of him for about two days through the most remote part of this sierra until we found him lodged in the hollow of a large, thick cork tree. He came out to meet us with great gentleness, with his garments now torn and his face so disfigured and burned by the sun, that we hardly recognized him, except that his clothes, though torn, convinced us, from the recollection we had of them, that he was the person we were looking for.

"He saluted us courteously, and in a few well-spoken words he told us not to wonder at seeing him going about in this way, as it was binding upon him

[6] *hack mule:* mule for hire.

[7] *I don't want a dog with a bell:* "I don't want anything that will cause me trouble."

in order that he might work out a penance which for his many sins had been imposed upon him. We asked him to tell us who he was, but we were never able to find out from him. We begged of him, too—when he was lacking food, which he could not do without—to tell us where we should find him, as we would bring it to him with all goodwill and eagerness; or if this were not to his liking, at least to come and ask it of us and not take it by force from the shepherds. He thanked us for the offer, begged pardon for the recent assault, and promised for the future to ask it in God's name without doing violence to anybody. As for a place to stay, he said he had no other than whatever chance offered where night happened to overtake him. His words ended in an outburst of weeping so bitter that those of us who were listening to him would have been made of stone if we hadn't joined him in it, comparing what we saw of him the first time with what we saw now; for as I said, he was a graceful and gracious youth, and in his polished language showed himself to be of good birth and courtly breeding. Rustics as we were that listened to him, his gentle bearing would be plain to coarseness itself.

"But in the middle of his conversation he stopped and became silent, keeping his eyes fixed on the ground for some time, during which we stood still waiting anxiously to see what would come of this trance; and with no little pity, for from his behavior, now staring at the ground with fixed gaze and eyes wide open without moving an eyelid, again closing them, tightening his lips and raising his eyebrows, we could see plainly that a fit of madness of some kind had come upon him. Before long he showed that what we imagined was the truth, for he arose in a fury from the ground where he had thrown himself and attacked the first person he found near him with such ferocity that if we had not dragged him off the other fellow, he would have beaten or bitten him to death. All the while, he was exclaiming, 'Oh faithless Fernando, here, here shall you pay the penalty of the wrong you have done me. These hands shall tear out that heart of yours, abode and dwelling of all iniquity, but of deceit and fraud above all.' To these he added other words, all in effect cursing this Fernando and branding him a traitor and villain.

"We forced him to release his hold with no little difficulty, and without another word he left us, and rushing off plunged in among these wilds and brambles, so as to make it impossible for us to follow him. From this we suppose that madness comes upon him from time to time, and that someone called Fernando must have done him a wrong of a grievous nature such as the condition it had brought him to seemed to show. This has all been now confirmed on those occasions—and there have been many—when he has crossed our path, at one time to beg the shepherds to give him some of the food they carry, at another to take it from them by force; for when there is a fit of madness upon him, even though the shepherds offer it freely, he will not accept it but snatches it from them with blows. But when he is in his senses he begs it for the love of God, courteously and civilly, and receives it with many thanks and not a few tears.

"To tell you the truth, sirs," continued the goatherd, "it was yesterday that we resolved, I and four of the lads, two of them our servants, and the other two friends of mine, to go in search of him until we find him, and when we do to take him, whether by force or of his own consent, to the town of Almodóvar, which is eight leagues from here, and see to his cure (if indeed what ails him can be cured), or learn when he is in his senses who he is, and if he has relatives who can be notified of his misfortune. This, sirs, is all I can say in answer to what you've asked me; and be sure that the owner of the articles you found is the one you saw pass by so nimbly and so naked."

Don Quixote had already described how he had seen the man go bounding along the mountainside; now he was filled with amazement at what he heard from the goatherd, and more eager than ever to discover who the unhappy madman was. In his heart he resolved, as he had done before, to search for him all over the mountain, not leaving a corner or cave unexamined until he had found him. But chance arranged matters better than he expected or hoped, for at that very moment, in a gorge on the mountain that opened where they stood, the youth he wished to find made his appearance, coming along talking to himself in a way that would have been unintelligible near at hand, much more at a distance. His dress was what has been described, save that as he drew near, Don Quixote noticed that a tattered leather jerkin[8] he wore was amber-tanned, from which he concluded that one who wore such garments could not be of very low rank.

As he approached, the youth greeted them in a harsh and hoarse voice but with great courtesy. Don Quixote returned his salutation with equal politeness, and dismounting from Rocinante advanced with well-bred bearing and grace to embrace him. He held him for a while close in his arms, as if he had known him for a long time. The other, whom we may call the Ragged One of the Sorry Countenance, as Don Quixote was of the Woeful Countenance, after submitting to the embrace pushed him back a little and, placing his hands on Don Quixote's shoulders, stood gazing at him as if seeking to see whether he knew him, not less amazed, perhaps, at the sight of the face, figure, and armor of Don Quixote than Don Quixote was at the sight of him. To be brief, the first to speak after embracing was the Ragged One, and he said what will be detailed below.

[8] *leather jerkin: coleto*, close-fitting vest or short-sleeved garment worn over the doublet.

CHAPTER XXIV

IN WHICH IS CONTINUED THE ADVENTURE OF THE SIERRA MORENA

The history relates that it was with the greatest attention that Don Quixote listened to the ragged Knight of the Sierra, who began by saying:

"Whoever you are, señor, for I know you not, I heartily thank you for the proofs of kindness and courtesy you have shown me. Would that I were in a condition to requite with more than goodwill what you have displayed toward me in the cordial reception you have given me; but my fate does not afford me any other means of returning kindnesses done me save the hearty desire to repay them."

"Mine," replied Don Quixote, "is to be of service to you, so much so that I had resolved not to leave these mountains until I had found you and learned of you whether there is any kind of relief to be found for that sorrow under which from the strangeness of your life you seem to labor and to search for you with all possible diligence, if search had been necessary. If your misfortune should prove to be one of those that close the door to any sort of consolation, it was my purpose to join you in lamenting and mourning over it, so far as I could; for it is still some comfort in misfortune to find one who can share it. And if my good intentions deserve to be acknowledged with any kind of courtesy, I entreat you, señor, by that which I perceive you possess in so high a degree, and likewise beseech you by whatever you love or have loved best in life, to tell me who you are and the cause that has brought you to live or die in these solitudes like a brute beast, dwelling among them in a manner so foreign to your condition as your dress and appearance show. I swear," added Don Quixote, "by the order of knighthood which I have received, and by my vocation of knight-errant, if you gratify me in this, to serve you with all the zeal my calling demands of me, either in relieving your misfortune if it admits of relief, or in joining you in lamenting it as I promised to do."

The Knight of the Forest, hearing him of the Woeful Countenance talk in this way, did nothing but stare at him and stare at him again, and again survey him from head to foot. When he had thoroughly examined him, he said to him, "If you have anything to give me to eat, for God's sake give it to me. After I have eaten, I will do all you ask in gratitude for the goodwill you have displayed toward me."

Sancho from his sack, and the goatherd from his pouch, furnished the Ragged One with the means of appeasing his hunger. What they gave him he ate like a half-witted being, so hastily that he took no time between mouthfuls, gorging rather than swallowing. While he ate, neither he nor they who observed him uttered a word. As soon as he had finished, he made signs to them to follow him, which they did, and he led them to a green patch which lay a little farther off round the corner of a rock.

On reaching it he stretched himself upon the grass, and the others did the same, all keeping silence, until the Ragged One, settling himself in his place, said, "If it is your wish, sirs, that I should disclose in a few words the surpassing extent of my misfortunes, you must promise not to break the thread of my sad story with any question or other interruption, for the instant you do so the tale I tell will come to an end."

These words of the Ragged One reminded Don Quixote of the tale his squire had told him, when he failed to keep count of the goats that had crossed the river and the story remained unfinished. But to return to the Ragged One, he went on to say, "I give you this warning because I wish to pass briefly over the story of my misfortunes, for recalling them to memory only serves to add fresh ones, and the less you question me the sooner shall I make an end of telling them, though I shall not omit to relate anything of importance in order fully to satisfy your curiosity."

Don Quixote gave the promise for himself and the others, and with this assurance he began as follows:

"My name is Cardenio, my birthplace one of the best cities of this Andalusia, my family noble, my parents rich, my misfortune so great that my parents must have wept and my family grieved over it without being able by their wealth to lighten it; for the gifts of fortune can do little to relieve reverses sent by Heaven. In that same country there was a heaven in which love had placed all the glory I could desire—such was the beauty of Luscinda, a damsel as noble and as rich as I, but of happier fortunes, and of less constancy than was due to so worthy a passion as mine. This Luscinda I loved, worshipped, and adored from my earliest and tenderest years, and she loved me in all the innocence and sincerity of childhood. Our parents were aware of our feelings, and were not sorry to notice them, for they saw clearly that as they ripened they must lead at last to a marriage between us, a thing that seemed almost prearranged by the equality of our families and wealth. We grew up, and with our growth grew the love between us, so that the father of Luscinda felt bound for propriety's sake to refuse me admission to his house, in this perhaps imitating the parents of that Thisbe so celebrated by the poets.[1] This refusal but added love to love and flame to flame; for though they enforced silence upon our tongues they could not impose it upon our pens, which can make known the heart's secrets to a loved one more freely than tongues. Many a time the presence of the object of love shakes the firmest will and strikes dumb the boldest tongue. Ah, heavens! How many letters did I write her, and

[1] *that Thisbe so celebrated by the poets:* In Ovid's telling, Pyramus and Thisbe are neighbors who fall in love at an early age. Forbidden by their rivalrous parents from seeing each other, the lovers continue their relationship by communicating through a crack in the wall that separates their homes.

how many modest, sweet replies did I receive! How many ditties and love songs did I compose in which my heart declared its feelings, described its ardent longings, reveled in its recollections and sported in its desires!

"At length, growing impatient and feeling my heart languishing with longing to see her, I resolved to put into execution and carry out what seemed to me the best mode of winning my desired and merited reward: to ask her of her father for my lawful wife, which I did. His answer to this was to thank me for the intention I showed to honor him and to regard myself as honored by the bestowal of his treasure; but that as my father was alive, it was his by right to make this demand, for if it were not in accordance with my father's full will and pleasure, Luscinda was not to be taken or given in secret. I thanked him for his kindness, reflecting that there was reason in what he said, and that my father would assent to it as soon as I should tell him. With that view I went the very same instant to let him know what my desires were.

"When I entered the room where he was, I found him with an open letter in his hand, which, before I could utter a word, he gave me, saying, 'By this letter you will see, Cardenio, the disposition Duke Ricardo has to favor you.' This Duke Ricardo, as you probably know already, sirs, is a grandee of Spain who has his seat in the best part of this Andalusia. I took and read the letter, which was couched in terms so flattering that even I myself felt it would be wrong in my father not to comply with the request the duke made in it, which was that he would send me immediately to him, as he wished me to become the companion, not servant, of his eldest son, and would take upon himself the charge of placing me in a position corresponding to the esteem in which he held me. On reading the letter my voice failed me, and still more when I heard my father say, 'Two days hence you will depart, Cardenio, in accordance with the duke's wish, and give thanks to God who is opening a road to you by which you may attain what I know you deserve.' To these words he added others of fatherly counsel.

"The time for my departure arrived. I spoke one night to Luscinda and told her all that had occurred, as I did also to her father, entreating him to allow some delay and to defer giving her in marriage until I should see what Duke Ricardo sought of me. He gave me the promise, and she confirmed it with vows and swoons unnumbered. At last, I presented myself to the duke and was received and treated by him so kindly that very soon envy began to do its work—the old servants growing jealous of me, regarding the duke's inclination to show me favor as an injury to themselves. But the one to whom my arrival gave the greatest pleasure was the duke's second son, Fernando by name, a gallant youth, of noble, generous, and amorous disposition, who very soon made so intimate a friend of me that it was remarked by everybody. For though the elder was attached to me and showed me kindness, he did not carry his affectionate treatment to the same length as Don Fernando.

"It so happened that, as between friends no secret remains unshared and as the favor I enjoyed with Don Fernando had grown into friendship, he made all his thoughts known to me, and in particular a love affair which troubled his mind a little. He was deeply in love with a peasant girl, a vassal of his father's, the daughter of wealthy parents,[2] and herself so beautiful, modest, discreet, and virtuous, that no one who knew her was able to decide in which of these respects she was most highly gifted or most excelled. The attractions of the fair peasant raised the passion of Don Fernando to such a point that, in order to gain his object and overcome her virtuous resolutions, he determined to pledge his word to her to become her husband, for to attempt it in any other way was to attempt an impossibility. Bound to him as I was by friendship, I strove by the best arguments and the most forcible examples I could think of to restrain and dissuade him from such a course. But seeing that I produced no effect, I resolved to make Duke Ricardo, his father, acquainted with the matter. Don Fernando, however, being sharp-witted and astute, anticipated my intention, for he perceived that by my duty as a good servant I was bound not to keep concealed a thing so much opposed to the honor of my lord the duke. And so to mislead and deceive me, he told me he could find no better way of effacing from his mind the beauty that so enslaved him than by absenting himself for some months. His design for this absence was for the two of us to go to my father's house under a pretense he would give the duke, his father: that he wished to look over and purchase some fine horses that were in my city, which produces the best in the world. When I heard him say so, even if his resolution had not been so worthy, I should have hailed it as one of the happiest that could be imagined, for I saw what a favorable opportunity it offered me of returning to see my Luscinda.

"With this thought and wish, I commended his idea and encouraged his design, advising him to put it into execution as quickly as possible, as, in truth, absence produced its effect in spite of the most deeply rooted feelings. I found out afterwards that when he said this to me, he had already enjoyed the peasant girl under the title of husband and was waiting for an opportunity of making it known without risk to himself, being in dread of what his father the duke would do when he came to know of his folly. It happened, then, that—as love in young men is for the most part nothing more than appetite, which, as its final object is enjoyment, comes to an end on obtaining it; and what seemed to be love takes to flight, for it cannot pass the limit fixed by nature, which fixes no limit to true love. What I mean to say is that after Don Fernando had enjoyed this peasant girl, his passion subsided and his eagerness cooled. If at first he feigned a wish to absent himself in order to cure his love, he was now in reality anxious to go to avoid keeping his promise.

"The duke gave him permission and ordered me to accompany him. We arrived at my city, and my father gave him the reception due his rank. I saw Luscinda without delay and, though it had not been dead or deadened, my love gathered

[2] *a peasant girl . . . of wealthy parents:* It may seem contradictory that a peasant (*labradora*) could come from a wealthy family, but it was not unusual for those Spaniards born outside the aristocracy to acquire wealth working the land, a phenomenon that could generate anxiety among those nobles of limited means. We have already encountered one wealthy peasant, Marcela (chap. 12), and in the second volume will be attending the wedding of another, Camacho the Rich (chap. 20).

fresh life. To my sorrow, I told the story of my love to Don Fernando, for I thought that in virtue of the great friendship he bore me I was bound to conceal nothing from him. I extolled her beauty, her grace, her wit, so warmly, that my praises excited in him a desire to see a damsel adorned by such attractions. To my misfortune I yielded to it, showing her to him one night by the light of a candle at a window where we used to talk to one another. When she appeared before him in her dressing gown, she drove all the beauties he had seen until then out of his recollection. Speech failed him, his head turned, he was spellbound, and in the end love-smitten, as you will see in the course of the story of my misfortune.

"To inflame still further his passion, which he hid from me and revealed to Heaven alone, it so happened that one day he found a note of hers entreating me to ask her of her father in marriage. So delicate, so modest, and so tender were her words that on reading them Don Fernando told me that in Luscinda alone were combined all the charms of beauty and understanding that were distributed among all the other women in the world. It is true (and I own it now), that though I knew what good cause Don Fernando had to praise Luscinda, it gave me uneasiness to hear these praises from his mouth, and I began to fear and mistrust him, for there was no moment when he was not ready to talk of Luscinda. He would bring up the subject himself, even if it was out of place, a circumstance that aroused in me an ill-defined jealousy. Not that I feared any change in the constancy or faith of Luscinda, but still my fate stirred in me a foreboding of what she assured me against. Don Fernando contrived always to read the letters I sent to Luscinda and her answers to me, under the pretense that he enjoyed the refinement of both. It so happened that Luscinda asked me for a book of chivalry to read that she was very fond of, *Amadís of Gaul*—"

Don Quixote no sooner heard a book of chivalry mentioned than he said, "Had your worship told me at the beginning of your story that Señora Luscinda was fond of books of chivalry, no higher praise would have been required to impress upon me the superiority of her understanding, for it could not have been of the excellence you describe had a taste for such delightful reading been lacking. As far as I am concerned, you need waste no more words in describing her beauty, worth, and intelligence; for on merely hearing of her interest, I declare her to be the most beautiful and the most intelligent woman in the world. I wish your worship had, along with *Amadís of Gaul*, sent her the worthy *Don Rugel of Greece*,[3] for I know Señora Luscinda would greatly relish Daraida and Garaya, and the wit of the shepherd Darinel, and his admirable bucolic verse, sung and delivered by him with such grace, cleverness, and ease. But a time may come when this omission can be remedied, and to rectify it nothing more is needed than for your worship to be so good as to come with me to my village, for there I can give you more than three hundred books which are the delight of my soul and the entertainment of my life—although it occurs to me that I have not got one of them now, thanks to the spite of wicked and envious enchanters. But pardon me for having broken the promise we made not to interrupt your discourse; for when I hear chivalry

[3] Don Rugel of Greece: eleventh in the *Amadís* cycle (Feliciano de Silva, 1535).

or knights-errant mentioned, I can no more help talking about them than the rays of the sun can help giving heat, or those of the moon moisture.[4] Pardon me, therefore, and proceed, for that is more to the purpose now."

As Don Quixote spoke, Cardenio's head fell to his breast, and he seemed plunged in deep thought. Though twice Don Quixote urged him to go on with his story, he neither looked up nor uttered a word in reply; but after some time he raised his head and said, "I cannot get rid of the idea, nor will anyone in the world take it from me or make me think otherwise, and he would be a blockhead who would hold to any other belief than that Master Elisabad—that knave—bedded Queen Madasima."[5]

"By thunder, that's not true!" cried Don Quixote in high wrath, turning upon him angrily, as his way was, "and it is an exceedingly great slander, or rather villainy. Queen Madasima was a very illustrious lady. It is not to be supposed that so exalted a princess would have made free with a quack. Whoever maintains the contrary lies like a great scoundrel, and I will let him know it, on foot or on horseback, armed or unarmed, by night or by day, or as he likes best."

Cardenio was looking at him steadily. His mad fit had now come upon him, and he had no inclination to go on with his story. Nor would Don Quixote have listened to it, so much had what he had heard about Madasima disgusted him. Strange to say, he stood up for her as if she were indeed his trueborn lady—to such a state had his unholy books brought him. As I said, Cardenio had now gone mad. When he heard himself called a liar, a scoundrel, and other insults, not relishing the mockery, he snatched up a stone that he found near him and with it delivered such a blow on Don Quixote's breast that he laid him on his back. Sancho Panza, seeing his master treated in this fashion, came at the madman with his fist; but the Ragged One received him in such a way that with a single punch he stretched Sancho at his feet, after which he climbed on top of him and laid into his ribs to his satisfaction. The goatherd, who came to the rescue, shared the same fate. When Cardenio had finished thrashing them all, he left them and quietly withdrew to his hiding place on the mountain. Sancho rose, enraged at having received such a beating without having done anything to deserve it. He ran to take vengeance on the goatherd, accusing him of not giving them warning that this man was at times taken with a mad fit; for if they had known, they would have been on their guard to protect themselves. The goatherd replied that he had said so, and that if Sancho had not heard him, that was no fault of his. Sancho retorted, and the goatherd rejoined, and the altercation ended in their seizing each other by the beard and exchanging such fisticuffs that if Don Quixote had not made peace between them, they would have knocked one another to pieces.

[4] *those of the moon moisture:* From the moon's power over the tides and its opposition to the sun, natural philosophers reasoned that the moon was cold and wet.

[5] *Master Elisabad—that knave—bedded Queen Madasima:* Master Elisabad, Amadís' tutor and personal physician, appears in various *Amadís* novels; however, there is no record of a Queen Madasima, nor of any affair involving Master Elisabad.

"Leave me alone, Sir Knight of the Woeful Countenance," said Sancho, grappling with the goatherd, "for this fellow is a peasant like myself, and no dubbed knight, and I can safely take satisfaction for the wrong done me, fighting with him hand to hand like an honest man."

"That is true," said Don Quixote, "but I know that he is not to blame for what has happened."

With this he pacified them and again asked the goatherd if it would be possible to find Cardenio, as he had the greatest interest in knowing the end of his story. The goatherd told him, as he had told him before, that there was no knowing for certain where his hiding place was; but that if he wandered about much in the vicinity he would not fail to find him, either in or out of his senses.

CHAPTER XXV

WHICH TREATS OF THE STRANGE THINGS THAT HAPPENED TO THE VALIANT KNIGHT OF LA MANCHA IN THE SIERRA MORENA, AND OF HIS IMITATION OF THE PENANCE OF BELTENEBROS

Don Quixote took leave of the goatherd, and once more mounting Rocinante ordered Sancho to follow him on his donkey, which he did very discontentedly. They proceeded slowly, making their way into the most rugged part of the mountain. Sancho all the while was dying to have a word with his master, and longing for him to begin the conversation, so that there should be no breach of the injunction laid upon him.

Unable to keep silence for very long, he said to him, "Señor Don Quixote, give me your worship's blessing to take my leave, for I'd like to go home at once to my wife and children. At least with them, I can talk and converse as much as I like. To ask me to go through these backwoods day and night and not speak to you when I have a mind is burying me alive. If we were lucky enough to have animals that could talk, like they did in the days of Guisopete,[1] it wouldn't be so bad, because I could talk to Rocinante about whatever came into my head, and so put up with my misfortune. But it tries a man's patience, and is downright harsh, for him to go seeking adventures all his life and get nothing but kicks and blanketings, brickbats and punches, and with all this to have to sew up his mouth without daring to say what's in his heart, as if he was mute."

"I understand you, Sancho," replied Don Quixote. "You are dying to have the interdict I placed upon your tongue lifted. Consider it removed, and say what you will while we are wandering these mountains."

"So be it," said Sancho. "Let me speak now, for God knows what will happen by-and-by. To take advantage of the permission at once, I ask, what made your worship stand up so for that Queen Magimasa—or whatever her name is—or what did it matter whether that abbot[2] was a friend of hers or not? If your worship had let it pass—for it wasn't for you to judge—it's my belief the madman would have gone on with his story, and the blow from the stone, and the kicks, and more than half a dozen punches in the face would have been spared."

[1] *Guisopete:* Sancho means *Isopete*, a popular collection of Aesop's fables.

[2] *abbot: abad*, corruption of "Elisabad" (see below).

"In faith, Sancho," answered Don Quixote, "if you knew as I do what an honorable and illustrious lady Queen Madasima was, I know you would say I had great patience that I did not break in pieces the mouth that uttered such blasphemies, for a very great blasphemy it is to say or imagine that a queen has been bedded by a surgeon. The truth of the story is that that Master Elisabad whom the madman mentioned was a man of great prudence and sound judgment and served as governor and physician to the queen. To suppose that she was his mistress is nonsense deserving very severe punishment; and as a proof that Cardenio did not know what he was saying, remember that when he said it he was out of his wits."

"That's what I say," said Sancho. "There was no reason to mind the words of a madman; for if good luck had not helped your worship and had sent that stone at your head instead of at your breast, in fine shape we would be for standing up for my lady, God confound her! By faith, Cardenio would have gotten away as a madman."

"Against men in their senses or against madmen," said Don Quixote, "every knight-errant is bound to stand up for the honor of women, whoever they may be, much more for queens of such high degree and dignity as Queen Madasima, for whom I have a particular regard on account of her agreeable qualities. For besides being extremely beautiful, she was very wise, and very patient in her misfortunes, of which she had many; and the counsel and society of Master Elisabad were a great help and support to her in enduring her afflictions with wisdom and longsuffering. Hence the ignorant and malicious rabble took occasion to say and think that she was his mistress. They lie, I say it once more, and will lie two hundred times more, all who think and say so."

"I don't think so, and I don't say so," said Sancho. "'Let them 'go where they will and sop it up with their own bread.' Lovers or not, they'll have God to give an account to. 'I come from my vineyard; I know nothing.' I'm not one to pry into the lives of others. 'He who buys and lies feels it in his purse.' What's more, 'naked was I born, naked I remain, nothing lost or gained.' If they were lovers, what's it to me? 'Many think there's smoke when there's no fire.' But 'who can put up a fence in the open plain'? What's more, they said of God—"

"Good God!" cried Don Quixote. "What nonsense you're stringing together! What has what we are talking about got to do with the proverbs you're threading one after the other? For God's sake, hold your tongue, Sancho, and from now on keep to prodding your donkey and don't meddle in what does not concern you; and understand with all your five senses that everything I have done, am doing, or shall do, is well founded on reason and in conformity with the rules of chivalry, for I understand them better than all others in the world who profess them."

"Señor," replied Sancho, "is it a good rule of chivalry that we should go astray through these mountains without path or road, looking for a madman who, when he is found, might take a fancy to finish what he began, not his story, but your worship's head and my ribs, and end by breaking them altogether?"

"Peace, I say again, Sancho," said Don Quixote, "for let me tell you it is not so much the desire of finding that madman that leads me into these regions as the desire to do among them a deed with which I shall win eternal name and fame throughout the known world. It shall be such that I shall thereby set the seal on all that can make a knight-errant perfect and famous."

"And is it very dangerous, this deed?"

"No," replied he of the Woeful Countenance, "though it may be that misfortune falls to us rather than victory.[3] All will depend on your diligence."

"On my diligence?" said Sancho.

"Yes," said Don Quixote, "for if you return soon from the place where I mean to send you, my penance will be soon over, and my glory will soon begin. But as it is not right to keep you any longer in suspense, waiting to see what comes of my words, I would have you know, Sancho, that the famous Amadís of Gaul was one of the most perfect knights-errant—I am wrong to say he was one; he stood alone, the first, the only one, the lord of all that were in the world in his time. A fig for Don Belianís and for all who say he equaled him in any respect, for my oath upon it, they are deceiving themselves! I say, too, that when a painter desires to become famous in his art, he endeavors to copy the originals of the loftiest painters he knows. The same rule holds good for all the most important crafts and callings that serve to adorn a republic. Thus must he who would be esteemed prudent and patient imitate Ulysses, in whose person and labors Homer presents to us a lively picture of prudence and patience;[4] as Virgil, too, shows us in the person of Æneas, the virtue of a pious son and the sagacity of a brave and skillful captain.[5] These authors do not represent or describe them as they were, but as they ought to be, so as to leave the example of their virtues to posterity.[6] In the same way, Amadís was the north star, daystar, sun of valiant and devoted knights, whom all we who fight under the banner of love and chivalry are bound to imitate. This then being so, I consider, friend Sancho, that the knight-errant who shall imitate him most closely will come nearest to reaching the perfection of chivalry. Now one of the instances in which this knight most conspicuously showed his prudence, worth, valor, endurance, fortitude, and love, was when he withdrew, rejected by Lady Oriana, to do penance upon the Peña

[3] *it may be that misfortune falls to us rather than victory:* literally, "it may be in the dice that we throw snake eyes instead of boxcars."

[4] *Ulysses . . . prudence and patience:* In the *Odyssey*, Ulysses (Greek, *Odysseus*) survives a ten-year journey home through cunning, endurance, and self-mastery.

[5] *Æneas . . . skillful captain:* On his return journey from Troy, Virgil's hero honors his father with a descent to the underworld before leading his people to Italy, where he defeats the Latins and founds Lavinium, Rome's mythic precursor.

[6] *These authors . . . to posterity:* Don Quixote picks up on two themes of Renaissance artistic theory. Art, which included the written art, was an imitative enterprise. The best artists continued in a tradition they first mastered before extending further through invention. The same notion of imitation held for the way artists represented reality. They were not to break with the world around them, nor were they to produce slavish representations. Their task, rather, was to assimilate their subject's forms and then improve upon them. When applied to the moral life, this idea of imitation called on the artist to lay bare a historical figure's virtues and vices, along with the consequences they entail.

Pobre, changing his name into that of Beltenebros, a name assuredly significant and appropriate to the life which he had voluntarily adopted.[7] So, as it is easier for me to imitate him in this than in cleaving giants asunder, cutting off serpents' heads, slaying dragons, routing armies, destroying fleets, and breaking enchantments, and as this place is so well suited for a similar purpose, I must not allow the opportunity to escape which now so conveniently offers me its forelock."[8]

"What exactly," said Sancho, "does your worship mean to do in such an out-of-the-way place as this?"

"Have I not told you," answered Don Quixote, "that I mean to imitate Amadís here, playing the victim of despair, the madman, the maniac, so as at the same time to imitate the valiant Don Roland, when at the fountain he had evidence of the fair Angelica having disgraced herself with Medoro and in his grief went mad and plucked up trees, troubled the waters of the clear springs, slew shepherds, destroyed flocks, burned down huts, leveled houses, dragged mares after him, and perpetrated a hundred thousand other outrages worthy of everlasting renown and record?[9] And though I have no intention of imitating Roland, or Orlando, or Rotolando—for he went by all these names—step by step in all the mad things he did, said, and thought, I will make a rough copy to the best of my power of all that seems to me most essential; but perhaps I shall content myself with the simple imitation of Amadís, who without giving way to any mischievous madness but merely to tears and sorrow, gained as much fame as the most famous."

"It seems to me," said Sancho, "that the knights who behaved in this way were provoked and had cause for those follies and penances. What cause has your worship for going mad? What lady has rejected you, or what evidence do you have to prove that Lady Dulcinea del Toboso has been up to any hanky-panky with a Moor or a Christian?"

"That's the point," replied Don Quixote, "and that's the beauty of this business of mine. No thanks or accolades are owed a knight-errant for going mad when he has cause. The key is to turn crazy without any provocation and leave my lady to wonder that if I do this without a motive, what would I do if I had one? Moreover, I have abundant cause in the long separation I have endured from my forever lady, Dulcinea del Toboso. For as you heard that shepherd Ambrosio say the other day, in absence all ills are felt and feared. And so, friend Sancho, waste no time in advising me against so novel, so happy, and so unheard-of an imitation. Mad I am, and mad I must be until you return with the answer to a letter that I mean to send by you to my lady Dulcinea. If it be such as my

[7] *Beltenebros . . . which he had voluntarily adopted*: The name the hermit gives Amadís recalls the Latin words for handsome (*bellus*) and obscurity (*tenebrae*). See footnote 15, page 112.

[8] *opportunity . . . offers me its forelock:* See footnote 8, page 187.

[9] *the valiant Don Roland . . . of everlasting renown and record:* As Don Quixote explains, Roland and Orlando are two names for the hero of Charlemagne's court who is the subject of *Orlando Furioso*. In Ariosto's epic poem, the protagonist descends into madness when he discovers a carving near a fountain that proclaims a love affair between the Saracen knight Medoro and Orlando's beloved, Angelica.

constancy deserves, my insanity and penance will come to an end; and if it be to the opposite effect, I shall become mad in earnest, and, being so, I shall suffer no more. Thus, in whatever way she may answer, I shall escape from the struggle and affliction in which you will leave me, enjoying in my senses the blessing you bear me, or as a madman not feeling the evil you bring me. But tell me, Sancho, do you have Mambrino's helmet safe? For I saw you take it up from the ground when that ungrateful wretch tried to break it in pieces but could not, by which the fineness of its temper may be seen."

To which Sancho answered, "As God lives, Sir Knight of the Woeful Countenance, I cannot endure or bear with patience some of the things your worship says. I'm beginning to suspect that everything you tell me about chivalry, and winning kingdoms and empires, and giving islands, and bestowing other rewards and dignities after the custom of knights-errant, must be all made up of wind and lies, and all pigments or figments, or whatever we might call them. For anyone who heard your worship calling a barber's basin Mambrino's helmet and couldn't see through the error in four days' time—what would he think except that the one who says and believes such things must have his brains addled? I have the basin in my sack all dented, and I'm taking it home to have it mended, to trim my beard in it—if, by God's grace, I'm allowed to see my wife and children someday."

"Look here, Sancho," said Don Quixote, "by him to whom you swore I now swear that you have the puniest mind of any squire that the world has or ever had. Is it possible that all this time you've been going about with me you haven't come to understand that all things belonging to knights-errant seem to be illusions and nonsense and ravings, and to go always by contraries? And not because it really is so, but because there is always a throng of enchanters in attendance upon us that alter everything with us, and turn things as they please, and according as they are disposed to aid or destroy us. Thus, what seems to you a barber's basin seems to me Mambrino's helmet, and to another it will seem something else. Rare foresight it was in the sage who is on my side to make what is really and truly Mambrino's helmet seem a basin to everybody. For if its true worth were apparent, all the world would pursue me to rob me of it; but when they see it is only a barber's basin they do not take the trouble to obtain it. This was plainly shown by him who tried to break it and left it on the ground without taking it; for by my faith, had he known it, he would never have left it behind. Keep it safe, my friend, for just now I have no need of it. Indeed, I shall have to take off all this armor and remain as naked as I was born, if I have a mind to follow Roland rather than Amadís in my penance."

Thus talking, they reached the foot of a high mountain which stood like an isolated peak among the others that surrounded it. Past its base there flowed a gentle brook; all around it spread a meadow so green and luxuriant that it was a delight to the eyes to look upon it; and forest trees in abundance, along with shrubs and flowers, added to the charms of the spot. It was this site that the Knight of the Woeful Countenance chose to perform his penance. As he beheld it, he exclaimed in a loud voice, as though he were out of his senses:

"This is the place, O heavens, that I designate to bewail the misfortune in which you yourselves have plunged me. This is the spot where the overflowings of my eyes shall swell the waters of yon little brook, and my deep and endless sighs shall stir unceasingly the leaves of these mountain trees, in testimony and token of the pain my persecuted heart is suffering. O rural deities, whoever you are that haunt this lone spot, give ear to the complaint of a wretched lover whom long absence and brooding jealousy have driven to bewail his fate among these wilds and complain of the hard heart of that fair and ungrateful one, the end and limit of all human beauty! O wood nymphs and dryads, who dwell in the thickets of the forest, so may the nimble wanton satyrs by whom you are vainly wooed never disturb your sweet repose, help me to lament my hard fate or at least weary not at listening to it! O Dulcinea del Toboso, day of my night, glory of my pain, guide of my path, star of my fortune, so may Heaven grant you in full all you seek of it, have regard for the place and condition to which absence from you has brought me, and make that return in kindness that is due to my fidelity! O lonely trees, that from this day forward shall bear me company in my solitude, give me some sign by the gentle movement of your boughs that my presence is not distasteful to you! O squire of mine, pleasant companion in my prosperous and adverse fortunes, fix well in your memory what you shall see me do here, so that you may relate and report it to the sole cause of all."

So saying, he dismounted from Rocinante, and in an instant relieved him of saddle and bridle; and giving him a slap on the haunches, said, "He gives you freedom who is bereft of it himself, O steed as excellent in deed as you are unfortunate in your lot. Begone where you will, for you bear written on your forehead that neither Astolfo's hippogriff[10] nor the famed Frontino that cost Bradamante so dear[11] could equal you in speed."

Seeing this Sancho said, "Good luck to him who has saved us the trouble of stripping the packsaddle off Dapple! As surely as I live, my donkey would not have gone without a slap on the haunches and something said in his praise. If he were here,[12] I wouldn't let anyone strip him because there would be no reason to. You wouldn't be able to find a victim of love or despair anywhere near him, for his master, which I was while it was God's pleasure, was nothing of the sort. In

[10] *Astolfo's hippogriff:* In *Orlando Furioso*, Ariosto introduces the hippogriff, a winged beast whose front half is an eagle and back half a horse. Astolfo's hippogriff carries him to Ethiopia.

[11] *Frontino that cost Bradamante so dear:* Also from *Orlando Furioso*, Frontino is the knight Ruggiero's horse, which the warrior Bradamante, his beloved, wins back for him in battle.

[12] *If he were here:* At this point in the first edition of the novel, Sancho begins to speak of his donkey as having been stolen from him—a loss that continues to vex him in the following chapter. Yet when we get to chapter 43, Dapple's trappings (and later Dapple himself) have inexplicably returned to Sancho's possession. A second edition published within a few months of the first added a scene in which Ginés de Pasamonte steals the donkey, but the rushed edits only introduced more plot inconsistencies. The case of the missing donkey will become a matter for conversation in chapter 3 of the second volume. See page 443.

truth, Sir Knight of the Woeful Countenance, if my departure and your worship's madness really do take place, it would be a good idea to saddle Rocinante again so that he can make up for the lack of Dapple, because it will save me time going and coming back. If I go on foot, I don't know when I'll get there or when I'll return, considering what a bad walker I am."

"Then I declare, Sancho," returned Don Quixote, "it shall be as you wish, for your plan does not seem to me a bad one, and three days hence you will depart, for I wish you to observe in the meantime what I do and say for her sake, that you may be able to tell it."

"What more do I have to see besides what I've already seen?" asked Sancho.

"How little you understand!" said Don Quixote. "I must now tear up my garments, scatter about my armor, knock my head against these rocks, and other like deeds, which you must witness."

"For the love of God," said Sancho, "be careful, your worship, how you give yourself those knocks on the head. You may come across such a rock, and in such a way, that the very first may put an end to the whole business of this penance. I should think, if knocks on the head really seem necessary to you and this deed can't be performed without them, you might be content—since the whole thing is pretended, counterfeit, and in jest—you might be content, I say, with giving them to yourself in the water, or against something soft, like cotton. Leave it all to me: I'll tell my lady that your worship knocked your head against the tip of a rock harder than a diamond."

"I thank you for your good intentions, friend Sancho," answered Don Quixote, "but I would have you know that all these things I am doing are not in jest but very much in earnest, for anything else would be a transgression of the ordinances of chivalry, which forbid us to tell any lie whatever under the penalties due to apostasy. To do one thing instead of another is just the same as lying; so my knocks on the head must be real, solid, and valid, without anything false or deceitful about them, and it will be needful to leave me some bandages to dress my wounds, since fortune has compelled us to do without the elixir we lost."

"It was worse losing the donkey," replied Sancho, "for with him bandages and all were lost. But I beg of your worship not to remind me again of that accursed liquor, for my soul, not to say my stomach, turns at hearing the very name of it. I beg of you, too, to count as past the three days you allowed me for seeing the mad things you do, for I consider them as already seen, judged, and without further appeals. I'll tell wonderful stories to my lady. So write the letter and send me off at once, for I long to return and take your worship out of this purgatory where I'm leaving you."

"Do you call it purgatory, Sancho?" said Don Quixote. "Rather call it hell, or even worse—if there be anything worse."

"For one who is in hell," said Sancho, "*nulla est retentio*,[13] as I have heard said."

[13] nulla est retentio: Sancho misremembers a line from the prayers of the Church's Office of the Dead: "Quia in inferno nulla est redemptio" (Salvation is impossible for the one in hell).

"I do not understand what *retentio* means," said Don Quixote.

"*Retentio*," answered Sancho, "means that whoever is in hell never comes nor can come out of it, which will be the opposite case with your worship, or my legs will be idle—that is, if I have spurs to enliven Rocinante. Let me get to El Toboso at once and into the presence of my lady Dulcinea, and I will tell her such things of the follies and madnesses—for it's all the same—that your worship has done and is still doing, that I'll make her softer than a glove though I find her harder than a cork tree; and with her sweet and honeyed answer I'll come back through the air like a witch, and take your worship out of this purgatory that seems to be hell but is not, as there is hope of getting out of it; which, as I have said, those in hell don't have, and I believe your worship will not say anything to the contrary."

"That is true," said he of the Woeful Countenance, "but how shall we manage to write the letter?"

"And the order for the donkey colt, too," added Sancho.

"All shall be included," said Don Quixote. "As there is no paper, it would be well done to write it on the leaves of trees, as the ancients did, or on tablets of wax—though that would be as hard to find just now as paper. But it has just occurred to me how it may be more than conveniently written, and that is in the notebook that belonged to Cardenio. You will take care to have it copied on paper, in a good hand, at the first village you come to where there is a schoolmaster, or if not, any sacristan will copy it. But see that you do not give it to any notary to copy, for they write a law hand that Satan could not make out."[14]

"What's to be done about the signature?" asked Sancho.

"The letters of Amadís were never signed," said Don Quixote.

"That is all very well," said Sancho, "but the order will need to be signed, and if it is copied they will say the signature is false, and I'll be left without donkey colts."

"The order will be signed in the same book," said Don Quixote, "and on seeing it my niece will give you no trouble about obeying it. As to the love letter, you may put by way of signature, 'Yours till death, the Knight of the Woeful Countenance.' It will be no great matter if it is in some other person's hand, for as well as I recollect, Dulcinea can neither read nor write, nor in the whole course of her life has she seen handwriting or letter of mine. My love and hers have been always platonic, not going beyond a modest look, and even that so seldom that I can safely swear I have not seen her four times in all these twelve years I have been loving her more than the light of these eyes that the earth will one day devour; and perhaps even of those four times she has not once noticed that I was looking at her. Such is the retirement and seclusion in which her father Lorenzo Corchuelo and her mother Aldonza Nogales have brought her up."

[14] *for they write a law hand that Satan could not make out:* Professions such as commerce, diplomacy, and law had recognizable styles of handwriting. Law hand was notoriously difficult to read.

"Ah, ha!" cried Sancho. "Lorenzo Corchuelo's daughter is Lady Dulcinea del Toboso, otherwise called Aldonza Lorenzo?"

"She it is," said Don Quixote, "and she it is that is worthy to be lady of the whole universe."

"I know her well," said Sancho, "and let me tell you she can fling a crowbar as well as the toughest lad in all the town. Lord, have mercy! She's a stout wench, fully grown and with hair on her chest. Any knight-errant who calls her his lady would have no one better to get him out of a pinch. Son of a bitch, is she ever hearty—and with a voice to match! I can tell you that one day she posted herself on the top of the belfry of the village to call some workers of theirs who were ploughing in a field of her father's, and though they were more than half a league off, they heard her as well as if they were at the foot of the tower. The best thing about her is she's not the least bit dainty. She's as easy as they come. She teases with everyone and grins and jokes at everything. So I say, Sir Knight of the Woeful Countenance, you not only may and ought to act like a madman for her sake, but you have every right to give in to despair and hang yourself. Anyone who finds out about it will say you did well, though the devil should take you. I wish I was on the road already, simply to see her. It's been a long time since I've seen her, and I bet she isn't what she used to be. Going out in the fields always, with all that the sun and the air do, spoil a woman's looks. I must confess the truth to your worship, Señor Don Quixote. Until now I've been under a great mistake, for I believed truly and honestly that Lady Dulcinea was some princess your worship was in love with, or some person great enough to deserve the rich presents you've sent her, such as the Biscayan and the galley slaves, and many more no doubt, for your worship must have won many victories in the time when I was not yet your squire. But all things considered, what good can it do Lady Aldonza Lorenzo—I mean Lady Dulcinea del Toboso—to have the vanquished your worship sends or will send coming to her and going down on their knees before her? Because maybe when they came, she'd be raking flax or threshing on the threshing floor, and they'd be ashamed to see her, and she'd laugh, or be annoyed by the present."

"I have told you many times, Sancho," said Don Quixote, "that you are a very great chatterer, and that with a blunt wit you are always striving at sharpness; but to show you what a fool you are and how reasoned I am, I would have you listen to a short story. You must know that a certain widow, fair, young, independent, and rich, and above all free and easy, fell in love with a sturdy strapping young lay brother. His superior came to know of it, and one day said to the worthy widow by way of brotherly remonstrance, 'I am surprised, señora, and not without good reason, that a woman of such high standing, so fair, and so rich as you are, should have fallen in love with such a mean, low, stupid fellow as So-and-so, when in this house there are so many masters, graduates, and divinity students from among whom you might choose as if they were as many pears, saying, 'This one I'll take, that I won't take.' She replied to him with great refinement and candor, 'My dear sir, you are very much mistaken, and your ideas are very old-fashioned, if you think that I have made a bad choice in So-and-so, fool as he seems. For what my interests are in him, he knows as much and more philosophy than Aristotle.' In the same way, Sancho, for what my interests are in Dulcinea del Toboso she is just as good as the most exalted princess on earth.

"It is not to be supposed that all those poets who sang the praises of ladies under the fancy names they give them had any such mistresses. Do you think that the Amarilises, the Filises, the Sylvias, the Dianas, the Galateas, the Fílidas,[15] and all the rest of them, that the books, the ballads, the barber shops, the theaters are full of, were really and truly ladies of flesh and blood and mistresses of those that glorify and have glorified them? Nothing of the kind! They only invent them for the most part to furnish a subject for their verses, and that they may pass for lovers, or for men valiant enough to be so. It is therefore enough for me to think and believe that the good Aldonza Lorenzo is fair and virtuous.

"As to her pedigree, it is very little matter, for no one will look into it for the purpose of conferring any order upon her, and I, for my part, count her the most exalted princess in the world. You should know, Sancho, if you do not, that two things alone beyond all others are incentives to love, and these are great beauty and a good name. These two things are to be found in Dulcinea in the highest degree, for in beauty no one equals her and in good name few approach her. To put the whole thing in a nutshell, I persuade myself that all I say is as I say, neither more nor less. I picture her in my imagination as I would have her to be, both in beauty and in rank. Helen does not approach her, nor does Lucretia come near her,[16] nor any other of the famous women of times past, Greek, Barbarian, or Latin. Let each say what he will, for if in this I am taken to task by the ignorant, I shall not be condemned by the critical."

"I say that your worship is entirely right," said Sancho, "and that I am an ass. But I don't know how the name of ass came into my mouth, for 'a rope is not to be mentioned in the house of him who has been hanged.' But let's see to the letter, and then, God be with you, I'll be off."

Don Quixote took out the notebook, and withdrawing a few paces off, very deliberately began to write the letter. When he had finished it he called to Sancho, saying he wished to read it to him and have him commit it to memory in case he lost it on the road; for with his bad luck anything could happen.

To which Sancho replied, "Write it two or three times there in the book and give it to me, and I will carry it very carefully. But to expect me to keep it in my memory is ridiculous, for I have such a bad one that I often forget my own name. For all that, I ask that you read it to me, as I should like to hear it, for it's sure to sound as pretty as it looks.

[15] *the Amarilises . . . the Fílidas:* Names of pastoral heroines, including *Galatea*, the protagonist of Cervantes' 1585 pastoral romance of the same name. Alonso Quixano has clearly read the books on the pastoral shelf of his library (see chap. 6).

[16] *Helen does not approach her, nor does Lucretia come near her:* Helen of Troy is the classical paragon of beauty, and Lucretia, who committed suicide after being raped by Tarquin, of chastity.

"Listen," said Don Quixote, "this is what it says:

Don Quixote's Letter to Dulcinea del Toboso

Sovereign and Exalted Lady,

He who is pierced by the point of absence, he who is wounded to the heart's core, sends you, sweetest Dulcinea del Toboso, the health that he himself enjoys not. If your beauty despises me, if your worth is not for me, if your scorn is my affliction, though I be sufficiently longsuffering, hardly shall I endure this anxiety, which, besides being oppressive, is protracted. My good squire Sancho will relate to you in full, fair ingrate, dear enemy, the condition to which I am reduced on your account. If it be your pleasure to give me relief, I am yours; if not, do as may be pleasing to you; for by ending my life I shall satisfy your cruelty and my desire.[17]

Yours till death,
The Knight of the Woeful Countenance

"On my father's life," said Sancho, when he heard the letter, "if that isn't the loftiest thing I ever heard! It's a wonder how your worship says everything you like in it, and how well you fit in 'The Knight of the Woeful Countenance' into the signature. I declare your worship is indeed the very devil, and there is nothing you don't know."

"Everything is needed for the calling I follow," said Don Quixote.

"Now then," said Sancho, "let your worship put the order for the three donkey colts on the other side, and sign it very clearly, so that they will recognize it at first sight."

"With all my heart," said Don Quixote.

Once he had written it, he read aloud the following:

Mistress Niece: In accordance with this bill of donkeys,[18] please pay to Sancho Panza, my squire, three of the five colts I left at home in your charge. Said colts are to be issued and paid for by the same number received here on account. Upon the presentation of this bill and confirmation of receipt, the order shall be considered duly completed. Recorded in the heart of the Sierra Morena, the twenty-seventh of August of the present year.

"That will do," said Sancho. "Now let your worship sign it."

"There is no need to sign it," said Don Quixote, "but merely to put my flourish, which is the same as a signature,[19] and enough for three donkeys, or even three hundred."

[17] *for by ending my life I shall satisfy your cruelty and my desire:* In the courtly love tradition, the spurned lover casts his beloved as his enemy for her refusal to favor him. Meanwhile, he wastes away from lovesickness (considered a physical illness). Only occasionally do the lovesick succumb to death. Grisóstomo's suicide presses the tradition beyond its accustomed bounds.

[18] *In accordance with this bill of donkeys:* Parody of the opening formula of a purchase order: "In accordance with this bill of exchange ..."

[19] *flourish . . . same as a signature:* Spanish signature conventions distinguish the characters of the person's name (signature) from decorative elements that may accompany it (flourish).

"I trust your worship," returned Sancho. "Let me go and saddle Rocinante, and be ready to give me your blessing, for I mean to go at once without seeing all the silly things your worship is going to do. I'll say I saw you do so many that she will not want any more."

"At any rate, Sancho," said Don Quixote, "I should like—and there is a reason for it—I should like you, I say, to see me stripped to the skin and performing a dozen or two follies, which I can get done in less than half an hour; for having seen them with your own eyes, you can then safely swear to however many more you might add. I can assure you that you will not tell of as many as I intend to perform."

"For the love of God, my master," said Sancho, "don't let me see your worship stripped, for it will grieve me to the point of tears. My head aches already with all the tears I shed last night for Dapple that I'm not fit for any fresh weeping. If it's your worship's pleasure that I should see some follies, do them in your clothes, keep them short, and let them be the ones that come quickest to mind. I myself want nothing of the kind, and, as I have said, it will save time for my return, which will be with the news your worship desires and deserves. If not, Lady Dulcinea had better watch out. If she doesn't answer reasonably, I swear as solemnly as I can that I'll get a fair answer out of her stomach with kicks and cuffs; for why should it be allowed that a knight-errant as famous as your worship should go mad without rhyme or reason for a ... ? Her ladyship had best not make me say it, for by God, I'll speak whatever's on my mind, come what may. I'm quite good at that! She doesn't know me well, because if she did, right now she'd be afraid."

"Right now, Sancho," said Don Quixote, "to all appearance you are no sounder in your wits than I."

"I may not be as crazy," answered Sancho, "but I'm certainly feistier. Putting that aside, what has your worship to eat until I come back? Will you go out on the road like Cardenio to force it from the shepherds?"

"Let not that matter trouble you," replied Don Quixote, "for even if I had need, I would eat nothing but the herbs and the fruits which this meadow and these trees may yield me. The beauty of this business of mine lies in not eating and in performing other mortifications."

"Goodbye, then," said Sancho. "Do you know what I'm afraid of? That I won't be able to find my way back to this spot where I'm leaving you, as it is such an out-of-the-way place."

"Observe the landmarks well," said Don Quixote, "for I will try not to go far from the vicinity, and I will even take care to mount the highest of these rocks so that I may discover you when you return; however, in order not to miss me and lose yourself, the best plan will be to cut some branches of the broom bushes that are so abundant around here, and as you go to lay them at intervals until you have come out upon the plain. These will serve you, after the fashion of the thread in the labyrinth of Theseus,[20] as marks and signs for finding me on your return."

[20] *thread in the labyrinth of Theseus:* Theseus tied one end of a ball of thread to the entrance of Minos' labyrinth and kept the other end with him as he ventured inward, enabling him to retrace his steps after he slayed the Minotaur.

"So I will," said Sancho Panza, and having cut some, he asked his master's blessing, and not without many tears on both sides, took his leave of him. Mounting Rocinante, of whom Don Quixote charged him earnestly to take as good care of as of his own person, he set out for the plain, strewing at intervals the broom branches as his master had counseled. And so he went his way, though Don Quixote pleaded with him to stay and watch him do just two follies.

He had not gone a hundred paces, however, when he returned and said, "I must say, señor, your worship has spoken rightly. In order to be able to swear without a weight on my conscience that I have seen you do follies, it would be well for me to see at least one, though in your worship's remaining here I have seen a very great one."

"Did I not tell you so?" said Don Quixote. "Wait, Sancho, and I will do them as quickly as you can say a Credo," and pulling off his breeches in all haste he stripped himself to his skin and his shirt.[21] Then, without more ado, he cut two capers in the air and did as many somersaults, heels over head, revealing such things to Sancho that his squire wheeled Rocinante around so he wouldn't have to see them a second time. He could now consider his conscience fully satisfied to swear that the master he left was insane; and so we will leave him to follow his road until his return, which was a quick one.

[21] *to his skin and his shirt:* Nothing was worn under the long undershirt, which accounts for Sancho's quick departure after he witnesses Don Quixote's somersaults.

CHAPTER XXVI

IN WHICH DON QUIXOTE CONTINUES HIS REFINED PERFORMANCE AS LOVER IN THE SIERRA MORENA

Returning to the proceedings of him of the Woeful Countenance, the history says that Don Quixote finished his capers and somersaults, naked from the waist down and clothed from the waist up, after which he observed Sancho depart without wishing to remain for any more follies. Finding himself alone, he climbed up to the top of a high rock and there set himself to consider what he had several times before considered without ever coming to any conclusion on the point, namely whether it would be better and more to his purpose to imitate the outrageous madness of Roland, or the melancholy madness of Amadís. Communing with himself, he said:

"What wonder is it if Roland was so good a knight and so valiant as everyone says he was, when, after all, he was enchanted, and nobody could kill him except by sticking a hairpin into the sole of his foot? And though he always wore shoes with seven iron soles,[1] cunning devices did not avail him against Bernardo del Carpio, who knew all about them and strangled him in his arms at Roncesvalles. But putting the question of his bravery aside, let us come to his losing his wits, for it is certain that he did lose them in consequence of the proofs he discovered at the fountain, and the intelligence the shepherd gave him of Angelica having slept more than two siestas with Medoro, a little curly-headed Moor and page to Agramante.[2] If he was persuaded that this was true and that his lady had wronged him, it is no wonder that he should have gone mad. As for me, how am I to imitate him in his madness, unless I can imitate him in the cause of it? For I will venture to swear that never in her life has my Dulcinea seen a Moor like him in his proper costume, no more than the mother who bore her. I would thus be plainly doing her a wrong if I were to pretend otherwise and go mad with the same kind of madness as the Frenzied Roland.

"On the other hand, I see that Amadís of Gaul, without losing his senses and without doing anything mad, acquired as much fame in love as the most famous; for according to his history, on finding himself rejected by his lady Oriana, who

[1] *he always wore shoes with seven iron soles:* Don Quixote confuses Roland with Ferragut, a character from a Carolingian ballad included in the Spanish translation of *Orlando Furioso,* who protects his vulnerable navel with seven plates of iron.

[2] *Medoro . . . page to Agramante:* Medoro was actually page to Dardinel of Almonte.

had ordered him not to appear in her presence until it should be her pleasure, all he did was to retire to the Peña Pobre in the company of a hermit. There he took his fill of weeping until Heaven sent him relief in the midst of his great grief and need. If this be true, as it is, why should I now take the trouble to strip stark naked or do mischief to these trees, which have done me no harm; or why am I to disturb the clear waters of these brooks, which will give me to drink whenever I wish? Long live the memory of Amadís and let him be imitated so far as is possible by Don Quixote of La Mancha, of whom it will be said, as was said of the other, that if he did not achieve great things, he died in attempting them. If I am not repulsed or rejected by my Dulcinea, it is enough for me to be absent from her, as I have said. And so now to business: Come to my memory, you deeds of Amadís, and show me how I am to begin to imitate you. I know already that what he chiefly did was to pray and commend himself to God. But what am I to do for a rosary, for I do not have one?"

And then it occurred to him how he might make one, and that was by tearing a great strip off the tail of his shirt which hung down, and making eleven knots on it, one bigger than the rest.[3] This served him for a rosary all the time he was there, during which he repeated countless Ave Marias. But what distressed him greatly was not having another hermit there to receive his confession and offer him consolation; and so he solaced himself by pacing up and down the little meadow and writing and carving on the bark of the trees and on the fine sand a multitude of poems, all in harmony with his sadness, some in praise of Dulcinea. When he was discovered there afterwards, the only ones completely legible that could be found were those that follow here:

Ye on the mountainside that grow,
Ye green things all, trees, shrubs, and bushes,
Are ye aweary of the woe
That this poor aching bosom crushes?
If it disturb you, and I owe
Some reparation, it may be a
Defense for me to let you know
Don Quixote's tears are on the flow,
And all for distant Dulcinea
Del Toboso.

As loyal a lover time can show,
Doomed for a ladylove to languish,
Among these solitudes doth go,
A prey to every kind of anguish.

[3] *one bigger than the rest:* Ten knots prompt the worshiper to pray an Ave Maria (Hail Mary). The eleventh knot, bigger than the rest, prompts an Our Father. A knotted rosary made from what is in effect the seat of one's underwear could be considered irreverent humor, even sacrilege. In the second edition of the novel (also 1605), the passage is rewritten so that Don Quixote strings together acorns to make a rosary.

Why Love should like a spiteful foe
Thus use him, he hath no idea,
But hogsheads full—this doth he know—
Don Quixote's tears are on the flow,
And all for distant Dulcinea
Del Toboso.

Adventure seeking doth he go
Up rugged heights, down rocky valleys,
But hill or dale, or high or low,
Mishap attendeth all his sallies:
Love still pursues him to and fro,
And plies his cruel scourge—ah me!
A punishment of endless woe;
Don Quixote's tears are on the flow,
And all for distant Dulcinea
Del Toboso.

The addition of "Del Toboso" to Dulcinea's name gave rise to no little laughter among those who found the above lines, for they suspected Don Quixote must have fancied that unless he added "del Toboso" when he introduced the name of Dulcinea the verse would be unintelligible, which was indeed the fact, as he himself afterwards admitted. He wrote many more poems, but, as has been said, these three were all that could be plainly and perfectly deciphered. In this way, and in sighing and calling on the fauns and satyrs of the woods to hear him, the nymphs of the streams to console him, and misty and mournful Echo[4] to answer him, as well as in looking for herbs to sustain him, he passed his time until Sancho's return. Had that return been delayed three weeks instead of three days, the Knight of the Woeful Countenance would have worn such an altered countenance that the mother who bore him would not have known him.

Here it will be well to leave him, wrapped up in sighs and verses, to relate how Sancho Panza fared on his mission.

Coming out upon the king's highway, Sancho made for El Toboso, and the next day reached the inn where the mishap of the blanket had befallen him. As soon as he recognized it, he felt as if he were once more flying through the air. He could not bring himself to enter, even though it was at an hour when he might well have done so; for it was dinnertime, and he longed to taste something hot, as it had been all cold fare with him for many days past. This craving drove him to draw near to the inn, still undecided whether to enter or not.

As he was hesitating, there came out two people who at once recognized him; and said one to the other, "Señor licentiate, is not he on the horse there

[4] *misty and mournful Echo:* After her beloved Narcissus died, the nymph Echo wasted away in sorrow until only her voice remained, echoing through hills and valleys.

Sancho Panza who, our adventurer's housekeeper told us, went off with her master as squire?"

"So it is," said the licentiate, "and that is our friend Don Quixote's horse."

If they knew him so well, it was because they were the priest and the barber of his own village, the same who had carried out the inquiry and trial of the books. As soon as they recognized Sancho Panza and Rocinante, being anxious to hear of Don Quixote, they approached, and calling him by his name the priest said, "Friend Sancho Panza, where is your master?"

Sancho recognized them at once and determined to keep secret the place and circumstances where and under which he had left his master, so he replied that his master was occupied in a certain place on a certain matter of great importance to him, which he could not disclose for all that was precious.[5]

"No, no," said the barber, "if you don't tell us where he is, Sancho Panza, we will suspect as we suspect already, that you have murdered and robbed him, for here you are mounted on his horse. I say that you must produce the master of this hack or else suffer the consequences."

"There is no need to threaten me," said Sancho, "for I am not a man to rob or murder anybody. Let his own fate, or God who made him, kill each one. My master is engaged very much to his liking doing penance off in those mountains." He then told them, all at once and without stopping, how he had left him, what adventures had befallen him, and how he was carrying a letter to Lady Dulcinea del Toboso, the daughter of Lorenzo Corchuelo, with whom he was head over heels in love.[6] They were both amazed at what Sancho Panza told them; for though they were aware of Don Quixote's madness and the nature of it, each time they heard of it they were filled with fresh wonder.

They then asked Sancho Panza to show them the letter he was carrying to Lady Dulcinea del Toboso. He said it was written in a notebook and that his master's directions were that he should have it copied on paper at the first village he came to. On this the priest said if he showed it to him, he himself would make a clean copy of it. Sancho put his hand into his breast in search of the notebook but could not find it, nor would he have found it had he kept searching until now. It had remained with Don Quixote, who had never given it to him, and Sancho had not thought of asking for it. When Sancho realized he could not find the book, his face grew deadly pale, and in great haste he again felt his body all over. Seeing plainly it was not to be found, he impulsively seized his beard with both hands and plucked away half of it, and followed immediately after by giving himself half a dozen punches to the face and nose till they were bathed in blood.

Seeing this, the priest and the barber asked him what had happened that he treated himself so roughly.

"What has happened to me," replied Sancho, "is that I have lost in an instant, from one hand to the other, three donkeys, each of them like a castle."

"How is that?" said the barber.

[5] *for all that was precious:* literally, "for the eyes in his head".

[6] *head over heels in love:* literally, "up to his liver in love".

"I have lost the notebook," said Sancho, "that contained the letter to Dulcinea and an order signed by my master that directed his niece to give me three donkey colts out of four or five he had at home." He then told them about the loss of Dapple.

The priest consoled him, telling him that when his master was found he would get him to renew the order and make a fresh draft on paper, as was usual and customary; for those made in notebooks were never accepted or honored.

Sancho was comforted with these words and said if that were so, the loss of Dulcinea's letter did not trouble him much, for he knew it almost by heart, and it could be taken down from him wherever and whenever they liked.

"Repeat it then, Sancho," said the barber, "and we will write it down afterwards."

Sancho Panza stopped to scratch his head to bring back the letter to his memory. He balanced himself now on one foot, now the other, one moment staring at the ground, the next at the sky. After having half gnawed off the end of a finger and kept them in suspense waiting for him to begin, he said after a long pause, "By God, señor licentiate, let the devil take what I can remember of the letter. But it did say at the beginning, 'Exalted and sullied Lady.'"

"It cannot have said *sullied*," said the barber, "but *serene* or *sovereign lady*."

"That's it," said Sancho. "Then, as well as I remember, it went on: 'He who is wounded, bruised, and sleepless kisses your worship's hands, most ungrateful and unknown beauty'; and it said something or other about health and sickness that he was sending her. From that it went tailing off until it ended with 'Yours till death, the Knight of the Woeful Countenance.'"

It gave the two no little amusement to see what a good memory Sancho had. They complimented him greatly upon it and begged him to repeat the letter a couple of times more so that they too might learn it by heart to write it out afterwards. Sancho repeated it three times, and as he did, uttered three thousand more absurdities. He then told them more about his master, but he never said a word about the blanketing that had befallen him in that inn, into which he refused to enter. He told them, moreover, how his lord, if he brought him a favorable answer from Lady Dulcinea del Toboso, was to set himself on a path to become an emperor, or at least a monarch; for it had been so settled between them, and with his personal worth and the might of his arm it was an easy matter to come to be one. And upon becoming an emperor, his lord was to arrange a marriage for him (for he would, of course, be a widower by that time) and was to give him as a wife one of the damsels of the empress, the heiress of some wealthy and powerful estate on the mainland, having nothing to do with islands of any sort, for he did not care for them now.

All this Sancho delivered with so much composure—wiping his nose from time to time—and with so little common sense that his two hearers were again filled with wonder at the force of Don Quixote's madness that could run away with this poor man's reason. They did not care to take the trouble of disabusing him of his error, as they considered that since it did not in any way hurt his conscience it would be better to leave him in it, and they would have all the more amusement in listening to his simplicities. And so they bade him pray to God for his lord's health, as it was a very likely and a very feasible thing for him in course of time to come to be an emperor, as he said, or at least an archbishop or some other dignitary of equal rank.

To which Sancho answered, "If fortune, sirs, should bring things about in such a way that my master should be inclined, instead of becoming an emperor, to become an archbishop, I should like to know what archbishops-errant commonly give their squires."

"They commonly give them," said the priest, "a simple benefice or cure or a position as sacristan, which provides them a decent fixed income—not counting the altar fees, which bring in much more."[7]

"But for that," said Sancho, "the squire must be unmarried and, at any rate, know how to help at Mass. If that's the case, woe is me, for I'm married already, and I don't know the first letter of the ABCs. What will become of me if my master gets it in his head to be an archbishop and not an emperor, as is customary with knights-errant?"

"Be not uneasy, friend Sancho," said the barber, "for we will entreat your master, and advise him, even pressing it upon him as a case of conscience, to become an emperor and not an archbishop, because it will be easier for him as he is more valiant than lettered."

"So I've thought," said Sancho, "though I can tell you he's fit for anything. What I mean to do for my part is to pray to our Lord to place him where it's best for him and where he'll be able to bestow on me the most rewards."

"You speak like a man of sense," said the priest, "and you will be acting like a good Christian; but what must now be done is to take steps to coax your master out of that useless penance you say he is performing. We had best turn into this inn to consider what plan to adopt, and also to dine, for it is now time."

Sancho said that they could go in but that he would wait there outside and that he would tell them afterwards the reason why he was unwilling and why it did not suit him to enter; but he begged them to bring him out something to eat, and to let it be hot, and also to bring barley for Rocinante. They left him and went in, and presently the barber brought him out something to eat. Later on, after they had between them carefully thought over what they should do to carry out their desires, the priest hit upon an idea very well adapted to humor Don Quixote and achieve their purposes. His notion, which he explained to the barber, was that he himself should assume the disguise of a wandering damsel, while the other should try as best he could to pass for a squire, and that they should thus proceed to where Don Quixote was. The priest, pretending to be an aggrieved and distressed damsel, would ask a favor of him, which as a valiant knight-errant he could not refuse to grant; and the favor he meant to ask him was

[7] *simple benefice or cure . . . which bring in much more:* The Church distinguishes auxiliary offices, which require minor orders (simple benefice) from those that involve spiritual care, which require major orders (cure). A *sacristan* is the church officer responsible for the maintenance of the sacristy, the room adjoining the altar where sacred vessels and vestments are stored.

that he should accompany her wherever she would lead him in order to redress a wrong that a wicked knight had done her. At the same time, she would entreat him not to require her to remove her mask, nor ask her any question regarding her circumstances until he had won her cause against the wicked knight. He had no doubt that Don Quixote would comply with any request made in these terms, and that in this way they might remove him and take him to his own village, where they would try to find out if his extraordinary madness admitted of any kind of cure.

CHAPTER XXVII

HOW THE PRIEST AND THE BARBER PROCEEDED WITH THEIR SCHEME; TOGETHER WITH OTHER MATTERS WORTHY OF RECORD IN THIS GREAT HISTORY

The priest's plan did not seem a bad one to the barber, but on the contrary so good that they immediately set about putting it into action. They borrowed a skirt and kerchief from the innkeeper's wife, leaving as her security a new cassock of the priest's; and the barber made a beard out of a clay-red oxtail in which the innkeeper used to stick his comb. The innkeeper's wife asked them what they wanted these things for, and the priest told her in a few words about the madness of Don Quixote, and how this disguise was intended to get him away from the mountain where he then was. The innkeeper and his wife immediately came to the conclusion that the madman was their guest, the man with the elixir and the master of the blanketed squire, and they told the priest all that had passed between him and them, not omitting what Sancho had been so silent about.

In the end, the innkeeper's wife dressed up the priest in a style that left nothing to be desired. She put on him a cloth skirt with black velvet stripes a palm broad, all slashed,[1] and a bodice of green velvet set off by a binding of white satin, which in addition to the skirt must have been made in the time of King Wamba.[2] The priest would not let them put a kerchief on him but instead put on his head a little quilted linen cap that he used for a nightcap. He bound his forehead with a strip of black silk, while with another he made a mask with which he concealed his beard and face very well. He then put on his hat, which was broad enough to serve him for an umbrella, and enveloping himself in his cloak seated himself sidesaddle on his mule. The barber mounted his mule with a beard down to the waist of mingled red and white, for it was, as has been said, the tail of a clay-red ox.

They took leave of all, and of the good Maritornes, who, sinner though she was, promised to pray a rosary of prayers that God might grant them success in such an arduous and Christian undertaking as the one they had before them. But hardly had he sallied forth from the inn when it struck the priest that he was

[1] *all slashed:* The black velvet stripes sown onto the skirt had vertical cuts made in them to reveal the fabric beneath.

[2] *King Wamba:* The Visigothic king Wamba reigned in the Iberian Peninsula from 672 to 680.

doing wrong in having clothed himself as he had, for it is an indecorous thing for a priest to dress himself that way, even though much might depend upon it. Saying so to the barber, he begged him to swap outfits, as it was fitter that the barber should be the distressed damsel, while he himself would play the squire's part, which would be less offensive to his dignity; otherwise, he was resolved to have nothing more to do with the matter, and let the devil take Don Quixote.

Just at this moment Sancho came up, and on seeing the pair in such costumes he was unable to restrain his laughter. The barber finally agreed to do as the priest wished, and, altering their plan, the priest went on to instruct him how to play his part and what to say to Don Quixote to induce him to come with them and give up his fancy for the place he had chosen for his idle penance. The barber told him he could manage it properly without any instruction, and as he did not care to dress himself up until they were near where Don Quixote was, he folded up the garments, the priest adjusted his beard, and the two set out under the guidance of Sancho Panza. For his part, Sancho went along telling them of the encounter with the madman they met in the sierra, saying nothing, however, about finding the valise and all that it contained; for though he was a simpleton, the lad was more than a little greedy.

The next day they reached the place where Sancho had laid the broom branches as marks to direct him to where he had left his master. When he recognized it, he told them that they had reached the entrance and that they would do well to dress themselves, if doing so was required to deliver his master; for they had already told him that proceeding in this way and dressing in this manner were of the utmost importance in order to rescue his master from the pernicious life he had adopted. They charged him strictly not to tell his master who they were or that he knew them, and should he ask if he had given the letter to Dulcinea (as ask he would), to say that he had. As she did not know how to read, Sancho was to tell him that she had given an answer by word of mouth, saying that she commanded him, on pain of her displeasure, to come and see her at once. They stressed that it was a very important matter for his master, because in this way and with what they meant to say to him, they felt sure of bringing him back to a better mode of life and inducing him to take immediate steps to become an emperor or monarch, for there was no fear of his becoming an archbishop.

All this Sancho listened to and firmly fixed in his memory. He thanked them heartily for intending to recommend his master to be an emperor instead of an archbishop, for he felt sure that when it came to bestowing rewards on their squires, emperors could do more than archbishops-errant. He said, too, that it would be best for him to go on before them to find Don Quixote and give him his lady's answer; for that perhaps might be enough to bring him away from the place without putting them to all this trouble. They approved of what Sancho proposed and resolved to wait for him until he brought back word of having found his master.

Sancho pushed on into the heart of the sierra, leaving them in a glen through which there flowed a peaceful little stream and where the rocks and trees afforded a refreshingly cool shade. It was an August day, with all the heat of one (and the heat in those parts is intense), and the hour was three in the afternoon. All of these things made the place more inviting and tempted them to wait there for Sancho's return. And so they did.

While they were resting in the shade, a voice unaccompanied by the notes of any instrument reached their ears, sweet and pleasing in its tone. They were not a little astonished, as it did not seem a likely place for one who sang so well; for though it is often said that shepherds of rare voice are to be found in the woods and fields, this is rather a flight of the poet's fancy than the truth. Still more surprised were they when they perceived that what they heard being sung were the verses not of a rustic shepherd but of a polished courtier. And so it proved, for the verses they heard were these:

What makes my quest of happiness seem vain?
Disdain.
What bids me to abandon hope of ease?
Jealousies.
What holds my heart in anguish of suspense?
Absence.
If that be so, then for my grief
Where shall I turn to seek relief,
When hope on every side lies slain
By Absence, Jealousies, Disdain?

What the prime cause of all my woe doth prove?
Love.
What at my glory ever looks askance?
Chance.
Whence is permission to afflict me given?
Heaven.
If that be so, I but await
The stroke of a resistless fate,
Since, working for my woe, these three,
Love, Chance, and Heaven, in league I see.

What must I do to find a remedy?
Die.
What is the lure for love when coy and strange?
Change.
What, if all fail, will cure the heart of sadness?
Madness.
If that be so, it is but folly
To seek a cure for melancholy:
Ask where it lies; the answer saith
In Change, in Madness, or in Death.[3]

[3] *What makes my quest of happiness . . . In Change, in Madness, or in Death:* In the first six verses of each stanza, a question posed in one verse is answered with a single word in the

The hour, the summer season, the solitude, the voice and skill of the singer—all contributed to the wonder and delight of the two listeners, who remained still waiting to hear something more. Finding, however, that the silence continued a while, they resolved to go in search of the musician who sang with so fine a voice. Just as they were about to do so, the same voice once more fell upon their ears, and they could not help but stop and listen. It sang this sonnet:

SONNET

When heavenward, holy Friendship, thou didst go
Soaring to seek thy home beyond the sky,
And take thy seat among the saints on high,
It was thy will to leave on earth below
Thy semblance, and upon it to bestow
Thy veil, wherewith at times hypocrisy,
Parading in thy shape, deceives the eye,
And makes its vileness bright as virtue show.
Friendship, return to us, or force the cheat
That wears it now, thy livery to restore,
By aid whereof sincerity is slain.
If thou wilt not unmask thy counterfeit,
This earth will be the prey of strife once more,
As when primeval discord held its reign.

The song ended with a deep sigh, and again the listeners remained waiting attentively for the singer to resume; but hearing that the music had now turned to sobs and heart-rending moans, they determined to find out who the unhappy being could be whose voice was as rare as his sighs were piteous. They had not proceeded far when on coming round a rock they discovered a man of the same aspect and appearance as Sancho had described to them when he told them the story of Cardenio. He, showing no astonishment when he saw them, stood still with his head bent down upon his breast like one in deep thought, without raising his eyes to look at them after the first glance when they suddenly came upon him.

The priest, who was aware of his misfortune and recognized him by the description, being a well-spoken man, approached him and in a few sensible words entreated him to abandon a life of such misery, lest he should end it there, which would be the greatest of all misfortunes. Cardenio was then in his right mind, free from any attack of that madness that so frequently carried him away. When he saw that they were dressed in a fashion so unusual among those who frequented those wilds, he could not help showing some surprise, especially when

---

next. The last four verses reflect on the verses preceding and end by gathering together the three single-word answers. The *ovillejo*, as this ten-verse stanza is called, is a complex poetic form. Cervantes is not remembered primarily as a poet; however, the *ovillejo* seems to be his invention, making its debut in these pages.

he heard them speak of his case as if it were a well-known matter (for the priest's words gave him to understand as much). And so he replied to them thus:

"I see plainly, sirs, whoever you may be, that Heaven, whose care it is to provide for the good, and even the wicked very often, here in this remote spot cut off from the company of others, sends me, though I deserve it not, those who seek to draw me away from this one to somewhere better, showing me by many forcible arguments how unreasonably I act in leading the life I do. But they, not knowing that if I escape from this evil I shall fall into another still greater, may consider me a weak-minded man, or, what is worse, one devoid of reason. Nor would it be any wonder, for I myself can perceive that the effect of the recollection of my misfortunes is so great and works so powerfully to my ruin, that in spite of myself I become at times like a stone, without feeling or consciousness, and I come to feel the truth of it when they tell me and show me proofs of the things I have done when the terrible fit overmasters me. All I can do is bewail my lot in vain, idly curse my destiny, and plead for my madness by telling how it was caused, to any that care to hear it. No reasonable beings on learning the cause will wonder at the effects, and if they cannot help me at least they will not blame me, and the repugnance they feel at my wild ways will turn into pity for my woes. If it be, sirs, that you are here with the same design as others have come with, before you proceed with your wise arguments, I entreat you to hear the story of my countless misfortunes, for perhaps when you have heard it you will spare yourselves the trouble you would take in offering consolation to a grief that is beyond its reach."

As the two of them desired nothing more than to hear from his own lips the cause of his suffering, they entreated him to tell it, promising not to do anything for his relief or comfort that he did not wish. Thereupon the unhappy gentleman began his sad story in nearly the same words and manner in which he had related it to Don Quixote and the goatherd a few days before, when, because of Master Elisabad and Don Quixote's scrupulous observance of what was due to chivalry, the tale was left unfinished, as this history has already recorded. They were fortunate that this time the mad fit kept off, allowing him to tell it to the end; and so, coming to the incident of the note that Don Fernando had found in a copy of *Amadís of Gaul*, Cardenio said that he remembered it perfectly. It read as follows:

Luscinda to Cardenio

> Every day I discover merits in you that oblige and compel me to hold you in higher estimation. If it be the case that you desire to relieve me of this obligation without cost to my honor, you may easily do so. I have a father who knows you and loves me dearly, who, without constraining my will in any way, shall grant what will be reasonable for you to have—if it be that you value me as you say and as I believe you do.

"As I told you, it was this letter that induced me to ask for Luscinda's hand in marriage. Because of this letter, Luscinda came to be regarded by Don Fernando as one of the most discreet and prudent women of the day, and because of it he formed a plan to ruin me before I could put my own into effect. I told Don Fernando that all Luscinda's father was waiting for was that my own father should ask her hand of him.[4] I dared not tell this to my father, fearing that he would not consent to do so—not because he did not know perfectly well the rank, goodness, virtue, and beauty of Luscinda, and that she had qualities that would do honor to any family in Spain, but because I was aware that he did not wish me to marry so soon before seeing what Duke Ricardo would do for me. In short, I told Don Fernando that I would not risk mentioning the matter to my father, not only on account of that difficulty but because of many others that daunted me. (I knew not well what they were, only that it seemed to me that what I desired was never to come to pass.) To all this, Don Fernando answered that he would take it upon himself to speak to my father and persuade him to speak to Luscinda's father.

"O ambitious Marius! O cruel Catiline! O wicked Sulla! O perfidious Ganelon! O treacherous Vellido! O vindictive Julián! O covetous Judas![5] Traitor, cruel, vindictive, and perfidious, how had this poor wretch failed in his fidelity, who with such candor opened to you the secrets and joys of his heart? What offense did I commit? What words did I utter, or what counsels did I give that had not the furtherance of your honor and welfare for their aim? Woe is me! Yet why do I complain? For sure it is that when misfortunes spring from the stars, they fall upon us from on high with such fury and violence that no power on earth can check their course nor human device stay their coming. Who could have thought that Don Fernando—a highborn gentleman, intelligent, bound to me by gratitude for my services, one that could win the object of his love wherever he might set his affections—would stain his conscience by robbing me of my one ewe lamb that was not even yet in my possession?[6] But laying aside these useless and unavailing reflections, let us take up the broken thread of my unhappy story.

"To proceed, then: Don Fernando found my presence an obstacle to the execution of his treacherous and wicked design, and so he resolved to send me to his elder brother under the pretext of asking money from him to pay for six horses. Purposely, and with the sole object of sending me away that he might the better carry out his infernal scheme, he had purchased these horses the very day he offered to speak to my father, the money for which he now desired me to fetch. Could I have anticipated this treachery? Could I by any chance have suspected it? Not at all. Instead, I offered with the greatest pleasure to go at once, happy about the good bargain that had been made.

[4] *that my own father should ask her hand of him:* that Cardenio's father should ask for Luscinda's hand in marriage on his son's behalf. Parental blessing of a marriage was expected, especially when reputational and property interests were at stake.

[5] *O ambitious Marius . . . O covetous Judas:* catalogue of notorious traitors and conspirators: figures of civil strife in ancient Rome (Gaius Marius, Catiline, Sulla); medieval Christians of legend (Ganelon, who betrayed Roland; Vellido Dolfos, who assassinated King Sancho II of Castille; Count Julián of Ceuta, who aided the Arabs and Berbers in their 711 invasion of the Iberian Peninsula); and Judas Iscariot, who betrayed Christ.

[6] *robbing me of my one ewe lamb . . . in my possession:* The prophet Nathan told a parable of a beloved ewe lamb to confront King David over his adultery with Bathsheba and murder of her husband (2 Samuel 12:1–4).

"That night I spoke with Luscinda and told her what had been agreed upon with Don Fernando, and how I had strong hopes of our fair and reasonable wishes being realized. She, as unsuspicious as I was of the treachery of Don Fernando, advised me to return speedily, as she believed the fulfilment of our desires would be delayed only so long as my father put off speaking to hers. I know not why it was that on saying this to me her eyes filled with tears, and there came a lump in her throat that prevented her from uttering a word of many more that it seemed to me she was trying to say to me. I was astonished at this unusual turn, which I never before observed in her, for we always conversed, whenever good fortune and my ingenuity gave us the chance, with the greatest joy and contentment, mingling tears, sighs, jealousies, doubts, or fears with our words. For my part, I praised my good fortune that Heaven should have given her to me for my mistress. I reveled in her beauty; I extolled her worth and her understanding. She paid me back tenfold by praising what she, in her love for me, thought worthy of praise. Besides all this, we had a hundred thousand trifles and doings of our neighbors and acquaintances to talk about. The utmost extent of my boldness was to take, almost by force, one of her fair white hands and raise it to my lips—as well as the narrow grating of the low window that separated us allowed me. The night before the unhappy day of my departure she wept, she groaned, she sighed, and she withdrew, leaving me uneasy and confused. I was overwhelmed at the sight of such strange and moving signs of grief and sorrow in Luscinda, but not to dash my hopes, I ascribed it all to the depth of her love for me and the pain that separation gives those who love tenderly. At last, I took my departure, sad and dejected, my heart filled with fancies and suspicions, but not knowing well what it was I suspected or fancied. These were plain omens pointing to the bitter outcome and misfortune that awaited me.

"I reached the place to which I had been sent, gave the letter to Don Fernando's brother, and was kindly received but not promptly dismissed, for he desired me to wait (very much against my will) eight days in some place where the duke his father was not likely to see me, as his brother wrote that the money was to be sent without his knowledge. All of this was a scheme of the treacherous Don Fernando, for his brother had no lack of money to enable him to dispatch me at once.

"The command was one that exposed me to the temptation of disobeying it, as it seemed to me impossible to endure life for so many days separated from Luscinda, especially after leaving her in the sorrowful mood I have described to you. Nevertheless, as a dutiful servant I obeyed, though I felt it would be at the cost of my well-being. Four days later there came a man in search of me with a letter he gave me, and which by the address I gathered to be from Luscinda, as the writing was hers. I opened it with fear and trepidation, persuaded that it must be something serious that had impelled her to write to me when at a distance, as she seldom did so when I was near. Before reading it, I asked the man who it was that had given it to him, and how long he had been upon the road. He told me that as he happened to be passing through one of the streets of the city at the noontime hour, a very beautiful lady called to him from a window, and with tears in her eyes said to him hurriedly, 'Brother, if you are a Christian, as you seem to be, for the love of God I entreat you to have this letter dispatched without a moment's delay to the place and person named in the address, all of which is well known. By this you will render a great service to our Lord. And that you may be at no inconvenience in doing so, take what is in this handkerchief.' And said he, 'with this she threw me a handkerchief out of the window in which were tied up a hundred reals and this gold ring that I bring here together with the letter I've given you. And then without waiting for any answer she left the window, though not before she saw me take the letter and the handkerchief and not until I, by signs, had let her know that I would do as she asked me. And so, seeing myself so well paid for the trouble I would have in bringing it to you, and knowing by the address that it was to you it was sent (for, señor, I know you very well), and also unable to resist that beautiful lady's tears, I resolved to trust no one else, but to come myself and give it to you. In sixteen hours from the time when it was given me, I've made the journey, which, as you know, is eighteen leagues.'

"While the good-natured improvised courier was telling me this, I was clinging to his every word, my legs trembling under me so that I could scarcely stand. At last, I opened the letter and read these words:

> The promise Don Fernando gave you to urge your father to speak to mine, he has fulfilled much more to his own satisfaction than to your advantage. I must tell you, señor, that he has asked for my hand in marriage, and my father, led away by what he considers Don Fernando's superiority over you, has favored his suit so earnestly, that in two days the betrothal[7] is to take place with such secrecy and so privately that the only witnesses are to be heaven above and a few members of the household. Picture to yourself the state I am in; judge if it be urgent for you to come. The outcome of this matter will show you whether I love you or not. God grant this may come to your hand before mine shall be forced to join itself with his who keeps so ill the faith that he has pledged.

"Such, in brief, were the words of the letter, words that made me set out at once without waiting any longer for reply or money. Now I saw clearly that it was not the purchase of horses but of his own pleasure that had made Don Fernando send me to his brother. The anger I felt against Don Fernando, along with the fear of losing the prize I had won by so many years of love and devotion, lent me wings, so that almost flying I reached home the next day, at an hour well suited for speaking with Luscinda. I arrived unobserved and left the mule on which I had come at the house of the worthy man who had brought me the letter. Fortune was pleased to be for once so kind that I found Luscinda at the grating that was the witness of our love. She recognized me at once, and I her, but not as she ought to have recognized me, or I her. But who is there in the world who can boast of having fathomed or understood the wavering mind and unstable nature

[7] *betrothal:* Early modern Spain distinguished the exchange of marital vows (betrothal, *desposorio*) from the festivities that celebrated the marital union (wedding, *boda*). Those festivities could come immediately after the betrothal, in the days or weeks following, or not at all.

of a woman? No one, to be sure. To proceed: as soon as Luscinda saw me she said, 'Cardenio, I am in my bridal dress, and the treacherous Don Fernando and my covetous father are waiting for me in the hall with the other witnesses, who shall be the witnesses of my death before they witness my betrothal. Be not distressed, my friend, but contrive to be present at this sacrifice. If it cannot be prevented by my words, I have a dagger concealed that will hinder more determined powers, putting an end to my life and giving you a first proof of the love I have borne and bear you.' I responded to her in haste and agitation, fearful lest I should not have time to reply, 'May your deeds give truth to your words, señora; and if you have a dagger to save your honor, I have a sword to defend you or kill myself if fortune be against us.'

"I do not believe she heard all these words, for I perceived that they called her away in haste, as the bridegroom was waiting. With this, the night of my sorrow set in, the sun of my happiness went down, I felt my eyes bereft of sight and my mind of reason. I could not bring myself to enter the house, nor was I capable of any movement; but when I considered how important it was that I should be present at what might take place on the occasion, I nerved myself as best I could and went in, for I well knew all the entrances and outlets. Besides, with the confusion that in secret pervaded the house no one took notice of me. Without being seen, I found an opportunity of placing myself in the recess formed by a window of the same hall[8] and concealed by the ends and borders of two tapestries, from between which I could, without being seen, see all that took place in there.

"Who could describe the convulsions my heart suffered as I stood there, the thoughts that came to me, the reflections that passed through my mind? They were such as cannot be told, nor were it well they should be. Suffice it to say that the bridegroom entered the hall in his usual dress, without ornament of any kind. As groomsman he had with him a cousin of Luscinda's. Except the servants of the house, there was no one else in the chamber. Soon afterwards Luscinda came out from an antechamber, attended by her mother and two of her damsels, arrayed and adorned as became her rank and beauty, and in full festival and ceremonial attire. My anxiety and distraction did not allow me to observe or notice in detail what she wore. I could only take note of the colors, which were crimson and white, and the glitter of the gems and jewels on her head dress and apparel, surpassed by the rare beauty of her lovely auburn hair, which, vying with the precious stones and the light of the four torches that stood in the hall, shone with a brighter gleam than all. O memory, mortal foe of my peace! Why bring before me now the incomparable beauty of that adored enemy of mine? Would it not be better, cruel memory, to replay before my imagination what she then did, so that stirred by an affront so glaring I may seek, if not vengeance, at least the end of my life? Be not weary, sirs, of listening to these digressions. My sorrow is not one of those that can or should be told tersely and in passing, for to me each incident seems to call for many words."

[8] *same hall:* the room of the house where the ceremony was to take place.

To this the priest replied that not only were they not weary of listening to him, but that the details he mentioned interested them greatly, being of a kind by no means to be omitted and deserving of the same attention as the main story.

"To proceed, then," continued Cardenio: "Everyone being assembled in the hall, the parish priest came in, and as he took the pair by the hand to perform the requisite ceremony, at the words, 'Do you, Señora Luscinda, take Señor Don Fernando, here present, for your lawful husband, as the holy Mother Church ordains?' I thrust my head and neck out from between the tapestries, and with eager ears and throbbing heart prepared to hear Luscinda's answer, awaiting in her reply the sentence of death or the grant of life. O that I had but dared at that moment to rush forward crying aloud, 'Luscinda, Luscinda! Consider what you are about to do! Remember what you owe me! Recall that you are mine and cannot be another's. Reflect that when you give your consent, the end of my life will come at the same instant. O treacherous Don Fernando! Robber of my glory, death of my life! What do you seek? Remember that you cannot as a Christian attain the object of your desires, for Luscinda is my bride, and I am her husband!'[9] Fool that I am! Now that I am far away and out of danger, I say I should have done what I did not do. Now that I have allowed my precious treasure to be robbed from me, I curse the robber, on whom I might have taken vengeance had I as much heart for it as I have for bewailing my fate. In short, as I was then a coward and a fool, little wonder is it if I am now dying shame-stricken, remorseful, and insane.

"The priest stood waiting for an answer from Luscinda, who for a long time withheld it. Just as I thought she was taking out the dagger to save her honor, or struggling for words to make some declaration of the truth on my behalf, I heard her say in a faint and feeble voice, 'I do.' Don Fernando said the same, and giving her the ring they stood linked by a knot that could never be loosed. The bridegroom then approached to embrace his bride; and she, pressing her hand upon her heart, fell fainting in her mother's arms.

"It only remains now for me to tell you the state I was in when in that consent that I heard I saw all my hopes mocked, the words and promises of Luscinda proved falsehoods, and the recovery of the prize I had that instant lost rendered impossible for ever. I stood stupefied, wholly abandoned, it seemed, by Heaven, declared the enemy of the earth that bore me, the air refusing me breath for my sighs, the water moisture for my tears. Fire alone gathered strength in me, such that my whole frame glowed with rage and jealousy. Everyone was thrown into confusion by Luscinda's fainting, and as her mother was unlacing her to give her

[9] *Luscinda is my bride, and I am her husband:* When Cardenio declares that Luscinda is his wife, his words are grounded in more than his earnest desire as a lover. Though he never commits to marrying her without parental approval, he draws rhetorical firepower from the widespread belief that a marital union was formed when a man and woman exchanged vows, even if in secret. When the Council of Trent took up the matter in 1563, it decided against the validity of what were called clandestine marriages. One of the reasons for the Council's opposition to them will become clear in the next chapter.

air, a sealed paper was discovered in her bosom, which Don Fernando seized at once and began to read by the light of one of the torches. As soon as he had read it, he seated himself in a chair, leaning his cheek on his hand in the attitude of one deep in thought, without taking any part in the efforts that were being made to recover his bride from her fainting fit.

"Seeing all the household in confusion, I ventured to come out, without regard to whether I was seen or not, and determined if I were seen, to do some frenzied deed that would prove to the world the righteous indignation of my breast, as I punished the faithless Don Fernando and even the swooning traitor with the inconstant heart. But my fate, doubtless reserving me for greater sorrows (if such there be), so ordained that the reason I have since lacked abounded to me in that moment. And so, without seeking to take vengeance on my greatest enemies (which might have been easily taken, as every thought of me was so far from their minds), I resolved to take it upon myself, and on myself to inflict the pain they deserved, perhaps with even greater severity than I should have dealt out to them had I then slain them. For sudden pain is soon over, but that which is protracted by tortures is ever slaying without ending life.

"In a word, I left the house and reached that of the man with whom I had left my mule. I made him saddle it for me, mounted without bidding him farewell, and rode out of the city, like another Lot, not daring to turn my head to look back upon it.[10] When I found myself alone in the open country, enveloped by the darkness of the night, and tempted by the stillness to give vent to my grief without apprehension or fear of being heard or seen, then I broke silence and lifted up my voice to heap curses upon Luscinda and Don Fernando, as if I could thus avenge the wrong they had done me. I called her cruel, ungrateful, false, thankless, but above all greedy, since the wealth of my enemy had blinded the eyes of her affection and turned it from me to set it on one to whom fortune had been more generous and liberal. And yet, amid this outburst of vitriol and condemnation, I found excuses for her, saying it was no wonder that a young girl in the seclusion of her parents' house, trained and schooled to obey them always, should have been ready to yield to their wishes when they offered her for a husband a gentleman of such distinction, wealth, and noble birth; that if she had refused to accept him she would have been thought out of her senses, or to have set her affection elsewhere, a suspicion injurious to her fair name and reputation. But then again, I said, had she declared I was her husband, they would have seen that in choosing me she had not chosen so poorly but that they might excuse her, for before Don Fernando had made his offer, they themselves could not have desired (if their desires had been ruled by reason) a more eligible husband for their daughter than I was; and she, before taking the last fatal step of giving her hand, might easily have said that I had already given her mine, for I should have come forward to support any assertion of hers to that effect. In short, I concluded

[10] *like another Lot, not daring to turn my head to look back upon it:* God rescued Lot's family from the destruction he was about to inflict on the cities of Sodom and Gomorrah but warned them not to look back as they fled (Genesis 19:17).

that feeble love, little reflection, great ambition, and a craving for rank had made her forget the words with which she had deceived me, encouraged and supported by my firm hopes and honorable passion.

"Thus soliloquizing and agitated, I journeyed onward for the remainder of the night. By daybreak I reached one of the passes of these mountains, among which I wandered for three days more without taking any path or road, until I came to some meadows lying on I know not which side of the mountains. There I inquired of some herdsmen in what direction the most rugged part of the sierra lay. They told me that it was in this vicinity, and I at once directed my course here, where I intended to end my life. But as I was making my way among these crags, my mule dropped dead through fatigue and hunger, or, as I think more likely, in order to have done with such a worthless burden as it bore in me. I was left on foot, worn out, famishing, without anyone to help me or any thought of seeking help. In this state I lay stretched on the ground, how long I know not, after which I rose up free from hunger, and found beside me some goatherds, who no doubt were the people who had relieved me in my need, for they told me how they had found me, and how my ravings and mad discourse showed plainly I had lost my reason. Since then I have been conscious that I am not always in full possession of my faculties, but am at times so deranged and crazed that I do a thousand mad things, tearing my clothes, crying aloud in these solitudes, cursing my fate, and idly calling on the dear name of her who is my enemy, and only seeking to end my life in lamentation; and when I recover my senses I find myself so exhausted and weary that I can scarcely move. Most commonly my dwelling is the hollow of a cork tree large enough to shelter this miserable body. The herdsmen and goatherds who frequent these mountains, moved by compassion, furnish me with food, leaving it by the wayside or on the rocks, where they think I may perhaps pass and find it. Even if I am out of my senses, nature teaches me what is required for my survival and gives me a craving and a will to meet my needs. At other times—so they tell me when they find me in my right mind—I set out upon the road, and though by force from the shepherds bringing it from the village to their huts. Thus do I pass the wretched life that remains to me, until it be Heaven's will to bring it to a close, or so to order my memory that I no longer recollect the beauty and treachery of Luscinda, or the wrong done me by Don Fernando. For if Heaven will do this without depriving me of life, I will turn my thoughts to some better end. If not, I can only implore it to have full mercy on my soul, for in myself I feel no power or strength to release my body from this strait in which I have of my own accord chosen to place it.

"Such, sirs, is the bitter story of my misfortune. Tell me if it be one that can be related with less emotion than you have seen in me; and do not trouble yourselves with urging or pressing upon me what reason suggests as likely to serve for my relief, for it will avail me as much as the medicine prescribed by a wise physician avails the sick man who will not take it. I have no wish for health without Luscinda, and since it is her pleasure to be another's when she rightly belongs to me, let it be my pleasure to be a prey to misery when I might have enjoyed happiness. She, by her inconstancy, sought to make my ruin irretrievable; I will strive to gratify her wishes by seeking destruction. Let my misfortune be an example to generations to come. I alone was deprived of the one comfort that the unfortunate have in abundance, for to them the impossibility of being consoled is itself a consolation, while to me it is the cause of greater sorrows and sufferings. I am convinced that even in death there will not be an end of them."

Here Cardenio brought to a close his long discourse and story, as full of misfortune as it was of love. But just as the priest was going to address some words of comfort to him, he was stopped by a voice that reached his ear, saying in melancholy tones what will be told in the Fourth Part of this narrative; for at this point the sage and meticulous historian Cide Hamete Benengeli brought the Third to a conclusion.

FOURTH PART OF THE INGENIOUS GENTLEMAN DON QUIXOTE DE LA MANCHA

CHAPTER XXVIII

WHICH TREATS OF THE STRANGE AND DELIGHTFUL ADVENTURE THAT BEFELL THE PRIEST AND THE BARBER IN THE SAME SIERRA

Happy and fortunate were the times when that most daring knight Don Quixote of La Mancha was sent into the world; for by reason of his having formed a resolution so honorable as that of seeking to revive and restore to the world the long-lost and almost defunct order of knight-errantry, we now enjoy in this age of ours (in such great need of uplifting entertainment), not only the charm of his true history, but also of the tales and episodes contained in it which are, in their way, no less pleasing, ingenious, and truthful, than the history itself. This history, to resume its thread—carded, spun, and wound—relates that just as the priest was going to offer consolation to Cardenio, he was interrupted by a voice that fell upon his ear saying in plaintive tones:

"O God! Is it possible I have found a place that may serve as a secret grave for this weary load of a body that I support so unwillingly? If the solitude these mountains promise deceives me not, it will be so. O unhappy me![1] How well suited is this stony wilderness to hear the complaints of my misfortune as they rise to heaven. How much more agreeable is its company than that of any human being, for there is none on earth to look to for counsel in doubt, comfort in sorrow, or relief in distress!"

All this was heard distinctly by the priest and those with him, and as it seemed to them to be uttered nearby, as indeed it was, they got up to look for the speaker. Before they had gone twenty paces they discovered behind a rock, seated at the foot of an ash tree, a youth in the dress of a peasant, whose face they were unable at the moment to see as he was leaning forward, bathing his feet in the brook that flowed past. They approached so silently that he did not perceive them, being fully occupied in bathing his feet, which were so fair that they looked like two pieces of shining crystal brought forth among the other stones of the brook. The whiteness and beauty of these feet struck them with surprise, for they did not seem to have been made to tread the soil or to follow the plough and the oxen as their owner's dress suggested. Finding they had not been noticed, the priest, who was in front, made a sign to the other two to conceal themselves behind some

[1] *O unhappy me:* The speaker uses the adjective *desdichada,* marked for gender.

fragments of rock that lay there. They did so, observing the youth closely. He had on a loose double-skirted dark brown jacket bound tight to his body with a white cloth. Along with these, he wore breeches and leggings of brown cloth, and on his head a brown montera.[2] His leggings were rolled up as far as the middle of the leg, which truly seemed to be of pure alabaster.

When he had finished bathing his beautiful feet, he wiped them with a towel he took from under the montera. His face lifted as he reached for his cap, and those who were watching him had an opportunity of seeing a beauty so exquisite that Cardenio said to the priest in a whisper, "As this is not Luscinda, it is no human creature but a divine being."

The youth then took off the montera, and shaking his head from side to side there broke loose and spread out a mass of hair that the beams of the sun might have envied. By this they knew that what had seemed a peasant was a lovely woman, indeed, the most beautiful the eyes of two of them had ever beheld—even Cardenio's, if his eyes had not seen and known Luscinda, for he afterwards declared that only the beauty of Luscinda could compare with this. The long golden tresses not only covered her shoulders, but such was their length and abundance, concealed her all round beneath their masses, such that except for her feet, nothing of her form was visible. She now used her hands as a comb, and if her feet had seemed like pieces of crystal in the water,[3] her hands looked like mounds of driven snow among her locks. All of this increased not only the admiration of the three beholders, but their eagerness to learn who she was.

With this object they resolved to show themselves. At the stir they made in getting to their feet, the fair damsel raised her head. Parting her hair from before her eyes with both hands, she looked to see who had made the noise, and the instant she saw them she started to her feet. Without waiting to put on her shoes or gather up her hair, she hastily snatched up a bundle of what seemed to be clothes that she had beside her, and, scared and alarmed, attempted to take flight. But before she had gone six paces she fell to the ground, her delicate feet being unable to bear the roughness of the stones.

Seeing this, the three hastened toward her, and the priest addressing her first said, "Stay, señora, whoever you may be, for those whom you see here only desire to be of service to you. You have no need to attempt a flight so heedless, for neither can your feet bear it, nor we allow it."

Taken by surprise and bewildered, she made no reply to these words. They, however, came toward her, and the priest taking her hand went on to say, "What your dress would hide, señora, is made known to us by your hair, a clear proof that it can be no insignificant cause that has disguised your beauty in a garb so

[2] *montera:* tall woven cap with a narrow brim.

[3] *if her feet had seemed like pieces of crystal in the water:* The emphasis on the beauty of the youth's feet may strike the modern reader as unusual. Conservative standards of dress, especially for women and the upper classes, meant that it was uncommon to see the exposed bodies of strangers. One of the enduring appeals of staging plays where women dressed as men was the titillation of seeing the silhouette of a woman's legs.

unworthy of it and sent it to such a desolate place as this where we have had the good fortune to find you, if not to relieve your distress, at least to offer you comfort. For no distress, so long as life lasts, can be so oppressive or reach such a height as to make the sufferer refuse to listen to comfort offered with good intention. And so, señora, or señor, or whatever you prefer to be, dismiss the fears that our appearance has caused you and make us acquainted with your good or evil fortunes, for from all of us together, or from each one of us, you will receive sympathy in your trouble."

While the priest was speaking, the disguised damsel stood as if spellbound, looking at them without opening her lips or uttering a word, just like a village rustic to whom something strange that he has never seen before has been suddenly shown. But when the priest addressed some further words to the same effect to her, sighing deeply she broke silence and said:

"Since the solitude of these mountains has been unable to conceal me, and the loosening of my disheveled tresses will not allow my tongue to deal in falsehoods, it would be idle for me now to make any further pretense of what, if you were to believe me, you would believe more out of courtesy than for any other reason. This being so, I say I thank you, sirs, for the offer you have made me, which places me under the obligation of complying with the request you have made; though I fear the account I shall give you of my misfortunes will leave you more disconsolate than softhearted, for you will be unable to suggest anything to remedy them or any consolation to alleviate them. However, that my honor may not be left a matter of doubt in your minds, now that you have discovered me to be a woman and see that I am young, alone, and in this dress—things that taken together or separately would be enough to destroy any good name—I feel bound to tell what I would willingly keep secret if I could."

All this she who was now seen to be a lovely woman delivered without any hesitation, with so much ease and in so sweet a voice that they were not less charmed by her intelligence than by her beauty. As they again repeated their offers and entreaties to her to fulfil her promise, she without further pressing, first modestly covering her feet and gathering up her hair, seated herself on a rock with the three placed around her, and after an effort to restrain some tears that came to her eyes, in a clear and steady voice began her story thus:

"In this Andalusia there is a town from which a duke takes a title that makes him one of those that are called Grandees of Spain. This nobleman has two sons, the elder heir to his dignity and, by all accounts, to his good qualities; the younger heir to I know not what, unless it be the treachery of Vellido and the falsehood of Ganelon. My parents are this lord's vassals, lowly in origin, but so wealthy that if birth had conferred as much on them as fortune, they would have had nothing left to desire, nor should I have had reason to fear trouble like that in which I find myself now; for it may be that my misfortune came about because of their misfortune in not having been nobly born. It is true they are not so low that they have any reason to be ashamed of their condition, but neither are they so high as to remove from my mind the impression that my mishap comes of their humble birth. They are, in short, peasants, plain homely people, without any taint of disreputable blood, and, as the saying is, old rusty Christians,[4] but so rich that by their wealth and openhanded way of life they are coming by degrees to earn the prestige of hidalgos, even knights.[5] With all this, the wealth and nobility they thought most of was in having me for their daughter, and as they have no other child to make their heir and are affectionate parents, I was one of the most indulged daughters that ever parents indulged.

"I was the mirror in which they beheld themselves, the staff of their old age, and the object in which, with submission to Heaven, all their wishes centered. My wishes were in accordance with theirs, for I knew their worth; and as I was mistress of their hearts, so was I also of their possessions. Through me they hired or dismissed their servants; through my hands passed the accounts and returns of what was sown and reaped. The oil mills, the winepresses, all of our flocks and herds, the beehives—everything in short that a rich farmer like my father has or can have, I had under my care, and I acted as steward and mistress with a diligence on my part and satisfaction on theirs that I cannot well describe to you. The leisure hours left to me after I had given the necessary orders to the head shepherds, overseers, and other laborers, I passed in such activities as are not only allowable but necessary for young girls, those that the needle, embroidery cushion, and spinning wheel usually afford; and if to refresh my mind I left them for a while, I found recreation in reading some devotional book or playing the harp, for experience taught me that music soothes the troubled mind and relieves weariness of spirit. Such was the life I led in my parents' house. If I have depicted it thus minutely, it is not out of ostentation, or to let you know that I am rich, but that you may see how, without any fault of mine, I have fallen from the happy condition I have described, to the misery I am in at present. The truth is that while I was leading this busy life in a retirement that might compare with that of a monastery and unseen as I thought by any except the servants of the house—for when I went to Mass it was so early in the morning, and I was so closely attended by my mother and the women of the household, and so thickly veiled and so shy, that my eyes scarcely saw more ground than I trod on—in spite of all this, the eyes of love, or idleness, more properly speaking, discovered me. These watchful eyes, which the lynx's cannot rival,[6] belonged to Don Fernando, for that is the name of the younger son of the duke I told of."

The moment the speaker mentioned the name of Don Fernando, Cardenio changed color and broke into a sweat, with such signs of emotion that the priest and the barber feared that one of the mad fits that they heard attacked him

[4] *old rusty Christians:* without the taint of Jewish or Moorish ancestry. See footnote 8, page 147.

[5] *hidalgos, even knights:* Hidalgo is the noble rank of Alonso Quixano, shared by an estimated 5–10 percent of the adult males of early modern Spain. The title of *caballero* (knight) was more prestigious, associated with military service and higher social standing. Far fewer men held the rank, and it could confer enhanced tax privileges.

[6] *the lynx's cannot rival:* The lynx was believed to possess the ability to see through solid objects.

sometimes was coming upon him. But Cardenio showed no further agitation and remained quiet, regarding the peasant girl with fixed attention, for he began to suspect who she was. She, without noticing the excitement of Cardenio, continued her story saying:

"Scarcely had he laid eyes on me, when, as he admitted afterwards, he was smitten with a violent love for me, as the manner in which it displayed itself plainly showed. But to shorten the long recital of my woes, I will pass over in silence all the schemes employed by Don Fernando for declaring his passion for me. He bribed all the household, he gave and offered gifts and presents to my parents. Every day was like a holiday or celebration in our street; by night no one could sleep for the music. The love letters that used to come into my hands (no one knew how) were innumerable, full of tender pleadings and pledges, containing more promises and oaths than there were letters in them. All of this not only did not soften me, but hardened my heart against him, as if he had been my mortal enemy, and as if everything he did to make me yield were done with the opposite intention. Not that the highbred bearing of Don Fernando was disagreeable to me, or that I found his insistence wearisome; for it gave me a certain sort of satisfaction to find myself so sought and prized by a gentleman of such distinction, and I was not displeased at seeing my praises in his letters (for however ugly we women may be, it strikes me that we are always pleased to hear ourselves called beautiful). Rather, my own sense of right was opposed to all this, as well as the repeated advice of my parents, who now very plainly perceived Don Fernando's purpose, for he cared very little if all the world knew it. They told me that they entrusted their honor and good name entirely to my virtuous nature, and bade me consider the disparity between Don Fernando and myself, from which I might conclude that his intentions, whatever he might say to the contrary, had for their aim his own pleasure rather than my advantage. If I were at all desirous of opposing an obstacle to his unreasonable suit, they were ready, they said, to marry me at once to anyone I preferred, either among the leading people of our own town or of any of those in the vicinity, for with their wealth and my good name, a match might be looked for in any quarter. This offer and their sound advice strengthened my resolution, and I never gave Don Fernando a word in reply that could hold out to him any hope of success, however remote.

"All my displays of modesty, which he must have taken for coyness, had apparently the effect of increasing his wanton appetite—for that is the name I give to his passion for me; had it been what he declared it to be, you would not now know, because there would have been no occasion to tell you about it. At length he learned that my parents were contemplating marriage for me in order to put an end to his hopes of having me as his own, or at least to secure additional protectors to watch over me, and this knowledge or suspicion made him act as you shall hear. One night, as I was in my chamber with no other companion than a damsel who waited on me, with the doors carefully locked lest my honor should be imperiled through any carelessness, I know not nor can conceive how it happened, but, with all this seclusion and these precautions and in the solitude and silence of my retirement, I found him standing before me, a vision that so astounded me that it deprived my eyes of sight and my tongue of speech. I had no power to utter a cry, nor, I think, did he give me time to utter one, as he immediately approached me, and taking me in his arms (for overwhelmed as I was, I was powerless, I say, to help myself), he began to make such professions to me that I know not how falsehood could have had the power of dressing them up to seem so like the truth. The traitor contrived that his tears should vouch for his words and his sighs for his sincerity.

"I, a poor young creature alone, ill versed among my people in matters such as this, began (I know not how) to think all these lying protestations true, though without being moved by his sighs and tears to anything more than pure compassion. And so, as the first feeling of bewilderment passed away and I began in some degree to recover myself, I said to him with more courage than I thought I could have possessed, 'If, as I am now in your arms, señor, I were in the claws of a fierce lion, and my deliverance could be obtained by doing or saying anything to the prejudice of my honor, it would no more be in my power to do or say it, than it would be possible to erase what is past. So then, if you hold my body clasped in your arms, I hold my soul secured by virtuous intentions, very different from yours, as you will see if you attempt to carry them into effect by force. I am your vassal, but I am not your slave. Your nobility neither has nor should have any right to dishonor or degrade my humble birth; and lowborn peasant as I am, I have my self-respect as much as you, a lord and gentleman. With me your violence will be to no purpose, your wealth will have no weight, your words will have no power to deceive me, nor your sighs or tears to soften me. Were I to see any of the things I speak of in him whom my parents gave me as a husband, his will should be mine, and mine should be bounded by his; and my honor being preserved (even though my inclinations were not) would willingly yield him what you, señor, would now obtain by force. This I say lest you should suppose that any but my lawful husband shall ever win any concession of me.' 'If that,' said this disloyal gentleman, 'be the only scruple you feel, fairest Dorotea' (for that is the name of this unhappy being), 'see here I give you my hand to be yours, and let Heaven, from which nothing is hid, and this image of Our Lady you have here, be witnesses of this pledge.'"

When Cardenio heard her say she was named Dorotea, he showed fresh agitation and felt convinced of the truth of his former suspicion. But he was unwilling to interrupt the story and wished to hear the end of what he, in large part, already knew, so he merely said, "You say that Dorotea is your name, señora? I have heard of another of the same name who can perhaps match your misfortunes. But proceed; as time permits I may tell you something that will astonish you as much as it will move you to pity."

Dorotea was struck by Cardenio's words as well as by his strange and miserable attire, and begged him if he knew anything concerning her to tell her at once. For if fortune had left her any blessing, it was the courage to bear whatever calamity might fall upon her, as she felt sure that none could reach her capable of increasing in any degree what she endured already.

"I would not let the occasion pass, señora," replied Cardenio, "of telling you what I think, if what I suspect were the truth, but so far there has been no opportunity, nor is it of any importance to you to know it."

"Be that as it may," replied Dorotea, "what happened in my story was that Don Fernando, taking an image that stood in the chamber, placed it as a witness of our betrothal, and with the most binding words and extravagant oaths gave me his promise to become my husband; though before he had made an end of his vows, I bade him consider well what he was doing, and think of the anger his father would feel at seeing him married to a peasant girl and one of his vassals. I told him not to let my beauty, such as it was, blind him, for beauty was not enough to furnish an excuse for his transgression. And if in the love he bore me he wished to do me any kindness, it would be to leave my lot to follow its course consistent with my condition; for marriages so unequal never bring happiness, nor does the enjoyment they begin with long endure.

"All this that I have now repeated I said to him, and much more that I cannot recollect, but it had no effect in persuading him to forego his purpose. He who has no intention of paying does not trouble himself about difficulties when he is striking the bargain. At the same time, I argued the matter briefly in my own mind, saying to myself, 'I shall not be the first who has risen through marriage from a lowly to a lofty station, nor will Don Fernando be the first whom beauty or, as is more likely, a blind attachment, has led him to choose a mate below his rank. Since I am introducing no new custom or practice, I may as well avail myself of the honor that chance offers me, for even though his inclination for me should not outlast the attainment of his desires, I shall be, after all, his wife before God. And if I attempt to repel him by scorn, I can see that when he finds his words to no avail he will resort to force, and I shall be left dishonored and without any means of proving my innocence to those who cannot know how innocently I have come to be in this position. For what arguments would persuade my parents that this gentleman entered my chamber without my consent?'

"These questions and answers passed through my mind in a moment. But the oaths of Don Fernando, the witnesses he appealed to, the tears he shed, and lastly the charms of his person and his highbred grace, which, accompanied by such signs of genuine love, might well have conquered a heart more independent and restrained than mine. All these things began to press on me as they sped me unawares to my ruin. I called my maid to me that there might be a witness on earth besides those in heaven. Again Don Fernando renewed and repeated his oaths, invoked as witnesses fresh saints in addition to the former ones, called down upon himself a thousand curses hereafter should he fail to keep his promise, shed more tears, redoubled his sighs and pressed me closer in his arms, from which he had never allowed me to escape. And so I was left by my maid, and ceased to be one, and he was proved to be a faithless traitor.

"The day that followed the night of my misfortune did not come so quickly, I suspect, as Don Fernando wished, for when desire has attained its object, the greatest pleasure is to fly from the scene of pleasure. I say so because Don Fernando made all haste to leave me. With the help of my crafty maid (who was indeed the one who had admitted him), he was on the street before daybreak. On taking leave of me he told me, though not with as much earnestness and fervor as when he came, that I might rest assured of his faith and of the sanctity and sincerity of his vows. To confirm his words, he took a costly ring from his finger and placed it upon mine. In short, he departed.

"Whether I was left sorrowful or happy, I know not. All I can say is, I was left agitated and troubled in mind by what had taken place, as if I were a stranger to myself. I had not the spirit, or else it did not occur to me, to chide my maid for the treachery she had been guilty of in concealing Don Fernando in my chamber, for as yet I was unable to make up my mind whether what had befallen me was for good or evil. I told Don Fernando at parting that as I was now his, he might see me on other nights in the same way until it should be his pleasure to let the matter become known. But except the following night he came no more, nor for more than a month could I catch a glimpse of him in the street or in church while I wearied myself with watching for him, although I knew he was in town and almost every day went out hunting, a pastime he was very fond of. I remember well how sad and dreary those days and hours were to me; I remember well how I began to doubt as they went by and even to lose confidence in the faith of Don Fernando; and I remember, too, how my maid heard those words in reproof of her audacity that she had not heard before and how I was forced to put a constraint on my tears and on the expression of my countenance so as not to give my parents cause to ask me why I was so melancholy and drive me to invent falsehoods in reply. But all this was suddenly brought to an end, for the time came when all such considerations were abandoned and there was no further place for noble deliberations, when my patience gave way and the secret of my heart became known abroad. This was because a few days later it was reported in town that Don Fernando had been married in a neighboring city to a maiden of rare beauty, the daughter of parents of distinguished position, though not so rich that her portion would entitle her to look for so highborn a match. It was said, too, that her name was Luscinda, and that at the betrothal some strange things had happened."

Cardenio heard the name of Luscinda, but he only shrugged his shoulders, bit his lips, bent his brows, and before long two streams of tears escaped from his eyes. Dorotea, however, did not interrupt her story, but went on in these words:

"This sad intelligence reached my ears, and instead of being struck with a chill, with such wrath and fury did my heart burn that I scarcely restrained myself from rushing out into the streets, crying aloud and proclaiming openly the perfidy and treachery of which I was the victim. But this transport of rage was for the time checked by a resolution I formed, to be carried out that night: to dress myself in this attire, which I got from a servant of my father's, a zagal,[7] as the farmers call them. To him I confided the whole of my misfortune and entreated him to accompany me to the city where I heard my enemy was. He, though he reproved me for my boldness and condemned my resolution, when he saw me

[7] *zagal:* young shepherd.

bent upon my purpose, offered to accompany me, as he said, to the end of the world. Without wasting time, I packed in a linen pillowcase a woman's dress, along with some jewels and money to provide for emergencies, and in the silence of the night, without letting my treacherous maid know, I left my house, accompanied by my servant and abundant anxieties. I set out on foot set for the city, borne, as it were, on wings by my eagerness to reach it, if not to prevent what I presumed to be already done, at least to call upon Don Fernando to tell me how his conscience had permitted it.[8]

"I reached my destination in two days and a half, and on entering the city inquired for the house of Luscinda's parents. The first person I asked gave me more in reply than I sought to know. He showed me the house and told me all that had occurred at the betrothal of the daughter of the family, an affair of such notoriety in the city that it was the talk of every knot of idlers in the street. He said that on the night of Don Fernando's betrothal with Luscinda, as soon as she had taken her vow to be his bride, she was overcome with a sudden fainting fit; and when the bridegroom approached to unlace the bosom of her dress to give her air, he found a piece of paper in her own handwriting, in which she declared that she could not be Don Fernando's bride because she was already Cardenio's, who, according to the man's account, was a gentleman of distinction of the same city; and that if she had accepted Don Fernando, it was only in obedience to her parents. In short, he said, the words of the paper made it clear she meant to kill herself once the ceremony was over and gave her reasons for ending her life—all of which was confirmed, it was said, by a dagger they found somewhere in her clothes. On seeing this, Don Fernando, persuaded that Luscinda had deceived, slighted, and disrespected him, lashed out at her while she was still in a swoon and tried to stab her with the dagger that had been found, and would have succeeded had not her parents and those who were present prevented him. It was said, moreover, that Don Fernando went away at once, and that Luscinda did not recover from her fainting spell until the next day, when she told her parents how she was really the bride of that Cardenio I have mentioned. I learned besides that Cardenio, it was said, had been present at the betrothal; and that upon seeing her betrothed contrary to his expectation, he had taken flight from the city in despair, leaving behind a letter declaring the wrong Luscinda had done him and his intention of going where no one should ever see him again.

"All this was a matter of notoriety in the city, and everyone spoke of it—especially when it became known that Luscinda was missing from her father's house and from the city, for she was not to be found anywhere, while her parents, half mad with worry, knew not what steps to take to recover her. What I learned revived my hopes, and I was better pleased not to have found Don Fernando than to find him married, for it seemed to me that the door to my relief was not yet entirely shut. I thought that perhaps Heaven had put this impediment in the way of the second marriage to lead him to recognize his obligations under the former one and reflect that as a Christian he was bound to consider his soul

[8] *how his conscience had permitted it*: "with what soul he had done it".

above all human objects. All this passed through my mind, and I tried to comfort myself without comfort, indulging in faint and distant hopes of cherishing that life that I now abhor.

"While I was in the city, uncertain what to do and unable to find Don Fernando, I heard notice given by the public crier offering a great reward to anyone who should find me, and giving the particulars of my age and of the very dress I wore; and I heard it said that the lad who came with me had taken me away from my father's house. I was cut to the heart to see how low my good name had fallen. It was not enough for my reputation to be tarnished by reports of my flight, but they had to add to it that I ran off with someone, a person so much beneath me and so unworthy of my consideration. The instant I heard the notice, I left the city with my servant, who now began to show signs of wavering in his loyalty to me. The same night, for fear of discovery, we entered the most thickly wooded part of these mountains. But as is commonly said, 'One evil calls up another,' and the end of one misfortune is apt to be the beginning of one still greater. So it proved in my case. For my worthy servant (until then so faithful and reliable), when he found me in this lonely spot, moved more by his own villainy than by my beauty, sought to take advantage of the opportunity which these wilds seemed to present him, and with little shame and less fear of God and respect for me, began to make overtures to me. Finding that I replied to the effrontery of his proposals with justly harsh language, he laid aside the entreaties which he had employed at first and began to use violence.

"But just Heaven, which seldom fails to watch over and aid good intentions, so aided mine that with my slight strength and with little exertion I pushed him over a precipice, where I left him, whether dead or alive I know not. Then, with greater speed than seemed possible in my terror and fatigue, I made my way into the mountains, without any other thought or purpose save that of hiding myself among them and escaping my father and those dispatched in search of me by his orders. It is now I know not how many months since with this object I came here, where I met a herdsman who hired me as his servant at a place in the heart of this sierra. All this time I have been serving him as shepherd, striving to remain always in the field to hide these locks that have now unexpectedly betrayed me. But all my care and pains were unavailing, for my master made the discovery that I was not a man, and was stirred with the same vile designs as my servant. As fortune does not always supply a remedy in cases of difficulty, and I had no precipice or ravine at hand down which to fling the master and cure his passion, as I had in the servant's case, I thought it a lesser evil to leave him and again conceal myself in this wilderness, rather than test my strength or ingenuity with him. So, as I say, once more I went into hiding to seek some place where I might with sighs and tears implore Heaven to have pity on my misery and grant me help and strength to escape from it, or let me die in this lonely place, leaving no trace of an unhappy being who, by no fault of hers, has furnished matter for gossip and scandal at home and abroad."

CHAPTER XXIX

WHICH TREATS OF THE DISCRETION OF THE LOVELY DOROTEA, ALONG WITH OTHER MATTERS OF GREAT DELIGHT AND ENTERTAINMENT*

"Such, sirs, is the true story of my sad adventures. Judge for yourselves now whether the sighs and lamentations you heard, and the tears that flowed from my eyes, had not sufficient cause even if I had indulged in them more freely. If you consider the nature of my misfortune, you will see that consolation is idle, as there is no possible remedy for it. All I ask of you is what you may easily and reasonably do: to show me where I may spend my life untroubled by the pressing fear that I will be discovered by those who seek me. For though the great love my parents bear me makes me feel sure of being kindly received by them, so great is my feeling of shame at the mere thought that I cannot present myself before them as they expect. I had rather banish myself from their sight forever than look them in the face knowing that they behold mine stripped of that purity they had a right to expect of me."

With these words she became silent, and the color that overspread her face showed plainly the pain and shame she was suffering at heart. In theirs, the listeners felt as much pity as wonder at her misfortunes.

Just as the priest was about to offer her some consolation and advice, Cardenio anticipated him saying, "So then, señora, you are the fair Dorotea, the only daughter of the rich Clenardo?"

Dorotea was astonished at hearing her father's name, and at the miserable appearance of him who mentioned it, for it has been already said how wretchedly clad Cardenio was. She said to him, "And who may you be, brother, who knows my father's name? For so far, if I remember rightly, I have not mentioned it in the whole story of my misfortunes."

"I am that unhappy being, señora," replied Cardenio, "whom, as you have said, Luscinda declared to be her husband. I am the unfortunate Cardenio, whom the wrongdoing of him who has brought you to your present condition has reduced to the state you see me in: bare, ragged, bereft of all human comfort, and what is worse, of reason, for I only possess it when Heaven is pleased for some short space to restore it to me. I, Dorotea, am he who witnessed the wrong done by Don Fernando, and waited to hear Luscinda pronounce the words of consent

* The titles for chapters 29 and 30 make more sense if inverted.

by which she owned herself his betrothed. I am he who lacked the courage to see how her fainting spell ended, or what came of the paper that was found in her breast, because my heart had not the fortitude to endure so many strokes of misfortune at once. And so I abandoned the house along with all patience and left a letter with my host, which I entreated him to place in Luscinda's hands. From there, I set off for these solitudes, resolved to end here the life I hated as if it were my mortal enemy.

"But fate would not rid me of it, contenting itself with robbing me of my reason, perhaps to preserve me for the good fortune I have had in meeting you. For if what you have just told us is true, as I believe it is, it may be that Heaven has yet in store for both of us a happier end to our calamities than we look for; because seeing that Luscinda cannot marry Don Fernando, being mine, as she has herself so openly declared, and that Don Fernando cannot marry her as he is yours, we may reasonably hope that Heaven will restore to us what is ours, as it is still validly binding and not yet alienated or destroyed.[1] And as our consolation springs from no distant hope or wild fancy, I entreat you, señora, to fix your noble mind, as I have resolved to do, on a new course, preparing yourself to welcome a brighter fortune. For I swear to you by the faith of a gentleman and a Christian not to desert you until I see you in possession of Don Fernando, and if I cannot by words induce him to recognize his obligation to you, in that case to avail myself of the right that my rank as a gentleman gives me and with just cause challenge him on account of the injury he has done you, not regarding my own wrongs, which I shall leave to Heaven to avenge, while I on earth devote myself to yours."

Cardenio's words left Dorotea in a greater state of wonder. Not knowing how to return thanks for such an offer, she attempted to kiss his feet, though Cardenio would not permit it. The licentiate replied for both, commending the sound reasoning of Cardenio and, above all, counseling and urging them to come with him to his village, where they might furnish themselves with what they needed and take measures to discover Don Fernando, restore Dorotea to her parents, or do what seemed to them most advisable. Cardenio and Dorotea thanked him and accepted his kind offer. The barber, who had been listening to all attentively and in silence, also shared some kindly words, and with no less goodwill than the priest, offered his services in any way that might be of use to them. He further explained to them in a few words the object that had brought them there, the strange nature of Don Quixote's madness, and how they were waiting for his squire, who had gone in search of him. Like the recollection of a dream, the quarrel he had had with Don Quixote came back to Cardenio's memory, and he described it to the others; but he was unable to say what the dispute was about.

At that moment they heard a shout and recognized it as coming from Sancho Panza, who, not finding them where he had left them, was calling to them aloud. They went to meet him, and in answer to their inquiries about Don Quixote, he told them how he had found him stripped to his shirt, lank, yellow, half dead

[1] *validly binding and not yet alienated or destroyed:* Cardenio uses the language of a legal right that has not yet been exhausted by a change in circumstances or the passage of time.

with hunger, and sighing for his lady Dulcinea. Although he had told him that she commanded him to leave that place and come to El Toboso, where she was expecting him, he had answered that he was determined not to appear in the presence of her beauty until he had done deeds to make him worthy of her favor. If this went on, Sancho said, he ran the risk of not becoming an emperor (as he was duty bound to become) or even an archbishop (which was the least he could be); for this reason, they ought to consider what was to be done to get him away from there.

In reply, the licentiate told him not to be uneasy, for they would lure him out in spite of himself. He then told Cardenio and Dorotea what they had proposed to do to cure Don Quixote, or at any rate take him home. Hearing this, Dorotea said that she could play the distressed damsel better than the barber, all the more so since she had with her the perfect dress for the part, and that they might entrust her with the many details the role demanded to further their scheme, for she had read a great many books of chivalry and knew exactly the style in which afflicted damsels requested favors of knights-errant.

"In that case," said the priest, "there is nothing more required than to set about it at once, for beyond a doubt fortune is declaring itself in our favor, since it has so unexpectedly begun to open a door for your relief and smoothed the way for us to our object."

Dorotea then took out of her pillowcase a dress of a fine worsted wool and a green mantle of some other beautiful fabric, and from a little box, a necklace and other jewels. In an instant, she so arrayed herself with these that she looked like a great and rich lady. All this and more, she said, she had taken from home in case of need, but that until then she had had no occasion to make use of it. They were all highly delighted with her grace, elegance, and beauty, and declared Don Fernando to be a man of very little taste when he rejected such charms.

But the one who admired her most was Sancho Panza, for it seemed to him (as it was indeed true) that in all the days of his life he had never beheld such a lovely creature. He asked the priest with great eagerness who this beautiful lady was and what she wanted in this out-of-the-way place.

"This fair lady, brother Sancho," replied the priest, "is no less a personage than the heiress in the direct male line of the great kingdom of Micomicón,[2] who has come in search of your master to request a favor of him, which is that he redress a wrong or injury that a wicked giant has done her. From the fame as a good knight that your master has acquired far and wide, this princess has come from Guinea[3] to seek him."

"A lucky seeking and a lucky finding!" said Sancho Panza at this, "especially if my master has the good fortune to redress that injury, right that wrong, and kill that son of a bitch of a giant your worship speaks of. And kill him he will

[2] *Micomicón:* See footnote 7, page 129.

[3] *Guinea:* Region of coastal West Africa bordered by the Atlantic Ocean to the south and the Sahel to the north. During Cervantes' lifetime, Portuguese trading colonies dominated the region.

if he meets him, unless, indeed, he happens to be a ghost, for my master has no power at all against ghosts. But one thing among others I would like to ask of you, señor licentiate, which is that to prevent my master taking a fancy to be an archbishop (which is what I'm afraid of), your worship would advise him to marry this princess at once. This way, he'll be disqualified from taking archbishop's orders, which will make it easy for him to come into his empire, and me to the end of my desires. I've been thinking over the matter carefully, and as far as I can make out, it won't suit me if my master becomes an archbishop because I'm no good for the Church since I'm married; and for me now, seeing as I have a wife and children, to set about obtaining dispensations[4] to allow me to earn an income in the Church would be an endless job. So, señor, everything depends on my master marrying this lady at once—for as yet I do not know her grace, and so I can't call her by her name."

"She is called Princess Micomicona," said the priest, "for as her kingdom is Micomicón, it is clear that must be her name."

"There's no doubt about that," replied Sancho, "for I've known many to take their name and title from the place where they were born and call themselves Pedro of Alcalá, Juan of Úbeda, and Diego of Valladolid. It may be that over there in Guinea queens have the same way of taking the names of their kingdoms."

"So it may," said the priest, "and as for your master's marrying, I will do all in my power toward it." With this Sancho was as much pleased as the priest was amazed at his simplicity and at seeing what a hold the absurdities of his master had taken of his imagination, for he had evidently persuaded himself that Don Quixote was going to be an emperor.

By this time Dorotea had seated herself upon the priest's mule, and the barber had fitted the oxtail beard to his face. They now told Sancho to conduct them to where Don Quixote was, warning him not to say that he knew either the licentiate or the barber, as his master's becoming an emperor entirely depended on his not recognizing them. Neither the priest nor Cardenio, however, thought fit to go with them—Cardenio, lest he should remind Don Quixote of the quarrel he had with him, and the priest, as there was no necessity for his presence just yet. So they allowed the others to go on before them, while they themselves followed slowly on foot. The priest made sure to instruct Dorotea how to act, but she said they should set their minds at ease, as everything would be done exactly as the books of chivalry required and described.

They had gone about three-quarters of a league when they discovered Don Quixote in a wilderness of rocks. He was by this time clothed but without his armor. As soon as Dorotea saw him and was told by Sancho that that was Don Quixote, she whipped her palfrey, the well-bearded barber following her. When they had approached him, her squire sprang from his mule and came forward to receive her in his arms, and she, dismounting with great ease of manner, advanced to kneel before the feet of Don Quixote. Though he took pains to raise her up, she, without rising, addressed him in this fashion:

[4] *obtaining dispensations:* A dispensation is a formal exception from canon law.

"From this spot I will not rise, valiant and dauntless knight, until your goodness and courtesy grant me a favor, which will redound to the honor and renown of your person and render a service to the most disconsolate and afflicted damsel that ever sun has seen. If the might of your strong arm is equal to the repute of your immortal fame, you are bound to aid this helpless being who, drawn by the aroma of your renowned name, has come from distant lands to seek your aid in her misfortunes."

"I will not answer a word, beauteous lady," replied Don Quixote, "nor will I listen to anything further concerning you, until you rise from the earth."

"I will not rise, señor," answered the afflicted damsel, "unless of your courtesy the favor I ask is first granted me."

"I grant and concede it," said Don Quixote, "provided it may be complied with without detriment or prejudice to my king, my country, or her who holds the key of my heart and freedom."

"It will not be to the detriment or prejudice of any of them, my worthy lord," said the afflicted damsel. Here Sancho Panza drew close to his master's ear and said to him very softly, "Your worship may very safely grant the favor she asks. It's nothing at all—only to kill a big giant. And the lady who asks it is the exalted Princess Micomicona, queen of the great kingdom of Micomicón of Ethiopia."

"Let her be who she may," replied Don Quixote, "I will do what is my bounden duty and what my conscience bids me, in conformity with what I have professed." Turning to the damsel he said, "Let your great beauty rise, for I grant the favor that you would ask of me."

"Then what I ask," said the damsel, "is that your magnanimous person accompany me at once whither I will conduct you, and that you promise not to engage in any other adventure or quest until you have avenged me of a traitor who, against all human and divine law, has usurped my kingdom."

"I repeat that I grant it," replied Don Quixote. "And so, lady, you may from this day forth lay aside the melancholy that distresses you and let your failing hopes gather new life and strength, for with the help of God and of my arm you will soon see yourself restored to your kingdom and seated upon the throne of your ancient and mighty realm, notwithstanding and despite the knaves who would deny it. And now shoulder to the grindstone, for 'in delay there is apt to be danger.'"

The distressed damsel attempted with great effort to kiss his hands, but Don Quixote, who was in all things a polished and courteous knight, would by no means allow it. Instead, he made her rise and embraced her with great courtesy and politeness, and ordered Sancho to arm him and to look to Rocinante's girths without a moment's delay. Sancho took down the armor, which was hung up on a tree like a trophy, and having seen to the girths, immediately set about arming his master.

As soon as he was in his armor, Don Quixote declared, "Let us be gone in the name of God to bring aid to this great lady."

The barber was all this time on his knees, at great pains to hide his laughter and not let his beard fall, for had it fallen their fine scheme might have come to nothing. Now that he saw that the favor was granted and Don Quixote was eager to set off and make good on his word, he rose and took his lady's hand, and the two of them placed her upon the mule. Don Quixote then mounted Rocinante, and the barber settled himself on his beast. Sancho was left to go on foot, which made him feel anew the loss of his Dapple and his sore need of him. But he bore it all with cheerfulness, being persuaded that his master was well down the path, if not on the verge, of becoming an emperor; for he had no doubt at all that he would marry this princess and, at the very least, become king of Micomicón.

The only thing that troubled him was the reflection that this kingdom was in the land of blacks, and that the people they would give him for vassals would all be black. But for this his imagination soon found a remedy. He said to himself, "What is it to me if my vassals are blacks? What more do I have to do than make a cargo of them and carry them to Spain, where I can sell them and get paid in cash, and with the money buy some title or office and live out my days in ease?[5] Nothing at all, unless you fall asleep or lack the talent or skill in business to sell three, six, or ten thousand vassals in the blink of an eye. By God, I'll make them disappear, one at a time or all together as I'm able. However black they might be, I'll turn them white or yellow![6] Come now, what a thumb-sucker I am!"[7]

And so he walked on, so determined and so content that he forgot all about the hardship of traveling on foot.

Cardenio and the priest were watching all this from among some bushes, not knowing how to join the others; but the priest, who was a great schemer, soon hit upon a way of carrying out their plan. With a pair of scissors he had in a case, he quickly cut off Cardenio's beard, put on him a gray capelet[8] of his own, and handed him a black cloak, leaving himself in his breeches and doublet.[9] Cardenio's appearance was so altered from what it had been that he would not have recognized himself in a mirror. Although the others had gone on ahead while they were disguising themselves, when their work was finished, they had no trouble getting to the king's highway before them, for the brambles and difficult crossings they encountered did not allow those on horseback to go as fast as those on foot. They then posted themselves on the level ground at the foot of the sierra.

As soon as Don Quixote and his companions emerged from the woods, the priest began to examine him very deliberately, making a show of trying to

[5] *What more do I . . . my days in ease:* Slavery was one of the bleak realities of early modern Spain, and as Sancho's scheme reveals, a source of wealth for those who traded in humans. Cervantes would have been familiar with the slave market in Seville, Spain's largest. The slavery Sancho contemplates here resembles the chattel slavery common to the New World, where sub-Saharan Africans were captured and subjected to forced labor with little possibility of returning home.

[6] *white or yellow:* the colors of silver and gold.

[7] *what a thumb-sucker I am:* "what a fool I am".

[8] *capelet:* over-the-shoulder cape extending to the mid-torso.

[9] *doublet: jubón,* close-fitting jacket worn in Europe from the late Middle Ages until the mid-seventeenth century. In Cervantes' Spain, it was short-waisted and considered everyday wear among men of substance.

recognize him. After having stared at him for some time, he hastened toward his friend with open arms exclaiming, "A happy meeting with the mirror of chivalry, my worthy compatriot Don Quixote of La Mancha, the flower and cream of high breeding, the protection and relief of the distressed, the quintessence of knights-errant!" And so saying, he clasped in his arms the knee of Don Quixote's left leg.

Don Quixote, astonished at the stranger's words and behavior, looked at him attentively, and at length recognized him, very much surprised to see him there, and made great efforts to dismount. This, however, the priest would not allow, to which Don Quixote said, "Permit me, señor licentiate, for it is not fitting that I should be on horseback and so reverend a person as your worship on foot."

"On no account will I allow it," said the priest. "Your mightiness must remain on horseback, for it is on horseback you achieve the greatest deeds and adventures that have been beheld in our age. As for me, an unworthy priest, it will serve me well enough to mount on the haunches of one of the mules of these gentlefolk who accompany your worship, if they have no objection, and I will consider myself mounted on the steed Pegasus,[10] or on the zebra or charger that bore the famous Moor Muzaraque, who to this day lies enchanted in the great hill of Zulema, a little distance from the great Complutum."[11]

"The thought didn't occur to me, señor licentiate," answered Don Quixote. "I know it will be the good pleasure of my lady the princess, out of love for me, to order her squire to give up the saddle of his mule to your worship, and he can sit behind, if the beast will bear it."

"It will, I am sure," said the princess, "and I am sure, too, that I need not order my squire, for he is too courteous and considerate to allow a churchman to go on foot when he might be mounted."

"That he is," said the barber, and at once alighting, he offered his saddle to the priest, who accepted it without much entreaty. Unfortunately, as the barber was mounting from behind, the mule, which happened to be a hired one (which is to say, inferior), lifted its hind hoofs and let fly a couple of kicks in the air. Had the kicks landed on Master Nicholas' chest or head, the beast would have left him wishing his expedition in search of Don Quixote to the devil. As it was, they took him by such surprise that he stumbled to the ground, giving so little heed to his beard that it fell off. All he could do when he found himself without it was to cover his face hastily with both hands and moan that his teeth were knocked out.

Don Quixote, when he saw the entire bushy beard detached from the face of the fallen squire without having taken his jaws or blood with it, exclaimed, "By the living God, this is a great miracle! It has knocked off and plucked away the beard from his face as if it had been deliberately shaved off."

[10] *steed Pegasus:* winged stallion of Greek mythology whom the hero Bellerophon tamed and rode in his exploits against ancient monsters such as the Chimera.

[11] *Moor Muzaraque ... Zulema, a little distance from the great Complutum:* Nothing is known of the Moor Muzaraque. Zulema is a hill south of Alcalá de Henares (the Roman Complutum), outside Madrid.

The priest, seeing the danger of discovery that threatened his scheme, at once pounced upon the beard and with it hurried to where Master Nicholas lay, still uttering moans. Bringing the barber's head to his breast, he put the beard on in an instant, muttering over him some words that he said were a certain special spell for sticking on beards, as they would see. As soon as he had reattached it he left him, and the squire appeared well bearded and whole as before. At this Don Quixote was astonished beyond measure. He begged the priest to teach him that spell when he had an opportunity, as he was persuaded its virtue must extend beyond the sticking on of beards; for it was clear that where the beard had been stripped off, the flesh must have been torn and lacerated, and if the spell could heal all that, it must be good for more than beards.

"And so it is," said the priest, and he promised to teach it to him at the first opportunity. They then agreed that for the present that the priest should mount and that the three should ride by turns until they reached the inn, which was probably about six leagues from where they were.

With three of them mounted (that is to say, Don Quixote, the princess, and the priest) and three on foot (Cardenio, the barber, and Sancho Panza), Don Quixote said to the damsel, "My lady, let your highness lead on whithersoever is most pleasing to you."

But before she could answer the licentiate said, "Toward what kingdom would your ladyship direct our course? Is it perchance toward that of Micomicón? It must be, or else I know little about kingdoms."

She, being ready on all points, understood that she was to answer "Yes," so she said "Yes, señor, my way lies toward that kingdom."

"In that case," said the priest, "we must pass right through my village. There your worship will take the road to Cartagena,[12] where you will be able to embark, fortune favoring. And if the wind is fair and the sea smooth and calm, in somewhat less than nine years you may come in sight of the great lake Meona, I mean Maeotis,[13] which is little more than a hundred days' journey this side of your highness' kingdom."

"Your worship is mistaken, señor," said she, "for it is not two years since I set out from it, and though I never had good weather, nevertheless I am here to behold what I so longed for, and that is my lord Don Quixote of La Mancha, whose fame came to my ears as soon as I set foot in Spain and impelled me to go in search of him, to commend myself to his courtesy, and entrust the justice of my cause to the might of his invincible arm."

"Enough! No more praise!" cried Don Quixote at this. "For I hate all flattery; and though this may not be so, still language of the kind is offensive to my chaste ears. I will only say, señora, that whether my arm has might or not, that which it may or may not have shall be devoted to your service even to death. And now,

[12] *Cartagena:* port city on Spain's southeast Mediterranean coast, base of the royal galleys.

[13] *Maeotis:* ancient name for the Sea of Azov, a shallow body of water in Eastern Europe that forms a northern extension of the Black Sea.

leaving this to its proper season, I would ask the señor licentiate to tell me what it is that has brought him into these parts, alone, unattended, and so lightly clad that I am filled with amazement."

"I will answer that briefly," replied the priest. "You must know then, Señor Don Quixote, that Master Nicholas, our friend and barber, and I were going to Seville to receive some money that a relative of mine who went to the Indies many years ago had sent me, and not such a small sum but that it was over sixty thousand *pesos ensayados*, which is worth twice that.[14] Passing by this place yesterday, we were attacked by four brigands, who stripped us right down to our beards, which they so stripped off that the barber found it necessary to put on a false one. Even this young man here," he said, pointing to Cardenio, "they left in a sorry state. But the best of it is (so it is being reported in these parts) that those who attacked us belong to a number of galley slaves who, they say, were set free almost on the very same spot by a man of such bravery that, in spite of the commissary and the guards, he released the lot of them. Beyond all doubt he must have been out of his senses, or he must be as great a scoundrel as they, or some man without heart or conscience to let the wolf loose among the sheep, the fox among the hens, the fly among the honey. He has defrauded justice, and opposed his king and lawful master, for he opposed his just commands. He has, I say, robbed the galleys of their feet, stirred up the Holy Brotherhood, which for many years past has been quiet, and, lastly, has done a deed by which his soul may be lost without any gain to his body."

Sancho had told the priest and the barber of the adventure of the galley slaves, which his master had achieved to his great fame. The priest in alluding to it thus made the most of the incident to see what would be said or done by Don Quixote, who changed color at every word, not daring to say that it was he who had been the liberator of those worthy people. "These, then," said the priest, "were they who robbed us; and God in his mercy pardon him who would not let them go to the punishment they deserved."

[14] *over sixty thousand* pesos ensayados, *which is worth twice that:* The *peso ensayado*, valued at 450 maravedis, was the accounting unit used in the Spanish Indies for large-scale transactions involving assayed bars of gold and silver, as well as the royal taxes levied on them. Due to the exchange rates the Crown imposed in Castile, precious metals were chronically undervalued relative to their market value elsewhere in Europe, prompting the outflow of these metals to foreign economies where they commanded higher prices.

CHAPTER XXX

WHICH TELLS OF THE CLEVER SCHEME ADOPTED TO EXTRICATE OUR LOVE-STRICKEN KNIGHT FROM THE SEVERE PENANCE HE HAD IMPOSED UPON HIMSELF

The priest had hardly ceased speaking when Sancho said, "In all truth, señor licentiate, the one who did that deed was my master; and it was not because I didn't tell him beforehand and warn him to be careful what he was doing, and that it was a sin to set them at liberty, seeing as they were all on the march because they were notorious scoundrels."

"Blockhead!" exclaimed Don Quixote at this. "It is no business or concern of knights-errant to inquire whether any persons in affliction, in chains, or oppressed that they may meet on the road go that way and suffer as they do because of their faults or because of their misfortunes. It only concerns them to aid them as persons in need of help, having regard to their sufferings and not to their villainy. I encountered a rosary or string of miserable and unfortunate people and did for them what my sense of duty demands of me. Let the rest be what it may. Whoever takes objection to it, excepting the sacred dignity of the señor licentiate and his honored person, I say he knows little about chivalry and lies like a filthy bastard, and I will have him understand this in further detail at the tip of my sword." So saying he settled himself in his stirrups and pressed down his morion,[1] for the barber's basin (which according to him was Mambrino's helmet), he carried hanging from the back of his saddle until he could repair the damage done to it by the galley slaves.

Dorotea, who was astute and quick-witted, by this time thoroughly understood Don Quixote's mad condition and that everyone except Sancho Panza was making fun of him. Not wanting to be excluded, she said to him, on observing his irritation, "Sir knight, remember the favor you have promised me, and that in accordance with it you must not engage in any other adventure, be it ever so pressing. Calm yourself, for if the licentiate had known that the galley slaves had been set free by that unconquered arm he would have stopped his mouth thrice over, or even bitten his tongue three times before he would have said a word that tended toward disrespect of your worship."

[1] *morion:* See footnote 22, page 28.

"That I swear heartily," said the priest, "and I would have even plucked a hair from my mustache."[2]

"I will hold my peace, señora," said Don Quixote, "and I will curb the natural anger that had arisen in my breast, and will proceed in peace and quietness until I have fulfilled my promise. But in return for this consideration I entreat you to tell me, if you have no objection to do so, what is the nature of your trouble, and how many, who, and what are the persons of whom I am to require due satisfaction and on whom I am to take vengeance on your behalf?"

"That I will do with all my heart," replied Dorotea, "if it will not be wearisome to you to hear of miseries and misfortunes."

"It will not be wearisome, señora," said Don Quixote.

To this Dorotea replied, "Well, if that is so, give me your attention."

As soon as she said this, Cardenio and the barber drew close to her side, eager to hear what sort of story the quick-witted Dorotea would invent for herself. Sancho did the same, for he was as much taken in by her as his master. She, having settled herself comfortably in the saddle, and with the help of coughing and other preliminaries having taken time to think, began with great liveliness of manner in this fashion:

"First of all, I would have you know, sirs, that my name is—" and here she stopped for a moment, for she forgot the name the priest had given her.

But he came to her relief, seeing what her difficulty was, and said, "It is no wonder, señora, that your highness should be confused and embarrassed in telling the tale of your misfortunes. Such afflictions often have the effect of depriving the sufferers of memory so that they do not even remember their own names, as is the case now with your ladyship, who has forgotten that she is called the Princess Micomicona, lawful heiress of the great kingdom of Micomicón. With this cue your highness may now recall to your sorrowful recollection all you may wish to tell us."

"That is the truth," said the damsel, "but I think from now on I shall have no need of any prompting, and I shall bring my true story safe into port. The tale is thus: The king my father, who was called Tinacrio the Sage,[3] was very learned in what they call magic arts and became aware by his craft that my mother, who was called Queen Jaramilla,[4] was to die before he did, and that soon after he too was to depart this life, and I was to be left an orphan without father or mother. All this, he declared, did not so much grieve him as his certain knowledge that a prodigious giant, the lord of a great island close to our kingdom, Pandafilando of the Wild Eye[5] by name—for it is averred that, though his eyes are properly placed and straight, he always looks askew as if he squinted, and this he does out

[2] *plucked a hair from my mustache:* Tugging at the end of one's mustache was a popular way to seal an oath or threat.

[3] *Tinacrio the Sage:* character from Pedro de la Sierra's sequel to *The Knight of Phoebus*.

[4] *Jaramilla:* diminutive of Jarama, river outside Madrid.

[5] *Pandafilando of the Wild Eye:* Pandafilando is an amalgam of underworld slang that suggests something like "Thieving Con Artist".

of malignity, to strike fear and terror into those he looks at. My father knew, I say, that this giant on becoming aware of my orphan condition would overrun my kingdom with a mighty force and strip me of everything, not leaving me even a small village to shelter me; but that I could avoid all this ruin and misfortune if I were willing to marry him. As far as he could see, however, he never expected that I would consent to a marriage so unequal. He said no more than the truth in this, for it has never entered my mind to marry that giant, or any other, let him be ever so great or enormous. My father said, too, that when he was dead and I saw Pandafilando about to invade my kingdom, I was not to wait and attempt to defend myself, for that would be ruinous to me, but that I should leave the kingdom entirely open to him if I wished to avoid the death and total destruction of my good and loyal vassals, for there would be no possibility of defending myself against the giant's devilish power. Instead, I should at once with some of my followers set out for Spain, where I should obtain relief in my distress on finding a certain knight-errant whose fame by that time would extend over the whole kingdom and who would be called, if I remember rightly, Don Azote[6] or Don Gigote."[7]

"*Don Quixote*, he must have said, señora," observed Sancho at this, "otherwise called the Knight of the Woeful Countenance."

"That's it," said Dorotea. "He said, moreover, that he would be tall of stature and lank featured and that on his right side under the left shoulder, or thereabouts, he would have a gray mole with hairs like bristles."

On hearing this, Don Quixote said to his squire, "Come here, Sancho my son, and help me to strip down, for I want to see if I am the knight that sage king foretold."

"What does your worship want to strip down for?" said Dorotea.

"To see if I have that mole your father spoke of," answered Don Quixote.

"There is no need to strip down," said Sancho, "for I know your worship has just such a mole on the middle of your backbone, which is the mark of a strong man."

"That suffices," said Dorotea, "for 'with friends we must not look too closely into trifles.' Whether it be on the shoulder or on the backbone matters little. It is enough if there is a mole, wherever it may be, for it is all the same flesh. No doubt my good father hit the mark in every particular, and I have hit the mark in commending myself to Don Quixote. He is surely the one my father spoke of, as the features of his countenance correspond with those assigned to this knight by that wide fame he has acquired not only in Spain but in all La Mancha; for I had scarcely landed at Osuna when I heard such accounts of his achievements that at once my heart told me he was the very one I had come in search of."

"But how did you land at Osuna, señora," asked Don Quixote, "when it is not a seaport?"[8]

[6] *Azote:* smack of the hand or blow with a lash.

[7] *Gigote:* stew made from roasted or fried pieces of meat, usually lamb, chopped up and served in a sauce.

[8] *Osuna . . . not a seaport:* Osuna, in Andalusia, is about fifty miles from the coast of Spain.

But before Dorotea could reply the priest anticipated her, saying, "The princess meant to say that after she had landed at Málaga the first place where she heard of your worship was Osuna."

"That is what I meant to say," said Dorotea.

"And that would be only natural," said the priest. "Will your majesty please proceed?"

"There is no more to add," said Dorotea, "save that in finding Don Quixote I have had such good fortune that I already regard myself queen and mistress of my entire dominions, since of his courtesy and magnanimity he has granted me the favor of accompanying me whithersoever I may conduct him, which will be only to bring him face to face with Pandafilando of the Wild Eye, that he may slay him and restore to me what has been unjustly usurped by him. All this must come to pass to the letter, since my good father Tinacrio the Sage foretold it. He likewise left it declared in writing in Chaldean or Greek characters (for I cannot read them), that if this knight he prophesied, after having cut the giant's throat, should be inclined to marry me I was to offer myself at once as his lawful wife without objection and yield him possession of my kingdom together with my person."

"What think you now, friend Sancho?" said Don Quixote at this. "Did you hear what she said? And did I not tell you so? See how we have already got a kingdom to govern and a queen to marry!"

"Cursed be the fool," said Sancho, "who doesn't marry her after slitting Señor Pandahilado's windpipe! Why, she's not a bad queen at all. I wish the fleas in my bed were more like her!" And so saying he slapped his sides and leaped for joy and then ran to seize the bridle of Dorotea's mule. Bringing it to a halt, he fell on his knees before her, begging her to give him her hand to kiss as a sign that he acknowledged her his queen and mistress.

Which of the bystanders could not have helped laughing to see the madness of the master and the simplicity of the servant? Dorotea, of course, gave her hand, and promised to make him a great lord in her kingdom, when Heaven should be so good as to permit her to recover and enjoy it, for which Sancho returned thanks in words that set them all laughing again.

"This, sirs," continued Dorotea, "is my story. It only remains to tell you that of all the attendants I took with me from my kingdom I have none left except this well-bearded squire, for all were drowned in a great tempest we encountered when in sight of port. He and I came to land on a couple of planks as if by a miracle. Indeed, the whole course of my life is a miracle and a mystery as you may have observed. If I have been tedious in any respect or not as precise as I ought, let the blame fall on what the licentiate said at the beginning of my tale, that constant and excessive troubles deprive the sufferers of their memory."

"They shall not deprive me of mine, exalted and worthy princess," said Don Quixote, "however great and unparalleled those troubles that I shall endure in your service may be. Here I confirm anew the favor I have promised you: I swear to go with you to the end of the world until I find myself in the presence of your fierce enemy, and with the help of God and the aid of my arm I will cut off his haughty head with the edge of this . . . I cannot say 'good sword,' thanks to Ginés de Pasamonte, who carried off mine"—this he said between his teeth, and then continued—"and when it has been cut off and you have been put in peaceful possession of your realm, it shall be left to your own decision to dispose of your person as may be most pleasing to you. For so long as my memory is occupied, my will enslaved, and my understanding enthralled by her.... I say no more. It is impossible for me for a moment to contemplate marriage, even with a phœnix."[9]

The last words of his master about not wanting to marry were so disagreeable to Sancho that raising his voice he exclaimed with great irritation, "On my word, Señor Don Quixote, I swear that you are out of your mind. How can your worship possibly object to marrying such an exalted princess as this? Do you think you're going to find the good fortune being offered to you now around every corner? Is my lady Dulcinea more beautiful, by any chance? Not her, not half as beautiful. I'll go as far as to say that she doesn't come up to the shoe of this lady here. A miserable chance I have of getting that county I'm waiting for if your worship goes looking for dainties at the bottom of the sea. In the devil's name, marry, marry, and take this kingdom that's been dropped into your lap. And when you are king, make me a marquis or governor of a province. As for the rest, let the devil take it."

Don Quixote could not endure to hear these blasphemies uttered against his lady Dulcinea. Lifting his spear, and without saying anything to Sancho or uttering a word, he gave him two such thwacks that he brought him to the ground. Had it not been that Dorotea cried out to spare him, he would have no doubt taken his life on the spot.

He said to Sancho after a pause, "Do you think, you scurvy peasant, that you will always be permitted to disrespect me,[10] that you are to be always offending and I always pardoning? Do not believe it, impious scoundrel, for beyond a doubt that is what you are, since you have set your tongue going against the peerless Dulcinea. Know you not, lout, vagabond, beggar, that were it not for the might she infuses into my arm I should not have strength enough to kill a flea? Tell me, scoffer with a viper's tongue, what do you think has won this kingdom and cut off this giant's head and made you a marquis—for all this I count as already accomplished and decided—but the might of Dulcinea, employing my arm as the instrument of her achievements? She fights in me and conquers in me, and I live and breathe in her, and owe my life and being to her.[11] You wicked bastard, how ungrateful you are! You see yourself raised from the dust of the earth to be a titled lord, and in return for so great a benefit you speak ill of the one who gave it you!"

Sancho was not so stunned that he failed to hear all his master said. Rising rather hurriedly, he ran to place himself behind Dorotea's palfrey, and from there he said to his master, "Tell me, señor: if your worship is resolved not to marry this great princess, it's obvious the kingdom will not be yours. And without the kingdom, how can you bestow rewards on me? That's what I'm complaining about.

[9] *phœnix:* symbol of all that is superlative.

[10] *disrespect me:* "stick your hand in my crotch".

[11] *I live and breathe in her, and owe my life and being to her:* See Acts 17:28: "In [God] we live and move and have our being."

Let your worship marry this queen without a second thought, now that we've got her here with us as if showered down from heaven. Afterwards, you can go back to my lady Dulcinea, for there must have been kings in the world who kept mistresses. As far as beauty is concerned, I'll hold my peace. If truth be told, I like them both, though I've never seen Lady Dulcinea."

"How have you never seen her, blasphemous traitor?" cried Don Quixote. "Have you not just now brought me a message from her?"

"I mean," said Sancho, "that I did not have a chance to look her over so carefully that I could notice her beauty in detail or her charms one by one. But from the glance I had, I like her."

"Now I forgive you," said Don Quixote. "I ask that you forgive me the injury I have done you; for our first impulses are not in our control."

"That I see," replied Sancho. "Just like with me the desire to speak is a first impulse. I can't help saying, at least once, what comes to mind."

"For all that, Sancho," said Don Quixote, "take heed of what you say, 'for the pitcher goes so often to the well ...'[12]—I need say no more."

"Well, then," said Sancho, "God is in heaven and sees every trick. He'll judge who does the most evil: me in not speaking right or your worship in not doing it."

"That is enough," said Dorotea. "Run, Sancho, and kiss your lord's hand and beg his pardon, and henceforward be more circumspect with your praise and abuse. Say nothing in disparagement of that Lady Toboso, of whom I know nothing save that I am her servant; and put your trust in God, for you will not fail to obtain some estate so that you may live like a prince."

Sancho advanced hanging his head and begged his master's hand, which Don Quixote presented to him with dignity, giving him his blessing as soon as he had kissed it. He then told him to go on ahead a little, as he had questions to ask and matters of great importance to discuss with him. Sancho obeyed, and when the two had gone some distance in advance, Don Quixote said to him, "Since your return I have had no opportunity or time to ask you many particulars touching your mission and the answer you have brought back. Now that chance has granted us the time and opportunity, deny me not the happiness you can give me by such good news."

"Let your worship ask what you will," answered Sancho. "I'll find a way out just like I found a way in. But I beg of you, señor, not to be so revengeful in the future."

"Why do you say that, Sancho?" said Don Quixote.

"I say it," he returned, "because those blows just now were more because of the quarrel the devil stirred up between us both the other night than for what I said against my lady Dulcinea, who I love and reverence as I would a relic—even if I'm not obliged to—for no other reason than that she's your worship's lady."

"Say no more on that subject for your life, Sancho," said Don Quixote, "for it is displeasing to me. I have already pardoned you, and you know the common saying, 'For a fresh sin, a fresh penance.'"

[12] *for the pitcher goes so often to the well ...:* "... that it finally breaks" (proverb).

While they went along conversing in this fashion, the priest observed to Dorotea that she had shown great cleverness, both in the story itself as in its conciseness, and the resemblance it bore to those of the books of chivalry. She said that she had many times amused herself reading them, but that she did not know where the provinces or seaports were, and so she had said without being sure that she had landed at Osuna.

"So I saw," said the priest, "and for that reason I made haste to say what I did, by which it was all set right. But is it not a strange thing to see how readily this unhappy gentleman believes all these figments and lies, simply because they are in the style and manner of the absurdities of his books?"

"So it is," said Cardenio, "and so strange and unheard of, that were one to attempt to invent and concoct it in fiction, I doubt if there would be any wit keen enough to imagine it."

"Another strange thing about it," said the priest, "is that, apart from the silly things that this worthy gentleman says in connection with his madness, when other subjects are brought up, he can discuss them in a perfectly rational manner, showing that his mind is quite clear and composed—so that, provided his chivalry is not touched upon, no one would take him to be anything but a man of thoroughly sound understanding."

While they were holding this conversation, Don Quixote continued his with Sancho, saying, "Friend Panza, let us forgive and forget our quarrels. Tell me now, dismissing anger and irritation, where, how, and when did you find Dulcinea? What was she doing? What did you say to her? What did she answer? How did she look when she was reading my letter? Who copied it out for you? And everything else in the matter that seems to you worth knowing, asking, and learning—neither adding nor falsifying to give me pleasure, nor depriving me of pleasure by cutting the story short."

"Señor," replied Sancho, "truth be told, nobody copied out the letter for me, for I carried no letter at all."

"It is as you say," said Don Quixote, "for the notebook in which I wrote it I found in my own possession two days after your departure, which gave me very great vexation, as I knew not what you would do on finding yourself without any letter. I was certain you would return from the place where you first missed it."

"That's what I would have done," said Sancho, "if I hadn't learned it by heart when your worship read it to me. I was able to repeat it to a sacristan, who took down my thoughts so precisely that he said in all the days of his life, though he had read many a letter of excommunication, he had never seen or read so pretty a letter as that."

"And do you still have it memorized, Sancho?" asked Don Quixote.

"No, señor," replied Sancho, "for as soon as I had repeated it, seeing there was no further use for the letter, I set about forgetting it. If I recollect anything, it's that part about 'Sullied,' I mean to say 'Sovereign Lady,' and the end 'Yours till death, the Knight of the Woeful Countenance.' Between those two parts, I put in 'my soul' and 'my life' and 'my eyes" some three hundred times."

CHAPTER XXXI

OF THE DELECTABLE DISCUSSION BETWEEN DON QUIXOTE AND SANCHO PANZA, HIS SQUIRE, TOGETHER WITH OTHER INCIDENTS

"All that is not unsatisfactory to me," said Don Quixote. "Go on. Did you reach her; and what was that queen of beauty doing? Surely you found her stringing pearls or embroidering some adornment in gold thread for this her enslaved knight."[1]

"I did not," said Sancho, "but I found her winnowing two bushels of wheat in the yard of her house."

"Then depend upon it," said Don Quixote, "the grains of that wheat were pearls when touched by her hands. Did you look, friend? Was it white wheat or brown?"

"Neither," said Sancho. "It was red."[2]

"Then, beyond a doubt, I promise you," said Don Quixote, "that, winnowed by her hands, it made the whitest bread. But go on. When you gave her my letter, did she kiss it? Did she place it on her head? Did she perform any ceremony befitting it? What did she do?"

"When I went to give it to her," replied Sancho, "she was hard at it thrashing a big pile of wheat in the sieve. She said to me, 'Lay the letter, friend, on the top of that sack, for I can't read it until I've finished sifting all this."

"Discreet lady!" said Don Quixote. "That was in order to read it at her leisure and enjoy it. Proceed, Sancho. While she was engaged in her work, what conversation did she hold with you? What did she ask about me, and what answer did you give? Make haste. Tell me all, and let not a drop be left behind in the inkwell."

"She didn't ask me anything," said Sancho. "But I told her how your worship was left doing penance in her service, naked from the waist up, off in these mountains like a savage, sleeping on the ground, not eating bread off a tablecloth and not combing your beard, weeping and cursing your fortune."

"In saying I cursed my fortune you spoke ill," said Don Quixote, "for rather do I bless it and shall bless it all the days of my life for having made me worthy of aspiring to love so lofty a lady as Dulcinea del Toboso."

"And so lofty is she," said Sancho, "that she's more than a hand's-breadth taller than me."

"What! Sancho," said Don Quixote, "did you measure yourself with her?"

[1] *adornment in gold thread for this her enslaved knight:* device or insignia worn by a knight.
[2] *red:* Red wheat was the least valued variety.

"I measured it like this," said Sancho. "When I was going to help her to put a sack of wheat on the back of a donkey, we came so close together that I could see she stood more than a good palm over me."

"Then it must be true," said Don Quixote, "that along with her imposing presence she is adorned with a thousand million charms of mind! But one thing you will not deny, Sancho: when you came close to her, did you not perceive a Sabæan odor,[3] an aromatic fragrance, a, I know not what, delicious, that I cannot find a name for—I mean a redolence, an exhalation, as if you were in the shop of some dainty glover?"[4]

"All I can say is," said Sancho, "that I did notice a little something, like the smell of a man. It must have been that she was all sweaty and greasy with hard work."

"It could not be that," said Don Quixote. "You must have been suffering from a head cold, or perhaps you smelled yourself. For I know well what would be the scent of that rose among thorns, that lily of the field, that liquid amber."

"Maybe so," replied Sancho. "There often comes from myself that odor, which in the moment seemed to come from her grace, Lady Dulcinea. But that's no wonder, for 'one devil is like another.'"

"Well then," continued Don Quixote, "she finished sifting the wheat and sent it to the mill. What did she do when she read the letter?"

"As for the letter," said Sancho, "she didn't read it, for she said she could neither read nor write. Instead, she tore it up into small pieces, saying that she did not want to let anyone read it out of fear that her secrets would get out, and that it was enough what I had related to her about the love your worship bore her and the extraordinary penance you were doing for her. To make an end of it, she told me to tell your worship that she kissed your hands and that she had a greater desire to see you than to write to you; and that therefore she entreated and commanded you, in sight of the present communication,[5] to come out of these woods, and to put an end to these absurdities, and to set out at once for El Toboso, unless something else of greater importance should happen, for she had a great desire to see your worship. She laughed heartily when I told her how your worship was called The Knight of the Woeful Countenance. I asked her if that Biscayan the other day had been there, and she told me he had and that he was an honest fellow. I also asked her about the galley slaves, but she said she had not seen any as yet."

"So far all goes well," said Don Quixote. "But tell me, what jewel was it that she gave you on taking your leave in return for your tidings of me? For it is a well-known ancient custom with knights and ladies errant to give the squires, damsels, or dwarfs who bring tidings of their ladies to the knights, or of their knights to the ladies, some rich jewel as a recompense for good news and acknowledgment of the message."

[3] *Sabæan odor:* The ancient kingdom of Sheba (Saba) in southern Arabia was renowned for its incense and perfumes.

[4] *dainty glover:* Glovers treated the leather used to make gloves with perfume.

[5] *in sight of the present communication:* a legal phrase.

"That is very likely," said Sancho, "and a good custom it was, to my mind. But that must have been in days gone by. These days it would seem to be the custom only to give a piece of bread and cheese—because that was what my lady Dulcinea handed me over the top of the yard when I took leave of her. It was sheep's milk cheese, to be precise."

"She is generous in the extreme," said Don Quixote, "and if she did not give you a jewel of gold, no doubt it must have been because she had not one on hand to give you. But 'gifts are good after Easter.'[6] I shall see her, and all shall be made right. But do you know what amazes me, Sancho? It seems to me you must have gone and come back through the air, for it took you little more than three days to go to El Toboso and return, though it is more than thirty leagues from here to there. I am inclined to think from this that the sage enchanter who is my friend and watches over my interests (for by necessity there is and must be one, or else I should not be a proper knight-errant), that this same wizard, I say, must have helped you travel without your knowledge. For some of these wizards will snatch up a knight-errant sleeping in his bed, and without his knowing how or in what way it happened, he wakes up the next day more than a thousand leagues away from the place where he went to sleep. If it were not for this, knights-errant would not be able to give aid to one another in peril, as they do at every turn.

"It may be that a knight is fighting in the mountains of Armenia with some dragon or ferocious monster or another knight and gets the worst of the battle and is at the point of death. When he least expects it, there appears on a cloud or chariot of fire another knight, a friend of his, who just before had been in England and who takes his part and delivers him from death. At night he finds himself in his own quarters dining very much to his satisfaction; and yet from one place to the other will have been two or three thousand leagues. All this is done by the craft and skill of the sage enchanters who take care of those valiant knights. So that, friend Sancho, I find no difficulty in believing that you may have gone from this place to El Toboso and returned in such a short time, since, as I have said, some friendly wizard must have carried you through the air without you perceiving it."

"That must have been it," said Sancho, "for in truth Rocinante went like a gypsy's donkey with quicksilver in his ears."[7]

"Quicksilver, indeed," said Don Quixote, "if not a legion of devils, folk that can travel and make others travel without being weary, whenever the whim seizes them. But putting this aside, what do you think I ought to do about my lady's command to go and see her? For though I feel I am bound to obey her summons, I feel too that I am prevented by the favor I have conceded to the princess who accompanies us, and the law of chivalry compels me to have regard for my word in preference to my desire. On the one hand, the longing to see my lady pursues and harasses me; on the other, my solemn promise and the glory

[6] *gifts are good after Easter:* "what is good now will still be good later".

[7] *gypsy's donkey with quicksilver in his ears:* Gypsy merchants were reputed to make the donkeys they were selling appear more vigorous by placing drops of mercury in their ears.

I shall win in this enterprise urge and call me. But what I think I shall do is to travel with all speed and reach quickly the place where this giant is, and on my arrival I shall cut off his head and establish the princess peacefully in her realm. Thereupon I shall return to behold the light that lightens my senses, to whom I shall make such excuses that she will be led to approve of my delay, for she will see that it entirely tends to increase her glory and fame. For all that I have won, am winning, or shall win by arms in this life, comes to me of the favor she extends to me and because I am hers."

"O what a sad state your worship's brains are in!" cried Sancho. "Tell me, señor, do you mean to travel all that way for nothing and to let slip through your hands so rich and noble a match as this, where the dowry is a kingdom that I have honestly heard reported is more than twenty thousand leagues all around, is generously stocked with what's needed to support human life, and is bigger than Portugal and Castile put together? Peace, for the love of God! Blush for what you've said. Excuse me for saying this, but take my advice: marry at once in the first village where there's a priest; if not, here is our licentiate who will do the business beautifully. Remember, I'm old enough to give advice, and the advice I'm giving fits perfectly. For 'a sparrow in the hand is better than a vulture on the wing,' and 'he who has the good and chooses the bad has good reason to complain when he isn't avenged.'"[8]

"Look here, Sancho," said Don Quixote. "If you are advising me to marry in order that I may become king when I slay the giant and be able to confer rewards on you and give you what I have promised, let me tell you that I shall be able to fulfill your wish very easily without marrying. Before going into battle I will make it a stipulation that if I come out victorious, even if I don't marry, they are to give me a portion of the kingdom so that I may bestow it upon whomever I choose. And when they give it to me, upon whom would you have me bestow it but you?"

"That's plain speaking," said Sancho. "But let your worship take care to choose a place on the seacoast, so that if I'm not pleased with my new life, I can ship off my black vassals and deal with them as I've said. Don't bother going to see my lady Dulcinea right now, your worship. Go and kill this giant, and let us finish off this business; for, by God, I have a feeling it will be one of great honor and profit."

"What you say is right, Sancho," said Don Quixote. "I will take your advice as to accompanying the princess before going to see Dulcinea, but I counsel you not to say anything to anyone, not even to those who are with us, about what we have considered and discussed. For as Dulcinea is so decorous that she does not wish her thoughts to be known, it is not right that I or anyone on my behalf should reveal them."

"Well if that's so," said Sancho, "how is it that your worship makes all those you conquer by your arm go present themselves before my lady Dulcinea, which is the same thing as signing your name to it that you love her and are her lover?

[8] *he who has the good . . . isn't avenged:* Sancho mangles a Spanish proverb beyond sense: "He who has the good and chooses the bad shouldn't complain when things go badly."

And considering that those who go are obliged to kneel before her and say they come from your worship to submit themselves to her, how can the thoughts of both of you be hidden?"

"How silly and simple you are!" said Don Quixote. "Do you not see, Sancho, that this tends to her greater exaltation? You must know that according to our way of thinking in chivalry, it is a high honor for a lady to have many knights-errant in her service, whose thoughts never go beyond serving her for her own sake and who look for no other reward for their great and true devotion than that she should be willing to accept them as her knights."

"It is with that kind of love," said Sancho, "I've heard preachers say we ought to love our Lord, for himself alone, without being moved by the hope of glory or the fear of punishment. For my part, though, I would rather love and serve him for what he can do."

"A devil of a bumpkin you are!" exclaimed Don Quixote. "But what astute things you say now and then. One would think you had gone to school."

"In faith, I can't even read."

Master Nicholas here called out to them to wait a while, as they wanted to halt and drink at a little spring that was there. Don Quixote drew up, not a little to the satisfaction of Sancho, for he was by this time weary of telling so many lies and in dread of his master catching him in one; for though he knew that Dulcinea was a peasant girl of El Toboso, he had never seen her in all his life.

Cardenio had now put on the clothes that Dorotea was wearing when they found her, and though they were not very good, they were far better than those he had left behind. They dismounted together by the side of the spring, and with what the priest had provided himself with at the inn, they all satisfied (though not very well) the keen appetite they brought with them.

While they were so employed, there happened to come by a youth passing on his way, who stopping to examine the party at the spring, the next moment ran to Don Quixote and clasping him round the legs, began to weep in great earnest, saying, "O señor, do you not recognize me? Look at me well. I am that lad Andrés who your worship released from the oak tree where I was tied."

Don Quixote recognized him, and taking his hand he turned to those present and said:

"That your worships may see how important it is to have knights-errant to redress the wrongs and injuries done by tyrannical and wicked men in this world, I may tell you that some days ago passing through a forest, I heard cries and piteous complaints as of a person in pain and distress. I immediately hastened, impelled by my bounden duty, to the quarter whence the plaintive accents seemed to me to proceed, and I found tied to an oak this lad who now stands before you, which in my heart I rejoice at, for his testimony will not permit me to depart from the truth in any detail. He was, I say, tied to an oak, naked from the waist up, and a scoundrel, whom I afterwards found to be his master, was lashing his flesh with the reins of his mare. As soon as I saw him, I asked the reason of so cruel a whipping. The boor replied that he was flogging him because he was his servant and because of carelessness that proceeded from dishonesty rather than stupidity. In reply this boy said, 'Señor, he flogs me only because I ask for my wages.' The master made I know not what speeches and excuses, which, though I listened to them, I did not accept. In short, I compelled the villain to unbind him, and to swear he would take him with him, and pay him real by real, and perfumed into the bargain. Is not all this true, Andrés my son? Did you not witness the authority with which I commanded him and the humility with which he promised to do all I enjoined, specified, and required of him? Answer without hesitation. Tell these gentlemen what took place, that they may ponder well the advantage there is in having knights-errant roam the countryside."

"All that your worship has said is quite true," answered the lad, "but the end of the business turned out just the opposite of what your worship supposes."

"What! The opposite?" cried Don Quixote. "Did not the villain pay you then?"

"Not only did he not pay me," replied the lad, "but as soon as your worship had left the forest and we were alone, he tied me up again to the same oak and gave me a fresh flogging, which left me like a flayed Saint Bartholomew. And every stroke he gave me he followed up with some joke about having made a fool of your worship. If it weren't for the pain I was suffering, I would have laughed at the things he said. In short, he left me in such a condition that I have been until now in a hospital getting cured of the injuries that wicked villain inflicted on me. For all this your worship is to blame; for if you had gone your own way and not come when you weren't called and not meddled in other people's business, my master would have been content with giving me one or two dozen lashes and would have then set me free and paid me what he owed me. But when your worship insulted him and called him so many useless names, his anger was kindled; and since he could not revenge himself on you, as soon as he saw you had left him, the storm burst on me so hard that I wonder if I'm ever going to grow up to be a man."

"The mischief," said Don Quixote, "lay in my going away. I should not have gone until I had seen you paid. I ought to have known well by long experience that there is no rogue who will keep his word if he finds it will not suit him to keep it. But you will remember, Andrés, that I swore if he did not pay you, I would seek him out and find him, though he were to hide in the belly of a whale."

"That's true," said Andrés, "but it's of no use."

"You shall see now whether it's of use or not," said Don Quixote; and so saying, he got up hastily and ordered Sancho to bridle Rocinante, who was grazing as they ate.

Dorotea asked him what he meant to do. He replied that he meant to go in search of that villain and punish him for such wicked behavior and see Andrés paid to the last maravedi, to the dismay of all the villains in the world. To this she replied that he must remember that in accordance with his promise he could not engage in any enterprise until he had completed hers; and that as he knew this better than anyone, he should restrain his zeal until his return from her kingdom.

"That is true," said Don Quixote, "and Andrés must have patience until my return as you say, señora. But I once more swear and promise not to cease until I have seen him avenged and paid."

"I have no faith in those oaths," said Andrés. "I would rather have now something to help me get to Seville than all the revenges in the world. If you have here anything to eat that I can take, give it me. God be with your worship and all knights-errant. And may their errands turn out as well for themselves as they have for me."

Sancho took out from his provisions a piece of bread and another of cheese. Giving them to the lad he said, "Here, take this, brother Andrés, for all of us have a share in your misfortune."

"Why, what share have you got?"

"This share of bread and cheese I'm giving you," answered Sancho. "God knows whether I'll miss it or not; for I would have you know, friend, that we squires to knights-errant have to bear a great deal of hunger and hard fortune and even other things more easily felt than told."

Andrés seized his bread and cheese, and seeing that nobody gave him anything more, bowed his head, and 'took hold of the road,' as the saying goes. It should be noted, however, that before leaving he said, "For the love of God, sir knight-errant, should you ever meet me again, even if you see them cutting me to pieces, do not help me or come to my rescue. Leave me to my misfortune; for it could not possibly be greater than the misfortune of being helped by your worship. May God curse you and every knight-errant the world has ever seen."

Don Quixote was about to get up to punish him, but the boy took to his heels at such a pace that no one attempted to follow. Andrés' story left Don Quixote feeling terribly embarrassed, and the others had to take great care to restrain their laughter so as not to add to his shame.

CHAPTER XXXII

WHICH TREATS OF WHAT BEFELL DON QUIXOTE'S PARTY AT THE INN

Their hearty meal being finished they saddled at once, and without any adventure worth mentioning they reached the inn (the object of Sancho Panza's fear and dread) on the following day. Although he had no desire to go inside the inn, it could not be avoided. When the innkeeper's wife, the innkeeper, their daughter, and Maritornes saw Don Quixote and Sancho coming, they went out to welcome the pair with signs of great contentment, which Don Quixote received with solemn expressions of approval. He bade them make up a better bed for him than the last time, to which the innkeeper's wife replied that if he paid better than he did the last time she would give him one fit for a prince. Don Quixote said he would, so they made up a tolerable one for him in the same garret as before. He lay down at once, battered and dazed.

No sooner was the door shut upon him than the innkeeper's wife made for the barber. Seizing him by the beard she said, "By my faith, you're not going to make a beard of my tail any longer. You must give my tail back to me. It's a shame the way that thing of my husband's goes tossing about on the floor—I mean the comb, which I used to stick in my good tail."[1]

But for all she tugged at it the barber would not give it up—until the licentiate told him to let her have it, as there was now no further need for their ruse. He could make himself known in his own character and tell Don Quixote that he had fled to this inn when those thieves the galley slaves robbed him. Should he ask for the princess' squire, they would tell him that she had sent him on before her to give notice to the people of her kingdom that she was coming and bringing with her the deliverer of them all. On hearing this, the barber cheerfully restored the tail to the innkeeper's wife. They likewise returned all the accessories they had borrowed to work Don Quixote's deliverance. Everyone at the inn was struck with wonder at Dorotea's beauty and even at the fine figure of the shepherd Cardenio. The priest requested that such fare as there was in the inn be prepared for them, and the innkeeper, in hope of better payment, served them up a tolerably good dinner. All this time Don Quixote was asleep, for they thought it best not to waken him, as sleeping would now do him more good than eating.

[1] *By my faith . . . in my good tail:* The tirade delivered by the innkeeper's wife is not without its innuendo.

When dinner was over, the company (which was the innkeeper, his wife, their daughter, Maritornes, and all the travelers) discussed Don Quixote's strange madness and the manner in which they had found him. The innkeeper's wife told them what had taken place between him and the mule driver; and then, looking around to see if Sancho was there—when she saw he was not—she gave them the whole story of his blanketing, which they received with no little amusement. But when the priest observed that it was the books of chivalry Don Quixote read that had addled his brain, the innkeeper said:

"I don't understand how that can be, for to my mind there is no better reading in the world. I have here two or three of them, with other writings that are the very life not only of myself but of many more. For when it is harvest time, the reapers flock here on holidays, and there is always one among them who can read and who takes up one of these books. We gather round him, thirty or more of us, and stay listening to him with a delight that makes our gray hairs grow young again. At least I can say for myself that when I hear of what furious and terrible blows the knights deliver, I am seized with the longing to do the same. I wish I could sit and listen to them night and day."

"And I just as much," said the innkeeper's wife, "because I never have a quiet moment in my house except when you are listening to someone reading, for then you are so distracted that for the time being you forget to scold."

"That's true," said Maritornes. "Faith, I relish hearing these things greatly too, for they are very pretty—especially when they describe some lady or another in the arms of her knight under the orange trees, and the dueña[2] who is keeping watch for them half dead with envy and fright. All this I say is as good as honey."

"And you, what do you think, young lady?" asked the priest, turning to the innkeeper's daughter.

"In all honesty, señor, I don't know," she said. "I listen, too, and to tell the truth, though I don't understand them, I like hearing them. But it's not the blows that my father enjoys that I like, but the laments the knights utter when they are separated from their ladies. Truly, they make me weep sometimes with the pity I feel for them."

"Then would you console them sometimes if they wept for you, young lady?" asked Dorotea.

"I don't know what I would do," said the girl. "I only know that some of those ladies are so cruel that they call their knights tigers and lions and a thousand other awful names. Jesus! I don't know what sort of people they are, so unfeeling and heartless, that rather than offer a glance to a worthy man they leave him to die or go mad. I don't know what the good is of being so fussy. If it's for honor's sake, why not marry them? That's all they want."

"Hush, child," said the innkeeper's wife. "It seems to me you know a great deal about these things. It's not fitting for girls to know or talk so much."

"As the gentleman asked me, I could not help answering him," said the girl.

[2] *dueña:* governess.

"Well then," said the priest, "bring me these books, señor innkeeper, for I should like to see them."

"With all my heart," he said, and going into his own room he brought out an old valise secured with a little chain, on opening which the priest found in it three large books and some manuscripts written in a very good hand. The first that he opened he found to be *Don Cirongilio of Thrace*, the second *Don Felixmarte of Hircania*, and the other *The History of the Great Captain Gonzalo Hernández de Córdoba*, with the *Life of Diego García de Paredes*.[3]

When the priest read the two first titles he looked over at the barber and said, "We need my friend's housekeeper and niece here now."

"Not necessary," said the barber. "I can do just as well to carry them to the yard or to the hearth. There is a very good fire going."

"What! Would your worship burn my books?" exclaimed the innkeeper.

"Only these two," said the priest, "*Don Cirongilio* and *Felixmarte*."

"Are my books, then, heretics or phlegmatics that you want to burn them?" asked the innkeeper.

"*Schismatics* you mean, friend," said the barber, "not *phlegmatics*."

"That's it," said the innkeeper. "If you want to burn any, let it be the one about the Great Captain and the other one about Diego García, for I would rather have a child of mine burned than either of the others."

"Brother," said the priest, "those two books are made up of lies and are full of folly and nonsense; but this book about the Great Captain is a true history and contains the deeds of Gonzalo Hernández de Córdoba, who by his many and great achievements earned the title all over the world of the Great Captain, a famous and illustrious name, and deserved by him alone. And this Diego García de Paredes was a distinguished knight of the city of Trujillo in Extremadura, a most gallant soldier. He had such physical strength that with one finger he stopped a mill wheel in full motion, and while he was posted with a great two-handed sword at the foot of a bridge, he kept the whole of an immense army from passing over it. He achieved such other exploits that if, instead of his relating them himself with the modesty of a knight and of one writing his own history, another writer without constraint or bias had recorded them, they would have thrown into oblivion all the deeds of the Hectors and Achilleses and Rolands."

"Tell that to my father!"[4] said the innkeeper. "As if stopping a mill wheel is something to be astonished at! By God your worship should read what I've read of

[3] Don Cirongilio of Thrace ... Life of Diego García de Paredes: The books in the valise tell stories of military exploits and battlefield heroism, yet fact and fiction are jumbled together. *Cirongilio* and *Felixmarte* are chivalric romances—fancies of the imagination. The third volume is a historical account of Gonzalo Hernández (or Fernández) de Córdoba (1453–1515), the Castilian general celebrated for his victories over the Moors in Granada and in the Italian campaigns. Editions published after 1580 appended the biography of one of his most famous subordinates, Diego García de Paredes (1468–1533), whose feats of strength on the battlefield earned him the epithet "the Spanish Samson". Though more grounded in history, these biographies also contain elements of heroic exaggeration.

[4] *Tell that to my father!*: "As if I care!"

Felixmarte of Hircania, how with one single backstroke he cleft five giants in two through the middle as if they had been made of bean pods like the little friars the children make.[5] Another time he attacked a very great and powerful army with more than one million six hundred thousand soldiers, all armed from head to foot, and he routed them all as if they had been flocks of sheep. And what do you say about the worthy Cirongilio of Thrace, who was so spirited and bold—as you can find out in this book? It says there that as he was sailing along a river there came up against him out of the water a fiery serpent, and he, as soon as he saw it, flung himself on it and got astride its scaly shoulders and squeezed its throat with both hands with such force that the serpent, realizing he was being choked, could do nothing but let itself sink to the bottom of the river, carrying with it the knight who would not let go his hold; and when they got down there he found himself among palaces and gardens so pretty that it was a wonder to see; and then the serpent changed itself into an aged man, who told him such things as were never heard.[6] Hold your peace, señor; for if you were to hear this you would go mad with delight. Two figs for your Great Captain and your Diego García!"

On hearing this Dorotea said in a whisper to Cardenio, "Our innkeeper is almost fit to play a second part to Don Quixote."

"I think so," said Cardenio, "for as he shows, he accepts it as a certainty that everything those books relate took place exactly as it is written down. The discalced friars[7] themselves could not persuade him to the contrary."

"But consider, brother," said the priest once more, "there never was any Felixmarte of Hircania in the world, nor any Cirongilio of Thrace, nor any of the other knights of the same sort that the books of chivalry talk of. The whole thing is the fabrication and invention of idle minds, devised by them for the purpose you describe of passing the time, as your reapers do when they read. I swear to you in all seriousness there never were any such knights in the world, and no such exploits or nonsense ever happened anywhere."

"Try that bone on another dog," said the innkeeper. "As if I didn't know how to count to five, or where my shoe pinches me! Don't think you can feed me that pap, for by God I don't have a foolish hair on my body. It's a fine joke for your worship to try and persuade me that everything these good books say is nonsense and lies when they are printed by the license of the Lords of the Royal Council, as if they were people who would allow such a lot of lies to be printed all together, and so many battles and enchantments that they take away one's senses."[8]

[5] *Bean pods like the little friars the children make:* Children would remove the seed from one end of a bean pod, which made it look like a hooded priest.

[6] *such things as were never heard:* The story the innkeeper relates is not to be found in *Cirongilio of Thrace*.

[7] *discalced friars:* Reformed branches of religious orders like the Discalced Carmelites (1562), whose members were known for going barefoot or in simple sandals, had a reputation for integrity.

[8] *printed by the license . . . take away one's senses:* The innkeeper rightly observes that for a book to be sold it had to receive official approval, but he assumes that approval guarantees that the book's contents are factual. He draws on two common presumptions about

"I have told you, friend," said the priest, "that this is done to distract our idle thoughts. Just as in well-ordered states, where games of chess, ball games, and billiards are allowed for the entertainment of those who are excused from or unable to work, so books of this kind are allowed to be printed on the rightful supposition that no one is so ignorant as to take any of them for true stories. If it were permitted me now and the present company desired it, I could say something about the qualities books of chivalry should possess to be good ones, which would be to the advantage and even to the enjoyment of some. I hope the time will come when I can communicate my ideas to someone who may be able to mend matters. In the meantime, señor innkeeper, believe what I have said; take your books, and come to terms with their truth or falsehood, and much good may they do you. God grant that you do not fall lame of the same foot your guest Don Quixote limps on."

"No fear of that," returned the innkeeper. "I won't be so crazy as to make a knight-errant of myself, for I see well enough that things are not now as they used to be in those days, when they say those famous knights roamed about the world."

Sancho had made his appearance in the middle of this conversation, and he was very much troubled and cast down to hear that knights-errant were things of the past and all the books of chivalry folly and lies. He resolved in his heart to wait and see what came of this journey of his master's, and if it did not turn out as happily as his master expected, he determined to leave him and go back to his wife and children and his ordinary work.

The innkeeper was carrying away the valise and the books when the priest said to him, "Wait—I want to see what those papers are that are written in such a good hand." The innkeeper took them out and handed them to him to read, and the priest saw they were a work of about eight sheets of manuscript. The title, written in large letters at the beginning, read *Novel of the Imprudent Meddler.*[9] The priest read three or four lines to himself and said, "I must say the title of this novel does not seem to me a bad one, and I feel an inclination to read it all."

To this the innkeeper replied, "Then your reverence will do well to read it, for I can tell you that some guests who have read it here have been greatly pleased with it and have begged me to let them take it; but I would not give it up, meaning to return it to the person who forgot the valise, books, and papers here, for perhaps he will return here some time or other. While I know I will miss the books, I certainly mean to return them, for though I'm an innkeeper, I'm still a Christian."

---

authority—the authority of the king and the authority of the written word—and then takes "authoritative" for "true". In the innkeeper's defense, we can say that there was no category for a book that tells a story that didn't actually take place but is plausible enough that it could have. That category is called fiction, and the innkeeper lives inside the book that comes closest to inventing it.

[9] Novel of the Imprudent Meddler: In Cervantes' day, "novel" (from the Italian *novella*) referred to a prose work of intermediate length—typically designed to be read in one or two sittings—that developed a single plot, often centered on amorous intrigue. Cervantes' *Exemplary Novellas* (1613) follow in this tradition, though they expand and subvert it in ways that anticipate the modern short story.

"You are very right, friend," said the priest. "But for all that, if the novel pleases me, you must let me copy it."

"With all my heart," replied the host.

While they were talking, Cardenio had taken up the novel and begun to read it. Forming the same opinion of it as the priest, he begged him to read it so that they all might hear.

"I would read it," said the priest, "if the time would not be better spent in sleeping."

"It will be rest enough for me," said Dorotea, "to while away the time by listening to some tale, for my spirits are not yet calmed enough to let me sleep when it would be seasonable."

"Well, in that case," said the priest, "I will read it, if only out of curiosity. Perhaps it may contain something pleasant."

Master Nicholas added his entreaties to the same effect, and Sancho too; seeing which, and considering that he would give pleasure to all and receive it himself, the priest said, "Well then, give me your attention, everyone, for the novel begins thus...."

CHAPTER XXXIII

IN WHICH IS RELATED *THE NOVEL OF THE IMPRUDENT MEDDLER*

In Florence, a rich and famous city of Italy in the province called Tuscany, there lived two noble and wealthy gentlemen, Anselmo and Lotario, such great friends that by way of distinction they were called by all that knew them "The Two Friends." They were unmarried, young, of the same age and of the same tastes, which was enough to account for the mutual friendship between them. Anselmo, it is true, was somewhat more inclined to seek pleasure in love than Lotario, for whom the pleasures of the hunt had more attraction; but on occasion Anselmo would forego his own tastes to yield to those of Lotario, and Lotario would surrender his to fall in with those of Anselmo, and in this way their inclinations kept pace one with the other with a concord so perfect that the best regulated clock could not surpass it.

Anselmo was madly in love with a beautiful, highborn maiden of the same city, the daughter of parents so estimable, and so estimable herself, that he resolved—with the approval of his friend Lotario, without whom he did nothing—to ask of them her hand in marriage. He did so, with Lotario being the bearer of the demand and conducting the negotiation so much to the satisfaction of his friend that in a short time he was in possession of the object of his desires. For her part, Camila was so happy in having won Anselmo for her husband, that she gave thanks unceasingly to Heaven and to Lotario, by whose means such good fortune had fallen to her. The first few days (those of a wedding being usually days of merrymaking), Lotario frequented his friend Anselmo's house as he had been accustomed, striving to do honor to him and to the occasion and to gratify him in every way he could. But when the wedding days were over and the succession of visits and congratulations had slackened, he began purposely to leave off going to the house of Anselmo. It seemed to him (as it naturally would to all men of sense), that one ought not to visit a friend's house after his marriage with the same frequency he did in his friend's bachelor days. For though true and genuine friendship cannot and should not be in any way doubted, still a married man's honor is a thing of such delicacy that even from brothers it can suffer injury, much more from friends.

Anselmo noted that Lotario's visits had diminished and reproached him sharply, saying that if he had known that marriage was to keep him from enjoying his friend's company as he used to, he would have never married; and that, if by the close relationship the two maintained while he was a bachelor they had earned such a sweet name as that of "The Two Friends," he should not allow a title so estimable and so gratifying to be lost over a needless anxiety to act with caution. He therefore entreated him (if such a phrase was allowable between them) to be once more master of his house and to come in and go out as before, assuring him that his wife Camila had no other desire or inclination than that which he would wish her to have, and that knowing how sincerely they loved one another she was grieved to see such coldness in him.

To all this and much more that Anselmo said to Lotario to persuade him to come to his house as he had been in the habit of doing, Lotario replied with so much prudence, sense, and judgment, that Anselmo was satisfied of his friend's good intentions, and it was agreed that on two days in the week and on holidays Lotario should come to dine with him. Although the two were satisfied with these terms, Lotario resolved to observe them no further than he considered to be in accordance with the honor of his friend, whose good name was more to him than his own. He said, and justly, that a married man upon whom Heaven had bestowed a beautiful wife should consider as carefully what friends he brought to his house as what female friends his wife associated with, for what cannot be done or arranged in the marketplace, at public festivals, or at Mass or other church visits (opportunities that husbands ought not always deny their wives), may be easily seen to in the house of a trusted female friend or relative.

Lotario said, too, that every married man should have some friend who would point out to him any negligence he might be guilty of in his conduct. For it will sometimes happen that owing to the deep affection the husband bears his wife, either he does not caution her, or, not to vex her, refrains from telling her to do or not to do certain things, doing or avoiding which may be a matter of honor or reproach to him. Errors of this kind he could easily correct if warned by a friend.

But where might one find such a friend as Lotario envisions, so wise, so loyal, and so true? Of a truth, I know not. Lotario alone fit the bill, for with the utmost care and vigilance he watched over the honor of his friend, and strove to diminish, stagger, and reduce the number of days for going to his house according to their agreement, lest the visits of a young man, wealthy, highborn, and with the attractions he was conscious of possessing, at the house of a woman so beautiful as Camila, should be regarded with suspicion by the inquisitive and malicious eyes of the idle public. For though his integrity and reputation might bridle slanderous tongues, still he was unwilling to hazard either his own good name or that of his friend. For this reason most of the days agreed upon Lotario devoted to some other business he pretended was unavoidable, so that a great portion of the day was taken up with complaints on one side and excuses on the other.

It happened, however, that on one occasion when the two were strolling together outside the city, Anselmo addressed the following words to Lotario:

"You may suppose, Lotario my friend, that I am unable to give sufficient thanks for the mercies God has rendered me in making me the son of such parents as mine were, and giving freely from his hand what are called the gifts of nature in addition to those of fortune, and above all for what he has done in giving me you for a friend and Camila for a wife—two treasures that I value, if not as highly as I ought, at least as highly as I am able. And yet, with all these good things, which are commonly all that men need to enable them to live happily, I am the most discontented and dissatisfied man in the whole world. For I know not for how long I have been harassed and oppressed by a desire so strange and so unusual, that I wonder at myself and blame and chide myself when I am alone, and strive to stifle it and hide it from my own thoughts—with no better success than if I were endeavoring deliberately to publish it to all the world. As it will soon be made known, I wish to confide it to your safe keeping, feeling sure that by this means, and by your readiness as a true friend to afford me relief, I shall soon find myself freed from the distress it causes me, and that your care will give me happiness in the same degree as my own folly has caused me misery."

Lotario was baffled by Anselmo's words, unable as he was to guess where such a lengthy preamble was leading. Though he tried to imagine what desire it could be that so troubled his friend, his conjectures were all far from the truth. To relieve the anxiety of his bewildered state, he told Anselmo that he was doing a flagrant injustice to their great friendship in seeking roundabout methods of confiding to him, for he well knew that he could trust his friend with his most hidden thoughts, whether for consolation if they were troubling him or for a solution that would put them into practice.

"That is the truth," replied Anselmo, "and with that confidence I will tell you, friend Lotario, that the desire that harasses me is that of knowing whether my wife Camila is as good and as perfect as I think her to be. I cannot satisfy myself of the truth on this point except by testing her in such a way that the trial may prove the purity of her virtue as the fire proves that of gold; for I am persuaded, my friend, that a woman is virtuous only in proportion as she is or is not tempted and that she alone is strong who does not yield to the promises, gifts, tears, and pleas of earnest lovers. What thanks does a woman deserve for being good if no one urges her to be bad, and what wonder is it that she is reserved and circumspect to whom no opportunity is given of going wrong and who knows she has a husband who will take her life the first time he catches her in an impropriety? I do not therefore hold her who is virtuous through fear or lack of opportunity in the same estimation as her who comes out of temptation and trial with a crown of victory.

"For these reasons and many others I could give you to justify the opinion I hold, I desire that my wife Camila should pass through this trial and be refined and tested by the fire of finding herself wooed and by one worthy to set his affections upon her. If she emerges victorious from this struggle, as I believe she will, I shall look upon my good fortune as unequaled. I shall be able to say that the cup of my desire is full and that the virtuous woman of whom the sage says 'Who shall find her?'[1] has fallen to my lot. If the result is contrary to what I expect, the satisfaction of knowing I have been right in my opinion will allow me to bear without complaint the pain that my so dearly bought experience will naturally cause me. And since nothing you may say in opposition to my wish will keep me from carrying it into effect, it is my desire, friend Lotario, that you agree to be the

[1] *Who shall find her:* a reference to Proverbs 31:10: "Who can find a good wife?"

instrument for effecting my desired purpose. I will arrange the opportunities for you to perform your part, and nothing shall be lacking of what I think necessary to pursue a virtuous, honorable, modest, and high-minded woman. I am induced to entrust this arduous task to you, among other reasons, by the consideration that if Camila is to be conquered by you, the conquest will not be pushed to extremes but only far enough to count as accomplished that which, from a sense of honor, should be left undone. In this way, I shall not be wronged in anything more than intention, and my wrong will remain buried in the integrity of your silence, which I know well will be as lasting as that of death in what concerns me. If, therefore, you would have me enjoy what can be called life, you will at once engage in this love struggle, not lukewarmly or sluggishly, but with the energy and zeal that my desire demands and with the trust our friendship guarantees."

Such were the words Anselmo addressed to Lotario, who listened to them with such attention that, except to say what has been already mentioned, he did not open his lips until the other had finished. When he saw that he had no more to say, he stared at him for a while, as one would stare at something never before seen that excited wonder and amazement. Lotario then said to him:

"I cannot persuade myself, Anselmo my friend, that what you have said to me is not in jest. Had I thought you were speaking seriously, I would not have allowed you to go so far, in order that I might put a stop to your long harangue by not listening to you. I truly suspect that either you do not know me, or I do not know you. But no, I know well you are Anselmo, and you know that I am Lotario. The problem is, it seems to me, that you are not the Anselmo you used to be and must have thought that I am not the Lotario I should be. For the things you have said to me are not those of that Anselmo who was my friend, nor are those things you demand of me what should be asked of the Lotario you know. True friends will prove their friends and make use of them, as a poet has said, *usque ad aras*[2]—by which he meant that they will not make use of their friendship in things that are contrary to God's will. If this, then, was a heathen's feeling about friendship, how much more should it be a Christian's, who knows that the divine must not be forfeited for the sake of any human friendship. And if a friend should go so far as to put aside his duty to Heaven to fulfil his duty to his friend, it should not be in matters that are trivial or of little moment but for those matters that affect the friend's life and honor. Now tell me, Anselmo, in which of these two areas are you endangered, that I should put myself at risk to gratify you and do a thing so detestable as what you ask of me? Neither, indeed. On the contrary, you ask of me, as far as I understand, to strive and labor to rob you of honor and life, and to rob myself of them at the same time. For if I take away your honor, it is plain I take away your life, as a man without honor is worse than dead; and if I am the instrument of so much wrong to you, as you would have me be, shall I, too, not be left without honor, and consequently without life? Listen

[2] usque ad aras: Latin, "all the way to the altar", that is, a friend whose loyalty extends to the limits of religion and moral obligation. The expression originates in classical moral philosophy.

to me, Anselmo my friend, and do not be impatient to answer me until I have said what is on my mind regarding the object of your desire, for there will be time enough left for you to reply and for me to hear."

"With pleasure," said Anselmo. "Say what you will."

Lotario then went on to say, "It seems to me, Anselmo, that your current temper of mind is like that of the Moors, who can never be brought to see the error of their creed by quotations from the Holy Scriptures, or by reasons that depend upon the examination of the understanding or are founded upon the articles of faith, but must have examples that are palpable, simple, intelligible, capable of proof, not admitting of doubt, with mathematical demonstrations that cannot be denied, like, 'If equals are taken from equals, the remainders are equal.' If they do not understand this in words (and indeed they do not), it has to be shown to them with the hands and set before their eyes, and even with all this no one succeeds in convincing them of the truth of our holy religion. This same mode of proceeding I shall have to adopt with you, for the desire that has sprung up in you is so absurd and remote from everything that has a semblance of reason, that I feel it would be a waste to spend my time reasoning with your simplicity (for at present I will call it by no other name). I am even tempted to leave you in your folly as a punishment for your pernicious desire; but the friendship I bear you, which will not allow me to desert you in such manifest danger of destruction, keeps me from dealing so harshly with you.

"That you may clearly see this, tell me, Anselmo, have you not asked me to force my suit upon a modest woman, sway one who is virtuous, make overtures to one who is pure-minded, pay court to one who is prudent? Yes, you have told me so. If you know, then, that you have a wife who is modest, virtuous, pure-minded, and prudent, what is it that you seek? And if you believe she will come forth victorious from all my attacks—as doubtless she will—what higher titles than those she possesses now do you think you can bestow upon her, or what more will she be afterwards than she is now? Either you do not hold her to be what you say, or you know not what you demand. If you do not hold her to be what you say, why do you seek to test her instead of treating her as guilty in the way that you deem best? But if she is as virtuous as you believe, it is a fruitless proceeding to put truth itself on trial, for after the trial, it will be esteemed as highly as it was before. Thus, it is conclusively proved that to attempt what may harm rather than benefit us is the work of unreasoning and reckless minds, all the more so when they are things that we are not forced or compelled to attempt, and that herald from afar that it is obvious madness to attempt them.

"Difficulties are attempted either for the sake of God or for the sake of the world, or for both. Those undertaken for God's sake are those that the saints attempt when they commit to live the lives of angels in human bodies; those undertaken for the sake of the world are those of the men who traverse such a vast expanse of water, such a variety of climates, so many strange countries, to acquire what are called the blessings of fortune; and those undertaken for the sake of God and the world together are those of brave soldiers, who no sooner do they see in the enemy's wall a breach as wide as a cannon ball could make, than, casting aside all fear, without hesitating or heeding the manifest peril that threatens them, borne onward by the desire of defending their faith, their country, and their king, they fling themselves dauntlessly into the midst of the thousand competing deaths that await them. Such are the things that men are known to attempt, and there is honor, glory, gain, in attempting them, however full of difficulty and peril they may be. But what you say you wish to attempt and carry out will not win you the glory of God nor the blessings of fortune nor fame among men. For even if you obtain what you desire, you will be no happier, richer, or more honored than you are right now. If it be otherwise, you will be reduced to misery greater than can be imagined, for there will be no advantage in reflecting then that no one is aware of the misfortune that has befallen you; it will suffice to torture and crush you that you know it yourself. In confirmation of this truth, let me recite a stanza composed by the famous poet Luigi Tansillo[3] at the end of the first part of his *Tears of Saint Peter*, which goes thus:

> The anguish and the shame but greater grew
>   In Peter's heart as morning slowly came;
> No eye was there to see him, well he knew,
>   Yet he himself was to himself a shame;
> Exposed to all men's gaze, or screened from view,
>   A noble heart will feel the pang the same;
> A prey to shame the sinning soul will be,
> Though none but heaven and earth its shame can see.

"Thus by keeping it secret you will not escape your sorrow, but rather you will shed tears unceasingly, if not tears of the eyes, tears of blood from the heart, like those shed by that simple doctor our poet tells us of, who underwent the trial of the goblet, which the wise Rinaldo, better advised, refused to do.[4] Though this may be a poetic fiction, it contains a moral lesson worthy of attention and study and imitation. How much more by what I am about to say will you be led to see the great error you wish to commit.

"Tell me, Anselmo, if Heaven or good fortune had made you master and lawful owner of a diamond of the finest quality, with an excellence and purity that satisfied every jeweler who saw it, all saying with a single voice and common consent that in purity, quality, and fineness, it was everything that a stone of the kind could possibly be; if you yourself were of the same belief, as knowing nothing to the contrary, would it be reasonable of you to desire to take that diamond and place it between an anvil and a hammer, and by mere force of blows and strength of arm try if it were as hard and as fine as they said? If you did, and if the stone should resist so silly a test, you would add nothing to its value or reputation. And if it were broken, as it might be, would not all be lost? Undoubtedly it

[3] *Luigi Tansillo:* Italian poet whose poem *Le lagrime de San Pietro* was published in Spanish translation in 1587.

[4] *like those shed . . . refused to do:* In an episode of *Orlando Furioso*, an enchanted goblet spills wine on the man who, having been unfaithful to his lady, attempts to drink from it.

would, leaving its owner to be counted as a fool in the opinion of all. Consider, then, Anselmo my friend, that Camila is a diamond of the finest quality, both in your estimation and in that of others, and that it is contrary to reason to expose her to the risk of being broken. For if she remains intact she cannot rise to a higher value than she now possesses, and if she gives way and is unable to resist, consider now how you will be deprived of her and with what good reason you will berate yourself for having been the cause of her ruin and your own. Remember there is no jewel in the world so precious as a chaste and virtuous woman, and that the whole honor of women consists in reputation. Considering that your wife's reputation is of the highest excellence you can imagine, why should you seek to call that truth in question?

"Remember, my friend, that woman is an imperfect animal, and that impediments are not to be placed in her way to make her trip and fall, but that they should be removed and her path left clear of all obstacles, so that without hindrance she may run her course freely to attain the desired perfection, which consists in being virtuous. Naturalists tell us that the ermine is a little animal which has a fur of purest white and that when the hunters wish to take it, they make use of this artifice: Having determined the places it frequents and passes, they block the way to them with mud, and then rousing it, drive it toward the spot. As soon as the ermine comes to the mud, it halts and allows itself to be taken captive rather than pass through the mire and spoil and sully its whiteness, which it values more than life and liberty. The virtuous and chaste woman is an ermine, and whiter and purer than snow is the virtue of modesty. He who wishes her not to lose it, but to keep and preserve it, must adopt a course different from that employed with the ermine. He must not put before her the mire of the gifts and attentions of insistent lovers, because perhaps—and even without a perhaps—she may not have sufficient virtue and natural strength in herself to pass through and tread under foot these impediments. They must be removed, and the brightness of virtue and the beauty of a good reputation must be put before her.

"A virtuous woman, too, is like a mirror of clear shining glass, liable to be tarnished and dimmed by every breath that touches it. She must be treated as relics are: adored, not touched. She must be protected and prized as one protects and prizes a fair garden full of roses and flowers, the owner of which allows no one to trespass or pluck a blossom. It is enough for others that from afar and through the iron grating they may enjoy its fragrance and its beauty. Finally, let me repeat to you some verses that come to my mind. I heard them in a modern comedy, and it seems to me they bear upon the point we are discussing. A prudent old man was giving advice to another (the father of a young girl) to lock her up, watch over her, and keep her in seclusion, and among other arguments he used these:

Woman is a thing of glass;
  But her brittleness 'tis best
  Not too curiously to test:
Who knows what may come to pass?

Breaking is an easy matter,
  And it's folly to expose
  What you cannot mend to blows;
What you can't make whole to shatter.

This, then, all may hold as true,
  And the reason's plain to see;
  For if Danaës there be,
There are golden showers too.[5]

"All that I have said to you so far, Anselmo, has been in reference to what concerns you. Now it is right that I should say something of what regards myself. If I am long-winded, pardon me, for the labyrinth into which you have entered and from which you would have me extricate you makes it necessary.

"You count me as your friend, and yet you would rob me of honor, a thing wholly inconsistent with friendship. This is not your only aim, for you would have me rob you of your honor, also. That you would rob me of it is clear, for when Camila sees that I pursue her, as you have asked of me, she will certainly regard me as an unscrupulous man devoid of honor, since I attempt and do a thing so unbecoming of my own position and your friendship. That you would have me rob you of your honor is beyond a doubt, for Camila, seeing that I press my suit upon her, will suppose that I have detected in her something unseemly that has encouraged me to make known to her my base desire; and if she holds herself dishonored, her dishonor touches you as belonging to her. Hence arises what so commonly takes place, that the husband of the adulterous woman, though he may not be aware of or have given any cause for his wife's failure in her duty, or, being careless or negligent, have had it in his power to prevent his dishonor, nevertheless is stigmatized by a vile and reproachful name. He thus comes to be regarded with eyes of contempt instead of pity by all who know of his wife's guilt, though they see that he is unfortunate not by his own fault but by the lust of a wicked consort. Let me tell you why, with good reason, dishonor attaches to the husband of the unchaste wife, though he may know not that she is so, nor is to blame, nor has done anything or given any provocation to make her so. Do not grow weary of listening to me, for it will be for your good:

"When God created our first parent in the earthly paradise, the Holy Scripture says that he infused sleep into Adam, and while he slept took a rib from his left side of which he formed our mother Eve. When Adam awoke and beheld her, he said, 'This is flesh of my flesh, and bone of my bone.' And God said, 'For this shall a man leave his father and his mother, and they shall be

[5] *For if Danaës . . . golden showers too:* Danaë's father imprisoned her in a bronze tower to thwart a prophecy that she would bear a son destined to kill him. Jupiter, however, was able to impregnate her by entering the chamber in the form of a golden rain shower. The source of the verses cited is unknown.

two in one flesh.'[6] Then was instituted the divine sacrament of marriage, with such ties that death alone can loose them. Such is the power and virtue of this miraculous sacrament that it makes two different people one and the same flesh. We witness something even greater when the virtuous are married, for though they have two souls they have but one will. Hence it follows that as the flesh of the wife is one and the same with her husband's, the stains that may come upon it or the injuries it incurs fall upon the husband's flesh, though he, as has been said, may have given no cause for them. For as the pain of the foot or any member of the body is felt by the whole body, because all is one flesh, as the head feels the hurt to the ankle without having caused it, so the husband, being one with her, shares the dishonor of the wife; and as all worldly honor or dishonor comes of flesh and blood, and the erring wife's is of that kind, the husband will have to bear his part of it and be held dishonored without knowing it. See, then, Anselmo, the peril you face in seeking to disturb the peace of your virtuous consort. See how your futile and imprudent curiosity would rouse passions that now repose peacefully in the breast of your chaste wife. Reflect that what you are staking everything to win is little, and what you will lose is so much that I leave it undescribed, not having the words to express it. But if all I have said is not enough to turn you from your vile purpose, you must seek some other instrument for your dishonor and misfortune; for such I will not consent to be, though I lose your friendship, the greatest loss that I can conceive."

Having said this, the wise and virtuous Lotario was silent. Anselmo, troubled in mind and deep in thought, was unable for a while to utter a word in reply. But at length he said:

"Lotario, my friend, I have listened attentively, as you have seen, to what you have chosen to say to me. In your arguments, examples, and analogies I have seen the great insight you possess and the perfection of true friendship you have reached. Likewise, I see and confess that if I am not guided by your opinion but follow my own, I am flying from the good and pursuing the evil. This being so, you must remember that I am now laboring under the infirmity that sometimes afflicts women, when the craving seizes them to eat clay, plaster, charcoal, and things even worse—things disgusting to look at, much more to eat—so that it will be necessary to resort to some artifice to cure me. This can be easily effected if only you will make a beginning, even though it be in a lukewarm and make-believe fashion, to pursue Camila, who will not be so yielding that her virtue will give way at the first attack. With this mere attempt, I shall rest satisfied, and you will have done what our friendship binds you to do, not only in giving me life, but in persuading me not to discard my honor. This you are obliged to do for one reason alone, that, being, as I am, resolved to put this test into practice, it is not for you to permit me to reveal my weakness to another, and so imperil the honor you strive to keep me from losing. If your honor may not stand as high in Camila's opinion as it ought while you are wooing her, that is of little or no importance. Before long, on finding in her that constancy we expect, you

[6] *When God created our first parent . . . in one flesh:* Genesis 2:21–24.

can tell her the plain truth as regards our ruse and so regain your place in her esteem. And as you are venturing so little, and by the venture can bring me so much satisfaction, do not refuse to undertake it, even if further difficulties present themselves to you; for as I have said, if you will only make a beginning, I will consider the matter decided."

Lotario did not know what further examples to offer or arguments to put forth in order to dissuade Anselmo from his purpose. Faced with Anselmo's fixed determination and his threat to confide his pernicious scheme to someone else, Lotario reasoned that he would avoid a greater evil if he resolved to gratify his friend and do what he asked, intending to manage the scheme in a way that would satisfy Anselmo without corrupting the mind of Camila. So in reply he told him not to communicate his purpose to any other, for he would undertake the task himself and would begin it as soon as he pleased. Anselmo embraced him warmly and affectionately and thanked him for his offer as if he had bestowed some great favor upon him. It was agreed between them to set about it the next day, Anselmo providing Lotario the place and time to converse alone with Camila, and furnishing him with money and jewels to offer and present to her. He suggested, too, that he should treat her to music and write poetry in her praise, and if he was unwilling to take the trouble of composing them, he offered to do it himself. Lotario agreed to everything with an intention very different from what Anselmo supposed, and with this understanding they returned to Anselmo's house, where they found Camila awaiting her husband anxiously and uneasily, for he was later than usual in returning that day.

Lotario went back to his own house and Anselmo remained in his, as much satisfied as Lotario was troubled in mind, for he could see no satisfactory way out of this ill-advised business. That night, however, he thought of a plan by which he might deceive Anselmo without any injury to Camila. The next day he went to dine with his friend and was welcomed by Camila, who received and treated him with great cordiality, knowing the affection her husband felt for him.

When dinner was over and the table cleared, Anselmo told Lotario to stay there with Camila while he attended to some pressing business, as he would return in an hour and a half. Camila begged him not to go, and Lotario offered to accompany him, but nothing could persuade Anselmo, who on the contrary pressed Lotario to remain waiting for him as he had a matter of great importance to discuss with him. At the same time, he told Camila not to leave Lotario alone until he came back. In short, he concocted such a fine story for the necessity, or folly, of his absence that no one could have suspected it was a pretense. Anselmo departed, and Camila and Lotario were left alone at the table, for the rest of the household had gone to dinner. Lotario stood alone on the battlefield, just as his friend desired, and facing an enemy who, by her beauty alone, could vanquish a squadron of armed knights. Judge whether he had good reason to fear.

But what he did was to lean his elbow on the arm of the chair and his cheek upon his hand, and, asking Camila's pardon for his ill manners, he said he wished to take a little nap until Anselmo returned. Camila in reply said he could rest more comfortably in the drawing room than in his chair and begged him to go and sleep there. But Lotario declined, and there he remained asleep until the return of Anselmo, who finding Camila in her own room and Lotario asleep, imagined that he had stayed away so long as to have afforded them time enough for conversation and even for sleep. He was all impatience until Lotario should wake up, that he might go out with him and ask him how he fared.

Everything happened as he wished. Lotario awoke, the two at once left the house, and Anselmo asked what he was anxious to know. Lotario in answer told him that he had not thought it advisable to declare himself entirely the first time, and therefore had only extolled the charms of Camila, telling her that all the city spoke of nothing else but her beauty and grace. This seemed to him an excellent way of beginning to gain her goodwill and render her disposed to listen to him with pleasure the next time, thus availing himself of the tactic the devil employs when he would deceive one who is on guard against temptation. For the angel of darkness transforms himself into an angel of light. Feigning the appearance of good, he does not reveal himself until he has achieved his purpose, unless his wiles are discovered at the beginning. All this gave great satisfaction to Anselmo. He said he would provide the same opportunity every day but without leaving the house, for he would find things to do at home so that Camila should not detect the plot.

Several days went by, and Lotario, without uttering a word to Camila, reported to Anselmo that he had talked with her and that he had never been able to draw from her the slightest indication that she would consent to anything dishonorable—not even a sign or shadow of hope. On the contrary, Lotario said, she threatened that if he did not give up his vile pursuit, she would take the matter to her husband.

"Fine work," said Anselmo. "Camila has thus far resisted words; we must now see how she will resist deeds. Tomorrow I will give you two thousand escudos in gold for you to offer or even give her, and as many more to buy jewels to lure her, for women, however chaste they may be, are fond of fine dress and fashionable attire, all the more so if they are beautiful. If she resists this temptation, I will rest satisfied and will give you no more trouble."

Lotario replied that now that he had begun, he would carry on the undertaking to the end, though he could foresee that he was to come out of it wearied and vanquished. The next day he received the four thousand escudos, and with them four thousand perplexities, for he did not know what to say for the latest falsehood. In the end he made up his mind to tell Anselmo that Camila stood as firm against gifts and promises as against words, and that there was no use in taking any further trouble, for the time was all spent in vain.

But chance, directing things in a different manner, so ordered that Anselmo, having left Lotario and Camila alone as on other occasions, shut himself into a chamber and through a keyhole set about watching and listening to what took place between them. He saw that for more than half an hour Lotario did not utter a word to Camila, nor would utter a word, though he were to be there for a century. Everything his friend had told him about Camila's responses, he realized, was all invention and lies. To ascertain if it were so, he came out, and calling Lotario aside asked him what news he had and in what mood he had found Camila. Lotario replied that he was not inclined to go on with the business, for she had answered him so angrily and harshly that he had no heart to say anything more to her.

"O Lotario, Lotario," said Anselmo, "how poorly do you meet your obligations to me and the great confidence I place in you! I have been just now watching through this keyhole, and I have seen that you have not said a word to Camila, from which I conclude that on the former occasions you have not spoken to her either. If this is so, as no doubt it is, why do you deceive me, or for what reason do you seek by cunning to deprive me of the means I might find of attaining my desire?"

Anselmo said no more, but he had said enough to cover Lotario with shame and confusion. Lotario, feeling as if it were a slight to his honor having been caught in a lie, swore to Anselmo that from that moment he would devote himself to making him happy without any deception, as his friend would see if he had the curiosity to spy on them—though he need not take the trouble, for the pains he would take to satisfy him would remove all suspicions from his mind. Anselmo believed him, and to provide him an opportunity more promising and less liable to surprise, he resolved to absent himself from his house for a week, traveling to the home of a friend of his who lived in a village not far from the city. To better account for his departure to Camila, he arranged that the friend should send him a very pressing invitation.

Unhappy, shortsighted Anselmo, what are you plotting, what are you devising, what are you scheming? Take heed that you are plotting against yourself, devising your own dishonor, scheming your own ruin. Your wife Camila is virtuous; you possess her in quiet and serenity. No one assails your happiness; her thoughts do not wander beyond the walls of your house. You are her heaven on earth, the object of her wishes, the fulfilment of her desires, the measure by which she measures her will, making it conform in all things to yours and Heaven's. If, then, the mine of her honor, beauty, virtue, and modesty yields to you without labor all the wealth it contains and you can wish for, why will you dig the earth in search of fresh veins, of new unknown treasure, risking the collapse of all, since it rests only on the feeble props of her weak nature? Know that from him who seeks the impossible, even the possible may with justice be withheld, as was better expressed by a poet who said:

'Tis mine to seek for life in death,
Health in disease seek I,
I seek in prison freedom's breath,
In traitors loyalty.

So Fate that ever scorns to grant
Or grace or boon to me,
Since what can never be I want,
Denies me what might be.[7]

[7] *'Tis mine to seek . . . what might be:* The source of these verses is unknown.

The next day Anselmo departed for the village, leaving instructions with Camila that during his absence Lotario would come to look after his house and dine with her, and that she was to treat him as she would himself. Camila was distressed at the orders her husband left her, as a discreet and right-minded woman would be, and told him to remember that it was not becoming that anyone should occupy his seat at the table during his absence; and if he acted this way from not feeling confident that she would be able to manage his house, let him try her this time, and he would find by experience that she was equal to greater responsibilities. Anselmo replied that it was his pleasure to have it so, and that she had only to submit and obey. Camila said she would do so, though against her will.

Anselmo departed, and the next day Lotario came to his house, where he was received by Camila with a friendly and modest welcome; but she never permitted Lotario to see her alone, for she was always attended by her servants, especially by a handmaid of hers, Leonela by name, to whom she was much attached (for they had been brought up together from childhood in her father's house) and whom she had kept with her after her marriage with Anselmo. The first three days Lotario did not speak to her, though he might have done so when they cleared the table and the servants retired to dine in haste—for such were Camila's orders. Leonela had further directions to dine earlier than Camila and never leave her side. She, however, having her thoughts set upon other things more to her taste and wishing to use the time and place for her own pleasures, did not always obey her mistress' commands but left them alone, as if they had ordered her to do so. It fell to Camila's modest bearing, her solemn countenance, and self-possessed manner to bridle Lotario's tongue.

The influence that the many virtues of Camila exerted in imposing silence on Lotario's tongue nonetheless proved mischievous for both of them; for if his tongue was silent, his thoughts were busy. He could dwell at leisure upon the perfections of Camila's goodness and beauty one by one, charms enough to soften a marble statue, how much more a heart of flesh. Lotario gazed upon her when he might have been speaking to her and thought how worthy she was of being loved. Little by little, this reflection began to assail his allegiance to Anselmo. A thousand times he thought of retreating from the city and going where Anselmo should never see him nor he see Camila, but the delight he found in gazing on her interposed and held him fast. He struggled within as he fought to repel and repress the pleasure he found in contemplating Camila. When alone, he blamed himself for his weakness, called himself a bad friend, even a bad Christian. He argued the matter and compared himself with Anselmo, always concluding that Anselmo's folly and presumption had been worse than his faithlessness, and that if he could excuse what he had in mind to do as easily before God as before man, he had no reason to fear any punishment for his offense.

In short, Camila's beauty and goodness, joined to the opportunity her blind husband had placed in his hands, laid waste to Lotario's loyalty. He now gave heed to nothing except the object toward which his inclinations led him. And so after Anselmo had been three days absent, during which time he had been carrying on a continual struggle with his desires, he began to make love to Camila so vehemently and with such impassioned pleas that she was overwhelmed with amazement, and could only rise from her seat and retire to her room without answering him a word. Yet the hope that always springs up with love was not weakened in Lotario by her rebuff; on the contrary, his passion for Camila increased. She, discovering in him what she had never expected, knew not what to do. Considering it neither safe nor proper to give him the opportunity of speaking to her again, she resolved to send that very night one of her servants with a letter to Anselmo, in which she addressed the following words to him:

CHAPTER XXXIV

IN WHICH IS CONTINUED *THE NOVEL OF THE IMPRUDENT MEDDLER*

> It is commonly said that an army looks badly without its general and a castle without its governor. I say that a young married woman looks still worse without her husband, unless there are very good reasons for his absence. I find myself so ill at ease without you, and so incapable of enduring this separation, that unless you return quickly I shall have to go for relief to my parents' house, even if I leave yours without a protector. For the protector you left me, if indeed he has deserved that title, has, I think, more regard to his own pleasure than to what concerns you. As you are a discerning man, I need say no more to you, nor indeed is it fitting I should say more.

Anselmo received this letter, and from it he gathered that Lotario had already begun his task and that Camila must have replied to him as he would have wished. Delighted beyond measure at such intelligence, he sent word to her not to leave the house on any account, as he would very shortly return. Camila was astonished at Anselmo's reply, which placed her in greater vexation than before, for she neither dared to remain in her own house, nor yet to go to her parents'; for in remaining her virtue was imperiled, and in going she was opposing her husband's commands.

At last, she decided upon what was the worse course for her, to remain, resolving not to flee from the presence of Lotario, that she might not give food for gossip to her servants. She now began to regret having written as she had to her husband, fearing he might imagine that Lotario had detected in her something dissolute that had impelled him to lay aside the respect he owed her; but confident of her innocence, she put her trust in God and in her own virtuous intentions, with which she hoped to resist silently Lotario's every advance without saying anything to her husband, so as not to involve him in any quarrel or trouble. She even began to consider how to make excuses for Lotario should Anselmo ask her what had induced her to write that letter. With these resolutions, more honorable than sound or beneficial, she remained the next day listening to Lotario, who pressed his suit so strenuously that Camila's firmness began to waver. Her virtue had enough to do to come to the rescue of her eyes and keep them from showing signs of a certain tender compassion that the tears and appeals of Lotario had awakened in her breast. Lotario observed all this, and it inflamed him all the more.

While Anselmo's absence allowed time and opportunity, Lotario was resolved to press the siege of the fortress; and so he assailed her self-regard with praises of her beauty, for there is nothing that more quickly reduces and levels the castle towers of a beautiful woman's vanity than vanity itself upon the tongue of flattery. With the utmost assiduity, in short, he tunneled through the rock of her purity and with such ammunition that had Camila been of bronze she must have fallen. He wept, he entreated, he promised, he flattered, he pleaded, he feigned—with so much feeling and apparent sincerity that he overthrew the virtuous resolves of Camila and won the triumph he least expected and most longed for.

Camila yielded; Camila fell. Little wonder that Lotario's friendship could not stand firm—a clear proof to us that love's passion is to be conquered only by fleeing from it, and that no one should engage in a struggle with an enemy so mighty; for divine strength is needed to overcome its human power. Leonela alone knew of her mistress' weakness, for the two false friends and new lovers were unable to conceal it. Lotario did not care to tell Camila the object Anselmo had in view, nor that he had provided him the opportunity of attaining such a result, lest she should undervalue his love and think that it was by chance and without intending it and not of his own design that he had pursued her.

A few days later Anselmo returned to his house and failed to notice what it had lost: that which he so lightly treated and so highly prized. He went at once to see Lotario and found him at home. They embraced each other, and Anselmo asked for the news of his life or his death.

"The news I have to give you, Anselmo my friend," said Lotario, "is that you possess a wife who is worthy to be the example and crown of all good wives. The words I have addressed to her have been borne away on the wind, my promises have been despised, my presents have been refused, such feigned tears as I shed have been turned into open ridicule. In short, as Camila is the essence of all beauty, so is she the treasure house where purity dwells, and gentleness and modesty abide with all the virtues that can confer praise, honor, and happiness upon a woman. Take back your money, my friend. Here it is—I have had no need to touch it, for the chastity of Camila yields not to things so vulgar as gifts or promises. Be content, Anselmo, and refrain from making further proof. As you have passed with dry feet through the sea of those doubts and suspicions that are and may be entertained of women, seek not to plunge again into the deep ocean of new embarrassments, or with another pilot make trial of the goodness and strength of the ship that Heaven has granted you for your passage across the sea of this world. You should instead consider yourself safe now in port. Moor yourself with the anchor of sound reflection, and rest in peace until you are called upon to pay that debt that no nobility on earth can escape paying."[1]

Anselmo was completely satisfied by Lotario's words and believed them as fully as if they had been spoken by an oracle. Nevertheless, he begged him not to give up the undertaking, if only for the sake of curiosity and amusement, though in the future he need not make use of the same fervent measures as before. All he wished him to do was to write some verses to her, praising her under the name

[1] *that debt that no nobility on earth can escape paying:* death.

of Cloris, for he would lead her to believe that Lotario was in love with a lady to whom he had given that name to enable him to sing her praises with the decorum due her modesty. If Lotario was unwilling to take the trouble of writing the verses, Anselmo would compose them himself.

"That will not be necessary," said Lotario, "for the muses are not such enemies of mine but that they visit me now and then in the course of the year. Do tell Camila what you have proposed about a pretended lover of mine. As for the verses, I will write them, and if not as good as the subject deserves, they shall be at least the best I can produce."

An agreement to this effect was made between the friends, the imprudent one and the treacherous one, and Anselmo returning to his house asked Camila the question she already wondered he had not asked before—what it was that had caused her to write the letter she had sent him. Camila replied that it had seemed to her that Lotario looked at her somewhat more freely than when he had been at home; but that now she was undeceived and believed it to have been only her own imagination, for Lotario now avoided seeing her or being alone with her. Anselmo told her she might be quite easy on the score of that suspicion, for he knew that Lotario was in love with a noble damsel in the city whom he celebrated under the name of Cloris, and that even if he were not, his fidelity and their great friendship left no room for fear. Had not Camila been informed by Lotario beforehand that this love for Cloris was a pretense and that he had told Anselmo of it in order to be able sometimes to give voice to the praises of Camila herself, no doubt she would have fallen into the despairing toils of jealousy; but being forewarned, she received the startling news without uneasiness.

The next day after the three had finished dining, Anselmo asked Lotario to recite something of what he had composed for his mistress Cloris; for as Camila did not know her, he might safely say what he liked.

"Even if she did know her," returned Lotario, "I would hide nothing, for when a lover praises his lady's beauty and charges her with cruelty, he casts no imputation upon her fair name. At any rate, all I can say is that yesterday I composed a sonnet on the ingratitude of this Cloris, which goes thus:

SONNET

At midnight, in the silence, when the eyes
Of happier mortals balmy slumbers close,
The weary tale of my unnumbered woes
To Cloris and to Heaven is wont to rise.
And when the light of day returning dyes
The portals of the east with tints of rose,
With undiminished force my sorrow flows
In broken accents and in burning sighs.
And when the sun ascends his star-girt throne,
And on the earth pours down his midday beams,

Noon but renews my wailing and my tears;
  And with the night again goes up my moan.
Yet ever in my agony it seems
To me that neither Heaven nor Cloris hears.

The sonnet pleased Camila, and still more Anselmo, for he praised it and said the lady was excessively cruel who was impassive before such obvious sincerity. On which Camila said, "Then all that love-smitten poets say is true?"

"As poets they do not tell the truth," replied Lotario, "but as lovers they are truthful insofar as words can express their feelings."

"There is no doubt of that," observed Anselmo, anxious to support and give credit to Lotario's ideas before Camila, who was as ignorant of his design as she was deep in love with Lotario. Thus taking delight in anything that was his, all the more so with the knowledge that his thoughts and writings were directed to her, the real Cloris, she asked him to repeat some other sonnet or verses if he recollected any.

"I do," replied Lotario, "but I do not consider this one as good as the first, or, more correctly speaking, less bad. You can easily judge, for it is this:

SONNET

  I know that I am doomed; death is to me
As certain as that thou, ungrateful fair,
Dead at thy feet shouldst see me lying, ere
My heart repented of its love for thee.
  If buried in oblivion I should be,
Bereft of life, fame, favor, even there
It would be found that I thy image bear
Deep graven in my breast for all to see.
  This like some holy relic do I prize
To save me from the fate my truth entails,
Truth that to thy hard heart its vigor owes.
  Alas for him that under lowering skies,
In peril o'er a trackless ocean sails,
Where neither friendly port nor polestar shows.

Anselmo praised this second sonnet too, as he had praised the first, and so he went on adding link after link to the chain with which he was binding himself and making his dishonor secure; for when Lotario was doing most to dishonor him, he told him he was most honored. Meanwhile, each step that Camila descended toward the depths of her abasement, she mounted, in his opinion, toward the summit of virtue and good repute.

It so happened that finding herself on one occasion alone with her maid, Camila said to her, "I am ashamed to think, my dear Leonela, how lightly I have valued myself that I did not compel Lotario to purchase by at least some expenditure of time that full possession of me that I so quickly yielded to him of my own free will. I fear he will look down on me as eager and obliging, not considering the irresistible influence he exerted on my will."

"Let not that trouble you, my lady," said Leonela, "for it does not take away the value of the thing given or make it the less precious to give it quickly if it is really valuable and worthy of being prized. It's often said that 'he who gives quickly, gives twice.'"

"They say also," said Camila, "that 'what costs little is valued less.'"

"That saying does not hold good in your case," replied Leonela, "for love, as I have heard say, sometimes flies and sometimes walks. With this one it runs; with that it moves slowly. Some it cools; others it burns. Some it wounds; others it kills. It begins the course of its desires, and at the same moment completes and ends it. In the morning it will lay siege to a fortress and by night will have taken it, for there is no power that can resist it. So what are you in dread of, what do you fear, when the same must have befallen Lotario, love having chosen the absence of my lord as the instrument for subduing you? It was absolutely necessary for love to complete then what it had resolved to do, without giving time to the occasion to let Anselmo return and by his presence compel the work to be left unfinished; for love has no better agent for carrying out his designs than opportunity; and he avails himself of opportunity in all his deeds, especially at the outset.

"All this I know well myself, more by experience than by hearsay. Someday, señora, I will enlighten you on the subject, for I too am of womanly flesh and blood. Moreover, Señora Camila, you did not surrender yourself or yield so quickly, but first you saw Lotario's whole soul in his eyes, in his sighs, in his words, his promises and his gifts, and by it and his good qualities realized how worthy he was of your love. This, then, being the case, do not let these scrupulous and prudish ideas trouble your imagination, but be assured that Lotario prizes you as you do him, and rest content and satisfied that as you are caught in the noose of love it is someone of worth and merit that has taken you, and someone that has not only the four S's that they say true lovers ought to have,[2] but a complete alphabet. Only listen to me and you will see how I can repeat it by rote. He is to my eyes and thinking, Amiable, Brave, Courteous, Distinguished, Elegant, Fond, Gallant, Honorable, Illustrious, Loyal, Manly, Noble, Open, Polite, Quick-witted, Rich, and the S's according to the saying, and then Tender, Veracious; X does not suit him, for it is a rough letter;[3] Y has been given already;[4] and Z, Zealous for your honor."

[2] *four S's that they say true lovers ought to have:* True lovers, according to a poetic tradition, are wise (*sabio*), exclusive (*solo*), diligent (*solícito*), and discreet (*secreto*).

[3] *X does not suit him, for it is a rough letter:* Leonela's dislike of the "sh" sound that the letter "X" represented at the time is consistent with Renaissance theories of beauty that classified sounds as rough or gentle. She also avoids having to come up with an "X" adjective. In Sebastián de Covarrubias' 1300-page dictionary (*Treasure of the Spanish or Castilian Language*, 1611), the words that start with "X" take up little more than two pages.

[4] *Y has been given already:* In the Spanish of the day, the letter "Y" sometimes represented the vowel "I".

Camila laughed at her maid's alphabet and gathered that she was more experienced in matters of love than she let on. She admitted as much, confessing to Camila that she was carrying on a love affair with a young man of good birth of the same city. Camila was uneasy at this, fearing that it might prove the means of endangering her honor. She asked whether their relationship had gone beyond words, and Leonela, with little shame and much effrontery said it had. For it has been well established that a lady's indiscretions make her servant shameless. When she sees her mistress take a false step, she thinks nothing of going astray herself, nor of its being known.

All that Camila could do was to entreat Leonela to say nothing of her actions to him whom she called her lover and to conduct her own affairs secretly lest they should come to the knowledge of Anselmo or Lotario. Leonela said she would, but the way she kept her word confirmed Camila's apprehension that through her maid she would lose her reputation. For this brazen and dissolute Leonela, when she perceived that her mistress' behavior was not what it used to be, had the audacity to bring her lover into the house, confident that even if her mistress saw him she would not dare to expose him. This mischief, among others, follows from the sins of mistresses: they make themselves the slaves of their own servants and are driven to help them cover up their foul and immoral deeds. Such was the case with Camila, who though she discovered, not once but many times, that Leonela was with her lover in some room of the house, not only did not dare to chide her, but provided her opportunities for concealing him and removed all difficulties, lest he should be seen by her husband.

She was unable, however, to prevent Lotario from seeing him leave the house early one morning. Not knowing who he was, Lotario at first took him for a ghost; but, as soon as he saw him hurry away, muffling his face with his cloak and concealing himself carefully and cautiously, he rejected this foolish idea, and adopted another, which would have been the ruin of all had not Camila found a remedy. It did not occur to Lotario that the man he had seen departing at such an untimely hour from Anselmo's house could have entered it on Leonela's account, nor did he even remember there was such a person as Leonela. All he could think was that as Camila had been easy work for him, so she had been with another. This further penalty the erring woman's sin brings with it, that her honor is distrusted even by him to whose overtures and persuasions she has yielded. He assumes that she will surrender more readily to others and believes without question every suspicion that comes into his mind. All Lotario's good sense seems to have failed him at this juncture; all his prudent maxims escaped his memory. Without leaving time for a rational thought, in his impatience and in the blindness of the jealous rage that gnawed his heart, dying to revenge himself upon Camila, who had done him no wrong, he hastened to Anselmo before he had risen and said to him:

"Know, Anselmo, that for several days past I have been struggling with myself, striving to withhold from you what it is no longer possible or right that I should keep concealed. Know that Camila's fortress has surrendered and is ready to submit to my will. If I have been slow to reveal this truth to you, it was in order to see if it were some passing whim of hers, or if she sought to test me and ascertain whether the love I began to make to her with your permission was made with a serious intention. I thought, as well, that she—if she were what she ought to be, and what we both believed her—would have before now informed you of my entreaties. But seeing that she delays, I believe the truth of the promise she has given me, which is that the next time you are absent from the house, she will grant me an interview in the chamber where you keep your jewels (and it was true that Camila used to meet him there). I do not wish you to rush precipitously to take vengeance, for the sin is as yet only committed in intention, and Camila's may change between now and the appointed time and repentance spring up in its place. As you have thus far always followed my advice wholly or in part, follow and observe this that I will give you now, so that having been truthfully informed and solemnly warned, you may satisfy yourself as to what may seem the best course. Pretend to absent yourself for two or three days, as you have been accustomed to do on other occasions, and arrange to hide yourself in the jewel chamber; for the tapestries and other things there to conceal you will serve you well. Then you will see with your own eyes and I with mine what Camila's purpose may be. If it be a guilty one, which may be feared rather than expected, with silence, prudence, and discretion you can yourself become the instrument of punishment for the wrong done to you."

Anselmo, who listened in rapt attention, was dumbfounded by Lotario's words. They came upon him at a time when he least expected to hear them, for he now looked upon Camila as having triumphed over the pretended attacks of Lotario and was beginning to enjoy the glory of her victory. He remained silent for a considerable time, looking on the ground with fixed gaze. At length, he said, "You have behaved, Lotario, as I expected of your friendship. I will follow your advice in everything. Do as you will, and keep this secret as you see it should be kept in circumstances so unexpected."

Lotario gave him his word, but after leaving him he repented altogether of what he had said to him, realizing how foolishly he had acted, as he might have revenged himself upon Camila in some less cruel and dishonorable way. He cursed his lack of sense, condemned his hasty resolution, and knew not what course to take to undo the mischief or find some ready escape from it. At last he decided upon revealing everything to Camila, and as there was no lack of opportunity for doing so, he found her alone the same day. But she, as soon as she had the chance of speaking to him, said, "Lotario my friend, I must tell you I have a sorrow in my heart that fills it so that it seems ready to burst. It will be a wonder if it does not; for the audacity of Leonela has now reached such a pitch that every night she conceals a lover of hers in this house and remains with him till morning, at the expense of my reputation, inasmuch as it is open to anyone to question it who may see him leaving my house at such unseasonable hours. But what distresses me is that I cannot punish or scold her, for her being privy to our intrigue bridles my mouth and keeps me silent about hers, while I am dreading that some catastrophe will come of it."

As Camila said this, Lotario at first imagined it was some device to delude him into the idea that the man he had seen going out was Leonela's lover and not hers; but when he saw how she wept and suffered and begged him to help her, he became convinced of the truth, and the conviction completed his confusion and remorse. Nonetheless, he told Camila not to distress herself, as he would take measures to put a stop to Leonela's insolence. At the same time, he told her what he had said to Anselmo, driven by the fierce rage of jealousy, and how he had arranged to hide himself in the jewel chamber that he might there see plainly how little she preserved her fidelity to him. He entreated her pardon for this madness and her advice as to how to repair it and escape safely from the intricate labyrinth in which his imprudence had trapped him.

Camila was struck with alarm at hearing what Lotario said, and with great anger and many shrewd words, she reproved him and rebuked his base design and the foolish and mischievous resolution he had made. But as woman has by nature a nimbler wit than man for good and for evil, though it is apt to fail when she sets herself deliberately to reason, Camila on the spur of the moment thought of a way to remedy what was to all appearance irremediable. She told Lotario to arrange for Anselmo to conceal himself the next day in the place he mentioned, for she hoped from his concealment to obtain the means of their enjoying themselves from then on without further disturbance. Without revealing her purpose to him entirely, she charged him to take care that after Anselmo was concealed to come to her when Leonela should call him; and to all she might say to him, he was to answer as he would have answered had he not known that Anselmo was listening. Lotario pressed her to explain her intention fully so that he might with more certainty and precaution take care to do what he saw to be needful.

"I tell you," said Camila, "there is nothing to take care of except to answer me what I shall ask you." For she did not wish to explain to him beforehand what she meant to do, fearing lest he should be unwilling to follow out an idea that seemed to her such a good one and should try or devise some other less practicable plan. At this, Lotario took his leave.

The following day, Anselmo, under pretense of going to his friend's country house, made his departure and then returned to conceal himself, which he was able to do easily, as Camila and Leonela were diligent in giving him the opportunity. And so he placed himself in hiding in the state of agitation it may be imagined of one expecting to see the vitals of his honor torn to pieces before his eyes and on the point of losing the supreme blessing he thought he possessed in his beloved Camila. Having made sure of Anselmo's being in his hiding place, Camila and Leonela entered the jewel chamber.

The instant she set foot in it, Camila said with a deep sigh, "Ah, dear Leonela! Would it not be better, before I do what I am unwilling you should know lest you should seek to prevent it, that you should take Anselmo's dagger, which I have asked of you, and with it pierce this vile heart of mine? But no—there is no reason that I should suffer the punishment of another's fault. I will first know what it is that the bold, licentious eyes of Lotario have seen in me that could have encouraged him to reveal to me a design so vile as that which he has disclosed to me, in contempt of his friend and of my honor. Go to the window, Leonela, and call him, for no doubt he is in the street waiting to carry out his wicked plan. Mine, cruel though it be, yet honorable, shall be carried out first."

"Ah, señora," said the crafty Leonela, who knew her part, "what is it you want to do with this dagger? Can it be that you mean to take your own life or Lotario's? Whichever you mean to do, it will lead to the loss of your reputation and good name. It is better to dissemble your wrong and not give this wicked man the chance of entering the house now and finding us alone. Consider, señora, we are weak women and he is a man, and determined. And as he comes with such a foul purpose, blinded and driven by passion, perhaps before you can put your plan into execution he may do what will be worse for you than taking your life.[5] Cursed be my master, Anselmo, for giving such authority in his house to this shameless fellow! And supposing you kill him, señora, as I suspect you mean to do, what shall we do with him when he is dead?"

"What, my friend?" replied Camila. "We shall leave him for Anselmo to bury; for it will be a fitting sport for him to have to shovel earth over his own infamy. Make haste and summon him, for all the time I delay in taking vengeance for my wrong seems to me an offense against the loyalty I owe my husband."

Anselmo heard all of this, and every word Camila uttered changed his mind, although when he realized that she was resolved to kill Lotario, his first impulse was to come out and show himself to avert such a disaster. He restrained himself, nevertheless, for he was eager to see the outcome of a resolution so bold and so virtuous, and he intended to come forth in time to prevent the deed.

Meanwhile, Camila, throwing herself upon a bed that was close by, fell into a swoon. Leonela began to weep bitterly, exclaiming, "Woe is me, that I should be fated to have dying here in my arms the flower of virtue upon earth, the crown of true wives, the pattern of chastity!"—with more to the same effect, so that anyone who heard her would have taken her for the most tender-hearted and faithful handmaid in the world, and her mistress for another persecuted Penelope.[6]

Camila was not long in recovering from her fainting fit. On coming to herself she said, "Why do you not go, Leonela, to summon that friend, the falsest to his friend the sun ever shone upon or night concealed? Away, run, haste, speed! Let not the fire of my wrath burn itself out with delay, nor the righteous vengeance I hope for melt away in threats and curses."

"I am on my way to call him, señora," said Leonela. "But you must first give me that dagger, lest while I am gone you should by means of it give cause to all who love you to weep for the rest of their lives."

[5] *he may do what will be worse for you than taking your life*: Rape was considered a grave dishonor in early modern Spain, and its victims were not always presumed innocent in the court of public opinion. The loss of reputation a woman faced for sexual misdeeds was especially acute in the upper strata of Spanish society.

[6] *persecuted Penelope*: Penelope kept 108 suitors at bay during her husband Odysseus' twenty-year absence from Ithaca.

"Go in peace, dear Leonela, I will not do so," said Camila, "for rash and foolish as I may be to your mind in defending my honor, I will not go to the lengths of Lucretia, who they say killed herself without having done anything wrong and without having first killed him on whom the guilt of her misfortune lay.[7] I shall die, if I am to die; but it must be after full vengeance upon him who has brought me here to weep over his offenses, which no fault of mine gave birth to."

A great deal of pleading was required on Camila's part before her maid would go to summon Lotario, but at last she went, and while awaiting her return Camila continued, as if speaking to herself, "Good God! Would it not have been more prudent to have repulsed Lotario, as I have done many a time before, than to allow him, as I am now doing, to think me unchaste and wicked, even for the short time I must wait until I undeceive him? No doubt it would have been better; but I should not be avenged, nor the honor of my husband vindicated, should he find so clear and easy an escape from the strait into which his depravity has led him. Let the traitor pay with his life for the temerity of his lascivious desire, and let the world know (if by chance it shall ever come to know) that Camila not only preserved her allegiance to her husband, but avenged him of the man who dared to wrong him. Still, I think it might be better to disclose this to Anselmo. But then I have called his attention to it in the letter I wrote to him in the country, and if he did nothing to prevent the mischief I there pointed out to him, I suppose it was that from pure goodness of heart and trustfulness he would not and could not believe that any thought against his honor could harbor in the breast of so staunch a friend. Nor indeed did I myself believe it for many days, nor should I have ever believed it if his insolence had not gone so far as to make it manifest by open presents, lavish promises, and ceaseless tears. But why do I argue thus? Does a bold determination stand in need of arguments? Surely not. Then let traitors be gone! Vengeance to my aid! Let the false one come, approach, advance, die, yield up his life, and then befall what may. Pure I came to him whom Heaven bestowed upon me, pure I shall leave him; and at the worst bathed in my own chaste blood and in the foul blood of the falsest friend that friendship ever saw in the world."

As she uttered these words, she paced the room holding the unsheathed dagger, with such irregular and disordered steps and such gestures that one would have supposed her to have lost her senses and taken her for some violent desperado instead of a delicate woman.

Anselmo, concealed behind some tapestries where he had hidden himself, beheld and was amazed at everything and already felt that what he had seen and heard was a sufficient answer to even greater suspicions. He would have been well pleased now if the proof provided by Lotario's coming were dispensed with, as he feared some sudden mishap. But as he was on the point of showing himself and coming forth to embrace and undeceive his wife, he paused as he saw Leonela returning, leading Lotario.

Camila when she saw him, drawing a long line in front of her on the floor with the dagger, said to him, "Lotario, pay attention to what I say to you. If by

[7] *Lucretia . . . her misfortune lay*: See footnote 16, page 193.

chance you dare to cross this line you see or even approach it, the instant I see you attempt it will be the instant I pierce my breast with this dagger I hold in my hand. Before you answer me a word, I desire you to listen to a few from me; afterwards, you may reply as it pleases you. First, I would like you to tell me, Lotario, if you know my husband Anselmo, and in what light you regard him; and secondly I wish to ascertain whether you know me, too. Answer me this, without embarrassment or reflecting deeply how you will respond, for these are no riddles I put to you."

Lotario was not so slow-witted but that from the first moment when Camila directed him to make Anselmo hide himself he understood what she intended to do. He accordingly matched her plan with such speed and cunning that between the two of them they made the lie look truer than truth. He thus responded to Camila: "I did not think, fair Camila, that you had called me to ask questions so remote from the object with which I come; but if you are doing so to postpone the promised reward, you may well put it off still longer, for the more the longing for happiness causes distress, the nearer comes the hope of gaining it. But lest you should say that I do not answer your questions, I say that I know your husband Anselmo, and that we have known each other from our earliest years. I will not speak of what you, too, know of our friendship, that I may not compel myself to testify against the wrong that love, the mighty excuse for greater errors, makes me inflict upon him. I know you and hold you in the same estimation as he does. Were it not so, I would not have, for a lesser prize, acted in opposition to what I owe to my station and the holy laws of true friendship, now broken and violated by me through that powerful enemy, love."

"If that is what you confess," returned Camila, "mortal enemy of all that rightly deserves to be loved, with what face do you dare to come before one whom you know to be the mirror that reflects another face—the face in which you ought to look to see how unworthily you wrong him? Woe is me! I now comprehend what has made you give so little heed to what you owe yourself. It must have been some liberty of mine, for I will not call it immodesty, as it did not proceed from any deliberate intention, but from some heedlessness such as women inadvertently commit when they think they have no occasion for reserve. If not, tell me, traitor, when did I by word or sign give a reply to your pleas that could awaken in you a shadow of hope of attaining your contemptible wishes? When were your professions of love not sternly and scornfully rejected and rebuked? When were your frequent pledges and still more frequent gifts believed or accepted? But as I am persuaded that no one can long persevere in an amorous pursuit without some hope to sustain him, I am willing to attribute to myself the blame of your indiscretion, for no doubt some thoughtlessness of mine has all this time nourished your fancy. I will therefore punish myself and inflict upon myself the penalty your guilt deserves. And that you may see that being so inhuman to myself I cannot possibly be otherwise to you, I have summoned you to be a witness of the sacrifice I mean to offer to the injured honor of my honored husband, wronged by you with all the determination you were capable of, and by me too through lack of caution in avoiding every occasion, if I have given any, of encouraging and sanctioning your base designs. My suspicion, I repeat, that some imprudence of mine has engendered these lawless thoughts is what causes me the most distress and is what I most desire to punish with my own hands, for were another executioner to punish me, my error might become more widely known. But before I do so, in my death I mean to inflict death, and take with me one who will fully satisfy my longing for the revenge I hope for and have before me. There shall I see, wherever *there* may be, the penalty meted out by inflexible, unswerving justice on him who has placed me in a position so desperate."

As she uttered these words, with incredible energy and speed she lunged at Lotario with the naked dagger. So intent did she appear on burying it in his breast, that he was almost in doubt whether these demonstrations were real or feigned, and he was obliged to make use of all his skill and strength to prevent her from striking him. To give this strange and corrupt farce the color of authenticity, Camila determined to stain her performance in her own blood. Realizing, or pretending to realize, that she could not wound Lotario, she said, "Fate, it seems, will not grant complete satisfaction to my just desire, but at least it cannot prevent me from satisfying it partially." With effort she managed to free the hand with the dagger that Lotario held in his grasp and took the weapon from him. Then directing the point to a place where it could not inflict a deep wound, she plunged it into her left side high up close to the shoulder, before allowing herself to fall to the ground as if in a swoon.

Leonela and Lotario stood amazed and astounded at this turn of events. Seeing Camila stretched on the ground and bathed in her blood, they were still uncertain as to the true nature of the act. Lotario, terrified and breathless, approached her quickly to pluck out the dagger; but when he saw how slight the wound was, he was relieved of his fears and once more marveled at the foresight, prudence, and astuteness of the fair Camila. The better to play his assigned part, he began to utter profuse and pathetic lamentations over her body as if she were dead, invoking curses not only on himself but also on him who had been the means of placing him in such a position. Knowing that his friend Anselmo heard him, he spoke in such a way as to make a listener feel much more pity for him than for Camila, even though he supposed her dead. Leonela took up her mistress in her arms and laid her on the bed, entreating Lotario to go in search of someone to attend to her wound in secret, and at the same time asking his advice and opinion as to what they should say to Anselmo about his lady's wound if he should chance to return before it was healed. He replied they might say what they liked, for he was not in a state to give advice that would be of any use; all he could tell her was to try and stanch the blood, as he was going where he should never more be seen; and with every appearance of deep grief and sorrow he left the house. When he found himself alone, and where there was nobody to see him, he crossed himself unceasingly, lost in wonder at the ingenuity of Camila and the fitting role played by Leonela. He reflected how convinced Anselmo would be that he had a second Portia[8]

[8] *Portia:* According to Plutarch, Portia (Brutus' wife) stabbed herself in the leg to prove to her husband that she would not reveal his secrets under torture.

for a wife, and he longed to meet with him so that they could rejoice together over the most craftily veiled truth and lie that could be imagined.

Leonela, as was said, stanched her lady's blood, which was no more than necessary to support her deception; and washing the wound with a little wine, she bound it up the best she could, telling her such things while she tended to her that, even if nothing else had been said before, would have been enough to assure Anselmo that he had in Camila a model of purity.

To Leonela's words Camila added her own, calling herself cowardly and weak-willed, since she lacked the resolve at the time she needed it most to rid herself of the life she so loathed. She asked her attendant's advice as to whether or not she ought to inform her beloved husband of all that had happened, but the other urged her to say nothing about it, for in doing so she would obligate him to take vengeance on Lotario, which he could not do but at great risk to himself; and it was the duty of the virtuous wife not to provoke her husband to a quarrel, but, on the contrary, to remove it as far as possible from him.

Camila replied that her opinion seemed quite sound and that she would follow her advice, but it would be necessary, all the same, to consider how she was to explain the wound to Anselmo, for he could not help seeing it. Leonela answered that she did not know how to tell a lie, even in jest.

"How then am *I* supposed to know, my dear?" asked Camila. "For I would not dare craft or keep up a falsehood if my life depended on it. If we can think of no escape from this difficulty, it will be better to tell him the plain truth than that he should find us out in a deceitful story."

"Do not be uneasy, señora," said Leonela. "Between now and tomorrow I will think of what we must say to him. Perhaps the wound being where it is, it can be hidden from his sight. Heaven will be pleased to aid us in a purpose so good and honorable. Compose yourself, señora, and endeavor to calm your excitement lest my lord find you agitated. Leave the rest to my care and to God's, who always supports good intentions."

Anselmo had with the deepest attention watched and listened as the tragedy of the death of his honor played out. The performers had acted with such wonderfully effective truth that it seemed as if they had become the realities of the parts they played. He longed for night and an opportunity of escaping from the house to go and see his good friend Lotario, and with him to rejoice over the precious pearl he had gained in having established his wife's purity. Both mistress and maid took care to give him time and opportunity to get away, and taking advantage of it, he made his escape and at once went in quest of Lotario.

It would be impossible to describe how he embraced him when he found him, the things he said to him in the joy of his heart, and the praises he bestowed upon Camila. Lotario listened to all of this without being able to show any pleasure, for he could not forget how deceived his friend was and how dishonorably he had wronged him. Though Anselmo could see that Lotario was not glad, still he imagined it was only because he had left Camila wounded and had been himself the cause of it; and so among other things, he told him not to be distressed about Camila's injury, for as they had agreed to hide it from him, the wound was evidently minor. That being so, he had no cause for fear but should henceforward be of good cheer and rejoice with him, since by his friend's skillful intervention Anselmo found himself raised to the greatest height of happiness that he could have ventured to hope for and desired no better pastime than writing poetry in praise of Camila that would preserve her name for all time to come. Lotario commended his purpose and promised on his own part to aid him in raising a monument so glorious.

And so Anselmo was left the most delightfully hoodwinked man the world has ever known. Persuaded he was accompanying the instrument of his glory, he himself led home by the hand the man who had been the utter destruction of his good name—whom Camila received with averted eyes, though with smiles in her heart. The deception was carried on for some time, until at the end of a few months Fortune turned her wheel and the evil that until then had been so skillfully concealed was published abroad, and Anselmo paid with his life the penalty of his imprudent meddling.

CHAPTER XXXV

WHEREIN *THE NOVEL OF THE IMPRUDENT MEDDLER* IS BROUGHT TO A CLOSE

There remained but little more of the novel to be read when Sancho Panza burst forth in wild excitement from the garret where Don Quixote lay, shouting, "Run, sirs, quick! Help my master, who is in the thick of the toughest, fiercest battle I ever laid eyes on. By the living God, he's given the giant, the enemy of my lady Princess Micomicona, such a slash that he's sliced his head clean off like it was a turnip."

"What are you talking about, brother?" said the priest, pausing as he was about to read the remainder of the novel. "Are you in your senses, Sancho? How the devil can it be as you say when the giant is two thousand leagues away?"

Here they heard a loud noise in the chamber and Don Quixote calling out, "Hold, thief, brigand, villain! I have got you now, and your scimitar shall be of no use!" Then it seemed as though he were slashing vigorously at the wall.

"Don't wait to listen," said Sancho, "but go in and stop them or help my master—though there is no need of that now, for no doubt the giant is dead by this time and giving account to God of his past wicked life. For I saw the blood flowing on the ground and the head cut off and fallen on one side, as big as a large wineskin."

"May I be cut to pieces," said the innkeeper at this, "if Don Quixote or Don Devil has not been slashing some of the skins of red wine that stand full at the head of his bed. The spilled wine must be what this good fellow takes for blood."

So saying he went into the room and the rest after him. There they found Don Quixote in the strangest attire in the world. He was in his undershirt, which was not long enough in front to cover his thighs completely and was six fingers shorter behind. His legs were very long and lean, covered with hair, and anything but clean; on his head he had a greasy little red cap that belonged to the innkeeper. Round his left arm he had rolled the blanket of the bed, to which Sancho (for reasons best known to himself) owed a grudge, and in his right hand he held his unsheathed sword, with which he was slashing about on all sides, uttering exclamations as if he were actually fighting some giant. The best of it was his eyes were not open, for he was fast asleep and dreaming that he was doing battle with the giant. For his imagination was so beset by the adventure he was going to accomplish that it made him dream he had already reached the kingdom of Micomicón and was engaged in combat with his enemy; and believing he was attacking the giant, he had given so many sword cuts to the wineskins that the whole room was full of wine. On seeing this, the innkeeper was so enraged that he fell on Don Quixote, and with his clenched fist began to pummel him in such a way that if Cardenio and the priest had not dragged him off, he would have brought the war of the giant to an end. In spite of everything, the poor gentleman never woke until the barber brought a great pot of cold water from the well and, with a single heave, flung it all over his body, on which Don Quixote woke up, but not so completely as to understand what was the matter.

Dorotea, seeing how short and scanty his attire was, would not go in to witness the battle between her champion and her opponent. As for Sancho, he went searching all over the floor for the head of the giant, and not finding it he said, "I see now that it's all enchantment in this house. The last time, on this very spot where I am now, I got ever so many thumps without knowing who gave them to me or being able to see anybody. And now this head isn't anywhere around here, though I saw it cut off with my own eyes and the blood running from the body like from a fountain."

"What blood and fountains are you talking about, enemy of God and his saints?" said the innkeeper. "Don't you see, you thief, that the blood and the fountain are only these wineskins here that have been stabbed and have left red wine swimming all over this room? May I see the soul of him who stabbed them swimming in hell!"

"I know nothing about that," said Sancho. "All I know is that if we don't find this head, I'll have the bad luck to have my county melt away like salt in water." Sancho awake was worse than his master asleep, so much had his master's promises affected him.

The innkeeper was beside himself at the nonchalant squire and his mischievous master. He swore that it would not be like the last time when they went without paying and that their privileges of chivalry would be of no excuse for either of them. They would compensate him, down to the cost of the plugs that would have to be put in the damaged wineskins.

The priest was holding Don Quixote's hands, who, imagining he had now ended the adventure and was in the presence of Princess Micomicona, knelt before the priest and said, "Exalted and beauteous lady, your highness may live from this day forth fearless of any harm this base being could do to you. I, too, from this day forth am released from the promise I gave you, since by the help of God on high and by the favor of her by whom I live and breathe, I have fulfilled it so successfully."

"Didn't I say so?" said Sancho on hearing this. "I wasn't drunk at all. Tell me if my master hasn't already salted that giant![1] As surely as the sunrise, my county is waiting for me!"

Who couldn't help but laugh at the absurdities of the pair, master and man? And laugh they did, all except the innkeeper, who cursed himself. At length the barber, Cardenio, and the priest managed with no small trouble to get Don Quixote on the bed, and he fell asleep with every appearance of excessive fatigue.

[1] *already salted that giant*: "so dead that he can be cured in salt".

They left him to sleep and came out to the gate of the inn to console Sancho Panza on not having found the head of the giant; but much more work had they to appease the innkeeper, who was furious at the sudden death of his wineskins.

His wife said, half scolding, half crying, "Cursed be the day and hour he came into my house, this knight-errant! Would that I had never set eyes on him, for he's cost me dear. The last time, he went off without paying for supper, bed, straw, or barley—for himself and his squire and a hack and a donkey. He said he was a knight adventurer—God send unlucky adventures to him and all the adventurers in the world—and therefore not bound to pay anything, for it was so settled by the statutes of knight-errantry. And then, all because of him, came the other gentleman who carried off my tail, and gave it back more than two cuartillos[2] the worse, all stripped of its hair, so that it is no use for my husband's purpose. Then, for the finishing touch, to burst my wineskins and spill my wine! I wish I saw his own blood spilled! But let him not deceive himself, for by my father's bones and my mother's eternal soul, if they don't pay me every last cuarto,[3] my name isn't my name, and I'm not my father's daughter."

All this and more to the same effect the innkeeper's wife delivered with great irritation. Her good maid Maritornes backed her up, while her daughter held her peace and smiled from time to time. The priest smoothed matters by promising to make good all losses to the best of his power, not only as regarded the wineskins but also the wine, and above all the depreciation of the tail, which they valued so highly. Dorotea comforted Sancho, telling him that she pledged herself, as soon as it should appear certain that his master had decapitated the giant and she found herself peacefully established in her kingdom, to bestow upon him the best county there was in it. With this Sancho consoled himself and assured the princess she might rely upon it that he had seen the head of the giant, and as further proof, it had a beard that reached to his waist. If it was not to be seen now, it was because everything that happened in that house was by enchantment, as he himself had proved the last time he had lodged there. Dorotea said she fully believed it and that he need not be uneasy, for all would go well and turn out as he wished.

With everyone appeased, the priest was eager to go on with the novel, as he saw there was but little more left to read. Dorotea and the others begged him to finish it, and he, as he was willing to please them and enjoyed reading it himself, continued the tale in these words:

And so it was that from the confidence Anselmo placed in Camila's virtue, he lived happy and carefree, while Camila was diligent in treating Lotario with contempt so that Anselmo might suppose her feelings toward him to be the opposite of what they were. The better to support the ruse, Lotario begged to be excused from coming to the house, as the displeasure with which Camila regarded his presence was plain to be seen. But the befooled Anselmo said he would on no

[2] *cuartillos:* The *cuartillo* was a copper alloy coin valued at a quarter of a real (8.5 maravedis).
[3] *cuarto:* copper coin valued at four maravedis.

account allow such a thing. And so in a thousand ways he became the author of his dishonor, believing that he was ensuring his happiness.

Meanwhile, the pleasure Leonela derived from feeling entitled to carry on her love affair reached new heights. Disregarding all other considerations, she gave in to her desires to the hilt, confident that her mistress would protect her and even advise her on how to continue without fear of discovery. At last one night Anselmo heard footsteps in Leonela's room, and on trying to enter to see who it was, he found that the door was held against him, which made him all the more determined to open it. Exerting his strength, he forced it open and entered the room in time to see a man leaping through the window into the street. He ran quickly to seize him or discover who he was, but he was unable to carry out either purpose, for Leonela flung her arms round him crying, "Be calm, señor! Do not give way to passion or follow him who has escaped. He belongs to me, so much so that he is my husband."

Anselmo would not believe it, but blind with rage drew a dagger and threatened to stab Leonela, ordering her to tell the truth or he would kill her. She, in her fear, not knowing what she was saying, exclaimed, "Do not kill me, señor, for I can tell you things more important than any you can imagine."

"Tell me then at once or you die," said Anselmo.

"It would be impossible for me now," said Leonela, "since I am so agitated. Leave me till tomorrow, and then you shall hear from me what will fill you with astonishment. Rest assured that he who leaped through the window is a young man of this city who has given me his hand in marriage."[4]

Anselmo was appeased with this and was content to wait during the length of time she asked of him, for he never expected to hear anything against Camila, so satisfied and sure of her virtue was he; and so he went out of the room and left Leonela locked in, telling her she could not come out until she had told him all she had to make known to him. He went at once to see Camila, and he told her everything that had passed between him and her handmaid and the promise she had given him to inform him of matters of great importance.

There is no need of saying whether Camila was agitated or not, for so great was her fear (well-founded to be sure) that Leonela would tell Anselmo all she knew of her faithlessness, she did not have the courage to wait and see if her suspicions were confirmed. That same night, as soon as she thought that Anselmo was asleep, she packed up the most valuable jewels she had and some money, and without being observed by anybody escaped from the house and went straightaway to Lotario's, to whom she related what had occurred, imploring him to hide her in a safe place or flee with her where they might be beyond Anselmo's reach. The state of confusion to which Camila reduced Lotario was such that he was unable to utter a word in reply, still less to decide what he should do. At length he resolved to hide her in a convent where a sister of his was prioress. Camila agreed to this, and with the speed the circumstances demanded, Lotario took her to the convent and left her there, and then himself left the city without letting anyone know of his departure.

[4] *given me his hand in marriage:* On clandestine marriage, see footnote 9, page 213.

Anselmo rose as soon as daylight came. In his eagerness to learn what Leonela had to tell him, he failed to notice that Camila was missing from his side, but hurried to the room where he had the maid locked in. He opened the door, entered, but found no Leonela. All he found was some sheets knotted to the window, a clear sign that she had let herself down from it and escaped. Downcast, he returned to tell Camila, but not finding her in bed or anywhere in the house he was lost in astonishment. He asked the servants of the house about her, but none of them could give him any explanation. As he was going in search of Camila, it happened by chance that he observed that her jewelry boxes were lying open and that the greater part of her jewels were gone. At this he became fully aware of his disgrace, and that Leonela was not the cause of his misfortune. Just as he was, half-dressed and overcome with grief, he went to see his friend Lotario to make known his sorrow to him. But when he was unable to find him, and when the servants reported that he had been absent from the house all night and had taken with him all the money he had, he felt as though he were losing his senses. To make matters complete, on returning to his own house he found it deserted and empty, not one of all his servants, male or female, remaining in it. He knew not what to think, or say, or do, and his reason seemed to be deserting him little by little.

He reviewed his position, and saw himself in a moment left without wife, friend, or servants, abandoned, he felt, by the heaven above him, and more than all robbed of his honor, for in Camila's disappearance he saw his own ruin. After long reflection he resolved at last to go to his friend's village, where he had stayed when he created the opportunities for his every misfortune that was set in motion. He locked the doors of his house, mounted his horse, and with a broken spirit set out on his journey. He had hardly gone halfway when, harassed by his reflections, he had to dismount and tie his horse to a tree, at the foot of which he threw himself, giving vent to piteous heartrending sighs. There he remained till nearly nightfall, when he observed a man approaching on horseback from the city. After greeting him, he asked what news there was from Florence.

The citizen replied, "The strangest that have been heard for many a day. It is reported abroad that Lotario, the great friend of the wealthy Anselmo, who lives near San Giovanni,[5] carried off last night Camila, Anselmo's wife, who has also disappeared. All this has been told by a maidservant of Camila's, whom the governor found last night lowering herself by a sheet from the windows of Anselmo's house. I know not indeed, precisely, how the affair came to pass. All I know is that the whole city is wondering at the occurrence, for no one could have expected a thing of the kind, seeing the great and intimate friendship that existed between them, so great, they say, that they were called 'The Two Friends.'"

"Is it known at all," said Anselmo, "what road Lotario and Camila took?"

"Not in the least," said the citizen, "though the governor has been very active in searching for them."

"God speed you, señor," said Anselmo.

[5] *San Giovanni:* Baptistery of Saint John.

"God be with you," said the citizen and went his way.

This disastrous news came near to robbing Anselmo not only of his senses but of his life. He got up as well as he was able and reached the house of his friend, who as yet knew nothing of his misfortune, but seeing him come pale, worn, and haggard, he gathered that he was suffering some heavy affliction. Anselmo at once begged to be allowed to retire to his room and to be given writing materials. His wish was complied with and he was left in bed and unattended, as he requested, with the door locked after him. Once he found himself alone, thoughts of his misfortune began so heavily to weigh on him that he soon recognized his life was drawing to a close, and therefore he resolved to leave behind a declaration of the cause of his strange end. He began to write, but before he had put down all he meant to say, his breath failed him and he yielded up his life, a victim of the pain brought by his imprudent meddling.

The master of the house, observing that it was now late and that Anselmo did not call, decided to go in and see if his friend's condition had worsened. He found Anselmo lying on his face, his body partly in the bed, partly on the writing table, on which he lay with the written paper open and the pen still in his hand. Having first called to him without receiving any answer, his host approached him. He took him by the hand, and when he found that it was cold, knew he was dead. Greatly surprised and distressed, he summoned the household to witness the sad fate that had befallen Anselmo. Then he read the paper, the handwriting of which he recognized as his, and which contained these words:

> A foolish and imprudent desire has robbed me of life. If the news of my death should reach Camila's ears, let her know that I forgive her, for she was not bound to perform miracles, nor ought I to have required her to perform them; and since I have been the author of my own dishonor, there is no reason why—

Thus far Anselmo had written, from which it could be inferred that at that point, before he could finish what he had to say, his life came to an end. The next day his friend gave notice of his death to his relatives, who had already learned of his misfortune, as well as the convent where Camila lay almost on the point of accompanying her husband on that inevitable journey—not on account of the news of his death, but because of those she received of her lover's departure. Although she considered herself a widow, it is said she refused either to abandon the convent or take the veil,[6] until not long afterwards, word reached her that Lotario had been killed in a battle in which Monsieur de Lautrec had been recently engaged with the Great Captain Gonzalo Fernández de Córdoba in the kingdom of Naples,[7] where her too late repentant lover had gone to live. On learning this, Camila took the veil and shortly afterwards died, worn out

[6] *take the veil:* take monastic vows to become a nun.

[7] *Lotario had been killed in a battle in which Monsieur de Lautrec . . . in the kingdom of Naples:* Lotario is killed in the Battle of Cerignola (1503), in which French forces that included the young Odet de Foix, Vicomte de Lautrec were defeated by the Spanish under Gonzalo Fernández de Córdoba. The account of the battle is included in the history book found in the valise along with the manuscript of *The Imprudent Meddler*.

by grief and melancholy. This was the end of all three, an end that came of a thoughtless beginning.

"I like this novel," said the priest, "but I cannot persuade myself of its truth; and if it has been invented, the author's invention is faulty, for it is impossible to imagine any husband so foolish as to try such a costly experiment as Anselmo's. If it had been represented as occurring between a lover and his mistress, it might pass; but between husband and wife there is something of an impossibility about it. As to the way in which the story is told, however, I have no fault to find."

CHAPTER XXXVI

WHICH TREATS OF THE STUPENDOUS BATTLE THAT DON QUIXOTE HAD WITH SOME WINESKINS,[1] WITH OTHER STRANGE OCCURRENCES THAT TOOK PLACE IN THE INN

At that moment the innkeeper, who was standing at the gate of the inn, exclaimed, "Here comes a fine troop of guests. If they stop here, we can say *gaudeamus*."[2]

"What people are they?" asked Cardenio.

"Four men," said the innkeeper, "riding *a la jineta*,[3] with lances and bucklers, and all with black veils. There is a woman in white with them riding sidesaddle, whose face is also veiled, and two attendants on foot."

"Are they very near?" asked the priest.

"So near," answered the innkeeper, "that here they come."

Hearing this Dorotea covered her face, and Cardenio retreated into Don Quixote's room. Hardly had they time to do so before the whole party the host had described entered the inn. The four that were on horseback, who were of highbred appearance and bearing, dismounted and came forward to take down the woman who rode sidesaddle, and one of them taking her in his arms placed her in a chair that stood at the entrance of the room where Cardenio had hidden himself. All this time neither she nor they had removed their veils or spoken a word, but when the woman was left in the chair, she gave a deep sigh and let her arms fall like one who was ill and weak. The attendants on foot then led the horses away to the stable.

Observing this, the priest, curious to know who these people in such dress and keeping such silence were, went to where the servants were standing and put the question to one of them, who answered him, "Faith, sir, I can't tell you who they are. I only know they seem to be people of distinction, particularly the one who advanced to take the lady you saw in his arms. I say so because all the rest show him respect, and nothing is done except what he directs and orders."

"And the lady, who is she?" asked the priest.

[1] *Which Treats . . . With Some Wineskins:* Narrated in the previous chapter. The incongruity is probably due to rushed edits before publication.

[2] *gaudeamus:* Latin, "let us rejoice", a call to celebrate.

[3] *riding* a la jineta: riding with short stirrups and close contact with the horse's sides for control.

"That I can't tell you either," said the servant, "for I haven't seen her face during the whole journey. I have indeed heard her sigh many times and utter such groans that she seems to be giving up the ghost every time; but it's no wonder if we don't know more than we have told you, as my comrade and I have only been in their company two days, for having met us on the road they begged and persuaded us to accompany them to Andalusia, promising to pay us well."

"And have you heard any of them called by his name?" asked the priest.

"No, indeed," replied the servant. "They all keep a marvelous silence on the road. Not a sound is to be heard among them except the poor lady's sighs and sobs, which make us pity her. We feel sure that wherever it is she's going, it's against her will, and as far as one can judge from her dress she's a nun or, what is more likely, about to become one. Perhaps it's because taking the vows is not of her own free will that she's so unhappy as she seems to be."

"That may well be," said the priest, and leaving them he returned to where Dorotea was.

She, hearing the veiled lady sigh and moved by natural compassion, drew near to her and said, "What are you suffering from, señora? If it is anything that women are familiar with and know how to relieve, I offer you my services with all my heart."

To this the unhappy lady made no reply, and though Dorotea repeated her offers more earnestly she still kept silence, until the gentleman with the veil, who, the servant said, was obeyed by the rest, approached and said to Dorotea, "Do not give yourself the trouble, señora, of making any offers to that woman, for it is her way to give no thanks for anything that is done for her. And do not try to make her answer unless you want to hear some lie from her lips."

"I have never told a lie," was the immediate reply of her who had been silent until now. "On the contrary, it is because I am so truthful and so ignorant of deceitful schemes that I am now in this miserable condition. This I call you yourself to witness, for it is my unstained truth that has made you false and a liar."

Cardenio heard these words clearly and distinctly, being quite close to the speaker, for there was only the door of Don Quixote's room between them. The instant he did so, uttering a loud exclamation he cried, "Good God! What is this I hear? What voice is this that has reached my ears?" Startled at the voice, the lady turned her head; and not seeing the speaker she stood up and attempted to enter the room. Observing this, the gentleman held her back, preventing her from moving a step. In her agitation and sudden movement, the silk with which she had veiled herself fell off and revealed a face that was a miracle of beauty, yet pale and terrified; for she kept turning her eyes everywhere she could direct her gaze, with an intensity that made her look as if she had lost her senses and gestures that excited the pity of Dorotea and all who beheld her, though they knew not their cause.

The gentleman grasped her firmly by the shoulders, and being so fully occupied with holding her back, he was unable to put a hand to his veil, which was falling off, as it soon did entirely. Dorotea, who was holding the lady in her arms, raising her eyes saw that he who likewise held her was her husband, Don

Fernando. As soon as she recognized him, with a prolonged plaintive cry drawn from the depths of her heart, she fell backwards fainting, and but for the barber being close by to catch her in his arms, she would have fallen completely to the ground. The priest at once hastened to uncover her face and throw water on it. As he did so, Don Fernando (for it was he who held the other in his arms) recognized her and stood as if death-stricken by the sight. He did not, however, relax his grasp of Luscinda (for it was she who was struggling to release herself from his hold), having recognized Cardenio by his voice, as he had recognized her. Cardenio also heard Dorotea's cry as she fell fainting, and imagining that it came from his Luscinda, burst forth in terror from the room. The first thing he saw was Don Fernando with Luscinda in his arms. Don Fernando, too, recognized Cardenio at once; and all three, Luscinda, Cardenio, and Dorotea, stood in silent amazement scarcely knowing what had happened to them.[4]

They gazed at one another without speaking, Dorotea at Don Fernando, Don Fernando at Cardenio, Cardenio at Luscinda, and Luscinda at Cardenio. The first to break silence was Luscinda, who thus addressed Don Fernando: "Leave me, Señor Don Fernando, for the sake of what you owe to yourself. If no other reason will induce you, leave me to cling to the wall of which I am the ivy, to the support from which neither your demands, nor your threats, nor your promises, nor your gifts have been able to detach me. See how Heaven, by ways strange and hidden from our sight, has brought me face to face with my true husband. Well you know by dear-bought experience that death alone will be able to efface him from my memory. May this plain declaration, then, lead you (as you can do nothing else) to turn your love into rage, your affection into resentment, and so to take my life; for if I yield it up in the presence of my beloved husband, I count it well bestowed. It may be by my death he will be convinced that I kept my faith to him to the last moment of life."

Meanwhile, Dorotea had come to herself and heard Luscinda's words, by which she recognized who she was. But seeing that Don Fernando did not yet release her or reply to her, she steeled her resolve as well as she could, rose, and knelt at his feet, and with a flood of bright and touching tears addressed him thus:

"If, my lord, the beams of that sun you hold eclipsed in your arms did not dazzle and rob your eyes of sight, you would have seen by this time that she who

[4] *The gentleman grasped her . . . knowing what had happened to them:* The scene is brimming with recognitions, as evidenced by the fivefold use of the verb *conocer* (to recognize). Aristotle taught that *anagnorisis*, the discovery of a hidden truth or recognition of a person's true identity, was a powerful element in drama. He paired this with the concept of *peripeteia*, a reversal of a character's circumstances that marks a turning point in the story. Scenes like this one, along with similar scenes in the coming chapters, are peppered with the language of wonder and appeals to the marvelous. The aesthetic theory of the day held that by crafting scenes of recognition and reversal, authors are able to generate a pleasing sense of wonder (*admiratio*) on the part of the reader. But the marvelous had to be contained in the realm of the plausible. Too many coincidences, too many turns of plot beyond belief, and the story would ring false, losing its power to captivate. The reader will have to decide how well Cervantes does in navigating between these two poles.

kneels at your feet is, so long as you will have it so, the unhappy and unfortunate Dorotea. I am that lowly peasant girl whom you, in your goodness or for your pleasure, chose to raise to the height where she could call herself yours. I am she who, in the seclusion of innocence, led a contented life until at the voice of your pleas and what seemed your true and tender passion, she opened the gates of her modesty and surrendered to you the keys of her liberty—a gift by you ungratefully received, as is clearly shown by my forced retreat to the place where you find me and by your appearance under the circumstances in which I see you. Nevertheless, I would not have you suppose that I have come here driven by my shame; it is only grief and sorrow at seeing myself forgotten by you that have led me. It was your will to make me yours, and you did so follow your will that now, even though you might wish otherwise, you cannot help being mine.

"Consider, my lord, whether the unsurpassed affection I bear you may compensate for the beauty and noble birth for which you would desert me. You cannot belong to the fair Luscinda because you are mine, nor can she be yours because she is Cardenio's. It will be easier, as a moment's reflection will show, to bend your will to love one who adores you, than to lead another who abhors you to love you truly. You sought me when I was vulnerable, you laid siege to my virtue, you were not ignorant of my station: well do you know how I yielded wholly to your will. There is no ground or reason for you to plead deception; that being so, if you are a Christian as you are a gentleman, why do you go to such straits to put off making me as happy at last as you did at first? And if you will not have me for what I am, your true and lawful wife, at least take and accept me as your slave, for so long as I am yours I will count myself happy and fortunate. Do not by deserting me let my shame become the talk of the gossips in the streets. Do not make the old age of my parents miserable; for the loyal services they as faithful vassals have ever rendered yours are not deserving of such a return. And if you think it will debase your blood to mingle it with mine, reflect that there is little or no nobility in the world that has not traveled the same road, and that in illustrious lineages it is not the woman's blood that is of account; and, moreover, that true nobility consists in virtue, and if you show yourself lacking in virtue by refusing me what you rightly owe me, then even I have higher claims to nobility than yours. To make an end, señor, these are my last words to you: whether you wish it or not, I am your wife. Your words are your witnesses, which must not and ought not be false if you pride yourself on that for the lack of which you scorn me.[5] The pledge you gave me testifies on my behalf, as does Heaven, which you yourself did call to witness the promise you made me; and if all this falls short, your own conscience will not fail to lift up its silent voice in the midst of your laughter, and vindicate the truth of what I say and mar your highest pleasures and joys."

All this and more the injured Dorotea delivered with such earnest feeling and such tears that everyone present, even those who came with Don Fernando, were moved to join her in them. Don Fernando listened to her without replying until, ceasing to speak, she gave way to such sobs and sighs that it would have been a

[5] *on that for the lack of which you scorn me:* noble birth.

heart of bronze that was not softened by the sight of her great sorrow. Luscinda stood looking at her with no less compassion for her sufferings than admiration for her intelligence and beauty, and would have gone to her to say some words of comfort but was prevented by Don Fernando's grasp, which held her fast.

He, overwhelmed with confusion and astonishment, after regarding Dorotea for some moments with a fixed gaze, opened his arms, and releasing Luscinda, exclaimed, "You have conquered, fair Dorotea, you have conquered; for it is impossible to have the heart to deny the united force of so many truths."

Luscinda, still light-headed, was on the point of falling to the ground when Don Fernando released her, but Cardenio, who stood near, having retreated behind Don Fernando to escape recognition, casting fear aside and without regard to what might happen, ran forward to support her. As he clasped her in his arms he said, "If Heaven in its compassion is willing to let you rest at last, mistress of my heart, true, constant, and fair, nowhere can you rest more safely than in these arms that now receive you, and received you once before, when fortune permitted me to call you mine."

At these words Luscinda looked up at Cardenio, at first coming to recognize him by his voice and then satisfying herself by her eyes that it was he. Hardly knowing what she did, and heedless of all considerations of decorum, she flung her arms around his neck and pressing her face close to his said, "Yes, my dear lord, you are the true master of this your slave, though a contrary fortune should again stand between us and fresh dangers threaten this life that hangs on yours."

A strange sight was this for Don Fernando and those that stood around, filled with surprise at an incident so unexpected. It appeared to Dorotea that Don Fernando changed color and looked as though he meant to take vengeance on Cardenio, for she observed him put his hand to his sword. The instant her suspicion was aroused, with incredible speed she clasped him round the knees, and kissing them and holding him so as to prevent his moving, she said while her tears continued to flow, "What is it you are thinking of doing, my only refuge, at this unexpected turn of events? You have your wife at your feet, and she whom you would have for your wife is in the arms of her husband. Reflect whether it would be right for you, whether it would even be possible for you, to undo what Heaven has done, or whether it would be becoming in you to seek to raise her to be your mate who in spite of every obstacle, and strong in her truth and constancy, is before your eyes, bathing with the tears of love the face and breast of her lawful husband. For God's sake I entreat you, for your own sake I implore you, let not this open demonstration rouse your anger; but rather so calm it as to allow these two lovers to live in peace and quiet without any interference from you, so long as Heaven permits them. In so doing, you will prove the generosity of your lofty, noble spirit, and the world shall see that reason has more influence over you than passion."

All the time Dorotea was speaking, Cardenio, though he held Luscinda in his arms, never took his eyes off Don Fernando, for he was determined, if he saw him make any hostile movement, to try and defend himself and resist as best he could all who might assail him, though it should cost him his life. But now Don

Fernando's friends, as well as the priest and the barber (who had been present the whole time, not to mention the worthy Sancho Panza), ran forward and gathered round Don Fernando. One and all, they entreated him to have regard for Dorotea's tears and not to allow her rightful expectations to be disappointed, since, as they firmly believed, what she said was true. Nor, they would have him consider, was it by accident as it might seem, but by a special disposition of Providence that they had all met in a place where no one would have expected to meet. The priest reminded him that only death could part Luscinda from Cardenio; that even if the sword were to separate them, they would think their death most happy; and that in a circumstance without remedy his wisest course was, striving for self-mastery, to show a generous spirit and freely allow the two to enjoy the happiness Heaven had granted them. He further called on him to turn his eyes upon the beauty of Dorotea, for then he would see that few if any could equal much less excel her, while to that beauty should be added her modesty and the surpassing love she bore him. But besides all this, he reminded him that if he prided himself on being a gentleman and a Christian, he could not do otherwise than keep his pledge; and that in doing so he would obey God and meet the approval of all sensible people, who hold it to be the privilege of beauty—even in one of humble birth, provided virtue accompany it—to be permitted to raise itself to the level of any rank, without any slur upon the one who places it on equal footing with himself; and furthermore that when the potent sway of passion asserts itself, so long as there be no mixture of sin in it, he is not to be blamed who gives way to it.

To be brief, they added to these such other forcible arguments that Don Fernando's manly heart (being after all nourished by noble blood) was touched and yielded to the truth, which he could not deny even had he wished it. As evidence of his submission and acceptance of the good advice offered him, he stooped down and embraced Dorotea, saying to her, "Rise, dear lady, for it is not right that the one I hold in my heart should be kneeling at my feet. If until now I have given no proof to my words, it may have been by Heaven's decree in order that, seeing the constancy with which you love me, I may learn to value you as you deserve. What I entreat of you is that you do not reproach me for my transgression and grievous wrongdoing; for the same cause and force that drove me to make you mine impelled me to struggle against being yours. To prove this, turn and look at the eyes of the now happy Luscinda, and you will see in them an excuse for all my errors. As she has found and gained the object of her desires, and I have found in you what satisfies all my wishes, may she live in peace and contentment as many happy years with her Cardenio as I pray Heaven will allow me to live with my Dorotea."

With these words he once more embraced her and pressed his face to hers with so much tenderness that he had to take great care to keep his tears from completing the proof of his love and repentance in the sight of all. Not so Luscinda, Cardenio, and almost all the others, for they shed so many tears, some at their own happiness, some at that of the others, that one would have supposed a heavy calamity had fallen upon them all. Even Sancho Panza was weeping, though afterwards he said he only wept because he saw that Dorotea was not, as he fancied, Queen Micomicona, of whom he expected such great rewards. Their wonder as well as their weeping lasted some time. Then Cardenio and Luscinda went and fell on their knees before Don Fernando, returning him thanks for the favor he had rendered them in language so grateful that he knew not how to answer them, and so he raised them up and embraced them with every mark of affection and courtesy.

He then asked Dorotea how she had managed to reach a place so far removed from her home, and she in a few fitting words told all that she had previously related to Cardenio, with which Don Fernando and his companions were so delighted that they wished the story had been longer, so charmingly did Dorotea describe her misadventures.

When she had finished, Don Fernando recounted what had befallen him in the city after he had found in Luscinda's bosom the paper in which she declared that she was Cardenio's wife and could never be his. He said he meant to kill her—and would have done so had he not been prevented by her parents—and that he left the house full of rage and shame, resolving to avenge himself when a more convenient opportunity arose. The next day he learned that Luscinda had disappeared from her father's house, and that no one could say where she had gone. Finally, at the end of some months he found out that she was in a convent and meant to remain there all the rest of her life, if she were not to share it with Cardenio.

As soon as he learned this, taking these three gentlemen as his companions, he arrived at her hiding place but avoided speaking to her, fearing that if it were known he was there, stricter precautions would be taken in the convent. Waiting for a time when the porter's lodge was open, he left two to guard the gate while he and the other entered the convent in search of Luscinda, whom they found in the cloisters in conversation with one of the nuns and carried off without giving her time to resist. They then reached a place with her where they could provide themselves with what they needed for taking her away, all of which they were able to do in complete safety, as the convent was in the country at a considerable distance from the city. He added that when Luscinda found herself in his power she fell into a swoon, and after regaining consciousness did nothing but weep and sigh without speaking a word. Thus in silence and tears they came to the inn, which for him was coming to heaven, where all the misfortunes of earth are brought to a certain and final end.

CHAPTER XXXVII

IN WHICH IS CONTINUED THE STORY OF THE FAMOUS PRINCESS MICOMICONA, WITH OTHER AMUSING ADVENTURES

To all this Sancho listened with no little sorrow of heart to see how his hopes of nobility were fading away and vanishing in smoke, how the fair Princess Micomicona had turned into Dorotea and the giant into Don Fernando—all while his master was sleeping tranquilly, completely unaware of all that had come to pass. Dorotea was unable to persuade herself that her present happiness was not all a dream. Cardenio was in a similar state of mind, and Luscinda's thoughts ran in the same direction. Don Fernando gave thanks to Heaven for the favor shown to him and for having been rescued from the intricate labyrinth in which he had been brought so near the destruction of his good name and of his soul. In short, everyone in the inn was full of contentment and satisfaction at the happy end of such a complicated and hopeless business. The priest in his wisdom made sound reflections upon the whole affair and congratulated each upon his good fortune. But the one who was in the highest spirits and good humor was the innkeeper's wife, because of the promise Cardenio and the priest had given her to pay for all the losses and damage she had sustained on Don Quixote's account.

Sancho, as has been already said, was the only one who was distressed, unhappy, and dejected; and so with a long face he went in to his master, who had just awoke, and said to him, "Sir Woeful Countenance, your worship may as well sleep as much as you want without bothering yourself about killing any giant or restoring her kingdom to the princess. For that's all over and settled now."

"I should think it was," replied Don Quixote, "for I have had the most prodigious and stupendous battle with a giant that I believe I have had in all my life. With one backstroke—*swish!*—I brought his head tumbling to the ground, and so much blood gushed forth from him that it ran in rivulets over the earth like water."

"Like red wine, your worship might better say," replied Sancho; "for I would have you know, if you don't know it, that the dead giant is a hacked-at wineskin, and the blood six arrobas[1] of red wine that it had in its belly. The cut-off head is the bitch that bore me—and the devil take it all."

"What are you talking about, fool?" said Don Quixote. "Are you in your right mind?"

[1] *arrobas:* See footnote 7, page 71.

"Let your worship get up," said Sancho, "and you will see the nice business you've made of it and what we have to pay, and you will see the queen turned into a private lady called Dorotea, and other things that will astonish you, if you understand them."

"I shall not be surprised at anything of the kind," returned Don Quixote, "for if you remember the last time we were here, I told you that everything that happened was a matter of enchantment. It would be no wonder if it were the same now."

"I could believe it all," replied Sancho, "if my blanketing was something of the same kind also. Only it wasn't, but real and genuine. I saw the innkeeper—who is here today—holding one end of the blanket and eagerly tossing me up to the skies, with a bellyful of laughs and all his might. When it comes to recognizing people, I hold for my part, simple and sinner as I am, that there is no enchantment about it at all, but a lot of bruising and bad luck."

"Nonetheless, God will give a remedy," said Don Quixote. "Hand me my clothes and let me go out, for I want to see these transformations and things you speak of."

Sancho fetched him his clothes; and while he was dressing, the priest gave Don Fernando and the others present an account of Don Quixote's madness and of the stratagem they had made use of to withdraw him from that Peña Pobre, where he imagined himself exiled because of his lady's scorn. He also described to them nearly all the adventures Sancho had mentioned. At this they marveled and laughed not a little, all of them in agreement that his was the strangest form of madness an addled mind could be capable of. The priest added that now that Señora Dorotea's good fortune prevented her from proceeding with their purpose, it would be necessary to devise or discover some other way of getting him home.

Cardenio proposed to carry out the scheme they had begun and suggested that Luscinda would act and support Dorotea's part sufficiently well.

"No," said Don Fernando, "that must not be, for I wish for Dorotea to proceed with her role. As long as the worthy gentleman's village is not very far off, I shall be happy if anything can be done for his relief."

"It is not more than two days' journey from here," said the priest.

"Even if it were more," said Don Fernando, "I would gladly travel so far for the sake of doing such a good work."

At that moment Don Quixote came out in full armor, with Mambrino's helmet (all dented as it was) on his head, his buckler on his arm, and leaning on his staff or spear. The strange figure he presented filled Don Fernando and the rest with amazement as they contemplated his lean, yellow face half a league long, his motley armor, and the solemnity of his deportment. They stood silently waiting to see what he would say.

He, fixing his eyes on the fair Dorotea, addressed her with great gravity and composure:

"I am informed by my squire here, fair lady, that your greatness has been annihilated and your being abolished, since, from a queen and lady of high degree as you used to be, you have been turned into a private maiden. If this has been done by the command of the wizard king your father, through fear that I should not provide you the aid you need and are entitled to, I may tell you he did not know and does not know half the Mass and was little versed in the annals of chivalry. For if he had read and gone through them as attentively and deliberately as I have, he would have found at every turn that knights of less renown than mine have accomplished things more difficult. It is no great matter to kill a whelp of a giant, however arrogant he may be, for only a few hours ago I myself was engaged with one. I will no more speak of it, that they may not say I am lying. Time, however, which reveals all, will tell the tale when we least expect it."

"You were engaged with a couple of wineskins, not a giant," said the innkeeper at this.

Don Fernando told him to hold his tongue and on no account interrupt Don Quixote, who continued, "I say in conclusion, high and disinherited lady, that if your father has brought about this metamorphosis in your person for the reason I have mentioned, you ought not to attach any importance to it; for there is no peril on earth through which my sword will not force a way, and with it, before many days are over, I will bring your enemy's head to the ground and place on yours the crown of your kingdom."

Don Quixote said no more and waited for the reply of the princess, who aware of Don Fernando's determination to carry on the ruse until Don Quixote had been conveyed to his home, with great ease of manner and gravity made answer, "Whoever told you, valiant Knight of the Woeful Countenance, that I had undergone any change or transformation did not tell you the truth, for I am the same as I was yesterday. It is true that certain strokes of good fortune, which have given me more than I could have hoped for, have made some alteration in me; but I have not therefore ceased to be what I was before or to entertain the same desire I have had all along of availing myself of the might of your valiant and invincible arm. And so in your kindness, señor, reinstate the father that begot me in your good opinion, and be assured that he was a wise and prudent man, since by his craft he found out such a sure and easy way of remedying my misfortune. For I believe, señor, that had it not been for you I should never have lit upon the good fortune I now possess. In this I am saying what is perfectly true, as most of these gentlemen who are present can fully testify. All that remains is to set out on our journey tomorrow, for today we could not make much progress. Regarding the rest of the happy outcome I am looking forward to, I trust to God and the valor of your heart."

So said the discreet Dorotea. On hearing her, Don Quixote turned to Sancho and said to him with an angry air, "I declare now, little Sancho, you are the greatest little villain in Spain. Tell me, thief and vagabond, did you not just now inform me that this princess had been turned into a maiden named Dorotea, and that the head which I am persuaded I cut off from a giant was the bitch that bore you, and other nonsense that put me in the greatest vexation I have ever been in all my life? I vow ..."—here he looked to heaven and clenched his teeth—"... I have a mind to exact a toll on you that will knock sense from here to eternity into the skull of every lying squire of a knight-errant."

"Let your worship calm down, señor," returned Sancho. "It may well be that I've been mistaken about the change of the lady Princess Micomicona. But as to the giant's head, or at least as to the slashing of the wineskins and the blood being red wine, I make no mistake, as sure as there is a God. The wounded wineskins are there at the head of your worship's bed, and the wine has made a lake of the room. If not, you'll see 'when it's time to fry the eggs'—I mean when his worship the innkeeper bills you for all the damage. As for the rest, I'm heartily glad that her ladyship the queen is as she was, for it concerns me as much as anyone."

"I tell you, Sancho," said Don Quixote, "you are a fool, I am sorry to say—and that's that."

"That will do," said Don Fernando. "Let us say no more about it. As her ladyship the princess proposes to set out tomorrow because it is too late today, so be it. We will pass the night in pleasant conversation, and tomorrow we will all accompany Señor Don Quixote; for we wish to witness the valiant and unparalleled achievements he is about to perform in the course of this mighty enterprise which he has undertaken."

"It is I who shall wait upon and accompany you," said Don Quixote. "I am much gratified by the favor that is bestowed upon me and the good opinion entertained of me, which I shall strive to justify or it shall cost me my life, or even more, if it can possibly cost me more."

Many were the compliments and expressions of politeness that passed between Don Quixote and Don Fernando, but they were brought to an end by a traveler who at that time entered the inn. He seemed from his attire to be a Christian recently arrived from the country of the Moors.[2] He was dressed in a short-skirted coat of blue cloth with half-sleeves and without a collar. His breeches were also of blue cloth, his cap of the same color, and he wore riding boots the color of ripe dates and had a Moorish cutlass slung from a baldric[3] across his chest. Behind him, mounted upon a donkey, there came a woman dressed in Moorish fashion, with her face veiled and a scarf on her head. She wore a little brocaded cap and a mantle that covered her from her shoulders to her feet. The man was of a robust and well-proportioned frame, in age a little over forty, rather swarthy in complexion, with a long mustache and a full beard. In short, his appearance was such that if he had been well dressed, he would have been taken for a person of quality and good birth.

On entering he asked for a room, and when they told him there was none in the inn,[4] he seemed distressed. Approaching her who by her dress seemed to be a Moor, he took her down from the saddle in his arms. Luscinda, Dorotea, the

[2] *country of the Moors:* the coastal region of western and central Africa known then as the Barbary Coast and today as the Maghreb. At the time, the region was a patchwork of regencies in the orbit of the Ottoman Empire (apart from the independent Sultanate of Morocco), interspersed with a few Spanish presidios, or fortified outposts.

[3] *baldric:* ornamented belt strapped over the shoulder.

[4] *there was none in the inn:* See Luke 2:7, where there's no room in the inn for Joseph and Mary.

innkeeper's wife, her daughter, and Maritornes, attracted by the strange (and to them entirely new) costume, gathered round her.

Dorotea, who was always kindly, courteous, and quick-witted, perceiving that both she and the man who had brought her were distressed at not finding a room, said to her, "Do not be troubled, señora, by the discomfort and lack of luxuries here, for it is the way of roadside inns to be without them. Still, if you will be pleased to share our lodging with us," she said pointing to Luscinda, "perhaps you will have found worse accommodation in the course of your journey."

To this the veiled lady made no reply. All she did was to rise from her seat, crossing her hands upon her breast, bowing her head and bending her body as a sign that she returned thanks. From her silence they concluded that she must be a Moor and unable to speak a Christian tongue.

At this moment the captive[5] came up, having been until now otherwise engaged, and seeing that they all stood around his companion and that she made no reply to what they addressed to her, he said, "Ladies, this damsel hardly understands my language and can speak none but that of her own country, for which reason she does not and cannot answer what has been asked of her."

"Nothing has been asked of her," returned Luscinda. "She has only been offered our company for this evening and a share of the quarters we occupy, where she shall be made as comfortable as the circumstances allow, with the goodwill we are bound to show all strangers that stand in need of it, especially if it is a woman to whom the service is rendered."

"On her part and my own, señora," replied the captive, "I kiss your hands, and I esteem highly, as I ought, the favor you have offered, which, on such an occasion and coming from people of your appearance, is, it is plain to see, a very great one."

"Tell me, señor," said Dorotea, "is this lady a Christian or a Moor? For her dress and her silence lead us to imagine that she is what we could wish she was not."

"In her dress and body, she is a Moor," said he, "but in her soul, she is a very great Christian, for she has the most earnest desire to become one."

"Then she has not been baptized?" returned Luscinda.

"There has been no opportunity for that," replied the captive, "since she left Algiers, her native country and home, and up to the present she has not found herself in any such imminent danger of death as to make it necessary to baptize her before she has been instructed in all the ceremonies our holy mother Church ordains.[6] But as God is pleased, before long she shall be baptized with the solemnity befitting her, which is higher than her dress or mine indicates."

By these words he excited a desire in all who heard him to know who the Moorish lady and the captive were, but no one ventured to ask just then, seeing that it was a fitter moment for helping them to rest themselves than for questioning them about their lives. Dorotea took the Moorish lady by the hand, and

[5] *captive:* in context, a slave ransomed from captivity in Muslim North Africa.

[6] *as to make it necessary . . . Church ordains:* To die unbaptized was understood as dying in a state of original sin, which resulted in eternal separation from God.

leading her to a seat at her side, requested her to remove her veil. She looked at the captive as if to ask him what they meant and what she was to do. He said to her in Arabic that they asked her to take off her veil, and thereupon she removed it and revealed a face so lovely, that to Dorotea she seemed more beautiful than Luscinda, and to Luscinda more beautiful than Dorotea. All those present felt that if any beauty could compare with theirs, it was the Moorish lady's, and there were even those who were inclined to give hers a slight advantage. And as it is the privilege and charm of beauty to win the heart and secure goodwill, everyone became eager to show kindness and attention to the lovely Moor.

Don Fernando asked the captive what her name was, and he replied that it was Lela Zoraida; but the instant she heard him, she guessed what the Christian had asked and said hastily, with some displeasure and energy, "No, not Zoraida. Maria, Maria!" giving them to understand that she was named "Maria" and not "Zoraida."

These words, and the touching earnestness with which she uttered them, drew more than one tear from some of the listeners, particularly the women, who are by nature tender-hearted and compassionate. Luscinda embraced her affectionately saying, "Yes, yes, Maria, Maria."

At this the Moor replied, "Yes, yes, Maria. Zoraida *macange*," which means "not Zoraida."

Night was now approaching, and by the orders of those who accompanied Don Fernando, the innkeeper had taken care and pains to prepare for them the best supper that was in his power. The hour therefore having arrived, they all took their seats at a long table, like one found in a refectory,[7] for round or square table there was none in the inn. The seat of honor at the head of it, they assigned—over his protests—to Don Quixote, who desired Lady Micomicona to place herself by his side, as he was her protector. Luscinda and Zoraida took their places next her, opposite to them were Don Fernando and Cardenio, next the captive and the other gentlemen, and by the side of the ladies, the priest and the barber. And so they dined in high enjoyment, which was increased when they observed Don Quixote leave off eating, and, moved by an impulse like that which made him deliver himself at such length when he dined with the goatherds, begin to address them:

"Verily, gentlemen, if we reflect upon it, great and marvelous are the things they see who make profession of the order of knight-errantry. Tell me, what being is there in this world, who entering the gate of this castle at this moment and seeing us as we are here, would suppose or imagine us to be what we are? Who would say that this lady who is beside me was the great queen that we all know her to be, or that I am that Knight of the Woeful Countenance, trumpeted far and wide by the mouth of Fame? There can be no doubt now that this art and calling surpasses all those that mankind has invented, and is the more deserving of being held in honor in proportion as it is the more exposed to peril. Away with those who assert that letters have the preeminence over arms. I will tell them, whosoever they may be, that they know not what they say. The reason that such persons commonly

[7] *refectory*: communal dining hall in a monastery or university.

assign, and upon which they chiefly rest, is that the labors of the mind are greater than those of the body, and that arms give employment to the body alone—as if the calling were a porter's trade, for which nothing more is required than sturdy strength; or as if, in what we who profess them call arms, there were not included acts of vigor for the execution of which high intelligence is requisite; or as if the soul of the warrior, when he has an army, or the defense of a city under his care, did not exert itself as much by mind as by body. Nay, see whether by bodily strength it be possible to learn or divine the intentions of the enemy, his plans, stratagems, or obstacles, or to ward off impending mischief. All these are the work of the mind, and in them the body has no share whatever.

"Since, therefore, arms have need of the mind, as much as letters, let us see now which of the two minds—that of the man of letters or that of the warrior—has most to do. This will be seen by the end and goal that each seeks to attain, for that purpose is the more estimable which has for its aim the nobler object. The end and goal of letters—I am not speaking now of divine letters, the aim of which is to raise and direct the soul to Heaven; for with an end so infinite no other can be compared—I speak of human letters, the end of which is to establish distributive justice, give to every man that which is his, and see and take care that good laws are observed: an end undoubtedly noble, lofty, and deserving of high praise, but not such as should be given to that sought by arms, which have for their end and object peace, the greatest boon that men can desire in this life. The first good news the world and mankind received was that which the angels announced on the night that was our day, when they sang in the air, 'Glory to God in the highest, and peace on earth to men of goodwill.'[8] The salutation which the great Master of heaven and earth taught his disciples and chosen followers when they entered any house was to say, 'Peace be on this house.'[9] And many other times he said to them, 'My peace I give unto you, my peace I leave you, peace be with you,'[10] a jewel and a precious gift given and left by such a hand, a jewel without which there can be no happiness either on earth or in heaven. This peace is the true end of war, and war is only another name for arms. This, then, being admitted, that the end of war is peace, and that so far it has the advantage of the end of letters, let us turn to the bodily labors of the man of letters, and those of him who follows the profession of arms, and see which are the greater."

Don Quixote delivered his discourse in such a manner and with such polished speech that for the time being he made it impossible for any of his hearers to consider him a madman. On the contrary, as they were mostly gentlemen, by nature inclined to arms, they listened to him with great pleasure as he continued:

"I say, then, that the trials of the student are these: first of all poverty—not that all are poor, but in order to put the case as strongly as possible. When I say that he endures poverty, I think nothing more need be said about his hard fortune, for

[8] *Glory to God . . . of goodwill:* Luke 2:14.

[9] *Peace be on this house:* Luke 10:5.

[10] *My peace . . . be with you:* John 14:27; 20:19.

he who is poor has no share of the good things of life. This poverty he suffers from in various ways, whether in hunger, or cold, or nakedness, or all together. But for all that it is not so extreme but that he gets something to eat, though it may be at somewhat unseasonable hours and from the leftovers of the rich; for the greatest misery of the student is what they themselves call 'going out for soup,'[11] and there is always some neighbor's brazier[12] or hearth for them, which, if it does not warm, at least tempers their cold. Lastly, they sleep comfortably at night under a roof. I will not go into other particulars, as for example their lack of shirts and scant supply of shoes, thin and threadbare garments, nor their habit of gorging themselves when good luck has treated them to a banquet of some sort. By this road that I have described, rough and hard, stumbling here, falling there, getting up to fall again, they reach the rank they desire, and that once attained, we have seen many who have passed these Syrtes[13] and Scyllas and Charybdises,[14] as if borne flying on the wings of favoring fortune. We have seen them, I say, ruling and governing the world from a chair, their hunger turned into satiety, their cold into comfort, their nakedness into fine raiment, their sleep on a mat into repose in holland and damask,[15] the justly earned reward of their virtue. Yet contrasted and compared with what the warrior undergoes, all that they experience falls far short of it, as I am now about to show."

[11] *going out for soup:* relying on charity to eat.

[12] *brazier:* box or bowl containing coals.

[13] *Syrtes:* treacherous sandbanks in the Gulf of Sidra, off the coast of Libya.

[14] *Scyllas and Charybdises:* mythical sea monsters on either side of the Strait of Messina, which separates Sicily from the Italian mainland.

[15] *holland and damask:* luxurious fabrics.

CHAPTER XXXVIII

WHICH TREATS OF THE CURIOUS DISCOURSE DON QUIXOTE DELIVERED ON ARMS AND LETTERS

Continuing his discourse, Don Quixote said:

"As we began in the student's case with poverty and all that it entails, let us see now if the soldier is richer, and we shall find that in poverty itself there is no one poorer; for he is dependent on his miserable pay, which comes late or never, or else on what he can plunder, seriously imperiling his life and conscience. Sometimes his nakedness will be so great that a torn-up doublet serves him for uniform and shirt.[1] In the depth of winter, he has to defend himself against the inclemency of the weather in the open field with nothing better than the breath of his mouth, which I need not say, coming from an empty place, must come out cold, contrary to the laws of nature. To be sure he looks forward to the approach of night to make up for all these discomforts on the bed that awaits him; only by his fault will it suffer from being narrow, for he can easily measure out on the ground as he likes and roll himself about in it to his heart's content without any fear of the sheets slipping away from him. Then, after all this, suppose the day and hour for taking his degree in his calling to have come; suppose the day of battle to have arrived, when they award him with a tassel in his cap to mend some bullet hole, perhaps, that has gone through his temples or left him with a crippled arm or leg.[2] Or if this does not happen, and merciful Heaven watches over him and keeps him safe and sound, it may be he will be in the same poverty he was in before, and he must go through more engagements and more battles, and come victorious out of all before he betters himself; but miracles of that sort are seldom seen. For tell me, sirs, if you have ever reflected upon it, by how much do those who have gained by war fall short of the number of those who have perished in it? No doubt you will reply that there can be no comparison, that the dead cannot be numbered, while the living who have been rewarded may be counted in the hundreds. All this is the reverse in the case of men of letters. For by methods licit or illicit, they all find means of support, so that though the soldier has more to

[1] *uniform and shirt:* Soldiers were responsible for providing their own uniform, arms, and equipment.

[2] *tassel in his cap . . . or leg:* Don Quixote compares the day of battle with a graduation ceremony, where the soldier receives his degree. The equivalent of the student's tassel in his graduation cap is a soldier's bandage from a battle wound.

endure, his reward is much less. But against all this it may be urged that it is easier to reward two thousand soldiers, for the former may be remunerated by giving them appointments, which must by necessity be conferred upon men of their calling, while the latter can only be recompensed out of the very property of the master they serve. But this impossibility only strengthens my argument.

"Putting this, however, aside, for it is a puzzling question for which it is difficult to find a solution, let us return to the superiority of arms over letters, a matter still undecided, so many are the arguments put forward on each side. Besides those I have mentioned, letters say that without them arms cannot maintain themselves, for war, too, has its laws and is governed by them, and laws belong to the domain of letters and men of letters. To this arms make answer that without them laws cannot be maintained, for by arms states are defended, kingdoms preserved, cities protected, roads made safe, seas cleared of pirates; and, in short, if it were not for them, states, kingdoms, monarchies, cities, ways by sea and land would be exposed to the violence and confusion which war brings with it, so long as it lasts and is free to make use of its privileges and powers. It is obvious that whatever costs most is valued and deserves to be valued most. To attain to eminence in letters costs a man time, sleepless nights, hunger, nakedness, headaches, indigestions, and other things of the sort, some of which I have already referred to. But for a man to come in the ordinary course of things to be a good soldier costs him all the student suffers, and in an incomparably higher degree, for at every step he runs the risk of losing his life. For what dread of want or poverty that can reach or harass the student can compare with what the soldier feels, who finds himself besieged in some stronghold and mounting guard in a watchtower, knows that the enemy is tunneling towards the post where he is stationed, and cannot under any circumstances retreat or flee from the imminent danger that threatens him? All he can do is to inform his captain of what is going on so that he may try to remedy it by a countermine,[3] and then stand his ground in fear and expectation of the moment when he will fly up to the clouds without wings and descend into the deep against his will.

"If this seems an insignificant risk, let us see whether it is equaled or surpassed by the encounter of two galleys stem to stem in the midst of the open sea, locked and entangled one with the other, when the soldier has no more standing room than two feet of the plank of the prow; and yet, though he sees before him threatening him as many ministers of death as there are cannon of the foe pointed at him—not a lance length from his body—and sees too that with the first heedless step he will go down to visit the depths of Neptune's bosom, still with dauntless heart, urged on by honor that nerves him, he makes himself a target for every harquebus[4] pointed at him, and struggles to cross that narrow path to the enemy's

[3] *countermine:* To neutralize the threat of a besieging army's tunnels, defenders dug their own to intercept the invader and collapse the enemy's works with explosives.

[4] *harquebus:* Matchlock long gun that was the standard firearm for Spanish soldiers during the sixteenth and early seventeenth centuries. When the trigger was pulled, a slow-burning match cord was lowered into the priming pan, igniting the gunpowder through

ship. What is still more marvelous, no sooner has one man sunk to where he will never rise from till the end of the world, than another takes his place; and if he too falls into the sea that waits for him like an enemy, another and another will succeed him without a moment's pause between their deaths. Such courage and daring are unsurpassed amid the perils of war.

Happy the blest ages that knew not the dread fury of those devilish engines of artillery, whose inventor I am persuaded is in hell receiving the reward of his diabolical invention, by which he made it easy for a base and cowardly arm to take the life of a gallant gentleman; and that, when he knows not how or whence, in the height of the ardor and enthusiasm that fire and animate brave hearts, there should come some random bullet, discharged perhaps by one who fled in terror at the flash when he fired off his accursed machine,[5] which in an instant puts an end to his aspirations and cuts off the life of one who deserved to live for ages to come.

Thus when I reflect on this, I am almost tempted to say that in my heart I repent of having adopted this profession of knight-errant in so detestable an age as we live in now; for though no peril can make me fear, still it gives me some uneasiness to think that gunpowder and tin[6] may rob me of the opportunity of making myself famous and renowned throughout the known earth by the might of my arm and the edge of my sword. But Heaven's will be done; if I succeed in my attempt, I shall be all the more honored, as I have faced greater dangers than the knights-errant of yore exposed themselves to."

All this lengthy discourse Don Quixote delivered while the others dined, forgetting to raise a morsel to his lips, though Sancho more than once told him to eat his supper, as he would have time enough afterwards to say all he wanted. It excited fresh pity in those who had heard him to see a man of apparently sound sense, and with rational views on every subject he discussed, so hopelessly deprived of all when his wretched and accursed chivalry was in question. The priest told him he was quite right in all he had said in favor of arms, and that he himself, though a man of letters and a university graduate, was of the same opinion.

They finished their supper, the table was cleared, and the hostess, her daughter, and Maritornes set to work preparing Don Quixote of La Mancha's garret, in which it was arranged that the women were to be lodged by themselves for the night. Don Fernando, meanwhile, begged the captive to tell them the story of his life, for it could not fail to be unusual and interesting, to judge by the hints he had given on his arrival in company with Zoraida. To this the captive replied that he would very willingly yield to his request, only he feared his tale would not

---

the touchhole and propelling a lead ball from the barrel. Cervantes served as a harquebusier (*arcabucero*) aboard the galley *Marquesa* at the Battle of Lepanto (1571).

[5] *accursed machine:* harquebus. Condemnation of the harquebus was common in early modern letters. Covarrubias' 1611 dictionary describes it as a "firearm forged in hell, invented by the devil".

[6] *tin:* one of the metals used to make bullets.

give them as much pleasure as he wished. Nevertheless, not to be unobliging, he would tell it. The priest and the others thanked him and added their entreaties.

Finding himself so pressed, the captive said there was no occasion to ask where a command had such weight, and added, "If your worships will give me your attention, you will hear a true story which, perhaps, fictitious ones constructed with ingenious and studied art cannot match." These words made them settle themselves in their places and fall into a great silence. Seeing them waiting on his words in hushed expectation, he began thus in a pleasant, quiet voice:

CHAPTER XXXIX

WHEREIN THE CAPTIVE RELATES HIS LIFE AND ADVENTURES

My family has its origin in a village in the mountains of León, where nature has been kinder and more generous to us than fortune, though in the general poverty of the region my father has passed for a man of means. He would have been so in reality had he been as clever in preserving his property as he was in spending it. This tendency of his to be liberal and spend freely he acquired from having been a soldier in his youth, for the soldier's life is a school in which the miser becomes free-handed and the free-handed prodigal; and if any soldiers are to be found who are tight-fisted, they are monsters of rare occurrence. My father went beyond liberality and bordered on prodigality, a habit by no means advantageous to a married man who has children to succeed to his name and position. He had three, all sons, and all of sufficient age to make choice of a profession. Finding that he was incapable of resisting his inclinations, he resolved to deprive himself of the instrument and cause of his prodigality and lavishness. That is, he decided to divest himself of his wealth, without which even Alexander would have seemed parsimonious.[1] And so calling us all three aside one day into a room, he addressed us in words somewhat to the following effect:

"My sons, to assure you that I love you, nothing more need be known or said than that you are my sons; and to encourage a suspicion that I do not love you, it is enough to know that I have been unable to resist spending your inheritance. Therefore, that you may for the future feel sure that I love you like a father and have no wish to ruin you like a stepfather, I propose to do with you what I have for some time now contemplated and after mature deliberation decided upon. You are now of an age to take your place in life, or at least to choose a calling that will bring you honor and profit when you are older. What I have resolved to do is to divide my property into four parts: three I will give to you, to each his portion without making any difference, and the other I will retain to live upon and support myself for whatever remainder of life Heaven may be pleased to grant me. But I wish each of you on taking possession of the share that falls to him to follow one of the paths I shall indicate. In this Spain of ours there is a proverb, to my mind very true—as they all are, being short aphorisms drawn from long practical experience. The one I refer to says, 'Church, sea, or royal

[1] *even Alexander would have seemed parsimonious:* Alexander the Great's generosity is legendary.

house,'[2] as much as to say, in plainer language, whoever wants to flourish and become rich, let him commit to the Church, or go to sea, adopting commerce as his calling, or go into the king's service in his household, for they say, 'Better a king's crumb than a lord's favor.' I say so because it is my will and pleasure that one of you should follow letters, another trade, and the third serve the king on the battlefield, for it is a difficult matter to gain admission to his service in his household, and if war does not bring much wealth it confers great distinction and fame. In a week's time, I will give you your full shares in money, without defrauding you of a cent, as you will see in the end. Now tell me if you are willing to follow out my idea and advice as I have laid it before you."

He called upon me as the eldest to answer. After urging him not to strip himself of his property but to spend it all as he pleased (for we were young men able to gain our living), I consented to comply with his wishes and said that mine were to follow the profession of arms and thereby serve God and my king. My second brother, having made the same proposal, decided upon going to the Indies to invest the portion that fell to him in trade. The youngest, and in my opinion the wisest, said he would rather commit to the Church or go to complete his studies at Salamanca.[3] As soon as we had come to an understanding and made choice of our professions, my father embraced us all, and in the short time he mentioned carried into effect what he had promised. When he had given to each his share, which as well as I remember was three thousand ducats apiece in cash (for an uncle of ours bought the estate and paid for it in ready money, not to let it go out of the family), we all three on the same day took leave of our good father. At the same time, as it seemed to me inhuman to leave my father with such scanty means in his old age, I induced him to take two of my three thousand ducats, as the remainder would be enough to provide me with all a soldier needed. My two brothers, moved by my example, gave him each a thousand ducats, so that there was left for my father four thousand ducats in money, besides three thousand (the value of the portion that fell to him), which he preferred to retain in land instead of selling it. Finally, as I said, we took leave of him, and of our uncle whom I have mentioned, not without sorrow and tears on both sides—they charging us to let them know whenever an opportunity offered how we fared, whether well or ill. We promised to do so, and when he had embraced us and given us his blessing, one set out for Salamanca, the other for Seville, and I for Alicante,[4] where I had heard there was a Genoese vessel taking in a cargo of wool for Genoa.

It is now some twenty-two years since I left my father's house, and all that time, though I have written several letters, I have had no news whatever of him or of my brothers. My own adventures during that period I will now relate briefly. I embarked at Alicante, reached Genoa after a prosperous voyage, and proceeded from there to Milan, where I provided myself with arms and a few soldier's

[2] *Church, sea, or royal house:* The full proverb is "Three things make a man prosper: the Church, the sea, and the royal house."

[3] *Salamanca:* University of Salamanca. See footnote 2, page 86.

[4] *Alicante:* Mediterranean seaport on the southeast coast of Spain.

accoutrements.[5] It was my intention to go from there and enlist in Piedmont, but as I was already on the road to Alessandria della Paglia, I learned that the great Duke of Alba was on his way to Flanders.[6] I changed my plans, joined him, served under him in the campaigns he undertook, was present at the deaths of Counts Egmont and Horn,[7] and was promoted to be ensign under a famous captain of Guadalajara, Diego de Urbina by name.[8] Some time after my arrival in Flanders, news came of the league that his Holiness Pope Pius V, of happy memory, had made with Venice and Spain against the common enemy, the Turk, who had just then with his fleet taken the famous island of Cyprus, which belonged to the Venetians, a loss deplorable and disastrous.[9] It was a known fact that the Most Serene Don Juan de Austria, natural brother of our good king Don Felipe,[10] was coming as commander-in-chief of the allied forces, and rumors were abroad of the vast warlike preparations that were being made, all of which stirred my heart and filled me with a longing to take part in the campaign that was expected. Though I had reason to believe, and almost certain promises, that on the first opportunity that presented itself I should be promoted to be captain, I preferred to leave all and set out for Italy, which I did. It was my good fortune that Don Juan had just arrived in Genoa, and was going on to Naples to join the Venetian fleet, as he afterwards did at Messina. I may say, in short, that I took part in that glorious expedition,[11] promoted by this time to be a captain of infantry, to which honorable charge my good luck rather than my merits raised me. That day—so fortunate for Christendom, because then all the nations of the

[5] *Milan, where I provided myself with arms and a few soldier's accoutrements:* Milan was renowned for the quality of its arms and armor.

[6] *Alessandria della Paglia . . . to Flanders:* In 1567 King Philip II of Spain sent the Duke of Alba to the Low Countries, at the time a Spanish possession, to quell a violent Protestant rebellion. His army was quartered in Alessandria della Paglia sometime in the summer of that year.

[7] *deaths of Counts Egmont and Horn:* The two prominent Catholic noblemen opposed Philip II's imposition of the Inquisition in the Spanish Netherlands and other authoritarian policies. Their execution for treason and heresy helped ignite the Dutch Revolt.

[8] *Diego de Urbina by name:* also Cervantes' captain in the Battle of Lepanto.

[9] *news came of the league . . . and disastrous:* The Holy League was a 1571 alliance brokered by Pope Pius V among the Catholic powers of Southern Europe to counter the advance of the Ottoman Turks in the eastern Mediterranean. The alliance was initially intended to aid the Venetian defenders of Cyprus, but the island fell to the Turks before the fleet could be assembled.

[10] *Don Juan of Austria, natural brother of our good king Don Felipe:* Don Juan of Austria (1547–1578) was a Spanish general and illegitimate son of Emperor Charles V.

[11] *that glorious expedition:* the Battle of Lepanto. On October 7, 1571, the fleet commissioned by the Holy League met the Ottoman navy in the Gulf of Corinth in what became the largest naval battle in Western history prior to the twentieth century. The engagement involved over 450 warships and 120,000 men. Though the Ottomans rebuilt their fleet within a year, the Holy League's decisive victory shattered the myth of Ottoman naval invincibility. The Ottomans would no longer threaten mainland Italy, and their influence in the western Mediterranean began to wane by century's end.

earth were disabused of the error under which they lay in imagining the Turks to be invincible on sea—on that day, I say, on which the Ottoman pride and arrogance were broken, among all that were there made happy (for the Christians who died that day were happier than those who remained alive and victorious) I alone was miserable; for instead of some naval crown that I might have expected had it been in Roman times, on the night that followed that famous day I found myself with fetters on my feet and manacles on my hands.

It happened in this way: El Uchalí,[12] the king of Algiers, a daring and successful corsair, having attacked and taken the leading Maltese galley (only three knights being left alive in it, and they badly wounded), the chief galley of Giovanni Andrea,[13] on board of which my company and I were placed, came to its relief. Doing as I was bound to do in such a case, I leaped on board the enemy's galley, which, pulling away from the one that had attacked it, prevented my men from following me. And so I found myself alone in the midst of my enemies, who were in such numbers that I was unable to resist. In short, I was taken, covered with wounds. El Uchalí, as you know, sirs, made his escape with his entire squadron, and I was left a prisoner in his power, the only forlorn one among so many filled with joy, and the only captive among so many free; for there were fifteen thousand Christians, all at the oar in the Turkish fleet, that regained their longed-for liberty that day.

They carried me to Constantinople, where the Grand Turk, Selim,[14] made my master General over the Sea for having done his duty in the battle and carried off as evidence of his bravery the standard of the Order of Malta.[15] The following year, which was the year seventy-two, I found myself at Navarino[16] rowing in the leading galley with the three lanterns.[17] There I observed how the opportunity to capture the whole Turkish fleet in harbor was lost. All the marines and janissaries[18] that belonged to it were certain that they were about to be attacked

[12] *El Uchalí:* also known as Uluç Ali, Occhiali, and Ali Pasha, Italian-born renegade who rose to the rank of Grand Admiral of the Ottoman fleet (*Kapudan Pasha*) and Governor-General (*Beylerbey*) of Algiers, an Ottoman regency. He commanded the left flank of the Ottoman fleet at Lepanto.

[13] *Giovanni Andrea:* Gianandrea Doria, Genoese admiral and great-nephew of the more famous admiral and statesman of the same name. He was criticized for allowing a gap to open in the Holy League's battle line at Lepanto, which Uluç Ali successfully exploited.

[14] *Constantinople, where the Grand Turk, Selim:* The once proud capital of the Eastern Roman Empire fell to the Ottoman Turks in 1453. Selim II, son of Suleiman the Magnificent, ruled over the Ottoman Empire 1566–1574.

[15] *carried off as evidence of his bravery the standard of the Order of Malta:* The standard of the Knights of Malta flew from the flagship of the flotilla.

[16] *Navarino:* present-day Pylos, on the southwest corner of Greece, where the Ottomans had rebuilt a naval fleet. Don Juan of Austria led an expedition to the site in 1572 and unsuccessfully laid siege to the garrison. Cervantes was among the soldiers who participated in the campaign.

[17] *three lanterns:* insignia flown by the Turkish admiral's flagship.

[18] *janissaries:* the Ottomans' elite infantry corps.

inside the very harbor and had their kits and *pasamaques*, or shoes, ready to flee at once on shore without waiting to be assailed—in so great fear did they stand of our fleet. But Heaven ordered it otherwise, not for any fault or neglect of the general who commanded on our side, but for the sins of Christendom, and because it was God's will and pleasure that we should always have instruments of punishment to chastise us. As it was, El Uchalí took refuge at Modon, which is an island near Navarino, and landing forces, fortified the mouth of the harbor and waited quietly until Don Juan withdrew. On this expedition the galley called the *Prize* was taken, whose captain was a son of the famous corsair Barbarossa. It was taken by the chief Neapolitan galley called the *She-Wolf*, commanded by that thunderbolt of war, that father of his men, that successful and unconquered captain Don Álvaro de Bazán, Marquis of Santa Cruz.[19] I cannot help telling you what took place at the capture of the *Prize*.

The son of Barbarossa was so cruel, and treated his slaves so badly, that when those who were at the oars saw that the *She-Wolf* galley was bearing down and gaining upon them, they all at once dropped their oars and seized their captain, who stood on the bridge at the end of the gangway shouting to them to row lustily; and passing him on from bench to bench, from the poop to the prow,[20] they so bit him that before he had got much past the mast his soul had already gone to hell. So great, as I said, was the cruelty with which he treated them, and the hatred with which they hated him.

We returned to Constantinople, and the following year, seventy-three, it became known that Don Juan had seized Tunis and taken the kingdom from the Turks, and placed Muley Hamet in possession, putting an end to the hopes which Muley Hamida, the cruelest and bravest Moor in the world, entertained of returning to reign there.[21] The Grand Turk took the loss greatly to heart, and with the cunning which all his race possess, he made peace with the Venetians, who were much more eager for it than he was. The following year, seventy-four, he attacked La Goletta[22] and the fort which Don Juan had left half built near Tunis. While all these events were occurring, I was laboring at the oar without any hope of freedom—at least I had no hope of obtaining it by ransom, for I was firmly resolved not to write to my father telling him of my misfortunes. At length La Goletta fell, and the fort fell, before which places there were seventy-five

[19] *Don Álvaro de Bazán, Marquis of Santa Cruz:* Don Álvaro de Bazán (1526–1588) was commander of the reserve fleet at Lepanto. He was reputed never to have lost a battle in his decades-long career.

[20] *from the poop to the prow:* from one end of the ship to the other.

[21] *Muley Hamet . . . to reign there:* Muley Hamida came to power in 1543 as king of an independent Tunis by overthrowing and blinding his father. In 1569 Uluç Ali conquered the kingdom and exiled Hamida. When the Spanish retook the city in 1573, they installed Muley Hamida's brother Muley Hamet as puppet ruler. Spain's strategic interest in Tunis stemmed from its proximity to Spanish-held Sicily and the fortress at nearby La Goletta.

[22] *La Goletta:* present-day La Goulette. It was a Spanish presidio located on an isthmus guarding the entrance to the Lake of Tunis, facing the city. Cervantes served in the vicinity some time before its fall.

thousand regular Turkish soldiers and more than four hundred thousand Moors and Arabs from all parts of Africa, and in the train of all this great host such munitions and engines of war and so many sappers[23] that with their hands they might have covered La Goletta and the fort with handfuls of earth. The first to fall was La Goletta, until then reckoned impregnable. It fell, not by any fault of its defenders (who did all that they could and should have done), but because experience proved how easily entrenchments could be made in the desert sand there; for while water used to be found at two palms depth, the Turks found none at two yards.[24] And so by means of a quantity of sandbags they raised their works so high that they commanded the walls of the fort, sweeping them as if from a cavalier,[25] so that no one was able to make a stand or maintain the defense.

It was a common opinion that our men should not have shut themselves up in La Goletta but should have waited in the open at the landing place. Those who say so talk idly and with little knowledge of such matters; for if in La Goletta and in the fort there were barely seven thousand soldiers, how could such a small number, however resolute, sally out and hold their own against numbers like those of the enemy? And how is it possible to help losing a stronghold that is not relieved, above all when surrounded by a host of determined enemies in their own country? Many thought and I thought so, too—that it was special favor and mercy that Heaven showed to Spain in permitting the destruction of that source and hiding place of mischief, that devourer, sponge, and moth of countless money, fruitlessly wasted there to no other purpose save preserving the memory of its capture by the invincible Charles V[26]—as if those stones were needed to uphold what is and will always be eternal. The fort also fell, but the Turks had to win it inch by inch, for the soldiers who defended it fought so gallantly and stoutly that the number of the enemy killed in twenty-two general assaults exceeded twenty-five thousand. Of three hundred that remained alive not one was taken unwounded—a clear and manifest proof of their gallantry and resolution, and how bravely they had defended themselves and held their post. A small fort or tower that was in the middle of the lagoon under the command of Don Juan Zanoguera, a Valencian gentleman and a famous soldier, capitulated upon terms. They took prisoner Don Pedro Puertocarrero, commandant of La Goletta, who had done all in his power to defend his fortress and took the loss of it so much to heart that he died of grief on the way to Constantinople, where they were carrying him as prisoner. They also took the commandant of the fort, Gabrio Serbelloni by name, a Milanese gentleman, a great engineer and

[23] *sappers:* soldiers who specialize in demolition.

[24] *for while water . . . at two yards:* The Turkish besiegers disproved the Spanish assumption that the water table of La Goletta was too high to permit trenching or heavy fortification. Exploiting this miscalculation, they successfully entrenched and fortified their positions around the Spanish fortress during the 1574 siege.

[25] *cavalier:* raised structure built within a larger fortification to provide elevated firepower over the surrounding defenses.

[26] *its capture by the invincible Charles V:* Charles V captured La Goletta in 1535. Neither he nor his son Philip II were able to extend Spain's direct rule of the region any further.

a very brave soldier. In these two fortresses perished many people of note, among whom was Pagano Doria, knight of the Order of Saint John, a man of generous disposition, as was shown by his extreme liberality to his brother, the famous Gianandrea Doria. What made his death the more lamentable was that he was slain by some Arabs to whom he entrusted himself seeing that the fort was now lost and who offered to conduct him in the disguise of a Moor to Tabarca, a small fort or station on the coast held by the Genoese employed in the coral fishery. These Arabs cut off his head and carried it to the commander of the Turkish fleet, who demonstrated to them the truth of our Castilian proverb that "though the treason may please, the traitor is hated," for they say he ordered those who brought him the present to be hanged for not having brought him alive.

Among the Christians who were taken in the fort was one named Don Pedro de Aguilar, a native of some place (I know not what) in Andalusia, who had been ensign in the fort, a soldier of great repute and rare intelligence, who had in particular a special gift for what they call poetry.[27] I say so because his fate brought him to my galley and to my bench, and made him a slave to the same master. Before we left the port, this gentleman composed two sonnets by way of epitaphs, one on La Goletta and the other on the fort. Indeed, I may as well repeat them, for I know them by heart, and I think they will be liked rather than disliked.

The instant the captive mentioned the name of Don Pedro de Aguilar, Don Fernando looked at his companions and they all three smiled. When he came to speak of the sonnets, one of them said, "Before your worship proceeds any further, I entreat you to tell me what became of that Don Pedro de Aguilar you have spoken of."

"All I know is," replied the captive, "that after having been in Constantinople two years, he escaped in the disguise of an Arnaut,[28] in the company of a Greek spy. Whether he regained his liberty or not I cannot tell. I suspect he did, because a year afterwards I saw the Greek in Constantinople, though I was unable to ask him what the result of the journey was."

"Well then, you are right," returned the gentleman, "for that Don Pedro is my brother, and he is now in our village in good health, rich, married, and with three children."

"Thanks be to God for all the mercies he has shown him," said the captive. "To my mind, there is no happiness on earth to compare with recovering lost liberty."

"And what is more," said the gentleman, "I know the sonnets my brother wrote."

"Then let your worship repeat them," said the captive, "for you will recite them better than I can."

"With all my heart," said the gentleman. "The one on La Goletta runs thus...."

[27] *Don Pedro de Aguilar ... call poetry:* Like the valise the mysterious guest leaves in Juan Palomeque's inn, the captive's tale mixes history and fable. Don Pedro de Aguilar is the only fictional character among the many historical figures mentioned in the military record of this chapter.

[28] *Arnaut:* Albanian.

CHAPTER XL

IN WHICH THE STORY OF THE CAPTIVE IS CONTINUED

SONNET

Blest souls, that, from this mortal husk set free,
In guerdon[1] of brave deeds beatified,
Above this lowly orb of ours abide
Made heirs of heaven and immortality,
With noble rage and ardor glowing ye,
Your strength, while strength was yours, in battle plied,
And with your own blood and the foeman's dyed
The sandy soil and the encircling sea.
It was the ebbing lifeblood first that failed
The weary arms; the stout hearts never quailed.
Though vanquished, yet ye earned the victor's crown:
Though mourned, yet still triumphant was your fall
For there ye won, between the sword and wall,
In heaven glory and on earth renown.

"That is it exactly, according to my recollection," said the captive.

"Well then, the one on the fort," said the gentleman, "if my memory serves me, goes thus:

SONNET

Up from this wasted soil, this shattered shell,
Whose walls and towers here in ruin lie,
Three thousand soldier souls took wing on high,
In the bright mansions of the blest to dwell.
The onslaught of the foeman to repel
By might of arm all vainly did they try,
And when at length 'twas left them but to die,
Wearied and few the last defenders fell.
And this same arid soil hath ever been
A haunt of countless mournful memories,
As well in our day as in days of yore.

[1] *guerdon:* reward.

But never yet to heaven it sent, I ween,[2]
From its hard bosom purer souls than these,
Or braver bodies on its surface bore."

The sonnets were not disliked, and the captive was cheered at the tidings they gave him of his comrade. Continuing his tale, he went on to say:

La Goletta and the fort being thus in their hands, the Turks gave orders to dismantle La Goletta, for the fort was reduced to such a state that there was nothing left to level. To do the work more quickly and easily, they mined it in three places; but nowhere were they able to blow up the part that seemed to be the least strong, that is to say, the old walls, while all that remained standing of the new fortifications that the Fratin[3] had made came to the ground with the greatest ease. The fleet finally returned victorious and triumphant to Constantinople, and a few months later my master died—El Uchalí, otherwise Uchalí Fartax, which means in Turkish "the scabby renegade," for that he was. It is the practice with the Turks to name people from some defect or virtue they may possess, the reason being that there are among them only four surnames belonging to families tracing their descent from the Ottoman house. The others, as I have said, take their names and surnames either from bodily blemishes or moral qualities.

This "scabby one" rowed at the oar as a slave of the Grand Signor[4] for fourteen years, and when over thirty-four years of age, in resentment at having been struck by a Turk while at the oar, turned renegade and renounced his faith[5] in order to be able to revenge himself. Such was his valor that, without owing his advancement to the base ways and means[6] by which most favorites of the Grand Signor rise to power, he came to be king of Algiers and afterwards General over

[2] *ween:* believe.

[3] *Fratin:* The Italian engineer Giacomo Palearo (nicknamed *il Fratino*, "The Little Friar") erected an additional layer of walls around the La Goletta presidio.

[4] *Grand Signor:* the sultan.

[5] *turned renegade and renounced his faith:* A slave who renounced his native religion and converted to Islam was set free and given expansive access to Ottoman society. Renegades like Uluç Ali rose to prominence as military and political leaders and became wealthy slaveholders. Their knowledge of European languages and geography was an asset to Ottoman expansion in the Mediterranean. The earthly price renegades paid came in the form of a stigma among their former people, usually Christian, sometimes Jews. Return home and reassimilation in society was a daunting process. Penitent renegades who returned to Spain were subjected to a rigorous investigation by the Inquisition, which sought evidence that their repentance for apostasy came to fruition while in Africa, a measure of sincerity. The case of the Murcian, whom the captive befriends in the following pages, offers a glimpse of the renegade's predicament.

[6] *base ways and means:* Among the vices alluded to is sodomy. The mentoring of renegade youths in the service of prominent Turks and Maghrebs, many of them renegades themselves, included sexual grooming. Such was the case with the Calabrian renegade Uluç Ali and his Venetian protégé, Hassan Pasha.

the Sea, which is the third place of trust in the realm. He was a Calabrian[7] by birth, a worthy man morally, and he treated his slaves with great humanity. He had three thousand of them, and after his death they were divided, as he directed by his will, between the Grand Signor (who is heir of all who die and shares with the children of the deceased) and his renegades.

I fell to the lot of a Venetian renegade who, when a cabin boy on board a ship, had been taken by Uchalí and was so much beloved by him that he became one of his most favored youths. He came to be the cruelest renegade I ever saw. His name was Hassan Pasha, and he grew very rich and became king of Algiers. With him I went there from Constantinople, rather glad to be so near Spain—not that I intended to write to anyone about my unhappy lot, but to try if fortune would be kinder to me in Algiers than in Constantinople, where I had attempted in a thousand ways to escape without ever finding a favorable time or chance. In Algiers I resolved to seek for other means of effecting the purpose I cherished so dearly. For the hope of obtaining my liberty never deserted me, and when in my plots and schemes and attempts the result did not match my expectations, without giving way to despair I immediately began to look out for or conjure up some new hope to support me, however faint or feeble it might be.

In this way I lived on immured in a building or prison called by the Turks a bagnio,[8] in which they confine the Christian captives, both those that are the king's as well as those belonging to private individuals, and also what they call those "of the Almacén," which is as much as to say the slaves of the municipality, who serve the city in the public works and other employments. Captives of this kind recover their liberty with great difficulty, for as they are public property and have no particular master, there is no one with whom to deal for their ransom, even though they may have the means.[9] To these bagnios, as I have said, some private individuals of the town are in the habit of bringing their captives, especially when they are to be ransomed, because there they can keep them in safety and comfort until their ransom arrives. Likewise, the king's captives that are on ransom do not go out to work with the rest of the crew, unless when their ransom is delayed, in which case, to make them write for it more urgently, they are compelled to work and go for wood, which is no light labor.

[7] *Calabrian:* The region of Calabria is the "toe" in the Italian Peninsula.

[8] *bagnio:* prison or barracks that housed enslaved Christians, particularly those not assigned to private service.

[9] *deal for their ransom . . . the means:* A slave's value in Algiers lay not primarily in labor but in ransom money, the cornerstone of the city's economy. Upon arrival, captives were interrogated and assigned a ransom price based on their perceived social standing and wealth back home. Nobles and military officers fetched the highest sums. Slaves were instructed to write letters to family members requesting funds, often far beyond their means. In Spain, the Trinitarian and Mercedarian orders—under royal patronage—raised supplementary funds. At least twice a year, friars visited Algiers to distribute alms and private donations, negotiate ransoms, and minister to the captives' spiritual and physical needs. They also carried letters, which kept open the lines of communication between captives and their family members.

I, however, was one of those on ransom, for when it was discovered that I was a captain, although I declared my scanty means and lack of fortune, nothing could dissuade them from including me among the gentlemen and those waiting to be ransomed. They put a chain on me, more as a sign that I was held for ransom than to keep me safe, and so I passed my life in that bagnio with several other gentlemen and prominent individuals similarly marked for ransom. Though at times (or rather almost always) we suffered from hunger and scanty clothing, nothing distressed us so much as hearing and seeing at every turn the unexampled and unheard-of cruelties my master inflicted upon the Christians. Every day he hanged a man, impaled one, cut off the ears of another—and all with so little provocation, or so entirely without any, that the Turks acknowledged he did it merely for the sake of doing it, and because he was by nature murderously disposed towards the whole human race. The only one that fared at all well with him was a Spanish soldier, something de Saavedra by name, to whom he never gave a blow himself nor ordered a blow to be given, nor addressed a hard word. What he did will dwell in the memory of the people there for many a year, and all to recover liberty. For the least of his many actions, we dreaded that he would be impaled, and he himself was in fear of it more than once. If only time permitted, I would tell you something now of what that soldier did, which would be far more fascinating than the narration of my own tale.[10]

To go on with my story: the courtyard of our prison was overlooked by the windows of the house belonging to a wealthy Moor of high position. These, as is usual in Moorish houses, were rather loopholes than windows, and were covered, moreover, with thick and close latticework. It so happened that one day I was on the terrace of our prison with three other comrades, we being alone, for all the other Christians had gone out to work. As we were passing the time by seeing how far we could leap with our chains, I chanced to raise my eyes, and from one of these little closed windows I saw a reed appear with a cloth attached to the end of it. It kept waving to and fro and moving, as if making signs to us to come and take it. We watched it, and one of those who were with me went and stood under the reed to see whether they would let it drop, or what they would do, but as he did so the reed was raised and moved from side to side, as if they meant to say "no" by a shake of the head. The Christian came back, and it was again lowered, making the same movements as before. Another of my comrades went, and with him the same happened as with the first. Then the third went forward, but with the same result as the first and second. Seeing this, I saw a chance to try my luck, and as soon as I came under the reed it was dropped and fell inside the bagnio at my feet. I moved to untie the cloth, in which I found a knot, and in

[10] *If only time permitted . . . my own tale:* During his five years of Algerian captivity, Cervantes organized four escape attempts, two of them elaborate in scope—all of them unsuccessful. In an inquest conducted by the Spanish Crown at the time of his ransom, fellow slaves testified that Cervantes had instructed them to blame him alone as the instigator if caught in order that they might avoid punishment. Why Cervantes was never subjected to the cruel death meted out to those who attempted escape remains a mystery.

this were ten cianis, which are coins of base gold current among the Moors, each worth ten reals of our money.

It is needless to say I rejoiced over this discovery. My joy was not less than my wonder as I tried to imagine how this good fortune could have come to us, but to me especially; for the evident unwillingness to drop the reed for any but me showed that it was for me the favor was intended. I took my welcome money, broke the reed, and returned to the terrace, and looking up at the window, I saw a very white hand thrust out that opened and shut very quickly. From this we gathered or fancied that it must be some woman living in that house that had done us this kindness. To show that we were grateful for it, we made salaams after the fashion of the Moors, bowing the head, bending the body, and crossing the arms on the breast. Shortly afterwards at the same window, a small cross made of reeds was held out and immediately withdrawn. This sign led us to believe that some Christian woman was a captive in the house, and that it was she who had been so good to us; but the whiteness of the hand and the bracelets we had observed made us dismiss that idea, though we thought it might be one of the Christian renegades whom their masters very often take as lawful wives, and gladly, for they prefer them to the women of their own nation. In all our conjectures, we were wide of the truth.

From that time forward, our sole occupation was watching and gazing at the window where the cross had appeared to us, as if it were our north star. At least two weeks passed without our seeing either it or the hand, or any other sign; and though we endeavored, meanwhile, with the utmost pains to find out who it was that lived in the house, and whether there were any Christian renegade in it, nobody could ever tell us anything more than that he who lived there was a rich Moor of high position, Hajji Morato by name, formerly governor of La Pata, an office of high dignity among them.[11] When we least thought it was going to rain any more cianis from that quarter, we saw the reed suddenly appear with another cloth tied in a larger knot attached to it, and this at a time when, as on the former occasion, the bagnio was deserted and unoccupied.

We made trial as before, each of the same three going forward before I did; but the reed was delivered to none but me, when on my approach it was lowered. I untied the knot and found forty Spanish gold escudos with a piece of paper written in Arabic, and at the end of the writing there was a large cross drawn. I kissed the cross, took the escudos, and returned to the terrace, and we all made our salaams. Again the hand appeared, I made signs that I would read the paper, and then the window was closed. We were all puzzled, though filled with joy at what had taken place. As none of us understood Arabic, great was our curiosity to know what the paper contained, and still greater the difficulty of finding someone to read it. At last I resolved to confide in a renegade, a native of Murcia, who professed a very great friendship for me and had given pledges that bound him to keep any secret I might entrust to him.

[11] *Hajji Morato . . . among them:* The historical Hajji Murād was a renegade of Slavic origin who rose to become the Ottoman Empire's ambassador to France in addition to the governor of the fortress of Al-Batha (*la Pata*), near Algiers.

It is the custom with some renegades, when they intend to return to Christian territory, to carry about them certificates from captives of repute testifying, in whatever form they can, that such and such a renegade is a worthy man who has always shown kindness to Christians and is eager to escape on the first opportunity that may present itself. Some obtain these testimonials with good intentions; others put them to a cunning use. For when they go to pillage on Christian territory, if they happen to be stranded or taken prisoners, they produce their certificates and say that from these papers may be seen the object they came for, which was to remain on Christian soil, and that it was to this end they joined the Turks in their foray. In this way they escape any immediate consequences and make their peace with the Church before it does them any harm, and then when they have the chance, they return to Barbary to become what they were before. There are others, however, who procure these papers and make use of them honestly and remain on Christian soil. This friend of mine was one of these renegades that I have described. He had certificates from all our comrades, in which we testified in his favor as strongly as we could. If the Moors had found the papers, they would have burned him alive.

I knew that he understood Arabic very well and could not only speak but also write it; but before I disclosed the whole matter to him, I asked him to read this paper to me, which I told him I had found by accident in a hole in my cell. He opened it and remained some time examining it and muttering to himself as he translated. I asked him if he understood it, and he told me he did perfectly well, and that if I wished him to tell me its meaning word for word, I must give him pen and ink that he might do it more satisfactorily. We at once gave him what he required, and he set about translating it bit by bit.

When he had finished, he said, "All that is here in Spanish is what the Moorish paper contains. You must bear in mind that when it says 'Lela Marien' it means 'Our Lady the Virgin Mary.'"[12]

We read the paper and it ran thus:

> When I was a child, my father had a slave who taught me to pray the Christian prayer[13] in my own language and told me many things about Lela Marien. The Christian died, and I know that she did not go to the fire but to Allah, because since then I have seen her twice, and she told me to go to the land of the Christians to see Lela Marien, who had great love for me. I know not how to go. I have seen many Christians, but except for you none has seemed to me to be a gentleman. I am young and beautiful and have plenty of money to take with me. See if you can find a way for us to escape. If you will, you shall be my husband there. If you will not, it will not distress me, for Lela Marien will find me someone to marry me. I myself have written this. Be careful to whom you give this to read: trust no Moor, for they are all perfidious. I am greatly troubled on this account, for I would not have you confide in anyone, because if my father found out he would at once fling me down a well and cover me with stones. I will attach a thread to the reed. Tie the answer

[12] *Lela Marien . . . Virgin Mary:* "Lela" is derived from an Amazigh (Berber) honorific that means "Lady". "Lela Marien" implies nothing about virginity.

[13] *the Christian prayer:* from context, probably the Hail Mary.

> to it, and if you have no one to write for you in Arabic, tell me by signs, for Lela Marien will make me understand you. She and Allah and this cross, which I often kiss as the captive taught me, protect you.

Judge, sirs, whether we had reason for surprise and joy at the words of this paper. Both one and the other were so great that the renegade surmised that the paper had not been found by chance but had been in reality addressed to one of us. He begged us, if what he suspected was the truth, to trust him and tell him all, for he would risk his life for our freedom. So saying, he took out from his breast a metal crucifix, and with many tears swore by the God the image represented—in whom, sinful and wicked as he was, he truly and faithfully believed—to be loyal to us and keep secret whatever we chose to reveal to him. For he thought and almost foresaw that by means of her who had written that paper, he and all of us would obtain our liberty, and he himself obtain the object he so much desired: his restoration to the bosom of the Holy Mother Church, from which by his own sin and ignorance he was now severed like a rotted limb. The renegade said this with so many tears and such signs of repentance that with one consent we agreed to tell him the whole truth of the matter; and so we gave him a full account of it all, without hiding anything from him. We pointed out to him the window at which the reed appeared, and he by that means took note of the house and resolved to find out with special care who lived in it. We agreed also that it would be advisable to answer the Moorish lady's letter, and the renegade without a moment's delay took down the words I dictated to him, which were exactly what I shall tell you, for nothing of importance that took place in this affair has escaped my memory—or ever will while life lasts. This, then, was the answer returned to the Moorish lady:

> May the true Allah protect you, my lady, and that blessed Marien, who is the true mother of God and who has put it into your heart to go to the land of the Christians because she loves you. Entreat her that she be pleased to show you how you can carry out the command she gives you, for she will, such is her goodness. On my own part, and on that of all these Christians who are with me, I promise to do all that we can for you, even to death. Fail not to write to me and inform me what you mean to do, and I will always answer you; for the great Allah has given us a Christian captive who can speak and write your language well, as you may see by this paper. Without fear, therefore, you can inform us of all that you wish. As to what you say, that if you do reach the land of the Christians you will be my wife, I give you my promise upon it as a good Christian; and know that the Christians keep their promises better than the Moors. Allah and Marien his mother watch over you, my lady.

The paper being written and folded, I waited two days until the bagnio was empty as before and then went to the usual place on the terrace to see if there was any sign of the reed, which was not long in making its appearance. As soon as I saw it, although I could not distinguish who held it out, I showed the paper as a sign to attach the thread, but it was already fixed to the reed, and to it I tied the paper. Shortly afterwards, our star once more made its appearance with the white flag of peace, the little bundle. It was dropped, and I picked it up, and found in the cloth, in gold and silver coins of all sorts, more than fifty escudos, which fifty times more strengthened our joy and doubled our hope of gaining our liberty. That very night our renegade returned and said he had learned that the Moor we had been told of lived in that house, that his name was Hajji Morato, that he was enormously rich, that he had one only daughter, the heiress of all his wealth, and that it was the general opinion throughout the city that she was the most beautiful woman in Barbary. Several of the viceroys who came there had sought her for a wife, but she had been always unwilling to marry. He had learned, moreover, that she had a Christian slave who was now dead. All of this agreed with the contents of the paper. We immediately took counsel with the renegade as to what means would have to be adopted in order to carry off the Moorish lady and bring us all to Christian territory. In the end it was agreed that for the present we should wait for a second communication from Zoraida (for that was the name of her who now desires to be called Maria) because we saw clearly that she and no one else could find a way out of all these difficulties. When we had decided upon this, the renegade told us not to be uneasy, for he would lose his life or else restore us to liberty. For four days the bagnio was filled with people, for which reason the reed for four days delayed its appearance, but at the end of that time, when the bagnio returned to its accustomed solitude, the reed appeared with the cloth so swollen that it promised a happy birth. Reed and cloth came down to me, and I found another paper and a hundred escudos in gold, without any other coins. The renegade was present, and in our cell we gave him the paper to read, which was to this effect:

> I cannot think of a plan, señor, for our going to Spain, nor has Lela Marien shown me one, though I have asked her. All that can be done is for me to give you plenty of money in gold from this window. With it, ransom yourself and your friends, and let one of you go to the land of the Christians, and there buy a vessel and come back for the others. I may be found in my father's garden, which is at the Babazon Gate[14] near the seashore, where I shall be all this summer with my father and my servants. You can carry me away from there by night without any danger and bring me to the vessel. Remember that you are to be my husband; otherwise, I will pray to Marien to punish you. If you cannot trust anyone to go for the vessel, ransom yourself and go, for I know you will return more surely than any other, as you are a gentleman and a Christian. Attempt to acquaint yourself with the garden. When I see you walking down below, I shall know that the bagnio is empty and I will give you an abundance of money. May Allah protect you, señor.

These were the words and contents of the second paper. On hearing them, each declared himself willing to be the ransomed one and promised to go and return with scrupulous good faith. I, too, made the same offer. But to all this the renegade objected, saying that he would not on any account consent to one of us being set free before all went together, as experience had taught him how poorly those who have been set free keep promises they made in captivity. Captives of

[14] *Babazon Gate:* gate on the eastern side of the fortified city that connected it with the harbor.

distinction frequently had recourse to this plan, he noted, paying the ransom of one who was to go to Valencia or Mallorca with money to enable him to outfit a boat and return for the others who had ransomed him, but who never came back; for recovered liberty and the dread of losing it again efface from the memory every obligation in the world. To prove the truth of what he said, he told us briefly what had happened to a certain Christian gentleman almost at that very time, the strangest case that had ever occurred even there, where astonishing and marvelous things are happening every instant. In short, he ended by saying that what could and ought to be done was to give the money intended for the ransom of one of us Christians to him, so that he might with it buy a vessel there in Algiers under the pretense of becoming a merchant and trader at Tetuan[15] and along the coast. When master of the vessel, it would be easy for him to find a way to get us all out of the bagnio and put us on board—especially if the Moorish lady gave, as she said, money enough to ransom everyone, because once free it would be the easiest thing in the world for us to embark even in open day. But the greatest difficulty was that the Moors do not allow any renegade to buy or own any craft, unless it is a large vessel for going on raiding expeditions, because they are afraid that anyone who buys a small vessel, especially if he is a Spaniard, only wants it for the purpose of escaping to Christian territory. This however he could get over by arranging with a Tagarin Moor[16] to take a share with him in the purchase of the vessel and in the profit on the cargo. With this cover, he could become master of the vessel, in which case he looked upon all the rest as accomplished.

Even though to my comrades and me it had seemed a better plan to send to Mallorca for the vessel, as the Moorish lady suggested, we did not dare to oppose him, fearing that if we did not do as he said, he would denounce us and place us in danger of losing our lives were he to reveal our dealings with Zoraida, for whose life we would have all given our own. We therefore resolved to put ourselves in the hands of God and in the renegade's. At the same time, an answer was given to Zoraida, telling her that we would do all she recommended, for she had given as good advice as if Lela Marien herself had delivered it, and that it depended on her alone whether we were to defer the business or carry it out at once. I also renewed my promise to be her husband. Thus the next day that the bagnio chanced to be empty, she at different times gave us by means of the reed and cloth two thousand gold escudos and a paper in which she said that the next Juma, that is to say Friday,[17] she was going to her father's garden, but that before she went she would give us more money. If it was not enough we were to let her know, as she would give us as much as we asked, for her father had so much he would not miss it, and besides she kept all the keys.

We at once gave the renegade five hundred escudos to buy the vessel, and with eight hundred I ransomed myself, giving the money to a Valencian merchant who happened to be in Algiers at the time and who had me released on

[15] *Tetuan:* city along the northern coast of Morocco (Romanized today as Tétouan).

[16] *Tagarin Moor:* Moor native to the Crown of Aragon.

[17] *Friday:* in Islam, day set aside for corporate worship, obligatory for men.

his word, pledging that on the arrival of the first ship from Valencia he would pay my ransom. For if he had given the money at once it would have made the king suspect that my ransom money had been for a long time in Algiers, and that the merchant had for his own advantage kept it secret. Indeed, my master alone was so mistrustful that I dared not on any account have the money paid down at once. The Thursday before the Friday on which the fair Zoraida was to go to the garden, she gave us a thousand escudos more and warned us of her departure, begging me, if I were ransomed, to find her father's garden at once and, by all means, to seek an opportunity of going there to see her. I answered in a few words that I would do so, and that she must remember to commend us to Lela Marien with all the prayers the captive had taught her. This having been done, steps were taken to ransom our three comrades so as to enable them to leave the bagnio, lest, seeing me ransomed and themselves not (though the money was forthcoming), they should make a disturbance about it and the devil should prompt them to do something that might injure Zoraida. For although knowing who they were might be sufficient to allay this concern, nevertheless I was unwilling to run any risk in the matter; and so I had them ransomed in the same way as I was, handing over all the money to the merchant so that he might with safety and confidence give security, without, however, confiding our arrangement and secret to him, which might have been dangerous.

CHAPTER XLI

IN WHICH THE CAPTIVE FURTHER RELATES HIS ADVENTURES

Before two weeks were over, our renegade had already purchased an excellent vessel with room for more than thirty people. To make the transaction safe and give it the color of legitimacy, he thought it well to make, as he did, a voyage to a place called Cherchell,[1] thirty leagues from Algiers on the Oran side, where there is an extensive trade in dried figs. Two or three times he made this voyage in company with the Tagarin already mentioned. (The Moors of Aragon are called *Tagarins* in Barbary, and those of Granada *Mudéjares*; but in the Kingdom of Fez they call the Mudéjares *Elches*, and they are the people the king chiefly employs in war.) To proceed: every time he passed with his vessel, he anchored in a cove that was not two crossbow shots from the garden where Zoraida was waiting. There the renegade, together with the two Moorish lads that rowed, would purposely station himself, either going through his prayers, or else rehearsing casually what he meant to perform in earnest. Thus he would go to Zoraida's garden and ask for fruit, which her father gave, not knowing him. But though, as he afterwards told me, he sought to speak to Zoraida and tell her who he was, and that by my orders he was to take her to the land of the Christians so that she might feel satisfied and at ease, he was never able to do so; for the Moorish women do not allow themselves to be seen by any Moor or Turk, unless their husband or father command them. With Christian captives, they are allowed to interact and converse, even more than might be considered proper. For my part, I would have been sorry if he had spoken to her, for perhaps it might have alarmed her to find her affairs talked of by renegades.

But God, who ordained otherwise, provided no opportunity for our renegade's well-meant purpose. He, seeing how safely he could go to Cherchell and return, and anchor when and how and where he liked, and that the Tagarin his partner had no will but his, saw that now that I was ransomed, all that was left to do was to find some Christians to row. And so he told me to look out for any I should be willing to take with me (over and above those who had been ransomed), and to arrange for them to join us the next Friday, which he decided upon for our departure. Following this I spoke to twelve Spaniards, all stout rowers, and such as could most easily leave the city. It was no easy matter to find so many just then, because there were twenty ships out on a raid, and

[1] *Cherchell:* port city to the west of Algiers on the way to the larger city of Oran.

they had taken all the rowers with them; and these would not have been found were it not that their master remained at home that summer without going to sea in order to finish a galliot[2] he had in dry dock. To these men I said nothing more than that the next Friday in the evening they were to come out furtively one by one and hang about Hajji Morato's garden, waiting for me there until I came. These directions I gave each one separately, with orders that if they saw any other Christians there, they were not to say anything to them except that I had directed them to wait at that spot.

This preliminary having been settled, another still more necessary step had to be taken, which was to let Zoraida know how matters stood that she might be prepared and forewarned so as not to be taken by surprise if we were suddenly to seize upon her before she thought the Christians' vessel could have returned. I determined, therefore, to go to the garden and try if I could speak to her. The day before my departure I went there under the pretense of gathering herbs.

The first person I met was her father, who addressed me in the language that all over Barbary and even in Constantinople is the medium between captives and Moors, and is neither Morisco nor Castilian, nor of any other nation, but a mixture of all languages,[3] by means of which we can all understand one another. In this sort of language, I say, he asked me what I wanted in his garden and to whom I belonged. I replied that I was a slave of Arnaut Mami[4] (for I knew for certain that he was a very great friend of his) and that I wanted some herbs to make a salad. He went on to ask me whether I was for ransom or not, and what my master demanded for me. While these questions and answers were proceeding, the fair Zoraida, who had already noticed me some time before, came out of the house in the garden; and as Moorish women are by no means particular about letting themselves be seen by Christians, or, as I have said before, at all coy, she had no hesitation in coming to where her father stood with me. Her father, moreover, seeing her approaching slowly, called to her to come.

It would be beyond my power now to describe to you the great beauty, the elegance, the rich adornments of my beloved Zoraida as she presented herself before my eyes. I will content myself with saying that more pearls hung from her fair neck, her ears, and her hair than she had hairs on her head. On her ankles, which as is customary were bare, she had *carcajes* (for so bracelets or anklets are called in Morisco) of the purest gold, set with so many diamonds that she told me afterwards her father valued them at ten thousand gold coins,[5] and those she had on her wrists were worth as much more. The pearls were in abundance and very fine, for the highest display and adornment of the Moorish women is

[2] *galliot:* small galley.

[3] *a mixture of all languages:* Lingua Franca. See footnote 13, page 149.

[4] *Arnaut Mami:* Albanian renegade, corsair, and Ottoman admiral. In a 1575 attack within sight of Catalonia, he took the Spanish galley *Sol* and enslaved the surviving passengers, among them Miguel de Cervantes, who was returning to Spain to petition for a military promotion.

[5] *gold coins:* doblas, perhaps Spanish doubloons or a North African coin.

decking themselves with rich pearls and seed-pearls; and of these there are therefore more among the Moors than among any other people. Zoraida's father had the reputation of possessing a great number, the purest in all Algiers, and of possessing also more than two hundred thousand Spanish escudos. She, who is mistress now of me only, was mistress of all this.

Whether thus adorned she would have been beautiful or not, and what she must have been in her prosperity, may be imagined from the beauty remaining to her after so many hardships; for it is well known that the beauty of some women has its times and its seasons, and is increased or diminished by chance causes; and naturally the emotions of the mind will heighten or impair it, though indeed more frequently they totally destroy it. In sum, she presented herself before me that day adorned with the utmost splendor and supremely beautiful; for me, at least, she was the most beautiful woman I had ever seen. When I thought besides of all I owed her, I felt as though I had before me some heavenly deity come to earth to bring me relief and happiness.

As she approached, her father told her in his own language that I was a captive belonging to his friend Arnaut Mami and that I had come for salad. She took up the conversation, and in that mixture of tongues I have spoken of she asked me if I was a gentleman and why I was not ransomed. I answered that I was already ransomed and that by the price it might be seen what value my master set on me, as they had given one thousand five hundred sultanis[6] for me.

To this she replied, "Had you been my father's, I can tell you that I would not have let him part with you for twice as much, for you Christians always tell lies about yourselves and make yourselves out to be poor to cheat the Moors."

"That may be, lady," said I, "but indeed I dealt truthfully with my master, as I do and mean to do with everybody in the world."

"And when do you depart?" asked Zoraida.

"Tomorrow, I think," said I, "for there is a vessel here from France that sails tomorrow, and I plan to take passage on her."

"Would it not be better," said Zoraida, "to wait for the arrival of ships from Spain and go with them and not with the French, who are not your friends?"[7]

"No," said I, "though if there were intelligence that a vessel were now coming from Spain it is true I might, perhaps, wait for it; however, it is more likely I shall depart tomorrow, for the longing I feel to return to my country and to those I love is so great that it will not allow me to wait for another opportunity, however more convenient, if it is delayed."

"No doubt you are married in your own country," said Zoraida, "and for that reason you are eager to go and see your wife."

[6] *sultanis:* The sultani was a gold coin circulated in the Ottoman Empire and its dependencies, comparable to a Spanish escudo.

[7] *the French, who are not your friends:* During the sixteenth century, the French Bourbon monarchy emerged as the principal rival of Habsburg Spain. The French Crown repeatedly allied itself with the Ottoman Turks (to the dismay of Christendom) as a counterweight to the Spanish Empire.

"I am not married," I replied, "but I have given my promise to marry on my arrival there."

"And is the lady beautiful to whom you have given it?" asked Zoraida.

"So beautiful," said I, "that to describe her worthily and tell you the truth, she looks very much like you."

At this her father laughed very heartily and said, "By Allah, Christian, she must be very beautiful if she looks like my daughter, who is the most beautiful woman in all this kingdom. Only look at her well and you will see I am telling the truth."

Zoraida's father as the better linguist helped to interpret most of these words and phrases, for though she spoke the bastard language that, as I have said, is employed there, she expressed her meaning more by signs than by words.

While we were still engaged in this conversation, a Moor came running up, exclaiming that four Turks had leapt over the fence or wall of the garden and were gathering the fruit, though it was not yet ripe. The old man was alarmed and Zoraida too, for the Moors commonly (and, so to speak, instinctively) have a dread of the Turks, but particularly of the soldiers, who are so insolent and domineering to the Moors under their power that they treat them worse than if they were their slaves.

Her father said to Zoraida, "Daughter, retire into the house and shut yourself in while I go and speak to these dogs; and you, Christian, pick your herbs and go in peace. And may Allah bring you safely to your own country."

I bowed, and he went away to look for the Turks, leaving me alone with Zoraida, who made as if she were about to retire as her father asked her. But the moment he was concealed by the trees of the garden, turning to me with her eyes full of tears she said, "*Amexi, cristiano, amexi?*" which is to say, "Are you leaving, Christian, are you leaving?"

I responded "Yes, señora, but not without you, come what may. Be on the watch for me on the next Juma, and do not be alarmed when you see us; for most assuredly, we will go to the land of the Christians."

This I said in such a way that she understood perfectly all that passed between us, and throwing her arm round my neck she began with feeble steps to move towards the house. But as chance would have it (and it might have been very unfortunate if Heaven had not otherwise ordained), just as we were moving on in the manner and position I have described, with her arm around my neck, her father, as he returned after having sent away the Turks, saw how we were walking, and we perceived that he saw us. Zoraida, ready and quick-witted, took care not to remove her arm from my neck, but on the contrary drew closer to me and laid her head on my breast, bending her knees a little and showing all the signs and tokens of fainting, while I at the same time made it seem as though I were supporting her against my will. Her father came running up to where we were, and seeing his daughter in this state asked what was the matter with her.

When she gave no answer, however, he said, "No doubt she has fainted in alarm at the entrance of those dogs," and taking her from mine he drew her to his own breast.

She sighing, her eyes still wet with tears, said again, "*Amexi, cristiano, amexi!*"—"Leave, Christian, leave!"

To this her father replied, "There is no need, daughter, for the Christian to go, for he has done you no harm, and the Turks have now gone. Feel no alarm—there is nothing to hurt you, for as I say, the Turks at my request have gone back the way they came."

"It was they who terrified her, as you have said, señor," said I to her father. "But since she tells me to go, I have no wish to displease her. Peace be with you, and with your leave I will come back to this garden for herbs if need be, for my master says there are nowhere better herbs for salad than here."

"Come back for any you have need of," replied Hajji Morato, "for my daughter does not speak thus because she is displeased with you or any Christian. She only meant that the Turks should go, not you—or that it was time for you to look for your herbs."

With this I at once took my leave of both, and she, looking as though her heart were breaking, retired with her father. While pretending to look for herbs, I made the round of the garden at my ease, and studied carefully all the approaches and outlets and the security of the house and everything that could be taken advantage of to make our task easy. Having done so I went and gave an account of all that had taken place to the renegade and my comrades, and looked forward with impatience to the hour when, all fear at an end, I should find myself in possession of the prize that fortune held out to me in the fair and lovely Zoraida.

At last the time passed, and the appointed day we so longed for arrived. With everyone following out the arrangement and plan that after careful consideration and many a long discussion we had decided upon, we succeeded as well as we could have wished. On the Friday following the day upon which I spoke to Zoraida in the garden, the renegade anchored his vessel at nightfall almost opposite the spot where I had found her. The Christians who were to row were ready and in hiding in different places round about, all waiting for me, anxious and elated, and eager to attack the vessel they had before their eyes; for they did not know the renegade's plan, but expected that they were to gain their liberty by force of arms and by killing the Moors who were on board the vessel. As soon, then, as my comrades and I made our appearance, all those that were in hiding saw us and came out to join us. It was now the time when the city gates are shut, and there was no one to be seen in all the surrounding countryside.

Now gathered together, we debated whether it would be better first to go for Zoraida or to make prisoners of the Moorish rowers who rowed in the vessel. While we were still in doubt, our renegade came up asking what was keeping us, as it was now time, with all the Moors off their guard and most of them asleep. We told him why we hesitated, but he said it was of more importance first to secure the vessel, which could be done with the greatest ease and without any danger, and then we could go for Zoraida. We all approved of what he said, and so without further delay, guided by him we made for the vessel. He, leaping on board first, drew his cutlass and said in Morisco, "Let no one make a move if he does not want it to cost him his life." By this time almost all the Christians were on board, and the Moors, who were fainthearted, hearing their captain speak in this way, were cowed; and without any one of them taking to his arms (and indeed they had few or hardly any) they submitted without saying a word to be bound by the Christians, who quickly secured them, threatening them that if they raised any kind of outcry, they would be all put to the sword.

This having been accomplished, and half of our party being left to keep guard over them, the rest of us, again taking the renegade as our guide, hastened towards Hajji Morato's garden. As good luck would have it, on trying the gate it opened as easily as if it had not been locked, and so in complete silence, we reached the house without being noticed by anyone. The lovely Zoraida was watching for us at a window, and as soon as she saw that there were people there, she asked in a low voice if we were "*Nizarani*,"[8] as much as to say or ask if we were Christians. I answered that we were and begged her to come down. As soon as she recognized me, she did not delay an instant, but without answering a word came down immediately, opened the door, and presented herself before us all, so beautiful and so richly attired that I cannot attempt to describe her. The moment I saw her I took her hand and kissed it, and the renegade and my two comrades did the same. The rest, who knew nothing of the circumstances, did as they saw us do, for it only seemed as if we were returning thanks to her and recognizing her as the giver of our liberty. The renegade asked her in the Morisco language if her father was in the house. She replied that he was and that he was asleep.

"Then it will be necessary to waken him and take him with us," said the renegade, "and everything of value in this beautiful estate."

"No," said she. "My father must not on any account be touched, and there is nothing in the house except what I shall take, and that will be quite enough to enrich and satisfy all of you. Wait a little and you shall see." So saying she went in, telling us she would return immediately and bidding us keep quiet without making any noise.

I asked the renegade what had passed between them, and when he told me, I declared that nothing should be done except in accordance with the wishes of Zoraida, who now came back with a little trunk so full of gold escudos that she could scarcely carry it. Unfortunately, her father awoke while this was going on, and hearing a noise in the garden, came to the window. At once realizing that all those who were there were Christians, raising a prodigiously loud outcry, he began to call out in Arabic, "Christians, Christians! Thieves, thieves!" by which cries we were all thrown into the greatest fear and confusion. The renegade, seeing the danger we were in and how important it was for him to carry out our plan before being heard, mounted with the utmost speed to where Hajji Morato was, and with him went some of our party. I, however, did not dare to leave Zoraida, who had fallen almost fainting in my arms.

To be brief, those who had gone upstairs acted so quickly that in an instant they came down, carrying Hajji Morato with his hands bound and a cloth tied over his mouth, which prevented him from uttering a word, warning him at the

[8] Nizarani: literally, "Nazarenes".

same time that to attempt to speak would cost him his life. When his daughter caught sight of him, she covered her eyes so as not to see him. Her father was horror-stricken, not knowing how willingly she had placed herself in our hands. It was now most essential for us to be on the move. Carefully and quickly we regained the vessel, where those who had remained on board were waiting, worried that some mishap had befallen us.

It was barely two hours after night set in when we were all on board the vessel, where the cords were removed from the hands of Zoraida's father and the cloth from his mouth. The renegade once more told him not to utter a word, or they would take his life. He, when he saw his daughter there, began to sigh piteously, and still more when he saw that I held her closely embraced and that she lay quiet without resisting or complaining or showing any reluctance. Nevertheless, he remained silent lest they should carry into effect the repeated threats the renegade had made to him.

Finding herself now on board, and that we were about to give way with the oars, Zoraida, seeing her father there, and the other Moors bound, had the renegade ask me to do her the favor of releasing the Moors and setting her father at liberty, for she would rather drown herself in the sea than permit a father who had loved her so dearly to be carried away captive before her eyes and on her account. The renegade repeated this to me, and I responded that I was very willing to do so; but he replied that it was not advisable, because if they were left there they would at once sound the alarm in the countryside and stir up the city, and lead to the dispatch of swift cruisers in pursuit and our being taken, by sea or land, without any possibility of escape. All that could be done was to set them free on the first Christian land we reached. On this point we all agreed; and Zoraida, to whom it was explained, together with the reasons that prevented us from doing at once what she desired, was satisfied likewise. Then in glad silence and with cheerful energy each of our stout rowers took his oar, and commending ourselves to God with all our hearts, we began our course for the island of Mallorca, the nearest Christian land.

Owing, however, to the Tramontana[9] rising a little, and the sea growing somewhat rough, it was impossible for us to keep a straight course for Mallorca, and we were compelled to coast in the direction of Oran, not without great uneasiness on our part lest we should be observed from the town of Cherchell, which lies on that coast, not more than sixty miles from Algiers. Moreover, we were afraid of meeting on that course one of the galliots that usually come with goods from Tetuan, although each of us for himself and all of us together felt confident that, if we were to meet a merchant galliot (as long as it were not a cruiser), not only should we not be lost, but that we should take a vessel in which we could more safely accomplish our voyage. As we pursued our course, Zoraida kept her head between my hands so as not to see her father, and I sensed that she was praying to Lela Marien to help us.

We might have made about thirty miles when daybreak found us some three harquebus shots from the shore, which seemed to us deserted and without anyone

[9] *Tramontana:* north wind.

to see us. For all that, however, by hard rowing we put out a little to sea, for it was now somewhat calmer, and having gained about two leagues the word was given to row by turns while we ate something, for the vessel was well provisioned. The rowers, however, said it was not a time to take any rest, that food should be served to those who were not rowing but that they would not leave their oars on any account. This was done, but now a stiff breeze began to blow, which obliged us to leave off rowing and make sail at once and steer for Oran, as it was impossible to take any other course. All this was done very promptly, and under sail we ran more than eight miles an hour without any fear, except that of coming across some vessel out on a raiding expedition. We gave the Moorish rowers some food, and the renegade comforted them by telling them that they were not held as captives, for we would set them free on the first opportunity.

The same was said to Zoraida's father, who replied, "Anything else, Christian, I might hope for or think likely from your generosity and good behavior, but do not think me so simple as to imagine you will give me my liberty; for you would have never exposed yourselves to the danger of depriving me of it only to restore it to me so generously, especially as you know who I am and the sum you may expect to receive on restoring it. If you will only name the price, I here offer you all you would ask for myself and for my unhappy daughter there—or else for her alone, for she is the greatest and most precious part of my soul."

As he said this, he began to weep so bitterly that he filled us all with compassion and forced Zoraida to look at him. When she saw him weeping, she was so moved that she rose from my feet and ran to throw her arms round him. Pressing her face to his, they both gave way to such an outburst of tears that several of us joined in their weeping. But when her father saw her in festive dress and with all her jewels about her, he said to her in his own language, "What means this, my daughter? Last night, before this terrible misfortune of ours befell us, I saw you in your everyday and indoor garments; and now, without having had time to dress, and without my bringing you any joyful news to furnish an occasion for you to adorn and bedeck yourself, you are arrayed in the finest attire it would be in my power to give you when fortune was most kind to us. Answer me this, for it causes me greater anxiety and surprise than even this misfortune itself."

The renegade interpreted to us what the Moor said to his daughter; she, however, returned him no answer. But when he observed in one corner of the vessel the little trunk in which she used to keep her jewels, which he well knew he had left in Algiers and had not brought to the garden, he was still more amazed, and asked her how that trunk had come into our hands and what there was in it.

To this the renegade, without waiting for Zoraida to reply, answered, "Do not trouble yourself by asking your daughter Zoraida so many questions, señor, for the one answer I will give you will serve for all: I would have you know that she is a Christian, and that it is she who has been the file for our chains and our deliverer from captivity. She is here of her own free will, as happy, I imagine, to find herself in this position as he who escapes from darkness into the light, from death to life, and from suffering to glory."

"Daughter, is this true what he says?" cried the Moor.

"It is," replied Zoraida.

"That you are in truth a Christian," said the old man, "and that you have given your father into the power of his enemies?"

To which Zoraida answered, "A Christian I am, but it is not I who have placed you in this position, for it never was my wish to leave you or do you harm, but only to do good to myself."

"And what good have you done yourself, daughter?" asked he.

"Ask Lela Marien to tell you," said she, "for she can answer you better than I."

The Moor had hardly heard these words when with incredible speed he flung himself headlong into the sea, where no doubt he would have been drowned had not the bulky, flowing garments he wore held him up for a little while on the surface of the water. Zoraida cried aloud to us to save him, and we all hastened to help. Seizing him by his robe, we drew him in half drowned and insensible, at which Zoraida was in such distress that she wept over him as piteously and bitterly as though he were already dead. We turned him on his stomach and he expelled a great quantity of water, and at the end of two hours came to himself. Meanwhile, the wind having changed, we were compelled to head for land and ply our oars to avoid being driven on shore; but it was our good fortune to reach a creek that lies on one side of a small promontory or cape, called by the Moors the Cape of the Cava Rumía, which in our language means "the wicked Christian woman." For it is a tradition among them that La Cava, through whom Spain was lost, lies buried at that spot, *cava* in their language meaning "wicked woman" and *rumía* "Christian."[10] Moreover, they count it unlucky to anchor there when necessity compels them, and they never do so otherwise. For us, however, it was not the resting place of the wicked woman but a haven of safety for our relief, so rough had the sea turned. We posted a lookout on shore, never letting the oars out of our hands, and ate of the provisions the renegade had stowed, imploring God and Our Lady with all our hearts to help and protect us that we might give a happy ending to a beginning so prosperous. At Zoraida's entreaty, orders were

[10] *Cape of the Cava Rumía, which in our language means "the wicked Christian woman" ... "Christian"*: According to legend, Rodrigo, the last of Spain's Visigothic kings, had an illicit sexual encounter with Florinda, the daughter of a noble vassal, after she was sent to court for her education. The nature of the encounter varies by the telling. Her reputation as a wicked Christian woman (*qahba rūmiyya* in Arabic—more precisely, "Christian whore") relies on the accounts in which she actively seduces King Rodrigo with her beauty. Marriage did not follow, which left Florinda and her family disgraced. To exact revenge, her father, Count Julián of Ceuta, aided the jihadist army that had advanced westward from Arabia and was seeking to extend Islamic rule across the Straits of Gibraltar. This much is true—that the invading Moors defeated Rodrigo in 711 at the Battle of Guadalete and established a political presence on the Iberian Peninsula that would endure in some form until 1492. The legend that the Cava Rumía is buried on the Barbary coast may have arisen from the phonetic similarity of Cava Rumía to the name of a Roman-era mausoleum. Historical details aside, the more interesting question is why Cervantes would juxtapose the fall of Visigothic Spain with the immigration story of a Muslim convert to Christianity and the Spanish slave she ransoms and weds.

given to set on shore her father and the other Moors who were still bound, for she could not endure, nor could her tender heart bear to see, her father in bonds and her fellow countrymen prisoners before her eyes. We promised her to do this at the moment of departure, for as it was uninhabited we ran no risk in releasing them at that place.

Our prayers were not so far in vain as to be unheard by Heaven, for after a while the wind changed in our favor and made the sea calm, inviting us once more to resume our voyage without fear. Seeing this we unbound the Moors, and one by one put them on shore, at which they were filled with amazement.

But when we came to free Zoraida's father, who had now completely recovered his senses, he said, "Why do you think, Christians, that this wicked woman rejoices at your giving me my liberty? Do you think it is because of the affection she bears me? Far from it! It is only because my presence hinders her from carrying out her base designs. And do not think the belief that your religion is better than ours has led her to change one for the other; it is only because she knows that immodesty is more freely practiced in your country than in ours." Then turning to Zoraida, while one of the other Christians and I held him fast by both arms, lest he should do some reckless act, he said to her, "Shameful girl, misguided maiden, where in your blindness and folly are you headed in the hands of these dogs, our natural enemies? Cursed be the hour when I begot you! Cursed the luxury and indulgence in which I reared you!"

Seeing that he was not likely soon to cease, I hurried to put him ashore. From there, he continued his curses and lamentations aloud, calling on Mohammed to pray to Allah to destroy us, to confound us, to make an end of us; and when, after having set sail, we could no longer hear what he said, we could see what he did, how he plucked out his beard and tore his hair and lay writhing on the ground. But once he raised his voice to such a pitch that we were able to hear what he said: "Come back, dear daughter, come back to shore! I forgive you of everything! Let those men have the money, for it is theirs now, and come back to comfort your sorrowing father, who will abandon his life to this deserted beach if you leave him."

All this Zoraida heard—and heard with sorrow and tears. All she could say in answer was, "Allah grant that Lela Marien, who is the reason I am a Christian, give you comfort in your sorrow, my father. Allah knows that I could not do otherwise than I have done, and that these Christians owe nothing to my will; for even had I wished not to accompany them but remain at home, it would have been impossible for me, so earnestly was my soul moved to carry out a design that seems as righteous to me as to you, dear father, it seems wicked."

But neither could her father hear her nor we see him when she said this; and so, while I consoled Zoraida, we turned our attention to our voyage, in which a fair wind so favored us that we made sure of finding ourselves off the coast of Spain by dawn of the following day. But as good seldom or never comes pure and unmixed without being attended or followed by some evil to cloud it, our fortune—or perhaps the curses that the Moor had hurled at his daughter, for whatever kind of father they may come from, these are always to be feared—brought it about that when we were now on the high sea and the night about three hours spent, as we were running with full sails and oars lashed (for the fair wind saved us the trouble of using them), we saw by the bright light of the moon a square-rigged vessel in full sail close to us, turning into the wind and standing across our course, so close that we had to strike sail to avoid running afoul of her, while they too put the helm hard up to let us pass. They came to the side of the ship to ask who we were, where we were headed, and where we came from, but as they asked this in French, our renegade said, "Let no one answer, for no doubt these are French corsairs who plunder all comers."

Acting on this warning no one answered a word, but after we had gone a little ahead, and the vessel was now lying to leeward, suddenly they fired two guns, and apparently both loaded with chain shot,[11] for with one they cut our mast in half and brought down both it and the sail into the sea, and the other, discharged at the same moment, sent a ball into our vessel amidships, staving her in completely, but without doing any further damage. Finding ourselves sinking, we began to shout for help and call upon those in the ship to pick us up, as we would soon be underwater. They then lay to, and lowering a skiff or boat, as many as a dozen Frenchmen, well-armed, with the matches lit on their harquebuses,[12] got into it and came alongside. Seeing how few we were and that our vessel was going down, they took us in, telling us that this had come to us through our incivility in not giving them an answer. Our renegade took the trunk containing Zoraida's wealth and dropped it into the sea without anyone noticing what he did.

In short we went on board with the Frenchmen, who, after having been informed of all that they wanted to know about us, plundered us of everything we had, as if they had been our bitterest enemies, and from Zoraida they took even the anklets she wore on her feet. But the distress they caused her did not distress me so much as the fear I was in that from robbing her of her rich and precious jewels they would proceed to rob her of the most precious jewel that she valued more than all.[13] The desires, however, of those people do not go beyond money, but of that their greed is insatiable, and on this occasion it was carried to such a pitch that they would have taken even the clothes we wore as captives if they had been worth anything to them. It was the opinion of some of them to throw us all into the sea wrapped up in a sail; for their purpose was to trade at some of the ports of Spain, holding themselves out as Bretons,[14] and if they brought us alive they would be punished as soon as the robbery was discovered. But the captain (who was the one who had plundered my beloved Zoraida) said he was satisfied with the prize he had gotten, and that he would not touch at any Spanish port, but pass the Straits of Gibraltar by night, or as best he could,

[11] *chain shot:* cannon shot made up of two balls chained together.

[12] *with the matches lit on their harquebuses:* that is, ready to fire. See footnote 4, page 309.

[13] *most precious jewel that she valued more than all:* her virginity.

[14] *Bretons:* At the time, the northwestern French province of Brittany was allied with Spain.

and make for La Rochelle, from which he had sailed.[15] And so they agreed by common consent to give us the skiff belonging to their ship and all we required for the short voyage that remained to us. This they did the next day when they came in view of the Spanish coast, at the sight of which all our sufferings and miseries were as completely forgotten as if we had never endured them—such is the joy of recovering lost liberty.

It was probably about midday when they placed us in the boat, giving us two kegs of water and some biscuit. The captain, moved by I know not what compassion, as the lovely Zoraida was about to embark, gave her some forty gold escudos, and would not permit his men to take from her those same garments she has on now. We got into the boat, returning them thanks for their kindness to us, and showing ourselves grateful rather than indignant. They put out to sea, steering for the straits. We, without looking to any compass save the land we had before us, set ourselves to row with such energy that by sunset we were so near that we might easily land, we thought, before the night was far advanced. But as the moon did not show that night, and the sky was clouded, and as we were unsure of our whereabouts, it did not seem to us a prudent thing to make for the shore, as several among us advised. They proposed that we run aground, even if it were on rocks and far from any habitation, for in this way we should be relieved from the fears we naturally felt of the raiding vessels of the Tetuan corsairs, who leave Barbary at nightfall and are on the Spanish coast by daybreak, where they are accustomed to take their fill of plunder and then go home to sleep in their own houses. But of the conflicting counsels, the one that was adopted was that we should approach gradually and land where we could if the sea were calm enough to permit us.

This was done, and a little before midnight we drew near to the foot of a lofty and very irregular mountain, not so close to the sea but that it left a narrow space on which to land conveniently. We ran our boat up on the sand, and all jumped out and kissed the ground, and with joyful tears corresponding to our great happiness we returned thanks to God our Lord for his incomparable goodness to us on our voyage. We took out of the boat the provisions it contained, drew it up on the shore, and then climbed a long way up the mountain, for even there we could not feel easy in our hearts or persuade ourselves that it was Christian soil that was now under our feet.

Dawn came, more slowly, I think, than we could have wished. We completed the ascent in order to see if from the summit any habitation or any shepherds' huts could be discovered, but strain our eyes as we might, we could make out neither dwelling, nor human being, nor path, nor road. We determined, however, to push on farther, certain that before long we were bound to see someone who could tell us where we were. What distressed me most was to see Zoraida going on foot over that rough ground; for though I once carried her on my shoulders, she was more wearied by my weariness than rested by the rest, and so she would

[15] *La Rochelle, from which he had sailed:* Huguenot (French Protestant) stronghold on the Bay of Biscay, infamous in the sixteenth century as a launching site for corsair raids.

never again allow me to undergo the exertion but went on very patiently and cheerfully while I led her by the hand. We had gone somewhat less than a quarter of a league when the sound of a little bell fell on our ears, a clear proof that there were flocks nearby. Looking around carefully to see if any were within view, we observed a young shepherd tranquilly and unsuspiciously whittling a stick with his knife at the foot of a cork tree. We called to him, and he, raising his head, sprang nimbly to his feet, for as we afterwards learned, the first who presented themselves to his sight were the renegade and Zoraida, and seeing them in Moorish dress he imagined that all the Moors of Barbary were upon him. Running with extraordinary swiftness into the woods before him, he began to raise a prodigious outcry, exclaiming, "The Moors—the Moors have landed! To arms, to arms!"

We were all thrown into confusion by these cries, not knowing what to do; but reflecting that the shouts of the shepherd would raise the country and that the coast guard[16] would come at once to see what was the matter, we agreed that the renegade must strip off his Turkish garments and put on a captive's jacket or coat, which one of our party gave him at once, though he himself was reduced to his shirt. And so commending ourselves to God, we followed the same road that we saw the shepherd take, expecting every moment that the coast guard would be down upon us. Nor did our expectation deceive us, for not two hours had passed when, coming out of the brushwood into the open ground, we saw some fifty mounted men swiftly galloping toward us. As soon as we saw them we stood still, waiting for them; but when they came close and discovered, instead of the Moors they were in search of, a band of poor Christians, they were taken aback. One of them asked if we might be the cause of the shepherd having raised the call to arms. I said "Yes," and as I was about to explain to him what had occurred, and where we came from and who we were, one of the Christians of our party recognized the horseman who had questioned us.

Before I could say anything more, he exclaimed, "Thanks be to God, sirs, who has brought us to this good place! For if I do not deceive myself, the ground we stand on is that of Vélez Málaga[17]—unless, indeed, all my years of captivity have erased from my memory that you, señor, who ask who we are, are Pedro de Bustamante, my uncle."

The Christian captive had hardly uttered these words, when the horseman threw himself off his horse and ran to embrace the young man, crying, "Nephew of my soul and life! I recognize you now. Long have I mourned you as dead, I, and my sister, your mother, and all your kin that are still alive, and whom God has been pleased to preserve that they may enjoy the happiness of seeing you. We knew long since that you were in Algiers, and from the appearance of your garments and those of all this company, I conclude that you have had a miraculous restoration to liberty."

[16] *coast guard: caballeria de la costa*, semi-professional mounted militia trained to patrol coastal communities and defend them from corsair incursions.

[17] *Vélez Málaga:* town on the southern coast of Andalusia, twenty miles east of the larger city of Málaga.

"It is true," replied the young man, "and in due time we will tell you all."

As soon as the horsemen understood that we were Christian captives, they dismounted from their horses, and each offered his to carry us to the city of Vélez Málaga, which was a league and a half distant. Some of them went to bring the boat to the city, we having told them where we had left it; others took us up behind them. Zoraida was placed on the horse of the young man's uncle. The whole town came out to meet us, for they had by this time heard of our arrival from one who had gone on in advance. They were not astonished to see liberated captives or captive Moors, for people on that coast are well used to see both one and the other; but they were wonderstruck at the beauty of Zoraida, which had been heightened both by the exertion of traveling and by the joy of finding herself on Christian soil, relieved of all fear of being lost. For this had brought such a glow to her face that, unless my affection for her were deceiving me, I would venture to say there was not a more beautiful creature in the world—at least, that I had ever seen.

We went straight to the church to give thanks to God for the mercies we had received. When Zoraida entered it, she said there were faces there like Lela Marien's. We told her they were her images. As well as he could, the renegade explained to her what they meant, that she might adore them as if each of them were the very same Lela Marien who had spoken to her. She, having great intelligence and a quick and clear instinct, understood at once all he said to her about them. From there they took us away and divided us all among different houses in the town; but as for the renegade, Zoraida, and myself, the Christian who came with us brought us to the house of his parents, who had a fair share of the gifts of fortune, and treated us with as much kindness as they did their own son.

We remained six days in Vélez, at the end of which the renegade, having informed himself of all that was required for him to do, set out for the city of Granada to restore himself to the sacred bosom of the Church through the medium of the Holy Inquisition.[18] The other released captives took their departures, each the way that seemed best to him, and Zoraida and I were left alone, with nothing more than the escudos that the Frenchman in his courtesy had bestowed upon Zoraida, out of which I bought the beast on which she rides. And with me for the present attending her as her father and squire and not as her husband,[19] she and I now journey with the intention of finding out whether my father is living, or if any of my brothers has had better fortune than mine has been—though, as Heaven has made me the companion of Zoraida, I think no other lot could be assigned to me, however happy, that I would rather have. The patience with which she endures the hardships that poverty brings with it, and the eagerness she shows to become a Christian, are such that they fill me with wonder and compel me to serve her all my life. And yet the happiness I feel in seeing myself hers, and

[18] *Granada to restore himself ... Holy Inquisition:* The regional tribunal over eastern Andalusia was headquartered in Granada, fifty-five miles northeast.

[19] *not as her husband:* In accordance with canon law, the captive and Zoraida cannot marry until the latter is baptized into the Catholic Church.

her mine, is disturbed and marred by not knowing whether I shall find any corner to shelter her in my own country, or whether time and death may not have made such changes in the fortunes and lives of my father and brothers that I shall hardly find anyone who recognizes me, if anyone is alive.

I have no more of my story to tell you, gentlemen. Whether it has been an entertaining or unusual one, let your better judgments decide. All I can say is that I would gladly have told it to you more briefly, though my fear of wearying you has made me leave out more than a few details.

CHAPTER XLII

WHICH TREATS OF WHAT FURTHER TOOK PLACE IN THE INN, AND OF SEVERAL OTHER THINGS WORTH KNOWING

With these words the captive fell silent, and Don Fernando said to him, "In truth, captain, the manner in which you have related this remarkable adventure has been such as befitted the novelty and strangeness of the matter. The whole story is uncommonly interesting; it abounds with incidents that fill the hearers with wonder and astonishment. So great is the pleasure we have found in listening that we should be glad if it were to begin again, even though tomorrow were to find us still occupied with the same tale."

Don Fernando, Cardenio, and the others offered to be of service to him in any way that lay in their power, and in words and language so kindly and sincere that the captain was much gratified by their goodwill. In particular Don Fernando offered, if he would go back with him, to get his brother the marquis to become godfather at the baptism of Zoraida, and on his own part to provide him with the means of making his appearance in his own country with the dignity and honor he was entitled to. For all this, the captive returned thanks very courteously, although he would not accept any of their generous offers.

By this time night closed in, and as it did, there came up to the inn a coach attended by some men on horseback, who demanded accommodation; to which the innkeeper's wife replied that there was not a hand's breadth of the whole inn unoccupied.

"Be that as it may," said one of those who had entered on horseback, "room must be found for his lordship the judge here."

Upon hearing this title, the innkeeper's wife was taken aback and said, "Señor, the fact is I have no beds. But if his lordship the judge carries one with him, as no doubt he does, he is welcome to come in, for my husband and I will give up our room to accommodate his worship."

"So be it," said the squire.

In the meantime, a man had gotten out of the coach whose dress indicated at a glance the office and post he held, for the long robe with ruffled sleeves he wore showed that he was, as his servant said, a royal magistrate.[1] He led by the hand a young girl in traveling dress, who appeared to be about sixteen years of age,

[1] *royal magistrate: oidor*. In the Spanish Empire, the *oidor* was a judge who served in the *Audiencia Real* (Royal Audience), the supreme court in its jurisdiction.

and of such a high-bred air, so beautiful and so graceful, that all were filled with admiration when she made her appearance, and but for having seen Dorotea, Luscinda, and Zoraida there in the inn, they would have fancied that a beauty like that of this maiden's would have been hard to find.

Don Quixote was present at the entrance of the judge with the young lady, and as soon as he saw him he said, "Your worship may with confidence enter and take your ease in this castle; for though the accommodation be scanty and poor, there are no quarters so cramped or inconvenient that they cannot make room for arms and letters—above all if arms and letters have beauty for a guide and leader, as letters represented by your worship have in this fair maiden, to whom not only ought castles throw themselves open and yield themselves up, but rocks should rend themselves asunder and mountains divide and bow themselves down to give her a reception. Enter, your worship, I say, into this paradise, for here you will find stars and suns to accompany the heaven your worship brings with you. Here you will find arms in their supreme excellence and beauty in its highest perfection."

The judge was struck with amazement at the language of Don Quixote, whom he scrutinized very carefully, no less astonished by his figure than by his speech. But before he could find words to answer him, he had a fresh surprise when he saw opposite to him Luscinda, Dorotea, and Zoraida, who, having heard of the new guests and of the beauty of the young lady, had come to see her and make her welcome. For their part, Don Fernando, Cardenio, and the priest greeted him in a more intelligible and polished style. In sum, the judge made his entrance in a state of bewilderment, both with what he saw and what he heard, and the fair ladies of the inn gave the fair damsel a cordial welcome. On the whole, he gathered that all who were there were people of quality, but with the figure, countenance, and bearing of Don Quixote he was at a loss to explain.

Every civility having been exchanged and the accommodation of the inn inquired into, it was settled, as it had been before settled, that all the women should retire to the garret that has been already mentioned and that the men should remain outside as if to guard them. And so the judge was very well pleased to allow his daughter (for such the damsel was) to go with the ladies, which she did very willingly; and with part of the innkeeper's narrow bed and half of what the judge had brought with him, they made a more comfortable arrangement for the night than they had expected.

From the moment the captive saw the judge, his heart had been racing, telling him that, somehow, this was his brother. He asked one of the servants who accompanied the judge what his name was, and whether he knew from what part of the country he came. The servant replied that he was called the Licentiate Juan Pérez de Viedma, and that he had heard it said he came from a village in the mountains of León. From this statement, and what he himself had seen, he felt convinced that this was his brother who had adopted letters by his father's advice. Excited and joyful, he called Don Fernando, Cardenio, and the priest aside and told them how the matter stood, assuring them that the judge was his brother. The servant had further informed him that he was now going to the

Indies with an appointment as judge of the Supreme Court of Mexico.[2] He had learned, likewise, that the young lady was his daughter, whose mother had died in giving birth to her, and that he was very rich in consequence of the dowry left to him with the daughter. He asked their advice as to what means he should adopt to make himself known or to determine beforehand whether, when he had made himself known, his brother would be ashamed of him on seeing him so poor or would receive him with a warm heart.

"Leave it to me to find out," said the priest, "though there is no reason for supposing, Señor Captain, that you will not be kindly received, because the worth and wisdom that your brother's bearing shows him to possess do not make it likely that he will prove haughty or insensible, or that he will be unsympathetic to the accidents of fortune."

"Still," said the captain, "I would not make myself known abruptly, but in some indirect way."

"I have told you already," said the priest, "that I will manage it in a way to satisfy us all."

By this time supper was ready, and they all took their seats at the table—except the ladies, who dined by themselves in their own room, and the captive. In the middle of supper, the priest said:

"I had a comrade of your worship's name, señor judge, in Constantinople, where I was a captive for several years, and that same comrade was one of the most valiant soldiers and captains in the whole Spanish infantry; but he had as large a share of misfortune as he had of gallantry and courage."

"And what was the captain's name, señor?" asked the judge.

"He was named Ruy Pérez de Viedma,"[3] replied the priest, "and he was born in a village in the mountains of León. He mentioned a circumstance connected with his father and his brothers that, had it not been told me by so truthful a man as he was, I should have set down as one of those fables the old women tell over the fire in winter. He said that his father had divided his property among his three sons and had addressed words of advice to them sounder than any of Cato's.[4] But I can say this much, that the choice he made of going to the wars was attended with such success that by his gallant conduct and courage, and without any help save his own merit, he rose in a few years to be an infantry captain and from there was set on the path to be given a senior command before long. But Fortune was against him, for where he might have expected her favor he lost it, and with it his liberty, on that glorious day when so many recovered theirs, at the battle of Lepanto. I lost mine at La Goletta, and after a variety of adventures we found ourselves comrades at Constantinople. From there he went to Algiers, where he met with one of the most extraordinary adventures that ever befell anyone in the world."

[2] *Supreme Court of Mexico: Audiencia de México.*

[3] *Ruy Pérez de Viedma:* The captive's name recalls that of Spain's epic hero, Ruy Díaz de Vivar, popularly known as El Cid.

[4] *sounder than any of Cato's:* See footnote 5, page 144.

Here the priest went on to relate briefly his brother's adventure with Zoraida. To all of this, the judge gave such an attentive hearing that never before had he been so much of a hearer.[5] The priest, however, only went so far as to describe how the Frenchmen plundered those who were in the boat, and the poverty and distress in which his comrade and the fair Moor were left, of whom he said he had not been able to learn their whereabouts—whether they had reached Spain or been carried to France by the Frenchmen.

The captain, standing a little to one side, was listening to all the priest said, and watching every movement of his brother, who, when he perceived the priest had reached the end of his story, gave a deep sigh and said with his eyes full of tears, "O, señor, if you only knew what news you have related and how personally it concerns me. The tears that spring from my eyes in spite of all my worldly wisdom and self-restraint betray the truth! That brave captain you speak of is my eldest brother, who, being of a bolder and loftier mind than my other brother or myself, chose the honorable and worthy calling of arms, which was one of the three careers our father proposed to us, as your comrade mentioned in that fable you thought he was telling you. I followed that of letters, in which God and my own exertions have raised me to the position in which you see me. My second brother is in Peru, so wealthy that with what he has sent to my father and me he has fully repaid the portion he took with him, and has even furnished my father's hands with the means of gratifying his natural generosity, while I too have been enabled to pursue my studies in a more becoming and creditable fashion, and so to attain my present standing. My father is still alive, though dying with anxiety to hear of his eldest son. He prays to God unceasingly that he may see him again before death closes his eyes.

"But with regard to him, I marvel that having so much common sense as he had, he should have neglected to give any account of himself, either of his troubles and sufferings or his prosperity, for if his father or any of us had known of his condition he need not have waited for that miracle of the reed to obtain his ransom. What now disquiets me is the uncertainty whether those Frenchmen may have restored him to liberty or murdered him to hide the robbery. All this will make me continue my journey, not with the satisfaction in which I began it, but in the deepest melancholy and sadness. O dear brother! If I only knew where you are now, I would hasten to seek you out and deliver you from your sufferings, though it were to cost me suffering myself! If only I could bring news to our old father that you are alive, even if you were in the deepest dungeon of Barbary. His wealth and my brother's and mine would rescue you from that place! O beautiful and generous Zoraida, would that I could repay your goodness to a brother! Would that I could be present at the new birth of your soul and at the wedding that would bring us so much happiness!"

All this and more the judge uttered with such deep emotion at the news he had received of his brother that all who heard him shared in it, showing their sympathy with his sorrow. The priest, seeing how well he had succeeded in

[5] *hearer: oidor*. The title *oidor* literally means "hearer".

carrying out his purpose and the captain's wishes, had no desire to keep them unhappy any longer, so he rose from the table, and going into the room where Zoraida was, he took her by the hand, with Luscinda, Dorotea, and the judge's daughter following her. The captain was waiting to see what the priest would do, when the latter, taking him with the other hand, advanced with both of them to where the judge and the other gentlemen were and said, "Let your tears cease to flow, señor judge, and the wish of your heart be gratified as fully as you could desire, for you have before you your worthy brother and your good sister-in-law. He whom you see here is Captain Viedma, and this is the fair Moor who has been so good to him. The Frenchmen I told you of have reduced them to the state of poverty you see that you may show the generosity of your kind heart."

The captain ran to embrace his brother, who placed both hands on his breast so as to have a good look at him, holding him a little way off, but as soon as he had fully recognized him he clasped him in his arms so closely, shedding such tears of heartfelt joy, that most of those present could not but join in them. The words the brothers exchanged, the emotion they showed, can scarcely be imagined, I believe, much less put down in writing. They told each other in a few words the events of their lives; they showed the true affection of brothers in all its strength. There the judge embraced Zoraida, putting all he possessed at her disposal; there he made his daughter embrace her, and the fair Christian and the lovely Moor drew fresh tears from every eye. There was Don Quixote observing all these strange proceedings attentively without uttering a word and attributing the whole to chimeras of knight-errantry. There they agreed that the captain and Zoraida should return with his brother to Seville and send news to his father of his having been delivered and found, so as to enable him to come and be present at the marriage and baptism of Zoraida; for it was impossible for the judge to put off his journey, as he was informed that in a month from that time the fleet was to sail from Seville for New Spain,[6] and to miss the passage would have been a great inconvenience to him.

In short, all were well pleased and happy with the captive's good fortune, and as now almost two-thirds of the night were past, they resolved to retire to bed for the remainder of it. Don Quixote offered to mount guard over the castle lest they should be attacked by some giant or other malevolent scoundrel, covetous of the great treasure of beauty the castle held. Those who understood him thanked him for this service, and they gave the judge an account of his extraordinary condition, with which he was not a little amused. Sancho Panza alone was fuming at the lateness of the hour for retiring to bed. He, of everyone, made himself the most comfortable, as he stretched himself on the trappings of his donkey, which, as will be told farther on, cost him so dear.

The ladies, then, having retired to their chamber, and the others having settled in with as little discomfort as they could, Don Quixote sallied out of the inn to act as sentinel of the castle as he had promised. It happened, however, that

[6] *the fleet was to sail from Seville for New Spain:* The West Indies fleet (*Flota de Indias*) departed Seville each spring bound for Veracruz.

a little before the approach of dawn a voice so musical and sweet reached the ladies' ears that it forced them all to listen attentively, but especially Dorotea, who had been awake, and by whose side Doña Clara de Viedma (for so the judge's daughter was called) lay sleeping. No one could imagine who it was that sang so sweetly, and the voice was unaccompanied by any instrument. At one moment it seemed to them as if the singer were in the courtyard, at another in the stable.

While they went on this way, very attentive yet perplexed, Cardenio came to the door and said, "Listen, whoever is not asleep, and you will hear the voice of a muleteer[7] enchanting as it chants."

"We are listening to it already, señor," said Dorotea.

Cardenio went away, and Dorotea, giving all her attention to the music, made out the words of the song to be these:

[7] *muleteer*: boy who takes care of mules.

CHAPTER XLIII

WHEREIN IS RELATED THE PLEASANT STORY OF THE MULETEER, TOGETHER WITH OTHER STRANGE THINGS THAT CAME TO PASS IN THE INN

Ah me, Love's mariner am I
On Love's deep ocean sailing;
I know not where the haven lies,
I dare not hope to gain it.

One solitary distant star
Is all I have to guide me,
A brighter orb than those of old
That Palinurus[1] lighted.

And vaguely drifting am I borne,
I know not where it leads me;
I fix my gaze on it alone,
Of all beside it heedless.

But overcautious prudery,
And coyness cold and cruel,
When most I need it, these, like clouds,
Its longed-for light refuse me.

Bright star, goal of my yearning eyes
As thou above me beamest,
When thou shalt hide thee from my sight
I'll know that death is near me.

The singer had gotten this far when it struck Dorotea that it was not fair to let Clara miss hearing such a sweet voice, so shaking her from side to side, she woke her saying, "Forgive me, child, for waking you. I do so that you may have the pleasure of hearing the finest voice you have heard perhaps in all your life."

Clara awoke quite drowsy, and not understanding Dorotea at first, asked her to repeat what she had said. Dorotea did so, and Clara became alert at once. But

[1] *Palinurus*: helmsman of Aeneas' ship in Virgil's *Aeneid*.

she had hardly heard two lines, as the singer continued, when a strange trembling seized her, as if she were suffering from a severe bout of quartan fever,[2] and throwing her arms round Dorotea she said, "Ah, dear lady of my soul and life! Why did you wake me? The greatest kindness fortune could do me now would be to close my eyes and ears so as neither to see or hear that unhappy musician."

"What are you talking about, child?" said Dorotea. "Why, they say this singer is a muleteer!"

"No, he is rather the lord of many places," replied Clara, "among them my heart, which he holds so firmly it shall never be taken from him, unless he is willing to surrender it."

Dorotea was amazed at the girl's ardent language, for it seemed to be far beyond such experience of life as her tender years gave any promise of. She said to her, "You speak in such a way that I cannot understand you, Señora Clara.[3] Explain yourself more clearly, and tell me what this talk about hearts and places is and this musician whose voice has so moved you. But do not tell me anything now; I do not want to lose the pleasure I get from listening to the singer by giving my attention to your distress, for I believe he is beginning to sing a new melody with new verses."

"Let him, in Heaven's name," returned Clara, and not to hear him she stopped both ears with her hands, at which Dorotea was again surprised. But turning her attention to the song, she found that it continued in this way:

Sweet Hope, my stay,
That onward to the goal of thy intent
Dost make thy way,
Heedless of hindrance or impediment,
Have thou no fear
If at each step thou findest death is near.

No victory,
No joy of triumph doth the faint heart know;
Unblest is he
That a bold front to Fortune dares not show,
But soul and sense
In bondage yieldeth up to indolence.

If Love his wares
Do dearly[4] sell, his right must be confessed;
What gold compares
With that whereon his stamp he hath imprest?

[2] *bout of quartan fever: cuartana,* form of malaria characterized by episodes of chills and sweating every third or fourth day.

[3] *Señora Clara:* The use of "Señorita" to refer to an unmarried woman was not yet common in Spanish.

[4] *dearly:* at a high price.

And all men know
What costeth little that we rate but low.

Love resolute
Knows not the word "impossibility";
And though my suit
Beset by endless obstacles I see,
Yet no despair
Shall hold me bound to earth while heaven is there.

Here the voice ceased and Clara's sobs began afresh, all of which excited Dorotea's curiosity to know what could be the cause of singing so sweet and weeping so bitter; so she again asked her what it was she was going to say before. On this Clara, afraid that Luscinda might overhear her, wound her arms tightly round Dorotea and, putting her mouth so close to her ear that she could speak without fear of being heard by anyone else, said:

"This singer, dear señora, is the son of a gentleman of Aragon, lord of two villages, who lives opposite my father's house in Madrid; and though my father had curtains on the windows of his house in winter and latticework in summer, in some way (I know not how) this gentleman, who was pursuing his studies, saw me—whether in church or elsewhere, I cannot tell—and, in short, fell in love with me. He made me to know it from the windows of his house, with so many signs and tears that I was forced to believe him, and even to love him, without knowing what it was he wanted of me. One of the signs he used to make me was to link one hand in the other, to show me he wished to marry me; and though I should have been glad if that could be, being alone and motherless I knew not whom to speak to. And so I left things as they were, showing him no favor, except that when my father was out, and his father as well, to raise the curtain or the lattice a little and let him see me plainly, at which he would show such delight that he seemed as if he were going mad.

"Meanwhile, the time for my father's departure arrived, which he found out about—though not from me, for I had never been able to tell him. He fell sick—of grief I believe—and so the day we were going away I could not see him to say farewell, except with my eyes. After we had been two days on the road, on entering the village inn a day's journey from here, I saw him at the inn door dressed as a muleteer, and so well disguised that if I did not carry his image graven on my heart, it would have been impossible for me to recognize him. But I did recognize him, and I was surprised and glad. He watched me, unsuspected by my father, from whom he always hides himself when he crosses my path on the road or at the inns where we stop; and as I know who he is, and reflect that for love of me he makes this journey on foot in such hardship, I am ready to die of sorrow.

"Where he sets his foot, there I set my eyes. I know not with what object he has come or how he could have gotten away from his father, who loves him beyond measure—because he has no other heir and because he is worthy of it, as you will agree when you see him. And moreover, I can tell you that everything he sings is out of his own head; for I have heard them say he is a great scholar and poet. What is more, every time I see him or hear him sing, I tremble all over and am terrified lest my father should recognize him and come to know of our love. I have never spoken a word to him in my life; and for all that, I love him so dearly that I could not live without him. This, dear señora, is all I have to tell you about the musician whose voice has delighted you so much. From it alone, you will easily gather that he is no muleteer but a lord of hearts and towns, as I told you already."

"Say no more, Doña Clara," said Dorotea at this, while she kissed her a thousand times over. "Say no more, I tell you, but wait till day comes, when I trust that God will so guide your affairs that they will have the happy ending such an innocent beginning deserves."

"Ah, señora," said Doña Clara, "what end can be hoped for when his father is of such lofty position, and so wealthy, that he would think I was not fit to be even a servant to his son, much less wife? And as to marrying without the knowledge of my father, I would not do it for all the world. I would not ask anything more than that this young man should go back and leave me. Perhaps with not seeing him, and the long distance we shall have to travel, the pain I suffer now may become easier, though I daresay the remedy I propose will do me very little good. I don't know how the devil this has come about, or how this love I have for him got into me—I such a young girl, and he such a mere boy. I truly believe we are the same age, and I am not sixteen yet; for I will be sixteen Michaelmas Day[5] next, my father says."

Dorotea could not help laughing to hear how like a child Doña Clara spoke. "Let us go to sleep now, señora," said she, "for what little of the night I imagine is left to us. God will soon send us daylight, and we will set everything right—or else a pox be upon me."

With this they fell asleep, and deep silence reigned all through the inn. The only people not asleep were the innkeeper's daughter and his wife's servant Maritornes. The two of them, knowing the weak point of Don Quixote's condition and that he was outside the inn mounting guard in armor and on horseback, resolved to play a trick on him—or at any rate to amuse themselves for a while by listening to his nonsense.

As it so happened, there was not a window in the whole inn that looked outwards except an opening in the wall of a hayloft through which they used to throw out the hay. At this opening the two semi-damsels[6] posted themselves and observed Don Quixote on his horse as he leaned on his spear and from time to time sent forth such deep and doleful sighs that he seemed to pluck up his soul by the roots with each of them. They could hear him, too, saying in a soft, tender, loving tone, "O my lady Dulcinea del Toboso, perfection of

[5] *Michaelmas Day:* September 29.

[6] *semi-damsels:* the one not fully a damsel because of her youth, the other because of her evening escapades.

all beauty, summit and crown of discretion, treasury of elegance, depositary of virtue, and finally, ideal of all that is good, honorable, and exquisite in this world! What is your grace doing now? Are you, perchance, mindful of your enslaved knight, who of his own free will has exposed himself to so great perils, and all to serve you? Give me tidings of her, O luminary of the three faces![7] Perhaps at this moment, envious of her countenance, you are watching her, either as she paces to and fro in a gallery of one of her sumptuous palaces, or as she leans over some balcony meditating how, while preserving her purity and magnificence, she may mitigate the tortures this wretched heart of mine endures for her sake, what glory should recompense my sufferings, what repose my toil, and lastly what death my life and what reward my services. And you, O Sun, that are now doubtless harnessing your steeds in haste to rise early and come forth to see my lady:[8] when you see her, I entreat you to salute her on my behalf. But take care when you see her and salute her that you kiss not her face; for I shall be more jealous of you than you were of that light-footed ingrate that made you sweat and run so on the plains of Thessaly, or on the banks of the Peneus (for I do not exactly recollect where it was you ran on that occasion) in your jealousy and love."[9]

Don Quixote had gone thus far in his pathetic speech when the innkeeper's daughter began to beckon to him saying, "Señor, come over here, please."

At these signals and voice Don Quixote turned his head and saw by the light of the moon, which was then in its full splendor, that someone was calling to him from the hole in the wall. To him this hole appeared to be a window, and what is more with a gilt grating, as rich castles (such as he believed the inn to be) ought to have. Thereupon it came into his imagination that, as on the former occasion, the fair damsel—the daughter of the lady of the castle, overcome by love for him—was once more seeking to win his affections. With this idea, not to show himself discourteous or ungrateful, he turned Rocinante's head and approached the opening, and when he saw the two wenches he said:

"I pity you, beauteous lady, that you should have directed your thoughts of love to a quarter from whence it is impossible that such a return can be made to you as is due to your great merit and gentle birth; for which you must not blame this unhappy knight-errant whom love renders incapable of submission to any other than her whom, the first moment his eyes beheld her, he made absolute mistress of his soul. Forgive me, noble lady, and retire to your apartment, and do not, by any further declaration of your passion, compel me to show myself more ungrateful. But if, out of the love you bear me, you should find that there is anything else in my power wherein I can gratify you, provided it be not love itself,

[7] *luminary of the three faces:* the moon.

[8] *O Sun . . . to see my lady:* Helios, the Greek sun god, travels across the sky in a chariot drawn by four horses. In later traditions, he is identified with Apollo.

[9] *light-footed ingrate . . . and love:* Daphne, nymph of the plains of Thessaly and daughter of the river god Peneus, spurned the advances of Apollo and was turned into a laurel tree after pleading to the gods for deliverance.

demand it of me. I swear to you by that sweet absent enemy of mine to grant it this instant, though it be that you require of me a lock of Medusa's hair, which was all snakes,[10] or even the very beams of the sun shut up in a vial."

"My mistress wants nothing of the sort, sir knight," said Maritornes at this.

"What then, discreet dueña,[11] is it that your mistress wants?" asked Don Quixote.

"Only one of your fair hands," said Maritornes, "to enable her to unburden on it the great passion, passion which has brought her to this opening, so much to the risk of her honor. For if the lord her father were to hear her, the least slice he would cut from her would be her ear."

"I should like to see that tried!" said Don Quixote. "But he had better keep himself in check, unless he would like to meet the most disastrous end that ever father in the world met for having laid hands on the tender limbs of a love-stricken daughter."

Maritornes felt sure that Don Quixote would present the hand she had asked for. Making up her mind what she was to do, she came down from the opening and went into the stable, where she took the halter of Sancho Panza's donkey and in all haste returned to the opening, just as Don Quixote had stood up on Rocinante's saddle in order to reach the grated window where he supposed the lovelorn damsel to be. Giving her his hand, he said, "Lady, take this hand, or rather this scourge of the evildoers of the earth. Take, I say, this hand which no other hand of woman has ever touched, not even hers who has complete possession of my entire body. I present it to you, not that you may kiss it, but that you may observe the contexture of the sinews, the close network of the muscles, the breadth and capacity of the veins, whence you may infer what must be the strength of the arm that has such a hand."

"We'll see about that," said Maritornes, and making a slip knot on the halter, she passed it over his wrist and then came down from the opening and tied the other end very firmly to the bolt on the door of the hayloft.

Don Quixote, feeling the roughness of the rope on his wrist, exclaimed, "Your grace seems to be grating rather than caressing my hand. Treat it not so harshly, for it is not to blame for the offense my resolution has given you, nor is it just to wreak all your vengeance on so small a part. Remember that one who loves so well should not revenge herself so cruelly."

But there was nobody now to listen to Don Quixote's words, for as soon as Maritornes had tied him, she and the other took off ready to die with laughing, leaving him bound in such a way that it was impossible for him to release himself.

He was, as has been said, standing on Rocinante, with his whole arm thrust into the opening and his wrist tied to the bolt of the door, and in mighty fear and dread of being left hanging by the arm if Rocinante were to stir one side

[10] *Medusa's hair, which was all snakes:* Medusa, one of the three monstrous sisters called Gorgons, had serpents for hair and, like her sisters, the power to turn to stone anyone who looked at her.

[11] *dueña:* See footnote 2, page 253.

or the other; so he did not dare to make the least movement, although from the patience and imperturbable disposition of Rocinante, he had good reason to expect that he would stand without budging for a whole century.

Finding himself bound, then, and that the ladies had retired, he began to fancy that all this was done by enchantment, as on the former occasion when in that same castle that enchanted Moor of a muledriver had thrashed him. He cursed in his heart his own lack of sense and judgment in venturing to enter the castle again after having come off so badly the first time, it being a settled point with knights-errant that when they have tried an adventure and have not succeeded in it, it is a sign that it is not reserved for them but for others, and that therefore they need not try it again. Nevertheless, he pulled his arm to see if he could release himself, but it had been tied so securely that all his efforts were in vain. It is true he pulled it gently lest Rocinante should move, but try as he might to seat himself in the saddle, he could do nothing but either stand upright or yank his hand.

It was then that he wished for the sword of Amadís, against which no enchantment whatever had any power. Then he cursed his ill fortune; then he magnified the loss the world would sustain by his absence while he remained there enchanted (which beyond all doubt he believed himself to be); then he once more took to thinking of his beloved Dulcinea del Toboso; then he called to his worthy squire Sancho Panza, who, buried in sleep and stretched upon the packsaddle of his donkey, was in that moment oblivious of the mother that bore him; then he called upon the sages Lirgandeo and Alquife[12] to come to his aid; then he invoked his good friend Urganda to bring him relief. And then, at last, morning found him in such a state of desperation and dismay that he was bellowing like a bull, for he had no hope that day would bring any remedy to his suffering, which he believed would last forever since he was enchanted. Of this he was convinced by seeing that Rocinante never stirred, much or little, and he felt persuaded that he and his horse were to remain in this state, without eating or drinking or sleeping, until the malign influence of the stars had passed, or until another, sager enchanter should disenchant him.

But he was very much deceived in this conclusion, for daylight had hardly begun to appear when there came up to the inn four men on horseback, well dressed and outfitted, with muskets across the pommels of their saddles. They called out and knocked loudly at the gate of the inn, which was still shut. Don Quixote saw this, and even from where he was, he did not fail to act as sentinel. And so he said in a loud and imperious tone, "Knights, or squires, or whatever you be, you have no right to knock at the gates of this castle; for it is plain enough that they who are within are either asleep, or else are not in the habit of throwing open the fortress until the sun's rays are spread over the whole surface of the earth. Withdraw to a distance, and wait till it is broad daylight, and then we shall see whether it will be proper or not to open to you."

[12] *Lirgandeo and Alquife:* Lirgandeo, narrator of *The Knight of Phoebus*, plays an analogous role to Cide Hamete Benengeli. On Alquife, see footnote 6, page 47.

"What the devil fortress or castle is this," said one, "to make us stand on such ceremony? If you are the innkeeper, order them to open for us. We are travelers who only want to feed our horses and go on, for we are in a hurry."

"Do you think, gentlemen, that I look like an innkeeper?" said Don Quixote.

"I don't know what you look like," replied the other, "but I know that you are talking nonsense when you call this inn a castle."

"A castle it is," returned Don Quixote, "indeed, one of the best in this whole province, and it has within it people who have had the scepter in the hand and the crown on the head."

"It would be better if it were the other way," said the traveler, "the scepter on the head and the crown in the hand.[13] But maybe there is within some company of actors, with whom it is a common thing to have those crowns and scepters you speak of; for in such a small inn as this, and where such silence is kept, I do not believe any people entitled to crowns and scepters are lodged."

"You know but little of the world," returned Don Quixote, "since you are ignorant of what commonly occurs in knight-errantry."

But the companions of the spokesman, growing weary of the dialogue with Don Quixote, renewed their knocks with great vehemence, so much so that the innkeeper (and not only he but everybody in the inn) awoke, and he got up to ask who knocked. It happened at this moment that one of the horses of the four who were seeking admittance went to smell Rocinante, who melancholy, dejected, and with drooping ears stood motionless, supporting his sorely stretched master; and as he was, after all, flesh, though he looked as if he were made of wood, he could not help giving way and in return smelling the one who had come to offer him attentions. He had hardly moved at all when Don Quixote lost his footing; and slipping off the saddle, he would have come to the ground but for being suspended by the arm, which caused him such agony that he believed either his wrist would be cut through or his arm torn off. He hung so near the ground that he could barely touch it with his feet, which was all the worse for him. For finding how close he was to being able to plant his feet firmly, he struggled and stretched himself as much as he could to gain a footing—much like those undergoing the torture of the strappado, when they are held just above the ground, who aggravate their own sufferings by their violent efforts to stretch themselves, deceived by the tantalizing hope that with just a little more they will reach the ground.[14]

[13] *crown in the hand:* perhaps a reference to the practice of branding infamous criminals with a crown on their hand.

[14] *strappado . . . reach the ground:* In the strappado (*garrucha*), the victim's hands were tied behind his back and the rope pulled over a pulley suspended above him. He would then be hoisted in the air and suddenly dropped, causing intense pain and often dislocating his shoulders.

CHAPTER XLIV

IN WHICH ARE CONTINUED THE UNHEARD-OF ADVENTURES IN THE INN

So loud, in fact, were Don Quixote's shouts that the innkeeper, opening the gate of the inn in all haste, came out in dismay and ran to see who was uttering such cries, just as those who were outside joined him. Maritornes, who had been by this time awakened by the same outcry, suspecting what it was, ran to the loft and, without anyone seeing her, untied the halter by which Don Quixote was suspended. Down he came to the ground in the sight of the innkeeper and the travelers, who approaching asked him what was the matter with him that he shouted so.

He, without replying a word, took the rope off his wrist, and rising to his feet leaped upon Rocinante, braced his buckler on his arm, put his spear in rest, and making a wide turn around the field came back at a half-gallop exclaiming, "Whoever shall say that I have been enchanted with just cause, provided my lady Princess Micomicona grants me permission to do so, I call him a liar, challenge him, and defy him to single combat."

The newly arrived travelers were amazed at Don Quixote's words, but the innkeeper dispelled their surprise by telling them who he was and not to mind him, as he was out of his senses. They then asked the innkeeper if by any chance a youth of about fifteen years of age had come to that inn, one dressed like a muleteer and of such and such an appearance, describing that of Doña Clara's lover. The innkeeper replied that there were so many people in the inn he had not noticed the person they were inquiring about.

But one of them, observing the coach in which the judge had come, said, "He is here no doubt, for this is the coach he is following. Let one of us stay at the gate, and the rest go in to look for him. It would be a good idea if one of us went round the inn, so he doesn't escape over the wall of the yard."

"So be it," said another; and while two of them went in, one remained at the gate and the other made the circuit of the inn. Observing this, the innkeeper was unable to guess the reason for which they were taking all these precautions, though he understood they were looking for the youth whose description they had given him.

It was by now broad daylight; and for that reason, as well as in consequence of the noise Don Quixote had made, everybody was awake and up, but particularly Doña Clara and Dorotea; for they had been able to sleep but badly that night, the one from agitation at having her lover so near her, the other from curiosity to see him. Don Quixote, when he saw that not one of the four travelers took any notice of him or replied to his challenge, was furious and ready to die with indignation and wrath; and if he could have found in the ordinances of chivalry that it was lawful for a knight-errant to engage in another enterprise when he had given his word and faith not to involve himself in any until he had made an end of the one to which he was pledged, he would have attacked the whole of them and made them answer him in spite of themselves. But considering that it would not become him, nor be right, to begin any new enterprise until he had established Micomicona in her kingdom, he was constrained to hold his peace and wait quietly to see what would be the upshot of the proceedings of those same travelers—one of whom found the youth they were looking for lying asleep by the side of a muleteer, without a thought of anyone coming in search of him, much less finding him.

The man laid hold of him by the arm, saying, "It becomes you well indeed, Señor Don Luis, to be dressed as you are; and how well the bed I find you in agrees with the luxury in which your mother reared you."

The youth rubbed his sleepy eyes and stared for a while at him who held him, but finally recognized him as one of his father's servants, at which he was so taken aback that for some time he could not find or utter a word.

Meanwhile, the servant went on to say, "There is nothing for it now, Señor Don Luis, but to submit quietly and return home, unless it is your wish that my lord, your father, should depart for the other world, for nothing else can be expected from the grief he is in at your absence."

"But how did my father know that I had taken this road and in this dress?" asked Don Luis.

"It was a student to whom you confided your intentions," answered the servant, "that revealed them, touched with pity at the distress he saw your father suffer on missing you. He therefore sent four of his servants in search of you, and here we all are at your service, better pleased than you can imagine that we shall return so soon and be able to restore you to those eyes that so yearn for you."

"That shall be as I please, or as Heaven orders," returned Don Luis.

"What can you please or Heaven order," said the other, "except to agree to go back? Anything else is impossible."

The entire conversation between the two was overheard by the muleteer at whose side Don Luis lay, and rising, he went to report what had taken place to Don Fernando, Cardenio, and the others, who had by this time dressed themselves. He told them how the man had addressed the boy as "Don,"[1] and what words had passed, and how he wanted him to return to his father, which the

[1] *Don:* The title "Don" (and the feminine "Doña") had been historically reserved for knights and high-ranking nobility. By the seventeenth century, however, it had become a broader marker of social distinction. Don Luis seems to have come by the title in the traditional way, as a member of the upper aristocracy. The commoner Clara, by contrast, referred to as "Doña Clara" (in the following paragraph), benefits from the elevated social standing conferred by her father's position as a prominent jurist.

youth was unwilling to do. With this, and what they already knew of the rare voice that Heaven had bestowed upon him, they all felt a great desire to know more particularly who he was, and even to help him if there was an attempt to use force against him. They therefore hastened to where he was still talking and arguing with his servant.

Dorotea at this moment came out of her room, followed by Doña Clara all in a tremor. Calling Cardenio aside, she told him in a few words the story of the musician and Doña Clara, and he at the same time told her what had happened, how his father's servants had come in search of him; but in telling her so, he did not speak low enough but that Doña Clara heard what he said, at which she was so much agitated that had not Dorotea hastened to support her she would have fallen to the ground. Cardenio then told Dorotea to return to her room, as he would set about to make the whole matter right, and they did as he asked.

The four men who had come in search of Don Luis had now come into the inn and surrounded him, urging him to return at once and without a moment's delay for his father's peace of mind. He replied that he could not do so on any account until he had concluded some business in which his life, honor, and heart were at stake. The servants pressed him, saying that most certainly they would not return without him, and that they would take him away whether he liked it or not.

"You shall not do that," replied Don Luis, "unless you take me dead—though however you take me, it will be without life."

By this time most of those in the inn had been attracted by the dispute, but particularly Cardenio, Don Fernando, his companions, the judge, the priest, the barber, and Don Quixote (for he now considered there was no need to mount guard over the castle any longer). Cardenio, being already acquainted with the young man's story, asked the men who wanted to take him away, what object they had in seeking to carry off this youth against his will.

"Our object," said one of the four, "is to save the life of his father, who is in danger of losing it through this gentleman's disappearance."

To this Don Luis exclaimed, "There is no need to talk about my personal affairs here. I am free, and I will return if I please. If not, none of you can compel me."

"Reason will compel your worship," said the man, "and if it has no power over you, it has power over us, to make us do what we came for, and what it is our duty to do."

"Let us hear what the whole matter is about," said the judge at this; but the man, who knew him as a neighbor of theirs, replied, "Do you not know this gentleman, señor judge? He is the son of your neighbor, who has run away from his father's house in dress quite unbecoming of his rank, as your worship may observe."

The judge then looked at him more carefully and recognized him. Embracing him, he said, "What childish folly is this, Señor Don Luis, or what can have been the cause that could have induced you to come here in this way, and in this outfit, which so ill becomes your condition?"

Tears came into the eyes of the young man, and he was unable to utter a word in reply to the judge, who told the four servants not to be uneasy, for everything would be satisfactorily settled. Then taking Don Luis by the hand, he drew him aside and asked the reason for his having come there.

But while he was questioning him they heard a loud outcry at the gate of the inn, the cause of which was that two of the guests who had spent the night there, seeing everybody busy about finding out what it was the four men wanted, had conceived the idea of going off without paying what they owed. But the innkeeper, who minded his own business more than other people's, caught them going out of the gate and demanded his due, abusing them for their dishonesty with such language that he drove them to reply with their fists; and so they began to beat him in such a style that the poor man was forced to cry out and call for help.

The innkeeper's wife and daughter could see no one else unoccupied who might give aid besides Don Quixote. The daughter said to him, "Sir knight, by the virtue God has given you, help my poor father, for two wicked men are beating him to a pulp."

To which Don Quixote very deliberately and phlegmatically replied, "Fair damsel, at the present moment your request is inopportune, for I am debarred from involving myself in any adventure until I have brought to a happy conclusion one to which my word has pledged me. But that which I can do for you is what I will now mention: run and tell your father to stand his ground as well as he can in this battle, and on no account to allow himself to be vanquished, while I go and request permission of Princess Micomicona to enable me to succor him in his distress. If she grants it, rest assured I will relieve him from it."

"Sinner that I am," exclaimed Maritornes, who stood by, "before you've got your permission, my master will be in the other world."

"Give me leave, señora, to obtain the permission I speak of," returned Don Quixote, "and if I get it, it will matter very little if he is in the other world, for I will rescue him from that place, though all its hosts oppose me. At any rate, I will give you such a revenge over those who shall have sent him there that you will be more than moderately satisfied."

Without saying anything more, he went and knelt before Dorotea, requesting her highness in knightly and errant phrase to be pleased to grant him permission to aid and succor the castellan of that castle, who now stood in grievous danger. The princess granted it graciously, and he at once, bracing his buckler on his arm and drawing his sword, hastened to the inn gate, where the two guests were still handling the innkeeper roughly.

But as soon as he reached the spot, he stopped short and stood still. Maritornes and the innkeeper's wife asked him why he hesitated to help their master and husband.

"I hesitate," said Don Quixote, "because it is not lawful for me to draw sword against persons of squirely condition. Call my squire Sancho to me, for this defense and vengeance are his affair and business."

Thus matters stood at the inn gate, where there was a very lively exchange of fisticuffs and punches, to the detriment of the innkeeper and the wrath of Maritornes and the innkeeper's wife and daughter, who were furious when they saw Don Quixote's cowardice and the hard treatment that their master, husband, and father was undergoing.

But let us leave him there, for he will surely find someone to help him. If not, let him suffer and hold his tongue who attempts more than his strength allows him to do. And let us go back fifty paces to see what Don Luis said in reply to the judge, whom we left questioning him privately as to his reasons for coming on foot and so shabbily dressed. To which the youth, pressing his hand in a way that showed his heart was troubled by some great sorrow, and shedding a flood of tears, answered:

"Señor, I have no more to tell you than that from the moment when, through Heaven's will and our being near neighbors, I first saw Doña Clara—your daughter and my lady—from that moment I made her the mistress of my will, and if yours, my true lord and father, offers no impediment, this very day she shall become my wife. For her I left my father's house, and for her I put on this disguise, to follow her wherever she may go, as the arrow seeks its mark or the sailor the north star. She knows nothing more of my passion than what she may have learned from having sometimes seen from a distance that my eyes were filled with tears. You know already, señor, the wealth and noble birth of my parents, and that I am their sole heir. If this is a sufficient inducement for you to venture to make me completely happy, accept me at once as your son; for if my father, influenced by other objects of his own, should disapprove of this happiness I have sought for myself, time has more power to undo and alter things than the human will."

With this the love-smitten youth was silent, while the judge, after hearing him, was astonished, perplexed, and surprised, both at the manner and intelligence with which Don Luis had confessed the secret of his heart, as at the position in which he found himself, not knowing what course to take in a matter so sudden and unexpected. All the answer, therefore, he gave him was to tell him to set his mind at ease for the present and arrange with his servants not to take him back that day so that there might be time to consider what was best for all parties. Don Luis eagerly kissed his hands, indeed, bathed them with his tears, in a way that would have touched a heart of marble, not to say that of the judge, who, as a shrewd man, had already perceived how advantageous the marriage would be to his daughter; though, were it possible, he would have preferred that it should be brought about with the consent of Don Luis' father, who he knew wished to bestow a title on his son.

The guests had by this time made peace with the innkeeper, for by persuasion and Don Quixote's fair words more than by threats, they had paid him what he demanded. Don Luis' servants were waiting for the end of the conversation with the judge and their master's decision, when the devil, who never sleeps, contrived that the barber, from whom Don Quixote had taken Mambrino's helmet and Sancho Panza the trappings of his donkey in exchange for those of his own, should at that moment enter the inn.

The said barber, as he led his donkey to the stable, observed Sancho Panza engaged in repairing something or other belonging to the packsaddle, which he recognized the moment he saw it. Making bold, he rushed at Sancho Panza, exclaiming, "Aha, sir thief, I have caught you! Hand over my basin and packsaddle and all the trappings that you robbed from me."

Sancho, finding himself so unexpectedly assailed, and hearing the abuse poured upon him, seized the packsaddle with one hand, and with the other landed a punch on the barber that bathed his teeth in blood. The barber, however, was not so ready to relinquish the prize he had made in the packsaddle. On the contrary, he raised such an outcry that everyone in the inn came running to know what the noise and quarrel meant. "Help in the name of the king and justice!" he cried. "This thief and highwayman wants to kill me for trying to recover my property."

"You lie," said Sancho, "I'm not a highwayman. It was in fair war my master Don Quixote won these spoils."

Don Quixote was standing by at the time, highly pleased to see his squire's offensive and defensive prowess, and from that time forth he held him to be a man of mettle[2] and in his heart resolved to dub him a knight on the first opportunity that presented itself, feeling sure that the order of chivalry would be fittingly bestowed upon him.

In the course of the altercation, the barber went on to say, among other things, "Gentlemen, this packsaddle is mine as surely as the death I owe to God; I know it as well as if I had given birth to it. Here in the stable is my donkey, who will not let me lie. Try it on him, and if it does not fit like a glove, call me a rascal. What's more, the same day I was robbed of this, they also robbed me of a new brass basin never yet put to use, which would fetch an escudo any day."

At this, Don Quixote could not keep himself from answering. Interposing himself between the two and separating them, he placed the packsaddle on the ground to lie there in sight until the truth was established and said, "Your worships may see clearly and plainly the error under which this worthy squire lies when he calls a basin which was, is, and shall be the helmet of Mambrino which I won from him in fair war and made myself master of by legitimate and lawful possession. With the packsaddle I do not concern myself; but I may tell you on that head that my squire Sancho asked my permission to strip off the caparison[3] of this vanquished poltroon's steed, and with it adorn his own. I allowed him, and he took it. As to its having been changed from a caparison into a packsaddle, I can give no explanation except the usual one, that such transformations take place in adventures of chivalry. To confirm all this, run, Sancho my son, and fetch hither the helmet which this good fellow calls a basin."

"Good grief, master!" said Sancho. "If we have no other proof of our case than what your worship puts forward, Mambrino's helmet is just as much a basin as this good fellow's caparison is a packsaddle."

"Do as I command you," said Don Quixote. "It cannot be that everything in this castle goes by enchantment."

[2] *man of mettle: hombre de pro*, epithet hearkening to the medieval Reconquista, a combination of Christian integrity and battlefield valor.

[3] *caparison:* a horse's decorative or protective trappings.

Sancho went to where the basin was kept and brought it back with him. When Don Quixote saw it, he took hold of it and said, "Your worships may see with what impudence this squire asserts that this is a basin and not the helmet I told you of. I swear by the order of chivalry I profess that this helmet is the identical one I took from him, without anything added to or taken from it."

"There's no doubt of that," said Sancho, "for from the time my master won it until now he hasn't used it in more than one battle, when he let loose those unlucky men in chains; and if it hadn't been for this basin-helmet[4] he would not have come out very well that time, for there was plenty of stone-throwing in that adventure."

[4] *basin-helmet:* Sancho diplomatically coins the term *baciyelmo*, a compound of *bacía* (basin) and *yelmo* (helmet).

CHAPTER XLV

IN WHICH THE DOUBTFUL QUESTION OF MAMBRINO'S HELMET AND THE PACKSADDLE IS FINALLY SETTLED, WITH OTHER ADVENTURES THAT OCCURRED IN TRUTH AND EARNEST

"What do you think now, gentlemen," said the barber, "of what these fine fellows say, when they want to claim this is a helmet?"

"Whoever says the contrary," said Don Quixote, "I will have him know that he lies if he is a knight, and if he is a squire that he lies again a thousand times."

Our own barber, who was present at all this (and who thoroughly understood Don Quixote's condition), took it into his head to back up his delusion and carry on the joke for the general amusement; so addressing the other barber he said:

"Señor barber, or whoever you are, you must know that I belong to your profession too, and have had a license to practice for more than twenty years. I know the implements of the barber craft, every one of them, perfectly well. I was likewise a soldier for some time in the days of my youth, and I know also what a helmet is, and a morion, and a headpiece with a visor, and other things pertaining to soldiering, that is, to the various kinds of soldiers' arms. I say—apart from a better opinion and always with submission to sounder judgments—that this piece we have now before us, which this worthy gentleman has in his hands, not only is no barber's basin, but is as far from being one as white is from black, and truth from falsehood. I say, moreover, that this, although it is a helmet, is not a complete helmet."

"Certainly not," said Don Quixote, "for half of it is missing, that is to say the beaver."

"It is quite true," said the priest, who saw the intent of his friend the barber.

Cardenio, Don Fernando, and his companions agreed with him. Even the judge, if his thoughts had not been so full of Don Luis' affair, would have helped to carry on the joke; but he was so taken up with the serious matters he had on his mind that he paid little or no attention to these facetious proceedings.

"For the love of God!" exclaimed the bamboozled barber at this. "Is it possible that such an honorable company can say that this is not a basin but a helmet? Why, this is a thing that would astonish a whole university, however learned it might be. Enough! If this basin is a helmet, why, then the packsaddle must be a horse's caparison, as this gentleman has said."

"To me it looks like a packsaddle," said Don Quixote. "But I have already said that with that question I do not concern myself."

"As to whether it is packsaddle or caparison," said the priest, "it is only for Señor Don Quixote to say; for in these matters of chivalry all these gentlemen and I bow to his authority."

"By God, gentlemen," said Don Quixote, "so many strange things have happened to me in this castle on the two occasions of my sojourn in it, that I will not venture to assert anything positively in reply to any question touching anything it contains; for it is my belief that everything that goes on within goes by enchantment. The first time, an enchanted Moor that dwells here gave me great trouble, nor did Sancho fare well among certain followers of his; and last night I was kept hanging by my arm for nearly two hours, without knowing how or why I came by such a mishap. So that now, for me to come forward to give an opinion in such a puzzling matter, would be to risk a rash decision. As regards the assertion that this is a basin and not a helmet, I have already given an answer; but as to the question whether this is a packsaddle or a caparison, I will not venture to give a positive opinion but will leave it to your worships' better judgment. Perhaps as you are not dubbed knights as I am, the enchantments of this place have nothing to do with you, and your faculties are unfettered, so that you can see things in this castle as they really and truly are and not as they appear to me."

"There can be no question," said Don Fernando to this, "but that Señor Don Quixote has spoken very wisely and that with us rests the decision of this matter. That we may have surer ground to stand on, I will take the votes of the gentlemen in secret and declare the result clearly and fully."

To those who were in on the secret of Don Quixote's condition, all of this was the source of great amusement; but to those who knew nothing about it, it seemed the greatest nonsense in the world, in particular to Don Luis' four servants, as well as to Don Luis himself and to three other travelers who had by chance entered the inn and had the appearance of officers of the Holy Brotherhood, as indeed they were. But the one who above all was at his wits' end was the barber, whose basin, there before his very eyes, had been turned into Mambrino's helmet and whose packsaddle he had no doubt whatever was about to become a rich caparison for a horse. Everyone laughed to see Don Fernando going from one to another collecting their votes and whispering to them to give him their private opinion whether the treasure over which there had been so much fighting was a packsaddle or a caparison.

After he had taken the votes of those who knew Don Quixote, he said aloud, "The fact is, my good fellow, that I am tired of collecting so many opinions, for I find that there is not one of whom I ask what I wish to know who does not tell me that it is absurd to say that this is the packsaddle of a donkey and not the caparison of a horse, indeed, of a thoroughbred horse. You must therefore give way, for in spite of you and your donkey, this is a caparison and no packsaddle. Your case has been stated and proved very badly on your part."

"May I have no part in heaven," said the poor barber, "if your worships are not all deceived; and may my soul appear before God as that thing appears to me a packsaddle and not a caparison. But, 'laws go ...'—I say no more.[1] And I am certainly not drunk, for I am fasting—apart from sin."

The simple talk of the barber provided no less amusement than the absurdities of Don Quixote, who now observed, "There is no more to be done now than for each to take what belongs to him, and to whom God has given it, may Saint Peter add his blessing."

One of the four servants said, "Unless this is a deliberate joke, I can't bring myself to believe that men who are, or seem to be, so intelligent as those present would dare to assert that this is not a basin, and that not a packsaddle; but as I see that they do assert it, I can only come to the conclusion that there must be something mysterious about insisting on what is so opposed to the evidence of experience and truth itself. For I swear by"—and here he completed the oath—"all the people in the world will not make me believe that this is not a barber's basin and that a jackass' packsaddle."

"It might easily be a jenny's," observed the priest.

"It's all the same," said the servant. "That's not the point—rather, whether it is or is not a packsaddle, as your worships say."

On hearing this, one of the newly arrived officers of the Brotherhood, who had been listening to the dispute and controversy, unable to restrain his anger and impatience, exclaimed, "It is a packsaddle as sure as my father is my father, and whoever has said or will say anything else must be drunk."

"You lie like a rascally bumpkin," returned Don Quixote; and lifting his spear, which he had never let out of his hand, he delivered such a blow at his head that, had the officer not dodged it, it would have stretched him at full length. The spear was shattered in pieces against the ground, and the rest of the officers, seeing their comrade assaulted, raised a shout, calling for help for the Holy Brotherhood. The innkeeper, who was of the fraternity, ran at once to fetch his staff of office and his sword, and took the side of his comrades. The servants of Don Luis clustered round him, lest he should escape from them in the confusion. Seeing the house turned upside down, the barber once more laid hold of his packsaddle, and Sancho did the same. Don Quixote drew his sword and charged at the officers. Don Luis cried out to his servants to leave him alone and go and help Don Quixote, along with Cardenio and Don Fernando, who were aiding him. The priest was shouting at the top of his voice, the innkeeper's wife was screaming, his daughter was wailing, Maritornes was weeping, Dorotea was aghast, Luscinda terror-stricken, and Doña Clara in a faint. The barber whacked Sancho, and Sancho pummeled the barber. Don Luis gave one of his servants—who ventured to catch him by the arm to keep him from escaping—a blow that bathed his teeth in blood. The judge defended Don Luis. Don Fernando had pinned down one of the officers and was kicking him heartily. The innkeeper raised his voice again calling for help for the Holy Brotherhood.

In short, the whole inn was nothing but cries, shouts, shrieks, confusion, terror, dismay, mishaps, sword cuts, fisticuffs, thwacks, kicks, and bloodshed. And

[1] *'laws go ...'—I say no more:* "laws go where kings wish", that is, kings act as they want.

in the midst of all this chaos, complication, and general entanglement, Don Quixote took it into his head that he had been plunged into the thick of the discord of Agramante's camp.[2]

In a voice that shook the inn like thunder, he cried out, "Hold all, let all sheathe their swords, let all be calm and attend to me if they value their lives!"

Everyone paused at the sound of his mighty voice, and he continued, "Did I not tell you, sirs, that this castle was enchanted, and that a legion or so of devils dwelt in it? In proof whereof I call upon you to behold with your own eyes how the discord of Agramante's camp has come hither and been transferred into the midst of us. See how they fight, here for the sword, there for the horse, on that side for the eagle, on this for the helmet. We are all fighting, and all at cross purposes. Come then, you, señor judge, and you, señor priest: let one represent King Agramante and the other King Sobrino,[3] and make peace among us; for by God Almighty it is a sorry business that so many persons of quality as we are should slay one another for such a trifling cause."

The officers, who did not understand Don Quixote's mode of speaking and found themselves roughly handled by Don Fernando, Cardenio, and their companions, were not to be appeased; the barber was, however, for both his beard and his packsaddle were the worse for the struggle. Sancho, like a good servant, obeyed the slightest word of his master, while Don Luis' four servants kept quiet when they saw how little they gained by not being so. The innkeeper alone insisted that they must punish the insolence of this madman, who at every turn raised a disturbance in the inn. At last the uproar was calmed, if only for a while. The packsaddle remained a caparison till judgment day; the basin remained a helmet and the inn a castle in Don Quixote's imagination.

All having been now pacified and reconciled by the persuasion of the judge and the priest, the servants of Don Luis began again to urge him to return with them at once. While he was discussing the matter with them, the judge took counsel with Don Fernando, Cardenio, and the priest as to what he ought to do in the matter, telling them how it stood and what Don Luis had said to him. It was eventually agreed that Don Fernando should tell Don Luis' servants who he was and that it was his wish that Don Luis should accompany him to Andalusia, where the marquis his brother would give him the honor due his merits; for it was easy to see that Don Luis had no present intention to return to his father, even if they threatened to tear him to pieces. On learning Don Fernando's rank and Don Luis' resolution, the four then settled it between themselves that three of them should return to tell his father what had taken place and that the other should remain to wait upon Don Luis and not leave him until they came back for him or his father's orders were known.

Thus, by the authority of Agramante and the wisdom of King Sobrino this web of disputes was resolved. But the enemy of concord and hater of peace,

[2] *discord of Agramante's camp:* In *Orlando Furioso,* the armies of Agramante lay siege to Paris until Saint Michael the Archangel sends personified Discord to sow strife among the Moorish king's allies.

[3] *King Sobrino:* wise Saracen king who pacifies the discord in Agramante's camp.

feeling himself slighted and made a fool of, and seeing how little he had gained after having involved them all in such an elaborate entanglement, resolved to try his hand once more by stirring up fresh quarrels and disturbances.

It came about in this way. The officers were pacified on learning the rank of those with whom they had been engaged and withdrew from the contest, considering that whatever the result might be they were likely to get the worst of the battle. But one of them, the one who had been thrashed and kicked by Don Fernando, recollected that among some warrants he carried for the arrest of certain delinquents he had one against Don Quixote, whom the Holy Brotherhood had ordered to be arrested for setting the galley slaves free, as Sancho had feared with very good reason.

With this in mind, then, he wished to satisfy himself as to whether Don Quixote's features matched his description. Taking out a parchment pouch from his breast, he lit upon the paper he was in search of, which he carefully set about reading (for he was not a quick reader). As he made out each word, he would fix his eyes on Don Quixote and compare the description in the warrant with his face, until he concluded that beyond all doubt he was the person described in it. As soon as he had satisfied himself, putting away his pouch, he took the warrant in his left hand and with his right seized Don Quixote by the collar so tightly that he did not allow him to breathe, and shouted aloud, "Help for the Holy Brotherhood! And that you may see I demand it in earnest, read this warrant which says this highwayman is to be arrested."

The priest took the warrant and saw that what the officer said was true and that the description matched Don Quixote's appearance. For his part, when Don Quixote found himself roughly handled by this villainous rogue, worked up to the highest pitch of wrath and with all his joints cracking with rage, he seized the officer by the throat with all the might of his two hands; and had the officer not been helped by his comrades, he would have yielded up his life before Don Quixote released his hold. The innkeeper, who was naturally inclined to support his brother officers, ran at once to aid them. The innkeeper's wife, when she saw her husband engaged in a fresh quarrel, lifted up her voice afresh, and its note was immediately caught up by Maritornes and her daughter, calling upon Heaven and all present for help. Sancho, seeing what was going on, exclaimed, "By the Lord, it is quite true what my master says about the enchantments of this castle, for it is impossible to live an hour in peace in it!"

Don Fernando separated the officer and Don Quixote, and to their mutual contentment made them relax the grip by which they held, the one the coat collar, the other the throat of his adversary. For all this, however, the officers did not cease to demand their prisoner and call on them to help and deliver him over bound into their power, as was required for the service of the king and of the Holy Brotherhood, on whose behalf they again demanded aid and assistance to carry out the capture of this robber and highwayman.

Don Quixote smiled when he heard these words and said very calmly, "Come now, base, ill-born brood, do you call it highway robbery to give freedom to those in bondage, to release the captives, to succor the miserable, to raise up the fallen, to relieve the needy? Infamous beings, who by your vile, groveling intellects deserve that Heaven should not make known to you the virtue that lies in knight-errantry or show you the sin and ignorance of your state when you refuse to respect the shadow, not to say the presence, of any knight-errant! Come now, band, not of officers, but of thieves—robbers with the license of the Holy Brotherhood—tell me who was the ignoramus who signed a warrant of arrest against such a knight as I am? Who was he that did not know that knights-errant are independent of all jurisdictions, that their law is their sword, their charter their prowess, and their edicts their will? Who, I say again, was the fool that knows not that there are no letters patent of nobility that confer such privileges or exemptions as a knight-errant acquires the day he is dubbed a knight, and devotes himself to the arduous calling of chivalry? What knight-errant ever paid poll tax, duty, queen's pin money, king's dues, toll, or ferry?[4] What tailor ever took payment of him for making his clothes? What castellan that received him in his castle ever made him pay for his stay? What king did not seat him at his table? What damsel was not enamored of him and did not yield herself up wholly to his will and pleasure? And, lastly, what knight-errant has there been, is there, or will there ever be in the world not bold enough to give, single-handed, four hundred blows to four hundred officers of the Holy Brotherhood if they stand in his way?"

[4] *poll tax, duty, queen's pin money, king's dues, toll, or ferry:* taxes either levied on an individual (poll tax, king's dues) or on merchandise (duty, queen's pin money, toll, ferry). Queen's pin money (*chapín de la reina*) derives its name from having once been collected to fund the queen's household expenses.

CHAPTER XLVI

OF THE END OF THE NOTABLE ADVENTURE OF THE OFFICERS OF THE HOLY BROTHERHOOD AND OF THE GREAT FEROCITY OF OUR WORTHY KNIGHT, DON QUIXOTE

While Don Quixote was talking in this way, the priest was attempting to persuade the officers that he was out of his senses, as they might gather by his deeds and his words, and that they need not press the matter any further, for even if they arrested him and carried him off, they would soon have to release him as a madman; to which the holder of the warrant replied that he had nothing to do with inquiring into Don Quixote's madness but only to execute his superior's orders, and that once taken they might let him go three hundred times if they liked.

"For all that," said the priest, "you must not take him away this time, nor, in my opinion, will he let himself be taken away."

In short, the priest used such arguments, and Don Quixote did such crazy things, that the officers would have been crazier than he was if they had not recognized that his wits were in short supply, and so they thought it best to stand down and even to act as peacemakers between the barber and Sancho Panza, who still continued their altercation with much bitterness. In the end they, as officers of justice, settled the question by arbitration in such a manner that both sides were, if not perfectly contented, at least to some extent satisfied: They exchanged the packsaddles, but not the girth straps or headstalls.[1] As to Mambrino's helmet, the priest, surreptitiously and without Don Quixote's finding out, paid eight reals for the basin, and the barber wrote out a receipt in which he renounced all claims to it then or thenceforth forevermore, amen.

These two disputes (the most serious and pressing) being settled, it only remained for Don Luis' servants to consent that three of them should return while one was left to accompany him where Don Fernando desired to take him. And as good luck and better fortune had already begun to solve difficulties and remove obstructions in favor of the lovers and brave souls of the inn, they were pleased to persevere and bring everything to a happy end; for the servants agreed to do as Don Luis wished, which gave Doña Clara such happiness that no one could have looked into her face just then without seeing the joy of her heart. Zoraida, though she did not fully comprehend all she saw, was alternately

[1] *headstalls:* The headstall is the part of the bridle that encircles the horse's head.

happy or sad, as she watched and studied the various faces, but particularly her Spaniard's, whom she followed with her eyes and clung to with her soul. The gift and compensation that the priest gave the barber had not escaped the innkeeper's notice, and he demanded the bill for Don Quixote's lodging, together with the amount of the damage to his wineskins and the loss of his wine, swearing that neither Rocinante nor Sancho's donkey should leave the inn until he had been paid to the very last cent. The priest settled everything amicably, and Don Fernando paid—though the judge had also very readily offered to defray the expenses. And all became so peaceful and quiet that the inn no longer reminded one of the discord of Agramante's camp, as Don Quixote said, but of the peace and tranquility of the days of Octavianus.[2] For all of which it was the universal opinion that their thanks were due to the priests' great zeal and eloquence, and to Don Fernando's incomparable generosity.

Finding himself now free and clear of so many disputes (his squire's as well as his own), Don Quixote considered that it would be advisable to continue the journey he had begun and bring to a close that great adventure for which he had been called and chosen. With this high resolve, he went and knelt before Dorotea, who would not allow him to utter a word until he had risen. To obey her, he rose and said, "It is a common proverb, fair lady, that 'diligence is the mother of good fortune,' and experience has often shown in important affairs that the earnestness of the negotiator brings the doubtful case to a successful end. But in nothing does this truth show itself more plainly than in war, where speed and agility forestall the devices of the enemy and win the victory before the foe has time to defend himself. All this I say, exalted and esteemed lady, because it seems to me that for us to remain any longer in this castle now is useless, and may be injurious to us in a way that we shall find out some day. For who knows but that your enemy the giant may have learned by means of secret and diligent spies that I am going to destroy him, and if the opportunity be given him he may seize it to fortify himself in some impregnable castle or stronghold, against which all my efforts and the might of my indefatigable arm may avail but little. Therefore, lady, let us, as I say, forestall his schemes by our activity, and let us depart at once in quest of fair fortune; for your highness is only kept from enjoying it as fully as you could desire by my delay in encountering your adversary."

Don Quixote held his peace and said no more, calmly awaiting the reply of the beauteous princess, who, with commanding dignity and in a style adapted to Don Quixote's own, replied to him in these words: "I give you thanks, sir knight, for the eagerness you, like a good knight to whom it is a natural obligation to succor the orphan and the needy, display to afford me aid in my sore trouble. Heaven grant that your wishes and mine may be realized, so that you may see that there are women in this world capable of gratitude. As to my departure, let it be forthwith, for I have no will but yours. Dispose of me entirely in accordance with your good pleasure; for she who has once entrusted to you the defense of her

[2] *days of Octavianus:* The emperor Octavian ushered in the Pax Romana, during which the Roman Empire enjoyed two centuries (27 B.C.–A.D. 180) of relative peace and stability.

person and placed in your hands the recovery of her dominions, must not think of offering opposition to that which your wisdom may ordain."

"On then in God's name," said Don Quixote, "for when a lady humbles herself before me, I will not lose the opportunity of raising her up and placing her on the throne of her ancestors. Let us depart at once, for the common saying that 'in delay there is danger' lends spurs to my desire to take the road; and as neither heaven has created nor hell seen any that can daunt or intimidate me, saddle Rocinante, Sancho, and get ready your donkey and the queen's palfrey, and let us take leave of the castellan and these gentlemen, and go hence this very instant."

Sancho, who was standing by all the time, said, shaking his head, "Ah, señor, señor, 'there is more mischief in the village than you hear about,' begging all good bodies' pardon."

"What mischief can there be in any village, or in all the cities of the world, you booby, that can hurt my reputation?" said Don Quixote.

"If your worship is angry," replied Sancho, "I'll hold my tongue and leave unsaid what as a good squire I am bound to say, and what a good servant should tell his master."

"Say what you will," returned Don Quixote, "provided your words be not meant to work upon my fears. For you, if you fear, are behaving like yourself; but I am like myself in not fearing."

"It's nothing of the kind, as I am a sinner before God," said Sancho; "it's only that I take it to be beyond doubt that this lady, who calls herself queen of the great kingdom of Micomicón, is no more queen than my mother. For if she was what she says, she wouldn't go rubbing noses[3] with someone you can find wherever you turn and around every corner."

Dorotea turned red at Sancho's words, for the truth was that her husband Don Fernando had now and then, when the others were not looking, gathered from her lips some of the reward his love had earned, and Sancho seeing this had considered that such freedom was more like a courtesan than a queen of a great kingdom.

She, however, being unable or not caring to answer him, allowed him to proceed, and he continued, "I say this, señor, because, if after we have traveled roads and highways, and passed bad nights and worse days, someone who is now enjoying himself in this inn is to reap the fruit of our labors, there is no need for me to be in a hurry to saddle Rocinante, put the blanket on the donkey, or get the palfrey ready, for it will be better for us to stay quiet. So, 'every hussy to her needle, and let's eat!'"[4]

Good God, how great was Don Quixote's indignation when he heard his squire's outrageous words! So great was it, that in a voice inarticulate with rage, with a stammering tongue and eyes that flashed living fire, he exclaimed, "Rascally clod, boorish, insolent, and ignorant, ill-spoken, foul-mouthed, impudent backbiter and slanderer! Have you dared to utter such words in my presence

[3] *rubbing noses:* kissing.

[4] *every hussy to her needle, and let's eat:* "Let everyone do as he pleases."

and in that of these illustrious ladies? Have you dared to harbor such gross and shameless thoughts in your muddled imagination? Begone from my presence, you born monster, storehouse of lies, hoard of untruths, garner of knaveries, inventor of scandals, publisher of absurdities, enemy of the respect due to royal personages! Begone, show yourself no more before me under pain of my wrath."

In so saying, he knitted his brows, puffed out his cheeks, gazed around him, and stamped on the ground violently with his right foot, showing in every way the rage that was pent up in his heart. At his words and furious gestures, Sancho was so intimidated and afraid that he would have been glad if the earth had opened up that instant and swallowed him, and his only thought was to turn round and make his escape from the angry presence of his master.

But the ready-witted Dorotea, who by this time so well understood Don Quixote's condition, said, to mollify his wrath, "Be not irritated at the absurdities your good squire has uttered, Sir Knight of the Woeful Countenance, for perhaps he did not utter them without cause. From his good sense and Christian conscience, it is not likely that he would bear false witness against anyone. We may therefore believe without any hesitation that since, as you say, sir knight, everything in this castle goes and is brought about by means of enchantment, Sancho, I say, may possibly have seen through this diabolical medium what he says he saw so much to the detriment of my modesty."

"I swear by God Omnipotent," exclaimed Don Quixote at this, "your highness has hit the nail on the head. Some vile illusion must have come before this sinner Sancho that made him see what it would have been impossible to see by any other means than enchantments; for I know well enough, from the poor fellow's goodness and harmlessness, that he is incapable of bearing false witness against anybody."

"True, no doubt," said Don Fernando, "for which reason, Señor Don Quixote, you ought to forgive him and restore him to your good graces[5] *sicut erat in principio*,[6] before illusions of this sort drive him out of his senses."

Don Quixote said he was ready to pardon him, and the priest went to get Sancho, who came in very humbly and fell on his knees, begging for the hand of his master. Having presented it to him and allowed him to kiss it, Don Quixote gave him his blessing and said, "Now, Sancho my son, you will be convinced of the truth of what I have many a time told you, that everything in this castle is done by means of enchantment."

"So it is, I believe," said Sancho, "except for that blanket business, which really happened by ordinary means."

"Do not believe it," said Don Quixote, "for had it been so, I would have avenged you that instant, or even now. But neither then nor now could I, nor have I seen anyone upon whom to avenge your wrong."

[5] *restore him to your good graces:* parody of a formula recited by subjects of the Inquisition who abjured their errors.

[6] sicut erat in principio: Latin, "as it was in the beginning", from the doxology *Gloria Patri* (Glory Be to the Father).

They were all eager to know what "that blanket business" was, and the innkeeper gave them a detailed account of Sancho's flights, at which they laughed not a little, and at which Sancho would have been no less embarrassed had not his master once more assured him it was all enchantment. For all that, his simplicity never reached such an extreme that he could persuade himself it was not the plain and simple truth, without any deception whatever about it, that he had been blanketed by beings of flesh and blood and not by imaginary phantoms, as his master believed and protested.

The illustrious company had now been two days in the inn; and as it seemed to them time to depart, they devised a plan so that, without giving Dorotea and Don Fernando the trouble of going back with Don Quixote to his village under pretense of restoring Queen Micomicona, the priest and the barber might carry him off with them as they proposed and the priest be able to treat his madness there. To further their plan, they arranged with the owner of an oxcart who happened to be passing that way to carry him after this fashion:

They constructed a kind of cage with wooden bars, large enough to hold Don Quixote comfortably; and then Don Fernando and his companions, the servants of Don Luis, and the officers of the Brotherhood, together with the innkeeper—by the directions and advice of the priest—covered their faces and disguised themselves, some in one way, some in another, so as to appear to Don Quixote quite different from the people he had seen in the castle. This done, in profound silence they entered the room where he lay sleeping and taking his rest from the recent scuffles, his dreams untroubled by what was about to happen. Advancing toward him, they seized him firmly and bound him fast hand and foot, so that when he awoke startled, he was unable to move and could only marvel and wonder at the strange figures he saw before him. He immediately succumbed to the idea his feverish imagination conjured up before him, and took it into his head that all these figures were ghosts of the enchanted castle, and that he himself was unquestionably enchanted, since he could neither move nor help himself—precisely what the priest, the concoctor of the scheme, expected would happen. Of those present, Sancho was the only one who was both in his senses and in his own proper character, and though he came very near to sharing his master's infirmity, he did not fail to recognize who these disguised figures were. But he did not dare open his lips until he saw what came of the assault and capture of his master; nor did the latter utter a word as he awaited the end of his misfortune, which came about when they brought in the cage, shut him up in it, and nailed the bars so firmly that they could not be easily burst open.

They then took him on their shoulders, and as they passed out of the room an awful voice—as awful as the barber (not he of the packsaddle but the other) was able to make it—was heard to say, "O Knight of the Woeful Countenance, let not this captivity in which you are placed afflict you, for this must needs be for the more speedy accomplishment of the adventure in which your great heart has engaged you; the which shall be accomplished when the raging Manchegan lion and the white Tobosan dove shall be linked together, having first humbled their haughty necks to the gentle yoke of matrimony. And from this marvelous union shall come forth to the light of the world brave whelps that shall rival the ravening claws of their valiant father. This shall come to pass ere the pursuer of the fleeing nymph shall in his swift natural course have twice visited the starry signs.[7] And you, O most noble and obedient squire that ever bore sword at side, beard on face, or nose to smell with, be not dismayed or grieved to see the flower of knight-errantry carried away thus before your very eyes; for soon, if it so please the Framer of the universe, you shall see yourself exalted to such a height that you shall not recognize yourself, and the promises which your good master has made you shall not prove false. I assure you, on the authority of the sage Mentironiana,[8] that you shall be paid your wages, as you shall see in due season. Follow then the footsteps of the valiant enchanted knight, for it is expedient that you should go to the destination assigned to both of you; and as it is not permitted to me to say more, God be with you. Where I go now, I alone know." As he brought the prophecy to a close, he raised his voice to a high pitch and then lowered it to such a soft tone that even those who knew it was all a joke were almost inclined to take what they heard seriously.

Don Quixote was comforted by the prophecy he heard, for he was able at once to decipher its meaning perfectly, understanding that it was promised to him that he should see himself united in holy and lawful matrimony with his beloved Dulcinea del Toboso, from whose blessed womb should proceed the whelps, his sons, to the eternal glory of La Mancha. Being thoroughly and firmly persuaded of this, he lifted up his voice, and with a deep sigh exclaimed, "O whoever-you-are who has foretold me so much good, I implore you that you entreat on my behalf that sage enchanter who takes charge of my interests that he leave me not to perish in this captivity in which they are now carrying me away, ere I see fulfilled promises so joyful and incomparable as those which have been now made me. For let this but come to pass, and I shall glory in the pains of my prison, find comfort in these chains wherewith they bind me, and regard this bed whereon they stretch me, not as a hard battlefield, but as a soft and happy nuptial couch. With respect to the consolation of Sancho Panza, my squire, I rely upon his goodness and rectitude that he will not desert me in good or evil fortune. If, by his ill luck or mine, it may not happen to be in my power to give him the island I have promised (or any equivalent for it), at least his wages shall not be lost; for in my will, which is already made, I have declared the sum that shall be paid to him, measured not by his many faithful services, but by the means at my disposal."

Sancho bowed his head very respectfully and kissed both his master's hands, for since they were tied together, he could not kiss just one. The apparitions then lifted the cage on their shoulders and set it down on the oxcart.

[7] *ere the pursuer of the fleeing nymph . . . twice visited the starry signs:* in two days. Apollo, the pursuer of Daphne (the fleeing nymph), also plays the role of sun in its daily circuit.

[8] *Mentironiana: mentira* (lie).

CHAPTER XLVII

OF THE STRANGE MANNER IN WHICH DON QUIXOTE OF LA MANCHA WAS CARRIED AWAY ENCHANTED, TOGETHER WITH OTHER REMARKABLE INCIDENTS

When Don Quixote saw himself caged and hoisted on the cart in this way, he said, "Many grave histories of knights-errant have I read; but never yet have I read, seen, or heard of their carrying off enchanted knights-errant in this fashion, or at the slow pace that these lazy, sluggish animals promise; for they always take them away through the air with marvelous swiftness, enveloped in a dark thick cloud or on a chariot of fire, or it may be on some hippogriff[1] or other beast of the kind. But to carry me off like this on an oxcart—by God, it puzzles me! Perhaps the chivalry and enchantments of our day take a different course from that of those in days gone by. It may be, too, that as I am a new knight in the world, and the first to revive the already forgotten calling of knight-adventurers, they may have newly invented other kinds of enchantments and other modes of carrying off the enchanted. What do you think of the matter, Sancho my son?"

"I don't know what to think," answered Sancho, "not being as well read as your worship in errant writings. But for all that, I would go so far as to swear that these apparitions on the loose around here are not quite catholic."[2]

"Catholic my father!" said Don Quixote. "How can they be Catholic when they are all devils that have taken fantastic shapes in order to come here and bring me to this condition? And if you wish to prove it, touch them and feel them, and you will find they have only bodies of air and no consistency except in appearance."

"By God, master," returned Sancho, "I have touched them already. That devil that goes about there so busily has firm flesh and another property very different from what I've heard said that devils have, for by all accounts they all smell like brimstone and other bad smells; but this one smells like amber from half a league off." (Sancho was here speaking of Don Fernando, who, like a gentleman of his rank, was very likely perfumed, as Sancho said.)

"Marvel not at that, Sancho my friend," said Don Quixote, "for let me tell you, devils are crafty. Even if they do carry perfumes about with them, they themselves have no scent because they are spirits; or if they give off a scent, they cannot smell of anything sweet but of something foul and fetid. The reason is that as they

[1] *hippogriff*: See footnote 10, page 189.

[2] *catholic*: aboveboard.

carry hell with them wherever they go and can get no ease whatever from their torments; and as a sweet scent is a thing that gives pleasure and enjoyment, it is impossible that they can smell sweet. If, then, this devil you speak of seems to you to smell of amber, either you are deceiving yourself, or he wants to deceive you by making you believe he is not a devil."

Such was the conversation that passed between master and man. Don Fernando and Cardenio, worried that Sancho would make a full discovery of their scheme (towards which he had already gone some way), resolved to hasten their departure. Calling the innkeeper aside, they directed him to saddle Rocinante and put the packsaddle on Sancho's donkey, which he did with great alacrity. In the meantime, the priest had arranged with the officers that they should accompany them as far as his village, he paying them so much a day. Cardenio hung the buckler on one side of the bow of Rocinante's saddle and the basin on the other, and by signs commanded Sancho to mount his donkey and take Rocinante's bridle, and at each side of the cart he placed two officers with their muskets. But before the cart was put in motion, out came the innkeeper's wife and daughter and Maritornes to bid Don Quixote farewell, pretending to weep with grief at his misfortune. Don Quixote said to them:

"Weep not, good ladies, for these mishaps are the lot of those who follow the calling I profess. If these reverses did not befall me, I should not esteem myself a famous knight-errant. Such things never happen to knights of little renown and fame, because nobody in the world thinks about them; to valiant knights they do, for these are envied for their virtue and valor by many princes and other knights who plot the destruction of the worthy by base means. Nevertheless, virtue is of herself so mighty, that in spite of all the dark arts that Zoroaster[3] its first inventor knew, she will come victorious out of every trial and shed her light upon the earth as the sun does upon the heavens. Forgive me, fair ladies, if, through inadvertence, I have in any way offended you; for intentionally and wittingly I have never done so to any. And pray to God that he would deliver me from this captivity to which some malevolent enchanter has consigned me. Should I find myself released from these bonds, know that the favors you have bestowed upon me in this castle shall be ever present in memory, that I may acknowledge, esteem, and requite them as they deserve."

While this was passing between the ladies of the castle and Don Quixote, the priest and the barber said farewell to Don Fernando and his companions, to the captain, his brother, and the ladies, now all made happy, and in particular to Dorotea and Luscinda. They all embraced one another and promised to let each other know how things went with them. Don Fernando directed the priest where to write to him so that he could be informed of what became of Don Quixote, assuring him that there was nothing that could give him more pleasure than to hear of it, and that he too, on his part, would send him word of everything he thought he would like to know, about his marriage, Zoraida's baptism, the fortune of Don

[3] *Zoroaster:* or Zarathustra, Iranian prophet and religious reformer who has been known to the West since antiquity as the inventor of magic and the fount of occult knowledge.

Luis, and Luscinda's return to her home. The priest promised to comply with his request to the letter, and they embraced once more and renewed their promises.

The innkeeper approached the priest and handed him some papers, saying he had discovered them in the lining of the valise in which the *Novel of the Impertinent Meddler* had been found. He could take them all if he liked, he told him, for their owner had not since returned and, as the innkeeper could not read, he did not want them for himself. The priest thanked him, and opening them he saw at the beginning of the manuscript the words *Novel of Rinconete and Cortadillo*, by which he gathered that it was a novel, and as that of *The Impertinent Meddler* had been good he concluded this would be so too, since they were both probably by the same author.[4] So he kept it, intending to read it when he had an opportunity.

He then mounted and his friend the barber did the same—both masked so as not to be recognized by Don Quixote—and set out following in the rear of the cart. The order of march was this: first went the cart with the owner leading it; at each side of it marched the officers of the Brotherhood, as has been said, with their muskets; then followed Sancho Panza on his donkey, leading Rocinante by the bridle; and behind all came the priest and the barber on their mighty mules, with faces covered (as was said before) and a grave and serious air, measuring their pace to suit the slow steps of the oxen. Don Quixote was seated in the cage, with his hands tied and his feet stretched out, leaning against the bars as silent and as patient as if he were a stone statue and not a man of flesh.

Thus slowly and silently they rode about two leagues, until they reached a valley that the carter[5] thought a convenient place for resting and feeding his oxen. He said so to the priest; but the barber was of the opinion that they ought to push on a little farther, since at the other side of a hill that appeared close by, he knew there was a valley that had more grass—much better than the one where they proposed to halt. The barber's suggestion was taken, and they continued their journey.

Just then the priest looked back and saw coming behind them six or seven mounted men, well-dressed and well-equipped, who soon overtook them, for they were traveling not at the sluggish, deliberate pace of oxen but like men who rode canons' mules and with the desire to quickly reach the inn, which was not a league off, so they could take their siesta. The speedy travelers came up with the slow, and they exchanged courteous salutations. One of the newcomers, who was, in fact, a canon of Toledo[6] and master of the others who accompanied him, observing the regular order of the procession—the cart, the officers, Sancho,

[4] Novel of Rinconete and Cortadillo ... *probably by the same author: Rinconete and Cortadillo* would be one of the twelve novellas that Cervantes published in 1613 in his collection of *Exemplary Novellas* (*Novelas ejemplares*).

[5] *carter:* owner of the oxcart and oxen.

[6] *canon of Toledo:* priest who serves in the governing body of a cathedral, responsible for liturgical functions and administrative duties. The Cathedral of Saint Mary of Toledo is the seat of the Archdiocese of Toledo, which has long claimed primacy in Spain.

Rocinante, the priest and the barber, and above all Don Quixote caged and confined—could not help asking what was the meaning of carrying the man in that fashion; though, from the badges of the officers, he already concluded that he must be some desperate highwayman or other malefactor whose punishment fell within the jurisdiction of the Holy Brotherhood.

One of the officers to whom he had put the question replied, "Let the gentleman himself tell you the meaning of his going like this, señor, for we do not know."

Don Quixote overheard the conversation and said, "By chance, gentlemen, are you versed and learned in matters of errant chivalry? Because if you are, I will tell you my misfortunes; if not, there is no good in my giving myself the trouble of relating them."

The priest and barber had approached as soon as they saw that the travelers were engaged in conversation with Don Quixote, for they were anxious to answer in such a way as to keep their ruse from being discovered.

The canon, replying to Don Quixote, said, "In truth, brother, I know more about books of chivalry than I do about Villalpando's *Elements of Logic*,[7] so if it is no more than that, you may safely tell me what you please."

"In God's name, then, señor," replied Don Quixote, "if that be so, I would have you know that I am held enchanted in this cage by the envy and fraud of wicked enchanters; for virtue is more persecuted by the wicked than loved by the good. I am a knight-errant, and not one of those whose names Fame has never thought of immortalizing in her record, but of those who, in defiance and in spite of envy itself and all that the magicians of Persia, the Brahmans of India, or Gymnosophists of Ethiopia[8] ever produced will place their names in the temple of immortality, to serve as examples and patterns for ages to come, whereby knights-errant may see the footsteps in which they must tread if they would attain the summit and crown of honor in arms."

"What Señor Don Quixote of La Mancha says is true," observed the priest, "for he goes enchanted in this cart, not from any fault or sins of his, but because of the malevolence of those to whom virtue is odious and valor hateful. This, señor, is the Knight of the Woeful Countenance, if you have ever heard him named, whose valiant achievements and mighty deeds shall be written on enduring bronze and imperishable marble, notwithstanding all the efforts of envy to obscure them and malice to hide them."

When the canon heard both the prisoner and the man who was at liberty talk in this way, he was ready to cross himself in his astonishment and could not

[7] *Villalpando's* Elements of Logic: The *Summa Summularum* (1557) was a treatise on dialectic used in universities. Its author, Gaspar Cardillo Villalpando, sought to recover Aristotelian logic from what he saw as its corruption by scholastic commentators. The dialogue that the canon and Don Quixote are about to have will rely heavily on what Aristotle and his followers in the sixteenth century had to say about literature.

[8] *the magicians ... Gymnosophists of Ethiopia:* ancient mystics and sages. The Gymnosophists were members of a philosophical sect associated with exotic wisdom traditions and Egyptian ascetic practices.

make out what had befallen him. All his attendants were in the same state of amazement.

Sancho Panza, who had drawn near to hear the conversation, now interjected in order to make everything plain, "Well, sirs, you may like or dislike what I'm going to say, but the fact of the matter is my master, Don Quixote, is just as much enchanted as my mother. He has his wits about him, he eats, he drinks, and he obeys nature's call—just like other men and just like he did yesterday before they caged him. And if that's the case, what do they mean by wanting me to believe that he's enchanted? For I have heard many a person say that enchanted people neither eat, sleep, nor talk; and my master, if you don't stop him, will talk more than thirty lawyers."

Then turning to the priest he exclaimed, "Ah, señor priest, señor priest! Do you think I don't recognize you? Do you think I don't guess and see the drift of these new enchantments? Well then, you should know that I would recognize you no matter how you covered your face; and I would be up to your tricks no matter how you hid them. After all, 'where envy reigns virtue cannot thrive,' and 'where there is greed there can be no generosity.' Fie on the devil! If it hadn't been for your worship, my master would be married to Princess Micomicona this minute, and I would be a count at least. I expected nothing less, not just because of the goodness of my master, him of the Woeful Countenance, but because of the greatness of my services. But I see now how true it is what they say in these parts, that 'the wheel of fortune turns faster than a millwheel,' and that 'those who were up yesterday are down today.' I'm sorry for my wife and children, for when they might fairly and reasonably expect to see their father return to them a governor or viceroy of some island or kingdom, they will see him come back a stableboy. I've said all this, señor priest, only to urge your paternity to listen to what your conscience says about the way you've mistreated my master. Take care that God doesn't call you to account in another life for making him a prisoner and charge against you all the good deeds that my lord Don Quixote leaves undone while he's behind bars."

"Well, trim my lantern!" exclaimed the barber at this. "So you are of the same fraternity as your master, are you, Sancho? By God, I'm beginning to see that you're going to need to keep him company in the cage and be put under a spell like him for having caught some of his illness and his chivalry. It's that island you dream about and all his promises that have gotten to you. Cursed be the hour when you conceived that baby."

"I haven't conceived anybody's baby!" returned Sancho. "And I'm no man to conceive, even if it was by the king himself. I may be poor, but I'm an old Christian, and I owe nothing to nobody. If I wish for an island, other people wish for worse. 'Everyone is the son of his own deeds.' Seeing as I'm a man, I may end up as pope, not to say governor of an island, especially as my master may win so many that he will not know who to give them to. Mind how you talk, master barber; for shaving isn't everything, and 'there's something different between Peter and Peter.'[9] I say this because we all know each other, and you shouldn't

[9] *there's something different between Peter and Peter:* "No two people are the same."

throw false dice with me. As to the enchantment of my master, God knows the truth. Let nothing more be said—it only makes it worse to stir it."

The barber chose not to answer Sancho lest by his plain speaking he should reveal what the priest and he himself were trying so hard to hide. With the same concern, the priest had asked the canon to ride on a little in advance, so that he might tell him the mystery of this man in the cage and other things that would amuse him. The canon agreed, and going on ahead with his servants, listened with attention to the account of the character, life, madness, and habits of Don Quixote, given to him by the priest, who described briefly the beginning and origin of his insanity, and told him the whole story of his adventures up to his being confined in the cage, together with the plan they had of taking him home to try if by any means they could discover a cure for his madness.

The canon and his servants were surprised anew when they heard Don Quixote's strange story. When it was finished he said, "Truly, señor priest, I for my part consider what they call books of chivalry to be harmful to the public; and though, led by an idle and shallow taste, I have read the beginnings of almost all that have been printed, I never could manage to read any one of them from beginning to end. It seems to me they are all more or less the same thing. One has nothing more in it than another; this no more than that. In my opinion this sort of writing and composition is of the same species as the tales they call Milesian, nonsensical stories that aim solely at giving amusement and not instruction, exactly the opposite of the apologue fables, which amuse and instruct at the same time.[10] And though it may be the chief object of such books to amuse, I do not know how they can succeed, when they are so full of such monstrous nonsense. For the enjoyment that takes life in the soul must come from the beauty and harmony that it contemplates in the things that the eye of the imagination brings before it. Nothing that has any ugliness or disproportion about it can give any pleasure. What beauty, then, or what proportion of the parts to the whole, or of the whole to the parts, can there be in a book or story where a lad of sixteen cuts down a giant as tall as a tower and makes two halves of him as if he were made of almond paste? When they want us to picture a battle, after having told us that there are a million combatants on the side of the enemy and only the book's hero opposed to them, we are expected to believe (whether we like it or not) that the said knight wins the victory by the single might of his strong arm. What, too, shall we say of the ease with which a future queen or empress gives herself over into the arms of some unknown wandering knight?

[10] *as the tales they call Milesian . . . at the same time:* Milesian tales refer to a genre of short, often erotic or sensational stories named after Miletus, the pleasure-loving town in Ancient Greece where Aristides, their supposed originator, purportedly set them. The inheritors of this tradition—from Apuleius' *Golden Ass* to Chaucer's "Miller's Tale" and Bocaccio's *Decameron*—captivate readers with fast-paced plots and racy details. In contrast, an *apologue* is a didactic tale that often uses allegorical figures or animals to convey its ethical instruction. Aesop's fables are the classical model, while in Spanish literature, *The Tales of Count Lucanor* (Don Juan Manuel, 1335) extend the tradition into medieval courtly culture.

What mind that is not wholly barbarous and uncultured can find pleasure in reading of how a great tower full of knights sails away across the sea like a ship with a fair wind and will be tonight in Lombardy and tomorrow morning in the land of Prester John of the Indies,[11] or some other place that Ptolemy never described nor Marco Polo saw?[12]

"If in answer to this, I am told that the authors of books of this kind write them as fiction[13] and therefore are not bound to regard niceties of truth, I would reply that fiction is all the better the more it looks like truth, and gives the more pleasure the more there is of the probable and possible about it. Plots in fiction should be wedded to the understanding of the reader and be constructed in such a way that, reconciling impossibilities, smoothing over difficulties, keeping the mind on the alert, they may surprise, interest, engage, and entertain, so that wonder and delight conjoined may keep pace one with the other. All of which he will fail to achieve who shuns verisimilitude and truth to nature, wherein lies the perfection of writing. I have never yet seen any book of chivalry that puts together a connected plot complete in all its parts, so that the middle agrees with the beginning, and the end with the beginning and middle. On the contrary, they construct them with such a multitude of members that it seems as though they meant to produce a chimera[14] or monster rather than a well-proportioned figure. And besides all this, they are harsh in their style, fantastical in their deeds, licentious in their romances, uncouth in their courtly speeches, wordy in their battles, silly in their arguments, absurd in their travels, and, in short, lacking in everything like intelligent art; for which reason they deserve to be banished from the Christian commonwealth as a worthless breed."

The priest listened to him attentively and felt that he was a man of sound understanding and that there was good reason in what he said. He told him that, being of the same opinion himself, and bearing a grudge against books of chivalry, he had burned all of Don Quixote's, which were many. He gave him an account of the inquiry he had made of them, of those he had condemned to the flames and those he had spared, with which the canon was not a little amused. Though he had said so much in condemnation of these books, the canon added that still he found one good thing in them, and that was the opportunity they afforded to a gifted intellect for displaying itself. For they presented a wide and spacious field over which the pen might range freely, describing shipwrecks, tempests, combats, battles, portraying a valiant captain with all the qualifications requisite to make one, showing him sagacious in foreseeing the wiles of the enemy, eloquent

[11] *Prester John of the Indies:* See footnote 6, page 9.

[12] *Ptolemy never described nor Marco Polo saw:* Ptolemy was an Alexandrian polymath of the second century A.D. whose *Geography* was the standard source on cartography and geography for over a millennium. The Venetian merchant Marco Polo wrote of his travels to East Asia via the Silk Road in the thirteenth century.

[13] *fiction:* The phrase that the canon uses is "the stuff of lies" (*cosas de mentira*), but he could have easily said "ficción", since at the time (and elsewhere in the novel) the word was synonymous with a lying tale.

[14] *chimera:* imaginary beast made up of parts from multiple animals.

in speech to encourage or restrain his soldiers, ripe in counsel, rapid in resolve, as bold in biding his time as in pressing the attack; now picturing some sad tragic incident, now some joyful and unexpected event; here a beauteous lady, virtuous, wise, and modest; there a Christian knight, brave and gentle; here a lawless, barbarous braggart; there a courteous prince, gallant and gracious; setting forth the devotion and loyalty of vassals, the greatness and generosity of nobles.

"Or again," said he, "the author may show himself to be an astronomer, or a skilled cosmographer, or musician, or one versed in affairs of state, and sometimes he will have a chance of coming forward as a magician if he likes. He can set forth the craftiness of Ulysses, the piety of Æneas, the valor of Achilles, the misfortunes of Hector, the treachery of Sinon, the friendship of Euryalus, the generosity of Alexander, the boldness of Cæsar, the clemency and integrity of Trajan, the fidelity of Zopyrus,[15] the wisdom of Cato, and in short all the faculties that serve to make an illustrious man perfect, now uniting them in one individual, again distributing them among many. If this is done with charm of style and ingenious invention, aiming at the truth as much as possible, he will assuredly weave a web of bright and varied threads that, when finished, will display such perfection and beauty that it will attain the worthiest object any writing can seek, which, as I said before, is to give instruction and pleasure combined. For the unrestricted range of these books enables the author to show his powers—epic, lyric, tragic, or comic—with all the charms that the sweet and pleasing arts of poetry and oratory are capable of; for the epic may be written in prose just as well as in verse."

[15] *Hector, the treachery of Sinon, the friendship of Euryalus ... Trajan, the fidelity of Zopyrus:* On the less obvious names: Hector was a Trojan prince of the *Iliad* who died in single combat against Achilles; Sinon, Greek agent in the *Aeneid* who persuaded the Trojans to accept the wooden horse left by the departing Greek armies; Euryalus, also from the *Aeneid*, Trojan warrior and devoted companion of Nisus; Trajan, Roman emperor (r. 98–117) celebrated by medieval theologians as one of the virtuous pagans; Zopyrus, according to Herodotus, Persian nobleman who helped Darius regain the rebellious city of Babylon from the inside by mutilating himself and posing as a defector.

CHAPTER XLVIII

IN WHICH THE CANON PURSUES THE SUBJECT OF THE BOOKS OF CHIVALRY, WITH OTHER MATTERS WORTHY OF HIS INTELLECT

"It is as you say, señor canon," said the priest. "For that reason those who have hitherto written such books deserve all the more censure for writing without paying any attention to good taste or the rules of art, by which they might guide themselves and become as famous in prose as the two princes of Greek and Latin poetry[1] are in verse."

"I myself, at any rate," said the canon, "was once tempted to write a book of chivalry in which all the points I have mentioned were to be observed; and if I must own the truth, I have written more than a hundred sheets.[2] To determine if they matched my own opinion of them, I showed them to people who were fond of this kind of reading, to learned and intelligent men as well as to ignorant people who cared for nothing but the pleasure of listening to nonsense, and from all I obtained flattering approval. Nevertheless, I proceeded no farther with it, not only because it seemed to me an occupation inconsistent with my profession, but because I perceived that the fools are more numerous than the wise; and, though it is better to be praised by the wise few than applauded by the foolish many, I have no mind to submit myself to the doubtful judgment of the benighted public, to whom the reading of such books falls for the most part.

"But what most of all made me stay my hand and even abandon the idea of finishing it was an argument I put to myself taken from the plays[3] that are acted nowadays, namely: If those that are now in vogue, both those that are pure

[1] *two princes of Greek and Latin poetry:* Homer and Virgil.

[2] *a hundred sheets:* since each sheet was written on both sides, two hundred pages.

[3] *plays:* The dialogue pivots from chivalric romances to theater—specifically, to the *comedia*, an extended work of drama that dealt with secular rather than sacred material. By the early seventeenth century, the *comedia* had become a dominant cultural form in Spain. The mode of experiencing these plays was as revolutionary as the content. Where theater was once confined to palaces, cloisters, and religious festivals, the *comedia* held its own as a commercial art form. Performances took place in a dedicated venue by a company of professional actors, were funded by ticket sales, and open to allcomers. Along with the chivalric romance, the *comedia* heralded the era of mass entertainment—exhilarating but also disorienting. The canon's condemnation of the state of theater in his day may sound elitist, yet he raises an enduring concern: that the drive for profit and public accolades rewards triviality and results in art of diminished beauty, truth, and goodness.

invention and those founded on history, are, all or most of them, downright nonsense and things that have neither head nor tail, and yet the public listens to them with delight and holds them up as worthy when they are so far from it; and if the authors who write them, and the actors who perform them, say that this is what they must be, for the public wants this and will have nothing else; and that those that follow rules and work out a plot according to the laws of art[4] will only find some half-dozen intelligent people to understand them, while all the rest remain blind to the merit of their composition; and that for themselves it is better to get bread from the many than praise from the few; then my book will fare the same way, after I have burnt off my eyebrows in trying to observe the principles I have spoken of, and I shall become like the tailor on the corner.[5] And though I have sometimes tried to convince theater producers that they are mistaken in this notion they have adopted, and that they would attract more people and get more credit by producing plays in accordance with the rules of art than by absurd ones, they are so thoroughly wedded to their own opinion that no argument or evidence can wean them from it.

"I remember saying one day to one of these obstinate fellows, 'Tell me, do you not recollect that a few years ago, there were three tragedies acted in Spain, written by a famous poet of these kingdoms, which were such that they filled all who heard them with admiration, delight, and interest, the ignorant as well as the wise, the masses as well as the elites, and brought in more money to the performers, these three alone, than thirty of the best that have been since produced?'

" 'No doubt,' replied the producer in question, 'you mean the *Isabela*, the *Filis*, and the *Alejandra*.'[6]

" 'Those are the ones I mean,' said I. 'See if they did not observe the principles of art, and if, by observing them, they failed to show their superiority and please all the world—so that the fault does not lie with the public that insists upon nonsense, but with those who don't know how to produce something else. *Ingratitude Revenged* was not nonsense, nor was there any in *The Numantia*, nor any to be found in *The Merchant Lover*, nor less in *The Friendly Fair Foe*,[7] nor in some others that have been written by certain gifted poets, to their own fame and renown, and to the profit of those that brought them out.' Some further remarks I added to these, with which, I think, I left him rather dumbfounded, but not so satisfied or convinced that I could disabuse him of his error."

[4] *laws of art:* precepts derived from classical writers, principally Aristotle, Horace, and Cicero.

[5] *tailor on the corner:* "The tailor on the corner sewed for nothing and threw in the thread to boot", a picture of futility.

[6] *the* Isabela, *the* Filis, *and the* Alejandra: plays by Lupercio Leonardo de Argensola (1559–1613).

[7] Ingratitude Revenged ... The Friendly Fair Foe: The playwrights are, respectively, Lope de Vega (1562–1635), Miguel de Cervantes, Gaspar de Aguilar (1561–1623), and Francisco de Tárrega (1554–1602). Of the roughly two dozen plays Cervantes wrote and saw performed during his time in Madrid in the 1580s, *The Numantia* (*La Numancia*) is one of only three that have survived.

"You have touched upon a subject, señor canon," observed the priest here, "that has awakened an old enmity I have against the plays in vogue at the present day, quite as strong as that which I bear to the books of chivalry; for while the drama, according to Tully,[8] should be the mirror of human life, the model of manners, and the image of the truth, those which are presented nowadays are mirrors of nonsense, models of folly, and images of lewdness. For what greater nonsense can there be in connection with what we are now discussing than for an infant to appear in swaddling clothes in the first scene of the first act, and in the second a grown-up bearded man? Or what greater absurdity can there be than putting before us a swashbuckling old man, a cowardly young man, a stableboy using fine language, a page giving sage advice, a king plying as a porter, a princess who is a kitchen maid? And then what shall I say of their attention to the time in which the action they represent may or can take place, save that I have seen a play where the first act began in Europe, the second in Asia, the third finished in Africa, and no doubt, had it been in four acts, the fourth would have ended in America, and so it would have been set in all four quarters of the globe? And if truth to life is the main thing the drama should keep in view, how is it possible for any average understanding to be satisfied when the action is supposed to take place in the time of King Pepin or Charlemagne and the principal figure portrayed in it is the emperor Heraclius, who entered Jerusalem with the cross and won the Holy Sepulcher, like Godfrey of Bouillon, there being years innumerable between the one and the other?[9] Or if the play is based on fiction and historical facts are introduced, or bits of what occurred to different people and at different times mixed up with it, all, not only without any semblance of probability, but with obvious errors that from every point of view are inexcusable? And the worst of it is, there are ignorant people who say that this is perfection, and that anything beyond this is mere affectation.

"And what will we say of sacred dramas? What miracles they invent in them! What apocryphal, ill-devised incidents, attributing to one saint the miracles of another! Even in secular plays they venture to introduce miracles without any reason or object except that they think some such miracle, or 'special effect' as they call it, will serve well to astonish stupid people and draw them to the play. All this tends to the prejudice of the truth and the corruption of history, nay more, to the reproach of the intellects of Spain; for foreigners who scrupulously observe the laws of drama look upon us as barbarous and ignorant, when they see the absurdity and nonsense of the plays we produce.

"It is not sufficient to argue that the chief object well-ordered governments have in view when they permit plays to be performed in public is to entertain the

[8] *Tully:* Marcus Tullius Cicero.

[9] *King Pepin or Charlemagne . . . Emperor Heraclius . . . Godfrey of Bouillon:* More than a century separates the reigns of the Frankish kings Pépin the Short (r. 751–768) and his son Charlemagne (r. 768–814) from the reign of the Byzantine emperor Heraclius, who was reputed to have recovered the true cross in 628 and restored it to Jerusalem the following year. Godfrey of Bouillon was one of the leaders of the First Crusade, which culminated with the capture of Jerusalem in 1099.

people with some harmless amusement and distract them somewhat from those evil habits that idleness is apt to engender; and that, as this may be attained by any sort of play, good or bad, there is no need to lay down laws, or bind those who write or act them to make them as they ought to be made, since, as I say, the object sought for may be secured by any sort. To this I would reply that the same end would be, beyond all comparison, better attained by means of good plays than by those that are not so; for after listening to an artistic and properly constructed play, the hearer will come away enlivened by its jests, instructed by its truths, awed by its story, his wits sharpened by its arguments, warned by its tricks, all the wiser for its examples, inflamed against vice, and in love with virtue. In all these ways, a good play will stimulate the mind of the hearer be he ever so boorish or dull; and of all impossibilities the greatest is that a play endowed with all these qualities will not entertain, satisfy, and please much more than one lacking in them, like the greater number of those which are commonly acted these days.

"Nor are the poets who write them to be blamed for this; for some there are among them who are perfectly well aware of their faults, and know what they ought to do; but as plays have become a marketable commodity, they say (and with truth) that the producers will not buy them unless they are after this fashion. For this reason, the poet tries to adapt himself to the requirements of the producer who is to pay him for his work. This truth may be seen by the countless plays that a most fertile mind of these kingdoms[10] has written, with so much brilliance, so much grace and gaiety, such polished poetry, such choice language, such profound reflections, and in a word, so rich in eloquence and elevation of style, that he has filled the world with his fame; and yet, in consequence of his desire to suit the taste of the producers, they have not all, as some of them have, come as near perfection as they ought.

"Others write plays with such heedlessness that, after they have been acted, the actors have to flee and go into hiding, afraid of being punished, as they often have been, for having acted something offensive to some king or other, or insulting to some noble family. All of these evils, and many more that I say nothing of, would be removed if there were some intelligent and sensible person at court to examine all plays before they were staged, not only those produced in the capital itself, but all that were intended to be acted in Spain; without whose approval, seal, and signature, no local magistracy should allow any play to be performed. In this way, producers would take care to send their plays to the court and could stage them in safety, and those who write them would be more careful and take more pains with their work, fearful of having to submit it to the strict examination of one who understood the matter. Thus would good plays be produced and

[10] *most fertile mind of these kingdoms:* Lope de Vega, whom Cervantes dubbed a "monster of nature", hit on the winning formula of a three-act play with a streamlined plot, a mix of nobles and commoners, tragedy and comedy, an emphasis on action over characterization, and a disregard of neo-Aristotelian purities. With his *comedia nueva,* he edged out playwrights like Cervantes who were more sensitive to classical theory. The plays of Cervantes' later years mark something of a surrender to the *comedia nueva*'s popularity.

the objects they aim at happily attained—not only the amusement of the people but the credit of the great minds of Spain, the interest and safety of the actors, and the trouble spared of inflicting punishment on them. And if the same person or some other were authorized to examine the newly written books of chivalry, no doubt some would appear with all the perfections you have described, enriching our language with the precious and charming treasure of their eloquence and driving the old books into obscurity before the light of the new—books of wholesome entertainment, not merely for the idle but for the very busiest. For the bow cannot be always bent, nor can weak human nature carry on without some appropriate pastime."

The canon and the priest had proceeded thus far with their conversation when the barber, coming forward, joined them and said to the priest, "This is the spot, señor licentiate, that I said was good for the oxen to enjoy fresh and plentiful pasture while we take our siesta."

"It seems good to me as well," returned the priest, and he told the canon what he proposed to do, on hearing which he too made up his mind to stop with them, drawn to the lovely valley that lay before their eyes. That he might enjoy the landscape as well as the conversation of the priest (to whom he had begun to take a liking) and also to learn about Don Quixote's adventures in greater detail, the canon desired some of his servants to go on to the inn, which was not far distant, and fetch from it what food there might be for the whole party, as he meant to rest for the afternoon where he was; to which one of his servants replied that the pack mule, which by this time ought to have reached the inn, carried provisions enough to make it unnecessary to get anything from the inn except barley.

"In that case," said the canon, "take all the beasts there, and bring back the pack mule."

While this was going on, Sancho, perceiving that he could speak to his master without having the priest and the barber (of whom he had his suspicions) present all the time, approached Don Quixote in his cage and said, "Señor, to clear my conscience I want to tell you the truth about your enchantment, which is that these two here with their faces covered are the priest of our village and the barber. I suspect they came up with this plan of carrying you off like this out of pure envy because your worship surpasses them in doing famous deeds. If this is the truth, it follows that you are not enchanted, but hoodwinked and made a fool of. To prove this, I want to ask you one thing; and if you answer me as I believe you will answer, you will be able to lay your finger on the trick, and you will see that you are not enchanted but driven mad."

"Ask what you will, Sancho my son," returned Don Quixote, "for I will satisfy you and respond wholeheartedly. As to what you say, that these who accompany us yonder are the priest and the barber, our neighbors and acquaintances, it is very possible that they may seem to be those same persons; but that they are so in reality and in fact, do not believe it on any account. What you are to understand and believe is that if they look like them, as you say, it must be that those who have enchanted me have taken this shape and likeness; for it is easy for enchanters to take any form they please, and they may have taken those of our friends in order to make you think as you do and lead you into a labyrinth of fancies from which you will find no escape, though you had the rope of Theseus.[11] They may also have done this to make me uncertain in my mind and unable to conjecture whence this evil comes to me; for if on the one hand you tell me that the barber and priest of our village are here in company with us, and on the other I find myself shut up in a cage and know in my heart that no power on earth that was not supernatural would have been able to shut me in, what would you have me say or think but that my enchantment is of a sort that transcends all I have ever read of in all the histories that deal with knights-errant that have been enchanted? So you may set your mind at rest as to the idea that they are what you say, for they are as much so as I am a Turk. But touching your desire to ask me something, say on, and I will answer you, though you should ask questions from now till tomorrow morning."

"For the love of Our Lady!" exclaimed Sancho, raising his voice. "Is it possible that your worship has so thick a skull and so small a brain that you can't see that what I say is the simple truth, that malice has more to do with your imprisonment and misfortune than enchantment? That being the case, I will prove plainly to you that you are not enchanted. If not, tell me now so that God may deliver you from this affliction and you may find yourself when you least expect it in the arms of my lady Dulcinea—"

"Leave off conjuring me," said Don Quixote, "and ask what you wish to know. I have already told you I will answer with all possible precision."

"I ask this," said Sancho; "what I would like to know and have you tell me, without adding or leaving out anything, but telling the whole truth as one expects it to be told, and as it is told, by all who profess arms, as your worship professes them, under the title of knights-errant—"

"I have told you I will not lie in any particular," said Don Quixote. "Finish your question; for in truth you weary me with all these oaths, requirements, and precautions, Sancho."

"Well, I rely on the goodness and truth of my master," said Sancho; "and so, because it has to do with what we're talking about, I would ask—speaking with all reverence—whether since your worship has been shut up and, as you think, enchanted in this cage, you have felt any desire or inclination to unburden yourself down below?"

"I do not understand this talk of unburdening down below," said Don Quixote; "explain yourself more clearly, Sancho, if you would have me give a direct answer."

"How is it possible," asked Sancho, "that your worship does not understand unburdening yourself down below? Why, it's the first thing schoolboys learn. Well then, I mean to ask whether you've had any desire to do what can't be avoided?"

"Ah! Now I understand you, Sancho," said Don Quixote. "Yes, often, and even this minute. Get me out of this bind, or else disaster awaits!"

[11] *rope of Theseus:* See footnote 20, page 195.

CHAPTER XLIX

WHICH TREATS OF THE INSIGHTFUL CONVERSATION THAT SANCHO PANZA HELD WITH HIS MASTER DON QUIXOTE

"Aha, I've caught you!" said Sancho. "This is what in my heart and soul I wanted to know. Come now, señor, can you deny what is commonly said around us when a person is in a foul mood, 'I don't know what ails so-and-so. He doesn't eat, or drink, or sleep, or gives a proper answer to any question. You would think he was enchanted'? From which it can be gathered that those who don't eat, drink, sleep, or do any of the natural acts I'm speaking about—that those people are enchanted; but not those that have the desire your worship has, and drink when drink is given them, and eat when there is anything to eat, and answer every question that's asked them."

"What you say is true, Sancho," replied Don Quixote; "but I have already told you there are many sorts of enchantments, and it may be that in the course of time they have been changed one for another. Now, it may be the way with enchanted people to do all that I do, though they did not do so before, so it is vain to argue or draw inferences against the usage of the time. I know and feel that I am enchanted, and that is enough to ease my conscience. It would weigh heavily on it if I thought I was not enchanted, and that in a fainthearted and cowardly way I allowed myself to remain in this cage, defrauding multitudes of the relief I might afford to those suffering and in distress, who at this very moment may be in great need of my aid and protection."

"For all that," replied Sancho, "I say that, for your greater and fuller satisfaction, it would be a good idea for your worship to try to get out of this prison (and I promise to do all in my power to help, and even to take you out of it), and see if you can once more mount your good Rocinante, who seems to be enchanted too, he is so melancholy and dejected; and then we might try our luck in looking for adventures again. If we come up short, there will be enough time to get back to the cage—which, on the faith of a good and loyal squire, I promise to shut myself up in along with your worship, if you are so unfortunate or if I am so stupid so as not to be able to carry out my plan."

"I am content to do as you say, brother Sancho," said Don Quixote. "When you see an opportunity for effecting my release I will obey you absolutely. But you will see, Sancho, how mistaken you are in your conception of my misfortune."

The knight-errant and the ill-errant squire kept up their conversation till they reached the place where the priest, the canon, and the barber, who had already dismounted, were waiting for them. The carter at once unyoked the oxen and left them to roam freely about the pleasant green spot, the freshness of which seemed to invite, not enchanted people like Don Quixote, but wide-awake, sensible folk like his squire, who begged the priest to allow his master to leave the cage for a little while; for if they did not let him out, the prison might not be as clean as the propriety of such a gentleman as his master required. The priest understood him and said he would very gladly comply with his request, only that he feared his master, finding himself at liberty, would take to his old ways and make off where nobody could ever find him again.

"I will answer for his not running away," said Sancho.

"And I also," said the canon, "especially if he gives me his word as a knight not to leave us without our consent."

Don Quixote, who was listening to all this, said, "I give my word. Moreover, one who is enchanted as I am cannot do as he likes with himself; for he who had enchanted him could prevent his moving from one place for three centuries, and if he attempted to escape would bring him back flying." With that being so, they could well release him, particularly as it would be to the advantage of all; for if they did not let him out, he protested, he would be unable to avoid offending their nostrils unless they kept their distance.

The canon took his hand, tied together as they both were, and on his word and promise they unbound him. Don Quixote was joyous beyond measure to find himself out of the cage. The first thing he did was to stretch himself all over; he then went to where Rocinante was standing and giving him a couple of slaps on the haunches said, "I still trust in God and in his blessed mother, O flower and mirror of steeds, that we shall soon see ourselves, both of us, as we wish to be—you with your master on your back, and I mounted upon you, following the calling for which God sent me into the world." And so saying, accompanied by Sancho, he withdrew to a retired spot, from which he came back much relieved and more eager than ever to put his squire's scheme into execution.

The canon gazed at him, wondering at the extraordinary nature of his madness, and that in all his remarks and replies he should show such excellent sense and only lose his stirrups, as has been already said, when the subject of chivalry was broached. And so, moved by compassion, he said to him, as they all sat on the green grass awaiting the arrival of the provisions:

"Is it possible, gentle sir, that the nauseous and idle reading of books of chivalry can have had such an effect on your worship as to upset your reason so that you fancy yourself enchanted, and the like, all as far from the truth as falsehood itself is? How can there be any human understanding that can persuade itself there ever was all that infinity of Amadises in the world, or all that multitude of famous knights, all those emperors of Trebizond, all those Felixmartes of Hircania, all those palfreys, damsels-errant, serpents, monsters, giants, marvelous adventures, enchantments of every kind, battles, prodigious encounters, splendid costumes, lovesick princesses, squires made counts, droll dwarfs, love letters, amorous flattery, swashbuckler women, and, in a word, all that nonsense the books of chivalry contain? For myself, I can only say that when I read them, so long as I do not stop to think that they are all lies and frivolity, they give me a certain amount of pleasure; but when I come to consider what they are, I fling the very best of them at the wall, and would fling it into the fire if there were one at hand, as richly deserving such punishment as cheats and impostors out of the range of ordinary toleration, and as founders of new sects and modes of life, and teachers that lead the ignorant public to believe and accept as truth all the folly they contain.

"Such is their audacity, they even dare to unsettle the wits of gentlemen of birth and intelligence, as is shown plainly by the way they have served your worship, when they have brought you to such a strait that you have to be shut up in a cage and carried on an oxcart as one would carry a lion or a tiger from place to place to make money by showing it. Come, Señor Don Quixote, have compassion on yourself, return to the fold of common sense, and make use of the liberal share of it that Heaven has been pleased to bestow upon you, employing your abundant gifts of mind in some other reading that may serve to benefit your conscience and add to your honor. And if, still led away by your natural bent, you desire to read books of achievements and of chivalry, read the Book of Judges in the Holy Scriptures, for there you will find grand reality and deeds as true as they are heroic. Lusitania had a Viriathus,[1] Rome a Cæsar, Carthage a Hannibal, Greece an Alexander, Castile a Count Fernán González, Valencia a Cid, Andalusia a Gonzalo Fernández, Extremadura a Diego García de Paredes, Jérez a Garci Pérez de Vargas, Toledo a Garcilaso, Seville a Don Manuel de León.[2] To read of their valiant deeds will entertain and instruct the loftiest minds and fill them with delight and wonder. Here, Señor Don Quixote, will be reading worthy of your sound understanding, from which you will rise learned in history, in love with virtue, strengthened in goodness, improved in manners, brave without rashness, prudent without cowardice—and all to the honor of God, your own advantage, and the glory of La Mancha, whence, I am informed, your worship derives your birth."

Don Quixote listened with the greatest attention to the canon's words, and when he found he had finished, after regarding him for some time, he replied to him:

"It appears to me, gentle sir, that your worship's discourse is intended to persuade me that there never were any knights-errant in the world, that all the books of chivalry are false, lying, mischievous, and useless to the commonwealth, and that I have done wrong in reading them, worse in believing them, and still worse in imitating them when I undertook to follow the arduous calling of

[1] *Viriathus:* Celtic-Iberian chieftain who resisted the Roman conquest of present-day Portugal.

[2] *Castile a Count Fernán González . . . Don Manuel de León:* Spanish heroes praised in widely circulated ballad sheets. Of those not already mentioned in the novel, Fernán González, Count of Castile, led the fight for Castilian independence from León in the tenth century; Garcilaso de la Vega, ancestor of the eponymous poet, beat back the Moors to the gates of Granada; the Sevillian knight Manuel Ponce de León, recovering from an injury, answered the king's call to bring him the head of the Moorish warrior Muza, whom he defeated in single combat.

knight-errantry which they set forth; for you deny that there ever were Amadises of Gaul or of Greece, or any other of the knights with whom the books are filled."

"It is all exactly as you state it," said the canon.

Don Quixote continued, "You also went on to say that books of this kind had done me great harm, inasmuch as they had addled my senses and shut me up in a cage, and that it would be better for me to reform and change my studies and read other, truer books which would afford more pleasure and instruction."

"Just so," said the canon.

"Well then," returned Don Quixote, "to my mind it is you who are the one that is out of his wits and enchanted, as you have ventured to utter such blasphemies against a thing so universally acknowledged and accepted as true that whoever denies it, as you do, deserves the same punishment which you say you inflict on the books that irritate you when you read them. For to try to persuade anybody that Amadís—and all the other knight-adventurers with whom the books are filled—never existed, would be like trying to persuade him that the sun does not yield light, or ice cold, or earth nourishment. What intelligent man in this world can persuade another that the story of Princess Floripes and Guy of Burgundy is not true, or that of Fierabras and the Mantible Bridge, which happened in the time of Charlemagne?[3] For by all that is good, it is as true as that it is daylight now; and if it is a lie, it must be a lie too that there was a Hector, or Achilles, or Trojan war, or Twelve Peers of France, or Arthur of England, who still lives changed into a raven and is unceasingly searched for in his kingdom. One might just as well try to make out that the history of Guarino Mezquino[4] or of the quest for the Holy Grail[5] is false, or that the loves of Tristan and Queen Iseult[6] are apocryphal, as well as those of Guinevere and Lancelot, when there are persons who can almost remember having seen Lady Quintañona, who was the best cupbearer in Great Britain. And so true is this that I recall a grandmother of mine on my father's side, whenever she saw any dueña in a venerable hood, used to say to me, 'Grandson, that woman looks like Lady Quintañona,' from which I conclude that she must have known her, or at least had managed to see some portrait of her.

"Then who can deny that the story of Pierres and the fair Magalona is true, when even to this day may be seen in the king's armory the peg with which the

[3] *story of Princess Floripes . . . Mantible Bridge, which happened in the time of Charlemagne:* two episodes from a French chivalric romance, *The History of Emperor Charlemagne and the Twelve Peers of France*, which blends sections of history with fiction. In the tale of the Mantible Bridge, a giant demands an extravagant tribute of thirty pairs of hunting dogs, along with one hundred maidens, falcons, and gold-shod horses. Not surprisingly, Don Quixote makes his argument about historical truth with an example of pure fancy.

[4] *history of Guarino Mezquino:* Italian chivalric romance (Andrea de Barberino, fifteenth century) filled with fantastical adventures.

[5] *Holy Grail:* chalice from which Christ drank at the Last Supper, or, in medieval legend, the chalice in which Joseph of Arimathea collected Christ's blood after his Crucifixion.

[6] *Tristan and Queen Iseult:* tragic story of illicit love that was passed from the British Isles to Spain through medieval French ballads.

valiant Pierres guided the wooden horse he rode through the air, and that it is slightly bigger than the pole of a cart?[7] And alongside of the peg is Babieca's saddle,[8] and at Roncesvalles there is Roland's horn, the size of a large beam.[9] From all this we may infer that there were Twelve Peers, and a Pierres, and a Cid, and other such knights—

> those, of whom they say,
> went out to seek adventure.[10]

"Or perhaps I shall be told, too, that there was no such knight-errant as the valiant Lusitanian Juan de Merlo,[11] who went to Burgundy and in the city of Arras fought with the famous lord of Charny, Mosén[12] Pierres by name, and afterwards in the city of Basel with Mosén Enrique de Remesten, coming out of both encounters covered with fame and honor; or adventures and challenges achieved and delivered, also in Burgundy, by the valiant Spaniards Pedro Barba and Gutierre Quixada (of whose family I come in the direct male line), when they vanquished the sons of the Count of San Polo. I shall be told, too, that Don Fernando de Guevara did not go in quest of adventures to Germany, where he engaged in combat with Micer[13] Jorge, a knight of the house of the Duke of Austria. I shall be told that the jousts of Suero de Quiñones, him of the 'Paso,' and the plots of Mosén Luis de Falces against the Castilian knight, Don Gonzalo de Guzmán, were mere mockeries; as well as many other achievements of Christian knights of these and foreign realms, which are so authentic and true, that, I repeat, he who denies them must be totally lacking in reason and good sense."

The canon was amazed to hear the medley of truth and fiction Don Quixote uttered. To see how well acquainted he was with everything relating or belonging to the achievements of his knight-errantry, he said in reply:

"I cannot deny, Señor Don Quixote, that there is some truth in what you say, especially as regards the Spanish knights-errant; and I am willing to grant too that the Twelve Peers of France existed, but I am not disposed to believe that they did all the things that Archbishop Turpin relates of them. For the truth of the matter

[7] *the story of Pierres . . . pole of a cart:* The story of the flying horse does not appear in the novel *History of the Fair Magalona, Daughter of the King of Naples, and Pierres, Son of the Count of Provence* but in *Clamades and Clarmonda*. It will be the basis for an episode in chapter 41 of the second volume.

[8] *Babieca's saddle:* It was popularly believed in Cervantes' day that a saddle in the Royal Armory in Madrid once belonged to El Cid's horse, Babieca. The collection also contained a sword that had been mistakenly inventoried in 1503 as Roland's.

[9] *Roland's horn, the size of a large beam:* The legend that Roland summoned his troops with an oliphant, a horn made from an elephant tusk, appears in medieval *chansons*.

[10] *those, of whom they say, / went out to seek adventure:* See footnote 1, page 69.

[11] *the valiant Lusitanian Juan de Merlo:* Don Quixote rounds out his diatribe with an appeal to historical figures. Juan de Merlo and the rest of the knights named in this paragraph lived in the fifteenth century. Their deeds are recorded in the *Chronicle of Juan II*.

[12] *Mosén:* "My Lord", Catalonian honorific used in the Crown of Aragon.

[13] *Micer:* "My Lord", Italian-derived honorific also used in the Crown of Aragon.

is they were knights chosen by the kings of France, and called 'Peers' because they were all equal in worth, rank, and prowess (at least if they were not, they ought to have been), and it was a kind of religious order like those of Santiago and Calatrava in the present day, in which it is assumed that those who take it are valiant knights of distinction and good birth. Just as we say now a Knight of Saint John or of Alcántara,[14] they used to say then a Knight of the Twelve Peers, because twelve equals were chosen for that military order. That there was a Cid, as well as a Bernardo del Carpio, there can be no doubt; but that they did the deeds people say they did, I hold to be very doubtful. In that other matter of the peg of Count Pierres that you speak of and say is near Babieca's saddle in the Armory, I confess my sin; for I am either so stupid or so short-sighted, that, though I have seen the saddle, I have never been able to see the peg, in spite of it being as big as your worship says it is."

"It is indeed there, beyond all doubt," said Don Quixote. "As further proof, they say it is enclosed in a cowhide sheath to keep it from rusting."

"All that may be," replied the canon, "but by the orders I have received, I do not remember seeing it. However, granting it is there, that is no reason why I am bound to believe the stories of all those Amadises and of all that multitude of knights they tell us about, nor is it reasonable that a man like your worship, so worthy, and with so many good qualities, and endowed with such a good understanding, should allow himself to be persuaded that such wild and crazy things as are written in those absurd books of chivalry are really true."

[14] *Santiago and Calatrava in the present day . . . Knight of Saint John or of Alcántara:* The orders of Santiago, Calatrava, and Alcántara are Spanish religious-military orders dating from the Middle Ages. The Order of Knights of the Hospital of Saint John of Jerusalem was founded in the Holy Land during the First Crusade.

CHAPTER L

OF THE THOUGHTFUL DEBATE DON QUIXOTE AND THE CANON HELD, TOGETHER WITH OTHER INCIDENTS

"A good joke, that!" returned Don Quixote. "Books that have been printed with the king's license and with the approval of those to whom they have been submitted,[1] read with universal delight and extolled by great and small, rich and poor, learned and ignorant, noble and common, in a word by people of every sort, of whatever rank or condition they may be—that these should be lies! And above all when they carry such an appearance of truth with them; for they tell us the father, mother, country, kindred, age, place, and the achievements, step by step and day by day, performed by such a knight or knights. Hush, sir, and do not utter such blasphemy! Trust me that I am advising you now to act as a sensible man should. Only read them, and you will see the pleasure you will derive from them.

"Come, tell me: Can there be anything more delightful than to see, as it were, here now displayed before us a vast lake of bubbling pitch with a host of snakes and serpents and lizards, and ferocious and terrible creatures of all sorts swimming about in it, while from the middle of the lake there comes a plaintive voice saying, 'Knight, whosoever you are who beholds this dread lake, if you would win the prize that lies hidden beneath these dusky waves, prove the valor of your stout heart and cast yourself into the midst of its dark burning waters, else you shall not be worthy to see the mighty wonders contained in the seven castles of the seven fairies that lie beneath this black expanse'; and then the knight, almost before the awful voice has ceased, without stopping to consider, without pausing to reflect upon the danger to which he is exposing himself, without even relieving himself of the weight of his massive armor, commending himself to God and to his lady, plunges into the midst of the boiling lake, and when he least expects it or knows what his fate is to be, he finds himself among flowery meadows, with which the Elysian fields[2] are not to be compared.

"The sky seems more transparent there, and the sun shines with a strange brilliancy, and a delightful grove of green leafy trees presents itself to the eyes and

[1] *the king's license . . . approval of those to whom they have been submitted:* All publications were submitted to a royal censor for approval. The king's license functioned as a rough equivalent to copyright.

[2] *Elysian fields:* paradise of the blessed in Greek mythology.

charms the sight with its verdure, while the ear is soothed by the sweet untutored melody of the countless birds of bright plumage that flit to and fro among the interlacing branches. Here he sees a brook whose limpid waters, like liquid crystal, ripple over fine sands and white pebbles that look like sifted gold and purest pearls. There he perceives a cunningly wrought fountain of variegated jasper and polished marble. Here another of rustic fashion where the little mussel shells and the spiral white and yellow mansions of the snail disposed in studious disorder, mingled with fragments of glittering crystal and mock emeralds, make up a work of varied aspect, where art, imitating nature, seems to have outdone it.

"Suddenly, there is presented to his sight a mighty castle or gorgeous palace with walls of massy gold, turrets of diamond and gates of jacinth. In short, so marvelous is its structure that though the materials of which it is built are nothing less than diamonds, carbuncles,[3] rubies, pearls, gold, and emeralds, the workmanship is still rarer. After having seen all this, what can be more agreeable than to see how a bevy of damsels comes forth from the gate of the castle in resplendent attire, such that, were I to set myself now to depict it as the histories describe it to us, I should never have done; and then how she who seems to be the first among them all takes by the hand the bold knight who had plunged into the boiling lake, and without addressing a word to him leads him into the rich palace or castle, and strips him as naked as when his mother bore him, and bathes him in lukewarm water, and anoints him all over with sweet-smelling ointments, and clothes him in a shirt of the softest sendal,[4] all scented and perfumed, while another damsel comes and throws over his shoulders a mantle which is said to be worth at the very least a city, if not more?

"How charming it is, then, when they tell us how, after all this, they lead him to another chamber where he finds the tables set out in such style that he is filled with amazement and wonder; to see how they pour out water for his hands distilled from amber and sweet-scented flowers; how they seat him on an ivory chair; to see how the damsels wait on him all in profound silence; how they bring him such a variety of dainties so temptingly prepared that the appetite is at a loss which to select; to hear strains of music while he dines, sung by whom or from what place he knows not. And then when the meal is over and the tables cleared, for the knight to recline in the chair, picking his teeth perhaps as usual, and a damsel, much lovelier than any of the others, to enter unexpectedly by the chamber door, and herself by his side, and begin to tell him all about the castle, and how she is held enchanted there, and other things that amaze the knight and astonish the readers who are perusing his history.[5]

"But I will not expatiate any further upon this, as it may be gathered from it that whatever part of whatever history of a knight-errant one reads, it will fill the reader, whoever he is, with delight and wonder. Take my advice, sir, and, as

[3] *carbuncles:* red garnets.

[4] *sendal:* sheer silk.

[5] *astonish the readers who are perusing his history:* As he does previously in chapter 21, Don Quixote sketches scenes that could come from many a chivalric romance.

I said before, read these books and you will see how they will banish any melancholy you may feel and raise your spirits should they be depressed. For myself I can say that since I have been a knight-errant I have become valiant, polite, generous, well-bred, magnanimous, courteous, dauntless, gentle, patient, and have learned to bear hardships, imprisonments, and enchantments; and though it is such a short time since I have seen myself shut up in a cage like a madman, I hope by the might of my arm (if Heaven aid me and fortune thwart me not) to see myself king of some kingdom where I may be able to show the gratitude and generosity that dwell in my heart. For by my faith, señor, the poor man is incapacitated from showing generosity to anyone, though he may possess that virtue in the highest degree; and gratitude that consists of disposition only is a dead thing, just as faith without works is dead.[6] For this reason I should be glad were fortune soon to offer me some opportunity of making myself an emperor, so as to show my heart in doing good to my friends, particularly to this poor Sancho Panza, my squire, who is the best fellow in the world. I would gladly give him a county I have been promising him for some time, only I am afraid he has not the capacity to govern his realm."

Sancho heard only these last words of his master, and said to him, "Work hard, Señor Don Quixote, to give me that county you've promised so often and I've looked forward to for so long, for I promise you there will be no lack of capacity in me to govern it. Even if there is, I have heard said there are men in the world who take leases on the estates of their lords, paying so much a year and taking charge of the government, while the lord, with his legs stretched out, enjoys the revenue they pay him, without bothering about anything else. That's what I'll do, and not haggle about the details, but wash my hands at once of the whole business and enjoy my rents like a duke. As for the rest, who cares?"

"That, brother Sancho," said the canon, "only holds good as far as the enjoyment of the revenue goes. The lord of the estate must also attend to the administration of justice, and here capacity and sound judgment come in, and above all a firm determination to find out the truth; for if this is lacking in the beginning, the middle and the end will always go wrong. In these matters, God commonly aids the honest intentions of the simple, just as he frustrates the evil designs of the crafty."

"I don't understand those philosophies," returned Sancho Panza. "All I know is I'd like to have my county as soon as I know how to govern it; for I have as much soul as the next person, and as much body as anyone, and I'll be as much king of my realm as any other of his; and being so I'll do as I like, and doing as I like I'll please myself, and pleasing myself I'll be content, and when a man is content he has nothing more to ask for, and when he has nothing more to ask for there's an end of it. So let the estate come, and God be with you; and 'we'll see each other later,' as one blind man said to the other."

"The philosophy you are speaking of, Sancho, is not a bad one," said the canon. "But for all that, there is a good deal to be said on this matter of counties."

[6] *faith without works is dead:* James 2:17.

To which Don Quixote returned, "I know not what more there is to be said; I only guide myself by the example set for me by the great Amadís of Gaul, when he made his squire count of the Ínsula Firme; and so, without any scruples of conscience, I can make a count of Sancho Panza, for he is one of the best squires that ever knight-errant had."

The canon was astonished at the methodical nonsense (if nonsense be capable of method) that Don Quixote uttered—at the way in which he had described the adventure of the knight of the lake, at the impression that the deliberate lies of the books he read had made upon him, and lastly he marveled at the simplicity of Sancho, who desired so eagerly to obtain the county his master had promised him.

By this time the canon's servants who had gone to the inn to fetch the pack mule had returned, and letting a carpet and the green grass of the meadow serve as a table, they seated themselves in the shade of some trees. There they ate in order that the carter might not be deprived of the advantage of the spot, as has been already said. As they were eating, they suddenly heard a loud noise and the sound of a bell that seemed to come from among some brambles and thick bushes that were close by, and the same instant they observed a beautiful goat—spotted all over in black, white, and brown—spring out of the thicket with a goatherd after it, calling to it and uttering the usual cries to make it stop or turn back to the fold. The fugitive goat, scared and frightened, ran towards the company as if seeking their protection, and then stood still.

The goatherd coming up seized it by the horns and began to talk to it as if it were possessed of reason and understanding: "Ah wanderer, wanderer, Spotty, Spotty! How have you gotten along all these days with this limp? What wolves have frightened you, my daughter? Won't you tell me what's the matter, my beauty? But what else can it be except that you are a *she* and can't keep still? A plague on your nature and the nature of those you take after! Come back, come back, my darling; and if you will not be so happy, at least you will be safe in the fold or with your companions. For if you—who ought to be their leader and guide—go wandering astray, what will become of them?"

The goatherd's talk amused all who heard it, but especially the canon, who said to him, "For your own sake, brother, take a rest and do not be in such a hurry to drive this goat back to the fold; for being a female, as you say, she will follow her natural instinct in spite of all you can do to prevent it. Have a little to eat and drink, and that will soothe your irritation. In the meantime, the goat will rest herself." And so saying, he handed him a piece of cold rabbit loin on a fork.

The goatherd took it with thanks, and drank and calmed himself, and then said, "I should be sorry if your worships took me for a simpleton for having spoken so seriously as I did to this animal; but the truth is there is a certain mystery in the words I used. I'm a peasant, but not so much of one that I don't know how to act toward men and beasts."

"That I can well believe," said the priest, "for I know already by experience that the woods breed men of learning, and shepherds' huts harbor philosophers."

"At the least, señor," returned the goatherd, "they shelter men of experience. And that you may see the truth of this with hard evidence (though I may seem to put myself forward without being asked), if it won't tire you, gentlemen, and you will give me your attention for a little while, I'll tell you a true story which will confirm this gentleman's word"—and he pointed to the priest—"as well as my own."

To this Don Quixote replied, "Seeing that this matter has a certain air of chivalry about it, I for my part, brother, will hear you most gladly, and so will all these gentlemen, from the high intelligence they possess and their love of curious novelties that interest, charm, and entertain the mind, as I feel quite sure your story will do. So begin, friend, for we are all prepared to listen."

"I'll pass," said Sancho. "This meat pie and I are headed to the brook there, where I plan to have my fill for three days; for I've heard my lord Don Quixote say that a knight-errant's squire should eat until he can hold no more whenever he has the chance, because it often happens that they end up by accident in a forest so thick that they cannot find a way out of it for six days; and if the man is not well filled or his saddlebag well supplied, there he may stay, as very often he does, turned into a mummy."

"You are in the right, Sancho," said Don Quixote. "Go where you wish and eat all you can, for I have had enough. All I require is to give my mind its refreshment, as I shall by listening to this good fellow's story."

"So shall we all," said the canon, who begged the goatherd to begin the promised tale.

The goatherd gave the goat he held by the horns a couple of slaps on the back, saying, "Lie down here beside me, Spotty. We have time enough to return to our fold." The goat seemed to understand him, for when her master had sat down, she stretched herself quietly beside him and looked up in his face to show him she was all attention to what he was going to say.

He began his story this way:

CHAPTER LI

WHICH TREATS OF WHAT THE GOATHERD RELATED TO THOSE WHO WERE CARRYING OFF THE VALIANT DON QUIXOTE

"Three leagues from this valley there is a village that, though small, is one of the richest in all the vicinity. In it there lived a farmer, a very worthy man, and so much respected that, although to be so is the natural consequence of being rich, he was even more respected for his virtue than for the wealth he had acquired. But what made him still more fortunate, as he said himself, was having a daughter of such exceeding beauty, rare intelligence, gracefulness, and virtue, that everyone who knew her and beheld her marveled at the extraordinary gifts with which Heaven and nature had endowed her. As a child she was beautiful, she continued to grow in beauty, and at the age of sixteen she was most lovely. The fame of her beauty began to spread abroad through all the villages around—but why do I say the villages around, merely, when it spread to distant cities, and even made its way into the halls of royalty and reached the ears of people of every class, who came from all sides to see her as if to see something rare and curious, or some miracle-working image?

"Her father watched over her and she watched over herself; for there are no locks, or guards, or bolts that can protect a young girl better than her own modesty. The wealth of the father and the beauty of the daughter led many neighbors as well as strangers to seek her for a wife; but he, as one might well be who had the disposal of so rich a jewel, was perplexed and unable to make up his mind to which of her countless suitors he should entrust her. I was one among the many who felt a desire so natural, and, as her father knew who I was, and I was of the same town, of pure blood, in the bloom of life, and very rich in possessions, I had great hopes of success.

"There was another of the same place and qualifications who also sought her, and this made her father's choice hang in the balance, for he felt that on either of us his daughter would be well bestowed. That he might escape from this state of perplexity, he resolved to refer the matter to Leandra (for that is the name of the rich damsel who has reduced me to misery), reflecting that as we were both equal it would be best to leave it to his dear daughter to choose according to her inclination—a course that is worthy of imitation by all fathers who wish to settle their children in life. I do not mean that they ought to leave them to make a choice of what is contemptible and bad, but that they should place before them what is good and then allow them to make a good choice as they please. I do not know which Leandra chose; I only know her father put off both of us with the tender age of his daughter and vague words that neither bound him nor dismissed us. My rival is called Anselmo and I myself Eugenio—that you may know the names of the personages that figure in this tragedy, the end of which is still in suspense, though it is plain to see it must be disastrous.

"About this time there arrived in our town one Vicente de la Roca, the son of a poor peasant of the same town, the said Vicente having returned from service as a soldier in Italy and various other parts. A captain who chanced to pass that way with his company had carried him off from our village when he was a boy of about twelve years, and now twelve years later the young man came back in a soldier's uniform, arrayed in a thousand colors with glass trinkets and fine steel chains all over.[1] Today he would appear in one fancy outfit, tomorrow in another; but all flimsy and gaudy, of little substance and less worth. The peasant folk, who are naturally malicious—and when they have nothing to do can be malice itself—noticed all this, and took inventory of his finery and jewelry, piece by piece, and discovered that he had three suits of different colors, with garters and stockings to match; but he made so many arrangements and combinations out of them, that if they had not counted them, anyone would have sworn that he had made a display of more than ten suits of clothes and twenty plumes. Do not look upon all this that I am telling you about the clothes as uncalled for or spun out, for it has a great deal to do with the story.

"He would seat himself on a bench under the great poplar in our plaza, and there he would keep us all hanging open-mouthed with the stories he told us of his exploits. There was no country on the face of the globe he had not seen, nor battle he had not been engaged in. He had killed more Moors than there are in Morocco and Tunis, and fought more single combats (according to his own account) than Gante and Luna, Diego García de Paredes,[2] and a thousand others he named, and out of every one he had come victorious without losing a drop of blood. On the other hand, he showed marks of wounds, which, though they could not be made out, he said were gunshot wounds received in various encounters and actions. Lastly, with monstrous impudence he would speak down to his equals[3] and even those who knew where he came from, and declare that his arm was his father and his deeds his pedigree, and that being a soldier he was as good as the king himself. To add to these swaggering ways, he dabbled in music, and played the guitar with such a flourish that some said he made it speak. Nor did his accomplishments end here, for he was something of a poet too, and on every trifle that happened in the town he made a ballad a league long.

[1] *soldier's uniform . . . all over:* Because soldiers' uniforms were not standardized, ostentation went unchecked.

[2] *Gante and Luna, Diego García de Paredes: Gante and Luna* may be a typesetter's error for *Garcilaso*. See footnote 2, page 403.

[3] *he would speak down to his equals:* literally, "he would use *vos* with his equals." The use of the second-person singular *vos* where *tú* was customary was a sign of contempt. See footnote 11, page 148.

"This soldier I have described, this Vicente de la Roca, this bravo, gallant, musician, poet, was often seen and watched by Leandra from a window of her house, which looked out on the plaza. The glitter of his showy attire took her fancy, his ballads bewitched her (for he gave away twenty copies of every one he made), the tales of his exploits he told about himself came to her ears; and in short, as the devil no doubt had arranged it, she fell in love with him before the possibility of making love to her had even suggested itself to him; and as in love affairs none are more easily carried out than those which have the inclination of the lady for an ally, Leandra and Vicente came to an understanding without any difficulty. Before any of her numerous suitors had any suspicion of her design, she had already put it into effect, having left the house of her dearly beloved father (for mother she had none), and disappeared from the village with the soldier, who came more triumphantly out of this undertaking than out of any of the large number he laid claim to. All the village and all who heard of it were amazed at the affair. I was aghast, Anselmo thunderstruck, her father full of grief, her relations indignant, the authorities all in a ferment, the officers of the Brotherhood in arms. They scoured the roads, they searched the woods and surrounding areas, and at the end of three days they found the impulsive Leandra in a mountain cave, stripped to her shift,[4] and robbed of all the money and precious jewels she had carried away from home with her.

"They brought her back to her unhappy father and questioned her about her misfortune. She confessed without pressure that Vicente de la Roca had deceived her, and under promise of marrying her had induced her to leave her father's house, as he meant to take her to Naples, the richest and most delightful city in the whole world. She, ill-advised and deluded, had believed him, robbed her father, and handed over everything to him the night she disappeared. Finally, he had carried her away to a rugged mountain and shut her up in the cave where they had found her. She said, moreover, that the soldier, without robbing her of her honor, had taken from her everything she had and left her in the cave, a thing that surprised everybody still further.

"It was not easy for us to credit the young man's continence, but she asserted it with such earnestness that it helped to console her distressed father, who thought nothing of what had been taken since the jewel that once lost can never be recovered had been left to his daughter. The same day that Leandra made her appearance her father removed her from our sight and took her away to shut her up in a convent in a town nearby, in the hope that time may wear away some of the disgrace she has incurred. Leandra's youth furnished an excuse for her fault, at least with those to whom it was of no consequence whether she was good or bad. But those who knew her intelligence and keen understanding did not attribute her failing to ignorance but to wantonness and the natural disposition of women, which is for the most part flighty and ill-regulated.

"With Leandra withdrawn from sight, Anselmo's eyes grew blind, or at any rate found nothing to look at that gave them any pleasure, and mine were in darkness

[4] *shift:* undershirt.

without a ray of light to direct them to anything enjoyable while Leandra was away. Our melancholy grew greater, our patience grew less; we cursed the soldier's finery and railed at the carelessness of Leandra's father. At last Anselmo and I agreed to leave the village and come to this valley. He, feeding a great flock of sheep of his own, and I a large herd of goats of mine, we pass our life among the trees, giving vent to our sorrows, together singing the fair Leandra's praises, or upbraiding her, or else sighing alone, and to heaven pouring forth our complaints in solitude. Following our example, many more of Leandra's lovers have come to these wild mountains and adopted our mode of life, and they are so numerous that one would fancy the place had been turned into the pastoral Arcadia, so full is it of shepherds and sheepfolds. Nor is there a spot in it where the name of the fair Leandra is not heard. Here one curses her and calls her capricious, fickle, and immodest; there another condemns her as frail and frivolous. This one pardons and absolves her; that one spurns and reviles her. One extols her beauty; another assails her character. In short, all abuse her, and all adore her, and to such a pitch has this general infatuation gone that there are some who complain of her scorn without ever having exchanged a word with her, and even some that bewail and mourn the raging fever of jealousy, for which she never gave anyone cause, for as I have already said, her misconduct was known before her passion. There is no nook among the rocks, no brookside, no shade beneath the trees that is not haunted by some shepherd telling his woes to the breezes. Wherever there is an echo it repeats the name of Leandra. The mountains ring with 'Leandra,' 'Leandra' murmur the brooks, and Leandra keeps us all bewildered and bewitched, hoping without hope and fearing without knowing what we fear.

"Of all this silly set, the one that shows the least and also the most sense is my rival Anselmo, for having so many other things to complain of, he only complains of separation; and to the accompaniment of a rebec,[5] which he plays admirably, he sings his complaints in verses that show his ingenuity. I follow another, easier, and to my mind wiser course, and that is to rail at the frivolity of women, at their inconstancy, their double dealing, their broken promises, their unkept pledges, and in short the scant reflection they show in fixing their affections and inclinations. This, sirs, was the reason for the words and arguments I used with this goat when I arrived here; for as she is a female, I have a contempt for her, though she is the best in all my fold.

"This is the story I promised to tell you, and if I have been longwinded in telling it, I will not be slow to serve you. My hut is close by, and I have fresh milk and tasty cheese there, as well as a variety of ripe fruit, no less pleasing to the eye than to the palate."

[5] *rebec:* small pear-shaped stringed instrument held against the chest or under the chin, played by bowing.

CHAPTER LII

OF THE QUARREL THAT DON QUIXOTE HAD WITH THE GOATHERD, TOGETHER WITH THE RARE ADVENTURE OF THE PENITENTS, WHICH WITH AN EXPENDITURE OF SWEAT HE BROUGHT TO A HAPPY CONCLUSION

The goatherd's tale gave great satisfaction to all the hearers, and the canon especially enjoyed it, for he had remarked with particular attention the manner in which it had been told, which was as far from the manner of a rustic goatherd as it was near to that of a polished courtier. He observed that the priest had been quite right in saying that the woods bred men of learning.

They all offered their services to Eugenio, but he who showed himself most liberal in this way was Don Quixote, who said to him, "Most assuredly, brother goatherd, if I found myself in a position to attempt any adventure, I would, this very instant, set out on your behalf, and would rescue Leandra from that convent (where no doubt she is kept against her will), in spite of the abbess and all who might try to prevent me, and would place her in your hands to deal with her according to your will and pleasure, observing, however, the laws of chivalry which lay down that no violence of any kind is to be offered to any damsel. But I trust in God our Lord that the might of one malignant enchanter may not prove so great but that the power of another better disposed may prove superior to it. I thus promise you my support and assistance, as I am bound to do by my profession, which is none other than to give aid to the weak and needy."

The goatherd eyed him, and noticing Don Quixote's sorry appearance and looks, he was filled with wonder and asked the barber, who was next to him, "Señor, who is this man who makes such a sight and talks in such a strain?"

"Who should it be," said the barber, "but the famous Don Quixote of La Mancha, the undoer of injustice, the righter of wrongs, the protector of damsels, the terror of giants, and the winner of battles?"

"That," said the goatherd, "sounds like what one reads in the books of the knights-errant, who did all that you say this man does, though it is my belief that either you are joking, or else this gentleman has empty lodgings in his head."

"You are a great scoundrel!" cried Don Quixote. "It is you who are empty and a fool. I am fuller than ever was the whoring bitch that bore you."[1] And passing

[1] *fuller than ever was the whoring bitch that bore you*: Don Quixote responds to the goatherd's slight about his empty head. "Fuller" (*lleno*) can also mean "pregnant".

from words to deeds, he picked up a loaf that was near him and threw it full in the goatherd's face, with such force that he flattened his nose. The goatherd, though he did not understand jokes, did understand that he was being mistreated in earnest. Paying no respect to carpet, tablecloth, or diners, he sprang upon Don Quixote and seized him by the throat with both hands. He would no doubt have throttled him had not Sancho Panza that instant come to the rescue, first grasping him by the shoulders, then flinging him down on the table, smashing plates, breaking glasses, and upsetting and scattering everything on it. Don Quixote, finding himself free, attempted to get on top of the goatherd, who, with his face covered with blood, and soundly kicked by Sancho, was on all fours feeling about for a table knife with which to take a bloody revenge. The canon and the priest, however, prevented him, while the barber somehow managed to get Don Quixote under the goatherd, who rained down upon him such a shower of fisticuffs that the poor knight's face streamed with blood as freely as his own.

The canon and the priest were bursting with laughter, the officers were leaping with delight, and both the one and the other urged them on as they do dogs that are locked together in a fight. Sancho alone was frantic, for he could not free himself from the grasp of one of the canon's servants, who kept him from going to his master's aid.

Just when everyone was in a pitch of high spirits and revelry (with the exception of the two combatants, who were mauling each other), they heard a trumpet sound a note so sorrowful that it made them all look in the direction from which the sound seemed to come. But the one that was most excited by hearing it was Don Quixote, who, though he was under the goatherd sorely against his will and something more than pretty well thrashed, said to him, "Brother devil (for it is impossible but that you must be one since you have had might and strength enough to overcome mine), I ask you to agree to a truce for but one hour; for the solemn note of yonder trumpet that falls on our ears seems to me to summon me to some new adventure." The goatherd, who was by this time tired of pummeling and being pummeled, released him at once, and Don Quixote, rising to his feet and turning his eyes to the vicinity where the sound had been heard, suddenly saw coming down the slope of a hill several men clad in white like penitents.[2]

It so happened that the clouds that year had withheld their moisture from the earth, and in all the villages of the district they were organizing processions, litanies, and flagellations, imploring God to open the hands of his mercy and send rain. To this end, the people of a nearby village were going in procession to a holy shrine that could be found on one side of the valley. Don Quixote, when he

[2] *penitents:* In Spanish Catholicism, a penitent (*disciplinante*) is a lay Christian who, in fulfillment of a vow or as an act of devotion, participates in a religious procession wearing a white robe and a conical hood that covers the head and face, leaving only openings for the eyes. Penitents often carry a candle, cross, or chain, and may walk barefoot or engage in acts of self-mortification as signs of humility and repentance.

saw the strange garb of the penitents, without reflecting how often he had seen it before, took it into his head that this was a case of adventure, and that it fell to him alone as a knight-errant to engage in it. He was all the more confirmed in this notion by the idea that a figure in mourning dress they carried with them was some illustrious lady that these villains and discourteous thieves were taking away by force.

As soon as this occurred to him, he ran with all speed to Rocinante, who was grazing in the field, and taking the bridle and the buckler from the saddlebow, he had him bridled in an instant. Calling to Sancho for his sword he mounted Rocinante, braced his buckler on his arm, and in a loud voice exclaimed to those who stood by, "Now, noble company, you shall see how important it is that there should be knights in the world professing the order of knight-errantry; now, I say, you shall see, by the deliverance of that worthy lady who is borne captive there, whether knights-errant deserve to be held in high regard."

So saying, he pressed his thighs against Rocinante (for he had no spurs), and at a full canter (for in all this true history we never read of Rocinante so much as trotting) went forth to face off with the penitents. The priest, the canon, and the barber ran to prevent him, but it was out of their power. Nor did he even stop for the shouts of Sancho calling after him, "Where are you going, Señor Don Quixote? What devils have possessed you to turn you against our Catholic faith? May the plague take me if that isn't a procession of penitents and the lady they are carrying on that litter the blessed figure of the immaculate Virgin![3] Take care what you are doing, señor, for this time it may be safely said that things are not what you think they are."

Sancho labored in vain, for his master was so bent on coming to quarters with the sheeted figures and releasing the lady in mourning that he did not hear a word; and even had he heard, he would not have turned back if the king had ordered him. He came up with the procession and reined in Rocinante, who was already anxious enough to slacken speed a little, and in a hoarse, excited voice he exclaimed, "You who hide your faces, perhaps because you are not good subjects, pay attention and listen to what I am about to say to you."

The first to halt were those who were carrying the figure, and one of the four ecclesiastics who were chanting a litany, struck by the strange sight of Don Quixote, the leanness of Rocinante, and the other ludicrous peculiarities he observed, said in reply to him, "Brother, if you have anything to say to us say it quickly, for these brethren are whipping themselves, and we cannot stop, nor is it reasonable we should stop to hear anything, unless indeed it is short enough to be said in two words."

"I will say it in one," replied Don Quixote, "and it is this: that at once, this very instant, you release that fair lady whose tears and sad countenance show plainly that you are carrying her off against her will, and that you have committed some

[3] *blessed figure of the immaculate Virgin:* Our Lady of Sorrows, a figure of the Virgin Mary clad in black or deep purple, depicted with a mournful expression and often with tears on her cheeks.

scandalous outrage against her. I, who was born into the world to redress all such like wrongs, will not permit you to advance another step until you have restored to her the liberty she pines for and deserves."

From these words all the hearers concluded that he must be a madman and began to laugh heartily. Their laughter acted like gunpowder on Don Quixote's fury, for drawing his sword without another word he made a rush at the litter. One of those who supported it, leaving the burden to his comrades, advanced to meet him, flourishing a forked stick that he had for propping up the litter when resting, and with this he caught a mighty cut Don Quixote made at him that severed it in two. But with the portion that remained in his hand he dealt such a thwack on the shoulder of Don Quixote's sword arm (which the buckler could not protect against the peasant's assault) that poor Don Quixote came to the ground in a sad plight.

Sancho Panza, who was coming on close behind puffing and blowing, seeing him fall, cried out to his assailant not to strike him again, for he was a poor enchanted knight who had never harmed anyone all the days of his life. What checked the peasant was not Sancho's shouting but the realization that Don Quixote did not stir hand or foot. Believing that he had killed him, he hastily rolled up his tunic to his waist and took to his heels across the country like a deer.

By this time all Don Quixote's companions had come up to where he lay. The penitents, seeing them come running, and with them the officers of the Brotherhood with their crossbows, sensed danger. They clustered around the figure, raised their hoods, and grasped their scourges, as the priests did their candles, and awaited the attack—resolved to defend themselves and even to take the offensive against their assailants if they could. Fortune, however, arranged the matter better than they expected, for all Sancho did was to fling himself on Don Quixote's body, raising over him the most doleful and laughable lamentation that ever was heard, for he believed his master was dead.

The priest was recognized by another priest who walked in the procession, and their recognition of one another set at rest the apprehensions of both parties. The first then told the other in two words who Don Quixote was, and he and the whole troop of penitents went to see if the poor gentleman was dead.

There they heard Sancho Panza saying, with tears in his eyes, "O flower of chivalry, that with one blow of a stick the course of your well-spent life has ended! O pride of your race, honor and glory of all La Mancha, nay, of all the world, which without you will be full of evildoers, no longer in fear of punishment for their misdeeds! Generous above all the Alexanders, since for only eight months of service you have given me the best island the sea girds or surrounds! Humble with the proud, haughty with the humble, encounterer of dangers, endurer of outrages, enamored without reason, imitator of the good, scourge of the wicked, enemy of the vile, in short, knight-errant, which is all that can be said!"[4]

[4] *all that can be said:* Whatever Sancho has learned in his service to Don Quixote, he has mastered the art of speaking like a knight-errant from a chivalric romance. (His one slip is praising Don Quixote's pride with the humble and humility with the proud, an inversion of

At the cries and moans of Sancho, Don Quixote came to himself, and the first word he said was, "He who lives separated from you, sweetest Dulcinea, has greater miseries to endure than these. Aid me, friend Sancho, to mount the enchanted cart, for I am not in a condition to press the saddle of Rocinante, as this shoulder is dashed to pieces."

"That I will do with all my heart, señor," said Sancho. "Let us return to our village with these gentlemen, who seek your good, and there we will prepare for making another sally, which may bring us more profit and fame."

"You are right, Sancho," returned Don Quixote. "It will be wise to let pass the malign influence of the stars which now prevails."

The canon, the priest, and the barber told him he would act very wisely in doing as he said; and so, highly amused at Sancho Panza's simplicities, they placed Don Quixote in the cart as before. The procession once more formed itself in order and proceeded on its road. The goatherd took his leave of the party. The officers of the Brotherhood declined to go any farther, and the priest paid what was due to them. The canon asked the priest to let him know how Don Quixote did, whether he was cured of his madness or still suffered from it, and then begged leave to continue his journey. In short, they all separated and went their ways, leaving to themselves the priest and the barber, Don Quixote, Sancho Panza, and the good Rocinante, who regarded everything with as great resignation as his master.

The carter yoked his oxen and made Don Quixote comfortable on a bundle of hay, and at his usual deliberate pace took the road the priest directed. At the end of six days, they reached Don Quixote's village and entered it about the middle of the day, which it so happened was a Sunday, and the people were all in the plaza, through which Don Quixote's cart passed. They all flocked to see what was in the cart, and when they recognized their townsman they were filled with amazement. A boy ran off to bring the news to his housekeeper and his niece that their master and uncle had come back all lean and yellow and stretched on a bundle of hay in an oxcart. It was piteous to hear the cries the two good ladies raised, how they beat their breasts and poured out fresh maledictions on those accursed books of chivalry—all of which was renewed when they saw Don Quixote coming in at the gate.

At the news of Don Quixote's arrival, Sancho Panza's wife came running, for she by this time knew that her husband had gone away with him as his squire. On seeing Sancho, the first thing she asked him was if the donkey was well. Sancho replied that he was, better than his master.

"Thanks be to God for being so good to me," she said. "Now tell me, my friend, what good has come of your squirings? What gown have you brought me back? What shoes for your children?"

---

a line from the *Aeneid.*) Salvador de Madariaga has called Sancho's progressive tendency to take on his master's traits, more pronounced in the next volume, the *quijotización* of Sancho. He sees a parallel *sanchificación* of Don Quixote—which, if present, is less pronounced.

"I bring nothing of that sort, my wife," said Sancho, "though I bring other things of more importance and value."

"I am very glad of that," returned his wife. "Show me these things of more value and importance, my friend; for I want to see them to cheer my heart, which has been so sad and heavy all these ages you have been away."

"I will show them to you at home, wife," said Sancho. "Be content for the present; for if it please God that we should again take to the road in search of adventures, you will soon see me a count, or governor of an island—and not one of those everyday islands, but the best that can be had."

"Heaven grant it, husband," said she, "for we have great need of it. But tell me, what's this about islands? I don't understand."

"'Honey is not for the mouth of the ass,'" returned Sancho. "You will see everything in good time, wife of mine. Just imagine how amazed you will be to hear yourself called 'your ladyship' by all your vassals."

"What are you talking about, Sancho, with these ladyships, islands, and vassals?" returned Juana Panza[5]—for so Sancho's wife was called, though they were not relations, for in La Mancha it is customary for wives to take their husbands' surnames.

"Don't be in such a hurry to know everything, Juana," said Sancho. "It is enough that I'm speaking the truth, so be silent.[6] But this much in passing I will tell you: there is nothing in the world more delightful than to be the honored squire of a knight-errant and a seeker of adventures. It's all too true that most of those adventures a fellow comes across don't end as pleasantly as he would like, for out of a hundred, ninety-nine will turn out backwards and upside down. I know it by experience, for out of some I came blanketed and out of others beaten. Still, for all that, it is a fine thing to be on the lookout for what might happen, crossing mountains, searching forests, climbing rocks, visiting castles, staying at inns for free, and the devil take the maravedi to pay."

While this conversation passed between Sancho Panza and his wife, Don Quixote's housekeeper and niece took him in, undressed him, and laid him in his old bed. He stared at them through heavy eyelids and could not make out where he was. The priest charged his niece to be very careful to make her uncle comfortable and to keep a watch over him lest he should make his escape from them again, telling her what they had been obliged to do to bring him home. On this the two of them once more lifted up their voices and renewed their maledictions upon the books of chivalry and implored Heaven to plunge the authors of such lies and nonsense into the midst of the bottomless pit. In a word, they were kept in anxiety and dread lest their uncle and master should slip away the moment he found himself somewhat better—which, as it turns out, is exactly what happened.

[5] *Juana Panza:* Sancho refers to her as "Mari Gutiérrez" and "Juana Gutiérrez" early on in the novel (see p. 60). She will be rechristened "Teresa Panza" in the next volume.

[6] *be silent:* literally "sew your mouth shut", or as we would say today, "zip your lips."

But the author of this history, though he has devoted research and industry to the discovery of the deeds achieved by Don Quixote in his third sally, has been unable to obtain any information respecting them, at any rate derived from authentic documents. Tradition has preserved in the memory of La Mancha nothing more than that Don Quixote, the third time he sallied forth from his home, traveled to Zaragoza, where he was present at some famous jousts that took place in that city,[7] and that there he had adventures worthy of his valor and great intelligence. Of his end and death he could learn no particulars, nor would he have found out anything, if good fortune had not brought to him an aged physician who had in his possession a leaden box, which, according to his account, had been discovered among the crumbling foundations of an ancient shrine that was being rebuilt.[8] In this box were found certain parchment manuscripts in Gothic script but in Castilian verse containing many of Don Quixote's achievements and setting forth the beauty of Dulcinea, the form of Rocinante, the fidelity of Sancho Panza, and the burial of Don Quixote himself, together with various epitaphs and eulogies on his life and character. But all that could be deciphered and read were those that the trustworthy author of this new and unparalleled history here presents.

The said author asks of those who read them nothing in return for the vast toil it has cost him in examining and searching the Manchegan archives in order to bring them to light, save that they give him the same credit that people of sense give to the books of chivalry so beloved by all. With this he will consider himself amply paid and fully satisfied, and will be encouraged to seek out and produce other histories, if not as truthful, at least equal in invention and not less entertaining.

The first words written on the parchment found in the leaden box were these:

[7] *famous jousts that took place in that city:* Beginning in the fifteenth century, Zaragoza, the capital of the Crown of Aragon, hosted tournaments to coincide with state events and civic celebrations.

[8] *leaden box . . . being rebuilt:* two historical events form the backdrop to this felicitous discovery. In 1588, during renovations of the former mosque (now cathedral) of Granada, a box was found in what had once been the minaret containing a bone, handkerchief, and a parchment written in a cryptic mix of Greek, Latin, and Arabic. When deciphered, the parchment told the legend of Saint Caecilius, who was reputed to have brought Christianity to the Iberian Peninsula and become the first bishop of Granada. In the years following, a series of circular lead plates were discovered in the Sacromonte caves outside Granada. The texts, written in Latin and an archaicized Arabic, claimed to be a Gospel account dictated by the Virgin Mary. It has since been theorized that the translators—Miguel de Luna and Alonso del Castillo, both Moriscos—fabricated the texts in an effort to legitimize Arabic as a sacred language and defend the place of Moriscos in Christian Spain.

THE ACADEMICIANS OF ARGAMASILLA,[9] A VILLAGE OF LA MANCHA, ON THE LIFE AND DEATH OF DON QUIXOTE OF LA MANCHA, *HOC SCRIPSERUNT*[10]

MONICONGO,[11] ACADEMICIAN OF ARGAMASILLA, ON THE TOMB OF DON QUIXOTE

EPITAPH

The scatterbrain that gave La Mancha more
Rich spoils than Jason's;[12] who a point so keen
Had to his wit, and happier far had been
If his wit's weathercock a blunter bore;
The arm renowned far as Gaeta's shore,[13]
Cathay,[14] and all the lands that lie between;
The muse discreet and terrible in mien[15]
As ever wrote on bronze in days of yore;
He who surpassed the Amadises all,
And who as naught the Galaors[16] accounted,
Supported by his love and gallantry:
Who made the Belianises sing small,
And sought renown on Rocinante mounted;
Here, underneath this cold stone, doth he lie.

PANIAGUADO,[17] ACADEMICIAN OF ARGAMASILLA, *IN LAUDEM DULCINEAE DEL TOBOSO*[18]

SONNET

She, whose full features may be here descried,
High-bosomed, with a bearing of disdain,
Is Dulcinea, she for whom in vain
The great Don Quixote of La Mancha sighed.

[9] *Academicians of Argamasilla:* Members of literary academies would gather to read aloud the compositions they had written on various topics or in each other's honor. Unsurprisingly, the hamlet of Argamasilla did not boast of one.

[10] Hoc scripserunt: Latin, "They wrote this."

[11] *Monicongo:* inhabitant of the Congo. Academicians were known to each other by humorous pseudonyms.

[12] *Rich spoils than Jason's:* treasures that Jason and the Argonauts brought home from Colchis, a kingdom located on the eastern Black Sea.

[13] *Gaeta's shore:* the coast of Naples.

[14] *Cathay:* northern China.

[15] *mien:* countenance.

[16] *Galaors:* Galaor was Amadís of Gaul's brother. See pages 26, 93–94.

[17] *Paniaguado:* Freeloader.

[18] In laudem Dulcineae del Toboso: Latin, "in praise of Dulcinea del Toboso".

For her, Toboso's queen, from side to side
He traversed the grim sierra, the champaign[19]
Of Aranjuez,[20] and Montiel's famous plain:
On Rocinante oft a weary ride.
Malignant planets, cruel destiny,
Pursued them both, the fair Manchegan dame,
And the unconquered star of chivalry.
Nor youth nor beauty saved her from the claim
Of death; he paid love's bitter penalty,
And left the marble to preserve his name.

CAPRICHOSO,[21] A MOST LEARNED ACADEMICIAN OF ARGAMASILLA, IN PRAISE OF ROCINANTE, STEED OF DON QUIXOTE OF LA MANCHA

SONNET[22]

On that proud throne of diamantine sheen,
Which the blood-reeking feet of Mars degrade,
The mad Manchegan's banner now hath been
By him in all its bravery displayed.
There hath he hung his arms and trenchant blade
Wherewith, achieving deeds till now unseen,
He slays, lays low, cleaves, hews; but art hath made
A novel style for our new paladin.
If Amadís be the proud boast of Gaul,
If by his progeny the fame of Greece
Through all the regions of the earth be spread,
Great Quixote crowned in grim Bellona's[23] hall
Today exalts La Mancha over these,
And above Greece or Gaul she holds her head.
Nor ends his glory here, for his good steed
Doth Brigliadoro and Bayard[24] far exceed;
As mettled steeds compared with Rocinante,
The reputation they have won is scanty.

[19] *champaign:* plain.

[20] *Aranjuez:* Don Quixote's travels in the 1605 volume do not take him anywhere close to Aranjuez, a town forty miles south of Madrid.

[21] *Caprichoso:* one who breaks artistic norms to pursue a fantastic vision.

[22] *Sonnet:* This sonnet has seventeen lines, rather than the customary fourteen. In Spanish Golden Age literature, the addition of a tercet to a sonnet (*soneto con estrambote*) generally served humorous ends, consistent with someone who styles himself *Caprichoso.*

[23] *Bellona's hall:* Bellona is the Roman goddess of war.

[24] *Brigliadoro and Bayard:* respective horses of Renaud de Montauban and Orlando Furioso.

BURLADOR,[25] ACADEMICIAN OF ARGAMASILLA, ON SANCHO PANZA

SONNET

The worthy Sancho Panza here you see;
A great soul once was in that body small,
Nor was there squire upon this earthly ball
So plain and simple, or of guile so free.
Within an ace of being count was he,
And would have been but for the spite and gall
Of this vile age, mean and illiberal,
That cannot even let a donkey be.
For mounted on an ass (excuse the word),
By Rocinante's side this gentle squire
Was wont his wandering master to attend.
Delusive hopes that lure the common herd
With promises of ease, the heart's desire,
In shadows, dreams, and smoke ye always end.

CACHIDIABLO,[26] ACADEMICIAN OF ARGAMASILLA, ON THE TOMB OF DON QUIXOTE

EPITAPH

The knight lies here below,
Ill-errant and bruised sore,
Whom Rocinante bore
In his wanderings to and fro.
By the side of the knight is laid
Stolid man Sancho, too,
Than whom a squire more true
Was not in the esquire trade.

TIQUITOC,[27] ACADEMICIAN OF ARGAMASILLA, ON THE TOMB OF DULCINEA DEL TOBOSO

EPITAPH

Here Dulcinea lies.
Plump was she and robust:
Now she is ashes and dust:
The end of all flesh that dies.

[25] *Burlador:* Trickster.
[26] *Cachidiablo:* Hobgoblin.
[27] *Tiquitoc:* Tick-tock, the sound made by certain wooden toys.

A lady of high degree,
With the port of a lofty dame,
And the great Don Quixote's flame,
And the pride of her village was she.

These were all the poems that could be deciphered. The rest, the writing being worm-eaten, were handed over to one of the academicians to theorize what they might have said. We have been informed that at the cost of many sleepless nights and much toil he has succeeded, and that he means to publish them in hopes of shedding light on Don Quixote's third sally.

Forse altro canterà con miglior plectro.[28]

FINIS

[28] Forse altro canterà con miglior plectro: Italian for "Perhaps another will sing with greater art", verse from *Orlando Furioso*. When Cervantes added this final flourish to his novel, he was likely hinting at his intention to write a sequel. He wouldn't have known when he submitted the manuscript to Juan de la Cuesta in 1604 that ten years later someone else would beat him to the press.

SECOND PART OF
THE INGENIOUS KNIGHT
DON QUIXOTE DE LA MANCHA
1615

THE AUTHOR'S PREFACE

My gracious heavens! How eagerly, most noble (or perhaps not-so-noble) reader, you must be looking forward to this preface, expecting to find here retaliation, vitriol, and abuse against the author of the second *Don Quixote*—I mean him who was, they say, begotten at Tordesillas and born at Tarragona.[1] Well, the truth is I am not going to give you that satisfaction; for though injuries stir up anger in humbler breasts, in mine the rule must allow for an exception. You would like me to call him an ass, a fool, and an impudent knave, but I have no such intention. Let his offense be his punishment, with his bread let him eat it, and there's an end of it.

What I cannot take lightly is that he charges me with being old and crippled,[2] as if it had been in my power to keep time from passing over me, or as if the loss of my hand had been brought about in some tavern and not on the grandest occasion that past or present has seen or the future can hope to see.[3] If my wounds have no beauty in the beholder's eye, they are, at least, honorable in the opinion of those who know where they were received; for the soldier cuts a finer figure dead in battle than alive in flight. So strong is my feeling that, if it were possible to live a different past, I would still prefer to have had my share in that mighty action than be free now from my wounds without having been present there. The marks the soldier bears on his face and breast are stars that give others a glimpse of heavenly honor, where worthy ambition receives its due praise; moreover, it is to be observed that it is not with gray hairs that one writes but with the understanding, and that commonly improves with years.

I resent as well that he calls me envious[4] and explains to me, as if I were ignorant, what envy is; for really and truly, of the two kinds there are, I only know

[1] *the second* Don Quixote *... born at Tarragona:* According to the title page of Avellaneda's sequel, the book was published in Tarragona by the "Licentiate Alonso Fernández de Avellaneda, native of the town of Tordesillas". See the Introduction.

[2] *he charges me with being old and crippled:* In his prologue, Avellaneda condemns Cervantes' supposed self-promotion and criticisms of other writers, quipping that he "has more tongue than hands". He jokes that Cervantes is a cranky old man—"as old as the Castle of San Cervantes" (probably the eleventh-century Castle of San Servando in Toledo)—without any friends, as evidenced by the fact that he couldn't find anyone to write dedicatory poems for Part I.

[3] *grandest occasion that past or present has seen or the future can hope to see:* Battle of Lepanto (1571), where Cervantes was hit with harquebus shot in the chest and left arm as he stormed an Ottoman ship. The wounds to his arm caused permanent disability. See page xii.

[4] *he calls me envious:* Avellaneda, ostensibly taking up the voice of Lope de Vega, insinuates that Cervantes writes out of envy of the more successful dramatist. Recall that in his

that which is holy, noble, and high-minded.[5] If that be so (as it is), I am not likely to attack a priest, above all if he further holds the rank of familiar of the Holy Office.[6] And if he said what he did on account of him on whose behalf it seems he spoke, he is entirely mistaken; for I worship the genius of that person, and admire his works along with his unceasing, virtuous dedication.[7] To be honest, I am grateful to this gentleman, the author, for saying that my novels are more satirical than exemplary yet still good; for they could not be so unless there was a little of everything in them.

I suspect you will say that I am taking a very humble approach, and keeping myself too much within the bounds of my moderation, from a feeling that additional suffering should not be inflicted upon a sufferer, and that what this gentleman has to endure must doubtless be very great, as he does not dare to come out into the open field and broad daylight but hides his name and disguises his country as if he had been guilty of some *lèse majesté*.[8] If you should happen to meet him, tell him on my behalf that I do not consider myself aggrieved; for I know well what the temptations of the devil are, and that one of the greatest is putting it into a man's head that he can write and print a book by which he will get as much fame as money and as much money as fame. To prove my point, I ask that you relate to him (in your own refined, charming way) the following story:

There was a madman in Seville who had the most ridiculous idea that ever madman in the world acted upon. It was this: he made a reed tube that was sharp at one end, and catching a dog in the street (or wherever it might be), he held one of its legs in place with his foot, while with his hand lifted up the other, and as best he could attached the tube where, by blowing, he made the dog as round as a ball. Then, holding it in this position, he gave it a couple of slaps on the belly and let it go, saying to the bystanders (and there were always plenty of them): "Do your worships really think that it is an easy thing to blow up a dog?"—Does your worship really think that it is an easy thing to write a book?

And if this story does not suit him, you may, dear reader, tell him this one, which is likewise about a madman and a dog:

In Córdoba there was another madman, who was in the habit of carrying a piece of marble slab or heavy stone on his head. Whenever he crossed paths with an unwary dog, he would come up close and drop the weight right on top of him; on which the dog in a rage, barking and howling, would run three streets without stopping. It so happened, however, that one of the dogs he dropped his load upon

---

dialogue with the Canon of Toledo, the priest laments that Lope de Vega has sacrificed his formidable talent at the altar of fame and financial gain. See footnote 10, page 388.

[5] *that which is holy, noble, and high-minded:* Saint Thomas Aquinas distinguishes the sin of envy from a zeal to emulate the righteous. *Summa Theologiae* II-II, Q. 36.

[6] *familiar of the Holy Office:* lay assistant to the Spanish Inquisition, which conferred exemption from certain taxes and laws. Lope was granted the office in 1608; he was ordained to the priesthood in 1614.

[7] *unceasing, virtuous dedication:* Cervantes' praise is mingled with irony. Prior to an existential crisis in 1611, Lope was notorious for his profligate life.

[8] lèse majesté: criminal offense against the dignity of a monarch.

was a capmaker's dog, of which his master was very fond. The stone came down hitting it on the head, and the dog raised a yell at the blow. The master, who saw the affair, was furious. Snatching up a yardstick, he rushed out at the madman and did not leave a sound bone in his body. At every stroke he gave him he said, "You dog, you thief! My hound! Don't you see, you brute, that this is a hunting dog?" And so, repeating the phrase "hunting dog" again and again, he sent the madman away beaten to a jelly.

The madman took the lesson to heart and vanished, and for more than a month never once showed himself in public; but after that he came out again with his old trick and a heavier load than ever. He came up to where there was a dog, and examining it very carefully without venturing to let the stone fall, he said, "This is a hunting dog. Beware!" In short, all the dogs he came across, be they mastiffs or terriers, he said were hunting dogs; and he let loose no more stones. Maybe it will be the same with this historian—that he will not venture another time to let loose the weight of his intellect in books, which, being inferior, are harder than stones.

Tell him, too, that I do not care a whit for the threat he holds out to me of depriving me of my profit by means of his book; for to borrow from the famous interlude "La Perendenga,"[9] I say in answer to him, "Long life to my lord the Veinticuatro, and Christ be with us all." Long life to the great Count of Lemos,[10] whose Christian charity and well-known generosity support me against all the strokes of my accursed fortune; and long life to the supreme benevolence of His Eminence of Toledo, Don Bernardo de Sandoval y Rojas.[11] What does it matter if there are no printing presses in the world, or if they print more books against me than there are letters in the *Coplas of Mingo Revulgo*![12] These two princes, unsought by any adulation or flattery of mine, of their own goodness alone, have taken it upon themselves to show me kindness and protect me, and in this I consider myself happier and richer than if Fortune had raised me to her greatest height in the ordinary way. The poor man may possess honor, but not the vicious; poverty may cast a cloud over nobility, but cannot hide it altogether; and as virtue by itself sheds a certain light, even though it be through the straits and chinks of penury, it wins the esteem of lofty and noble spirits, and in consequence their protection.

You need say no more to him, nor will I say anything more to you, except to ask you to bear in mind that this Second Part of *Don Quixote* I offer you is cut by the same craftsman and from the same cloth as the First, and that in it I present to you Don Quixote further developed, and at length dead and buried, so that

[9] *"La Perendenga":* lost theater piece. The title is a slang term for a prostitute.

[10] *the great Count of Lemos:* See the dedication below.

[11] *Don Bernardo de Sandoval y Rojas:* Bernardo de Sandoval y Rojas (1546–1618) was the Cardinal-Archbishop of Toledo and influential patron who provided political and financial support to Cervantes during the last five years of the author's life.

[12] Coplas of Mingo Revulgo: collection of satiric poems written in the second half of the fifteenth century.

no one may dare to tell any more tales about him, for those already produced are sufficient. It is enough, too, that an honorable man has given an account of all his witty lunacies without desiring to revisit them; for abundance, even of good things, prevents them from being valued; and scarcity, even in the case of what is bad, confers a certain value.

I almost forgot to tell you that you should expect the *Persiles*[13] soon, which I am now finishing—and also the Second Part of *Galatea*.[14]

[13] Persiles: *The Labors of Persiles and Sigismunda*, Byzantine novel Cervantes completed four days before his death in April 1616, published posthumously the following year.

[14] *Second Part of* Galatea: sequel to Cervantes' pastoral romance, *The Seven Books of La Galatea* (1585). No trace of this sequel has been found.

DEDICATION

TO THE COUNT OF LEMOS:[1]

Recently, when I sent Your Excellency a copy of my plays that have been published but not staged,[2] I said (if I remember correctly) that Don Quixote was putting on his spurs to go and render homage to Your Excellency. Now, I say that "with his spurs, he is on his way." Should he reach his destination, I consider I shall have rendered some service to Your Excellency, as from many parts I am urged to send him off, so as to dispel the loathing and disgust caused by another Don Quixote who, under the name of *The Second Part*, has run masquerading through the whole world.

The one who has desired most to see him has been the great emperor of China, who wrote me a letter in Chinese a month ago and sent it by a special courier. He asked me—or to be truthful, he begged me—to send him a copy, for he intended to found a college where the Spanish tongue would be taught, and it was his wish that the book to be read should be the history of Don Quixote. He also added that I should go and be the rector of this college. I asked the bearer if His Majesty had set aside any money to offset my travel expenses. He answered, "No, it had not even occurred to him."

"Then, brother," I replied, "you can return to your China post haste (or at whatever haste you are inclined to go), as I am not fit for so long a travel. In addition to being ill,[3] I am very much without money, while emperor for emperor and monarch for monarch, I have at Naples the great Count of Lemos, who, without so many petty titles of colleges and rectorships, sustains me, protects me, and shows me more favor than I can wish for."[4]

Thus I gave him his leave and I beg mine from you, offering Your Excellency *The Labors of Persiles and Sigismunda*, a book I shall finish within four months,

[1] *Count of Lemos:* Pedro Fernández de Castro (1576–1622), seventh Count of Lemos and Viceroy of Naples (1610–1616), was a sought-after patron among Golden Age writers. The 1615 *Don Quixote* is the second of three works Cervantes dedicated to him.

[2] *plays that have been published but not staged: Eight Plays and Eight Interludes Never Before Performed* (1615).

[3] *ill:* Cervantes would die six months after these lines were published.

[4] *more favor than I can wish for:* In 1610, Cervantes had applied unsuccessfully to serve in the count's retinue in Naples. On the surface, his dedications to the Count of Lemos brim with admiration, and yet his yarn about the emperor of China—along with his admission that he is "very much without money"—undercuts Cervantes' praise for being generously supported.

Deo volente,[5] and which will be either the worst or the best that has been composed in our language—I mean of those intended for entertainment. I repent of having called it the worst, for in the opinion of friends, it is sure to attain the summit of all possible greatness. May Your Excellency return in the good health I wish for you. *Persiles* will be ready to kiss your hand and I your feet, being as I am, Your Excellency's most humble servant.

From Madrid, this last day of October of the year one thousand six hundred and fifteen.

At the service of Your Excellency:

MIGUEL DE CERVANTES SAAVEDRA

[5] Deo volente: literally, "God willing".

CHAPTER I

OF THE INTERVIEW THE PRIEST AND THE BARBER HAD WITH DON QUIXOTE ABOUT HIS MALADY

Cide Hamete Benengeli, in the Second Part of this history and third sally of Don Quixote, says that the priest and the barber went nearly a month without seeing him, lest they should recall or bring back to his recollection what had taken place. They did not, however, fail to visit his niece and housekeeper and charge them to treat him with the greatest care—to give him food that would strengthen him and such things as were good for the heart and the brain, from which, it was plain to see, all his misfortune proceeded. The niece and housekeeper replied that they had done so, and would continue to do so, with unfailing attention, for they could tell that their master was little by little beginning to show signs of being in his right mind. This gave great satisfaction to the priest and the barber, for they felt confirmed in having taken the right course when they carried him off enchanted on the oxcart, as has been described in the First Part of this great and most detailed history, in the last chapter thereof. They resolved, therefore, to pay him a visit and test the improvement in his condition, although they thought it almost impossible that there could be any. It was agreed that they would not touch upon any point connected with knight-errantry so as not to run the risk of reopening wounds that were still so tender.

When they came to see him, they found him sitting up in bed in a green flannel shirt and red Toledo cap,[1] and so withered and dried up that he looked as if he had been turned into a mummy. They were very cordially received by him; they asked him about his health, and he talked to them about himself very naturally and in very fine language. In the course of their conversation they fell to discussing what they call statecraft[2] and systems of government, correcting this abuse and condemning that, reforming one practice and abolishing another, each of the three making himself a new legislator, a modern Lycurgus or a second Solon.[3] So completely did they remodel the State, that they seemed to have thrust it into a furnace and taken out something quite different from what they had put in. On all the subjects they dealt with, Don Quixote spoke so reasonably

[1] *Toledo cap:* nightcap with a pointed or tapering end.

[2] *statecraft:* politics.

[3] *a modern Lycurgus or a second Solon:* ancient lawgivers synonymous with sound government.

that the two examiners were fully convinced that he was quite recovered and in his full senses.

The niece and housekeeper were present at the conversation and could not find words enough to express their thanks to God at seeing their master so clear in his mind. The priest, however, changing his original plan, which was to avoid touching upon matters of chivalry, resolved to test Don Quixote's recovery once and for all and see whether it was genuine or not. And so, from one subject to another, he came at last to talk of the news that had come from court. Among other things, he said it was considered certain that the Turk was approaching with a powerful fleet, and that no one knew what his purpose was or when the great storm would burst. In light of this concern, which almost every year seemed to call Christendom to arms, his Majesty had made provision for the security of the coasts of Naples and Sicily and the island of Malta.

To this Don Quixote replied, "His Majesty has acted like a prudent warrior in providing for the safety of his realms in time, so that the enemy may not find him unprepared; but if my advice were taken, I would recommend him to adopt a measure which at present, no doubt, his Majesty is very far from thinking of."

The moment the priest heard this he said to himself, "God keep you in his hand, poor Don Quixote, for it seems to me you are about to hurl yourself from the height of your madness into the profound abyss of your simplicity."

The barber, who had the same suspicion as the priest, asked Don Quixote what would be his advice as to the measures that he said ought to be adopted; for perhaps it might prove to be one that would have to be added to the list of the many impertinent suggestions that people were in the habit of offering to princes.[4]

"Mine, master shaver," said Don Quixote, "will not be impertinent, but, on the contrary, pertinent."

"I don't mean that," said the barber, "but that experience has shown that all or most of the measures which are proposed to his Majesty are either impossible, or absurd, or injurious to the king and to the kingdom."

"Mine, however," replied Don Quixote, "is neither impossible nor absurd, but the easiest, the most reasonable, the readiest, and most expeditious that could suggest itself to any arbitrista's mind."

"You take a long time to tell it, Señor Don Quixote," said the priest.

"I would not want to tell it here and now," said Don Quixote, "only to have it reach the ears of the lords of the Council tomorrow morning and someone else carry off the thanks and rewards of my trouble."

[4] *many impertinent suggestions that people were in the habit of offering to princes:* A class of reformer had arisen in late sixteenth-century Spain known as the *arbitrista*—a policy expert who identified economic, demographic, or political problems affecting the nation and proposed remedies in a written report, or *arbitrio,* that he presented to the royal court for consideration. While some *arbitrios* were well-informed, many were utopian and impractical, prompting writers like Cervantes and Francisco de Quevedo to satirize the *arbitristas* as pedantic theorists whose schemes were inadequate to address Spain's deepening crises.

"For my part," said the barber, "I give my word here and before God that I will not repeat what your worship says, to king, rook,[5] or earthly man—an oath I learned from the ballad of the priest, who, in the Introit, told the king about the thief who had robbed him of the hundred gold escudos and his swiftest mule."[6]

"I am not versed in stories," said Don Quixote, "but I know the oath is a good one, because I know the barber to be an honest fellow."

"Even if he were not," said the priest, "I will vouch for him that in this matter he will be as silent as a mute, under pain of paying any penalty that may be pronounced."

"And who will be security for you, señor priest?" asked Don Quixote.

"My profession," replied the priest, "which is to keep secrets."

"By thunder!" cried Don Quixote at this. "What more has his Majesty to do but to command, by public proclamation, all the knights-errant that are scattered over Spain to assemble on a fixed day in the capital? For even if no more than half a dozen come, there may be one among them who alone will suffice to destroy the entire might of the Turk. Pay close attention and follow me. Is it, pray, any new thing for a single knight-errant to demolish an army of two hundred thousand men, as if they all had but one throat or were made of almond paste? Tell me, rather, how many histories are there filled with these marvels? If only (in an evil hour for me—I don't speak for anyone else) the famous Don Belianís were alive now or anyone of the innumerable progeny of Amadís of Gaul! If any of these were alive today and were to come face to face with the Turk, by my faith, I would not like to be in the Turk's place. But God will have regard for his people, and will provide someone, who, if not so valiant as the knights-errant of yore, at least will not be inferior to them in spirit. God knows what I mean, and I say no more."

"Alas!" exclaimed the niece at this. "May I die if my master does not want to turn knight-errant again!"

To which Don Quixote replied, "A knight-errant I shall die, and let the Turk come down or go up when he likes, and in as strong a force as he can. Once more I say, God knows what I mean."

But here the barber said, "I ask your worships to give me leave to tell a short story of something that happened in Seville, which, since it fits like a glove, I should like greatly to tell it." Don Quixote gave him leave, and the rest prepared to listen. He began thus:

"In the madhouse at Seville there was a man whom his relations had placed there for being out of his mind. He was a graduate of Osuna in canon law; but even if he had been a graduate of Salamanca, it was the opinion of most people that he would have been mad all the same. This graduate, after some years of

[5] *rook:* castle in the game of chess.

[6] *ballad of the priest . . . his swiftest mule:* In the ballad, the thief who robs the priest on the road warns him to tell no man or woman of the theft. Later, when the priest is saying Mass before the king, he notices the thief in the pews and denounces him as he sings the Introit to the liturgy.

confinement, took it into his head that he was sane and in his full senses, and under this impression wrote to the Archbishop, entreating him earnestly and in very polished language, to have him released from the misery in which he was living; for by God's mercy he had now recovered his lost reason, though his relations, in order to enjoy his property, kept him there, and, in spite of the truth, would make him out to be mad until his dying day.

"The Archbishop, moved by repeated sensible, well-written letters, directed one of his chaplains to inquire of the director of the asylum about the truth of the licentiate's statements, and to have an interview with the madman himself, and, if it should appear that he was in his senses, to take him out and restore him to liberty. The chaplain did so, and the director assured him that the man was still mad, and that though he often spoke like a highly intelligent person, he would in the end break out into nonsense that in quantity and quality offset all the sensible things he had said before, as might be easily tested by talking to him. The chaplain resolved to try the experiment, and obtaining access to the madman conversed with him for an hour or more, during the whole of which time he never uttered a word that was incoherent or absurd, but, on the contrary, spoke so rationally that the chaplain was compelled to believe him to be sane. Among other things, he said the director was against him in order not to lose the presents his relations sent him for reporting him still mad but with lucid intervals; and that the worst foe he had in his misfortune was his large property, for in order to enjoy it, his enemies disparaged and threw doubts upon the mercy our Lord had shown him in turning him from a brute beast into a man. In short, he spoke in such a way that he cast suspicion on the director, and made his relations appear greedy and heartless and himself so rational that the chaplain determined to take him away with him, so that the Archbishop might see him and determine for himself the truth of the matter.

"Yielding to this conviction, the worthy chaplain begged the director to have the clothes in which the licentiate had entered the house given to him. The director again warned him about what he was doing, as the licentiate was beyond doubt still mad; but all his cautions and admonitions were unavailing to dissuade the chaplain from taking him away. The director, seeing that it was the order of the Archbishop, obeyed, and they dressed the licentiate in his own clothes, which were new and decent. He, as soon as he saw himself clothed like one in his senses, and divested of the appearance of a madman, entreated the chaplain to permit him in charity to go and take leave of his comrades the madmen. The chaplain said he would go with him to see what madmen there were in the house; so they went upstairs, and with them some of those who were present.

"Approaching a cage in which there was a furious madman, though just at that moment calm and quiet, the licentiate said to him, 'Brother, tell me if there is anything I can do for you, for I am going home, as God has been pleased, in his infinite goodness and mercy, without any merit of mine, to restore me my reason. I am now cured and in my senses, for with God's power nothing is impossible. Have strong hope and trust in him, for as he has restored me to my original condition, so likewise he will restore you if you trust in him. I will take care to send you some good things to eat. Be sure you eat them, for I would have you know I am convinced, as one who has gone through it, that all this madness of ours comes of having the stomach empty and the brains full of wind. Take courage! Take courage! For despondency in misfortune breaks down health and brings on death.'

"To all these words of the licentiate another madman in a cage opposite that of the furious one was listening; and raising himself up from an old mat on which he lay stark naked, he asked in a loud voice who it was that was going away cured and in his senses. The licentiate answered, 'It is I, brother, who am going. I have now no need to remain here any longer, for which I return infinite thanks to Heaven that has had so great mercy upon me.'

"'Mind what you are saying, licentiate; don't let the devil deceive you,' replied the madman. 'Keep quiet, stay where you are, and you will save yourself the trouble of coming back.'

"'I know I am cured,' returned the licentiate, 'and that I shall not have to come back again.'

"'You cured!' said the madman. 'Well, we shall see. God be with you. But I swear to you by Jupiter, whose majesty I represent on earth, that for this crime alone, which Seville is committing today in releasing you from this house, and treating you as if you were in your senses, I shall have to inflict such a punishment on it as will be remembered for ages and ages, amen. Do you not know, you miserable little licentiate, that I can do it, being, as I say, Jupiter the Thunderer, who holds in my hands the fiery bolts with which I am able and am willing to threaten and lay waste the world? But in one way only will I punish this ignorant town, and that is by not raining upon it, nor on any part of its district or territory, for three whole years, to be reckoned from the day and moment when this threat is pronounced. You free, you cured, you in your senses! And I mad, I disordered, I bound! I will as soon think of sending rain as of hanging myself.'

"Those present stood listening to the words and exclamations of the madman. But our licentiate, turning to the chaplain and seizing him by the hands, said to him, 'Do not be uneasy, señor; attach no importance to what this madman has said. For if he is Jupiter and will not send rain, I, who am Neptune, the father and god of the waters, will rain as often as it pleases me and may be needful.'

"The governor and the bystanders laughed, and at their laughter the chaplain was half ashamed, and he replied, 'For all that, Señor Neptune, it will not do to anger Señor Jupiter. Remain where you are, and some other day, when there is a better opportunity and more time, we will come back for you.' So they stripped the licentiate, and he was left where he was. And that's the end of the story."

"So that's the story, master barber," said Don Quixote, "which fit so much like a glove that you could not help telling it? Master shaver, master shaver! How blind is the one who cannot see through cheesecloth. Is it possible that you do not know that the comparisons made between mind and mind, valor and valor, beauty and beauty, birth and birth, are always odious and unwelcome? I, master barber, am not Neptune, the god of the waters, nor do I try to make anyone take me for an astute man, for I am not one. My only intent is to convince the world of the mistake it makes in not reviving the happy time when the order of knight-errantry was in the field. But our depraved age does not deserve to enjoy such a blessing as those ages enjoyed when knights-errant took upon their shoulders the defense of kingdoms, the protection of damsels, the succor of orphans and minors, the chastisement of the proud, and the recompense of the humble. With the knights of these days, for the most part, it is the damask, brocade, and rich fabrics they wear, which rustle as they go, not the chain mail of their armor. No knight nowadays sleeps in the open field exposed to the inclemency of heaven, and in full panoply from head to foot. No one now does battle with fatigue, so to speak, as the knight-errant used to do, with his feet still in the stirrups and leaning upon his lance. No one now, emerging from the forest, braves distant mountains and from there treads the barren, lonely shore of the sea—mostly a tempestuous and stormy one—and finding on the beach a little boat without oars, sail, mast, or tackling of any kind, in the intrepidity of his heart flings himself into it and commits himself to the wrathful billows of the deep sea, that one moment lift him up to heaven and the next plunge him into the depths; and opposing his breast to the irresistible gale, finds himself, when he least expects it, three thousand leagues and more away from the place where he embarked; and leaping ashore in a remote and unknown land has adventures that deserve to be written, not on parchment, but in bronze.

"But now sloth triumphs over energy, indolence over exertion, vice over virtue, arrogance over courage, and theory over practice in arms, which flourished and shone only in the golden ages and in knights-errant. For tell me, who was more virtuous and more valiant than the famous Amadís of Gaul? Who more discreet than Palmerín of England? Who more gracious and mild than Tirante el Blanco? Who more courtly than Lisuarte of Greece? Who more slashed or slashing than Don Belianís? Who more intrepid than Perión of Gaul? Who more ready to face danger than Felixmarte of Hircania? Who more sincere than Esplandián? Who more impetuous than Don Cirongilio of Thrace? Who more furious than Rodamonte? Who more prudent than King Sobrino? Who more daring than Reinaldos? Who more invincible than Roland? And who more gallant and courteous than Ruggiero, from whom the dukes of Ferrara of the present day are descended, according to Turpin in his cosmography?[7]

"All these knights, and many more that I could name, señor priest, were knights-errant, the light and glory of chivalry. My proposal[8] would be for his Majesty to deploy these, or those like them. In doing so, he would find himself well served and would save great expense, and the Turk would be left tearing his beard. Yet I will stay where I am, since the chaplain will not take me away.

[7] *more gallant and courteous . . . in his cosmography:* In *Orlando Furioso*, Ariosto imagines the knight Ruggiero as the progenitor of the House of Este, which ruled Ferrara and other territories from 1240 to 1597. Archbishop Turpin—based on the historical bishop of Rheims of the eighth century—was transformed in medieval epic into a warrior-prelate and, by Cervantes' time, was ridiculed as a chronicler of the fantastic and untrue.

[8] *proposal: arbitrio.*

If Jupiter, as the barber has told us, will not send rain, here am I, and I will rain when I please. I say this so that Master Basin may know that I understand him."

"Honestly, Señor Don Quixote," said the barber, "I didn't mean it like that. So help me God, my intention was good, and your worship ought not take offense."

"As to whether I ought to take offense or not," returned Don Quixote, "I myself am the best judge."

Hereupon the priest observed, "I have hardly said a word yet. I would gladly be relieved of a doubt, arising from what Don Quixote has said, that worries and works my conscience."

"The señor priest has leave for more than that," returned Don Quixote, "so he may declare his doubt, for it is not pleasant to carry a doubt in one's conscience."

"Well then, with that permission," said the priest, "I say my doubt is that in no way can I persuade myself that the whole pack of knights-errant you, Señor Don Quixote, have mentioned, were really and truly persons of flesh and blood that ever lived in the world. On the contrary, I suspect it to be all fiction, fable, and falsehood, and dreams told by men awakened from sleep, or rather still half asleep."

"That is another mistake," replied Don Quixote, "into which many have fallen who do not believe that there ever were such knights in the world. I have often, with many people and on many occasions, tried to expose this almost universal error to the light of truth. Sometimes I have not been successful in my purpose, sometimes I have, supporting it upon the shoulders of the truth. That truth is so clear that I can almost say I have with my own eyes seen Amadís of Gaul, who was a man of lofty stature, fair complexion, with a handsome though black beard, of a countenance between gentle and stern in expression, sparing of words, slow to anger, and quick to put it to rest. As I have depicted Amadís, so I could, I think, portray and describe all the knights-errant that are in all the histories in the world. For by the knowledge I have that they were what their histories describe, and by the deeds they did and the dispositions they displayed, it is possible, with the aid of sound philosophy, to deduce their features, complexion, and stature."

"How big, in your worship's opinion, might the giant Morgante[9] have been, Señor Don Quixote?" asked the barber.

"With regard to giants," replied Don Quixote, "opinions differ as to whether there ever were any or not in the world; but the Holy Scripture, which cannot err by a jot from the truth, shows us that there were, when it gives us the history of that great Philistine Goliath, who was seven cubits and a half in height,[10] which is a huge size. Likewise, in the island of Sicily, there have been found leg bones and arm bones so large that their size makes it plain that their owners were giants, and as tall as great towers. Geometry puts this fact beyond a doubt. But, for all that, I cannot speak with certainty as to the size of Morgante, though I suspect he cannot have been very tall. I am inclined to be of this opinion because I find in the history in which his deeds are described in detail that he frequently

[9] *giant Morgante:* See footnote 18, page 27.

[10] *seven cubits and a half in height:* Goliath was *six* cubits and a half in height (1 Samuel 17:4).

slept under a roof, and as he found houses to contain him, it is clear that his bulk could not have been anything excessive."

"Quite true," said the priest, who, taking great pleasure in hearing such nonsense, asked him what ideas he had about the features of Reinaldos of Montalban, and Don Roland and the rest of the Twelve Peers of France, for they were all knights-errant.

"As for Reinaldos," replied Don Quixote, "I venture to say that he was broad-faced, of ruddy complexion, with roguish and somewhat prominent eyes, excessively punctilious and touchy, and given to the society of thieves and wastrels. With regard to Roland, or Rotolando, or Orlando (for the histories call him by all these names), I firmly believe that he was of middle height, broad-shouldered, rather bowlegged, swarthy-complexioned, red-bearded, with a hairy body and a severe expression of countenance, a man of few words, but very polite and well-bred."

"If Roland was not a more graceful person than your worship has described," said the priest, "it is no wonder that the fair Lady Angelica rejected him and left him for the refinement, liveliness, and grace of that budding-bearded little Moor to whom she surrendered herself.[11] She showed her sense in falling in love with the gentle softness of Medoro rather than the roughness of Roland."

"That Angelica, señor priest," returned Don Quixote, "was an inconstant damsel, flighty and somewhat wanton, and she left the world as full of her follies as of the fame of her beauty. She treated with scorn a thousand gentlemen, men of valor and wisdom, and took up with a smooth-faced sprig of a page, without fortune or fame, except such reputation for gratitude as the affection he bore his friend got for him. The great poet who sang her beauty, the famous Ariosto, not caring to sing her adventures after her contemptible surrender (which were probably not shining examples of virtue), left her where he says:

> How she received the scepter of Cathay,
> Some bard of defter quill may sing some day;[12]

and this was no doubt a kind of prophecy, for poets are also called *vates*, that is to say diviners;[13] Its truth was made plain, for since then a famous Andalusian poet has lamented and sung her tears, and another well-known poet of singular talent, a Castilian, has sung her beauty."[14]

"Tell me, Señor Don Quixote," said the barber here, "among all those who praised her, has there been no poet to write a satire on this Lady Angelica?"

[11] *budding-bearded little Moor to whom she surrendered herself*: See footnote 9, page 187.

[12] *some bard of defter quill may sing some day:* the same verse that Cervantes quotes at the end of Part I (see p. 416).

[13] *diviners:* those gifted in divination, the ability to discover hidden knowledge through supernatural power.

[14] *Its truth was made plain . . . her beauty:* The first is a book in Alonso Quixano's library, Luis Barahona de Soto's *The Tears of Angelica* (1586); the second is Lope de Vega's *The Beauty of Angelica* (1602).

"I can well believe," replied Don Quixote, "that if Sacripante or Roland had been poets they would have cut the damsel down to size; for it is naturally the way with poets who have been scorned and rejected by their ladies, whether fictitious or not, in short by those whom they select as the ladies of their thoughts, to avenge themselves in satires and libels—a vengeance, to be sure, unworthy of generous hearts. But up to the present I have not heard of any defamatory verse against Lady Angelica, who turned the world upside down."

"Strange," said the priest.

But at this moment they heard the housekeeper and niece, who had previously left the conversation, exclaiming aloud in the courtyard, and at the noise they all ran out.

CHAPTER II

WHICH TREATS OF THE NOTABLE ALTERCATION SANCHO PANZA HAD WITH DON QUIXOTE'S NIECE AND HOUSEKEEPER, TOGETHER WITH OTHER AMUSING MATTERS

The history relates that the outcry Don Quixote, the priest, and the barber heard came from the niece and housekeeper exclaiming to Sancho, who was trying to force his way in to see Don Quixote while they held the door against him, "What does the vagabond want in this house? Be off to your own, brother, for it is you, and no one else, who deludes my master, and leads him astray, and takes him tramping about the country."

To which Sancho replied, "Devil's own housekeeper! I'm the one deluded, and led astray, and taken tramping about the country, and not your master! He has carried me all over the world, and you are very mistaken. He took me away from home by a trick, promising me an island, which I'm still waiting for."

"May evil islands choke you, you detestable Sancho," said the niece. "What are islands?[1] Is it something to eat, you glutton and food fiend?"

"It is not something to eat," replied Sancho, "but something to govern and rule, and better than four cities or four judgeships at court."

"All the same," said the housekeeper, "you won't enter here, you bag of mischief and sack of knavery. Go govern your house and dig your seed patch, and give up looking for islands, or highlands."

The priest and the barber listened with great amusement to the words of the three; but Don Quixote, uneasy lest Sancho should blab and blurt out a whole heap of mischievous nonsense and touch upon points that might not be altogether to his credit, called to him and made the other two hold their tongues and let him come in. Sancho entered, and the priest and the barber took their leave of Don Quixote, of whose recovery they despaired when they saw how wedded he was to his crazy ideas and how saturated with the foolishness of his benighted chivalry. The priest said to the barber, "You will see, my friend, that when we are least thinking of it, our gentleman will be off once more for another flight."

"I have no doubt of it," returned the barber; "but I do not wonder so much at the madness of the knight as at the simplicity of the squire, who has such a firm

[1] *What are islands:* The niece's confusion is understandable. The word Don Quixote uses for "island" in Part I, which Sancho repeats, is not the common Spanish word *isla* but the Latinate *ínsula*.

belief in all that about the island, that I wonder if any amount of reasoning would get it out of his head."

"God help them," said the priest. "Let us be on the lookout to see what comes of all these absurdities of the knight and squire, for it seems as if they had both been cast in the same mold. The madness of the master would be worthless without the simplicity of the man."

"Too true," said the barber. "I should like very much to know what the pair are talking about at this moment."

"I promise you," said the priest, "the niece or the housekeeper will tell us afterwards, for they are not the kind to fail to listen."

Meanwhile, Don Quixote had shut himself up in his room with Sancho, and when they were alone he said to him, "It grieves me greatly, Sancho, that you should have said, and still say, that I took you from your cottage, when you know that I did not remain in my house. We sallied forth together, we took the road together, we wandered abroad together; we have had the same fortune and the same luck. If they blanketed you once, they pummeled me a hundred times, and that is the only advantage I have of you."

"That was only reasonable," replied Sancho, "for by what your worship says, misfortunes belong more properly to knights-errant than to their squires."

"You are mistaken, Sancho," said Don Quixote, "according to the maxim *quando caput dolet*, etc."[2]

"I don't understand any language but my own," said Sancho.

"I mean to say," said Don Quixote, "that when the head suffers all the members suffer; and so, being your lord and master, I am your head, and you are a part of me, since you are my servant. Therefore, any evil that affects or shall affect me should give you pain, and what affects you give pain to me."

"So it ought to be," said Sancho. "But when I was blanketed as a member, my head was on the other side of the wall, looking on while I was flying through the air, and did not feel any pain whatever. If the members are obliged to feel the suffering of the head, the head should be obliged to feel the sufferings of the members."

"Do you mean to say now, Sancho," said Don Quixote, "that I was not suffering when they were blanketing you? If you do, you must not say so or think so, for I felt more pain then in spirit than you did in body. But let us put that aside for the present, for we shall have opportunities enough for considering and settling the point. Tell me, Sancho my friend, what do they say about me in the village here? What do the common people think of me? What about the hidalgos and knights?[3] What do they say of my valor, of my achievements, of my courtesy? How do they treat the task I have undertaken in reviving and restoring to the world the now forgotten order of chivalry? In short, Sancho, I would have you tell me all that has come to your ears on this subject. You are to tell me without

[2] quando caput dolet, *etc.*: *caetera membra dolent*. Don Quixote goes on to translate the Latin maxim.

[3] *hidalgos and knights*: See footnote 29, page 28.

adding anything to the good or taking away anything from the bad; for it is the duty of loyal vassals to tell the truth to their lords just as it is and in its proper shape, not allowing flattery to add to it or any vain deference to lessen it. I would have you know, Sancho, that if the naked truth, undisguised by flattery, came to the ears of princes, times would be different, and other ages would be reckoned iron ages more than ours, which I hold to be the golden of these latter days. Profit by this advice, Sancho, and report to me clearly and faithfully the truth of what you know touching on what I have demanded of you."

"That I will do with all my heart, master," replied Sancho, "provided your worship will not be angered at what I say, since you wish me to relate the matter in all its nakedness, without putting any more clothes on it than when it came to my attention."

"I will not be angered at all," returned Don Quixote. "You may speak freely, Sancho, and without any beating about the bush."

"Well then," said he, "first of all, I have to tell you that the common people consider your worship a mighty great madman, and me no less a fool. The hidalgos say you haven't been content to remain a hidalgo and so you've taken the title 'Don' and had the gall to make a knight of yourself,[4] with no more than four grapevines and a couple of acres of land and never a shirt to your back. The knights say they don't want to have hidalgos acting as if they were the same as them, particularly those squire hidalgos who polish their own shoes and darn their black stockings with green silk."

"That," said Don Quixote, "does not apply to me, for I always go well dressed and never patched. Ragged I may be, but ragged more from the wear and tear of arms than of time."

"As to your worship's valor, courtesy, accomplishments, and deeds, there are a variety of opinions. Some say, 'crazy but entertaining'; others, 'brave but unlucky'; others, 'courteous but meddling,' and then they go into such a number of things that they don't leave a whole bone either in your worship or in myself."

"Recollect, Sancho," said Don Quixote, "that wherever virtue exists in an eminent degree it is persecuted. Few or none of the famous men that have lived escaped being calumniated by malice. Julius Cæsar, the boldest, wisest, and bravest of captains, was charged with being ambitious, and not particularly cleanly in his dress or pure in his morals. Of Alexander, whose deeds won him the name of Great, they say that he was somewhat of a drunkard. Of Hercules, him of the many labors, it is said that he was given to the pleasures of the flesh. Of Don Galaor, the brother of Amadís of Gaul, it was whispered that he was quarrelsome, and of his brother that he was a whimperer. For this reason,

[4] *you've taken the title 'Don' and had the gall to make a knight of yourself:* See footnote 29, page 28. It was not yet common for hidalgos to style themselves "Don", especially among those of limited means. Don Quixote's aristocratic pretensions are aided by a subtle difference in the titles of the two volumes. In the 1605 novel he is *The Ingenious Gentleman (Hidalgo) Don Quixote de la Mancha*, whereas in the 1615 sequel Cervantes upgrades him to *The Ingenious Knight (Caballero) Don Quixote de la Mancha.*

Sancho, among all these calumnies against good men, mine may be overlooked, since they are no more than you have said."

"But, on my life, that's just it!"

"Is there more, then?" asked Don Quixote.

"There's the tail to be skinned yet,"[5] said Sancho. "So far everything is cakes and fancy bread.[6] If your worship really wants to know all about the slanders they are saying about you, I will fetch you someone this minute who can tell you the whole of them without missing a crumb. Last night the son of Bartholomew Carrasco, who has been studying at Salamanca, came home after having been made a bachelor,[7] and when I went to welcome him, he told me that your worship's history is already going around in books, with the title of *The Ingenious Gentleman Don Quixote de la Mancha*. He says they mention me in it by my own name of Sancho Panza, and Lady Dulcinea del Toboso too, along with other things that happened to us when we were alone, so that I crossed myself in my wonder how the historian who wrote them down could have known them."

"I assure you, Sancho," said Don Quixote, "the author of our history must be some sage enchanter; for to such as them, nothing they choose to write about is hidden."

"A sage and an enchanter, you say!" exclaimed Sancho. "Why, the bachelor Samson Carrasco—the fellow I just mentioned—says the author of the history is called Cide Hamete Berenjena."

"That is a Moorish name," said Don Quixote.

"That may be so," replied Sancho, "for I've heard say that most Moors are great lovers of eggplant."[8]

"You must have mistaken the surname of this 'Cide'—which means in Arabic 'Lord'—Sancho," observed Don Quixote.

"Very likely," replied Sancho, "but if your worship wishes me to fetch the bachelor, I'll go for him in a twinkling."

"You will do me a great pleasure, my friend," said Don Quixote, "for what you have told me has left me dumbfounded. I shall not eat a morsel that will agree with me until I have heard all about it."

"Then I am off for him," said Sancho. And leaving his master he went in quest of the bachelor, with whom he returned in a short time; and the three together had a very entertaining conversation.

[5] *There's the tail to be skinned yet:* "The worst is yet to come."

[6] *So far everything is cakes and fancy bread:* "I've only mentioned the good part."

[7] *having been made a bachelor:* awarded a *bachillerato*, the undergraduate degree akin to an associate's degree. It preceded a *licenciatura*, a closer analog to today's bachelor's degree.

[8] *eggplant: berenjena.*

CHAPTER III

OF THE LAUGHABLE CONVERSATION THAT PASSED BETWEEN DON QUIXOTE, SANCHO PANZA, AND THE BACHELOR SAMSON CARRASCO

Don Quixote remained very deep in thought, waiting for the bachelor Carrasco, from whom he was to hear how he himself had been put into a book as Sancho said. He could not persuade himself that any such history could be in existence, for the blood of the enemies he had slain was not yet dry on the blade of his sword, and now they wanted to make out that his mighty achievements were going about in print. For all that, he fancied some sage, either a friend or an enemy, might, by the aid of magic, have given them to the press—if a friend, in order to magnify and exalt them above the most famous ever achieved by any knight-errant; if an enemy, to bring them to naught and degrade them below the meanest ever recorded of any low squire, though as he said to himself, the achievements of squires never were recorded. If, however, it were a fact that such a history was in existence, it must necessarily, being the story of a knight-errant, be grandiloquent, lofty, imposing, magnificent, and true.

With this he comforted himself somewhat, though it made him uncomfortable to think that the author was a Moor, judging by the title of "Cide," and that no truth was to be looked for from Moors, as they are all impostors, cheats, and schemers. He was afraid he might have dealt with his love affairs in some indecorous fashion, which might tend to the discredit and prejudice of the purity of his lady Dulcinea del Toboso. He would have had him set forth the fidelity and respect he had always observed towards her, spurning queens, empresses, and damsels of all sorts, and keeping in check the first impulses of his natural desires. Turning over and over again these and many other thoughts, he was found by Sancho and Carrasco, whom Don Quixote received with great courtesy.

The bachelor, though he was called Samson, was of no great bodily size. Nevertheless, he was a very great wag. He was of a sallow complexion, but very sharp-witted, somewhere about twenty-four years of age, with a round face, a flat nose, and a large mouth—all indications of a mischievous disposition and a love of fun and jokes. Of this he gave a sample as soon as he saw Don Quixote, by falling on his knees before him and saying, "Let me kiss your mightiness' hand, Señor Don Quixote of La Mancha, for by the habit of Saint Peter I wear (though I have no more than the first four orders [1]), your worship is one of the most famous knights-errant that have ever been, or will be, all the world over. A blessing on Cide Hamete Benengeli, who has written the history of your great deeds, and a double blessing on that lover of books who took the trouble of having it translated out of the Arabic into our Castilian vulgar tongue for the universal entertainment of the people!"

Don Quixote made him rise and said, "So then, it is true that there is a history of me, and that it was a Moor and a sage who wrote it?"

"So true is it, señor," said Samson, "that it is my belief that there are more than twelve thousand volumes of the said history in print this very day. Only ask Portugal, Barcelona, and Valencia, where they have been printed. There is even a report that it is being printed at Antwerp.[2] I am persuaded there will not be a country or language without a translation of it."[3]

Hearing this, Don Quixote observed, "One of the things that ought to give most pleasure to a virtuous and eminent man is to find himself during his lifetime in print and published, with his good name on the tongues of all people—I say good name, for if it be the opposite, then there is no death to be compared to it."

"If it is a matter of good name and fame," said the bachelor, "your worship alone surpasses all the knights-errant; for the Moor in his own language, and the Christian in his, have taken care to set before us your gallantry, your high courage in encountering dangers, your fortitude in adversity, your patience under misfortunes as well as wounds, the purity and continence of the platonic loves of your worship and my lady Doña Dulcinea del Toboso—"

"I never heard my lady Dulcinea called *Doña*," observed Sancho at this; "nothing more than 'Lady Dulcinea del Toboso.' So here already the history is wrong."

"That is not an objection of any importance," replied Carrasco.

"Certainly not," said Don Quixote. "But tell me, señor bachelor, what deeds of mine are most extolled in this history?"

"On that point," replied the bachelor, "opinions differ, as tastes do. Some swear by the adventure of the windmills that your worship took to be Briareuses[4] and giants; others by that of the fulling mills. One praises the description of the two armies that afterwards took the appearance of two droves of sheep; another that of the dead body on its way to be buried in Segovia. A third says the

[1] *though I have no more than the first four orders:* The bachelor has received the four minor orders of doorkeeper (*ostiarius*), reader (*lector*), exorcist (*exorcista*), and acolyte (*acolytus*), which entitle him to dress as a secular priest—in a cassock and with a clerical tonsure.

[2] *Only ask Portugal . . . at Antwerp:* By 1615, there were editions of the first volume produced in Madrid, Lisbon, and Valencia (1605); Brussels (1607); and Milan (1610). Despite Samson's report, Antwerp would not print the novel until 1673.

[3] *there will not be a country or language without a translation of it:* The first translation of the novel into another language was into English, Thomas Shelton's 1612 *The History of the Valorous and Wittie Knight-Errant Don-Quixote of the Mancha.* It would form the basis of *The History of Cardenio* (1613), a lost play attributed to William Shakespeare and John Fletcher, based on the interpolated tale of Cardenio in the Sierra Morena.

[4] *Briareuses:* See footnote 2, page 61.

liberation of the galley slaves is the best of all, and a fourth that nothing matches the affair with the Benedictine giants, and the battle with the valiant Biscayan."

"Tell me, señor bachelor," said Sancho at this point, "does the adventure with the Yanguesans come in, when our good Rocinante went hankering after what wasn't meant for him?"

"The sage has left nothing in the inkwell," replied Samson. "He tells all and sets down everything, even to the cartwheels that the worthy Sancho performed on the blanket."

"I didn't perform any cartwheels on the blanket," returned Sancho; "in the air I did, and more of them than I liked."

"There is no biography in the world, I suppose," said Don Quixote, "that has not its ups and downs, all the more so when the subjects are knights-errant, for their histories can never be entirely made up of prosperous adventures."

"For all that," replied the bachelor, "there are those who have read the history who say they would have been glad if the author had left out some of the countless beatings that were inflicted on Señor Don Quixote in various encounters."

"That's where the truth of the history comes in," said Sancho.

"At the same time, they might fairly have passed them over in silence," observed Don Quixote; "for there is no need of recording events which do not change or affect the truth of a history if they tend to bring the hero of it into contempt. Æneas was not in truth as pious as Virgil represents him, nor Ulysses so wise as Homer describes him."

"True enough," said Samson; "but it is one thing to write as a poet, another to write as a historian. The poet may describe or sing things, not as they were, but as they ought to have been; but the historian has to write them down, not as they ought to have been, but as they were, without adding anything to the truth or taking anything from it."

"Well then," said Sancho, "if this señor Moor has aimed to tell the truth, no doubt my beatings are right there alongside my master's; for they never took the measure of his worship's shoulders[5] without doing the same for my whole body. But I have no right to wonder at that, for as my master himself says, the members must share the pain of the head."

"You are a sly dog, Sancho," said Don Quixote. "I would swear that you have no lack of memory when you want to use it."

"If I were to try to forget the thwacks they gave me," said Sancho, "my bruises wouldn't allow it, for they are still fresh on my ribs."

"Hush, Sancho," said Don Quixote, "and don't interrupt the bachelor, whom I entreat to go on and relate everything that is said about me in this history."

"And about me," said Sancho, "for they say, too, that I am one of the principal presonages in it."

"*Personages*, not *presonages*, friend Sancho," said Samson.

"So we have another fusspot about words, do we?" said Sancho. "Keep on that way and we won't get to the end in a lifetime."

[5] *took the measure of his worship's shoulders:* beat with a yardstick.

"May God shorten mine, Sancho," returned the bachelor, "if you are not the second person in the history. There are even some who would rather hear you talk than the cleverest to be found in the whole book; though there are some, too, who say you showed yourself exceedingly gullible in believing there was any possibility that you would govern that island offered you by Señor Don Quixote."

"'The sun has not yet sunk beneath the garden wall,'"[6] said Don Quixote. "When Sancho is somewhat more advanced in life, with the experience that years bring, he will be fitter and better qualified for being a governor than he is at present."

"By God, señor," said Sancho, "if I can't govern the island at this age, I won't be able to govern it at Methuselah's age.[7] The problem is that my island is off somewhere dillydallying (where, I don't know), not that I'm short of the brains to govern it."

"Leave it to God, Sancho," said Don Quixote, "for all will turn out well, perhaps better than you think. No leaf on the tree stirs but by God's will."

"That is true," said Samson; "and if it be God's will, there will be no shortage of a thousand islands, much less one, for Sancho to govern."

"I've seen governors in these parts," said Sancho, "that didn't measure up to the sole of my shoe, and for all that they are called 'your lordship' and served with silver dishes."

"Those are not governors of islands," observed Samson, "but of other governments of an easier kind. Those that govern islands must at least know grammar."

"I could manage the *gram*[8] well enough," said Sancho; "but as for the *mar* I'll pass, since I don't know what it is. But leaving this matter of the government in God's hands, to send me wherever it may be most to his service, I may tell you, Señor Bachelor Samson Carrasco, I couldn't be more delighted that the author of this history spoke of me in a way that gives no offense; for on the faith of a true squire, if he had said anything about me that was at all unbecoming an Old Christian such as I am, the deaf would have heard of it."

"That would be working miracles," said Samson.

"Miracles or no miracles," said Sancho, "let everyone mind how he speaks or writes about people, and not put down higgledy-piggledy the first thing that comes into his head."

"One of the faults they find with this history," said the bachelor, "is that its author inserted in it a novel called *The Impertinent Meddler*—not that it is bad or poorly written, but that it is out of place and has nothing to do with the history of his worship Señor Don Quixote."

"I'll bet that son-of-a-dog has mixed apples and oranges,"[9] said Sancho.

[6] *The sun has not yet sunk beneath the garden wall:* "There is still time."

[7] *Methuselah's age*: Methuselah was a biblical patriarch who lived 969 years, making him the oldest person mentioned in the Bible (Genesis 5:27).

[8] gram: a grass used as fodder.

[9] *apples and oranges:* literally, "cabbages with baskets".

"Then, I say," said Don Quixote, "the author of my history was no sage, but some ignorant chatterer, who, in a haphazard and heedless way, set about writing it, let it turn out as it may— just as Orbaneja, the painter of Úbeda, used to do, who, when they asked him what he was painting, answered, 'Whatever it turns out to be.' Sometimes he would paint a rooster in this fashion, and so unlike one that he had to write alongside of it in Gothic letters,[10] 'This is a rooster.' So it will be with my history, which will require a commentary to make it intelligible."

"No fear of that," returned Samson, "for it is so plain that there is nothing in it to puzzle over. The children turn its pages, the young people read it, the grown men understand it, the old folk praise it. In a word, it is so read and dogeared and quoted by people of all sorts, that whenever they see a skinny old hack, they say, 'There goes Rocinante.' Those that are most likely to read it are the pages, for there is not a lord's antechamber where there is not a *Don Quixote* to be found. One takes it up if another lays it down; this one pounces upon it, and that one begs for it. In short, your history is the most delightful and least harmful entertainment that has ever been seen, for there is not to be found in the whole of it even the semblance of an immodest word or a thought that is other than Catholic."

"To write in any other way," said Don Quixote, "would not be to write truth but falsehood, and historians who have recourse to falsehood ought to be burned, like those who coin false money. I know not what could have led the author to have recourse to novels and irrelevant stories, when he had so much to write about in mine; no doubt he must have gone by the proverb 'with straw or hay, etc.,'[11] for by merely setting forth my thoughts, my sighs, my tears, my lofty purposes, my enterprises, he might have made a volume as large or larger than all the works of El Tostado[12] would make up. In fact, the conclusion I arrive at, señor bachelor, is, that to write histories, or books of any kind, there is need of great judgment and a mature understanding. To give expression to humor, and write in a strain of graceful pleasantry, is the gift of great geniuses. The cleverest character in comedy is the fool, for he who would have people take him for a fool must not be one. History is in a measure a sacred thing, for it should be true, and where the truth is, there God is. But notwithstanding this, there are some who write and toss off books as if they were fritters."

"No book is so bad that it is without any good," said the bachelor.

"No doubt of that," replied Don Quixote; "but it often happens that those who have acquired and attained a well-deserved reputation by their writings lose it entirely or damage it in some degree when they have them published."[13]

[10] *Gothic letters:* large capital letters appropriate for a monument.

[11] *with straw or hay, etc.:* "with straw or hay, my hunger at bay" ("Anything will do.").

[12] *El Tostado:* Alfonso de Madrigal (ca. 1410–1455), theologian whose complete works took up twenty-four folio volumes in a 1615 edition.

[13] *when they have them published:* Literary works, such as those shared at literary academies, might circulate in manuscript without ever being published. See footnote 9, page 413.

"The reason for that," said Samson, "is that as printed works are examined at leisure, their faults are easily seen; and the greater the fame of the writer, the more closely they are scrutinized. Men famous for their genius, great poets, illustrious historians, are always, or most commonly, envied by those who take a particular delight and pleasure in criticizing the writings of others without having produced any of their own."

"That is no wonder," said Don Quixote; "for there are many theologians who are no good for the pulpit but excellent in detecting the defects or excesses of those who preach."

"All that is true, Señor Don Quixote," said Carrasco; "but I wish such fault-finders were more lenient and less exacting, and did not pay so much attention to the spots on the bright sun of the work they grumble at. For if *aliquando bonus dormitat Homerus,*[14] they should remember how long he remained awake to shed the light of his work with as little shade as possible. Perhaps it may be that what they find fault with may be moles, which sometimes heighten the beauty of the face that bears them; and so I say very great is the risk to which he who publishes a book exposes himself, for of all impossibilities the greatest is to write one that will satisfy and please all readers."

"The book that relates my history must have pleased few," said Don Quixote.

"Quite the contrary," said the bachelor; "for as *stultorum infinitum est numerus,*[15] innumerable are those who have relished your history. But some have brought a charge against the author's memory, considering that he forgot to say who the thief was who stole Sancho's Dapple; for it is nowhere stated but only to be inferred from the text that he was stolen, and a little farther on we see Sancho mounted on the same donkey without any reappearance of it.[16] They say, too, that he forgot to relate what Sancho did with those hundred escudos that he found in the valise in the Sierra Morena, as he never alludes to them again. There are many who would be glad to know what he did with them, or what he spent them on, for it is one of the serious omissions of the work."

"Señor Samson, I am not in the mood now for going into accounts or explanations," said Sancho. "An uneasy stomach has come over me, and unless I doctor it with a couple sips of the good stuff, I'll see no better than Saint Lucy.[17] I have it at home, and my old woman is waiting for me. After dinner I'll come back, and will answer you and all the world every question you may choose to ask—whether it's about the loss of the donkey or how I spent the hundred escudos." And without another word or waiting for a reply, he made off for home.

[14] aliquando bonus dormitat Homerus: "Sometimes even the worthy Homer nods off", that is, errs—adapted from Horace's *Ars Poetica.*

[15] stultorum infinitum est numerus: "There is an infinite number of fools" (Ecclesiastes 1:15 in the Latin Vulgate).

[16] *who the thief was who stole . . . any reappearance of it:* See footnote 12, page 189.

[17] *I'll see no better than Saint Lucy:* In medieval accounts of the martyr Lucia of Syracuse, her Roman executioners gouged out her eyes before putting her to death for her faith.

Don Quixote begged and entreated the bachelor to stay and do penance[18] with him. The bachelor accepted the invitation and remained, and a couple of young pigeons were added to the ordinary fare. They talked chivalry over their meal, while Carrasco humored his host. The banquet came to an end, and they took their afternoon siesta. Then Sancho returned, and their conversation was resumed.

[18] *do penance:* dine.

CHAPTER IV

IN WHICH SANCHO PANZA GIVES A SATISFACTORY REPLY TO THE DOUBTS AND QUESTIONS OF THE BACHELOR SAMSON CARRASCO, TOGETHER WITH OTHER MATTERS WORTH KNOWING AND TELLING

Sancho came back to Don Quixote's house, and returning to the recent subject of conversation, he said, "As to what Señor Samson said, that he would like to know by who, or how, or when my donkey was stolen, I say in reply that the same night we went into the Sierra Morena, fleeing from the Holy Brotherhood after that unlucky adventure of the galley slaves and the other adventure of the corpse that was going to Segovia, my master and I took refuge deep in the woods, and there, my master leaning on his lance, and I seated on my Dapple, battered and weary from our recent fighting, we fell fast asleep—just as if we had been on four feather mattresses. I, in particular, slept so sound, that, whoever he was, he was able to come and prop me up on four stakes, which he put under the four corners of the packsaddle in such a way that he left me mounted on it and took away Dapple from under me without my feeling a thing."

"That is an easy matter," said Don Quixote, "and it is no new occurrence, for the same thing happened to Sacripante at the siege of Albracca. The famous thief, Brunello, by the same contrivance, took his horse from between his legs."[1]

"Day came," continued Sancho, "and I had barely stretched my legs when the stakes gave way and I fell to the ground with a mighty crash. I looked around for the donkey but could not see him. The tears rushed to my eyes and I raised such a lamentation that, if the author of our history has not put it in, he may depend upon it he has left out a good thing. Some days after (I don't know how many) when I was traveling with her ladyship Princess Micomicona, I saw my donkey. Mounted upon him, dressed as a gypsy, was that Ginés de Pasamonte, the great rogue and rascal that my master and I freed from the chain."

"That is not where the mistake is," replied Samson. "It is that before the donkey has turned up, the author speaks of Sancho as being mounted on it."

"I don't know what to say to that," said Sancho, "unless the historian made a mistake, or perhaps it might be a blunder of the printer's."

[1] *the same thing happened to Sacripante . . . between his legs:* In *Orlando Innamorato*, the dwarf Brunello uses a magic ring that makes him invisible and unfastens the saddle of Sacripante's horse, stealing it from beneath the sleeping king.

"No doubt that's it," said Samson. "But what became of the hundred escudos? Did they vanish?"

To which Sancho answered, "I spent them for my own good—and my wife's, and my children's. Those escudos are the reason my wife has been able to bear so patiently all my wanderings on highways and byways in the service of my master Don Quixote. For if after all this time I had come back to the house penniless and without the donkey, I would have had an ugly future to look forward to. If anyone wants to know anything more about me, here I am, ready to answer the king himself in person. Whether I took or didn't, spent or didn't— that's no one's business; for the whacks that were given me in these journeys were to be paid for in money, and even if they were valued at no more than four maravedis apiece, another hundred escudos would not pay me for half of them. Let everyone be honest about his past and not call white black or black white; for each of us is as God made him, and very often worse."

"I will take care," said Carrasco, "to impress upon the author of the history that, if he prints it again, he must not forget what the worthy Sancho has said—if he wishes to raise it a good span higher."

"Is there anything else to correct in the history, señor bachelor?" asked Don Quixote.

"No doubt there is," replied he, "but not anything that will be of the same importance as those I have mentioned."

"By any chance, does the author promise a second part?" asked Don Quixote.

"He does promise one," replied Samson, "but he says he has not found it, nor does he know who has it; and so we cannot say whether it will appear or not. As some say, moreover, that no second part has ever been good,[2] and others that enough has been already written about Don Quixote, it is thought there will be no second part; though some, who are jovial rather than saturnine,[3] say, 'Let us have more Quixotic adventures![4] Let Don Quixote charge and Sancho chatter, and come what may, we will be content.'"

"What does the author mean to do?" asked Don Quixote.

"What?" replied Samson. "Why, as soon as he has found the history, which he is now searching for with extraordinary diligence, he will at once send it to the press, moved more by the profit that may accrue to him from doing so than by any thought of praise."

At this Sancho observed, "The author looks for money and profit, does he? It will be a wonder if he succeeds, for everything will be rush, rush like the tailor on Easter Eve; and works done in a hurry are never finished as perfectly

[2] *no second part has ever been good:* Sequels to popular literary works were common in Golden Age Spain, and not only of chivalric romances. There were also continuations of pastoral romances and picaresque novels—often without any involvement by the original author.

[3] *jovial rather than saturnine:* more influenced by the astrological sign of Jupiter (Jove) than Saturn.

[4] *Quixotic adventures:* literally, *quijotadas*, coined word reflecting the novel's popularity.

as they ought to be. Let master Moor, or whatever he is, pay attention to what he's doing, and my master and I will give him enough to write about in the way of adventures and accidents of all sorts, as would make up not only one second part, but a hundred. The good man probably thinks we're fast asleep in the straw here, but let him hold up our feet to be shod and he'll see which foot it is we go lame on. All I say is, that if my master would take my advice, we would be now in the field, redressing outrages and righting wrongs, as is the use and custom of the good knights-errant."

Sancho had hardly uttered these words when the neighing of Rocinante fell upon their ears, which Don Quixote accepted as a happy omen, and he resolved to make another sally in three or four days from that time. Announcing his intention to the bachelor, he asked his advice as to where he ought to commence his expedition. The bachelor replied that in his opinion he ought to go to the kingdom of Aragon, and the city of Zaragoza, where there were to be certain solemn jousts at the festival of Saint George,[5] at which he might win renown above all the knights of Aragon, which would be winning it above all the knights of the world. He commended his very praiseworthy and gallant resolution, but admonished him to proceed with greater caution in encountering dangers, because his life did not belong to him, but to all those who had need of him to protect and aid them in their misfortunes.

"That's just the thing that bothers me, Señor Samson," said Sancho here. "My master will attack a hundred armed men like a hungry boy would half a dozen melons. Body of the world,[6] señor bachelor! There's a time to advance and a time to retreat. It shouldn't always be 'Santiago, and attack, Spain!'[7] What's more, I've heard it said (and I think by my master himself, if I remember rightly) that the center of bravery lies between the extremes of being cowardly and reckless. That being so, I don't want him to flee without having good reason, or to attack when the odds make it better not to. But above all, I warn my master that if he is going to take me with him, it must be on the condition that he is to do all the fighting, and that I'm not to be called on to do anything except what concerns keeping him clean and comfortable. In this area, I'll see that he's taken good care of. But to expect me to draw a sword, even against country bandits with hatchets and hoods, is a waste of a thought.

"I don't set up to be a fighting man, Señor Samson, but only the best and most loyal squire that ever served knight-errant; and if my master Don Quixote, in consideration of my many faithful services, is pleased to give me some island of the many his worship says we may stumble on in these parts, I will take it as a great favor. If he doesn't give it to me, I was born like everyone else, and a man must not live in dependence on anyone except God. What's more, my bread will taste just as good—and maybe even better—without a government than if I were

[5] *the festival of Saint George:* celebrated April 23 in honor of the patron saint of Aragon.

[6] *Body of the world:* mild oath that uses a euphemism for the name of Christ.

[7] *Santiago, and attack, Spain:* Christian battle cry during the Reconquista, invoking Saint James (Santiago), the patron saint of Spain.

a governor. Anyway, how do I know that the devil hasn't prepared some stumbling block for me with these governments, to make me lose my footing and fall and knock my teeth out? Sancho I was born, and Sancho I mean to die. But for all that, if Heaven made me a fair offer of an island or something else of the kind, without much trouble and without much risk, I'm not such a fool as to refuse it. For they say, too, 'When you're offered a heifer, run with a halter' and 'When good luck comes knocking, invite it in to stay.'"

"Brother Sancho," said Carrasco, "you have spoken like a professor. But for all that, put your trust in God and in Señor Don Quixote, for he will give you a kingdom, not merely an island."

"It's all the same to me," replied Sancho; "though I can tell you, Señor Carrasco, that my master would not be throwing the kingdom he might give me into a sack with holes; for I have felt my own pulse, and I judge myself sound enough to rule kingdoms and govern islands. More than once, I've told my master as much."

"Take care, Sancho," said Samson; "honors change manners, and perhaps when you find yourself a governor you won't even recognize the mother that bore you."

"That may hold for those born in the gutter," said Sancho, "but not for those like me who have the fat of an Old Christian four fingers thick on their souls. Take a good look at me and you'll see if I would ever be ungrateful."

"May God grant it," said Don Quixote. "We shall see when the government comes. Indeed, I seem to see it already."

He then begged the bachelor, if he were a poet, to do him the favor of composing some verses for him conveying the farewell he meant to take of his lady Dulcinea del Toboso, and to see that a letter of her name was placed at the beginning of each line, so that at the end of the verses, "Dulcinea del Toboso" might be read by putting together the first letters. The bachelor replied that although he was not one of the famous poets of Spain (there being, it was said, only three and a half), he would not fail to compose the requested verses; though he saw a great difficulty in the task, as the letters which made up the name were seventeen; so, if he made four stanzas of four verses each, there would be a letter over, and if he made them of five, what they called *décimas* or *redondillas*, there were three letters short. Nevertheless, he would try to drop a letter as well as he could, so that the name "Dulcinea del Toboso" might fit into four ballad stanzas.

"It must be, by some means or other," said Don Quixote, "for unless the name stands there plain and manifest, no woman would believe the verses were made for her."

They agreed upon this, and that the departure should take place in three days from that time. Don Quixote charged the bachelor to keep it a secret, especially from the priest and Master Nicholas, and from his niece and the housekeeper, lest they should hinder his praiseworthy and valiant design. Carrasco gave his word and then took his leave, charging Don Quixote to inform him of his good or evil fortunes whenever he had an opportunity. And thus they bade each other farewell, and Sancho went away to make the necessary preparations for their expedition.

CHAPTER V

OF THE SHARP-WITTED AND ENTERTAINING CONVERSATION THAT PASSED BETWEEN SANCHO PANZA AND HIS WIFE TERESA PANZA, AND OTHER MATTERS WORTHY OF BEING DULY RECORDED

The translator of this history, when he came to write this fifth chapter, noted that he considered it apocryphal, because in it Sancho Panza speaks in a style unlike that which might have been expected from his limited intelligence, and says things so subtle that he does not think it possible he could have conceived them; however, desirous of doing what his task imposed upon him, he was unwilling to leave it untranslated, and therefore he went on to say:

Sancho came home in such high spirits that his wife could recognize his giddiness a bowshot off—so much so that it made her ask him, "What have you brought, friend Sancho, that makes you so happy?"

To which he replied, "Wife of mine, if it were God's will, I would be very glad not to be as happy as I look."

"I don't understand you, husband," said she, "and I don't know what you mean by saying you would be glad, if it were God's will, not to be happy; for fool as I am, I don't know how someone can find pleasure in not having it."

"Listen to me, Teresa," replied Sancho, "I am happy because I've made up my mind to go back in the service of my master Don Quixote, who means to go out a third time seeking adventures. I am going with him again because circumstances require it, and also because I'm encouraged by the hope that I may find another hundred escudos like those we have spent, though it makes me sad to have to leave you and the children. If God would be pleased to let me have my daily bread in the comfort of my home, without taking me out into the byways and crossroads—and he could do it with no trouble just by willing it—it is clear my happiness would be more solid and lasting, for the happiness I have is mingled with sorrow at leaving you; so that I was right in saying I would be glad, if it were God's will, not to be happy."

"Look here, Sancho," said Teresa; "ever since you latched on to a knight-errant you talk in such a roundabout way that there's no understanding you."

"It is enough that God understands me, wife," replied Sancho, "for he is the understander of all things. There we'll leave the matter. But mind, sister, you must look to Dapple carefully for the next three days, so that he may be fit to take arms: double his feed, and see to the packsaddle and other harness, for it's not a wedding we're headed to, but to go around the world and tussle with giants and dragons and monsters, and hear hissings and roarings and bellowings and howlings. And even all this would be a bed of roses if we didn't have to face Yanguesans and enchanted Moors."

"I know well enough, husband," said Teresa, "that squires-errant don't eat their bread for nothing, and so I will be always praying to our Lord to deliver you speedily from such a hard fortune."

"I can tell you, wife of mine," said Sancho, "if I did not expect to see myself governor of an island before long, I would drop dead on the spot."

"Don't do that, husband of mine," said Teresa. "'Let the hen live, though it be with her pip.'[1] Live, and let the devil take all the governments in the world. You came out of your mother's womb without a government, you have lived until now without a government, and when it is God's will you will go (or, rather, be carried) to your grave without a government. How many there are in the world who live without a government, and continue to live all the same, and are counted as people. 'The best sauce in the world is hunger,' and as the poor are never without that, they always eat with relish. But mind, Sancho, if by good luck you should find yourself with some government, don't forget me and your children. Remember that Sanchico is now fully fifteen, and it is right he should go to school, if his uncle the abbot has a mind to have him trained for the Church. Consider, too, that your daughter Mari Sancha will not die of grief if we marry her; for I have my suspicions that she is as eager to get a husband as you to get a government; and, after all, 'a daughter looks better poorly married than well whored.'"

"By my faith," replied Sancho, "if God brings me to get any sort of a government, I intend, my good woman, to make such a high match for Mari Sancha that there will be no approaching her without calling her 'my lady.'"

"Better not to, Sancho," returned Teresa. "Marry her to her equal, that's the safest plan; for if you take her out of her clogs and put her in high-heeled shoes, out of her gray flannel petticoat into silken gowns, out of the plain 'Marica' and 'you'[2] into 'Doña So-and-so' and 'my lady,' the girl won't know where she is, and at every turn she will fall into a thousand blunders that will show the thread of her coarse homespun."

"Hush, silly woman," said Sancho. "Give her two or three years of practice, and dignity and decorum will fit her like a glove. If not, what does it matter? Let her be 'my lady,' and never mind what happens."

"Keep to your own station, Sancho," replied Teresa. "Don't try to raise yourself higher. Remember the proverb that says, 'Wipe the nose of your neighbor's son, then invite him in to stay.'[3] A fine thing it would be, indeed, to marry our Maria to some great count or grand gentleman, who, when he felt like it, would abuse her and call her a peasant and clodhopper's daughter and spinning

[1] *pip:* swelling in the throat or crop of a hen.

[2] *you: tú*, the informal form of the second-person singular.

[3] *Wipe the nose of your neighbor's son, then invite him in to stay*: "When the boy next door grows up, marry him off to your daughter."

wench. Not in my lifetime, husband! I haven't brought up my daughter to be treated like that. You bring home the money, Sancho, and leave marrying her to me. There is Lope Tocho, our friend Juan Tocho's son—a stout, sturdy young fellow—and I can see he doesn't look sour at the girl. With him, one of our own sort, she will be well married, and we'll always have her under our eyes and be all one family—parents and children, grandchildren and sons-in-law—and the peace and blessing of God will dwell among us. So don't you go marrying her in those courts and grand palaces where they won't know what to make of her, or she what to make of herself."

"Why, you beast of a Barabbas' wife!"[4] said Sancho. "What do you mean by trying, without rhyme or reason, to keep me from marrying my daughter to someone who will give me grandchildren that will be called 'your lordship'? Look here, Teresa, I have always heard my elders say that the one that doesn't know how to take advantage of luck when it comes to him has no right to complain if it passes him by. Now that luck is knocking at our door, it won't do to shut it out. When we have a wind at our backs, we should let it carry us along."

(It is this sort of talk, and what Sancho says below, that made the translator of the history say he considered this chapter apocryphal.)

"Don't you see, you brute," continued Sancho, "that it will be good for me to fall into some profitable government so we'll be lifted out of the mire and so I can marry Mari Sancha to whom I like. Picture yourself called 'Doña Teresa Panza,' and sitting in church on a fine carpet and cushions and draperies, in spite and in the face of all the noble ladies of the town. And you would stay as you are, growing neither greater nor less, like a figure in a tapestry. Let us say no more about it, for Sanchica shall be a countess, say what you will."

"Are you sure of what you're saying, husband?" replied Teresa. "Even so, I'm afraid this rank of countess for my daughter will be her ruin. You do as you like, make a duchess or a princess of her, but I can tell you it will not be with my will and consent. Brother, I have always been a lover of equality, and I can't bear to see people putting on airs without reason. They called me Teresa at my baptism, a plain, simple name, without any additions or tags or fringes of Dons or Doñas. Cascajo was my father's name, and as I am your wife, I am called Teresa Panza, though by right I ought to be called Teresa Cascajo. But 'kings go where laws wish,'[5] and I am content with this name without having the 'Don' put on top of it to make it so heavy that I can't carry it. I don't want to make people talk about me when they see me go dressed like a countess or governor's wife; for they will say at once, 'See what airs the hussy gives herself! Only yesterday she was spinning flax and would go to Mass with the tail of her skirt over her head instead of a mantle,[6] and there she goes today in a hooped gown with her broaches and

[4] *Barabbas' wife:* Barabbas was the insurrectionist whom the crowds demanded that Pilate pardon instead of Jesus (Matthew 27:21; Acts 3:14).

[5] *kings go where laws wish:* Teresa mixes up the saying "laws go where kings wish".

[6] *with the tail of her skirt over her head instead of a mantle:* Women were obliged to enter church with their heads covered. Those too poor to afford a mantle (*mantilla*) would use the edge of their outer skirt.

airs, as if we didn't know her!' If God keeps me in my seven senses,[7] or five, or whatever number I have, I am not going to bring myself to such a state. You go, brother, and be a government or an islander and swagger as much as you like. But by the soul of my mother, neither my daughter nor I are going to stir a step from our village. 'A respectable woman has a broken leg and keeps at home' and 'for a virtuous young lady, a busy day is as good as a holiday.' Be off to seek your fortune with your Don Quixote, and leave us to our misfortunes, for God will mend them as we deserve it. And by the way, I don't know who attached the 'Don' to his name, which neither his father nor grandfather ever had."

"I declare you have a devil of some sort in your body!" said Sancho. "God help you, what a lot of things you've strung together, one after the other, without head or tail! What have Cascajo and the broaches and the proverbs and the airs to do with what I'm saying? Look here, fool and simpleton (for so I may call you when you don't understand my words and run away from good fortune), if I had said that my daughter was to throw herself down from a tower, or go roaming the world, as the Infanta Doña Urraca wanted to do,[8] you would be right in disagreeing with my intentions. But if in an instant, in less than the twinkling of an eye, I put the 'Don' and 'my lady' on her back, and take her out of the stubble and place her under a canopy, on a dais, and on a couch, with more velvet cushions than all the Almohadas of Morocco[9] ever had in their family, why won't you consent and fall in line with my wishes?"

"Do you know why, husband?" replied Teresa. "Because of the proverb that says 'The one who covers you, discovers you.' People only throw a hasty glance at a poor man. On a rich man, they fix their eyes; and if that rich man was poor once upon a time, then you have the sneering and murmuring and spite of backbiters. And in the streets here they swarm as thick as bees."

"Look here, Teresa," said Sancho, "and listen to what I'm about to say to you. Maybe you have never heard this in all your life. I didn't come up with the idea myself, because what I'm going to tell you are the opinions of his reverence the preacher who preached in this town last Lent. He said (if I remember rightly) that those things that our eyes see in the present linger in our memory much longer and more forcibly than things past."[10]

[7] *seven senses:* Memory and common sense were often added to the traditional five.

[8] *as the Infanta Doña Urraca wanted to do:* According to a ballad, when the daughter of King Fernando I of Castile learned that only her brothers were to receive an inheritance, she threatened to leave home and give up her body at whim "to Moors for money and Christians for free".

[9] *Almohadas of Morocco:* Sancho means Almohades, the Almohad Caliphate, a Berber Muslim dynasty from North Africa that ruled Moorish Spain during the twelfth and thirteenth centuries. *Almohadas* are cushions or pillows, one of Arabic's many contributions to Spanish.

[10] *those things that our eyes see in the present . . . more forcibly than things past:* According to the prevailing theory, a memory was formed when patterns of light entering through the eyes left a physical impression on the soul, like a seal on wax. As time passed, the impression began to break down or was overwritten.

(On account of the observations that Sancho makes here, the translator says he regards this chapter as apocryphal, inasmuch as they are beyond Sancho's capacity.)

"It follows, then," he continued, "that when we see any person well dressed and cutting a fine figure with rich garments and a retinue of servants, it's as if we are impelled to respect him. Even if our memory at the same moment recalls to us some lowly condition we have seen him in—whether it was poverty or low birth—it's now a thing of the past, without any existence. The only thing that has any existence is what we see before us. And if this person who fortune has raised from his original lowly state—these were the very words the reverend father used—to his present height of prosperity, is well-bred, generous, courteous to all, without seeking to vie with those whose nobility is of ancient date, depend upon it, Teresa, no one will remember what he was, and everyone will respect what he is—except, of course, the envious, from whom no fair fortune is safe."

"I do not understand you, husband," replied Teresa. "Do as you like, and don't break my head with any more speechifying and rhetoric. If you have revolved to do what you say—"

"*Resolved*, you should say, woman," said Sancho, "not *revolved*."

"Don't you go nitpicking me, husband," said Teresa; "I speak as God pleases and don't talk in pretty pictures. I say if you're bent on having a government, take your son Sancho with you, and start teaching him how to hold one; for sons ought to inherit and learn the trades of their fathers."

"As soon as I have the government," said Sancho, "I will send for him right away, and I will send you money—which I'll have plenty of—for there is never any shortage of people to lend to governors when they are in need. All I ask is that you dress him so as to hide what he is and make him look like what he is to be."

"You send the money," said Teresa, "and I'll dress him up for you as fine as you please."

"Then we are agreed that our daughter is to be a countess," said Sancho.

"The day I see her a countess," replied Teresa, "it will be the same to me as if I was burying her. But once more I say, do as you please, for we women are born to this burden of being obedient to our husbands, even if they are fools." With this she began to weep in earnest, as if she already saw Sanchica dead and buried.

Sancho consoled her by saying that though he was to make her a countess, he would put it off as long as possible.

Here their conversation came to an end, and Sancho went back to see Don Quixote and make arrangements for their departure.

CHAPTER VI

OF WHAT TOOK PLACE BETWEEN DON QUIXOTE AND HIS NIECE AND HOUSEKEEPER—ONE OF THE MOST IMPORTANT CHAPTERS IN THE WHOLE HISTORY

While Sancho Panza and his wife, Teresa Cascajo, held the above implausible conversation, Don Quixote's niece and housekeeper were not idle, for by a thousand signs they began to guess that their uncle and master meant to give them the slip the third time and once more return to what was for them his ill-errant chivalry. They labored by all the means in their power to divert him from his awful design; but it was all preaching in the desert and hammering cold iron.

During this time, among many other words that passed between them, the housekeeper said, "In truth, master, if you do not keep still and stay quiet at home, and give over roaming mountains and valleys like a troubled spirit, looking for what they say are called adventures, but what I call misfortunes, I shall have to make complaint to God and the king with loud supplication to send some remedy."

To which Don Quixote replied, "What answer God will give to your complaints, housekeeper, I know not, nor what his Majesty will answer either; I only know that if I were king I should decline to answer the numberless silly petitions they present every day; for one of the greatest among the many troubles kings have is being obliged to listen to all and answer all, and therefore I should be sorry that any affairs of mine should worry him."

Whereupon the housekeeper said, "Tell us, señor, at his Majesty's court are there no knights?"

"There are," replied Don Quixote, "and plenty of them; and it is right there should be, to set off the dignity of the prince, and for the greater glory of the king's majesty."

"Then might not your worship," said she, "be one of those that, without stirring a step, serve their king and lord in his court?"

"You must understand, my friend," said Don Quixote, "all knights cannot be courtiers, nor can all courtiers be knights-errant, nor need they be. There must be all sorts in the world; and though we may be all knights, there is a great difference between one and another. The courtiers, without leaving their chambers or the threshold of the court, range the world over by looking at a map, without its costing them a cent, and without suffering heat or cold, hunger or thirst; but we, the true knights-errant, measure the whole earth with our own feet, exposed to the sun, to the cold, to the air, to the inclemencies of heaven, by day and night, on foot and on horseback. Nor do we only know enemies in pictures, but in their own real shapes. At all risks and on all occasions we attack them, without any regard to childish points or rules of single combat, whether one has or has not a shorter lance or sword, whether one carries relics or any secret weapon about him, whether or not the sun is to be divided and portioned out,[1] and other niceties of the sort that are observed in set combats of man to man, that you know nothing about, but I do. You must know besides, that the true knight-errant, though he may see ten giants that not only touch the clouds with their heads but pierce them, and that walk about, each of them, on two tall towers by way of legs, and whose arms are like the masts of mighty ships, and each eye like a great mill wheel, and glowing brighter than a glass furnace, must not on any account be dismayed by them. On the contrary, he must attack and fall upon them with a gallant bearing and a fearless heart, and, if possible, vanquish and destroy them, even though they have for armor the shells of a certain fish that they say are harder than diamonds, and in place of swords wield trenchant blades of Damascus steel or clubs studded with spikes also of steel, such as I have more than once seen. All this I say, housekeeper, that you may see the difference there is between the one sort of knight and the other. It would be well if there were no prince who did not set a higher value on this second, or more properly speaking first, kind of knight-errant; for as we read in their histories, there have been some among them who have been the salvation, not merely of one kingdom, but of many."

"Ah, señor!" here exclaimed the niece. "Don't you realize that all this you are saying about knights-errant is fable and fiction? Their histories, if indeed they were not burned, would deserve, each of them, to have a sambenito[2] put on it, or some mark by which it might be known as infamous and a corrupter of good manners."

"By the God that gives me life," said Don Quixote, "if you were not my born niece, the daughter of my own sister, I would inflict such a punishment upon you for the blasphemy you have uttered that it would be heard all the world round. Is it truly possible that a girl that hardly knows how to handle a dozen lace bobbins dares to wag her tongue and criticize the histories of knights-errant? What would Señor Amadís say if he heard of such a thing? He, however, no doubt would forgive you, for he was the most humble-minded and courteous knight of his time, and moreover a great protector of damsels. But some there are that might have heard you, and it would not have been well for you in that case. For they are not all courteous or mannerly; some are ill-conditioned scoundrels. Nor is it everyone that calls himself a gentleman that is so in all respects. Some are gold, others

[1] *the sun is to be divided and portioned out:* to position the combatants so that neither is facing the sun.

[2] *sambenito:* penitential garment worn by Inquisition heretics. It was draped over the shoulders like a scapular and bore symbols or inscriptions indicating the wearer's heresy.

pyrite; all look like gentlemen, but not all can stand the touchstone of truth.[3] There are men of low rank who strain themselves to bursting to pass for gentlemen, and high gentlemen who, one would fancy, were dying to pass for men of low rank. The former raise themselves by their ambition or by their virtues; the latter debase themselves by their idleness or vices. One has need of experience and discernment to distinguish these two kinds of gentlemen, so much alike in name and so different in conduct."

"God bless me!" said the niece. "That you should know so much, uncle—enough, if need be, to get up into a pulpit and go preach in the streets—and yet that you should fall into a delusion so great and a folly so manifest as to try to make yourself out vigorous when you are old, strong when you are sickly, able to put straight what is crooked when you yourself are bent by age, and, above all, a knight when you are not one; for though hidalgos may be so, poor men are nothing of the kind!"[4]

"There is a great deal of truth in what you say, niece," returned Don Quixote. "I could tell you things about noble pedigrees that would astonish you; but, not to mix up things human and divine, I refrain. Heed this brief word, my dears, about nobility. All the lineages in the world can be reduced to four kinds, which are these: those that had humble beginnings and went on spreading and extending themselves until they attained surpassing greatness; those that had great beginnings and maintained them, and still maintain and uphold the greatness of their origin; those, again, that from a great beginning have ended in a point like a pyramid, having reduced and lessened their original greatness till it has come to nought, like the point of a pyramid, which, relative to its base or foundation, is nothing; and then there are those—and it is they that are the most numerous—that have had neither an illustrious beginning nor a remarkable mid-course, and so will have an end without a name, like an ordinary plebeian line.

"Of the first—those that had a humble origin and rose to the greatness they still preserve—the Ottoman house may serve as an example, which from a humble and lowly shepherd, its founder, has reached the height at which we now see it.[5] For examples of the second sort of lineage, that began with greatness and maintains it still without adding to it, there are the many princes who have inherited the dignity and maintain themselves in their inheritance without increasing or diminishing it, keeping peacefully within the limits of their states. Of those that began great and ended in a point, there are thousands of examples, for all the Pharaohs and Ptolemies of Egypt,[6] the Cæsars of Rome, and the whole

[3] *touchstone of truth:* Jewelers determined the purity of gold by rubbing it on a touchstone, a dark stone related to flint, and examining the color and quality of the streak it left.

[4] *knight . . . nothing of the kind:* A hidalgo could be knighted (made a *caballero*), but he needed sufficient wealth to maintain the lifestyle expected of a noble.

[5] *the Ottoman house . . . now see it:* The Ottoman dynasty was traditionally said to have been founded by the shepherd Osman Ghazi in the thirteenth century.

[6] *Ptolemies of Egypt:* The Ptolemaic dynasty was founded by Ptolemy, one of Alexander the Great's generals and bodyguards, following Alexander's death in 323 B.C. It ruled Egypt until 30 B.C., when the territory was annexed by the Roman Empire.

throng (if I may apply such a word to them) of countless princes, monarchs, lords, Medes, Assyrians, Persians, Greeks, and barbarians—all these lineages and lordships have ended in a point and come to nothing, they themselves as well as their founders. It would be impossible now to find one of their descendants, and even should we find one, it would be in some lowly and humble condition. Of plebeian lineages I have nothing to say, save that they merely serve to swell the number of those that live, without any eminence to entitle them to any fame or praise beyond this.

"From all I have said I would have you gather, my poor innocents, that great is the confusion among lineages, and that only those are seen to be great and illustrious that show themselves so by the virtue, wealth, and generosity of their possessors. I have said virtue, wealth, and generosity, because a great man who is vicious will be a great example of vice, and a rich man who is not generous will be merely a miserly beggar; for the possessor of wealth is not made happy by possessing it, but by spending it, and not by spending as he pleases, but by knowing how to spend it well. The poor gentleman has no way of showing that he is a gentleman but by virtue, by being affable, well-bred, courteous, gentle-mannered, and kindly—not haughty, arrogant, or censorious—but above all by being charitable. By two maravedis given with a cheerful heart to the poor, he will show himself as generous as he who distributes alms with bell-ringing, and no one that perceives him to be endowed with the virtues I have named, even though he know him not, will fail to recognize and set him down as one of good blood. It would be strange were it not so. Praise has ever been the reward of virtue, and those who are virtuous cannot fail to receive commendation.

"There are two roads, my daughters, by which men may reach wealth and honors: one is that of letters, the other that of arms. I have more of arms than of letters in my composition, and, judging by my inclination to arms, was born under the influence of the planet Mars.[7] I am, therefore, in a measure constrained to follow that road, and by it I must travel in spite of all the world. It will be labor in vain for you to urge me to resist what Heaven wills, fate ordains, reason requires, and, above all, my own inclination favors. Knowing as I do the countless toils that are the accompaniments of knight-errantry, I know, too, the infinite blessings that are attained by it. I know that the path of virtue is very narrow, and the road of vice broad and spacious.[8] I know their ends and goals are different, for the broad and easy road of vice ends in death, and the narrow and toilsome one of virtue in life, and not transitory life, but in that which has no end. I know, as our great Castilian poet says, that

[7] *born under the influence of the planet* Mars: Alonso Quixano was born when the planet Mars, identified with the Roman god of war, was ascendant. The belief that heavenly bodies had power over human inclinations was still widespread, though among intellectuals it was increasingly contested.

[8] *the path of virtue is very narrow, and the road of vice broad and spacious:* See Matthew 7:13–14: "The gate is wide and the way is easy, that leads to destruction.... The gate is narrow and the way is hard, that leads to life."

It is by rugged paths like these they go
That scale the heights of immortality,
Unreached by those that falter here below."[9]

"Woe is me!" exclaimed the niece. "My lord is a poet, too! He knows everything, and he can do everything. I will bet, if he chose to turn mason, he could make a house as easily as a cage."

"I can tell you, niece," replied Don Quixote, "if these chivalrous thoughts did not engage all my faculties, there would be nothing that I could not do, nor any sort of knickknack that would not come from my hands, particularly cages and toothpicks."

At this moment there came a knocking at the door, and when they asked who was there, Sancho Panza answered that it was he. The instant the housekeeper realized who it was, she ran to hide herself so as not to see him—so greatly did she loathe him. The niece let him in, and his master Don Quixote came forward to receive him with open arms. The pair shut themselves up in his room, where they had another conversation not inferior to the previous one.

[9] *great Castilian poet . . . here below:* from the "First Elegy" of Garcilaso de la Vega (c. 1501–1536), hailed as the Prince of Castilian Poets. Quotations from Garcilaso are frequent in Part II.

CHAPTER VII

OF WHAT PASSED BETWEEN DON QUIXOTE AND HIS SQUIRE, TOGETHER WITH OTHER VERY NOTABLE INCIDENTS

The instant the housekeeper saw Sancho Panza shut himself in with her master, she guessed what they were up to. Suspecting that the result of their conversation would be a resolve to undertake a third sally, she seized her mantle, and in deep anxiety and distress, ran to find the bachelor Samson Carrasco, as she thought that, being a well-spoken man and a new friend of her master's, he might be able to persuade him to give up any such crazy notion.

She found him pacing the patio of his house. Perspiring and in a flutter, she fell at his feet the moment she saw him.

Carrasco, seeing how distressed and overcome she was, said to her, "What is this, mistress housekeeper? What has happened to you? One would think you were about to breathe your last."

"It's nothing, Señor Samson," said she, "only that my master is breaking out. Without a doubt, he's breaking out!"

"And where is he breaking out, señora?" asked Samson. "What part of his body has he burst?"

"He's not breaking out anywhere except at the door of his madness," she replied. "I mean, dear señor bachelor, that he is going to run off again—and this will be the third time—to hunt all over the world for what he calls 'ventures,' though I can't make out why he gives them that name. The first time he was brought back to us slung across the back of a donkey and bruised all over. The second time he came in an oxcart, shut up in a cage and convinced that he was enchanted. The poor creature was in such a state that the mother that bore him would not have known him: lean, yellow, with his eyes sunk deep in the back of his skull. To bring him round again, ever so little, cost me more than six hundred eggs. God knows, so does everyone else. My hens, too—they won't let me tell a lie."

"That I can well believe," replied the bachelor, "for they are so good, so fat, and so well-bred that they would not say one thing for another, though they were to burst for it. In short then, mistress housekeeper, that is all, and there is nothing except the matter of what is feared Don Quixote may do?"

"No, señor," said she.

"Well then," returned the bachelor, "don't be uneasy, but go home in peace. Get me ready something hot for breakfast, and while you are on the way say the prayer of Saint Apollonia,[1] that is, if you know it. I will come presently, and what wonders you will see"

"Woe is me!" cried the housekeeper. "Is it the prayer of Saint Apollonia you would have me say? That would do if my master had a toothache; but the infirmity he has is in his brain."

"I know what I am saying, mistress housekeeper. There is no need to argue with me, for you know I am a bachelor of Salamanca, and one can't be more of a bachelor than that," replied Carrasco. With this the housekeeper went home, and the bachelor went to look for the priest and arrange with him what will be told in its proper place.

While Don Quixote and Sancho were shut up together, they had a discussion that the history records with the utmost truth and exactitude. Sancho said to his master, "Señor, I have adduced my wife to let me go with your worship wherever you choose to take me."

"*Induced*, you should say, Sancho," said Don Quixote, "not *adduced*."

"Once or twice, as well as I remember," replied Sancho, "I have asked your worship not to mend my words, as long as you understand what I mean by them; and if you don't understand them to say 'Sancho, or devil, I don't understand you.' If I don't make my meaning plain, then you may correct me, for I am so focile—"

"I don't understand you, Sancho," said Don Quixote at once. "I know not what 'I am so focile' means."

"'So focile' means 'I'm so much like that,'" replied Sancho.

"I understand you still less now," said Don Quixote.

"Well, if you can't understand me," said Sancho, "I don't know how to put it. I know nothing else, God help me."

"Ah, I think I'm catching on," said Don Quixote. "You mean to say you are so *docile*, tractable, and gentle that you will respect what I say to you, and submit to what I teach you."

"I'd bet," said Sancho, "that from the very beginning you understood me and knew what I meant, but you wanted to fluster me so that you could hear me make a couple hundred more blunders."

"Maybe so," replied Don Quixote. "But to come to the point, what does Teresa say?"

"Teresa says," replied Sancho, "that I should keep a close eye on your worship and 'let documents speak and mouths be still,' for 'he who cuts the cards shouldn't shuffle,' since 'one *take* is better than two *I'll give you*'s.' To which I say, 'rare is the advice of a woman, and foolish the man who ignores it.'"

"And so say I," said Don Quixote. "Continue, Sancho my friend. Go on—you're speaking pearls today."

"The fact is," continued Sancho, "that, as your worship knows better than I do, all of us must face death. 'Today we are, and tomorrow we are not,' and 'the lamb goes to slaughter as soon as the sheep,' and nobody can promise himself

[1] *the prayer of Saint Apollonia:* Saint Apollonia, as the housekeeper correctly points out below, is the patron saint of those suffering from toothaches. Samson's joke may be that the prayer should be said for him, since his teeth are aching for breakfast.

more hours of life in this world than God may be pleased to give him. For 'Death is deaf,' and 'when it comes knocking at our life's door, it is always urgent,' and neither prayers, nor struggles, nor scepters, nor miters, can keep it back—as is commonly said and reported, and as they tell us from the pulpits every day."

"All that is very true," said Don Quixote; "but I cannot make out what you're driving at."

"What I'm driving at," said Sancho, "is that your worship must settle on a fixed salary for me, to be paid monthly while I am in your service, and that the wages should be paid to me out of your estate. I do not want to serve in return for rewards,[2] which come late, come up short, or don't come at all. May God grant me my fair share. To be blunt, I would like to know what my fair share is to be, whether much or little; for 'the hen sits on one egg,' and 'many littles make a much,' and 'so long as one gains, there is nothing lost.' To be sure, if it happens that your worship should give me that island you've promised me—which I neither believe nor expect—I am not so ungrateful or grasping that I wouldn't be willing to have the revenue of the island valued and taken from my wages in due promotion."

"Sancho, my friend," replied Don Quixote, "sometimes proportion may be as good as promotion."

"I see," said Sancho. "I'll bet I should have said *proportion*, and not *promotion*. But it is no matter, since your worship has understood me."

"And so well understood," returned Don Quixote, "that I have seen into the depths of your thoughts and know the mark you are aiming at with the countless arrows of your proverbs. Look here, Sancho, I would readily fix your wages if I had ever found any instance in the histories of the knights-errant to show or indicate, by the slightest hint, what their squires used to get monthly or yearly; but I have read all or the best part of their histories, and I cannot remember reading of any knight-errant having assigned fixed wages to his squire. I only know that they all served for rewards, and that when they least expected it, if good luck attended their masters, they found themselves recompensed with an island or something equivalent to it, or at the least they were left with a title and lordship. If with these hopes and additional inducements you, Sancho, are pleased to return to my service, well and good; but to suppose that I am going to upend from the foundations the ancient usage of knight-errantry is futile. And so, my Sancho, get you back to your house and explain my intentions to your Teresa. If she likes and you like to serve for rewards under me, *bene quidem*;[3] if not, we remain friends. For 'if the dovecote does not lack food, it will not lack doves.' Bear in mind, my son, that 'a good hope is better than a bad holding, and a good claim better than a bad return.' I speak in this way, Sancho, to show you that I can shower down proverbs just as well as you. In short, I mean to say, and I do say, that if you do not care to work for rewards and run the same chance that I run, God be with you and make you a saint; for I shall find plenty of squires more obedient and solicitous, and not so wearisome and talkative as you are."

[2] *rewards*: See 3-40, n. 60 (I.20).

[3] bene quidem: Latin, "well agreed".

When Sancho heard his master's firm resolve, a cloud darkened the sky above him and the wings of his heart drooped, for he had been convinced that his master would not set off without him for all the wealth in the world. As he stood there dumbfounded and melancholy, Samson Carrasco came in with the housekeeper and niece, who were anxious to hear by what arguments he was about to dissuade their master from going to seek adventures. The arch wag Samson came forward, and embracing him as he had done before, said with a loud voice, "O flower of knight-errantry! O shining light of arms! O honor and mirror of the Spanish nation! May God Almighty in his infinite power grant that any person or persons who would impede or hinder your third sally find no way out of the labyrinth of their schemes nor ever accomplish what they most desire!"

And then, turning to the housekeeper, he said, "Mistress housekeeper may just as well leave off saying the prayer of Saint Apollonia, for I know it is the inexorable will of the heavenly spheres that Señor Don Quixote shall proceed to put into execution his new and lofty designs. I should lay a heavy burden on my conscience if I did not call upon this knight to hold back no more the might of his strong arm and the virtue of his valiant spirit too long kept in check, for by his inactivity he is defrauding the world of the redress of wrongs, of the protection of orphans, of the honor of virgins, of the aid of widows, and of the support of wives—and other matters of this kind appertaining, belonging, proper, and peculiar to the order of knight-errantry. On, then, my lord Don Quixote, beautiful and brave, let your worship and highness set out today rather than tomorrow. If anything is required for the execution of your purpose, here am I ready in person and purse to supply it; and were there a need to attend your magnificence as squire, I should esteem it the happiest good fortune."

At this, Don Quixote, turning to Sancho, said, "Did I not tell you, Sancho, there would be squires enough and to spare for me? See now who offers to become one, no less than the illustrious bachelor Samson Carrasco—the perpetual joy and delight of the courts of the Salamancan schools, sound in body, discreet, patient under heat or cold, hunger or thirst, with all the qualifications requisite to make a knight-errant's squire. But Heaven forbid that to gratify my own inclination I should shake or shatter this pillar of letters and vessel of the sciences and cut down this towering palm of the fair and liberal arts. Let this new Samson remain in his own country, and, bringing honor to it, honor at the same time the gray heads of his venerable parents; for I will be content with any squire that comes to hand, as Sancho does not deign to accompany me."

"I do deign!" cried Sancho, deeply moved and with tears in his eyes. "Master of mine, let it not be said of me, 'the bread eaten and the company dispersed.' For I come of no ungrateful stock, as all the world knows, but particularly my own village, in which my Panza ancestors made their home. Furthermore, I know and have learned, by many good words and deeds, your worship's desire to show me favor. If I've been haggling about my wages, it was only to please my wife; for when she gets it in her head to press a point, no hammer can drive in the hoops of a barrel like she drives a fellow to do what she wants. But mind you, 'a man must be a man, and a woman a woman'; and as it's undeniable that I'm a man everywhere, I ought to be one in my own house too, come what may. So there's nothing more to do but for your worship to make your will with its codicil[4] in such a way that it can't be provoked, and let us set out at once, to save Señor Samson's soul from suffering, as he says his conscience obliges him to persuade your worship to sally out upon the world a third time. And so I offer again to serve your worship faithfully and loyally, as well and better than all the squires that served knights-errant in times past or present."

The bachelor was filled with amazement when he heard Sancho's phraseology and manner of speaking, for though he had read the First Part of Don Quixote's history he never thought that Sancho could be so comical as he was there described. But now, hearing him talk of a "will and codicil that could not be *provoked*," instead of "will and codicil that could not be *revoked*," he believed all he had read of him, and set him down as one of the greatest simpletons of modern times; and he said to himself that two such lunatics as master and man the world had never seen.

At last Don Quixote and Sancho embraced each another and made friends, and by the advice and with the approval of the great Carrasco, who was now their oracle, it was arranged that their departure should take place in three days, by which time they could have everything ready that was needed for the journey and could also look for a closed helmet, which Don Quixote said he must by all means take. Samson offered him one on behalf of a friend whom he knew would not refuse him, though it was dingy with rust and mildew rather than bright and clean like burnished steel.

The curses that the housekeeper and niece heaped on the bachelor were past counting. They tore their hair, they clawed their faces, and in the style of the hired mourners that were once in fashion, they raised a lamentation over the departure of their master and uncle as if it had been his death. Samson's intention in persuading him to sally forth once more was to do what the history relates farther on—all by the advice of the priest and barber, with whom he had previously discussed the subject.

To conclude, then, Don Quixote and Sancho spent the next three days supplying themselves with what they considered necessary; Sancho made peace with his wife, while Don Quixote made peace with his niece and housekeeper. Finally, at nightfall, unseen by anyone except the bachelor, who thought fit to accompany them half a league out of the village, they took to the road for El Toboso. Don Quixote sat astride his good Rocinante and Sancho his old Dapple, the saddlebag furnished with items of the edible sort and the purse with money that Don Quixote gave him for emergencies. Samson embraced Don Quixote and entreated him to keep him apprised of his good or evil fortunes, so that he might rejoice over the former or condole with him over the latter, as the laws of friendship required. Don Quixote promised him he would do so. And so Samson returned to the village, and the other two set out for the great city of El Toboso.

[4] *codicil:* supplement to a will that clarifies, modifies, or revokes provisions in the original document without replacing it entirely.

CHAPTER VIII

WHEREIN IS RELATED WHAT BEFELL DON QUIXOTE ON HIS WAY TO SEE HIS LADY DULCINEA DEL TOBOSO

"Blessed be Allah the all-powerful!" proclaims Hamete Benengeli on beginning this eighth chapter. "Blessed be Allah!" he repeats three times. He pronounces these benedictions (so he tells us) because he has finally set Don Quixote and Sancho on the road, and the readers of his delightful history can be assured that the achievements and antics of Don Quixote and his squire are about to begin. He urges them, moreover, to forget the former chivalric deeds of the ingenious gentleman and to fix their eyes on those that are to come, which now begin on the road to El Toboso, as the others began on the plains of Montiel. Nor is it much to ask when one considers all that he promises. And so he continues in this way:

Don Quixote and Sancho were left alone, and the moment Samson took his departure, Rocinante began to neigh and Dapple to sigh, which, by both knight and squire, was accepted as a good sign and a very happy omen; though, if the truth is to be told, the sighs and brays of Dapple were louder than the neighings of the hack, from which Sancho inferred that his good fortune was to outstrip that of his master, building, perhaps, upon some judicial astrology[1] that he may have known, though the history says nothing about it. All that can be said is that when he stumbled or fell, he was heard to say he wished he had not left home, for by stumbling or falling there was nothing to be got but a damaged shoe or a broken rib. And, fool as he was, he was not far from the truth.

Don Quixote said to him, "Sancho, my friend, night is drawing on upon us as we go, and more darkly than will allow us to reach El Toboso by daylight. There I am resolved to go before I engage in another adventure, and there I shall obtain the blessing and generous permission of the peerless Dulcinea, with which permission I expect and feel assured that I shall conclude and bring to a happy termination every perilous adventure; for nothing in life makes knights-errant more valorous than finding themselves favored by their ladies."

"So I believe," replied Sancho. "But I think it will be difficult for your worship to speak with her (or see her, at any rate) where you will be able to receive her blessing—unless, indeed, she throws it over the wall of the yard where I saw her the

[1] *judicial astrology:* the study of the stars to predict the future, what is known simply as astrology today.

time before, when I took her the letter that told of the ridiculous things your worship was doing in the heart of the Sierra Morena."

"Did you take that for a yard wall, Sancho," said Don Quixote, "where, or beyond which, you saw that never sufficiently extolled grace and beauty? It must have been the gallery, corridor, or portico of some rich and royal palace."

"It might have been all that," returned Sancho, "but to me it looked like a wall, unless my memory fails."

"At all events, let us go there, Sancho," said Don Quixote. "Provided that I see her, it is the same to me whether it be over a wall, or at a window, or through the chink of a door, or the grate of a garden. For any beam of the sun of her beauty that reaches my eyes will give light to my reason and strength to my heart, so that I shall be unmatched and unequaled in wisdom and valor."

"Well, to tell the truth, señor," said Sancho, "when I saw that sun of Lady Dulcinea del Toboso, it was not bright enough to throw out beams at all. It must have been the case that—since her grace was sifting that wheat I told you of—the thick dust she raised came before her face like a cloud and dimmed it."

"What? Do you still persist, Sancho," said Don Quixote, "in saying, thinking, believing, and maintaining that my lady Dulcinea was sifting wheat, an occupation entirely at variance with what is and should be the employment of persons of distinction, who are brought up and reserved for other pursuits that show their rank a bowshot off? You have forgotten, O Sancho, those lines of our poet wherein he paints for us how, in their crystal abodes, those four nymphs employed themselves who rose from their beloved Tagus and seated themselves in a verdant meadow to embroider those cloths which the ingenious poet there describes to us, how they were worked and woven with gold and silk and pearls.[2] Something of this sort must have been the employment of my lady when you saw her, only that the spite which some wicked enchanter seems to have against everything of mine changes all those things that give me pleasure, and turns them into shapes unlike their own. So I fear that in that history of my achievements which they say is now in print, if it turns out that its author was some sage who is an enemy of mine, he will have put one thing for another, mingling a thousand lies with one truth, and amusing himself by relating incidents which have nothing to do with the account of a true history. O envy, root of all countless evils and canker of the virtues! All the vices, Sancho, bring some kind of pleasure with them; but envy brings nothing but irritation, bitterness, and rage."

"So I say too," replied Sancho. "I suspect in that legend or history of us that the bachelor Samson Carrasco told us he saw, my honor goes dragged in the dirt, knocked about, up and down, sweeping the streets, as they say. And yet on the faith of an honest man, I never spoke ill of any enchanter, and I'm not so well off that I could be envied. To be sure, I can be pretty sly, and I have more than a bit of rogue in me. But all that is covered by the great cloak of my simplicity, always natural and never acted. If I had no other good quality than that I have

[2] *those lines of our poet . . . gold and silk and pearls:* Don Quixote again refers to Garcilaso de la Vega, this time to his *Third Eclogue*.

always believed, firmly and truly, in God and all that the holy Roman Catholic Church teaches, and that I am a mortal enemy of the Jews, the historians ought to have mercy on me and treat me well in their writings. But let them say what they like. 'Naked was I born, naked I remain, nothing lost or gained.' I don't give a fig about being put into a book and passed on from hand to hand over the world. Let them say what they like of me."

"That, Sancho," returned Don Quixote, "reminds me of what happened to a famous poet of our own day, who, having written a bitter satire against all the courtesans of note,[3] did not include or name in it a certain lady of whom it was questionable whether she was a courtesan or not. She, seeing she was not in the list of the poet, asked him what he had seen in her that he did not include her along with the others, telling him he must add to his satire and put her in the next edition, or else face the consequences. The poet did as she asked him and left her without a shred of reputation, and she was satisfied by getting fame, though it was infamy. In keeping with this is what they relate of that shepherd who set fire to the famous temple of Diana,[4] by repute one of the seven wonders of the world, and burned it with the sole object of making his name live on for ages to come; and, though it was forbidden to name him either in speech or in writing, lest the object of his ambition should be attained, nevertheless it became known that he was named Herostratus. And something of the same sort happened with the great emperor Charles V and a gentleman in Rome. The emperor was eager to see that famous temple of the Rotunda,[5] called in ancient times the temple of all the gods, but today, more properly, 'of all the saints,' which is the best preserved building of all those of pagan construction in Rome, and the one which best sustains the reputation of mighty works and magnificence of its founders. It is in the form of a half orange, of enormous dimensions and well lighted, though no light penetrates it save that which is admitted by a window, or rather round skylight, at the top. It was from this that the emperor examined the building. A Roman gentleman stood by his side and explained to him the skillful construction and ingenuity of its exquisite construction and unparalleled architecture. When they left the skylight he said to the emperor, 'A thousand times, your Sacred Majesty, the impulse came upon me to seize your Majesty in my arms and fling myself down from that skylight, so as to leave behind me in the world a name that would last forever.' 'I am thankful to you for not carrying such an evil thought into effect,' said the emperor, 'and I shall give you no opportunity in the future of again putting your loyalty to the test. I

[3] *courtesans of note:* literally, "lady courtesans" (*damas courtesanas*), prostitutes who catered to élite men. The satire is probably Vicente Espinel's *Satire Against the Ladies of Seville* (c. 1578).

[4] *the famous temple of Diana:* The temple of Artemis (Diana in Roman mythology) was located in Ephesus. Herostratus set fire to it in 356 B.C., though it was later rebuilt.

[5] *that famous temple of the Rotunda:* the Pantheon, Roman temple whose present construction dates to the second century A.D. It was rededicated as the Basilica of Saint Mary and the Martyrs in 609.

therefore forbid you ever to speak to me or to be where I am; and he followed up these words by bestowing on him a generous gift.'

"My meaning, Sancho, is that the desire of acquiring fame is a very powerful motive. What do you think it was that flung Horatius in full armor down from the bridge into the depths of the Tiber?[6] What burned the hand and arm of Mucius?[7] What impelled Curtius to plunge into the deep burning gulf that opened in the midst of Rome?[8] What, in opposition to all the omens that declared against him, made Julius Cæsar cross the Rubicon?[9] And to come to more modern examples, what scuttled the ships, and left stranded and cut off in the New World the gallant Spaniards under the command of the most courteous Cortés?[10] All these and a variety of other great exploits are, were, and will be the work of fame that mortals desire as a reward and portion of the immortality their famous deeds deserve; though we Catholic Christians and knights-errant look more to that future glory that is everlasting in the ethereal regions of heaven than to the vanity of the fame that is to be acquired in this present transitory life—a fame that, however long it may last, must ultimately expire along with the world itself, which has its own appointed end. So that, O Sancho, in what we do we must not overstep the bounds which the Christian religion we profess has assigned to us. We must slay pride by slaying giants, envy by generosity and nobleness of heart, anger by calmness of demeanor and equanimity, gluttony and sloth by the spareness of our diet and the length of our vigils, lust and lewdness by the loyalty we preserve to those whom we have made the mistresses of our thoughts, indolence by traversing the world in all directions seeking

[6] *flung Horatius ... depths of the Tiber:* The Roman officer Publius Horatius Cocle single-handedly held back an invading army of Etruscans at the Pons Sublicius, a wooden bridge over the Tiber, until the Roman soldiers behind him could demolish it to protect the city of Rome. Once the bridge collapsed, he jumped into the river and—depending on the account—either swam to safety or drowned, sacrificing himself for Rome.

[7] *What burned the hand and arm of Mucius:* The Roman youth Gaius Mucius Scaevola—possibly legendary—was captured in a failed raid on an Etruscan encampment outside Rome. To prove his bravery to his captors, he held his hand in a fire without flinching. The Etruscans were amazed by his iron will and released him.

[8] *What impelled Curtius ... midst of Rome:* According to Roman legend, after an earthquake in 362 B.C. opened up a chasm in the Roman Forum, an augur declared that the fissure would not close until the Romans offered to the gods their most precious possession. While the city's leaders debated the meaning of the prophecy, the young soldier Marcus Curtius, mounted in full battle regalia, proclaimed that Rome's most precious possession was its youth. He then leaped into the chasm, which immediately closed over him.

[9] *What, in opposition ... cross the Rubicon:* In 49 B.C., Julius Caesar led a legion south across the Rubicon River into the heart of Italy, defying the Roman Senate. The event, interpreted as an act of war, precipitated the fall of the Roman Republic and rise of imperial rule.

[10] *left stranded and cut off the gallant Spaniards ... most courteous Cortés:* When Hernán Cortés landed on the shores of Mexico in 1519, he ordered all eleven of his expedition's ships to be destroyed so that his soldiers would have no option but to march inland and pursue the conquest.

opportunities of making ourselves, besides Christians, famous knights. Such, Sancho, are the means by which we reach those extremes of praise that fair fame carries with it."

"All that your worship has said so far," said Sancho, "I have understood quite well. Still, I would be glad if your worship would dissolve a doubt for me, which has just this minute come into my mind."

"*Resolve*, you mean, Sancho," said Don Quixote. "Say on, in God's name, and I will answer as well as I can."

"Tell me, señor," Sancho went on to say, "those Julys or Augusts, and all those venturous knights that you say are now dead—where are they now?"

"The heathens," replied Don Quixote, "are, no doubt, in hell; the Christians, if they were good Christians, are either in purgatory or in heaven."

"Very good," said Sancho. "Now I want to know—the tombs where the bodies of those hoity-toity lords are, do they have silver lamps before them, or are the walls of their chapels decorated with crutches, shrouds, locks of hair, legs and eyes in wax?[11] What are they decorated with?"

To which Don Quixote answered, "The tombs of the heathens were generally sumptuous temples. The ashes of Julius Cæsar's body were placed on top of a stone pyramid of vast size, which they now call in Rome Saint Peter's needle.[12] The emperor Hadrian had for a tomb a castle as large as a good-sized village, which they called the *Moles Adriani*, and is now the Sant'Angelo Castle in Rome.[13] The queen Artemisia buried her husband Mausolus in a tomb which was considered one of the seven wonders of the world.[14] But none of these tombs, or of the many others of the heathens, were ornamented with shrouds or any of those other offerings and tokens that show that those who are buried there are saints."

"That's the point I'm coming to," said Sancho. "Now tell me, which is the greater work, to bring a dead man to life or to kill a giant?"

"The answer is easy," replied Don Quixote. "It is a greater work to bring to life a dead man."

"I've got you now!" declared Sancho. "In that case, the fame of those who bring the dead to life, who give sight to the blind, cure cripples, restore health to the sick, and before whose tombs there are lamps burning, and whose chapels are

[11] *walls of their chapels ornamented with crutches . . . and eyes in wax:* Sancho envisions the votive offerings left by those who have been healed or protected after calling on the aid of a saint.

[12] *Saint Peter's needle:* The Vatican Obelisk is an Egyptian obelisk located in St. Peter's Square. According to a medieval legend, Julius Caesar's ashes were contained in a bronze globe that crowned the monument. When the obelisk was relocated in 1586, the globe was opened and found to be empty.

[13] *Sant'Angelo Castle in Rome:* The Castel Sant'Angelo, used as the Vatican prison in Cervantes' time, was originally built as a mausoleum for Hadrian in the first century.

[14] *The queen Artemisia . . . of the world:* The Mausoleum at Halicarnassus, in present-day Turkey, was built in the fourth century B.C. as the tomb of Mausolus, a satrap of the Persian Empire. It is the origin of the word "mausoleum", an above-ground burial structure.

filled with devout folk on their knees adoring their relics is a better fame in this life and in the other than the fame that all the heathen emperors and knights-errant that have ever been in the world have left or may leave behind them?"

"That I grant, too," said Don Quixote.

"Then this fame, these rewards, these privileges, or whatever you call it," said Sancho, "belong to the bodies and relics of the saints who, with the approval and permission of our holy mother Church, have lamps, candles, shrouds, crutches, pictures, eyes, and legs given to increase devotion and add to their own Christian reputation. Kings carry the bodies or relics of saints on their shoulders, and kiss bits of their bones, and enrich and adorn their oratories[15] and favorite altars with them."

"What would you have me infer from all you have said, Sancho?" asked Don Quixote.

"My meaning is," said Sancho, "let us set about becoming saints, and we will obtain more quickly the good fame we're striving after. For you know, señor, yesterday or the day before yesterday (it's so recent I can talk like this) they canonized and beatified two little barefoot friars,[16] and it is now considered the greatest good luck to kiss or touch the iron chains they used to tie up and torture their bodies, and they are held in greater veneration, so it is said, than the sword of Roland in the armory of our lord the king,[17] may God preserve him. So that, señor, it is better to be a humble little friar of no matter what order, than a valiant knight-errant. With God a couple dozen penitential lashings do more than two thousand lance thrusts, whether they are given to giants, monsters, or dragons."

"All that is true," returned Don Quixote, "but we cannot all be friars, and many are the ways by which God takes his own to heaven. Chivalry is a religion; there are sainted knights in glory."

"Yes," said Sancho, "but I have heard say that there are more friars in heaven than knights-errant."

"That," said Don Quixote, "is because those in religious orders are more numerous than knights."

"The errants are many," said Sancho.

"Many," replied Don Quixote, "but few those who deserve the name of knights."

With these and similar conversations they passed the night and the following day, without anything worth mention happening to them, at which Don Quixote was not a little dejected; but at length, the next day at dusk they caught sight of the great city of El Toboso.[18] On their first glimpse, Don Quixote's

[15] *oratories:* private chapels.

[16] *they canonized and beatified two little barefoot friars:* It's unclear to whom Sancho is referring.

[17] *the sword of Roland in the armory of our lord the king:* See footnote 8, page 395.

[18] *the great city of El Toboso:* It is estimated that El Toboso had about nine hundred residents at the time.

spirits rose and Sancho's fell, for he did not know where Dulcinea's house was, nor in all his life had he ever seen her, any more than his master. They were therefore both uneasy, the one to see her, the other at not having seen her, and Sancho was at a loss to know what he was to do when his master sent him to El Toboso. In the end, Don Quixote made up his mind to enter the city at nightfall, and they waited until the time came among some oak trees that were nearby. When the moment they had agreed upon arrived, they made their entrance into the city, where something happened to them that may be fairly called something.

CHAPTER IX

WHEREIN IS RELATED WHAT WILL BE SEEN THERE

'Twas at the very midnight hour more or less when Don Quixote and Sancho emerged from the woods and entered El Toboso. The town was in deep silence, for all the inhabitants were asleep, and stretched on the broad of their backs, as the saying goes. The night was fairly clear, though Sancho would have preferred it to have been pitch black, so that the darkness could provide an excuse for his blundering. All around nothing was to be heard except the barking of dogs, which deafened Don Quixote's ears and troubled Sancho's heart. Now and then a donkey brayed, pigs grunted, cats meowed, and the various noises they made seemed louder in the silence of the night—all of which the lovelorn knight took to be of evil omen.

Nevertheless, he said to Sancho, "Sancho, my son, lead on to the palace of Dulcinea, it may be that we shall find her awake."

"What palace am I supposed to lead you to, for pity's sake," said Sancho, "when what I saw her highness in was nothing but a very little house?"

"Most likely she had withdrawn at that moment into some small apartment of her palace," said Don Quixote, "to amuse herself with damsels, as great ladies and princesses are accustomed to do."

"Señor," said Sancho, "if, in spite of me, your worship insists that the house of my lady Dulcinea is a palace, do you really think this is an hour to find the door open? And will it be right for us to go knocking till they hear us and open the door, making a disturbance and confusion all through the household? Do you suppose we're going to the house of our wenches, like lovers who come and knock and go in at any hour, however late it may be?"

"Let us first find the palace once and for all," replied Don Quixote, "and then I will tell you, Sancho, what we had best do. But look, Sancho, for either I see badly, or that dark mass in outline over there should be Dulcinea's palace."

"Then let your worship lead the way," said Sancho. "Perhaps it is. Yet even if I saw it with my eyes and touched it with my hands, I would believe it as much as I believe it's daylight now."

Don Quixote took the lead, and having gone some two hundred paces he came upon the mass that was casting a shadow, and found it was a great tower. He then realized that the building in question was no palace but the main church of the town. He said, "It's the church we have come upon, Sancho."

"So I see," said Sancho, "and God grant we may not come upon our graves. It is no good sign to be wandering through a graveyard at this time of night—and that after my telling your worship, if I'm not mistaken, that the house of this lady will be at the end of an alley."

"The curse of God on you for a blockhead!" exclaimed Don Quixote. "Where have you ever heard of castles and royal palaces being built at the end of alleys?"

"Señor," replied Sancho, "every country has a way of its own. Perhaps here in El Toboso it is the custom to build palaces and grand buildings in alleys. I entreat your worship to let me search among these streets or alleys before me. It may be that in some corner or other I stumble on this palace—and would to God I found it chewed to bits for making such miserable fools of us."

"Speak respectfully of what belongs to my lady, Sancho," said Don Quixote. "Let us keep the feast in peace and not throw the rope after the bucket."[1]

"I'll hold my tongue," said Sancho, "but how am I to take it patiently when your worship wants me—having only once seen the house of our mistress—to remember where it was and find it in the middle of the night, when your worship can't find it, who must have seen it thousands of times?"

"You will drive me to desperation, Sancho," said Don Quixote. "Look here, heretic, have I not told you a thousand times that I have never once in my life seen the peerless Dulcinea or crossed the threshold of her palace, and that I am enamored solely by hearsay and by the great reputation she bears for beauty and discretion?"

"I hear it now," returned Sancho, "and I may tell you that if you have not seen her, no more have I."

"That cannot be," said Don Quixote, "for you once said, on bringing back the answer to the letter I sent by you, that you saw her sifting wheat."

"Don't dwell on that, señor," said Sancho. "I must tell you that my seeing her and the answer I brought you back were by hearsay too, for I can no more tell who Lady Dulcinea is than I can punch a hole in the sky."

"Sancho, Sancho," said Don Quixote, "there are times for jests and times when jests are out of place. If I tell you that I have neither seen nor spoken to the lady of my heart, it is no reason for you to say you have not spoken to her or seen her, when the contrary is the case, as you well know."

While the two were engaged in this conversation, they noticed someone with a pair of mules approaching the spot where they stood, and from the noise the plough made, as it dragged along the ground, they guessed him to be some laborer who had gotten up before daybreak to go to his work, and so it proved to be. He came along singing the ballad that goes

Ill did ye fare, ye men of France,
In Roncesvalles chase—[2]

"May I die, Sancho," said Don Quixote, when he heard him, "if any good will come to us tonight! Do you not hear what that field hand is singing?"

[1] *Let us keep the feast in peace and not throw the rope after the bucket*: "Let's not argue or take matters to an extreme."

[2] *In Roncesvalles chase*: See footnote 16, page 27.

"I do," said Sancho, "but what has Roncesvalles chase to do with us? He could just as well be singing the ballad of Calaínos,[3] for any good or ill that can come to us in our business."

By this time the laborer had come near, and Don Quixote asked him, "Can you tell me, worthy friend, and God speed you, whereabouts here is the palace of the peerless princess Doña Dulcinea del Toboso?"

"Señor," replied the lad, "I'm a stranger, and I've been only a few days in the town doing farm work for a rich farmer. In that house opposite there live the priest of the village and the sacristan, and both or either of them will be able to give your worship some account of this lady princess, for they have a list of all the people of El Toboso; though it is my belief there is not a princess living in the whole of it. Many ladies there are, of quality, and in her own house each of them may be a princess."

"Well, then, the lady I am inquiring for will be one of these, my friend," said Don Quixote.

"Maybe so," replied the lad. "God be with you, for here comes the daylight." And without waiting for any more of his questions, he whipped on his mules.

Sancho, seeing his master downcast and somewhat dissatisfied, said to him, "Señor, daylight will be here before long, and it will not do for us to let the sun find us in the street. It will be better for us to leave the city and for your worship to hide in the countryside nearby. I'll come back in the daytime, and I won't leave a crumb in the whole village that I haven't looked under for the house, castle, or palace of my lady—and hard luck for me if I don't find it. Once I do find it, I'll speak to her grace and tell her where and how your worship is waiting for her to arrange some plan for you to see her without any damage to her honor and reputation."

"Sancho," said Don Quixote, "you have delivered a thousand sentences condensed in the compass of a few words. I thank you for the advice you have given me and take it most gladly. Come, my son, let us go look for some place where I may hide, while you return, as you say, to seek and speak with my lady, from whose discretion and courtesy I look for favors more than miraculous."

Sancho was in a fever to get his master out of the town, lest he should discover the falsehood of the reply he had brought to him in the Sierra Morena on behalf of Dulcinea. For this reason, he hastened their departure, which they took at once, and two miles out of the village they found a wooded area where Don Quixote could hide himself. Meanwhile, Sancho returned to the city to speak to Dulcinea, in which embassy things befell him that demand fresh attention and a new chapter.

[3] *ballad of Calaínos:* According to the ballad, the princess of Seville refused to marry the Moor Calaínos until he brought her the heads of three Christian warriors—among them Roland, who killed him in battle. The expression "verses from Calaínos" (*coplas de Calaínos*) came to refer dismissively to an inconsequential statement.

CHAPTER X

WHEREIN IS RELATED THE CRAFTY DEVICE SANCHO ADOPTED TO ENCHANT LADY DULCINEA, AND OTHER INCIDENTS AS LUDICROUS AS THEY ARE TRUE

When the author of this great history comes to relate what is set down in this chapter, he says he would have preferred to pass it over in silence, fearing it would not be believed; for here Don Quixote's madness reaches the confines of the greatest that can be conceived—and even goes a couple bowshots beyond the greatest. Nevertheless, though still under the same fear and apprehension, he has recorded the episode without adding to it or leaving out a particle of the truth and entirely disregarding the charges of falsehood that might be brought against him. And he was right in doing so, for the truth may be brittle but will not break and always rises above falsehood as oil above water.

Thus he continues with his story, relating that as soon as Don Quixote had found a hiding place in a thicket or oak grove near El Toboso, he ordered Sancho to return to the city and not come into his presence again without having first spoken on his behalf to his lady—to request of her, if it were her good pleasure, that she allow herself to be seen by her enslaved knight and to deign to bestow her blessing upon him so that he might thereby hope for a favorable conclusion to all his undertakings and difficult enterprises. Sancho agreed to execute the task according to the instructions and to bring back an answer as good as the one he brought back before.

"Go, my son," said Don Quixote, "and be not dazed when you find yourself exposed to the light of that sun of beauty you go to seek. Happy are you above all the squires in the world! Note well, and let it not escape your memory, how she receives you—if she changes color while you are giving her my message; if she is agitated and disturbed at hearing my name; if she cannot rest upon her cushion should you perchance find her seated in the sumptuous state chamber proper to her rank; and should she be standing, observe if she poises herself now on one foot, now on the other; if she repeats two or three times the reply she gives you; if her disposition passes from gentle to austere, from harsh to tender; if she raises her hand to smooth her hair, though it be not disarranged. In short, my son, observe all her actions and motions, for if you will report them to me as they were, I will gather what she hides in the recesses of her heart as regards my love. For I would have you know, Sancho, if you know it not, that with lovers the outward actions and motions they give way to when their loves are in question are the faithful messengers that carry the news of what is going on in the depths of their hearts. Go, my friend, may better fortune than mine attend you and bring you a happier result than that which I await in dread in this dreary solitude."

"I will go and return quickly," said Sancho. "Cheer up that little heart of yours, my master, for at the present moment you seem to have one no bigger than a hazelnut. Remember what they say: 'A stout heart breaks bad luck,' and 'Where there's no smoke, there's no fire.' And what's more, they say, 'The rabbit jumps up where it's least expected.' I say this because, if we could not find my lady's palaces or castles tonight, now that it's daylight I expect to find them when I least expect it. Once I've found them, leave it to me how to handle her."

"Your proverbs, Sancho," said Don Quixote, "are always to the purpose, no matter what the circumstance. May God's purpose for me be good fortune in what I desire."

With this, Sancho wheeled about and gave Dapple the stick. Don Quixote, resting in his stirrups and leaning against his lance, remained behind on his horse, filled with sad and troubled forebodings. There we will leave him and accompany Sancho, who parted from his master no less serious and troubled; so much so, that as soon as he emerged from the woods, and after looking around to confirm that Don Quixote was not within sight, he dismounted from his donkey and sat down at the foot of a tree, where he began to converse with himself, saying: "Now, brother Sancho, tell me where your worship is going. Are you going to look for some donkey that has been lost? Not at all. Then what are you looking for? I am looking for no more or less than a princess, and in her for the sun of beauty and heavenly canopy combined. And where do you expect to find all this, Sancho? Where? Why, in the great city of El Toboso. Well then, on whose behalf are you going to look for her? On behalf of the famous knight Don Quixote of La Mancha, who rights wrongs, gives food to those who thirst and drink to the hungry. That's all very well, but do you know where her house is, Sancho? My master says it's some royal palace or grand castle. By chance, have you ever seen her? Neither I nor my master ever saw her. And does it strike you that it might be understandable if the people of El Toboso, when they found out that you were here with the intention of snatching their princesses and disturbing their ladies, were to come and smash your ribs and not leave a whole bone in you? They would certainly have very good reason, if they did not see that I am under orders, and that

'you are a messenger, my friend,
no blame belongs to you.'[1]

Don't you trust to that, Sancho, for Manchegan folk are as hot-tempered as they are honest and won't put up with nonsense from anybody. By the Lord, no sooner

[1] *you are a messenger, my friend,/no blame belongs to you:* Verses repeated in several ballads about Bernardo del Carpio and Fernán González.

they get scent of you than you're doomed. So be off, you scoundrel! Let the lightning bolt fall ...[2] Why should I go searching for a three-footed cat to please another man, especially when looking for Dulcinea will be like looking for the right Marica in Ravenna or bachelor in Salamanca?[3] The devil, the devil and nobody else, has mixed me up in this business!"

Such was Sancho's soliloquy, and all the conclusion he could come to was to say to himself again, "Well, there's a remedy for everything except death, under whose yoke we must all pass when life is finished, whether we like it or not. I have a thousand proofs that this master of mine is a madman fit to be tied, and for that matter, I'm not far behind him; for if there's any truth in the proverb that runs 'Tell me the company you keep, and I'll tell you who you are,' or the other, 'Not with whom you are bred, but with whom you are fed,' then I'm a greater fool than he is to follow him and serve him. Well now, if he is crazy (and he is), and with a madness that tends to take one thing for another, white for black and black for white—as happened when he said the windmills were giants and the monks' mules dromedaries, flocks of sheep armies of enemies, and much more to the same tune—it will not be very hard to make him believe that some country girl, the first I come across here, is Lady Dulcinea. If he doesn't believe it, I'll swear it; and if he swears, I'll swear again. If he persists, I'll persist still more, so that, come what may, I'll get the best of him. Maybe, by holding out in this way, I can put a stop to his sending me on any more missions of this kind. Or maybe he will think (as I suspect he will) that one of those wicked enchanters he says despises him has changed her form for the sake of doing him wrong and injuring him."

With this reflection Sancho set his mind at ease, considering the business as good as settled, and he remained where he was till the afternoon to make Don Quixote think he had time enough to go to El Toboso and return. So favorably did things turn out for him that as he got up to mount Dapple, he observed coming from El Toboso towards the spot where he stood three peasant girls on three colts, or fillies—for the author does not make the point clear, though it is more likely they were jennies,[4] the usual mount with village girls; but as it is of no great consequence, we need not stop to prove it.

To be brief, the instant Sancho saw the peasant girls, he returned full speed to seek his master, whom he found sighing and uttering a thousand passionate lamentations. When Don Quixote saw him, he exclaimed, "What news, Sancho, my friend? Am I to mark this day with a white or black stone?"[5]

[2] *Let the lightning bolt fall . . . :* ". . . on Tamayo's house." (That is, "Let someone else deal with this problem.")

[3] *like looking for the right Marica in Ravenna or bachelor in Salamanca:* that is, "like looking for a needle in a haystack". "Marica" is a diminutive form of "Maria", a common name in an Italian city like Ravenna.

[4] *jennies:* female donkeys, which were considered more docile and reliable than male donkeys.

[5] *white or black stone:* The custom of marking a good day with a white stone and a bad day with a black stone dates to antiquity.

"Your worship," replied Sancho, "had better mark it in red, like the words on the walls of universities,[6] so that everyone may see it plainly."

"Then you bring good news," said Don Quixote.

"So good," replied Sancho, "that your worship has only to spur Rocinante and get out into the open field to see Lady Dulcinea del Toboso, who, along with two damsels of hers, is coming to see your worship."

"Holy God! What are you saying, Sancho, my friend?" exclaimed Don Quixote. "Take care you are not deceiving me or seeking by false joy to cheer my real sadness."

"What could I get by deceiving your worship," returned Sancho, "especially when it will so soon be shown whether I tell the truth or not? Come, señor, push on, and you will see our mistress coming, robed and adorned like the princess she is. She and her damsels are all one glow of gold, all bunches of pearls, diamonds, and rubies, all cloth of brocade of more than ten borders—with their hair loose on their shoulders like so many sunbeams playing with the wind. And besides all that, they come mounted on three dappled cackneys, the finest sight you ever saw."

"*Hackneys*, you mean, Sancho," said Don Quixote.

"There is not much difference between *cackneys* and *hackneys*," said Sancho. "But no matter what they come on, there they are, the finest ladies one could wish for, especially my lady Princess Dulcinea, who staggers the senses."

"Let us go, Sancho, my son," said Don Quixote, "and in recompense for this news, as unexpected as it is good, I bestow upon you the best spoil I shall win in the first adventure I may have. If that does not satisfy you, I promise you the foals I shall have this year from my three mares, which as you know are in foal on our village common."

"I'll take the foals," said Sancho, "for it is not quite certain that the spoils of the first adventure will be good ones."

By this time they had emerged from the woods and saw the three village lasses close at hand. Don Quixote looked all along the road to El Toboso, and as he could see nobody except the three peasant girls, he was thoroughly puzzled. He asked Sancho if he had left them behind outside the city.

"How outside the city?" returned Sancho. "Are your worship's eyes in the back of your head that you can't see that the ladies are the ones coming this way, shining like the very sun at noonday?"

"I see nothing, Sancho," said Don Quixote, "but three country girls on three jackasses."

"May God deliver me from the devil!" cried Sancho. "And can it be that your worship takes three hackneys (or whatever they're called) as white as the driven snow for jackasses? By the Lord God, I'll tear my beard if that's the case!"

"Well, I can only say, Sancho, my friend," said Don Quixote, "that it is as plain they are jackasses—or jennies—as that I am Don Quixote and you Sancho Panza. At any rate, they seem to me to be so."

[6] *in red, like the words on the walls of universities:* A successful candidate for a doctorate or professorship was announced with a *vítor*, a red ochre monogram painted on the wall of a university building.

"Hush, señor," said Sancho. "Don't talk that way. Open your eyes and come and pay your respects to the lady of your thoughts, who is close upon us now."

With these words he advanced to receive the three village lasses and, dismounting from Dapple, caught hold of one of the donkeys of the three country girls by the halter. Dropping on both knees on the ground, he said, "Queen and princess and duchess of beauty, may it please your haughtiness and greatness to receive into your favor and goodwill your captive knight who stands there turned into marble stone, and quite stupefied and benumbed at finding himself in your magnificent presence. I am Sancho Panza, his squire, and he the vagabond knight Don Quixote of La Mancha, otherwise called 'The Knight of the Woeful Countenance.'"

Don Quixote had by this time placed himself on his knees beside Sancho, and, with eyes starting out of his head and a puzzled gaze, was regarding her whom Sancho called queen and lady; and as he could see nothing in her except a village girl, and not a very attractive one, for she was platter-faced and snub-nosed, he was perplexed and bewildered, and did not venture to open his lips. The country girls, at the same time, were astonished to see these two men, so different in appearance, on their knees, preventing their companion from going on.

She who had been stopped, breaking silence, said angrily and testily, "Get the hell out of the way and let us pass. We're in a hurry."

To which Sancho returned, "O princess and universal lady of El Toboso, is not your magnanimous heart softened by seeing the pillar and prop of knight-errantry on his knees before your sublimated presence?"

On hearing this, one of the others exclaimed, "So we get a nice brushing down and a carrot, do we? Look how the little lords have come to sweet-talk the village girls—as if we here couldn't butter your bums just as well. You go your way and let us go ours, and you'll be the better for it."

"Get up, Sancho," said Don Quixote at this. "I see that fortune, 'with evil done to me unsated still,'[7] has taken possession of all the roads by which any comfort may reach this wretched soul that I carry in my flesh. And you, highest perfection of excellence that can be desired, utmost limit of grace in human shape, sole relief of this afflicted heart that adores you—though the malign enchanter that persecutes me has brought clouds and cataracts on my eyes, and to them, and them only, transformed your unparalleled beauty and changed your features into those of a poor peasant girl—if it so be that he has not at the same time changed mine into those of some monster to render them loathsome in your sight, refuse not to look upon me with tenderness and love, seeing in this submission that I make on my knees to your transformed beauty the humility with which my soul adores you."

"Tell it to my grandfather!" cried the girl. "I wasn't born for dainties. If you want our gratitude, get out of the way and let us pass."

Sancho stood aside and let her go, immensely pleased to have gotten so nicely out of the predicament he was in. The instant the village lass who had done duty

[7] *with evil done to me unsated still:* from Garcilaso's *Third Eclogue.*

for Dulcinea found herself free, prodding her "cackney" with a spike she had at the end of a stick, she set off at full speed across the field. The donkey, however, feeling the point more acutely than usual, began to buck so hard that it flung Lady Dulcinea to the ground; seeing which, Don Quixote ran to raise her up, and Sancho to fix and girth the packsaddle, which also had slipped under the donkey's belly. The packsaddle being secured, as Don Quixote was about to lift up his enchanted mistress in his arms and put her upon her beast, the lady, getting up from the ground, saved him the trouble. Going back a little, she took a short run, and putting both hands on the haunches of the donkey she dropped into the saddle more lightly than a falcon and sat astride as if she were a man. When Sancho saw this, he exclaimed, "By Roque,[8] our lady is lighter than a feather! She could teach the most experienced Cordovan or Mexican how to mount. She cleared the high back of the saddle in one jump, and without spurs she's making the hackney run like a zebra. Her damsels are not far behind her—all of them are flying like the wind." This was the truth, for as soon as they saw Dulcinea mounted, they pushed on after her and sped away without looking back for more than half a league.

Don Quixote followed them with his eyes, and when they were no longer in sight, he turned to Sancho and said, "What say you, Sancho? Do you see how the enchanters despise me? See to what a length the malice and spite they bear me go, when they seek to deprive me of the happiness I would feel to see my lady as she is. Alas, I was born to be an example of misfortune, and the bull's eye at which the arrows of adversity are aimed. Observe too, Sancho, that these traitors were not content with transforming my Dulcinea, but they transformed her into a shape as mean and ill-favored as that of the village girl yonder. At the same time, they robbed her of that which is such a peculiar property of ladies of distinction, that is to say, the sweet fragrance that comes of being always among perfumes and flowers. For I must tell you, Sancho, that when I approached to seat Dulcinea upon her hackney (as you say it was, though to me it appeared a donkey), she gave me a whiff of raw garlic that made my head reel and poisoned my very heart."

"O scum of the earth!" cried Sancho at this. "O miserable, spiteful enchanters! O that I could see you all strung by the gills, like sardines on a twig! How great is your knowledge, how great your power, and your works greater still! It ought to have been enough for you, you scoundrels, to have changed the pearls of my lady's eyes into oak galls[9] and her hair of purest gold into the bristles of a red ox's tail—in short, all her features from fair to foul—without meddling with her smell. By it alone we have found out what was hidden underneath that ugly bark; though, to tell the truth, I never saw her ugliness, but only her beauty, which was raised to the highest pitch of perfection by a mole she had on her right lip, like a mustache, with seven or eight red hairs like threads of gold, and more than a palm long."

"From the correspondence which exists between those of the face and those of the body," said Don Quixote, "Dulcinea must have another mole resembling it

[8] *By Roque*: See footnote 6, page 42.

[9] *oak galls*: swelling outgrowths that form on oak trees.

on the thick of the thigh of the side on which she has the one on her face.[10] But hairs of the length you have mentioned are very long for moles."

"Well, all I can say is there they were as plain as could be," replied Sancho.

"I believe it, my friend," returned Don Quixote; "for nature bestowed nothing on Dulcinea that was not perfect and well-finished. Indeed, if she had a hundred moles like the one you have described, in her they would not be moles but moons and shining stars. But tell me, Sancho, that which seemed to me to be a pack-saddle as you were fixing it, was it a flat saddle or a side saddle?"

"It was neither," replied Sancho; "it was a jineta saddle[11] draped with a cloth worth half a kingdom, so rich was it."

"And that I could not see all this, Sancho!" said Don Quixote. "Once more I say, and will say a thousand times, I am the most unfortunate of men."

Sancho—the rascal—had enough to do to hide his laughter, at hearing the simplicity of the master he had so exquisitely hoodwinked. At length, after a good deal more conversation had passed between them, they remounted their beasts and followed the road to Zaragoza, which they expected to reach in time to take part in a certain grand festival which is held every year in that illustrious city. But before they got there things happened to them, so many, so important, and so strange that they deserve to be recorded and read, as will be seen farther on.

[10] *From the correspondence . . . on her face:* According to a folk belief, moles on the body were found in symmetry.

[11] *jineta saddle:* lightweight saddle with high pommels and short stirrups.

CHAPTER XI

OF THE STRANGE ADVENTURE WHICH THE VALIANT DON QUIXOTE HAD WITH THE CART OF "THE PARLIAMENT OF DEATH"

Dejected beyond measure did Don Quixote pursue his journey, turning over in his mind the cruel trick the enchanters had played on him in changing his lady Dulcinea into the vile shape of the country girl, nor could he think of any way of restoring her to her original form. These reflections so absorbed him, that without being aware of it he let go of Rocinante's bridle, who, perceiving the liberty that was granted him, stopped at every step to nibble the fresh grass with which the plain abounded.

Sancho recalled his master from his reverie. "Melancholy, señor," said he, "was made not for beasts but for men; but if men give way to it too much they turn to beasts. Keep yourself in check, your worship; return to your old self. Gather up Rocinante's reins, cheer up, rouse yourself, and show that gallant spirit that knights-errant ought to have. Why so downcast? Why all the brooding? Are we here or in France?[1] The devil take all the Dulcineas in the world; for the well-being of a single knight-errant is worth more than all the enchantments and transformations on earth."

"Hush, Sancho," said Don Quixote in a weak and faint voice. "Hush and utter no blasphemies against that enchanted lady; for I alone am to blame for her misfortune and hard fate. Her calamity has come of the hatred the wicked bear me."

"So say I," returned Sancho. "'Who once beheld her beauteous form, how could his tender heart not mourn.'"[2]

"You may well say that, Sancho," replied Don Quixote, "as you saw her in the full perfection of her beauty; for the enchantment does not go so far as to distort your vision or hide her loveliness from you. Against me alone and against my eyes is the strength of its venom directed. Nevertheless, there is one thing which has occurred to me, and that is that you did ill describe her beauty to me, for as well as I recollect, you said that her eyes were pearls; but eyes that are like pearls are rather the eyes of a sea bream than of a lady. I am persuaded that Dulcinea's must be green emeralds, full and soft, with two rainbows for eyebrows. Take away those pearls from her eyes and transfer them to her teeth. Beyond a doubt, Sancho, you have taken the one for the other, the eyes for the teeth."

[1] *Are we here or in France?*: That is, "Where's your head?"

[2] *Who once beheld her beauteous form, how could his tender heart not mourn*: adaptation of an old proverb.

"Very likely," said Sancho, "for her beauty bewildered me as much as her ugliness did your worship. But let us leave it all to God, who alone knows what is to happen in this vale of tears, in this evil world of ours, where there is hardly a thing to be found without some mixture of wickedness, deceit, and rascality. Yet one thing, señor, troubles me more than all the rest, and that is thinking what is to be done when your worship conquers some giant, or some other knight, and orders him to go and present himself before the beauty of Lady Dulcinea. Where is this poor giant or this poor wretch of a vanquished knight to find her? I can see them now wandering all over El Toboso, staring blankly like straw dummies[3] and asking for my lady Dulcinea; and even if they meet her in the middle of the street they won't know her any more than they would know my father."

"Perhaps, Sancho," returned Don Quixote, "the enchantment does not go so far as to deprive conquered and presented giants and knights of the power of recognizing Dulcinea. We will try by experiment with one or two of the first I vanquish and send to her, whether they see her or not, by commanding them to return and give me an account of what happened to them in this respect."

"I declare, I think what your worship has proposed is excellent," said Sancho. "With this plan, we'll find out what we want to know. If it's only from your worship that she is hidden, the misfortune will be more yours than hers. But so long as Lady Dulcinea is well and happy, we on our part will make the best of it and get on as well as we can, seeking our adventures and leaving Time to take his own course; for he is the best physician for these and greater ailments."

Don Quixote was about to reply to Sancho Panza, but he was prevented by a cart crossing the road full of the most diverse and strange personages that could be imagined. He who led the mules and acted as driver was a hideous demon. The cart was open to the sky, without a canopy or support posts. The first figure that presented itself to Don Quixote's eyes was that of Death itself with a human face. Next to it was an angel with large painted wings, and at one side an emperor with a crown (to all appearance of gold) on his head. At the feet of Death was the god called Cupid, without his blindfold, but with his bow, quiver, and arrows. There was also a knight in full armor, except that he had no morion or helmet but only a hat decked with plumes of various colors. Along with these there were others with a variety of costumes and faces. All this, unexpectedly encountered, took Don Quixote somewhat aback and struck terror into the heart of Sancho; but Don Quixote quickly recovered, heartened that some new perilous adventure was presenting itself to him. With this assurance, and with a spirit prepared to face any danger, he planted himself in front of the cart and in a loud and menacing tone, exclaimed, "Carter, coachman, devil, or whatever you may be, tell me at once who you are, where you are going, and who these people are you carry in your wagon, which looks more like Charon's boat[4] than an ordinary cart."

[3] *straw dummies: bausanes*, straw figures placed in battlements to deceive the attacker into believing that the castle was more heavily defended.

[4] *Charon's boat:* It was the job of Charon to ferry the dead across the rivers Acheron and Styx to their eternal home in Hades.

To which the devil, stopping the cart, answered quietly, "Señor, we are actors who belong to Angulo el Malo's company.[5] We have been performing the play[6] *The Parliament of Death* this morning—it being the eighth day of Corpus Christi—in a village beyond that hill, and we have to perform it this afternoon in that village which you can see from here. As it is so close by, and to save the trouble of undressing and dressing again, we are traveling in the costumes in which we perform. That lad there appears as Death, that other as an angel, that woman (the producer's wife) plays the queen, this one the soldier, that the emperor, and I the devil. I am one of the principal characters of the play, for in this company I take the leading parts. If you want to know anything more about us, ask me and I will answer with the utmost precision, for since I am a devil I know a little about everything."

"By the faith of a knight-errant," replied Don Quixote, "when I saw this cart I imagined some great adventure was presenting itself to me; but I declare one must touch with the hand what appears to the eye if illusions are to be avoided. God speed you, good people. Keep your festival, and remember, if you demand of me anything by which I can render you a service, I will do it gladly and willingly, for since childhood I have been fond of theater, and in my youth a keen lover of the actor's art."

While they were talking, fate so willed that one of the company, a jester toting a great number of bells and three inflated ox-bladders at the end of a stick, joined them. Approaching Don Quixote, the clown began to brandish his stick, bang the ground with the bladders, and prance about with great jingling of the bells—all of which so startled Rocinante that, in spite of Don Quixote's efforts to rein him in, he took the bit between his teeth and set off across the plain with greater speed than the bones of his anatomy ever gave any promise of.

Sancho, who thought his master was in danger of being thrown, jumped off Dapple and ran in all haste to help him; but by the time he reached him he was already on the ground. Beside him was Rocinante, who had come down with his master—the usual upshot of Rocinante's fits of boldness and high spirits.

No sooner had Sancho dismounted his beast to go and help Don Quixote than the dancing devil with the bladders jumped up on Dapple, and beating the animal with them, more by the fright and the noise than by the pain of the blows, made him fly across the fields towards the village where they were going to hold their festival. With his master on the ground and his donkey on the run, Sancho was unsure which of the two crises he should attend to first; but in the end, like a good squire and good servant, he let his love for his master prevail over his

[5] *Angulo el Malo's company:* A historical figure, Andrés de Angulo (known as "el Malo") was a theater producer and actor active in the final decades of the sixteenth century.

[6] *play:* literally, "auto". The auto sacramental was a genre of liturgical drama performed during the festival of Corpus Christi, a celebration of the Real Presence of Christ in the Eucharist. These one-act plays had a moralizing or catechizing purpose, usually incorporating at some point praise of the Eucharist, and were performed in the open air. There is evidence of a sacramental play of this title (*Las cortes de la muerte*) authored by Lope de Vega.

affection for his donkey—though every time he saw the bladders rise in the air and come down on the hind quarters of his Dapple he felt the pains and terrors of death, and he would have rather had the blows fall on the apples of his own eyes than on the least hair of his donkey's tail. In this trouble and perplexity, he came to where Don Quixote lay in a far sorrier plight than he cared to see, and having helped him to mount Rocinante, he said to him, "Señor, the devil has carried off my Dapple."

"What devil?" asked Don Quixote.

"The one with the bladders," said Sancho.

"Then I will recover him," said Don Quixote, "even if he is shut up with him in the deepest and darkest dungeons of hell. Follow me, Sancho, for the cart goes slowly, and with its own mules I will make good the loss of Dapple."

"You need not take the trouble, señor," said Sancho. "Temper your anger, for as I now see, the devil has let Dapple go and he is coming back to where he was." And so it turned out, for having fallen down with Dapple, in imitation of Don Quixote and Rocinante, the devil made off on foot to the town, and the donkey came back to his master.

"For all that," said Don Quixote, "it will be well to visit the discourtesy of that devil upon some of those in the cart, even if it were the emperor himself."

"Don't think of it, your worship," returned Sancho. "Take my advice and never meddle with actors, for they are a favored class. I myself have known an actor arrested for two murders who came off scot-free. Remember that, as they are merry people who live to entertain, everyone supports, protects, and values them, above all when they are those of the royal companies with a license,[7] all or most of whom in their dress and appearance look like princes."

"All the same," said Don Quixote, "that devil of an actor must not go off boasting, even if the whole human race favors him."

So saying, he made for the cart, which was now very near the town, shouting out as he went, "Stay! Halt, you merry, festive crew! I would like to teach you how to treat donkeys and animals that serve the squires of knights-errant for steeds."

So loud were Don Quixote's shouts that those in the cart heard and understood them, and, guessing by the words what the speaker's intention was, Death in an instant jumped out of the cart, with the emperor, the devil driver, and the angel after him; nor did the queen or the god Cupid stay behind. All of them armed themselves with stones and formed a line, prepared to receive Don Quixote with the sharp edges of their pebbles. Don Quixote, when he saw them drawn up in such a gallant array with uplifted arms ready for a mighty discharge of stones, checked Rocinante and began to consider in what way he could attack them with the least danger to himself.

As he halted Sancho came up, and seeing him disposed to attack this well-ordered squadron, said to him, "It would be the height of madness to attempt such an enterprise. Consider, señor, that when a creek full of stones are aimed

[7] *royal companies with a license:* Privileged theater troupes were licensed by the Royal Council.

at your head there's no defensive armor in the world to protect you except what you'll find under the cover of a brass bell. Besides, one should remember that it is rashness, not valor, for a single man to attack an army that has Death in it, and where emperors fight in person, with angels, good and bad, to help them. If this consideration will not make you think twice, perhaps it will to know for certain that among all these, though they look like kings, princes, and emperors, there is not a single knight-errant."

"Now indeed, Sancho," said Don Quixote, "you have put your finger on what may and should turn me from the resolution I had already formed. I cannot and must not draw sword, as I have many a time before told you, against anyone who is not a dubbed knight. It is for you, Sancho, if you will, to take vengeance for the wrong done to your Dapple. I will help you from here by shouts and sound advice."

"There is no reason to take vengeance on anyone, señor," replied Sancho; "for it is not the part of good Christians to revenge wrongs. I will arrange it with my donkey to leave his grievance to my goodwill and pleasure, and that is to live in peace as long as Heaven grants me life."

"Well," said Don Quixote, "if that is your determination, good Sancho, sensible Sancho, Christian Sancho, honest Sancho, let us leave these phantoms alone and turn to the pursuit of better and worthier adventures; for from what I see of this country, we cannot fail to find plenty of marvelous ones in it."

He at once wheeled about, Sancho ran to take possession of his Dapple, Death and his flanking squadron returned to their cart and pursued their journey, and thus the dread adventure of the Cart of Death ended happily, thanks to Sancho's advice to his master, who, the very next day, would encounter a lovelorn knight-errant. And that would lead to an adventure no less thrilling than the last.

CHAPTER XII

OF THE STRANGE ADVENTURE WHICH BEFELL THE VALIANT DON QUIXOTE WITH THE BOLD KNIGHT OF THE MIRRORS

The night following the day of the encounter with Death, Don Quixote and his squire passed under some tall shady trees, and Don Quixote at Sancho's persuasion ate a little from the provisions carried by Dapple. Over their supper Sancho said to his master, "Señor, what a fool I should have looked if I had chosen for my reward the spoils of the first adventure your worship achieved, instead of the foals of the three mares. After all, 'a sparrow in the hand is better than a vulture on the wing.' "

"Nonetheless, Sancho," replied Don Quixote, "if you would have let me attack them as I wanted, at the very least the emperor's gold crown and Cupid's painted wings would have come to you as spoils, for I should have taken them by force and given them into your hands."

"The scepters and crowns of those play-actor emperors," said Sancho, "weren't pure gold, but only foil of brass or tin."

"That is true," said Don Quixote, "for it would not be right that the accessories of the drama should be real, instead of being mere fictions and semblances, like the drama itself; towards which, Sancho—and, as a necessary consequence, towards those who perform and produce it—I wish that you were favorably disposed, for they are all instruments of great good to the commonwealth, placing before us at every step a mirror in which we may see vividly displayed the activity of human life; nor is there any likeness that shows us more faithfully what we are and ought to be than the play and the players. Come, tell me, have you not seen a play acted in which kings, emperors, pontiffs, knights, ladies, and many other personages were introduced? One plays the villain, another the knave, this one the merchant, that the soldier, one the sharp-witted fool, another the foolish lover; and when the play is over, and they have taken off the costumes they wore in it, all the actors become equal."

"Yes, I've seen that," said Sancho.

"Well then," said Don Quixote, "the same thing happens in the comedy of this bustling world, where some play emperors, others popes, and, in short, all the characters that can be brought into a play. But when it is over, that is to say when life ends, death strips them all of the garments that distinguish one from the other, and all are equal in the grave."

"A fine comparison," said Sancho; "though not so new but that I've heard it many and many a time.[1] There is also that other one about the game of chess—how, so long as the game lasts, each piece has its own particular job, and when the game is finished they are all mixed, jumbled up, shaken together, and stowed away in the bag, which is much like ending life in the grave."

"Each day, Sancho, you are less of a simpleton and more of a sage," said Don Quixote.

"Some of your worship's good sense is bound to stick to me," said Sancho. "Land that of itself is barren and dry will eventually yield good fruit if you dung it and till it. What I mean is that your worship's conversation has been the dung that has fallen on the barren soil of my dry mind, which has been tilled in the time I have been in your service and society. With this help, I hope to yield fruit in abundance, of a kind that will not fall away or slip from those paths of good breeding that your worship has made in my parched understanding."

Don Quixote laughed at Sancho's affected phraseology. What he said about his improvement seemed true to his master, for now and then he spoke in a way that surprised him; though always, or mostly, when Sancho attempted learned or courtly speech, he wound up tumbling off the summit of his simplicity into the abyss of his ignorance. Where he showed his culture and memory to the greatest advantage was in his fondness for proverbs, whether or not they had any bearing on the subject at hand, as has been seen already and will be further observed in the course of this history.

In conversation of this kind they passed a good part of the night, until Sancho felt a desire to let down the curtains of his eyes, as he used to say when he wanted to go to sleep. Stripping Dapple of his trappings, he left him at liberty to graze his fill. He did not remove Rocinante's saddle, since his master's express orders were that so long as they were in the field or not sleeping under a roof, Rocinante was not to have his saddle taken off. For among knights-errant, it was the ancient usage established and observed to take off the bridle and hang it on the saddlebow. But to remove the saddle from the horse—never! Sancho acted accordingly and gave him the same liberty he had given Dapple, between whom and Rocinante there was a singular friendship. Of such a tender nature their friendship was that it is handed down by tradition from father to son that the author of this true history devoted some special chapters to it, which, in order to preserve the decorum due to a history so heroic, he did not insert therein. At times, nonetheless, he forgets this resolution of his and describes how eagerly the two beasts would scratch one another when they were together and how, when

[1] *I've heard it many and many a time:* As Sancho correctly points out, Don Quixote is not the first to compare our lives to a play or the theater to the drama of life. The *Theatrum mundi* metaphor was a commonplace of the early modern world. In Shakespeare's *As You Like It* (1599), Jaques' monologue beginning "All the world's a stage, / And all the men and women merely players" divides the life of man into seven acts, or ages. Later in the century, Pedro Calderón de la Barca's sacramental play *The Grand Theater of the World* (1655), portrayed God as a cosmic empresario who assigns roles to human actors.

they were tired or full, Rocinante would lay his neck across Dapple's, stretching half a yard or more on the other side. The two of them would stand thus, gazing thoughtfully on the ground, for three days—or at least so long as they were left alone and hunger did not drive them to go and look for food. I may add that they say the author left it on record that he likened their friendship to that of Nisus and Euryalus and Pylades and Orestes.[2] If this was the case, we should not help but wonder how firm the friendship must have been between these two peaceful animals—shaming men, who preserve friendships with one another so badly. This was why it was said,

> For friend no longer is there friend;
> The reeds turn lances now.[3]

And someone else has sung,

> From friend to friend, a bug, etc.[4]

Let no one think that the author was far off the mark when he compared the friendship of these animals to that of men; for men have received many lessons from beasts and learned many important things—such as enemas from the stork, herbal purges and gratitude from the dog, watchfulness from the crane, foresight from the ant, modesty from the elephant, and loyalty from the horse.[5]

Sancho at last fell asleep at the foot of a cork tree, while Don Quixote dozed beneath a sturdy oak. A short time only had elapsed when a noise that Don Quixote heard coming from behind awoke him. Rising up startled, he listened and looked in the direction the noise came from and made out two men on horseback, one of whom, letting himself drop from the saddle, said to the other, "Dismount, my friend, and take the bridles off the horses, for so far as I can see, this place will furnish grass for them, and the solitude and silence my lovesick thoughts require." As he said this he stretched himself upon the ground, and as he flung himself down, the armor in which he was clad rattled, whereby Don Quixote concluded that he must be a knight-errant. Going over to Sancho, who was asleep, he shook him by the arm and with no small difficulty brought him

[2] *Nisus and Euryalus and Pylades and Orestes:* paragons of friendship in Greek mythology. On Nisus and Euryalus, see footnote 15, page 384. Pylades and Orestes were cousins raised together in the court of Agamemnon; their relationship was so close that they were often described as brothers.

[3] *For friend . . . turn lances now:* Lines from a ballad reprinted in Ginés Pérez de Hita's *History of the Civil Wars of Granada*, published at the turn of the seventeenth century.

[4] *From friend to friend, a bug, etc.*: "From friend to friend, a bug in the eye." The origin of the saying is disputed, but it is used to caution against placing too much trust in a friend.

[5] *men have received . . . from the horse:* Central to the providential instinct of the premodern world was the belief that nature contained a storehouse of wisdom for human benefit—both what we would call today scientific knowledge as well as moral examples. The traits cited are found in Pliny's *Natural History* (though in Pliny it is an Egyptian ibis that administers itself an enema). In Cervantes' time, these lessons were widely disseminated in miscellanies and emblem books.

back to his senses, and said in a low voice to him, "Brother Sancho, we have got an adventure."

"May God send us a good one," said Sancho. "And where may her ladyship the adventure be?"

"Where, Sancho?" replied Don Quixote. "Turn your eyes and look, and you will see stretched out there a knight-errant, who, it strikes me, is not terribly happy, for I saw him fling himself off his horse and throw himself on the ground with a certain air of dejection, and his armor rattled as he fell."

"Well," said Sancho, "how does your worship gather that there is to be an adventure?"

"I do not mean to say," returned Don Quixote, "that it is a complete adventure, but that it is the beginning of one, for it is in this way adventures begin. But listen, for it seems he is tuning a lute or guitar, and from the way he is spitting and clearing his throat he must be getting ready to sing something."

"Faith, you're right," said Sancho. "No doubt he is some lovelorn knight."

"There is no knight-errant that is not," replied Don Quixote. "But let us listen to him, for if he sings, by that thread we shall unravel the ball of his thoughts, because out of the abundance of the heart the mouth speaks."[6]

Sancho was about to reply to his master when the Knight of the Forest's voice (which was neither very bad nor very good) stopped him. Listening attentively, the pair heard him sing this

SONNET

Your pleasure, prithee, lady mine, unfold;
Declare the terms that I am to obey;
My will to yours submissively I mold,
And from your law my feet shall never stray.
Would you I die, to silent grief a prey?
Then count me even now as dead and cold;
Would you I tell my woes in some new way?
Then shall my tale by Love itself be told.
The unison of opposites to prove,
Of the soft wax and diamond hard am I;
But still, obedient to the laws of love,
Here, hard or soft, I offer you my breast,
Whate'er you grave or stamp thereon shall rest
Indelible for all eternity.

With an "Ah me!" that seemed to be drawn from the inmost recesses of his heart, the Knight of the Forest brought his song to an end, and shortly afterwards exclaimed in a melancholy and piteous voice, "O fairest and most ungrateful woman on earth! Is it possible, most serene Casildea de Vandalia, that you will suffer this your captive knight to waste away and perish in ceaseless

[6] *out of the abundance of the heart the mouth speaks:* reference to Matthew 12:34.

wanderings and crushing toils? It is not enough that I have compelled all the knights of Navarre, all the Leonese, all the Tartesians,[7] all the Castilians, and finally all the knights of La Mancha, to confess that you are the most beautiful in the world?"

"Not so," said Don Quixote at this, "for I am of La Mancha, and I have never confessed anything of the sort, nor could I nor should I confess a thing so much to the prejudice of my lady's beauty. Take note, Sancho, that this knight is raving. But let us listen; perhaps he will tell us more about himself."

"That he will," returned Sancho, "for he seems to be in a mood to bewail for a month at a stretch."

But this was not the case, for the Knight of the Forest, hearing voices near him, instead of continuing his lamentation, stood up and exclaimed in a distinct but courteous tone, "Who goes there? What manner of men are you? Do you belong to the number of the happy or of the miserable?"

"Of the miserable," answered Don Quixote.

"Then come to me," said he of the Forest, "and rest assured that it is to misery itself and affliction itself you come."

Don Quixote, finding himself answered in such a soft and courteous manner, went over to him, and so did Sancho.

The sorrowful knight took Don Quixote by the arm, saying, "Sit down here, sir knight; for it is to me a sufficient proof that you are a knight, and of those that profess knight-errantry, to have found you in this place, where solitude and a chill air, the natural couch and proper retreat of knights-errant, keep you company."

To which Don Quixote answered, "A knight I am of the profession you mention, and though sorrows, misfortunes, and calamities have made my heart their abode, the compassion I feel for the misfortunes of others has not been thereby banished from it. From what you have just now sung, I gather that your misfortunes spring from love—I mean from the love you bear that fair ingrate you named in your lament."

In the meantime, they had seated themselves together on the hard ground peaceably and sociably, just as if, at the first light of dawn, they were not going to break each other's heads.

"Are you, sir knight, in love perchance?" asked he of the Forest of Don Quixote.

"By mischance I am," replied Don Quixote, "though the ills arising from well-bestowed affections should be esteemed favors rather than misfortunes."

"That is true," returned he of the Forest, "if scorn did not muddy our reason and understanding, for if disdain is excessive it looks like revenge."

"I was never scorned by my lady," said Don Quixote.

"Certainly not," said Sancho, who stood close by, "for my lady is as gentle as a lamb and softer than butter."

"Is this your squire?" asked he of the Forest.

"He is," said Don Quixote.

[7] *Tartesians:* Andalusians.

"I never yet saw a squire," said he of the Forest, "who ventured to speak when his master was speaking; at least, there is mine, who is as grown up as his father, and there is no evidence that he has ever opened his lips when I am speaking."

"By my faith then," said Sancho, "I have spoken and am fit to speak in the presence of one as much or even—but never mind—it only makes it worse to stir it."

The Squire of the Forest took Sancho by the arm, saying to him, "Let us two go where we can talk squirely as much as we please, and leave these gentlemen our masters to fight it out over the story of their loves. Depend upon it, daybreak will find them still at it."

"By all means," said Sancho. "I will tell your worship who I am so that you can see whether I'm able to hold my own among the most talkative squires."

With this the two squires withdrew to one side, and between them there passed a conversation as comical as that which passed between their masters was serious.

CHAPTER XIII

IN WHICH IS CONTINUED THE ADVENTURE OF THE KNIGHT OF THE FOREST, TOGETHER WITH THE STIMULATING DIALOGUE THAT TOOK PLACE BETWEEN THE TWO SQUIRES

The knights and the squires made two parties, these telling the story of their lives, the others the story of their loves; but the history relates first of all the conversation of the servants and afterwards takes up that of the masters. We read that, withdrawing a little from the others, he of the Forest said to Sancho, "A hard life it is we lead and live, señor, we that are squires to knights-errant. Verily, we eat our bread by the sweat of our faces, which is one of the curses God laid on our first parents."[1]

"We could also say," added Sancho, "that we eat it by the chill of our bodies; for who gets more heat and cold than the miserable squires of knights-errant? All in all, it wouldn't be so bad if we had something to eat, for 'troubles are lighter when there's bread.' But sometimes we go a day or two without dining on anything except the wind in our face."

"All that," said he of the Forest, "may be endured when we have hopes of reward; for unless the knight-errant he serves is extremely unlucky, after a while the squire will at least find himself rewarded with a fine government of some island or some fair county."

"I," said Sancho, "have already told my master that I'll be content with the government of some island, and he is so noble and generous that he has promised it to me many a time."

"I," said he of the Forest, "shall be satisfied with a canonry[2] for my services. Indeed, my master has already bequeathed me one, and what a plum it is!"

"Your master, no doubt," said Sancho, "is a churchly knight[3] and can bestow rewards of that sort on his good squire, but mine is only a layman—though I remember some well-spoken (but, to my mind, malicious) people tried to persuade him to become an archbishop. He, however, would not be anything but an emperor. I was trembling the whole time with the worry that he might decide to go into the Church, not finding myself fit to hold an office in it; for I may tell you, though I may seem a man, I'm no better than a beast for the Church."

[1] *we eat our bread . . . our first parents:* the curse laid on Adam and Eve after the Fall (Genesis 3:19).

[2] *canonry:* the office of canon. See footnote 6, page 379.

[3] *churchly knight: caballero a lo eclesiástico,* a phrase of Sancho's invention.

"Well, you are wrong there," said he of the Forest. "Those island governments are not all as good as you might think. Some are corrupt, some are poor, some are dull. In short, the highest and choicest of them brings with it a heavy burden of troubles that the unhappy fellow whose lot it's fallen to bears on his shoulders. Far better would it be for us who have adopted this accursed service to go back to our own houses, and there employ ourselves in pleasanter occupations—in hunting or fishing, for instance; for what squire in the world is there so poor as not to have a hack, a couple of greyhounds, and a fishing rod to amuse himself with in his own village?"

"I'm not without any of those things," said Sancho. "To be sure I don't have a hack, but I have a donkey that's worth my master's horse twice over. May God send me a bad Easter—and may it be the next one coming—if I ever swap one animal for the other, even if I were to get four bushels of barley to boot. You might laugh at the value I put on my Dapple—for dapple is the color of my beast. As to greyhounds, I have all I could want, for there are enough and to spare in my town. Anyway, hunting is more fun when it's with someone else's dogs."

"In all earnestness, sir squire," said he of the Forest, "I've made up my mind to be done with the nonsense of these knights and go back to my village and bring up my children. I have three, like three Oriental pearls."

"I have two," said Sancho, "that might be presented before the Pope himself, especially a girl who I'm raising to be a countess, if it please God, though her mother doesn't approve."

"And how old is this fine woman being reared to be a countess?" asked he of the Forest.

"Fifteen, a couple of years more or less," answered Sancho, "but she's as tall as a lance, fresh as an April morning, and as strong as a porter."

"With traits like those, she would make a good wood nymph, not just a countess," said he of the Forest. "Son of a bitch! That little wench must be hearty as hell."

To which Sancho answered, more than a little irritated, "She is no bitch, nor was her mother, nor will either of them be, please God, while I live. Speak more civilly. If I may say so, your worship's speech does not befit one trained to serve knights-errant, who are the height of courtesy."

"O how little you know about compliments, sir squire," returned he of the Forest. "Why, don't you know that when a horseman delivers a good lance thrust at the bull in the plaza, or when anyone does anything very well, the people are accustomed to say, 'Son of a bitch! That fellow was incredible!' and that what seems to be an insult is high praise? Disown sons and daughters, señor, who fail to do things worthy of such compliments being heaped on their parents."

"I do disown them," replied Sancho, "and with that kind of reasoning, you might as well call me and my children and my wife a whole pack of bitches, for whatever they do or say deserves the same overwhelming praise. I pray to God to deliver me from my mortal sin so that I may see them once more, or (what amounts to the same thing) to deliver me from this perilous calling of squire I've fallen into a second time—all because I was baited and tricked by a purse with a hundred ducats I found one day in the heart of the Sierra Morena. The devil is always putting a bag full of doubloons[4] in front of my eyes, here, there, everywhere, until I imagine at every turn I'm putting my hand on it, hugging it, and carrying it home with me, making investments, getting interest, and living like a prince. So long as I think of this, I make light of all the hardships I endure with this simpleton of a master of mine, who, I well know, is more of a madman than a knight."

"That's why they say, 'Greed bursts the bag,'" said he of the Forest; "but if you want to talk about madmen, there is not a greater one in the world than my master. He belongs with those of whom they say, 'The problems of others kill the ass.' For in order that another knight may recover the senses he's lost, he makes a madman of himself and goes looking for something that, when he finds it, may well end up flying back in his face."

"And is he in love by any chance?" asked Sancho.

"He is," said of the Forest, "with one Casildea de Vandalia, the most heartless and hearty[5] lady the whole world could produce; but that heartlessness is not the only foot he limps on. He has greater schemes rumbling in his bowels, as will be clear before many hours are over."

"'There's no road so smooth but it has some pothole in it,'" said Sancho. "'In other houses they cook beans, but in mine it's by the potful.'[6] Madness is bound to have more followers and servants than good sense; but if there is any truth in the common saying that 'to have companions in trouble gives some relief,' I may take consolation from you knowing that you serve a master as crazy as my own."

"Crazy but valiant," replied he of the Forest, "and more of a sneak than either crazy or valiant."

"Mine isn't like that," said Sancho. "I mean, there isn't a sneaky thing about him. No, he has a heart of gold.[7] He never thinks of doing harm to anyone, only good to all. There is no malice in him whatsoever; a child could persuade him that it is night at noonday. It's because of this simplicity that I love him like I love my own heartstrings, and I can't bring myself to leave him, no matter how crazy he acts."

"For all that, brother and señor," said he of the Forest, "'If the blind lead the blind, both risk falling into the pit.' We're better off beating a hasty retreat and returning home; for those who go looking for adventures don't always find good ones."

Sancho had begun to spit frequently, and his spittle had a rather thick and dry look to it. When the compassionate Squire of the Forest saw it, he said, "It

[4] *doubloons:* A doubloon (*doblón*) was worth considerably more than a ducat—approximately six ducats if it was a *doblón de a cuatro.*

[5] *heartless and hearty:* literally, "rawest and well-roasted". *Crudo* (raw) could mean "cruel" in Golden Age poetry.

[6] *In other houses they cook beans, but in mine it's by the potful:* "As crazy as your master may be, mine is even crazier."

[7] *he has a heart of gold:* literally, "he has a soul like a jug."

seems to me that with all this talk of ours, our tongues are sticking to the roofs of our mouths. I have a pretty good loosener hanging from the saddlebow of my horse." Getting up he came back the next minute with a large wineskin and an empanada half a yard across—this is no exaggeration, for the empanada was stuffed with a white rabbit so big that Sancho, as he handled it, thought it was stuffed not merely with kid but with goat.[8]

Looking it over, Sancho said, "And do you carry this with you, señor?"

"Well, what were you expecting?" said the other. "Do you think I'm one of those measly squires made of water and wool? I carry better provisions on the back of my horse than what a general takes with him when he goes on a march."

Sancho, who ate without needing to be persuaded, and in mouthfuls the size of the knots on horses' fetters, said, "You are a trusty squire, well outfitted, magnificent, and grand, as this banquet shows, which, if it hasn't come here by magic art, certainly has the look of it. I, on the other hand, unlucky beggar, have nothing more in my saddlebag than a scrap of cheese so hard you could beat a giant's brains out with it, and to keep it company, a few dozen carob beans and as many more hazelnuts and walnuts. I have the poverty of my master to thank for it, and the idea he has and the rule he follows, that knights-errant are not to maintain themselves on anything except dried fruits and the herbs of the field."

"By my faith, brother," said he of the Forest, "my stomach is not made for thistles, or wild pears, or roots from the woods. Let our masters have their opinions about chivalry and eat what their laws of chivalry tell them to. I carry a basket filled with food and this wineskin hanging from the saddlebow, whatever they may say. It is such an object of worship with me, and I love it so, that there is hardly a moment when I'm not holding it in my embrace and kissing it."

And so saying he thrust it into Sancho's hands, who raising it aloft pointed it to his mouth and gazed at the stars for a quarter of an hour. When he had done drinking, he let his head fall on one side, and giving a deep sigh, he exclaimed, "Son of a bitch! That is what I call fine wine!"

"There, you see?" said he of the Forest, hearing Sancho's exclamation. "You praised the wine by calling it a son of a bitch."

"Well," said Sancho, "I own it, and I grant that it's no dishonor to call anyone a son of a bitch when it's to be understood as praise. But tell me, señor, on your mother's life, is this wine from Ciudad Real?"

"What a wine taster you are!" said he of the Forest. "Indeed, it comes from nowhere else; and it's been aged for a few years to boot."

"Say no more," said Sancho. "And don't think for a minute that I wouldn't have guessed where it came from. What would you say if I told you, sir squire, that I had such a keen natural instinct in judging wines that you only had to let me smell one and I could identify its region, its kind, its flavor, its vintage, the containers it's been stored in, and everything else having to do with it? But it's

[8] *the empanada was stuffed . . . with goat:* To prepare a rabbit empanada, the animal would be deboned, stuffed with a thick chunk of bacon, coated in a dressing of olive oil, vinegar, and herbs, and then breaded in a batter of butter, eggs, and flour before being baked.

no wonder, for I have had in my family, on my father's side, the two best wine tasters that have been known in La Mancha for many a long year. To prove it I'll tell you now something that happened to them. They gave the two of them some wine out of a cask to try, asking their opinion about its condition, its quality, and the smoothness or boldness of the wine. One of them tried it with the tip of his tongue; the other did no more than bring it to his nose. The first said the wine had a taste like iron; the second said it had a stronger taste like cordovan.[9] The owner said the cask was clean and that nothing had been added to the wine that would have given it a taste of either iron or leather. Nevertheless, these two great wine tasters stood by what they said. Time went by, the wine was sold, and when they came to clean out the cask, they found in it a small key hanging from a cordovan strap. Tell me now if someone who comes from the same stock doesn't have a right to give his opinion in these matters."

"That's why I say," said he of the Forest, "we should give up going in quest of adventures. If we have loaves, why look for cakes? Let's return to our homes, for God will find us there if it be his will."

"Until my master reaches Zaragoza," said Sancho, "I'll remain in his service. After that, we'll see."

The end of it was that the two squires talked so much and drank so much that sleep had to tie their tongues and stay their thirst, for to quench it was impossible. And so the pair of them fell asleep clinging to the now nearly empty wineskin and with half-chewed bits of food in their mouths. There we will leave them for the present to relate what passed between the Knight of the Forest and him of the Woeful Countenance.

[9] *cordovan:* cordovan leather.

CHAPTER XIV

WHEREIN IS CONTINUED THE ADVENTURE OF THE KNIGHT OF THE FOREST

Among the things that passed between Don Quixote and the Knight of the Wood, the history tells us that he of the Forest said to Don Quixote, "In sum, sir knight, I would have you know that my destiny, or, more properly speaking, my choice, led me to fall in love with the peerless Casildea de Vandalia. I call her peerless because she has no peer, whether it be in bodily stature or in the supremacy of rank and beauty. This same Casildea I speak of requited my honorable passion and gentle aspirations by compelling me—as his stepmother did Hercules[1]—to engage in many perils of various sorts, at the end of each promising me that, with the end of the next, the object of my hopes should be attained. But my labors have gone on increasing link by link until they are past counting, nor do I know what will be the last one that is to be the beginning of the fulfillment of my chaste desires.

"On one occasion she bade me go and challenge the famous giantess of Seville, La Giralda by name,[2] who is as mighty and strong as if made of bronze and, though never stirring from one spot, is the most restless and changeable woman in the world. I came, I saw, I conquered, and I made her stay quiet and behave herself, for nothing but north winds blew for more than a week. Another time I was ordered to lift those ancient stones, the mighty Bulls of Guisando,[3] an enterprise that might more fitly be entrusted to porters than to knights. Again, she bade me fling myself into the Cabra Chasm[4]—an unparalleled and awful danger—and bring her a minute account of all that is concealed in those gloomy depths. I stopped the motion of the Giralda, I lifted the Bulls of Guisando, I flung myself into the chasm and brought to light the secrets of its abyss. Yet my hopes are as dead as dead can be, and her scorn and her commands as alive as ever.

[1] *as his stepmother did Hercules:* Juno, Hercules' stepmother, had King Eurystheus impose a sentence of twelve labors on Hercules as atonement for a murderous rampage the hero had committed in a fit of madness.

[2] *La Giralda by name:* What was once the minaret of the Great Mosque of Seville and later the bell tower of the Seville Cathedral was crowned in 1568 with a bronze weather-vane depicting a female allegory of triumphant Christianity.

[3] *Bulls of Guisando:* set of four granite sculptures from pre-Roman times depicting bulls or wild hogs, located near Ávila.

[4] *Cabra Chasm:* vertical cave, long believed to be one of the entrances to hell, in the side of the Picacho de la Sierra de Cabra, a mountain near Córdoba.

"To be brief, last of all she has commanded me to go through all the provinces of Spain and compel all the knights-errant wandering therein to confess that she surpasses all women alive today in beauty, and that I am the most valiant and the most deeply enamored knight on earth; in support of which claim I have already traveled over the greater part of Spain and have there vanquished several knights who have dared to contradict me. But what I most plume and pride myself upon is having vanquished in single combat that most famous knight Don Quixote of La Mancha and made him confess that my Casildea is more beautiful than his Dulcinea. In this one victory I hold myself to have conquered all the knights in the world. For this Don Quixote that I speak of has vanquished them all, and I having vanquished him, his glory, his fame, and his honor have passed and are transferred to my person; for

> The more the vanquished hath of fair renown,
> The greater glory gilds the victor's crown.[5]

Thus, the innumerable achievements of the said Don Quixote are now set down to my account and have become mine."

Don Quixote was amazed when he heard the Knight of the Forest, and was a thousand times on the point of telling him he lied, and had the words on the tip of his tongue; but he restrained himself as well as he could in order to force him to confess the lie with his own lips. So he said to him quietly, "As to what you say, sir knight, about having vanquished most of the knights of Spain, or even of the whole world, I say nothing; but that you have vanquished Don Quixote of La Mancha I consider doubtful. It may have been some other that resembled him, although there are few like him."

"Preposterous!" declared he of the Forest. "By the heaven above us, I fought Don Quixote, overcame him, and made him yield. He is a man of tall stature, gaunt features, long, lank limbs, with hair turning gray, an aquiline nose rather hooked, and large black drooping whiskers. He does battle under the name of 'The Knight of the Woeful Countenance,' and he has for squire a peasant called Sancho Panza. He presses the loins and rules the reins of a famous steed called Rocinante. Lastly, he has for the mistress of his will a certain Dulcinea del Toboso, once upon a time called Aldonza Lorenzo, just as I call mine Casildea de Vandalia because her name is Casilda and she is of Andalusia. If all these tokens are not enough to vindicate the truth of what I say, here is my sword, that will compel incredulity itself to give credence to it."

"Calm yourself, sir knight," said Don Quixote, "and give ear to what I am about to tell you. I would have you know that this Don Quixote you speak of is the greatest friend I have in the world—so much so that I may say I regard him in the same light as my own person; and from the precise and clear indications you have given I cannot but think that he must be the very one you have vanquished. On the other hand, I see with my eyes and feel with my hands that

[5] *The more . . . the victor's crown:* quoted loosely from *La Araucana*, epic poem of Spain's subjugation of Chile (Alonso de Ercilla, published in parts from 1569 to 1589).

it is impossible it can have been the same; unless indeed it be that, as he has many enemies who are enchanters, and one in particular who is always persecuting him, one of these may have taken his shape in order to allow himself to be vanquished so as to defraud him of the fame that his exalted achievements as a knight have earned and acquired for him throughout the known world. In confirmation of this, I must tell you, too, that it is but ten hours since these said enchanters his enemies transformed the shape and person of the fair Dulcinea del Toboso into a foul and coarse village lass. In the same way they must have transformed Don Quixote. If all this does not suffice to convince you of the truth of what I say, here is Don Quixote himself, who will maintain it by arms, on foot or on horseback or in any way you please."

So saying he stood up and laid his hand on his sword, waiting to see what the Knight of the Forest would do, who in an equally calm voice said in reply, "'Pledges don't distress a good payer'[6]—he who has succeeded in vanquishing you once when transformed, Sir Don Quixote, may fairly hope to subdue you in your own proper shape. But as it is not becoming for knights to perform their feats of arms in the dark, like highwaymen and bullies, let us wait till daylight, that the sun may behold our deeds. The conditions of our combat shall be that the vanquished shall be at the victor's disposal, to do all that he may enjoin, provided the injunction be such as shall be becoming a knight."

"I am more than satisfied with these conditions and terms," replied Don Quixote.

Having spoken thus, they went over to where their squires lay and found them snoring, in the same posture as when sleep had overtaken them. They roused them and ordered them to get the horses ready, for at sunrise they were to engage in a bloody and arduous single combat; at which news Sancho was aghast and thunderstruck, trembling for the safety of his master because of the mighty deeds he had heard the Squire of the Forest ascribe to his. But without a word the two squires went in quest of their mounts; for by this time the three horses and the donkey had sniffed each other out and were all together.

On the way, he of the Forest said to Sancho, "You must know, brother, that it is the custom with the fighting men of Andalusia, when they are seconds in any quarrel, not to stand idle with folded arms while the principals fight. I say this to remind you that while our masters are fighting, we, too, have to fight and smash each other to bits."

"That custom, sir squire," replied Sancho, "may hold good among those bullies and fighting men you talk of, but certainly not among the squires of knights-errant—at least, I have never heard my master speak of any custom of the sort, and he knows all the laws of knight-errantry by heart. Even if I admit it to be true that there's some express law requiring squires to fight while their masters are fighting, I don't mean to obey it, but to pay the penalty that may be laid on peacefully minded squires like myself; for I am sure it cannot be more than two

[6] *Pledges don't distress a good payer:* "He who is in the right has no fear of following through on his word."

pounds of wax,[7] and I would rather pay that, for I know it will cost me less than the bandage I'll have to buy to mend my head, which I consider broken and split already. There's another thing that makes it impossible for me to fight: that I have no sword, for I never carried one in my life."

"I know a good remedy for that," said he of the Forest. "I have here two linen sacks of the same size. You will take one, and I the other, and we will fight at sack blows with equal arms."

"If that's the way, so be it with all my heart," said Sancho, "for that sort of battle will serve to knock the dust out of us instead of hurting us."

"That will not do," said the other. "To keep the wind from blowing them away, we must put into the bags half a dozen nice smooth pebbles, all of the same weight. In this way we'll be able to whack each other without doing ourselves any harm or mischief."

"On my father's body!" exclaimed Sancho. "See to it that you stuff those bags with sable fur and carded cotton balls[8] so that our heads won't be broken and our bones beaten to jelly. But even if they are filled with cocoons from the silkworm, I can tell you, señor, I am not going to fight. Let our masters fight as they wish, and let us drink and live. Time will not fail to claim our lives without our going to look for reasons for them to end before the proper time comes when they grow ripe and fall to the ground."

"Nonetheless," returned he of the Forest, "we must fight, even if it's only for half an hour."

"By no means," said Sancho. "I am not going to be so discourteous or so ungrateful as to have any quarrel, be it ever so small, with someone I've eaten and drunk with. Besides, who the devil would arrange a fight for no reason?"

"I have the perfect solution," said he of the Forest. "Before we begin the battle, I'll come up to your worship very quietly and smack you three or four times. With that I'll rouse your anger, though you were sleeping sounder than a dormouse."

"To match that plan," said Sancho, "I have another that's not far behind it. I will take a club, and before your worship comes near enough to rouse my anger, I'll send your anger so sound to sleep with whacks that it won't wake up unless it's in the other world, where it is known that I'm not a man to let my face be handled by anyone. Let each one mind his own affairs—though the better way would be to let each one's anger sleep, for 'no man knows another's heart,' and 'a man may go out for wool and come back shorn.' 'God gave his blessing to peace and his curse to quarrels'; for if 'a hunted cat, surrounded and hard pressed, turns into a lion,' God knows what I, who am a man, may turn into. And so from this time forth I warn you, sir squire, that all the harm and mischief that may come of our quarrel will be put down to your account."

[7] *two pounds of wax:* As a member of a religious confraternity, Sancho would be familiar with such a fine for failure to follow a confraternity's internal regulations. The wax, measured by the pound, was used for candles to light religious festivals or funerals.

[8] *sable fur and carded cotton balls:* Fur from the sable, a species of marten, was highly prized. Carding is the process of disentangling and collecting cotton fibers for subsequent processes like spinning.

"Very good," said he of the Forest. "God will send the morning, and all shall be right."

By now brightly plumed birds of all sorts had begun to warble in the trees, and with their varied and gladsome notes seemed to welcome the rosy dawn as she revealed the beauty of her countenance at the gates and balconies of the east, shaking from her locks a profusion of liquid pearls. Bathed in this dulcet moisture, the plants likewise seemed to shed and shower down a pearly spray. The willows distilled sweet manna, the fountains laughed, the brooks babbled, the woods rejoiced, and the meadows arrayed themselves in all their glory at her coming. But hardly had the light of day made it possible to make out and distinguish things, when the first object that presented itself to the eyes of Sancho Panza was the Squire of the Forest's nose, which was so large that it almost overshadowed his whole body. It is recorded, in fact, that it was of enormous size, hooked in the middle, covered with warts, and of a mulberry color like an eggplant. It hung down two fingers' length below his mouth, and the size, the color, the warts, and the bend of it, made his face so hideous that Sancho, as he looked at him, began to tremble hand and foot like a child in convulsions. He vowed in his heart to let himself be smacked two hundred times rather than be provoked to fight that monster.

Don Quixote examined his adversary and found that he already had his helmet on and visor lowered, so that he could not see his face. He observed, however, that he was a sturdily built man but not very tall in stature. Over his armor he wore a surcoat or cassock of what seemed to be the finest cloth of gold, bespangled all over with glittering mirrors like little moons, which gave him an extremely gallant and splendid appearance. Above his helmet fluttered a great quantity of plumes, green, yellow, and white, and his lance, which was leaning against a tree, was very long and bulky, and had a steel point more than a palm in length.

Don Quixote observed all and took note of all, and from what he saw he concluded that the said knight must be a man of great strength, but he did not for all that give way to fear like Sancho Panza. On the contrary, with a composed and dauntless air, he said to the Knight of the Mirrors,[9] "If, sir knight, your great eagerness to fight has not banished your courtesy, by it I would entreat you to raise your visor a little, in order that I may see if the comeliness of your countenance corresponds with that of your constitution."

"Whether you come victorious or vanquished out of this emprise, sir knight," replied he of the Mirrors, "you will have more than enough time and leisure to see me. If I do not now comply with your request, it is because it seems to me I should do a serious wrong to the fair Casildea de Vandalia in wasting time while I stopped to raise my visor before compelling you to confess what you are already aware I maintain."

"Well then," said Don Quixote, "while we are mounting you can at least tell me if I am that Don Quixote whom you said you vanquished."

[9] *Knight of the Mirrors:* In the chivalric romances, it is not uncommon for a knight to take on a new name with a change in circumstances.

"To that we answer you," said he of the Mirrors, "that you are as like the very knight I vanquished as one egg is like another. But since you say enchanters persecute you, I will not venture to say positively whether you are the said person or not."

"That," said Don Quixote, "is enough to convince me that you are under a deception; however, to relieve you of it entirely, let our horses be brought to us, and in less time than it would take you to raise your visor—if God, my lady, and my arm stand me in good stead—I shall see your face, and you shall see that I am not the vanquished Don Quixote you take me to be."

With this, cutting short the conversation, they mounted. Don Quixote wheeled Rocinante round in order to take a proper distance to charge back upon his adversary, while he of the Mirrors did the same. But Don Quixote had not moved away twenty paces when he heard himself called by the other, and, each returning halfway, he of the Mirrors said to him, "Remember, sir knight, that the terms of our combat are that the vanquished, as I said before, shall be at the victor's disposal."

"I am aware of it already," said Don Quixote, "provided what is commanded and imposed upon the vanquished be things that do not transgress the limits of chivalry."

"That is understood," replied he of the Mirrors.

At this moment the extraordinary nose of the squire presented itself to Don Quixote's view, and he was no less amazed than Sancho at the sight—so much so that he set him down as a monster of some kind or a human being of some new species or unearthly breed. Sancho, seeing his master step back to run his course, was not keen to be left alone with him of the nose, fearing that with one whack with his nostrils the battle would be all over for him and he would be left stretched on the ground, either by the blow or with fright. So he ran after his master, holding on to Rocinante's stirrup leather, and when it seemed to him time to turn about, he said, "I implore of your worship, señor, before you turn to charge, to help me up into this cork tree. From there I'll be able to see better than I would from the ground the brave encounter your worship is going to have with this knight."

"It seems to me rather, Sancho," said Don Quixote, "that you wish to mount to the top of the stands in order to see the bulls without danger."

"To tell the truth," returned Sancho, "that squire's monstrous nose has scared the wits out of me, and I'm terrified to be near him."

"It is," said Don Quixote, "such a nose that were I not who I am it would terrify me too. Come then, I will help you up where you wish."

While Don Quixote waited for Sancho to climb the cork tree, he of the Mirrors took as much ground as he considered necessary, and, supposing Don Quixote to have done the same, without waiting for the sound of a trumpet or any other signal to direct them, he wheeled his horse (which was not more agile or better-looking than Rocinante), and at his top speed—an easy trot—he proceeded to charge his enemy. Seeing him, however, engaged in helping Sancho up a tree, he drew rein and halted midway, for which his horse was very grateful, as he was already unable to move. Don Quixote, imagining that his foe was coming down upon him flying, drove his spurs vigorously into Rocinante's lean flanks and made him speed along in such style that the history tells us that on this occasion only was he known to have done something close to running, for on all others it was a simple trot with him. With this unparalleled fury he bore down where he of the Mirrors stood digging his spurs into his horse up to the buttons,[10] without being able to make him stir a finger's length from the spot where he had come to a standstill in his course.

At this fortuitous moment, Don Quixote came upon his adversary, stymied by his horse and occupied with his lance, which he either could not manage or had no time to lay in rest. Don Quixote paid no attention to these difficulties, but in perfect safety to himself and without any risk met him of the Mirrors with such force that he brought him to the ground in spite of himself over the haunches of his horse, and with so heavy a fall that he lay to all appearance dead, not stirring hand or foot.

The instant Sancho saw him fall he slid down from the cork tree and made all haste to where his master was. Don Quixote, dismounting from Rocinante, went and stood over him of the Mirrors, and unlacing his helmet to see if he was dead, and to give him air if he should happen to be alive, he saw—who can say what he saw, without filling all who hear it with astonishment, wonder, and awe? He saw, the history says, the very countenance, the very features, the very look, the very physiognomy, the very effigy, the very image … of the bachelor Samson Carrasco! As soon as he saw it, he called out in a loud voice, "Make haste here, Sancho, and behold what you will see but not believe. Quick, my son, and learn what magic can do and wizards and enchanters are capable of."

Sancho came up, and when he saw the countenance of the bachelor Carrasco, he fell to crossing himself a thousand times and blessing himself as many more. All this time the prostrate knight showed no signs of life. Sancho said to Don Quixote, "It is my opinion, señor, just to be safe, that your worship should take and thrust your sword into the mouth of this fellow here who looks like the bachelor Samson Carrasco. Perhaps you will kill one of your enchanter enemies inside him."

"Your advice is not bad," said Don Quixote, "for of enemies the fewer the better."

He was drawing his sword to carry into effect Sancho's counsel and suggestion, when the squire of the Mirrors came up, now without the nose which had made him so hideous, and cried out in a loud voice, "Be careful what you do, Señor Don Quixote! That's your friend the bachelor Samson Carrasco you have at your feet, and I am his squire!"

"And the nose?" said Sancho, seeing him without the hideous feature he had before.

The squire replied, "I have it here in my pocket," and putting his hand into his right pocket, he pulled out a masquerade nose of varnished pasteboard of

[10] *up to the buttons:* The strap holding the spur to the boot was fastened to a metal button at the edge of the spur bracket.

the make already described. Sancho, examining him more and more closely, exclaimed aloud in a voice of amazement, "Holy Mary, be good to me! If it isn't Tom Cecial, my neighbor and friend!"

"Why, to be sure I am!" returned the now unnosed squire. "Tom Cecial I am, my friend and companion Sancho Panza; and I'll tell you presently the secrets, tricks, and schemes that brought me here. In the meantime, I beg of your master not to touch, mistreat, wound, or slay the Knight of the Mirrors lying at his feet; because he is beyond all doubt the reckless and ill-advised bachelor Samson Carrasco, our fellow townsman."

Don Quixote observed now that he of the Mirrors had begun to revive. Holding the naked point of his sword over his face, he said to him, "You are a dead man, knight, unless you confess that the peerless Dulcinea del Toboso excels your Casildea de Vandalia in beauty. In addition to this you must promise, if you should survive the loss of this battle, to go to the city of El Toboso and present yourself before her on my behalf. There she will deal with you according to her good pleasure. If she leaves you free to do yours, you are in like manner to return and seek me out—the trail of my mighty deeds will serve you as a guide to lead you to where I may be—and tell me what has passed between you and her. Said conditions, in accordance with what we stipulated before our combat, do not transgress the just limits of knight-errantry."

"I confess," said the fallen knight, "that the dirty, tattered shoe of Lady Dulcinea del Toboso is better than the ill-combed though clean beard of Casildea; and I promise to go and to return from her presence to yours and to give you a full and detailed account of all you demand of me."

"You must also confess and believe," added Don Quixote, "that the knight you vanquished was not and could not be Don Quixote of La Mancha, but someone else in his likeness, just as I confess and believe that you, though you seem to be the bachelor Samson Carrasco, are not so, but some other resembling him, whom my enemies have here put before me in his shape in order that I may restrain and moderate the vehemence of my wrath and make a gentle use of the glory of my victory."

"I confess, affirm, and believe everything to be as you believe, affirm, and claim it," responded the crippled knight. "Let me rise, I entreat you—if indeed the shock of my fall will allow me, for it has left me in a sorry plight."

Don Quixote helped him to rise with the assistance of his squire Tom Cecial, from whom Sancho never took his eyes and to whom he put questions, the replies to which furnished clear proof that he was really and truly the Tom Cecial he said. But the impression made on Sancho's mind by what his master said about the enchanters having changed the face of the Knight of the Mirrors into that of the bachelor Samson Carrasco would not permit him to believe what he saw with his eyes. In sum, both master and man remained under the delusion.

Down in the mouth and out of luck, he of the Mirrors and his squire parted from Don Quixote and Sancho with the intention to look for some village where the bachelor could have his ribs treated and plastered. Don Quixote and Sancho resumed their journey to Zaragoza, where the history leaves them in order to tell who the Knight of the Mirrors and his long-nosed squire were.

CHAPTER XV

WHEREIN IT IS MADE KNOWN WHO THE KNIGHT OF THE MIRRORS AND HIS SQUIRE WERE

Elated and vainglorious in the highest degree did Don Quixote go forth having won a victory over such a valiant knight as he fancied him of the Mirrors to be, and one from whose knightly word he expected to learn whether the enchantment of his lady remained in force; inasmuch as the said vanquished knight was bound, under the penalty of ceasing to be one, to return and render him an account of what took place between the two of them. Don Quixote was of one mind, but he of the Mirrors of another, for in that moment he had no thought of anything else but to find some village where he could have his wounds treated, as has been said already.

Now then, the history tells us that when the bachelor Samson Carrasco recommended Don Quixote to resume the knight-errantry he had laid aside, it was in consequence of having been previously in conclave with the priest and the barber on the means to be adopted to induce Don Quixote to stay at home in peace and quiet without worrying himself with his ill-starred adventures. At this meeting it was decided by the unanimous vote of all—and on the special advice of Carrasco—that Don Quixote should be allowed to go, as it seemed impossible to restrain him. Samson would sally forth to meet him as a knight-errant and do battle with him (for there would be no difficulty about a cause) and vanquish him—that being looked upon as an easy matter. It would then be agreed and settled that the vanquished was to be at the mercy of the victor. Once Don Quixote was vanquished, the bachelor knight was to command him to return to his village and home and not leave it for two years, or until he received further orders from him. There was no doubt that Don Quixote would unhesitatingly obey rather than contravene or fail to observe the laws of chivalry. During the period of his seclusion, he might perhaps forget his folly, or there might be an opportunity of discovering some ready remedy for his madness.

Carrasco undertook the task, and Tom Cecial, Sancho Panza's friend and neighbor, a jolly, feather-brained fellow, offered himself as his squire. Carrasco armed himself in the fashion described, and Tom Cecial, that he might not be recognized by his neighbor when they met, fitted over his own natural nose the false masquerade one that has been mentioned. They followed the same route Don Quixote took and almost caught up with him in time to be present at the adventure of the Cart of Death and then finally encountered them in the forest, where all that the sagacious reader has been reading about took place. And had it not been for the extraordinary fancies of Don Quixote, which led him to believe that the bachelor was not the bachelor, señor bachelor would have been incapacitated forever from taking his degree of licentiate—all because "he did not find nests where he thought to find birds."[1]

Tom Cecial, seeing their desires come to naught and the sorry end of their expedition, said to the bachelor, "Well, Señor Samson Carrasco, we're served right. It's easy enough to plan and set about an enterprise, but it's often a difficult matter to come well out of it. Don Quixote a madman, and we sane; he goes off laughing, safe and sound, and you are left sore and sorry! I'd like to know now which one is crazier, the one who is so because he can't help it, or the one who is so of his own choice?"

To which Samson replied, "The difference between the two kinds of madmen is, that the one who is mad by nature will be one always, while the one who is mad of his own accord can leave off being one whenever he likes."

"In that case," said Tom Cecial, "I was a madman of my own accord when I volunteered to become your squire, and of my own accord I'll leave off being one and go home."

"That's your own business," returned Samson, "but to suppose that I am going home without giving Don Quixote a thrashing is absurd. It is not any wish that he may recover his senses that will make me hunt him out now, but a desire for vengeance. The sore pain I am in with my ribs won't let me entertain more charitable thoughts."

Thus discoursing, the two proceeded until they reached a town where it was their good luck to find a bonesetter, with whose help the unfortunate Samson was cured. Tom Cecial left him and went home, while the bachelor stayed behind planning his revenge. The history will return to him again at the proper time, so as not to omit making merry now with Don Quixote.

[1] *he did not find nests where he thought to find birds:* "Things turned out the opposite of what he expected."

CHAPTER XVI

OF WHAT BEFELL DON QUIXOTE WITH A DISCREET GENTLEMAN OF LA MANCHA

Don Quixote pursued his journey in the high spirits, satisfaction, and pride already described, imagining himself the world's most valorous knight-errant of the age because of his recent victory. All the adventures that could befall him from that time forth he regarded as already undertaken and brought to a happy conclusion. He made light of enchantments and enchanters; he thought no more of the countless drubbings that had been administered to him in the course of his knight-errantry, nor of the volley of stones that had knocked out half his teeth, nor of the ingratitude of the galley slaves, nor of the audacity of the Yanguesans and the shower of stakes that fell upon him. In short, he said to himself that if he could discover any means or design to disenchant his lady Dulcinea, he would not envy the highest fortune that the most fortunate knight-errant of yore ever reached or could reach.

He was going along entirely absorbed in these fancies, when Sancho said to him, "Isn't it odd, señor, that I still have before my eyes that monstrously enormous nose of my neighbor, Tom Cecial?"

"Do you then believe, Sancho," said Don Quixote, "that the Knight of the Mirrors was the bachelor Carrasco and his squire Tom Cecial your neighbor?"

"I don't know what to say about that," replied Sancho. "All I know is that the details he gave me about my own house, wife, and children, nobody else but him could have given me; and the face, once the nose was off, was the very face of Tom Cecial, as I have seen it many a time in my town and next door to my own house; and the sound of the voice was just the same."

"Let us reason the matter, Sancho," said Don Quixote. "Come now, by what process of thinking can it be supposed that the bachelor Samson Carrasco would come out as a knight-errant, in arms offensive and defensive, to fight with me? Have I ever been his enemy? Have I ever given him any reason to hold a grudge against me? Am I his rival, or does he profess arms, that he should envy the fame I have acquired in them?"

"Well, but what are we to say, señor," returned Sancho, "about that knight, whoever he is, being so like the bachelor Carrasco and his squire so like my neighbor Tom Cecial? And if that's enchantment, as your worship says, was there no other pair in the world for them to take the likeness of?"

"It is all," said Don Quixote, "a scheme and plot of the malignant magicians that persecute me, who, foreseeing that I was to be victorious in the conflict, arranged that the vanquished knight should display the countenance of my friend the bachelor in order that the friendship I bear him should interpose to stay the edge of my sword and might of my arm and temper the just wrath of my heart; so that he who sought to take my life by fraud and falsehood should save his own. As proof, Sancho, you know already by experience, which cannot lie or deceive, how easy it is for enchanters to change one countenance into another, turning fair into foul and foul into fair; for it is not two days since you saw with your own eyes the beauty and elegance of the peerless Dulcinea in all its perfection and natural harmony, while I saw her in the repulsive and mean form of a coarse country wench, with cataracts in my eyes and a foul smell in her mouth. After the perverse enchanter dared to perform so wicked a transformation, it is no wonder that he would carry out that of Samson Carrasco and your neighbor in order to snatch the glory of victory from my grasp. For all that, however, I console myself, for in whatever shape he may have been, I, after all, have been victorious over my enemy."

"God knows the truth about everything," said Sancho. Aware as he was that he had been the mastermind behind Dulcinea's transformation, he was not satisfied with his master's illusions; but he chose not to reply lest he should say something that might reveal his trickery.

As they were engaged in this conversation, they were overtaken by a man who was following the same road behind them. He was mounted on a very handsome speckled mare and dressed in a cloak of fine green cloth finished with triangles in a tawny velvet;[1] his riding cap was of the same velvet. His mare was outfitted for travel in the jineta fashion,[2] likewise in green and mulberry. He carried a Moorish cutlass hanging from a broad green and gold baldric,[3] with leggings of the same material. The spurs were not gilt but a lacquered green, and so brightly polished that, matching as they did the rest of his apparel, they looked finer than if they had been of pure gold.

As the traveler approached, he saluted them courteously. Spurring his mare, he was about to pass them without stopping when Don Quixote called out to him, "Gallant sir, if your worship is going our way and has no occasion for speed, I would be honored if we joined company."

"In truth," replied the gentleman on the mare, "I would not pass you so hastily but for fear that your horse might turn restive in the company of my mare."

"You'll have no difficulty keeping your mare in check, señor," said Sancho in reply to this, "for our horse is the most virtuous and well-behaved horse in the world. He's never done anything wrong on these occasions, and the only time he misbehaved, my master and I suffered for it sevenfold. I say again, your worship may pull up if you like; for if she was offered to him on a silver platter, the horse wouldn't hanker after her."

[1] *finished with triangles in a tawny velvet:* The triangle appliqué at the hem permitted the rider greater freedom of movement. For men of rank, black was the color of dress at court, while travel wear tended to be in bright colors.

[2] *in the jineta fashion:* See footnote 3, page 293.

[3] *baldric:* belt for the sword worn across the shoulder.

The traveler drew rein, amazed at the figure and bearing of Don Quixote, who rode without his helmet, which Sancho carried like a valise in front of Dapple's packsaddle. If the man in green examined Don Quixote closely, still more closely did Don Quixote examine the man in green, who struck him as being a man of intelligence. In appearance he was about fifty years of age, with but few gray hairs, an aquiline cast of features, and an expression between somber and light-hearted. His dress and bearing showed him to be a man of good condition. What the gentleman in green thought of Don Quixote of La Mancha was that a man of that appearance and manner he had never yet seen. He marveled at the length of his hair, his lofty stature, his lean and sallow face, his armor, his demeanor, and his gravity—a figure such as had not been seen in those regions for many a long day.

Don Quixote saw very plainly the attention with which the traveler was regarding him and read curiosity in his amazement. Courteous as he was and ready to please everybody, before the other could ask him any question he anticipated him by saying, "The appearance I present to your worship being so strange and so out of the ordinary, I should not be surprised if it filled you with wonder; but you will cease to wonder when I tell you, as I do, that I am one of the knights of

> those, of whom they say,
> go out to seek adventure.[4]

I have left my home, I have mortgaged my estate, I have given up my comforts, and committed myself to the arms of Fortune, to bear me whithersoever she may please. My desire was to bring to life again knight-errantry, now dead, and for some time past, stumbling here, falling there, now coming down headlong, now raising myself up again, I have carried out a great portion of my design, defending widows, protecting maidens, and giving aid to wives, orphans, and minors—the proper and natural duty of knights-errant. Therefore, because of my many valiant and Christian achievements, I have been already found worthy to make my way in print to well-nigh all, or most, of the nations of the earth. Thirty thousand volumes of my history have been printed, and it is on the way to be printed thirty thousand thousands of times, if Heaven does not put a stop to it. In short, to sum up all in a few words, or in a single one, I may tell you I am Don Quixote of La Mancha, otherwise called 'The Knight of the Woeful Countenance;' for though self-praise is degrading, I must perforce sound my own sometimes, that is to say, when there is no one at hand to do it for me. So that, gentle sir, neither this horse, nor this lance, nor this shield, nor this squire, nor all these arms put together, nor my sallow countenance, nor my severe leanness will henceforth astonish you, now that you know who I am and what profession I follow."

With these words Don Quixote held his peace. Considering the time he took to answer, the man in green seemed to be at a loss for a reply. After a long pause, however, he said to him, "You were right when you saw curiosity in my amazement, sir knight, but you have not succeeded in removing the astonishment I

[4] *those, of whom they say, / go out to seek adventure*: Don Quixote quotes variations of this couplet in Part I.

feel at seeing you; for although you say, señor, that knowing who you are ought to remove it, it has not done so. On the contrary, now that I know, I am left more astonished and wonderstruck than before. How is it possible that there are knights-errant in the world these days and histories of real chivalry printed? I cannot persuade myself that there can be anyone on earth nowadays who aids widows, or protects maidens, or defends wives, or gives help to orphans; nor should I believe it had I not seen it in your worship with my own eyes. Blessed be Heaven! For by means of this history of your noble and genuine chivalrous deeds, which you say has been printed, the countless stories of fictitious knights-errant with which the world is filled, so much to the injury of morality and the prejudice and discredit of good histories, will have been driven into oblivion."

"There is a good deal to be said on that point," said Don Quixote, "as to whether the histories of the knights-errant are fictitious or not."

"Why, is there anyone who doubts that those histories are false?" asked the man in green.

"I doubt it," replied Don Quixote, "but never mind that just now. If our journey lasts long enough, I trust in God I shall show your worship that you do wrong in going with the stream of those who regard it as a matter of certainty that they are not true."

From this last observation of Don Quixote's, the traveler began to suspect that he was some madman and was waiting for him to confirm it by something further. But before they could turn to any new subject, Don Quixote begged him to tell him who he was, since he himself had rendered account of his station and life. To this, he in the green cloak replied "I, Sir Knight of the Woeful Countenance, am a hidalgo by birth, native of the village where, please God, we are going to dine today. I am more than fairly well off, and my name is Don Diego de Miranda. I spend my life with my wife, children, and friends. My pastimes are hunting and fishing, but I keep neither hawks nor greyhounds, nothing but a tame partridge and an intrepid ferret.[5] I have six dozen or so books,[6] some in our mother tongue, some Latin, some of them history, others devotional. Those of chivalry have not as yet crossed the threshold of my door. I am more given to turning over the profane than the devotional, so long as they are books of honest entertainment that charm by their style and attract and interest by the inventiveness they display, though of these there are very few in Spain. Sometimes I dine with my neighbors and friends; often I invite them to dine with me. My banquets are fastidious and well served, with nothing lacking. I have no taste for gossip, nor do I allow gossip in my presence. I do not pry into my neighbors' lives, nor have I lynx-eyes for what others do. I hear Mass every day. I share my goods with the poor, making no display of good works, lest I let hypocrisy

[5] *nothing but a tame partridge and an intrepid ferret:* The partridge served as a decoy; the ferret was used to flush rabbits from their burrows.

[6] *six dozen or so books:* In wealth and status, Don Diego de Miranda and Don Quixote seem to be similarly situated; however, for Don Diego's six dozen books, Don Quixote boasts of owning more than three hundred (see p. 181).

and vainglory—those enemies that subtly take possession of the most watchful heart—find an entrance into mine. I strive to make peace between those whom I know to be quarreling. I am the devoted servant of Our Lady, and my trust is ever in the infinite mercy of God our Lord."

Sancho listened with the greatest attention to the account of the gentleman's life and occupation; and thinking it a good and a holy life and that he who led it ought to work miracles, he threw himself off Dapple and, running in haste, seized his right stirrup and kissed his foot again and again with a devout heart and almost with tears.

Seeing this, the gentleman asked him, "What are you doing, brother? Why these kisses?"

"Let me kiss you," said Sancho, "for I think your worship is the first saint in the saddle I ever saw all the days of my life."

"I am no saint," replied the gentleman, "but a great sinner. You are the saint, brother, for you must be a good fellow, as your simplicity shows."

Sancho went back and regained his packsaddle, having coaxed a laugh from his master's profound melancholy and excited fresh amazement in Don Diego. Don Quixote then asked him how many children he had and observed that one of the things wherein the ancient philosophers, who were without the true knowledge of God, placed the *summum bonum*[7] was in the gifts of nature, in those of fortune, in having many friends, and many and good children.

"I, Señor Don Quixote," answered the gentleman, "have one son, without whom I might count myself happier than I am, not because he is a bad son, but because he is not so good as I could wish. He is eighteen years of age. He has been for six years at Salamanca studying Latin and Greek, and when I wished him to turn to the study of other sciences I found him so wrapped up in that of poetry—if that can be called a science—that there is no getting him to take kindly to the law, which I wished him to study,[8] or to theology, the queen of them all. I would like him to be an honor to his family, as we live in days when our kings liberally reward learning that is virtuous and worthy; for learning without virtue is a pearl on a dunghill. He spends the whole day in settling whether Homer expressed himself correctly or not in such and such a line of the *Iliad*, whether Martial[9] was indecent or not in such and such an epigram, whether such and such lines of Virgil are to be understood in this way or in that. In short, all his talk is of the works of these poets, and those of Horace, Persius, Juvenal, and Tibullus.[10] Of the moderns in our own language he makes no great account;

[7] summum bonum: highest good.

[8] *the law, which I wished him to study:* At the turn of the seventeenth century, approximately half the students enrolled at the University of Salamanca were studying law.

[9] *Martial:* first-century A.D. Roman writer of epigrams, pithy statements in poetic form. His obscene humor is notorious.

[10] *Horace, Persius, Juvenal, and Tibullus:* All four of these Roman poets lived within a couple decades of the life of Christ. Ideas from Horace's *Ars Poetica* surface in the Canon of Toledo's literary theory (Part I, chap. 47). Persius and Juvenal were satirists. Tibullus was known for his elegies. Don Diego's son has pursued a course of study in the humanities

but with all his seeming indifference to Spanish poetry, just now his thoughts are absorbed in composing a gloss on four lines that have been sent him from Salamanca, which I suspect are for some poetical tournament."[11]

To all this Don Quixote said in reply, "Children, señor, are portions of their parents' bowels, and therefore, be they good or bad, are to be loved as we love the souls that give us life. It is for the parents to guide them from infancy in the ways of virtue, propriety, and worthy Christian conduct, so that when grown up they may be the staff of their parents' old age and the glory of their posterity. To force them to study this or that science I do not think wise, though it may be no harm to persuade them. When there is no need to study for the sake of *pane lucrando*[12] and it is the student's good fortune that Heaven has given him parents who provide him with it, it would be my advice to them to let him pursue whatever science they may see him most inclined to; and though that of poetry is less useful than pleasurable, it is not one of those that bring discredit upon the possessor.

"Poetry, señor hidalgo, is, as I take it, like a tender young maiden of supreme beauty, to array, bedeck, and adorn whom is the task of several other maidens, who are all the rest of the sciences. She must avail herself of the help of all, and all derive their luster from her. But this maiden will not bear to be handled, nor dragged through the streets, nor exposed either at the corners of the marketplaces or in the closets of palaces. She is the product of an alchemy of such virtue that he who is able to practice it will turn her into pure gold of inestimable worth. He that possesses her must keep her within bounds, not permitting her to break out in ribald satires or soulless sonnets. She must on no account be offered for sale, unless, indeed, it be in heroic poems, moving tragedies, or lively and ingenious comedies. She must not be touched by the buffoons, nor by the ignorant vulgar, incapable of comprehending or appreciating her hidden treasures. And do not suppose, señor, that I apply the term vulgar here merely to plebeians and the lower orders; for everyone who is ignorant, be he lord or prince, may and should be included among the vulgar.[13] He, then, who shall embrace and cultivate poetry under the conditions I have named, shall become famous, and his name honored throughout all the civilized nations of the earth.

"With regard to what you say, señor, of your son having no great opinion of Spanish poetry, I am inclined to think that he is not quite right there, and for this reason: the great poet Homer did not write in Latin, because he was a Greek, nor did Virgil write in Greek, because he was a Latin. In short, all the ancient

---

(*studiae humanitatis*), which prized the original language of classical texts as models of eloquence and the ideas they expressed as the highest achievements in human thought. Originating in Italy, humanism came to Spanish universities in the late fifteenth century.

[11] *gloss . . . some poetical tournament:* In this kind of poetry competition, the contestant was tasked to compose a poem of four stanzas, each of which would culminate in a verse from the four-verse poem the jury had chosen.

[12] pane lucrando: Latin, "to earn one's bread".

[13] *vulgar:* The noun *vulgo* usually referred to the masses, or common people. Don Quixote explains that he is taking the word in a sense more familiar to English speakers, as someone or something lacking in good taste.

poets wrote in the language they imbibed with their mother's milk, and never went in quest of foreign ones to express their sublime conceptions. That being so, the usage should rightly extend to all nations. The German poet should not be undervalued because he writes in his own language, nor the Castilian, nor even the Biscayan, for writing in his. Your son, señor, I suspect, is not prejudiced against Spanish poetry but against those poets who are mere Spanish versifiers, without any knowledge of other languages or sciences to adorn and give life and vigor to their natural inspiration. Yet even in this he may be wrong, for according to a true belief, a poet is born one—that is to say, the poet by nature comes forth a poet from his mother's womb. Following the bent that Heaven has bestowed upon him, without the aid of study or art, he produces things that show how truly he spoke who said, '*Est Deus in nobis*,' etc.[14] At the same time, I say that the poet by nature who calls in art to his aid will be a far better poet and will surpass him who tries to rely upon his knowledge of art alone. The reason is that art does not surpass nature but only brings it to perfection. Thus, nature combined with art, and art with nature, will produce a perfect poet.

"To bring my argument to a close, I would say then, señor hidalgo, let your son go on as his star leads him, for being so studious as he seems to be, and having already successfully surmounted the first step of the sciences, which is that of the languages, with their help he will by his own exertions reach the summit of humane letters, which so well becomes a secular knight,[15] and adorns, honors, and distinguishes him, as much as the miter[16] does the bishop, or the gown the learned jurist. If your son write satires that sully the honor of others, chide and correct him and tear them up; but if he compose discourses in which he rebukes vice in general, in the style of Horace and with elegance like his, commend him; for it is legitimate for a poet to write against envy and reprove the envious in his verse, and the other vices too, provided he does not single out individuals. There are, however, poets who, for the sake of saying something spiteful, would run the risk of being banished to the coast of Pontus.[17] If the poet is pure in his morals, he will be pure in his verses too. The pen is the tongue of the soul, and as the thought engendered is there, so will be the things that it writes down. When kings and princes observe this marvelous science of poetry in wise, virtuous, and thoughtful subjects, they honor, value, exalt them, and even crown them with the leaves of that tree which lightning strikes not,[18] as if

[14] Est Deus in nobis, *etc.*: "Est deus in nobis: agitante calescius in illo." ("A god dwells within us: when he stirs, we grow warm", Ovid, *Fasti* VI).

[15] *secular knight:* literally, "knight of sword and cape".

[16] *miter:* ceremonial headdress of a bishop or abbot.

[17] *banished to the coast of Pontus:* In A.D. 8, Ovid was banished from the city of Rome and exiled to the remote town of Tomis on the Black Sea (Latin, *Pontus Euxinus*). According to one theory, *The Art of Love*, his poetic manual instructing a man how to find and keep a woman, offended the emperor.

[18] *tree which lightning strikes not:* It was believed that Apollo protected the laurel tree from lightning strikes. In antiquity, a laurel wreath was the prize for winning an athletic or literary contest.

to show that they whose brows are honored and adorned with such a crown are not to be assailed by anyone."

He of the green cloak was filled with astonishment at Don Quixote's argument, so much so that he began to abandon the notion he had taken up about his being crazy. But in the middle of the discourse, it being not very much to his taste, Sancho had turned aside out of the road to ask for a little milk from some shepherds who were milking their ewes close by. Just as the gentleman was about to renew the conversation—with which he was highly pleased—Don Quixote raised his head and observed a cart covered with royal flags coming along the road they were traveling. Persuaded that this must be some new adventure, he called aloud to Sancho to come and bring him his helmet. Sancho, hearing himself called, left the shepherds and, prodding Dapple vigorously, came up to his master, who was about to face a rash and terrifying adventure.

CHAPTER XVII

WHEREIN IS SHOWN THE FURTHEST POINT THAT THE UNMATCHED COURAGE OF DON QUIXOTE COULD POSSIBLY REACH IN THE HAPPILY CONCLUDED ADVENTURE OF THE LIONS

The history relates that when Don Quixote called out to Sancho to bring him his helmet, Sancho was buying some cottage cheese the shepherds agreed to sell him, and agitated by his master's great haste did not know what to do with it or what to carry it in. So as not to lose the cottage cheese (which he had already paid for), he thought it best to throw it into his master's helmet, and acting on this bright idea he went to see what his master wanted with him.

Don Quixote, as he approached, exclaimed to him, "Give me that helmet, my friend, for either I know little of adventures, or what I observe yonder is one that calls upon me to arm myself."

He of the green cloak on hearing this looked in all directions but could see nothing except a cart coming towards them with two or three small flags, which led him to conclude it must be carrying treasure of the king's, and he said as much to Don Quixote. He, however, would not believe him, being always convinced that everything that happened to him must be adventures and still more adventures.

Don Quixote replied to the gentleman, "'He who is prepared has his battle half fought.' Nothing is lost by my preparing myself, for I know by experience that I have enemies, visible and invisible, and I know not when, where, at what moment, or in what shapes they will attack me."

Turning to Sancho, he called for his helmet; and Sancho, as he had no time to take out the cottage cheese, had to give it just as it was. Don Quixote took the helmet and, without noticing what was in it, thrust it down in hot haste upon his head; but as the cottage cheese was pressed and squeezed, the whey began to run all over his face and beard, which so startled him that he cried out to Sancho, "Sancho, what is this? I think my skull is softening, or my brains are melting, or I am sweating from head to foot! If I am sweating it is not indeed from fear. I am convinced beyond a doubt that the adventure which is about to befall me is a terrible one. Give me something to wipe myself with, if you have it, for this profuse sweat is blinding me."

Sancho held his tongue and gave him a cloth, and gave thanks to God at the same time that his master had not found out what was the matter. Don Quixote then wiped himself and took off his helmet to see what it was that made his head feel so cool. Seeing all that white mash inside his helmet he put it to his nose, and as soon as he had smelled it, he exclaimed, "By the life of my lady Dulcinea del Toboso, it is cottage cheese you have put here, you treacherous, impudent, ill-mannered squire!"

To which, with great composure and pretended innocence, Sancho replied, "If it is cottage cheese let me have it to eat, your worship. No, let the devil eat it, for he must have put it there. Would I dare to sully your helmet? Ha, you've finally caught me! Faith, sir, by the light God gives me, it seems I must have enchanters too that persecute me, being an extension of your worship. They must have put that filth there to provoke your patience to anger and make you batter my ribs as you often do. Well, this time, they're off the mark, for I trust to my master's good sense to see that I have no cottage cheese or milk or anything of the sort. If I did I would put it in my stomach, not in the helmet."

"Perhaps so," said Don Quixote. All this the gentleman was observing, and with astonishment; all the more so when, after having wiped himself clean—head, face, beard, and helmet—Don Quixote put the helmet on, and settling himself firmly in his stirrups, easing his sword in the scabbard, and grasping his lance, he cried, "Now, come who will, here am I, ready to take on Satan himself in person!"

By this time the cart with the flags had come up, unattended by anyone except the driver on a mule and a man sitting in front. Don Quixote planted himself before it and cried out, "Whither are you going, brothers? What cart is this? What have you got in it? What flags are those?"

To this the driver replied, "The cart is mine. What is in it is a pair of wild caged lions, which the governor of Oran[1] is sending to court as a present to his Majesty. The flags are our lord the king's, to show that what is here is his property."

"And are the lions large?" asked Don Quixote.

"So large," replied the man who sat at the door of the cart, "that larger, or as large, have never crossed from Africa to Spain. I am the lionkeeper, and I have brought over others but never any like these. They are male and female. The male is in that first cage and the female in the one behind, and they are hungry now, for they have eaten nothing today, so let your worship stand aside, for we must make haste to the place where we are to feed them."

Hereupon, smiling slightly, Don Quixote exclaimed, "Come at me with baby lions, would they? Baby lions at such a time as this? By God, those gentlemen who send them here shall see if I am a man to be frightened by lions. Get down, my good fellow, and as you are the lionkeeper, open the cages and release those beasts to me. In the midst of this field I will let them know who Don Quixote of La Mancha is, in spite and in the teeth of the enchanters who send them to me."

"I see," said the hidalgo to himself at this. "Our worthy knight has shown who he is. The cottage cheese, no doubt, has softened his skull and melted his brains."

[1] *Oran:* Spanish-controlled outpost on the coast of North Africa near Algiers.

At this instant Sancho came up to him saying, "Señor, for God's sake do something to keep my master Don Quixote from taking on those lions; for if he does, they'll tear us all to pieces here."

"Is your master then so mad," asked the gentleman, "that you believe and are afraid he will fight such fierce animals?"

"He is not mad," said Sancho, "but he is bold."

"I will prevent it," said the gentleman, and going over to Don Quixote, who was insisting that the lionkeeper open the cages, he said to him, "Sir knight, knights-errant should attempt adventures which have the hope of a successful outcome, not those which entirely lack it; for valor that encroaches on the domain of recklessness has more of insanity about it than courage. Moreover, these lions do not come to oppose you, nor do they dream of such a thing. They are going as presents to his Majesty, and it will not be right to stop them or delay their journey."

"Señor hidalgo," replied Don Quixote, "you go and mind your tame partridge and your intrepid ferret, and leave each of us to manage his own business. This is mine. I know whether these gentlemen the lions are coming for me or not." Then turning to the lionkeeper he exclaimed, "By all that's good, sir scoundrel, if you don't open the cages this very instant, I'll pin you to the cart with this lance."

The driver, seeing the determination of this armored apparition, said to him, "Please your worship, for charity's sake, señor, let me unyoke the mules and place myself in safety along with them before the lions are turned out. If the lions kill them on my watch I'll be ruined for life, for all I possess is this cart and these mules."

"O man of little faith!"[2] retorted Don Quixote. "Get down, unyoke, and do what you wish. You will soon see that you are exerting yourself for nothing and that you might have spared yourself the trouble."

The driver got down and with all speed unyoked the mules. The lionkeeper called out at the top of his voice, "I call all here to witness that against my will and under compulsion I open the cages and let the lions loose, and that I warn this gentleman that he will be accountable for all the harm and mischief which these beasts may do, and for my salary and privileges as well. You, gentlemen, place yourselves in safety before I open, for I know they will do me no harm."

Once more the gentleman tried to persuade Don Quixote not to do such a mad thing, as it was tempting God to engage in such folly. To this, Don Quixote replied that he knew what he was doing. The gentleman in return entreated him to reflect, for he was aware that he was under a delusion.

"Well, señor," answered Don Quixote, "if you do not like to be a spectator of this tragedy, as in your opinion it will be, spur your flea-bitten mare and retreat to safety."

Hearing this, Sancho with tears in his eyes entreated him to give up an enterprise compared with which the one of the windmills, and the awful one of the fulling mills, and, in fact, all the feats he had attempted in the whole course

[2] *O man of little faith:* See Matthew 14:31, where Jesus told Peter he had "little faith" after losing faith while walking on the water to meet Jesus.

of his life, were cakes and fancy bread. "Look, señor," said Sancho, "there's no enchantment here, nor anything of the kind, for between the bars and chinks of the cage I've seen the claw of a real lion, and judging by it I wager that the lion the claw belongs to must be bigger than a mountain."

"Fear, at any rate," replied Don Quixote, "will make him look bigger to you than half the world. Withdraw, Sancho, and leave me. If I die here you know our old compact: you will go to Dulcinea—I say no more." To these he added some further words that banished all hope of his giving up his insane project. He of the green cloak would have offered resistance, but he found himself ill-matched as to arms and did not think it prudent to come to blows with a madman, for such Don Quixote now showed himself to be in every respect. The latter, renewing his commands to the lionkeeper and repeating his threats, gave warning to the gentleman to spur his mare, Sancho his Dapple, and the driver his mules—all attempting to get away from the cart as far as they could before the lions broke loose.

Sancho was weeping over his master's death, for this time he firmly believed it would be brought by the lions' claws. He cursed his fate and called it an unlucky hour when he thought of taking service with him again; but with all his tears and lamentations he did not forget to thrash Dapple so as to put a good space between himself and the cart. The lionkeeper, seeing that the fugitives were now some distance off, once more entreated and warned him as before. Don Quixote replied that he heard him and that he need not trouble himself with any further warnings or entreaties, as they would be fruitless, and bade him make haste.

During the delay that occurred while the lionkeeper was opening the first cage, Don Quixote was considering whether it would not be well to do battle on foot instead of on horseback. He finally resolved to fight on foot, fearing that Rocinante might take fright at the sight of the lions. He therefore sprang off his horse, flung his lance aside, braced his buckler on his arm, and drawing his sword, advanced slowly with marvelous spirit and a resolute courage to plant himself in front of the cart, commending himself with all his heart to God and to his lady Dulcinea.

It is to be observed that on coming to this passage, the author of this true history breaks out into exclamations: "O valiant Don Quixote, high-mettled beyond extolling! Mirror, wherein all the heroes of the world may see themselves! A second Don Manuel de León,[3] formerly the glory and honor of Spanish knighthood! In what words shall I describe this dread exploit, by what language shall I make it credible to ages to come, what eulogies are there not fitting for you, though they be hyperboles piled on hyperboles! On foot, alone, undaunted, high-souled, with but a simple sword, and that no trenchant blade of the perrillo stamp,[4] a shield, but no bright polished steel one, there you stood, biding and awaiting the two fiercest lions that Africa's jungles ever bred! Let your own deeds be your praise, valiant Manchegan, and here I leave them as they stand, lacking the words wherewith to glorify them!"

[3] *Don Manuel de León:* See footnote 2, page 393.

[4] *perrillo stamp:* The fifteenth-century armorer Julián del Rey was renowned for his short, wide swords stamped with the figure of a little dog (*perrillo*).

Here the author's outburst came to an end, and he proceeded to take up the thread of his story, saying that the lionkeeper, seeing that Don Quixote had taken up his position and that it was impossible for him to avoid letting out the male without incurring the enmity of the fiery and daring knight, flung open the doors of the first cage, containing, as has been said, the lion, which was now seen to be of enormous size, and grim and hideous appearance. The first thing he did was to turn round in the cage in which he lay, protrude his claws, and stretch himself thoroughly. He next opened his mouth and yawned very leisurely, and with near two palms' length of tongue that he had thrust forth, he licked the dust out of his eyes and washed his face. Having done this, he put his head out of the cage and looked all round with eyes like glowing coals, a spectacle and demeanor to strike terror into temerity itself. Don Quixote merely observed him with fixed stare, longing for him to leap from the cart and come to close quarters with him, when he hoped to hack him to pieces. So far did his unparalleled madness go.

But the noble lion, more courteous than arrogant, not troubling himself about silly bravado, after having looked all round, as has been said, turned about and presented his hindquarters to Don Quixote, then very coolly and tranquilly lay down again in the cage. Seeing this, Don Quixote ordered the keeper to take a stick to him and provoke him to make him come out.

"That I won't do," said the lionkeeper, "for if I anger him, the first he'll tear to pieces will be myself. Be satisfied, sir knight, with what you have done, which leaves nothing more to be said on the score of courage, and do not seek to tempt fortune a second time. The lion has the door open; he's free to come out or not to come out. But as he has not come out so far, he will not come out today. Your worship's great courage has been fully manifested already. No brave champion, so it strikes me, is bound to do more than challenge his enemy and wait for him on the field. If his adversary doesn't come, the disgrace is on him, and he who waits for him carries off the victor's crown."

"That is true," said Don Quixote. "Close the door, my friend, and let me have, in the best form you can, what you have seen me do by way of testimony: to wit, that you opened for the lion, that I waited for him, that he did not come out, that I still waited for him, and that still he did not come out, and lay down again. I am not bound to do more. Away with enchantments, and may God uphold the right, the truth, and genuine chivalry! Close the door as I bade you, while I signal to the fugitives that have left us that they may learn this exploit from your lips."

The lionkeeper obeyed, and Don Quixote, fixing on the point of his lance the cloth he had wiped his face with after the deluge of cottage cheese, proceeded to recall the others, who still continued to flee, looking back at every step—all in a body, with the hidalgo bringing up the rear. Sancho, however, happening to observe the signal of the white cloth, exclaimed, "May I die if my master has not overcome the wild beasts, for he is calling to us."

They all stopped and saw that it was Don Quixote who was making signals. Shaking off some of their fear, they approached slowly until they were near enough to hear distinctly Don Quixote's voice calling to them. They returned at length to the cart, and as they came up, Don Quixote said to the driver, "Yoke your mules once more, brother, and continue your journey; and you, Sancho, give him two gold escudos for himself and the lionkeeper to compensate for the delay they have incurred through me."

"That will I give with all my heart," said Sancho. "But what has become of the lions? Are they dead or alive?"

The lionkeeper then in full detail and bit by bit described the end of the contest, exalting to the best of his power and ability the bravery of Don Quixote, at the sight of whom the lion quailed and would not and dared not come out of the cage, although he had held the door open ever so long; and after having told the knight that it was tempting God to provoke the lion in order to force him out, which he wished to have done, very reluctantly and altogether against his will, he had allowed the door to be closed.

"What do you think about that, Sancho?" said Don Quixote. "Are there any enchantments that can prevail against true valor? The enchanters may be able to rob me of good fortune, but of fortitude and courage they cannot."

Sancho paid the escudos, the driver yoked his mules, the lionkeeper kissed Don Quixote's hands for the gift bestowed upon him and promised to give an account of the valiant exploit to the king himself, as soon as he saw him at court.

"If by chance," said Don Quixote, "his Majesty should happen to ask who performed it, you are to say 'The Knight of the Lions'; for it is my desire that into this new name the name I have hitherto borne of Knight of the Woeful Countenance be from this time forward altered and transformed. In this I follow the ancient usage of knights-errant, who changed their names when they pleased or when it suited their purpose."

The cart went its way, and Don Quixote, Sancho, and he of the green cloak went theirs.

All this time, Don Diego de Miranda had not spoken a word, being entirely taken up with observing and noting all that Don Quixote did and said. The opinion he formed was that Don Quixote was a sane man gone mad and a madman with a touch of sanity. The First Part of his history had not yet reached him, for had he read it, the amazement with which his words and deeds filled him would have vanished, as he would then have understood the nature of his madness; but knowing nothing of it, he took him to be rational one moment and crazy the next, for what he said was sensible, elegant, and well expressed, and what he did, absurd, rash, and foolish. Said he to himself, "What could be madder than putting on a helmet full of cottage cheese and then persuading oneself that enchanters are softening one's skull? Or what could be greater rashness and folly than wanting to fight lions tooth and nail?"

Don Quixote roused him from these reflections and this soliloquy by saying, "No doubt, Señor Don Diego de Miranda, you set me down in your mind as a fool and a madman, and it would be no wonder if you did, for my deeds do not argue anything else. But for all that, I would have you take notice that I am neither so mad nor so foolish as I must have seemed to you. A gallant knight shows his advantage when under the eyes of his sovereign he brings his lance to bear adroitly upon a fierce bull in the midst of a spacious plaza. A knight shows his advantage when arrayed in glittering armor he paces the lists before the ladies in some joyous tournament, and all those knights show their advantage when they entertain, enliven, and, if we may say so, honor the courts of their princes by warlike exercises, or what resemble them. But to greater advantage than all these does a knight-errant show himself when he traverses deserts, solitudes, crossroads, forests, and mountains, in quest of perilous adventures, bent on bringing them to a happy and successful conclusion, all to win a glorious and lasting renown. To greater advantage, I maintain, does the knight-errant show himself when he brings aid to some widow in a lonely waste, than the court knight dallying with some city damsel.

"All knights have their own special parts to play. Let the courtier devote himself to the ladies, let him add luster to his sovereign's court by his liveries, let him entertain poor gentlemen with the sumptuous fare of his table, let him arrange jousts and marshal tournaments and prove himself noble, generous, magnificent, and above all a good Christian. In so doing he will fulfill the duties that are especially his. But let the knight-errant explore the corners of the earth and penetrate the most intricate labyrinths, at each step let him attempt impossibilities, on desolate plains let him endure the burning rays of the midsummer sun and the bitter inclemency of the winter winds and frosts. Let no lions daunt him, no monsters terrify him, no dragons make him quail; for to seek these, to attack those, and to vanquish all are in truth his main duties.

"I, then, as it has fallen to my lot to be a member of knight-errantry, cannot avoid attempting all that to me seems to come within the sphere of my duties. Thus it was my bounden duty to attack those lions that I just now attacked, although I knew it to be the height of rashness; for I know well what valor is, that it is a virtue that occupies a place between two vicious extremes, cowardice and temerity. But it will be a lesser evil for him who is valiant to rise till he reaches the point of rashness than to sink until he reaches the point of cowardice; for as it is easier for the prodigal than for the miser to become generous, so it is easier for a rash man to prove truly valiant than for a coward to rise to true valor. Believe me, Señor Don Diego, in attempting adventures it is better to lose by a card too many than by a card too few;[5] for to hear it said, 'such a knight is rash and daring,' falls far better on the ears than 'such a knight is timid and cowardly.'"

"I confess, Señor Don Quixote," said Don Diego, "that everything you have said and done is proved correct by the test of reason itself; and I believe, if the laws and ordinances of knight-errantry should be lost, they might be found in your worship's breast as in their own proper depository and archive. But let us make haste and reach my village, where you shall take rest after your recent exertions; for if they have not been of the body they have been of the spirit, and these sometimes tend to produce bodily fatigue."

"I take the invitation as a great favor and honor, Señor Don Diego," replied Don Quixote. And pressing forward at a quicker pace than before, they reached at about two in the afternoon the village and house of Don Diego, or as Don Quixote called him, "The Knight of the Green Cloak."

[5] *it is better to lose by a card too many than by a card too few*: The expression comes from the card game *veintiuno*, today known as blackjack.

CHAPTER XVIII

OF WHAT HAPPENED TO DON QUIXOTE IN THE CASTLE OR HOUSE OF THE KNIGHT OF THE GREEN CLOAK, TOGETHER WITH OTHER MATTERS OUT OF THE ORDINARY

Don Quixote found Don Diego de Miranda's house built in village style, with his coat of arms in rough stone over the street door. In the courtyard was the storeroom and at the entrance the cellar, and all around there were clay vats,[1] which coming from El Toboso,[2] brought back to his memory his enchanted and transformed Dulcinea. With a sigh—and not thinking of what he was saying or in whose presence he was—he exclaimed,

> O treasures sweet, now to my sorrow found!
> Once sweet and welcome when God willed it so.[3]

O Tobosan vats, how you bring back to my memory the treasure sweet of my bitter regrets!"

The student poet, Don Diego's son, who had come out with his mother to receive him, heard this exclamation, and both mother and son were filled with amazement at the extraordinary figure he presented. Dismounting from Rocinante, Don Quixote advanced with great politeness to ask permission to kiss the lady's hand, while Don Diego said, "Señora, receive with your accustomed kindness Señor Don Quixote of La Mancha, whom you see before you, a knight-errant, and the bravest and wisest in the world."

The lady, whose name was Doña Christina, received him with every sign of goodwill and great courtesy, and Don Quixote placed himself at her service with an abundance of well-chosen and polished phrases. Almost the same civilities were exchanged between him and the student, who listening to Don Quixote, took him to be a sensible, clear-headed person.

(Here the author describes minutely everything belonging to Don Diego's home, putting before us in his picture the whole contents of a rich gentleman-farmer's house. But the translator of the history thought it best to pass over these

[1] *clay vats: tinajas*. The *tinaja* is a large earthenware vessel used to store liquids such as water, wine, or oil. It may be buried up to its neck to keep its contents cool.

[2] *coming from El Toboso:* El Toboso was known for its pottery.

[3] *O treasures sweet . . . God willed it so:* The opening of Garcilaso de la Vega's "Sonnet X". In Garcilaso's poem, the lyric voice addresses a memento the absent beloved has left behind—if faithful to the inspiration from Virgil, a lock of her hair.

and other details of the same sort in silence, as they did not align with the main purpose of the story, the strong point of which is truth rather than dull digressions.)

They led Don Quixote into a room, and Sancho removed his armor, leaving him in Walloon breeches[4] and a chamois leather doublet, all stained with the rust of his armor. His collar was of the Walloon style[5] as worn by students (without starch or lace), his leggings buff-colored, and his shoes polished. He wore his good sword, which hung in a sealskin baldric, for he had suffered for many years, they say, from an ailment of the kidneys;[6] and over all he threw a long cloak of good gray cloth. But before anything else, he had washed his head and face with five or six buckets of water (for as regard the number of buckets there is some dispute), and still the water remained whey-colored, thanks to Sancho's greediness and purchase of that unlucky cottage cheese that turned his master so white.

Thus arrayed, and with an easy and gallant air, Don Quixote passed into another room, where the student was waiting to entertain him while the table was being set; for on the arrival of so distinguished a guest, Doña Christina was anxious to show that she knew how and was able to give a becoming reception to those who came to her house.

While Don Quixote was taking off his armor, Don Lorenzo (for so Don Diego's son was called) took the opportunity to ask his father, "What are we to make of this gentleman you have brought home to us, sir? For his name, his appearance, and your describing him as a knight-errant have completely puzzled my mother and me."

"I don't know what to say, my son," replied Don Diego. "All I can tell you is that I have seen him act the acts of the greatest madman in the world and heard him make observations so sensible that they efface and undo all he does. Talk to him and take the measure of his wits, and as you are astute, form the most reasonable conclusion you can as to his wisdom or folly; though, to tell the truth, I am more inclined to take him to be mad than sane."

With this Don Lorenzo went away to entertain Don Quixote as has been said, and in the course of the conversation that passed between them Don Quixote said to Don Lorenzo, "Your father, Señor Don Diego de Miranda, has told me of the rare abilities and subtle intellect you possess, and, above all, that you are a great poet."

"A poet, it may be," replied Don Lorenzo, "but a great one, by no means. It is true that I am somewhat given to poetry and to reading good poets, but not so much so as to justify the title of 'great' which my father gives me."

"I do not dislike that modesty," said Don Quixote, "for there is no poet who is not conceited and does not think he is the best poet in the world."

"There is no rule without an exception," returned Don Lorenzo. "There may be some who are poets and yet do not think they are."

[4] *Walloon breeches: valones*, wide, puffed-out trousers often gathered at the knee.

[5] *Walloon style:* large, flat collar without adornment.

[6] *for he had suffered . . . of the kidneys:* Since antiquity, it was believed that the body parts of seals had medical or talismanic properties.

"Very few," said Don Quixote. "But tell me, what verses are those which you are now composing and which your father tells me keep you so restless and absorbed? If it is a gloss, I know something about glosses, and I should like to hear them. If they are for a poetical tournament, try to win the second prize; for the first is always awarded by favor or personal standing, the second by simple justice. And so the third comes to be the second, and the first, reckoning in this way, will be third—in the same way that licentiate degrees are conferred at the universities. But for all that, the title of first is a great distinction."

"So far," said Don Lorenzo to himself, "I should not take you to be a madman; but let us go on." So he said to him, "Your worship has apparently attended school. What subjects have you studied?"

"That of knight-errantry," said Don Quixote, "which is as good as that of poetry, and even a finger or two above it."

"I don't know what subject that is," said Don Lorenzo, "and until now I've never heard of it."

"It is a subject," said Don Quixote, "that comprehends in itself all or most of the subjects in the world, for he who professes it must be a jurist and must know the rules of justice, distributive and commutative,[7] so as to give to each one what belongs to him and is due to him. He must be a theologian, so as to be able to give a clear and distinctive reason for the Christian faith he professes, wherever it may be asked of him.[8] He must be a physician, and above all an herbalist, so that in a wilderness or wasteland he will know the herbs that have the property of healing wounds, for a knight-errant must not go looking for someone to cure him at every step. He must be an astronomer, so as to know by the stars how many hours of the night have passed, and what clime and quarter of the world he is in. He must know mathematics, for at every turn some occasion for them will present itself to him. This is not to leave out that he must be adorned with all the virtues, cardinal and theological.[9] To come down to lesser details, he must, I say, be able to swim as well as Nicholas or Nicolao the Fish[10] could, as the story goes. He must know how to shoe a horse and repair his saddle and bridle. To return to higher matters, he must be faithful to God and to his lady. He must be pure in thought, decorous in words, generous in works, valiant in deeds, patient in suffering, compassionate toward the needy, and, lastly, an upholder of the truth though its defense should cost him his life. Of all these qualities, great and small, is a true knight-errant made up. Judge then, Señor Don Lorenzo,

[7] *distributive and commutative:* Distributive justice concerns the fair allocation of resources and burdens within a community proportionate to each person's merit or need. Commutative justice governs exchanges between individuals to ensure equality and reciprocity. The concepts originate in Aristotle's *Nicomachean Ethics*.

[8] *give a clear and distinctive reason . . . asked of him:* See 1 Peter 3:15: "Always be prepared to make a defense to any one who calls you to account for the hope that is in you."

[9] *virtues, cardinal and theological:* To the four cardinal virtues of temperance, justice, prudence, and fortitude—drawn from Aristotelian philosophy—the Church added the theological virtues of faith, hope, and love.

[10] *Nicholas or Nicolao the Fish:* merman from a Sicilian folktale.

whether it be a contemptible subject which the knight who studies and professes it has to learn, and whether it may not compare with the very loftiest that are taught in the schools and colleges."

"If such is the case," replied Don Lorenzo, "this subject, I admit, surpasses them all."

"How, 'if such is the case'?" asked Don Quixote.

"What I mean to say," said Don Lorenzo, "is that I doubt whether there are now—or ever were—any knights-errant, and adorned with such virtues."

"Many a time," replied Don Quixote, "have I said what I now say once more, that the majority of the world is of the opinion that there never were any knights-errant in it; and as it is my opinion that, unless Heaven by some miracle brings home to them the truth that there were and are, all the pains one takes will be in vain (as experience has often proved to me), I will not now stop to disabuse you of the error you share with the multitude. All I shall do is to pray to Heaven to deliver you from it and show you how beneficial and necessary knights-errant were in days of yore and how useful they would be today if only they were in vogue; but now, because of the sins of the people, sloth, indolence, gluttony, and luxury are triumphant."

"Our guest has broken out on our hands," said Don Lorenzo to himself at this point. "But for all that, he is a fascinating madman, and I should be a silly fool to doubt it."

Here, being summoned to dinner, they brought their conversation to a close. Don Diego asked his son what he had been able to make out as to the wits of their guest. To which he replied, "All the doctors and skilled scribes in the world could not make sense of the scrawl of his madness; he is a madman by turns, full of lucid intervals."

They went in to dinner, and the meal was such as Don Diego said on the road he was in the habit of giving to his guests: fastidious, plentiful, and tasty. But what pleased Don Quixote most was the marvelous silence that reigned throughout the house, for it was like a Carthusian monastery.[11]

When the table had been cleared, grace said[12] and their hands washed, Don Quixote earnestly pressed Don Lorenzo to repeat to him his verses for the poetry tournament, to which he replied, "So as not to be like those poets who, when they are asked to recite their verses, refuse, and when they are not asked for them vomit them up, I will repeat my gloss. I expect no prize for it, having composed it merely as a mental exercise."

"A discerning friend of mine," said Don Quixote, "was of the opinion that no one ought to waste labor in glossing verses. The reason he gave was that the gloss can never rise to the level of the text, and that it generally wanders away from the meaning and purpose aimed at in the glossed verses; moreover, that the laws of glossing were too strict, as they did not allow questions, nor 'said he,' nor

[11] *Carthusian monastery:* See footnote 4, page 92.

[12] *grace said:* Church Fathers such as Athanasius, John Chrysostom, and Jerome instructed Christians to give thanks before and after a meal.

'I say,' nor turning verbs into nouns or altering the construction—not to speak of other restrictions and limitations that fetter gloss writers, as you no doubt know."

"Truly, Señor Don Quixote," said Don Lorenzo, "I wish I could catch your worship in a mistake, but I cannot, for you slip through my fingers like an eel."

"I don't understand what you say or mean by slipping," said Don Quixote.

"I will explain myself another time," said Don Lorenzo. "For the present, attend to the glossed verses and the gloss, which run thus:

Could *was* become an *is* for me,
Then would I ask no more than this;
Or could, for me, the time that is
Become the time that is to be!—

GLOSS

Dame Fortune once upon a day
To me was bountiful and kind;
But all things change; she changed her mind,
And what she gave she took away.
O Fortune, long I've begged of thee;
The gifts thou gavest me restore,
For, trust me, I would ask no more,
Could 'was' become an 'is' for me.

No other prize I seek to gain,
No triumph, glory, or success,
Only the long-lost happiness,
The memory whereof is pain.
One taste, methinks, of bygone bliss
The heart-consuming fire might stay;
And, so it come without delay,
Then would I ask no more than this.

I ask what cannot be, alas!
That time should ever be, and then
Come back to us, and be again,
No power on earth can bring to pass;
For fleet of foot is he, I wis,[13]
And idly, therefore, do we pray
That what for aye hath left us may
Become for us the time that is.

Perplexed, uncertain, to remain
'Twixt hope and fear, is death, not life;
'Twere better, sure, to end the strife,

[13] *wis*: know.

And dying, seek release from pain.
And yet, thought were the best for me.
Anon[14] the thought aside I fling,
And to the present fondly cling,
And dread the time that is to be."

When Don Lorenzo had finished reciting his gloss, Don Quixote stood up and in a loud voice, almost a shout, exclaimed as he grasped Don Lorenzo's right hand in his, "By the highest heavens, noble youth, you are the best poet on earth, and deserve to be crowned with laurel, not by Cyprus or by Gaeta—as a certain poet, God forgive him, said[15]—but by the Academies of Athens, if they still flourished, and by those of Paris, Bologna, and Salamanca, which flourish now.[16] Heaven grant that the judges who rob you of the first prize—that Phœbus may pierce them with his arrows and the Muses never cross the thresholds of their doors. Repeat me some of your long-measure verses,[17] señor, if you will be so good, for I want thoroughly to feel the pulse of your rare genius."

Is there any need to say that Don Lorenzo enjoyed hearing himself praised by Don Quixote, even though he looked upon him as a madman? O power of flattery, how far reaching you are, and how wide are the bounds of your pleasing jurisdiction! Don Lorenzo gave a proof of it, for he complied with Don Quixote's entreaty and repeated to him this sonnet on the myth of Pyramus and Thisbe.

SONNET

The lovely maid, she pierces now the wall;
Heart-pierced by her young Pyramus doth lie;
And Love spreads wing from Cyprus isle[18] to fly,
A chink to view so wondrous great and small.
There silence speaketh, for no voice at all
Can pass so strait[19] a strait; but love will ply
Where to all other power 'twere vain to try;
For love will find a way whate'er befall.
Impatient of delay, with reckless pace
The rash maid wins the fatal spot where she
Sinks not in lover's arms but death's embrace.

[14] *Anon:* presently, after a while.

[15] *by Cyprus or by Gaeta—as a certain poet, God forgive him, said:* The identity of the poet, and with it the allusion to Cyprus and Gaeta, remain a mystery.

[16] *Paris, Bologna, and Salamanca, which flourish now:* at the time, the three most prestigious universities on the Continent.

[17] *long-measure verses:* Spanish poetics distinguishes short-measure verses (*versos de arte menor*), of eight syllables per line or fewer, and long-measure verses (*verses de arte mayor*), which exceed eight syllables. The most common long-measure verse length is eleven syllables, characteristic of the Golden Age sonnet, including the one that follows.

[18] *Cyprus isle:* Cyprus is the consecrated isle of Venus, mother of the winged Cupid.

[19] *strait:* narrow.

So runs the strange tale, how the lovers twain[20]
One sword, one sepulcher, one memory,
Slays and entombs and brings to life again.[21]

"Blessed be God," said Don Quixote when he had heard Don Lorenzo's sonnet, "that among the hosts there are of hackneyed poets I have found one consummate one, which, señor, the art of this sonnet proves to me that you are!"

For four days was Don Quixote most sumptuously entertained in Don Diego's house, at the end of which time he asked his permission to depart, telling his host he thanked him for the kindness and hospitality he had received in his house, but that, as it did not become knights-errant to give themselves up for long to idleness and luxury, he was anxious to fulfill the duties of his calling in seeking adventures, of which he was informed there was an abundance in that region, where he hoped to employ his time until the day came round for the jousts at Zaragoza, for that was his proper destination. First of all, he meant to enter the Cave of Montesinos, of which so many marvelous things were reported all through the country, and at the same time to investigate and explore the origin and true source of the seven lakes commonly called the Lakes of Ruidera.[22]

Don Diego and his son commended his laudable resolution and invited him to furnish himself with all he wanted from their house and belongings, as they would most gladly be of service to him; which, indeed, his personal worth and honorable profession made incumbent upon them.

The day of his departure finally came, as welcome to Don Quixote as it was sad and sorrowful to Sancho Panza, who was very well satisfied with the abundance of Don Diego's house and was loath to return to the starvation of the woods and wilds and the meager provisions of his saddlebag. This, however, he filled and packed with what he considered needful.

On taking leave, Don Quixote said to Don Lorenzo, "I know not whether I have told you already, but if I have, I tell you once more that if you wish to spare yourself fatigue and toil in reaching the inaccessible summit of the temple of fame, you have nothing to do but to turn aside out of the ever-so-narrow path of poetry and take the still narrower one of knight-errantry, wide enough, however, to make you an emperor in the twinkling of an eye."

[20] *lovers twain:* the two lovers.

[21] *The lovely maid . . . to life again:* As told in Ovid's *Metamorphoses*, the ill-fated Pyramus and Thisbe are neighbors from rival families who fell in love with each other. Forbidden to pursue a relationship, they communicated through a crack in the wall of their adjoining homes. The night that they arranged to meet under a mulberry tree, Thisbe was forced to flee from a lioness. Pyramus arrived and, finding only her cloak, took her for dead and killed himself. When Thisbe returned and discovered the dead body of her lover, she also committed suicide.

[22] *the Cave of Montesinos . . . the lakes of Ruidera:* The Lagunas de Ruidera, in eastern La Mancha, form a chain of caves, waterfalls, and lakes created by water from underground aquifers and surface tributaries of the Upper Guadiana River flowing through travertine limestone deposits across uneven terrain. The dissolved minerals give the water a vibrant blue-green hue. Today the region is protected as a national park.

In this speech Don Quixote submitted the final evidence for a verdict on his madness, but still better in what he added when he said, "God knows I would gladly take Don Lorenzo with me to teach him how to spare the humble and trample the proud under foot,[23] virtues that are part and parcel of the profession I belong to; but since his tender age does not allow of it, nor his praiseworthy pursuits permit it, I will simply content myself with impressing it upon your worship that you will become famous as a poet if you are guided by the opinion of others rather than by your own. No fathers or mothers ever think their own children ugly, and this sort of deception prevails still more strongly in the case of the offspring of the mind."

Both father and son were amazed afresh at the strange medley Don Quixote talked, at one moment sense, at another nonsense, and at his unflinching resolve to carry on in quest of his ill-fated adventures, the end of his every desire. Offers of service and civilities were renewed, and then, with the gracious permission of the lady of the castle, they took their departure, Don Quixote on Rocinante and Sancho on Dapple.

[23] *spare the humble and trample the proud under foot:* In the episode of the penitents in Part I, Sancho inverts this phrase from Virgil's *Aeneid* when he pronounces a eulogy over what he believes to be his master's dead body (see p. 409).

CHAPTER XIX

IN WHICH IS RELATED THE ADVENTURE OF THE ENAMORED SHEPHERD, ALONG WITH OTHER TRULY ENTERTAINING INCIDENTS

Don Quixote had gone but a short distance beyond Don Diego's village, when he fell in with a couple of either priests or students and a couple of peasants, mounted on four beasts of the donkey variety. One of the students carried, wrapped up in a piece of green buckram[1] serving as portmanteau, what seemed to be a little white linen of fine quality and a couple of pairs of ribbed stockings; the other carried nothing but a pair of new fencing foils with pommels.[2] The peasants carried various articles that showed they were on their way from some large town where they had bought them and were taking them home to their village. Both students and peasants were struck with the same amazement that everybody felt who saw Don Quixote for the first time and were dying to know who this man, so different from ordinary men, could be. Don Quixote saluted them, and after learning that their road was the same as his, made them an offer of his company and begged them to slacken their pace, as their young donkeys traveled faster than his horse. Then, to gratify them, he told them in a few words who he was and the calling and profession he followed, which was that of a knight-errant seeking adventures in all parts of the world. He informed them that his own name was Don Quixote of La Mancha, and that he was called, by way of surname, the Knight of the Lions.

All this was Greek or gibberish to the peasants, but not so to the students, who very soon perceived the crack in Don Quixote's head; for all that, however, they regarded him with admiration and respect. One of them said to him, "If you, sir knight, have no fixed road, as it is the way with those who seek adventures not to have any, let your worship come with us. You will see one of the finest and richest weddings that up to this day has ever been celebrated in La Mancha, or for many a league round."

Don Quixote asked him if it was some prince's that he spoke of it in this way. "Not at all," said the student. "It is the wedding of a farmer and a farmer's daughter, he the richest in all this country, and she the fairest that mortal has ever set

[1] *buckram:* coarse cotton or linen fabric used to stiffen garments or bind books.

[2] *pommels:* The pommel is the rounded or decorative piece at the end of a sword's hilt. It provides balance, keeps the hand from slipping, and gives the sword distinctive ornamentation.

eyes on. The festivities with which it is to be attended will be something extraordinary, for it will be celebrated in a meadow adjoining the town of the bride, who is called by repute Quiteria the fair, as the bridegroom is called Camacho the rich. She is eighteen, and he twenty-two. They are evenly matched, though some of the well-informed, who know all the pedigrees in the world by heart, insist that the family of the fair Quiteria is better than Camacho's—but no one minds that nowadays, for wealth can solder many a crack.[3]

"At any rate, Camacho is free-handed, and it is his fancy to enclose the whole meadow with boughs and cover it overhead, so that the sun will have hard work if he tries to get in to reach the grass that covers the soil. He has provided dancers too, not only sword dancers but also bell dancers, for in his own town there are those who jingle the bells to perfection; of shoe dancers[4] I say nothing, for he has hired a veritable multitude of them. But none of these things, nor of the many others I have omitted to mention, will do more to make this a memorable wedding than the part which I suspect the despairing Basilio will play in it.

"This Basilio is a youth of the same village as Quiteria, and he lived in the house next door to that of her parents, of which circumstance Love took advantage to reenact for the world the long-forgotten loves of Pyramus and Thisbe. For Basilio loved Quiteria from his earliest years, and she responded to his passion with countless modest proofs of affection, so that the loves of the two children, Basilio and Quiteria, were the talk and the amusement of the town. As they grew up, Quiteria's father made up his mind to refuse Basilio his accustomed freedom of access to the house, and so to relieve himself of constant doubts and suspicions, he arranged a match for his daughter with the rich Camacho, as he did not approve of marrying her to Basilio, who had not so large a share of the gifts of fortune as of nature. For if the truth is told ungrudgingly, he is the most agile youth we know, a mighty bar thrower,[5] a first-rate wrestler, and a great ballplayer. He runs like a deer and leaps better than a goat, bowls nine-pins as if by magic, sings like a lark, plays the guitar so as to make it speak, and, above all, handles a sword as well as the best."

"For that excellence alone," said Don Quixote at this, "the youth deserves to marry, not merely the fair Quiteria, but Queen Guinevere herself were she alive now, in spite of Lancelot and all who would try to prevent it."

"Tell that to my wife," said Sancho, who had until now listened in silence, "for she won't hear of anything but each one marrying his equal, holding to the proverb 'every mare with her pair.' My own preference is that this good Basilio—for

[3] *for wealth can solder many a crack:* The insinuation is that Camacho is descended from New Christians (see footnote 8, page 147).

[4] *not only sword dancers but also bell dancers . . . shoe dancers:* Sword dancers kept time by clashing their swords together in rhythmic patterns. Bell dancers marked the beat with jingling bells attached to their feet or hands. Shoe dancers slapped their shoes in time with the music.

[5] *mighty bar thrower:* Like Aldonza Lorenzo (see p. 192), Basilio excels at this rustic sport, in which the winner is the person who can throw a metal bar the farthest and have it land point-first into the ground.

I'm beginning to take a liking to him already—should marry this lady Quiteria. Blessings in this life and the next—I mean the opposite—on anyone who would keep those who love each other from marrying."[6]

"If all those who loved each other were to marry," said Don Quixote, "it would deprive parents of the right to marry their children to the proper person and at the proper time; and if it was left to daughters to choose husbands as they pleased, one would be for choosing her father's servant, and another someone she has seen passing in the street and fancies to be gallant and dashing, though he may be a drunken bully. Love and affection easily blind the eyes of the judgment, so much wanted in choosing one's way of life. The matrimonial choice is very liable to error, and it needs great caution and the special favor of Heaven to make it a good one. He who has to make a long journey will, if he is wise, seek a trustworthy and pleasant companion to accompany him before he sets out. Why, then, should not he do the same who has to make the whole journey of life down to the final destination of death, more especially when the companion has to be his companion in bed, at board, and everywhere, as the wife is to her husband? The companionship of one's wife is no article of merchandise, which, after it has been bought, may be returned, bartered, or exchanged. It is an inseparable accident[7] that lasts as long as life lasts; it is a noose that, once draped around the neck, becomes a Gordian knot,[8] which, if the scythe of Death does not cut it, there is no untying. I could say a great deal more on this subject were I not prevented by the anxiety I feel to know if the señor licentiate has anything more to tell about the story of Basilio."

To this the bachelor (or as Don Quixote called him, licentiate[9]) replied, "I have nothing further to say but that from the moment Basilio learned that the fair Quiteria was to be married to Camacho the rich, he has never been seen to smile, or heard to utter a rational word. He always goes about moody and dejected, talking to himself in a way that shows plainly he is out of his senses. He eats little and sleeps little. All he eats is fruit, and when he sleeps, if he sleeps at all, it is in the field on the hard earth like a brute beast. Sometimes he gazes at the sky; at other times he fixes his eyes on the earth in such an abstracted way that he might be taken for a clothed statue with its costume stirred by the wind. In short, he shows such signs of a heart crushed by suffering, that all we who know him believe that when tomorrow the fair Quiteria says 'I do,' it will be his death sentence."

[6] *Blessings in this life . . . from marrying:* Sancho's ironic way to express his opinion that those who prevent lovers from marrying can go to hell.

[7] *inseparable accident:* A marital bond is not essential to a person's nature (like having a soul), yet it is nonetheless inseparable from the person who marries. The distinction between accidental and essential properties comes from Aristotle.

[8] *Gordian knot:* a knot that cannot be untied. In the ancient Phrygian city of Gordium, a prophecy held that whoever could untie an intricate knot tied to an oxcart would be destined to rule all Asia. Instead of trying to disentangle it, Alexander the Great cut through the knot with his sword.

[9] *bachelor . . . licentiate:* On the distinction between the two university degrees, see footnotes 4–5, pages 137–38.

"God will find a remedy," said Sancho, "for 'God who gives the wound gives the medicine.' Nobody knows what is to come. 'There is many an hour between today and tomorrow, and in any one of them the house may fall.' 'I've seen the rain coming down and the sun shining at the same time.' 'He who goes to bed in good health may not awake the next day.' And tell me, is there anyone who can boast that he's driven a nail into the wheel of fortune? No, sir. Between a woman's 'yes' and 'no' I wouldn't try to fit the head of a pin, for there would not be room for it. If you tell me Quiteria loves Basilio heart and soul, then I'll give him a sack of good luck; for love, I've heard say, looks through spectacles that make copper seem like gold, poverty wealth, and bleary eyes[10] pearls."

"What are you driving at, Sancho? Curses on you!" exclaimed Don Quixote. "When you take to stringing proverbs and sayings together, the only one who can understand you is Judas himself—and may he take you with him! Tell me, you animal, what do you know about nails or wheels or anything else?"

"Well, if you don't understand me," replied Sancho, "it's no wonder my words are taken for nonsense. It's no matter—I understand myself, and I know my words haven't been all that foolish. The problem, señor, is that your worship is always scribbling with everything I say, for that matter, everything I do."

"*Quibbling*, not *scribbling*," said Don Quixote, "you corrupter of honest language, God confound you!"

"Don't get angry with me, your worship," returned Sancho. "You know I haven't been brought up at court or trained at Salamanca, to know whether I'm adding or dropping a letter or two in my words. By God, it's not fair to force a man from Sayago to speak like a Toledan;[11] and there might even be Toledans who don't always hit the mark when it comes to polished talk."

"That is true," said the licentiate, "for those who have been bred up in the Tanneries and Zocodover[12] cannot talk like those who are almost all day pacing the cathedral cloisters, and yet they are all Toledans. Pure, correct, elegant, and lucid language comes from courtiers with keen judgment,[13] even if they were born in Majalahonda[14]—I say keen judgment, because there are many who lack it, and keen judgment is the grammar of good language, cultivated through practice. I, sirs, for my sins have studied canon law at Salamanca, and I rather plume myself on expressing my meaning in clear, plain, and intelligible language."

"If you did not plume yourself more on your dexterity with those foils you carry than on your dexterity of tongue," said the other student, "you would have been the head of your class instead of the tail."

"Look here, bachelor Corchuelo," returned the licentiate, "you have the most mistaken idea in the world about skill with the sword, if you think it useless."

[10] *bleary eyes: lagañas*, the crust that forms over the eyes during sleep.

[11] *a man from Sayago to speak like a Toledan:* Sayagués, named for Sayago, a town in Aragon, was the name given to the rustic speech of the stock bumpkin character in Golden Age theater. Toledo was the cultural capital of Castile.

[12] *Tanneries and Zocodover:* disreputable neighborhoods of Toledo.

[13] *keen judgment: discreción*. See footnote 18, page 103.

[14] *Majalahonda:* now called Majadahonda, a town ten miles northwest of Madrid.

"It is no idea on my part, but an established truth," replied Corchuelo; "and if you wish me to prove it to you by experience, you have swords there, and the moment is opportune. I have a steady hand and a strong arm, and these joined with my resolve—which is not small—will make you confess that I am not mistaken. Dismount and put in practice your positions and circles and angles and science, for I hope to make you see stars at noonday with my brute swordsmanship, in which, next to God, I place my trust that the man is yet to be born who will make me turn my back, and that there is not one in the world I will not compel to give ground."

"As to whether you turn your back or not, I do not concern myself," replied the swordsman, "though it might be that your grave would be dug on the spot where you planted your foot the first time—I mean that you would be stretched dead there for despising skill with the sword."

"We shall soon see," replied Corchuelo, who immediately dismounting his donkey, drew out in a fury one of the swords the licentiate carried on his beast.

"It must not be this way," said Don Quixote at this point. "I will be the arbiter of this fencing match and judge this oft disputed matter." And dismounting from Rocinante and grasping his lance, he planted himself in the middle of the road, just as the licentiate, with an easy, graceful bearing and step, advanced toward Corchuelo, who came on against him, shooting fire from his eyes, as the saying goes. The other two of the company, the peasants, without dismounting from their donkeys, served as spectators of the mortal tragedy. The slashes, straight thrusts, downstrokes, diagonal slashes and two-handed blows[15] that Corchuelo delivered were past counting and came thicker than hail. He attacked like an angry lion, but he was met by a tap on the mouth from the pommel of the licentiate's sword that checked him in the midst of his furious onset and made him kiss it as if it were a relic, though not as devoutly as relics are customarily kissed.

The end of it was that the licentiate by thrusts made him pay every one of the buttons of the short cassock he wore, tore the skirts into strips like the tentacles of an octopus, knocked off his hat twice, and so completely tired him out, that in vexation, anger, and rage, he took the sword by the hilt and flung it away with such force, that one of the peasants, who was a notary, went after it and later made an affidavit that the bachelor sent it nearly three-quarters of a league—testimony that serves to establish with all certainty that force is overcome by skill.

Corchuelo sat down wearied, and Sancho approaching him said, "By my faith, señor bachelor, if your worship takes my advice, you will never challenge anyone to fence again, only to wrestle and throw the bar, for you have the youth and strength for that. But as for these sword masters as they call them, I've heard say they can put the point of a sword through the eye of a needle."

"I am satisfied with having tumbled off my donkey," said Corchuelo, "and with having had the truth I was so ignorant of proved to me by experience."

Getting up he embraced the licentiate, and they were better friends than ever. And not caring to wait for the notary who had gone for the sword, as they saw he

[15] *slashes . . . and two-handed blows:* each a recognized fencing stroke.

would be a long time about it, they resolved to push on so as to reach Quiteria's village, to which they all belonged, in good time.

During the remainder of the journey the licentiate held forth to them on the excellences of swordsmanship with such conclusive arguments and such figures and mathematical proofs that all were convinced of the value of the science and Corchuelo cured of his obstinacy.

It had grown dark, but before they reached the town it seemed to them all as if there was a heaven full of countless glittering stars in front of it. They heard, too, the pleasant mingled notes of a variety of instruments—flutes, drums, psalteries,[16] pipes, and tambourines—and as they drew near they noticed that the trees of a leafy bower that had been constructed at the entrance of the town were filled with lights unaffected by the wind, for the breeze at the time was so gentle that it had not power to stir the leaves on the trees. The musicians were there entertaining the wedding guests, wandering through the pleasant grounds in separate bands, some dancing, others singing, others playing the various instruments already mentioned. In short, it seemed as though all through the meadow delight itself danced, while happiness leaped through the air. Several other people were engaged in building raised benches from which people might conveniently see the plays and dances that were to be performed the next day on the spot dedicated to the celebration of the marriage of Camacho the rich and the funeral rites of Basilio.

Don Quixote would not enter the village, although the peasant as well as the bachelor pressed him. He excused himself on the grounds, amply sufficient in his opinion, that it was the custom of knights-errant to sleep in the fields and woods in preference to towns, even were it under gilded ceilings. And so he turned aside a little out of the road, very much against Sancho's will, as the fine lodging he had enjoyed in the castle or house of Don Diego came back to his mind.

[16] *psalteries:* An ancestor of the zither and dulcimer, the psaltery is played by plucking strings stretched over a fretless board.

CHAPTER XX

WHEREIN AN ACCOUNT IS GIVEN OF THE WEDDING OF CAMACHO THE RICH, ALONG WITH WHAT BECAME OF BASILIO THE POOR

Scarce had the fair Aurora given bright Phœbus time to dry the liquid pearls upon her golden locks with the heat of his fervent rays, when Don Quixote, shaking off sloth from his limbs, sprang to his feet and called to his squire Sancho, who was still snoring. Seeing this, Don Quixote addressed him thus before he roused him: "Happy are you above all the dwellers on the face of the earth, for without envying or being envied, you sleep with tranquil mind; neither do enchanters persecute nor enchantments affright. Sleep, I say, and will say a hundred times—without any jealous thoughts of your mistress to make you keep ceaseless vigils, or any cares as to how you are to pay the debts you owe or find tomorrow's food for yourself and your needy little family to interfere with your repose. Ambition breaks not your rest, nor does this world's empty pomp disturb you, for the utmost reach of your anxiety is to provide for your donkey, since upon my shoulders you have laid the support of yourself, the counterpoise and burden that nature and custom have imposed upon masters. The servant sleeps and the master lies awake thinking how he is to feed him, advance him, and reward him. The distress of seeing the sky turn brazen and withhold its needful moisture from the earth is not felt by the servant but by the master, who in time of scarcity and famine must support the one who has served him in times of plenty."

To all this Sancho made no reply because he was asleep, nor would he have awakened as soon as he did had not Don Quixote brought him to his senses with the butt of his lance. He awoke at last, drowsy and lazy, and casting his eyes about in every direction observed, "If I'm not mistaken, there is a scent coming from that bower far more like fried bacon than rushes[1] or thyme. A wedding that begins with smells like that—cross my heart—ought to be plentiful and free-handed."

"Enough, you glutton," said Don Quixote. "Come, let us go and witness this wedding ceremony and see what the rejected Basilio does."

"Let him do what he likes," returned Sancho. "If he weren't so poor, he would be marrying Quiteria. There's nothing more to the matter than a fellow without a cent who wants to marry up in the clouds. Faith, señor, it's my opinion the

[1] *rushes:* probably the rush daffodil, or jonquil, whose heavily fragrant white or yellow flowers provided an aromatic oil used in perfumes.

poor man should be content with what he can get and not go looking for dainties at the bottom of the sea. I'd bet my arm that Camacho could bury Basilio in reals. If that's the case, as no doubt it is, what a fool Quiteria would be to refuse the fine dresses and jewels Camacho must have given her and will give her and take Basilio's bar-throwing and swordplay. They won't give a pint of wine at the tavern for a good toss of the bar or a neat thrust of the sword. Talents and accomplishments that can't be turned into money—let Count Dirlos[2] have them; but when those gifts fall to one that has hard cash, I wish my condition of life was as enticing as they are. On a good foundation you can raise a good building, and the best foundation in the world is money."

"For the love of God, Sancho," said Don Quixote here, "bring your harangue to an end. It is my belief that if you were allowed to continue every one you began, you would have no time left for eating or sleeping, for you would spend it all in talking."

"If your worship had a good memory," replied Sancho, "you would remember the articles of our agreement before we started from home this last time. One of them was that I was to be allowed to say all I liked, so long as it wasn't against my neighbor or your worship's authority. So far, it seems to me, I haven't violated that article."

"I remember no such article, Sancho," said Don Quixote; "and even if it were so, I desire you to hold your tongue and come along; for the instruments we heard last night are already beginning to enliven the valleys again, and no doubt the marriage will take place in the cool of the morning and not in the heat of the afternoon."

Sancho did as his master asked him, and putting the saddle on Rocinante and the packsaddle on Dapple, they both mounted and at a leisurely pace entered the bower. The first thing that presented itself to Sancho's eyes was a whole ox spitted on a whole elm tree, and in the fire at which it was to be roasted there was burning a middling-sized mountain of firewood. Six stewpots that stood round the blaze had not been made in the ordinary mold of common pots, for they were six half wine jars, each fit to hold the contents of a slaughterhouse. They swallowed up whole sheep and hid them away in their insides without showing any more sign of them than if they were pigeons. Countless were the rabbits already skinned and the plucked fowls that hung on the trees for burial in the pots, numberless the wildfowl and game of various sorts suspended from the branches that the air might keep them cool. Sancho counted more than sixty wineskins of over six gallons each—all filled, as it proved afterwards, with full-bodied wines. There were, besides, piles of the whitest bread, like the heaps of grain one sees on the threshing floors. There was a wall made of cheeses arranged like open brickwork, and two cauldrons full of oil—bigger than those of a dyer's shop—served for cooking fritters, which when fried were taken out with two mighty shovels and plunged into another cauldron of prepared honey that stood close by. Of cooks,

[2] *Count Dirlos:* hero from the ballad tradition who clears his name after being falsely accused of treason.

men and women, there were over fifty, all clean, brisk, and blithe. In the capacious belly of the ox were a dozen soft little sucking pigs, which, sewn up there, served to give it tenderness and flavor. The spices of different kinds did not seem to have been bought by the pound but by the arroba, and all lay open to view in a great chest. In short, all the preparations made for the wedding were in rustic style, but abundant enough to feed an army.

Sancho observed everything, contemplated everything, and everything won his heart. The first to captivate his fancy were the pots, out of which he would have very gladly helped himself to a healthy kettleful. Then he was smitten with the wineskins, and, lastly, the produce of the frying pans—if such imposing cauldrons may indeed be called frying pans. Unable to control himself or bear it any longer, he approached one of the busy cooks and with civil but hungry words asked permission to soak a scrap of bread in one of the pots; to which the cook answered, "Brother, today is not one of those days where hunger has any sway, thanks to the rich Camacho. Get down and look around for a ladle and skim off a hen or two, and may they make a fine meal."

"I don't see one," said Sancho.

"Wait," said the cook, "sinner that I am. How finnicky and helpless you are!" So saying he grabbed a bucket and, plunging it into one of the half vats, took out three hens and a couple of geese and said to Sancho, "Eat hearty, friend, and take the edge off your appetite with these skimmings until dinnertime comes."

"I have nothing to put them in," said Sancho.

"Well then," said the cook, "take spoon and all; for Camacho's wealth and happiness supply everything."

While Sancho fared thus, Don Quixote was watching the entrance at one end of the bower, of some twelve farmers, all in festive dress, mounted on twelve beautiful mares with rich, handsome trappings and many little bells attached to their front straps. They marshaled in regular order and ran not one but several courses over the meadow, with jubilant shouts and cries of "Long live Camacho and Quiteria! He as rich as she is fair, and she the fairest on earth!"

Hearing this, Don Quixote said to himself, "It is easy to see these folk have never seen my Dulcinea del Toboso, for if they had they would be more restrained in their praises of this Quiteria of theirs."

Shortly after this, several bands of dancers of various kinds began to enter the bower at different places, and among them one of sword dancers composed of some twenty-four lads of a gallant and high-spirited appearance, clad in the finest and whitest of linen, and with headscarves embroidered in various colors with fine silk. One of those on the mares asked an active youth who led them if any of the dancers had been wounded. "As yet, thank God, no one has been wounded," said he. "We are all safe and sound."

At once he fell in with the rest of his comrades, and they executed so many turns and with such great dexterity, that although Don Quixote was well used to see dances of the same kind, he thought he had never seen any so good as this. He also admired another that came in composed of fair young maidens, none of whom seemed to be under fourteen or over eighteen years of age, all clad in a rich cloth of green, with their locks partly braided, partly flowing loose, but all of such bright gold as to vie with the sunbeams. Around their necks they wore garlands of jasmine, roses, amaranth, and honeysuckle. Leading them was a venerable old man and an aged matron, quicker in their step than their years would suggest; the music of a Zamoran gaita[3] accompanied them. With bright faces and nimble feet, they proved the best dancers in the world.

Following these there came an artistic dance of the kind they call "speaking dances." It was made up of eight nymphs in two rows, with the god Cupid leading one and Wealth the other, the former adorned with wings, bow, quiver and arrows, the latter in a rich dress of gold and silk of several colors. The nymphs that followed Love bore their names written on white parchment in large letters on their backs. POETRY was the name of the first, KEEN JUDGMENT of the second, BIRTH of the third, and COURAGE of the fourth. Those that followed Wealth were distinguished in the same way. The badge of the first announced LIBERALITY, that of the second LARGESS, the third TREASURE, and the fourth PEACEFUL POSSESSION. In front of them all came a wooden castle carried by four wild men, all clad in ivy and hemp stained green, and looking so natural that they nearly terrified Sancho. On the front of the castle and on each of the four sides of its frame it bore the inscription MODESTY CASTLE. Four skillful drum and flute players accompanied them on their instruments.

The dance began with Cupid, who, after performing two figures, raised his eyes and aimed his bow at a damsel who stood between the turrets of the castle, and thus addressed her:

I am the mighty God whose sway
Is potent over land and sea.
The heavens above us own me—nay,
The shades below acknowledge me.
I know not fear, I have my will,
Whate'er my whim or fancy be;
For me there's no impossible,
I order, bind, forbid, set free.

Having concluded the stanza, he shot an arrow at the top of the castle and went back to his place. Wealth then came forward and performed two more figures. As soon as the drums went quiet, he said:

But mightier than Love am I,
Though Love it be that leads me on,
Than mine no lineage is more high,
Or older, underneath the sun.
To use me rightly few know how,
To act without me fewer still.
For I am Wealth, and I vow
For evermore to do thy will.

[3] *Zamoran gaita:* probably a double-reed woodwind instrument similar to the oboe.

Wealth withdrew, and Poetry came forward, and when she had performed her figures like the others, fixing her eyes on the damsel of the castle, she said:

With many a fanciful conceit,
Fair Lady, winsome Poesy
Her soul, an offering at thy feet,
Presents in sonnets unto thee.
If thou my homage wilt not scorn,
Thy fortune, watched by envious eyes,
On wings of poesy upborne
Shall be exalted to the skies.

Poetry withdrew, and Liberality advanced on the side of Wealth, and after having gone through her figures, said:

To give, while shunning each extreme,
The sparing hand, the over-free,
Therein consists, so wise men deem,
The virtue Liberality.
But thee, fair lady, to enrich,
Myself a prodigal I'll prove,
A vice not wholly shameful, which
May find its fair excuse in love.

In the same manner all the characters of the two bands advanced and retired, and each performed its figures and recited its verses, some of them graceful, some burlesque—but Don Quixote's memory (though he had an excellent one) only carried away those that have been just quoted. Everyone then mingled together, forming chains and breaking off again with graceful, unconstrained gaiety. Whenever Love passed in front of the castle he shot his arrows up at it, while Wealth hurled balls of gilt clay[4] against its walls. At length, after they had danced a good while, Wealth took out a great purse, made of the skin of a large striped cat and to all appearance full of money, and flung it at the castle. With the force of the blow the boards fell apart and tumbled down, leaving the damsel exposed and unprotected. Wealth and the characters of his band advanced and, throwing a great gold chain over her neck, pretended to take her and lead her away captive. On seeing this, Love and his supporters acted as if they were about to snatch her away from them, the whole action being to the accompaniment of the drums and in the form of a regular dance. The wild men made peace between them, and with great dexterity readjusted and fixed the boards of the castle, and the damsel once more ensconced herself within. With this the dance concluded, to the great delight of the audience.

Don Quixote asked one of the nymphs who it was that had composed and arranged it. She replied that it was a beneficiary[5] of the town who had an

[4] *balls of gilt clay: alcancía*. The *alcancía*, the forerunner of the piggy bank, was a clay sphere filled with coins and sealed. In some traditions it was painted gold. When struck or dropped, the *alcancía* would break and scatter the coins inside.

[5] *beneficiary*: recipient of a church benefice.

admirable talent for devising those sorts of things. "I will wager," said Don Quixote, "that the same bachelor or beneficiary is a greater friend of Camacho's than of Basilio's, and that he is better at satire than at vespers.[6] How cleverly he has fit Basilio's charms and Camacho's riches into the dance!"

Sancho Panza, who was listening to all this, exclaimed, "'The king is my rooster.'[7] I stick to Camacho."

"It is quite obvious that you are a rube, Sancho," said Don Quixote, "and of the kind that cries, 'Long life to the conqueror.'"

"I don't know what kind I am," returned Sancho, "but I know very well that I'll never get such elegant skimmings off Basilio's pots as the ones here I've got off Camacho's." He showed him the bucketful of geese and hens, and grabbing one began to eat with great zest and appetite, saying, "A fig for Basilio's charms! You're worth what you have, and you have what you're worth. As a grandmother of mine used to say, 'There are only two families in the world, the Haves and the Have Nots.' She stuck to the Haves. To this day, Señor Don Quixote, 'A man is more likely to reach for *have* than *know*. 'A donkey covered with gold looks better than a horse with a packsaddle.' So I say once more I'm sticking with Camacho and the bountiful skimmings from his pots full of geese and hens and rabbits. As for Basilio's skimmings, if any ever come to hand, or even to foot, they'll be nothing but dishwater."

"Have you finished your harangue, Sancho?" asked Don Quixote.

"Of course I've finished it," replied Sancho, "because I see your worship is offended. If it wasn't for that, I'd have three days' worth of material to work with."

"May God grant I see you mute before I die, Sancho," said Don Quixote.

"At the rate we are going," said Sancho, "I'll be the one chewing mud before your worship dies. Maybe then I'll be so mute that I won't say a word till the end of the world, or at least till the day of judgment."

"Even should that happen, Sancho," said Don Quixote, "your silence will never match all you have spoken, are speaking, and will speak in this life; moreover, it naturally stands to reason that my death will come before yours. I therefore never expect to see you mute, not even when you are drinking or sleeping, and that is all I can say."

"In good faith, señor," replied Sancho, "there's no trusting that fleshless one, I mean Death, who's as ready to devour the lamb as the sheep, and, as I have heard our priest say, treads with equal foot upon the lofty towers of kings and the lowly huts of the poor.[8] That lady is mightier than she is dainty. She's not a bit squeamish; she devours all and makes room for all, and fills her saddlebag with people of all kinds, ages, and ranks. She is no reaper who takes a siesta. At all times she is reaping and cutting down, the dry grass as well as the green. She

[6] *vespers:* evening prayer of the Liturgy of the Hours, marked by the chanting or recitation of the Psalms and Magnificat.

[7] *The king is my rooster:* "I'm rooting for the big guy." The expression comes from cockfighting.

[8] *as I have heard our priest say . . . of the poor:* The priest was quoting Horace, verses that Cervantes' friend likewise cites in the preface to Part I. See footnote 10, page 10.

never seems to chew, but gobbles up and swallows everything put before her. She has a canine appetite that is never satisfied. And though she has no belly, there's no mistaking she has the dropsy,[9] with a thirst to drink the lives of everything that lives, just like someone would drink a jug of cold water."

"Say no more, Sancho," said Don Quixote at this. "Stand still and don't risk a fall.[10] In truth what you have said about death in your rustic phrasing is what a good preacher might have said. I tell you, Sancho, with your sagacity and native talent, you could take a pulpit in hand and go about the world preaching fine sermons."

"'He preaches well who lives well,'" said Sancho, "and I know no more theology than that."

"Nor need you," said Don Quixote, "but I cannot conceive or make out how it is that, the fear of God being the beginning of wisdom,[11] you, who fear a lizard more than you fear God, know so much."

"Stick to judging your chivalries, señor," returned Sancho, "and don't set yourself up to judge other men's fears or braveries. I am as respectable a fearer of God as any son of my neighbor. Leave me to make short work of these skimmings, for all the rest is only idle talk that we'll be called to account for in the other world."[12]

So saying he began a fresh attack on his bucket, with such a hearty appetite that he aroused Don Quixote's, who no doubt would have helped him had he not been prevented by what must be related below.

[9] *dropsy:* edema, the accumulation of fluid in the body's tissue.

[10] *Stand still and don't risk a fall:* "Quit while you're ahead."

[11] *the fear of God being the beginning of wisdom:* Psalm 111:10; Proverbs 1:7.

[12] *idle talk that we'll be called to account for in the other world:* See Matthew 12:36, where Jesus says, "On the day of judgment men will render account for every careless word they utter."

CHAPTER XXI

IN WHICH CAMACHO'S WEDDING IS CONTINUED, WITH OTHER ENJOYABLE INCIDENTS

While Don Quixote and Sancho were engaged in the discussion set forth in the last chapter, they heard loud shouts and a great noise, which were made by the men on the mares as they went at full gallop, shouting, to receive the bride and bridegroom. The two of them were approaching with musical instruments and pageantry of all sorts around them and accompanied by the priest and the relatives of both and all the most distinguished people of the surrounding villages. When Sancho saw the bride, he exclaimed, "By my faith, she's not dressed like a country girl, but like some fine court lady. Lord Almighty! As well as I can make out, the beads on that necklace must be some kind of coral, and her green Cuenca cloth is thirty-pile velvet;[1] and then the white linen trimming—by my oath, but it's satin! Look at her hands—jet[2] rings on them! A pox on me if they're not gold rings, and real gold, and set with pearls as white as cottage cheese—every one of them worth an arm and a leg! Son of a bitch, take a look at her hair! If that's not a wig, I never saw longer tresses and with such a golden gleam all the days of my life. And try finding fault with how elegantly she carries herself; try criticizing her figure. You'd have to say she was like a walking palm tree loaded with clusters of dates[3]—that's just what the trinkets hanging from her hair and neck look like. I swear in my heart she's a brave girl—fit to pass over the Flemish banks."[4]

Don Quixote laughed at Sancho's unschooled compliments and thought that, apart from his lady Dulcinea del Toboso, he had never seen a more beautiful woman. The fair Quiteria appeared somewhat pale, which was, no doubt,

[1] *thirty-pile velvet:* The most prized velvet was three-pile, woven with two warps and a single weft, which produced a dense, lustrous fabric.

[2] *jet:* black gemstone formed from fossilized wood subjected to intense geological pressure.

[3] *walking palm tree loaded with clusters of dates:* echo of descriptions of the beloved in the Song of Songs, e.g., 7:7-8.

[4] *fit to pass over the Flemish banks:* Three interpretations of this curious phrase lead roughly to the same place: (1) If the Flemish banks are the dangerous shoals off the coast of Belgium, then Quiteria has the courage to face the trials of an unhappy marriage; (2) if the Flemish banks are the financial institutions that held many of the Spanish Crown's loans, then she is the treasure that can redeem a great debt—a broad praise of her worth; (3) bed frames could be made from Flemish wood. In this case, she is worthy of the nuptial bed and brave enough to share it with a man she doesn't love.

because of the bad night brides always spend getting themselves ready for their wedding on the following day. They advanced toward a platform that stood on one side of the meadow decked with boughs and carpets, where they were to take their vows, and from which they were to behold the dances and plays.

But as they took their places, they heard a loud outcry behind them and a voice exclaiming, "Wait just a moment, you rash, inconsiderate people!"

At these words everyone turned round and saw that the speaker was a man clad in what appeared to be a loose black coat decorated with crimson patches shaped like flames. He was crowned, as was presently seen, with a crown of gloomy cypress, and in his hand he held a long staff. As he approached, he was recognized by all as the gallant Basilio. Everyone waited anxiously to see what would come of his words, in dread of some catastrophe in consequence of his appearance at such a moment. He came up at last weary and breathless and, planting himself in front of the bridal pair, drove his staff—which had a steel spike at the end—into the ground. And with a pale face and eyes fixed on Quiteria, he addressed her thus in a hoarse, trembling voice:

"Well do you know, ungrateful Quiteria, that according to the holy law we acknowledge, so long as you live you can take no husband.[5] Nor are you ignorant that I have never failed to observe the respect due to your honor—in my hopes that time and my own exertions would improve my fortunes. Yet you, casting off all you owe to my true love, would surrender what is mine to another whose wealth serves to bring him not only good fortune but supreme happiness. Now, to crown this happiness—not that I think he deserves it, but inasmuch as Heaven is pleased to bestow it upon him—I will, with my own hands, do away with the one obstacle that could interfere with it: I will remove myself from between the two of you. Long live the rich Camacho! Many a happy year may he live with the ungrateful Quiteria! And let the poor Basilio die, Basilio whose poverty clipped the wings of his happiness and brought him to the grave!"

So saying, he seized the staff he had driven into the ground and, leaving one half of it fixed there, revealed it to be a sheath that concealed a medium-sized sword. The hilt (as it may be called) being planted in the ground, Basilio, with cool composure and unflinching determination, threw himself upon it. In an instant, the bloody point and half the steel blade appeared at his back—the unhappy man falling to the earth bathed in his blood, transfixed by his own weapon.

His friends at once ran to his aid, filled with grief at his misery and sad fate. Don Quixote, dismounting from Rocinante, hastened to support him and took him in his arms, and found he had not yet ceased to breathe. They were about to draw out the rapier, but the priest who was standing by objected to its being

[5] *according to the holy law we acknowledge, so long as you live you can take no husband:* Basilio implies that he and Quiteria have already exchanged marital vows in secret. Following the Council of Trent's 1563 decree, a valid marriage required that the local parish publicly announce during three successive Masses the couple's intent to marry. If no canonical impediments were raised (such as bigamy or consanguinity), the couple would exchange vows before at least two witnesses and a priest, who pronounced a blessing.

withdrawn before he had confessed him, as the instant of its withdrawal would be that of this death. Basilio, however, reviving slightly, said in a weak voice, as though in pain, "If you would consent, cruel Quiteria, to give me your hand as my bride in this last fatal moment, I might still hope that my rashness would find pardon, as by its means I attained the bliss of being yours."

Hearing this the priest bade him think of the welfare of his soul rather than of the cravings of the body, and in all earnestness implore God's pardon for his sins and for his rash resolve; to which Basilio replied that he was determined not to confess unless Quiteria first gave him her hand in marriage, for that happiness would compose his mind and give him courage to make his confession.

Don Quixote, hearing the wounded man's entreaty, exclaimed aloud that what Basilio asked was just and reasonable, and moreover a request that might be easily complied with; and that it would be as much to Señor Camacho's honor to receive Señora Quiteria as the widow of the brave Basilio as if he received her directly from her father.

"In this case," said the priest, "it will be only to say 'I do,' and no consequences can follow the utterance of the words, for the nuptial couch of this marriage must be the grave."

Camacho was listening to all this, stunned and bewildered and not knowing what to say or do. But so urgent were the entreaties of Basilio's friends—imploring him to allow Quiteria to give him her hand so that his soul, leaving this life in despair, should not be lost—that they moved, indeed, forced him, to say that if Quiteria were willing to give it he was satisfied, as it was only putting off the fulfillment of his wishes for a moment. At once everybody assailed Quiteria and pressed her, some with prayers, and others with tears, and others with persuasive arguments, to give her hand to poor Basilio; but she, harder than marble and more unmoved than any statue, seemed unable or unwilling to utter a word. Nor would she have given any reply had not the priest urged her to decide quickly what she meant to do, as Basilio now had his soul at his teeth, and there was no time for hesitation.

On this the fair Quiteria, to all appearance distressed, grieved, and repentant, advanced without a word to where Basilio lay, his eyes already turned in his head, his breathing short and painful, murmuring the name of Quiteria between his teeth, and by all appearances about to die like a heathen and not like a Christian. Quiteria approached him, and kneeling, asked for his hand by signs without speaking.

Basilio opened his eyes and, gazing fixedly at her, said, "O Quiteria, why have you turned compassionate at a moment when your compassion will serve as a dagger to rob me of life? I have not now the strength left either to bear the happiness you give me in accepting me as yours, or to suppress the pain that is rapidly drawing the dread shadow of death over my eyes. What I entreat of you, O fatal star to me, is that the hand you demand of me and would give me be not given out of hollow acquiescence or to deceive me afresh, but that you confess and declare that without any constraint upon your will you give it to me as to your lawful husband. For it is not fitting that you should toy with me at such a moment as this or have recourse to falsehoods with one who has dealt so truly by you."

While uttering these words he showed such weakness that the bystanders expected each return of faintness would take his life with it. Then Quiteria, overcome with modesty and shame, holding in her right hand the hand of Basilio, said, "No force could bend my will. As freely, therefore, as it is possible for me to do so, I give you the hand of a lawful wife. Take yours if you give it to me of your own free will, untroubled and unaffected by the calamity your rash act has brought upon you."

"Yes, I give it," said Basilio, "not agitated or distracted, but with unclouded reason that Heaven is pleased to grant me, thus do I give myself to be your husband."

"And I give myself to be your wife," said Quiteria, "whether you live many years or they carry you from my arms to the grave."

"For one so badly wounded," observed Sancho at this point, "this young man has quite a bit to say. They should make him put an end to this romantic talk and attend to his soul; for to my thinking he has it more on his tongue than at his teeth."

Basilio and Quiteria having thus joined hands, the priest, deeply moved and with tears in his eyes, pronounced the blessing upon them and implored Heaven to grant an easy passage to the soul of the newly wedded man. He, the instant he received the blessing, started nimbly to his feet and with incredible ease pulled out the rapier that had been sheathed in his body.

All the bystanders were astounded, and some (more simple than inquiring) began shouting, "Miraculous, miraculous!"

But Basilio replied, "Not 'miraculous, miraculous'! Ingenious, Ingenious!"

The priest, perplexed and amazed, went over to examine the wound with both hands and found that the blade had passed, not through Basilio's flesh and ribs, but through a hollow iron tube full of blood, which he had skillfully fixed in place, the blood, as was afterwards learned, having been so prepared as not to congeal. In short, the priest and Camacho and most of those present saw they were tricked and made fools of. The bride showed no signs of displeasure at the deception; on the contrary, hearing them say that the marriage, being fraudulent, would not be valid, she said that she confirmed it anew, from which they all concluded that the affair had been planned by agreement and understanding between the two. At this Camacho and his supporters felt so keenly the disgrace that they decided to revenge themselves by violence. A great number of them drawing their swords attacked Basilio, in whose protection as many more swords were in an instant unsheathed, while Don Quixote taking the lead on horseback, with his lance over his arm and well covered with his shield, made everyone give way before him. Sancho, who never found any pleasure or enjoyment in such misdeeds, retreated to the vats from which he had taken his delectable skimmings, considering that, as a holy place, it would be respected.

"Hold, sirs, hold!" cried Don Quixote in a loud voice. "We have no right to take vengeance for wrongs that love may do to us. Remember that love and war are the same thing, and as in war it is allowable and common to make use of wiles and stratagems to overcome the enemy, so in the contests and rivalries of love the tricks and devices employed to attain the desired end are justifiable, provided they be not to the discredit or dishonor of the loved object. Quiteria belonged to Basilio and Basilio to Quiteria by the just and beneficent disposal of Heaven. Camacho is rich and can purchase his pleasure when, where, and however it pleases him. Basilio has but this ewe lamb,[6] and no one, however powerful he may be, shall take her from him. These two whom God has joined man cannot separate.[7] He who attempts to do so must first pass the point of this lance." So saying he brandished the weapon with such skill and resolve that he overawed all who did not know him.

The impression that Quiteria's rejection made on Camacho's mind was so potent that it banished her at once from his thoughts; and so the counsels of the priest, who was a wise and kindly disposed man, prevailed with him, and by their means he and his supporters were pacified. To prove it, they put away their swords, railing against Quiteria's weak will rather than Basilio's crafty mind. Camacho reasoned that if Quiteria as a maiden had such a love for Basilio, she would have loved him too as a married woman, and that he ought to thank Heaven more for having taken her than for having bestowed her on him.

With Camacho and his armed companions consoled, those on Basilio's side were appeased; and the rich Camacho, to show that he not only felt no resentment for the ruse but thought nothing of it, desired the festival to go on just as if he had really gotten married. Neither Basilio, however, nor his bride, nor their followers would take any part in it, and they departed for Basilio's village; for the poor, if they are virtuous and sensible, have those who follow, honor, and uphold them, just as the rich have those who flatter and wait on them.

With them they took Don Quixote, praising him as the pinnacle of manliness.[8] Sancho alone had a cloud on his soul, for he found himself debarred from awaiting Camacho's splendid feast, which lasted until night. Thus dragged off, he moodily followed his master as he accompanied Basilio's party and left behind him the flesh pots of Egypt,[9] though in his heart he took them with him. The nearly finished skimmings he carried in the bucket conjured up visions before his eyes of the glorious bounty he was losing. And so, vexed and dejected though not hungry, without dismounting from Dapple, he followed in the footsteps of Rocinante.

[6] *Basilio has but this ewe lamb:* See footnote 6, page 209.

[7] *These two whom God has joined man cannot separate:* Matthew 19:6.

[8] *pinnacle of manliness:* literally, "a worthy man with hair on his chest".

[9] *flesh pots of Egypt:* See Exodus 16:2–3, where the Israelites "murmured against Moses and Aaron in the wilderness, and said to them 'Would that we had died by the hand of the Lord in the land of Egypt, when we sat by the fleshpots and ate bread to the full.'"

CHAPTER XXII

WHEREIN IS RELATED THE GRAND ADVENTURE OF THE CAVE OF MONTESINOS IN THE HEART OF LA MANCHA, WHICH THE VALIANT DON QUIXOTE BROUGHT TO A SUCCESSFUL END

Many and great were the attentions shown to Don Quixote by the newly married couple, who felt themselves under an obligation to him for coming forward in defense of their cause. They exalted his wisdom to the same height as his courage, holding him to be a Cid in arms and a Cicero in eloquence. The worthy Sancho enjoyed himself for three days at the expense of the two, from whom they learned that the sham wound was not a scheme arranged with the fair Quiteria, but a device of Basilio's, who counted on exactly the result they had seen. He confessed, it is true, that he had confided his idea to some of his friends, so that at the proper time they might aid him in his purpose and insure the deception's success.

"That," said Don Quixote, "is not and ought not to be called deception which aims at virtuous ends." The marriage of lovers he maintained to be a most excellent end, reminding them, however, that love has no greater enemy than hunger and constant want; for love is all gaiety, enjoyment, and happiness, especially when the lover is in the possession of the object of his love, and poverty and want are their declared enemies. He said this to persuade Señor Basilio to abandon the practice of those accomplishments he was skilled in, for though they brought him fame, they brought him no money, and apply himself to the acquisition of wealth by legitimate industry, which will never fail those who are prudent and persevering. "The poor man who is a man of honor (if indeed a poor man can be a man of honor) has a jewel when he has a fair wife, but if she is taken from him, his honor is taken from him and obliterated. The fair woman who is a woman of honor, and whose husband is poor, deserves to be crowned with the laurels and crowns of victory and triumph. Beauty by itself attracts the desires of all who behold it. The royal eagles and birds of towering flight swoop down upon it as on a delectable lure; but if beauty is accompanied by want and penury, then the ravens and the kites and other birds of prey assail it, and she who stands firm against such attacks well deserves to be called the crown of her husband.[1]

[1] *well deserves to be called the crown of her husband:* See Proverbs 12:4: "A good wife is the crown of her husband."

"Remember, O prudent Basilio," added Don Quixote, "it was the opinion of a certain sage (I know not whom) that there was not more than one good woman in the whole world; and his advice was that each one should be convinced in his mind that this one good woman was his own wife, and in this way he would live happy. I myself am not married, nor, so far, has it ever entered my thoughts to be so. Nevertheless, I would venture to give advice to anyone who might ask it, as to the mode in which he should seek a wife such as he would be content to marry. The first thing I would recommend him would be to look to a good name rather than to wealth, for a good woman does not win a good name merely by being good but by letting it be seen that she is so. Intemperance in the open does much more damage to a woman's honor than depravity in secret. If you take a good woman into your house, it will be an easy matter to keep her good, and even to make her still better. But if you take a bad one you will find it hard work to mend her, for it is no very easy matter to pass from one extreme to another. I do not say it is impossible, but I look upon it as difficult."

Sancho, listening to all this, said to himself, "This master of mine, when I say anything that has weight and substance, says I could take a pulpit in hand and go about the world preaching fine sermons. But I say of him that, when he begins stringing sayings together and giving advice not only could he take a pulpit in hand, but two on each finger, and go into the marketplaces to his heart's content. Devil take you for a knight-errant, how many things you know! I used to think in my heart that all he knew about was what belonged to his chivalry, but there's not a fire he doesn't have a poker in."

Sancho muttered this half aloud, and his master overheard him and asked, "What are you muttering there, Sancho?"

"I'm not saying anything or muttering anything," said Sancho; "I was only saying to myself that I wish I had heard what your worship has just said before I married. Perhaps I'd say now, 'The ox left to roam licks himself well.'"[2]

"Is your Teresa so bad then, Sancho?"

"She is not very bad," replied Sancho; "but she is not very good either—at least, she's not as good as I would like."

"You do wrong, Sancho," said Don Quixote, "to speak ill of your wife; for after all she is the mother of your children."

"The score is even," returned Sancho. "She speaks ill of me whenever she gets it in her head, especially when she's jealous; and Satan himself couldn't put up with her then."

Don Quixote and Sancho ended up remaining three days with the newly married couple, by whom they were entertained and treated like kings. Don Quixote begged the fencing licentiate to find him a guide to show him the way to the Cave of Montesinos, as he had a great desire to enter it and see with his own eyes if the wonderful tales that were told of it all over the country were true. The licentiate said he would get him a cousin of his own, an illustrious scholar, and one very much given to reading books of chivalry, who would have great

[2] *The ox left to roam licks himself well:* "He who is free can do as he pleases."

pleasure in conducting him to the mouth of the very cave, and would show him the Lakes of Ruidera, which were likewise famous all over La Mancha and even all over Spain. He assured Don Quixote that he would find him entertaining, for he was a youth who could write books good enough to be printed and dedicated to princes. The cousin arrived at last, leading a donkey in foal, with a packsaddle covered with a multicolored rug or saddle pad. Sancho saddled Rocinante, got Dapple ready, and stocked his own packsaddle, which supplemented the cousin's, likewise well filled. And so, commending themselves to God and bidding farewell to all, they set out, taking the road for the famous Cave of Montesinos.

On the way Don Quixote asked the cousin of what sort and character his pursuits, avocations, and studies were, to which he replied that he was by profession a humanist, and that his pursuits and studies were in writing books for publication, all of great utility and no less entertainment to the nation. One was called *The Book of Liveries*, in which he described seven hundred and three liveries, with their colors, mottoes, and emblems,[3] from which the knights of the court might pick and choose any they desired for festivals and celebrations, without having to go begging for them from anyone or wracking their brains, as the saying is, to have them appropriate to their objects and purposes.

"For," said he, "I give the jealous, the rejected, the forgotten, the absent what will suit them, and fit them without fail. I have another book, too, which I plan to call *Metamorphoses, or the Spanish Ovid*, one of rare and original invention, which imitates Ovid in burlesque style. I show in it who the Giralda of Seville and the Angel of the Magdalena were,[4] who the sewer of Vecinguerra in Córdoba was named for,[5] as well as the Bulls of Guisando,[6] the Sierra Morena, the Leganitos and Lavapiés fountains in Madrid, not forgetting the Piojo, the Cano Dorado, and the Priora fountains[7]—all with their allegories, metaphors, and changes, so that they are amusing, interesting, and instructive, all at once. Another book I have I call *The Supplement to Polydore Vergil*,[8] which treats of the invention of things, and is a work of great erudition and research, for I establish and elucidate elegantly some things of great importance that Polydore failed to mention. He forgot to tell us who was the first man in the world that had a head cold and who was the

[3] *liveries, with their colors, mottoes, and emblems:* For courtly festivities, knights would adorn themselves with stylized outfits whose colors, emblems, and accompanying verses (mottoes), conveyed allegorical meaning. A livery might represent classical material, the theological virtues, or a natural cycle like the four seasons.

[4] *who the Giralda of Seville and the Angel of the Magdalena were:* Both of these are weathervanes, the former atop the Seville Cathedral (see footnote 2, page 497) and the latter formerly above La Magdalena Church in Salamanca.

[5] *who the sewer of Vecinguerra in Córdoba was named for:* The sewer, which runs into the Guadalquivir River, was named for Vicente Guerra, a hero of the Reconquista.

[6] Bulls of Guisando: See footnote 3, page 497.

[7] *Leganitos and . . . the Priora fountains:* fountains in Madrid, still preserved in place names.

[8] The Supplement to Polydore Vergil: The cousin plans to write a supplement to *On the Invention of Things* (1499), a history of discoveries, inventions, and origins by the Italian humanist Polydore Vergil of Urbino (c. 1470–1555).

first to try ointments for the French disease,[9] but I explain it in exhaustive detail and quote more than twenty-five authors in proof of it. So you may conclude that I have labored to good purpose and that the book will be of service to the whole world."

Sancho, who had been very attentive to the cousin's words, said to him, "Tell me, señor—and God give you luck in publishing your books—can you tell me (as you certainly can, since you know so much) who was the first man that scratched his head? To my thinking, it must have been our father Adam."

"So it must have been," replied the cousin, "for there is no doubt but Adam had a head and hair; and being the first man in the world he would have scratched himself sometimes."

"I think so, too," said Sancho. "But now tell me, who was the first tumbler in the world?"

"Really, brother," answered the cousin, "I could not at this moment say positively without having investigated it. I will look it up when I go back to where I have my books and will satisfy you the next time we meet, for this will not be the last."

"Look here, señor," said Sancho, "don't give yourself any trouble about it, for I have just this minute hit upon what I asked you. The first tumbler in the world, you must know, was Lucifer, when they cast or pitched him out of heaven; for he came tumbling into the bottomless pit."

"You are right, friend," said the cousin.

Don Quixote said, "Sancho, that question and answer are not your own; you have heard them from someone else."

"Hold your peace, señor," said Sancho. "Faith, if I get a mind to asking questions and answering, I'll go on from now till tomorrow morning. To be sure, to ask foolish things and answer nonsense I don't need to go looking for help from my neighbors."

"You have said more than you are aware of, Sancho," said Don Quixote, "for there are some who weary themselves out in learning and proving things that, after they are known and proved, are not worth a fig to the understanding or memory."

In this and other pleasant conversation the day went by. That night they lodged in a small village from which it was not more than two leagues to the Cave of Montesinos—so the cousin told Don Quixote, adding that if he was determined to enter it, it would be necessary for him to provide himself with ropes so that he might be tied and lowered into its depths. Don Quixote said that even if it reached to the bottomless pit he meant to see where it went, so they bought about a hundred fathoms of rope.[10] The next day at two in the afternoon they arrived at the cave, the mouth of which was spacious and wide but full of thorn and wild fig bushes and brambles and briars, so thick and matted that they completely blocked and covered it over.

[9] *French disease: morbo gálico*. The *morbo gálico* is syphilis, most likely introduced not by the French but by sailors from Christopher Columbus' voyages to the New World.

[10] *hundred fathoms of rope:* about six hundred feet.

On coming within sight of it, the cousin, Sancho, and Don Quixote dismounted. The first two immediately tied the latter very securely with the ropes. As they were girding and swathing him Sancho said, "Be careful what you do down there, my master. Don't go burying yourself alive or get yourself in a position where you'll be like a bottle hung to cool in a well. It's no affair or business of your worship's to become the explorer of this cave, which must be worse than a Moorish dungeon."

"Tie me and hold your peace," said Don Quixote, "for such an undertaking as this, friend Sancho, was reserved for me."

The guide added, "I beg of you, Señor Don Quixote, to observe carefully and examine with a hundred eyes everything that is there inside. Perhaps there will be some things for me to put into my book of *Transformations*."

"'The drum is in hands that will know how to beat it well,'" said Sancho Panza.

When he had said this and the tying was finished (which was not over the armor but only over the doublet) Don Quixote observed, "It was careless of us not to have provided ourselves with a small cowbell to be tied on the rope close to me, the sound of which would show that I was still descending and alive. But as that is out of the question now, let it be in God's hand to guide me."

He then fell on his knees and in a low voice offered up a prayer to heaven, imploring God to aid him and grant him success in this to all appearance perilous and untried adventure, and then exclaimed aloud, "O mistress of my actions and movements, illustrious and peerless Dulcinea del Toboso, if it so be that the prayers and supplications of this fortunate lover can reach your ears, by your incomparable beauty I entreat you to listen to them, for they but ask you not to refuse me your favor and protection now that I stand in such need of them. I am about to precipitate, to sink, to plunge myself into the abyss that is here before me, only to let the world know that while you favor me there is no impossibility I will not attempt and accomplish."

With these words he approached the cavern and discovered that it was impossible to let himself down or effect an entrance except by sheer force or cleaving a passage. So drawing his sword he began to demolish and cut away the brambles at the mouth of the cave, at the noise of which a vast multitude of crows and grackles flew out of it so thick and so fast that they knocked Don Quixote down—and if he had been as much of a believer in augury as he was a Catholic Christian, he would have taken it as a bad omen and declined to bury himself in such a place. He got up, however, and as there came no more crows, or nightbirds like the bats that flew out at the same time with the crows, the cousin and Sancho giving him rope, he lowered himself into the depths of the dread cavern.

As he entered it Sancho sent his blessing after him, making a thousand crosses over him and saying, "God, and the Peña de Francia, and the Trinity of Gaeta guide you,[11] flower and cream of knights-errant. Down you go, O bravest man

[11] *the Peña de Francia, and the Trinity of Gaeta guide you:* The Sanctuary of Our Lady of the Rock (La Peña de Francia), in the vicinity of Salamanca, was probably named for French immigrants who settled nearby during the Middle Ages. The Sanctuary of the Holy Trinity, overlooking the sea at Gaeta, near Naples, was a popular devotional site for sailors.

on earth, heart of steel, arm of brass. Once more, may God guide you and send you back safe, sound, and unhurt to the light of this world you are leaving to bury yourself in the darkness you seek there." The cousin offered up almost the same prayers and supplications.

Don Quixote kept calling to them to give him rope and more rope, and they let it out little by little. By the time the calls (which came out of the cave as out of a pipe) ceased to be heard, they had let down the hundred fathoms of rope. They were inclined to pull Don Quixote up again, as they could give him no more rope; however, they waited about half an hour, at the end of which time they began to gather in the rope again with great ease and without feeling any weight, which made them wonder if Don Quixote had remained below. Persuaded that it was so, Sancho wept bitterly and hauled away in a great hurry in order to settle the question. When, however, they had come to what seemed more than eighty fathoms they felt a weight, at which they were greatly delighted. At last, at ten fathoms more, they saw Don Quixote distinctly.

Sancho called out to him, saying, "Welcome back, señor! We had begun to think you were going to stay there for a generation."

But Don Quixote answered not a word. Drawing him out entirely, they saw that he had his eyes shut and every appearance of being fast asleep.

They stretched him on the ground and untied him, but still he did not awaken. It wasn't until they rolled him back and forth and shook and pulled him about for some time that he revived, stretching himself just as if he were waking up from a deep and sound sleep. Looking about he said, "God forgive you, friends. You have taken me away from the sweetest and most delightful existence and spectacle that ever human being enjoyed or beheld. Now indeed do I know that all the pleasures of this life pass away like a shadow and a dream, or fade like the flower of the field. O ill-fated Montesinos! O sore-wounded Durandarte! O unhappy Belerma! O tearful Guadiana, and O hapless daughters of Ruidera who show in your waves the tears that flowed from your beauteous eyes!"

The cousin and Sancho Panza listened with deep attention to Don Quixote's words, which he uttered as though with immense pain he were drawing them up from his very bowels. They begged him to explain himself and tell them what he had seen in that hell down there.

"*Hell* do you call it?" said Don Quixote. "Call it by no such name, for it does not deserve it, as you shall soon see."

He then asked them to give him something to eat, as he was very hungry. They spread the cousin's saddle pad on the grass and covered it with the stores of the saddlebag, and all three, as friends and comrades, made a dinner and supper of it all in one. When their meal was finished, Don Quixote of La Mancha said, "Let no one rise. Attend to me, my sons, both of you."

CHAPTER XXIII

OF THE WONDERFUL THINGS THAT THE INCOMPARABLE DON QUIXOTE SAID HE BEHELD IN THE DEPTHS OF THE CAVE OF MONTESINOS, THE IMPOSSIBILITY AND MAGNITUDE OF WHICH HAVE LED THIS ADVENTURE TO BE DEEMED APOCRYPHAL

It was about four in the afternoon when the sun, veiled in clouds, with subdued light and tempered beams, permitted Don Quixote to relate, without heat or inconvenience, what he had beheld in the cave of Montesinos to his two illustrious hearers. He began as follows:

"A matter of some twelve or fourteen times a man's height down in this pit, on the righthand side, there is a recess, roomy enough to contain a large cart with its mules. A little light reaches it through some chinks or crevices, communicating with it and open to the surface of the earth. This recess I perceived when I was already growing weary and irritable at finding myself hanging suspended by the rope, traveling downwards into that dark region without any certainty or knowledge of where I was going, so I resolved to enter it and rest myself for a while. I called out, telling you not to let out more rope until I bade you, but you must not have heard me. I then gathered in the rope you were sending me, and making a coil of it I seated myself on top, ruminating on what I was to do to lower myself to the bottom, having no one to hold me up.

"As I was thus deep in thought and perplexity, suddenly and without provocation a profound sleep fell upon me, and when I least expected it—I know not how—I awoke and found myself in the midst of the most beautiful, delightful meadow that nature could produce or the most fertile human imagination conceive. I opened my eyes, I rubbed them, and found I was not asleep but thoroughly awake. Nevertheless, I felt my head and breast to satisfy myself whether it was I myself who was there or some unsubstantial phantom. Touch, feeling, the collected thoughts that passed through my mind—all convinced me that I was the same then and there that I am this moment. There then presented itself to my sight a stately royal palace or castle, with walls that seemed built of clear transparent crystal. Through two great doors that opened wide therein, I saw coming forth and advancing toward me a venerable old man, clad in a long gown of purple serge[1] that trailed upon the ground. Over his shoulders and breast he

[1] *serge:* twill fabric with diagonal ridges, typically made from wool.

wore a green satin collegiate hood, and covering his head a black Milanese cap. His snow-white beard fell below his waist. He carried no weapons whatsoever, nothing but rosary beads, each greater than a large hazelnut, and every tenth bead like a sizeable ostrich egg. His bearing, his gait, his dignity, and imposing presence held me spellbound and wondering.

"He approached me, and the first thing he did was to embrace me closely. Then he said, 'For a long time now, O valiant knight Don Quixote of La Mancha, we who are here enchanted in these solitudes have been hoping to see you, that you may make known to the world what is shut up and concealed in this deep cave, called the Cave of Montesinos, which you have entered—an achievement reserved for your invincible heart and stupendous courage alone to attempt. Come with me, illustrious sir, and I will show you the marvels hidden within this transparent castle, whereof I am the governor and perpetual warden; for I am Montesinos himself, from whom the cave takes its name.'[2]

"The instant he told me he was Montesinos, I asked him if the story they told in the world here above was true—that he had taken out the heart of his great friend Durandarte from his breast with a little dagger and carried it to Lady Belerma, as his friend had commanded him when at the point of death.[3] He said in reply that they spoke the truth in every respect except as to the dagger, for it was not a dagger, nor little, but a grooved poniard sharper than an awl."[4]

"That poniard must have been made by Ramón de Hoces of Seville,"[5] said Sancho.

"I know not," said Don Quixote. "It could not have been by that poniard maker, however, because Ramón de Hoces was a man of yesterday, and the matter of Roncesvalles, where this fateful encounter occurred, was long ago. But the question is of no great importance, nor does it affect or make any alteration in the truth or substance of the story."

"That is true," said the cousin. "Continue, Señor Don Quixote, for I am listening to you with the greatest pleasure in the world."

[2] *I am Montesinos himself, from whom the cave takes its name:* The identification of a cave near the Ruidera Lakes with the legendary French paladin Montesinos, made famous in Spanish ballads, predates Cervantes.

[3] *he had taken out the heart . . . point of death:* Montesinos, Durandarte, and Belerma originally came from French chivalric literature but took on their life (literally, in the case of Durandarte) in Spanish oral traditions. According to early modern Spanish ballads, when the Frankish rearguard was routed by a Basque ambush at the Battle of Roncesvalles (778), one of the casualties was the knight Durandarte, the personified sword of the paladin Roland. As he was about to succumb to his battle wounds, Durandarte asked his cousin Montesinos to cut out his heart and present it to Belerma, his beloved, as a final token of his love. The grief-stricken, yet faithful Montesinos fulfilled the dramatic request, carrying his cousin's heart to Belerma in a silver box.

[4] *grooved poniard sharper than an awl:* What Montesinos suggests is a tool longer than a dagger that was used by cobblers or basket weavers.

[5] *Ramón de Hoces of Seville:* The identity of this person, whether historical or fictional, is unclear.

"And with no less do I tell the tale," said Don Quixote. "To proceed—the venerable Montesinos led me into the crystal palace, where, in a lower chamber, strangely cool and entirely of alabaster, was an elaborately wrought marble tomb. Upon it I beheld, stretched at full length, a knight, not of bronze or marble or jasper (as are seen on other tombs), but of actual flesh and bone. His right hand—which seemed to me rather hairy and sinewy, a sign of great strength in its owner—lay on the side of his heart. But before I could put any question to Montesinos, he, seeing me gazing at the tomb in amazement, said to me, 'This is my friend Durandarte, flower and mirror of the true lovers and valiant knights of his time. He is held enchanted here, as I myself and many others are, by the French enchanter Merlin,[6] who, they say, was the devil's son; but my belief is that he was not the devil's son, but that he knew, as the saying is, a point more than the devil. How or why he enchanted us, no one knows, but time will tell, and I suspect that time is not far off. What I marvel at is—which I know to be as sure as that it is now day—that Durandarte ended his life in my arms, and that, after his death, I took out his heart with my own hands. Indeed, it must have weighed more than two pounds, for according to naturalists, he who has a large heart is more largely endowed with valor than he who has a small one. Yet as this is the case, and as the knight really did die, how comes it that he now moans and sighs from time to time, as if he were still alive?'

"As he said this, the wretched Durandarte cried out in a loud voice:

'O cousin Montesinos!
'Twas my last request of thee,
When my soul hath left the body,
And that lying dead I be,
With thy poniard or thy dagger
Cut the heart from out my breast,
And bear it to Belerma.
This was my last request.'

"On hearing this, the venerable Montesinos fell on his knees before the unhappy knight, and with tearful eyes exclaimed, 'Long since, Señor Durandarte, my beloved cousin, long since have I done what you bade me on that sad day when I lost you. I took out your heart as well as I could, not leaving the smallest bit of it in your breast, I wiped it with a lace handkerchief, and I took the road to France with it, having first laid you in the bosom of the earth with tears enough to wash and cleanse my hands of the blood that covered them after wandering among your bowels. As further proof, O cousin of my soul, at the first village I came to after leaving Roncesvalles, I sprinkled a little salt upon your heart to keep it sweet, and bring it, if not fresh, at least pickled, into the presence of Lady Belerma, whom, together with you, myself, Guadiana your squire, the dueña Ruidera and her seven

[6] *the French enchanter Merlin:* Merlin, who is a central figure in the Arthurian legends, is of Welsh origin, though medieval French poets incorporated him into romances that expanded his role as a wise enchanter.

daughters and two nieces, and many more of your friends and acquaintances, the sage Merlin has been keeping enchanted here these many years. And although more than five hundred have gone by, not one of us has died. Ruidera and her daughters and nieces alone are missing, and these, because of the tears they shed, Merlin—out of the compassion he must have felt for them—changed into so many lakes, which to this day in the world of the living and in the province of La Mancha are called the Lakes of Ruidera. The seven daughters belong to the kings of Spain and the two nieces to the knights of a very holy order called the Order of Saint John. Guadiana your squire, likewise bewailing your fate, was changed into a river of his own name, but when he came to the surface and beheld the sun of another heaven, so great was his grief at finding he was leaving you, that he plunged into the bowels of the earth; however, as he cannot help following his natural course, he from time to time comes forth and shows himself to the sun and the world. The aforesaid lakes send him their waters, and with these, and others that come to him, he makes a grand and imposing entrance into Portugal. But for all that, go where he may, he shows his melancholy and sadness, and takes no pride in breeding delectable choice fish, only coarse and tasteless ones, very different from those of the golden Tagus.

"'All this that I tell you now, my cousin, I have told you many times before, and as you make no answer, I fear that either you do not believe me or do not hear me. God knows what grief I feel from this. I have now news to give you, which, if it serves not to alleviate your sufferings, will not in any way increase them. Know that you have here before you—and open your eyes to see—that great knight of whom the sage Merlin has prophesied so many things. Don Quixote of La Mancha I mean, who has again, and to better purpose than in past times, revived in these days knight-errantry, long since forgotten, and by whose intervention and aid it may be we shall be disenchanted; for great deeds are reserved for great men.'"

"'If that is not to be,' cried the wretched Durandarte in a low and feeble voice, 'if that is not to be ... then, O cousin, I say, "Be patient and shuffle the deck!"'" And turning over on his side, he relapsed into his former silence without uttering another word.

"There was now heard a great outcry and lamentation, accompanied by deep sighs and bitter sobs. I looked around, and through the crystal wall I saw passing through another chamber a procession of two rows of fair damsels all clad in mourning, and with white turbans of Turkish fashion on their heads. Behind, in the rear of these, there came a lady, for so from her dignity she seemed to be, also clad in black, with a white veil so long and ample that it swept the ground. Her turban was twice as large as the largest of any of the others; her eyebrows met, her nose was rather flat, her mouth was large but with ruddy lips, and her teeth, of which at times she allowed a glimpse, were seen to be sparse and crooked, though as white as peeled almonds. She carried in her hands a fine cloth, and in it (as well as I could make out) a heart that had been mummified, so parched and shriveled was it.

"Montesinos told me that all those forming the procession were the attendants of Durandarte and Belerma, who were enchanted there with their master and mistress, and that the last, she who carried the heart in the cloth, was Lady

Belerma, who, with her damsels, four days in the week went in procession singing, or rather weeping, dirges over the body and miserable heart of his cousin; and that if she appeared to me somewhat unattractive or not so beautiful as fame reported her, it was because of the bad nights and worse days that she passed in that enchantment, as I could see by the great dark circles round her eyes, and her sickly complexion.

"'Her sallowness, and the rings round her eyes,' said he, 'are not caused by the monthly ill common to women, for she has not known it in many months, even years, but by the grief her own heart suffers because of that which she holds in her hand perpetually, and which recalls to her memory the sad fate of her lost lover. Were it not for this, hardly would the great Dulcinea del Toboso, so celebrated in all these parts, and even in the world, match her in beauty, grace, and charm.'

"'Belay you!' exclaimed I at this. 'Tell your story as you ought, Señor Don Montesinos, for you know very well that "all comparisons are odious," so that there is no reason to compare one person with another. The peerless Dulcinea del Toboso is what she is, and the lady Doña Belerma is what she is and has been, and that's enough.'

"To which he answered, 'Forgive me, Señor Don Quixote. I confess I was wrong and spoke unadvisedly in saying that Lady Dulcinea could scarcely come up to Lady Belerma; for it were enough for me to have learned—by what means I know not—that you are her knight, to make me bite my tongue out before I compared her to anything save heaven itself.'

"After this apology which the great Montesinos made me, my heart recovered itself from the shock I had received in hearing my lady compared with Belerma."

"I'm amazed," said Sancho, "that your worship didn't jump on the old coot and bruise every one of his bones with kicks, then pluck his beard till there wasn't a hair left."

"No, Sancho, my friend," said Don Quixote, "it would not have been right for me to do that, for we are all bound to pay respect to the aged, even if they are not knights, but especially to those who are and who are enchanted. I only know that in the many other questions and answers we exchanged, I gave him as good as he brought."

"I cannot understand, Señor Don Quixote," remarked the cousin here, "how it is that your worship, in such a short space of time as you have been below there, could have seen so many things, and said and answered so much."

"How long has it been since I went down?" asked Don Quixote.

"Barely more than an hour," replied Sancho.

"That cannot be," returned Don Quixote, "because night overtook me while I was there, and day came, and it was night again and day again three times; so that, by my reckoning, I have been three days in those remote regions hidden from our eyes."

"My master must be right," replied Sancho. "Seeing that everything that's happened to him is by enchantment, maybe what seems to us an hour would seem three days and nights there."

"That's it," said Don Quixote.

"And did your worship eat anything all that time, señor?" asked the cousin.

"I never touched a morsel," answered Don Quixote, "nor did I feel hunger or think of it."

"And do the enchanted eat?" asked the cousin.

"They neither eat," said Don Quixote, "nor are they subject to the greater excrements, though it is thought that their nails, beards, and hair grow."

"And do the enchanted sleep, señor?" asked Sancho.

"Certainly not," replied Don Quixote. "At least, during those three days I was with them, not one of them closed an eye, nor did I either."

"The proverb, 'Tell me what company you keep, and I'll tell you who you are,' is to the point here," said Sancho. "Your worship keeps company with enchanted people that are always fasting and keeping watch. What wonder is it, then, that you don't eat or sleep while you're with them? But forgive me, señor, if I say that everything you've told us so far—may God take me (I was about to say the devil), if I believe the slightest bit."

"What!" said the cousin. "Has Señor Don Quixote, then, been lying? Why, even if he wished it, he has not had time to imagine and put together such a host of lies."

"I don't believe my master lies," said Sancho.

"If not, what do you believe?" asked Don Quixote.

"I believe," replied Sancho, "that this Merlin, or those enchanters who enchanted the whole crew your worship says you saw and talked to down there, stuffed your imagination or your mind with all these tales you've been treating us to, and all that are still to come."

"All that might be, Sancho," replied Don Quixote, "but it is not so. Everything that I have told you I saw with my own eyes and touched with my own hands. But what will you say when I tell you now how, among the countless other marvelous things Montesinos showed me—of which at leisure and at the proper time I will give you an account in the course of our journey, for they would not all be appropriate here—he showed me three country girls who went skipping and capering like goats over the pleasant fields there. The instant I beheld them I knew one to be the peerless Dulcinea del Toboso and the other two those same country girls that were with her and that we spoke to on the road from El Toboso. I asked Montesinos if he knew them, and he told me he did not, but he thought they must be some enchanted ladies of distinction, for it was only a few days before that they had made their appearance in those meadows; but I was not to be surprised at that, because there were a great many other ladies there of times past and present, enchanted in various strange shapes, and among them he had recognized Queen Guinevere and her dueña Quintañona, she who poured out the wine for Lancelot 'when from Brittany he came.'"[7]

When Sancho Panza heard his master say this, he was ready to take leave of his senses or die with laughter; for as he knew the real truth about the pretended

[7] *Queen Guinevere . . . 'when from Brittany he came'*: from a ballad Don Quixote quotes several times in Part I.

enchantment of Dulcinea, in which he himself had been the enchanter and concocter of the whole story, he made up his mind at last that, beyond all doubt, his master was stark mad. So he said to him, "It was an evil hour, a worse season, and a sorrowful day, when your worship, my dear master, went down to the other world, and an unlucky occasion when you met with Señor Montesinos, who has sent you back to us like this. You were well enough here above in your full senses, such as God had given you, quoting from books and giving advice at every turn, and not as you are now, talking the greatest nonsense that can be imagined."

"Because I know you, Sancho," said Don Quixote, "I do not heed your words."

"Nor I your worship's," said Sancho, "even if you beat me or kill me for those I've spoken and will speak if you don't correct and mend your own. But tell me, while we're still on good terms, how or by what did you recognize the lady our mistress. And if you spoke to her, what did you say, and what did she answer?"

"I recognized her," said Don Quixote, "because she was wearing the same garments she wore when you pointed her out to me. I spoke to her, but she did not utter a word in reply. On the contrary, she turned her back on me and took to flight, at such a pace that an arrow could not have overtaken her. I wished to follow her, and would have done so had not Montesinos recommended me not to take the trouble as it would be useless, particularly as the time was drawing near when it would be necessary for me to leave the cavern. He told me, moreover, that in course of time he would let me know how he and Belerma and Durandarte, and all who were there, were to be disenchanted.

"But of all I saw and took note of down there, what gave me the most pain was that while Montesinos was speaking to me, one of the two companions of the hapless Dulcinea approached me without my having seen her coming, and with tears in her eyes said to me, in a soft, agitated voice, 'My lady Dulcinea del Toboso kisses your worship's hands, and entreats you to do her the favor of letting her know how you are; and, being in great need, she also entreats your worship as earnestly as she can to be so good as to lend her half a dozen reals, or as much as you may have on hand, with this new cotton petticoat I have here as security. She promises to repay them in short order.'

"I was amazed and taken aback by such a message. Turning to Señor Montesinos I asked him, 'Is it possible, Señor Montesinos, that persons of distinction under enchantment can be in need?' To which he replied, 'Believe me, Señor Don Quixote, that which is called need is to be met with everywhere, and penetrates all quarters and reaches everyone, and does not spare even the enchanted. As Lady Dulcinea del Toboso sends to borrow those six reals, and the security is to all appearance a good one, there is nothing for it but to give them to her, for no doubt she must be in some great strait.' 'I will take no security of her,' I replied, 'nor yet can I give her what she asks, for all I have is four reals,' which I gave. (They were those which you, Sancho, gave me the other day to bestow in alms upon the poor I met along the road.) I said, 'Tell your mistress, my dear, that I am grieved to the heart because of her distresses and wish I was a Fugger[8] to remedy them. I would have her know that I cannot be, and ought not be in health while deprived of the happiness of seeing her and enjoying her discreet conversation, and that I implore her as earnestly as I can to allow herself to be seen and addressed by this her captive servant and forlorn knight. Tell her, too, that when she least expects it she will hear it announced that I have taken an oath and vow after the fashion of that which the Marquis of Mantua took to avenge his nephew Valdovinos, when he found him at the point of death in the heart of the mountains, which was, not to eat bread off a tablecloth (and other inconsequential matters which he added) until he had avenged him.[9] I will take the same to have no rest, and to roam the seven regions of the earth more thoroughly than the Infante Don Pedro of Portugal ever roamed them, until I have disenchanted her.'[10] 'All that and more, you owe my lady,' was the damsel's answer to me, and taking the four reals, instead of making me a curtsey she cut a caper, springing two full yards into the air."

"O blessed God!" exclaimed Sancho aloud at this, "is it possible that such a person can exist in this world, and that enchanters and enchantments can have such power in it to change my master's good sense into an everlasting madness! O señor, señor, for God's sake, consider who you are! Think of your honor, and give no credit to this nonsense that has left you weak and witless."

"You talk this way because you love me, Sancho," said Don Quixote, "and not being experienced in the things of the world, you assume that whatever has any difficulty about it is impossible. But time will pass, as I said before, and I will tell you some of the things I saw down there which will make you believe what I have related now, the truth of which allows neither reply nor question."

[8] *Fugger:* The House of Fugger, a family of bankers and merchants based in Augsburg, was synonymous with wealth during the sixteenth and seventeenth centuries. Charles V was able to finance his election as Holy Roman Emperor in 1514 thanks to an enormous loan from the Fugger bank.

[9] *taken an oath and vow . . . avenged him:* from a ballad Don Quixote quotes several times in Part I.

[10] *roam the seven regions . . . until I have disenchanted her:* The *Book of Infante Dom Pedro of Portugal, Who Traveled the Four Regions of the World* (1547) was a semi-legendary travelogue that recounted the journeys of Infante Dom Pedro (1392–1499), son of King João I of Portugal. Early versions told of his travels through Europe and the Holy Land, but the 1547 edition incorporated fantastic elements, such as a visit to the mythical court of Prester John.

CHAPTER XXIV

IN WHICH ARE RELATED A THOUSAND TRIFLES, AS TRIVIAL AS THEY ARE NECESSARY TO THE RIGHT UNDERSTANDING OF THIS GREAT HISTORY

He who translated this great history from the original written by its first author, Cide Hamete Benengeli, says that on coming to the chapter giving the adventures of the Cave of Montesinos he found written in the margin of it, in Hamete's own hand, these exact words:

"I cannot convince myself that everything that is written in the preceding chapter actually happened to the valiant Don Quixote. All the adventures that have occurred up to the present I consider to have been possible and probable;[1] but as for this one of the cave, I see no way of accepting it as true, as it passes all reasonable bounds. For me to believe that Don Quixote could lie, he being the most truthful gentleman and the noblest knight of his time, is impossible. He would not tell a lie even if he were to be shot through with arrows. On the other hand, I reflect that he related the story with all the circumstances detailed, and that he could not in so short a space have fabricated such a vast edifice of absurdities. If, then, this adventure seems apocryphal, it is no fault of mine. And so, without affirming its falsehood or its truth, I write it down. Decide for yourself, O prudent reader. I am not bound, nor is it in my power, to do more. They say it is well-established, however, that at the time of his death he retracted the story and said he had invented it, judging it to be comparable to the adventures he had read of in his histories."

He then goes on to say:

The cousin was amazed as much at Sancho's boldness as at his master's patience and concluded that the good temper the latter displayed arose from the happiness he felt at having seen his lady Dulcinea, even enchanted as she was. Otherwise, the words and language Sancho had addressed to him would have deserved a thrashing. Indeed, he seemed to him to have been rather impudent to his master, to whom he now observed, "I, Señor Don Quixote of La Mancha, look upon the time I have spent in traveling with your worship as very well employed, for I have gained four things in the course of it. The first is that I

[1] *possible and probable*: In his *Poetics*, Aristotle teaches that the poet is not required to relate what has happened but "what is possible according to the law of probability and necessity."

have made your acquaintance, which I consider great good fortune. The second, that I have learned what the Cave of Montesinos contains, together with the transformations of Guadiana and the Lakes of Ruidera, which will be of use to me for the *Spanish Ovid* that I have in hand. The third, to have discovered how old playing cards are, that they were in use at least in the time of Charlemagne, as may be inferred from the words you say Durandarte uttered when, at the end of that long spell while Montesinos was talking to him, he woke up and said, 'Be patient and shuffle the deck.' This expression he could not have learned while he was enchanted, but only before he had become so, in France, and in the time of the aforesaid emperor Charlemagne. This little tidbit is just the thing for me for that other book I am writing, the *Supplement to Polydore Vergil on the Invention of Antiquities*. I doubt he ever thought of including the invention of cards in his book, as I mean to do in mine. It will be a matter of great importance, particularly when I can cite so grave and veracious an authority as Señor Durandarte. The fourth thing is that I have ascertained the source of the Guadiana River, heretofore unknown to mankind."

"You are right," said Don Quixote, "but I should like to know, if by God's favor they grant you a license to print those books of yours—which I doubt—to whom do you mean to dedicate them?"

"There are lords and grandees in Spain to whom they can be dedicated," said the cousin.

"Not many," said Don Quixote. "Not that they are unworthy of it, but because they do not want to accept books and incur the obligation of making an appropriate return of what is due to the author's labor and courtesy. One prince I know who makes up for all the rest, and more—how much more, if I ventured to say, I might stir up envy in many a noble breast.[2] But let us put this aside for some more convenient time, and let us go and look for some place to shelter ourselves for the night."

"Not far from here," said the cousin, "there is a shrine where a hermit lives. They say he was once a soldier and has the reputation of being a good Christian and a very intelligent and charitable man. Close to the shrine he has a small house which he built at his own cost, but though small it is large enough to receive guests."

"Do you think this hermit has any hens?" asked Sancho.

"Few hermits are without them," said Don Quixote, "for those we see nowadays are not like the hermits of the Egyptian deserts who were clad in palm leaves and lived on the roots of the earth. But do not think that by praising these I am disparaging the others. All I mean to say is that the penances of those of the present day do not match the asceticism and austerity of former times. It does not follow from this that they are not all worthy—at least I think them so. At the worst, the hypocrite who pretends to be good does less harm than the open sinner."

[2] *One prince . . . a noble breast:* The prince intended is most likely the dedicatee of Part II, the Count of Lemos.

At that moment they saw approaching them a man on foot, proceeding at a rapid pace and beating a mule loaded with lances and halberds.[3] When he came up to them, he saluted them and passed on without stopping.

Don Quixote called to him, "Stay, good fellow. You seem to be making more haste than suits that mule."

"I cannot stop, señor," answered the man. "The arms you see I carry here are to be used tomorrow, so I must not delay. God be with you. But if you want to know what I am carrying them for, I mean to lodge tonight at the inn that is beyond the shrine. If you are going the same road you will find me there, and I will tell you some unusual things. Once more God be with you."

He urged on his mule at such a pace that Don Quixote had no time to ask him what these unusual things were that he meant to tell them. And as he was somewhat inquisitive, and always tortured by his anxiety to learn something new, he decided to set out at once and go and pass the night at the inn instead of stopping at the shrine, where the cousin wanted them to stay.

Accordingly, they mounted and all three took the direct road for the inn, which they reached a little before nightfall. On the road the cousin proposed that they go up to the shrine for a little something to drink. The instant Sancho heard this he steered his Dapple toward it, and Don Quixote and the cousin did the same; but it seems Sancho's bad luck so ordered it that the hermit was not at home, for so a lay sister they found at the shrine told them. They called for some of the best. She replied that her master had none, but that if they liked cheap water she would give it with great pleasure.

"If I felt like water," said Sancho, "there are wells along the road where I could have had all I wanted. Ah, Camacho's wedding, and plentiful house of Don Diego, how often I miss you!"

Leaving the shrine, they pushed on toward the inn, and a little farther they came upon a youth who was pacing along in front of them at no great speed, so that they overtook him. He carried a sword over his shoulder, and slung on it what must have been a bundle of his clothes— probably his breeches or pantaloons, and his cloak and a shirt or two. He had on a velvet jacket, which in places was shiny like satin, and had his shirt out.[4] His stockings were of silk, and his shoes square-toed as they wear them at court. His age might have been eighteen or nineteen. He was of a merry countenance, and to all appearance of an active disposition, and he went along singing seguidillas[5] to beguile the tedium of the road. As they overtook him, he was just finishing one, which the cousin memorized. They say it ran thus—

[3] *halberds:* The halberd is a polearm topped with a spike, an ax blade, and often a hook or thorn on the reverse side.

[4] *which in places was shiny like satin, and had his shirt out:* indications of the youth's poverty. The velvet has shiny spots where it is worn thin. He wears his shirt out to cover up that he is not wearing breeches over his stockings.

[5] *seguidillas:* light-hearted poems of alternating five- and seven-syllable verses.

Off to battle I go
With no wealth but my song;
Had I money at all,
I would stay safe at home.

The first to address him was Don Quixote, who said, "You travel very lightly, my gallant friend. May we ask where you are bound, if it is your pleasure to tell us?"

To which the youth replied, "The heat and my poverty are the reason of my traveling so lightly, and it is to war that I am bound."

"How poverty?" asked Don Quixote. "The heat one can understand."

"Señor," replied the youth, "in this bundle I carry velvet pantaloons to match my jacket. If I wear them out on the road, I will not be able to make a decent appearance in them in the city, and I haven't the means to buy others. For this reason, as well as to keep myself cool, I'm making my way in this fashion to overtake some companies of infantry that are not twelve leagues off, where I will enlist. There will be no shortage of baggage trains to travel with after that to the port of departure, which they say will be Cartagena.[6] I would rather have the king for a master and serve him in battle than serve a court pauper."

"Are you getting a bonus?" asked the cousin.

"If I had been in the service of some grandee of Spain or person of distinction," replied the youth, "I should have been sure to get it, for that is the advantage of serving good masters—that out of the servants' hall men end up as second lieutenants or captains or get additional pay. But I, to my misfortune, always served upstarts and office seekers, whose wages and food allowance were so scanty that half his pay went to keep his collar starched. It would be a miracle indeed if a volunteer page ever got anything like a reasonable bonus."

"Tell me, for heaven's sake," asked Don Quixote, "is it possible, my friend, that all the time you served you never obtained any livery?"[7]

"They gave me two," replied the page, "but just as when one leaves a religious community before making a profession, they strip him of the dress of the order and give him back his own clothes, so did my masters return me mine. As soon as the business that brought them to court was finished, they went home and took back the liveries they had given merely for show."

"As the Italians would say, what remarkable *spilorceria*!"[8] said Don Quixote. "But for all that, consider yourself happy in having left court with as worthy an object as you have, for there is nothing on earth more honorable or profitable than serving, first of all God, and then one's king and natural lord, particularly in the profession of arms, by which, if not more wealth, at least more honor is to be won than by letters, as I have said many a time. For though letters may have founded more great houses than arms, still those founded by arms have

[6] *Cartagena:* port on the southeast coast of Spain, the base of operations for military expeditions in Italy and the wider Mediterranean.

[7] *livery:* servant's uniform.

[8] spilorceria: stinginess.

an indefinable superiority over those founded by letters, and a definite splendor belonging to them that distinguishes them above all.

"Bear in mind what I am now about to say to you, for it will be of great use and comfort to you in time of trouble: Do not let your mind dwell on the adversities that may befall you; for the worst of all is death, and if it be a good death, the best of all is to die. They asked the valiant Roman emperor Julius Cæsar what was the best death. He answered that which is unexpected—the death that comes suddenly and unforeseen. Though he answered like a pagan, and one without the knowledge of the true God, yet, as far as sparing our feelings is concerned, he was right. For suppose you are killed in the first engagement or skirmish, whether struck by a cannon ball or blown up by a mine, what does it matter? It is only dying, then everything is over. According to Terence, a soldier looks better dead in battle than alive and safe in flight.[9] The good soldier wins fame in proportion as he is obedient to his captains and those in command over him. Remember, my son, that it is better for the soldier to smell of gunpowder than of civet,[10] and that if old age should come upon you in this honorable calling, though you may be covered with wounds and crippled and lame, it will not come upon you without honor, and of a nature that poverty cannot lessen—especially now that provisions are being made to support and relieve old and disabled soldiers.[11] For it is not right to deal with them after the fashion of those who set free and get rid of their black slaves when they are old and useless. Turning them out of their houses under the pretense of making them free, they make them slaves to hunger, from which they cannot expect to be released except by death. For the present I will say no more than that you get up behind me on my horse as far as the inn and dine with me there. Tomorrow you can pursue your journey, and God give you as good speed as your intentions deserve."

The page did not accept the invitation to mount, though he did agree to dine with him at the inn. They say here that Sancho said to himself, "God be with you, my master. Is it possible that a man who can say so many good things as he has said just now can say that he saw the impossible absurdities he reports about the Cave of Montesinos? Well, well, time will tell."

Just as night was falling, they reached the inn. To Sancho's delight, his master took it for an actual inn, and not, as usual, for a castle. As soon as they entered, Don Quixote asked the innkeeper about the man with the lances and halberds, and was told that he was in the stable seeing to his mule—which was what Sancho and the cousin proceeded to do for their beasts, giving the best manger and the best place in the stable to Rocinante.

[9] *According to Terence ... in flight:* The maxim does not appear in any of Terence's surviving works.

[10] *civet:* yellowish substance used to make perfume, extracted from the mammal of the same name.

[11] *provisions are being made to support and relieve old and disabled soldiers:* In reality, the first pension system for Spanish soldiers would not be set up until the 1760s.

CHAPTER XXV

IN WHICH IS SET DOWN THE BRAYING ADVENTURE, AND THE ENTERTAINING ADVENTURE OF THE PUPPETEER, TOGETHER WITH THE MEMORABLE PREDICTIONS OF THE DIVINING MONKEY

Don Quixote's bread would not bake (as the popular saying goes) until he had heard the curious things promised by the man who carried the weaponry. He went to seek him where the innkeeper said he was and having found him, asked him to tell by all means what he had to say in answer to the question he had asked him on the road.

"The tale of my wonders must be taken more leisurely and not standing," said the man. "Let me finish foddering my beast, good sir, and then I'll tell you things that will astonish you."

"Don't wait for that," said Don Quixote. "I'll help you with everything."

And so he did, sifting the barley for him and cleaning out the manger, a degree of humility that made the other feel bound to tell him with a good grace what he had asked. So seating himself on a bench, with Don Quixote beside him and the cousin, the page, Sancho Panza, and the innkeeper for a senate and audience, he began his story in this way:

"You must know that in a village four leagues and a half from this inn, it so happened that one of the village councilmen, by the schemes and wiles of a servant girl of his (it's too long a tale to tell), lost a donkey; and though he did all he possibly could to find it, it was all to no purpose. A fortnight might have gone by, so the story goes, since the donkey had been missing, when, as the councilman who had lost it was standing in the plaza, another councilman of the same town said to him, 'Congratulate me for good news, brother. Your donkey has turned up.' 'That I will, and well, brother,' said the other. 'But tell us, where has he turned up?' 'In the forest,' said the finder; 'I saw him this morning without packsaddle or harness of any sort, and so lean that it touched one's heart to see him. I tried to drive him before me and bring him to you, but he is already so wild and skittish that when I went near him, he took off into the thickest part of the forest. If you have a mind that we two should go back and look for him, let me put up this jenny at my house and I'll be back at once.' 'You will be doing me a great kindness,' said the donkey's owner, 'and I'll try to pay it back in the same coin.'

"It is with all these details, and in the very same way I am telling it now, that those who know all about the matter tell the story. Well then, the two councilmen set off on foot, arm in arm, for the forest, and coming to the place where they hoped to find the donkey, they could not find him, nor was he to be seen anywhere about, search as they might. Seeing, then, that there was no sign of him, the councilman who had seen him said to the other, 'Look here, brother; a plan has occurred to me, by which, beyond a doubt, we shall manage to locate the animal, even if he is stowed away in the bowels of the earth, not to say the forest. It is this: I can bray to perfection, and if you can ever so little, the thing's as good as done.' 'Ever so little, you say, brother?' said the other. 'By God, I'll not take second to anybody, not even to the donkeys themselves.' 'We'll soon see,' said the second councilman, 'for my plan is that you should go on one side of the forest, and I the other, so as to go all round about it. Every now and then, you will bray and I will bray; and it cannot be but that the donkey will hear us and answer us if he is in the forest.' To which the owner of the donkey replied, 'It is an excellent plan, I declare, brother, and worthy of your great genius.'

"The two separated as agreed, and it so turned out that they brayed almost at the same moment. Each, deceived by the braying of the other, ran to look, imagining that the donkey had turned up at last. When they came in sight of one another, the one with the missing donkey said, 'That was surely my donkey that brayed, was it not?' 'No, it was I,' said the other. 'Well then, I can tell you, brother,' said the donkey's owner, 'that between you and a donkey there is not the slightest difference as far as braying goes, for I never in all my life saw or heard anything more natural.' 'Those praises and compliments belong to you more justly than to me, brother,' said the one who had devised the plan; 'for by the God that made me, you could outdo by a couple brays the most accomplished brayer in the world. Your tone is deep, you hold your voice with good time and pitch, and your finishing notes come thick and fast. Verily, I confess myself beaten and yield the victor's palm to you for this rare accomplishment.' 'Well then,' said the owner, 'I'll set a higher value on myself in the future, and consider that I know how to do something with refinement, for though I always thought I brayed well, I never supposed I came up to the pitch of perfection you say.' 'And I say too,' said the second, 'that there are rare gifts going to waste in the world, and that they are ill bestowed upon those who don't know how to make use of them.' 'Ours,' said the donkey's owner, 'unless it is in cases like this we have now in hand, cannot be of any service to us, but even in this may God grant that they can be of some use.'

"So saying they separated and took to their braying once more, but at every turn they continued to deceive one another. Finally, when they came to meet each other again, they arranged for a signal (so as to know that it was they and not the donkey) to give two brays, one after the other. In this way, doubling the brays at every step, they made the complete circuit of the forest. But the lost donkey never gave them an answer or even the sign of one. How could the poor unlucky brute have answered, when, in the thickest part of the forest, they found him devoured by wolves? As soon as he saw him his owner said, 'I was wondering why he didn't answer, for if he wasn't dead he'd have brayed when he heard us, or he'd have been no donkey; but for the sake of having heard you bray to such perfection, brother, I count the trouble I have taken to look for him well spent, even though I have found him dead.' 'I yield to you on that score,' said the other. 'If the abbot sings well, the acolyte is not much behind him.'

With this, they returned disconsolate and hoarse to their village, where they told their friends, neighbors, and acquaintances what had befallen them in their search for the donkey, each praising to the heavens the other's talent in braying. The whole story came to be known and spread abroad through the villages in the region. And the devil, who never sleeps, with his love for sowing dissensions and scattering discord everywhere, blowing mischief about and making quarrels out of nothing, contrived to make the people of the other towns fall to braying whenever they saw anyone from our village, as if to throw the braying of our councilmen in our faces. Then the boys took to it, which was the same thing as it getting into the hands and mouths of all the devils of hell. Braying spread from one town to another in such a way that the men of the braying town are as easy to be known as blacks are to be known from whites. The miserable joke has gone so far that several times the scoffed have come out in arms and in a body to do battle with the scoffers, and neither prince nor pauper, fear nor shame, can mend matters. Tomorrow or the day after, I believe, the men of my town—that is, of the braying town—are going to take the field against another village two leagues away from ours, one of those that persecute us most. So that we may show up well prepared, I have bought these lances and halberds you have seen. These are the curious things I said that I would tell you about. If you don't think them so, I have no others to share."

With this the worthy fellow brought his story to a close.

Just at this moment there came in at the gate of the inn a man entirely clad in chamois leather, hose, breeches, and doublet, who said in a loud voice, "Señor innkeeper, do you have a room? The divining monkey and the puppet show of the rescue of Melisendra have arrived."

"Well, I'll be!" cried the innkeeper. "It's Master Pedro! We're in for a grand night." (I forgot to mention that the said Master Pedro had his left eye and nearly half his cheek covered with a patch of green taffeta, a sign that he had an ailment on that side.) "Your worship is welcome, Master Pedro," continued the innkeeper. "But where are the monkey and the puppet show? I don't see them."

"They are close at hand," said the man in chamois leather. "I came on ahead to find out if there was any room."

"I'd make the Duke of Alba[1] himself clear out to make room for Master Pedro," said the innkeeper. "Bring in the monkey and the puppet show. There's company in the inn tonight that will pay to see it and the talented monkey."

[1] *Duke of Alba:* Fernando Álvarez de Toledo, third Duke of Alba (1507–1582), general who led the successful military campaign that secured Phillip II's claim to the Portuguese throne. He was less successful in restoring order in the Spanish Netherlands. See footnote 6, page 314.

"So be it by all means," said the man with the patch. "I'll lower the price and be well satisfied if I only pay my expenses. Let me go back now and hurry on the cart with the monkey and the puppet show." With this he went out of the inn.

Don Quixote at once asked the innkeeper who this Master Pedro was, what the puppet show was, and what this monkey was he had with him. The innkeeper replied, "He is a famous puppeteer, who for some time past has been going about this Mancha de Aragón,[2] exhibiting a puppet show of the rescue of Melisendra by the famous Don Gaiferos, one of the best and best-represented stories that have been seen in this part of the kingdom for many a year. He also has with him a monkey with the most extraordinary gift ever seen in a monkey or imagined in a human being; for if you ask him anything, he listens attentively to the question and then jumps on his master's shoulder, and pressing close to his ear tells him the answer, which Master Pedro then delivers. He says a great deal more about things past than about things to come; and though he does not always hit the truth in every case, most of the time he is not far off, so that he makes us think he's got the devil in him. He gets two reals for every question if the monkey answers—I mean, if his master answers for him after he has whispered into his ear. It is believed, then, that this Master Pedro is very rich. He's an *hombre galante* as they say in Italy, and *bon compaño*,[3] and leads the finest life in the world. He talks more than six, drinks more than a dozen, and all by his tongue, his monkey, and his puppet show."

Master Pedro now came back, and in a cart followed the puppet show and the monkey—a big one, without a tail and with buttocks as bare as felt, but not vicious-looking. As soon as Don Quixote saw him, he asked him, "Can you tell me, sir fortune-teller, *Qué peje pillamo?*[4] What is to become of us? See, here are my two reals," and he bade Sancho give them to Master Pedro.

But Master Pedro answered for the monkey and said, "Señor, this animal does not give any answer or information touching things that are to come. Of things past he knows something, and more or less of things present."

"Good grief!" said Sancho. "I wouldn't give a fig to be told what's past with me, for who knows that better than I do myself? And to pay for being told what I know would be beyond foolish. But since you know things present, here are my two reals. Tell me, most excellent sir monkey, what is my wife Teresa Panza doing now? How is she keeping busy?"

Master Pedro refused to take the money, saying, "I will not receive payment in advance or until the service has been first rendered." With his right hand he then proceeded to give a couple slaps on his left shoulder, and with one jump the monkey perched himself upon it and, putting his mouth to his master's ear,

[2] *Mancha de Aragón:* eastern region of La Mancha, stretching from Cuenca south to Albacete.

[3] hombre galante ... bon compaño: a "gallant man" and "good company"—phrases that Cervantes renders in language as much Spanish as it is Italian.

[4] Qué peje pillamo: Written in Italian as *Che pesce pigliamo?* ("What fish are we to catch?"). Don Quixote explains his meaning in the question that follows.

began chattering his teeth rapidly. After having kept this up as long as one would be saying a credo, with another jump he brought himself to the ground. The same moment Master Pedro ran in great haste and fell upon his knees before Don Quixote and, embracing his legs, exclaimed, "These legs do I embrace as I would embrace the two pillars of Hercules, O illustrious reviver of knight-errantry, so long consigned to oblivion! O never-yet-duly-extolled knight, Don Quixote of La Mancha, courage of the faint-hearted, prop of the tottering, arm of the fallen, staff and counsel of all who are unfortunate!"

Don Quixote was thunderstruck, Sancho astounded, the cousin staggered, the page astonished, the man from the braying town agape, the innkeeper in perplexity, and, in short, everyone amazed at the words of the puppeteer, who went on to say, "And you, worthy Sancho Panza, the best squire and squire to the best knight in the world! Be of good cheer, for your good wife Teresa is well. She is at this moment sifting a pound of flax. To be more precise, she has in her left hand a jug with a broken spout that holds a good drop of wine, with which she solaces herself at her work."

"That I can well believe," said Sancho. "She's a lucky one, and—her jealousy aside—I wouldn't trade her for the giantess Andandona, who by my master's account was a very clever and worthy woman.[5] My Teresa is one of those that won't let themselves be deprived of anything, even if it's at the expense of her heirs."

"I confess now," said Don Quixote, "that he who reads much and travels much sees and knows a great deal. I say so because what amount of persuasion could have persuaded me that there are monkeys in the world that can divine as I have seen now with my own eyes? For I am that very Don Quixote of La Mancha this worthy animal refers to, though he has gone rather too far in my praise. But whatever I may be, I thank Heaven that it has endowed me with a tender and compassionate heart, always disposed to do good to all and harm to none."

"If I had money," said the page, "I would ask Señor Monkey what will happen to me in the pilgrimage I'm making."

To this Master Pedro, who had by this time risen from Don Quixote's feet, replied, "I have already said that this little beast gives no answer as to the future; but if he did, not having money would be of no consequence, for to oblige Señor Don Quixote, here present, I would give up all the profits in the world. And now, because I have promised it, and to afford him pleasure, I will set up my puppet show and offer entertainment to all who are in the inn, without any charge whatever."

As soon as he heard this, the innkeeper, delighted beyond measure, pointed out a place where the puppet show might be set up, which was done at once.

Don Quixote was not very well satisfied with the divinations of the monkey, as he did not think it proper that a monkey should divine anything, either past or future; so while Master Pedro was arranging the show, he withdrew with Sancho to a corner of the stable, where, without being overheard by anyone, he

[5] *Andandona . . . worthy woman:* The giantess, a character in *Amadís of Gaul,* is in fact a fearsome enchantress who aids her son Arcaláus in his schemes against Amadís.

said to him, "Look here, Sancho, I have been seriously thinking over this monkey's extraordinary gift, and have come to the conclusion that beyond doubt this Master Pedro, his master, has a pact—tacit or express—with the devil."

"If the packet is express from the devil," said Sancho, "there's no doubt it's a very dangerous packet. But what good can it do Master Pedro to have such packets?"

"You do not understand me, Sancho," said Don Quixote. "I only mean he must have made some agreement with the devil to infuse this power into the monkey, that he may earn a living, and after he has grown rich he will give him his soul, which is what the enemy of mankind wants. This I am led to believe by observing that the monkey only answers about things past or present, and the devil's knowledge extends no further. The future he knows only by guesswork, and that not always. It is reserved for God alone to know the times and the seasons,[6] and for him there is neither past nor future; all is present.

"This being as it is, it is clear that this monkey speaks by the spirit of the devil. I am astonished they have not denounced him to the Holy Office, that they might interrogate and force out of him by whose power it is that he practices divination. It is certain this monkey is not an astrologer; neither his master nor he has read, nor knows how to read, those cards they call judiciary,[7] which are now so common in Spain that there is not a silly girl, a page, or an old cobbler who will not try to lay out cards as readily as pick up a jack from the ground—bringing to nought the marvelous truth of the science by their lies and ignorance. I know of a lady who asked one of these card readers whether her little lap dog would get pregnant and have pups, and how many and of what color the little pups would be. To which the señor astrologer, after having laid out his cards, answered that the dog would get pregnant and give birth to three pups, one green, another bright red, and the third multicolored, provided she conceived between eleven and twelve either of the day or night, and on a Monday or Saturday. But as things turned out, two days after this, the dog died of overeating, and the señor planet ruler earned the reputation in that place of being a most profound astrologer, which is common to most of these planet rulers."

"All the same," said Sancho, "I'd be obliged if your worship would have Master Pedro ask his monkey whether what happened to your worship in the Cave of Montesinos is true. For my part—begging your worship's pardon—I'm convinced that the whole thing was a sham, or at any rate something you dreamt."

"That may be," replied Don Quixote. "Still, I will do what you suggest, though I have my own scruples about doing so."

Master Pedro soon came in looking for Don Quixote to tell him the show was now ready and to come and see it, for it was worth seeing. Don Quixote explained his wish and begged him to ask his monkey at once to tell him whether certain

[6] *It is reserved for God alone to know the times and the seasons:* See Acts 1:7, where Jesus tells his apostles, "It is not for you to know times or seasons which the Father has fixed by his own authority."

[7] *those cards they call judiciary:* tarot cards.

things which had happened to him in the Cave of Montesinos were dreams or realities, for to him they appeared to be a little of both.

Upon this Master Pedro, without answering, went back to fetch the monkey, and, having placed it in front of Don Quixote and Sancho, said: "See here, Señor Monkey, this gentleman wishes to know whether certain things which happened to him in the cave called the Cave of Montesinos were false or true." On his making the usual sign, the monkey climbed onto his left shoulder and seemed to whisper in his ear. Master Pedro then said, "The monkey says that the things you saw or that happened to you in that cave are partly false and partly true. He knows this only and no more as regards the question. If your worship wishes to know something else, on Friday next he will answer all that may be asked him. His powers are at present exhausted and will not return to him till Friday, as he has said."

"Did I not say, señor," said Sancho, "that I could not bring myself to believe that what your worship said about the adventures in the cave was entirely true, not even the half of it?"

"The course of events will tell, Sancho," replied Don Quixote. "Time, which reveals all things, leaves nothing that it does not drag into the light of day, though it be buried in the bosom of the earth. But enough of that for the present. Let us go and see Master Pedro's puppet show, for I am sure there must be something novel in it."

"Something!" exclaimed Master Pedro. "This show of mine has sixty thousand novel things in it. Let me tell you, Señor Don Quixote, it is one of the best-worth-seeing things in the world today. But *operibus credite et non verbis*.[8] I'm off to work, for it's getting late, and we have a great deal to do and say and show."

Don Quixote and Sancho obeyed him and went to where the puppet theater was already set up and uncovered, surrounded by lighted wax candles, which made it look splendid and bright. When they took their seats, Master Pedro ensconced himself inside the theater, for it was he who had to work the puppets. A boy, a servant of his, posted himself outside to act as interpreter and explain the mysteries of the exhibition, having a wand in his hand to point to the puppets as they came out. And so, all who were in the inn being arranged in front of the puppet theater, some of them standing, and Don Quixote, Sancho, the page, and cousin, accommodated with the best places, the interpreter began to say what he will hear or see who reads or hears the next chapter.

[8] operibus credite et non verbis: Latin, "Believe in deeds, not in words", maxim that echoes the Latin Vulgate of John 10:38.

CHAPTER XXVI

IN WHICH IS CONTINUED THE ENTERTAINING ADVENTURE OF THE PUPPETEER, TOGETHER WITH OTHER THINGS IN TRUTH QUITE GOOD

"All were silent, Tyrians and Trojans...."[1] I mean, all who were watching the show were hanging on the lips of the interpreter of its wonders, when drums and trumpets were heard to sound inside it and cannon to go off. The noise was soon over, and then the boy lifted up his voice and said, "This true story which is here represented to your worships is taken word for word from the French chronicles and from the Spanish ballads that everybody—down to the boys in the streets—knows by heart.[2] Its subject is the rescue by Señor Don Gaiferos of his wife Melisendra, when a captive in Spain at the hands of the Moors in the city of Sansueña, for so they called then what is now called Zaragoza.

"Here you may see how Don Gaiferos is playing backgammon, just as they sing it—

> At tables playing Don Gaiferos sits,
> For Melisendra is forgotten now.

And that personage who appears there with a crown on his head and a scepter in his hand is the emperor Charlemagne, the supposed father of Melisendra, who, angered to see his son-in-law's idleness and neglect, comes in to berate him. Observe with what vehemence and energy he berates him. You would fancy he was going to give him half a dozen raps with his scepter. Indeed, there are authors who say he did give them, and sound ones too. After having said a great deal to Don Gaiferos about imperiling his honor by not securing the release of his wife, he declares, so the tale goes:

> I've said enough; see to it now.

Observe, too, how the emperor turns away and leaves Don Gaiferos fuming. You see now how in a burst of anger, he flings the table and the board far from him, calls

[1] *All were silent, Tyrians and Trojans....*: "... hushed and alert, they gave heed", opening verses of Book II of *The Aeneid* in a popular Spanish translation, where Aeneas begins his account of the destruction of Troy for Queen Dido and her court in Carthage.

[2] *true story ... knows by heart*: Spanish ballads told of the rescue of the princess Melisendra, daughter of Charlemagne, after Moors kidnapped her and carried her off to their stronghold in Zaragoza. Seven years pass before her husband, Gaiferos, sets off to rescue her, and only because Charlemagne shames him into abandoning his life of ease in Paris.

in haste for his armor, and asks his cousin Don Roland for the loan of his sword, Durindana.[3] See how Don Roland refuses to lend it, offering him his company in the difficult enterprise he is undertaking. But the brave Gaiferos in his anger will not accept it and tells him that he alone will suffice to rescue his wife, be she imprisoned deep in the center of the earth. With this he retires to arm himself and set out on his journey at once.

"Now let your worships turn your eyes to that tower that appears here, which is supposed to be one of the towers of the alcazar of Zaragoza, now called the Aljafería.[4] The lady who appears on that balcony dressed in Moorish fashion is the peerless Melisendra. Many a time from that place would she gaze upon the road to France and seek consolation in her captivity by thinking of Paris and her husband. Observe, too, a new incident which now occurs, such as perhaps never was seen. Do you not see that Moor, who silently and stealthily, with his finger to his lips, approaches Melisendra from behind? Observe now how he imprints a kiss upon her lips, and what a hurry she is in to spit and wipe them with the white sleeve of her smock, and how she bewails herself and tears her fair hair as though it were to blame for the wrong. Observe, too, that the stately Moor who is in that corridor is King Marsilio of Sansueña, who, having seen the Moor's insolence, at once orders him (though a kinsman and a great favorite of his) to be seized and given two hundred lashes, while carried through the streets of the city according to custom

with criers going before him
and cudgels from behind.[5]

Now you see them come out to execute the sentence, although the offense has been scarcely committed; for among the Moors there are no indictments nor remands as with us."

Here Don Quixote called out, "Boy, boy, go straight on with your story, and don't run into curves and slants. To establish a fact definitively requires a great many proofs and confirmations."

Master Pedro said from within, "Don't get lost in details, boy. Do as the gentleman bids you; it's the best plan. Stick to plainchant, and don't try for counterpoint, for it's apt to break down from being over fine."

"I will," said the boy, and he went on to say, "This figure that you see here on horseback, covered with a Gascon cloak,[6] is Don Gaiferos himself. Here his wife, now avenged of the insult of the amorous Moor, takes her stand on the

[3] *Durindana:* name in Italian epics for Roland's sword.

[4] *Aljafería:* fortified palace built by the Moors in the second half of the eleventh century. After the Christians recaptured Zaragoza in 1118, it became the residence of the Christian kings of Aragon.

[5] *with criers ... from behind:* Criers announce the prisoner's crime, while the constables that follow beat him with their staffs. The verses come from an unrelated ballad by Francisco de Quevedo.

[6] *Gascon cloak:* pleated cape with a hood and circular or semi-circular cut, which allowed a traveler to protect himself from the elements.

battlements of the tower with a calmer and more tranquil countenance. She addresses her husband, supposing him to be some traveler, and holds with him all that conversation and dialogue in the ballad that goes—

> If you, sir knight, to France are bound,
> Oh! for Gaiferos ask—

which I do not repeat here because wordiness is apt to produce boredom. Suffice it to observe how Don Gaiferos reveals himself, and that by her joyful gestures Melisendra shows us she has recognized him. What is more, we see how she lowers herself from the balcony to place herself on the haunches of her good husband's horse.

"Alas, unhappy lady! The edge of her skirt has caught on one of the bars of the balcony and she is left hanging in the air, unable to reach the ground. But see how merciful Heaven sends aid in our sorest need. Don Gaiferos advances, and without minding whether the rich skirt is torn or not, he seizes her and by force brings her to the ground. Then with one jerk, he sets her on the haunches of his horse—astride like a man—and bids her hold on tight and clasp her arms round his neck, crossing them on his breast so as not to fall, for Lady Melisendra was not used to that style of riding. You see, too, how the neighing of the horse reveals how happy he is with the gallant and beautiful burden he bears in his lord and lady. You see how they wheel round and leave the city, and in joy and gladness take the road to Paris.

"Go in peace, O peerless pair of true lovers! May you reach your longed-for country in safety, and may fortune interpose no impediment to your prosperous journey. May the eyes of your friends and kinsmen behold you enjoying in peace and tranquility the remaining days of your life. And may they be as many as those of Nestor!"[7]

Here Master Pedro called out again and said, "Simplicity, boy! None of your high flights. 'All affectation is bad.'"

The interpreter made no answer but went on to say, "There was no shortage of idle eyes, which observe everything, to see Melisendra descend from the balcony and mount. Word was brought to King Marsilio, who at once gave orders to sound the alarm. See what a stir there is, and how the city is drowned with the sound of the bells pealing in the towers of all the mosques."

"No, no," said Don Quixote at this point. "On the matter of the bells Master Pedro is quite inaccurate, for the Moors do not use bells, only kettledrums and a kind of reed pipe somewhat like our chirimía.[8] To ring bells this way in Sansueña is beyond doubt a great absurdity."

On hearing this, Master Pedro stopped ringing and said, "Don't get lost in details, Señor Don Quixote, or insist on taking things to such extremes that we

[7] *Nestor:* Greek hero of the Trojan War whose reign as king of Pylos stretched over three generations.

[8] *chirimía:* loud, piercing woodwind instrument popular in early modern Spain, in the same family as the modern oboe.

never get to the end of them. Are there not almost every day a thousand comedies performed all around us full of thousands of inaccuracies and absurdities, and for all that, they have a successful run and are listened to not only with applause, but with admiration and all the rest of it? Go on, boy, and speak as you wish. So long as I fill my moneybag, it doesn't matter if I show as many inaccuracies as there are particles in a sunbeam."

"True enough," said Don Quixote.

The boy went on, "See what a numerous and glittering crowd of horsemen leaves the city in pursuit of the two faithful lovers, what a blowing of trumpets there is, what sounding of horns, what beating of drums and tabors.[9] I fear they will overtake them and bring them back tied to the tail of their own horse, which would be a dreadful sight."

Don Quixote, seeing such a swarm of Moors and hearing such a din, thought it would be right to aid the fugitives. Standing up, he exclaimed in a loud voice, "Never while I live will I allow an outrage to be committed in my presence against such a famous knight and fearless lover as Don Gaiferos. Halt, ill-born rabble! Follow him not nor pursue him, or you will have to reckon with me in battle!" And doing as he said, he drew his sword and with one leap landed in front of the puppet theater, where with unparalleled speed and fury he began to shower down blows on the puppet troop of Moors, knocking over some, decapitating others, maiming this one and demolishing that. Among many more, he delivered one downstroke that—if Master Pedro had not shrunk back, ducked, and curled into a ball—would have sliced off his head as easily as if it had been made of almond paste.

Master Pedro was shouting, "Get a hold of yourself, Señor Don Quixote! Can't you see they're not real Moors you're knocking down and killing and destroying, but only little pasteboard figures! Look—sinner that I am!—how you're wrecking and ruining all that I'm worth!"

But in spite of this, Don Quixote did not cease to discharge a continuous rain of cuts, slashes, downstrokes, and backstrokes. At last, in less than the space of two credos, he brought the whole theater to the ground, with all its fittings and figures demolished and cut to pieces, King Marsilio badly wounded, and the emperor Charlemagne with his crown and head split in two. The whole audience was thrown into confusion, the monkey fled to the roof of the inn, the cousin was frightened, and even Sancho Panza himself was in great fear, for as he swore after the storm was over, he had never seen his master in such a furious passion.

The complete destruction of the show being thus accomplished, Don Quixote became a little calmer and said, "I wish I had here before me now all those who do not or will not believe how useful knights-errant are in the world. Just think, if I had not been here present, what would have become of the brave Don Gaiferos and the fair Melisendra! Depend upon it, by this time those dogs[10]

[9] *tabors:* atabales. The *atabal* was a small kettledrum.

[10] *dogs:* derogatory term for Muslims.

would have overtaken them and inflicted some outrage upon them. So then, long live knight-errantry beyond everything living on earth this day!"

"A long and happy life," said Master Pedro at this in a feeble voice, "and a quick death for me, for I am so unfortunate that I can say with King Don Rodrigo—

Yesterday was I lord of Spain;
Today I've not a turret left
That I may call mine own.[11]

Not half an hour—no, barely a minute ago—I saw myself lord of kings and emperors, with my stables filled with countless horses, and my trunks and bags with endless finery. Now I find myself ruined and laid low, destitute and a beggar, and above all without my monkey, for by my faith, I'll have to sweat my teeth off[12] before I catch him—and all through the reckless fury of sir knight here, who, they say, protects the fatherless, rights wrongs, and does other charitable deeds; but whose generous intentions have come up short in my case only, blessed and praised be the highest heavens! Truly, the Knight of the Woeful Countenance he must be to have worked such woe on my puppets."

Sancho Panza was touched by Master Pedro's words. He said to him, "Don't weep and lament, Master Pedro. You're breaking my heart. You should know that my master Don Quixote is so catholic and conscientious a Christian that, if it becomes clear to him that he's done you any wrong, he'll own it and be willing to pay and make you whole—and then some."

"Only let Señor Don Quixote pay me for some part of the work he has destroyed," said Master Pedro. "I will be content, and his worship will ease his conscience, for he cannot be saved who keeps what is another's against the owner's will and makes no restitution."

"That is true," said Don Quixote, "but at present I am not aware that I have anything of yours, Master Pedro."

"What!" returned Master Pedro. "These relics lying here on the bare hard ground—what scattered and shattered them but the invincible strength of that mighty arm? And who did those bodies belong to but me? And how did I earn my living by but by them?"

"Now am I fully convinced," said Don Quixote, "of what I had many a time before believed, that the enchanters who persecute me do nothing more than put figures like these before my eyes and then transform them into whatever they wish. With the utmost sincerity, I assure you gentlemen who now hear me that to me everything that has taken place here seemed to take place literally—that Melisendra was Melisendra, Don Gaiferos Don Gaiferos, Marsilio Marsilio, and Charlemagne Charlemagne. That was why my anger was roused, and to be faithful to my calling as a knight-errant I sought to give aid and protection to

[11] *Yesterday was I lord of Spain . . . mine own:* The ballad tells of the fall of Visigothic Spain to the Moors in 711.

[12] *sweat my teeth off:* euphemism for "sweat my tail off".

those who fled. With this good intention I did what you have seen. If the result has been the opposite of what I intended, it is no fault of mine but of those wicked beings that persecute me. And yet for all that, I am willing to pay the penalty for this error of mine, though it did not proceed from malice. Let Master Pedro decide what he wants for the spoiled puppets. I will pay on the spot in good and current Castilian money."

Master Pedro made him a bow saying, "I expected no less of the exemplary Christianity of the valiant Don Quixote of La Mancha, true helper and protector of all destitute and needy vagabonds. Our innkeeper gentleman and the great Sancho Panza will be the arbitrators and appraisers between your worship and me of what these damaged puppets are worth or may be worth."

The innkeeper and Sancho consented, then Master Pedro picked up from the ground King Marsilio of Zaragoza with his head off and said, "Here you see how impossible it is to restore this king to his former state. I am therefore of the opinion, saving your better judgments, that for his death, decease, and demise, four reals and a half may be given me."

"Proceed," said Don Quixote.

"Well then, for this split from top to bottom," continued Master Pedro, taking up the halves of Emperor Charlemagne, "it would not be much if I were to ask five reals and a quarter."

"That's not a little," said Sancho.

"Nor is it much," said the innkeeper. "Make it even, and say five reals."

"Let him have the whole five and a quarter," said Don Quixote, "for the sum total of this notable disaster does not stand on a quarter more or less. Make an end of it quickly, Master Pedro, for it's getting close to dinnertime, and I'm beginning to get hungry."

"For this figure," said Master Pedro, "without a nose and missing an eye, who is the fair Melisendra, I ask—and my demand is reasonable—two reals and twelve maravedis."

"It would be nothing short of disastrous," said Don Quixote, "if Melisendra and her husband are not by this time at the French border, if not beyond, for the horse they rode on seemed to me to fly rather than gallop. There is no use trying to sell me a cat for a rabbit by presenting me with a noseless Melisendra when she is now, if all has gone well, in France enjoying a life of ease at her husband's side. May God look after each of us, Master Pedro, and let us all proceed fairly and honestly. Now go on."

Master Pedro, sensing that Don Quixote was beginning to wander and return to his original delusion, was not inclined to let him slip away, so he said to him, "This cannot be Melisendra, but must be one of the damsels that waited on her; so if I'm given sixty maravedis for her, I'll be content and sufficiently paid."

And so he went on, putting values on ever so many more smashed puppets, which, after the two arbitrators had adjusted them to the satisfaction of both parties, came to forty reals and three-quarters. Over and above this sum, which Sancho promptly disbursed, Master Pedro asked for two reals for his trouble in catching the monkey.

"Let him have them, Sancho," said Don Quixote, "not to get the monkey, but to drink his cares away. I would give two hundred reals this minute for the good news to anyone who could tell me positively that the lady Doña Melisandra and Señor Don Gaiferos were now in France and with their own people."

"No one could tell us that better than my monkey," said Master Pedro, "but there's no devil that could catch him now. All the same, I suspect that affection and hunger will drive him to come looking for me tonight. God will send the morning, and we shall see."

In short, the puppet show tempest passed over, and all dined in peace and good company at Don Quixote's expense, for he was the height of generosity. Before daylight, the man with the lances and halberds departed, and soon after daybreak the cousin and the page came to bid Don Quixote farewell, the former returning home, the latter resuming his journey, toward which, to help him, Don Quixote gave him twelve reals. Master Pedro did not care to get into any more arguments with Don Quixote, whom he knew very well; so he rose before the sun, and having gotten together the remains of his show and caught his monkey, he too went off to seek his adventures. The innkeeper, who did not know Don Quixote, was as much astonished at his ravings as at his generosity.

To conclude, Sancho, by his master's orders, paid him very liberally, and taking leave of him they departed the inn at about eight in the morning and took to the road, where we will leave them to pursue their journey. This is necessary in order to allow certain other matters to be set forth that are relevant to this remarkable history.

CHAPTER XXVII

IN WHICH IT IS SHOWN WHO MASTER PEDRO AND HIS MONKEY WERE, TOGETHER WITH THE MISHAP DON QUIXOTE HAD IN THE BRAYING ADVENTURE, WHICH DID NOT TURN OUT AS HE WOULD HAVE LIKED OR AS HE HAD EXPECTED

Cide Hamete, the chronicler of this great history, begins this chapter with these words, "I swear as a Catholic Christian...." His translator says regarding this that Cide Hamete's swearing as a Catholic Christian, he being a Moor (as no doubt he was), only meant that just as a Catholic Christian taking an oath swears, or ought to swear what is true and tell the truth in what he avers, so he was telling the truth as much as if he swore as a Catholic Christian in all he chose to write about Don Quixote—especially in explaining who Master Pedro was and who the divining monkey was that amazed so many villages with his divinations.

He relates, then, that he who has read the First Part of this history will remember well Ginés de Pasamonte whom, with other galley slaves, Don Quixote set free in the Sierra Morena—a kindness for which he afterwards got poor thanks and worse payment from that malicious, ill-mannered set. This Ginés de Pasamonte (Don Ginesillo de Parapilla, as Don Quixote called him) was the one who stole Dapple from Sancho Panza. The failure of the printers to include the how and the when of this matter in the First Part has puzzled a good many people, who attribute to the bad memory of the author what was the error of the press. In fact, Ginés stole him while Sancho Panza was asleep on his back, adopting the device that Brunello had recourse to when he stole Sacripante's horse from between his legs at the siege of Albracca;[1] and, as has been told, Sancho afterwards recovered him. This Ginés, then, afraid of being caught by the officers of justice, who were looking for him to punish him for his misconduct and innumerable crimes (which were so many and so great that he himself wrote a long book giving an account of them), resolved to shift his quarters to the kingdom of Aragon,[2] cover up his left eye, and take up puppeteering; for this trade, as well as sleight of hand, he knew how to perform to perfection.

[1] *adopting the device . . . of Albracca:* See footnote 1, page 445.

[2] *shift his quarters to the kingdom of Aragon:* Castile and Aragon were sovereign jurisdictions in early modern Spain.

As it happened, he bought the monkey from some ransomed Christians returning from Barbary, which he taught to climb on to his shoulder when he made a certain sign and to whisper, or appear to do so, in his ear. Thus prepared, before entering any village where he was bound with his puppet show and monkey, he would inform himself at the nearest village—or from the most likely person he could find—as to what particular things had happened there, and to whom. Keeping them well in mind, the first thing he did was to perform his puppet show, sometimes one story, sometimes another, but all lively, amusing, and familiar. As soon as the show was over he brought forward the accomplishments of his monkey, assuring the public that he divined all the past and the present, but as to the future he had no skill. For each question answered he asked two reals, though for some questions he gave a discount, depending on how he judged the mood of his questioners. When he occasionally came to houses where things that he knew of had happened to the people living there, even if they did not ask him a question, not caring to pay for it, he would make the sign to the monkey and then declare that it had said such and such, which fitted the case exactly. In this way he acquired prodigious fame and amassed a great following. On other occasions, being very crafty, he would answer in such a way that the answers suited the questions; and as no one cross-questioned him or pressed him to tell how his monkey divined, he hoodwinked them all and filled his purse.

The moment he entered the inn he recognized Don Quixote and Sancho, and with that knowledge it was easy for him to astonish them and all who were there; but it would have cost him dear had Don Quixote brought down his hand a little lower when he cut off King Marsilio's head and destroyed all his horsemen, as related in the preceding chapter.

So much for Master Pedro and his monkey.

Now let me return to Don Quixote of La Mancha. After he had left the inn, he determined to visit first the banks of the Ebro[3] and its surroundings before entering the city of Zaragoza, for he had ample time to spare before the jousts began. With this object in mind, he followed the road and traveled along it for two days, without meeting any adventure worth committing to writing, until on the third day, as he was ascending a hill, he heard a great noise of drums, trumpets, and harquebuses. At first he imagined some regiment of soldiers was passing that way, and to see them he spurred Rocinante and mounted the hill. On reaching the top, he saw at the foot of it what must have been over two hundred men, armed with weapons of various kinds—lances, crossbows, partisans,[4] halberds, and pikes, a few harquebuses, and a great many bucklers. He descended the slope and approached the squadron close enough to see distinctly the flags, make out the colors, and distinguish the devices they bore, especially one on a

[3] *Ebro:* From its headwaters in the Cantabrian Mountains, the Ebro River flows southeast, cutting through the heart of Aragon and emptying into the Mediterranean in Catalonia. Zaragoza is the largest city on its banks.

[4] *partisans:* Similar to the halberd, the partisan is a polearm fitted with a long, flat blade that has smaller spiked blades thrusting out on either side of the base.

standard or ensign of white satin, on which there was painted in a very lifelike style a donkey of the Sardinian variety,[5] with its head up, its mouth open and its tongue out, as if it were in the act and attitude of braying. Surrounding it were inscribed in large characters these two lines—

They brayed not in vain,
Our magistrates twain.

From this device Don Quixote concluded that these people must be from the braying town, and he said so to Sancho, explaining to him what was written on the standard. At the same time, he observed that the man who had told them about the matter was wrong in saying that the two men who brayed were councilmen, for according to the lines on the standard they were magistrates.[6]

To which Sancho replied, "Señor, that's nothing to fuss about, for maybe the councilmen who brayed became magistrates of their town afterwards, and so they may go by both titles. Anyway, it has nothing to do with the truth of the story whether the brayers were magistrates or councilmen, provided at least that they did bray; for a magistrate is just as likely to bray as a councilman."

In short, Don Quixote and Sancho concluded that the taunted town had turned out to do battle with some other that had taunted it more than was appropriate for a good neighbor.

Don Quixote proceeded to join them, not a little to Sancho's disquiet, for he was never fond of getting mixed up in such affairs. The members of the squadron received him into their midst, taking him to be someone who was on their side. Don Quixote, putting up his visor, advanced with a self-possessed and noble bearing to the standard with the donkey, and all the chief men of the army gathered round him to look at him, staring with the usual amazement that everybody felt on seeing him for the first time.

Don Quixote, noticing that they examined him so attentively and that none of them spoke to him or asked him any questions, determined to take advantage of their silence. And so breaking his own, he lifted up his voice and said, "Worthy sirs, I entreat you as earnestly as I can not to interrupt a speech I wish to address to you, until you find it displeases or wearies you; and if that comes to pass, on the slightest hint you give me I will put a seal upon my lips and a gag upon my tongue."

They urged him to say what he liked, for they would listen to him willingly.

With this permission Don Quixote continued, saying: "I, sirs, am a knight-errant whose calling is that of arms, and whose profession is to protect those who require protection and give help to such as stand in need of it. Some days ago I became acquainted with your misfortune and the cause which impels you to take up arms at every turn to revenge yourselves upon your enemies. Having many

[5] *Sardinian variety:* small breed of donkey indigenous to the island of Sardinia.

[6] *councilman . . . magistrates:* A councilman (*regidor*) was an administrative official who formed part of the council (*ayuntamiento*) that governed a city, whereas a magistrate (*alcalde*) was primarily a judicial official, responsible for maintaining civic order.

times thought over this matter, I find that, according to the laws of combat, you are mistaken in holding yourselves insulted. For a private individual cannot insult an entire community unless it is by challenging it collectively as a traitor, because he cannot tell who in particular is guilty of the treason for which he challenges it. Of this we have an example in Don Diego Ordoñez de Lara, who challenged the whole town of Zamora because he did not know that Vellido Dolfos alone had committed the treachery of slaying his king.[7] He thus challenged them all, and the vengeance and the reply concerned all. Though, to be sure, Señor Don Diego went rather too far, indeed very much beyond the limits of a challenge; for he had no occasion to challenge the dead, or the waters, or the fish, or the loaves of bread,[8] and all the rest of it as set forth. But let that pass, for when anger overflows there's no father, governor, or bridle to check the tongue.

"It being the case, then, that no one person can insult a kingdom, province, city, state, or entire community, it is clear there is no reason for going out to avenge the challenge of such an insult, inasmuch as it is not one. A fine thing it would be if the clockers were to be up in arms at every moment with everyone who called them by that name, or the casserole makers, eggplant growers, whalers, soap makers, or the bearers of all the other names and titles that are always in the mouths of boys and riffraff![9] It would be a nice business indeed if all these illustrious cities were to get in a huff and revenge themselves and go about perpetually making sackbuts of their swords in every petty quarrel![10] No, I say! God forbid!

"There are four things for which sensible men and well-ordered States ought to take up arms, draw their swords, and risk their persons, lives, and properties. The first is to defend the Catholic faith; the second, to defend one's life, which is in accordance with natural and divine law; the third, in defense of one's honor, family, and property; the fourth, in the service of one's king in a just war; and if to these we choose to add a fifth—which may be included in the second—in defense of one's country. To these five, as it were, capital causes, there may be added some others that may be just and reasonable, and make it a duty to take up arms. But to take them up for trifles and things to laugh at and be amused by rather than offended makes it appear as though he who did so was altogether lacking in

[7] *Don Diego Ordoñez de Lara . . . his king:* In 1072 Sancho II of Castile and León besieged the city of Zamora, which harbored rebellious nobles loyal to his sister Urraca. According to ballads, a Zamoran nobleman named Vellido Dolfos snuck out of the city and pretended to defect to King Sancho's side. Under the pretext of showing the king a secret entrance to the city, he lured Sancho away from his camp and then assassinated him with a dagger he had hidden among some rocks. Afterwards, Don Diego Ordoñez de Lara, a partisan of Sancho, challenged the city to release the assassin.

[8] *loaves of bread:* In the ballad, the loaves of bread (*panes*) that Don Diego challenges are probably a metonymy for the wheat fields that surround the city.

[9] *clockers . . . and riffraff:* Spanish cities and villages had nicknames based on common professions or landmarks.

[10] *making sackbuts of their swords in every petty quarrel:* The act of continually drawing a sword from its sheath resembles the sliding action of a sackbut, predecessor of the trombone.

common sense. Moreover, to take an unjust revenge—and there cannot be any just one—is directly opposed to the sacred law that we acknowledge, wherein we are commanded to do good to our enemies and to love those that hate us,[11] a command which, though it seems quite difficult to obey, is only so to those who have in them less of God than of the world, and more of the flesh than of the spirit. For Jesus Christ—God and true man, who never lied, and could not and cannot lie—said as our lawgiver that his yoke was easy and his burden light.[12] He would not, therefore, have laid any command upon us that was impossible to obey. Thus, sirs, you are bound to hold your peace by human and divine law."

"The devil take me," said Sancho to himself at this, "if my master isn't a theologian. And if he isn't, he's as much like a theologian as one egg is like another."

Don Quixote stopped to take a breath, and, observing that silence was still preserved, had a mind to continue his discourse. He would have done so had not Sancho's cleverness interfered; for seeing his master pause, he took the lead saying, "My lord Don Quixote of La Mancha, who once was called the Knight of the Woeful Countenance but now is called the Knight of the Lions, is a gentleman of great discretion, who knows Latin and his mother tongue like a bachelor. In all of his dealings and counsel, he proceeds like a good soldier and has all the laws and ordinances of what they call combat at his fingertips. You therefore have nothing to do but to let yourselves be guided by what he says, and I'll take the blame if it's wrong. Besides this, you have been told that it is foolish to take offense at merely hearing a bray. I remember when I was a boy I brayed as often as I felt like it. I was a brayer without equal, so elegant and so natural that when I brayed all the donkeys in town would bray in reply. But for all that I was never less than the son of my parents, who were greatly respected; and though I was envied because of this gift by more than one of the high and mighty boys in my town, I couldn't have cared less. To show you that I'm telling the truth, wait and listen, for this art, like swimming, once learned is never forgotten." Then taking hold of his nose, he began to bray so vigorously that all the surrounding valleys resounded.

One of the men who stood near him, however, thought that Sancho was mocking them. He lifted up a long staff he had in his hand and brought down on him such a blow that Sancho dropped helpless to the ground. Don Quixote, seeing him so roughly handled, attacked the man who had struck him, lance in hand, but so many thrust themselves between them that he could not avenge him. Far from it, finding a shower of stones rained upon him, and crossbows and harquebuses unnumbered leveled at him, he wheeled Rocinante round and, as fast as his best gallop could take him, fled from the midst of them. At the same time he commended himself to God with all his heart to deliver him out of this peril, in dread every step of a bullet coming in at his back and out at his breast, and every moment taking a breath to see whether the air had gone out from him.

The members of the squadron were satisfied with seeing him flee and did not fire on him. They set Sancho (scarcely restored to his senses) on his donkey and

[11] *commanded to do good to our enemies and to love those that hate us:* Matthew 5:44.

[12] *said, as our lawgiver, that his yoke was easy and his burden light:* Matthew 11:30.

let him go after his master—not that he was sufficiently in his wits to guide the beast. It was left to Dapple to follow the footsteps of Rocinante, from whom he could not remain a moment separated. Don Quixote having got some way off looked back and, seeing Sancho coming, waited for him, as he perceived that no one followed him.

The armed villagers stood their ground till night, and as the enemy did not come out to battle, they returned to their town exulting. Had they been aware of the ancient custom of the Greeks, they would have erected a monument there.

CHAPTER XXVIII

OF MATTERS THAT BENENGELI SAYS HE WHO READS THEM WILL UNDERSTAND IF HE READS THEM CAREFULLY

When the brave man flees, it is because treachery is made manifest, and it befits the prudent to guard themselves for better occasions. This proved to be the case with Don Quixote, who, giving way before the fury of the villagers and the hostile intentions of the angry squadron, took to flight and, without a thought to Sancho or the danger in which he was leaving him, retreated to such a distance as he thought made him safe. Sancho, lying across his donkey, followed him as has been said and at length came up, having by this time recovered his senses. When he joined him, he let himself fall off Dapple at Rocinante's feet, sore, bruised, and beaten.

Don Quixote dismounted to examine his wounds, but finding him whole from head to foot he said to him, hot with anger, "In an evil hour did you take to braying, Sancho! Where did you learn that it is a good idea to mention rope in the house of a man that has been hanged? When braying is the tune, what counterpoint is to be expected but beatings? Give thanks to God, Sancho, that they signed the cross on you with a stick and did not mark you *per signum crucis*[1] with a cutlass."

"I'm not up to answering," said Sancho, "for I feel as if I was speaking through my back.[2] Let's mount and get away from here. I'll keep from braying but not from saying that knights-errant flee and leave their good squires to be ground to dust at the hands of their enemies."

"He does not flee who retreats," returned Don Quixote. "I would have you know, Sancho, that the valor that is not based upon a foundation of prudence is called rashness, and the exploits of the rash man are to be attributed to good fortune rather than to courage. I own that I retreated, but not that I fled. Therein I have followed the example of many valiant men who have reserved themselves for better times. The histories are full of instances of this, but as it would not be any good to you or pleasure to me, I will not recount them to you now."

Sancho was by this time mounted with the help of Don Quixote, who then himself mounted Rocinante, and at a leisurely pace they proceeded to take

[1] per signum crucis: Latin, "by the sign of the cross"; in context, a slash to the face.

[2] *speaking through my back:* through his open wounds, from which it was believed vapors were released.

shelter in a poplar grove that was in sight about a quarter of a league off. Every now and then Sancho gave vent to deep sighs and dismal groans, and when Don Quixote asked him what caused such acute suffering, he replied that, from the end of his backbone up to the nape of his neck, he was in such pain that it nearly drove him out of his senses.

"The cause of that pain," said Don Quixote, "must be, no doubt, that the staff with which they beat you being long and straight struck you all over your back where all the parts that are sore are located. Had it struck you any more, you would be sorer still."

"By God," said Sancho, "your worship has relieved me of a great doubt, and cleared up the point for me in lovely phrases! On my body! Is the cause of my pain such a mystery that there's any need to tell me I am sore everywhere the staff hit me? If it was my ankles that hurt me there might be a reason to guess why they did, but it doesn't take much to guess that I'm sore where they beat me. By my faith, my master, 'the ills of others hang by a hair.'[3] Every day I discover more and more what little I have to hope for from keeping company with your worship. If this time you've allowed me to be drubbed, the next time—or a hundred times more—we'll have the blanketings from the other day all over again, and all the rest of the shenanigans which, if they've cost me my back today, will eventually cost me an arm and a leg. I would be better off—if I wasn't an ignorant brute that will never do any good in his life—I would be better off, I say, to go home to my wife and children and support them and bring them up on what God may please to give me, instead of following your worship along roads that lead nowhere and paths that are none at all, with little to drink and less to eat. And when it comes to sleeping ... ! 'Measure out seven feet on the ground, brother squire, and if that's not enough for you, take as many more, for you can have it all your own way and stretch yourself to your heart's content.' O that I could see burned and turned to ashes the first man that took up knight-errantry, or at least the first who chose to be squire to such fools as all the knights-errant of past times must have been! I say nothing of those of the present day because, as your worship is one of them, I respect them, and because I know your worship knows a point more than the devil in what you say and think."

"I would lay a good wager with you, Sancho," said Don Quixote, "that now that you are talking on without anyone to stop you, you don't feel a pain in your whole body. Talk away, my son; say whatever comes into your head or mouth. For so long as you feel no pain, the irritation your impertinences give me will be my pleasure; and if you are so anxious to go home to your wife and children, God forbid that I should prevent you. You have my money. See how long it is since we left our village this third time, and how much you can and ought to earn every month, and pay yourself out of your own hand."

"When I worked for Tom Carrasco, the father of the bachelor Samson Carrasco that your worship knows," replied Sancho, "I used to earn two ducats a month besides my food. I can't tell what I can earn with your worship, though

[3] *the ills of others hang by a hair:* "We give little thought to the problems of others."

I know a knight-errant's squire has a harder time of it than the one who works for a farmer. After all, those of us who work for farmers—however much we toil during the day—at the worst, at night, we have a pot of stew and sleep in a bed, which I have not slept in since I've been in your worship's service, if it wasn't the short time we were in Don Diego de Miranda's house and the feast I had with the skimmings I took off Camacho's pots, and what I ate, drank, and slept in Basilio's house. All the rest of the time I've been sleeping on the hard ground under the open sky, exposed to what they call the inclemencies of heaven, keeping life in me with scraps of cheese and crusts of bread, and drinking water either from the brooks or from the springs we come to on these bypaths we travel."

"I admit, Sancho," said Don Quixote, "that all you say is true. How much, do you think, ought I to give you over and above what Tom Carrasco gave you?"

"I think," said Sancho, "that if your worship was to add on two reals a month I'd consider myself well paid—that is, as far as the wages of my labor go. But to make up to me for your worship's pledge and promise to me to give me the government of an island, it would be fair to add six reals more, which makes thirty in all."

"Very good," said Don Quixote. "It is twenty-five days since we left our village, Sancho, so calculate the prorated amount to determine how much I owe you in total, and pay yourself, as I said before, out of your own hand."

"On my body!" said Sancho. "Your worship is very much mistaken in your accounting. For when it comes to the promise of the island we should count from the day your worship promised it to this present hour."

"Well, how long is it, Sancho, since I promised it to you?" asked Don Quixote.

"If I remember rightly," said Sancho, "it has to be over twenty years, three days—more or less."

Don Quixote gave himself a great slap on the forehead and began to laugh heartily before saying, "Why, my wanderings in the Sierra Morena and the whole course of our sallies have lasted barely two months. How can you say, Sancho, that I promised you the island twenty years ago? I believe now that you would have all the money of mine in your possession go to your wages. If so, and if that be your pleasure, I give it to you now once and for all. Much good may it do you, for so long as I see myself rid of such a good-for-nothing squire, I'll be glad to be left a pauper. But tell me, you perverter of the squirely rules of knight-errantry, where have you ever seen or read that any knight-errant's squire made terms with his lord, 'you must give me so much a month for serving you'? Immerse yourself, scoundrel, rogue, monster—for such I take you to be—immerse yourself, I say, into the *mare magnum*[4] of their histories; and if you find that any squire ever said or thought what you have said now, I will let you nail it on my forehead and give me, over and above, four sound slaps in my face. Turn the rein or halter of your Dapple, and begone home. You shall not take a single step further in my company. O bread thanklessly received! O promises ill-bestowed! O man more beast than human! Now, when I was about to raise you to such a position, that,

[4] mare magnum: Latin, "great sea".

in spite of your wife, they would call you 'my lord,' you are leaving me? You are going now when I had a firm and fixed intention of making you lord of the best island in the world? Well, as you yourself have said before, 'honey is not for the mouth of the ass.' Ass you are, ass you will be, and ass you will perish when your life has run its course. And I am sure that it will come to its close before you realize what a beast you are."

Sancho regarded Don Quixote earnestly while he was giving him this dressing down, and was so touched by remorse that tears came to his eyes. In a piteous and broken voice he said to him, "My master, I confess that all I need to be a complete ass is a tail. If your worship will only pin one on me, I'll consider it well placed, and I'll serve you as an ass all the remaining days of my life. Forgive me and have pity on my folly, and remember how little I know. If I talk too much, it's more from suffering than hard feelings; but 'he who sins and mends, his soul to God commends.'"

"I would have been surprised, Sancho," said Don Quixote, "if you didn't include some bit of a proverb in your speech. Well, well, I forgive you, provided you mend and not show yourself in the future so fond of your own interest. Try to be of good cheer and take heart, and encourage yourself to look forward to the fulfillment of my promises, which, by being delayed, does not become impossible."

Sancho said he would do so and keep his spirits up as best he could. They then entered the forest, where Don Quixote settled himself at the foot of an elm, and Sancho at the foot of a beech (for trees of this kind and others like them always have feet but no hands). Sancho passed the night in pain, for with the evening dews the blows of the staff made themselves felt all the more. Don Quixote passed it in his never-failing meditations. For all that, they had some winks of sleep, and with the appearance of daylight they pursued their journey in quest of the banks of the famous Ebro, where things befell them that will be related in the following chapter.

CHAPTER XXIX

OF THE FAMOUS ADVENTURE OF THE ENCHANTED BOAT

By stages already described or left undescribed, two days after leaving the forest Don Quixote and Sancho reached the river Ebro. The sight of it was a great delight to Don Quixote as he contemplated and gazed upon the charms of its banks, the clearness of its stream, the gentleness of its current, and the abundance of its crystal waters. The pleasant view revived a thousand tender thoughts in his mind. Above all, he dwelt upon what he had seen in the Cave of Montesinos; for though Master Pedro's monkey had told him that of those things part was true, part false, he clung more to their truth than to their falsehood—the very reverse of Sancho, who held them all to be downright lies.

As they were thus proceeding, they discovered a small boat without oars or any other rigging that lay at the water's edge tied to the trunk of a tree growing on the bank. Don Quixote looked around and seeing nobody, he dismounted from Rocinante without more ado and ordered Sancho to get down from Dapple and tie both beasts securely to the trunk of a poplar or willow that stood there.

Sancho asked him the reason of this sudden dismounting and tying. Don Quixote answered, "You must know, Sancho, that this boat is irresistibly beckoning me to enter it. It can have no other purpose. In it I am to go to give aid to some knight or other person of distinction in need, no doubt in some sore strait; for this is the way of the books of chivalry and of the enchanters who appear and speak in them. When a knight is involved in some difficulty from which he cannot be delivered save by the hand of another knight, though they may be at a distance of two or three thousand leagues or more one from the other, they either take him up on a cloud, or they provide a boat for him to get into, and in less than the twinkling of an eye they carry him where they will and where his help is required. And so, Sancho, this boat is placed here for the same purpose; this is as true as that it is now day. Before this one passes, tie Dapple and Rocinante together, and then may it be in God's hand to guide us. For I would not hold back from embarking, though barefoot friars were to beg me."

"If it's going to be like that," said Sancho, "and your worship is set on giving in to these—I don't know if I should call them absurdities—at every turn, there's nothing to do but to obey and keep my head down, bearing in mind the proverb, 'Do as your master bids you, and join him at his table.'[1] All the same, for the sake

[1] *Do as your master bids you, and join him at his table:* "Obey, and your master will reward you."

of clearing my conscience, I want to warn your worship that in my opinion this boat isn't enchanted but belongs to some of the fishermen on this river, for they catch the best shad in the world here."

Sancho said this as he tied up the beasts, his heart heavy with sorrow, and left them to the care and protection of the enchanters. Don Quixote told him not to be uneasy about deserting the animals, "for he who would transport the two of them over such longinquous roads and regions would take care to feed their beasts."

"I don't understand that part about *logiquous*," said Sancho. "In all my life I've never heard such a word."

"*Longinquous*," replied Don Quixote, "means far off. It is no wonder you don't understand it, for you are not bound to know Latin, like some who pretend to know it and don't."

"They are tied now," said Sancho. "What should we do next?"

"What?" cried Don Quixote. "Cross ourselves and weigh anchor. I mean, embark and cut the moorings by which the boat is held." He leaped into the boat, with Sancho following, and cut the line. The boat began to drift away slowly from the bank.

When Sancho saw himself somewhere around two yards out in the river, he began to tremble and give himself up for lost; but nothing distressed him more than hearing Dapple bray and seeing Rocinante struggling to get loose. He said to his master, "Dapple is braying in despair at our leaving him, and Rocinante is trying to escape and jump in after us. O beloved friends, peace be with you! May the madness that is taking us from you, seen for what it is, return us to your company!"

With this he fell to weeping so bitterly that Don Quixote said to him, greatly irritated, "What are you afraid of, you cowardly creature? What are you crying about, heart of butter? Who pursues you? Who is troubling you, you tame little mouse? What do you lack that would make you needy in the very heart of abundance? Are you, perchance, tramping barefoot over the Riphaean Mountains[2] instead of seated on a bench like an archduke on the tranquil stream of this pleasant river, from which in a short space we shall come out upon the broad sea? By now we must have traversed seven or eight hundred leagues. If I had here an astrolabe to take the altitude of the pole,[3] I could tell you how many we have traveled, though either I know little, or we have already crossed or shall shortly cross the equinoctial line[4] which parts the two opposite poles midway."

"And when we come to that line your worship speaks of," said Sancho, "how far will we have gone?"

"Very far," said Don Quixote, "for of the three hundred and sixty degrees that this terraqueous globe contains—as computed by Ptolemy, the greatest

[2] *Riphaean Mountains:* legendary mountains in classical geography that were depicted as the northern boundary of the known world.

[3] *astrolabe to take the altitude of the pole:* The astrolabe, an instrument mapping the celestial sphere on two planes, allowed the user to calculate the altitude angle of the celestial pole above the horizon (altitude of the pole), a value that corresponds to the observer's latitude.

[4] *equinoctial line:* the equator.

cosmographer known[5]—we will have traveled one-half when we come to the line I spoke of."

"By God," said Sancho, "your worship gives me a nice authority for what you say, putrid Dolly something transmogrified, or whatever it is."

Don Quixote laughed at the interpretation Sancho put upon "computed," and the name of the cosmographer Ptolemy, and he said, "You should know, Sancho, that with the Spaniards and those who embark at Cádiz for the East Indies, one of the signs they have to show them when they have passed the equinoctial line I told you of is that the lice die upon everyone on board the ship. Not a single one is left or to be found in the whole vessel if they gave its weight in gold for it. So, Sancho, you may as well pass your hand down your thigh, and if you come upon anything alive we will be no longer in doubt. If not, then we have crossed."

"I don't believe a bit of it," said Sancho. "Still, I'll do as your worship asks me, though I don't know what need there is for trying these experiments, for I can see with my own eyes that we haven't moved five yards away from the bank or shifted two yards from where the animals stand. For there are Rocinante and Dapple in the very same place where we left them, and watching a point as I'm doing now, I swear by all that's good that we're not stirring or moving at the pace of an ant."

"Try the test I told you of, Sancho," said Don Quixote, "and pay attention to nothing else, for you know nothing about colures, lines, parallels, zodiacs, ecliptics, poles, solstices, equinoxes, planets, signs, bearings[6]—the measures of which the celestial and terrestrial spheres are composed. If you were acquainted with these things, or any portion of them, you would see clearly how many parallels we have cut, what signs we have seen, and what constellations we have left behind and are now leaving behind. But again I tell you, feel and hunt, for I am certain you are cleaner than a sheet of smooth white paper."

Sancho felt, and passing his hand gently and carefully down to the hollow of his left knee, he looked up at his master and said, "Either the test is a false one, or we have not come to where your worship says—not anywhere close."

"Why, how so?" asked Don Quixote. "Have you come upon anything?"

"Plenty of anythings!" replied Sancho, and shaking his fingers he washed his whole hand in the river along which the boat was quietly gliding in midstream, not moved by any occult intelligence or invisible enchanter, but simply by the current, just there smooth and gentle.

They now came in sight of some large watermills that stood in the middle of the river. The instant Don Quixote saw them he cried out, "Do you see over

[5] *terraqueous globe . . . greatest cosmographer known:* The writings of the Greco-Roman polymath Claudius Ptolemy (second century A.D.) established the geocentric model of the cosmos that held sway until the Copernican Revolution. In his *Geography*, a guide to drawing maps, Ptolemy underestimated the earth's circumference by forty-three hundred miles. This miscalculation led Christopher Columbus to believe that Asia lay much closer to Europe when sailing westward. The term "terraqueous globe" refers to the earth as composed of land (*terra*) and water (*aqua*).

[6] *colures . . . bearings:* astronomical terms used to chart the heavens according to the Ptolemaic cosmos.

there, my friend? There stands the castle or fortress, where no doubt there is some imprisoned knight, or ill-used queen, or infanta or princess in whose aid I am brought hither."

"What the devil city, fortress, or castle is your worship talking about, señor?" asked Sancho. "Don't you see that those are watermills in the middle of the river for grinding wheat?"

"Hold your peace, Sancho," said Don Quixote. "Though they look like watermills they are not so. I have already told you that enchantments transform things and change their proper shapes. I do not mean to say they really change them from one form into another but that it seems as though they did, as experience proved in the transformation of Dulcinea, sole refuge of my hopes."

By this time, the boat, having reached the middle of the stream, began to move less slowly than before. The millers from the watermills, when they saw the boat coming down the river and on the point of being sucked in by the draft of the wheels, hurriedly ran out, several of them, with long poles to stop it. Being all mealy, with faces and garments covered with flour, they presented a sinister appearance. They raised loud shouts, crying, "Devils of men, where are you going? Are you mad? Do you want to drown yourselves or dash yourselves to pieces on these waterwheels?"

"Did I not tell you, Sancho," said Don Quixote at this, "that we had reached the place where I am to show what the might of my arm can do? See what ruffians and villains come out against me. See what monsters oppose me. See what hideous countenances come to frighten us! You shall soon see, scoundrels!" Then standing up in the boat he began in a loud voice to hurl threats at the millers, exclaiming, "Ill-intentioned and worse-counseled rabble, restore to liberty the person you hold in bondage in this your fortress or prison—high or low or of whatever rank or quality he be—for I am Don Quixote of La Mancha, otherwise called the Knight of the Lions, for whom, by the disposition of Heaven above, it is reserved to bring this adventure to a happy conclusion."

So saying he drew his sword and began making passes in the air at the millers, who, hearing but not understanding all this nonsense, attempted to stop the boat, which was now getting into the rushing channel of the waterwheels. Sancho fell upon his knees devoutly appealing to Heaven to deliver him from such imminent peril, which it did by the actions and agility of the millers, who, pushing against the boat with their poles, stopped it—not, however, without upsetting and throwing Don Quixote and Sancho into the water. Lucky it was for Don Quixote that he could swim like a goose, though the weight of his armor carried him twice to the bottom. Had it not been for the millers, who dove in and hoisted them both out, it would have been Troy[7] with the two of them.

As soon as they were landed, both more drenched than thirsty, Sancho went down on his knees and with clasped hands and eyes raised to heaven, prayed a long and fervent prayer to God to deliver him evermore from his master's rash whims and undertakings. The fishermen, the owners of the boat, which the mill

[7] *Troy:* byword for catastrophe.

wheels had knocked to pieces, now came up, and seeing it smashed they proceeded to strip Sancho and to demand payment for it from Don Quixote. But he with great calmness, just as if nothing had happened him, told the millers and fishermen that he would pay for the boat most cheerfully, on condition that they delivered up to him, free and unhurt, the person or persons that were imprisoned in that castle of theirs.

"What persons or what castle are you talking about, madman? Do you intend to carry off the people who come to grind wheat in these watermills?"

"That's enough," said Don Quixote to himself. "It would be preaching in the desert to attempt by entreaties to induce this rabble to do any virtuous action. In this adventure two mighty enchanters must have encountered one another, and one frustrates what the other attempts. One provided the boat for me, and the other upset me. God help us, this world is all machinations and schemes at cross purposes one with the other. I can do no more." Then turning toward the watermills, he said aloud, "Friends, whoever you be that are immured in that prison, forgive me that, to my misfortune and yours, I cannot deliver you from your misery. This adventure is doubtless reserved and destined for some other knight."

So saying he settled scores with the fishermen and paid fifty reals for the boat, which Sancho handed to them very much against his will, saying, "With a couple more boat businesses like this, we'll have sunk our whole capital."

The fishermen and the millers stood staring in amazement at the two figures, so very different to all appearance from ordinary men, and were wholly unable to make out the drift of the observations and questions Don Quixote addressed to them. Concluding that they were madmen, they left them and betook themselves, the millers to their mills, and the fishermen to their huts. Don Quixote and Sancho returned to their beasts and to their beastly moods.

So ended the adventure of the enchanted boat.

CHAPTER XXX

OF DON QUIXOTE'S ADVENTURE WITH A FAIR HUNTRESS

They reached their beasts in low spirits and with long faces, knight and squire—Sancho particularly, for with him whatever touched the money stash touched his heart, and when anything was taken from it he felt as if he was robbed of the apple of his eyes. In sum, without exchanging a word, they mounted and left behind the famous river, Don Quixote absorbed in thoughts of his love, Sancho in thoughts of growing richer, which at that time seemed to him far from likely. For fool as he was, he saw clearly enough that the bulk of his master's actions were utterly senseless; and he began to cast about for an opportunity of retiring from his service and going home without providing any explanation or even saying farewell. Fortune, however, ordered matters after a fashion very much the opposite of what he contemplated.

It so happened that the next day around sunset, on coming out of a forest, Don Quixote cast his eyes over a green meadow, and at the far end of it observed some people, and as he drew nearer saw that it was a hawking party. Coming closer, he distinguished among them a handsome lady on a pure white palfrey or hackney caparisoned with green trappings and a silver-mounted sidesaddle. The lady was also wearing green, and so richly and splendidly dressed that splendor itself seemed personified in her. On her left hand she bore a hawk, proof to Don Quixote's mind that she must be some great lady and the mistress of the whole hunting party, which was the truth.

He said to Sancho, "Run Sancho, my son, and say to that lady on the palfrey with the hawk that I, the Knight of the Lions, kiss the hands of her exalted beauty, and if her excellence will grant me leave I will go and kiss them in person and place myself at her service for whatever may be in my power and her highness may command. Mind how you speak, Sancho, and take care not to let any of your proverbs into your message."

"You've got a likely one here to let any in!" said Sancho. "To think of saying that to me! Why, this isn't the first time in my life I've carried messages to high and exalted ladies."

"Beside the one you took to Lady Dulcinea," said Don Quixote, "I know of no other you have carried, at least in my service."

"That's true," replied Sancho, "but 'pledges don't distress a good payer,' and 'in a house where there's plenty, supper is soon ready.' I mean there's no need to tell or warn me about anything. I'm ready for it all and know a little about everything."

"That I believe, Sancho," said Don Quixote. "Go and good luck to you, and God speed you."

Sancho went off at top speed, forcing Dapple out of his regular pace, and came to where the fair huntress was standing. Dismounting, he knelt before her and said, "Fair lady, that knight that you see there, the Knight of the Lions by name, is my master. I am a squire of his, and at home they call me Sancho Panza. This same Knight of the Lions, who was called not long ago the Knight of the Woeful Countenance, sends me to say may it please your highness to give him leave that, with your permission, approbation, and consent, he may come and carry out his wishes, which are, as he says and I believe, to serve your exalted loftiness and beauty. If you give it, your ladyship will do a thing which will redound to your honor, and he will receive a most distinguished favor and happiness."

"You have indeed, squire," said the lady, "delivered your message with all the formalities such messages require. Rise up, for it is not right that the squire of a knight so great as he of the Woeful Countenance, of whom we have heard a great deal here, should remain on his knees. Rise, my friend, and bid your master welcome to the services of myself and the duke my husband, in a country house we have here."

Sancho got up, charmed as much by the beauty of the good lady as by her highbred air and courtesy, but above all by what she had said about having heard of his master, the Knight of the Woeful Countenance; for if she did not call him Knight of the Lions it was no doubt because he had so lately taken the name.

"Tell me, brother squire," asked the duchess (whose title, however, is not known), "this master of yours, is he not one of whom there is a history being circulated in print called *The Ingenious Gentleman Don Quixote of La Mancha*, who has for the lady of his heart a certain Dulcinea del Toboso?"

"He is the same, señora," replied Sancho. "And that squire of his who figures, or ought to figure in that history under the name of Sancho Panza is myself, unless they've changed me in the cradle, I mean in the press."

"I am rejoiced at all this," said the duchess. "Go, brother Panza, and tell your master that he is welcome to my estate, and that nothing could happen to me that could give me greater pleasure."

Sancho returned to his master mightily pleased with this gratifying answer and told him all the great lady had said to him, lauding to the skies in his rustic phrase her rare beauty, her great elegance, and her courtesy. Don Quixote drew himself up briskly in his saddle, fixed himself in his stirrups, settled his visor, gave Rocinante the spur, and with an easy bearing advanced to kiss the hands of the duchess, who, having sent to summon the duke her husband, told him while Don Quixote was approaching all about the message. As both of them had read the First Part of this history (and from it were aware of Don Quixote's mad infirmity), they awaited him with the greatest delight and desire to make his acquaintance, intending to humor him and agree with everything he said. As long as he stayed with them, they determined to treat him as a knight-errant, with all the accustomed ceremonies in the books of chivalry they had read, for they themselves were very fond of them.

Don Quixote now came up with his visor raised, and as it appeared that he was about to dismount, Sancho made haste to go and hold his stirrup for him. But in getting down off Dapple he was so unlucky as to hitch his foot in one of the ropes of the packsaddle in such a way that he was unable to free it and was left hanging by it with his face and chest on the ground. Don Quixote, who was not used to dismount without having the stirrup held, fancying that Sancho had by this time come to hold it for him, threw himself off with a lurch and brought Rocinante's saddle after him (which was no doubt badly girthed), and saddle and he both came to the ground—not without discomfiture to him and abundant curses muttered between his teeth against the unlucky Sancho, who had his foot still in the shackles.

The duke ordered his huntsmen to go to the help of knight and squire, and they raised Don Quixote, sorely shaken by his fall. He, limping, advanced as best he could to kneel before the noble pair. This, however, the duke would by no means permit. On the contrary, dismounting from his horse, he went and embraced Don Quixote saying, "I am grieved, Sir Knight of the Woeful Countenance, that your first experience on my property should have been such an unfortunate one as we have seen; but the carelessness of squires is often the cause of worse accidents."

"That which has happened to me in meeting you, mighty prince," replied Don Quixote, "cannot be unfortunate, even if my fall had not stopped short of the depths of the bottomless pit, for the glory of having seen you would have lifted me up and delivered me from it. My squire (God's curse upon him) is better at unloosing his tongue in talking impertinences than in tightening the girths of a saddle to keep it steady. But however I may be, fallen or raised up, on foot or on horseback, I shall always be at your service and that of my lady the duchess, your worthy consort, worthy queen of beauty and paramount princess of courtesy."

"Gently, Señor Don Quixote of La Mancha," said the duke; "where my lady Doña Dulcinea del Toboso is, it is not right that other beauties should be praised."

Sancho, by this time released from his entanglement, was standing by, and before his master could answer he said, "There's no denying my lady Dulcinea del Toboso is very beautiful. You couldn't say it enough. But 'the rabbit jumps up where one least expects it.' I've heard say that what we call nature is like a potter that makes clay vessels, and he who makes one lovely vessel can also make two, or three, or a hundred. I say so because, by my faith, my lady the duchess is in no way behind my mistress, Lady Dulcinea del Toboso."

Don Quixote turned to the duchess and said, "Your highness may conceive that never had knight-errant in this world a more talkative or humorous squire than I have. He will prove the truth of what I say, if your loftiness is pleased to accept my services for a few days."

To which the duchess answered, "That worthy Sancho is humorous I consider a very good thing, because it is a sign that he is shrewd; for humor and wit, Señor Don Quixote, as you very well know, do not take up their abode with dull minds. As good Sancho is humorous and witty, I here set him down as shrewd."

"And talkative," added Don Quixote.

"So much the better," said the duke, "for many humorous things cannot be said in few words. But not to lose time in talking, come, great Knight of the Woeful Countenance—"

"Of the Lions, your highness must say," said Sancho, "for there is no Woeful Countenance or any such character now."

"So be it: He of the Lions," continued the duke. "I say, let Sir Knight of the Lions come to a castle of mine close by, where he shall be given that reception which is due to so exalted a personage, and which the duchess and I are accustomed to give to all knights-errant who come there."

By this time Sancho had fixed and girthed Rocinante's saddle, and Don Quixote having gotten on his back and the duke having mounted a fine horse, they placed the duchess in the middle and set out for the castle. The duchess desired Sancho to come to her side, for she found infinite enjoyment in listening to his witticisms. Sancho required no pressing, but pushed himself in between them and the duke, who thought it rare good fortune to receive in their castle such a knight-errant and such an erring squire.

CHAPTER XXXI

WHICH TREATS OF MANY AND GREAT MATTERS

Supreme was the satisfaction that Sancho felt at seeing himself, to his mind, in the favor and confidence of the duchess, for he looked forward to finding in her castle what he had found in Don Diego's house and in Basilio's. Ever fond of the good life, he seized by the forelock any opportunity for a feast when it presented itself.

The history informs us that before they reached the country house or castle, the duke went on in advance and instructed all his servants how they were to treat Don Quixote; and so the instant he came up to the castle gates with the duchess, two grooms or stableboys, clad in what they call morning gowns of fine crimson satin reaching to their feet, came out, and catching Don Quixote in their arms before he saw or heard them, said to him, "Your highness should go and take my lady the duchess off her horse."

Don Quixote obeyed, and great bandying of compliments followed between the two over the matter. In the end the duchess' determination carried the day, and she refused to dismount from her palfrey except in the arms of the duke, saying she did not consider herself worthy to impose so unnecessary a burden on so great a knight. At length the duke came out to take her down, and as they entered a spacious courtyard two fair damsels came forward and threw over Don Quixote's shoulders a large mantle of the finest scarlet cloth.

In an instant, all the galleries that looked on the courtyard were filled with the servants of the household, crying, "Welcome, flower and cream of knight-errantry!" All or most of them flung perfumed water from little bottles over Don Quixote and the duke and duchess. At all of this Don Quixote was greatly astonished, and for the first time he was thoroughly convinced that he was a genuine knight-errant and not a pretend one, now that he saw himself treated in the same way as he had read of such knights being treated in days of yore.

Sancho, deserting Dapple, hung on to the duchess and entered the castle, but feeling some twinges of conscience at having left the donkey alone, he approached a respectable dueña[1] who had come out with the rest to receive the duchess, and in a low voice he said to her, "Señora González, or whatever your grace's name may be—"

"My name is Doña Rodríguez de Grijalba," replied the dueña. "What is your will, brother?"

[1] *dueña:* older woman who serves as governess in a noble household.

To which Sancho answered, "I should be glad if your worship would do me the favor to go out to the castle gate, where you will find a gray donkey of mine. If you please, have them put him in the stable, or put him there yourself, for the poor little beast is jittery by nature and not all that used to being alone."

"If the master is as shrewd as the man," said the dueña, "we're in for trouble. Be off with you, brother, and bad luck to you and him who brought you here. Go look after your donkey yourself, for we, the dueñas of this house, are not used to work of that kind."

"Well, to be honest," returned Sancho, "I've heard my master, who knows all about the mysteries of the past, telling the story of Lancelot—

When from Brittany he came,
Upon him ladies waited,
And dueñas on his hack.

And when it comes to my donkey, I wouldn't trade him for Señor Lancelot's hack."

"If you're a jester, brother," said the dueña, "keep your witticisms for some place where they'll be appreciated and paid for. From me you're going to get nothing but a fig."[2]

"In any event, it will be a very ripe one," said Sancho, "for if points are counted in years, you won't lose the game."

"You son of a bitch!" cried the dueña, aglow with anger. "Old or not, I'm accountable to God, not to you, you garlic-stuffed scoundrel!" She said it so loud, that the duchess heard it and, turning round and seeing the dueña so excited and with eyes aflame, asked who it was she was arguing with.

"With this good fellow here," said the dueña, "who has insisted that I go and put a donkey of his at the castle gate into the stable, holding it up to me as an example that they did this I don't know where—that some ladies waited on a Lancelot and dueñas on his hack. And if that weren't enough, he called me old to boot."

"I should have considered that the greatest affront that could be offered me," the duchess responded. Addressing Sancho, she said to him, "You must know, friend Sancho, that Doña Rodríguez is very youthful and that she wears that hood more for authority and custom's sake than because of her years."

"May all the rest of mine be unlucky," said Sancho, "if I meant it that way. I only spoke because of the great affection I have for my donkey, and I thought I could not commend him to a more kindhearted person than Lady Doña Rodríguez."

Don Quixote, who was listening, said to him, "Is this proper conversation for this place, Sancho?"

"Señor," replied Sancho, "everyone must mention what he wants wherever he may be. I thought of Dapple here, and I spoke of him here. If I had thought of him in the stable, I would have spoken there."

[2] *fig:* obscene gesture made with the thumb held up between the index and middle fingers.

At this the duke observed, "Sancho is quite right, and there is no reason at all to find fault with him. Dapple shall be fed to his heart's content, and Sancho may rest easy, for he shall be treated like his master."

While this conversation—amusing to all except Don Quixote—was proceeding, they ascended the staircase and ushered Don Quixote into a chamber hung with rich cloth of gold and brocade. Six damsels relieved him of his armor and waited on him like pages, all of them prepared and instructed by the duke and duchess as to what they were to do and how they were to treat Don Quixote, so that he might see and believe they were treating him like a knight-errant. When his armor was removed, there stood Don Quixote in his tight-fitting breeches and chamois doublet, lean, lanky, and long, with cheeks that seemed to be kissing each other inside—such a figure, that if the damsels waiting on him had not taken care to restrain their amusement (which was one of the particular directions their master and mistress had given them), they would have burst with laughter.

They asked permission to undress him so that they could put a shirt on him, but he would not on any account, saying that modesty became knights-errant just as much as valor. He said, however, they could give the shirt to Sancho. But afterwards, when the two were shown to a room with a sumptuous bed, Don Quixote decided to undress and wear the shirt himself.

Finding himself alone with his squire, he said to him, "Tell me, you newfledged buffoon and old booby, do you think it right to offend a dueña so venerable and so worthy of respect as her? Was that a time for you to think about your Dapple, or are these noble personages likely to let the beasts fare badly when they treat their owners in such elegant style? For God's sake, Sancho, restrain yourself, and don't show the thread so as to let them see what a coarse, boorish cloth you're made of. Remember, you sinner, the master is the more esteemed the more respectable and well-bred his servants are. One of the greatest advantages that princes have over other men is that they have servants as good as themselves to wait on them. Do you not see—shortsighted being that you are, and unlucky mortal that I am—that if they perceive you to be a coarse peasant or a dull blockhead, they will suspect me to be some impostor or swindler? No, Sancho friend, no. Keep clear, keep clear, I say, of these stumbling blocks; for he who loses his footing as a chatterbox and jokester collapses as a wretched buffoon the first time he trips. Bridle your tongue; weigh your words before they escape your mouth. Bear in mind we are now in a place where, by God's help and the strength of my arm, we shall come forth greatly advanced in fame and fortune."

Sancho promised him with much earnestness to keep his mouth shut, and to bite off his tongue before he uttered a word that was not altogether appropriate and well considered, and told him that he could set his mind at ease on that point. Never on his account would it be discovered who they really were.

Don Quixote dressed himself, put on his baldric with his sword, threw the scarlet mantle over his shoulders, placed on his head a montera[3] of green satin that the damsels had given him, and thus arrayed passed out into the great hall,

[3] *montera:* See footnote 2, page 220.

where he found the damsels drawn up in double file, the same number on each side, all with the implements necessary for him to wash his hands, which they presented to him with profuse obeisances and ceremonies. Then came twelve pages, together with the chief steward, to lead him to dinner, as his hosts were already waiting for him.

They placed him in their midst, and with much pomp and stateliness they conducted him into another room, where there was a sumptuous table set for only four. The duchess and the duke came out to the doorway of the room to receive him, and with them a somber priest. He was one of those who rule noblemen's houses; one of those who, not being born princes themselves, never know how to teach those who are how to behave as such; one of those who would have the greatness of great people measured by their own narrowness of mind; one of those who, when they try to introduce economy into the household they rule, lead it into stinginess. One of this kind, I say, must have been the somber churchman who came out with the duke and duchess to receive Don Quixote.

A vast number of polite speeches were exchanged, and at length, taking Don Quixote between them, they proceeded to sit down at the table. The duke pressed Don Quixote to take the head of the table, and, though he refused, the entreaties of the duke were so many that he had to accept.

The priest took his seat opposite to him, and the duke and duchess those at the sides. All this time Sancho stood by, gaping with amazement at the honor he saw shown to his master by these illustrious people. Observing all the ceremonies and entreaties that had passed between the duke and Don Quixote to induce him to take his seat at the head of the table, he said, "If your worship will give me leave, I will tell you a story of what happened in my village about this matter of seats."

The moment Sancho said this Don Quixote trembled, believing beyond any doubt that he was about to say something foolish. Sancho glanced at him, and guessing his thoughts, said, "Don't be afraid of my going astray, señor, or saying anything that isn't on the mark. I haven't forgotten the advice your worship gave me just now about talking too much or too little, well or badly."

"I have no recollection of anything, Sancho," said Don Quixote. "Say what you will. Only say it quickly."

"Well then," said Sancho, "what I'm going to say is so true that my master Don Quixote, who is here present, will keep me from lying."

"Lie as much as you want for all I care, Sancho," said Don Quixote, "for I am not going to stop you. But consider what you are about to say."

"I have so considered and reconsidered," said Sancho, "that 'the bellringer can rest content,'[4] as will be seen by what follows."

"It would be well," said Don Quixote, "if your highnesses would order them to throw out this idiot, for he is about to talk a heap of nonsense."

"By the life of the duke, Sancho shall not be taken away from me for a moment," said the duchess. "I am very fond of him, for I know he is very discreet."

[4] *the bellringer can rest content*: "There will be no need to sound an alarm."

"Discreet be the days of your holiness," said Sancho, "for the good opinion you have of my judgment, even if I don't deserve it. But the story I want to tell is this: There was an invitation given by a gentleman of my town, a very rich one, and one of distinction, for he was one of the Álamos of Medina del Campo, and married to Doña Mencía de Quiñones, the daughter of Don Alonso de Marañón, Knight of the Order of Santiago, who was drowned at Herradura. He was the one there was a quarrel about years ago in our village, which my master Don Quixote was mixed up in, to the best of my belief—the one where Tomasillo the mischief-maker, the son of Balbastro the blacksmith, ended up getting wounded. Isn't all this true, my master? As you live, say so, so that these gentlefolk may not take me for some lying chatterer."

"So far," said the priest, "I take you to be more a chatterer than a liar; but I don't know what I shall take you for by-and-by."

"You cite so many witnesses and proofs, Sancho," said Don Quixote, "that I have no choice but to say you must be telling the truth. Go on, and make the story short, for you're on your way not to finish it in two days."

"He is not to make it short," said the duchess. "On the contrary, for my gratification, he is to tell it as he knows it, though he should not finish it these six days. And if he took so many, they would be to me the pleasantest I ever spent."

"Well then, sirs, I say," continued Sancho, "that this same gentleman, who I know as well as I do my own hands, for it's not a bowshot from my house to his, invited a poor but respectable farmer—"

"Get on, brother," said the churchman. "At the rate you are going you will not make an end of your story short of the world to come."

"I'll make an end halfway there, please God," said Sancho. "And so I say this farmer, coming to the house of the gentleman I spoke of that invited him—rest his soul, he's now dead. What's more, he died the death of an angel, so they say. I wasn't there, for just at that time I had gone to the harvest in Tembleque—"

"As you live, my son," said the churchman, "make haste back from Tembleque, and finish your story without burying the gentleman, unless you want to make more funerals."

"Well then, it so happened," said Sancho, "that as the pair of them were going to sit down to dine—I think I can see them now plainer than ever—"

Great was the enjoyment the duke and duchess derived from the irritation the worthy churchman showed at the long-winded, halting way Sancho had of telling his story, while Don Quixote was chafing with rage and vexation.

"So, as I was saying," continued Sancho, "as the pair of them were going to sit down to dine, as I said, the farmer insisted upon the gentleman's taking the head of the table, and the gentleman insisted upon the farmer's taking it, as his orders should be obeyed in his house. But the farmer, who prided himself on his politeness and good breeding, would not on any account, until the gentleman, his patience wearing thin, put his hands on his shoulders and forced him to sit down, saying, 'Sit down, you stupid lout, for wherever I sit will be the head to you.' That's the story, and I do believe that it hasn't been brought out of place."

Don Quixote turned a thousand colors, which, on his sunburnt face, mottled it till it resembled jasper. The duke and duchess suppressed their laughter so as not altogether to mortify Don Quixote, for they saw through Sancho's impertinence. To change the conversation and keep Sancho from uttering more absurdities, the duchess asked Don Quixote what news he had of Lady Dulcinea, and if he had sent her any presents of giants or miscreants lately, for he could not but have vanquished a good many.

To which Don Quixote replied, "Señora, my misfortunes, though they had a beginning, will never have an end. I have vanquished giants, and I have sent her rogues and miscreants. But where are they to find her if she is enchanted and turned into the ugliest peasant wench that can be imagined?"

"I don't know," said Sancho Panza; "to me she seems the fairest creature in the world. At any rate, in nimbleness and jumping she won't give in to a tumbler. By my faith, señora duchess, she leaps from the ground on to the back of a donkey like a cat."

"Have you seen her enchanted, Sancho?" asked the duke.

"Have I seen her?" said Sancho. "Why, who the devil was it but me that first thought of the enchantment business? She's as much enchanted as my father."

The priest, when he heard them talking of giants and rogues and enchantments, began to suspect that this must be Don Quixote of La Mancha, whose story the duke was always reading. He had often reproved him for it, telling him it was foolish to read such fooleries. Becoming convinced that his suspicion was correct, addressing the duke, he said very angrily to him, "Señor, your excellency will have to give account to God for what this good man does. This Don Quixote, or Don Simpleton, or whatever his name is, cannot, I imagine, be such a blockhead as your excellency would have him, holding out encouragement to him to go on with his vagaries and follies." Then turning to address Don Quixote he said, "And you, numbskull, who put it into your head that you are a knight-errant, and that you vanquish giants and capture miscreants? Go your ways in a good hour, and in a good hour be it said to you. Go home and bring up your children if you have any, and attend to your business, and give up going wandering about the world, gaping and making a laughingstock of yourself to all who know you and all who don't. Where, in heaven's name, have you discovered that there are or ever were knights-errant? Where are there giants in Spain or miscreants in La Mancha, or enchanted Dulcineas, or all the rest of the silly things they tell about you?"

Don Quixote listened attentively to the reverend gentleman's words, and as soon as he perceived he had done speaking, without regarding the presence of the duke and duchess, he sprang to his feet with angry looks and an agitated countenance and said—

But the reply deserves a chapter to itself.

CHAPTER XXXII

OF THE REPLY DON QUIXOTE GAVE HIS CRITIC, WITH OTHER INCIDENTS, SERIOUS AND COMICAL

Don Quixote, then, having risen to his feet, trembling from head to foot like a man dosed with mercury,[1] said in a rushed, agitated voice, "The surroundings in which I find myself, the personages before me, and the respect I have and have always had for the profession to which your worship belongs, bind the hands of my just indignation. Not only for these reasons but because I know, as everyone knows, that the weapon of a man in a gowned profession[2] is the same as a woman's—the tongue—I will with mine engage in equal combat with your worship, from whom one might have expected good advice instead of foul abuse. Pious, well-meant reproof requires a different demeanor and arguments of another kind. At any rate, to have reproved me in public, and so roughly, exceeds the bounds of proper reproof, for that comes better with gentleness than with rudeness; and it is not seemly to call the sinner roundly a blundering fool without knowing anything of the sin that is reproved.

"Come, tell me, for which of the stupidities you have observed in me do you condemn and abuse me and bid me go home and look after my house and wife and children, without knowing whether I have any? Is nothing more needed than to barge into other people's houses to rule over the masters—and that, perhaps, after having been brought up in the austerity of some university boarding house and without having ever seen more of the world than may lie within twenty or thirty leagues round—to presume to lay down the laws of chivalry willy-nilly, and to pass judgment on knights-errant? Is it, perchance, an idle occupation, or is the time wasted that is spent roaming the world in quest, not of its enjoyments, but of those arduous toils whereby the good mount upwards to their uncorrupted abode? If gentlemen, great lords, nobles, men of high birth, were to rate me as a fool I should take it as an irreparable insult; but I care not a fig if bookworms, who have never entered upon or trod the paths of chivalry should think me foolish. Knight I am, and knight I will die, if such be the pleasure of the Most High.

"Some take the broad road of overweening ambition, others that of mean and servile flattery, others that of deceitful hypocrisy, and some that of true religion.

[1] *like a man dosed with mercury:* Mercury exposure can cause uncontrollable shaking.
[2] *gowned profession:* scholars and clergy.

But I, led by my star, follow the narrow path of knight-errantry, and in pursuit of that calling I despise wealth, but not honor. I have redressed injuries, righted wrongs, punished scoffers, vanquished giants, and crushed monsters. I am in love, for no other reason than that it is incumbent on knights-errant to be so; but though I am, I am no carnal-minded lover, but of those whose love is chaste and platonic. My intentions are always directed to worthy ends, which are to do good to all and evil to none. If the man with this vision, this purpose, and this toil deserves to be called a fool, it is for your highnesses to say, O most excellent duke and duchess."

"By God, that's good!" said Sancho. "Say no more in your own defense, your worship and my master, for there's nothing more in the world to say—or to think or insist on, for that matter. Besides, when this gentleman denies as he has that there are or ever have been any knights-errant in the world, is it any wonder that he doesn't know what he's talking about?"

"Perhaps, brother," said the priest, "you are that Sancho Panza spoken of to whom your master has promised an island?"

"Yes, I am," said Sancho, "and what's more, I deserve it as much as anyone. I'm of the kind—'Keep company with the good, and you will be like them,' and of those, 'Not who you're raised with but who you graze with,' and of those, 'Lean on a tree for aid, and enjoy the blessing of its shade.' I have leaned on a good master, and for months I've been going about with him, and please God I'll be just like him one day. Long life to him and long life to me, for he'll have no shortage of empires to rule, and I'll have no shortage of islands to govern."

"Certainly not, Sancho my friend," said the duke, "for in the name of Señor Don Quixote I confer upon you the government of an island of no small importance that I have to spare."

"Get down on your knees, Sancho," said Don Quixote, "and kiss the feet of his excellency for the favor he has bestowed upon you."

Sancho obeyed, and on seeing this the priest stood up from the table in a rage and exclaimed, "By the gown I wear, I am almost inclined to say that your excellency is as great a fool as these sinners. How can they not be insane when those of us in our senses applaud their insanity! I leave your excellency with them, for so long as they are in the house, I will remain in my own and spare myself the trouble of reproving what I cannot remedy." And without uttering another word or eating another morsel, he went off, the entreaties of the duke and duchess being entirely unavailing to stop him—not that the duke could manage many words through his laughter over the priest's unseemly outburst.

When he had done laughing, he said to Don Quixote, "You have replied on your own behalf so nobly, Sir Knight of the Lions, that there is no occasion to seek further satisfaction for what seems to be an offense but is really none at all; for as women cannot cause an offense, no more can priests, as you very well know."[3]

[3] *for what seems to be an offense . . . as you very well know:* The duke alludes to the customs of the honor code, which Don Quixote expands upon in his reply. On the distinction between an offense (*agravio*) and insult or indignity (*afrenta*), see footnote 11, page 110.

"That is true," said Don Quixote, "and the reason is that he who is not liable to offense cannot give offense to anyone. Women, children, and priests, as they cannot defend themselves, though they may receive offense cannot be insulted, because between the offense and the insult there is, as your excellency very well knows, this difference: the insult comes from one who is capable of offering it, who delivers it, and who maintains it.[4] The offense may come from any quarter without carrying insult. To take an example: a man is standing unsuspectingly in the street and ten others come up armed and beat him; he draws his sword and acquits himself like a man, but the number of his antagonists makes it impossible for him to effect his purpose and avenge himself. This man suffers an offense but not an insult. Another example will make the same thing plain: a man is standing with his back turned; another comes up and strikes him and, after striking him, takes to flight without waiting an instant; the other pursues him but does not overtake him. He who received the blow received an offense, but not an insult, because an insult must be maintained. If he who struck him, though he did so on the sly, had drawn his sword and stood and faced him, then he who had been struck would have received offense and insult at the same time—offense because he was struck treacherously, insult because he who struck him maintained what he had done, standing his ground without taking to flight. And so, according to the laws of the accursed duel, I may have received offense but not insult, for neither women nor children can maintain it, nor can they wound, nor have they any way of standing their ground. It is just the same with those connected with religion; for these three sorts of persons are without arms offensive or defensive, and so—though naturally they are bound to defend themselves—they have no right to offend anybody. While I said just now I might have received offense, I say now certainly not, for he who cannot receive an insult can still less give one; for which reasons I ought not to feel, nor do I feel aggrieved at what that good man said to me. I only wish he had stayed a little longer, that I might have shown him the mistake he makes in supposing and maintaining that there are not and never have been any knights-errant in the world. Had Amadís or any of his countless descendants heard him say as much, I am sure it would not have gone well with his worship."

"I'll swear to that," said Sancho. "They would have given him a slash that would have left him wide open from top to bottom like a pomegranate or a ripe melon. Likely fellows they were to put up with jokes like that! By my cross, if Reinaldos of Montalban had heard that little man's words I have no doubt he would've given him such a spank on the mouth that he wouldn't be able to speak for the next three years. Just let him try to stand in their way and see what happens to him!"

The duchess, as she listened to Sancho, was ready to die with laughter, and in her own mind she set him down as more comical and dimwitted than his master—and there were a good many just then who were of the same opinion.

Don Quixote finally calmed down, and dinner came to an end. As the table was being cleared, four damsels came in, one of them with a silver basin, another

[4] *who maintains it:* who defends his words or actions with arms.

with a jug[5] also of silver, a third with two fine white towels on her shoulder, and the fourth with her arms bared to the elbows, and in her white hands (for white they certainly were) a ball of Neapolitan soap.[6] The damsel with the basin approached, and with arch composure and impudence, thrust it under Don Quixote's chin, who, wondering at such a ceremony, said never a word, supposing it to be the custom of that country to wash beards instead of hands. He therefore stretched his beard out as far as he could, and at the same instant the jug began to pour and the damsel with the soap rubbed his beard briskly, raising snowflakes, for the soap lather was no less white, not only over the beard, but all over the face, and over the eyes of the submissive knight, so that he was obliged to keep them shut. The duke and duchess, who had not known anything about this, waited to see what came of this strange washing. The damsel playing barber, when she had him a hand's breadth deep in lather, pretended that there was no more water, and asked the one with the jug to go and fetch some, while Señor Don Quixote waited. She did so, and Don Quixote was left the strangest and most ludicrous figure that could be imagined.

All those present (and there were a good many) were watching him, and as they saw him there with half a yard of neck—and that uncommonly brown—his eyes shut, and his beard full of soap, it was a great wonder that they could restrain their laughter, and did so only by great discretion. The damsels who had concocted the joke kept their eyes down, not daring to look at their master and mistress. The duke and duchess struggled by turns to contain their anger and knew not what to do—whether to punish the audacity of the girls or to reward them for the amusement they had received from seeing Don Quixote in such a plight.

At length the damsel with the jug returned, and they made an end of washing Don Quixote. The one who carried the towels very deliberately wiped him and dried him, all four together making him a profound obeisance and curtsey. They were about to go when the duke, lest Don Quixote should see through the joke, called out to the one with the basin saying, "Come and wash me, and take care that there is water enough." The girl, sharp-witted and prompt, came and placed the basin for the duke as she had done for Don Quixote, and they soon had him well soaped and washed, and having wiped him dry they made their obeisance and retired. It was learned afterwards that the duke had sworn that if they had not washed him as they had Don Quixote he would have punished them for their impudence, which they adroitly atoned for by soaping him as well.

Sancho observed the ceremony of the washing very attentively and said to himself, "My goodness! If it were only the custom in this country to wash squires' beards too as well as knights'—for by God and upon my soul I need it badly. If they gave me a shave with the razor besides, I'd take it as a still greater kindness."

"What are you mumbling to yourself, Sancho?" asked the duchess.

"I was saying, señora," he replied, "that in the courts of other princes, when they clear the table, I've always heard it said that they give you water for your

[5] *jug: aguamanil*, jug with a long spout specifically used for handwashing.

[6] *Neapolitan soap:* aromatic, olive-oil-based paste produced in Naples, used for personal grooming.

hands, but not soap for your beard. That just shows that 'the more you live the more you see.' On the other hand, they say, 'He who lives a long life must suffer much evil'—though to get a washing like this is pleasure, not pain."

"Don't be uneasy, friend Sancho," said the duchess; "I will take care that my damsels wash you and even put you in the tub if necessary."

"I'll be content with the beard," said Sancho, "at any rate for the present. As for the future, God has decreed what is to be."

"Attend to worthy Sancho's request, steward," said the duchess, "and do exactly what he wishes."

The steward replied that Señor Sancho should be obeyed in everything. With that he went away to dinner and took Sancho along with him, while the duke and duchess and Don Quixote remained at the table discussing a great variety of things, but all bearing on the calling of arms and knight-errantry.

The duchess begged Don Quixote, as he seemed to have a vivid memory, to conjure before her mind's eye the beauty and features of Lady Dulcinea del Toboso, for judging by the report trumpeted abroad of her beauty, she felt sure she must be the fairest creature in the world, nay, in all La Mancha.

Don Quixote sighed on hearing the duchess' request and said, "If I could pluck out my heart and lay it on a plate on this table here before your highness' eyes, it would spare my tongue the pain of telling what can hardly be thought of, for in it your excellency would see her portrayed in full. But why should I attempt to depict in detail, and feature by feature, the beauty of the peerless Dulcinea, the burden being one worthy of other shoulders than mine—an enterprise wherein the brushes of Parrhasius, Timantes, and Apelles, and the chisel of Lysippos[7] ought to be employed, to paint it in pictures and carve it in marble and bronze, and Ciceronian and Demosthenian eloquence to sound its praises?"

"What does *Demosthenian* mean, Señor Don Quixote?" asked the duchess. "It is a word I never heard in all my life."

"Demosthenian eloquence," said Don Quixote, "means the eloquence of Demosthenes,[8] as Ciceronian means that of Cicero, who were the two most eloquent orators in the world."

"So it is," said the duke. "You have betrayed your ignorance with such a question. In any event, Señor Don Quixote would greatly gratify us if he would describe her to us, for I dare say that even in an outline or sketch she would be something to make the fairest envious."

[7] *Parrhasius, Timantes, and Apelles, and the chisel of Lysippos:* The painters Parrhasius of Ephesus, Timantes of Cythnus, and Apelles of Kos, along with the sculptor Lysippos—all of whom flourished around the fourth century B.C.—were among the most celebrated artists of Ancient Greece. None of their original works survive, though their reputations endure through copies and literary accounts.

[8] *Demosthenes:* Demosthenes (384–322 B.C.) was an Athenian statesman whose speeches roused his countrymen against the encroachment of Philip of Macedon and his son Alexander the Great. Plutarch relates that Demosthenes overcame a speech impediment by practicing his orations with pebbles in his mouth.

"I would certainly do so," said Don Quixote, "had she not been blurred to my mind's eye by the misfortune that fell upon her a short time ago, one of such a nature that I am more ready to weep over it than to describe it. For your highnesses must know that, going a few days back to kiss her hands and receive her blessing and permission for this third sally, I found her altogether a different being from the one I sought. I found her enchanted and changed from a princess into a peasant, from fair to foul, from an angel into a devil, from fragrant to pestiferous, from refined to rustic, from a dignified lady into a jumping tomboy, and, in a word, from Dulcinea del Toboso into a coarse Sayago[9] wench."

"Good God!" exclaimed the duke aloud at this. "Who could have done the world such an injury? Who could have robbed it of the beauty that gladdened it, of the grace and gaiety that charmed it, of the modesty that was its pride?"

"Who?" replied Don Quixote. "Who could it be but some malignant enchanter of the many that persecute me out of envy—that accursed race born into the world to obscure and bring to naught the achievements of the good and glorify and exalt the deeds of the wicked. Enchanters have persecuted me, enchanters persecute me still, and enchanters will continue to persecute me until they have sunk me and my lofty chivalry in the deep abyss of oblivion. They injure and wound me where they know I feel it most. For to deprive a knight-errant of his lady is to deprive him of the eyes he sees with, of the sun that gives him light, of the food whereby he lives. Many a time before have I said it, and I say it now once more: a knight-errant without a lady is like a tree without leaves, a building without a foundation, or a shadow without the body that casts it."

"There is no denying it," said the duchess. "But still, if we are to believe the history of Don Quixote that has come to light lately to general applause, it is to be inferred—if I mistake not—that you never saw Lady Dulcinea, and that she is nothing in the world but an imaginary lady, one that you yourself conceived and gave birth to in your mind, and adorned with whatever charms and perfections you chose."

"There is a good deal to be said on that point," said Don Quixote. "God knows whether there is any Dulcinea or not in the world, or whether she is imaginary or not imaginary; these are things the proof of which must not be pushed to extreme lengths. I have not conceived nor given birth to my lady, though I behold her as is fitting of a lady who contains in herself all the qualities to make her famous throughout the world: beautiful without blemish, dignified without haughtiness, tender and yet modest, gracious from courtesy and courteous from good breeding, and lastly, of exalted lineage—because beauty shines forth and excels with a higher degree of perfection in those of good blood than in the fair of lowly birth."

"That is true," said the duke; "but Señor Don Quixote will give me leave to say what I am constrained to say by the story of his exploits that I have read, from which it is to be inferred that, granting there is a Dulcinea in El Toboso, or elsewhere, and that she is in the highest degree beautiful as you have described her to us, as regards the loftiness of her lineage she is not on par with the Orianas,

[9] *Sayago:* See footnote 11, page 533.

Alastrajareas, Madasimas,[10] or others of their kind, with whom, as you well know, the histories abound."

"To that I may reply," said Don Quixote, "that Dulcinea is the daughter of her own works, that virtues rectify blood, and that lowly virtue is more to be regarded and esteemed than exalted vice. Dulcinea, besides, has that within her that may raise her to be a crowned and sceptered queen. For the merit of a fair and virtuous woman is capable of performing greater miracles, and by virtue, though not formally, she possesses in herself higher fortunes."

"I declare, Señor Don Quixote," said the duchess, "that in all you say, you go most cautiously, with a heavy foot and sounding line in hand, as the saying goes. Henceforth I will believe, and I will take care that everyone in my house believes—even my lord the duke if needs be—that there is a Dulcinea in El Toboso, that she is living today, and that she is beautiful and nobly born and deserves to have such a knight as Señor Don Quixote in her service. That is the highest praise that is in my power to give her or that I can think of. But I cannot help entertaining a misgiving and admitting a certain grudge against Sancho Panza. The misgiving is this: that the aforesaid history declares that the said Sancho Panza, when he carried a letter on your worship's behalf to the said lady Dulcinea, found her sifting a sack of wheat; and it says in particular that it was red wheat,[11] a detail that makes me doubt the loftiness of her lineage."

To this Don Quixote answered, "Señora, your highness must know that everything or almost everything that happens to me transcends the ordinary limits of what happens to other knights-errant—whether it be that it is directed by the inscrutable will of destiny or by the malice of some jealous enchanter. Now it is an established fact that all or most famous knights-errant have some special gift: one, that of being impervious to enchantment; another, that of being made of such invulnerable flesh that he cannot be wounded—as was the famous Roland, one of the twelve peers of France, of whom it is related that he could not be wounded except in the sole of his left foot, and that it must be with the point of a thick pin and not with any other sort of weapon whatever; and so, when Bernardo del Carpio slew him at Roncesvalles, finding that he could not wound him with steel, he lifted him up from the ground in his arms and strangled him,[12] calling to mind the death which Hercules inflicted on Antæus, the fierce giant that they say was the son of Terra.[13]

"I would infer from what I have mentioned that perhaps I may have some gift of this kind—not that of being invulnerable, because experience has many times

[10] *Orianas, Alastrajareas, Madasimas:* Oriana is Amadís of Gaul's beloved and the daughter of King Lisuarte of Great Britain. Madasima, queen of the Island of the Vermillion Tower, is also a character in *Amadís of Gaul* and the subject of a dispute between Cardenio and Don Quixote in Part I, chapter 24. Alastrajarea, wife of Prince Anastrax, appears in *Florisel of Niquea*, tenth in the *Amadís* cycle.

[11] *red wheat:* See footnote 2, page 245.

[12] *the famous Roland . . . and strangled him:* Don Quixote recapitulates a story he tells in Part I (see p. 27).

[13] *Hercules inflicted on Antæus . . . of Terra:* See footnote 17, page 27.

proved to me that I am of tender flesh and not at all impenetrable; nor that of being impervious to enchantment, for I have already seen myself thrust into a cage, in which all the world would not have been able to confine me except by force of enchantments. But as I delivered myself from that one, I am inclined to believe that there is no other that can hurt me. And so, these enchanters, seeing that they cannot exert their vile craft against my person, revenge themselves on what I love most and seek to rob me of life by mistreating that of Dulcinea in whom I live. Therefore, I am convinced that when my squire carried my message to her, they transformed her into a peasant girl, engaged in such a mean occupation as sifting wheat. I have already said, however, that the wheat was not red wheat, nor wheat at all, but grains of orient pearl.

"As a proof of all this, I must tell your highnesses that, coming to El Toboso a short time back, I was altogether unable to discover the palace of Dulcinea. The next day, although Sancho my squire saw her in her own proper shape (which is the fairest in the world), to me she appeared to be a coarse, ill-favored farm wench, and by no means a well-spoken one—she who is propriety itself. And so, as I am not and (so far as one can judge) cannot be enchanted, she is the one who is enchanted, beset, altered, changed, and transformed. In her have my enemies revenged themselves upon me, and for her shall I live in ceaseless tears, until I see her in her pristine state.

"I have mentioned this lest anybody should take issue with what Sancho said about Dulcinea's winnowing or sifting; for as they changed her before my eyes, it is no wonder if they changed her before his. Dulcinea is illustrious and wellborn, and of one of the noble families of El Toboso, which are many, ancient, and good. Therein, most assuredly, not small is the share of the peerless Dulcinea, through whom her town will be famous and celebrated in ages to come, as Troy was through Helen and Spain through La Cava, though with a better title and tradition.[14]

"On another score, I would have your graces understand that Sancho Panza is one of the most amusing squires that ever served knight-errant. Sometimes there is a simplicity about him so acute that it is a diversion to try and make out whether he is simple or clever. He has mischievous tricks that mark him as a rogue and blundering ways that prove him to be a fool. He doubts everything and believes everything. When I fancy he is on the point of coming down headlong from sheer stupidity, he comes out with something so wise that he soars up to the heavens. All in all, I would not trade him for any other squire, though I were given a city to boot. I am therefore in doubt whether it would be wise to send him to the government your highness has bestowed upon him, though I perceive in him a certain aptitude for the work of governing. We need only smooth over the rough spots in his understanding, and he would manage any government as easily as the king does his taxes; moreover, we know already by ample experience that it does not require much cleverness or much learning to be a governor, for

[14] *Troy was through Helen and Spain through La Cava:* Troy and Spain were lost over the beauty of these women. On La Cava, see footnote 10, page 337.

there are a hundred round about us that scarcely know how to read and yet govern like falcons.[15] The main point is that they should have good intentions and be desirous of doing right in all things, for they will never be at a loss for persons to advise and direct them in what they have to do, like those knight-governors who, being unschooled, pronounce sentences with the aid of an adviser. My advice to him will be to take no bribe and surrender no right. I have some other little matters I have been ruminating over that shall be produced in due season for Sancho's benefit and the advantage of the island he is to govern."

The duke, duchess, and Don Quixote had reached this point in their conversation when they heard voices and a great hubbub in the palace, and Sancho burst abruptly into the room all glowing with anger, with a dishcloth for a bib. He was followed by several servants, or, more properly speaking, kitchen boys and other underlings, one of whom carried a small trough full of water, which from its color and impurity was plainly dishwater. The one with the trough pursued him everywhere he went, attempting with the utmost persistence to thrust it under his chin, while another kitchen boy seemed anxious to wash his beard.

"What is all this, brothers?" asked the duchess. "What is this? What do you want to do to this good man? Do you forget he is a governor-elect?"

To which the barber kitchen boy replied, "The gentleman will not let himself be washed as is customary, and as my lord and the señor his master have been."

"Yes, I will," said Sancho, in a great rage, "but I'd like it to be with cleaner towels, clearer soap, and hands not so dirty. There's not so much difference between me and my master that he should be washed with angels' water and I with devil's lye. The customs of countries and princes' palaces are only good so long as they aren't disagreeable; but the way of washing they have here is worse than doing penance. I have a clean beard, and I don't need any of those amenities. Anyone who tries to wash me or touch a hair of my head, I mean to say my beard—speaking with all due respect—I'll give him such a punch that I'll leave my fist print in his skull. These kinds of cirimonies and soapings are more like jokes than any reception a host might give."

The duchess was ready to die with laughter when she saw Sancho's rage and heard his words; but it was no pleasure to Don Quixote to see him so sloppily outfitted with the dingy towel and with the hangers-on from the kitchen all around him. Making a low bow to the duke and duchess, as if to ask their permission to speak, he addressed the rabble in a dignified tone: "Ho there, sir knights! Let your worships leave that youth alone, and go back to where you came from—or anywhere else if you like. My squire is as clean as any other person, and those troughs might as well be narrow, thin-necked vessels to him. Take my advice and leave him alone, for neither he nor I are ones for joking."

Sancho took up the speech from Don Quixote and went on, "No, let them come and try their jokes on the country bumpkin, for it's about as likely I'll put up with them as that it's now midnight! Let them bring me a comb here—or

[15] *falcons:* an obscure reference. The *girifalte* (gyrfalcon) is the largest bird of the falcon family, and in urban slang, a thief.

what they please—and curry[16] this beard of mine. If they get anything out of it that's an offense to cleanliness, they can clip me to the skin."

Upon this, the duchess, laughing all the while, said, "Sancho Panza is right and always will be in all he says. He is clean, and, as he says himself, he does not need to be washed. If our ways do not please him, that is his business. Besides, you promoters of cleanliness have been excessively careless and thoughtless—I would even say audacious—to bring troughs and wooden utensils and kitchen dishrags, instead of basins and jugs of pure gold and holland towels to such a person and such a beard. But after all, you are ill-conditioned and ill-bred, and spiteful as you are, you cannot help showing the grudge you have against the squires of knights-errant."

The mischievous servants, and even the steward who came with them, took the duchess to be speaking in earnest, so they removed the dishcloth from Sancho's neck and, bewildered and ashamed, went off and left him; whereupon Sancho, seeing himself safe from what seemed to him extreme danger, ran and fell on his knees before the duchess, saying, "From great ladies great favors may be looked for. This which your grace has done me today cannot be requited with less than wishing I was dubbed a knight-errant, to devote myself all the days of my life to the service of so exalted a lady. I am a farm laborer, my name is Sancho Panza, I am married, I have children, and I am serving as a squire. If in any one of these ways I can serve your highness, I will not be longer in obeying than your grace in commanding."

"It is easy to see, Sancho," replied the duchess, "that you have learned to be polite in the school of politeness itself. I mean to say it is easy to see that you have been nursed in the bosom of Señor Don Quixote, who is, of course, the cream of good breeding and flower of ceremony—or *cirimony*, as you would say. Fair be the fortunes of such a master and such a servant, the one the north star of knight-errantry, the other the daystar of squirely fidelity! Rise, Sancho, my friend. I will repay your courtesy by taking care that my lord the duke makes good to you the promised gift of the government as soon as possible."

With this, the conversation came to an end, and Don Quixote retired to take his siesta; but the duchess begged Sancho, unless he had a very great desire to sleep, to come and spend the afternoon with her and her damsels in a very cool chamber. Sancho replied that, though he certainly had the habit of sleeping four or five hours in the heat of the day in summer, to serve her excellence he would try with all his might not to sleep even one that day; and that he would come in obedience to her command. With that he went off. The duke gave fresh orders with respect to treating Don Quixote as a knight-errant, without departing even in the smallest particular from the style in which, as the stories tell us, they used to treat the knights of old.

[16] *curry:* to comb the coat of an animal.

CHAPTER XXXIII

OF THE DELECTABLE DISCOURSE THAT THE DUCHESS AND HER DAMSELS HELD WITH SANCHO PANZA, WELL WORTH READING AND NOTING

The history records that Sancho did not sleep that afternoon, but in order to keep his word came after dinner to visit the duchess, who, finding enjoyment in listening to him, made him sit down beside her on a low seat,[1] though Sancho, out of pure good breeding, did not want to sit down. The duchess, however, told him he was to sit down as governor and talk as squire, as in both respects he was worthy of even the chair of the Cid Ruy Diaz Campeador.[2] Sancho shrugged his shoulders, obeyed, and sat down, and all the duchess' damsels and dueñas gathered round him, waiting in profound silence to hear what he would say.

It was the duchess, however, who spoke first, saying, "Now that we are alone, and that there is nobody here to overhear us, I should be glad if the señor governor would relieve me of certain doubts I have, arising from the history of the great Don Quixote that is now in print. One of them is that, inasmuch as worthy Sancho never saw Dulcinea—I mean Lady Dulcinea del Toboso—nor took Don Quixote's letter to her, for it was left in the memorandum book in the Sierra Morena, how did he dare to invent the answer and all that about finding her sifting wheat, the whole story being a deception and falsehood, and so much to the prejudice of the peerless Dulcinea's good name, a thing that is not at all becoming the character and fidelity of a good squire?"

At these words, Sancho, without uttering one in reply, got up from his chair and, with noiseless steps, his body bent and his finger on his lips, went all around the room lifting up the curtains. This done, he came back to his seat and said, "Señora, now that I have seen that there is no one listening to us on the sly—apart from these bystanders—I will answer what you have asked me, and all you may ask me without fear or concern. The first thing I have to say is that for my own part I hold my master Don Quixote to be stark mad, though sometimes he says things that, to my mind—and indeed everybody's that listens to him—are so wise and run in such a straight furrow that Satan himself could not have said them better. But

[1] *low seat:* A wealthy noblewoman like the duchess would receive guests on a dais (*estrado*), where she would be seated on cushions. She asks Sancho to sit on a low-backed chair beside her, a sign of confidence and intimacy.

[2] *chair of the Cid Ruy Diaz Campeador:* allusion to a ballad in which El Cid defeats King Búcar of Morrocco and sends a marble bench of his as a gift to King Alonso VI of Castile.

for all that, really, and beyond all question, it's my firm belief that he's cracked. Well then, as this is clear to my mind, I can get him to believe things without a head or tail, like that story about the answer to the letter, and the other one from six or eight days ago that isn't in the histories yet—I mean, the one about the enchantment of my lady Dulcinea; for I made him believe she's enchanted, though there's no more truth in it than over the hills of Úbeda."[3]

The duchess begged him to tell her about the enchantment or deception, so Sancho told the whole story exactly as it had happened, which amused his listeners more than a little. Then resuming, the duchess said, "In consequence of what worthy Sancho has told me, a misgiving forms in my mind, and there comes a kind of whisper to my ear that says, 'If Don Quixote is mad, crazy, and cracked, and Sancho Panza his squire knows it, and, notwithstanding, serves and follows him, and goes trusting to his empty promises, there can be no doubt he must be still madder and more foolish than his master. That being so, it will be cast in your teeth, señora duchess, if you give this Sancho an island to govern; for how will he who does not know how to govern himself know how to govern others?'"

"By God, señora," said Sancho, "that concern is well-founded. Your grace may put it plainly, or however you like. I know what you say is true. If I were wise I would have left my master long ago. But this has been my fate, this my bad luck: I can't help but follow him. We're from the same village; I've eaten his bread and I'm fond of him. He's been appreciative and gave me his donkey colts. Above all I'm loyal—so it's impossible for anything to separate us except the pickaxe and shovel.[4] If your highness doesn't wish to give me the government you promised, God made me from even less,[5] and maybe your not giving it to me will be all the better for my conscience, for though I'm a fool I know the proverb, 'To her hurt the ant sprouted wings.' It may be that Sancho the squire will get to heaven sooner than Sancho the governor. 'They make as good bread here as in France,' and 'every cat is gray at night,' and 'unhappy the man who hasn't had breakfast come two in the afternoon,' and 'there's no stomach a hand's breadth bigger than another,' and 'every one of them can be filled with straw or hay,' as the saying goes, and 'the little birds of the field have God for their provider,' and 'four yards of Cuenca cloth keep you warmer than four yards of Segovia serge,' and 'when we leave this world and are put underground the prince travels the same narrow path as the journeyman,' and 'the Pope's body takes up no more feet of earth than the sacristan's, though one is more exalted than the other.' For when we enter our graves we settle in and make ourselves small, or rather they settle us in and make us small in spite of us. And then good night.

"So I say once more, if your ladyship does not wish to give me the island because I'm a fool, I'll take care to give myself no trouble about it like a wise man.

[3] *no more truth in it than over the hills of Úbeda:* The sense is that "nothing could be further from the truth", though Sancho's use of this idiomatic expression isn't clear.

[4] *pickaxe and shovel*: tools used to dig a grave.

[5] *God made me from even less:* The full proverb is "From even less God made us, who made us from nothing."

I've heard it said that 'behind the cross there's the devil,' and that 'all that glitters is not gold,' and that from among the oxen, the ploughs, and yokes, Wamba the farmer was taken to be made king of Spain, and from among brocades, and pleasures, and riches, Rodrigo was taken to be devoured by snakes, if the verses from the old ballads don't lie."

"To be sure, they don't lie!" exclaimed Doña Rodríguez, the dueña, who was one of those listening. "Why, there's a ballad that says they put King Rodrigo alive into a tomb full of toads, snakes, and lizards, and that two days afterwards the king, in a plaintive and feeble voice, cried out from inside the tomb—

They gnaw me now, they gnaw me now,
There where I most did sin.[6]

That being the case, the gentleman has good reason to say he would rather be a field hand than a king, if vermin are to eat him."

The duchess could not help laughing at the simplicity of her dueña, or wondering at the language and proverbs of Sancho, to whom she said, "Worthy Sancho knows very well that once a knight has made a promise he strives to keep it, though it should cost him his life. My lord and husband the duke, though not a knight of the errant variety, is nonetheless a knight for that reason, and will keep his word about the promised island in spite of the world's envy and malice. Let Sancho be of good cheer; for when he least expects it he will find himself seated on the throne of his island and of dignity itself, and will take possession of his government that he may exchange it for another of three-layered brocade.[7] The charge I give him is to be careful how he governs his vassals, bearing in mind that they are all loyal and wellborn."

"As to governing them well," said Sancho, "there's no need of charging me to do that, for I'm kind-hearted by nature and full of compassion for the poor. 'There's no stealing bread from him who kneads and bakes.'[8] By my faith, they better not roll loaded dice with me. 'I'm an old dog, and I know one call from another.' I'm sure to wake up at the right moment, and I don't let cobwebs cover my eyes, because 'I know where my shoe pinches me.' I say so, because with me the good will have help and support, and the bad neither footing nor access. It seems to me that in governments a good beginning is everything. Maybe, after having been governor for a couple weeks, I'll take a liking to the work and know more about it than the field labor I've been raised to do."

"You are right, Sancho," said the duchess, "for 'no one is born educated,' and 'bishops are made out of men and not out of stones.' But to return to the subject we were discussing just now, the enchantment of Lady Dulcinea, I look upon it

[6] *where I most did sin:* The sin condemned in the ballad "The Penitence of King Rodrigo" is licentiousness.

[7] *that he may exchange it for another of three-layered brocade:* that Sancho may use the government as a stepping-stone to one even greater.

[8] *There's no stealing bread from him who kneads and bakes:* "One should think twice about trying to deceive someone experienced."

as certain, and something more than evident, that Sancho's idea of tricking his master—making him believe that the peasant girl was Dulcinea and that if he did not recognize her it must be because she was enchanted—was all a device of one of the enchanters that persecute Don Quixote. For in truth and earnest, I know from good authority that the coarse country wench who jumped up on the donkey was and is Dulcinea del Toboso, and that worthy Sancho, though he fancies himself the deceiver, is the one that is deceived. There is no more reason to doubt the truth of this than of anything else we never saw. Señor Sancho Panza must know that we too have enchanters here who are well disposed toward us and tell us what goes on in the world, plainly and distinctly, without subterfuge or deception. Believe me, Sancho, that agile country lass was and is Dulcinea del Toboso, who is as much enchanted as the mother that bore her. When we least expect it, we shall see her in her own proper form, and then Sancho will be disabused of the error he is under at present."

"All that's very possible," said Sancho Panza. "I'm willing to believe now my master's story about what he saw in the Cave of Montesinos, where he says he saw Lady Dulcinea del Toboso in the very same dress that I said I had seen her in when I enchanted her to please myself. It must be all exactly the other way, as your ladyship says, because nobody should suppose that out of my poor mind such a cunning trick could be concocted in a moment. And don't think my master is so crazy that by my weak and insignificant powers he could be persuaded to believe something so fanciful. But, señora, your excellency must not therefore take me for a bad-natured fellow, for a dolt like me isn't going to see into the thoughts and plots of those vile enchanters. I invented all that to escape my master's scolding, and not with any intention of hurting him. If it's turned out differently, there's a God in heaven who judges our hearts."

"Quite true," said the duchess; "but tell me, Sancho, what is this you say about the Cave of Montesinos, for I should like to know."

Thereupon Sancho related to her, word for word, what has been said already touching that adventure. Having heard it, the duchess said, "From this occurrence it may be inferred that, as the great Don Quixote says he saw there the same country wench Sancho saw on the way from El Toboso, it is, no doubt, Dulcinea, and that there are some very active and exceedingly thorough enchanters about."

"So say I," said Sancho. "If my lady Dulcinea is enchanted, so much the worse for her. I'm not going to pick a fight with my master's enemies, who seem to be many and spiteful. Let the truth be known that the one I saw was a country wench, and I set her down to be a country wench. If that was Dulcinea, it ought not to be left at my doorstep, and I shouldn't be called to answer for it or take the consequences. But no, they insist on nagging at me at every step—'Sancho said it, Sancho did it, Sancho here, Sancho there,' as if Sancho was nobody at all and not the same Sancho Panza that's now going all over the world in books—so Samson Carrasco told me, and he's no less than a graduate of Salamanca. People like that can't lie, except when the whim seizes them or they have some very good reason for it. So there's no occasion for anybody to pick a fight with me; and then I have a good character, and as I've heard my master say, 'A good name is better than great riches.'[9] Just let them stick me into this government and they'll see wonders, for the man who's been a good squire will be a good governor."

"All of good Sancho's observations," said the duchess, "are maxims worthy of Cato[10]—or at any rate, out of the very heart of Michael Verino himself, who *florentibus occidit annis*.[11] In fact, to speak in his own style, 'Under a bad cloak there's often a good drinker.'"

"Truth be told, señora," said Sancho, "I've drunk more than a little in my life. I drink when I'm thirsty—I'm no hypocrite. I drink when I have the hankering, and when I don't. I'll take a drink when it's offered to me so I don't look fussy or rude; for when a friend drinks to your health, what heart can be so hard as not to return the favor? But 'when I put on my pants, I don't get them dirty.'[12] Besides, squires to knights-errant mostly drink water, for they are always wandering in the woods, forests and meadows, mountains and crags, without a drop of wine to be had if they gave their eyes for it."

"So I believe," said the duchess. "And now let Sancho go and take his siesta, and we will talk afterwards at greater length, and settle how he may soon go and stick himself into the government, as he says."

Sancho once more kissed the duchess' hand and entreated her to let good care be taken of his Dapple, for he was the light of his eyes.

"What Dapple is this?" asked the duchess.

"My donkey," said Sancho, "which, not to call him by that name, I'm accustomed to call Dapple. I begged this lady dueña here to take care of him when I came into the castle, and she got as angry as if I had said she was ugly or old, though it ought to be more natural and proper for dueñas to feed donkeys than to put on airs in great halls. As God lives, I know a gentleman from my village who had it out for these ladies."

"He must have been a scoundrel," said the dueña Doña Rodríguez. "If he had been a gentleman and wellborn, he would have exalted them higher than the top of the moon."

"That will do," said the duchess. "No more of this. Hush, Doña Rodríguez, and let Señor Panza rest easy and leave the treatment of Dapple in my charge, for as he is a treasure of Sancho's, I'll place his care on my shoulders."

"It will be enough for him to be placed in the stable," said Sancho. "Neither he nor I are worthy to rest a moment on your highness' shoulders, and I'd as soon stab myself as agree to it; for though my master says that in civilities 'it is better to lose by a card too many than a card too few,' when it comes to civilities of the ass and donkey variety, we should proceed with caution and stay in the middle of the road."

[9] *A good name is better than great riches:* Proverbs 22:1.

[10] *maxims worthy of Cato:* See footnote 5, page 144.

[11] *Michael Verino himself, who* florentibus occidit annis: Latin, "died in the flower of youth". The precocious Florentine humanist Michael Verino, who composed a book of Latin maxims modeled on the *Distichs of Cato,* died at age seventeen in 1483. At Verino's funeral, fellow humanist Angelo Poliziano pronounced the words cited by the duchess.

[12] *when I put on my pants, I don't get them dirty:* "I don't drink to excess."

"Take him to your government, Sancho," said the duchess, "and there you will be able to make as much of him as you like, and even release him from work and pension him off."

"Don't think, señora duchess, that you've said anything absurd," said Sancho. "I've seen more than two asses go off to governments. For me to take mine with me would be nothing new."

Sancho's words made the duchess laugh again and gave her fresh amusement, and dismissing him to his siesta she went away to tell the duke the conversation she had had with him. Between the two, they arranged to play an extraordinary prank on Don Quixote that would be entirely in the style of knight-errantry. In that same style they played several on him of a piece, so clever that they form the best adventures this great history contains.

CHAPTER XXXIV

WHICH RELATES HOW THE WAY IN WHICH THE PEERLESS DULCINEA DEL TOBOSO WAS TO BE DISENCHANTED WAS LEARNED, WHICH IS ONE OF THE RAREST ADVENTURES IN THIS BOOK

Great was the pleasure the duke and duchess took in their conversations with Don Quixote and Sancho Panza. More assured than ever of their plan to play pranks on them that would have the appearance of adventures, they took as their basis of action what Don Quixote had already told them about the Cave of Montesinos in order to devise a memorable one. But what the duchess marveled at above all was that Sancho's simplicity could be so great as to make him believe as absolute truth that Dulcinea had been enchanted, when it was he himself who had been the enchanter and trickster in the business. Having, therefore, instructed their servants in everything they were to do, six days afterwards they took him out to hunt, with as great a retinue of huntsmen and beaters[1] as a crowned king.

They presented Don Quixote with a hunting suit and Sancho with another of the finest green cloth, but Don Quixote declined to put his on, saying that he must soon return to the hard pursuit of arms and could not carry wardrobes or luggage with him. Sancho, however, took what they gave him, meaning to sell it at the first opportunity.

The appointed day having arrived, Don Quixote armed himself, while Sancho arrayed himself and, having mounted on his Dapple (for he would not give him up, though they offered him a horse), placed himself in the midst of the troop of huntsmen. The duchess came out splendidly attired. Don Quixote, out of pure courtesy and politeness, held the rein of her palfrey, though the duke wanted not to allow him. At last they reached a forest that lay between two high mountains, where—after occupying various posts, ambushes, and paths, and distributing the party in different positions—the hunt began with great noise, shouting, and hallooing, so that, between the baying of the hounds and the blowing of the horns, they could not hear one another. The duchess dismounted, and with a sharp spear in her hand posted herself where she knew the wild boars were in the habit of passing. The duke and Don Quixote likewise dismounted and placed themselves one at each side of her. Sancho took up a position in the rear of all without dismounting from Dapple, whom he dared not desert lest some mischief should befall him.

[1] *beaters:* members of a hunting party who drew game out into the open by beating bushes with sticks or making noises.

Scarcely had they taken their stand in a line with several of their servants, when they saw a huge boar, closely pressed by the hounds and followed by the huntsmen, making toward them, grinding his teeth and tusks, and dripping foam from his mouth. As soon as he saw him Don Quixote, bracing his shield on his arm and drawing his sword, advanced to meet him. The duke with his spear did the same. The duchess would have gone in front of them all had not the duke prevented her.

Sancho alone, deserting Dapple at the sight of the mighty beast, took to his heels as hard as he could and tried in vain to climb a tall oak. As he was clinging to a branch, however, halfway up in his struggle to reach the top, the bough—such was his bad luck and hard fate—gave way, and caught in his fall by a broken limb of the oak, he hung suspended in the air unable to reach the ground. Finding himself in this position, and that the green coat was beginning to tear, and reflecting that if the fierce animal came that way he might be able to get at him, he began to utter such cries and call for help so earnestly that all who heard him and did not see him felt sure he must be in the teeth of some wild beast.

In the end the tusked boar fell pierced by the blades of the many spears they held in front of him. Don Quixote, turning round at the cries of Sancho (for he knew by them that it was he), saw him hanging from the oak head downwards, with Dapple, who did not forsake him in his distress, close beside him. (Cide Hamete observes here that he seldom saw Sancho Panza without seeing Dapple, or Dapple without seeing Sancho Panza. Such was their attachment and loyalty one to the other.) Don Quixote went over and unhooked Sancho, who, as soon as he found himself on the ground, looked at the tear in his hunting coat and was grieved to the heart, for he thought he had inherited an estate in that suit.

Meanwhile they had slung the mighty boar across the back of a mule, and having covered it with rosemary sprigs and myrtle branches, they carried it off as the spoils of victory to some large tents that had been pitched in the middle of the forest. There they found the tables laid and dinner served, in such grand and sumptuous style that it was easy to see the rank and magnificence of those who had provided it.

Sancho, as he showed the tears in his damaged suit to the duchess, observed, "If we had been hunting rabbits, or after small birds, my coat would have been safe from being in the plight it's in. I don't know what pleasure a person finds in lying in wait for an animal that may take your life with his tusk if he gets at you. I recollect having heard an old ballad sung that says,

> By bears may you be devoured,
> As was Favila of renown."

"Favila," said Don Quixote, "was a Gothic king, who, going hunting, was devoured by a bear."[2]

[2] *Favila . . . by a bear:* Favila, son of Pelayo and second king of Asturias, was reputedly mauled by a bear during a hunt in 739. Sancho quotes from a poem in which the speaker pronounces a series of curses against a servant who stole his cloak.

"Just so," said Sancho. "I'm not in favor of kings and princes placing themselves in such dangers for the sake of a pleasure which, as I see it, ought not to be one, since it consists of killing an animal that has done no harm whatever."

"Quite the contrary, Sancho. You are wrong there," said the duke, "for hunting is more suitable and necessary for kings and princes than for anybody else. The hunt is the very image of war. It has stratagems, wiles, and crafty devices for overcoming the enemy in safety. In it extreme cold and intolerable heat must be borne, indolence and sleep are despised, the bodily powers are invigorated, the limbs of him who engages in it are made supple, and, in a word, it is a pursuit which may be followed without injury to anyone and with enjoyment to many. The best of it is, it is not for everybody, as field sports of other kinds are—except hawking, which also is only for kings and great lords. Reconsider your opinion therefore, Sancho, and when you are governor take to hunting, and you will find the good of it."

"Not me," said Sancho. "A good governor should have a broken leg and keep at home. A fine thing it would be if, after people had been to the trouble of coming to look for him on business, the governor was off in the forest enjoying himself. A government like that would be on its way downhill. By my faith, señor, hunting and amusements are more fit for idlers than for governors. What I intend to amuse myself with is playing cards as often as I can and bowling on Sundays and holidays. These hunts don't suit my nature or agree with my conscience."

"God grant it may turn out so," said the duke, "because 'it's a long step from saying to doing.'"

"Be that as it may," said Sancho, "'pledges don't distress a good payer,' and 'he who God helps does better than he who gets up early,' and 'it's the guts that move the feet and not the feet the guts.' I mean to say that if God gives me help and I do my duty honestly, no doubt I'll govern better than a monarch. Just 'let them put a finger in my mouth, and they'll see whether I can bite or not.'"

"The curse of God and all his saints upon you, accursed Sancho!" exclaimed Don Quixote. "When will the day come—as I have often said to you—when I shall hear you make one single coherent, rational remark without proverbs? Pray, your highnesses, leave this fool alone, for he will grind down your souls under, not two, but two thousand proverbs, and will continue to drag them in at the wrong times and for the wrong reasons for as long as God gives him health—or me, for that matter, if I cared to listen to them."

"Sancho Panza's proverbs," said the duchess, "though more in number than the Greek Commander's,[3] are not therefore less to be esteemed for the conciseness of the maxims. For my own part, I can say they give me more pleasure than others that might be better suited to the occasion."

[3] *Greek Commander's:* Hernán Núñez de Toledo (d. 1553), known as *el Comendador Griego* ("the Greek Commander") for his role as commander of the Order of Santiago and expertise in classical language, was a professor of Greek at the universities of Alcalá and Salamanca. He compiled a vast collection of proverbs—some eighty-five hundred in Romance languages—and published them in a critical edition that was released posthumously in 1555.

In pleasant conversation of this kind they passed out of the tent and into the forest. The day was spent in visiting some of their hunting posts and blinds, and then night closed in—not as brilliantly or serenely as might have been expected of the season (for it was then midsummer), but bringing with it a kind of haze that greatly aided the project of the duke and duchess.

As night began to fall, and a little after twilight set in, suddenly the whole forest on all four sides seemed to be on fire. Shortly after—here, there, on all sides—a vast number of trumpets and other military instruments were heard, as if several troops of cavalry were passing through the woods. The blaze of the fire and the noise of the warlike instruments almost blinded the eyes and deafened the ears of those that stood by, and indeed of all who were in the forest. Then there were heard repeated cries after the fashion of the Moors when they rush to battle. Trumpets and clarions brayed, drums beat, fifes played—so unceasingly and so fast that he could not have had any senses who did not lose them with the confused din of so many instruments. The duke was astounded, the duchess amazed, Don Quixote wondering, Sancho Panza trembling, and indeed, even they who were aware of the cause were frightened. In their fear, silence fell upon them, and a mounted courier, in the figure of a demon passed in front of them, blowing, in lieu of a bugle, a huge hollow horn that gave out a horrible hoarse note.

"Ho there, brother courier!" cried the duke. "Who are you? Where are you going? What troops are these that appear to be passing through this forest?"

To which the courier replied in a harsh, discordant voice, "I am the devil, and I am in search of Don Quixote of La Mancha. Those who are coming this way are six troops of enchanters, who are bringing on a triumphal car the peerless Dulcinea del Toboso. She comes under enchantment, together with the gallant Frenchman Montesinos, to give instructions to Don Quixote as to how the said lady may be disenchanted."

"If you were the devil, as you say and as your appearance indicates," said the duke, "you would have recognized the said knight Don Quixote of La Mancha, for you have him here before you."

"By God and upon my conscience," said the devil, "I didn't notice, for my mind is occupied with so many different things that I forgot my main reason for coming."

"This demon must be an honest fellow and a good Christian," said Sancho. "If he wasn't, he wouldn't swear by God and his conscience. I feel sure now there must be good people even in hell itself."

Without dismounting, the demon then turned to Don Quixote and said, "The unfortunate but valiant knight Montesinos sends me to you, Knight of the Lions (would that I saw you in their claws), bidding me tell you to wait for him wherever I may find you, as he brings with him the one whom they call Dulcinea del Toboso, that he may show you what is needful in order to disenchant her. As I came for no more, I need stay no longer. May demons of my stripe be with you, and good angels with these gentlefolk." So saying he blew his huge horn, turned about, and went off without waiting for a reply from anyone.

They all felt fresh wonder, but particularly Sancho and Don Quixote—Sancho, to see how, in spite of the truth, they insisted that Dulcinea was enchanted; Don

Quixote, because he could not be sure whether what had happened to him in the Cave of Montesinos was true or not.

While he was deep in these cogitations, the duke said to him, "Do you mean to wait, Señor Don Quixote?"

"Why would I not?" replied he. "Here will I wait, fearless and firm, though all hell should come to attack me."

"Well, I—if I see another devil or hear another horn like the last one—will wait here as much as in Flanders," said Sancho.

Night now closed in more completely, and many lights began to flit through the woods, just as those fiery exhalations from the earth, which look like shooting stars to our eyes, flit through the sky.[4] A frightful noise, too, was heard, like that made by the solid wheels the oxcarts usually have, whose harsh, ceaseless creaking, they say, puts to flight any bears or wolves in their path. In addition to all this commotion, there came a further disturbance that heightened the tumult, for now it seemed as if in truth, on all four sides of the forest, four skirmishes or battles were going on at the same time. In one quarter resounded the dull noise of a terrible cannonade; in another numberless harquebuses were being discharged. Close by, one could almost hear the shouts of the combatants; and farther away, the Moorish lelilies[5] resounded again and again.

In a word, the bugles, the horns, the clarions, the trumpets, the drums, the cannon, the harquebuses, and above all the tremendous noise of the carts arose together in a din so confused and horrific that Don Quixote had need to summon up all his courage to brave it; but Sancho's gave way, and he fell fainting on the duchess' lap, who let him lie there and promptly bade them throw water in his face. This was done, and he came to himself by the time one of the carts with the creaking wheels reached them.

It was drawn by four plodding oxen all draped in black cloth. On each horn they had fixed a large lighted wax candle, and on the top of the cart was constructed a raised seat, on which sat a venerable old man with a beard whiter than snow itself, and so long that it fell below his waist. He was dressed in a long robe of black buckram,[6] for as the cart was thickly set with a multitude of candles it was easy to make out everything that was on it. Leading it were two hideous demons, also clad in buckram, with countenances so frightful that Sancho, having once seen them, shut his eyes so as not to see them again.

As soon as the cart came opposite the spot, the old man rose from his lofty seat and, standing up, said in a loud voice, "I am the sage Lirgandeo."[7] And without another word the cart then passed on.

[4] *fiery exhalations . . . through the sky:* According to Aristotle, the earth emits hot, dry vapors into the atmosphere, where they may ignite and produce phenomena like meteors and shooting stars.

[5] *Moorish lelilies:* battle cries or celebratory exclamations. The Spanish word *lelilí* roughly approximates the sound of the Arabic phrase "lā ilāha illā Allāh" ("There is no god but Allah"), the central affirmation of Islam.

[6] *buckram:* See footnote 1, page 530.

[7] *Lirgandeo:* See footnote 12, page 356.

Behind it came another of the same kind, with another aged man enthroned, who, stopping the cart, said in a voice no less solemn than that of the first, "I am the sage Alquife, the great friend of Urganda the Unknown," and passed on.

Then another cart came by at the same pace, but the occupant of the throne was not old like the others, but a man stalwart and robust, and of a forbidding countenance, who as he came up said in a voice far hoarser and more devilish, "I am the enchanter Arcaláus, the mortal enemy of Amadís of Gaul and all his kindred," and then passed on.

Having gone a short distance, the three carts halted and the monotonous noise of their wheels ceased. Soon after they heard another, not noise, but sound of sweet, harmonious music, of which Sancho was very glad, taking it to be a good sign. He said to the duchess, from whom he did not stir a step or for a single instant, "Señora, where there's music there can be no evil."[8]

"Nor where there are lights and it is bright," said the duchess.

To which Sancho replied, "Fire gives light, and it's bright where there are bonfires, as we see by the ones that are all around us and that might burn us. But music is a sign of celebration and merrymaking."

"That remains to be seen," said Don Quixote, who was listening to all that passed.

And he was right, as will be shown in the following chapter.

[8] *where there's music there can be no evil:* According to popular belief, music frightened off evil spirits.

CHAPTER XXXV

WHEREIN IS CONTINUED THE INSTRUCTION GIVEN TO DON QUIXOTE REGARDING THE DISENCHANTMENT OF DULCINEA, TOGETHER WITH OTHER MARVELOUS INCIDENTS

They saw advancing toward them, to the sound of this pleasing music, what they call a triumphal car,[1] drawn by six gray mules draped in white linen, on each of which was mounted a penitent,[2] robed also in white, with a large lighted wax candle in his hand. The car was twice or, perhaps, three times as large as the former ones, and in front and on the sides stood twelve more penitents, all as white as snow and all with lighted candles—a spectacle to excite fear as well as wonder.

On a raised throne was seated a nymph dressed in layer upon layer of a sheer silvery fabric, each embroidered with unnumbered sequins glittering in gold, which made her appear, if not richly, at least brilliantly appareled. Her face was covered with thin, transparent sendal,[3] the texture of which did not prevent the fair features of a maiden from being distinguished, while the numerous lights made it possible to judge of her beauty and of her years, which seemed to be not less than seventeen but not yet to have reached twenty. Beside her was a figure in a flowing robe reaching to the feet, while the head was covered with a black veil.

The instant the car was opposite the duke and duchess and Don Quixote, the music of the clarions ceased, and then that of the lutes and harps in the triumphal car. The figure in the robe rose up, then loosening its robe and removing the veil from its face, disclosed to their eyes the shape of Death itself, fleshless and hideous—at which sight Don Quixote felt uneasy, Sancho quavered, and the duke and duchess showed no little trepidation. Having risen to its feet, this living death, in a sleepy voice and with a tongue hardly awake, held forth as follows:

> I am that Merlin who the legends say
> The devil had for father, and the lie

[1] *triumphal car:* Renaissance artists revived the classical tradition of the triumphal procession, a celebration of a victorious general returning from battle, and centered their depictions in painting, poetry, and courtly spectacle on the grand triumphal car. The vehicle was reimagined as a richly ornamented chariot or cart, often drawn by exotic animals and commemorating allegorical victories.

[2] *penitent:* See footnote 2, page 407.

[3] *sendal:* fine silk used for ceremonial clothing.

Hath gathered credence with the lapse of time.
Of magic prince, of Zoroastric[4] lore
Monarch and treasurer, with jealous eye
I view the efforts of the age to hide
The gallant deeds of doughty errant knights,
Who are, and ever have been, dear to me.
Enchanters and magicians and their kind
Are mostly hard of heart. Not so am I;
For mine is tender, soft, compassionate,
And its delight is doing good to all.
In the dim caverns of the gloomy Dis,[5]
Where, tracing mystic lines and characters,
My soul abideth now, there came to me
The sorrow-laden sighs of her, the fair,
The peerless Dulcinea del Toboso.
I knew of her enchantment and her fate,
From highborn dame to peasant wench transformed
And touched with pity, first I turned the leaves
Of countless volumes of my devilish craft,
And then, in this grim, grisly skeleton
Myself encasing, hither have I come
To show where lies the fitting remedy
To give relief in such a piteous case.
O thou, the pride and pink of all that wear
The adamantine steel! O shining light,
O beacon, north star, path and guide of all
Who, scorning slumber and the lazy down,
Adopt the toilsome life of bloodstained arms!
To thee, great hero who all praise transcends,
La Mancha's luster and Iberia's star,
Don Quixote, wise as brave, to thee I say—
For peerless Dulcinea del Toboso
Her pristine form and beauty to regain,
'Tis needful that thy esquire Sancho shall,
On his own sturdy buttocks bared to heaven,
Three thousand and three hundred lashes lay,
And that they smart and sting and hurt him well.
Thus have the authors of her woe resolved.
And for this cause, I make my presence known.

"By all that's good," exclaimed Sancho at this, "I'll just as soon give myself three stabs with a dagger as three lashes, let alone three thousand. If that's how

[4] *Zoroastric*: of the Zoroastrian religion, synonymous with dark magical arts.
[5] *Dis*: hell, or the underworld; also, the ruler of the underworld in Roman mythology.

to disenchant—to the devil with it! I don't see what my rear end has got to do with enchantments. By God, if Señor Merlin hasn't found out some other way of disenchanting Lady Dulcinea del Toboso, she can go to her grave enchanted."

"I'll take you, Don Bumpkin stuffed with garlic," said Don Quixote, "and tie you to a tree as naked as when your mother brought you forth, and give you not just three thousand three hundred, but six thousand six hundred lashes—and so well laid on that they won't be gotten rid of if you try three thousand three hundred times. Don't answer me a word or I'll tear your soul out."

On hearing this Merlin said, "That will not do, for the lashes worthy Sancho has to receive must be given of his own free will and not by force, and at whatever time he pleases, for he is bound to no statute of limitations. Yet it is permitted, if he wishes to commute the sentence by half, that the lashes be given by another's hand, even if it is a weighty one."

"Not any hand, my own or anybody else's, weighty or weighable is going to touch me," said Sancho. "Was I the one who gave birth to Lady Dulcinea del Toboso that my rear end should pay for her wandering eye? My master, who does have a share in her—for he's always calling her 'my life' and 'my soul,' and his breath and support—he's the one who can and should whip himself for her and take all the trouble that's needed for her disenchantment. But for me to whip myself? Abernuncio!"[6]

As soon as Sancho had done speaking the nymph in silver that was at the side of Merlin's ghost stood up, and removing the thin veil from her face revealed one that seemed to all something more than exceedingly beautiful; and with manly self-assurance and in a voice not very much like a lady's, addressing Sancho directly, said, "You wretched squire, soul of a pitcher, heart of a cork tree, with bowels of flint and pebbles! If, you impudent thief, they commanded you to throw yourself down from some lofty tower; if, enemy of mankind, they asked you to swallow a dozen toads, two lizards, and three adders; if they wanted you to slay your wife and children with a murderous sharpened scimitar, it would be no wonder for you to show yourself disdainful and squeamish. But to dwell on three thousand three hundred lashes, what every poor little orphan gets every month—it is enough to amaze, astonish, astound the compassionate hearts of all who hear it, nay, all who will come to hear it in the course of time.

"Turn, O miserable, hard-hearted animal, turn, I say, those skittish mule's eyes upon mine, the likeness of radiant stars, and you will see them weeping stream upon stream and river upon river, tracing furrows, tracks, and paths over the fair fields of my cheeks. Let it move you, you crafty, vicious monster, to see my blooming youth—still in its adolescence, for I am not yet twenty—wasting and withering away beneath the husk of a rude peasant wench. If I do not appear in that shape now, it is a special favor Señor Merlin here has granted me, to the sole end that my beauty may soften you; for the tears of beauty in distress turn rocks into cotton and tigers into lambs.

[6] *Abernuncio:* "No way." Popular corruption of *Abrenuntio* ("I renounce"), spoken by a godparent during the baptismal rite to reject Satan and his dominion on behalf of the child.

"Lay into that hide of yours, you great untamed brute; rouse your lusty vigor, which only urges you to eat and eat, and set free the softness of my flesh, the gentleness of my nature, and the fairness of my face. And if you will not relent or act promptly, do so for the sake of that poor knight you have beside you—I mean your master, whose soul I can this moment see, how he has it stuck in his throat not ten fingers from his lips, and only waiting for your inflexible or yielding reply to make its escape by his mouth or go back again into his stomach."

Don Quixote on hearing this felt his throat, and turning to the duke he said, "By God, señor, Dulcinea says true—I have my soul stuck here in my throat like the nut of a crossbow."[7]

"What say you to this, Sancho?" said the duchess.

"I say, señora," returned Sancho, "what I said before: as for the lashes, abernuncio!"

"*Abrenuncio*, you should say, Sancho, and not as you do," said the duke.

"Let me alone, your highness," said Sancho. "I'm not in the mood right now to deal with the finer points or a letter more or less. These lashes that are supposed to be given to me—or that I'm supposed to give myself—have upset me so much that I don't know what I'm saying or doing. But something I'd like to know about this lady, my lady Dulcinea del Toboso, is where she learned this way she has of asking for favors. She comes to ask me to tear up my flesh with lashes, and she calls me 'soul of a pitcher,' and 'great untamed brute,' and a string of vile names that the devil's welcome to. Is my flesh bronze? Or is it anything to me whether she's enchanted or not? What basket of white linen has she brought with her, what shirts, handkerchiefs, or socks—not that I wear any—to persuade me? No, nothing but one piece of abuse after another, even though she knows the proverb they use around here that 'a donkey loaded with gold goes lightly up a mountain,' and that 'gifts break rocks,' and 'pray hard and hammer harder,' and that 'one *take* is better than two *I'll give you's*.'"

"Then there's my master, who ought to stroke my back and pet me to turn this wool of mine into carded cotton. He says if he gets hold of me, he'll tie me naked to a tree and double the count of lashes on me. These fine, pitiful people should consider that it's not merely a squire, but a governor they are asking to whip himself and not to pile on insults. Let them learn—plague take them—the right way to ask and beg and behave themselves; for 'not all times are alike' and people aren't always in a good mood. I'm about to burst with grief right now after seeing my green coat torn, and here they come asking me to whip myself of my own free will, when I'm about as likely to do that as become an Indian chief."

"Well then, the fact is, friend Sancho," said the duke, "that unless you become softer than a ripe fig, you shall not take hold of that government. It would be a nice thing for me to send my islanders a cruel governor with flinty bowels, who won't yield to the tears of afflicted damsels or to the prayers of wise and powerful

[7] *nut of a crossbow:* grooved roller that holds a crossbow string under tension until its release.

enchanters and sages of old. In short, Sancho, either you are to whip yourself or they are to whip you, or you shall not be governor."

"Señor," said Sancho, "can I not have two day's grace to think about what's best for me?"

"No, certainly not," said Merlin. "Here, this minute and on the spot, the matter must be settled. Either Dulcinea will return to the Cave of Montesinos and to her former condition of peasant wench, or else in her present form shall be carried to the Elysian fields, where she will remain waiting until the number of stripes is completed."

"Now then, good Sancho," said the duchess. "Show courage and gratitude for your master Don Quixote's bread you have eaten. We are all bound to oblige and please him for his benevolent disposition and lofty chivalry. Consent to this whipping, my son, and let's leave the devil to himself and fear to the wretched, for 'a stout heart breaks bad luck,' as you very well know."

To this Sancho replied with an irrelevant remark, which he addressed to Merlin: "Will your worship tell me, Señor Merlin—when that courier devil came up he gave my master a message from Señor Montesinos, charging him to wait for him here, as he was coming to arrange how Lady Doña Dulcinea del Toboso was to be disenchanted. But up to the present we haven't seen Montesinos, or anything like him."

To which Merlin answered, "The devil, Sancho, is an ignoramus and a great scoundrel. I am the one who sent him to look for your master, but not with a message from Montesinos but from myself. Montesinos is in his cave expecting, or more properly speaking, waiting for his disenchantment; for he has yet to skin the tail.[8] If he owes you anything, or you have any business to transact with him, I'll bring him to you and leave him where you wish. For the present, make up your mind to consent to this penance, and believe me it will be very good for you, for soul as well for body—for your soul because of the charity with which you will perform it; for your body because I know that you are of a sanguine complexion and it will do you no harm to draw a little blood."[9]

"There's no shortage of doctors in the world. Even the enchanters are doctors," said Sancho. "Nevertheless, since everybody is telling me the same thing—though I can't see it myself—I say that I am willing to give myself the three thousand three hundred lashes, provided I can lay them on whenever I want, without any limit on days or times. I will try and get out of debt as quickly as I can so that the world can enjoy the beauty of Lady Dulcinea del Toboso, who is apparently (contrary to what I thought) beautiful after all. It must be a condition, too, that I am not to be under obligation to draw blood with the scourge, and that if any of the lashes happen to be fly flappers,[10] they will count. *Item:*[11] In case I should make any mistake in the

[8] *he has yet to skin the tail:* "The hardest part remains."

[9] *sanguine complexion . . . a little blood:* According to humoral theory, people with a sanguine complexion have an excess of blood in circulation.

[10] *fly flappers:* light swats, as if to shoo away flies.

[11] Item: term used to mark sections in a document.

tally, Señor Merlin, since he knows everything, is to keep count and let me know how many remain or are over the number."

"There will be no need to let you know of any over," said Merlin, "because when you reach the full number, Señora Dulcinea will at once, and that very instant, be disenchanted, and will come in her gratitude to seek out the worthy Sancho and thank him, and even reward him for the good work. You therefore have no cause to be uneasy about stripes too many or too few. Heaven forbid I should cheat anyone of even a hair of his head."

"Well then, it's in God's hands," said Sancho. "I give in to my bad luck. I mean, I accept the penance on the conditions laid down."

Hardly had Sancho uttered these last words when the music of the clarions struck up once more, and again a host of harquebuses were discharged. Don Quixote hung on Sancho's neck kissing him again and again on the forehead and cheeks. The duchess and the duke expressed the greatest satisfaction, the car began to move on, and as it passed the fair Dulcinea bowed to the duke and duchess and made a low curtsey to Sancho.

And now bright smiling dawn came on apace. The flowers of the field, revived, raised up their heads, and the crystal waters of the brooks, murmuring over the gray and white pebbles, hastened to pay their tribute to the expectant rivers. The glad earth, the unclouded sky, the fresh breeze, the clear light—each and all showed that the day that came treading on the skirts of morning would be calm and bright. The duke and duchess, pleased with their hunt and at having carried out their plans so cleverly and successfully, returned to their castle, resolved to continue with their pranks. For to them there was no reality that could provide them more amusement.

CHAPTER XXXVI

IN WHICH IS RELATED THE STRANGE AND UNPARALLELED ADVENTURE OF THE DISTRESSED DUEÑA, ALIAS COUNTESS TRIFALDI, TOGETHER WITH A LETTER THAT SANCHO PANZA WROTE TO HIS WIFE, TERESA PANZA

The duke had a majordomo[1] of a very fun-loving and impertinent turn. It was he that played the part of Merlin, made all the arrangements for the recent adventure, composed the verses, and found a page to represent Dulcinea. Now, with the assistance of his master and mistress, he dreamed up another of the strangest and most comical schemes that can be imagined.

The duchess asked Sancho the next day if he had made a beginning with the task of penance he had to perform for the disenchantment of Dulcinea. He said he had, and had given himself five lashes overnight.

The duchess asked him what he had given them with.

He said with his hand.

"That," said the duchess, "is more like giving oneself slaps than lashes. I am sure the sage Merlin will not be satisfied with such tenderness. Worthy Sancho must make a scourge with thorns or a cat-o'-nine tails that will make itself felt, for 'it's with blood that letters are mastered.'[2] The release of so great a lady as Dulcinea will not be granted so easily or at such a paltry price. Remember, Sancho, that works of charity done in a lukewarm and half-hearted way are without merit and of no avail."[3]

To this Sancho replied, "If your ladyship will give me a proper scourge or cord, I'll lay it on, so long as it doesn't hurt too much. You must know—bumpkin that

[1] *majordomo:* chief steward, the official over domestic affairs, including staff, finances, provisioning, and protocol.

[2] *it's with blood that letters are mastered:* "No pain, no gain."

[3] *Remember, Sancho . . . of no avail:* This piece of advice caused consternation among Inquisition censors. It was suppressed in the 1616 Valencian edition of the novel and would not reappear in Spanish editions until the 1830s. According to the Catholic theology of the time, the merit of charitable works depended not only on the act itself but also on the disposition of the will. Theologians disagreed on the extent to which works of charity done out of a weak or sluggish will were meritorious.

I am—my flesh is more cotton than hemp, and it won't do any good for me to harm myself for the sake of somebody else."

"So be it by all means," said the duchess. "Tomorrow I'll give you a scourge that will be just the thing for you, and will accommodate itself to the tenderness of your flesh, as if it was its own sister."

Then said Sancho, "Your highness should know, dear lady of my soul, that I have a letter written to my wife, Teresa Panza, giving her an account of all that's happened to me since I left her. I have it here in my breast, and there's nothing left to do but to put the address on it. I'd be glad if your discretion would read it. I think it fits the governor style—I mean, the way governors ought to write."

"And who dictated it?" asked the duchess.

"Who should have dictated but me, sinner as I am?" returned Sancho.

"And did you write it yourself?" asked the duchess.

"That I didn't," said Sancho, "for I can neither read nor write, though I can sign my name."

"Let us see it," said the duchess, "for we may be certain that you will display in it the quality and quantity of your wit."

Sancho took out an unsealed letter from his breast, and the duchess, taking it, found it ran in this fashion:

SANCHO PANZA'S LETTER TO HIS WIFE, TERESA PANZA

> If I was well whipped, at least I rode in style;[4] if I've gotten a good government, it's at the cost of a good whipping. This will not make sense right now, my Teresa. Eventually, you will understand what it means. You need to know, Teresa, that I have decided that you will ride in a coach, for that is a matter of importance, because every other way of going is going on all fours. You are a governor's wife; take care that nobody speaks evil of you behind your back. I am sending you here a green hunting suit that my lady the duchess gave me. Alter it to make a skirt and bodice for our daughter. My master Don Quixote (if I am to believe what I hear in these parts) is a sane madman and an entertaining idiot—and I'm in no way behind him. We have been in the Cave of Montesinos, and the sage Merlin has laid hold of me for the disenchantment of Dulcinea del Toboso, who is called Aldonza Lorenzo over there. With three thousand three hundred lashes minus five that I'm to give myself, she will be left as entirely disenchanted as the mother that bore her. Do not say anything about this to anyone; for if you make your affairs public, some will say they are white, and others will say they are black.
>
> I will leave here in a few days for my government, where I am going with a mighty great desire to make money. They tell me all new governors set out with the same desire. I will size it up and let you know if you should come and live with me or not. Dapple is well and sends you his regards. I have no intention of leaving him behind, even if they took me away to be Grand Turk. My lady the duchess kisses your hands a thousand times. Send her back two thousand, for as my master says, "nothing costs less or is cheaper than civility." God has not been pleased to provide another valise for me with another hundred escudos, like the one the other

[4] *If I was well whipped, at least I rode in style:* This obscure saying may have originally described a criminal paraded through town on the back of a donkey.

day. But never mind, my Teresa, the bellringer's in a safe place, and everything will come out in the wash with the government. The only thing is that I am very worried about what they tell me—that once I've tasted it I will eat my hands off after it. If that's the case, it will not come very cheap to me—though the maimed and one-armed do get a benefice of their own in the alms they beg for, so that one way or another you will be rich and in luck. God give it to you as he can and keep me to serve you.

From this castle, the 20th of July, 1614.

Your husband the governor,
SANCHO PANZA

When she had finished reading the letter, the duchess said to Sancho, "On two points the worthy governor goes rather astray: one is in saying or hinting that this government has been bestowed upon him for the lashes that he is to give himself, when he knows (and he cannot deny it) that when my lord the duke promised it to him nobody ever dreamed of such a thing as lashes; the other is that he shows himself here to be very greedy. I would not have him a money-seeker, for 'greed bursts the bag,' and the greedy governor does ungoverned justice."

"I don't mean it that way, señora," said Sancho. "If you think the letter doesn't run as it should, we can tear it up and make another. It might be a worse one if it's left to my brains."

"No, no," said the duchess, "this one will do. I wish the duke to see it."

With this they headed to a garden where they were to dine, and the duchess showed Sancho's letter to the duke, who was highly delighted with it. They dined, and after the table had been cleared and they had amused themselves for a while with Sancho's rich conversation, the melancholy sound of a fife and harsh discordant drum made itself heard. Everyone appeared to be set on edge by this dull, confused, martial harmony—especially Don Quixote, who could not remain in his seat in such a pitch of anxiety. As to Sancho, it is needless to say that fear drove him to his usual refuge, the side or the skirts of the duchess. In all truth, the sound they heard was a most plaintive and melancholy one.

While they nervously waited, they saw advancing towards them through the garden two men clad in mourning robes so long and flowing that they trailed upon the ground. As they marched, they beat two great drums, which were likewise draped in black, and beside them came the fife player, black and somber like the others. Following these came a personage of gigantic stature enveloped rather than clad in a gown of the deepest black, the skirt of which was of prodigious dimensions. Over the gown, girdling or crossing his figure, he had a broad baldric which was also black, and from which hung a huge gem-encrusted scimitar in a black scabbard. He had his face covered with a gossamer black veil, through which might be glimpsed a very long beard as white as snow. He advanced, keeping step to the sound of the drums with great gravity and dignity. In short, his stature, his measured steps, his somber demeanor, and his retinue might well have struck with astonishment, as they did, all who beheld him without knowing who he was.

With this pomp and solemnity he advanced to kneel before the duke, who, with the others, awaited him standing. The duke, however, would not on any account allow him to speak until he had risen. The prodigious scarecrow obeyed and, standing up, removed the veil from his face, revealing the most fearsome, the longest, the whitest, and the thickest beard that human eyes had ever beheld. Then drawing up a grave, sonorous voice from the depths of his broad, capacious chest, and fixing his eyes on the duke, he said:

"Most high and mighty señor, my name is Trifaldín[5] of the White Beard. I am squire to the Countess Trifaldi, otherwise called the Distressed Dueña, on whose behalf I bear a message to your highness. May your magnificence be pleased to grant her leave and permission to come and tell you her trouble, which is one of the strangest and most wonderful that the mind most familiar with trouble in the world could have imagined. But first she desires to know if the valiant and never vanquished knight Don Quixote of La Mancha is in this your castle, for she has come in quest of him on foot and without breaking her fast from the kingdom of Candaya to your realms here—a thing which may and ought to be regarded as a miracle or set down to enchantment. She is even now at the gate of this fortress or palace, and only waits for your permission to enter. I have spoken."

With that he coughed, stroked down his beard with both his hands, and stood very tranquilly waiting for the duke's response, which was to this effect: "Many days ago, worthy squire Trifaldín of the White Beard, we heard of the misfortune of my lady the Countess Trifaldi, whom the enchanters have caused to be called the Distressed Dueña. Bid her enter, O stupendous squire, and tell her that the valiant knight Don Quixote of La Mancha is here. From his generous disposition, she may safely promise herself every protection and assistance. You may tell her, too, that if my aid is necessary it will not be withheld, for I am bound to give it to her by my knightly station, which involves the protection of women of all kinds, especially widowed, wronged, and distressed ladies, such as her ladyship seems to be."

On hearing this Trifaldín bent his knee to the ground, and making a sign to the fifer and drummers to strike up, he turned and marched out of the garden to the same notes and at the same pace as when he entered, leaving them all amazed at his bearing and solemnity.

Turning to Don Quixote, the duke said, "Well then, renowned knight, the mists of malice and ignorance are unable to hide or obscure the light of valor and virtue. I say so, because your excellency has been barely six days in this castle, and already the unhappy and the afflicted come in quest of you from lands far distant and remote—and not in coaches or on dromedaries, but on foot and fasting, confident that in that mighty arm they will find a cure for their sorrows and troubles thanks to your great achievements, which are circulated all over the known earth."

[5] *Trifaldín:* In the *Orlando* poems of Boiardo and Ariosto, there is a character named "Trufaldino" (*Trufaldín* in Spanish translations), which derives from the Italian verb *trufar* (to deceive, outwit).

"I wish, señor duke," replied Don Quixote, "that blessed churchman, who at dinner the other day showed such ill-will and bitter spite against knights-errant, were here now to see with his own eyes whether such knights are needed in the world. At the least, he would learn at close distance that those suffering any extraordinary affliction or sorrow, in extreme cases and unusual misfortunes, do not go looking for a remedy in the houses of jurists or village sacristans. Nor do they go to the knight who has never ventured beyond the limits of his own town, or to the indolent courtier who only seeks for news to pass along, instead of striving to do deeds and exploits for others to relate and record. Relief in distress, help in need, protection for damsels, consolation for widows—these are to be found in no persons better than in knights-errant. I give unceasing thanks to Heaven that I am one, and regard any misfortune or suffering that may befall me in the pursuit of so honorable a calling as endured to good purpose. Let this dueña come and ask what she will, for I will work her relief by the might of my arm and the dauntless resolution of my bold heart."

CHAPTER XXXVII

WHEREIN IS CONTINUED THE REMARKABLE ADVENTURE OF THE DISTRESSED DUEÑA

The duke and duchess were extremely happy to see how readily Don Quixote fell in with their scheme. For his part, Sancho observed, "I hope this señora dueña won't be putting any difficulties in the way of the promise of my government. I've heard a Toledo apothecary who talked like a goldfinch say that where dueñas were mixed up nothing good could come of it. My God, how he hated them, that apothecary! And so what I'm thinking is, if all dueñas (of whatever variety or condition they might be) are plagues and busybodies, what must the distressed ones be like, as they've said this Countess Three-Skirts or Three-Trains[1] is—for where I come from, skirts or trains, trains or skirts, it's all one."

"Hush, friend Sancho," said Don Quixote. "Since this lady dueña comes in quest of me from such a distant land she cannot be one of those the apothecary meant. Moreover, this is a countess, and when countesses serve as dueñas it is in the service of queens and empresses, for in their own houses they are mistresses paramount and have other dueñas to wait on them."

To this Doña Rodríguez, who was present, answered, "My lady the duchess has dueñas in her service that might be countesses if it was the will of fortune. But 'laws go where kings wish.' Let nobody speak ill of dueñas, above all of aged maiden ones. Though I am not one myself, I know well the advantage a maiden dueña has over one that is a widow. But 'he who sheared us has kept the shears.'"[2]

"For all that," said Sancho, "there's so much to be sheared from dueñas—so my barber said— that 'it would be better not to stir the rice, even if it sticks.'"[3]

"These squires," returned Doña Rodríguez, "are always our enemies. As they are the haunting spirits of the antechambers and watch us at every step, whenever they are not saying their prayers (and that's often enough) they spend their time tattling about us, digging up our bones, and burying our good name. They can be condemned to the galleys for all I care. We will live in spite of them, and in great houses too, though we die of hunger and cover our flesh (delicate or not) in a widow's black garments, as one covers or hides a dunghill on a procession day. By my faith, if time and circumstances permitted, I could prove, not only to those here present, but to all the world, that there is no virtue that is not to be found in a dueña."

[1] *Three-Skirts or Three-Trains: faldas.* A *falda* is a skirt or the train of a long dress.

[2] *he who sheared us has kept the shears:* "He who mistreated us may yet mistreat others."

[3] *it would be better not to stir the rice, even if it sticks:* "It would be better to drop the matter."

"I have no doubt," said the duchess, "that my good Doña Rodríguez is right, and very much so. But she would do well to bide her time for fighting her own battle and that of the rest of the dueñas, so as to confound the slander of that vile apothecary and root out the prejudice in the great Sancho Panza's mind."

To this Sancho replied, "Ever since my sails were filled with that governorship, I haven't wished for a squirely wind to blow my way, and I don't care a wild fig for all the dueñas in the world."

They would have carried on this dueña dispute had they not heard the notes of the fife and drums once more, from which they concluded that the Distressed Dueña was making her entrance. The duchess asked the duke if it would be proper to go out to receive her, as she was a countess and a person of rank.

"In respect of her being a countess," said Sancho, before the duke could reply, "I am for your highnesses going out to receive her; but in respect of her being a dueña, it is my opinion you shouldn't budge."

"Who asked you to meddle in this, Sancho?" said Don Quixote.

"Who, señor?" said Sancho. "I meddle because I have a right to meddle, as a squire who has learned the rules of courtesy in the school of your worship, the most courteous and well-bred knight in the whole world of courtliness. In matters like this, as I have heard your worship say, 'as much is lost by a card too many as by a card too few,' and 'to the careful listener, few words.'"

"Sancho is right," said the duke. "We'll see what the countess is like, and by that measure the courtesy that is due to her."

The drums and fife now made their entrance as before; and here the author brought this short chapter to an end and began the next, following up the same adventure, which is one of the most notable in the history.

CHAPTER XXXVIII

WHEREIN IS TOLD THE DISTRESSED DUEÑA'S TALE OF HER MISFORTUNES

Following the melancholy musicians there filed into the garden as many as twelve dueñas in two lines, all dressed in ample mourning robes of what looked like milled serge, with headdresses of fine white muslin[1] so long that they allowed only the border of the robe to be seen. Behind them came Countess Trifaldi, the squire Trifaldín of the White Beard leading her by the hand, clad in the finest unnapped black baize, such that if it had a nap, every tuft would have been as large as a Martos garbanzo.[2] The train (or skirt, or whatever it might be called) ended in three points, which were carried by three pages, likewise dressed in mourning, forming an elegant geometrical figure with the three acute angles made by the three points. From this, all who saw the peaked skirt concluded that it must be because of it the countess was called Trifaldi, as though to say "The Countess of the Three Skirts." Benengeli likewise says it was so, though that by her right name she was called Countess Lobuna, because wolves bred in great numbers in her country; and if, instead of wolves, they had been foxes, she would have been called Countess Zorruna,[3] as it was the custom in those parts for lords to take distinctive titles from the thing or things most abundant in their dominions. This countess, however, in favor of the novelty of her skirt, dropped Lobuna and took up Trifaldi.

The twelve dueñas and the lady came forward at a processional pace, their faces being covered with black veils—not gossamer ones like Trifaldín's, but so thick that they allowed nothing to be seen through them. As soon as the band of dueñas was fully in sight, the duke, the duchess, and Don Quixote stood up, as well as all who were watching the slow-moving procession. The twelve dueñas halted and formed a path along which La Dolorida[4] advanced, Trifaldín still holding her hand. On seeing this the duke, the duchess, and Don Quixote went some twelve paces forward to meet her.

[1] *headdresses of fine white muslin:* appropriate to widows.

[2] *finest unnapped black baize . . . a Martos garbanzo:* Napping is a finishing process that raises the fibers on the fabric to create a soft, fuzzy surface, often used on coarse cloths like flannel and baize to imitate the appearance of felt. The comparison of the tufts to garbanzos—famously cultivated in Martos, a town in Andalusia—underscores the fabric's coarseness and weight.

[3] *Countess Lobuna . . . Countess Zorruna: lobo* (wolf); *zorro* (fox).

[4] *La Dolorida:* The Distressed One.

She then, kneeling on the ground, said in a voice hoarse and rough, rather than fine and delicate, "May it please your highnesses not to offer such courtesies to this your servant, I should say to this your handmaid, for I am in such distress that I shall never be able to respond in kind, because my strange and unparalleled misfortune has carried off my good sense—I know not where. It must be a long way off, for the more I look for it the less I find it."

"He would be bereft of good sense, señora countess," said the duke, "who did not perceive your worth by your person, for at a glance it may be seen it deserves all the cream of courtesy and flower of polite usage." And raising her up by the hand, he led her to a seat beside the duchess, who likewise received her with great civility. Don Quixote remained silent, while Sancho was dying to see the faces of Trifaldi and one or two of her many dueñas. But there was no possibility of it until they themselves revealed them of their own accord and free will.

All kept still, waiting to see who would break silence, which the Distressed Dueña did in these words: "I am confident, most mighty lord, most fair lady, and most discreet company, that my most miserable misery will be accorded a reception no less dispassionate than generous and pitying in your most valiant breasts, for it is one that is enough to melt marble, soften diamonds, and mollify[5] the steel of the most hardened hearts in the world. But ere it is proclaimed to your hearing (not to say your ears), I would fain be enlightened whether there be present in this society, circle, or company, that knight immaculatissimus,[6] Don Quixote de la Manchissima, and his squirissimus Panza."

"The Panza is here," said Sancho, before anyone could reply, "and Don Quixotissimus too. And so, most distressedest Dueñissima, you can say what you willissimus, for we are all readissimus to do you any servissimus."

On this Don Quixote rose and, addressing the Distressed Dueña, said, "If your sorrows, afflicted lady, can indulge in any hope of relief from the valor or might of any knight-errant, here are mine, which, feeble and limited though they be, shall be entirely devoted to your service. I am Don Quixote of La Mancha, whose calling it is to give aid to the needy of all sorts. That being so, it is not necessary for you, señora, to make any appeal to benevolence, or deal in preambles, only to tell your woes plainly and straightforwardly; for you have hearers that will know how, if not to remedy them, to sympathize with them."

On hearing this, the Distressed Dueña made as though she would throw herself at Don Quixote's feet, and actually did fall before them and said, as she strove to embrace them, "Before these feet and legs I cast myself, O unconquered knight, as before the foundations and pillars of knight-errantry, for that is what they truly are. These feet I desire to kiss, for upon their steps hangs and depends the sole remedy for my misfortune, O valorous errant, whose veritable achievements leave behind and eclipse the fabulous ones of the Amadises, Esplandians, and Belianises!" Then turning from Don Quixote to Sancho Panza and grasping his hands, she said, "O most loyal squire that ever served knight-errant in this

[5] *mollify:* soften.

[6] *immaculatissimus:* very unblemished.

present age or ages past, whose goodness is more extensive than the beard of Trifaldín, my companion here of present, well may you boast that in serving the great Don Quixote, you are serving, summed up in one, the whole host of knights that have ever borne arms in the world. I conjure[7] you, by what you owe to your most loyal goodness, that you be my kind intercessor with your master, so that he speedily may give aid to this most humble and most unfortunate countess."

To this Sancho answered, "As to my goodness, señora, being as long and as great as your squire's beard, it hardly matters to me. May I have my soul well bearded and mustached when it comes time to leave this life behind—that's the point. About beards here below, I care little or nothing. But without all these fancy phrases, I will beg my master—because I know he loves me, and, besides, he needs me right now for a certain business—to give aid to your worship as far as he can. Unpack your woes and lay them before us. Leave us to deal with them, for we'll be all of one mind."

The duke and duchess, as it was they who had suggested this adventure, were ready to burst with laughter at all this, and between themselves they commended the clever acting of Trifaldi, who, returning to her seat, said:

"Queen Doña Maguncia[8] reigned over the famous kingdom of Candaya, which lies between the great Trapobana and the Southern Sea, two leagues beyond Cape Comorin.[9] She was the widow of King Archipiela,[10] her lord and husband, and of their marriage they brought forth the Princess Antonomasia,[11] heiress of the kingdom. This Princess Antonomasia was reared and grew up under my care and direction, I being the oldest and highest in rank of her mother's dueñas. Time passed, and the young Antonomasia reached the age of fourteen, and such a perfection of beauty that nature could not raise it higher. Think not that her intelligence was childish. She was as intelligent as she was fair, and she was fairer than all the world—and is so still, unless the envious Fates and hard-hearted sisters three have cut the thread of her life.[12] But they have not done so, for Heaven will not suffer so great a wrong to Earth as would be to pluck unripe the grapes of the fairest vineyard on its surface.

"Of this beauty, to which my poor feeble tongue has failed to do justice, countless princes— not only of that country but of others—were enamored, among them a private gentleman[13] at court who dared to raise his thoughts to the heaven

[7] *conjure:* charge.

[8] *Maguncia:* Mainz, German city on the left bank of the Rhine River.

[9] *between the great Trapobana . . . beyond Cape Comorin:* The fictitious kingdom is situated somewhere in the Indian Ocean near Sri Lanka (Trapobana) and the tip of the Indian subcontinent (Cape Comorin).

[10] *Archipiela:* shortened form of *archipiélago* (archipelago).

[11] *Antonomasia:* figure of speech in which a quality of a person stands in for his name, such as "The Bard" for Shakespeare.

[12] *envious Fates and hard-hearted sisters three have cut the thread of her life:* The Fates span Western mythologies but are most known in Greek sources as the three sister goddesses who weave the destiny of each human on a loom from birth to death.

[13] *private gentleman:* nobleman who does not hold a political office.

of so great beauty, trusting to his youth, his gallant bearing, his numerous accomplishments and graces, and his quickness and readiness of wit. For I may tell your highnesses, if I am not wearying you, that he played the guitar so as to make it speak, and he was, besides, a poet and a great dancer, and he could make birdcages so well that, by making them alone, he might have gained a livelihood had he found himself reduced to utter poverty. Gifts and graces of this kind are enough to bring down a mountain, not to say a tender young girl. But all his gallantry, wit, and gaiety, all his graces and accomplishments, would have been of little or no avail towards gaining the fortress of my pupil had not the impudent thief taken the precaution of gaining me over first.

"The villain and heartless vagabond first sought to win my goodwill and purchase my compliance so as to get me, like a treacherous warden, to deliver up to him the keys of the fortress I had in charge. In a word, he gained an influence over my mind and overcame my resolutions with I know not what trinkets and jewels he gave me. But it was some verses I heard him singing one night from a grated window that opened on the street where he lived, that, more than anything else, made me give way and led to my fall. If I remember rightly, they ran thus:

From that sweet enemy of mine
  My bleeding heart hath had its wound;
  And to increase the pain I'm bound
To suffer and to make no sign.[14]

"The lines seemed pearls to me and his voice sweet as syrup. Afterwards (I may say ever since then, looking at the misfortune into which I have fallen), I have thought that poets, as Plato advised, ought to be banished from all well-ordered states[15]—at least the amatory ones, for they write verses, not like those about the Marquis of Mantua,[16] that delight and draw tears from the women and children, but subtle conceits that pierce the heart like soft thorns, and like the lightning strike it, leaving one's clothing unharmed.

"Another time he sang:

Come Death, so subtly veiled that I
  Thy coming know not, how or when,
  Lest it should give me life again
To find how sweet it is to die.[17]

—and other verses and love songs of the same kind, which enchant when sung and fascinate when written. And what shall I say when they condescend to

[14] *From that sweet enemy . . . make no sign:* fragment of a late fifteenth-century poem, popular in Spanish translation, by the Italian Serafino de' Ciminelli.

[15] *as Plato advised . . . well-ordered states:* from Books III and X of the *Republic.*

[16] *those about the Marquis of Mantua:* the ballad that Don Quixote acts out in his delirium of Part I, chapter 5.

[17] *Come Death . . . sweet it is to die:* adapted from a poem by the Comendador Juan Escrivá, published in the *Cancionero general* (1511).

compose a sort of verse that was at that time in vogue in Candaya, which they call seguidillas?[18] Then hearts leap, laughter breaks forth, the body grows restless, and all the senses turn quicksilver. And so I say, sirs, that these troubadours richly deserve to be banished to the Isles of Lizards.[19] Though it is not they that are at fault, but the simpletons that extol them and the fools that believe in them. Had I been the faithful dueña I should have been, his stale conceits would have never moved me, nor should I have been taken in by such phrases as 'in death I live,' 'in ice I burn,' 'in flames I shiver,' 'hopeless I hope,' 'I go and stay,' and paradoxes of that sort which their writings are full of. And then when they promise the Phœnix of Arabia, the crown of Ariadne, the horses of the Sun, the pearls of the South, the gold of Tibar, and the balsam of Panchaia![20] Then do they let their pens fly, for it costs them little to make promises they have no intention or power of fulfilling.

"But where am I wandering to? Woe is me, unfortunate being! What madness or folly leads me to speak of the faults of others when there is so much to be said about my own? Again, woe is me, hapless that I am! It was not poetry that conquered me, but my own simplicity; it was not music that made me yield, but my own imprudence. My great ignorance and little caution opened the way and cleared the path for Don Clavijo's advances—for that was the name of the gentleman I have referred to. And so, with my help as go-between, he found his way many a time into the chamber of the deceived Antonomasia (deceived not by him but by me) under the title of a lawful husband; for sinner though I was, I would not have allowed him to approach the edge of the sole of her slippers without being her husband. No, no, not that! Marriage must come first in any business of the kind that I oversee.

"There was one difficulty in this case, which was that of inequality of rank—Don Clavijo being a private gentleman and Princess Antonomasia, as I said, heiress to the kingdom. The entanglement remained for some time a secret, kept hidden by my cunning precautions, until I noticed a certain expansion of waist in Antonomasia that must before long reveal it, the dread of which made us all there take counsel together. It was agreed that before the mischief came to light, Don Clavijo should ask Antonomasia to be his wife before the vicar,[21] in the form of a written agreement made by the princess she become his lawful spouse—this drafted by my intellect in such binding terms that the might of Samson could not have broken it. The necessary steps were taken; the vicar saw the

[18] *seguidillas:* See footnote 5, page 564.

[19] *Isles of Lizards:* fanciful deserted islands.

[20] *the crown of Ariadne . . . pearls of the south, the gold of Tibar, and the balsam of Panchaia:* Each is a mythical prize of renown: the crown of Ariadne is the constellation of seven stars that Venus gave Ariadne on marrying her son Bacchus; the pearls of the South are pearls from the Indian Ocean; the gold of Tibar is Arabian gold, considered the finest in the world; the balsam of Panchaia is the utopian island from ancient Greek history, perhaps present-day Bahrain. On the horses of the Sun, see footnote 8, page 354.

[21] *vicar:* representative of an ecclesiastic of superior rank.

agreement and took the lady's confession. She openly confessed, and he ordered her into the custody of a very worthy bailiff of the court."[22]

"Are there bailiffs in the court of Candaya, too," said Sancho at this, "and poets and seguidillas? I swear, the world must be the same all over. But hurry up, Señora Trifaldi. It's late, and I'm dying to know the end of this long story."

"I will," replied the countess.

[22] *he ordered her into the custody of a very worthy bailiff of the court:* Prior to the Council of Trent's *Tametsi* decree (1563) outlawing clandestine marriage, the freely given promise to marry made by the contracting man and woman constituted a valid marriage in the eyes of the Church. Litigation arose when one party—typically the woman or her family—alleged that the marriage had been entered into under compulsion, which could expose the man to charges of seduction and kidnapping. After Princess Antonomasia makes the declaration that she has entered into the marriage freely, she is placed in custody for her protection so that the investigation can proceed without the risk of Don Clavijo abducting her.

CHAPTER XXXIX

IN WHICH TRIFALDI CONTINUES HER MARVELOUS AND MEMORABLE STORY

By every word that Sancho uttered, the duchess was as much delighted as Don Quixote was driven to desperation. He ordered him to hold his tongue, and La Dolorida went on to say:

"At length, after much questioning and answering, as the princess held to her story without changing or varying her previous declaration, the vicar gave his decision in favor of Don Clavijo, and she was delivered over to him as his lawful wife—which Queen Doña Maguncia, Princess Antonomasia's mother, so took to heart that within the space of three days we buried her."

"She died, no doubt," said Sancho.

"Obviously," said Trifaldín. "They don't bury living people in Candaya, only the dead."

"Señor Squire," said Sancho, "a man in a swoon has been known to be buried before now in the belief that he was dead. It struck me that Queen Maguncia ought to have swooned rather than died, for in life a great many things may be remedied, and the princess' folly was not so great that she needed to react so strongly. If the lady had married some page of hers or some other servant of the house, as many others have done (so I've heard), then the mischief would have been past curing. But to marry such an elegant, accomplished gentleman as has been just now described to us—even if, even if it was foolish, it was not as foolish as you think. For according to the rules of my master here—and he won't let me tell a lie—just as men of letters can rise to be bishops, so gentlemen knights, especially if they are errant, can rise to be kings and emperors."

"You are right, Sancho," said Don Quixote. "With a knight-errant, if he has but two fingers' breadth of good fortune, he has the potential to become the mightiest lord on earth. But let Señora La Dolorida proceed. I suspect that she has yet to tell us the bitter part of this so far sweet story."

"The bitter is indeed to come," said the countess, "and so bitter that wolfsbane is sweet and oleander savory in comparison.[1] The queen, then, being dead and not in a swoon, we buried her. Hardly had we covered her with earth, hardly had we said our last farewells, when—*quis talia fando temperet a lachrymis?*[2]—

[1] *wolfsbane is sweet and oleander savory in comparison:* Wolfsbane and oleander are highly toxic if ingested.

[2] quis talia fando temperet a lachrymis?: "Who, in speaking of such things, could hold back his tears?" (*Aeneid* II, 6–8).

over the queen's grave there appeared, mounted upon a wooden horse, the giant Malambruno, Maguncia's first cousin, who besides being cruel is an enchanter. He, to revenge the death of his cousin, punish the audacity of Don Clavijo, and in wrath at the insolence of Antonomasia, left them both enchanted by his art on the grave itself—she being changed into a bronze ape and he into a terrifying crocodile of some unknown metal, while between the two there stands a pillar, also of metal, with certain characters in the Syriac language[3] inscribed upon it. These being translated into Candayan, and now into Castilian, contain the following sentence:

> THE TWO RASH LOVERS SHALL NOT RECOVER THEIR FORMER SHAPE UNTIL THE VALIANT MANCHEGAN COMES TO DO BATTLE WITH ME IN SINGLE COMBAT. THE FATES RESERVE THIS UNPARALLELED ADVENTURE FOR HIS MIGHTY VALOR ALONE.

"This done, he drew from its sheath a huge, broad scimitar, and seizing me by the hair, he made as though he meant to cut my throat and shear my head clean off. I was terror-stricken, my voice stuck in my throat, and I was in the deepest distress. Nevertheless, I summoned up my strength as well as I could, and in a trembling and piteous voice I addressed such words to him as induced him to stay the infliction of a punishment so severe. He then caused all the dueñas of the palace—those that are here present—to be brought before him; and after having dwelt upon the enormity of our offense and denounced dueñas, their characters, their evil ways and worse intrigues—laying to the charge of all what I alone was guilty of—he said he would not inflict on us the penalty of death, but with another punishment of a slow nature which would be in effect civil death[4] forever. The very instant he ceased speaking, we all felt the pores of our faces opening and pricking us, as if with the points of needles. We at once put our hands to our faces and found ourselves in the state you now see."

Here La Dolorida and the other dueñas raised the veils with which they were covered and revealed faces all bristling with beards, some red, some black, some white, and some grizzled, at which spectacle the duke and duchess made a show of being filled with wonder. Don Quixote and Sancho were overwhelmed with amazement and the bystanders lost in astonishment, while Trifaldi went on to say: "Thus did that malevolent villain Malambruno punish us, covering the tenderness and softness of our faces with these rough bristles. Would to Heaven he had swept off our heads with his enormous scimitar instead of obscuring the light of our countenances with these wool-combings that cover us! For if we consider the matter carefully, sirs—and what I am now going to say I would say with eyes flowing like fountains, only that the thought of our misfortune and the oceans they have already wept keep them as dry as barley spears, and so I say it without tears—where, I ask, is a dueña with a beard to go? What father or mother will pity her? Who will help her? If even when she has smooth skin and

[3] *Syriac language:* Aramaic language in which early Christian texts are preserved, hence its archaic mystique.

[4] *civil death:* here, a miserable existence. See footnote 17, page 164.

a face tortured by a thousand kinds of washes and cosmetics, she can hardly get anyone to love her, what will she do when she reveals a face turned into a forest? Oh dueñas, my companions! It was an unlucky day when we were born and an ill-starred hour when our fathers begot us!"

And as she said this, she showed signs of being about to faint.

CHAPTER XL

OF MATTERS TOUCHING ON THIS ADVENTURE AND MEMORABLE HISTORY

Verily and truly, all those who find pleasure in histories like this one ought to show their gratitude to Cide Hamete, its original author, for the scrupulous care he has taken to set before us all its minute particulars, not leaving anything (however insignificant it may be) that he does not make clear and plain. He portrays the thoughts, he reveals the aspirations, he answers implied questions, clears up doubts, sets objections at rest, and, in a word, makes plain the smallest points the most inquisitive can desire to know. O renowned author! O happy Don Quixote! O illustrious Dulcinea! O comical Sancho! All and each, may you endure countless ages for the delight and amusement of those here living!

The history goes on to say that when Sancho saw La Dolorida faint, he exclaimed, "I swear by the faith of an honest man and the eternal glory of all my ancestors the Panzas—never did I see or hear of, nor has my master related or conceived in his mind, such an adventure like this. By a thousand devils (not to curse you for being an enchanter and a giant),[1] could you find no other punishment for these sinners besides bearding them? Would it not have been better—it would have been better for them—to have taken off half their noses from the middle upwards, even though they'd have snuffled when they spoke, than to have put beards on them? I'll bet they don't have the means of paying anybody to shave them."

"That is the truth, señor," said one of the twelve. "We have not the money to get ourselves shaved, and so some of us have taken to using sticking-plasters and adhesive patches as an economical remedy, for by applying them to our faces and plucking them off with a jerk we are left as bare and smooth as the bottom of a stone mortar. There are, to be sure, women in Candaya that go about from house to house to remove down, trim eyebrows, and make cosmetics for the use of the women, but we, the dueñas of my lady, would never let them in, for most of them give off the stench of go-betweens, being past their prime as principals.[2] If we are not relieved by Señor Don Quixote, we shall be carried to our graves with beards."

"I will pluck out my own in the land of the Moors," said Don Quixote, "if I don't cure yours."

[1] *By a thousand devils . . . and a giant:* The accustomed oath is "By God." Sancho may be hesitant to curse someone with occult power.

[2] *stench of go-betweens . . . as principals:* Too old to be the protagonists of love affairs (perhaps as prostitutes), they now work as procuresses.

At this moment Trifaldi recovered from her swoon and said, "The ring of that promise, valiant knight, reached my ears in the midst of my swoon and has been the means of reviving me and bringing back my senses. And so once more I implore you, illustrious errant, indomitable sir, to let your gracious promises be turned into deeds."

"There shall be no delay on my part," said Don Quixote. "Resolve what I must do, señora, for my heart is most eager to serve you."

"It is the case," replied La Dolorida, "that it is five thousand leagues (a couple more or less) from here to the kingdom of Candaya if you go by land; but if you go through the air and in a straight line, it is three thousand two hundred and twenty-seven. You must know, too, that Malambruno told me that whenever fate provided the knight our deliverer, he himself would send him a steed far better and with fewer defects than a horse for hire. For it will be that same wooden horse on which the valiant Pierres carried off the fair Magalona. The said horse is guided by a peg he has in his forehead that serves for a bridle, and flies through the air with such rapidity that you would think the very devils were carrying him. According to ancient tradition, this horse was made by Merlin. He lent him to Pierres, who was a friend of his and who made long journeys with him and, as has been said, carried off the fair Magalona, bearing her through the air on its haunches and making all who beheld them from the earth gape with astonishment. Merlin never lent him save to those whom he loved or those who paid him well. Since the great Pierres, we know of no one having mounted him until now.[3]

"From him Malambruno stole this horse by his magic art, and he has him now in his possession. He makes use of him in his journeys which he constantly makes through different parts of the world. He is here today, tomorrow in France, and the next day in Potosí.[4] The best of it is the said horse neither eats nor sleeps nor wears out shoes, and goes at an ambling pace through the air without wings, so that he whom he has mounted upon him can carry a cup full of water in his hand without spilling a drop, so smoothly and easily does he go, for which reason the fair Magalona enjoyed riding him greatly."

"For going smoothly and easily," said Sancho at this, "give me my Dapple, though he can't go through the air. But on the ground, I'll back him against all the amblers in the world."

They all laughed, and La Dolorida continued, "This same horse—if it be that Malambruno is disposed to put an end to our sufferings—will be here before us ere the night shall have advanced half an hour; for he announced to me that the sign he would give me whereby I might know that I had found the knight I was in quest of would be to send me the horse wherever he might be, speedily and promptly."

[3] *For it will be that same wooden horse . . . until now:* Trifaldi's story draws primarily on Adenet le Roi's *Cleomadès* (late thirteenth century), translated into Spanish in the sixteenth century as *Historia del valeroso caballero Clamades y la hermosa Clarmonda*, which features an escape on a flying wooden horse. It also echoes motifs from *The History of Pierres of Provence and the Fair Magalona*, a romance involving the lovers' escape on horseback.

[4] *Potosí:* city in present-day Bolivia, famed for nearby silver mines.

"And how many is there room for on this horse?" asked Sancho.

"Two," said La Dolorida, "one in the saddle, and the other on the haunches. Generally, these two are knight and squire, when there is no damsel that is being carried off."

"I'd like to know, Señora Dolorida," said Sancho, "what is the name of this horse?"

"His name," said La Dolorida, "is not the same as Bellerophon's horse that was called Pegasus; or Alexander the Great's, called Bucephalus; or Orlando Furioso's, the name of which was Brigliador; nor yet Bayard, the horse of Reinaldos of Montalban; nor Frontino like Ruggiero's; nor Bootes or Peritoa, as they say the horses of the sun were called;[5] nor is he called Orelia, like the horse on which the unfortunate Rodrigo, the last king of the Goths, rode to battle where he lost his life and his kingdom."[6]

"I'll bet," said Sancho, "that since they haven't given him one of these famous names of well-known horses, they haven't given him the name of my master's, Rocinante, which for being suitable to the purpose, surpasses every one that's been mentioned."

"That is true," said the bearded countess. "Still, it fits him very well, for he is called Clavileño[7] the Swift, which name is in accordance with his being made of wood, with the peg he has in his forehead, and with the swift pace at which he travels. And so, as far as a name goes, he may compare with the famous Rocinante."

"I have nothing to say against his name," said Sancho. "But with what sort of bridle or halter is he managed?"

"I have said already," said the Trifaldi, "that it is with a peg, by turning which to one side or the other the knight who rides him makes him go as he pleases, either through the upper air, or skimming and almost sweeping the earth, or else in that middle course that is sought and followed in all well-ordered actions."[8]

"I'd like to see him," said Sancho. "But to think I'm going to mount him, either in the saddle or on the haunches, is to ask pears of the elm tree. A fine joke that is! I can hardly keep my seat on Dapple, and on a packsaddle softer than silk itself, and here they'd have me hold on to wooden haunches without any pad or cushion! By God, I have no intention of bruising myself to get rid of anyone's beard. Let each one shave himself as best he can. I'm not going to accompany my master on any such long journey. Anyway, I can give no more help to shaving these beards than I can to disenchanting my lady Dulcinea."

[5] *Bootes or Peritoa, as they say the horses of the sun were called:* The names given for the horses pulling Phaeton's chariot do not match those found in sources like Ovid. "Bootes" is in reference to "Boötes", a constellation associated in Greek mythology with the plow. "Peritoa" may be a corruption of "Pirithous", friend of the hero Theseus.

[6] *Rodrigo . . . life and his kingdom:* Rodrigo's horse is given a name in early modern Spanish ballads.

[7] *Clavileño: clavija* (peg); *leño* (wood).

[8] *that middle course . . . well-ordered actions:* Classical moral theory, most prominent in Aristotle, advocated the *via media*, or golden mean—a life lived in moderation.

"Yes, you can, my friend," replied Trifaldi, "and so much, that without you, so I understand, we shall be able to do nothing."

"In the king's name!" exclaimed Sancho. "What do squires have to do with the adventures of their masters? Do they get all the fame for their accomplishments, while we get stuck with the work? On my body! If the historians would only say, 'Such-and-such a knight finished such and such an adventure, but with the help of so-and-so, his squire, without which it would have been impossible for him to accomplish it.' But no, they just write, 'Don Paralipomenon[9] of the Three Stars accomplished the adventure of the six monsters,' without mentioning any such person as his squire—who was there the whole time—just as if he didn't exist. Once more, sirs, I say that my master can go alone, and much good may it do him. I'll stay here in the company of my lady the duchess. Maybe when he comes back, he will find Señora Dulcinea's cause well advanced, for in my free time, I intend to give myself such a whipping that the hair won't grow back over the scars."

"For all that, you must go if it is necessary, my good Sancho," said the duchess, "for they are worthy people who ask you. These ladies must not be left with bushy faces because of your idle fears. That would be a terrible outcome."

"In the king's name, once more!" said Sancho. "If this charitable work were to be done for the sake of orphan girls or damsels in confinement, a man might expose himself to some hardships. But to bear it for the sake of stripping beards off dueñas? Devil take it! I'd sooner see them all bearded, from the highest to the lowest, and from the most prim and proper to the sauciest."

"You are very hard on dueñas, Sancho my friend," said the duchess. "You incline very much to the opinion of the Toledo apothecary, but you are quite wrong to do so. There are dueñas in my house that may serve as paragons of dueñas. Here is my Doña Rodríguez, who will not allow me to say otherwise."

"Your excellency may say it if you like," said Rodríguez, "for God knows the truth of everything. Whether we dueñas are good or bad, bearded or smooth, we are our mothers' daughters like other women. As God sent us into the world, he knows why he did. On his mercy I rely, and not on anybody's beard."

"Well, Señora Rodríguez, Señora Trifaldi, and present company," said Don Quixote, "I trust in Heaven that it will look with kindly eyes upon your troubles, for Sancho will do as I bid him. Only let Clavileño come, and let me find myself face to face with Malambruno—I am certain no razor will shave you more easily than my sword shall shave Malambruno's head off his shoulders. 'God bears with the wicked, but not for ever.'"

"Ah!" cried La Dolorida at this. "May all the stars of the celestial regions look down upon your greatness with benign eyes, valiant knight, and shed all prosperity and courage upon your heart, that it may be the shield and safeguard of the abused and downtrodden race of dueñas, detested by apothecaries, sneered at by squires, and tricked by pages. A pox upon the hussy that in the flower of

[9] *Paralipomenon:* In the Latin Vulgate, First and Second Chronicles are known by their Greek name, the Books of Paralipomenon.

her youth would not sooner become a nun than a dueña! Unfortunate beings that we are, we dueñas! Though we may be descended in the direct male line from Hector of Troy himself, our mistresses never fail to address us as inferiors[10] if they think it makes queens of them. O giant Malambruno, though you are an enchanter, you are true to your promises. Send us now the peerless Clavileño, that our misfortune may be brought to an end; for if the hot weather sets in and these beards of ours are still there, alas for our lot!"

Trifaldi said this in such a pathetic way that she drew tears from the eyes of everyone. Even Sancho's filled up. And he resolved in his heart to accompany his master to the uttermost ends of the earth, if doing so were necessary to remove the wool from those venerable faces.

[10] *address us as inferiors:* literally, "use *vos* with us", the second-person singular form directed to social inferiors. See footnote 11, page 148.

CHAPTER XLI

OF THE ARRIVAL OF CLAVILEÑO AND THE END OF THIS PROTRACTED ADVENTURE

Night came, and with it the appointed time for the arrival of the famous horse Clavileño. His delay was already beginning to make Don Quixote uneasy, for it struck him that, as Malambruno was so long about sending it, either he himself was not the knight for whom the adventure was reserved, or else Malambruno did not dare to meet him in single combat.

But lo! Suddenly there came into the garden four wild men all clad in green ivy and carrying on their shoulders a great wooden horse. They placed it on its feet on the ground, then one of the wild men said, "Let the knight who has the courage to mount this machine do so."

Here Sancho exclaimed, "Don't expect me to mount it, for I don't have the courage, and I'm not a knight."

"And let the squire, if he has one," continued the wild man, "take his seat on its haunches, and let him trust the valiant Malambruno; for by no sword save his, nor by the malice of any other, shall he be assailed. He has but to turn this peg in the horse's neck, and it will bear them through the air to where Malambruno awaits them. But lest the vast elevation of their course should make them giddy, their eyes must be covered until the horse neighs, which will be the sign of their having completed their journey." With these words, leaving Clavileño behind them, the wild men withdrew with the same dignified bearing as when they entered.

As soon as La Dolorida saw the horse, she exclaimed almost in tears to Don Quixote, "Valiant knight, the promise of Malambruno has proved trustworthy. The horse has come, our beards are growing, and by every hair in them we here implore you to shave and shear us, as you need do no more than mount him with your squire and make a happy beginning with your new journey."

"That I will do, Señora Countess Trifaldi," said Don Quixote. "Most gladly and with right goodwill, without delaying for a cushion or to put on my spurs so as not to lose time. Such is my desire to see you and all these dueñas shaved clean."

"That I won't do," said Sancho, "with goodwill or bad will or any will at all. If this shaving can't be done without my climbing onto this horse's haunches, my master had better look for another squire to go with him, and these ladies for some other way of making their faces smooth. I'm no witch to have a taste for flying through the air. What would my islanders say when they heard their governor was strolling out and about on the winds? And another thing, seeing that it's three thousand something leagues from here to Candaya, if the horse gets tired, or the giant loses his temper, it will take us half a dozen years to get back, and there won't be an isle or island in the world that will recognize me. And so as it is a common saying 'in delay there's danger,' and 'when they offer you a heifer, run with a halter,' these ladies' beards must excuse me. 'Saint Peter is very well in Rome'—what I mean is, I'm quite content to stay in this house and be treated to one favor after another, which I hope will end with the master of it making me a governor."

"Friend Sancho," said the duke at this, "the island that I have promised you will neither run off nor vanish. It has roots so deeply buried in the bowels of the earth that it will be no easy matter to pluck it up or shift it from where it is. You know as well as I do that there is no sort of office of any importance that is not obtained by a payment of some kind, great or small. Well then, the payment I look to receive for this government is that you go with your master Don Quixote and bring this memorable adventure to a conclusion. Whether you return on Clavileño as quickly as his speed seems to promise or adverse fortune brings you back on foot traveling as a pilgrim from hostel to hostel and from inn to inn, you will always find your island upon your return where you left it, your islanders with the same eagerness they have always had to receive you as their governor, and me with the same goodwill as ever. Doubt not the truth of this, Señor Sancho, for to do so would be to do a grievous wrong to my desire to serve you."

"Say no more, señor," said Sancho. "I am a poor squire and not one to carry around so many courtesies unreturned. Let my master mount it, then put a blindfold over my eyes and commit me to God's care. Just let me know whether I should commend myself to our Lord or call on the angels to protect me once we go soaring up into the sky."[1]

To this Trifaldi answered, "Sancho, you may freely commend yourself to God or whomever you like; for though he is an enchanter, Malambruno is a Christian and works his enchantments with great sagacity, taking very good care not to provoke anyone."

"Well then," said Sancho, "may God and the most holy Trinity of Gaeta[2] be my help!"

"Since the memorable adventure of the fulling mills," said Don Quixote, "I have never seen Sancho in such a fright as now. Were I as superstitious as others, his abject fear would cause me some little trepidation of spirit. But come here, Sancho, for with the leave of these gentlemen and ladies, I would say a word or two to you in private."

Drawing Sancho aside among the trees of the garden and seizing both his hands he said, "You see now, brother Sancho, the long journey we have before us. God knows when we shall return or what leisure or opportunities this enterprise will allow us. I wish you therefore to retire now to your chamber, as

[1] *Just let me know . . . into the sky:* Sancho is concerned that invoking God's aid directly will nullify the witchcraft powering Clavileño's flight.

[2] *the most holy Trinity of Gaeta:* See footnote 11, page 552.

though you were going to fetch something required for the road, and in short order give yourself but five hundred lashes of the three thousand three hundred to which you are bound; it will be all to the good. To make a beginning of something is to have it half finished."

"By God," said Sancho, "your worship must be out of your senses! This is like the saying, 'You see me pregnant, and you want me a virgin.' Just as I'm about to go sitting on a bare board, your worship wants me to flay my backside! What your worship is asking is unreasonable. Let's be off to shave these dueñas. On our return, I give you my word that I will fulfill my obligation, and do it so quickly that I'll make you a happy man. I can say no more."

"Well, I will comfort myself with that promise, my good Sancho," replied Don Quixote, "and I believe you will keep it; for indeed, though you are stupid, your honesty is unimpeachable."

"I'm not a peach," said Sancho; "I'm well-tanned. But even if I was somewhere in between, I'd still keep my word."

With this they went back to mount Clavileño, and as they were about to do so Don Quixote said, "Cover your eyes, Sancho and mount; for one who sends for us from lands so far distant cannot mean to deceive us for the sake of the paltry glory to be derived from deceiving persons who trust in him. Though all should turn out to the contrary of what I hope, no malice will be able to dim the glory of having undertaken this exploit."

"Let's be off, señor," said Sancho, "for I've taken the beards and tears of these ladies deeply to heart. I swear off every tasty morsel until I've seen them restored to their former smoothness. Mount, your worship, and blindfold yourself, for if I'm to go on its haunches, it's plain that the rider in the saddle must mount first."

"That is true," said Don Quixote, and taking a handkerchief out of his pocket, he begged La Dolorida to cover his eyes very carefully. But after having the blindfold put on he removed it, saying, "If my memory does not deceive me, I have read in Virgil of the Palladium of Troy, a wooden horse the Greeks offered to the goddess Pallas, which carried a brood of armed knights who were afterwards the destruction of Troy.[3] It would be as well to see first what Clavileño has in his stomach."

"There is no occasion," said La Dolorida. "I will vouch for him, and I know that Malambruno has nothing tricky or treacherous about him. You may mount without any fear, Señor Don Quixote. May it be on my head if any harm befalls you."

Don Quixote thought that to say anything further with regard to his safety would be putting his courage in an unfavorable light; and so, without further debate, he mounted Clavileño and tried the peg, which turned easily. As he

[3] *I have read . . . of Troy:* Don Quixote's memory does not serve him well here. The Palladium was not the wooden horse but a sacred image of Pallas Athena that was believed to safeguard Troy while it remained in the city. According to tradition, Odysseus and Diomedes stole the wooden statue before the city fell. Athena did lend the Athenians the art to build the wooden horse, which was presented to her as a votive offering.

had no stirrups and his legs hung down, he looked like a figure painted in some Roman triumph or embroidered on a Flemish tapestry.[4]

Quite reluctantly and very slowly, Sancho proceeded to mount. After settling himself as well as he could on the horse's haunches, he found them rather hard and not at all soft. He asked the duke if it would be possible to oblige him with a pad of some kind or a cushion—even if it came from his lady's dais or the bed of one of the pages—as the haunches of that horse were more like marble than wood. On this Trifaldi observed that Clavileño would not bear any kind of harness or trappings, and that his best plan would be to sit sidesaddle, as in that way he would not feel the hardness so much.

Sancho did so, and bidding them farewell, allowed a blindfold to be put over his eyes. But immediately afterwards he uncovered them again and, looking tenderly and tearfully on those in the garden, asked them to help him in his present trial, each with a Paternoster and an Ave Maria, so that God would provide people to pray for them if they found themselves in another such strait.

At this Don Quixote exclaimed, "Are you on the gallows, thief, or drawing your final breath, to use pitiful entreaties of that sort? Cowardly, spiritless creature, are you not in the very place the fair Magalona occupied and from which she descended, not into the grave but to become queen of France, unless the histories lie? And I who am here beside you, may I not put myself on par with the valiant Pierres, who pressed this very spot that I now press? Cover your eyes, cover your eyes, abject animal, and let not your fear escape your lips, at least in my presence."

"Blindfold me," said Sancho. "Since you won't let me commend myself or be commended to God, is it any wonder if I'm afraid there is a legion of devils around here that is going to carry us off to Peralvillo?"[5]

They were then blindfolded, and Don Quixote, finding himself settled to his satisfaction, felt for the peg. As soon as he placed his fingers on it, all the dueñas and everyone who stood by lifted up their voices exclaiming, "God guide you, valiant knight! God be with you, intrepid squire! Up, up! Cleave the air more swiftly than an arrow! Now begin to amaze and astonish all who are gazing at you from the earth! Hold on tight, valiant Sancho—you're tottering! Be careful not to fall off, for your fall will be worse than that rash youth's who tried to steer the chariot of his father the Sun!"[6]

As Sancho heard the voices, clinging tightly to his master and winding his arms round him, he said, "Señor, how can they say that we're going up so high, if their voices reach us here and they seem to be right next to us?"

[4] *he had no stirrups . . . on a Flemish tapestry:* Stirrups did not come into use until the time of Charlemagne.

[5] *Peralvillo:* The village of Peralvillo in La Mancha was one of the sites where the Holy Brotherhood executed criminals.

[6] *that rash youth's who tried to steer the chariot of his father the Sun:* Phaeton, son of the sun god Helios, rashly attempted to drive his father's chariot across the sky. Lacking the proper skill to control the fiery horses, he veered too far from the earth, freezing some lands, and too close, scorching others into deserts. Zeus ended his flight with a lightning bolt, and his lifeless body plunged into the river Eridanus.

"Don't mind that, Sancho," said Don Quixote. "As affairs of this kind and flights like this are out of the common course of things, you can see and hear as much as you like a thousand leagues off. But don't squeeze me so tight, or you will upset me. I really don't know what you have to be uneasy or frightened about, for I can safely swear I never mounted a smoother-going steed all the days of my life. One would think we had never stirred from one place. Banish fear, my friend, for indeed everything is going as it ought, and we have the wind astern."

"That's true," said Sancho, "for such a strong wind comes against me on this side that it seems as if people were blowing on me with a thousand pair of bellows." Which was the case: they were puffing at him with a great pair of bellows. For the whole adventure was so well planned by the duke, the duchess, and their majordomo that nothing was left out to make it perfectly successful.

Don Quixote, now feeling the blast, said, "Beyond a doubt, Sancho, we must have already reached the second region of the air, where the hail and snow are generated. The thunder, the lightning, and the thunderbolts are engendered in the third region, and if we go on ascending at this rate, we shall shortly plunge into the region of fire.[7] I know not how to regulate this peg so as not to mount up where we shall be burned."

And now they began to warm their faces from a distance with tow[8] (which could be easily set on fire and extinguished again) attached to the end of a cane. On feeling the heat Sancho said, "May I die if we're not already in that fiery place, or very close to it, for a good part of my beard has been singed. I have a mind, señor, to take off my blindfold and see where it is we are."

"Do nothing of the kind," said Don Quixote. "Remember the true story of the licentiate Torralba, who, by devilish power, went flying through the air on a stick while his eyes were shut. In twelve hours, he reached Rome and dismounted at Tor di Nona (which is a street in the city), and saw the whole sack and storming and the death of Bourbon, and was back in Madrid the next morning, where he gave an account of all he had seen.[9] He said, moreover, that as he was going through the air, the devil bade him open his eyes; he did so and saw himself so near the body of the moon—so it seemed to him—that he could have laid hold of it with his hand, and that he did not dare to look at the earth lest he should be seized with dizziness. So that, Sancho, it will not do for us to remove our blindfolds, for he who has us in charge will be responsible for us. Perhaps we are gaining in altitude and mounting up to enable us to descend at one swoop on the

[7] *second region of the air ... region of fire:* A popular interpretation of the Ptolemaic cosmos conceived of the sublunar realm (the atmosphere from the earth to the moon) as successive regions of air, cold, water, and fire.

[8] *tow:* loose fibers of flax, hemp, or jute, which were used in ropemaking, upholstery, and paper production.

[9] *licentiate Torralba ... all he had seen:* Dr. Eugenio Torralba, a physician from Cuenca, was investigated by the Inquisition for sorcery after he claimed to have traveled through the air to see the Sack of Rome, a brutal event in which imperial forces under Charles V looted the city on May 6, 1527. Charles III, Duke of Bourbon, an imperial general, was killed while scaling the city walls.

kingdom of Candaya, as the falcon does on the heron so as to seize it, however high it may soar. And though it seems to us not half an hour since we left the garden, believe me we must have traveled a great distance."

"I don't know how that can be," said Sancho. "All I know is that if Señora Magellan or Magalona was satisfied with these haunches, she must not have had a very tender body."

The duke, the duchess, and all in the garden were listening to the conversation of the two heroes and were beyond measure amused by it. Desirous now to put the finishing touch on this rare and well-contrived adventure, they set fire to Clavileño's tail with some tow. The horse, being full of firecrackers, immediately blew up with a prodigious noise and brought Don Quixote and Sancho Panza to the ground half singed.

By this time, the bearded band of dueñas—Trifaldi and all—had vanished from the garden. Those that remained lay stretched out on the ground as if in a swoon. Don Quixote and Sancho got up rather shaken and, looking around, were filled with amazement at finding themselves in the same garden from which they had started, with so many people lying on the ground. Their astonishment was increased when at one side of the garden they observed a tall lance planted in the ground, and hanging from it by two cords of green silk a smooth white parchment on which there was the following inscription in large gold letters:

> THE ILLUSTRIOUS KNIGHT DON QUIXOTE OF LA MANCHA HAS, BY MERELY ATTEMPTING IT, BROUGHT TO A CONCLUSION THE ADVENTURE OF COUNTESS TRIFALDI, OTHERWISE CALLED THE DISTRESSED DUEÑA. MALAMBRUNO IS NOW SATISFIED ON EVERY POINT, THE CHINS OF THE DUEÑAS ARE NOW SMOOTH AND CLEAN, AND KING DON CLAVIJO AND QUEEN ANTONOMASIA ARE IN THEIR ORIGINAL FORM. WHEN THE SQUIRELY FLAGELLATION SHALL HAVE BEEN COMPLETED, THE WHITE DOVE SHALL FIND HERSELF DELIVERED FROM THE PESTIFEROUS FALCONS THAT PERSECUTE HER AND IN THE ARMS OF HER BELOVED MATE. SUCH IS THE DECREE OF THE SAGE MERLIN, ARCH ENCHANTER OF ENCHANTERS.

As soon as Don Quixote had read the inscription on the parchment he understood clearly that it referred to the disenchantment of Dulcinea. Returning hearty thanks to Heaven that he had with so little danger achieved so grand an exploit as to restore to their former complexion the countenances of those venerable dueñas, he advanced towards the duke and duchess, who had not yet come to themselves.

Taking the duke by the hand, he said, "Be of good cheer, worthy sir, be of good cheer. All is over. The adventure has been completed and without any harm done, as the note attached to this post shows plainly."

The duke came to himself slowly, like one recovering consciousness after a heavy sleep. The duchess and all who had fallen to the ground around the garden did the same, with such demonstrations of wonder and amazement that they would have almost persuaded one that what they pretended so skillfully in jest had really happened to them. The duke read the placard with half-shut eyes and then ran to embrace Don Quixote with open arms, declaring him to be the best knight that had ever been seen in any age. Sancho kept looking around for La Dolorida to see what her face looked like without the beard, and if she was as lovely as her elegant person promised. But they told him that the instant Clavileño descended flaming through the air and came to the ground, the whole band of dueñas with Trifaldi vanished, and that they were already shaved, without so much as stubble left.

The duchess asked Sancho how he had fared on that long journey, to which Sancho replied, "I felt, señora, that we were flying through the region of fire, as my master told me, and I wanted to uncover my eyes for a bit; but my master, when I asked permission to take off my blindfold, wouldn't let me. But since I have a little bit of a curious streak and a wish to know things that are forbidden and kept from me, quietly and without anyone seeing me, I pulled the handkerchief that was covering my eyes just a little to the side, close to my nose, and from underneath looked towards the earth. It seemed to me that the whole thing was no bigger than a grain of mustard, and that the men walking on it were hardly any bigger than hazelnuts. So you can imagine how high we were at that point."

To this the duchess said, "Sancho, my friend, consider what you're saying. You must not have seen the earth, but only the men walking on it; for if the earth looked to you like a grain of mustard and each man like a hazelnut, one man alone would have covered the whole earth."

"That's true," said Sancho, "but for all that I got a glimpse of a bit of one side of it, and saw it all."

"Mind you, Sancho," said the duchess, "with a bit of one side, one does not see the whole of what one looks at."

"I don't know about that way of looking at things," said Sancho. "I only know that your ladyship will do well to keep in mind that since we were flying by enchantment, I might have seen the whole earth and all the men by enchantment whatever way I looked. If you won't believe this, you won't believe either how, lifting the blindfold almost to my eyebrows, I found myself so close to the sky that there wasn't a palm and a half between me and it. And by everything that I can swear by, señora, it's huge! It so happened we came near where the seven goats are,[10] and by God and upon my soul—being a goatherd back home in my younger days—as soon as I saw them, I had this itch to spend a little time with them. If I hadn't given into it, I think I'd have burst! So here I was, and what do you think I did? Without saying anything to anybody, not even to my master, slowly and without making a noise I got down from Clavileño and played with the goats—which are like violets, as pretty as flowers—for almost three-quarters of an hour. And Clavileño never stirred or moved from one spot."

"And while the good Sancho was playing with the goats," said the duke, "how did Señor Don Quixote entertain himself?"

To which Don Quixote replied, "As all these things and such like occurrences are out of the ordinary course of nature, it is no wonder that Sancho says what he does. For my own part, I can only say that I did not uncover my eyes either above or below, nor did I see sky or earth or sea or shore. It is true I felt that I was passing through the region of the air, and even that I touched that of fire; but

[10] *where the seven goats are:* the constellation Pleiades.

that we passed farther I cannot believe. For the region of fire being between the heaven of the moon and the last region of the air, we could not have reached that heaven where the seven goats that Sancho speaks of are without being burned. And as we were not burned, either Sancho is lying, or Sancho is dreaming."

"I am neither lying nor dreaming," said Sancho. "Just ask me what those goats looked like, and you'll see by that whether I'm telling the truth or not."

"Tell us then, Sancho," said the duchess.

"Two of them," said Sancho, "are green, two blood-red, two blue, and one a little bit of everything."

"That must be a new kind of goat," said the duke. "In this earthly region of ours we have no such colors—I mean goats of such colors."

"That's plain to see," said Sancho. "There's obviously a difference between the goats of heaven and the goats on earth."

"Tell me, Sancho," said the duke, "did you see any he-goat among those goats?"

"No, señor," said Sancho, "but I have heard it said that none ever went past the horns of the moon."[11]

They did not wish to ask him anything more about his journey, for they saw he was well on his way to go rambling all over the heavens giving an account of everything that went on there, without having ever stirred from the garden. Such, in short, was the end of the adventure of the Distressed Dueña, which gave the duke and duchess laughing matter not only for the time being, but for all their lives, and Sancho something to talk about for centuries, if he had lived so long.

But Don Quixote, coming close to him, said in a whisper, "Sancho, as you would have us believe what you saw in heaven, I would like you to believe me as to what I saw in the Cave of Montesinos. I say no more."

[11] *he-goat . . . horns of the moon:* The exchange between the duke and Sancho plays on the double entendre of "he-goat" (*cabrón*, cuckold) and "horns" (*cuernos*, the sign of a cuckold).

CHAPTER XLII

OF THE COUNSEL DON QUIXOTE GAVE SANCHO PANZA BEFORE HE SET OUT TO GOVERN THE ISLAND, TOGETHER WITH OTHER WELL-CONSIDERED MATTERS

The duke and duchess were so well pleased with the successful and comical result of the adventure of La Dolorida, that they resolved to carry on the joke, seeing what a fit subject they had to deal with for making it all pass for reality. So having laid their plans and given instructions to their servants and vassals how to deal with Sancho in his government of the promised island, the next day (the one following Clavileño's flight), the duke told Sancho to prepare himself to go and be governor, for his islanders were already looking out for him as for the showers of May.

Sancho knelt before him and said, "Ever since I came down from heaven, ever since I looked down from its height and beheld the earth and saw how little it is, the desire I once had to be a governor has not been nearly as strong. For what is grand about being ruler on a grain of mustard, or what dignity or authority is there in governing half a dozen men the size of hazelnuts (for as far as I could see, there were no more on the whole earth)? If your lordship would be so good as to give me the smallest bit of heaven, even if it was no more than half a league, I'd rather have that than the best island in the world."

"Recollect, Sancho," said the duke, "I cannot give a bit of heaven—no, not so much as the breadth of my nail—to anyone. Rewards and favors of that kind are reserved for God alone. What I can give, I give you—and that is a real, genuine island, compact, well proportioned, and uncommonly fertile and fruitful, where, if you know how to use your opportunities, you may, with the help of the world's riches, gain those of heaven."[1]

"Well then," said Sancho, "bring me the island. I'll try and be such a governor that, in spite of the scoundrels, I'll go to heaven. And it's not from any craving I have to step out of my proper place and better myself, but from a desire to find out what it tastes like to be a governor."

"Once you find out, Sancho," said the duke, "you'll eat your fingers off after the government,[2] so sweet a thing is it to command and be obeyed. Depend

[1] *if you know . . . gain those of heaven:* echo of the Parable of the Unjust Steward (Luke 16:1–9) and Parable of the Talents (Matthew 25:14–30).

[2] *you'll eat your fingers off after the government:* "You'll do your utmost."

upon it, when your master comes to be emperor (as he will beyond a doubt from the course his affairs are taking), it will be no easy matter to wrest the office from him, and he will be sore and sorry at heart to have been so long without becoming one."

"Señor," said Sancho, "it is my belief that it's a good thing to be in charge, even if it's only over a herd of cattle."

"May I be buried with you, Sancho,"[3] said the duke, "but you know everything. I hope you will make as good a governor as your sagacity promises. That is all I have to say. Now take note that tomorrow is the day you must set out for the government of the island. This evening they will provide you with the proper attire for you to wear, and all things requisite for your departure."

"Let them dress me how they want," said Sancho. "However I'm dressed, I'll be Sancho Panza."

"That's true," said the duke, "but one's dress must be suited to the office or rank one holds. It would not do for a jurist to dress like a soldier, or a soldier like a priest. You, Sancho, shall go partly as a lawyer, partly as a captain, for in the island I am giving you, arms are needed as much as letters, and letters as much as arms."

"I know very little about letters," said Sancho. "I don't even know my A B C's. But it will be enough for me to have the Christus[4] in my memory to be a good governor. As for arms, I'll handle those they give me till I drop, and then, God be my help!"

"With so good a memory," said the duke, "Sancho cannot go wrong in anything."

Here Don Quixote joined them; and learning what had passed, and how soon Sancho was to go to his government, he with the duke's permission took him by the hand and led him to his room for the purpose of giving him advice as to how he was to conduct himself in office. As soon as they had entered the chamber, he closed the door after him and almost by force made Sancho sit down at his side. In a calm voice, he addressed him:

"I give infinite thanks to Heaven, friend Sancho, that, before I have met with any good luck, fortune has come forward to meet you. I, who counted upon my good fortune to discharge the recompense of your services, find myself still waiting for advancement, while you, before the time and contrary to all reasonable expectation, see yourself blessed in the fulfillment of your desires. Some will bribe, beg, solicit, rise early, entreat, and persist, without attaining the object of their pursuit. Another comes, and without knowing why or wherefore, finds himself invested with the place or office so many have sought. It is here that the common saying applies, 'In every pursuit, there is good luck as well as bad luck.' You, who, to my thinking, are beyond all doubt a simpleton, without early rising or night watching or taking any trouble, with the mere breath of knight-errantry

[3] *May I be buried with you:* "You and I are of one mind."

[4] *Christus:* cross printed at the beginning of spelling books. Sancho implies that Christian faith, even without book learning, is enough to govern well.

that has been breathed upon you, sees yourself without more ado governor of an island, as though it were a mere matter of course. This I say, Sancho, that you attribute not the favor you have received to your own merits, but give thanks to Heaven, which disposes matters beneficently, and secondly thanks to the great power the profession of knight-errantry contains in itself. With a heart, then, inclined to believe what I have said to you, attend, my son, to your Cato[5] here who would counsel you and be your north star and guide to direct and pilot you to a safe haven out of this stormy sea in which you are about to engulf yourself. For offices and great trusts are nothing more than a mighty gulf of troubles.

"First of all, my son, you must fear God, for in the fear of him is wisdom,[6] and being wise you cannot err in anything.

"Secondly, you must keep in view who you are, striving to know yourself,[7] the most difficult thing to know that the mind can imagine. If you know yourself, it will follow that you will not puff yourself up like the frog that tried to make himself as large as the ox.[8] And if you do, the recollection of having kept pigs in your own country will serve as the ugly feet for the plumes of your folly."[9]

"That's the truth," said Sancho, "but that was when I was a boy. Afterwards, when I was something more of a man, it was geese I kept, not pigs. But to my thinking that has nothing to do with it, for not everyone who is a governor comes from kingly stock."

"True," said Don Quixote, "and for that reason those who are not of noble origin should take care that the dignity of the office they hold be accompanied by a mild gentleness, which, wisely employed, will save them from the sneers of malice that no station escapes.

"Glory in your humble birth, Sancho, and be not ashamed of saying you are peasant-born; for when it is seen that you are not embarrassed, no one will attempt to embarrass you. Pride yourself upon being of lowly virtue rather than a lofty sinner. Countless are they who, born of inferior parentage, have risen to the highest dignities, pontifical and imperial. Of the truth of this, I could give you examples enough to weary you.

"Remember, Sancho, if you make virtue your aim, and take pride in doing virtuous actions, you will have no cause to envy those who have princes and lords for fathers and grandfathers; for blood is an inheritance, but virtue an acquisition, and virtue has in itself alone a worth that blood does not possess.

"This being so, if it should happen that anyone of your relatives should come to see you when you have established yourself in your island, you are not to repel or slight him, but on the contrary to welcome him, entertain him, and make much of him; for in so doing you will be approved of Heaven (which is not

[5] *Cato:* Don Quixote sees himself as one of the Roman senators, father and son, renowned for their wisdom and defense of tradition.

[6] *fear God, for in the fear of him is wisdom:* Psalm 111:10; Proverbs 9:10.

[7] *know yourself:* maxim inscribed at the Temple of Apollo in Delphi.

[8] *puff yourself up . . . as the ox:* In Aesop's fable, the frog's envy eventually led him to burst.

[9] *ugly feet for the plumes of your folly:* Also from Aesop, the peacock prided himself on the beauty of his feathers, but his vanity was dashed when he saw his ugly feet.

pleased that any should despise what it has made), and will comply with the laws of well-ordered nature.

"If you bring your wife with you (and it is not well for those that administer governments to be long without their wives), teach and instruct her, and strive to smooth down her natural roughness; for all that may be gained by a wise governor may be lost and wasted by a boorish, stupid wife.

"If by chance you become a widower—a thing which may happen—and in virtue of your office seek a consort of higher degree, do not choose one to serve you as a hook or fishing rod, or as a hood for your cape.[10] Verily, I tell you, for all the judge's wife receives, the husband will be held accountable on the Day of Judgment, where he will have to repay fourfold in death the items that in life he did not claim as his own.

"Never hold to arbitrary laws, which are highly prized by ignorant men who pride themselves on cleverness.

"Let the tears of the poor man find with you more compassion, but not more justice, than the pleadings of the rich.

"Strive to lay bare the truth, not only amid the promises and presents of the rich man, but amid the sobs and entreaties of the poor as well.

"When there is an appropriate place for equity, press not the utmost rigor of the law against the guilty; for the reputation of the stern judge stands not higher than that of the compassionate one.

"If you ever permit the staff of justice to sway, let it be not by the weight of a gift, but by that of mercy.

"If it should happen to you to give judgment in the cause of one who is your enemy, turn your thoughts away from your injury and fix them on the justice of the case.

"Let not your passion blind you in another man's cause, for the errors you will thus commit will be most frequently irremediable. If not, they may only be remedied at the expense of your good name and even of your fortune.

"If a beautiful woman comes to seek justice of you, shield your eyes from her tears and your ears from her lamentations and consider deliberately the merits of her demand—lest you have your reason swept away by her weeping and your integrity by her sighs.

"Abuse not by word him whom you must punish in deed, for the pain of punishment is enough for the unfortunate without the addition of your invective.

"Bear in mind that the culprit who comes under your jurisdiction is but a miserable man subject to all the propensities of our depraved nature. So far as may be in your power, show yourself lenient and forbearing; for though the attributes of God are all equal, to our eyes that of mercy is brighter and loftier than that of justice.

[10] *hook . . . of your cape:* Don Quixote counsels against a public official's using his wife as a means of receiving illicit gifts, while he pretends to be beyond bribery. He combines two proverbs: "It is neither the hook nor the fishing rod but the bait that entices" and "I refuse, I refuse ... but toss it in the hood of my cape." The latter would be voiced by a friar happy to receive alms but squeamish about touching the money.

"If you follow these precepts and rules, Sancho, your days will be long, your fame eternal, your reward abundant, your felicity unutterable. You will marry your children as you wish; they and your grandchildren will bear titles. You will live in peace and concord with all men; and when life draws to a close, death will come to you in calm and ripe old age, and the light and loving hands of your great-grandchildren will close your eyes.

"What I have thus far addressed to you are instructions for the adornment of your mind. Listen now to those which are to serve for the adornment of your body."

CHAPTER XLIII

OF THE SECOND SET OF COUNSELS DON QUIXOTE GAVE SANCHO PANZA

Who, hearing the foregoing discourse of Don Quixote, would not have taken him for a person of great good sense and greater rectitude of purpose? As has been frequently observed in the course of this great history, he talked nonsense only when he touched on chivalry. In discussing all other subjects, he showed that he had a clear and unbiased understanding; so that at every turn his acts belied his intellect, and his intellect belied his acts. In the case of these second counsels that he gave Sancho, he showed himself to have a lively wit and displayed his wisdom prominently, but also his folly.

Sancho listened to him with the deepest attention and endeavored to fix his counsels in his memory, as one who meant to store them up and draw on them in order to bring the full promise of his government to a happy result.

Don Quixote then went on to say:

"With regard to the mode in which you should govern your person and your house, Sancho, the first charge I have to give you is to be clean and trim your nails, not letting them grow as some do, whose ignorance makes them fancy that long nails are an ornament to their hands, as if those excrescences they neglect to trim were not nails but the talons of a lizard-catching kestrel—a filthy and unnatural abuse.

"Do not go about untucked and sloppy, Sancho; for slovenly attire is a sign of an unstable mind, unless indeed the slovenliness is by design, as was the common opinion in the case of Julius Cæsar.[1]

"Set about discretely to determine what your office is worth. If it will allow you to bestow liveries[2] on your servants, give them respectable and serviceable ones, rather than showy and extravagant ones, then divide them between your servants and the poor. That is to say, if you can clothe six pages, clothe three of them and three poor men. Thus you will have pages for heaven and pages for earth. The vainglorious never think of this new mode of bestowing liveries.

"Eat neither garlic nor onions, lest they catch a whiff of your boorish origin.

"Walk slowly and speak deliberately, but not in such a way as to make it seem you are listening to yourself, for all affectation is bad.

[1] *case of Julius Cæsar:* Suetonius wrote that Julius Caesar wore his toga loosely belted, which was considered effeminate or unconventional. The elderly general Sulla was reported to have warned, "Beware the badly belted youth."

[2] *liveries:* uniforms.

"Eat a sparing dinner and an even more sparing supper; for the health of the whole body is forged in the workshop of the stomach.

"Be temperate in drinking, bearing in mind that wine in excess keeps neither secrets nor promises.

"Take care, Sancho, not to chew on both sides, nor to eruct in anyone's presence."

"*Eruct?*" said Sancho. "I don't know what that means."

"To *eruct*, Sancho," said Don Quixote, "means to *belch*, which is one of the filthiest words in the Spanish language, though a very expressive one. Therefore delicate natures have had recourse to the Latin, and instead of *belch* say *eruct*, and instead of *belches* say *eructations*. If some do not understand these terms it matters little, for custom will bring them into use in the course of time, so that they will be readily understood. This is the way a language is enriched—by custom and the public rule."

"In truth, señor," said Sancho, "one of the counsels and cautions I mean to commit to memory is this one, not to belch, since I'm constantly doing it."

"*Eruct*, Sancho, not *belch*," said Don Quixote.

"I will say *eruct* from now on, and I swear not to forget it," said Sancho.

"Likewise, Sancho," said Don Quixote, "you must not mingle so many proverbs in your discourse as you do; for though proverbs are short maxims, you drag them in so often by the head and shoulders that they sound more like nonsense than maxims."

"God alone can fix that," said Sancho. "I have more proverbs in me than a book, and when I speak they come so thick together into my mouth that they fight among themselves to get out. That's why my tongue lets fly the first ones it finds, even if they aren't right for the purpose. But I'll be careful from now on to use ones that befit the dignity of my office; for 'in a house where there's plenty, supper is soon cooked,' and 'whoever cuts the cards doesn't shuffle,' and 'the bellringer's in a safe place,' and 'giving and keeping require brains.'"

"Go on, Sancho!" said Don Quixote. "Pack, tack, string proverbs together. Nobody is stopping you! 'My mother beats me, and I make fun of her.'[3] Here I am counseling you to avoid proverbs, and in a second you have unleashed a whole litany of them, which have as much to do with what we are talking about as 'over the hills of Úbeda.' Mind, Sancho, I do not say that a proverb aptly brought in is objectionable; but to pile up and string together proverbs at random makes conversation dull and vulgar.

"When you ride on horseback, do not sit at the very back of the saddle, nor carry your legs stiff or sticking out from the horse's belly, nor yet sit so loosely that one would suppose you were on Dapple; for how one rides a horse makes gentlemen of some and grooms of others.

"Be moderate in your sleep, for he who does not rise early does not get the benefit of the day. Remember, Sancho, diligence is the mother of good fortune. Indolence, its opposite, never yet attained the object of an honest ambition.

[3] *My mother beats me, and I make fun of her:* "I persist in doing wrong despite correction."

"The last counsel I will give you now, though it does not tend to bodily improvement, I would have you carry carefully in your memory, for I believe it will be no less useful to you than those I have given you already, and it is this: never engage in a dispute about families, at least in the way of comparing them one with another; for necessarily one of those compared will be better than the other, and you will be hated by the one you have disparaged and get nothing in any shape from the one you have exalted.

"Your attire shall be full-length breeches, a long jerkin, and a cape a trifle longer; loose breeches[4] by no means, for they are becoming neither for gentlemen nor for governors.

"For the present, Sancho, this is all that has occurred to me to advise you. As time goes by and occasions arise, my instructions shall follow—if you take care to keep me informed of your circumstances."

"Señor," said Sancho, "I see well enough that all these things your worship has said to me are good, holy, and profitable. But what use will they be to me if I don't remember one of them? To be sure, the ones about not letting my nails grow and marrying again if I have the chance won't slip out of my head. But all that other hash, muddle, and jumble—I don't and can't recollect any more of it than of last year's clouds. So it must be given to me in writing; for even though I can't either read or write, I'll give it to my confessor, to drive it into me and remind me of it whenever it's necessary."

"Oh, sinner that I am!" cried Don Quixote. "How bad it looks in governors not to know how to read or write. Let me tell you, Sancho, when a man does not know how to read, or is left-handed, it argues one of two things: either that he was the son of exceedingly mean and lowly parents, or that he himself was so incorrigible and ill-conditioned that neither good company nor good teaching could make any impression on him. It is a great defect that you labor under, and therefore I would have you learn, at the very least, to sign your name."

"I can sign my name well enough," said Sancho, "for when I was the chief steward of the brotherhood[5] in my village I learned to make certain letters, like the marks on bales of goods,[6] which they told me made out my name. Besides I can pretend my right hand is maimed and make someone else sign for me, for 'there's a remedy for everything except death.' And as I'll have the authority and the staff, I can do as I like. Besides, 'he who has the magistrate for his father ...'[7]—I'll be governor, and that's higher than a magistrate. Just come

[4] *full-length breeches ... loose breeches:* Don Quixote advocates formalwear: breeches and stockings of the same fabric (*calza entera*), a close-fitting jacket with sleeves (*ropilla larga*), and a collared cape (*herreruelo*). Loose breeches (*gregüescos*)—baggy knee-length trousers known in English as "Spanish breeches"—were matched with stockings and considered less formal.

[5] *steward of the brotherhood:* See footnote 15, page 158.

[6] *certain letters, like the marks on bales of goods:* Bales of goods were marked with hastily written initials or symbols, sometimes chalked or painted, to indicate ownership, origin, or destination.

[7] *he who has the magistrate for his father ...:* "... the judgment goes his way."

and see what happens to them! Let them belittle and abuse me—'they'll come for wool and go home shorn,' and 'blessings come looking for those God loves,' and 'the empty talk of the rich passes for wisdom in this world.' And as I'll be rich, being a governor—and at the same time generous, as I mean to be—no one will find fault with me. 'If you make yourself honey, the flies will devour you.'[8] 'You're worth what you have,' as my grandmother used to say, and 'there is no revenge on the powerful.'"

"God's curse upon you, Sancho!" exclaimed Don Quixote at this. "Sixty thousand devils fly away with you and your proverbs! For the last hour you have been stringing them together and inflicting the pangs of torture on me with every one of them. Those proverbs will bring you to the gallows one day, I promise you. Your subjects will take the government from you, or they will rise up and revolt. Tell me, where do you pick them up, you ignoramus? How do you apply them, you blockhead? With me, to utter one and make it apply properly, I have to sweat and labor as if I were digging."

"By God, my master," said Sancho, "your worship is making a fuss about nothing. Why the devil should you be annoyed if I make use of what belongs to me? I have nothing else, no other inheritance except proverbs and more proverbs. Here are three that just now came into my head, ready to be plucked like pears in a basket. But I won't repeat them, for 'blessed silence, your name is Sancho.'"[9]

"That you are not, Sancho," said Don Quixote. "For not only are you not blessed silence, but you are cursed speaking and cursed arguing. Still, I would like to know what three proverbs have just now come into your mind, for I have been turning over my own—and it is a good one—and none occurs to me."

"What can be better," said Sancho, "than 'never stick your thumbs between two back teeth,'[10] and 'to "Get out of my house!" and "What do you want with my wife?" there's no answer,' and 'whether you hit a rock with a pitcher or a pitcher with a rock, it's bad for the pitcher'? All of them fit like a glove. For no one should argue with his governor, or someone in authority over him, because he'll be the worse for it, like the one who puts his finger between two back teeth (and if they aren't back teeth it makes no difference, so long as they are teeth). And to whatever the governor might say there's no answer, any more than to 'Get out of my house!' and 'What do you want with my wife?' As for the one about the stone and the pitcher, a blind man could see that. It's necessary then that 'he who sees the speck in another's eye should see the beam in his own,'[11] so that it won't be said of him, 'the corpse was horrified at the sight of a slit

[8] *If you make yourself honey, the flies will devour you:* "Play nice, and you'll be taken advantage of."

[9] *blessed silence, your name is Sancho:* The saying was "Blessed silence, your name is holy (*santo*)" until the sixteenth century, when "Sancho" became a common substitute.

[10] *never stick your thumbs between two back teeth:* "don't meddle in a dispute between family members."

[11] *who sees the speck in another's eye should see the beam in his own:* Matthew 7:3.

throat.'[12] And your worship knows well that 'the fool knows more in his own house than the wise man in another's.'"

"No, Sancho," said Don Quixote, "the fool knows nothing, either in his own house or in anybody else's, for no wise structure of any sort can stand on a foundation of folly. But let us say no more about it, Sancho, for if you govern badly, yours will be the fault and mine the shame. I comfort myself with having done my duty in advising you as earnestly and as wisely as I could, and thus I am released from my obligations and my promise. God guide you, Sancho, and govern you in your government, and deliver me from the misgiving I have that you will turn the whole island upside down, a thing I might easily prevent by explaining to the duke who you are and telling him that fat little body of yours is nothing else but a sack full of proverbs and sauciness."

"Señor," said Sancho, "if your worship thinks I'm not fit for this government, I give it up on the spot; for the mere black of the nail of my soul[13] is more precious to me than my whole body. I can live just as well as simple Sancho on bread and onions than as governor on partridges and capons. What's more, 'while we're asleep we're all equal, great and small, rich and poor.' But if your worship looks into it, you will see it was your worship alone that put me on to this business of governing. I don't know any more about the government of islands than a buzzard does. And if there's any reason to think that because of my being a governor the devil will get hold of me, I'd rather go as Sancho to heaven than governor to hell."

"By God, Sancho," said Don Quixote, "for those last words you have uttered alone, I judge that you deserve to be governor of a thousand islands. You have good natural instincts, without which no knowledge is worth anything. Commend yourself to God, and try not to swerve in the pursuit of your main object—I mean, always make it your aim and fixed purpose to do right in all matters that come before you, for Heaven always helps good intentions. And now let us go to dinner, for I think my lord and lady are waiting for us."

[12] *the corpse was horrified at the sight of a slit throat:* "an imperfect person should not be scandalized by another's imperfections."

[13] *mere black of the nail of my soul:* the smallest part.

CHAPTER XLIV

HOW SANCHO PANZA WAS CONDUCTED TO HIS GOVERNMENT, AND OF THE STRANGE ADVENTURE THAT BEFELL DON QUIXOTE IN THE CASTLE

It is reputed that in the original version of this history, when Cide Hamete came to write this chapter, his translator did not translate it as Benengeli had written it. This was a kind of protest the Moor lodged against himself for having taken up a story so dry and of so little variety as the story of Don Quixote.[1] For he found himself forced to speak perpetually of him and Sancho, without venturing to indulge in digressions and episodes more serious and more interesting. He said, too, that to go on—with mind, hand, and pen always restricted to writing about a single subject and speaking through the mouths of only a few characters—was intolerable drudgery, the result of which was never equal to the author's labor. To avoid this pitfall, the author had availed himself in the First Part of the device of novels like *The Impertinent Meddler* and *The Captive Captain*, which stand, as it were, apart from the story, the others found there being incidents that occurred to Don Quixote himself and could not be omitted. He also thought, he says, that many, engrossed with interest in the exploits of Don Quixote, would take no interest in the novels, and pass them over hastily or impatiently without noticing the elegance and art of their composition, which would be obvious to see were they published by themselves, without any connection to the harebrained adventures of Don Quixote or the buffoonery of Sancho. Therefore in this Second Part he thought it best not to insert novels outright, either separate or interwoven, but only episodes with the semblance of novels—these arising out of the circumstances of the facts present and employed sparingly, with no more words than necessary to make them plain. And as he confines and restricts himself to the narrow limits of the narrative, though his mind is well able to deal with the whole universe, he requests that his labors may not be despised, and that credit be given him, not only for what he writes, but for what he has refrained from writing.

And so he goes on with his story, saying that the day Don Quixote gave his counsels to Sancho, the same afternoon after dinner, he handed them to him in writing so that he might get someone to read them to him. They had scarcely been given to him, however, when he let them drop, and they fell into the hands

[1] *It is reputed . . . of Don Quixote:* No shortage of ink has been spilled over the perplexities of these opening lines.

of the duke, who showed them to the duchess. They were both amazed afresh at the madness and wit of Don Quixote.

To carry on the joke, then, the same evening they dispatched Sancho with a large following to the village that was to serve him for an island. It happened that the person who had charge of him was a majordomo of the duke's, a very clever man with a keen sense of humor—and there can be no humor without cleverness—and the one who played the part of Countess Trifaldi in the comical way that has been already described. Thus qualified, and instructed by his master and mistress as to how to deal with Sancho, he carried out their scheme admirably.

Now it came to pass that as soon as Sancho saw this majordomo, he noted a resemblance in his features to those of Trifaldi. Turning to his master, he said to him, "Señor, either the devil will carry me off here on this spot, righteous and believing, or your worship must admit to me that the face of this majordomo of the duke's here is the very face of La Dolorida."

Don Quixote observed the majordomo attentively, and having done so, said to Sancho, "There is no reason why the devil should carry you off, Sancho, either righteous or believing—and what you mean by that I know not. The face of La Dolorida is that of the majordomo, but for all that the majordomo is not La Dolorida; for his being so would involve a very great contradiction. But this is not the time for going into questions of this nature, which would be involving ourselves in an inextricable labyrinth. Believe me, my friend, we must pray earnestly to our Lord that he deliver us both from wicked wizards and enchanters."

"It's no joke, señor," said Sancho, "for before this I heard him speak, and it sounded exactly like the voice of Trifaldi echoing in my ears. Well, I'll hold my peace, but I'm going to be on the lookout from now on for any sign that might confirm or disprove this suspicion."

"As well you should do, Sancho," said Don Quixote. "Let me know all you discover and all that befalls you in your government."

Sancho at last set out attended by a great number of people. He was dressed like a scholar, cloaked in a robe of tawny watered camlet,[2] with a montera cap of the same material, and mounted *a la jineta* upon a mule. Behind him, in accordance with the duke's orders, followed Dapple with brand new trappings and silk ornaments. From time to time, Sancho turned round to look at his donkey, so well pleased to have him with him that he would not have changed places with the emperor of Germany. On taking leave, he kissed the hands of the duke and duchess and received his master's blessing, which Don Quixote gave him with tears, and he received blubbering.

Gentle reader, let the worthy Sancho go in peace, and good luck to him. Be on the lookout for two bushels of laughter, which the account of how he behaved himself in office will give you. In the meantime, turn your attention to what

[2] *tawny watered camlet:* Camlet, a costly fabric prized for its durability and sheen, was woven from a blend of goat hair, silk, and wool. Watered camlet was pressed with engraved rollers while damp to create a rippled pattern.

happened to his master the same night. If you do not laugh here, at the very least you will stretch your mouth with a grin; for Don Quixote's adventures must be greeted either with wonder or with laughter.

It is related that as soon as Sancho had gone, Don Quixote was overcome with loneliness, and had it been possible for him to revoke the mandate and take away the government from him he would have done so. The duchess observed his dejection and asked him why he was melancholy, because, she said, if it was for the loss of Sancho, there were squires, dueñas, and damsels in her house who would wait upon him to his heart's content.

"The truth is, señora," replied Don Quixote, "that I do feel the loss of Sancho, but that is not the main cause of my looking sad. Of all the offers your excellency makes me, I accept only the goodwill with which they are made. As to the remainder, I entreat of your excellency to permit me to wait upon myself in my chamber."

"Indeed, Señor Don Quixote," said the duchess, "that must not be. Four of my damsels, as beautiful as flowers, shall wait upon you."

"To me," said Don Quixote, "they will not be flowers, but thorns to pierce my heart. They, or anything like them, shall as soon enter my chamber as grow wings. If your highness wishes to gratify me still further, though I deserve it not, let me have my way and wait upon myself in my own room; for I place a barrier between my inclinations and my virtue, and I do not wish to break this rule through the generosity your highness is disposed to display towards me. In short, I will sleep in my clothes sooner than allow anyone to undress me."

"Say no more, Señor Don Quixote, say no more," said the duchess. "I assure you I will give orders that not even a fly—not to say a damsel—shall enter your room. Let me not be the one to undermine the propriety of Señor Don Quixote, for it strikes me that among his many virtues the one that is preeminent is that of modesty. Your worship may undress and dress in private and in your own way, as you please and when you please, for there will be no one to hinder you. In your chamber you will find all the basins requisite to supply the demands of one who sleeps with his door locked, to the end that no natural needs compel you to open it.[3] May the great Dulcinea del Toboso live a thousand years, and may her fame extend all over the surface of the globe, for she deserves to be loved by a knight so valiant and so virtuous; and may kind Heaven infuse zeal into the heart of our governor Sancho Panza to finish off his whipping speedily, so that the world may once more enjoy the beauty of so grand a lady."

To which Don Quixote replied, "Your highness has spoken like what you are—from the mouth of a noble lady nothing bad can come. Dulcinea will be more fortunate and better known to the world by your highness' praise than by all the eulogies the greatest orators on earth could bestow upon her."

"Now then, Señor Don Quixote," said the duchess, it is nearly suppertime, and the duke is probably waiting. Come let us go to supper and retire to rest early, for the journey you made yesterday from Candaya was not such a short one but that it must have caused you some fatigue."

[3] *all the basins:* washbasin and chamber pot.

"I feel none, señora," said Don Quixote, "for I would go so far as to swear to your excellency that in all my life I never mounted a quieter beast, or one with a softer step than Clavileño. I don't know what could have induced Malambruno to discard a steed so swift and so gentle, and burn it so recklessly as he did."

"One can imagine," said the duchess, "that repenting of the evil he had done to Trifaldi and company, and others, and the crimes he must have committed as a wizard and enchanter, he resolved to do away with all the instruments of his craft. And so he burned Clavileño as the chief instrument—that which kept him most restless, wandering from land to land. By its ashes and the trophy of the placard, the valor of the great Don Quixote of La Mancha is established forever."

Don Quixote renewed his thanks to the duchess and, having had supper, retired to his chamber alone, refusing to allow anyone to enter with him to wait on him—such was his fear of encountering temptations that might lead him to forget his chaste fidelity to his lady Dulcinea; for he had always present in his mind the virtue of Amadís, that flower and mirror of knights-errant. He locked the door behind him, and by the light of two wax candles undressed himself. But as he was taking off his stockings—O disaster unworthy of such a personage!—there came the sound not of sighs (nor of anything else that might bely his delicacy or good breeding), but of some two dozen stitches being ripped in one of his stockings, leaving it to look like a window-lattice. The worthy gentleman was beyond measure distressed, and at that moment he would have given an ounce of silver to have had a bit of green silk there (I say green silk because the stockings were green).

Here Cide Hamete exclaimed in his manuscript, "O poverty, poverty! I know not what could have possessed the great Cordovan poet to call you 'holy gift ungratefully received.'[4] Although a Moor, I know well enough from the exchanges I have had with Christians that holiness consists in charity, humility, faith, obedience, and poverty. But for all that, I say he must have a great deal of godliness who can find any satisfaction in being poor—unless, indeed, it is the kind of poverty one of their greatest saints refers to, saying, 'possess all things as though you possessed them not,'[5] which is what they call poverty in spirit. But you, that other poverty—for it is of you I am speaking now—why do you love to subdue gentlemen and men of good birth more than others? Why do you compel them to smear the cracks in their shoes with soot, and to have the buttons of their coats, one of silk, another of horsehair, and another of glass? Why must their ruffs be always crinkled like endive leaves, and not starched and shaped?"[6] (From this we may observe the antiquity of starched and shaped ruffs.) He then goes on: "Poor

[4] *the great Cordovan poet . . . 'holy gift ungratefully received'*: The poet is Juan de Mena; the quote is from his allegorical poem *Laberinto de Fortuna* (1444).

[5] *one of their greatest saints refers to, saying, 'possess all things as though you possessed them not,'*: an echo of the Apostle Paul's words in 1 Corinthians 7:29–31.

[6] *ruffs be always . . . endive leaves, and not starched and shaped:* The ruff (*lechugilla*, resembling *lechuga*, lettuce) was a frilled cambric or lace collar that came into fashion in the mid-sixteenth century. It required a professional to pleat, starch, and maintain. The *cuello escarolado* (collar resembling endive, *escarola*) was a variant noted for its tight pleats, or flutes, that was less formal and capable of being prepared at home.

wellborn gentleman, spoon-feeding his honor while he dines miserably and in secret, making a hypocrite of the toothpick with which he sallies out into the street after eating nothing to oblige him to use it! Poor fellow, I say, with his fragile honor, imagining that people notice from a mile away his patched shoe, his sweat-stained hat, his threadbare cloak, and his empty stomach!"

All this was brought home to Don Quixote by the run in his stocking. He comforted himself, however, when he noticed that Sancho had left behind a pair of traveling boots,[7] which he resolved to wear the next day. At last he went to bed, out of spirits and heavy at heart, both because he missed Sancho and because of the irreparable disaster to his stockings, the stitches of which he would have even mended with silk of another color, which is one of the greatest signs of poverty a gentleman can show in the course of his never-failing embarrassments. He snuffed out the candles, but the night was warm and he could not sleep, so he rose from his bed and cracked open a grated window that looked out on a beautiful garden. As he did so he saw and heard people walking and talking in the garden. He set himself to listen attentively, and those below raised their voices so that he could hear these words:

"Press me not to sing, Emerencia, for you know that ever since this stranger entered the castle and my eyes beheld him, I cannot sing but only weep. Besides, my lady is a light rather than a heavy sleeper, and I would not for all the wealth of the world have her find us here. Even if she were asleep and did not waken, my singing would be in vain if this new Æneas, who has come into these parts to spurn me,[8] sleeps on and wakens not to hear it."

"Be not concerned, dear Altisidora," replied a voice. "The duchess is no doubt asleep, along with everybody in the house save the lord of your heart and disturber of your soul; for just now I perceived that he opened the grated window of his chamber, so he must be awake. Sing, my poor sufferer, in a soft, sweet tone to the accompaniment of your harp. Even if the duchess hears us, we can lay the blame on the heat of the night."

"That is not the point, Emerencia," replied Altisidora. "It is that I do not wish for my song to lay bare my heart, that I should be thought a light and wanton maiden by those who know not the mighty power of love. But let come what may! Better a blush on the cheeks than a sore in the heart." Here, a harp gently touched made itself heard.

As he listened to all this, Don Quixote was in a state of breathless amazement, for immediately the countless adventures like this—with windows, gratings, gardens, serenades, lovemakings, and swoons—that he had read of in his silly books of chivalry, came to his mind. He at once concluded that one of the duchess' damsels was in love with him, and that her modesty forced her to keep her passion secret. He trembled lest he should fall and made an inward resolution not to

[7] *traveling boots:* tall boots that would hide the tear in his stocking.

[8] *new Æneas, who has come into these parts to spurn me:* Returning from Troy, Aeneas stopped in Carthage, where he won the heart of Queen Dido. After he abandoned her to continue his journey, she committed suicide.

yield. Commending himself with all his might and soul to his lady Dulcinea he made up his mind to listen to the music. To let them know he was there he gave a pretended sneeze, at which the damsels were not a little delighted, for all they wanted was that Don Quixote should hear them.

So having tuned the harp, Altisidora, running her hand across the strings, began this ballad:

O thou that art above in bed,
Between the holland sheets,
A-lying there from night till morn,
With outstretched legs asleep;

O thou, most valiant knight of all
The famed Manchegan breed,
Of purity and virtue more
Than gold of Araby;

Give ear unto a suffering maid,
Well-grown but evil-starred,
For those two suns of thine have lit
A fire within her heart.

Adventures seeking thou dost rove,
To others bringing woe;
Thou scatterest wounds, but, ah, the balm
To heal them dost withhold!

Say, valiant youth, and so may God
Thy enterprises speed,
Didst thou the light mid Libya's sands[9]
Or Jaca's crags[10] first see?

Did scaly serpents give thee suck?
Who nursed thee when a babe?
Wert cradled in the forest rude,
Or gloomy mountain cave?

O Dulcinea may be proud,
That plump and lusty maid;
For she alone hath had the power
A tiger fierce to tame.

And she for this shall famous be
From Tagus to Jarama,

[9] *Libya's sands:* Libya was believed to teem with venomous reptiles.
[10] *Jaca's crags:* mountain peaks on the southern edge of the Pyrenees near Jaca (Aragon).

From Manzanares to Genil,
Pisuerga to Arlanza.[11]

My petticoat I fain would give
Could I but take her place,
The brightest and the best I have,
Adorned with golden lace.

O for to be the happy fair
Held in those arms so stout,
Or even by thy pillow tasked
To pick thy dandruff out!

I rave—to favors such as these
Unworthy to aspire;
It were enough to rub thy feet
For one so mean as I.

What caps, what slippers silver-laced,
Would I on thee bestow!
What damask breeches make for thee;
What fine long holland cloaks!

And I would give thee pearls that should
As big as oak galls[12] show;
So matchless that each one might well
Be called the great "Alone."[13]

Manchegan Nero, look not down
From thy Tarpeian Rock[14]
Upon this burning heart, nor add
The kindling of thy wrath.

A virgin soft and young am I,
Not yet fifteen years old;
(I'm only three months past fourteen,
I swear upon my soul).

I hobble not nor do I limp,
All blemish I'm without,

[11] *From Tagus ... to Arlanza:* The Jarama and Manzanares flow into the Tagus in Castile; the Genil into the Guadalquivir in Andalusia; and the Arlanza into the Pisuerga in León.

[12] *oak galls:* See footnote 9, page 479.

[13] *Alone:* possibly the nickname of a pearl owned by the Spanish Habsburgs.

[14] *Manchegan Nero ... Tarpeian Rock:* See footnote 16, page 101.

And as I walk my lily locks
Are trailing on the ground.

And though my nose is rather flat,[15]
And though my mouth is wide,
My teeth like topazes exalt
My beauty to the sky.

Thou knowest that my voice is sweet,
That is if thou dost hear;
And I am molded in a form
Somewhat below the mean.

These charms, and many more, are thine,
Spoils to thy quiver famed;
A damsel of this house am I,
Altisidora named.

Here the song of the heart-stricken Altisidora came to an end, while the warmly courted Don Quixote began to feel alarm. With a deep sigh he said to himself, "O that I should be such an unlucky knight that no damsel can set eyes on me but falls in love with me! O that the peerless Dulcinea should be so unfortunate that they cannot let her enjoy my incomparable constancy in peace! What do you want of her, you queens? Why do you persecute her, you empresses? Why do you pursue her, you virgins of ages fourteen to fifteen? Leave the unhappy being to triumph, rejoice, and glory in the lot that love has been pleased to bestow upon her in delivering over my heart and yielding to her my very soul. O love-smitten throng, know that to Dulcinea only I am dough and sugar paste, flint to all others; for her I am honey, for you bitter aloe. For me Dulcinea alone is beautiful, wise, virtuous, graceful, and high-bred, and all others are ugly, foolish, frivolous, and lowborn. Nature sent me into the world to be hers and no other's. Altisidora may weep or sing, the lady for whose sake they beat me in the castle of the enchanted Moor may give way to despair,[16] but I must be Dulcinea's, boiled or roasted[17]—pure, courteous, and chaste, in spite of all the magic-working powers on earth."

With that he shut the window with a bang, and as much out of temper and out of sorts as if some great misfortune had befallen him stretched himself on his bed, where we will leave him for the present, as the great Sancho Panza, who is about to inaugurate his famous government, now demands our attention.

[15] *my nose is rather flat:* Women with a flat nose (like Maritornes in Part I) had a reputation for licentiousness.

[16] *the lady for whose sake . . . to despair:* Don Quixote recalls the indignities of Part I, chapter 17.

[17] *boiled or roasted:* "one way or the other".

CHAPTER XLV

OF HOW THE GREAT SANCHO PANZA TOOK POSSESSION OF HIS ISLAND, AND OF HOW HE MADE A BEGINNING IN GOVERNING

O perpetual revealer of the antipodes,[1] torch of the world, eye of heaven, sweet stimulator of wine coolers![2] Thymbraeus here, Phœbus there,[3] now archer, now physician, father of poetry, inventor of music; you, who always rise and, notwithstanding appearances, never set! To you, O Sun, by whose aid man begets man,[4] to you I appeal to brighten my clouded mind that I may be able to proceed with scrupulous exactitude in giving an account of the great Sancho Panza's government. For without you, I feel weak, feeble, and uncertain.

To come to the point, then—Sancho with all his attendants arrived at a village of some one thousand inhabitants, and one of the largest the duke possessed. They informed him that it was called the island of Barataria, either because the name of the village was Baratario, or because of the duplicity[5] with which the government had been conferred upon him. On reaching the gates of the town (which was a walled one), the town council came out to meet him, the bells rang out a peal, and the inhabitants showed every sign of general satisfaction. With great pomp they conducted him to the principal church to give thanks to God, and then with mock ceremonies they presented him with the keys of the town and acknowledged him as perpetual governor of the island of Barataria.

The attire, the beard, and the fat, squat figure of the new governor amazed all those who were not in on the secret, and even all who were—and they were not a few. Finally, leading him out of the church they carried him to the judgment seat and seated him on it.

[1] *antipodes:* diametrically opposite places on the surface of the earth. The apostrophe that follows is to the sun.

[2] *sweet stimulator of wine coolers:* On a hot day, *cantimploras* (earthenware canteens filled with wine or water) would be placed in a draft or covered with a damp rag to keep cool. Shaking the canteen before drinking evenly distributed the coolest parts.

[3] *Thymbraeus here, Phœbus there:* epithets of Apollo, the sun god. A temple in the city of Thymbra, near Troy, was dedicated to him.

[4] *by whose aid man begets man:* In *Generation of Animals*, Aristotle taught that the man provides the "vital heat" necessary to give life and form to the shapeless matter that the woman carries in her womb.

[5] *duplicity: barato*, tip given to an onlooker in a gambling establishment; more broadly, a term for deception.

The duke's majordomo said to him, "It is an ancient custom in this island, señor governor, that he who comes to take possession of this famous island is required to answer a question which shall be put to him, and which must be a somewhat knotty and difficult one. By his answer, the people take the measure of their new governor's intelligence, and hail with joy or lament his arrival accordingly."

While the majordomo was making this speech, Sancho was gazing at several large letters inscribed on the wall opposite his seat, and as he could not read, he asked what it was that was painted on the wall.

The answer was, "Señor, there it is written and recorded the day on which your lordship took possession of this island. The inscription says,

> THIS DAY, THE SO-AND-SO OF SUCH-AND-SUCH A MONTH AND YEAR, SEÑOR DON SANCHO PANZA TOOK POSSESSION OF THIS ISLAND. MANY YEARS MAY HE ENJOY IT."

"And who do they call *Don* Sancho Panza?" asked Sancho.

"Your lordship," replied the majordomo, "for no other Panza but the one who is now seated in that chair has ever entered this island."

"Well then, let me tell you, brother," said Sancho, "I don't have a Don, and there has never been one in my family. My name is plain Sancho Panza. Sancho was my father's name, and Sancho was my grandfather's, and they were all Panzas, without any Dons or Doñas tacked on. I suspect that in this island there are more Dons than stones. But never mind—God knows what I mean, and maybe if my government lasts four days I'll weed out these Dons that no doubt are as great a nuisance as mosquitos, they're so many. Let the majordomo go on with his question, and I'll give the best answer I can, whether the people lament it or not."

At this moment there came to the tribunal two men, one in the dress of a peasant farmer and the other of a tailor, for he had a pair of scissors in his hand. The tailor said, "Señor governor, this farmer and I come before your worship on account of this good man coming to my shop yesterday (for with apologies to all present, I'm a licensed tailor, God be thanked[6]). Putting a piece of cloth into my hands, he asked me, 'Señor, will there be enough in this cloth to make me a cap?' I measured the cloth and said there would. He probably suspected—as I supposed, and I supposed right—that I wanted to steal some of the cloth, an idea fed by his ill will and the bad opinion people have of tailors. He asked if there would be enough for two. I guessed what he was up to and said 'yes.' He, insisting on carrying further his malicious purpose, went on adding cap after cap, and I 'yes' after 'yes,' until we got as far as five. He has just this moment come for them. I gave him the caps, but he won't pay me for my work. Instead, he asks me to pay *him*, or else return his cloth."

"Is all this true, brother?" asked Sancho.

[6] *with apologies . . . be thanked:* The tailor has passed his apprenticeship after being examined by the local tailors' guild. An apology is customary when an infelicity has been uttered—an indication of the poor reputation of tailors.

"Yes," replied the man. "But will your worship make him show the five caps he's made me?"

"With all my heart," said the tailor. And drawing his hand from under his cloak, he showed five caps on his five fingertips and said, "Here are the caps this good man asks for. By God and upon my conscience I don't have a scrap of cloth left, and I'll let the work be examined by the inspectors of the trade."

Everyone present laughed at the number of caps and the novelty of the lawsuit. Sancho set himself to think for a moment and then said, "It seems to me that in this case it is not necessary to deliver longwinded arguments, but only to use the judgment of an honest man. And so my decision is that the tailor lose the work and the farmer the cloth, and that the caps go to the prisoners in jail. Let that be the end of it."

If the previous decision about the cattle dealer's purse excited the bystanders' admiration, this provoked their laughter.[7] The governor's orders were nonetheless executed.

There now presented themselves before him two elderly men, one of whom carried a cane stalk[8] for a walking stick. The one without a walking stick said, "Señor, some time ago I lent this good man ten escudos in gold to gratify him and do him a service, on the condition that he was to return them to me whenever I should ask for them. A long time passed before I asked for them, for I would not cause him any more trouble to return them than what he was in when I first lent them. But thinking he was getting careless about repaying me, I asked for them once and several times. Not only will he not give them back, but he denies that he owes them and says I never lent him any such escudos, or if I did, that he repaid them. I have no witnesses either of the loan or the repayment, for he never repaid me. I would like your worship to put him under oath, and if he swears he returned them to me, I forgive him the debt here and before God."

"What do you say to this, good old man, you with the walking stick?" asked Sancho.

To which the old man replied, "I admit, señor, that he lent them to me, but let your worship lower your staff,[9] and as he leaves it to my oath, I'll swear that I gave them back and paid him really and truly."

The governor lowered the staff, and as he did so the old man handed his walking stick to the other old man to hold for him while he swore, as if he found it in his way. He then laid his hand on the cross of the staff, saying that it was true the ten escudos that were demanded had been lent to him but that he had with his own hand given them back into the hand of the other, and that he, not remembering, was always asking for them.

[7] *If the previous decision . . . their laughter:* The lawsuit involving the cattle dealer's purse will be told further on.

[8] *cane stalk: cañaheja,* which probably refers to the giant fennel plant, known for its sturdy, hollow stalk.

[9] *staff:* A magistrate's staff was the symbol of his office. The old man asks to take his oath with his hand on the cross at the top of the staff.

Seeing this the great governor asked the creditor what answer he had to give to what his opponent said. He said that no doubt his debtor had told the truth, for he believed him to be an honest man and a good Christian—that he must have forgotten when and how he had given him back the escudos, and that from that time forth he would make no further demand on him.

The debtor took his walking stick again, and bowing his head left the tribunal. Observing this—how, without another word, he went off—and observing too the resignation of the plaintiff, Sancho buried his head in his breast and remained for a short space in deep thought, with the forefinger of his right hand on his brow and nose. Then he raised his head and had them call back the old man with the walking stick, for he had already left. They brought him back, and as soon as Sancho saw him, he said, "Honest man, give me that walking stick. I need it for a moment."

"Willingly," said the old man. "Here it is señor," and he put it into his hand.

Sancho took it and, handing it to the other old man, said to him, "Go, and God be with you. You are now paid."

"I, señor?" returned the old man. "Why, is this cane stalk worth ten gold escudos?"

"Yes," said the governor, "or if not I am the greatest idiot in the world. Now you will see whether I have the brains to govern a whole kingdom." He ordered the cane to be broken in two—there, in the presence of all. It was done, and in the middle of it they found ten gold escudos.

Everyone was filled with amazement and looked upon their governor as another Solomon. They asked him how he had come to the conclusion that the ten escudos were in the cane stalk. He replied that observing how the old man who swore gave the walking stick to his opponent while he was taking the oath, and swore that he had really and truly given him the escudos, and how as soon as he had done swearing he asked for the walking stick again, it came into his head that the money demanded must be inside it. From this he said it might be seen that God sometimes guides those who govern in their judgments, even though they may be fools. Besides, he had himself heard his village priest mention just such another case, and he had so good a memory that, if it was not that he forgot everything he wished to remember, there would not be such a memory in all the island. To conclude, the old men went off, one crestfallen and the other in high contentment; all who were present were astonished, and he who was recording the words, deeds, and movements of Sancho could not make up his mind whether he was to take him for a simpleton or sage.

As soon as this case was disposed of, there came to the tribunal a woman holding on with a tight grip to a man dressed like a well-to-do farmer. She came forward making a great outcry exclaiming, "Justice, señor governor, justice! If I don't get it on earth, I'll go looking for it in heaven. Señor governor of my soul, this wicked man caught me in the middle of the fields here and used my body as if it was a filthy rag, and—woe is me!—took from me what I had kept safe these twenty-three years and more, defending it against Moors and Christians, natives and strangers. And I always as hard as an oak, and keeping myself as pure as a salamander in the fire[10] or wool among the brambles,[11] for this good man to come now with his clean hands to handle me!"

"It remains to be proved whether this fine fellow has clean hands or not," said Sancho. Turning to the man, he asked him what he had to say in answer to the woman's charge.

He, all in confusion, answered, "Sirs, I am a poor swine farmer. This morning I left the village to sell four pigs (begging your pardon),[12] and between the taxes and the buyers' hard bargaining, they got out of me a little less than what they're worth. As I was returning to my village, I happened to meet this good lady on the road, and the devil—who makes a confounded mess of everything—yoked us together. I paid her fairly, but she wasn't content with that. She laid hold of me and never let go till she brought me here. She says I raped her, but she lies by the oath I swear, or am ready to swear. And that's the whole truth and every crumb of it."

The governor asked him if he had any money in silver on him. He said he had about twenty ducats in a leather purse in his breast. The governor asked him to take it out and hand it to the complainant; he obeyed trembling. The woman took it, and making a thousand bows to all and praying to God for the long life and health of the señor governor who had such regard for distressed orphans and virgins, she hurried out of court with the purse clutched in both hands, first looking, however, to see if the money it contained was silver.

As soon as she was gone, Sancho said to the farmer, whose tears were already starting and whose eyes and heart were following his purse, "Good fellow, go after that woman and take the purse from her, by force even, and come back with it here." He did not say this to one who was a fool or deaf, for the man was off like a flash of lightning and ran to do as he was told.

All the bystanders waited anxiously to see the end of the case. Presently both man and woman came back at even closer grips than before, she with the purse rolled up in the lap of her skirt, and he struggling hard to take it from her, but all in vain against the woman's defense. Meanwhile, the woman was crying out, "Justice from God and the world! Look at the shamelessness of this villain, señor governor. In the middle of town, in the middle of the street, he wanted to take the purse your worship commanded him to give me."

"And did he take it?" asked the governor.

"Take it?" said the woman. "I'd let my life be taken from me sooner than this purse. A pretty child I'd be! They'll have to throw some other cat in my face than this disgusting brute. Pincers and hammers, mallets and chisels won't pry it out of my hands. No, not even lions' claws. They'll have to take the soul out of my body first!"

[10] *salamander in the fire:* It was believed that the salamander could pass through fire without being burned.

[11] *wool among the brambles*: perhaps an allusion to the expression "little wool, and that among brambles", to refer to someone whose meager property is pledged to others.

[12] *four pigs (begging your pardon):* "Pigs" (*puercos*) was considered an inappropriate word in polite company. See page 32.

"She's right," said the man. "I admit that I'm beaten and powerless. My strength wasn't enough to take it from her," and he let go his hold of her.

Upon this the governor said to the woman, "Let me see that purse, my worthy and sturdy woman." She handed it to him at once. The governor returned it to the man and said to the unforced mistress of force, "Sister, if you had shown as much, or only half as much spirit and resolve in defending your body as you have shown in defending that purse, the strength of Hercules could not have forced you. Be off with God speed, and bad luck to you. And don't show your face in all this island, or within six leagues of it on any side under pain of two hundred lashes. Be off at once, I say, you shameless, cheating shrew." The woman was cowed and went off disconsolately, hanging her head.

The governor said to the man, "Honest man, go home with your money, and God speed you. And for the future, if you don't want to lose it, see that you don't take it into your head to yoke with anybody." The man thanked him as clumsily as he could and went his way, and the bystanders were again filled with admiration at their new governor's judgments and sentences.

All this, having been taken down by his chronicler, was at once dispatched to the duke, who was awaiting it with great eagerness.

And here let us leave the good Sancho; for his master, sorely troubled in mind by Altisidora's music, has pressing claims upon us now.

CHAPTER XLVI

OF THE TERRIBLE BELL AND CAT FRIGHT THAT DON QUIXOTE RECEIVED IN THE COURSE OF THE ENAMORED ALTISIDORA'S LOVE SUIT

We left Don Quixote wrapped up in the reflections brought on by the music of the enamored maiden Altisidora. He went to bed with them, and just like fleas they would not let him sleep or get a moment's rest—no less than did his torn stockings. But as Time is fleet-footed and no obstacle can stay his course, he came riding on the hours, and morning very soon arrived. Seeing this, Don Quixote quitted the soft down, and, not at all sluggish, dressed himself in his chamois suit and put on his traveling boots to hide the embarrassment of his stockings. He threw over himself his scarlet mantle, put on his head a montera of green velvet trimmed with silver edging, flung across his shoulder the baldric with his good trenchant sword, took up a large rosary that he always carried with him, and with great solemnity and precision of step proceeded to the antechamber where the duke and duchess were already dressed and waiting for him.

As he passed through a gallery, Altisidora and the other damsel, her friend, were lying in wait for him. The moment Altisidora saw him she pretended to faint, while her friend caught her in her lap and began hastily unlacing the bosom of her dress.

Don Quixote observed it, and approaching them said, "I know very well what this seizure arises from."

"I know not from what," replied the friend, "for Altisidora is the healthiest damsel in all this house. I have never heard her complain all the time I have known her. A plague on all the knights-errant in the world, if they are all ungrateful! Go away, Señor Don Quixote, for this poor child will not come to herself again so long as you are here."

To which Don Quixote returned, "Do me the favor, señora, to let a lute be placed in my chamber tonight. I will comfort this poor maiden to the best of my power; for in the early stages of love a prompt disillusion is an approved remedy." With this he retired, so as not to be judged by any who might see him there.

He had scarcely withdrawn when Altisidora, recovering from her swoon, said to her companion, "The lute must be left for him, for no doubt he intends to provide us with some music. Coming from him, it can't be bad."

They went at once to inform the duchess of what was going on, and of the lute Don Quixote asked for. She, delighted beyond measure, plotted with the duke and her two damsels to play a prank on him that would be amusing but harmless.

In high glee they waited for night, which came quickly as the day had come. As for the day, the duke and duchess spent it in charming conversation with Don Quixote. It should also be noted that sometime that day the duchess dispatched a page of hers (who in the forest had played the part of the enchanted Dulcinea) to Teresa Panza. He carried with him the letter from her husband Sancho Panza, along with the bundle of clothing that he had laid aside to be sent to her, and was charged to bring a full account of all that transpired in her presence.

When eleven o'clock came, Don Quixote found a vihuela[1] in his chamber. He tried it out, opened the window, and observed that some people were walking in the garden. After passing his fingers over the frets of the guitar and tuning it as well as he could, he spat and cleared his throat. Then, with a voice a little hoarse but full-toned, he sang the following ballad, which he had himself that day composed:

Mighty Love the hearts of maidens
Doth unsettle and perplex,
And the instrument he uses
Most of all is idleness.
Sewing, stitching, any labor,
Having always work to do,
To the poison Love instilleth
Is the antidote most sure.
And to proper-minded maidens
Who desire the matron's name
Modesty's a marriage portion,
Modesty their highest praise.
Men of prudence and discretion,
Courtiers gay and gallant knights,
With the wanton damsels dally,
But the modest take to wife.
There are passions, transient, fleeting,
Loves in hostelries declared,
Sunrise loves, with sunset ended,
When the guest hath gone his way.
Love that springs up swift and sudden,
Here today, tomorrow flown,
Passes, leaves no trace behind it,
Leaves no image on the soul.
Painting that is laid on painting
Maketh no display or show;
Where one beauty holds possession,
There no other can take hold.

[1] *vihuela:* The *vihuela* was a guitar-shaped instrument with frets and a flat back, played by plucking. Native to Spain, it differed from the lute—more popular elsewhere in Europe—which had a rounded back.

Dulcinea del Toboso
Painted on my heart I wear;
Never from its tablets, never,
Can her image be erased.
The quality of all in lovers
Most esteemed is constancy;
'Tis by this that love works wonders,
This exalts them to the skies.

Don Quixote had gotten this far with his song (to which the duke, the duchess, Altisidora, and nearly the whole household of the castle were listening), when all of a sudden from a gallery directly over his window they let down a cord with more than a hundred bells attached to it, and immediately after that emptied a great sack full of cats, which also had bells of a smaller size tied to their tails. Such was the din of the bells and the meowing of the cats, that though the duke and duchess were the pranksters, they themselves were startled by it, while Don Quixote stood paralyzed with fear.

As luck would have it, two or three of the cats made their way in through the grated window of his chamber and, running from one side to the other, made it seem as if there was a legion of devils on the loose. They extinguished the candles that were burning in the room and rushed about seeking some way of escape. The cord with the large bells never ceased rising and falling, and most of the people in the castle, ignorant of what was going on, were at their wits' end.

Don Quixote sprang to his feet and drawing his sword began making passes at the grating, shouting out, "Be gone, malignant enchanters! Be gone, you witchcraft-working rabble! I am Don Quixote of La Mancha, against whom your evil machinations will not avail nor have any power." And turning upon the cats that were running about the room, he made several lunges at them. They made a dash for the grated window and escaped—except one, which, finding itself hard pressed by the slashes of Don Quixote's sword, flew at his face and held on to his nose by its claws and teeth, causing him such pain that he cried out as loud as he could. The duke and duchess hearing this, and guessing what it was, ran with all haste to his room.

As the poor gentleman was striving with all his might to detach the cat from his face, they opened the door with a master key and went in with lights, where they witnessed the unequal combat. The duke ran forward to part the combatants, but Don Quixote cried out aloud, "Let no one take him from me! Leave me hand to hand with this demon, this wizard, this enchanter. I will teach him—I myself—who Don Quixote of La Mancha is." The cat, however, indifferent to these threats, snarled and held on. At last the duke pulled it off and flung it out the window.

Don Quixote was left with a face as full of holes as a sieve and a nose in not very good condition, greatly vexed that they did not let him finish the battle he had been so stoutly fighting with that villain of an enchanter. They sent for some oil of Aparicio,[2] and Altisidora herself with her own fair hands bandaged his wounds. As she did so, she said to him in a low voice. "All these mishaps have befallen you, hardhearted knight, for the sin of your insensibility and obstinacy. God grant that your squire Sancho forget to whip himself, so that that your dearly beloved Dulcinea may never be released from her enchantment and you may never come to her bed—at least while I who adore you am alive."

To all this Don Quixote made no answer except to heave deep sighs. Afterwards, he stretched himself on his bed, thanking the duke and duchess for their kindness, not because he stood in any fear of that bell-ringing rabble of enchanters in cat shape, but because he recognized their good intentions in coming to his rescue. The duke and duchess left him to rest and withdrew greatly grieved at the unfortunate result of their prank, as they never thought the adventure would have fallen so heavy on Don Quixote or cost him so dear.

It turned out costing him five days of confinement to his bed, during which he had another adventure, pleasanter than the recent one, which his chronicler will not relate just now in order that he may turn his attention to Sancho Panza, who was proceeding in his government with great diligence and no shortage of comedy.

[2] *oil of Aparicio:* ointment attributed to the sixteenth-century Morisco healer Aparicio de Zubia. When applied directly to the skin, it helped reduce inflammation, soothe pain, and prevent infection. The closely guarded formula included St. John's wort, turpentine, and rosemary.

CHAPTER XLVII

WHEREIN IS CONTINUED THE ACCOUNT OF HOW SANCHO PANZA CONDUCTED HIMSELF IN HIS GOVERNMENT

The history says that from the court of justice they carried Sancho to a sumptuous palace, where in a spacious chamber there was a table laid out with royal magnificence. The clarions sounded as Sancho entered the room, and four pages came forward to present him with water for his hands, which Sancho received with great dignity. The music ceased, and Sancho seated himself at the head of the table, for there was only a single chair and no more than one place setting. A personage (afterwards revealed to be a physician) took his place standing at Sancho's side with a whalebone wand in his hand. They then removed a fine white cloth covering fruit and a great variety of dishes. Someone who looked like a student said grace, and a page tied a laced bib on Sancho, while another who played the part of head butler set a dish of fruit before him. But hardly had he tasted a morsel when the man with the wand touched the plate with it, and they took it away from Sancho's presence with the utmost celerity. The butler brought him another dish, and Sancho proceeded to try it; but before he could get to it, not to say taste it, the wand had already touched it and a page had carried it off with the same promptness as the fruit. Sancho seeing this was puzzled and, looking from one to another, asked if this dinner would have to be eaten by sleight of hand.

To this the man with the wand replied, "It is not to be eaten, señor governor, except as is usual and customary in other islands where there are governors. I, señor, am a physician, and I am paid a salary in this island to serve its governors as such. I have a much greater regard for their health than for my own, studying day and night and making myself acquainted with the governor's constitution in order to be able to cure him when he falls sick. My principal responsibility is to attend at his dinners and suppers to allow him to eat what appears to me to be fit for him, and to keep from him what I think will do him harm and be injurious to his stomach. For this reason, I ordered that plate of fruit to be removed as being too moist. That other dish I ordered to be removed as being too hot and containing many spices that stimulate thirst; for he who drinks much kills and consumes the radical moisture wherein life consists."[1]

[1] *radical moisture wherein life consists:* according to Galenic theory, the innate vital moisture that sustains life, gradually consumed over time.

"Well then," said Sancho, "that dish of roast partridges over there that looks so well-seasoned won't do me any harm."

To this the physician replied, "Those my lord the governor shall not eat so long as I live."

"Why not?" asked Sancho.

"Because," replied the doctor, "our master Hippocrates, the north star and beacon of medicine, says in one of his aphorisms: *omnis saturatio mala, perdicis autem pessima*, which means 'all overindulgence is bad, but that of partridge is the worst.'"[2]

"In that case," said Sancho, "let señor doctor decide which of the dishes on the table will do me the most good and the least harm, and let me eat it without his tapping it with his stick. For by the life of the governor—and so may God allow me to enjoy it—I'm dying of hunger. In spite of the doctor and all he may say, to deny me food is the way to take my life instead of prolonging it."

"Your worship is right, señor governor," said the physician. "Therefore, it is my opinion that your worship should not eat of those stewed rabbits there, because it is a furry kind of food. If that veal were not roasted and served with pickles, you might try it. But it is out of the question."

"That great big steaming dish over there," said Sancho, "seems to me to be an olla podrida.[3] With such a variety of things to be found in an olla podrida, I'm sure to come across something tasty and good for me."

"*Absit*,"[4] said the doctor. "Away with such a base thought! There is nothing in the world less nourishing than an olla podrida. Save them for the canons, the college rectors, and the peasants' weddings, but let us find no olla podrida at a governor's table, where everything present should be prepared with all refinement and care. The reason for this is that always, everywhere, and by everybody, simple medicines are more esteemed than compound ones. We cannot go wrong with those that are simple, while in the compound we may go wrong by merely altering the quantity of the things that comprise them. I am of the opinion that what the governor should eat now in order to preserve and strengthen his health is a hundred or so wafers[5] and a few thin slices of quince paste, which will settle his stomach and help his digestion."

Sancho on hearing this sat back in his chair and surveyed the doctor intently, and in a solemn tone asked him what his name was and where he had studied.

He replied, "My name, señor governor, is Doctor Pedro Recio de Agüero.[6] I am a native of a place called Tirteafuera, which lies between Caracuel and

[2] omnis saturatio mala, perdicis autem pessima ... *partridge is the worst:* The doctor modifies an aphorism attributed to Hippocrates, substituting "bread" (*panis*) with "partridges" (*perdicis*).

[3] *olla podrida:* stew made with a variety of meats, beans, and vegetables. The name of the dish has passed into English as a synonym for "hodgepodge".

[4] Absit: Latin, "Far be it from me."

[5] *wafers: suplicaciones*, tube-shaped wafers named for the stick (*palillo de suplicación*) used to shape the dough.

[6] *Recio de Agüero: recio* (harsh); *agüero* (omen).

Almodóvar del Campo, on the right-hand side,[7] and I have the degree of doctor from the University of Osuna."[8]

To which Sancho, glowing with rage, returned, "Then let Doctor Pedro Recio de Mal Agüero,[9] native of Tirteafuera, a place that's on the right-hand side as we go from Caracuel to Almodóvar del Campo, graduate of Osuna, get out of my presence at once; or else I swear by the sun, I'll take a club to every doctor on this island, beginning with you, until there's not one left—at least no more of the ignorant ones. As to the learned, wise, sensible physicians, I'll revere them as divine persons. Once more I say, let Pedro Recio get out of here or I'll take this chair I am sitting on and break it over your head. And if they call me to account for it, I'll clear myself by saying I served God by killing a bad doctor—a public executioner. Now give me something to eat, or else take your government; for a trade that doesn't feed its master isn't worth two beans."

The doctor was stunned when he saw the governor in such a passion, and he would have made a *tirteafuera* out of the room but that the same instant a post horn[10] sounded in the street. The butler, going to the window, turned back and said, "It's a courier from my lord the duke, no doubt with some dispatch of importance."

The courier came in sweating and agitated and, taking a piece of paper from his breast, placed it in the governor's hands. Sancho handed it to the majordomo and asked him to read the address, which ran thus:

> To Don Sancho Panza, Governor of the Island of Barataria, into his own hands or those of his secretary.

Sancho, when he heard this said, "Which of you is my secretary?"

"I am, señor," said one of those present, "for I can read and write. I'm also a Biscayan."[11]

"With that addition," said Sancho, "you might be secretary to the emperor himself. Open this paper and see what it says." The newly minted secretary obeyed, and having read the contents said the matter was one to be discussed in private. Sancho ordered everyone to leave the chamber except the majordomo and the butler. The doctor and the others withdrew, and then the secretary read the letter, which was as follows:

> It has come to my knowledge, Señor Don Sancho Panza, that certain enemies of mine and of the island are planning to make a furious attack upon it some night,

[7] *Tirteafuera . . . right-hand side:* village in La Mancha, southwest of Ciudad Real. Cervantes plays on the similarity between *Tirteafuera* and the expression *Tírate afuera* ("Be gone").

[8] *degree of doctor from the University of Osuna:* minor university that did not have a medical school. The madman of Seville, from the story that the barber tells at the opening of Part II, is also an Osuna graduate.

[9] *Mal Agüero:* "Bad Omen".

[10] *post horn:* coiled brass instrument with cupped mouthpiece that couriers used to announce their arrival or departure.

[11] *Biscayan:* The Basque secretary—loyal, cautious in speech, and a capable writer—was proverbial in early modern Spain.

I know not when. It behooves you to be on the alert and keep watch, lest they catch you by surprise. I also know by trustworthy spies that four people have entered the town in disguise in order to take your life, because they stand in dread of your keen mind. Keep your eyes open and be heedful of who approaches to address you, and eat nothing that is presented to you. I will take care to send you aid if you find yourself in difficulty, but in all things you will act as may be expected of your judgment.

From this place, the Sixteenth of August, at four in the morning.

Your friend,
THE DUKE

Sancho was astonished, and those who stood by pretended to be so too. Turning to the majordomo he said to him, "What we have to do first, and it must be done at once, is to lock up Doctor Recio; for if anyone wants to kill me it's him, and the worst way of all—a slow death from hunger."

"Likewise," said the butler, "it is my opinion your worship should not eat anything that is on this table, for the meal was a present from some nuns; and as they say, 'Behind the cross there's the devil.'"

"I don't deny it," said Sancho. "For the present, give me a piece of bread and four pounds or so of grapes. No poison can come in them. The fact is I can't go on without eating, and if we are to be prepared for these battles that are threatening us we must be well provisioned; for 'it's the gut that leads the heart and not the heart that leads the gut.' You, secretary, answer my lord the duke and tell him that all his commands will be obeyed to the letter, as he directs; and say from me to my lady the duchess that I kiss her hands, and that I beg of her not to forget to send my letter and bundle to my wife Teresa Panza by a messenger. I will take it as a great favor and will not fail to serve her in all that may be within my power. While you're at it, you can include a kiss of the hand to my master Don Quixote, so that he can see I'm grateful. As a good secretary and a good Biscayan you can add whatever you like and whatever suits. And now clear this table and give me something to eat, and I'll be ready to meet all the spies and assassins and enchanters that come against me or my island."

At this moment a page entered saying, "Here is a farmer on business, who wants to speak to your lordship on a matter of great importance, he says."

"It's very strange," said Sancho, "the ways of these men on business. Is it possible they can be such fools not to see that a time like this is no time for coming on business? Those of us who govern and those of us who are judges—are we not men of flesh and blood, and are we not to be allowed a little rest; or do they think we're made of marble? By God and on my conscience, if the government remains in my hands (and I have a feeling it won't), I'm going to put more than one man on business in his place. Now then, tell this good man to come in, but first make sure that he's not some spy or one of my assassins."

"No, my lord," said the page, "for he looks like a worthy fellow. Either I know very little, or he is as good as good bread."

"There is nothing to be afraid of," said the majordomo, "for we are all here."

"Would it be possible, butler," said Sancho, "now that Doctor Pedro Recio is not here, to let me eat something with some substance to it, even if it's just a piece of bread and an onion?"

"Tonight at supper," said the butler, "the shortcomings of the dinner shall be made right, and your lordship shall be fully contented."

"God grant it," said Sancho.

The farmer now came in, a fine-looking man, who one could tell from a thousand leagues off was an honest fellow and a good soul. The first thing he said was, "Who here is the lord governor?"

"Who should it be," said the secretary, "but the one who is seated in the chair?"

"Then I humble myself before him," said the farmer, and kneeling before him he asked for his hand to kiss it. Sancho refused, and told him to stand up and say what he wanted. The farmer obeyed and then said, "I am a farmer, señor, a native of Miguelturra, a village two leagues from Ciudad Real."

"Another Tirteafuera!" said Sancho. Go on, brother. I know Miguelturra very well, I can tell you, for it's not very far from my own town."

"The case is this, señor," continued the farmer. "By God's mercy, I am married by the license and customs of the holy Roman Catholic Church. I have two sons, students: the younger is studying to become a bachelor, and the elder to be a licentiate. I am a widower, for my wife died, or more properly speaking, a bad doctor killed her, giving her a purge when she was with child. If it had pleased God that the child had been born and was a boy, I would have had him study to be a doctor so that he might not be jealous of his brothers the bachelor and the licentiate."

"So you're saying that if your wife had not died, or had not been killed, you would not now be a widower?" asked Sancho.

"No, señor, certainly not," said the farmer.

"I'm glad we cleared that up," said Sancho. "Keep going, brother, for it's closer to bedtime than business time."

"Well then," said the farmer, "this son of mine who is going to be a bachelor fell in love with a maiden in my town named Clara Perlerina, the daughter of Andrés Perlerino, a very rich farmer. This name of Perlerines does not come to them by their ancestry, but because all the family are paralytics,[12] and for a better name they call them Perlerines. Though to tell the truth, the maiden is as lovely as an Oriental pearl, and like a flower of the field—if you look at her on the right side; on the left not so much, for on that side she is missing an eye that she lost by smallpox. And though her face is covered with deep pits, those who love her say that they aren't pits but the graves where the hearts of her lovers are buried. She is so cleanly that, not to soil her face, she carries her nose turned up, as they say, so that one would fancy it was running away from her mouth. In spite of all this, she is exceedingly attractive. She has a wide mouth, and except for the ten or twelve teeth and molars she's missing, she might set a new standard in beauty. I have nothing to add about her lips, for they are so fine and delicate

[12] *paralytics: perláticos*, those suffering from palsy (*perlesía*), the loss of voluntary movement.

that, if lips could be spun into thread, you could make a skein of them. Being of a different color from ordinary lips, they are near miraculous, all mottled with blue and green and an eggplant color. Let my lord the governor pardon me for painting in such detail the charms of the one who will eventually be my daughter; for I love her, and I see nothing wrong with her."

"Paint what you will," said Sancho. "I enjoy your painting. If I had eaten dinner, there could be no dessert more to my taste than your portrait."

"The dessert has yet to be served," said the farmer, "but it's coming sooner than you think. I will tell you, señor, if I could paint her gracefulness and her tall figure, it would astonish you; but that can't be because she is bent double with her knees up to her mouth. For all that it's easy to see that if she could stand up, she'd knock her head against the ceiling. Also, she would have given her hand to my bachelor before now, only that she can't stretch it out because it's withered. But still, one can see its elegance and fine form by its long furrowed nails."

"That will do, brother," said Sancho. "Consider you have painted her from head to foot. What is it you want now? Come to the point without all this beating around the bush, and all these odds and ends."

"I want your worship, señor," said the farmer, "to do me the favor of giving me a letter of recommendation to the girl's father, begging him to be so good as to let this marriage take place, as we are not poorly matched either in the gifts of fortune or of nature. For to tell the truth, señor governor, my son is demon-possessed, and there is not a day but the evil spirits torment him three or four times. From having once fallen into the fire, he has his face puckered up like a piece of parchment, and his eyes watery and always running. But he has the disposition of an angel, and if it was not for his habit of hitting and punching himself, he'd be a saint."

"Is there anything else you want, good man?" asked Sancho.

"There's another thing I'd like," said the farmer, "but I'm afraid to mention it. Well, I'm going to get it off my chest. After all, I can't let it be rotting inside me, come what may. I mean, señor, that I'd like your worship to give me three hundred or six hundred ducats to add to my bachelor's portion, to help him in setting up house. For it's clear they must live by themselves, without being subject to meddling from their fathers-in-law."

"See if there's anything else you'd like," said Sancho, "and don't hold back from mentioning it out of bashfulness or modesty."

"No, indeed there is not," said the farmer.

The moment he said this the governor started to his feet, and seizing the chair he had been sitting on he exclaimed, "By all that's good, you smug little Don Hayseed, if you don't get out of here at once and hide yourself from my sight, I'll lay your head open with this chair. You sly son of a bitch, you devil's own painter, coming to me at this time of day to ask for six hundred ducats! How should I have them, you stinking brute? And why should I give them to you if I had them, you sneak of a fool? What do I have to do with Miguelturra or the entire Perlerines family tree? Get out I say, or by the life of my lord the duke I'll do as I said. You're not from Miguelturra. You're some rascal sent here from hell to tempt me. Why, you louse, I haven't had the government half a day, and you want me to have six hundred ducats already!"

The butler made signs to the farmer to leave the room, which he did with his head down, and to all appearance in terror lest the governor should carry his threats into effect, for the rogue knew very well how to play his part.

But let us leave Sancho in his wrath, and peace be with them all; and let us return to Don Quixote, whom we left with his face bandaged and doctored after the feline injuries, of which he was not cured for eight days. On one of these days there befell him what Cide Hamete promises to relate with that exactitude and truth with which he is accustomed to set forth everything connected with this great history, however minute it may be.

CHAPTER XLVIII

OF WHAT BEFELL DON QUIXOTE WITH DOÑA RODRÍGUEZ, THE DUCHESS' DUEÑA, TOGETHER WITH OTHER OCCURRENCES WORTHY OF RECORD AND ETERNAL REMEMBRANCE

Exceedingly moody and dejected was the sorely wounded Don Quixote, with his face bandaged and marked, not by the hand of God, but by the claws of a cat, mishaps incidental to knight-errantry.

Six days he remained without appearing in public, until one night as he lay awake thinking of his misfortunes and of Altisidora's pursuit of him, he perceived that someone was opening the door of his room with a key. At once he made up his mind that the infatuated damsel was coming to make an assault upon his chastity and put him in danger of failing in the fidelity he owed to his lady Dulcinea del Toboso. "No," said he, firmly persuaded of the truth of his idea (and he said it loud enough to be heard), "the greatest beauty upon earth shall not avail to make me renounce my adoration of her whom I bear stamped and engraved in the core of my heart and the secret depths of my bowels—be you transformed, my lady, into a clumsy country wench or into a nymph of golden Tagus weaving a web of silk and gold, be you the captive of Merlin or Montesinos. Where'er thou art, thou art mine, and where'er I am, I must be thine."

The very instant he uttered these words, the door opened. He stood up on the bed wrapped from head to foot in a yellow satin coverlet,[1] with a nightcap on his head, and his face and mustache tied up (his face because of the scratches, and his mustache to keep his whiskers from drooping and falling down), giving him the appearance of the most extraordinary scarecrow that could be conceived. He kept his eyes fixed on the door, and just as he was expecting to see the lovelorn Altisidora make her appearance, he saw a most venerable dueña enter. She was wearing a veil with fringe, white in color and so long that it enveloped her from head to foot. Between the fingers of her left hand, she held a short lighted candle, while with her right she shaded it to keep the light from her eyes, which were covered by spectacles of great size. She advanced with noiseless steps, treading very carefully.

Don Quixote kept an eye upon her from his watchtower. After observing her attire and noting her silence, he concluded that it must be some witch or

[1] *coverlet:* bedspread.

sorceress that was coming in such a costume to cast a spell on him, and he began hurriedly crossing himself. Still, the specter advanced and, on reaching the middle of the room, looked up and saw the frenzy with which Don Quixote was crossing himself.

If he was scared by seeing such a figure as hers, she was terrified at the sight of his; for the moment she saw his tall yellow form with the coverlet and the bandages that disfigured him, she gave a loud scream and exclaimed, "Jesus! What's this I see?"

In her fright, the candle fell from her hands. Finding herself in the dark, she turned round to run off, but stumbling on her skirts in her consternation, she measured her length with a mighty fall.

Don Quixote in his trepidation began saying, "I conjure you, phantom—or whatever you are—tell me who you are and what you want of me. If you are a soul in torment, say so, and all that my powers can do I will do for you. I am a Catholic Christian and love to do good to all the world, and to this end I have embraced the order of knight-errantry to which I belong, the province of which extends to doing good even to souls in purgatory."

The unfortunate dueña hearing herself thus conjured, by her own fear guessed Don Quixote's and in a low plaintive voice answered, "Señor Don Quixote—if you are indeed Don Quixote—I am no phantom or specter or soul in purgatory, as you seem to think, but Doña Rodríguez, dueña of honor to my lady the duchess. I come to you with one of those grievances that your worship is in the business of redressing."

"Tell me, Señora Doña Rodríguez," said Don Quixote, "have you by chance come to act as a go-between? Because I must tell you I am not available for anyone's benefit, thanks to the peerless beauty of my lady Dulcinea del Toboso. In short, Señora Doña Rodríguez, if you will leave aside any love messages, you may go and light your candle and come back, and we will discuss all the commands you have for me and whatever you wish, saving only, as I said, all seductive communications."

"I carry nobody's messages, señor," said the dueña. "Little do you know me. I am hardly advanced enough in years to take to any such childish tricks. God be praised my body still has its vigor, and all my teeth and molars in my mouth, except one or two that the colds, so common in this Aragon country, have robbed me of. But wait a little while I go and light my candle; I will return immediately and lay my sorrows before you as before one who relieves those of all the world." And without staying for an answer she went out of the room and left Don Quixote tranquilly meditating while he waited for her.

A thousand thoughts at once suggested themselves to him on the subject of this new adventure. It struck him as being ill done and worse advised on his part to expose himself to the danger of breaking his pledged faith to his lady. Said he to himself, "Who knows but that the devil, being wily and cunning, may be trying now to entrap me with a dueña, having failed with empresses, queens, duchesses, marchionesses, and countesses. Many a time have I heard it said by men of sense that he will sooner offer you a flat-nosed wench than a woman with a pleasing profile; and who knows but this silence and seclusion may prove the opportunity to awaken my sleeping desires and lead me in these my latter years to fall where I have never stumbled. In cases like this, it is better to flee than to await the battle. But I must be out of my senses to think and utter such nonsense; for it is impossible that a white-hooded dueña, spindly and bespectacled, could excite a wanton sentiment in the world's most indifferent heart. Is there any dueña on earth with fair flesh? Is there any dueña in the wide world that is not short-tempered, wrinkled, and prudish? Be gone, then, dueña crew, undelightful to all mankind. Oh, but that lady did well who, they say, set two statues of dueñas with spectacles and lace cushions at the end of her reception room, as if at work, and the figures gave the place as much of an air of propriety as if they had been real dueñas."

So saying he leaped off the bed, intending to close the door and not allow Señora Rodríguez to enter. But as he went to shut it, Señora Rodríguez returned with a lighted candle, and having a closer view of Don Quixote with the coverlet around him and his bandages and nightcap, she was alarmed afresh. Retreating a couple of paces, she exclaimed, "Am I safe, sir knight? For I don't look upon it as a sign of very great virtue that your worship should have gotten up out of bed."

"I may well ask the same, señora," said Don Quixote, "and I do ask: shall I be safe from being assailed and forced?"

"Of whom and against whom do you demand that security, sir knight?" asked the dueña.

"Of you and against you I ask it," replied Don Quixote. "For I am not marble, nor are you bronze, nor is it now ten o'clock in the morning, but midnight (or a little past it, I imagine), and we are in a room more secluded and private than the cave must have been where the treacherous and daring Æneas enjoyed the fair, soft-hearted Dido. But give me your hand, señora. I require no better protection than my own continence and my own sense of propriety, as well as that which is inspired by that venerable headdress." So saying he kissed his right hand, then took hers in his own, she yielding hers to him with the same ceremony.[2] (Here Cide Hamete inserts a parenthesis in which he says that to have seen the two of them hand in hand as they went from the door to the bed, he would have given the best of his two mantles.[3])

Don Quixote finally got into bed, and Doña Rodríguez took her seat on a chair at a little distance without taking off her spectacles or setting aside the candle. Don Quixote wrapped himself completely in the bedcovers, leaving nothing but his face visible.

As soon as they had both regained their composure, he broke silence saying, "Now, Señora Doña Rodríguez, you may unburden yourself of all that is buried

[2] *So saying . . . same ceremony:* As written, each one kisses his own hand before taking the other's. This may reflect a copyist's error, an obscure custom, or one of Cervantes' whimsical flourishes.

[3] *mantles: almalafas*. The *almalafa* was an enveloping outer wrap worn by Spanish Muslims and their descendants, banned in a 1567 royal decree.

in your sorrowful heart and afflicted bowels. By me you shall be listened to with chaste ears and aided by compassionate exertions."

"I believe it," replied the dueña. "From your worship's gentle and winning presence, only such a Christian answer could be expected. The fact is, Señor Don Quixote, that though you see me seated in this chair, here in the middle of the kingdom of Aragon, and in the attire of a despised outcast dueña, I am from the Oviedo region of Asturias, and of a family with which many of the best of the province are connected by blood.[4] My unkind fate and the improvidence of my parents (who, I know not how, were unseasonably reduced to poverty), brought me to the court of Madrid, where as a provision and to avoid greater misfortunes, my parents placed me as a handmaid in the service of a noblewoman—and I would have you know that for sewing hems and backstitches, I have never been surpassed by any in all my life. My parents left me in service and returned to their own country, and a few years later went, no doubt, to heaven, for they were exceedingly faithful Catholic Christians. I was left an orphan with nothing but the miserable wages and paltry gifts that are given to such maids in palaces.

"About this time, without any encouragement on my part, one of the squires of the household fell in love with me, a man somewhat advanced in years, full-bearded and personable, and above all as good a gentleman as the king himself, for he came of mountain stock. We did not carry on our relationship with such secrecy but that they came to the knowledge of my lady, and she, not to have any fuss about it, had us married with the full sanction of the holy mother Roman Catholic Church. From this marriage a daughter was born who put an end to my good fortune, if I had any—not that I died in childbirth, for I passed through it safely and in due season, but because shortly afterwards my husband died of a certain shock he received. Had I time to tell you of it, I know your worship would be surprised."

Here she began to weep bitterly and said, "Pardon me, Señor Don Quixote, if I am unable to control myself, for every time I think of my unfortunate husband my eyes fill up with tears. God bless me, with what an air of dignity he used to carry my lady behind him on a stout mule as black as jet! For in those days they did not use coaches or litters, as they say they do now, but ladies rode on the croup[5] behind their squires. This much at least I cannot help telling you, that you may observe the good breeding and punctiliousness of my worthy husband. Turning once into the Calle de Santiago in Madrid, which is rather narrow, he came upon one of the magistrates of the Court, with two constables before him, emerging from it. As soon as my good squire saw him, he wheeled his mule about and made as if he would turn and accompany him.[6] My lady, who was riding behind him, said to him in a low voice, 'What are you doing, you idiot? Don't you see that I am here?' The magistrate like a polite man pulled up his horse and said to him, 'Proceed, señor, for it is I, rather, who ought to escort my lady

[4] *Oviedo region of Asturias . . . by blood:* Asturias, in northwest Spain, was the cradle of the Reconquista, where Spain's most noble families traced their Visigothic lineage.

[5] *croup:* rump.

[6] *as if he would turn and accompany him:* a sign of respect.

Doña Casilda'—for that was my mistress' name. Still my husband, cap in hand, persisted in trying to accompany the magistrate. Seeing this, my lady, filled with rage and vexation, pulled out a large pin (or, I rather think, a bodkin[7]) out of her needle case and drove it into his back with such force that my husband gave a loud yell, and writhing fell to the ground with his lady. Her two footmen ran to pick her up, and the magistrate and the bailiffs did the same.

The Guadalajara Gate was all in a commotion—I mean the idlers congregated there. My mistress came back on foot, and my husband hurried away to a barber's shop protesting that he was run right through the guts. My husband's courtesy was noised abroad to such an extent that the boys mocked him openly in the street. On this account (and because he was somewhat shortsighted), my lady dismissed him, and I am convinced beyond a doubt that grief over this brought on his death. I was left a helpless widow, with a daughter on my hands growing in beauty like the seafoam. Eventually, however, as I had the character of being an excellent needlewoman, my lady the duchess (then recently married to my lord the duke), offered to take me with her to this kingdom of Aragon, and my daughter also, and here as time went by my daughter grew up and with her all the graces in the world. She sings like a lark, dances at balls as lightly as thought and in the open air like someone spellbound, reads and writes like a schoolmaster, and does sums like a miser. Of her cleanliness I say nothing, for the running water is not purer. Her age is now, if my memory serves me, sixteen years five months and three days—one more or less.

"To come to the point, the son of a very rich farmer from a village of my lord the duke's not very far from here fell in love with my little girl. How I know not, they came together, and under the promise of marrying her he made a fool of my daughter, and will not keep his word. Though my lord the duke is aware of it (for I have complained to him, not once but many and many a time, and entreated him to order the farmer to marry my daughter), he turns a deaf ear and will scarcely listen to me—the reason being that as the deceiver's father is so rich, and lends him money, and is constantly putting up security for his debts, he does not wish to offend or annoy him in any way. Now, señor, I want your worship to take it upon yourself to redress this wrong either by entreaty or by arms; for by what all the world says, you came into it to redress grievances and right wrongs and help the unfortunate. Let your worship put before you the unprotected condition of my daughter, her youth, and all the perfections I have said she possesses. Before God and on my conscience, out of all the damsels my lady has, there is not one that comes up to the sole of her shoe. The one they call Altisidora, who they look upon as the most charming and elegant of them, put in comparison with my daughter, does not come within two leagues of her. For I would have you know, señor, all that glitters is not gold. That same little Altisidora is more of a hussy than a beauty, and more impudent than modest. Besides that, she's not in fine form, for she has such a disagreeable breath that one cannot bear to be near her

[7] *bodkin:* thick metal needle used to pierce fabric or leather, thread ribbons through tight spaces, or mark patterns for embroidery.

for a moment. Even my lady the duchess ... but I'll hold my tongue, for they say that walls have ears."

"On my life, Doña Rodríguez, what ails my lady the duchess?" asked Don Quixote.

"Well, if you insist," replied the dueña, "I cannot help answering the question and telling the whole truth. Señor Don Quixote, have you observed how attractive my lady the duchess is, that complexion of hers like the smoothness of a polished sword, those two cheeks of milk and scarlet—the one like the sun and the other like the moon—that lively step with which she treads or rather seems to spurn the earth, so that one would fancy she went radiating health wherever she passed? Well, let me tell you she may thank God for this, first of all, and next two drains she has, one in each leg, by which all the evil humors—of which the doctors say she is full—are discharged."[8]

"Blessed Virgin!" exclaimed Don Quixote. "Is it possible that my lady the duchess has drains of that sort? I would not have believed it if the barefoot friars had told me; but as the lady Doña Rodríguez says so, it must be so. Surely such incisions, and in such places, do not discharge humors, but liquid amber. Verily, I do believe now that this practice of draining humors is a very important matter for one's health."

Don Quixote had hardly said this, when the chamber door flew open with a loud bang. With the start the noise gave her, Doña Rodríguez let the candle fall from her hand, and the room was left as dark as a wolf's mouth, as the saying is. Suddenly the poor dueña felt two hands seize her by the throat, so tightly that she could not cry out, while someone else, without uttering a word, very briskly hoisted up her petticoats and, with what seemed to be a slipper, began to lay into her so fiercely that anyone would have felt pity for her. Although Don Quixote did pity her, he never stirred from his bed, but stayed quiet, apprehensive that his turn for a drubbing might be coming. Nor was the apprehension an idle one; for leaving the dueña (who did not dare to cry out) well basted, the silent executioners fell upon Don Quixote. Stripping him of his sheet and coverlet, they pinched him so fast and so hard that he was driven to defend himself with his fists, and all this in marvelous silence. The battle lasted nearly half an hour, and then the ghosts fled. Doña Rodríguez gathered up her skirts and, bemoaning her fate, went out without saying a word to Don Quixote, while he, sorely pinched, puzzled, and dejected, remained alone. There we will leave him, wondering who could have been the perverse enchanter who had reduced him to such a state. But that shall be told in due season, for Sancho claims our attention, and the methodical arrangement of the story demands it.

[8] *drains ... are discharged:* Consistent with premodern humoral medical theory, incisions were made in the body to drain excess humors—what we know now is blood and the various fluids produced by a topical infection. To prevent the wound from healing, physicians would make repeated incisions, treat the wound with irritants, or insert substances into the opening like wax beads or garbanzos. In early modern Spain, drains were most commonly opened in a woman's thighs to treat infertility.

CHAPTER XLIX

OF WHAT HAPPENED TO SANCHO IN MAKING THE ROUND OF HIS ISLAND

We left the great governor angered and irritated by that portrait-painting rogue of a farmer who, instructed by the majordomo, as the majordomo was by the duke, was playing a prank on him. Sancho—foolish, boorish, and rotund as he was—held his own against them all, saying to those around him and to Doctor Pedro Recio, who as soon as the private business of the duke's letter was disposed of had returned to the room, "Now I see plainly enough that judges and governors have to be made of bronze not to resist the demands of the applicants that at all times and seasons insist on being heard and helped, and their own affairs and no others attended to, come what may. And if the poor judge does not hear them and settle the matter—either because he cannot or because it is not the time set apart for hearing them—they immediately start to abuse him, run him down, gnaw at his bones, and even pick holes in his pedigree. You silly, stupid applicant, don't be in a hurry! Wait for the proper time and season for doing business. Don't come at the dinner hour, or at bedtime; for judges are only flesh and blood, and must give to their nature what she naturally demands of them—all except myself, for in my case I give her nothing to eat, thanks to Señor Doctor Pedro Recio Tirteafuera here, who would have me die of hunger, and declares this death to be life. May God give the same life to him and all his kind—I mean the bad doctors. The good ones deserve palms and laurels."

All who knew Sancho Panza were astonished to hear him speak so elegantly, and did not know what to attribute it to unless it was that public office and sober responsibility either sharpen or dull a man's wits. At last Doctor Pedro Recio Agüero of Tirteafuera promised to let him have supper that night, even if it violated all the aphorisms of Hippocrates. With this the governor was satisfied and looked forward to the approach of night and suppertime with great eagerness. Though time, to his mind, stood still and made no progress, nevertheless the hour he so longed for came, and they gave him a beef salad with onions and some boiled calves' feet quite far gone. He fell to it with greater relish than if they had given him francolins[1] from Milan, pheasants from Rome, veal from Sorrento, partridges from Morón, or geese from Lavajos.

Turning to the doctor at supper he said to him, "Look here, señor doctor, for the future don't trouble yourself about giving me dainty things or choice dishes to

[1] *francolins:* probably the black francolin, a gamebird of the pheasant family, raised in captivity as a delicacy for the Spanish élite.

eat, for it will be only taking my stomach off its hinges. It's accustomed to goat, cow, bacon, jerky, turnips, and onions. If by any chance it's given these palace dishes, it takes them squeamishly, and sometimes with loathing. What the head butler had best do is to serve me with what they call ollas podridas (and the rottener they are the better they smell). He can put whatever he likes into them, so long as it's good to eat. I'll be obliged to him and will repay him some day. But let nobody play pranks on me, for 'either we are or we are not.'[2] Let's live and eat in peace and good company, for 'when God sends the dawn, he sends it for all.' I mean to govern this island without giving up a right or taking a bribe. 'Let every man keep his eyes open, and watch out for the arrow.' I can tell them 'the devil's in Cantillana ...'[3] and if they drive me to it they'll see something that will astonish them. Otherwise, 'if you make yourself honey, the flies will eat you.'"[4]

"Of a truth, señor governor," said the butler, "your worship is in the right about everything you have said. I promise you in the name of all the inhabitants of this island that they will serve your worship with all zeal, affection, and goodwill, for the mild kind of government you have already given a sample of leaves them no ground for doing or thinking anything to your worship's disadvantage."

"I believe it," said Sancho, "and they would be great fools if they did or thought otherwise. Once more I say, see to my feeding and my Dapple's, for that's what matters most. When the hour comes let's make the rounds,[5] for it is my intention to purge this island of every kind of corruption and of all good-for-nothing layabouts. I would have you know that lazy idlers are the same thing in a State as the drones in a hive: they eat up the honey that the worker bees make. I mean to protect the laborer, to preserve the privileges of the hidalgos, to reward the virtuous, and above all to respect religion and honor its ministers. What do you say to that, my friends? Do I have a point, or am I spouting nonsense?"

"There is so much in what your worship says, señor governor," said the majordomo, "that I am filled with wonder when I see a man like your worship, entirely without learning (for I believe you have none at all), say such things, and so full of sound maxims and sage remarks—very different from what was expected of your worship's intelligence by those who sent us or by us who came here. Every day we see something new in this world: mockeries become realities, and mockers find themselves mocked."

Night came, and with the permission of Doctor Pedro Recio, the governor had supper. They then got ready to make the rounds, and he set off with the majordomo, the secretary, the head butler, the chronicler charged with recording his deeds, and constables and notaries enough to form a fair-sized squadron. In the midst marched Sancho with his staff, as fine a sight as one could wish to see. Only a few streets of the town had been traversed when they heard a noise as of

[2] *either we are or we are not:* "we should act naturally."

[3] *the devil's in Cantillana . . . :* ". . . and the bishop's in Brenes" ("there's always something going on somewhere").

[4] *if you make yourself honey, the flies will eat you:* See footnote 8, page 671.

[5] *make the rounds:* patrol the city after curfew.

a clashing of swords. They hurried to the spot, and found that the combatants were but two, who seeing the authorities approaching stood still. One of them exclaimed, "Help, in the name of God and the king! Are men to be allowed to rob in the middle of this town and rush out and attack people in the very streets?"

"Be calm, my good man," said Sancho, "and tell me what the cause of this quarrel is; for I am the governor."

Said the other combatant, "Señor governor, I will tell you in a very few words. Your worship must know that this gentleman has just now won more than a thousand reals in that gambling house opposite—and God knows how. I was there, and decided more than one doubtful point in his favor, very much against what my conscience told me. He collected his winnings, and when I expected him to give me at least an escudo or so for a tip—what is usual and customary to give men of quality of my kind who stand by to see fair or foul play, back up swindles, and prevent quarrels—he pocketed his money and left the house. Indignant at this I followed him and, speaking to him fairly and civilly, asked him to give me something, even if it were only eight reals. He knows I am an honest man and that I have neither profession (for my parents never taught me any) nor property (for my parents left me none). But the rogue, who is a greater thief than Cacus and a greater sharper than Andradilla,[6] would not give me more than four reals; so your worship may see how little shame and conscience he has. By my faith if you had not come up, I'd have made him disgorge his winnings and taught him a lesson he wouldn't forget."

"What do you say to this?" asked Sancho. The other replied that all his antagonist said was true, and that he did not choose to give him more than four reals because he very often gave him money; and that those who expected tips ought to be civil and take what is given to them in good cheer and not make any claim against winners unless they know them for certain to be sharpers and their winnings to be unfairly won; and there could be no better proof that he himself was an honest man than his having refused to give anything; for sharpers always pay something to the lookers-on who know them.

"That is true," said the majordomo. "Let your worship consider what is to be done with these men."

"What is to be done," said Sancho, "is this: you, the winner, whether you're good, bad, or indifferent, give this assailant of yours a hundred reals at once, and you must disburse thirty more for the poor prisoners; and you who have neither profession nor property, and linger about the island in idleness, take these hundred reals now, and sometime tomorrow leave the island under sentence of banishment for ten years—and under pain of completing it in another life if you violate the sentence, for I'll hang you on a gibbet, or at least the hangman will by my orders. Not a word from either of you, or I'll make him feel the weight of my hand."

The one paid down the money and the other took it, and the latter left the island, while the other went home. Then the governor said, "Either I'm not good

[6] *greater sharper than Andradilla:* The identity of this sharper (gambling cheat) is unknown.

for much, or I'll get rid of these gambling houses, for it strikes me they bring nothing but trouble."

"This one at least," said one of the notaries, "your worship will not be able to get rid of, for a great man owns it, and what he loses every year is beyond all comparison more than what he makes by the cards. On the minor gambling houses your worship may exercise your power, and it is they that do the most harm and shelter the most barefaced practices; for in the houses of lords and gentlemen of quality the notorious sharpers dare not attempt to play their tricks. As the vice of gambling has become common, it is better that men should play in houses of repute than in some tradesman's, where they catch an unlucky fellow in the small hours of the morning and skin him alive."

"I am quite aware, notary, that there is a good deal to be said on that point," said Sancho.

And now a bailiff[7] came up with a young man in his grasp and said, "Señor governor, this youth was coming towards us, and as soon as he saw the officers of justice he turned round and ran like a deer—a sure proof that he must be some evildoer. I ran after him, and had it not been that he stumbled and fell, I should never have caught him."

"What did you run for, fellow?" asked Sancho.

To which the young man replied, "Señor, it was to avoid answering all the questions that officers of justice ask."

"What are you by trade?"

"A weaver."

"And what do you weave?"

"Lance heads, with your worship's good leave."

"Joking with me are you—like some second-rate jester? How charming. And where were you going just now?"

"To get some fresh air, señor."

"And where does one get some fresh air on this island?"

"Wherever it blows."

"Very nice. Your answers are always on point, you smart young fellow. Take notice now that I am the air, and that I blow upon you astern and am sending you to jail. Ho there! Lay hold of him and take him away. I'll make him sleep there tonight without air."

"By God," said the young man, "your worship will make me sleep in jail just as soon as make me king."

"Why shouldn't I make you sleep in jail?" said Sancho. "Don't I have the power to arrest you and release you whenever I like?"

"All the power your worship has," said the young man, "won't be able to make me sleep in jail."

"How? Not able?" said Sancho. "Take him away at once where he'll see his mistake with his own eyes, even if the jailer is willing to exercise a little

[7] *bailiff: corchete,* low-level law enforcement officer responsible for arrests and maintaining order. The *corchete* was subordinate to a constable (*alguacil*).

interested generosity on his behalf. I'll lay a penalty of two thousand ducats on him if he lets him stir a step from the prison."

"That's ridiculous," said the young man. "The fact of the matter is that all the men on earth won't make me sleep in prison."

"Tell me, you devil," said Sancho, "do you have some angel to deliver you and take off the irons I'm going to order them to put on you?"

"Now, señor governor," said the young man in a lively manner, "let's be reasonable and come to the point. Suppose that your worship orders me to be taken to prison and have irons and chains put on me. Suppose that they lock me in a cell, that the jailer is threatened with heavy penalties if he lets me out, and that he obeys your orders. Still, if I choose not to sleep and decide to remain awake all night without closing an eye, will your worship with all your power be able to make me sleep if I don't want to?"

"No, truly," said the secretary. "The fellow has made a good point."

"So then," said Sancho, "it would be entirely of your own choice you would keep from sleeping—not to oppose my will?"

"No, señor," said the youth, "certainly not."

"Well then, go, and God be with you," said Sancho. "Be off home to bed, and God give you a good night's rest, for I don't want to rob you of it. But for the future, let me advise you not to joke with the authorities, because you may come across someone who will bring down the joke on your skull."

The young man went his way, and the governor continued his round. Shortly afterwards two bailiffs came up with a man in custody and said, "Señor governor, this person who seems to be a man is not so, but a woman—and not an unattractive one—in man's clothes." They raised two or three lanterns to her face, and by their light they distinguished the features of a woman to all appearance of the age of sixteen or a little more, with her hair gathered into a gold and green silk net, and fair as a thousand pearls. They scanned her from head to foot and observed that she had on red silk stockings with garters of white taffeta fringed with gold and pearl. Her breeches were of green and gold fabric, and under an open jacket or smock of the same material she wore a doublet of the finest white and gold cloth; her shoes were white and such as men wear. She carried no sword at her belt, but only a richly ornamented dagger, and on her fingers she had several handsome rings. In short, the girl seemed fair to look at in the eyes of all. None of those who beheld her recognized her. The townspeople said they could not imagine who she was. Those who were in on the secret of the pranks that were to be played on Sancho were the ones who were most surprised, for this incident or discovery had not been arranged by them. They watched anxiously to see how the affair would end.

Sancho was fascinated by the girl's beauty. He asked her who she was, where she was going, and what had induced her to dress herself in that outfit. She, with her eyes fixed on the ground, answered in modest confusion, "I cannot tell you, señor, before so many people what it is of such consequence to me to have kept secret. One thing I wish to be known—that I am no thief or evildoer, but only an unhappy young lady whom the power of jealousy has led to cast aside the respect due to modesty."

Hearing this the majordomo said to Sancho, "Make the people stand back, señor governor, that this lady may say what she wishes with less embarrassment."

Sancho gave the order, and everyone except the majordomo, the head butler, and the secretary stood aside. Finding herself then in the presence of no more, the damsel went on to say, "I am the daughter, sirs, of Pedro Pérez Mazorca, the tax collector on wool in this town, who is in the habit of coming very often to my father's house."

"That doesn't make sense," said the majordomo. "I know Pedro Pérez very well, and I know he has no child at all, either son or daughter. Besides, you say he is your father, yet you then add that he comes very often to your father's house."

"I had already noticed that," said Sancho.

"I am confused just now, sirs," said the damsel, "and I don't know what I'm saying. The truth is that I am the daughter of Diego de la Llana, whom you all probably know."

"Now that makes sense," said the majordomo. "I know Diego de la Llana, and know that he is a gentleman of position and a rich man, and that he has a son and a daughter, and that since he was left a widower nobody in all this town can speak of having seen his daughter's face; for he keeps her so closely shut up that he does not give even the sun a chance of seeing her. For all that, it is reported that she is extremely beautiful."

"It is true," said the damsel, "and I am that daughter. Whether the report lies or not as to my beauty, you, sirs, will have decided by this time, as you have seen me." With this she began to weep bitterly.

On seeing this the secretary leaned over to the head butler's ear and said to him in a low voice, "Something serious has no doubt happened to this poor maiden, that she goes wandering from home in such a dress and at such an hour, and one of her rank too."

"There can be no doubt about it," returned the butler, "and moreover her tears confirm your suspicion."

Sancho gave her the best comfort he could and entreated her to tell them without any fear what had happened to her, as they would all earnestly and by every means in their power attempt to relieve her.

"The fact is, sirs," said she, "that my father has kept me shut up these ten years, for that is how long it's been since the earth received my mother. Mass is said at home in a sumptuous chapel, and all this time I have seen nothing but the sun in the heaven by day, and the moon and the stars by night. Nor do I know what streets are like, or plazas, or churches, or even men, except my father and a brother I have—and Pedro Pérez the tax collector, whom, because he came frequently to our house, I took it into my head to call my father, to avoid naming my own. This seclusion and the restrictions laid upon my going out—even if it were only to church—have kept me unhappy for many a day and month past. I longed to see the world, or at least the town where I was born, and it did not seem to me that this wish was inconsistent with the respect highborn maidens should have for themselves. When I heard them talking of bullfights taking place, and mock battles put on, and plays performed, I asked my brother, who is a year younger than me, to tell me what sort of things these were, and many more that I had never seen. He explained them to me as well as he could, but the only effect was to kindle in me a still stronger desire to see them. At last, to cut short the story of my ruin, I begged and entreated my brother—O that I had never made such an entreaty—" And once more she gave way to a burst of weeping.

"Proceed, señora," said the majordomo, "and finish your story of what has happened to you, for your words and tears are keeping us all in suspense."

"I have only a little more to say, though many a tear to shed," said the damsel, "for ill-placed desires can only be paid for in some such way."

The maiden's beauty had made a deep impression on the head butler's heart. He again raised his lantern for another look at her and thought they were not tears she was shedding but seed pearl or dew of the meadow. Indeed, he exalted them still higher and made Oriental pearls of them, fervently hoping her misfortune might not be so great a one as her tears and sobs seemed to indicate. The governor was losing patience at the length of time the girl was taking to tell her story and told her not to keep them waiting any longer; for it was late, and there still remained a good deal of the town to be gone over.

She, with broken sobs and half-suppressed sighs, went on to say, "My misfortune, my misadventure, is simply this—that I entreated my brother to dress me up as a man in a suit of his clothes and take me some night, when our father was asleep, to see the whole town. He, overcome by my entreaties, consented, and dressing me in this suit and himself in clothes of mine that fitted him as if made for him—for he has not a hair on his chin, and might pass for a very beautiful young girl—tonight, about an hour ago, more or less, we left the house, and guided by our youthful and foolish impulse we made the circuit of the whole town. Then, as we were about to return home, we saw a great troop of people coming, and my brother said to me, 'Sister, this must be the round, stir your feet and put wings to them, and follow me as fast as you can, or else we'll be recognized—and that would be a bad business for us,' and so saying he turned about and began, I cannot say to run but to fly. In less than six paces I fell from fright, and then the officer of justice came up and carried me before your worships, where I find myself put to shame before all these people as capricious and wicked."

"So then, señora," said Sancho, "no other mishap has befallen you? It wasn't jealousy that made you leave home, as you said at the beginning of your story?"

"Nothing has happened me," said she. "It was not jealousy that brought me out, but merely a longing to see the world, which did not go beyond seeing the streets of this town."

The appearance of the bailiffs with her brother in custody, whom one of them had overtaken as he ran away from his sister, now fully confirmed the truth of what the damsel said. He had nothing on but a rich petticoat and a short blue damask cloak with fine gold lace. His head was uncovered and adorned only with its own hair, which looked like rings of gold, so bright and curly was it. The governor, the majordomo, and the butler went aside with him, and, unheard by his sister, asked him how he came to be in that dress. He, with no less shame and embarrassment, told exactly the same story as his sister, to the great delight of the lovestruck butler.

The governor, however, said to them, "To be perfectly honest, young lady and gentleman, this is no more than a childish escapade. There was no need for all this delay and all these tears and sighs to explain your little adventure. If you had said, 'We are so-and-so, and we escaped from our father's house like this in order to wander around, out of mere curiosity and with no other purpose,' there would have been an end of the matter, without these silly tears and sobs and all the rest of it."

"That is true," said the damsel, "but you see the confusion I was in was so great it did not let me behave as I ought."

"No harm has been done," said Sancho. "Come, we will leave you at your father's house; it may be that they haven't even missed you. The next time, don't be so childish or eager to see the world. For 'a respectable young lady should have a broken leg and keep at home,' and 'the woman and the hen by roaming about are soon lost, and 'she who is eager to see is also eager to be seen.' I say no more."

The youth thanked the governor for his kind offer to take them home, and they directed their steps towards the house, which was not far off. On reaching it the youth threw a pebble up at a grating, and immediately a female servant who was waiting for them came down and opened the door. They went in, leaving the party marveling as much at their grace and beauty as at the desire they had to see the world by night and without leaving the village—a whim they attributed to their youth.

The head butler was left with a heart pierced through and through, and he made up his mind on the spot to ask the damsel's hand in marriage from her father the following day, certain she would not be refused of him as he was a servant of the duke's. Even to Sancho, schemes of marrying the youth to his daughter Sanchica suggested themselves, and he resolved to open the negotiation at the proper season, persuading himself that no husband could be refused to a governor's daughter. And so the night's round came to an end, and a couple of days later the government itself, whereby all his plans were overthrown and swept away, as will be seen farther on.

CHAPTER L

WHEREIN IS SET FORTH WHO THE ENCHANTERS AND EXECUTIONERS WERE WHO FLOGGED THE DUEÑA AND PINCHED DON QUIXOTE, AND ALSO WHAT BEFELL THE PAGE WHO CARRIED THE LETTER TO TERESA PANZA, SANCHO PANZA'S WIFE

Cide Hamete, the painstaking investigator of the minute points of this true history, says that when Doña Rodríguez left her room to go to Don Quixote's, another dueña who slept with her observed her, and as all dueñas are fond of prying, listening, and sniffing, she followed her so silently that the good Rodríguez never noticed. As soon as the dueña saw her enter Don Quixote's room, not to fail in a dueña's notorious habit of tattling, she hurried off that instant to report to the duchess how Doña Rodríguez was in Don Quixote's room with him. The duchess told the duke and asked him to let her and Altisidora go and see what the said dueña wanted with Don Quixote.

The duke gave them leave, and the two of them cautiously and quietly crept to the door of the room and posted themselves so close to it that they could hear all that was said inside. But when the duchess heard how Rodríguez had made public the Aranjuez of her drains[1] she could not restrain herself, nor Altisidora either. And so, filled with rage and thirsting for vengeance, they burst into the room, tormenting Don Quixote and flogging the dueña in the manner already described; for indignities that offend their charms and self-esteem greatly provoke the anger of women and make them eager for revenge. The duchess told the duke what had happened, and he was much amused by it. She, to proceed with her design of entertaining herself with Don Quixote and playing pranks on him, dispatched the page who had played the part of Dulcinea in the negotiations for her disenchantment (which Sancho Panza in the cares of government had forgotten all about) to Teresa Panza his wife with her husband's letter and another from herself, and also a great string of fine coral beads as a present.

Now the history says this page was very sharp and quick-witted. Eager to serve his lord and lady, he set off very willingly for Sancho's village. As he approached

[1] *Aranjuez of her drains:* Since the late sixteenth century, the Royal Palace of Aranjuez, south of Madrid, has boasted of gardens watered by fountains (*fuentes*)—the same word translated as "drains".

it, he observed a number of women washing in a brook and asked them if they could tell him whether a woman lived there of the name of Teresa Panza, wife of one Sancho Panza, squire to a knight called Don Quixote of La Mancha. Hearing the question, a young girl who was washing stood up and said, "Teresa Panza is my mother, Sancho is my father, and the knight is our master."

"Well then, miss," said the page, "come and show me where your mother is, for I bring her a letter and a present from your father."

"That I will with all my heart, señor," said the girl, who seemed to be about fourteen, more or less. Leaving the clothes she was washing to one of her companions, and without putting anything on her head or feet (for she was bare-legged and had her hair hanging about her), away she skipped in front of the page's horse, saying, "Come, your worship, our house is at the entrance of the town, and my mother is there, very sorrowful at not having had any news of my father in many days."

"Well," said the page, "I am bringing her such good news that she will have reason to thank God."

At last, skipping, running, and capering, the girl reached the town, but before going into the house she called out at the door, "Come out, Teresa my mother, come out, come out. There's a gentleman here with letters and other things from my good father."

At these words, her mother Teresa Panza came out spinning a bundle of flax. She wore a gray petticoat (so short that one would have thought that "they to her shame had cut it short"[2]), a gray bodice of the same fabric, and a smock. The woman was not very old, though plainly past forty, strong, healthy, vigorous, and sun-worn. Seeing her daughter and the page on horseback, she exclaimed, "What's this, child? What gentleman is this?"

"A servant of my lady, Doña Teresa Panza," replied the page. Matching words to actions, he flung himself off his horse and with great humility advanced to kneel before Señora Teresa, saying, "Let me kiss your hand, Señora Doña Teresa, as the lawful and only wife of Señor Don Sancho Panza, rightful governor of the island of Barataria."

"Oh, señor, get up! Don't do that!" cried Teresa. "I'm no court lady, but only a poor country woman, the daughter of a clodhopper, and the wife of a squire-errant and not of any governor at all."

"You are," said the page, "the most worthy wife of a most arch-worthy governor. As proof of what I say, accept this letter and this present." As he said this, he took out of his pocket a string of coral beads with gold clasps and placed it on her neck, adding, "This letter is from his lordship the governor. Another letter I bring with these coral beads is from my lady the duchess, who sends me to your worship."

Teresa stood lost in astonishment, and her daughter just as much. The girl said, "May I die if our master Don Quixote's not at the bottom of this. He must have given father the government or county he so often promised him."

[2] *they to her shame had cut it short:* line from a ballad that refers to the practice of cutting short the skirts of prostitutes to shame them.

"That is the truth," said the page, "for it is through Señor Don Quixote that Señor Sancho is now governor of the island of Barataria, as will be seen by this letter."

"Will your worship read it to me, noble sir?" asked Teresa. "For though I can spin I can't read—not a scrap."

"Me neither," said Sanchica, "but wait a bit, and I'll go and fetch someone who can read it, either the priest himself or the bachelor Samson Carrasco. They'll come gladly to hear any news of my father."

"There is no need to fetch anybody," said the page, "for though I can't spin, I can read. I'll read it." And so he read it through, but as it has been already related, it is not inserted here. He then took out the other one from the duchess, which ran as follows:

Friend Teresa,

Your husband Sancho's good qualities, of heart as well as of head, induced and compelled me to request my husband the duke to give him the government of one of his many islands. I am told he governs like a gyrfalcon,[3] which makes me very happy—and, consequently, the duke as well. I am very thankful to Heaven that I have not made a mistake in choosing him for this government; for I would have Señora Teresa know that a good governor is hard to find in this world. May God make me as good as Sancho's way of governing.

Herewith I send you, dear one, a string of coral interspersed with gold beads. I wish they were Oriental pearls, but "he who gives you a bone does not wish to see you dead."[4] A time will come when we shall become acquainted and meet each other, but God knows the future. Commend me to your daughter Sanchica, and tell her from me to ready herself, for I mean to make a high match for her when she least expects it.

They tell me there are large acorns in your village; send me a couple of dozen or so, and I shall value them greatly as coming from your hand. Write to me at length to assure me of your health and well-being. If there is anything you stand in need of, simply open your mouth to ask, and that shall be the measure.

May God keep you.

From this place.

Your loving friend,
THE DUCHESS

"Ah, what a good, simple, humble lady!" said Teresa when she heard the letter. "May I be buried with ladies of that kind—not the gentlewomen we have in this town, who think because they're gentlewomen the wind must not touch them, and go to church with as much airs as if they were queens, no less, and seem to think they are disgraced if they look at a farmer's wife! See here how this good lady—though she's a duchess—calls me 'friend' and treats me as if I was her

[3] *gyrfalcon:* See footnote 15, page 614.

[4] *he who gives you a bone does not wish to see you dead:* "a gift, no matter how small, is a sign of goodwill."

equal. May I see her equal with the tallest belltower in La Mancha! As for the acorns, señor, I'll send her ladyship a peck[5] and such big ones that people from all over will come to marvel at them. And now, Sanchica, see that the gentleman is comfortable. Put up his horse, get some eggs out of the stable, and cut plenty of bacon, and let's give him his dinner like a prince. Between the good news he has brought and his fine face, he deserves it all. Meanwhile, I'll run out and give the neighbors the news of our good fortune, along with father priest and Master Nicholas the barber, who are and always have been such friends of your father's."

"That I will, mother," said Sanchica. "But mind you give me half of that necklace. I don't think my lady the duchess could have been so stupid as to send it all to you."

"It is all for you, my child," said Teresa. "But let me wear it round my neck for a few days; for in truth it seems to make my heart glad."

"You will be glad too," said the page, "when you see the bundle there in this portmanteau. It is a suit of the finest cloth, which the governor only wore one day out hunting and now sends to Señora Sanchica."

"May he live a thousand years," said Sanchica, "and the one who brings it as many—no, two thousand, if necessary."

With this Teresa hurried out of the house with the letters, and with the string of beads round her neck, and went along thrumming the letters as if they were a tambourine. By chance coming across the priest and Samson Carrasco she broke out into a dance and cried out, "Faith, no one will call us poor now! We've got a little government! Just let the finest of fine ladies come stare me down. I'll put her in her place!"

"What's all this, Teresa Panza?" they asked. "What madness is this, and what papers are those?"

"The only madness," said she, "is that these are the letters of duchesses and governors, and what I have on my neck are fine coral beads for Ave Marias and Paternosters of beaten gold.[6] And I am a governess!"

"God help us," said the priest. "We don't understand you, Teresa, or know what you are talking about."

"There, you may see it yourselves," said Teresa, and she handed them the letters.

The priest read them out for Samson Carrasco to hear. Samson and he regarded one another with looks of astonishment at what they had read, and the bachelor asked who had brought the letters. Teresa in reply told them to come with her to her house and they would see the messenger, a most elegant youth, who had brought another present which was worth as much more. The priest took the coral beads from her neck and examined them again and again. Having satisfied himself as to their fineness, he fell to wondering afresh and said, "By the gown I wear, I don't know what to say or think of these letters and presents. On the one

[5] *peck: celemín*, Spanish dry measure equivalent to one to two gallons.

[6] *fine coral beads for Ave Marias and Paternosters of beaten gold:* Teresa compares the necklace to a rosary, likening the small coral beads to Ave Marias (Hail Marys) and the large gold beads to Paternosters (Our Fathers). See footnote 3, page 198.

hand I can see and feel the fineness of these coral beads, and on the other I read how a duchess sends to ask for a couple dozen acorns."

"Square that if you can," said Carrasco. "Well, let's go and speak with the messenger to see if we can learn something about this new mystery."

They did so, and Teresa returned with them. They found the page sifting a little barley for his horse and Sanchica cutting a slice of bacon to go with the scrambled eggs for his dinner. His looks and his handsome apparel pleased them both greatly. After they had saluted him courteously and he them, Samson asked him to give them his news—both of Don Quixote and of Sancho Panza—for though they had read the letters from Sancho and her ladyship the duchess, they were still puzzled and could not make out what was meant by Sancho's government, and above all of an island, when all or most of those in the Mediterranean belonged to his Majesty.

To this the page replied, "As to Señor Sancho Panza's being a governor there is no doubt whatever; but whether it is an island or not that he governs, with that I have nothing to do. Suffice it that it is a town of more than a thousand inhabitants. With regard to the acorns I may tell you my lady the duchess is so humble and unassuming that—not to speak of sending to ask for acorns from a peasant woman—she has been known to ask one of her neighbors to lend her a comb. I would have your worships know that the ladies of Aragon, though they are just as illustrious, are not so punctilious and haughty as the Castilian ladies. They treat people with greater sincerity."

In the middle of this conversation, Sanchica came in with her skirt full of eggs. She said to the page, "Tell me, señor, does my father wear fitted breeches[7] since he was made governor?"

"I have not noticed," said the page, "but no doubt he wears them."

"Oh my God!" exclaimed Sanchica. "What a sight it must be to see my father in tights! Isn't it strange that ever since I was born I've wanted to see my father in fitted breeches?"

"As things go, you will see that if you live," said the page. "God willing, he is well on his way to traveling with a sunshade if he can hold out in the government two months more."

The priest and the bachelor could see plainly enough that the page was a jokester, but the fineness of the coral beads and the hunting suit that Sancho sent (for Teresa had already shown it to them) did away with the impression. They could not help laughing at Sanchica's wish, and still more when Teresa said, "Señor priest, ask around if there's anybody here going to Madrid or Toledo who could buy me a hoopskirt,[8] a proper fashionable one of the best quality; for there's no denying I must do honor to my husband's government as well as I can. If it comes down to it, I'll go to Court myself in the best coach I can find;

[7] *fitted breeches: calzas atacadas*, close-fitting breeches extending from the waist to the knees, where they were fastened with ties or buttons.

[8] *hoopskirt: verduagdo* (origin of the English "farthingale"), bell-shaped skirt stiffened with hoops of wood, rope, or whalebone, worn under gowns to create volume.

for she who has a governor for her husband may very well have a coach of her own to keep."

"And why not, mother!" said Sanchica. "God, I wish it were tomorrow already—even if people said when they saw me seated in the coach with my mother, 'Take a look at that nobody, that garlic-muncher's daughter, how comfortably she goes along in her coach, like a she-pope.' They can trudge through the mud; I'll travel in my coach with my feet off the ground. Bad luck to backbiters all over the world. 'Let the rest of them tease—I'll be warm and at ease!' Do I say right, mother?"

"To be sure you do, my child," said Teresa. "All this good luck—and even more—my good Sancho predicted to me. You'll see, my daughter. He won't stop till he's made me a countess. To start on the right foot is everything in luck. As I've heard your good father say many a time (for besides being your father he's the father of proverbs too), 'When they offer you a heifer, run with a halter.' When they offer you a government, take it. When they give you a county, seize it. When they hold out something good, snatch it. Otherwise, you'll go to bed and miss out when good fortune and happiness come knocking at your door!"

"And what do I care," added Sanchica, "whether anybody says when he sees me holding my head up—'the dog saw himself in hempen breeches ...'[9] and the rest of it."

Hearing this the priest said, "I do believe these Panzas are born with a sackful of proverbs in their insides, every one of them. I never saw one that doesn't pour them out at all times and on all occasions."

"That is true," said the page, "for Señor Governor Sancho utters them at every turn. Though a great many of them are off the mark, they still amuse one, and my lady the duchess and the duke praise them highly."

"Then you still insist that all this about Sancho's government is true, señor," said the bachelor, "and that there actually is a duchess who sends him presents and writes to him? Because we, although we have handled the present and read the letters, don't believe it and suspect it to be something in the line of our fellow townsman Don Quixote, who fancies that everything is done by enchantment. For this reason I am almost ready to say that I'd like to touch and feel your worship to see whether you are a mere ambassador of the imagination or a man of flesh and blood."

"All I know, sirs," replied the page, "is that I am a real ambassador, and that Señor Sancho Panza is in fact a governor, and that my lord and lady the duke and duchess can give, and have given him this same government, and that I have heard it said that Sancho Panza is acquitting himself valiantly there. Whether there is any enchantment in all this or not, it is for your worships to settle between you. That's all I know by the oath I swear—and that's by the life of my parents whom I have still alive and love dearly."

"It may be so," said the bachelor, "but *dubitat Augustinus*."[10]

[9] *the dog saw himself in hempen breeches* . . . : ". . . and didn't recognize his companions."

[10] dubitat Augustinus: Latin, "Augustine doubts"—Scholastic shorthand used in theological and legal argumentation.

"Doubt who will," said the page; "what I have told you is the truth, and that will always rise above falsehood as oil above water. If not, *operibus credite, et non verbis.*[11] Let one of you come with me, and he will see with his eyes what he does not believe with his ears."

"It's for me to make that trip," said Sanchica. "Take me with you, señor, behind you on your horse. I'll go with all my heart to see my father."

"Governors' daughters," said the page, "must not travel along the roads alone, but accompanied by coaches and litters and a great number of attendants."

"By God," said Sanchica, "I can go just as well mounted on a jenny as in a coach. What a dainty girl you must take me for!"

"Hush, girl," said Teresa. "You don't know what you're talking about. The gentleman is quite right, for 'as the occasion, so the behavior.' When it was Sancho it was 'Sancha'; when it is governor it's 'señora.' I don't know if I'm explaining myself well."

"Señora Teresa says more than she is aware of," said the page. "Now give me something to eat and let me go at once, for I mean to return this evening."

"Come and do penance with me,"[12] said the priest at this, "for Señora Teresa has more will than means to serve so worthy a guest."

The page refused, but had to consent at last for his own sake. The priest took the page home with him very gladly in order to have an opportunity of questioning him at leisure about Don Quixote and his doings. The bachelor offered to write the letters in reply for Teresa; but she did not want to let him mix himself up in her affairs, for she thought him something of a mischief-maker. And so she gave a cake and a couple of eggs to a young acolyte who was a penman, and he wrote for her two letters, one for her husband and the other for the duchess, dictated out of her own head, which are not the worst inserted in this great history, as will be seen farther on.

[11] *operibus credite, et non verbis*: See footnote 8, page 573.

[12] *Come and do penance with me*: See footnote 18, page 444.

CHAPTER LI

OF THE PROGRESS OF SANCHO'S GOVERNMENT, AND OTHER SUCH ENTERTAINING MATTERS

Day came after the night of the governor's round, a night that the head butler passed without sleeping (such were his thoughts of the face, charms, and beauty of the disguised damsel), while the majordomo spent what was left of it in writing an account to his lord and lady of all Sancho said and did, being as much amazed at his sayings as at his doings, for there was a mixture of shrewdness and simplicity in all his words and deeds. The señor governor got up, and by Doctor Pedro Recio's directions they made him breakfast out of a little fruit compote and four sips of cold water—which Sancho would have readily exchanged for a piece of bread and a bunch of grapes. But seeing that he had no say in the matter, he submitted with no little sorrow of heart and discomfort of stomach, Pedro Recio having persuaded him that a light and delicate diet enlivened the wits, which was essential for people placed in command and in high offices, where they have to employ not only the bodily powers but those of the mind as well.

By means of this sophistry Sancho was made to endure hunger, and hunger so keen that in his heart he cursed the government and even him who had given it to him. In spite of his hunger and his fruit compote, he undertook to deliver judgments that day. The first thing that came before him was a question that was submitted to him by a stranger, in the presence of the majordomo and the other attendants. It was in these words: "Señor, a large river separated two districts of one and the same realm—I ask that your worship pay close attention, for this is an important case and a rather knotty one. Well then, on this river there was a bridge, and at one end of it a gallows and a kind of tribunal, where four judges commonly sat to administer the law which the lord of river, bridge, and realm had enacted. The law was to this effect: 'If anyone crosses this bridge from one side to the other he shall declare on oath where he is going and with what purpose. If he swears truly, he shall be allowed to pass, but if falsely, he shall be put to death by being hanged on the gallows erected there, without possibility of pardon.' Though the law and its severe penalty were known, many people crossed, but in their declarations it was easy to see at once they were telling the truth, and the judges let them pass freely. It happened, however, that one man, when they came to take his declaration, swore no more in the oath he took than that he was going to die upon the gallows that stood there. The judges held a consultation over the oath and said, 'If we let this man pass freely, he has sworn falsely, and by the law he ought to die; but if we hang him, as he swore he was going to die on that gallows, and therefore swore the truth, by the same law he ought to go free.' It is asked of your worship, señor governor, what are the judges to do with this man? For they are utterly confounded, and having heard of your worship's acute and exalted intellect, they have sent me to entreat your worship on their behalf to give your opinion on this thoroughly puzzling case."

To this Sancho answered, "Those gentlemen the judges that sent you to me might have spared themselves the trouble, for I have more ignorance than insight in me. But repeat the case over again so I can understand it. Maybe I can hit the nail on the head."

The questioner repeated again and again what he had said before, and then Sancho said, "It seems to me I can set the matter right in a moment, and in this way: the man swears that he is going to die upon the gallows, but if he dies upon it, he has sworn the truth, and by the law enacted deserves to go free and pass over the bridge; but if they don't hang him, then he has sworn falsely, and by the same law deserves to be hanged."

"It is as the señor governor says," said the messenger. "As regards a complete understanding of the case, there is nothing left to desire or hesitate about."

"Well then I say," said Sancho, "that they should let the part of this man pass that has sworn truly, and hang the part that has lied. In this way the terms of the crossing will be complied with down to the letter."

"But then, señor governor," replied the questioner, "the man will have to be divided into two parts, and if he is divided of course he will die. In this way, none of the requirements of the law will be carried out, and it is absolutely necessary to comply with it."

"Look here, my good sir," said Sancho; "either I'm a numbskull or this passenger has the same reason for dying as for living and passing over the bridge; for if the truth saves him the falsehood equally condemns him. That being the case, it is my opinion you should say to the gentlemen who sent you to me that since the arguments for condemning him and for absolving him are exactly balanced, they should let him pass freely, as it is always more praiseworthy to do good than to do evil. I would give this signed with my name if I knew how to sign. What I've said in this case is not out of my own head, but one of the many precepts I recall that my master Don Quixote gave me the night before I left to become governor of this island. It was this: that when there was any doubt about the justice of a case I should lean to mercy. And it is God's will that I should remember it now, for it fits this case as if it was made for it."

"That is true," said the majordomo. "I maintain that Lycurgus himself, who gave laws to the Lacedemonians,[1] could not have pronounced a better decision than the great Panza has given. Let the morning's audience close with this, and I will see that the señor governor has dinner entirely to his liking."

"That's all I ask for—fair play," said Sancho. "Give me my dinner, and then let it rain cases and questions on me. I'll settle them in a twinkling."

[1] *Lycurgus himself, who gave laws to the Lacedemonians:* See footnote 3, page 425.

The majordomo kept his word, for he felt it against his conscience to kill so wise a governor by hunger—particularly as he intended to have done with him that same night, carrying out the last prank he was commissioned to play on him.

It came to pass that after he had dined that day—in opposition to the rules and aphorisms of Doctor Tirteafuera—as they were clearing the table there came a courier with a letter from Don Quixote for the governor. Sancho ordered the secretary to read it to himself, and if there was nothing in it that demanded secrecy to read it aloud. The secretary did so, and after he had skimmed the contents he said, "It may well be read aloud, for what Señor Don Quixote writes to your worship deserves to be printed or written in letters of gold. It is as follows—"

DON QUIXOTE OF LA MANCHA'S LETTER TO SANCHO PANZA, GOVERNOR OF THE ISLAND OF BARATARIA

When I was expecting to hear of your stupidities and blunders, friend Sancho, I have received news of your displays of good sense, for which I give special thanks to Heaven, which can raise the poor from the dunghill and make wise men of fools.[2] They tell me you govern as if you were a man, and are a man as if you were a beast—so great is the humility with which you conduct yourself. But I would have you bear in mind, Sancho, that very often it is fitting and necessary for the authority of office to resist the heart's humility; for the seemly attire of one who is invested with serious duties should be such as they require and not measured by what his own humble tastes may lead him to prefer. Dress well—a stick dressed up does not look like a stick. I do not say you should wear trinkets or fine raiment, or that being a judge you should dress like a soldier, but that you should array yourself in the apparel your office requires, and that at the same time it be neat and handsome.

To win the goodwill of the people you govern there are two things, among others, that you must do: one is to be civil to all (this, however, I told you before), and the other to take care that food is abundant, for there is nothing that vexes the heart of the poor more than hunger and high prices. Do not make many proclamations; but those you make take care that they be good ones, and above all that they be observed and carried out. For proclamations that are not observed are the same as if they did not exist; rather, they encourage the idea that the prince who had the wisdom and authority to make them had not the power to enforce them. Laws that threaten and are not enforced come to be like the log, the king of the frogs, that frightened them at first, but that in time they despised and mounted upon.[3] Be a father to virtue and a stepfather to vice. Do not always be strict, nor yet always lenient, but observe a mean between these two extremes—for that is the aim of wisdom.[4] Visit the jails, the slaughter houses, and the markets; for the presence of

[2] *Heaven, which can raise the poor from the dunghill and make wise men of fools*: See Psalm 113:7–8 (God "raises the poor from the dust, and lifts the needy from the ash heap, to make them sit with princes").

[3] *the log, the king of the frogs . . . mounted upon:* In one of Aesop's fables, the frogs grow tired of governing themselves and petition Zeus for a king. He sends them a log, which lands in the marsh with a terrifying crash. When the frogs realize that the log does nothing and poses no threat, they grow bold and climb onto it, mocking its passivity.

[4] *mean between these two extremes . . . aim of wisdom:* See footnote 8, page 652.

the governor is of great importance in such places. It comforts the prisoners who are in hopes of a speedy release, it is the bane of the butchers who have then to give just weight, and it is the terror of the market women for the same reason.

Let it not be seen that you are (even if by chance it is true, which I do not believe) covetous, a chaser of women, or a glutton; for when the people and those that have dealings with you become aware of your special weakness they will bring their batteries to bear upon you in that quarter, till they have brought you down to the depths of perdition. Consider and reconsider, study and review the advice and instructions I gave you before your departure to your government, and you will see that in them, if you follow them, you will have a help at hand to lighten the troubles and difficulties that beset governors at every step. Write to your lord and lady and show yourself grateful to them, for ingratitude is the daughter of pride, and one of the greatest sins we know of. He who is grateful to those who have been good to him shows that he will be so to God also, who continually bestows on him abundant blessings.

My lady the duchess sent off a messenger with your suit and another present to your wife Teresa Panza; we expect the answer any moment now.

I have been somewhat indisposed because of a certain cat-scratching I received, not very much to the benefit of my nose. But it was nothing; for if there are enchanters who maltreat me, there are also some who defend me. Let me know if the majordomo who is with you had any share in the Trifaldi performance, as you suspected; and keep me informed of everything that happens to you, as the distance is so short—all the more as I am thinking of giving up very soon this idle life I am now leading, for I was not born for it. Something has occurred to me which I am inclined to think will put me out of favor with the duke and duchess; but though I am sorry for it I do not care, for after all I must obey my calling rather than their pleasure, in accordance with the common saying, *amicus Plato, sed magis amica veritas*.[5] I quote this Latin to you because I assume that since you have become a governor you have learned it. Farewell. God keep you from being an object of pity to anyone.

Your friend,
DON QUIXOTE OF LA MANCHA

Sancho listened to the letter with great attention, and it was praised and considered wise by all who heard it. He then got up from the table and, calling his secretary, shut himself up with him in his room, and without putting it off any longer, he set about at once answering his master Don Quixote. He had the secretary write down what he told him without adding or taking out anything, which he did. The answer was to the following effect:

SANCHO PANZA'S LETTER TO DON QUIXOTE OF LA MANCHA

The pressure of business is so great on me that I have no time to scratch my head or even to cut my nails—and they have gotten so long that only God can help me. I say this, master of my soul, so that you won't be surprised if I have not until now sent you word of how things are going with me—good or bad—in this government,

[5] amicus Plato, sed magis amica veritas: Latin, "Plato is a friend, but the truth is a greater friend." The aphorism may be of Scholastic origin—a distillation of Aristotle's teaching that the truth must be honored above friendship.

in which I am suffering more hunger than when we two were wandering through the woods and wilds.

My lord the duke wrote the other day to warn me that certain spies had come to this island to kill me; but up to the present I have not discovered any except a certain doctor who receives a salary in this town for killing all the governors that come here. His name is Doctor Pedro Recio, and he is from Tirteafuera. You can see what a name he has to make me dread dying under his hands. This doctor says about himself that he does not cure diseases when there are any, but rather prevents them coming. The medicines he uses are diet and more diet until he brings the person down to bare bones—as if being thin was not worse than coming down with a fever.

In short he is killing me with hunger, and I am dying of exasperation. When I thought I was coming to this government to get my meat hot and my drink cool, and take my ease between holland sheets on feather beds, I find I have come to do penance like a hermit. As I don't do it willingly, I suspect that in the end the devil will carry me off.

So far I have not handled any taxes or taken any bribes. I don't know what to think of it. They tell me here that when governors come to this island, they have plenty of money either given to them or lent to them by the townspeople, and that this is the usual custom not only here but with everyone else who goes into governing.

Last night going the rounds, I came upon a beautiful damsel in man's clothes, and a brother of hers dressed like a woman. My head butler has fallen in love with the girl and in his own mind has chosen her for a wife, so he says, and I have chosen the youth for a son-in-law. Today we are going to explain our intentions to the father of the two, who is one Diego de la Llana, a hidalgo and as much of an Old Christian as you could ask for.

I have visited the marketplaces, as your worship advises me. Yesterday I found a stall keeper selling new hazelnuts and discovered that she had mixed a fanega[6] of old empty rotten nuts with a fanega of new ones. I confiscated all of it for the children of the orphanage, who will know how to distinguish them well enough, and I sentenced her not to come into the marketplace for a fortnight. They told me I did bravely. I can tell your worship it is commonly said in this town that there are no people worse than the market women, for they are all shameless, impudent and corrupt, and I can well believe it from what I have seen of them in other towns.

I am very glad my lady the duchess has written to my wife Teresa Panza and sent her the present your worship speaks of. I will make sure to show myself grateful when the time comes. Kiss her hands for me, and tell her I said that she has not thrown her favor into a sack with a hole in it, as I will prove to her. I would not wish your worship to have any disagreement with my lord and lady; for if you fall out with them it is plain it must do me harm. As you have advised me to be grateful, it's not right for your worship not to be grateful to those who have shown you such kindness and have treated you so hospitably in their castle.

That part about the cat-scratching I don't understand, but I suppose it must be one of the evil deeds the wicked enchanters are always doing to your worship. You can tell me more about it when we see each other. I wish I could send your worship something, but I don't know what to send other than some very clever little tubes

[6]*fanega:* unit of dry volume equivalent to 1.6 bushels.

they make in this island to work with bladders.[7] I'll find something to send if the office remains with me, one way or another. If my wife Teresa Panza writes to me, pay the postage and send me the letter, for I have a very great desire to hear how my house and wife and children are doing.

And so, may God deliver your worship from spiteful enchanters and bring me well and peacefully out of this government—which I doubt, for I expect to take leave of it and my life together from the way Doctor Pedro Recio treats me.

Your worship's servant,
SANCHO PANZA THE GOVERNOR

The secretary sealed the letter, and immediately dismissed the courier; and Sancho's pranksters put their heads together and arranged how he was to be thrown out of the government. Sancho spent the afternoon drawing up certain ordinances relating to the good government of what he imagined to be an island. He decreed that foodstuffs were not to be hoarded in the State.[8] He permitted wine to be imported from any and every place, provided the region it came from was declared so that a price might be set for it according to its quality, reputation, and the estimation in which it was held. Anyone who watered down his wine or changed the name was to forfeit his life for it. He reduced the prices of all manner of shoes, boots, and stockings—but of shoes in particular, as they seemed to him to run extravagantly high. He established a fixed rate for servants' wages, which were becoming recklessly exorbitant. He laid extremely heavy penalties on those who sang lewd or loose songs either by day or night. He decreed that no blind man should sing of any miracle in verse, unless he could produce authentic evidence that it was true, for it was his opinion that most of the ditties the blind men sing are made up, to the detriment of the true ones. He established and installed a constable for the poor, not to harass them, but to examine them and see whether they really were so; for many a sturdy thief or drunkard goes about under cover of a make-believe crippled limb or a sham sore. In a word, he made so many good rules that to this day they are preserved there and are called THE CONSTITUTIONS OF THE GREAT GOVERNOR SANCHO PANZA.

[7] *clever little tubes they make in this island to work with bladders:* perhaps as festive toys or comic props, like the bladder-stick carried by the jester from *The Parliament of Death* (see p. 483).

[8] *foodstuffs were not to be hoarded in the State:* The provision is designed to curb price gouging—buying up a certain commodity to create artificial scarcity, then taking advantage of the temporary monopoly to resell it at an inflated price.

CHAPTER LII

WHEREIN IS RELATED THE ADVENTURE OF THE SECOND DISTRESSED OR AFFLICTED DUEÑA, OTHERWISE CALLED DOÑA RODRÍGUEZ

Cide Hamete relates that Don Quixote, being now cured of his scratches, felt that the life he was leading in the castle was entirely inconsistent with the order of chivalry he professed. He therefore determined to ask the duke and duchess to permit him to take his departure for Zaragoza, as the time of the festival was now drawing near, and he hoped to win there the suit of armor that is the accustomed prize at festivals such as this one.

As he dined one day with the duke and duchess, just as he was about to carry his resolution into effect and ask for their permission, lo and behold there came in through the door of the great hall two women (as they afterwards proved to be), draped in mourning from head to foot, one of whom approaching Don Quixote flung herself full length at his feet, pressing her lips to them, and uttering moans so sad, so deep, and so doleful that she put all who heard and saw her into a state of bewilderment. Though the duke and duchess supposed it must be some prank their servants were playing on Don Quixote, still the earnest way the woman sighed and moaned and wept puzzled them and left them uncertain, until Don Quixote, touched with compassion, raised her up and made her unveil herself and remove the mantle from her tearful face. She complied and revealed what no one could have ever anticipated, for she revealed the countenance of Doña Rodríguez, the dueña of the house—the other female in mourning being her daughter, who had been jilted by the rich farmer's son. All who knew her were filled with astonishment, and the duke and duchess more than any; for though they thought her foolish and simple-minded, they did not think her capable of something so ridiculous. Doña Rodríguez, at length, turning to her master and mistress said to them, "Will your excellencies be pleased to permit me to speak to this gentleman for a moment? It is necessary I should do so in order to resolve a matter that affects me, brought on by the effrontery of a villainous peasant."

The duke said that for his part he gave her leave, and that she might speak with Señor Don Quixote as much as she liked.

She then, turning to Don Quixote and addressing herself to him, said, "A few days ago, valiant knight, I gave you an account of the injustice and treachery of a wicked farmer to my dearly beloved daughter, the unhappy damsel here before you, and you promised me to take her part and right the wrong that has been done her. It has now come to my hearing that you are about to depart from this castle in quest of such fair adventures as God may vouchsafe to you. Therefore, before you take the road, I ask that you challenge this brazen rustic, and compel him to marry my daughter in fulfillment of the promise he gave to become her husband before he seduced her; for to expect that my lord the duke will do me justice is to ask pears from the elm tree, for the reason I stated privately to your worship. So may our Lord grant you good health and forsake us not."

To these words Don Quixote replied very gravely and solemnly, "Worthy dueña, hold back your tears, or rather dry them, and spare your sighs, for I take it upon myself to obtain redress for your daughter, for whom it would have been better not to be so quick to believe lovers' promises, which are for the most part easily made and very slowly performed. And so, with my lord the duke's leave, I will at once go in quest of this inhuman youth, and will find him out and challenge him and slay him, if it be that he refuses to keep his promised word; for the chief object of my profession is to spare the humble and chastise the proud—I mean, to help the distressed and destroy the oppressors."

"There is no need," said the duke, "for your worship to take the trouble of seeking out the rustic of whom this worthy dueña complains, nor is there any need, either, for asking my leave to challenge him. I admit him duly challenged, and will take care that he is informed of the challenge, accepts it, and comes to answer it in person at this castle of mine, where I shall provide to both a fair field, observing all the conditions which are usually and properly observed in such trials, in addition to observing justice on both sides, as all princes who offer a free field to combatants within the limits of their lordships are bound to do."

"Then with that assurance and your highness' good leave," said Don Quixote, "I hereby for this one time waive my privilege of noble blood, and come down and put myself on a level with the lowly birth of the wrongdoer, making myself equal with him and enabling him to enter into combat with me. And so, I challenge and defy him, though absent, on the plea of his malfeasance in breaking faith with this poor damsel, who was a maiden and now by his misdeed is none, and say that he shall fulfill the promise he gave her to become her lawful husband, or else stake his life upon the question."

Then plucking off a glove, he threw it down in the middle of the hall. The duke picked it up, saying, as he had said before, that he accepted the challenge in the name of his vassal, and fixed six days thence as the time, the courtyard of the castle as the place, and for arms the customary ones of knights, lance and shield and full armor, with all the other accessories, without trickery, guile, or charms of any sort, and examined and passed by the judges of the field. "But first of all," he said, "it is requisite that this worthy dueña and unworthy damsel should place their claim for justice in the hands of Don Quixote; for otherwise nothing can be done, nor can the said challenge be brought to a lawful outcome."

"I do so place it," replied the dueña.

"And I too," added her daughter, full of tears and covered with shame and confusion.

This declaration having been made, and the duke having settled in his own mind what he would do in the matter, the ladies in black withdrew, and the duchess gave orders that for the future they were not to be treated as servants of hers, but as lady adventurers who came to her house to demand justice. So they gave them a room to themselves and waited on them as they would on strangers—to the consternation of the other female servants, who did not know where the folly and imprudence of Doña Rodríguez and her unfortunate daughter would end.

And now, to complete the enjoyment of the feast and bring the dinner to a satisfactory conclusion, lo and behold the page who had carried the letters and presents to Teresa Panza, the wife of Governor Sancho Panza, entered the hall. The duke and duchess were very well pleased to see him, being anxious to know the result of his journey. But when they asked him, the page said in reply that he could not give it before so many people or in a few words. He begged their excellencies to be pleased to let it wait for a private opportunity, and in the meantime amuse themselves with these letters. Taking out the letters, he placed them in the duchess' hand. One bore by way of address, LETTER FOR MY LADY THE DUCHESS SO-AND-SO OF I DON'T KNOW WHERE; and the other: TO MY HUSBAND SANCHO PANZA, GOVERNOR OF THE ISLAND OF BARATARIA, WHOM GOD PROSPER LONGER THAN ME. The duchess' bread would not bake, as the saying is, until she had read the letter addressed to her. Having looked it over herself and seen that it might be read aloud for the duke and all present to hear, she read out as follows:

TERESA PANZA'S LETTER TO THE DUCHESS

The letter your highness wrote me, my lady, gave me great pleasure. In all truth, I had been eagerly expecting it. The string of coral beads is lovely, and my husband's hunting suit does not fall short of it. The whole village is very much pleased that your ladyship has made a governor of my good man Sancho—though nobody believes it, particularly the priest, Master Nicholas the barber, and the bachelor Samson Carrasco. But I don't care for that, for so long as it is true (as it is), they may all say what they like. To tell the truth, if the coral beads and the suit had not come, I would not have believed it either; for in this village everybody considers my husband a numbskull, and except for governing a flock of goats, they cannot imagine what sort of government he can be fit for. God grant it and direct him accordingly as he sees the needs of his children.

I am resolved with your worship's leave, lady of my soul, to make the most of this fine day and go in style to Court in a coach, so that I can make everyone who already envies me burst their eyes out. And so I beg your excellency to order my husband to send me some money—and to let it be enough to talk about, because expenses at Court are quite great. A loaf costs a real, and meat thirty maravedis a pound, which is unbelievable. If he does not want me to go, let him tell me in time, for I am itching to be off. My friends and neighbors tell me that if my daughter and I make a grand impression at Court, my husband will come to be known far more by me than I by him, for plenty of people will be sure to ask, "Who are those ladies in that coach?" and some servant of mine will answer, "The wife and daughter of Sancho Panza, governor of the island of Barataria." In this way Sancho will become known, and I'll be thought well of—and on to Rome.[1]

[1] *on to Rome:* "the sky's the limit."

I am as disappointed as disappointed can be that they have gathered no acorns this year in our village. What I am sending your highness is about half a peck that I went to the woods to gather one by one myself. I could find no bigger ones; I wish they were as large as ostrich eggs.

Let your high mightiness not forget to write to me. I will be sure to answer and let you know how I'm doing, along with whatever news there might be around here, where I remain, praying our Lord to have your highness in his keeping and not to forget me.

Sancha my daughter, and my son, kiss your worship's hands.

She who would rather see your ladyship than write to you,

Your servant,
TERESA PANZA

Everyone was greatly amused by Teresa Panza's letter, but particularly the duke and duchess. The duchess asked Don Quixote's opinion whether they might open the letter that had come for the governor, which she suspected must be very good. Don Quixote said that to gratify them he would open it, and did so, and found that it read as follows:

TERESA PANZA'S LETTER TO HER HUSBAND SANCHO PANZA

I got your letter, Sancho of my soul, and I promise you and swear as a Catholic Christian that I was within two fingers' breadth of going crazy I was so happy. I can tell you, brother, when I came to hear that you were a governor I about dropped dead from pure joy—and you know they say that sudden joy kills as well as great sorrow. As for Sanchica your daughter, she wet herself she was so happy. There I was with the suit you sent in front of me, the coral beads my lady the duchess sent me round my neck, the letters in my hands, and the fellow who brought them standing by—in spite of all this, I truly believed that what I saw and touched was all a dream. Who could have thought that a goatherd would come to be a governor of islands? You know, my friend, what my mother used to say, 'One must live long to see much.' I say this because I expect to see more if I live longer; for I don't expect to stop until I see you a landlord or a tax collector, which are offices where (though the devil carries off the ones who abuse them) they still make and handle money. My lady the duchess will tell you the desire I have to go to Court. Consider the matter and let me know your pleasure; I will try to do you honor by going in a coach.

Neither the priest, nor the barber, nor the bachelor, nor even the sacristan can believe that you are a governor. They say the whole thing is a delusion or something enchanted—like everything belonging to your master Don Quixote. Samson says he must go in search of you and drive the government out of your head and the madness out of Don Quixote's skull. I only laugh, look at my string of beads, and think about the dress I am going to make for our daughter out of your suit. I sent some acorns to my lady the duchess; I wish they had been gold. Send me some strings of pearls if they are in fashion in that island.

Here is the news from the village: La Berrueca has married her daughter to a good-for-nothing painter, who came here to paint whatever he could find. The council gave him an order to paint his Majesty's arms over the door of the town-hall. He asked for two ducats, which they paid him in advance. He worked for eight days, and at the end of them had painted nothing, and then said he wasn't about to waste his time painting trinkets. He returned the money, and for all that he has married as if he were a good workman. To be sure he has now laid aside his paintbrush and taken a shovel in hand, and goes to the field like a gentleman.

Pedro Lobo's son has received the first orders and tonsure, with the intention of becoming a priest.[2] Minguilla (Mingo Silvato's granddaughter) found out and has taken him to court on account of his having given her a promise of marriage. Evil tongues say she is carrying his child, but he firmly denies it.

There are no olives this year, and there is not a drop of vinegar to be found in the whole village.

A company of soldiers passed through here. When they left, they took away with them three of the girls from the village. I will not tell you who they are. Perhaps they will come back; they will be sure to find those who will take them for wives with all their blemishes, good or bad.

Sanchica is making lace. She earns eight maravedis a day clear, which she puts into a moneybox to go towards her house furnishings; but now that she is a governor's daughter you will contribute to her dowry without her working for it.

The fountain in the plaza has run dry. A flash of lightning struck the pillory, and I couldn't care less.

I expect an answer to this letter, and to find out your decision about my going to Court. And so may God keep you longer than me, or as long, for I would not leave you in this world without me.

Your wife,
TERESA PANZA

The letters were applauded, laughed over, relished, and admired. To top it off, the courier arrived, bringing the letter Sancho sent to Don Quixote. This, too, was read aloud, and it raised some doubts as to the governor's simplicity. The duchess withdrew to hear from the page about his adventures in Sancho's village, which he narrated at full length without leaving a single circumstance unmentioned. He gave her the acorns, and also a cheese Teresa had given him that was particularly good—even better than those from Tronchón.[3] The duchess received it with the greatest delight, in which we will leave her, to describe the end of the government of the great Sancho Panza, flower and mirror of all governors of islands.

[2] *first orders . . . a priest:* See footnote 4, page 137.

[3] *those from Tronchón:* Sheep's cheese from Tronchón, a town in Aragon, was greatly esteemed.

CHAPTER LIII

OF THE TROUBLED END AND CONCLUSION SANCHO PANZA'S GOVERNMENT CAME TO

To suppose that the things of this life will continue forever in the same state is an idle fancy. On the contrary, everything in it seems to go in a circle, round and round. Spring gives way to summer, summer to fall, fall to autumn, autumn to winter, and winter to spring. And so time rolls along on a never-ceasing wheel. Man's life alone, swifter than time, speeds onward to its end without any hope of renewal—save for that other life, which is endless and boundless. Thus declares Cide Hamete, the Mahometan philosopher. For there are many that by the light of nature alone, without the light of faith, have an understanding of the transience and instability of this present life and the endless duration of that eternal life we hope for. But our author is here speaking of the rapidity with which Sancho's government came to an end, melted away, disappeared, vanished as it were in smoke and shadow.

As he lay in bed on the night of the seventh day of his government—sated, not with bread and wine, but with delivering judgments and giving opinions and making laws and proclamations—just as sleep, in spite of hunger, was beginning to close his eyelids, he heard such a noise of bell-ringing and shouting that one would have thought the whole island was going under. He sat up in bed and listened intently to try to make out what could be the cause of so great an uproar. Yet not only was he unable to discover what it was, but as countless drums and trumpets now helped to swell the din of the bells and shouts, he was more bewildered than ever, and filled with fear and terror. Getting up he put on a pair of slippers because of the dampness of the floor, and without throwing a dressing gown or anything of the kind over him he rushed out of the door of his room, just in time to see approaching along a corridor a band of more than twenty people with lighted torches and naked swords in their hands, all shouting out, "To arms, to arms, señor governor, to arms! The enemy is in the island in countless numbers, and we are lost unless your skill and valor come to our defense."

Keeping up this noise, tumult, and uproar, they came to where Sancho stood dazed and thunderstruck by what he saw and heard, and as they approached one of them called out to him, "Arm yourself at once, your lordship, if you would not have yourself destroyed and the whole island lost."

"What do I have to do with arming?" said Sancho. "What do I know about arms or defense? It's better to leave all that to my master Don Quixote, who will settle matters and make everything safe in two winks. Sinner that I am, God help me, I don't know anything about this kind of trouble."

"Ah, señor governor," said another, "what sloth this is! Arm yourself! Here are arms for you, offensive and defensive. Come out to the plaza and be our leader and captain. It falls upon you by right, for you are our governor."

"Arm me then, in God's name," said Sancho. They at once produced two large shields[1] they had come provided with, and placed them upon him over his shirt, without letting him put on anything else—one shield in front and the other behind. Passing his arms through openings they had made, they bound him tight with ropes, leaving him walled and boarded up as straight as a spindle and unable to bend his knees or stir a single step. In his hand they placed a lance, which he leaned on to keep himself from falling. When they had finished arming him, they told him to march forward, lead them on, and stir them to action; for with him as their guide, lamp, and morning star, they were sure to bring the undertaking to a successful conclusion.

"How am I supposed to march, unlucky soul that I am," said Sancho, "when I can't even move my joints? These boards bound so tight to my body won't let me. What you should do is carry me in your arms and lay me across or set me upright in a doorway. I'll hold it either with this lance or with my body."

"On, señor governor!" cried another. "It is fear more than the boards that keeps you from moving. Make haste, rouse yourself, for there is no time to lose. The enemy is increasing in numbers, the shouts grow louder, and the danger is pressing."

Urged by these exhortations and reproaches, the poor governor attempted to advance, but he fell to the ground with such a crash that he thought he had fallen to pieces. There he lay like a tortoise enclosed in its shell, or a side of pork pressed between two kneading troughs,[2] or a boat bottom up on the beach. Nor did the band of pranksters feel any compassion for him when they saw him down—so far from it that, extinguishing their torches, they began to shout afresh and to renew the calls to arms with such energy, trampling on poor Sancho and slashing at him over the shield with their swords in such a way that, if he had not gathered himself together in a ball and drawn in his head between the shields, it would have fared badly with the poor governor.

Squeezed into that narrow space he lay, sweating and sweating again, and commending himself with all his heart to God to deliver him from his present peril. Some stumbled over him, others fell upon him, and there was one who took up a position on top of him for some time, and from there as if from a watchtower issued orders to the troops, shouting out, "Here, our side! Here the enemy is thickest! Hold the breach there! Shut that gate! Barricade those ladders! Here with your pitch and resin fireballs and kettles of boiling oil! Barricade the streets with feather beds!"

In short, he mentioned in his zeal every little detail, and every implement and engine of war by means of which an assault upon a city is fended off, while the

[1] *large shields: pavéses*. The *pavés* was a large convex shield, usually made of wood, with a rectangular or oval shape. It was commonly used to provide full-body protection to crossbowmen and archers.

[2] *side of pork pressed between two kneading troughs:* fatback set out to cure.

bruised and battered Sancho, who heard and suffered all, said to himself, "O if it would only please the Lord to let the island be lost at once, and I could see myself either dead or free from this torture!"

Heaven heard his prayer, and when he least expected it, he heard voices exclaiming, "Victory, victory! The enemy retreats in defeat! Come, señor governor, get up! Come and enjoy the victory and divide the spoils that have been won from the foe by the might of your invincible arm."

"Lift me up," said the wretched Sancho in a pitiful voice. They helped him get up, and as soon as he was on his feet he said, "You can nail the enemy I've beaten to my forehead. I don't want to divide the spoils of the foe; I only beg of some friend—if I have one—to give me a sip of wine, for I'm parched with thirst, and to wipe off my sweat, for I'm turning to water."

They rubbed him down, fetched him wine and unfastened the shields, and he seated himself on his bed, where with fear, agitation, and fatigue he fainted away. Those who had been in on the prank were now sorry they had pushed it so far; however, the anxiety his fainting away had caused them was relieved by his returning to himself. He asked what time it was; they told him it was already daybreak. He said no more, and in silence began to dress himself, while everyone watched him, waiting to see what the haste with which he was putting on his clothes meant.

He got himself dressed at last, and then, slowly (for he was badly bruised and could not go fast) he proceeded to the stable, followed by all who were present. Going up to Dapple, he embraced him and gave him a loving kiss on the forehead, and said to him, not without tears in his eyes, "Come along, comrade, friend, and partner in my toils and sorrows. When I was with you and had no cares to trouble me except mending your harness and feeding your little frame, happy were my hours, my days, and my years. But since I left you, and mounted the towers of ambition and pride, a thousand miseries, a thousand troubles, and four thousand anxieties have entered into my soul."

All the while he was speaking in this strain, he was fixing the packsaddle on the donkey, without a word from anyone. Then having Dapple saddled, he got up on him with great pain and difficulty. Addressing himself to the majordomo, the secretary, the head butler, and Pedro Recio the doctor and several others who stood by, he said, "Make way, gentlemen, and let me go back to my old freedom. Let me go look for my past life, and raise myself up from this present death. I was not born to be a governor or protect islands or cities from the enemies that choose to attack them. Ploughing and digging, vinedressing and pruning are more in my way than defending provinces or kingdoms. 'Saint Peter is very well in Rome'—I mean each of us is best following the trade he was born to. A scythe fits my hand better than a governor's scepter. I'd rather have my fill of gazpacho than be subject to the misery of a meddling doctor who kills me with hunger; I'd rather lie in summer under the shade of an oak, and in winter wrap myself in a double sheepskin jacket in freedom, than go to bed between holland sheets and dress in sables under the restraint of a government. God be with your worships, and tell my lord the duke that 'naked I was born, naked I remain, nothing lost or gained.'—I mean that without a cent I came into this government, and without a cent I go out of it, very different from the way governors commonly leave other islands. Stand aside and let me go. I need to plaster myself, for I believe every one of my ribs is crushed, thanks to the enemies that have been trampling over me tonight."

"That is unnecessary, señor governor," said Doctor Recio, "for I will give your worship a tonic against falls and bruises that will soon make you as sound and strong as ever. And as for your diet, I promise your worship to behave better and let you eat plentifully of whatever you like."

"You spoke too late," said Sancho. "I'd as soon turn Turk as stay any longer. Those jokes won't work a second time. By God I'd as soon remain in this government—or take another, even if it was offered me between two plates—as fly to heaven without wings. I come from a long line of Panzas, and they are every one of them stubborn. Once they say 'odds,' odds it must be, no matter if it's evens, in spite of all the world. Here in this stable I leave the ant's wings that lifted me up into the air for the swallows and other birds to eat me.[3] Let's take to level ground and our feet once more. If they're not shod in fancy cordovan shoes, they won't lack for a pair of sturdy alpargatas[4]—'every mare with her pair,' and 'don't stretch your legs beyond the edge of your sheets.' Now let me pass, for it's growing late with me."

To this the majordomo said, "Señor governor, we would let your worship go with all our hearts, though it deeply grieves us to lose you, for your wisdom and Christian conduct naturally make us wish that you remain. But it is well known that every governor, before he leaves the place where he has been governing, is bound first to render an account. Let your worship do so for the ten days you have held the government, and then you may go and the peace of God go with you."

"No one can demand it of me," said Sancho, "except whoever my lord the duke appoints. I am going to meet him, and to him I will render an exact one. Besides, when I go forth naked as I do, there is no other proof needed to show that I have governed like an angel."

"By God the great Sancho is right," said Doctor Recio. "We should let him go, for the duke will be beyond measure glad to see him."

They all agreed to this and allowed him to go, first offering to keep him company and furnish him with all he wanted for his own comfort and for the journey. Sancho said he did not want anything more than a little barley for Dapple, and half a cheese and half a loaf for himself. The distance being so short, there was no need for any better or bulkier provisions. They embraced him, and he with tears embraced them all in return, leaving them filled with wonder not only at his remarks but at his firm and prudent resolution.

[3] *ant's wings . . . to eat me*: Sancho alludes to a proverb he cites earlier: "To her hurt the ant sprouted wings" (see p. 617).

[4] *alpargatas:* canvas shoes with rope soles.

CHAPTER LIV

WHICH DEALS WITH MATTERS RELATING TO THIS HISTORY AND NO OTHER

The duke and duchess resolved to proceed with the challenge that Don Quixote, for the reason already mentioned, had given their vassal. As the young man was in Flanders (where he had fled to escape having Doña Rodríguez for a mother-in-law), they arranged to substitute him with a footman from Gascony[1] named Tosilos, carefully instructing him first in all he had to do.

Two days later the duke told Don Quixote that four days hence his opponent would present himself on the battlefield armed as a knight and would maintain that the damsel lied by half a beard[2]—indeed, a whole beard—if she declared that he had given her a promise of marriage. Don Quixote was greatly pleased at the news, assured that he would do wonders in combat. He considered it rare good fortune that an opportunity should have arisen for letting his noble hosts see what the might of his strong arm was capable of. And so in high spirits and satisfaction he awaited the end of the four days, which measured by his impatience seemed spinning themselves out into four hundred centuries.

Let us pass over them (as we pass over other things), and let us join Sancho, half joyful, half sad, as he journeyed to reunite with his master. With no other company but Dapple, he was happier than in being governor of all the islands in the world. Now then, it so happened that before he had gone a great way from the island he had governed (and whether he had governed an island, city, town, or village, he never troubled himself to inquire), he saw coming along the road he was traveling six pilgrims with staffs, foreigners of the kind that beg for alms in song. They fell into line as they drew near and, lifting up their voices together, began to sing in their own language something that Sancho could not understand—with the exception of a word that sounded plainly "alms," from which he gathered that it was alms they asked for in their song. Being, as Cide Hamete says, remarkably charitable, he took out of his saddlebag the half loaf and half cheese he had been provided with and gave his food to them, explaining by signs that he had nothing else to give away. They received it very gladly, but exclaimed, "Geld! Geld!"[3]

"I don't understand what you want from me, good people," said Sancho.

[1] *Gascony:* region of southwest France that includes the cities of Bordeaux and Biarritz.

[2] *lied by half a beard:* formulaic oath used to initiate a challenge.

[3] *Geld:* German for "money".

At this one of them took a purse from his breast and showed it to Sancho, by which he gathered they were asking for money. Sancho put his thumb to his throat and spread his hand upwards, giving them to understand that he didn't have a cent on him, and urging Dapple forward he broke through their line. As he was passing, one of them who had been examining him very closely rushed toward him and, flinging his arms round him, exclaimed in a loud voice and good Spanish, "God bless me! What's this I see? Is it possible I'm holding in my arms my dear friend, my good neighbor Sancho Panza? There's no doubt about it, for I am not asleep, and I'm not drunk."

Sancho was surprised to hear himself called by his name and find himself embraced by a foreign pilgrim. He stared at him silently, but he was still not able to recognize him. The pilgrim, perceiving his confusion, cried, "How can it be, Sancho Panza, that you don't recognize your neighbor Ricote, the Morisco[4] shopkeeper from your village?"

Looking at him more carefully, Sancho began to recall his features, and at last recognized him perfectly. Without getting off the donkey, he threw his arms round his neck saying, "Who the devil could have guessed who you were, Ricote, dressed like a vagabond? Tell me now, who's turned you into a Frenchy,[5] and what made you so bold to come back to Spain, where if they catch you and recognize you, you'll have a heavy price to pay?"

"As long as you don't betray me, Sancho, I'm safe," said the pilgrim. "No one is going to recognize me in this outfit. But let's turn off the road and go into that poplar grove over there where my comrades are going to eat and rest. They will want you to join them in their meal, for they are very good fellows. I'll have time enough to tell you then all that's happened to me since I left our village in obedience to his Majesty's edict, which has hung heavily over my unhappy people, as you have heard."[6]

Sancho complied, and after Ricote spoke to the other pilgrims, the group withdrew to the poplar grove they saw, turning a considerable distance from the road. They threw down their staffs and took off their pilgrim's capes[7] so that they were left in shirtsleeves. All of them were good-looking young fellows, except Ricote, who was a man somewhat advanced in years. Each carried with him a provisions sack, and each sack appeared to be well filled—at least with what would attract someone thirsty, and from a good two leagues off. They stretched themselves on

[4] *Morisco:* See footnote 5, page 70.

[5] *Frenchy: franchote*, derogatory term for foreigners of any nation.

[6] *his Majesty's edict . . . as you have heard:* Over the period 1609–1614, the Spanish Crown forcibly removed some three hundred thousand Moriscos from Spain, region by region. Philip III and his chief minister, the Duke of Lerma, had become convinced that the descendants of Spanish Muslims could neither sincerely embrace the Catholic faith nor fully assimilate the dominant culture. Moreover, the Crown feared that Moriscos were conspiring with Spain's enemies (such as the Ottoman Empire, Morocco, and France) to create internal strife and possibly incite an uprising.

[7] *pilgrim's capes: mucetas* or *esclavinas*. The *muceta* or *esclavina*, still worn by Catholic prelates, is a short cape made of cloth or leather, draped over the shoulders.

the ground, and making a tablecloth of the grass they spread upon it bread, salt, knives, walnuts, scraps of cheese, and well-picked hambones, which, if they were past gnawing were not past sucking. They also set out a black delicacy called caviar, which is made from fish eggs, ideal for stimulating thirst. Nor was there any lack of olives—dry, it is true, and without any seasoning—but for all that tasty and filling. But what made the best show on the banquet field were half a dozen wineskins, for each pilgrim produced his own from his provisions sack. Even the good Ricote, who from a Morisco had transformed himself into a German or Dutchman, took out his, which in size might have vied with the five others.

They began to eat with very great relish and very leisurely, savoring every bite—very small, every one of them, which they took up on the point of the knife—and then all at the same moment raised their arms and wineskins aloft, the spouts placed in their mouths and all eyes fixed on heaven just as if they were taking aim at it. In this pose they remained ever so long, wagging their heads from side to side as if in acknowledgment of the pleasure they were enjoying while they decanted the bowels of the bottles into their own stomachs.

Sancho beheld everything, "and nothing gave him pain"[8]—so far from it, acting on the proverb he knew so well, "when in Rome, do as the Romans do," he asked Ricote for his wineskin and took aim like the rest of them, and with no less enjoyment. Four times did the wineskins bear being uplifted, but the fifth it was all in vain, for by then they were drier and more sapless than a rush, which made the good cheer that had been kept up so far begin to flag.

Every now and then one of them would take Sancho's right hand in his own saying, "*Español y tudesqui, tuto uno: bon compaño.*"

Sancho would answer, "*Bon compaño, jura Di!*"[9] He would then go off into a fit of laughter that lasted an hour, without a thought for the moment of anything that had befallen him in his government; for cares have very little sway over us while we are eating and drinking.

At length, their wine having come to an end, drowsiness began to overtake them, and they dropped asleep on their very table and tablecloth. Ricote and Sancho alone remained awake, for they had eaten more and drunk less. Ricote drew Sancho aside and they seated themselves at the foot of a beech, leaving the pilgrims buried in sweet sleep; and without once falling into his own Morisco tongue,[10] Ricote spoke as follows in pure Castilian:

"You know well, neighbor and friend Sancho Panza, how the edict his Majesty commanded to be issued against those of my nation struck us all with terror and dismay. At least it did to me, to such an extent that I think before the time granted us for leaving Spain had expired, the full force of the penalty had already

[8] *and nothing gave him pain:* opening lines of a ballad most recently referenced in Altisidora's amorous lament (see p. 679): "See Nero at Tarpeia, and Rome consumed in flames;/ Young and old are screaming, but nothing gives him pain."

[9] Español y tudesqui … jura Di: The pilgrims say in *lingua franca*: "A Spaniard and Germans, all are one: good company." Sancho responds, "Good company, by God!"

[10] *his own Morisco tongue:* Arabic.

fallen on me and my children.[11] I decided, then, and I think wisely—just like one who knows that at a certain date the house he lives in will be taken from him and so makes arrangements for a new home—I decided, I say, to leave town myself, alone and without my family, and go seek out some place to take them to at our convenience and not in the rushed way in which the others took their departure. For I saw very plainly, and so did all the older men among us, that the proclamations were not mere threats, as some said, but fixed laws that would be enforced at the appointed time.

"What made me believe this was what I knew of the vile and foolish plans our people were devising, plans of such a nature that I think it was divine inspiration that moved his Majesty to carry out a resolution so noble. Not that we were all guilty, for some were true and steadfast Christians. But they were so few that they couldn't compare with those who were not; and it was not wise to nourish a viper at the breast by harboring enemies inside the house.

"In short it was with just cause that we were condemned to be banished, a mild and lenient punishment in the eyes of some, but to us the most terrible that could be inflicted on us. Wherever we are, we weep for Spain. After all, we were born there, and it's our native country. Nowhere do we find the welcome that we, in our unhappy condition, long for. In Barbary and every part of Africa where we counted upon being received, welcomed, and favored, it is there they insult and mistreat us most. We failed to realize what good fortune we had until we lost it. Such is the longing nearly all of us have to return to Spain, that most of those who like myself know the language—and there are many who do—come back to it and leave their wives and children forsaken abroad, so great is their love for it. I know from experience the meaning of the saying, 'Sweet is the love of one's country.'

"I left our village, as I said, and went to France, but though they gave us a kind reception there I was anxious to see all I could. I crossed into Italy and reached Germany. There it seemed to me we might live with more freedom, as the inhabitants pay no attention to trifles. Everyone lives as he likes, for in most parts they enjoy liberty of conscience.[12] I took a house in a town near Augsburg and then joined these pilgrims, who are in the habit of coming to Spain in great numbers every year to visit the shrines there, which they look upon as their Indies and a sure and certain source of gain. They travel nearly all

[11] *At least it did . . . on me and my children:* Edicts of expulsion were issued against the Moriscos of La Mancha in July 1610 (Moriscos who had resettled from Granada) and March 1611 (all remaining Moriscos) with a grace period of two months. Enforcement of Spain's expulsion edicts continued until August 1614.

[12] *for in most parts they enjoy liberty of conscience:* If by "liberty of conscience" Ricote means "freedom of religion", his characterization is inaccurate. At the dawn of the seventeenth century, most German governments permitted only one religious confession to be practiced: Roman Catholic, Lutheran, or Calvinist. Islam, Ricote's ancestral faith, was not tolerated. His mention of Augsburg, however, is historically apt: the free imperial city was one of the few German jurisdictions where Catholics and Protestants coexisted legally and peacefully.

over it, and there is no town they leave without being 'well fed and watered,' as the saying is, and with a real, at least in change. They come off at the end of their travels with more than a hundred escudos saved, which, exchanged for gold, they smuggle out of the kingdom—in the hollow of their staffs or in the patches of their pilgrim's capes or by some other device of their own—and carry to their own country in spite of the guards at the posts and crossings where they are searched.[13]

"My purpose now, Sancho, is to carry away the treasure I left buried, which, since it is outside the town, I'll be able to do without risk, and to write—or cross over from Valencia—to my daughter and wife, who I know are in Algiers, and find a way to bring them to some French port and then to Germany, there to await what it may be God's will to do with us. For I am well aware, Sancho, that Ricota my daughter and Francisca Ricota my wife are Catholic Christians, and though I am not so much so, I'm still more of a Christian than a Moor. It has long been my prayer that God would open the eyes of my understanding and show me how I am to serve him. Yet what amazes me and I cannot understand is why my wife and daughter should have gone to Barbary rather than to France, where they could live as Christians."

To this Sancho replied, "Ricote, it wasn't in their hands to choose where they went. Your wife's brother, Juan Tiopieyo, took them, and being a true Moor he went where he thought best. I can tell you another thing: it's my belief you're wasting your time going to look for what you've left buried, for we heard that a great many pearls and gold coins that your brother-in-law and your wife were carrying out of the country were taken from them."[14]

"That may be," said Ricote, "but I know they didn't touch my buried treasure, because I didn't tell them where it was for fear that something might happen to it. And so if you will come with me, Sancho, and help me dig it up and conceal it, I'll give you two hundred escudos you can use to provide for your needs—and you know that I know your needs are many."

"I would do it," said Sancho, "but I'm not at all greedy. This very morning I let a position slip through my hands that would have enabled me to cover the walls of my house in gold and dine off silver before six months were over. For this reason—and because I feel I would be guilty of treason to my king if I helped his enemies—I wouldn't go with you if instead of promising me two hundred escudos you gave me four hundred right now."

"And what position is this you've given up, Sancho?" asked Ricote.

"I've given up being governor of an island," said Sancho, "and such a one, faith, as you won't find the like of easily."

"And where is this island?" asked Ricote.

[13] *hundred escudos saved . . . where they are searched:* The German pilgrims come to Spain to acquire gold, likely attracted by the abundance of New World bullion and favorable exchange conditions, with plans to profit from its resale abroad. For a related phenomenon with silver, see footnote 14, page 237.

[14] *were taken from them:* Moriscos fleeing the country were easy targets for highwaymen.

"Where?" said Sancho. "Two leagues from here. It's called the island of Barataria."

"Nonsense, Sancho!" said Ricote. "Islands are way out in the sea. There are no islands on the mainland."

"How can you say that?" said Sancho. "I tell you, friend Ricote, I left it this morning. Yesterday I was governing there as I pleased like a Sagittarius.[15] But for all that I gave it up, for it seemed to me a dangerous job, being a governor."

"And what have you gained from governing?" asked Ricote.

Sancho replied, "I've gained the knowledge that I'm no good for governing, unless it's a drove of cattle, and that the riches that are earned from these governments come at the cost of your rest and sleep, and even your food; for in islands the governors must eat little, especially if they have doctors to look after their health."

"I don't understand you, Sancho," said Ricote. "It all seems to me nonsense what you're saying. Who would give you islands to govern? Is there any shortage in the world of men more qualified than you are to be governors? Hold your peace, Sancho. Come back to your senses, and consider whether you will come with me as I said to help me to take away the treasure I left buried—for it may certainly be called a treasure, it's so great—and I will give you something to live on, as I told you."

"And I have told you already, Ricote, that I will not," said Sancho. "Be content that I'm not going to betray you, and go your way in God's name and let me go mine. I know that 'well-gotten gain will be lost, but ill-gotten gain will be lost along with its owner.'"

"I won't argue with you, Sancho," said Ricote. "But tell me this, were you in our village when my wife and daughter and brother-in-law left it?"

"I was," said Sancho, "and I can tell you that your daughter left it looking so lovely that all the village turned out to see her, and everybody said she was the fairest creature in the world. She wept as she went, and embraced all her friends and acquaintances and those who came out to see her, and she begged them all to commend her to God and Our Lady his mother—and in such a touching way that it made me weep myself, though I'm not often given to tears. Faith, many a one would have liked to hide her or go out on the road and carry her off, but the fear of going against the king's command kept them back. The one who showed himself most moved was Don Pedro Gregorio, the rich young heir you know of. They say he was deeply in love with her, and since she left he hasn't been seen in our village again. We all suspect he's gone after her to steal her away, but so far nothing has been heard of it."

"I always had a suspicion that gentleman had a passion for my daughter," said Ricote, "but as I felt sure of my Ricota's virtue it gave me no anxiety to know that he loved her. You must have heard it said, Sancho, that Morisco women seldom or never give their hearts to Old Christians; and my daughter—who,

[15] *Sagittarius:* perhaps an oblique reference to the centaur Chiron, tutor to Achilles, whom Homer praised as the "wisest and most just of all the centaurs".

to my mind, was more concerned about being a Christian than being in love—wouldn't trouble herself about the attentions of this heir."

"God grant it," said Sancho, "for it would be bad for both of them. But let me be off now, friend Ricote, for I want to reach the place where my master Don Quixote is staying tonight."

"God be with you, brother Sancho," said Ricote. "My comrades are beginning to stir, and it is also time for us to continue our journey."

They embraced each other, then Sancho mounted Dapple as Ricote leaned upon his staff. And so they parted.

CHAPTER LV

OF WHAT BEFELL SANCHO ON THE ROAD, AND OTHER THINGS THAT CANNOT BE SURPASSED

The length of time he delayed with Ricote prevented Sancho from reaching the duke's castle that day, though he was within half a league of it when a somewhat dark and cloudy night overtook him. As it was summertime, this did not trouble him much, and he turned off the road intending to wait for morning. But his bad luck and hard fate so willed it that as he was searching for a place to make himself as comfortable as possible, he and Dapple fell into a deep, dark hole that lay among some very old buildings. As he fell he commended himself with all his heart to God, imagining that he was not going to stop until he reached the depths of the bottomless pit. But it did not turn out so, for at a little more than three times a man's height Dapple touched bottom, and Sancho found himself sitting on top of him without any wound or injury whatsoever.

He felt himself all over and held his breath to see whether he was in good shape or had a hole punctured in him anywhere.[1] Finding himself whole and in perfect health, he was profuse in his thanks to God our Lord for the mercy that had been shown him, for he had been certain that he was smashed into a thousand pieces. He also felt along the sides of the pit with his hands to see if it was possible to get out of it without help, but he found they were quite smooth and provided no hold anywhere—at which he was greatly distressed, especially when he heard Dapple's plaintive and tender cries. Little wonder that Dapple complained, for in truth he was in a very bad way.

"Alas," said Sancho, "what unexpected accidents happen at every turn to those who live in this miserable world! Who would have said that the man who only yesterday was sitting on a throne, governor of an island, giving orders to his servants and his vassals, would find himself today buried in a pit without a soul to help him, or servant or vassal to come to his relief? Here we are to perish with hunger, my donkey and myself, if we don't die first—he from his bruises and injuries, and I from grief and sorrow. No matter what happens, I won't be as lucky as my master Don Quixote of La Mancha when he went down into the cave of that enchanted Montesinos. There he found people to fuss over him more than if he had been in his own house. It was as if he was welcomed to a table laid out and a

[1] *held his breath . . . anywhere:* According to popular belief, one's life and breath could escape through surface wounds.

bed waiting for him. There he saw fair and pleasant visions, but here, I imagine, I'll see toads and snakes.

"Unlucky wretch that I am, what an end my foolish dreams have come to! When it's Heaven's will that I'm found, they'll remove my bones from this place picked clean, white, and polished, and my good Dapple's with them. It may be from them that they figure out who we are—at least those who have heard that Sancho Panza never left his donkey's side, nor his donkey Sancho Panza's. Unlucky wretches, I say again, that our hard fate should not let us die in our own country and among our own people, where if there was no help for our misfortune, at any rate there would be someone to grieve for it and to close our eyes as we passed away! O comrade and friend, how poorly have I repaid your faithful services! Forgive me, and entreat Fortune as well as you can to deliver us out of this miserable predicament we're both in. I promise to put a crown of laurel on your head to make you look like a poet laureate and to double your feed."

In this strain did Sancho bewail himself. His donkey listened to him but answered him never a word—such was the distress and anguish the poor beast found himself in. At length, after a night spent in bitter moanings and lamentations, day came, and by its light Sancho determined that it was wholly impossible to escape out of that pit without help. He fell to bemoaning his fate and uttering loud shouts to find out if there was anyone within hearing; but all his shouting was only crying in the wilderness, for there was not a soul anywhere in the vicinity to hear him. Then, at last, he gave himself up for dead.

Dapple was lying on his back, and Sancho helped him to his feet, a position that he could scarcely maintain. Taking a piece of bread out of his saddlebag, which had shared their fortunes in the fall, he gave it to the donkey—to whom it was not unwelcome—saying to him, as if he understood him, "With bread all sorrows are less."

He noticed then on one side of the pit an opening large enough to fit a person if he bent over and crouched. Sancho went over to it and entered, squeezing himself through, and found it wide and spacious on the inside, which he was able to see because a ray of sunlight that penetrated what might be called the roof showed everything plainly. He observed too that it opened and widened into another spacious cavity. When he saw this, he made his way back to where the donkey was, and with a stone began to pick away the clay from the hole until in a short time he had made room for the beast to pass easily. This accomplished, taking him by the halter, he proceeded to pass through the cavern to see if there was any outlet at the other end. He advanced—sometimes in the dark, sometimes without light, but never without fear.

"God Almighty help me!" he said to himself. "What is a misadventure for me would have made a great adventure for my master Don Quixote. No doubt he would take these depths and dungeons for flowery gardens or the palaces of Galiana[2] and would have been confident that he would come out of this darkness

[2] *palaces of Galiana:* common expression for the most luxurious place imaginable. Galiana was the wife of a Moorish governor of Toledo, whose summer villa and gardens stood outside the city on the banks of the Tagus River.

and imprisonment into some flower-filled meadow. But I, unlucky as I am, hopeless and spiritless, expect at every step another pit deeper than the first to open under my feet and swallow me up for good. 'Welcome evil, if you come alone.'"

In this way and with these reflections he judged that he traveled a little more than half a league when at last he saw a dim light that looked like daylight and found its way in on one side, showing that this road, which appeared to him the road to the other world, led to some opening.

Here Cide Hamete leaves him and returns to Don Quixote, who in high spirits and satisfaction was looking forward to the day fixed for the battle he was to fight with the thief who had robbed Doña Rodríguez's daughter of her honor, for whom he hoped to obtain satisfaction for the wrong and injury shamefully done to her. It happened that having sallied forth one morning to practice and train for what he would have to do in the encounter he expected to find himself engaged in the next day, as he was putting Rocinante through his paces or pressing him to the charge, he brought his feet so close to a pit that but for reining him in tightly it would have been impossible for him to avoid falling into it. He pulled him up without a fall, and coming a little closer examined the hole without dismounting. As he was looking, he heard loud cries proceeding from it, and by listening attentively was able to make out that the one who uttered them was saying, "Hello up there! Is there any Christian who hears me or any charitable gentleman who will take pity on a sinner buried alive, on an unfortunate disgoverned governor?"

It struck Don Quixote that it was the voice of Sancho Panza he heard, at which he was taken aback and amazed. Raising his own voice as much as he could, he cried out, "Who is down there? Who is that who cries out?"

"Who should be here, or who should cry out," was the answer, "but the wretched Sancho Panza, governor of the island of Barataria—for his sins and for his misfortune—and formerly squire of the famous knight Don Quixote of La Mancha?"

When Don Quixote heard this, he was doubly astonished and even more stupefied, for it came to his mind that Sancho must be dead and that his soul was in torment down below. Carried away by this idea he exclaimed, "I conjure you by everything that as a Catholic Christian I can conjure you by, tell me who you are. If you are a soul in torment, tell me what you would have me do for you; for as my profession is to give aid and succor to those that need it in this world, it will also extend to aiding and succoring the distressed of the other, who cannot help themselves."

"In that case," answered the voice, "your worship who speaks to me must be my master Don Quixote of La Mancha. Even from the tone of the voice it's obvious that it can be nobody else."

"Don Quixote I am," replied Don Quixote, "he whose profession it is to aid and succor the living and the dead in their necessities. I ask, then, that you tell me who you are, for you are keeping me in suspense; because, if you are my squire Sancho Panza and are dead—since the devils have not carried you off, and you are by God's mercy in purgatory—our holy mother the Roman Catholic Church has intercessory means sufficient to release you from the pains you are in. I for my part will plead with her to that end, so far as my substance will go. Without further delay, therefore, declare yourself, and tell me who you are."

"By all that's good," was the answer, "and by the birth of whoever your worship chooses, I swear, Señor Don Quixote of La Mancha, that I am your squire Sancho Panza, and that I have never died all my life; but that, having given up my government for reasons that would require more time to explain, I fell last night into this pit where I am now. Dapple is my witness and won't let me lie. For added proof, he's here with me."

Nor was this all. It seemed as if the donkey understood what Sancho said, because at that moment he began to bray so loudly that the whole cave resounded.

"Unmistakable evidence!" exclaimed Don Quixote. "I know that bray as well as if I was the donkey's mother—and your voice too, my Sancho. Wait while I go to the duke's castle, which is nearby, and I will bring someone to take you out of this pit into which your sins no doubt have brought you."

"Go, your worship," said Sancho, "and come back quick for God's sake. I can't bear being buried alive any longer, and I'm dying of fear."

Don Quixote left him and headed to the castle to tell the duke and duchess what had happened to Sancho. They were more than a little astonished at the news. While they could easily understand his having fallen—aware of the other entrance to the cave, which had been in existence there from time immemorial—they could not imagine how he had left the government without their receiving any intimation of his coming. To be brief, they fetched ropes and tackle, and with much labor and the help of many hands, they pulled Dapple and Sancho Panza out of the darkness into the light of day.

A student who saw him remarked, "That's the way all bad governors should come out of their governments, as this sinner comes out of the depths of the pit—dead with hunger, pale, and, as far as I can tell, without a cent."

Sancho overheard him and said, "It's been eight or ten days, brother heckler, since I took up the government of the island they gave me, and all that time I never had a bellyful of food—no, not for an hour. Doctors persecuted me, enemies crushed my bones, and I had no opportunity to take bribes or levy taxes. If that's the case (as it is), I don't think I deserve to come out like this. But 'man proposes and God disposes.' God knows what's best, and what suits each one best. 'As the occasion, so the behavior,' and 'never say, "I won't drink this water,"' and 'where you think there's smoke, there's no fire.' God knows my meaning, and that's enough. I could say more, but I won't."

"Do not be angry or annoyed at what you hear, Sancho," said Don Quixote, "or there will never be an end of it. Keep a clear conscience and let them say what they like; for trying to stop slanderers' tongues is like trying to put gates on the open plain. If a governor comes out of his government rich, they say he has been a thief; and if he comes out poor, that he has been a failure and a blockhead."

"They'll be pretty sure this time," said Sancho, "to set me down for a fool rather than a thief."

Thus talking, and surrounded by boys and a crowd of people, they reached the castle, where in one of the corridors the duke and duchess stood waiting for them. Sancho would not go up to see the duke until he had first put up Dapple in the stable, for he said he had passed a very bad night in his last lodging. He then went upstairs to see his lord and lady. Kneeling before them, he said:

"Because it was your highnesses' pleasure—not because I deserved it—I went to govern your island of Barataria, which 'I entered naked, and naked I remain; nothing lost or gained.' Whether I have governed well or badly, I have had witnesses who will say what they think fit. I have answered questions, I have resolved disputes, and always dying of hunger, for this was the wish of Doctor Pedro Recio of Tirteafuera, the island and governor doctor. Enemies attacked us by night and put us in a great bind, but the people of the island say they came off safe and victorious by the might of my arm. May God give them as much health as there's truth in what they say.

"In short, during that time I have weighed the cares and responsibilities governing brings with it, and I've learned by experience that my shoulders can't bear them. They are no load for my loins or arrows for my quiver. And so, before the government threw me over, I preferred to throw the government over. Yesterday morning I left the island as I found it, with the same streets, houses, and roofs it had when I entered it. I asked no loan of anybody, nor did I try to fill my pocket. Though I meant to make some useful laws, I made hardly any, since I was afraid they would not be kept; for in that case it amounts to the same thing to make them as not to make them. I left the island, as I said, without any escort except my donkey. I fell into a pit, I pushed on through it, until this morning by the light of the sun I saw an outlet—but not so easy a one but that, had not Heaven sent me my master Don Quixote, I'd have stayed there till the end of the world.

"So now my lord and lady duke and duchess, here is your governor Sancho Panza, who in only ten days of governing has come to realize that he would not give anything to be governor—not just of an island, but of the whole world. That point being settled, kissing your worships' feet, and imitating the game the children play when they say, 'Jump and give it to me,' I'm taking a jump out of the government and moving on to the service of my master Don Quixote. For even though the bread I eat in his service comes with distress, at least I eat my fill; and for my part, so long as I'm full, it's all the same to me whether it's with carrots or partridges."

Here Sancho brought his long speech to an end, Don Quixote having been the whole time in dread of his uttering a host of absurdities. When he found him conclude with so few, he thanked Heaven in his heart. The duke embraced Sancho and told him he was terribly sorry he had given up the government so soon, but that he would see that he was provided with some post or another on his estate less onerous and more profitable. The duchess also embraced him and gave orders that he should be taken good care of, as it was plain to see he had been badly treated and worse bruised.

CHAPTER LVI

OF THE PRODIGIOUS AND UNPARALLELED BATTLE THAT TOOK PLACE BETWEEN DON QUIXOTE OF LA MANCHA AND THE FOOTMAN TOSILOS IN DEFENSE OF DOÑA RODRÍGUEZ'S DAUGHTER

The duke and duchess had no reason to regret the prank that had been played on Sancho Panza in giving him the government—especially as their majordomo returned the same day and gave them a minute account of almost every word and deed that Sancho uttered or did during the time. He concluded with an eloquent description of the attack on the island and Sancho's fear and departure, with which they were not a little amused.

After this the history goes on to say that the day fixed for the battle arrived, and that the duke—after having repeatedly instructed his footman Tosilos how to deal with Don Quixote so as to vanquish without killing or wounding him—gave orders to have the heads removed from the lances, telling Don Quixote that Christian charity, on which he plumed himself, could not permit the battle to be fought with so much risk and danger to life; and that he must be content with the offer of a battle in the open field on his territory (though even that was against the decree of the holy Council, which prohibits all such challenges[1]) and not push such an arduous venture to its extreme limits. Don Quixote agreed to let his excellency arrange all matters connected with the affair as he pleased, as on his part he would obey him in everything.

The dread day having arrived, then, and the duke having ordered a spacious stand to be erected facing the court of the castle for the judges of the field and the appellant dueñas, mother and daughter, vast crowds flocked from all the surrounding villages and hamlets to see the novel spectacle of the battle—nobody in those parts, dead or alive, having ever seen or heard of such a thing. The first person to enter the field and the lists was the master of ceremonies, who surveyed and paced the whole ground to see that there was nothing unfair or concealed to make the combatants stumble or fall. Then the dueñas entered and seated themselves, enveloped in mantles covering their eyes—nay even

[1] *against the decree of the holy Council, which prohibits all such challenges:* In 1563 the Council of Trent issued a decree against dueling, condemning it as contrary to the Christian ethic of humility and forgiveness. Violators were threatened with excommunication.

their bosoms—and displaying no slight emotion as Don Quixote appeared in the lists. Shortly afterwards, accompanied by several trumpets and mounted on a powerful steed that came thundering into the courtyard, the great footman Tosilos made his appearance on one side with his visor down and stiffly cased in a suit of stout, shining armor. His horse was easily recognized as a Friesian[2]—broad-backed and dapple-gray, and with an arroba of wool clinging to each of his legs. The gallant combatant came well primed by his master the duke as to how he was to bear himself against the valiant Don Quixote of La Mancha, being warned that he must on no account slay him, but to attempt to veer off from the first encounter so there would be no risk of killing him—as he was sure to do if he met him full tilt.

He crossed the courtyard at a walk, and coming to where the dueñas were seated stopped to look at the one who demanded him for a husband. The marshal of the field summoned Don Quixote, who had already presented himself in the courtyard. Standing by Tosilos' side, he addressed the dueñas, asking if they consented to have Don Quixote of La Mancha do battle for their right. They said they did, and that whatever he should do in that behalf they declared rightly done, final, and valid.

By this time the duke and duchess had taken their places in a gallery commanding the enclosure, which was filled to overflowing with a multitude of people eager to see this perilous and unparalleled encounter. The conditions of the combat were that if Don Quixote proved the victor, his antagonist was to marry the daughter of Doña Rodríguez; but if he should be vanquished, his opponent was released from the promise claimed against him and any other related obligations. The master of ceremonies portioned out the sun to them[3] and stationed each on the spot where he was to stand. The drums beat, the sound of the trumpets filled the air, the earth trembled under foot, the hearts of the gazing crowd beat anxiously—some hoping for a happy outcome, some fearful of disaster. Lastly, Don Quixote, commending himself with all his heart to God our Lord and to Lady Dulcinea del Toboso, stood waiting for them to give the signal to begin the charge. Our footman, however, had his mind set on a very different matter. His only thought was of what I am now going to relate.

It seems that as he stood contemplating the woman who would be his enemy, he was struck with the thought that she was the most beautiful woman he had ever seen in his life; and the little blind boy whom in our streets they commonly call Love had no intention to miss the opportunity of triumphing over a footman's heart and adding it to the list of his trophies. And so, stealing gently upon him unseen, he drove an arrow two yards long into the poor footman's left side and pierced his heart through and through—which he was able to do quite at his ease, for Love is invisible and comes in and goes out as he likes, without anyone calling him to account for what he does.

[2] *Friesian:* horse breed, originating in the Dutch province of Friesland, known for its strength, high-stepping gait, and long hair on the lower legs.

[3] *portioned out the sun to them:* See footnote 1, page 455.

Well then, when they gave the signal to charge, our footman was in an ecstasy, musing upon the beauty of the one whom he had already made mistress of his liberty, and so he paid no attention to the sound of the trumpet—unlike Don Quixote, who was off the instant he heard it, and, at the highest speed Rocinante was capable of, set out to meet his enemy, his good squire Sancho shouting lustily as he saw him start, "God guide you, cream and flower of knights-errant! God give you the victory, for you have the right on your side!"

But though Tosilos saw Don Quixote coming at him, he never stirred a step from the spot where he was posted. Instead of charging, he called loudly to the marshal of the field, to whom he said when he came up to see what he wanted, "Señor, the purpose of this battle is to decide whether or not I marry that lady, isn't it?"

"Just so," was the answer.

"Well then," said the footman, "My conscience is convicting me, and I would lay a heavy burden on it if I were to go any further with this battle. I therefore declare that I yield myself vanquished, and that I am willing to marry the lady at once."

The marshal of the field was lost in astonishment at Tosilos' words, and as he was one of those who was privy to the whole scheme, he did not know what to say in reply. Don Quixote pulled up mid-route when he saw that his enemy was not coming on to the attack. The duke could not make out the reason why the battle did not go on; but the marshal of the field went over to let him know what Tosilos said. When the duke found out, he was astonished and extremely angry. In the meantime, Tosilos advanced to where Doña Rodríguez sat, and said in a loud voice, "Señora, I am willing to marry your daughter. I have no wish to obtain by strife and fighting what I can obtain in peace and without any risk to my life."

The valiant Don Quixote heard him and said, "As that is the case, I am released and absolved from my promise. Let them marry by all means, and as God our Lord has given her, may Saint Peter add his blessing."

The duke had now come down to the castle courtyard, and going up to Tosilos he said to him, "Is it true, sir knight, that you yield yourself vanquished, and that moved by scruples of conscience you wish to marry this damsel?"

"It is, señor," replied Tosilos.

"And he does well," said Sancho, "for 'what you give to the mouse, give to the cat, and it will save you trouble.'"

Tosilos meanwhile was trying to unlace his helmet. He begged them to come to his aid at once, as his power of breathing was failing him and he could not remain so long shut up in that confined space. They removed it in all haste, revealing his footman features for everyone to see. At the sight, Doña Rodríguez and her daughter raised a mighty outcry, exclaiming, "This is a trick! This is a trick! They have foisted Tosilos, my lord the duke's footman, on us in place of the real husband. The justice of God and the king against such fraud, not to say villainy!"

"Do not distress yourselves, ladies," said Don Quixote, "for this is no fraud or villainy. Or if it is, it is not the duke who is at the bottom of it, but those wicked enchanters who persecute me, and who, jealous of my reaping the glory of this victory, have turned your husband's features into those of this person, who you say is a footman of the duke's. Take my advice, and marry him—notwithstanding the malice of my enemies—for beyond a doubt he is the one you wish for a husband."

When the duke heard this, his anger nearly vanished in a fit of laughter. He said, "The things that happen to Señor Don Quixote are so extraordinary that I am ready to believe this footman of mine is not one. But let us adopt this plan and device: let us put off the marriage for, say, a fortnight, and let us keep this person about whom we are uncertain in close confinement. Perhaps in the course of that time he may return to his original shape. For the spite which the enchanters entertain against Señor Don Quixote cannot last so long, especially as it is of so little advantage to them to carry out these deceptions and transformations."

"Oh, señor," said Sancho, "those scoundrels are very used to changing whatever concerns my master from one thing into another. A knight that he overcame some time back, called the Knight of the Mirrors, they turned into the shape of the bachelor Samson Carrasco of our town and a great friend of ours. And they have turned my lady Dulcinea del Toboso into a common country wench. I suspect this footman will have to live and die a footman all the days of his life."

Here Rodríguez's daughter exclaimed, "Let this man that claims me for a wife be whoever he may. I am grateful to him all the same, for I had rather be the lawful wife of a footman than the cheated mistress of a gentleman—though the man who played me false is nothing of the kind."

In sum, the whole affair ended with Tosilos being shut up until it was seen how his transformation turned out. Everyone hailed Don Quixote as victor, but the greater number were vexed and disappointed at finding that the combatants they had been so anxiously waiting for had not battered one another to pieces—just as the boys are disappointed when the man they are waiting to see hanged does not come out because the prosecution or the court has pardoned him. The people dispersed, the duke and Don Quixote returned to the castle, they locked up Tosilos, Doña Rodríguez and her daughter were thrilled to see that however the matter ended it would be in marriage, and Tosilos hoped for no less.

CHAPTER LVII

WHICH TREATS OF HOW DON QUIXOTE TOOK LEAVE OF THE DUKE, AND OF WHAT FOLLOWED WITH THE CLEVER AND IMPUDENT ALTISIDORA, ONE OF THE DUCHESS' DAMSELS

Don Quixote felt that the time was right to abandon the life of idleness he was leading in the castle; for he considered that he was depriving the world of himself by remaining shut up and inactive amid the countless luxuries and enjoyments his hosts lavished upon him as a knight; moreover, he was of the belief that he would have to render a strict account to Heaven for that indolence and seclusion. And so one day he asked the duke and duchess to grant him permission to take his departure. They granted it, admitting at the same time that they were very sorry he was leaving them.

The duchess gave Sancho Panza the letters his wife had written, and he shed tears over them, saying, "Who would have thought that the grand hopes that the news of my government bred in my wife Teresa Panza's breast would end with my going back to more lousy adventures with my master Don Quixote of La Mancha? Still, I'm glad to see my Teresa did what was right by sending the acorns, for if she hadn't sent them, I would have been sorry, and she would have shown herself ungrateful. It makes me feel better that they can't call the present a bribe, since I had already received the government when she sent them, and it's only reasonable that those who have had something nice done for them should show their gratitude—even if it's with something small. After all, I went into the government naked, and I come out of it naked; so I can say with a safe conscience (and that's no small matter), 'naked I was born, naked I remain, nothing lost or gained.'"

Thus did Sancho soliloquize on the day of their departure, while Don Quixote (who had the night before taken leave of the duke and duchess) made his appearance at an early hour in full armor in the courtyard of the castle. The whole household of the castle was watching him from the corridors, and the duke and duchess, too, came out to see him. Sancho was mounted on his Dapple, with his saddlebag, valise, and supply of provisions—supremely happy because the duke's majordomo, the same person who had acted the part of Trifaldi, had given him a little purse with two hundred gold escudos to meet the necessary expenses on the road. But of this Don Quixote knew nothing as yet.

While all were observing him, as has been said, suddenly from among the dueñas and handmaidens the clever and impudent Altisidora lifted up her voice and said in pathetic tones:

Give ear, cruel knight;
Draw rein; where's the need
Of spurring the flanks
Of that ill-broken steed?
From what art thou flying?
No dragon I am,
Not even a sheep,
But a tender young lamb.
Thou hast jilted a maiden
As fair to behold
As nymph of Diana
Or Venus of old.
Bireno,[1] *Æneas—what worse shall I call thee?*
Barabbas go with thee! All evil befall thee!

In thy claws, ruthless robber,
Thou bearest away
The heart of a meek
Loving maid for thy prey,
Three headscarves thou stealest,
And garters a pair,
From legs than the whitest
Of marble more fair;
And the sighs that pursue thee
Would burn to the ground
Two thousand Troy Towns,
If so many were found.
Bireno, Æneas—what worse shall I call thee?
Barabbas go with thee! All evil befall thee!

May no bowels of mercy
To Sancho be granted,
And thy Dulcinea
Be left still enchanted,
May thy falsehood to me
Find its punishment in her,
For in my land the just
Often pays for the sinner.
May thy grandest adventures
Discomfitures prove,
May thy joys be all dreams,
And forgotten thy love.

[1] Bireno: knight from *Orlando Furioso* who abandons his wife on a desert island after he grows tired of her.

Bireno, Æneas—what worse shall I call thee?
Barabbas go with thee! All evil befall thee!

May thy name be abhorred
For thy conduct to ladies,
From London to England,
From Seville to Cádiz;
May thy cards be unlucky,
Thy hands contain ne'er a
King, seven, or ace
When thou playest primera;[2]
When thy corns are removed
May it be to the quick;
When thy molars are drawn
May the roots of them stick.
Bireno, Æneas—what worse shall I call thee?
Barabbas go with thee! All evil befall thee!

All the while that the unhappy Altisidora was bewailing herself in the above strain, Don Quixote stood staring at her; and without uttering a word in reply he turned round to Sancho and said, "Sancho my friend, I charge you by the life of your forefathers to tell me the truth: Have you by any chance taken the three headscarves and the garters this lovesick maid speaks of?"

To this Sancho answered, "The three headscarves I have, but the garters—as much as 'over the hills of Úbeda.'"[3]

The duchess was amazed at Altisidora's audacity. She knew that she was bold, lively, and impudent, but not so much so as to put on this brazen performance. Not being prepared for the joke, her astonishment was all the greater.

The duke had a mind to keep up the sport, so he said, "It does not seem to me appropriate, sir knight, that after having received the hospitality that has been offered you in this very castle, you should have ventured to carry off no fewer than three headscarves, not to mention my handmaid's garters. It shows a bad heart and does not match your reputation. Restore her garters, or else I defy you to mortal combat, for I am not afraid of wily enchanters changing or altering my features as they changed his who encountered you into those of my footman Tosilos."

"God forbid," said Don Quixote, "that I should draw my sword against your illustrious person from which I have received such great favors. The headscarves I will restore, as Sancho says he has them. As to the garters that is impossible, for I do not have them, neither has he. If your handmaiden here will look in her hiding places, depend upon it she will find them. I have never been a thief, my lord duke, nor do I mean to be so long as I live, if God cease not to have me in

[2] *primera:* card game, similar to modern poker, in which kings, sevens, and aces are high-value cards.

[3] *over the hills of Úbeda:* See footnote 3, page 617.

his keeping. This damsel by her own confession speaks as one in love, for which I am not to blame, and therefore need not ask pardon—either of her or of your excellency, whom I entreat to have a better opinion of me, and once more to give me leave to pursue my journey."

"And may God so prosper it, Señor Don Quixote," said the duchess, "that we may always hear good news of your exploits. God speed you—for the longer you stay, the more you inflame the hearts of the damsels who behold you. As for this damsel of mine, I will so chastise her that she will not transgress again, either with her eyes or with her words."

"O valiant Don Quixote, one word and no more I ask you to hear," said Altisidora, "and that is that I beg your pardon about the theft of the garters; for by God and upon my soul I am wearing them. I've fallen into the same blunder as the man who went looking for his donkey when the whole time he was mounted on it."

"Didn't I say so?" said Sancho. "I'm a likely one to hide thefts! Why, if I was interested in stealing something, I had plenty of opportunities in my government."

Don Quixote bowed his head and saluted the duke and duchess and all the bystanders; and wheeling Rocinante round, Sancho following him on Dapple, he rode out of the castle, setting his course for Zaragoza.

CHAPTER LVIII

WHICH TELLS HOW ADVENTURES CAME CROWDING ON DON QUIXOTE IN SUCH NUMBERS THAT THEY GAVE EACH OTHER NO TIME TO BREATHE

When Don Quixote saw himself in the open country, free and unburdened from the attentions of Altisidora, he felt at his ease, in fresh spirits to take up the pursuit of chivalry once more. Turning to Sancho, he said, "Freedom, Sancho, is one of the most precious gifts that Heaven has bestowed upon men. No treasures that the earth holds buried or the sea conceals can compare with it. For freedom, as for honor, life may and should be ventured. Captivity, on the other hand, is the greatest evil that can fall to the lot of man. I say this, Sancho, because you have seen the luxury, the abundance we have enjoyed in this castle we are leaving. Yet amid those sumptuous banquets and snow-cooled beverages I felt as though I were undergoing the straits of hunger, because I did not enjoy them with the same freedom as if they had been my own. For the sense of being under an obligation to return benefits and favors received is a restraint that checks the independence of the spirit. Happy is he to whom Heaven has given a piece of bread for which he is not bound to give thanks to any but Heaven itself!"

"For all your worship says," said Sancho, "it's not becoming that there should be no thanks on our part for the two hundred gold escudos that the duke's majordomo has given me in a little purse I carry next my heart, like a poultice or ointment, for whatever needs might turn up. We aren't always going to find castles where they'll entertain us. We may even end up at a roadside inn where we get thrashed."

In conversation of this kind, the knight and squire errant were pursuing their journey, when, after they had gone a little more than half a league, they spied some dozen men dressed like laborers stretched upon their cloaks on the grass of a green meadow eating their dinner. They had beside them what appeared to be white sheets concealing some objects under them, standing upright or lying flat, and arranged at intervals. Don Quixote approached the diners, and saluting them courteously first, he asked them what it was those cloths covered.

"Señor," answered one of the party, "under these cloths are some images carved in relief intended for a display we are putting up in our village. We carry them covered so that they won't lose their shine, and on our shoulders that they won't be broken."

"With your good leave," said Don Quixote, "I should like to see them; for images that are carried so carefully no doubt must be fine ones."

"I should think they were!" said the other. "Let the money they cost speak for that. Truth be told, there is not one of them that hasn't set us back more than fifty ducats. So that your worship may judge, wait a moment and you will see with your own eyes." And getting up from his dinner he went and uncovered the first image, which proved to be one of Saint George[1] on horseback with a serpent coiled at his feet and the lance thrust down its throat with all that fierceness that is usually depicted. The image was one blaze of gold, as the saying is.

On seeing it Don Quixote said, "That knight was one of the best knights-errant that heaven's army ever owned. He was called Don Saint George, and he was moreover a defender of maidens. Let us see this next one."

The man uncovered it, and it was seen to be that of Saint Martin[2] on his horse, dividing his cloak with the beggar. The instant Don Quixote saw it he said, "This knight too was one of the Christian adventurers, but I believe he was generous rather than valiant, as you may observe, Sancho, by his dividing his cloak with the beggar and giving him half of it. No doubt it was winter at the time, for otherwise he would have given him the whole of it, so charitable was he."

"It was not that, most likely," said Sancho, "but that he was mindful of the proverb that says, 'For giving and keeping there's need of brains.'"

Don Quixote laughed and asked them to take off the next cloth, underneath which was seen an image of the patron saint of Spain seated on horseback, his sword stained with blood, trampling on Moors and treading heads underfoot. On seeing it Don Quixote exclaimed, "Now this is a knight, and of Christ's own squadrons. This one is called Don Saint James the Moorslayer,[3] one of the bravest saints and knights the world ever had or heaven has now."

They then raised another cloth that appeared to be covering Saint Paul falling from his horse, with all the details that are usually given in depictions of his conversion.[4] When Don Quixote saw it, rendered in such lifelike style that one would have said Christ was speaking and Paul answering, "This," he said, "was in his time the greatest enemy that the Church of God our Lord had, and the

[1] *Saint George:* According to tradition, George of Lydda (d. 303) was a member of the Praetorian Guard who was martyred for refusing to recant the Christian faith. In the popular medieval story depicted in the image, a cruel dragon extorted a tribute of livestock from a village. After the villagers ran out of animals, they were forced to surrender themselves. The saint arrived just in time to rescue a princess who was about to be offered as a sacrifice.

[2] *Saint Martin:* Martin of Tours (d. 397) abandoned a career in the Roman military for a life in the Church, rising to become third bishop of Tours. His legendary charity is exemplified by the story of him dividing his military cloak with a beggar while he was still a catechumen.

[3] *Don Saint James the Moorslayer:* Santiago Matamoros, name given to the Apostle James the Great in depictions of his miraculous appearance in the legendary Battle of Clavijo, where he aided Christian warriors fighting to reconquer Spain from the Moors.

[4] *Saint Paul falling from his horse . . . his conversion:* Saint Paul, originally known as the Pharisee Saul of Tarsus, was struck blind by a vision of Christ as he traveled to Damascus to persecute Christians, an encounter that led to his conversion and subsequent apostolic ministry (Acts 9:1–9; 26:12–18). Images commonly depict him falling from his horse.

greatest champion it will ever have—a knight-errant in life, a steadfast saint in death, an untiring laborer in the Lord's vineyard, a teacher of the Gentiles, whose school was heaven, and whose instructor and master was Jesus Christ himself."

There were no more images, so Don Quixote had them covered again, and said to those who brought them, "I take it as a happy omen, brothers, to have seen what I have; for these saints and knights were of the same profession as myself, which is the calling of arms. Only there is this difference between them and me—they were saints and fought with divine weapons; I am a sinner and fight with human ones. They won heaven by force of arms, for heaven suffers violence.[5] I ... I do not yet know what I have won with my sufferings. But if my Dulcinea del Toboso were to be released from hers, perhaps with mended fortunes and a mind restored to itself, I might direct my steps in a better path than I am following at present."

"May God hear and sin be deaf," said Sancho to this.

The men were filled with wonder, both at the figure and the words of Don Quixote, though they did not understand one half of what he meant by them. They finished their dinner, took their images on their backs, and bidding farewell to Don Quixote resumed their journey.

Sancho was amazed afresh at the extent of his master's knowledge—as much as if he had never known him—for it seemed to him that there was no story or event in the world that he had not at his fingertips and fixed in his memory. He said to him, "In truth, my master, if what happened to us today is to be called an adventure, it has been one of the sweetest and pleasantest that have befallen us in the whole course of our travels. We have come out of it unbruised and undismayed. We have neither drawn sword, nor have our bodies been beaten into the ground, nor have we been left hungry. Blessed be God that he has let me see such a thing with my own eyes!"

"You say well, Sancho," said Don Quixote, "but remember all times are not alike nor do they always unfold the same way. These things the vulgar commonly call omens—which are not based upon any natural reason—will by him who is wise be esteemed and reckoned merely as happy accidents. One of these believers in omens will get up one morning, leave his house, and meet a friar of the order of the blessed Saint Francis, and, as if he had met a griffin, he will turn about and go home. With another Mendoza[6] the salt is spilled on his table, and gloom is spilled over his heart, as if nature was obliged to give warning of coming misfortunes by means of such trivial things as these. The wise man and the Christian should not trifle with what it may please Heaven to do. Scipio on coming to Africa stumbled as he leaped on shore. His soldiers took it as a bad omen; but he, clasping the soil with his arms, exclaimed, 'You cannot escape me, Africa, for I hold you tight between my arms.'[7] Thus, Sancho, meeting those images has been to me a most happy occurrence."

[5] *heaven suffers violence:* echo of Matthew 11:12.

[6] *Mendoza:* "superstitious person". The noble Mendoza family was synonymous with superstition.

[7] *Scipio on coming ... my arms:* Suetonius attributes the quote to Julius Caesar.

"I can well believe it," said Sancho, "but I wish your worship would tell me what the reason is that Spaniards, when they are about to go into battle and call on that Saint James the Moorslayer, say 'Santiago and close Spain!'[8] Is Spain really open, that someone needs to close it? What does that custom mean?"

"You are very simple, Sancho," said Don Quixote. "God, you see, gave that great Knight of the Red Cross[9] to Spain as her patron saint and protector, especially in those hard struggles the Spaniards had with the Moors. For this reason, they invoke and call upon him as their defender in all their battles. In these he has been seen many a time beating down, trampling under foot, destroying and slaughtering the Hagarene[10] squadrons in the sight of all—of which fact I could give you many examples recorded in truthful Spanish histories."

Sancho changed the subject and said to his master, "Señor, I'm amazed at how forward Altisidora, the duchess' handmaid, was. The one they call Love must have pierced and wounded her something fierce. They say he's a little blind fellow who, though his eyes are bleary (or more properly speaking sightless), if he aims at a heart, however small it is, hits it and pierces it through and through with his arrows. I have heard it said too that the arrows of Love are blunted by a maiden's modesty and reserve. But with this Altisidora it seems they are sharpened rather than blunted."

"Bear in mind, Sancho," said Don Quixote, "that love is influenced by no consideration, recognizes no restraints of reason, and is of the same nature as death, which assails alike the lofty palaces of kings and the lowly huts of shepherds. When it takes entire possession of a heart, the first thing it does is to banish fear and meekness from it; and so without embarrassment Altisidora declared her passion, which made me feel shame rather than pity."

"That's some incredible cruelty and ingratitude!" exclaimed Sancho. "I can only say for myself that the very tiniest loving word of hers would have conquered me and made me her slave. Son of a bitch! What a heart of marble you have, what bronze innards, what mortar in your soul! But I can't imagine what it is that this damsel saw in your worship that could have conquered and captivated her like that. What gallant figure was it, what swagger, what grace, what good looks—which of these things by itself, or what all together could have made her fall in love with you? For indeed and in truth many a time I stop to look at your worship from the sole of your foot to the topmost hair of your head, and I see more to frighten than to make a person fall in love. I've heard it said that beauty is the first and main thing that excites love, and as your worship has none at all, I don't know what the poor creature fell in love with."

[8] *Santiago and close Spain:* The battle cry Sancho references is "Santiago y cierra, España", an invocation of the saint's aid as Christians charged their Moorish foes during the Reconquista. "Cierra", which commonly means "close", here functions as a command for troops to close ranks or charge the enemy.

[9] *Knight of the Red Cross:* Santiago Matamoros was typically depicted with the cross of the military order named in his honor.

[10] *Hagarene:* As early as Josephus, Arabs were believed to have descended from Ishmael, the son of the patriarch Abraham by his concubine Hagar (Genesis 16; 21:8–21)—a lineage invoked by Christians in anti-Muslim polemics.

"Recollect, Sancho," replied Don Quixote, "there are two kinds of beauty: one of the mind, the other of the body. That of the mind displays and exhibits itself in intelligence, in modesty, in honorable conduct, in generosity, in good breeding. All these qualities are possible and may exist in an ugly man. When it is this kind of beauty and not that of the body that is the attraction, love is apt to spring up suddenly and violently. I, Sancho, perceive clearly enough that I am not beautiful, but at the same time I know I am not hideous. It is enough for an honest man not to be a monster to be an object of love, if only he possesses the endowments of mind I have mentioned."

While engaged in this discourse they were making their way through a forest that lay beyond the road, when suddenly, without expecting anything of the kind, Don Quixote found himself caught in some nets of green cord stretched from one tree to another. Unable to conceive what it could be, he said to Sancho, "Sancho, it strikes me this affair of these nets will prove one of the strangest adventures imaginable. May I die if the enchanters that persecute me are not trying to entangle me in them and delay my journey, by way of revenge for my obduracy toward Altisidora. Well, let me assure them that if these nets, instead of being green cord, were made of the hardest diamonds—or stronger than that with which the jealous god of blacksmiths enmeshed Venus and Mars[11]—I would break them as easily as if they were made of rushes or cotton threads."

But just as he was about to press forward and break through it all, suddenly from among some trees two shepherdesses of surpassing beauty presented themselves to his sight—or at least damsels dressed like shepherdesses, save that their shepherd's coats and skirts were of fine brocade; that is to say, the skirts were a richly embroidered fabric of silk and gold. Their hair, which in its golden brightness vied with the beams of the sun itself, fell loose upon their shoulders and was crowned with garlands twined with green laurel and red amaranth.[12] Their years to all appearance were not under fifteen nor above eighteen.

Such was the spectacle that filled Sancho with amazement, fascinated Don Quixote, made the sun halt in his course to behold them, and held all four in a strange silence. One of the shepherdesses, at length, was the first to speak and said to Don Quixote, "Hold, sir knight, and do not break these nets. They are not spread here to do you any harm, but only for our amusement. As I know you will ask why they have been set out, and who we are, I will tell you in a few words. In a village some two leagues from here, where there are many hidalgos and people of substance, it was agreed upon by a number of friends and relations to come with their wives, sons and daughters, neighbors, friends and kinsmen, and take our recreation here, which is one of the pleasantest spots in the whole region, setting up a new pastoral Arcadia[13] among ourselves, we maidens dressing as shepherdesses

[11] *nets . . . which the jealous god of blacksmiths enmeshed Venus and Mars:* Vulcan trapped his wife Venus and her lover Mars in an unbreakable, invisible net he fashioned.

[12] *twined with green laurel and red amaranth:* Taken together, laurel and amaranth symbolize unfading glory and immortality.

[13] *Arcadia:* pastoral utopia of classical and Renaissance literature, named after a province in the central Peloponnese.

and the youths as shepherds. We have prepared two eclogues, one by the famous poet Garcilaso, the other by the most excellent Camões,[14] in its own Portuguese tongue, but we have not as yet acted them. Yesterday was the first day of our coming here. We have a few of what they say are called field tents pitched among the trees on the bank of an ample brook that nourishes all these meadows. Last night we spread these nets in the trees here to snare the innocent little birds that, startled by the noise we make, may fly into them. If you please to be our guest, señor, you will be welcomed heartily and courteously, for here in this place neither care nor sorrow shall enter."

She held her peace and said no more, and Don Quixote answered, "Of a truth, fairest lady, Actaeon when he unexpectedly beheld Diana bathing in the stream[15] could not have been more fascinated and wonderstruck than I at the sight of your beauty. I commend your mode of entertainment and thank you for the kindness of your invitation. If I can serve you, you may command me with full confidence of being obeyed, for my profession is none other than to show myself grateful and ready to serve persons of all conditions, but especially persons of quality such as your appearance indicates. And if instead of taking up but a small space, these nets took up the whole surface of the globe, I would seek out new worlds through which to pass, so as not to break them. So that you may give some degree of credence to this grandiose language of mine, know that it is no less than Don Quixote of La Mancha that makes this declaration to you, if indeed it be that such a name has reached your ears."

"Ah, friend of my soul!" instantly exclaimed the other shepherdess. "What great good fortune has befallen us! Do you see this gentleman we have before us? Well, let me tell you that he is the most valiant, the most devoted, and the most courteous gentleman in all the world—unless a history of his achievements that has been printed and I have read is telling lies and deceiving us. I will lay a wager that this good fellow who is with him is one Sancho Panza his squire, whose witticisms none can equal."

"That's true," said Sancho. "I am that same witty squire you speak of, and this gentleman is my master Don Quixote of La Mancha, the same that's in the history you're referring to."

"Oh, my friend," said the other, "let us entreat him to stay, for it will give our fathers and brothers infinite pleasure. I too have heard just what you have told me of the valor of the one and the witticisms of the other. What is more, they say of him that he is the most constant and loyal lover that was ever heard of, and that his lady is one Dulcinea del Toboso, to whom all over Spain the palm of beauty is awarded."

"And justly awarded," said Don Quixote, "unless, indeed, your unequaled beauty makes it a matter of doubt. But spare yourselves the trouble, ladies, of

[14] *Camões:* Luis de Camões (d. 1580), Portuguese poet best known for his epic *The Lusiads*. His eclogues appear in the posthumous poetry collection *Rimas* (1595).

[15] *Actaeon when he unexpectedly beheld Diana bathing in the stream:* When the hunter Actaeon accidentally stumbled on Diana and her nymphs bathing in a stream, the goddess changed him into a stag, leaving him to be devoured by his hunting dogs.

pressing me to stay, for the urgent calls of my profession do not allow me to take rest under any circumstances."

At that moment there came up to the place where the four stood a brother of one of the two shepherdesses, like them in shepherd costume, and as richly and festively dressed as they were. They told him that their companion was the valiant Don Quixote of La Mancha and the other Sancho his squire, of whom he knew already from having read their history. The gallant shepherd offered him his services and begged Don Quixote to accompany him to their tents. Don Quixote had no choice but to give in and comply.

The shepherds now set about flushing out the birds, and the nets were filled with a variety of them, which, deceived by the net's color, fell into the danger they were flying from. Upwards of thirty people, all gaily attired as shepherds and shepherdesses, assembled on the spot and were at once informed who Don Quixote and his squire were, at which they were not a little delighted, as they knew of him already through his history. They returned to their tents, where they found tables laid out—choicely, plentifully, and neatly furnished. They treated Don Quixote as a person of distinction, giving him the place of honor. All kept their eyes on him and were full of wonder at his presence. When the meal was finished, Don Quixote with great composure lifted up his voice and said:

"One of the greatest sins that men are guilty of is—some will say pride—but I say ingratitude, going by the common saying that hell is full of ingrates. This sin, so far as it has lain in my power, I have endeavored to avoid ever since I have enjoyed the faculty of reason. If I am unable to requite good deeds that have been done me by other deeds, I substitute the desire to do so. And if that is not enough, I make them known publicly; for he who declares and makes known the good deeds done to him would repay them by others if it were in his power, and for the most part those who receive are the inferiors of those who give. Thus, God is superior to all because he is the supreme giver, and the offerings of man fall short by an infinite distance of being a full return for the gifts of God. But gratitude in some degree makes up for this deficiency and shortcoming.

"I, therefore, grateful for the favor that has been extended to me here and unable to make a return in the same measure, restricted as I am by the narrow limits of my power, offer what I can and what I have to offer in my own way. And so I declare that for two full days I will maintain in the middle of this highway leading to Zaragoza that these ladies here present disguised as shepherdesses are the fairest and most courteous maidens in the world, excepting only the peerless Dulcinea del Toboso, sole mistress of my thoughts—be it said without offense to those who hear me, ladies and gentlemen."

On hearing this Sancho, who had been listening with great attention, cried out in a loud voice, "Is it possible there is anyone in the world who will dare to take an oath that this master of mine is a madman? Tell me, gentlemen shepherds, is there a village priest, however wise or learned he may be, who could say what my master has said; or is there knight-errant, whatever renown he may have as a man of valor, that could offer what my master has offered now?"

Don Quixote turned to Sancho and with a countenance glowing with anger said to him, "Is it possible, Sancho, there is anyone in the whole world who will say you are not a fool, with a lining to match, and I know not what impertinent and obnoxious trimmings? Who asked you to meddle in my affairs or to inquire whether I am a wise man or a blockhead? Hold your peace—answer me not a word. Saddle Rocinante if he is unsaddled, and let us go put my offer into execution; for with the right that I have on my side you may consider as vanquished all who shall venture to question it." And in a great rage, and showing his anger plainly, he rose from his seat, leaving the company lost in astonishment and unsure whether they should regard him as a madman or a rational being.

In the end, though they sought to dissuade him from involving himself in such a challenge, assuring him that they admitted his gratitude as fully established and needed no fresh proofs to be convinced of his valiant spirit, as those related in the history of his exploits were sufficient—nevertheless, Don Quixote persisted in his resolve. Mounting on Rocinante, bracing his buckler on his arm, and grasping his lance, he posted himself in the middle of a king's highway that was not far from the green meadow. Sancho followed on Dapple, together with all the members of the pastoral gathering, eager to see what the outcome of his vainglorious and extraordinary undertaking would be.

Don Quixote, having planted himself in the middle of the road as has been said, rent the air with words to this effect: "All you travelers and wayfarers, knights, squires, people on foot or on horseback, who pass this way or shall pass in the course of the next two days—know that Don Quixote of La Mancha, knight-errant, is posted here to maintain by arms that the beauty and courtesy enshrined in the nymphs that dwell in these meadows and groves surpass all upon earth, putting aside the lady of my heart, Dulcinea del Toboso. Therefore, let him who thinks otherwise step forward, for here I await him."

Twice he repeated the same words, and twice they fell unheard by any adventurer. But fate, that was guiding affairs for him from better to better, so ordered it that shortly afterwards there appeared on the road a crowd of men on horseback, many of them with lances in their hands, all riding in a compact body and in great haste. No sooner had those who were with Don Quixote seen them than they turned about and withdrew to some distance from the road, for they knew that if they stayed some harm might come to them. But Don Quixote with intrepid heart stood his ground, while Sancho Panza shielded himself with Rocinante's hindquarters. The troop of lancers came up, and one of them who was in advance began shouting to Don Quixote, "Get out of the way, you son of the devil, or these bulls will knock you to pieces!"

"Rabble!" returned Don Quixote. "I care nothing for bulls, be they the fiercest that the Jarama breeds on its banks.[16] Confess at once, scoundrels, that what I have declared is true—else you will have to deal with me in combat."

[16] *bulls, be they the fiercest that the Jarama breeds on its banks:* Bulls raised in the Jarama River Valley were prized for their ferocity and speed. The finest were selected for bullfighting spectacles put on in nearby Madrid.

The herdsman had no time to reply, nor Don Quixote to get out of the way even if he wished; and so the drove of fierce bulls and tame bullocks, together with the crowd of herdsmen and others who were taking them to be penned up in a village where they were to be run the next day, passed over Don Quixote and over Sancho, Rocinante and Dapple, hurling them all to the earth and rolling them over on the ground. Sancho was left crushed, Don Quixote rattled, Dapple battered, and Rocinante in no very sound condition.

At length, however, they all got up. Don Quixote in great haste, stumbling here and falling there, took off running after the drove, shouting out, "Hold! Stay, you vile rabble! A single knight awaits you, and he is not of the temper or opinion of those who say, 'For a fleeing enemy, make him a silver bridge.'" The retreating party in their haste, however, did not stop or heed his menaces any more than last year's clouds. Weariness brought Don Quixote to a halt, and more enraged than avenged he sat down on the road to wait until Sancho, Rocinante, and Dapple came up. When they reached him, master and man mounted once more, and without going back to bid farewell to the mock or imitation Arcadia, they continued their journey—more in humiliation than good cheer.

CHAPTER LIX

WHEREIN IS RELATED THE STRANGE THING, WHICH MAY BE REGARDED AS AN ADVENTURE, THAT HAPPENED TO DON QUIXOTE

A clear, limpid spring that they discovered in a cool grove relieved Don Quixote and Sancho of the dust and fatigue due to the unpolite behavior of the bulls. By the side of this spring, having turned Dapple and Rocinante loose without halter or bridle, the forlorn pair, master and man, seated themselves. Sancho had recourse to the larder of his saddlebag and took out of it what he called a light meal. Don Quixote rinsed his mouth and bathed his face, by which cooling process his flagging energies were revived. Out of pure vexation he remained without eating, and out of pure politeness Sancho did not venture to touch a morsel of what was before him, but waited for his master to take the first bite. Seeing, however, that Don Quixote, absorbed in thought, was forgetting to carry the bread to his mouth, he trampled all good breeding under foot and without a word began to stow away in his paunch the bread and cheese that came to his hand.

"Eat, Sancho my friend," said Don Quixote. "Support life, which is of more consequence to you than to me, and leave me to die under the pain of my thoughts and pressure of my misfortunes. I was born, Sancho, to live dying, and you to die eating. To prove the truth of what I say, look at me, printed in histories, famed in arms, courteous in behavior, honored by princes, courted by maidens. Yet after all that, when I looked forward to palms, triumphs, and crowns, won and earned by my valiant deeds, I have this morning seen myself trampled on, kicked, and crushed by the feet of unclean and filthy animals. This thought blunts my teeth, paralyzes my jaws, cramps my hands, and robs me of all appetite for food—so much so that I have a mind to let myself die of hunger, the cruelest death of all deaths."

"So then," said Sancho, munching hard all the time, "your worship does not agree with the proverb that says, 'Let Martha die, but let her die with a full belly.' I for one have no mind to kill myself; so far from that, I mean to do as the cobbler does, who stretches the leather with his teeth until he makes it reach as far as he wants. I'll stretch out my life by eating until it reaches the end Heaven has fixed for it. Let me tell you, señor, there's no greater folly than to think of dying of despair[1] as your worship does. Take my advice: lie down after you eat

[1] *dying of despair:* committing suicide.

something and sleep a while on this green grassy mattress, and you will see that when you wake up you'll feel a little bit better."

Don Quixote took his words to heart, for it struck him that Sancho's reasoning was more like a philosopher's than a blockhead's. And he said, "Sancho, if you will do for me what I am going to tell you, my relief would be more assured and my heaviness of heart not so great. It is this: go aside a little while I am sleeping in accordance with your advice and, making bare your backside to the air, give yourself three or four hundred lashes with Rocinante's reins, on account of the more than three thousand you are to give yourself for Dulcinea's disenchantment. For it is a great pity that the poor lady should be left enchanted through your carelessness and negligence."

"There is a good deal to be said on that point," said Sancho. "Let us both go to sleep now, and after that, God has decreed what will happen. Your worship should be aware that for a man to whip himself in cold blood is a hard thing, especially if the stripes fall on an ill-nourished and worse-fed body. Let my lady Dulcinea have patience, and when she is least expecting it, she will see me made into a sieve with whipping, and 'until death it's all life'—I mean that I still have life in me and the desire to make good what I have promised."

Don Quixote thanked him and ate a little; Sancho ate a good deal. Then they both lay down to sleep, leaving those two inseparable friends and comrades, Rocinante and Dapple, to their own devices and to feed unrestrained upon the abundant grass with which the meadow was furnished. They woke up rather late, mounted once more, and resumed their journey, pushing on to reach an inn that was in sight, about a league off. I say an inn, because Don Quixote called it so, contrary to his usual practice of calling all inns castles.

They reached it and asked the innkeeper if they could lodge there. He said yes, with as much comfort and as good fare as they could find in Zaragoza. They dismounted, and Sancho stowed away his larder in a room of which the innkeeper gave him the key. He took the beasts to the stable, fed them, and came back to see what orders Don Quixote, who was seated on a bench at the door, had for him, giving special thanks to Heaven that this inn had not been taken for a castle by his master.

When suppertime came, they retired to their room. Sancho asked the innkeeper what he had to give them for supper. To this the innkeeper replied that his mouth should be the measure. He had only to ask what he would; for that inn was provided with the birds of the air and the fowl of the earth and the fish of the sea.

"There's no need of all that," said Sancho. "If they'll roast us a couple of chickens we'll be satisfied, for my master is delicate and eats little, and I'm not much of a glutton."

The innkeeper replied he had no chickens, for the kites[2] had stolen them.

"Well then," said Sancho, "let señor innkeeper tell them to roast a young hen, and make it tender."

[2] *kites:* The red kite is a medium-sized raptor with a forked tail, native to Europe. They are generally scavengers, though they are known to carry off small animals like rodents or perhaps a chick.

"Young hen, my father!" cried the innkeeper. "To be completely honest, just yesterday I sent over fifty to the city to sell. But aside from young hens, ask what you will."

"In that case," said Sancho, "you won't have any shortage of veal or kid."

"At the moment," said the innkeeper, "there's none in the house, for it's all been eaten. But next week there will be enough and to spare."

"Much good that does us," said Sancho. "I'll lay a bet that whatever you're lacking is made up for by all the bacon and eggs you have."

"By God," said the innkeeper, "my guest has quite the sense of humor. I tell him I have no hens, young or old, and he wants me to have eggs! Talk of other delicacies, if you please, and don't ask for hens again."

"On my body!" said Sancho. "Let's settle the matter. Say at once what you have, and let us have no more words about it."

"In truth and earnest, señor guest," said the innkeeper, "all I have is a couple of cowheels like calves' feet, or a couple of calves' feet like cowheels. They are boiled with garbanzos, onions, and bacon, and at this moment they are crying 'Come eat me, come eat me!'"

"I mark them for mine on the spot," said Sancho. "Don't let anybody touch them. I'll pay better for them than anyone else, for I could not ask for anything more to my taste. It's all the same to me whether they are feet or heels."

"Nobody will touch them," said the innkeeper, "for the other guests I have, being people of high quality, bring their own cook and butler and larder with them."

"If you come to people of quality," said Sancho, "there's nobody more so than my master. But the calling he follows does not allow for larders or storerooms. We lay ourselves down in the middle of a meadow and fill ourselves with acorns and medlars."[3]

Here ended Sancho's conversation with the innkeeper, Sancho not caring to carry it any further by answering him; for the innkeeper had already asked him what the calling or profession was that his master followed.

Suppertime having arrived, then, Don Quixote retired to his room, the innkeeper brought in the stewpot just as it was, and he sat down to dine very heartily. It seems that in the room next to Don Quixote's, which had nothing but a thin partition to separate it, he overheard these words, "As you live, Señor Don Jerónimo, while they are bringing supper, let us read another chapter of the *Second Part of Don Quixote of La Mancha.*"[4]

[3] *medlars:* The medlar (*níspero*) is a small tree in the rose family whose fruit resembles a crab apple.

[4] Second Part of Don Quixote of La Mancha: The official title is *Second Volume of the Ingenious Gentleman Don Quixote de la Mancha, Which Contains His Third Sally and Is the Fifth Part of His Adventures*. The author is listed as "the Licentiate Alonso Fernández de Avellaneda, native of the village of Tordesillas", almost certainly a pseudonym. The printing license was issued in July 1614, the same month that Sancho posts a letter to his wife in chapter 36 (see pp. 635–36). Though the evidence is circumstantial, it is likely that Cervantes did not have knowledge of the unauthorized sequel until he had written some forty or fifty chapters of his own continuation. With Avellaneda's *Quixote* now introduced into the narrative, references will be frequent.

The instant Don Quixote heard his own name he started to his feet and listened with open ears to catch what they said about him. He heard the Don Jerónimo who had been addressed say in reply, "Why would you have us read that nonsense, Don Juan, when it is impossible for anyone who has read the First Part of the history of Don Quixote of La Mancha to take any pleasure in reading this Second Part?"

"For all that," said the one addressed as Don Juan, "we shall do well to read it, for there is no book so bad that it does not contain something good. What displeases me most is that it represents Don Quixote as now cured of his love for Dulcinea del Toboso."[5]

On hearing this Don Quixote, full of wrath and indignation, lifted up his voice and said, "Whoever he may be who says that Don Quixote of La Mancha has forgotten or can forget Dulcinea del Toboso, I will teach him with equal arms that what he says is very far from the truth. Neither can the peerless Dulcinea del Toboso be forgotten, nor can forgetfulness have a place in Don Quixote. His motto is constancy, and his profession to maintain it with his life and never wrong it."

"Who is this that answers us?" asked those in the next room.

"Who should it be," said Sancho, "but Don Quixote of La Mancha himself, who will make good on all he's said and all he will say; for 'pledges don't distress a good payer.'"

Sancho had hardly uttered these words when two gentlemen, for such they seemed to be, entered the room. One of them, throwing his arms round Don Quixote's neck, said to him, "Your appearance cannot leave any question as to your name, nor can your name fail to identify your appearance. Unquestionably, señor, you are the real Don Quixote of La Mancha, north star and daystar of knight-errantry, despite and in defiance of him who has sought to usurp your name and bring to naught your achievements, as the author of this book which I here present to you has done."

With this he put a book that his companion was carrying into Don Quixote's hands. Don Quixote took the book and without replying began to leaf through it. But he soon returned it saying, "In the little I have seen, I have discovered three things in this author that deserve to be censured. The first is some words that I have read in the preface; the next that the language is Aragonese, for sometimes he writes without articles;[6] and the third, which above all stamps him as ignorant, is that he goes wrong and departs from the truth in the most important part of the history, for here he says that my squire Sancho Panza's wife is called Mari Gutiérrez, when she is called nothing of the sort, but Teresa

[5] *it represents Don Quixote as now cured of his love for Dulcinea del Toboso:* In Avellaneda's sequel, Dulcinea spurns Don Quixote, who thenceforward calls himself "The Love-Cured Knight".

[6] *The language is Aragonese . . . without articles:* If Don Quixote means grammatical articles, the criticism is unfounded. There is nothing about article usage in Avellaneda's sequel peculiar to Aragonese Spanish.

Panza.[7] When a man errs on such an important point as this there is good reason to fear that he is in error on every other point in the history."

"A fine historian he is!" exclaimed Sancho at this. "He must know all about our business when he calls my wife Teresa Panza, Mari Gutiérrez. Take a look at the book again, señor, and see if I'm in it and if he's changed my name."

"From your talk, friend," said Don Jerónimo, "no doubt you are Sancho Panza, Señor Don Quixote's squire."

"Yes, I am," said Sancho, "and I'm proud of it."

"Faith, then," said the gentleman, "this new author does not handle you with the decency that displays itself in your person. He makes you out to be an overeater and a simpleton, and not in the least bit funny—a very different being from the Sancho described in the First Part of your master's history."

"God forgive him," said Sancho. "He might have left me in my corner without troubling his head about me. 'Let him who knows how ring the bells,' and 'Saint Peter is very well in Rome.'"

The two gentlemen pressed Don Quixote to come into their room and have supper with them, as they knew very well there was nothing in that inn fit for a personage like him. Don Quixote, who was always polite, yielded to their request and dined with them. Sancho stayed behind with the stew, and invested with plenary authority seated himself at the head of the table—and with him the innkeeper, for he was no less fond of cowheel and calves' feet than Sancho was.

While at supper Don Juan asked Don Quixote what news he had of Lady Dulcinea del Toboso, whether she was married, had given birth, or was with child, or whether, still in her maidenhood and preserving all modesty and delicacy, she cherished the remembrance of Señor Don Quixote's tender passion.

To this he replied, "Dulcinea is a maiden still and my passion more firmly rooted than ever. Our communication is as unsatisfactory as before, and her beauty transformed into that of a foul country wench." He then proceeded to give them a full and particular account of Dulcinea's enchantment and of what had happened to him in the Cave of Montesinos, together with what the sage Merlin had prescribed for her disenchantment, namely the scourging of Sancho.

Exceedingly great was the amusement the two gentlemen derived from hearing Don Quixote recount the strange incidents of his history; and if they were amazed by his absurdities, they were equally amazed by the elegant style in which he delivered them. On the one hand, they regarded him as a man of keen mind; on the other, he gave all signs of being a lunatic. They could not make up their minds where between wisdom and folly they ought to place him.

Sancho having finished his supper—and having left the innkeeper passed out next to the wine bottle—returned to the room next door where his master was. As he came in he said, "May I die, sirs, if the author of this book of your worships

[7] *Mari Gutiérrez . . . called nothing of the sort, but Teresa Panza:* In all fairness, Sancho refers to his wife once as Mari Gutiérrez (and Juana Gutiérrez also). See page 60.

has any hopes of being on good terms with us. If he insists on calling me a glutton (according to what your worships say), I would appreciate it if he didn't call me a drunkard too."

"But he does," said Don Jerónimo. "I cannot remember, however, in what way, though I know his words are offensive, and what is more, lying, as I can see plainly by the physiognomy of the worthy Sancho before me."

"Believe me," said Sancho, "the Sancho and the Don Quixote of this history must be different people from the ones that appear in the history Cide Hamete Benengeli wrote, who are ourselves: my master—valiant, wise, and true in love; and me—simple, funny, and neither a glutton or a drunkard."

"I believe it," said Don Juan, "and were it possible, an order should be issued that no one should have the presumption to deal with anything relating to Don Quixote, save his original author Cide Hamete—just as Alexander commanded that no one should presume to paint his portrait save Apelles."[8]

"Let him who will paint me," said Don Quixote. "But let him not abuse me, for patience will often give way when insults are heaped upon it."

"None can be offered to Señor Don Quixote," said Don Juan, "that he himself will not be able to avenge, if he does not ward it off with the shield of his patience, which, I take it, is great and strong."

A considerable portion of the night passed in conversation like this, and though Don Juan wished Don Quixote to read more of the book to see what it was all about, he was not to be prevailed upon, saying that he treated it as read and pronounced it utterly silly. Furthermore, were it to reach its author's ears that Don Quixote had the book in his hand, he did not want him to flatter himself with the idea that he had read it. For our thoughts, and still more our eyes, should keep distant from what is obscene and filthy.

They asked him where his travels were taking him. He replied to Zaragoza, to take part in the harness jousts[9] that were held in that city every year. Don Juan told him that the new history described how Don Quixote (let him be who he might) took part there in a tilting at the ring,[10] utterly devoid of invention, poor in mottoes, very poor in costume, though rich in stupidities.

"For that very reason," said Don Quixote, "I will not set foot in Zaragoza. By that means I shall expose to the world the lie of this new historian, and people will see that I am not the Don Quixote he speaks of."

"You will do quite right," said Don Jerónimo. "There are other jousts in Barcelona in which Señor Don Quixote may display his prowess."

[8] *Apelles:* The anecdote about the fourth-century B.C. Greek painter arises in Pliny's *Natural History*.

[9] *harness jousts:* The harness joust (*justa del arnés*) was a martial spectacle popular in early modern Spain, often associated with royal events or civic celebrations, as in Zaragoza. Participants performed in courtly games wearing full-plate armor, the "harness" being the name for the suit of armor.

[10] *tilting at the ring:* courtly game in which a mounted knight riding at a full gallop tried to aim a lance through a small ring suspended by a cord.

"That is what I mean to do," said Don Quixote. "And as it is now time, I pray your worships to give me leave to retire to bed, and to place and retain me among the number of your greatest friends and servants."

"And me too," said Sancho. "Maybe I'll be good for something."

With this they exchanged farewells, and Don Quixote and Sancho retired to their room, leaving Don Juan and Don Jerónimo amazed to see the medley he made of his good sense and insanity. They felt thoroughly convinced that these two, and not those their Aragonese author described, were the genuine Don Quixote and Sancho. Don Quixote rose early and bade farewell to his hosts by knocking at the partition of the other room. Sancho paid the innkeeper magnificently and recommended him either to say less about the provisions of his inn or to provision it better.

CHAPTER LX

OF WHAT HAPPENED TO DON QUIXOTE ON HIS WAY TO BARCELONA

It was a fresh morning giving promise of an equally fresh day as Don Quixote left the inn, first of all taking care to find out the most direct road to Barcelona without touching Zaragoza—so anxious was he to make out this new historian, who they said abused him so, to be a liar.

As it turned out, nothing worthy of being recorded happened to him for six days. At the end of that time, having turned aside out of the road, he was overtaken by night in a thicket of either oak or cork trees (for on this point Cide Hamete is not as precise as he usually is on other matters).

Master and man dismounted from their beasts, and as soon as they had settled themselves at the foot of the trees, Sancho, who had enjoyed a good midday meal, let himself pass straightaway through the gates of sleep. But Don Quixote, whom his thoughts, far more than hunger, kept awake, could not close an eye, and roamed in fancy to and fro through all sorts of places. At one moment, it seemed to him that he was in the Cave of Montesinos and saw Dulcinea transformed into a country wench, skipping and mounting upon her donkey. Again, the words of the sage Merlin were sounding in his ears, setting forth the conditions to be observed and the exertions to be made for the disenchantment of Dulcinea.

He lost all patience when he considered the laziness and meager charity of his squire Sancho; for to the best of his belief he had only given himself five lashes, a paltry number in light of the vast number required. At this thought he felt such vexation and anger that he reasoned the matter thus: "If Alexander the Great cut the Gordian knot,[1] saying, 'Cutting amounts to the same thing as untying,' and yet did not fail to become lord paramount of all Asia, neither more nor less could happen now in Dulcinea's disenchantment if I scourge Sancho against his will. For if it is the condition of the remedy that Sancho shall receive some three thousand lashes, what does it matter to me whether he inflicts them himself, or someone else inflicts them, when the essential point is that he receives them, let them come from whatever quarter they may?"

With this idea he went over to Sancho, having first taken Rocinante's reins and arranged them so as to be able to flog him with them, and began to untie

[1] *Alexander the Great cut the Gordian knot:* See footnote 8, page 532. The following quote comes from Quinto Curcio.

the laces by which his breeches were held up—the common belief being he had but one in front.[2]

But the instant he approached him, Sancho woke up in his full senses and cried out, "What is this? Who's touching me and untying my breeches?"

"It is I," said Don Quixote, "and I come to overcome your shortcomings and relieve my own distresses. I come to whip you, Sancho, and wipe out some portion of the debt you have undertaken. Dulcinea is perishing, you are living on regardless, I am dying of hope deferred. Therefore lower your breeches of your own will, for it is mine, here in this retired spot, to give you at least two thousand lashes."

"Not a bit of it," said Sancho. "Let your worship keep quiet, or else by the living God the deaf shall hear us. The lashes I committed to must be voluntary and not forced on me, and right now I have no interest in whipping myself. It should be enough that I gave you my word to flog and swat myself when I have the inclination."

"It will not do to leave it to your courtesy, Sancho," said Don Quixote, "for you are hard of heart and, though a peasant, tender of flesh." So saying, he attempted forcibly to untie him.

Seeing this Sancho got up and lunged at his master. First gripping him with all his might in his arms and then catching his heel, Sancho made him trip and stumble to the ground on his back. He pressed his right knee into Don Quixote's chest and held his hands in his own so that he could neither move nor breathe.

"How now, traitor!" exclaimed Don Quixote. "Do you revolt against your master and natural lord? Do you rise against him who gives you his bread?"

"I neither topple king, nor raise up king," said Sancho. "I only stand up for myself, for I am my own lord.[3] If your worship promises to be quiet and not to try to whip me now, I'll let you go free and unhindered; if not—

Traitor and Doña Sancha's foe,
Thou diest on the spot."[4]

Don Quixote gave his promise, and swore by the life of his thoughts not to touch so much as a hair of his garments, and to leave him entirely free and to his own discretion to whip himself whenever he pleased.

Sancho rose and went off some distance from the spot, but as he was about to lean against a tree he felt something touch his head. Putting up his hands, he encountered somebody's two feet with shoes and stockings on them. He trembled with fear and made for another tree, where the very same thing happened to him. He then began to cry out, calling on Don Quixote to come and protect

[2] *untie the laces . . . in front:* In addition to a stiffened waistband, *gregüescos* were often held up by laces threaded through the eyelets of the breeches and doublet.

[3] *I neither topple . . . my own lord:* lines attributed to Bertrand du Guesclin, knight who intervened in the civil war between Peter of Castile and his rebellious illegitimate brother, Henry of Trastámara, during the 1360s.

[4] *Traitor and Doña Sancha's foe, / Thou diest on the spot:* adapted from a ballad about the Seven Infantes of Lara.

him. Don Quixote did so, and asked what had happened to him and what he was afraid of. Sancho replied that all the trees were full of men's feet and legs. Don Quixote felt them and guessed at once what it was.

He said to Sancho, "You have nothing to be afraid of, for these feet and legs that you feel but cannot see belong no doubt to some outlaws and highwaymen that have been hanged on these trees. The authorities in these parts are accustomed to hang them up by twenties and thirties when they catch them; whereby I conjecture that I must be near Barcelona."[5] And it was, in fact, as he supposed. With the first light they looked up and saw that the fruit hanging on those trees were the bodies of highwaymen.

And now day dawned, and if the dead outlaws had scared them, their hearts were no less troubled by upwards of forty living ones, who all of a sudden surrounded them, and in the Catalan tongue ordered them to stand and wait until their captain arrived. Don Quixote was on foot, with his horse unbridled and his lance leaning against a tree—in short, completely defenseless. He thought it best therefore to fold his arms and bow his head and reserve himself for a more favorable occasion. The highwaymen made haste to search Dapple, and did not leave him a single thing of all he carried in the packsaddle and the valise. Lucky it was for Sancho that the duke's escudos and those he brought from home were in a belt that he wore around himself. For all that, these good folk would have stripped him—and even looked to see what he had hidden between the skin and flesh—but for the arrival at that moment of their captain.

The captain looked about thirty-four years of age, strongly built, above middle height, of stern aspect and swarthy complexion. He was mounted on a powerful horse, and had on a coat of mail, with four of the pistols they call *pedreñales*[6] in that country at his waist. When he saw that his squires (for so they call those who follow that trade) were about to search Sancho Panza, he ordered them to desist and was at once obeyed, so the money belt escaped. He wondered to see the lance leaning against the tree, the shield on the ground, and Don Quixote in armor and dejected, with the saddest and most melancholy face that sadness itself could produce. Going up to him he said, "Be not so cast down, good man, for you have not fallen into the hands of any inhuman Osiris,[7] but into Roque Guinart's,[8] which are more merciful than cruel."

[5] *I must be near Barcelona:* Catalonia at the turn of the seventeenth century was plagued with rival gangs of highwaymen (*bandoleros*) who held up travelers and raided undefended villages. *Bandolerismo* was a complex phenomenon, arising from weak central authority, factionalism among the nobility, and local feuds. Outlaws enjoyed protection across all levels of Catalonian society—rural and urban alike—and even from some royal officials. An honor-based vendetta culture made it difficult to end the cycles of violence.

[6] pedreñales: From *pedernal* (flint), the *pedreñal* was a medium-barrel firearm using an early flint ignition system. In early modern Spain, it was the weapon of choice among rural outlaws.

[7] *Osiris:* Busiris, Egyptian king from Greek mythology who had one foreigner sacrificed each year.

[8] *Roque Guinart's:* Perot Roca Guinarda was a notorious Catalonian *bandolero*. In 1611 King Philip III pardoned him on the condition that he leave Spain for ten years.

"The cause of my dejection," returned Don Quixote, "is not that I have fallen into your hands, O valiant Roque, whose fame is bounded by no limits on earth, but that my carelessness should have been so great that your soldiers should have caught me unbridled. For it is my duty, according to the rule of knight-errantry I profess, to be always on the alert and at all times my own sentinel. Let me tell you, great Roque, had they found me on my horse with my lance and shield, it would not have been very easy for them to reduce me to submission. For I am Don Quixote of La Mancha, he who has filled the whole world with his achievements."

Roque Guinart now gathered that Don Quixote's weakness was more akin to madness than to bravado; and though he had sometimes heard him spoken of, he never regarded the things attributed to him as true, nor could he persuade himself that such a condition could overmaster the heart of man. He was extremely glad, therefore, to meet him and test at close quarters what he had heard of him at a distance. So he said to him, "Despair not, valiant knight, nor regard as adverse fate the position in which you find yourself. It may be that by these slips your crooked fortune will make itself straight; for Heaven by strange circuitous ways, mysterious and incomprehensible to man, raises up the fallen and makes rich the poor."

Don Quixote was about to thank him, when they heard behind them a noise as of a troop of horses. There was, however, but one, riding on which at a furious pace came a youth who looked about twenty years of age, clad in green damask edged with gold, and breeches and a loose frock, with a hat looped up in the Walloon fashion, tight-fitting polished boots, gilt spurs, dagger and sword, and in his hand a short-barreled musket and a pair of pistols at his waist.

Roque turned round at the noise and caught sight of this striking figure, which drawing near addressed him thus: "I came in quest of you, valiant Roque, to find in you if not a remedy at least relief in my misfortune. Not to keep you in suspense, for I see you do not recognize me, I will tell you who I am. I am Claudia Jerónima, the daughter of Simón Forte, your good friend and special enemy of Clauquel Torrellas, who is yours also as being of the faction opposed to you. You know that this Torrellas has a son who is called—or at least who was called until two hours ago—Don Vicente Torrellas. To cut short the tale of my misfortune, I will tell you in a few words what this youth has brought upon me. He saw me, he courted me, I listened to him, and, unknown to my father, I loved him; for there is no woman, however secluded she may live or close she may be kept, who will not have opportunities and to spare for following her headlong impulses. In a word, he pledged himself to be my husband, and I promised to be his wife, without carrying matters any further. Yesterday I learned that, forgetful of his pledge to me, he was about to marry another, and that he was to go this morning to the betrothal, news which overwhelmed me and exhausted my patience. My father not being at home I was able to adopt this attire you see, and urging my horse to speed I overtook Don Vicente about a league from here, where, without waiting to utter reproaches or hear excuses, I fired this musket at him, and these two pistols besides. To the best of my belief, I must have lodged more than two bullets in his body, opening doors to let my honor go free, enveloped in his blood. I left him there in the hands of his servants, who did not dare and were not able to interfere in his defense. I come to seek from you a letter of safe conduct to France, where I have relatives with whom I can live; and also to implore you to protect my father, so that Don Vicente's numerous kinsmen may not venture to wreak their lawless vengeance upon him."

Roque, filled with amazement at the fair Claudia's gallant bearing, high spirit, and fine figure, along with her tale, said to her, "Come, señora, let us go and see if your enemy is dead; then we will consider what will be best for you."

Don Quixote, who had been listening to what Claudia said and Roque Guinart said in reply to her, exclaimed, "Nobody need trouble himself with the defense of this lady, for I take it upon myself. Give me my horse and arms, and wait for me here. I will go in quest of this knight, and dead or alive I will make him keep his word pledged to so great beauty."

"Nobody need have any doubt about that," said Sancho, "for my master has quite a knack for matchmaking. Only a few days ago he forced another man to marry, who in the same way backed out of his promise to another maiden; and if it had not been for his persecutors the enchanters changing the man's proper shape into a footman's, that maiden would not be one anymore."

Roque, who was more occupied with the fair Claudia's story than the words of master or man, did not hear them. Ordering his squires to restore to Sancho everything they had stripped from Dapple, he directed them to return to the place where they had been quartered during the night, and then set off with Claudia at full speed in search of the wounded or slain Don Vicente. They reached the spot where Claudia met him, but found nothing there save freshly spilled blood. Looking all around, however, they spotted some people on the slope of a hill above them, and concluded, as indeed it proved to be, that it was Don Vicente, whom either dead or alive his servants were removing to attend to his wounds or to bury him. They made haste to overtake them, which, as the party moved slowly, they were able to do with ease. They found Don Vicente in the arms of his servants, whom he was entreating in a broken feeble voice to leave him there to die, as the pain of his wounds would not permit him to go any farther. Claudia and Roque threw themselves off their horses and advanced toward him. The servants were startled by the appearance of Roque, and Claudia was moved by the sight of Don Vicente.

Going up to him half tenderly, half sternly, she seized his hand and said to him, "Had you given me this hand according to our compact, you would have never come to this strait."

The wounded gentleman opened his all but closed eyes, and recognizing Claudia said, "I see clearly, fair and mistaken lady, that it is you that has slain me, a punishment not merited or deserved by my feelings toward you, for never did I mean to, nor could I wrong you in thought or deed."

"It is not true, then," said Claudia, "that you were going this morning to marry Leonora, the daughter of the rich Balvastro?"

"Assuredly not," replied Don Vicente. "My cruel fortune must have carried those tidings to you to drive you in your jealousy to take my life. To assure yourself of this, press my hands and take me for your husband if you will; I have no better satisfaction to offer you for the wrong you imagine you have received from me."

Claudia wrung his hands, and her own heart was so wrung that she lay fainting on the bleeding breast of Don Vicente, whom a death spasm seized the same instant. Roque was in perplexity and knew not what to do; the servants ran to fetch water to sprinkle on their faces, and brought some and bathed them with it. Claudia recovered from her swoon, but not so Don Vicente from the paroxysm that had overtaken him, for his life had come to an end. On perceiving this, Claudia, when she had convinced herself that her beloved husband was no more, rent the air with her sighs and made the heavens ring with her lamentations. She tore her hair and scattered it to the winds; she beat her face with her hands and showed all the signs of grief and sorrow that could be conceived to come from an afflicted heart. "Cruel, reckless woman!" she cried. "How easily you were moved to carry out a thought so wicked! O furious force of jealousy, to what desperate lengths do you lead those that give you lodging in their breasts! O husband, whose unhappy fate in being mine has borne you from the marriage bed to the grave!"

So vehement and so piteous were Claudia's lamentations that they drew tears from Roque's eyes, unaccustomed as they were to shed them on any occasion. The servants wept, Claudia swooned away again and again, and the whole place seemed a field of sorrow and an abode of misfortune. In the end Roque Guinart directed Don Vicente's servants to carry his body to his father's village, which was close by, for burial. Claudia told him she meant to go to a monastery of which an aunt of hers was abbess, where she intended to spend her life with a better and everlasting spouse. He applauded her pious resolution and offered to accompany her wherever she wished, vowing to protect her father against the kinsmen of Don Vicente and all the world, should they seek to injure him. Claudia would not on any account allow him to accompany her. Thanking him for his offers as well as she could, she took leave of him in tears. Don Vicente's servants carried away his body, and Roque returned to his comrades. So ended the love of Claudia Jerónima—but what wonder, when it was the insuperable and cruel might of jealousy that wove the fabric of her sad story?

Roque Guinart found his squires at the place where he had ordered them to go, and Don Quixote on Rocinante in the midst of them delivering a harangue in which he urged them to give up a mode of life so full of peril, to the soul as well as to the body. But as most of them were Gascons,[9] rough lawless fellows, his speech did not make much of an impression on them. Roque on coming up asked Sancho if his men had returned and restored to him the treasures and jewels they had stripped off Dapple. Sancho said they had, but that three headscarves that were worth three cities were missing.

"What are you talking about, man?" said one of the bystanders; "I have them, and they aren't worth three reals."

"That is true," said Don Quixote, "but my squire values them at the rate he says, as having been given me by the person who gave them."

[9] *Gascons:* See footnote 1, page 734.

Roque Guinart ordered them to be restored at once, and making his men fall in line he directed all the clothing, jewelry, and money that they had taken since the last distribution to be produced. After making a hasty valuation and reducing what could not be divided into money, he made shares for the whole band so equitably and carefully, that in no case did he exceed or fall short of strict distributive justice.

When this had been done and all were left satisfied, Roque observed to Don Quixote, "If this scrupulous exactness were not observed with these fellows, there would be no living with them."

Hearing this Sancho remarked, "From what I've seen here, justice is such a good thing that there is no doing without it, even among thieves."

One of the squires heard this, and raising the butt-end of his harquebus would no doubt have broken Sancho's head with it had not Roque Guinart called out to him to restrain himself. Sancho was frightened out of his wits, and vowed not to open his lips so long as he was in the company of these people.

At this instant one or two of those squires posted as sentinels on the roads, to watch who came along and report what he saw to their chief, came up and said, "Señor, there is a great troop of people not far off coming along the road to Barcelona."

To which Roque replied, "Have you made out whether they are of the sort that are after us, or of the sort we are after?"

"The sort we are after," said the squire.

"Well then, away with you all," said Roque, "and bring them here to me at once without letting one of them escape."

They obeyed, and Don Quixote, Sancho, and Roque, left by themselves, waited to see what the squires brought. While they were waiting, Roque said to Don Quixote, "It must seem strange to Señor Don Quixote this life we live—strange adventures, strange incidents, and all full of danger. I do not wonder that it should seem so, for in truth I must admit there is no mode of life more restless or anxious than ours. What led me into it was a certain thirst for vengeance, which is strong enough to disturb the quietest hearts. I am by nature tender-hearted and kindly, but as I said, the desire to revenge myself for a wrong that was done to me so outstrips my better impulses that I keep on in this way of life in spite of what my conscience tells me. As deep calls to deep[10] and sin to sin, revenges have linked themselves together, and I have taken upon myself not only my own but those of others. It pleases God, however, that, though I see myself in this maze of entanglements, I do not lose all hope of escaping from it and reaching a safe port."

Don Quixote was amazed to hear Roque utter such admirable and sound sentiments, for he did not think that among those who followed such trades as robbing, murdering, and waylaying, there could be anyone capable of a virtuous thought. He said in reply, "Señor Roque, the beginning of health lies in knowing the disease and in the sick man's willingness to take the medicines which the physician prescribes. You are sick, you know what ails you. Heaven, or more

[10] *deep calls to deep:* echo of Psalm 42:7.

properly speaking God, who is our physician, will administer medicines that will cure you, and cure gradually, and not of a sudden or by a miracle. I say further that discerning sinners are nearer to their reformation than simpletons. As your worship has shown good sense in your remarks, all you have to do is to keep up a good heart and trust that the weakness of your conscience will be strengthened. If you have any desire to shorten the journey and put yourself easily in the way of salvation, come with me, and I will show you how to become a knight-errant, a calling wherein so many hardships and mishaps are encountered that if they are taken as penances, they will in short order lodge you in heaven."

Roque laughed at Don Quixote's exhortation, but changing the conversation he related the tragic outcome of Claudia Jerónima, at which Sancho was extremely grieved; for he had not been displeased by the young woman's beauty, boldness, and spirit.

The squires now returned from their raid, bringing with them two gentlemen on horseback, two pilgrims on foot, and a coach full of women with some six servants on foot and on horseback in attendance on them, and a couple of muleteers whom the gentlemen had with them. The squires made a ring around them, both victors and vanquished maintaining profound silence, waiting for the great Roque Guinart to speak. He asked the gentlemen who they were, where they were going, and what money they carried with them.

"Señor," replied one of them, "we are two captains of the Spanish infantry. Our companies are in Naples, and we are on our way to embark in four galleys which they say are in Barcelona under orders for Sicily. We have about two or three hundred escudos, with which we are, according to our notions, rich and contented, for a soldier's poverty does not allow a more extensive treasure."

Roque asked the pilgrims the same questions he had put to the captains, and was answered that they were going to take ship for Rome, and that between them they might have about sixty reals. He asked also who was in the coach, where they were bound, and what money they had. One of the men on horseback replied, "The persons in the coach are my lady Doña Guiomar de Quiñones, wife of the regent of the Vicaría in Naples[11]—her little daughter, a handmaid, and a dueña. We six servants are in attendance upon her, and the money amounts to six hundred escudos."

"So then," said Roque Guinart, "we have got here nine hundred escudos and sixty reals. My soldiers must number some sixty. See how much there falls to each, for arithmetic is not my strong suit."

As soon as the robbers heard this, they raised a shout of "Long life to Roque Guinart, in spite of the lladres[12] that seek his ruin!"

The captains showed plainly that they were upset, the regent's lady was downcast, and the pilgrims did not at all enjoy seeing their property confiscated.

[11] *regent of the Vicaría in Naples:* The *Vicaría* referred to the government of the Viceroyalty of Naples, at the time a Spanish possession. The regent was a high-ranking judicial official who presided over the viceroyalty's principal criminal court.

[12] *lladres:* Catalan for "thieves".

Roque kept them in suspense in this way for a while, but he had no desire to prolong their distress, which might be seen a bowshot off.

Turning to the captains he said, "Sirs, will your worships be pleased of your courtesy to lend me sixty escudos, and her ladyship the regent's wife eighty, to satisfy this band that follows me, for 'it is by his singing the abbot gets his dinner.' You then may at once proceed on your journey, free and unhindered, with a letter of safe conduct which I will give you, so that if you come across any other bands of mine that I have scattered in these parts, they may do you no harm. I have no intention of doing injury to soldiers, or to any woman, especially one of quality."

Profuse and hearty were the expressions of gratitude with which the captains thanked Roque for his courtesy and generosity, for such they regarded his leaving them their own money. Señora Doña Guiomar de Quiñones wanted to throw herself out of the coach to kiss the feet and hands of the great Roque, but he would not permit it on any account—so far from that, he begged her pardon for the wrong he had done her under pressure of the inexorable necessities of his unfortunate calling. The regent's lady ordered one of her servants to give the eighty escudos that had been assessed as her share at once, for the captains had already paid down their sixty. The pilgrims were about to give up the whole of their pittance, but Roque told them to keep quiet.

Turning to his men he said, "Of these escudos two fall to each man and twenty remain over; let ten be given to these pilgrims, and the other ten to this worthy squire that he may be able to speak favorably of this adventure." And then having brought to him writing materials, with which he always went provided, he gave them in writing a letter of safe conduct to the leaders of his bands. After bidding them farewell, he let them go free and filled with admiration at his magnanimity, his generous disposition, and his unusual conduct, and inclined to regard him as an Alexander the Great rather than a notorious robber.

One of the squires observed in his mixture of Gascon and Catalan, "This captain of ours would make a better friar than highwayman. If he wants to be so generous another time, let it be with his own property and not ours."

The unlucky soul did not speak so low but that Roque overheard him and, drawing his sword, split his head open, saying, "That's the way I punish the insolent and unruly." They were all taken aback, and not one of them dared to utter a word, such deference did they pay him. Roque then withdrew to one side and wrote a letter to a friend of his in Barcelona, telling him that the famous Don Quixote of La Mancha, the knight-errant of whom there was so much talk, was with him, and was, he assured him, the wisest and most comical man in the world. Four days from that date, that is to say, on Saint John the Baptist Day,[13] he promised to deposit him in full armor mounted on his horse Rocinante, together with his squire Sancho on a donkey, in the middle of the beach along the city. He asked also that notice be given of this to his friends the Nyerros, that they

[13] *Saint John the Baptist Day:* either the day that commemorated his birth (June 24) or beheading (August 29).

might be entertained by his company. He wished, he said, that his enemies the Cadells[14] could be deprived of this pleasure, but that was impossible, because the absurdities and insights of Don Quixote and the antics of his squire Sancho Panza could not help giving general pleasure to all the world. He dispatched the letter by one of his squires, who, exchanging the dress of a highwayman for that of a peasant, made his way into Barcelona and gave it to the person to whom it was directed.

[14] *his friends the Nyerros . . . his enemies the Cadells:* The rival Nyerro and Cadell families dominated political and social life in Catalonia during the late sixteenth and early seventeenth centuries. The influence of the two noble families extended into royal government, and both relied on patronage networks that were maintained by banditry. The Nyerros tended to be aligned with aristocratic interests, while the Cadells supported the interests of urban centers and the peasantry.

CHAPTER LXI

OF WHAT HAPPENED TO DON QUIXOTE ON ENTERING BARCELONA, TOGETHER WITH OTHER MATTERS THAT PARTAKE OF THE TRUE RATHER THAN OF THE CLEVER

Don Quixote spent three days and three nights with Roque, and had he spent three hundred years he would have found enough to observe and wonder at in his mode of life. At daybreak they were in one place, at dinnertime in another. Sometimes they fled without knowing from whom, at other times they lay in wait not knowing for what. They slept standing, breaking their slumbers to shift from place to place. There was nothing but sending out spies and scouts, posting sentinels and blowing out the match cords of harquebuses,[1] though they carried but few, for almost all used pedreñales. Roque spent his nights in some place or another apart from his men, that they might not know where he was, for the many proclamations the viceroy of Barcelona had issued against his life kept him in fear and uneasiness, and he did not venture to trust anyone, afraid that even his own men would kill him or deliver him up to the authorities—of a truth, a weary miserable life! At length, by unfrequented roads, shortcuts, and secret paths, Roque, Don Quixote, and Sancho, together with six squires, set out for Barcelona. They reached the beach on Saint John's Eve during the night. Roque, after embracing Don Quixote and Sancho (to whom he presented the ten escudos he had promised but had not until then given), left them with many expressions of goodwill on both sides.

Roque went back, while Don Quixote remained on horseback, just as he was, waiting for day. It was not long before the countenance of the fair Aurora began to show itself at the balconies of the east, gladdening the grass and flowers, if not the ear—though to gladden that too there came at the same moment a sound of clarions and drums, a din of bells, a tramp, tramp, and cries of "Clear the way!" of runners[2] that seemed to come from the city.

The dawn made way for the sun, which with a face broader than a buckler began to rise slowly above the low line of the horizon. Don Quixote and Sancho gazed all around them. They beheld the sea, a sight they had never before seen. It struck them as exceedingly spacious and broad, much more so

[1] *blowing out the match cords of harquebuses:* See footnote 4, page 309.

[2] *runners:* heralds who cleared a path for the processions and festivities of Saint John the Baptist Day.

than the Lakes of Ruidera, which they had seen in La Mancha. They saw the galleys along the beach, which, striking their awnings,[3] displayed themselves decked with streamers and pennons that trembled in the breeze and kissed and swept the water, while on board the bugles, trumpets, and clarions were sounding and filling the air far and near with melodious warlike notes. Then they began to move and execute a kind of skirmish upon the calm water, while a vast number of horsemen on fine horses and in showy liveries, emerging from the city, engaged on their side in a somewhat similar movement. The soldiers on board the galleys kept up a ceaseless fire, which they on the walls and forts of the city returned. The heavy cannon rent the air with the tremendous noise they made, to which the gangway guns of the galleys replied. The bright sea, the smiling earth, the clear air (though at times darkened by the smoke of the guns)—all seemed to fill the whole multitude with unexpected delight. Sancho could not make out how it was that those great masses that moved over the sea had so many feet.

And now the horsemen in livery came galloping up with shouts and outlandish cries and cheers to where Don Quixote stood amazed and wondering. One of them, he to whom Roque had sent word, addressing him exclaimed, "Welcome to our city, mirror, beacon, north star, and daystar of all knight-errantry in its widest extent! Welcome, I say, valiant Don Quixote of La Mancha—not the false, the fictitious, the apocryphal one, that these latter days have offered us in lying histories, but the true, the legitimate, the real one that Cide Hamete Benengeli, flower of historians, has described to us!"

Don Quixote made no answer, nor did the horsemen wait for one, but wheeling again with all their followers, they began prancing around Don Quixote, who, turning to Sancho, said, "These gentlemen have plainly recognized us. I will wager they have read our history, and even that newly printed one by the Aragonese."

The cavalier who had addressed Don Quixote again approached him and said, "Come with us, Señor Don Quixote, for we are all of us your servants and great friends of Roque Guinart's."

To this Don Quixote returned, "If courtesy breeds courtesy, yours, sir knight, is daughter or very nearly akin to the great Roque's. Carry me where you please. I will have no will but yours, especially if you deign to employ it in your service."

The cavalier replied with words no less polite, and then with everyone closing in around him, they set out for the city to the music of the clarions and the drums. As they were entering it, the wicked one (who is the author of all mischief) and the boys (who are wickeder than the wicked one) contrived that a couple of these audacious, irrepressible urchins should force their way through the crowd. With one of them lifting up Dapple's tail and the other Rocinante's, they inserted a

[3] *striking their awnings:* The ship's awning was a canvas or sailcloth covering held up on a frame over the central deck, designed to shield officers and crew from the elements. It could be raised or struck (lowered) depending on weather, ceremonial protocol, or preparations for battle.

handful of furze[4] under each. The poor beasts felt the strange spurs and added to their anguish by pressing their tails tight, so much so that, cutting a multitude of capers, they flung their masters to the ground. Don Quixote, covered with shame and embarrassment, ran to pluck the plume from his poor nag's tail, while Sancho did the same for Dapple. His guides tried to punish the audacity of the boys, but there was no possibility of doing so, for they hid themselves among the hundreds of others that were following them. Don Quixote and Sancho mounted once more, and with the same music and acclamations reached their guide's house, which was large and stately—in short, that of a rich gentleman. There for the present we will leave them, for such is Cide Hamete's pleasure.

[4] *furze:* thorny evergreen shrub.

CHAPTER LXII

WHICH DEALS WITH THE ADVENTURE OF THE ENCHANTED HEAD, TOGETHER WITH OTHER TRIVIAL MATTERS THAT CANNOT BE LEFT UNTOLD

Don Quixote's host was one Don Antonio Moreno by name, a gentleman of wealth and intelligence, and very fond of amusing himself in any fair and good-natured way. Having Don Quixote in his house, he set about devising modes of making him exhibit his madness in some harmless fashion; for jokes that cause pain are not jokes, and no pastime is worth anything if it hurts another. The first thing he did was to have Don Quixote take off his armor and lead him (in that tight chamois suit we have already described and depicted more than once) to a balcony that overlooked one of the main streets of the city, in full view of the crowd and of the boys, who gazed at him as they would at a monkey. The cavaliers in livery rode before him again—as though it were for him alone that they wore it and not to enliven the day's festival. Sancho was in high delight, for it seemed to him that (how, he knew not) he had stumbled upon another Camacho's wedding, another house like Don Diego de Miranda's, another castle like the duke's.

Some of Don Antonio's friends dined with him that day, and all showed honor to Don Quixote and treated him as a knight-errant. He, becoming puffed up and exalted in consequence, could not contain himself for satisfaction. Such were Sancho's witticisms that all the servants of the house, and all who heard him, were kept hanging upon his lips. During the meal Don Antonio said to him, "We hear, worthy Sancho, that you are so fond of *manjar blanco* and meatballs, that if you have any left, you keep them in your pocket for the next day."[1]

"No, señor, that's not true," said Sancho, "for I am more cleanly than gluttonous, and my master Don Quixote here knows well that we two are used to live for a week on a handful of acorns or nuts. To be sure, if it so happens that they offer me a heifer, I run with a halter—I mean, I eat what I'm given, and make use of opportunities as I find them. But whoever says that I'm an overeater or not cleanly, let me tell him that he's wrong. I'd put it in a different way if I didn't respect the honorable beards at this table."

[1] *Sancho, that you are so fond of* manjar blanco *and meatballs . . . in your pocket for the next day:* Sancho does this in Avellaneda's sequel (chap. 12). *Manjar blanco* was a sweet paste made from creamed chicken, ground almonds, sugar, and a thickener such as rice flour or breadcrumbs. It was shaped into balls for presentation.

"Indeed," said Don Quixote, "Sancho's moderation and cleanliness in eating might be inscribed and graved on brass plates, to be kept in eternal remembrance in ages to come. It is true that when he is hungry there is a certain appearance of voracity about him, for he eats at a great pace and chews with both jaws; but cleanliness he is always mindful of. When he was governor, he learned how to eat daintily—so much so that he eats grapes, and even pomegranate seeds, with a fork."

"What?" cried Don Antonio. "Has Sancho been a governor?"

"I have," said Sancho, "of an island called Barataria. I governed it to perfection for ten days. During that time, I had no rest and learned to look down on all the governments in the world. I got out of it by running for my life. And then I fell into a pit where I gave myself up for dead. It's only by a miracle that I escaped alive."

Don Quixote then gave them a minute account of the whole affair of Sancho's government, with which he greatly amused his hearers.

When dinner was finished Don Antonio, taking Don Quixote by the hand, went with him into a secluded room in which there was nothing in the way of furniture except a table, apparently of jasper, resting on a pedestal of the same material. Upon this table rested a head, after the fashion of the busts of Roman emperors, which seemed to be of bronze. Don Antonio traversed the whole apartment with Don Quixote and walked round the table several times. He then said, "Now that I am satisfied that no one is listening to us, Señor Don Quixote, and that the door is shut, I will tell you of one of the rarest adventures—or more properly speaking strange things—that can be imagined, on condition that you will keep what I say to you in the remotest recesses of secrecy."

"I swear it," said Don Quixote, "and for greater security I will put a tombstone over it. For I would have you know, Señor Don Antonio" (he had by this time learned his name), "that you are addressing one who, though he has ears to hear, has no tongue to speak. You may safely transfer whatever you have in your breast into mine, and rely upon it that you have consigned it to the depths of silence."

"In reliance upon that promise," said Don Antonio, "I will astonish you with what you shall see and hear, and relieve myself of some of the vexation it gives me to have no one to whom I can confide my secrets, for they are not of a kind to be entrusted to everybody."

Don Quixote was puzzled, wondering what could be the object of such precautions; whereupon Don Antonio taking his hand passed it over the bronze head and the whole table and the pedestal of jasper on which it stood, and then said, "This head, Señor Don Quixote, has been designed and fabricated by one of the greatest magicians and wizards the world ever saw, a Pole by birth, I believe, and a pupil of the famous Escotillo of whom such marvelous stories are told.[2] He was here in my house, and in exchange for a thousand escudos that I gave him he constructed this head, which has the power of answering whatever questions are put to its ear. He observed the points of the compass, he traced figures, he studied

[2] *famous Escotillo of whom such marvelous stories are told:* The identity of this magician, if historical, is unknown.

the stars, he watched favorable moments, and at length brought it to the perfection we shall see tomorrow—for on Fridays it is mute, and this being Friday we must wait till the next day. In the interval, your worship may consider what you would like to ask it. I know by experience that in all its answers it tells the truth."

Don Quixote was amazed at the head's power and was inclined to disbelieve Don Antonio; but seeing what a short time he had to wait to test the matter, he did not choose to say anything except to thank him for having revealed to him so great a secret. They then left the room, Don Antonio locked the door, and they headed to the chamber where the rest of the gentlemen were assembled. In the meantime, Sancho had recounted to them several of the adventures and incidents that had happened to his master.

That afternoon they took Don Quixote out for a stroll, not in his armor but in street attire, with a cape of tawny cloth upon him, which at that season would have made ice itself sweat.[3] Orders were left with the servants to entertain Sancho so as not to let him leave the house. Don Quixote was mounted, not on Rocinante, but upon a tall mule of easy pace and handsomely caparisoned. They put the cape on him, and on the back—without his noticing—they stitched a parchment on which they wrote in large letters, THIS IS DON QUIXOTE OF LA MANCHA. As they set out upon their excursion the placard attracted the eyes of all who chanced to see him, and as they read out, "This is Don Quixote of La Mancha," Don Quixote was amazed to see how many people gazed at him, called him by his name, and recognized him.

Turning to Don Antonio, who rode at his side, he observed to him, "Great are the privileges knight-errantry bestows, for it makes him who professes it known and famous in every region of the earth. See, Don Antonio, the very boys of this city know me without ever having seen me."

"True, Señor Don Quixote," returned Don Antonio, "for as fire cannot be hidden or kept secret, virtue cannot escape being recognized; and that which is attained by the profession of arms shines distinguished above all others."

It came to pass, however, that as Don Quixote was proceeding amid the acclamations that have been described, a Castilian, reading the inscription on his back, cried out in a loud voice, "The devil take you for a Don Quixote of La Mancha! How did you get here without dying from the countless beatings your ribs have taken? You're crazy! If you were crazy all alone and kept your madness to yourself, it wouldn't be so bad. But you have the gift of making idiots and fools of everyone who has anything to do with you or say to you. Just look at these gentlemen keeping you company! Go home, you fool, and look after your affairs and your wife and children, and give up these stupidities that are eating away at your brain and skimming off your wits."

"Go your own way, brother," said Don Antonio, "and don't offer advice to those who don't ask you for it. Señor Don Quixote is in his full senses, and we

[3] *cape of tawny . . . ice itself sweat:* The cape of tawny cloth (*balandrán*) was a long, flowing cape made from a semicircular piece of wool, fastened by decorative braids. It was considered winter wear for men of status.

who keep him company are not fools. Virtue is to be honored wherever it may be found. Go, and bad luck to you, and don't meddle where you are not wanted."

"By God, your worship is right," replied the Castilian, "for to advise this good man is to kick against the goads.[4] Still, it fills me with pity that the sound mind they say this idiot has in everything should be drained away through the channel of his knight-errantry. May the bad luck your worship speaks of follow me and all my descendants if from this day forth—though I should live longer than Methuselah—I ever give advice to anybody, even if he asks me for it."

The advice-giver went his way, and they continued their stroll. But so great was the press of the boys and people to read the placard, that Don Antonio was forced to remove it as if he were taking off something else.

Night came and they went home, where there was a dancing party for the ladies, for Don Antonio's wife, a fun-loving noblewoman known for her beauty and wit, had invited some friends of hers to come and do honor to her guest and amuse themselves with his strange delusions. Several of them came, they dined sumptuously, and the dance began at about ten o'clock. Among the ladies were two of a mischievous turn, and though perfectly modest, they were somewhat free in playing tricks for harmless diversion's sake. These two were so indefatigable in taking Don Quixote out to dance that they tired him out, not only in body but in spirit. It was a sight to see the figure Don Quixote made—long, lank, lean, and yellow, his garments clinging tight to him, ungainly, and above all anything but agile.

The young ladies flirted with him surreptitiously, and he on his part surreptitiously repelled them. But finding himself hard pressed by their flirtation, he lifted up his voice and exclaimed, "*Fugite, partes adversæ!*[5] Leave me in peace, unwelcome thoughts! Be gone with your desires, ladies, for she who is queen of mine, the peerless Dulcinea del Toboso, suffers none but hers to lead me captive and subdue me." So saying he sat down on the floor in the middle of the room, worn out and broken down by the exertion of the dance.

Don Antonio directed him to be carried off to bed. The first that laid hold of him was Sancho, saying as he did so, "In an evil hour you took to dancing, my master. Do you think all mighty men of valor are dancers, and all knights-errant made for the ballroom? If you do, I can tell you you're mistaken. There's many a man that would rather undertake to kill a giant than cut a caper. If you were shoe dancing,[6] I could take your place, for I can shoe dance like a gyrfalcon. But I'm no good in a ballroom." With these and other observations Sancho set the whole room laughing, and then put his master to bed, covering him up well so that he might sweat out any chill caught after his dancing.

The next day Don Antonio decided to put the enchanted head to the test. With Don Quixote, Sancho, and two friends of his (in addition to the two ladies that had tired out Don Quixote at the ball, who had remained for the night with

[4] *kick against the goads:* echo of Acts 26:14.

[5] Fugite, partes adversæ: Latin, "Begone, hostile powers"—from the Catholic rite of exorcism.

[6] *shoe dancing:* See footnote 4, page 531.

Don Antonio's wife), he locked himself up in the chamber where the head was. He explained to them the property it possessed and entrusted the secret to them, telling them that now for the first time he was going to test the power of the enchanted head. Except for Don Antonio's two friends, no one else was privy to the mystery of the enchantment; and if Don Antonio had not first revealed it to them, they would have been inevitably reduced to the same state of amazement as the rest, so artfully and skillfully was it contrived.

The first to approach the ear of the head was Don Antonio himself. In a low voice—but not so low as not to be audible to all—he said to it, "Head, tell me by the power you possess, what am I at this moment thinking?"

The head, without any movement of the lips, answered in a clear and distinct voice, so as to be heard by all, "I do not judge thoughts."

All were thunderstruck at this, and all the more so as they saw that there was nobody anywhere near the table or in the whole room that could have answered.

"How many of us are here?" asked Don Antonio once more.

He was answered in the same way softly, "You and your wife, with two friends of yours and two of hers, and a famous knight named Don Quixote of La Mancha, and a squire of his, Sancho Panza by name."

Now there was fresh astonishment; now everyone's hair was standing on end with awe. Don Antonio stepped away from the head and exclaimed, "This suffices to show me that I have not been deceived by him who sold you to me, O sage head, talking head, answering head, wonderful head! Let someone else go and ask what question he likes of it."

As women are commonly impulsive and inquisitive, the first to come forward was one of the two friends of Don Antonio's wife. Her question was, "Tell me, Head, what should I do to be very beautiful?"

The answer she got was, "Be very modest."

"I have no more to ask," said the fair questioner.

Her companion then came up and said, "I would like to know, Head, whether or not my husband loves me."

The answer given to her was, "Consider how he treats you, and you may guess."

The married lady went off saying, "That answer did not need a question. Of course the treatment one receives shows the disposition of him from whom it is received."

Then one of Don Antonio's two friends advanced and asked it, "Who am I?"

"You know," was the answer.

"That is not what I am asking you," said the gentleman. "Tell me if you recognize me."

"Yes, I recognize you. You are Don Pedro Noriz," was the reply.

"I do not seek to know more," said the gentleman, "for this is enough to convince me, O Head, that you know everything."

As he stepped away, the other friend came forward and asked it, "Tell me, Head, what are my eldest son's wishes?"

"I have said already," was the answer, "that I cannot judge wishes; however, I can tell you that your son's wish is to bury you."

"That's like 'what I see with my eyes, I point out with my finger,'"[7] said the gentleman, "so I ask no more."

Don Antonio's wife came up and said, "I don't know what to ask you, Head; I would only like to know if I will have many years to enjoy my good husband."

The answer she received was, "You will, for his vigor and his temperate habits promise many years of life, which by their intemperance others so often cut short."

Then Don Quixote came forward and said, "Tell me, you that answer, was that which I describe as having happened to me in the Cave of Montesinos the truth or a dream? Will Sancho's whipping be accomplished without fail? Will Dulcinea's disenchantment be carried out?"

"As to the question of the cave," was the reply, "there is much to be said. There is something of both in it. Sancho's whipping will proceed leisurely. Dulcinea's disenchantment will come to its due end."

"I seek to know no more," said Don Quixote. "Let me but see Dulcinea disenchanted, and I will consider that all the good fortune I could wish for has come upon me all at once."

The last questioner was Sancho, and his questions were, "Head, will I by any chance have another government? Will I ever escape from the hard life of a squire? Will I get back to see my wife and children?"

To which the answer came, "You will govern in your house. If you return to it, you will see your wife and children. On ceasing to serve, you will cease to be a squire."

"Good grief!" cried Sancho Panza. "I could have told myself that. The prophet Perogrullo[8] couldn't have added anything more."

"What answer do you want, you beast?" said Don Quixote. "Is it not enough that the replies this head has given suit the questions put to it?"

"Yes, it is enough," said Sancho, "but I would have liked it to have made itself plainer and told me more."

The questions and answers came to an end here, but not the wonder with which all were filled—all except Don Antonio's two friends who were in on the secret. This Cide Hamete Benengeli thought fit to reveal at once, not to keep the world in suspense with the belief that the head had some strange magical mystery in it. He says, therefore, that on the model of another head, the work of an engraver, which he had seen in Madrid, Don Antonio made this one at home for his own amusement and to astonish the ignorant. Its mechanism was as follows:

The table was of painted wood and varnished to imitate jasper, and the pedestal on which it stood was of the same material, with four eagles' claws projecting from it to support the weight more steadily. The head—which resembled a bust or figure of a Roman emperor and was colored like bronze—was hollow inside,

[7] *That's like 'what I see with my eyes, I point out with my finger'*: "That's obvious."

[8] *prophet Perogrullo*: humorous figure from Spanish tradition, famous for truisms such as "If it is cold, it is not hot."

as was the table, into which it was fitted so exactly that no trace of the joining was visible. The pedestal of the table was also hollow and connected to the neck and chest of the head, and the whole display was connected to another room underneath the chamber in which the head stood. Through the entire cavity in the pedestal, table, chest, and neck of the bust, there passed a tin tube carefully adjusted and concealed from sight. In the room below connected to the one above was placed the person who was to answer, with his mouth to the tube, and the voice, as in an ear-trumpet, passed from above downwards, and from below upwards, the words coming clearly and distinctly. It was impossible, thus, to detect the trick.

A nephew of Don Antonio's, a smart, quick-witted student, was the answerer. As he had been told beforehand by his uncle who the people were that would come with him that day into the chamber where the head was, it was an easy matter for him to answer the first question at once and correctly. The others he answered by guesswork, and, being clever, cleverly. Cide Hamete adds that this marvelous contrivance stood for some ten or twelve days; but that, as it became noised abroad through the city that he had in his house an enchanted head that answered all who asked questions of it, Don Antonio, fearing it might come to the ears of the watchful sentinels of our faith, explained the matter to the Inquisitors, who commanded him to break it up and have done with it, lest the ignorant masses should be scandalized. Nevertheless, Don Quixote and Sancho continued to insist that the head was enchanted and capable of answering questions, though more to Don Quixote's satisfaction than Sancho's.

The gentlemen of the city, to gratify Don Antonio and also to commemorate Don Quixote's visit and give him an opportunity of displaying his folly, arranged for a tilting at the ring to be held six days from that time. This, however, as will be explained later, did not take place.

Don Quixote had the desire to take a stroll through the city quietly and on foot, for he feared that if he went on horseback the boys would follow him; so he and Sancho and two servants that Don Antonio gave him set out for a walk. It came to pass that going along one of the streets, Don Quixote lifted up his eyes and saw written in very large letters over a door, Books printed here. He was vastly pleased at this, for until then he had never seen a printing office, and he was curious to know what it was like. He entered with all his following, and saw them printing sheets in one place, correcting proofs in another, typesetting here, revising there—in short, all the work that is to be seen in great printing offices. He went up to one station and asked what they were up to there. The workmen told him, he watched them with wonder, and passed on.

He approached one man among others and asked him what he was doing. The workman replied, "Señor, this gentleman here" (pointing to a man of prepossessing appearance and a somewhat somber look) "has translated an Italian book into our Spanish tongue, and I am setting it up in type for the press."

"What is the title of the book?" asked Don Quixote.

The author replied, "Señor, in Italian the book is called *Le bagatelle*."

"And what does *Le bagatelle* mean in our Spanish?" asked Don Quixote.

"*Le bagatelle*," said the author, "is as though we should say in Spanish *Los juguetes*.[9] But though the book is humble in name, it has good solid matter in it."

"I," said Don Quixote, "have some little smattering of Italian, and I plume myself on singing some of Ariosto's stanzas. But tell me, señor—I do not say this to test your ability, but merely out of curiosity—have you ever come across the word *pignatta* in your book?"

"Yes, often," said the author.

"And how do you render that in Spanish?"

"How should I render it," returned the author, "but by *olla*?"[10]

"On my body!" exclaimed Don Quixote. "How proficient you are in the Italian language! I would lay a good wager that where they say in Italian *piace* you say in Spanish *place*, and where they say *più* you say *más*, and you translate *su* by *arriba* and *giù* by *abajo*."[11]

"Of course that's how I translate them," said the author. "Those are their proper equivalents."

"I would venture to swear," said Don Quixote, "that your worship is not known in the world, which always begrudges its reward to choice intellects and praiseworthy labors. What talents lie wasted there! What genius thrust away into corners! What worth left neglected! Still, it seems to me that translation from one language into another—unless it is from the queens of languages, the Greek and the Latin—is like looking at Flemish tapestries from the wrong side. Though the figures are visible, they are full of threads that make them indistinct, and they do not show the clarity and color of the right side. Translation from easy languages bespeaks neither ingenuity nor command of words, any more than transcribing or copying out one document from another. But I do not mean by this to draw the inference that no credit is to be allowed for the work of translating, for a man may employ himself in worse ways and less profitable to himself. And this judgment makes an exception for two famous translators, Doctor Cristóbal de Figueroa, in his *The Shepherd Fido*, and Don Juan de Jáuregui, in his *Aminta*, wherein by their splendid work they leave in doubt which is the translation and which the original.[12] But tell me, are you printing this book at your own risk, or have you sold the copyright to some bookseller?"[13]

"I print at my own risk," said the author. "I expect to make at least a thousand ducats by this first run of two thousand copies. At six reals apiece, they will disappear in a twinkling."

[9] Los juguetes: trifles.

[10] olla: cooking pot.

[11] *they say in Italian . . . you say* abajo: pleases (*piace/place*), more (*più/más*), up (*su/arriba*), down (*giù/abajo*).

[12] *And this judgment . . . the original:* Cristóbal de Figueroa published a Spanish translation of Battista Guarini's *Il Pastore Fido*, a pastoral tragicomedy, in 1602; Juan de Jáuregui's Spanish translation of the pastoral drama *Aminta*, by Torquato Tasso, followed in 1607.

[13] *are you printing . . . copyright to some bookseller:* A *privilegio* (copyright) from the king gave the author the exclusive right to publish a book during a period of time. Authors like Cervantes commonly sold the *privilegio* to a printer or bookseller to avoid the risk that sales would not offset publication costs.

"A fine calculation you are making!"[14] said Don Quixote. "It is plain you are ignorant of printers' schemes and how they look out for each other. I promise you when you find yourself saddled with two thousand copies you will feel so beaten and bruised that it will astonish you, particularly if the book is a little out of the ordinary and not in any way entertaining."

"What?" cried the author. "Would your worship have me give it to a bookseller who will give three maravedis for the copyright and think he is doing me a favor? I don't print my books to win fame in the world, for I am known in it already by my works. I want to make money, without which reputation is worthless."

"God send your worship good luck," said Don Quixote.

He moved on to another station, where he saw them correcting[15] a sheet of a book with the title *Light of the Soul*.[16] Noticing it, he observed, "Books like this, though there are many of the kind, are the ones that deserve to be printed, for sinners are plentiful these days, and lights unnumbered are needed for all that are in darkness."

He passed on and saw they were also correcting a book. When he asked its title, they told him it was called, *The Second Part of the Ingenious Gentleman Don Quixote of La Mancha*, by someone from Tordesillas.

"I have heard of this book already," said Don Quixote. "Verily and on my conscience, I thought it had been by this time burned to ashes as a meddlesome intruder. But its Martinmas will come to it as it does to every pig.[17] For fictions have the more merit and charm about them the more nearly they approach the truth or what looks like it; and true stories, the truer they are the better they are."

So saying he walked out of the printing office with a certain amount of displeasure on his face. That same day Don Antonio arranged to take him to see the galleys that were anchored near shore, at which Sancho was in high delight, as he had never seen any all his life. Don Antonio sent word to the commandant of the galleys that he intended to bring his guest, the famous Don Quixote of La Mancha, of whom the commandant and all the citizens had already heard, that afternoon to see them. What happened on board of them will be told in the next chapter.

[14] *A fine calculation you are making:* At six reals apiece, a run of two thousand copies would indeed bring in one thousand ducats if every copy were sold; however, the translator would still need to reimburse the printer for production costs and pay a commission to booksellers.

[15] *correcting:* proofreading and resetting type for the sheet to be reprinted.

[16] Light of the Soul: A catechism with this title (*Luz del alma cristiana*) was published in 1554 and reprinted several times in the following decades.

[17] *But its Martinmas will come to it as it does to every pig:* It was the tradition to slaughter pigs on Saint Martin's Day (November 11).

CHAPTER LXIII

OF THE MISHAP THAT BEFELL SANCHO PANZA WHEN HE VISITED THE GALLEYS, AND THE STRANGE ADVENTURE OF THE FAIR MORISCO

Profound were Don Quixote's reflections on the pronouncements of the enchanted head, not one of them hitting on the secret of the contrivance, but all concentrated on the promise, which he regarded as a certainty, of Dulcinea's disenchantment. This he turned over in his mind again and again with great satisfaction, fully persuaded that he would shortly see its fulfillment. As for Sancho, though he hated being a governor, as has been said, still he had a longing to be giving orders and once more finding himself obeyed—such is the misfortune that authority, even in jest, brings with it.

To resume, that afternoon their host Don Antonio Moreno and his two friends, along with Don Quixote and Sancho, went to the galleys. The commandant had been already made aware of his good fortune in seeing two such famous persons as Don Quixote and Sancho. The instant they came to the shore, all the galleys rolled back their awnings and the clarions rang out. A skiff covered with rich carpets and cushions of crimson velvet was immediately lowered into the water, and as Don Quixote stepped on board of it, the leading galley fired her gangway gun, and the other galleys did the same. As he mounted the starboard ladder, the whole crew saluted him exclaiming, "Hu, hu, hu," three times—as is the custom when a personage of distinction comes on board a galley. The general, for so we shall call him, a Valencian gentleman of rank, gave him his hand and embraced him, saying, "I shall mark this day with a white stone[1] as one of the happiest I can expect to enjoy in my lifetime, a token of that occasion on which I saw Señor Don Quixote of La Mancha, in whom is contained and condensed all that is worthy in knight-errantry."

Don Quixote, delighted beyond measure with such a lordly reception, replied to him in words no less courteous. The party proceeded to the poop deck,[2] which was very handsomely decorated, and seated themselves on the bulwark benches.[3] The boatswain[4] passed along the gangway and signaled with his whistle for the crew members to take off their shirts, which they did in an instant.

[1] *white stone:* See footnote 5, page 476.
[2] *poop deck:* raised superstructure at the back of the ship, typically housing officers.
[3] *bulwark benches:* benches built along the inner sides of the ship's bulwarks.
[4] *boatswain:* officer in charge of the oarsmen.

Sancho, seeing such a number of men stripped to the skin, was taken aback, and still more when he saw them roll back the awning so briskly that it seemed to him as if all the devils were at work at it. But all this was cakes and fancy bread compared to what I am about to relate.

Sancho was seated on the stanchion,[5] close to the lead rower on the righthand side. He, previously instructed in what he was to do, took hold of Sancho, hoisting him up in his arms, and the whole crew, who were standing ready, beginning on the right, proceeded to pass him down, whirling him along from hand to hand and from bench to bench with such rapidity that it took the sight out of poor Sancho's eyes, and he was quite sure that the devils themselves were handling him; nor did they finish with him until they had sent him back along the left side and deposited him on the poop deck. The poor fellow was left bruised and breathless and all in a sweat, and unable to comprehend what it was that had happened to him.

Don Quixote, when he saw Sancho's wingless flight, asked the general if this was a usual ceremony with those who came on board the galleys for the first time; if so, as he had no intention of adopting their profession, he was not about to perform such feats of agility, and if anyone offered to lay hold of him to whirl him about, he vowed to God he would kick his soul out of his body. As he said this, he stood up and clapped his hand upon his sword. At this instant they rolled up the awning and lowered the yard[6] with a prodigious rattle. Sancho thought heaven was coming off its hinges and going to fall on top of him, and full of terror he buried his head between his knees; nor were Don Quixote's knees altogether under control, for he too shook a little, squeezed his shoulders together, and lost color. The crew then hoisted the yard with the same rapidity and clatter as when they lowered it, all the while keeping silence as though they had neither voice nor breath. The boatswain gave the signal to weigh anchor, and leaping upon the middle of the gangway, he began to lay on to the shoulders of the crew with his kurbash[7] or whip, and to haul out gradually to sea.

When Sancho saw so many red feet (for such he took the oars to be) moving all together, he said to himself, "These are the real enchanted things, not the ones my master talks about. What can those wretches have done to be whipped like that; and how does that one man who goes along there whistling dare to whip so many? If you ask me, this is hell—or at least purgatory!"

Don Quixote, observing how attentively Sancho regarded what was going on, said to him, "Ah, Sancho my friend, how quickly and conveniently might you finish off Dulcinea's disenchantment, if you would strip to the waist and take your place among those gentlemen! Amid the pain and sufferings of so many you would hardly feel your own; moreover, perhaps the sage Merlin would allow each of these lashes, being laid on with a good hand, to count for ten of those which you must give yourself at last."

[5] *stanchion:* post supporting the awning and securing the lines leading to auxiliary sails.
[6] *yard:* lateen yard; horizontal crossbeam supporting the sail.
[7] *kurbash:* See footnote 19, page 165.

The general was about to ask what these lashes were and what Dulcinea's disenchantment was, when a sailor exclaimed, "Monjui[8] is signaling that there's an oared vessel off the coast to the west."

On hearing this the general sprang upon the gangway crying, "Don't let her give us the slip, my boys! No doubt it's some corsair brigantine from Algiers that the watchtower has spotted." The three other galleys immediately came alongside the flagship to receive their orders. The general commanded that two put out to sea while he with the other kept in shore, so that in this way the vessel could not escape them. The crews plied the oars driving the galleys so furiously that they seemed to fly. The two that had put out to sea, after a couple of miles sighted a vessel which, so far as they could make out, they judged to be one of fourteen or fifteen banks,[9] and so she proved. As soon as the vessel sighted the galleys, she began to flee in the hope of making her escape by her speed; but the attempt failed, for the flagship was one of the fastest vessels afloat and overtook her so rapidly that those aboard the brigantine saw clearly there was no possibility of escaping. The rais[10] therefore would have no choice but to have them drop their oars and give themselves up so as not to provoke the captain in command of our galleys to anger.

But chance, directing things otherwise, so ordered that just as the flagship came close enough for those on board the vessel to hear the shouts from her calling on them to surrender, two *Toraquis* (that is to say, two Turks), both drunk, who with a dozen more were on board the brigantine, discharged their muskets, killing two of the soldiers that lined the sides of our vessel. Seeing this the general swore he would not leave one of those he found on board the vessel alive; but as he bore down furiously upon her, she slipped away from him underneath the oars. The galley shot a good way ahead; those on board the vessel saw their case was desperate, and while the galley was coming about they set sail, and by sailing and rowing once more tried to sheer off. But their activity did not do them as much good as their rashness did them harm, for the galley, catching up with them in a little more than half a mile, threw her oars over them and took the whole of them alive.

The other two galleys now joined company and all four returned with the prize to the beach, where a vast multitude stood waiting for them, eager to see what they brought back. The general anchored close in, and saw that the viceroy of the city was on shore. He ordered the skiff to push off to fetch him, and the yard to be lowered for the purpose of hanging without delay the rais and the rest of the men taken on board the vessel, about thirty-six in number, all stout fellows and most of them Turkish musketeers.

He asked which one was the rais of the brigantine, and was answered in Spanish by one of the prisoners (who afterwards proved to be a Spanish renegade[11]),

[8] *Monjui:* Montjüich, prominent hill overlooking Barcelona's harbor where a watchtower allowed scouts to monitor for seaborne invaders.

[9] *fourteen or fifteen banks:* benches of rowers.

[10] *rais:* title for the captain of a ship associated with the Ottoman Turks or North African Muslims.

[11] *renegade:* See footnote 5, page 320.

"This young man, señor, that you see here is our rais." He pointed to one of the handsomest and most gallant-looking youths that could be imagined. The youth was perhaps not even twenty years of age.

"Tell me, dog," said the general, "what led you to kill my soldiers when you saw it was impossible for you to escape? Is that how to show respect to a flagship? Do you not know that rashness is not valor? Faint prospects of success should make men bold, but not rash."

The rais was about to reply, but the general could not at that moment listen to him, as he had to turn to receive the viceroy, who was now coming on board the galley, and with him certain of his attendants and some townspeople.

"You have had a good chase, señor general," said the viceroy.

"Your excellency shall soon see how good by the game strung up to this yard," replied the general.

"How so?" returned the viceroy.

"Because," said the general, "against all law, reason, and usages of war they have killed on my hands two of the best soldiers on board these galleys, and I have sworn to hang every man that I have taken, but above all this youth who is the rais of the brigantine." He pointed to him as he stood with his hands already bound and the rope round his neck, awaiting his death.

The viceroy looked at him, and seeing him so well-favored, so graceful, and so submissive, he felt a desire to spare his life, the comeliness of the youth furnishing him at once with a letter of recommendation. He therefore questioned him saying, "Tell me, rais, are you a Turk, a Moor, or a renegade?"

To which the youth replied, also in Spanish, "I am neither Turk, nor Moor, nor renegade."

"What are you then?" said the viceroy.

"A Christian woman," replied the youth.

"A woman and a Christian, in such attire and in such circumstances! It is more marvelous than credible," said the viceroy.

"Stay the execution of my sentence," said the youth. "Your vengeance will not lose much by waiting while I tell you the story of my life."

What heart could be so hard as not to be softened by these words—at least enough to listen to what the unhappy youth had to say? The general invited him to say what he pleased, but not to expect pardon for his flagrant offense. With this permission, the youth began in these words:

"Born of Morisco parents, I am of that nation, more unhappy than wise, upon which of late a sea of woes has poured down. In the course of our misfortune, I was carried to Barbary by two uncles of mine, for it was in vain that I declared I was a Christian, as in fact I am—not a mere pretended one, or outwardly, but a true Catholic Christian. It availed me nothing with those charged with our grim banishment to protest this, nor would my uncles believe it. On the contrary, they treated it as a lie I concocted to enable me to remain behind in the land of my birth. And so, more by force than of my own will, they took me with them.

"I had a Christian mother, and a father who was a man of keen judgment and a Christian too. I imbibed the Catholic faith with my mother's milk, I was well brought up, and neither in word nor in deed did I, to my knowledge, show any sign of being a Morisco. As I grew in these virtues—for such I hold them to be—so did I grow in beauty, if indeed I possess any. Great as was the seclusion in which I lived, it was not so great but that a young gentleman, Don Gaspar Gregorio by name,[12] eldest son of a gentleman who is lord of a village near ours, found opportunities to observe me. How he saw me, how we met, how his heart was lost to me and mine not kept from him would take too long to tell, especially at a moment when I am in dread of the cruel cord that threatens to interpose itself between my tongue and my throat. I will only say, therefore, that Don Gregorio chose to accompany me in our banishment.

"He joined company with the Moriscos who were going forth from other villages, for he knew their language very well, and on the voyage he struck up a friendship with my two uncles who were carrying me with them; for my father, like a wise and far-sighted man, as soon as he heard the first edict for our expulsion, left our village and departed in search of some refuge for us abroad. He left hidden and buried—at a spot of which I alone have knowledge—a large quantity of pearls and precious stones of great value, together with a sum of money in gold cruzados[13] and doubloons. He charged me on no account to touch the treasure, if by any chance they expelled us before his return. I obeyed him, and with my uncles, as I have said, and others of our kindred and neighbors, passed over to Barbary. The place where we took up our residence was Algiers, much the same as if we had taken it up in hell itself.

"The king heard of my beauty and report told him of my wealth, which was in some degree fortunate for me. He summoned me before him and asked me what part of Spain I came from and what money and jewels I had. I mentioned the place, and told him the jewels and coins were buried there; but that they might easily be recovered if I myself went back for them. All this I told him, in dread lest my beauty and not his greed should influence him. While he was in conversation with me, they brought him word that in my company was one of the handsomest and most graceful youths that could be imagined. I knew at once that they were speaking of Don Gaspar Gregorio, whose comeliness surpasses the most highly vaunted beauty. I was troubled when I thought of the danger he was in, for among those barbarous Turks a fair youth is more esteemed than a woman, be she ever so beautiful.[14] The king immediately ordered that he be brought before him, that he might see him and asked me if what they said about the youth was true. I then, almost as if inspired by heaven, told him it was, but that I would have him know he was not a man, but a woman like myself, and I entreated him to allow

[12] *Don Gaspar Gregorio by name*: apparently an alternate name for "Don Pedro Gregorio" (see p. 739).

[13] *cruzados:* The cruzado was a Portuguese gold coin stamped with a cross, commonly valued at around four hundred Portuguese reals.

[14] *for among those barbarous Turks a fair youth . . . be she ever so beautiful:* The sexual proclivities of Turks and the Muslim men of North Africa is a recurring theme in the literature of Cervantes and other Spanish writings of the era.

me to go and dress her in her proper attire, so that her beauty might be seen to perfection and that she might present herself before him with less embarrassment. He ordered me to go by all means and said that the next day we should discuss the plan to be adopted for my return to Spain to carry away the hidden treasure.

"I saw Don Gaspar, I told him the danger he was in if he let it be seen he was a man, I dressed him as a Moorish woman, and that same afternoon I brought him before the king, who was charmed when he saw him and resolved to keep the damsel and make a present of her[15] to the Grand Señor.[16] To avoid the risk she might run among the women of his seraglio,[17] and distrustful of himself, he commanded her to be placed in the house of some noble Moorish ladies who would protect and attend to her. There he was taken at once. What we both suffered—for I cannot deny that I love him—may be left to the imagination of those who are separated if they love one another dearly. The king then arranged that I should return to Spain in this brigantine, and that two Turks, those who killed your soldiers, should accompany me. There also came with me this Spanish renegade" (and here she pointed to him who had first spoken), "whom I know to be secretly a Christian, and to be more desirous of being left in Spain than of returning to Barbary. The rest of the crew of the brigantine are Moors and Turks, who merely serve as rowers. The two Turks, greedy and insolent, instead of obeying the orders we had to land me and this renegade in Christian dress—with which we came provided—on the first Spanish soil we came to, chose to run along the coast and make some prize[18] if they could, fearing that if they put us ashore first, we might, in case of some accident befalling us, make it known that the brigantine was at sea; thus, if there happened to be any galleys on the coast, they might be taken.

"We sighted this shore last night, and knowing nothing of these galleys, we were discovered. The result is what you have seen. To sum up, there is Don Gregorio in woman's dress, among women, in imminent danger of his life; and here am I with hands bound, in expectation, or rather in dread, of losing my life, of which I am already weary. Here, sirs, ends my sad story, as true as it is unhappy. All I ask of you is to allow me to die like a Christian,[19] for as I have already said, I am not to be charged with the offense of which those of my nation are guilty."

She stood silent, her eyes filled with moving tears, accompanied by many more from the bystanders. The viceroy, touched with compassion, went up to her without speaking and untied the cord that bound the hands of the Moorish girl.

While the Morisco Christian was telling her strange story, an elderly pilgrim, who had come on board the galley at the same time as the viceroy, kept his eyes

[15] *her:* Ana Félix briefly switches from masculine to feminine pronouns to refer to Don Gregorio, consistent with what the king believes Don Gregorio's gender to be.

[16] *Grand Señor:* Grand Turk.

[17] *seraglio:* harem.

[18] *make some prize:* capture another ship and take spoils.

[19] *die like a Christian:* die in a state of grace; have access to a priest who will administer the last rites, which included the sacraments of penance and the Eucharist.

fixed upon her. The instant she ceased speaking he threw himself at her feet, and embracing them said in a voice broken by sobs and sighs, "O Ana Félix, my unhappy daughter, I am your father Ricote come back to look for you, unable to live without you, my very soul!"

At these words, Sancho opened his eyes and raised his head, which he had been holding down, brooding over his unlucky excursion. Looking at the pilgrim he recognized in him that same Ricote he met the day he abandoned his government and was certain that this was his daughter. She being now unbound embraced her father, mingling her tears with his, while he addressing the general and the viceroy said, "This, sirs, is my daughter, more unhappy in her adventures than in her name. Ana Félix is her name,[20] surnamed Ricote, celebrated as much for her beauty as for my wealth. I left my native land in search of some shelter or refuge for us abroad, and having found one in Germany I returned in this pilgrim's dress, in the company of some other German pilgrims, to seek my daughter and take up a large quantity of treasure I had left buried. I did not find my daughter; the treasure I did find and have with me. Now, in this strange and roundabout way you have seen, I find the treasure that more than all makes me rich—my beloved daughter. If our mild fault and her tears and mine can, in accordance with your sound sense of justice, open the door to clemency, extend it to us, for we never had any intention of injuring you, nor do we sympathize with the aims of our people, who have been justly banished."

"I know Ricote well," said Sancho at this, "and I know too that what he says about Ana Félix being his daughter is true. As to those other particulars about going and coming, and having good or bad intentions, I say nothing."

While all present stood amazed at this strange occurrence, the general said, "Any one of your tears would not allow me to keep my oath. Live, fair Ana Félix, all the years that Heaven has allotted you. But these rash, insolent fellows must pay the penalty of the crime they have committed."

With that he gave orders to have the two Turks who had killed his two soldiers hanged at once at the yardarm. The viceroy, however, begged him earnestly not to hang them, as their behavior smacked more of madness than of bravado. The general yielded to the viceroy's request, for revenge is not easily taken in cold blood.

They then tried to devise some scheme for rescuing Don Gaspar Gregorio from the danger in which he had been left. Ricote offered for that purpose more than two thousand ducats that he had in pearls and gems. They proposed several plans, but none so good as the one suggested by the renegade already mentioned, who offered to return to Algiers in a small vessel of about six banks, manned by Christian rowers, as he knew where, how, and when he could and should land, nor was he ignorant of the house where Don Gaspar was staying.

The general and the viceroy had doubts about placing confidence in the renegade and entrusting him with the Christians who were to row, but Ana Félix

[20] *more unhappy . . . Ana Félix is her name:* "Felix" is Latin for "fortunate" or "happy"—the source of the Spanish cognate *feliz.*

said she could answer for him, and her father promised to pay the ransom of the Christians if by any chance they should be captured. This, then, being agreed upon, the viceroy landed, and Don Antonio Moreno took the fair Morisco and her father home with him, the viceroy charging him to give them the best reception and welcome in his power, while on his own part he offered all that his house contained for their entertainment—so great was the goodwill and charity that Ana Félix's beauty instilled in his heart.

CHAPTER LXIV

TREATING OF THE ADVENTURE THAT BROUGHT DON QUIXOTE MORE UNHAPPINESS THAN ALL THAT HAD HITHERTO BEFALLEN HIM

The wife of Don Antonio Moreno, so the history says, was extremely happy to see Ana Félix in her house. She welcomed her with great kindness, charmed as much by her beauty as by her intelligence, for in both respects the fair Morisco was richly endowed. All the people of the city flocked to see her, as though they had been summoned by the ringing of the bells.

Don Quixote told Don Antonio that the plan adopted for releasing Don Gregorio was not a good one, for its risks were greater than its advantages, and that it would be better to land himself with his arms and horse in Barbary. He would carry Don Gregorio off in spite of the whole Moorish host, as Don Gaiferos carried off his wife Melisendra.[1]

"Remember, your worship," observed Sancho on hearing him say so, "Señor Don Gaiferos carried off his wife from the mainland and took her by land to France. But here, even if we manage to carry off Don Gregorio, we don't have a way of bringing him to Spain, since there's the sea in the middle."

"There's a remedy for everything except death," said Don Quixote. "If they bring the vessel close to shore we shall be able to get on board, though all the world should strive to prevent us."

"Your worship makes it sound very simple," said Sancho, "but 'from word to deed there's much in between.' I side with the renegade, for he seems to me an honest, good-hearted fellow."

Don Antonio then said that if the renegade did not prove successful, the great Don Quixote's proposed expedition to Barbary should be adopted.

Two days afterwards the renegade put to sea in a light vessel of six oars, on each side manned by a brave crew, and two days later the galleys set sail eastward, the general having begged the viceroy to let him know all about the release of Don Gregorio and about Ana Félix. The viceroy promised to do as he requested.

One morning as Don Quixote went out for a stroll along the beach, arrayed in full armor (for as he often said, "his armor was his only gear, his only rest the fray," and he never was without it for a moment), he saw coming toward

[1] *as Don Gaiferos carried off his wife Melisendra:* the subject of Master Pedro's puppet show (see chap. 26).

him a knight, also in full armor, with a shining moon painted on his shield. On approaching sufficiently near to be heard, the knight said in a loud voice, addressing himself to Don Quixote, "Illustrious knight, and never-sufficiently-extolled Don Quixote of La Mancha, I am the Knight of the White Moon, whose unheard-of achievements you will perhaps recall. I come to do battle with you and prove the might of your arm, to the end that I make you acknowledge and confess that my lady, let her be who she may, is incomparably fairer than your Dulcinea del Toboso. If you acknowledge this fairly and openly, you shall escape death and save me the trouble of inflicting it upon you; if you fight and I vanquish you, I demand no other satisfaction than that, laying aside arms and abstaining from going in quest of adventures, you withdraw and betake yourself to your own village for the space of a year and live there without putting hand to sword, in peace and quiet and beneficial repose—this being necessary for the prosperity of your estate and the salvation of your soul. If you vanquish me, my head shall be at your disposal, my arms and horse your spoils, and the renown of my deeds transferred and added to yours. Consider which will be your best course, and give me your answer speedily, for this day is all the time I have for the dispatch of this business."

Don Quixote was amazed and astonished, not only at the Knight of the White Moon's arrogance but at his reason for issuing the challenge. With calm dignity he answered him, "Knight of the White Moon, of whose achievements I have never heard until now, I will venture to swear you have never seen the illustrious Dulcinea; for had you seen her I know you would have taken care not to make this demand, because the mere sight of her would have removed all doubt from your mind that there ever has been or can be a beauty to be compared with hers. And so, not saying you lie, but merely that you are not correct in what you state, I accept your challenge with the conditions you have proposed, and at once, that the day you have fixed may not expire. From your conditions I except only that of the renown of your achievements being transferred to me, for I know not of what sort they are nor what they may amount to. I am satisfied with my own, such as they be. Take, therefore, the side of the field you choose, and I will do the same; and 'to whom God shall give it, may Saint Peter add his blessing.'"

The Knight of the White Moon had been seen from the city, and the viceroy was informed how he was in conversation with Don Quixote. The viceroy, supposing it must be some fresh adventure concocted by Don Antonio Moreno or some other gentleman of the city, hurried out at once to the beach accompanied by Don Antonio and several other gentlemen, just as Don Quixote was wheeling Rocinante round in order to take up the necessary distance. When the viceroy saw that the two of them were evidently preparing to come to the charge, he put himself between them, asking what it was that led them to engage in combat all of a sudden in this way. The Knight of the White Moon replied that it was a question of precedence of beauty, and briefly told him what he had said to Don Quixote and how the conditions of the challenge agreed upon on both sides had been accepted. The viceroy went over to Don Antonio and asked in a low voice if he knew who the Knight of the White Moon was, or if it was some prank they were playing on Don Quixote. Don Antonio replied that he neither knew who he was nor whether the challenge was in jest or in earnest. This answer left the viceroy in a state of perplexity, not knowing whether he ought to let the combat go on or not; but unable to persuade himself that it was anything but a joke he stepped aside, saying, "Gallant knights, if there is no other remedy except to confess or die, and Don Quixote is inflexible and your worship of the White Moon still more so, I leave the matter in God's hands and you to your combat."

He of the White Moon thanked the viceroy in courteous and well-chosen words for the permission he gave them, and so did Don Quixote, who, commending himself with all his heart to Heaven and to his Dulcinea (as was his custom on the eve of any combat that awaited him), proceeded to take a little more distance, as he saw his antagonist was doing the same. Then, without blast of trumpet or other instrument of war to give them the signal to charge, both at the same instant wheeled their horses. He of the White Moon being the swifter met Don Quixote after having traversed two-thirds of the course. There, he collided so violently that, without touching him with his lance (for he held it high, as if on purpose), he hurled Don Quixote and Rocinante to the earth in a perilous fall.

The knight sprang upon him at once. Placing his lance over Don Quixote's visor, he said to him, "You are vanquished, sir knight, nay dead unless you admit the conditions of our combat."

Don Quixote, bruised and stupefied, without raising his visor said in a weak and feeble voice, as if he were speaking from the tomb, "Dulcinea del Toboso is the fairest woman in the world, and I the most unfortunate knight on earth. It is not fitting that my weakness should defraud these words of their truth. Run your lance through me, sir knight, and take my life, for you have taken away my honor."

"By no means will I do so," said he of the White Moon. "Let the fame of Lady Dulcinea's beauty live on, undimmed as ever. All I require is that the great Don Quixote retire to his own home for a year, or for so long a time as shall by me be enjoined upon him, as we agreed before engaging in this combat."

The viceroy, Don Antonio, and several others who were present heard all this, and heard too how Don Quixote replied that so long as nothing in prejudice of Dulcinea was demanded of him, he would observe all the rest like a true and loyal knight. With Don Quixote's confession given, he of the White Moon wheeled about, and making obeisance to the viceroy with a bow of the head, rode away into the city at a half gallop. The viceroy ordered Don Antonio to follow after him and by some means or other find out who he was. They raised Don Quixote up and uncovered his face, and found him pallid and bathed with sweat. Rocinante, who was thoroughly ravaged, was for the present unable to stir.

Sancho did not know what to say or do, so overcome was he with despair. He felt as if he had been dreaming, that the entire encounter had been a piece of enchantment. Here was his master defeated and bound not to take up arms for a year. He saw the light of the glory of his achievements obscured, the hopes of his recent promises swept away like smoke before the wind. Rocinante, he feared, was crippled for life, and his master's bones shattered along with his madness,[2] if such a feat were possible. In the end they carried him into the city on a litter, which the viceroy sent for, and there the viceroy himself returned, eager to find out who this Knight of the White Moon was who had left Don Quixote in such a sad plight.

[2] *his master's bones shattered along with his madness:* The text plays on *dislocado* (dislocated) and *deslocado* (cured of madness).

CHAPTER LXV

WHEREIN IS MADE KNOWN WHO THE KNIGHT OF THE WHITE MOON WAS, ALONG WITH DON GREGORIO'S RELEASE AND OTHER EVENTS

Don Antonio Moreno followed the Knight of the White Moon, and a number of boys followed him as well—rather, pursued him—until they caught up with him at an inn in the heart of the city. Don Antonio, eager to make his acquaintance, entered also. A squire came out to meet the knight and remove his armor. He then shut himself into a lower room, but not before Don Antonio followed him inside, for he would not let any bread bake until he found out who he was.

Seeing that the gentleman would not leave him, he of the White Moon said, "I know very well, señor, what you have come for: it is to find out who I am. As there is no reason why I should conceal it from you, while my servant here is taking off my armor I will tell you the truth of the matter, without leaving out anything. You must know, señor, that they call me the bachelor Samson Carrasco. I am of the same village as Don Quixote of La Mancha, whose madness and folly make all of us who know him feel pity for him. I am one of those who have felt it most. Persuaded that his chance of recovery lay in rest and remaining at home and in his own house, I devised a scheme for keeping him there. Three months ago I went out to meet him as a knight-errant, under the assumed name of the Knight of the Mirrors, intending to engage him in combat and defeat him without hurting him, making it the condition of our combat that the vanquished should be at the disposal of the victor. What I meant to demand of him—for I regarded him as vanquished already—was that he should return to his own village and not leave it for a whole year, by which time he might be cured.

But fate ordered otherwise, for he was the one who vanquished and unhorsed me, and so my plan failed. He went his way, and I came back conquered, covered with shame, and sorely bruised by my fall, which was a particularly violent one. This did not quench my desire to meet him again and defeat him, as you have seen today. And as he is so scrupulous in his observance of the laws of knight-errantry, he will, no doubt, in order to keep his word, obey the injunction I have laid upon him. This, señor, is how the matter stands, and I have nothing more to tell you. I implore of you not to betray me or tell Don Quixote who I am, so that my honest endeavors may be successful and that a man of excellent wits—were he only rid of the fooleries of chivalry—may get them back again."

"O señor," said Don Antonio, "may God forgive you the wrong you have done the whole world in trying to bring the most entertaining madman in it back to his senses. Do you not see, señor, that what is gained by Don Quixote's sanity can never match the amusement that his buffoonery brings? My belief is that all the señor bachelor's pains will be of no avail to bring a man so hopelessly cracked to his senses again; and if it were not uncharitable, I would say may Don Quixote never be cured, for by his recovery we lose not only his antics, but his squire Sancho Panza's too, any one of which is enough to turn melancholy itself into merriment. Nevertheless, I'll hold my peace and say nothing to him, and we'll see whether I am right in my suspicion that Señor Carrasco's efforts will be fruitless."

The bachelor replied that, in any event, the state of things looked promising, and he hoped for a happy result from it; and putting his services at Don Antonio's commands he took his leave of him. He had his armor packed at once upon a mule and departed the city that very day on the horse he had ridden into battle, returning to his home without meeting any adventure that requires recounting in this true history.

Don Antonio reported to the viceroy what Carrasco told him, and the viceroy was not very well pleased to hear it, for with Don Quixote's retirement there was an end to the amusement of everyone who knew anything about his mad doings.

Six days did Don Quixote remain in bed, dejected, melancholy, moody, and out of sorts, brooding over the unhappy event of his defeat. Sancho attempted to comfort him, and among other things he said to him, "Hold your head up, señor, and cheer up if you can. Give thanks to Heaven that if you've had a tumble to the ground you didn't come out of it with a broken rib. As you know, 'where they give, they take,' and 'where there's fire, there's not always smoke,'—a fig for the doctor, for there's no need of him to cure this ailment. Let's go home and put an end to going around in search of adventures in strange lands and places. Rightly looked at, I'm the one who's the bigger loser, though it's your worship who's had the worse treatment. When I gave up my government, I gave up every desire to be a governor again. But I didn't give up the dream of being made a count—and that will never come to pass if your worship gives up becoming a king by renouncing the calling of chivalry. And so my hopes are going to turn into smoke."

"Peace, Sancho," said Don Quixote. "You have seen that my seclusion and retirement is not to exceed a year. I shall soon return to my honored calling, and I shall not be at a loss for a kingdom to win and a county to bestow on you."

"May God hear it and sin be deaf," said Sancho. "I have always heard it said that 'a good hope is better than a bad holding.'"

As they were talking Don Antonio entered the room. With an expression of great joy, he announced, "Reward me for my good news, Señor Don Quixote! Don Gregorio and the renegade who went for him have come ashore. Ashore do I say? They are by this time in the viceroy's house and will be here immediately."

Don Quixote cheered up a little and said, "In truth I am almost ready to say I should have been glad had it turned out just the other way, for it would have obliged me to cross over to Barbary, where by the might of my arm I should have restored to liberty not only Don Gregorio, but all of Barbary's Christian captives. But what am I saying, miserable being that I am? Am I not he that has been conquered? Am I not he that has been overthrown? Am I not he who must not take up arms for a year? Then what am I making professions for? What am I bragging about, when it is fitter for me to handle the distaff than the sword?"

"No more of that, señor," said Sancho. "'Let the hen live, though it be with her pip.'[1] 'Today for you and tomorrow for me.' In this business of encounters and whacks one shouldn't pay them any mind, for 'he who falls today may get up tomorrow,' unless, of course, he chooses to stay in bed—I mean gives in to weakness and doesn't pluck up fresh spirit for fresh battles. Let your worship get up now to receive Don Gregorio; for the household seems to be in a bustle, and no doubt he's arrived by this time."

And so it proved, for as soon as Don Gregorio and the renegade had given the viceroy an account of the voyage there and back, Don Gregorio, eager to see Ana Félix, came with the renegade to Don Antonio's house. When they carried him off from Algiers, he had been wearing a woman's outfit; on board the vessel, however, he exchanged it for that of a captive who escaped with him. In whatever dress he might be, Don Gregorio looked like someone to be loved and served and esteemed, for he was exceptionally handsome, and to judge by appearances some seventeen or eighteen years of age. Ricote and his daughter came out to welcome him, the father with tears, the daughter with a modest blush. They did not embrace each other, for deep love is likely to be accompanied by self-restraint. Seen side by side, the combined beauty of Don Gregorio and Ana Félix were the wonder of all who were present. It was silence that spoke for the lovers at that moment, and their eyes were the tongues that declared their pure and happy feelings.

The renegade explained the measures and means he had adopted to rescue Don Gregorio. For his part, Don Gregorio showed that his intelligence was in advance of his years, describing briefly and without unnecessary detail the peril and embarrassment he found himself in among the women with whom he had sojourned. To conclude, Ricote liberally recompensed and rewarded both the renegade and the men who had rowed; and the renegade was reconciled with the Church and reconfirmed, and from a rotten limb became by penance and repentance a clean and sound one.

Two days later the viceroy discussed with Don Antonio the steps they should take to enable Ana Félix and her father to stay in Spain, for it seemed to them there could be no objection to a daughter who was so good a Christian and a father, to all appearance, so well-intentioned remaining there. Don Antonio offered to arrange the matter at the capital, where he was compelled to go on some other business, hinting that many a difficult affair was settled there with the help of favors and bribes.

"By no means," said Ricote, who was present during the conversation. "It will not do to rely on favors or bribes, because with the great Don Bernardino de

[1] *pip:* See footnote 1, page 450.

Velasco, Count of Salazar, to whom his Majesty has entrusted our expulsion,[2] neither entreaties nor promises, bribes nor appeals to compassion, are of any use; for though it is true he mingles mercy with justice, still, seeing that the whole body of our nation is tainted and corrupt, he cauterizes the wound with fire rather than soothing it with ointment. Thus, by prudence, sagacity, care, and the fear he inspires, he has borne on his mighty shoulders the weight of this great policy and carried it into effect, all our schemes, plots, demands, and wiles, being ineffectual to blind his Argus eyes.[3] He remains ever on the watch, lest one of us should remain behind in concealment and like a hidden root come in course of time to sprout and bear poisonous fruit in Spain, now cleansed and relieved of the fear in which our vast numbers kept it. Heroic resolve of the great Philip the Third, and unparalleled wisdom to have entrusted it to Don Bernardino de Velasco!"[4]

"At any rate," said Don Antonio, "when I am there I will make all possible efforts, and let Heaven do as pleases it best. Don Gregorio will come with me to relieve the anxiety that his parents must be suffering on account of his absence. Ana Félix will remain in my house with my wife, or in a monastery. And I know the viceroy will be glad that the worthy Ricote should stay with him until we see what terms I can negotiate."

The viceroy agreed to all that was proposed; but Don Gregorio on learning what had passed declared he could not and would not on any account leave Ana Félix; however, as it was his purpose to go and see his parents and devise some way of returning for her, he agreed to the proposed arrangement. Ana Félix remained with Don Antonio's wife, and Ricote in the viceroy's house.

The day of Don Antonio's departure came and two days later that of Don Quixote and Sancho, for Don Quixote's fall did not permit him to set out on the road any sooner. There were tears and sighs, swoons and sobs, at the parting between Don Gregorio and Ana Félix. Ricote offered Don Gregorio a thousand escudos if he would have them, but he would not take any except five, which Don Antonio lent him and he promised to repay at court. So the two of them took their departure, and Don Quixote and Sancho afterwards, as has been already said—Don Quixote without his armor and in traveling clothes, and Sancho on foot, Dapple being loaded with the armor.

[2] *Don Bernardino de Velasco . . . entrusted our expulsion:* Bernardino Fernández de Velasco (d. 1621) occupied administrative offices under King Phillip III on the Council of War and Council of Finance. The king placed him in charge of the Morisco expulsion in 1609, a task he carried out with unrelenting zeal.

[3] *Argus eyes:* Argus Panoptes, one-hundred-eyed giant charged with guarding Io, was priestess of the goddess Hera.

[4] *He remains . . . entrusted it to Don Bernardino de Velasco:* Ricote's full-throated defense of the Morisco expulsion is consistent with the pro-expulsion speeches of other characters in Cervantes' literature. His defense stands apart, however, for praising in effusive terms what has brought immense suffering on the Morisco and his family.

CHAPTER LXVI

WHICH TREATS OF WHAT HE WHO READS WILL SEE, OR WHAT HE WHO HAS IT READ TO HIM WILL HEAR

As he left Barcelona, Don Quixote turned his gaze to the place where he had fallen. "Here was my Troy,"[1] said he. "Here my misfortune, not my cowardice, robbed me of all the glory I had won; here Fortune made me the victim of her caprices; here the luster of my achievements was dimmed. Here, in a word, fell my happiness never to rise again."

"Señor," said Sancho on hearing this, "it's becoming of brave hearts to be patient in adversity just as much as to be glad in prosperity. I've learned this from experience, for if when I was a governor I was happy, now that I'm a squire and on foot I'm not sad. What's more, I've heard it said that the lady who goes by the name Fortune is a flighty drunk, and more importantly, blind. She doesn't see what she does, or know who she knocks down or raises up."

"You have become quite a philosopher, Sancho," said Don Quixote. "You speak very sensibly; I know not who taught you. But I can tell you there is no such thing as Fortune in the world, nor does anything which takes place here, be it good or bad, come about by chance, but by Heaven's special providence[2]—hence the common saying that 'each man is the maker of his own Fortune.' I have been that of mine, but not with the proper amount of prudence. My over-confidence has therefore laid me low; for I ought to have reflected that Rocinante's feeble strength could not resist the mighty bulk of the Knight of the White Moon's horse. In short, I took a risk, I did my best, I was overthrown; but though I lost my honor I did not lose, nor can I lose the virtue of keeping my word. When I was a knight-errant, daring and valiant, I supported my achievements by hand and deed, and now that I am a humble squire I will make good my words by keeping the promise I have given. Forward then, Sancho my friend, let us go to keep the year of the novitiate[3] in our own country, and in that seclusion we shall gather fresh strength to return to the calling of arms, never far from my mind."

[1] *Here was my Troy*: expression of lament over total devastation, as the fall of Troy was for the vanquished Trojans.

[2] *Heaven's special providence*: Special providence describes God's direct sovereignty over individuals and historical events, guiding them to their appointed ends.

[3] *novitiate*: probation.

"Señor," returned Sancho, "traveling on foot is not such a pleasant thing that it makes me feel disposed or tempted to make long marches. Let's leave this armor hung up on some tree, instead of someone who's been hanged. With me on Dapple's back and my feet off the ground we'll arrange the legs of the journey as your worship pleases to measure them out; but to suppose that I'm going to travel on foot and make long days of it is a waste of thought."

"You say well, Sancho," said Don Quixote. "Let my armor be hung up as a trophy, and under it or around it we will carve on the trees what was inscribed on the trophy of Roland's armor—

These let none move
Who dareth not his might with Roland prove."[4]

"I like the sound of it," said Sancho. "And if we weren't going to miss Rocinante down the road, it would be just as well to leave him hung up too."

"And yet I had rather not have either him or the armor hung up," said Don Quixote, "lest it be said, 'for good service a bad return.'"

"Your worship is right," said Sancho, "for as the wise have said, 'the fault of the donkey must not be laid on the packsaddle.' Since the fault here is your worship's, punish yourself and don't let your anger break out against the already battered and bloody armor, or Rocinante's gentle way, or my tender feet, trying to make them travel more than is reasonable."

In conversation of this kind the two of them spent the rest of the day, and the next four as well, without anything occurring to interrupt their journey. On the fifth day as they entered a village, they found a great number of people at the door of an inn enjoying themselves, as it was a holiday.

Upon Don Quixote's approach a peasant called out, "One of these two gentlemen who are coming here, and who don't know the parties, will tell us what we ought to do about our wager."

"That I will certainly do," said Don Quixote, "and according to the merits of the case, if I am able to understand it."

"Well, here it is, worthy sir," said the peasant. "A man of this village who is so fat that he weighs eleven arrobas[5] challenged another, a neighbor of his, who doesn't weigh more than five,[6] to run a race. The agreement was that they were to run a distance of a hundred paces with equal weights; and when the challenger was asked how the weights were to be made equal he said that the other, as he weighed five arrobas, should put six in iron on his back, and that in this way the eleven arrobas of the thin man would equal the eleven arrobas of the fat one."

"No, no," cried Sancho, before Don Quixote had a chance to answer. "Only a few days ago I resigned from being a governor and a judge, as all the world knows. I'm qualified to settle these questions and give an opinion in all manner of disputes."

[4] *These let none . . . with Roland prove:* See footnote 8, page 94.

[5] *eleven arrobas:* about 280 pounds.

[6] *five:* about 125 pounds.

"Answer in God's name, Sancho my friend," said Don Quixote, "for I am not fit to give crumbs to a cat, my wits are so confused and upset."

With this permission Sancho said to the peasants who stood clustered around him, waiting with open mouths for the decision to come from his, "Brothers, what the fat man is asking is unreasonable and doesn't have a shadow of justice in it. If it's true, as they say, that the challenged may choose the weapons, the other has no right to choose what will prevent and keep him from winning. My decision, therefore, is that the fat challenger prune, peel, thin, trim and lighten himself—that is, that he take six arrobas of his flesh off his body, here or there, as he pleases, and as suits him best. Being reduced in this way to a weight of five arrobas, he'll make himself even with the five of his opponent, and they'll be able to run on equal terms."[7]

"Well, I'll be!" said one of the peasants when he heard Sancho's decision. "The gentleman has spoken like a saint and given judgment like a canon. I'd wager that the fat man wouldn't part with a single ounce of his flesh, let alone six arrobas."

"The best plan will be for them not to run," said another, "so that the thin man doesn't break down under the weight, and the fat one doesn't strip himself of his flesh. Let half the wager be spent on wine, and let's take these gentlemen to the tavern where they serve the good stuff—and 'I'll wear the cloak when it rains!'"[8]

"I thank you, sirs," said Don Quixote; "but I cannot stop for an instant, for sad thoughts and unhappy circumstances oblige me to seem discourteous and to travel in haste."

And spurring Rocinante he pushed on, leaving them wondering at what they had seen and heard, at his strange figure and at the shrewdness of his servant, for such they took Sancho to be.

One of the peasants observed, "If the servant is so clever, imagine what the master is like! I'll bet if they're going to Salamanca to study, they'll end up as judges in the capital in no time. For there's no surer calling than to study night and day until, with a little help and some good luck, before a man knows it he has a staff in his hand or a miter on his head."[9]

That night master and man camped out in the open field, a clear sky above them. The next day as they were pursuing their journey, they saw coming toward them a man on foot with a knapsack around his neck and a short lance in his hand—the accustomed trappings of a letter carrier. As soon as he came close to Don Quixote, he quickened his pace and half running came up to him, and embracing his right thigh (for he could reach no higher), exclaimed with evident delight, "O Señor

[7] *A man of this village who is so fat. . . . :* The riddle first appears in *De singulari certamine* (Andrea Alciato, 1544), but by the early seventeenth century had become widespread.

[8] *I'll wear the cloak when it rains:* "I'll suffer the consequences", used here ironically.

[9] *staff in his hand or a miter on his head:* The staff symbolizes the office of a mayor or governor, the miter of a bishop.

Don Quixote of La Mancha, what happiness will fill the heart of my lord the duke when he learns that your worship is coming back to his castle, for he is still there with my lady the duchess!"

"I do not recognize you, friend," said Don Quixote, "nor will I know who you are unless you tell me."

"I'm Tosilos, my lord the duke's footman, Señor Don Quixote," replied the courier. "The fellow who refused to fight your worship over marrying Doña Rodríguez's daughter."

"God bless me!" exclaimed Don Quixote. "Is it possible that you are the one whom my enemies the enchanters changed into the footman you speak of in order to rob me of the honor of that battle?"

"Nonsense, good sir!" said the courier. "There was no enchantment or transformation at all. I entered the lists just as much the footman Tosilos as I came out of them the footman Tosilos. I resolved to marry without fighting, for the girl had won my heart. But things turned out very differently, for as soon as your worship left the castle, my lord the duke ordered that I be given a hundred strokes with the stick for having acted contrary to the orders he gave me before I entered into combat. The end of the matter is that the girl has become a nun, Doña Rodríguez has gone back to Castile, and I am now on my way to Barcelona with a packet of letters for the viceroy, which my master is sending him. If your worship would like a swallow of something potent, though warm, I have a gourd here full of the best, and some scraps of Tronchón cheese[10] that will serve as an appetizer—to wake up your thirst if it happens to be asleep."

"I accept the offer," said Sancho. "Let's make nice work of everything you have. Pour out, good Tosilos, in spite of all the enchanters in the Indies."

"You are indeed the greatest glutton in the world, Sancho," said Don Quixote, "and the greatest ignoramus walking the earth not to see that this courier is enchanted and this Tosilos an impostor. Remain with him and take your fill. I will go on slowly and wait for you to catch up to me."

The footman laughed, unsheathed his gourd, took the scraps out of his knapsack, and selecting a small loaf of bread he and Sancho seated themselves on the green grass, and in peace and good company finished off the contents of the knapsack down to the bottom, so thoroughly that they licked the wrapper over the bundle of letters, merely because it smelled like cheese.

Tosilos said to Sancho, "Beyond a doubt, Sancho my friend, that master of yours must be crazy."

"Must be?" said Sancho. "He owes[11] nothing to anyone and pays for everything, especially when the coin is madness. I see things plainly enough, and so I tell him plainly enough. But what's the use, especially now that he's been finished off? For he's been defeated by the Knight of the White Moon."

[10] *Tronchón cheese:* See footnote 3, page 729.

[11] *owes:* Sancho picks up the verb *deber*, which Tosilos uses as "must be" and responds with it in the sense of "owes".

Tosilos begged him to tell what had happened, but Sancho replied that it would not be good manners to leave his master waiting for him. Some other day if they met there would be time enough for that. Then getting up, after shaking his doublet and brushing the crumbs out of his beard, he drove Dapple on before him, bidding farewell to Tosilos and rejoining his master, who was waiting for him under the shade of a tree.

CHAPTER LXVII

OF THE RESOLUTION DON QUIXOTE FORMED TO BECOME A SHEPHERD AND TAKE TO A LIFE IN THE FIELDS DURING HIS PROMISED YEAR OF RETIREMENT, WITH OTHER EVENTS TRULY DELECTABLE AND HAPPY

If a multitude of reflections weighed on Don Quixote before he had been overthrown, a great many more weighed on him after his fall. He was under the shade of a tree, as has been said, and there, like flies to honey, thoughts came harassing and stinging him. Some of them turned upon the disenchantment of Dulcinea, others upon the life he was about to lead in his forced retirement. Sancho came up and spoke in high praise of the generous disposition of the footman Tosilos.

"Is it possible, Sancho," said Don Quixote, "that you still think he is a real footman? Apparently, it has escaped your memory that you have seen Dulcinea transformed into a peasant wench and the Knight of the Mirrors into the bachelor Carrasco—all the work of the enchanters that persecute me. But tell me now, did you ask this Tosilos, as you call him, what has become of Altisidora? Did she weep over my absence, or has she already consigned to oblivion the amorous thoughts that used to afflict her when I was present?"

"The thoughts I had," replied Sancho, "didn't leave any room for asking fool's questions. On my body, señor! Is your worship in a condition now to search out other people's thoughts, especially thoughts about love?"

"Look here, Sancho," said Don Quixote, "there is a great difference between what is done out of love and what is done out of gratitude. A knight may very possibly fall out of love, but it is impossible, strictly speaking, for him to be ungrateful. Altisidora, to all appearances, loved me truly. She gave me the three headscarves you know about. She wept at my departure, she cursed me, she abused me. Casting shame to the winds, she bewailed herself in public. All these are signs that she adored me, for the wrath of lovers always ends in curses. I had no hopes to give her, nor treasures to offer her, for mine are given to Dulcinea, and the treasures of knights-errant are like those of the fairies—illusory and deceptive.[1] All I can give her is the place in my memory I keep for her, without prejudice, however, to that which I hold devoted to Dulcinea, whom you wrong by your delay in whipping

[1] *like those of the fairies—illusory and deceptive:* According to folklore, a fairy's treasure disappears as soon as it is touched by a human.

yourself and scourging that flesh—would that I saw it eaten by wolves—which would rather keep itself for the worms than for the relief of that poor lady."

"Señor," replied Sancho, "if the truth be told, I cannot persuade myself that whipping my backside has anything to do with disenchanting the enchanted. It's like saying, 'If your head aches, rub ointment on your knees.' At any rate I'll make bold to swear that in all the histories dealing with knight-errantry that your worship has read you have never come across anybody being disenchanted by whipping. But for better or for worse, I'll whip myself when I feel like it and there's a convenient time to scourge myself."

"God grant it," said Don Quixote, "and Heaven give you grace to take it to heart and own the obligation you are under to help my lady, who is yours also, inasmuch as you are mine."

As they pursued their journey talking in this way they came to the very same spot where they had been trampled by the bulls. Don Quixote recognized it and said to Sancho, "This is the meadow where we came upon those elegant shepherdesses and gallant shepherds who were trying to revive and imitate the pastoral Arcadia there, an idea as novel as it was ingenious. In emulation of them—if it so be that you approve of it, Sancho—I would have us become shepherds, at least for the time I have to live in retirement. I will buy some sheep and everything else requisite for the pastoral calling. I will take the name of the shepherd Quixótiz and you the shepherd Panzino, and together we will roam the woods and groves and meadows singing songs here, lamenting in elegies there, drinking of the crystal waters of the springs or limpid brooks or flowing rivers. The oaks will yield us their sweet fruit with bountiful hand, the trunks of the hard cork trees a seat, the willows shade, the roses perfume, the widespread meadows carpets tinted with a thousand dyes. The clear, pure air will give us breath, the moon and stars lighten the darkness of the night for us. Song shall be our delight, lamenting our joy. Apollo will supply us with verses and love with conceits whereby we shall make ourselves famed forever, not only in this age but in ages to come."

"Yes, sir," said Sancho, "that squares with my notions of the good life—and even corners them. Besides, I'll bet that no sooner than the bachelor Samson Carrasco and Master Nicholas the barber see it, they'll want to follow suit and become shepherds along with us. God grant it gets in the priest's head to join the sheepfold too—he's so fun-loving and fond of a good time."

"You've spoken soundly, Sancho," said Don Quixote. "The bachelor Samson Carrasco, if he enters the pastoral fraternity (as no doubt he will), may call himself the shepherd Samsonino, or perhaps the shepherd Carrascón. Nicholas the barber may call himself Niculoso, as old Boscán formerly was called Nemoroso.[2] As for the priest, I don't know what name we can fit to him unless it is something derived from his title, and we call him the shepherd Curiambro.[3] For the

[2] *Boscán formerly was called Nemoroso:* It has been traditional to identify the shepherd Nemoroso in Garcilaso's *Eclogues* with Garcilaso's friend and fellow poet Juan Boscán (d. 1542).

[3] *Curiambro:* derived from *cura* (priest).

shepherdesses whose lovers we shall be, we can pick names as we would pears. Since my lady's name does just as well for a shepherdess as for a princess, I need not trouble myself to look for one that will suit her better. To your lady, Sancho, you can give her what name you will."

"I don't intend to give her any but Teresona," said Sancho, "which will go well with her stout figure and with her own name, as she's called Teresa. What's more, when I sing her praises in my poems I'll show how chaste my love is, for I'm not going to look 'for better bread than ever came from wheat' in other men's houses. It won't do for the priest to have a shepherdess, for the sake of a good example. If the bachelor chooses to have one, the world's his oyster."

"God bless me, Sancho my friend!" said Don Quixote. "What a life we shall lead! What shawms[4] and Zamoran gaitas[5] shall delight our ears, what tabors, tambourines, and rebecs![6] And if the albogues are heard amid this varied music, nearly all the pastoral instruments will be there."

"What are *albogues?*" asked Sancho. "I've never seen or heard of them in all my life."

"*Albogues*," said Don Quixote, "are brass plates similar to candlestick holders that when struck against one another on the hollow side make a noise which, if not very pleasing or harmonious, is not disagreeable and accords very well with the rustic notes of the gaita and tabor. The word *albogues* is Morisco, as are all those in our Spanish tongue that begin with *al-*, for example, *almohaza, almorzar, alfombra, alguacil, alhucema, almacén, alcancía*, and others of the same kind, of which there are not many more.[7] Our language has only three that are Morisco and end in *-í*, which are *borceguí, zaquizamí*,[8] and *maravedí. Alhelí* and *alfaquí*[9] show themselves to be Arabic, not only by the *al-* at the beginning as by the *-í* they end with. I mention this in passing, the chance allusion to *albogues* having reminded me of it. It will be of great assistance to us in the perfect practice of this calling that I am something of a poet, as you know, and that in addition the bachelor Samson Carrasco is an accomplished one. Of the priest I say nothing; but I will wager he has some spice of the poet in him, and no doubt Master

[4] *shawms:* The shawm (*churumbela*) is a double-reed woodwind in the oboe family.

[5] *Zamoran gaitas:* See footnote 3, page 539.

[6] *tabors ... rebecs:* The tabor is a small snare drum that hangs from a strap on the player's left arm, allowing him to drum the instrument with a stick in his right hand while he plays a flute held in his left hand. For rebecs, see footnote 6, page 81.

[7] *The word* albogues ... *not many more:* It is estimated that 8 percent of Spanish words, around four thousand, derive from Arabic, the language that the Muslim conquerors brought to the Iberian Peninsula in the eighth century. Words that begin with the prefix "al-" are generally Arabic in origin. Of the words Don Quixote names, *almorzar* (to have lunch or a snack) is the only one not drawn from Arabic. He also lists a comb for grooming horses (*almohaza*), carpet (*alfombra*), constable (*alguacil*), lavender plant (*alhucema*), warehouse (*almacén*), and money box (*alcancía*).

[8] borceguí, zaquizamí: a midcalf boot and attic, respectively. Scholars today are not as confident as Don Quixote about the Arabic origin of *borceguí.*

[9] Alhelí *and* alfaquí: respectively, the wallflower and a scholar of Islamic law.

Nicholas too, for all barbers, or most of them, are guitar players and versifiers. I will bewail my separation; you shall glorify yourself as a constant lover. The shepherd Carrascón will play the rejected one, and the priest Curiambro whatever may please him best. And so it will go as happily as the heart could wish."

To this Sancho answered, "I am so unlucky, señor, that I'm afraid the day will never come when I'll see myself in such a calling. O what polished spoons I'll make when I'm a shepherd![10] What migas,[11] custards, garlands, and shepherding knickknacks! And if I don't earn a reputation for my wisdom, at least I'll be famous for my ingenuity. My daughter Sanchica will bring our dinner out to the pasture. But watch out! She's good-looking, and there are shepherds out there with more mischief than innocence in them. I don't want her to 'come for wool and go back shorn.' True love and raw desire are just as common in the fields as in the cities, and in shepherds' huts as in royal palaces. 'Do away with the cause, and you do away with the sin.' 'If eyes don't see, hearts don't break,' and 'a hasty retreat is better than a good man's prayers.'"

"A truce to your proverbs, Sancho!" exclaimed Don Quixote. "Any one of those you have uttered would suffice to explain your meaning. Many a time have I recommended you not to be so lavish with proverbs and to exercise some moderation in delivering them, but it seems to me that 'it is only preaching in the desert.' 'My mother beats me, and I make fun of her.'"[12]

"It seems to me," said Sancho, "that your worship is like the saying that goes, 'Said the frying pan to the kettle, "Get away, blackie!"' You scold me for using proverbs, and then you string them together two at a time."

"Observe, Sancho," replied Don Quixote, "my proverbs suit the purpose, and when I quote them they fit like a ring to the finger; you bring them in by the head and shoulders, in such a way that you drag them in, rather than introduce them. If I am not mistaken, I have told you already that proverbs are short maxims drawn from the experience and observation of our wise men of old; but the proverb that is not to the purpose is a piece of nonsense and not a maxim. But enough of this—as nightfall is drawing on, let us retire some little distance from the king's highway to pass the night. God knows what is in store for us tomorrow."

They turned aside, and ate late and poorly, very much against Sancho's will, who turned over in his mind the hardships attendant upon knight-errantry in woods and forests, even though at times abundance presented itself in castles and houses, as at Don Diego de Miranda's, at the wedding of Camacho the Rich, and at Don Antonio Moreno's. He reflected, however, that it could not always be day, nor always night. And so that night he passed in sleeping, and his master in waking.

[10] *what polished spoons I'll make when I'm a shepherd:* Sancho either dreams of the wooden spoons he will carve or the food he will eat with them.

[11] *migas:* literally, "breadcrumbs", dish still common in Spain, made from fried breadcrumbs seasoned with meat, garlic, and paprika.

[12] *My mother beats me, and I make fun of her:* See footnote 3, page 669.

CHAPTER LXVIII

OF THE SWINISH ADVENTURE THAT BEFELL DON QUIXOTE

The night was rather dark, for though there was a moon in the sky it was not in a place where she could be seen; for sometimes Lady Diana goes on a stroll to the antipodes[1] and leaves the mountains all black and the valleys in darkness. Don Quixote obeyed nature so far as to sleep his first sleep, but he did not go on to the second—very different from Sancho, who never had any second, because with him sleep lasted from night till morning, in which he showed what a sound constitution and few cares he had.[2]

Don Quixote's cares kept him restless, so much so that he awoke Sancho and said to him, "I am amazed, Sancho, at the indifference of your temperament. I suppose you are made of marble or hard bronze, incapable of any emotion or feeling whatever. I lie awake while you sleep, I weep while you sing, I am faint with fasting while you are sluggish with a full belly. It is the duty of good servants to share the sufferings and feel the sorrows of their masters, if it be only for the sake of appearances. See the calmness of the night, the solitude of our surroundings, inviting us to break our slumber and keep watch. Rise as you live, and retire a little distance, and with a good heart and cheerful courage give yourself three or four hundred lashes that they may be accounted to Dulcinea's disenchantment. This I earnestly beg of you, for I have no desire to come to blows with you a second time, as I know you have a heavy hand. As soon as you have laid them on we will pass the rest of the night, I singing my separation, you your constancy, making the first beginning of the pastoral life we are to follow in our village."

"Señor," replied Sancho, "I'm no monk to get up out of the middle of my sleep and scourge myself, and I certainly don't think that a fellow can go from the pain of whipping to the other extreme of making music. Let me sleep, your worship, and stop harassing me about whipping myself, or else you'll make me swear never to touch a hair of my shirt, let alone my flesh."

[1] *Lady Diana goes on a stroll to the antipodes:* The moon, of which Diana is goddess, is in the antipodes when it is on the far side of the earth.

[2] *Don Quixote obeyed . . . few cares he had:* Biphasic sleep, the practice of sleeping in two shifts, was the norm in pre-industrial Europe. The first sleep lasted from some time after sunset until around midnight, when people would awaken to do chores, socialize, or engage in religious devotion. After a couple hours of activity, they returned to bed and slept until sunrise, the second sleep. In this scene, Don Quixote and Sancho depart from the norm, each in his own way.

"O hard heart!" cried Don Quixote. "O pitiless squire! O bread ill-bestowed and favors ill-acknowledged, both those I have done and those I mean to do for you! Because of me you have seen yourself a governor, and because of me you see yourself in immediate expectation of being a count or obtaining some other equivalent title, for I—*post tenebras spero lucem*."[3]

"I don't know what that is," said Sancho. "All I know is that so long as I'm asleep I have neither fear nor hope, trouble nor glory. Blessings on him that invented sleep, the cloak that covers over all a man's thoughts, the food that removes hunger, the drink that drives away thirst, the fire that warms the cold, the cold that tempers the heat, and, to conclude, the universal coin with which everything is bought, the weight and balance that makes the shepherd equal with the king and the fool with the wise man. Sleep, I have heard say, has only one fault—that it is like death. For between a sleeping man and a dead man there is very little difference."

"Never have I heard you speak so elegantly as now, Sancho," said Don Quixote, "from which I begin to see the truth of the proverb you sometimes quote, 'Not with whom you are bred, but with whom you are fed.'"

"By my life, my master," said Sancho, "I'm not the one stringing together proverbs now. They drop in pairs from your worship's mouth faster than from mine. There's only one difference between mine and yours: yours are well-timed and mine are untimely. Either way, they're all proverbs."

At this point they became aware of a harsh, indistinct noise that seemed to spread through all the valleys around. Don Quixote stood up and laid his hand upon his sword; Sancho crouched under Dapple and put the bundle of armor on one side of him and the donkey's packsaddle on the other, in fear and trembling as great as Don Quixote's excitement. Each instant the noise increased and came nearer to the two terrified men—or at least to one, for as to the other, his courage is known to all.

The fact of the matter was that a group of men were taking some six hundred pigs to sell at a fair and were on their way with them at that hour. So great was the noise the pigs made and their grunting and snorting, that they deafened Don Quixote and Sancho's ears, and they could not make out what it was. The widespread grunting drove came on in a surging mass, and without showing any respect for Don Quixote's dignity or Sancho's, passed right over the pair of them, demolishing Sancho's entrenchments, and not only upsetting Don Quixote but sweeping Rocinante off his feet into the bargain. With the barrage of unclean beasts bearing down upon them, packsaddle and armor, Dapple and Rocinante, Sancho and Don Quixote were left trampled on the ground and in disarray.

Sancho got up as well as he could and begged his master to give him his sword, saying he wanted to kill half a dozen of those exceedingly rude swine, for he had by this time realized what they were.

[3] post tenebras spero lucem: Latin, "After darkness I await the light" (Job 17:12 in the Vulgate). The motto was adopted by Juan de la Cuesta, Cervantes' publisher, and appears on the title pages of both the 1605 and 1615 *Don Quixote* novels.

"Let them be, my friend," said Don Quixote. "This insult is the penalty of my sin, and it is the righteous punishment of Heaven that jackals should devour a vanquished knight, that wasps should sting him, and swine trample him under foot."

"I suppose it's also the punishment of Heaven," said Sancho, "that flies should bite the squires of vanquished knights, and lice feast on them, and hunger assault them. If we squires were the sons of the knights we serve—or their very near relations—it would be no wonder if we were afflicted for their misdeeds down to the fourth generation.[4] But what do the Panzas have to do with the Quixotes? In any event, let's lie down again and sleep what little of the night there's left. God will send us dawn and everything will be all right."

"Sleep, Sancho," returned Don Quixote, "for you were born to sleep as I was born to watch. During the time that remains until dawn I will give free rein to my thoughts, and unburden them in a little madrigal that, unknown to you, I composed in my head last night."

"I would wager," said Sancho, "that not too many thoughts are needed to write poems. Let your worship versify as much as you like and I'll sleep as much as I can."

Without further delay, taking as much of the ground as he desired, he curled up and fell into a sound sleep, undisturbed by bonds, debts, or troubles of any kind. Don Quixote, propped up against the trunk of a beech or a cork tree (for Cide Hamete does not specify what kind of tree it was) sang in this strain to the accompaniment of his own sighs:

When in my mind
I muse, O Love, upon thy cruelty,
To death I flee,
In hope therein the end of all to find.

But drawing near
That welcome haven in my sea of woe,
Such joy I know,
That life revives, and still I linger here.

Thus life doth slay,
And death again to life restoreth me;
Strange destiny,
That deals with life and death as with a play![5]

He accompanied each verse with many sighs and not a few tears, just like one whose heart was pierced with grief at his defeat and his separation from Dulcinea.

At length daylight came, and the sun struck Sancho's eyes with its beams. He awoke, shook off his sleep, and stretched his lazy limbs, and seeing the havoc the

[4] *down to the fourth generation:* See, e.g., Exodus 34:7; Deuteronomy 5:9.

[5] *When in my mind . . . death as with a play:* Don Quixote recites a Spanish adaptation of a poem from *Gli Asolani* (1505), by the Italian courtier Pietro Bembo.

pigs had made with his provisions he cursed the drove—and more besides. The two of them then resumed their journey.

As evening closed in, they saw coming toward them some ten men on horseback and four or five on foot. Don Quixote's heart beat quick and Sancho's quailed with fear, for the men approaching them carried lances and bucklers, and were prepared for battle. Don Quixote turned to Sancho and said, "If I could make use of my weapons, and my promise had not tied my hands, I would count this host that comes against us as cakes and fancy bread. But perhaps it may prove something different from what we apprehend."

The men on horseback now approached and, raising their lances, surrounded Don Quixote in silence, pointing them at his back and breast and menacing him with death. One of those on foot, putting his finger to his lips as a sign to him to be silent, seized Rocinante's bridle and drew him off the road. The others drove Sancho and Dapple before them, all maintaining a strange silence, and followed in the steps of the one who led Don Quixote. Two or three times Don Quixote attempted to ask where they were taking him and what they wanted, but the instant he began to open his lips they threatened to close them with the points of their lances. Sancho fared the same way, for the moment he seemed about to speak one of those on foot punched him with a goad, and Dapple likewise, as if he too wanted to talk.

Night set in, they quickened their pace, and the fears of the two prisoners grew greater, especially as they heard themselves assailed with—

"Get on, you troglodytes!"[6]
"Silence, you barbarians!"
"March, you cannibals!"
"No murmuring, you Scythians!"[7]
"Don't open your eyes, you murderous Polyphemes,[8] you bloodthirsty lions!"

And names similar to these with which their captors harassed the ears of the wretched master and man.

Sancho went along saying to himself, "Us tortoise eyes? Us barbers and cannonballs? I don't like these names at all. 'It's in a bad wind our grain is being winnowed.'[9] 'Misfortune is raining down on us like sticks on a dog.' I hope these ugly names are the worst of this adventure."

Don Quixote rode completely dazed, unable with the aid of all his wits to make out what could be the meaning of these abusive names they called them. The only conclusion he could arrive at was that there was no good to be hoped for and much evil to be feared. About an hour after midnight, they reached a

[6] *troglodytes:* brutes.

[7] *Scythians:* See footnote 23, page 130.

[8] *Polyphemes:* Polyphemus was a cyclops from Greek mythology.

[9] *It's in a bad wind our grain is being winnowed:* In a whirlwind or gust, it's difficult to separate the wheat and chaff.

castle, which Don Quixote saw at once was the duke's, where they had been but a short time before.

"Good God!" he cried when he recognized the mansion. "What does this mean? It is all courtesy and good manners in this house. But with the defeated, good turns into evil, and evil into worse."

They entered the main courtyard of the castle and found it decorated and outfitted in a style that added to their amazement and doubled their fears, as will be seen in the following chapter.

CHAPTER LXIX

OF THE STRANGEST AND MOST EXTRAORDINARY ADVENTURE THAT BEFELL DON QUIXOTE IN THE WHOLE COURSE OF THIS GREAT HISTORY

The horsemen dismounted, and together with the men on foot, they lifted up Sancho and Don Quixote without a moment's delay and carried them into the courtyard. All around there were burning nearly a hundred torches fixed in sockets, besides some five hundred lamps in the corridors, so that in spite of the night, which was quite dark, the lack of daylight was unnoticeable. In the middle of the court was a bier, raised about two yards above the ground and covered completely by an immense canopy of black velvet. On the steps all around it, white wax candles burned in more than a hundred silver candlesticks. Upon the bier was seen the dead body of a damsel so lovely that by her beauty she made death itself look beautiful. She lay with her head resting upon a brocaded cushion and crowned with a garland of various sweet-smelling flowers. Her hands were crossed upon her breast, and between them rested a branch of a yellow victory palm.[1]

On one side of the courtyard was erected a stage, and upon two chairs there were seated two people, who, with crowns on their heads and scepters in their hands, appeared to be kings of some kind, whether real or mock ones. By the side of this stage, which was reached by steps, were two other chairs on which the men carrying the prisoners seated Don Quixote and Sancho, all in silence, and by signs giving them to understand that they too were to be silent—which, however, they would have been without any signs, for their amazement at all they saw held them tongue-tied.

And now two people of distinction—who were at once recognized by Don Quixote as his hosts the duke and duchess—ascended the stage attended by a great entourage and seated themselves on two sumptuous chairs close to what appeared to be the two kings. Who would not have been amazed at this? Nor was this all, for Don Quixote realized that the dead body on the bier was that of the fair Altisidora. As the duke and duchess mounted the stage, Don Quixote and Sancho rose and made them a profound obeisance, which they returned by bowing their heads slightly.

[1] *victory palm:* In Christian iconography, the palm is a symbol of virginity, a victory palm because the bearer has conquered temptation.

An official then came over to them and, approaching Sancho, threw over him a robe of black buckram painted all over with flames of fire. And taking off his cap, he put upon his head a coroza, such as those wear who have been sentenced by the Holy Office.[2] The official whispered in his ear that if he dared open his lips, they would either gag him or take his life. Sancho surveyed himself from head to foot and saw himself all ablaze with flames; but as they did not burn him, he did not care two cents for them. He took off the coroza, and seeing it painted with demons he put it on again, saying to himself, "Well, so far the flames haven't burned me, and the demons haven't carried me off." Don Quixote surveyed him too, and though fear had gotten the better of his faculties, he could not help smiling to see the figure Sancho made.

And now as if from underneath the bier there arose a low sweet sound of flutes, which, coming unbroken by human voice (for there silence itself kept silence), had a soft and soothing effect. All of a sudden there appeared beside the pillow of the apparently dead body a fair youth in a toga, who, to the accompaniment of a harp that he himself played, sang in a sweet and clear voice these two stanzas:

While fair Altisidora, who the sport
  Of cold Don Quixote's cruelty hath been,
Returns to life, and in this magic court
  The dames in sables come to grace the scene,
And while her matrons all in seemly sort
  My lady robes in baize and bombazine,[3]
Her beauty and her sorrows will I sing
With defter pick than touched the Thracian string.[4]

But not in life alone, methinks, to me
  Belongs the office; Lady, when my tongue
Is cold in death, believe me, unto thee
  My voice shall raise its tributary song.
My soul, from this strait prison house set free,
  As o'er the Stygian lake[5] it floats along,
Thy praises singing still shall hold its way,
And make the waters of oblivion stay.[6]

At this point one of the two that looked like kings exclaimed, "Enough, enough, divine singer! It would be an endless task to put before us now the death

[2] *threw over him a robe . . . by the Holy Office:* Sancho's outfit recalls the penitential garments of those condemned by the Inquisition: the *sambenito* (black scapular painted with flames or demons) and the *coroza* (conical hat, often painted to match the *sambenito*).

[3] *baize and bombazine:* coarse fabrics, the latter associated with mourning.

[4] *Thracian string:* Orpheus, the musician who charmed creatures from Olympus to Hades, was from Thrace.

[5] *Stygian lake:* Souls must cross the Styx on their way to Hades.

[6] *But not in life alone . . . waters of oblivion stay:* This octave comes from Garcilaso de la Vega's *Third Eclogue*.

and the charms of the peerless Altisidora, not dead as the ignorant world imagines, but living in the voice of fame and in the penance which Sancho Panza, here present, must undergo to restore her to the long-lost light. For this reason, O Rhadamanthus, you who sit in judgment with me in the murky caverns of Dis,[7] who knows all that the inscrutable fates have decreed regarding what must be done to revive this damsel, declare these things at once so that the happiness we look forward to from her restoration be no longer delayed."

No sooner had Minos, Rhadamanthus' fellow judge, said this, than Rhadamanthus rising up announced:

"Hear ye, officials of this house, high and low, great and small! Approach one and all and imprint upon Sancho's face twenty-four smacks, and give him twelve pinches and six pin pricks in the back and arms. For upon this ceremony depends the restoration of Altisidora."

On hearing this Sancho broke silence and cried out, "By all that's good, I'll as soon let my face be smacked or handled as turn Moor. On my life, what has pawing my face got to do with this damsel's resurrection? 'The old lady took a fancy to the chard ...'[8] They enchant Dulcinea, and whip me to disenchant her. Altisidora dies of ailments God was pleased to send her, and to bring her to life again they have to give me twenty-four smacks, poke holes in my body with pins, and bruise my arms with pinches! Try those jokes on my brother-in-law. 'I'm an old dog, and I know one call from another.'"

"You shall die!" exclaimed Rhadamanthus in a loud voice. "Relent, you tiger! Humble yourself, proud Nimrod![9] Suffer and be silent! No impossibilities are asked of you. It is not for you to inquire into the difficulties in this matter. Smacked you must be, pricked you shall see yourself, and with pinches you must be made to howl. Heed these words, o servants, and obey my orders; or by the word of an honest man, you shall see the end you were born for."

At this some six dueñas, advancing across the court, made their appearance in procession, one after the other, four of them with spectacles, and all with their right hands uplifted, revealing four fingers' width of their forearms to make their hands look longer, as is the fashion nowadays. No sooner had Sancho caught sight of them than, bellowing like a bull, he exclaimed, "I would gladly let myself be manhandled by all the world, but allow dueñas to touch me? Never! Scratch my face, like they did to my master in this very castle. Run my body through with sharpened daggers. Pinch my arms with red-hot pincers. I'll bear it all in patience to serve these ladies and gentlemen. But I won't let dueñas touch me, not even if the devil were carrying me away!"

[7] *O Rhadamanthus ... of Dis:* In Greek mythology, the demigod Rhadamanthus, along with his brother Minos, judged the dead. Dis, originally a name for Pluto, came to refer to his realm in the underworld. On Dis, footnote 5, page 629.

[8] *The old lady took a fancy to the chard ... :* "... and left not a leaf, soft or hard." Sancho employs the saying to criticize the appetite that others have to satisfy themselves at his expense.

[9] *Nimrod:* hunter descended from Noah (Genesis 10:8–9). According to tradition, he oversaw the construction of the Tower of Babel, and his name became synonymous with God-defying hubris.

Here Don Quixote, too, broke silence, saying to Sancho, "Have patience, my son, and gratify these noble people. Give all thanks to Heaven that it has infused such virtue into your person, that by your sufferings you can disenchant the enchanted and restore to life the dead."

The dueñas were now close to Sancho, and he, having become more docile and reasonable, settling himself well in his chair presented his face and beard to the first, who gave him a smack very sharply delivered, and then made him a low curtsey.

"Less politeness and less lotion, señora dueña," said Sancho. "By God, your hands smell like vinegar-wash."[10]

To summarize, all of the dueñas smacked him, and several others of the household pinched him; but what he could not stand was being pricked by pins. Clearly out of patience, he started up from his chair and, seizing a lighted torch that stood near him, fell upon the dueñas and the whole set of his tormentors, exclaiming, "Begone, you ministers of hell! I'm not made of bronze not to feel these bizarre tortures."

At that moment Altisidora, who was probably tired of having been lying on her back so long, turned on her side. Upon seeing this, the bystanders cried out almost with one voice, "Altisidora is alive! Altisidora lives!"

Rhadamanthus ordered Sancho to set aside his wrath, as the object they had in view had now been attained. When Don Quixote saw Altisidora move, he went on his knees to Sancho saying to him, "Now is the time, my bosom son, more than my squire, for you to give yourself some of those lashes you are bound to receive for the disenchantment of Dulcinea. Now, I say, is the time when your virtue is ripe and endowed with efficacy to work the good expected of you."

To which Sancho answered, "As I see it, that's one trick on top of another—and not honey on pancakes. A nice thing it would be for a whipping to come now, on top of pinches, smacks, and pin pricks! What's next, to tie a huge stone around my neck and toss me into a well? That's not nearly as bad as having to be the cow at the wedding to cure other people's ailments.[11] Leave me alone—or else by God I'll turn this place upside down, come what may."

Altisidora had by this time sat up on the bier, and as she did so the clarions sounded, accompanied by flutes, and the voices of all present exclaimed, "Long life to Altisidora! Long life to Altisidora!"

The duke and duchess and the kings Minos and Rhadamanthus stood up, and everyone, together with Don Quixote and Sancho, advanced to receive her and usher her off the bier. She, making as though she were recovering from a swoon, bowed her head to the duke and duchess and to the kings, and looking sideways at Don Quixote, said to him, "God forgive you, heartless knight! Because of your cruelty I have been more than a thousand years, by my reckoning, in the other world. And to you, O most compassionate squire that ever

[10] *vinegar-wash:* A popular cosmetic used to whiten the hands and face used vinegar as a base.

[11] *the cow at the wedding to cure other people's ailments:* cow slaughtered to feed the wedding guests.

sun has seen, I render thanks for the life I am now in possession of. From this day forth, friend Sancho, count as yours six blouses of mine, which I bestow upon you to make as many shirts for yourself. If they are not all quite new, at least they are all clean."

Sancho kissed her hands in gratitude, kneeling, and with the coroza in his hand. The duke commanded that they take it from him and give him back his cap and doublet and remove the flaming robe. Sancho begged the duke to let them give him the robe and hat, as he wanted to take them home as a souvenir of his extraordinary adventure. The duchess responded that she would indeed let him have them, for he was well aware what a great friend of his she was. The duke then gave orders that the courtyard should be cleared, that all should retire to their chambers, and that Don Quixote and Sancho should be conducted to their old quarters.

CHAPTER LXX

WHICH FOLLOWS CHAPTER SIXTY-NINE AND DEALS WITH MATTERS INDISPENSABLE FOR THE CLEAR UNDERSTANDING OF THIS HISTORY

Sancho slept that night in a cot in the same chamber with Don Quixote, which he would have gladly avoided if he could, for he knew very well that with questions and answers his master would not let him sleep—and he was in no mood for much talking, as he still felt the pain of his late martyrdom, which interfered with his freedom of speech. It would have been more to his taste to sleep in a hovel alone than in that luxurious chamber with company.

So well founded did his apprehension prove, and so correct were his suspicions, that scarcely had his master got into bed when he said, "What do you think of tonight's adventure, Sancho? Great and mighty is the power of coldhearted disdain, for you with your own eyes have seen Altisidora slain, not by arrows, nor by the sword, nor by any warlike weapon, nor by deadly poisons, but by the mere thought of the sternness and scorn with which I have always treated her."

"She's welcome to die as often as she wants and however she wants," said Sancho, "provided she leaves me alone, for never in my life have I made her love me or scorned her. As I've said before, I have no idea how the health of a girl like Altisidora, flightier than she is wise, has anything to do with the sufferings of Sancho Panza. It's finally becoming clear to me that there are enchanters and enchantments in the world. May God deliver me from them since I can't deliver myself. And so I beg of your worship to let me sleep and not ask me any more questions, unless you want me to throw myself out the window."

"Sleep, Sancho my friend," said Don Quixote, "if the pin pricks and pinches you have received and the smacks administered to you will allow it."

"No pain was equal to the insult of the smacks," said Sancho, "for the simple reason that it was dueñas, confound them, that gave them to me. But once more I entreat your worship to let me sleep, for sleep is relief from misery to those who are miserable when awake."

"Be it so, and God be with you," said Don Quixote.

They fell asleep, both of them, and Cide Hamete, the author of this great history, took this opportunity to relate what it was that induced the duke and duchess to contrive the elaborate plot that has been described. The bachelor Samson Carrasco, he says, not forgetting how he as the Knight of the Mirrors had been vanquished and overthrown by Don Quixote, which defeat and overthrow upset all his plans, resolved to try his hand again, hoping for better luck than he had before. And so, having learned where Don Quixote was from the page who brought the letter and present to Sancho's wife, Teresa Panza, he secured new armor and another horse, and put a white moon upon his shield; and to carry his arms he had a mule led by a peasant—not by Tom Cecial, his former squire, for fear he should be recognized by Sancho or Don Quixote.

He came to the duke's castle, and the duke informed him of the route Don Quixote had taken with the intention of being present at the jousts at Zaragoza. He told him, too, of the pranks he had played on him, and of the scheme to disenchant Dulcinea at the expense of Sancho's backside. Finally, he gave him an account of the trick Sancho had played on his master, making him believe that Dulcinea was enchanted and turned into a country wench; and of how his wife the duchess had persuaded Sancho that it was he himself who was deceived, inasmuch as Dulcinea was really enchanted. Hearing all this, the bachelor laughed not a little and marveled not only at the astuteness and simplicity of Sancho but at the length to which Don Quixote's madness went.

The duke begged of him if he found Don Quixote—whether he defeated him or not—to return that way and let him know the result. This the bachelor did. He set out in quest of Don Quixote, and not finding him at Zaragoza, he went on. How he fared has been already told. He returned to the duke's castle and told him everything: what the conditions of the combat were and how Don Quixote, like a loyal knight-errant, was now returning to keep his promise of retiring to his village for a year, by which time, said the bachelor, he might perhaps be cured of his madness. For that was the object that had led him to adopt these disguises, as it was a sad thing for a gentleman as intelligent as Don Quixote to lose his wits. With this he took his leave of the duke and went home to his village to wait there for Don Quixote, who was coming after him.

Thereupon the duke seized the opportunity of playing this prank on him, so much did he enjoy everything connected with Sancho and Don Quixote. He had the roads about the castle far and near—everywhere he thought Don Quixote was likely to pass on his return—occupied by large numbers of his servants on foot and on horseback, who were to bring him to the castle, by fair means or foul, if they met him. They did meet him, and sent word to the duke, who, having already settled what was to be done, as soon as he heard of his arrival, ordered the torches and lamps in the court to be lit and Altisidora to be placed on the bier with all the pomp and ceremony that has been described, the whole affair being so well arranged and acted that it differed but little from reality. (Cide Hamete adds that for his part he considers the concocters of the joke as crazy as the victims of it, and that the duke and duchess were not two fingers' breadth removed from looking like fools themselves for taking such pains to make a mockery of a pair of fools.)

Returning to this pair, one was sleeping soundly and the other lying awake occupied with his passing thoughts when daylight came to them, bringing with it the desire to rise; for the lazy down was never a delight to Don Quixote, victor or vanquished. Altisidora, brought back from death to life as Don Quixote supposed, following the designs of her lord and lady, entered the chamber crowned with the garland she had worn on the bier and in a robe of white taffeta embroidered with gold flowers, her hair flowing loose over her shoulders, and leaning upon a staff of fine black ebony. Don Quixote, disconcerted and tongue-tied by her appearance, was unable to make any show of courtesy, but instead shrank back and nearly covered himself completely with the sheets and quilt on the bed.

Altisidora seated herself on a chair at the head of the bed, and, after a deep sigh, said to him in a tender yet feeble voice, "When noblewomen and modest maidens trample honor under foot, and loosen their tongues to break through every impediment, publishing abroad the inmost secrets of their hearts, they find themselves in the cruelest of circumstances. Such a one am I, Señor Don Quixote of La Mancha, crushed, conquered, love-smitten, but yet patient under suffering and virtuous, and so much so that my heart broke with grief and I lost my life. For the last two days I have been dead, slain by the thought of the cruelty with which you have treated me, obdurate knight—'O harder thou than marble to my pleas'[1]—or at least believed to be dead by all who saw me. Had it not been that Love, taking pity on me, entrusted my recovery to the sufferings of this good squire, there I should have remained in the other world."

"Love would have been better off entrusting the sufferings to my donkey, and I would have been much obliged," said Sancho. "But tell me, señora—and may Heaven send you a tenderer lover than my master—what did you see in the other world? What goes on in hell? For of course that's where somebody who dies in despair[2] is bound for."

"To tell you the truth," said Altisidora, "I must not have died outright, for I did not go into hell. Had I gone in, it is very certain I should never have come out again, do what I might. The truth is, I came to the gate, where some dozen or so of the devils were playing tennis, all in breeches and doublets, with collars trimmed with Flemish lace, and ruffles of the same material that served them for cuffs, with four fingers' breadth of the forearms exposed to make their hands look longer. In their hands they held racquets made of fire. But what amazed me still more was that books, apparently full of wind and rubbish, served them for balls—a strange and marvelous thing. This, however, did not astonish me so much as to observe that, although with players it is usual for the winners to be glad and the losers sorry, there in that game all were growling, all were snarling, and all were cursing one another."

"That's no wonder," said Sancho, "for devils, whether they're playing or not, can never be content, win or lose."

"Very likely," said Altisidora. "But there is another thing that surprises me too—I mean, surprised me then—and that was that no ball outlasted the first throw or was of any use a second time. It was astonishing the constant succession there was of books, new and old. To one of them—a brand new, well-bound one—they gave such a stroke that they knocked the guts out of it and

[1] *O harder thou than marble to my pleas*: from Garcilaso de la Vega's *First Eclogue*.

[2] *in despair*: See footnote 13, page 96.

scattered the pages about. 'Take a look at what book that is,' said one devil to another. The other replied, 'It's the *Second Part of the History of Don Quixote of La Mancha*, not by Cide Hamete, the original author, but by an Aragonese somebody who claims to be from Tordesillas.' 'Get it away from me,' said the first, 'into the depths of hell and out of my sight.' 'Is it that bad?' said the other. 'It's so bad,' said the first, 'that if I had set about deliberately to make it worse, I could not have done it.' They then went on with their game, knocking other books about. I, having heard them mention the name of Don Quixote, whom I love and adore so, took care to retain this vision in my memory."

"A vision it must have been, beyond doubt," said Don Quixote, "for I have no equal in the world. This history has been going about here for some time from hand to hand, but it does not stay long in any, for everyone gives it a taste of his foot. I am not disturbed to hear that I am wandering in a fantastic shape in the darkness of the pit or in the daylight above, for I am not the one that history treats of. If the history is good, faithful, and true, it will live for ages; but if it is bad, the journey from its birth to its burial will not be a long one."

Altisidora was about to proceed with her complaint against Don Quixote, when he said to her, "I have several times told you, señora, that it grieves me you should have set your affections upon me, as from mine they can only receive gratitude, but no return. I was born to belong to Dulcinea del Toboso, and the fates, if there are any, dedicated me to her. To suppose that any other beauty can take the place she occupies in my heart is to suppose an impossibility. This frank declaration should suffice to make you retire within the bounds of your modesty, for no one can bind himself to do what is impossible."

Hearing this, Altisidora, with a show of anger and agitation, exclaimed, "On your life, Don Codfish, you have a soul made of mortar; your heart is like the pit of a date! You are more stubborn and hard-headed than a country bumpkin who thinks he knows what he's talking about. If I ever come at you, I'll tear your eyes out. Do you really believe, Don Defeated, Don Beaten-with-Sticks, that I died for your sake? All that you've seen tonight has been make-believe. I'm not the kind of woman to let my fingernail suffer for a camel like you, much less die!"

"That I can well believe," said Sancho. "All that stuff about lovers pining to death is ridiculous. They may talk about it, but as for doing it—tell that to Judas!"

While they were talking, the poet-musician who had sung the two stanzas recently noted entered the room, and making a profound obeisance to Don Quixote said, "Will your worship, sir knight, consider retaining me in the number of your most faithful servants? I have long been a great admirer of yours, both because of your fame and because of your achievements."

"Please tell me who your worship is," replied Don Quixote, "so that my courtesy may be equal to your merits." The young man replied that he was the musician and poet of the night before. "Truly," said Don Quixote, "your worship has a most excellent voice; but what you sang did not seem to me very much to the purpose, for what have Garcilaso's stanzas to do with this lady's death?"

"Don't let that surprise you," returned the musician. "With the unschooled poets of our age, the way for everyone is to write as he pleases and pilfer where he chooses, whether it is appropriate to the matter or not. And nowadays there is no nonsense they sing or write that is not chalked up to poetic license."

Don Quixote was about to reply, but was prevented by the duke and duchess, who came in to see him. With them there followed a long and delightful conversation, in the course of which Sancho said so many witty and insightful things that he left the duke and duchess wondering not only at his simplicity but at his astuteness. Don Quixote begged their permission to take his departure that same day, inasmuch as for a vanquished knight like himself it was fitter he should live in a pigsty than in a royal palace. They gave it very readily, and the duchess asked him if Altisidora was in his good graces.

He replied, "Señora, let me tell your ladyship that this damsel's ailment comes entirely of idleness. The cure for it is honest and constant employment. She herself has told me that lace is worn in hell. As she must know how to make it, let it never be out of her hands. When she is occupied in turning the needle to and fro, the image or images of what she loves will not turn to and fro in her thoughts. This is the truth, this is my opinion, and this is my advice."

"Mine too," added Sancho. "Never in all my life have I seen a lacemaker that died of love. When damsels are at work, their minds are more set on finishing their tasks than on thinking about love. I speak from my own experience. When I'm digging, I never think of my old woman—I mean my Teresa Panza, whom I love better than my own eyelashes."

"You say well, Sancho," said the duchess. "I will take care that my Altisidora employs herself henceforward in needlework of some sort, for she is extremely skilled at it."

"There is no need to resort to that remedy, señora," said Altisidora. "The mere thought of the cruelty with which this feather-headed villain has treated me will suffice to blot him from my memory without any other device. With your highness' leave I will retire, not to have before my eyes—I won't say his woeful countenance—but his ugly, abominable face!"

"That reminds me of the common saying, 'He who heaps scorn is nearest to forgive,'" said the duke.

Altisidora then, pretending to wipe away her tears with a handkerchief, made an obeisance to her master and mistress and left the room.

"I see bad luck in your future, poor damsel," said Sancho. "Bad luck I see. You've cast your lot with a soul as dry as straw and a heart as hard as oak. Had it been me, in faith, 'another rooster would have crowed for you.'"

So the conversation came to an end, and Don Quixote dressed himself and dined with the duke and duchess, and set out the same afternoon.

CHAPTER LXXI

OF WHAT PASSED BETWEEN DON QUIXOTE AND HIS SQUIRE SANCHO ON THE WAY TO THEIR VILLAGE

The vanquished and afflicted Don Quixote went along very downcast in one respect and very happy in another. His sadness arose from his defeat, and his contentment from the thought of the power that Sancho possessed, as had been proved by the resurrection of Altisidora—though it was with difficulty he could persuade himself that the love-smitten damsel had really been dead. Sancho went along anything but cheerful, for it grieved him that Altisidora had not kept her promise of giving him the blouses.

Turning this over in his mind he said to his master, "Surely, señor, I'm the most unlucky doctor in the world. There's many a physician that, after killing the sick man he was supposed to cure, demands payment for his services, even if all he's done is sign a little list of medicines that the pharmacist—not the doctor—puts together. That's how the shakedown works. With me on the other hand, somebody else's health costs me drops of blood, smacks, pinches, pin-pricks, and whippings—and nobody gives me a cent. Well, I swear by all that's good if they put another patient into my hands, they'll have to grease them for me before I do any curing. As they say, 'it's by his singing the abbot gets fed.' I'm not going to believe that Heaven has given me this power for me to be dealing it out to others free of charge."

"You're right, Sancho my friend," said Don Quixote. "Altisidora has behaved very badly in not giving you the blouses she promised; and although your power is *gratis data*[1]—as it has cost you no study whatever, any more than such study as your personal sufferings may be—I can say for myself that if you had desired payment for the lashes required to disenchant Dulcinea, I would have already paid you handsomely. I am not sure, however, whether payment will befit the cure, and I would not have the reward interfere with the medicine. Nonetheless, I doubt there would be anything lost by trying it. Consider how much you would like, Sancho, and whip yourself at once. You may pay yourself in cash with your own hand, since you hold onto my money."

At this proposal Sancho opened his eyes and his ears a palm's breadth wide, and in his heart very readily agreed to whip himself. He said to his master, "Very

[1] gratis data: Latin, "given free".

well then, señor, I will consent to gratify your worship's wishes if I'm to benefit by it. My love for my wife and children leaves me no choice but to look selfish. Let your worship say how much you will pay me for each lash I give myself."

"If, Sancho," replied Don Quixote, "your recompense were consistent with the importance and nature of the cure, the treasures of Venice, indeed, the mines of Potosí,[2] would be insufficient to pay you. See what you have of mine, and put a price on each lash."

"In all," said Sancho, "there are three thousand three hundred, and then some. Of these, I've given myself about five; the rest remain. Let's count the five against the remainder and stick with the three thousand three hundred. At a quarter real apiece—I won't take less, though the whole world should order me—that makes three thousand three hundred quarter reals. The three thousand are one thousand five hundred half reals, which make seven hundred fifty reals. And the three hundred make a hundred fifty half reals, which come to seventy-five reals, which added to the seven hundred fifty make eight hundred twenty-five reals in all.[3] I will deduct these from what I have belonging to your worship, and I'll return home rich and content, though well whipped, for 'there's no catching trout ...'[4]—but I say no more."

"O blessed Sancho! O dear Sancho!" exclaimed Don Quixote. "How we shall be bound to serve you, Dulcinea and I, all the days of our lives that Heaven may grant us! If she returns to her former self—and it cannot be but that she will—her misfortune will have been good fortune, and my defeat a most happy triumph. Now tell me Sancho, when will you begin the scourging? If you will make short work of it, I will add a hundred reals to the bargain."

"When?" replied Sancho. "This very night without fail. Let your worship arrange for us to spend it under the stars, and I'll lay into my hide."

Night, longed for by Don Quixote with the greatest eagerness in the world, came at last, though it seemed to him that the wheels of Apollo's chariot had broken down and that the day was drawing itself out longer than usual—just as is the case with lovers, for whom the passing hours never keep pace with their desires. They made their way at length among some pleasant trees that stood a little distance from the road, and there leaving unoccupied Rocinante's saddle and Dapple's packsaddle, they stretched themselves on the green grass and dined off Sancho's provisions. Sancho then made a sturdy but flexible whip out of Dapple's halter and bridle and retreated about twenty paces from his master among some beech trees.

[2] *the treasures of Venice, indeed, the mines of Potosí:* The Republic of Venice was one of the wealthiest states in Europe due to its extensive Mediterranean commerce. The mines of Potosí, Bolivia, were the source of much of the silver that enriched the Spanish Empire. To this day, to say in Spanish that something is worth a *potosí* is to say that it is worth a fortune.

[3] *eight hundred twenty-five reals in all:* Sancho's math is impeccable; 825 reals would be the equivalent of about fifty-two escudos. As a point of comparison, Ricote offers Sancho two hundred escudos to help him dig up his family treasure (see p. 738).

[4] *there's no catching trout ...:* "... in dry breeches." ("No pain, no gain.")

Don Quixote, seeing him march off with such determination and energy, said to him, "Take care, my friend, not to cut yourself to pieces. Allow the lashes to wait their turn, and do not be in so great a hurry that you run out of breath midway. I mean, do not beat yourself so harshly that you cause your life to fail you before you've reached the desired number. So that you may not lose by a card too many or too few, I will station myself apart and count on my rosary here the lashes you give yourself. May Heaven help you as your good intention deserves."

"'Pledges don't distress a good payer,'" said Sancho. "I intend to lay it on in a way that hurts without killing me. I figure that's where the essence of this miracle is."

He then stripped himself from the waist upwards, and snatching up the whip he began to lay into himself and Don Quixote to count the lashes. He might have given himself six or eight when he began to realize that this was no small joke and that its price very low. Holding back for a moment, he told his master that he had been rushed into a bad deal. Each of those lashes, he said, ought to be paid for at the rate of half a real instead of a quarter.

"Go on, Sancho my friend, and be not disheartened," said Don Quixote, "for I double the stakes on the price."

"In that case," said Sancho, "let it be in God's hand, and let the lashes come raining down!"

But the rascal no longer laid them on his back. He laid them on the trees instead, and with such groans every now and then that one would have thought at each of them his soul was being plucked up by the roots.

Don Quixote, touched to the heart, and fearing he might make an end of himself, and that through Sancho's imprudence he might fall short of his own object, said to him, "As you live, my friend, let the matter rest where it is, for the remedy seems to me a very rough one, and it will be well to have patience. 'Zamora was not won in an hour.' If I have not counted wrong, you have given yourself over a thousand lashes. That is enough for the present. 'The donkey,' to use a homely expression, 'bears the load, but not the overload.'"

"No, no, señor," replied Sancho. "Let it never be said of me, 'The money paid, the arm broken.'[5] Go back a little farther, your worship, and let me give myself at least a thousand lashes more. If I can go at it a couple more times like this, we'll have finished off the order, and there will even be fabric to spare."

"As you are in such a willing mood," said Don Quixote, "may Heaven aid you. Lay on and I'll retire."

Sancho returned to his task with so much zeal that he soon had the bark stripped off several trees, such was the severity with which he whipped himself. One time, raising his voice, and giving a beech a tremendous lashing, he cried out, "Here dies Samson, and all with him!"[6]

[5] *The money paid, the arm broken:* refers to being paid for a job and then refusing to do it on the pretext of a broken arm.

[6] *Here dies Samson, and all with him:* Loose adaptation of Judges 16:30, when Samson brought down the temple of Dagon on himself and the Philistines.

At the sound of his piteous cry and of the stroke of the cruel lash, Don Quixote ran to him at once, and seizing the twisted halter that served him for a kurbash, said to him, "Heaven forbid, Sancho my friend, that to please me you should lose your life, which is needed for the support of your wife and children. Let Dulcinea wait for a better opportunity, and I will content myself with a hope soon to be realized. Have patience until you have gained fresh strength so as to finish off this business to the satisfaction of all."

"If that's what your worship wants, señor," said Sancho, "so be it. But throw your cloak over my shoulders; I'm sweating and I don't want to catch a cold. It's a risk that novice penitents run."

Don Quixote obeyed and, stripping himself, covered Sancho, who slept until the sun woke him. They then resumed their journey, which for the time being they brought to an end at a village that lay three leagues farther on. They dismounted at an inn, which Don Quixote recognized as such and did not take to be a castle with moat, turrets, portcullis, and drawbridge; for ever since he had been vanquished, he talked more rationally about everything, as will be shown presently.

They lodged him in a room on the ground floor, where in place of leather hangings there were pieces of painted serge such as they commonly use in villages. On one of them was painted by some very poor hand the Abduction of Helen, when the bold guest carried her off from Menelaus.[7] On the other was the story of Dido and Æneas, she on a high tower, as though she were signaling with half a sheet to her fugitive guest who was out at sea making his escape in a frigate or brigantine. Don Quixote noticed in the two stories that Helen did not go very reluctantly, for she had a sly smile on her face, while the fair Dido was shown shedding tears the size of walnuts.

As he looked at them, he observed, "Those two ladies were very unfortunate not to have been born in this age, and I unfortunate above all men not to have been born in theirs. Were I to have laid my hands on those gentlemen, Troy would not have been burned or Carthage destroyed, for it would have been only for me to slay Paris, and all these misfortunes would have been avoided."

"I'll bet you," said Sancho, "that before long there won't be a tavern, roadside inn, hostel, or barber shop where the story of our doings won't be found in paintings. But I'd like it painted by the hand of a better painter than the one who painted these."

"You're right, Sancho," said Don Quixote. "This painter is like Orbaneja, a painter in Úbeda,[8] who when they asked him what he was painting, would say, 'Whatever it turns out to be.' If he chanced to paint a rooster he would write under it, 'This is a rooster,' for fear they might think it was a fox. The painter or writer—for it's all the same—who published the history of this new *Don Quixote* that has come out must have been one of this sort, I think, Sancho,

[7] *when the bold guest carried her off from Menelaus:* In some accounts, Paris abducts Helen and carries her off to Troy after he meets her and falls in love with her while he is a guest in Menelaus' house.

[8] *Orbaneja, a painter in Úbeda:* Don Quixote has told this story earlier (see p. 442).

for he painted or wrote 'whatever it turns out to be.' Or perhaps he is like a poet named Mauleón that was at court some years ago, who would answer without thinking whatever he was asked. When someone asked him what *Deum de Deo* meant, he replied *Dé donde diere*.[9] But putting this aside, tell me, Sancho, have you a mind to lay on another round tonight, and would you rather have it indoors or in the open air?"

"Honestly, señor," said Sancho, "for what I'm going to give myself, it's all the same to me whether it's in a house or in the fields. That said, I think I'd like it to be among trees; for they make good company and are a wonderful aid to help me bear my pain."

"It should not be done that way, Sancho my friend," said Don Quixote. "Instead, so that you may recover strength, we must save it for our own village; for at the latest we shall get there the day after tomorrow."

Sancho said he might do as he pleased, but that for his own part he would like to finish off the business quickly before his blood cooled and while the mill was still grinding—because "in delay there's danger," and "pray hard and hammer harder," and "one *take* is better than two *I'll give you*'s," and "better a sparrow in the hand than a vulture on the wing."

"For God's sake, Sancho, no more proverbs!" exclaimed Don Quixote. "It seems to me you are becoming *sicut erat*[10] again. Speak in a plain, simple, straightforward way, as I have often told you, and 'one loaf will be worth a hundred.'"[11]

"I don't know why I have such bad luck," said Sancho, "but I can't give an answer without using a proverb, and I don't know a proverb that won't serve for an answer. But I'll try to improve if I can."

And so for the present the conversation ended.

[9] Deum de Deo ... Dé donde diere: *Deum de Deo* (Latin, "God from God", from the Nicene Creed); *Dé donde diere* (Spanish, "Strike where you can").

[10] sicut erat: *sicut erat in princpio* (Latin, "as it was in the beginning")—from the Gloria Patri.

[11] *one loaf will be worth a hundred:* "You'll be the better for it."

CHAPTER LXXII

OF HOW DON QUIXOTE AND SANCHO REACHED THEIR VILLAGE

All that day Don Quixote and Sancho remained at the inn waiting for night, the one to finish off his task of scourging in the open country, the other to see it fulfilled, for therein lay the fulfillment of his desires. Meanwhile there arrived at the inn a traveler on horseback with three or four servants, one of whom said to the man who appeared to be the master, "Here, Señor Don Álvaro Tarfe, your worship may take your siesta today. The lodgings look clean and cool."

When he heard this Don Quixote said to Sancho, "Look here, Sancho. When I was leafing through that book of the Second Part of my history, I think in passing I came upon this name of Don Álvaro Tarfe."

"Very likely," said Sancho. "We had better let him dismount. Afterwards, we can ask about it."

The gentleman dismounted, and the innkeeper gave him a room on the ground floor opposite Don Quixote's, which was adorned with painted serge hangings of the same variety. The newly arrived gentleman put on summer clothing and came out to the entrance of the inn, which was wide and cool. There he addressed Don Quixote, who was pacing up and down, asking him, "In what direction is your worship bound, gentle sir?"

"To a village near this one which is my own," replied Don Quixote. "And your worship, where are you bound for?"

"I am going to Granada, señor," said the gentleman, "to my own country."

"And a fine country it is," said Don Quixote. "But will your worship do me the favor of telling me your name, for I would wager that knowing it will be more of consequence to me than I could put into words."

"My name is Don Álvaro Tarfe," replied the traveler.

To which Don Quixote returned, "I have no doubt whatever that your worship is that Don Álvaro Tarfe who appears in print in the *Second Part of the History of Don Quixote of La Mancha*, lately printed and published by a new author."

"I am the same," replied the gentleman, "and that Don Quixote, the principal personage in the said history, was a very great friend of mine. It was I who took him away from home—or at least induced him to travel to some jousts that were to be held at Zaragoza, where I was going myself. In all truth, I showed him kindness on many an occasion and saved him from having his back touched up by the executioner because of his extreme rashness."[1]

[1] *saved him . . . because of his extreme rashness:* In chapter 8 of Avellaneda's sequel, Don Quixote is taken into custody for attempting to free a thief (who he thinks is a knight)

"Tell me, Señor Don Álvaro," said Don Quixote, "am I at all like that Don Quixote you speak of?"

"No indeed," replied the traveler, "not a bit."

"And that Don Quixote," said ours, "did he have with him a squire called Sancho Panza?"

"He did," said Don Álvaro, "but though he was known to be quite funny, I never heard him say anything that had any humor in it."

"That I can well believe," said Sancho at this, "for not everyone is born with a sense of humor. That Sancho your worship speaks of, gentle sir, must be a huge scoundrel, a bore, and a thief, all rolled into one. I am the real Sancho Panza, and I have more wisecracks in me than if they came raining down. Your worship can find out for yourself. Follow me for a year or so, and you'll discover that they fall from me at every turn. So many are they and so funny that, even though I don't know what I'm saying half the time, I make everybody in earshot break out into laughter. And the real Don Quixote of La Mancha, the famous, the valiant, the wise, the lover, the righter of wrongs, the guardian of minors and orphans, the protector of widows, the slayer of damsels,[2] he who has for his sole mistress the peerless Dulcinea del Toboso, is this gentleman before you, my master. All other Don Quixotes and all other Sancho Panzas are dreams and hoaxes."

"By God, I believe it!" said Don Álvaro. "You have uttered more wisecracks, my friend, in the few words you have spoken than the other Sancho Panza in all the words I ever heard from him—and they were not a few. He was more greedy than well-spoken, and more dull than funny. I'm convinced that the enchanters who persecute Don Quixote the Good have been trying to persecute me with Don Quixote the Bad. With all that, I don't know what to say, for I am ready to swear I left him shut up in the Casa del Nuncio in Toledo,[3] yet here another Don Quixote turns up, though a very different one from mine."

"I don't know whether I am good," said Don Quixote, "but I can safely say that I am not 'the Bad.' To prove it, let me tell you, Señor Don Álvaro Tarfe, that I have never in my life been to Zaragoza; instead, when it was told me that this imaginary Don Quixote had been present at the jousts in that city, I declined to enter it, in order to drag his falsehood before the face of the world. And so I went on straight to Barcelona, the treasure house of courtesy, haven of strangers, refuge of the poor, home of the valiant, champion of the wronged, ideal setting for lifelong friendships, and city unrivaled in location and beauty. And though the adventures that befell me there are not by any means matters of enjoyment, but rather of regret, I do not regret them, simply because I have seen it. In a word, Señor Don Álvaro Tarfe, I am Don Quixote of La Mancha, the one touted by fame, and not the unlucky one that has attempted to usurp my name and deck

---

on his way to be flogged. Don Álvaro Tarfe rescues Don Quixote from having a similar sentence of flogging carried out on him.

[2] *slayer of damsels:* presumably, Altisidora.

[3] *Casa del Nuncio in Toledo:* insane asylum founded by papal nuncio in the century.

himself out in my ideas. I entreat your worship by your duty as a gentleman to be so good as to make a declaration before the magistrate of this village that you never in all your life saw me until now, and that neither am I the Don Quixote in the published *Second Part*, nor this Sancho Panza, my squire, the one your worship knew."

"That I will do most willingly," replied Don Álvaro, "though it amazes me to find two Don Quixotes and two Sancho Panzas at once, as much alike in name as they differ in demeanor. Again I declare that I did not see what I saw, and that what happened to me did not happen."

"No doubt your worship is enchanted, like my lady Dulcinea del Toboso," said Sancho. "Would to heaven your disenchantment depended on me giving myself another three thousand and something lashes like what I'm giving myself for her, for I'd lay them on free of charge."

"I don't understand that part about the lashes," said Don Álvaro. Sancho replied that it was a long story to tell, but he would tell him if they happened to be traveling the same road.

By now dinnertime arrived, and Don Quixote and Don Álvaro dined together. The magistrate of the village came by chance into the inn together with a notary, and Don Quixote laid a petition before him, showing that it was requisite for his rights that Don Álvaro Tarfe, the gentleman there present, should make a declaration before him that he did not know Don Quixote of La Mancha, also there present, and that he was not the one that was in print in a history entitled *Second Part of Don Quixote of La Mancha*, by one Avellaneda of Tordesillas. The magistrate then put it in legal form, and the affidavit was made with all the formalities required in such cases. At this Don Quixote and Sancho were in high delight—as if such an affidavit was of any great importance to them, and as if their words and deeds did not plainly show the difference between the two Don Quixotes and the two Sanchos. Many civilities and offers of service were exchanged by Don Álvaro and Don Quixote, in the course of which the great Manchegan displayed such good taste that he disabused Don Álvaro of the error he was under. Don Álvaro, for his part, felt convinced he must have been enchanted, now that he had been brought in contact with two such opposite Don Quixotes.

Evening came, they set out from the village, and after about half a league two roads branched off, one leading to Don Quixote's village, the other the road Don Álvaro was to follow. In this short interval Don Quixote told him of his unfortunate defeat and of Dulcinea's enchantment and the remedy, all of which threw Don Álvaro into fresh amazement. Embracing Don Quixote and Sancho, he went his way, and Don Quixote went his.

Don Quixote spent the night among trees again in order to give Sancho an opportunity of working out his penance, which he did in the same fashion as the night before—at the expense of the bark of the beech trees much more than of his back, of which he took such good care that the lashes would not have knocked off a fly had one landed on him. The duped Don Quixote did not miss a single stroke of the count, and he found that together with those of the night before they made up three thousand twenty-nine. The sun apparently had got up early to witness the sacrifice, and with his light they resumed their journey, discussing Don Álvaro's deception, and saying how well done it was to have taken his declaration before a magistrate with all the appropriate formalities.

That day and night they traveled on, nor did anything worth mentioning happen to them, unless it was that in the course of the night Sancho finished off his task, at which Don Quixote was beyond measure joyful. He watched for daylight, to see if along the road he would cross paths with his now disenchanted lady Dulcinea. As he pursued his journey, there was no woman he met that he did not approach to see if she was Dulcinea del Toboso, as he held it absolutely certain that Merlin's promises could not fail.

Full of these thoughts and longings, they ascended a hill from which they could see their village. When he caught his first glimpse of it, Sancho fell on his knees exclaiming, "Open your eyes, longed-for home, and see how your son Sancho Panza comes back to you, if not very rich, very well whipped. Open your arms and receive, too, your son Don Quixote, who, if he comes vanquished by the arm of another, comes victor over himself, which, as he himself has told me, is the greatest victory anyone can desire. With full pockets do I return to you, for 'though I was well whipped, at least I rode in style.'"[4]

"Have done with these fooleries," said Don Quixote. "Let us push on straight and get home, where we may give free range to our fancies and settle our plans for our future pastoral life."

With this they descended the slope and directed their steps to their village.

[4] *though I was well whipped, at least I rode in style:* See footnote 4, page 635.

CHAPTER LXXIII

OF THE OMENS THAT MET DON QUIXOTE AS HE ENTERED HIS VILLAGE, ALONG WITH OTHER INCIDENTS THAT EMBELLISH AND GIVE CREDIT TO THIS GREAT HISTORY

At the entrance of the village, so says Cide Hamete, Don Quixote saw two boys arguing on the village threshing floor, one of whom said to the other, "Take it easy, Periquillo. You'll never see it again as long as you live."

Don Quixote heard this, and he said to Sancho, "Did you not hear, friend, what that boy said, 'You shall never see it again as long as you live'?"

"Well," said Sancho, "what does it matter what the boy said?"

"What does it matter?" said Don Quixote. "Do you not see that, applied to the object of my desires, the words mean that I am never more to see Dulcinea?"

Sancho was about to answer, when he was distracted with the sight of a rabbit that was tearing across the plain pursued by several greyhounds and hunters. In its terror it ran to take shelter and hide itself under Dapple. Sancho caught it alive and presented it to Don Quixote, who was saying, "*Malum signum, malum signum!*[1] A rabbit flees, greyhounds chase it, Dulcinea does not appear."

"Your worship's a strange man," said Sancho. "Let's assume that this rabbit is Dulcinea, and these greyhounds chasing it the malignant enchanters who turned her into a country wench. She runs off, I catch her and put her into your worship's hands, and you hold her in your arms and cherish her. What bad sign is that, or what ill omen is there to be found here?"

The two boys who had been arguing came over to look at the rabbit, and Sancho asked one of them what their disagreement was about. He was answered by the one who had said, "You'll never see it again as long as you live," that he had taken a cage full of crickets from the other boy, and did not mean to give it back to him as long as he lived.[2]

Sancho took out four quartos[3] from his pocket and gave them to the boy for the cage, which he placed in Don Quixote's hands, saying, "There, señor! There are the omens broken and destroyed. They have no more to do with our affairs, to my thinking, fool as I am, than with last year's clouds. If I remember rightly,

[1] malum signum: an evil sign.

[2] *cage full of crickets from the other boy . . . he lived:* Cage (*jaula*) is feminine, which makes it grammatically possible for Don Quixote to hear "la" and think "her".

[3] *quartos:* See footnote 24, page 28.

I've heard the priest of our village say that it does not become Christians or sensible people to give any heed to these silly things. Even you yourself said the same thing to me some time ago, telling me that all Christians who believed in omens were fools. But there's no need to dwell on it more. Let's push on and go into our village."

The hunters came up and asked for their rabbit, which Don Quixote gave them. They then went on, and at the entrance of the town on a meadow they came upon the priest and the bachelor Samson Carrasco busy with their breviaries.[4] (It should be mentioned that Sancho had thrown, by way of a saddle pad, over Dapple and over the bundle of armor, the buckram robe painted with flames that they had put on him at the duke's castle the night Altisidora came back to life. He had also set the coroza on Dapple's head—the oddest transformation and decoration that ever donkey in the world underwent.) Don Quixote and Sancho were at once recognized by the priest and the bachelor, who came toward them with open arms. Don Quixote dismounted and received them with a warm embrace. The boys, with their eagle eyes, spied out the donkey's hat and came running to see it, calling out to one another, "Come here, boys, and see Sancho Panza's donkey fitted finer than Mingo,[5] and Don Quixote's horse, scrawnier than ever."

At length, flanked by the boys and accompanied by the priest and the bachelor, they made their entrance into the town. They proceeded to Don Quixote's house, at the door of which they found his housekeeper and niece, who had already received news of his arrival. News had been brought to Teresa Panza, Sancho's wife, as well. She, disheveled and half dressed, dragging Sanchica her daughter by the hand, ran out to meet her husband. But seeing him not nearly as dressed up as she thought a governor ought to be, she said to him, "How is it you come back looking like this, husband, on foot and footsore? You cut a figure more like someone ungoverned than governor."

"Hold your tongue, Teresa," said Sancho. "Sometimes there's fire but no smoke. Let's go into the house. I have wonders to tell. What's most important is that I bring money, earned by my own ingenuity and without harming a soul."

"Bring the money in, my good husband," said Teresa, "no matter whether you earned it this way or that. However you may have gotten it, you'll not have brought any new practice into the world."

Sanchica embraced her father and asked him if he brought her anything, for she had been waiting for him like May showers. He took hold of her by the waist, and his wife by the hand, while the daughter led Dapple. They all headed to their house, on their way leaving Don Quixote in his, in the hands of his niece and housekeeper, and in the company of the priest and the bachelor.

Don Quixote at once, without any regard to time or season, withdrew in private with the bachelor and priest, and in a few words told them of his defeat and of the

[4] *breviaries:* The breviary is a book of devotional material to be prayed, recited, and sung at various times during the day (the canonical hours). As a novitiate priest, it would be fitting for Samson Carrasco to join the village priest.

[5] *fitted finer than Mingo:* popular expression of unknown origin.

obligation he was under not to leave his village for a year—which he meant to keep to the letter without departing a hair's breadth from it, as became a knight-errant bound by scrupulous good faith and the laws of knight-errantry. He told them also of how he thought of becoming a shepherd for that year and taking his recreation in the solitude of the fields, where he could with perfect freedom give range to his thoughts of love while he followed the virtuous pastoral calling. He asked of them—if they did not have a great deal to do and were not prevented by more important business—to agree to be his companions, for he would buy sheep enough to qualify them as shepherds. The most important point of the whole affair, he informed them, was settled, for he had given them names that would fit them to a T. The priest asked what they were. Don Quixote replied that he himself was to be called the shepherd Quixótiz, the bachelor the shepherd Carrascón, the priest the shepherd Curiambro, and Sancho Panza the shepherd Panzino.

Both of them were astounded at the new turn in Don Quixote's madness; however, lest he should once more sneak out of the village in pursuit of his chivalry, and trusting that in the course of the year he might be cured, they gave their approval to his new project, applauded his crazy idea as a brilliant one, and offered themselves as companions in the pursuit.

"What's more," said Samson Carrasco, "as all the world knows, I'm a renowned poet. At every opportunity I will be composing poems—pastoral or courtly, as it may come into my head—to pass away our time in those secluded regions where we shall be roaming. But what is most needful, sirs, is that each of us should choose the name of the shepherdess he means to glorify in his verses, and that we should not leave a tree, be it ever so hard, without marking and carving her name on it, as is the habit and custom of love-smitten shepherds."

"That's the very thing," said Don Quixote. "Of course, I am relieved from searching for the name of an imaginary shepherdess, for there's the peerless Dulcinea del Toboso, the glory of these brooksides, the ornament of these meadows, the mainstay of beauty, the cream of all the graces, and, in a word, the being to whom all praise is appropriate, be it ever so hyperbolical."

"Very true," said the priest, "but the rest of us will have to look around for gentle shepherdesses that square with our designs—indeed that corner them."

"And," added Samson Carrasco, "if they fail us, we can call them by the names of the ones in print that the world is filled with: Fílidas, Amarilises, Dianas, Fléridas, Galateas, Belisardas;[6] for as they sell them in the marketplaces we may fairly buy them and make them our own. If my lady (or I should say my shepherdess) happens to be called Ana, I'll sing her praises under the name of Anarda, and if Francisca, I'll call her Francenia, and if Lucía, Lucinda—it all amounts to the same thing. And Sancho Panza, if he joins this fraternity, may glorify his wife Teresa Panza as Teresaina."

Don Quixote laughed at the adaptation of the name, while the priest heaped praise upon the worthy and honorable resolution he had made and again offered

[6] *Fílidas . . . Belisardas:* shepherdesses from well-known pastoral novels, including the protagonist of Cervantes' *La Galatea* (1585).

to accompany him all the time that he could spare from his obligations. And so they took their leave of him, advising and beseeching him to take care of his health and rest as much as he could.

It so happened that his niece and housekeeper overheard the entire conversation among the three of them, and as soon as the men were gone, the two went in to see Don Quixote. The niece said, "What's this, uncle? Now that we were thinking you had come back for good to lead a quiet, respectable life here at home, are you going to wander into another maze and play 'little shepherd, coming here, little shepherd going there?'[7] Truth be told, 'the barley grass is too hard now for piping.'"[8]

"And," added the housekeeper, "will your worship be able to spend his days out in the field, enduring the heats of summer, the chills of winter, and the howling of the wolves? Not you. That's a job for hardy men, bred and seasoned for such work almost from the time they were in swaddling clothes. Why, evil for evil, it's better to be a knight-errant than a shepherd! Look here, señor. Take my advice—and I'm not giving it to you with a stomach full of bread and wine, but fasting, and with fifty years behind me—stay at home, look after your affairs, go often to confession, be good to the poor. And may it be upon my soul if any evil comes to you."

"Hold your peace, my daughters," said Don Quixote. "I know very well what my duty is. Help me to bed, for I don't feel very well; and rest assured that, knight-errant now or wandering shepherd to be, I shall never fail to look after your interests, as my actions will prove to you."

The good daughters—which the housekeeper and niece undoubtedly were—helped him to bed, where they gave him something to eat and made him as comfortable as possible.

[7] *little shepherd . . . going there:* verses from a folk song.

[8] *the barley grass is too hard now for piping:* Children would make whistles with barley grass before it dried out. The niece is commenting on her uncle's age.

CHAPTER LXXIV

OF HOW DON QUIXOTE FELL ILL, OF THE WILL HE MADE, AND HOW HE DIED

As nothing that is man's can last forever, but all tends ever downwards from its beginning to its end, above all man's life, and as Don Quixote's enjoyed no special dispensation from Heaven to suspend its course, his life came to a close when he least expected it. For whether it was from the melancholy that his defeat caused him or because Heaven so willed it, a fever settled upon him and kept him in his bed for six days, during which he was often visited by his friends the priest, the bachelor, and the barber, while his good squire Sancho Panza never left his bedside.

Persuaded that what kept him in this state was grief at finding himself vanquished and the object of his heart—the liberation and disenchantment of Dulcinea—unattained, his friends strove by all the means in their power to cheer him up. The bachelor bid him take heart, get out of bed, and begin his pastoral life, for which he himself, he said, had already composed an eclogue that would take the shine off everything Sannazaro[1] had ever written. He had also bought with his own money two exceptional dogs to guard the flock, one called Barcino and the other Butrón, which a herdsman in Quintanar had sold him. But for all this Don Quixote could not shake off his sadness.

His friends called in the doctor, who felt his pulse and was not very pleased with it. He said that to be safe it would be wise for him to attend to the health of his soul, as the health of his body was in danger. Don Quixote heard this calmly—not so his housekeeper, his niece, and his squire, who fell weeping bitterly, as if he was already lying dead before them. The doctor's opinion was that melancholy and grief were bringing him to his end. Don Quixote begged them to leave him alone, as he had a wish to sleep a little. They obeyed, and he slept at one stretch, as the saying is, more than six hours, so that the housekeeper and niece thought he was going to sleep forever.

But at the end of that time he woke up, and in a loud voice exclaimed, "Blessed be Almighty God for the abundant goodness he has shown me! In truth his mercies are boundless, and the sins of men can neither cut them short nor hold them back."

The niece listened with attention to her uncle's words, and they struck her as more coherent than what usually came from him, at least during his illness, so

[1] *Sannazaro:* Jacopo Sannazaro (1458–1530), father of Renaissance pastoral poetry.

she asked, "What are you saying, señor? Has something new happened? What mercies or what sins of men are you talking about?"

"The mercies, niece," said Don Quixote, "are those that God has this moment shown me. I said that the course of his mercies is not hindered by my sins. My reason is now free and clear, rid of the dark shadows of ignorance that my unhappy, constant study of those detestable books of chivalry cast over it. Now I see through their absurdities and deceptions. My only regret is that the destruction of my illusions has come so late that it leaves me no time to make some amends by reading other books that might be a light to my soul.[2] Niece, I feel myself at the point of death, and I would like to meet it in such a way as to show that I have not lived such a bad life that I should leave behind me the name of a madman; for though I have been one, I do not wish that the fact should be made plainer at my death. Call in to me, my dear, my good friends the priest, the bachelor Samson Carrasco, and Master Nicholas the barber, for I wish to confess and make my will."

But his niece was saved the trouble by the entrance of the three.

The instant Don Quixote saw them he exclaimed, "Congratulate me, good sirs: I am no longer Don Quixote of La Mancha, but Alonso Quixano, whose way of life won for him the name of Good. Now am I the enemy of Amadís of Gaul and of the whole countless troop of his descendants. Odious to me now are all the profane stories of knight-errantry. Now I see my folly and the peril into which reading them brought me. Now, by God's mercy schooled into my right senses, I loathe them."

When the three heard him speak in this way, they had no doubt whatever that some new insanity had taken possession of him. Said Samson, "Is that what you say, Señor Don Quixote, now that we have news of Lady Dulcinea being disenchanted? Just as we are on the point of becoming shepherds, to pass our lives singing like a band of princes—are you now thinking of turning hermit? Hush, for heaven's sake. Be serious, and let's have no more nonsense."

"All that nonsense," said Don Quixote, "that until now has been real only in its power to harm me will, with Heaven's help, turn death to my benefit. Sirs, I sense that I am rapidly drawing near the end. A truce to jesting. Let me have a confessor to confess me and a notary to make my will; for in extremities like this, a man must not trifle with his soul. While the priest is hearing my confession, let someone go for the notary."

They looked at one another, wondering at Don Quixote's words, and although they were unsure, they were inclined to believe him. One of the signs that led them to conclude he was dying was this sudden and complete return to his senses after having been mad;[3] for to the words already quoted he added many more, so well expressed, so Christian, and so rational, as to banish all doubt and convince them that he was of sound mind.

[2] *light to my soul:* See footnote 16, page 791.

[3] *One of the signs . . . having been mad:* One of the popular beliefs about madness was that those who suffered from it regained their sanity when they were near death.

The priest turned them all out, and, left alone with him, heard his confession. The bachelor went for the notary and returned shortly afterwards with him and with Sancho, who, having already learned from the bachelor the condition his master was in, and finding the housekeeper and niece weeping, began to blubber and shed tears.

When the confession was over, the priest came out saying, "Alonso Quixano the Good is indeed dying, and is indeed in his right mind. We may now go in to see him while he makes his will."

This news gave a tremendous impulse to the brimming eyes of the housekeeper, niece, and Sancho Panza his good squire, making the tears burst from their eyes and a host of sighs from their hearts; for truly, as has been said more than once, whether as simply Alonso Quixano the Good or as Don Quixote of La Mancha, Don Quixote was always of a gentle disposition and kindly in all his ways. For this reason, he was beloved not only by those of his own house but by all who knew him.

The notary came in with the rest, and as soon as the preamble of the will had been set out and Don Quixote had commended his soul to God with all the usual Christian formalities, coming to the bequests, he said, "*Item:*[4] it is my will that, regarding certain moneys in the hands of Sancho Panza (whom in my madness I made my squire), inasmuch as between him and me there have been certain accounts and debits and credits, no claim be made against him, nor any account demanded of him in respect of them; but that if anything remains over and above, after he has paid himself what I owe him, the balance, which will be but little, shall be his, and much good may it do him. If, when I was mad, I had a share in giving him the government of an island, now that I am in my senses, I would give him the government of a kingdom were it in my power. The simplicity of his character and the fidelity of his conduct deserve no less." Then turning to Sancho, he said, "Forgive me, my friend, for the opportunity I have given you to act as mad as I have, making you fall into the same error I myself fell into—that there were and still are knights-errant in the world."

"Ah!" said Sancho weeping. "Don't die, master! Take my advice and live many years. The most foolish thing a man can do in this life is to let himself die without rhyme or reason, without anybody killing him, or any hands but melancholy's making an end of him. Come now, don't be lazy. Get up from your bed and let's head off to the fields dressed like shepherds as we agreed. Maybe behind some bush we'll find Lady Dulcinea disenchanted, as fine as fine can be. If you're dying from grief over having been defeated, put the blame on me. Say you were knocked down because I did a poor job saddling Rocinante. Besides, you must have seen in your books of chivalry that it's a common thing for knights to knock each other off their horses. The one who's conquered today will be conqueror tomorrow."

"Very true," said Samson. "Good Sancho Panza's view of these matters is quite right."

[4] Item: See footnote 11, page 632.

"Not so fast, sirs," said Don Quixote. "'No birds may be found in last year's nests.'[5] I was mad; now I am in my senses. I was Don Quixote of La Mancha, I am now, as I said, Alonso Quixano the Good. May my repentance and sincerity restore me to the esteem in which you once held me. Let us proceed, Master Notary:

"*Item:* I bequeath my estate in its entirety, without particular enumeration, to my niece Antonia Quixana, here present, after whatever is necessary to satisfy the bequests I have made has been deducted from the most available part of it. The first disbursement I desire to be made is the payment of the wages I owe for the time my housekeeper has served me, with an additional twenty ducats for a dress. The priest and the bachelor Samson Carrasco, now present, I appoint my executors.

"*Item:* It is my wish that if Antonia Quixana, my niece, desires to marry, she is to marry a man of whom it shall be first ascertained by a thorough investigation that he does not know what books of chivalry are. If it should be proved that he does, and if, in spite of this, my niece insists upon marrying him, and does marry him, then she shall forfeit the whole of what I have left her, which my executors shall devote to works of charity as they please.

"*Item:* I entreat the aforesaid gentlemen my executors, if any happy chance should lead them to discover the author who is said to have written a history now going about under the title of *Second Part of the Deeds of Don Quixote of La Mancha*, that they beg of him on my behalf as earnestly as they can to forgive me for having been, without intending it, the cause of his writing so many and such monstrous absurdities as he has written in it; for I leave this world with a sense of remorse for having given him cause to write them."

With this he closed his will, and feeling a fainting spell coming on, he stretched himself out at full length on the bed. Everyone was overtaken with concern and came to his aid. During the three days he lived after the day he made his will, he fell into a swoon quite often. Anxiety continued to reign at the house, yet the niece still ate, the housekeeper still drank, and Sancho Panza still enjoyed himself; for the thought of inherited property lessens—if not sweeps away—the grief that the heir might otherwise feel when the deceased has gone on.

At last Don Quixote's end came, but not until he had received the sacraments and had in full and forcible terms expressed how much he despised the books of chivalry. The notary was there at the time, and he said that in no book of chivalry had he ever read of any knight-errant dying in his bed so serenely and so like a Christian as Don Quixote, who amid the tears and lamentations of all present yielded up his spirit—that is to say died.

When the priest saw that his life had ended, he asked the notary to bear witness that Alonso Quixano the Good, commonly called Don Quixote of La Mancha, had passed from this present life and died naturally. He explained that he desired this affidavit in order to remove the possibility of any other author save Cide Hamete Benengeli bringing him to life again falsely and making interminable stories out of his achievements.

[5] *No birds may be found in last year's nests:* "Times have changed."

Such was the end of the Ingenious Gentleman of La Mancha, whose village Cide Hamete would not indicate precisely in order to leave all the towns and villages of La Mancha to contend among themselves for the right to adopt him and claim him as a son, as the seven cities of Greece contended for Homer.[6] The lamentations of Sancho and the niece and housekeeper are omitted here, as well as the new epitaphs upon his tomb.[7] Samson Carrasco, however, contributed the following lines:

A doughty gentleman lies here;
A stranger all his life to fear;
Nor in his death could Death prevail,
In that last hour, to make him quail.

He for the world but little cared;
And at his feats the world was scared;
A crazy man his life he passed,
But in his senses died at last.

Then said the most sage Cide Hamete to his pen, "Rest here, hung from this rack[8] and by this wire, O my pen—whether of skillful make or clumsy cut I know not. Here shall you remain long ages hence, unless presumptuous or malignant storytellers take you down to profane you. But before they touch you, warn them as best you can with these words:

'Hold off, you weaklings! Hold your hands!
Adventure it let none,
For this exploit, my lord the king,
Was meant for me alone.[9]

For me alone was Don Quixote born, and I for him. It was his to act, mine to write. We two together make but one, notwithstanding and in spite of that pretended Tordesillescan writer who has ventured, or might further venture with his coarse, sputtering ostrich quill to write the achievements of my valiant knight. It is no burden for his shoulders, nor subject for his graceless wit.'

"If perchance you should make his acquaintance,[10] warn him to leave at rest where they lie the weary, moldering bones of Don Quixote, and not to attempt to carry him off—in opposition to all the privileges of death—to Old Castile,

[6] *seven cities of Greece contended for Homer:* Tradition holds that Smyrna, Chios, Colophon, Salamis, Rhodes, Argos, and Athens each claimed to be Homer's birthplace.

[7] *new epitaphs upon his tomb:* in addition to the epitaphs by the academicians of Argamasilla (see pp. 413–16).

[8] *this rack:* An *espetera* (rack) is a board mounted on the kitchen wall, fitted with hooks for hanging pots and cooking utensils.

[9] *For this exploit, my lord the king, / Was meant for me alone:* adapted from a ballad on the siege of Granada.

[10] *If perchance you should make his acquaintance:* Cide Hamete continues to address his pen directly, counseling the pen what to do if it should meet Avellaneda.

making him rise from the grave where in all reality he lies stretched at full length, powerless to make any third expedition or new sally.[11] For the two that he has already made—so much to the enjoyment and approval of everybody to whom they have become known, in these as well as in foreign realms—are quite sufficient for the purpose of turning into ridicule the whole of those made by all the knights-errant.

"In so doing you shall discharge your Christian calling, giving good counsel to one that bears ill-will toward you. And I shall remain satisfied, proud to have been the first who has ever enjoyed the fruit of his writings, as was my wish.[12] For my desire has been no other than to deliver over to the detestation of mankind the false and foolish tales of the books of chivalry, which, thanks to the history of my true Don Quixote, are even now tottering, and doubtless doomed to fall forever. *Vale*."[13]

[11] *to Old Castile . . . new sally:* Avellaneda concludes his sequel alluding to a subsequent sally Don Quixote makes into Old Castile (roughly corresponding to the modern region of Castilla y León), where he takes on a new squire who is later revealed to be a prostitute fleeing the man who impregnated her.

[12] *And I shall remain . . . as was my wish:* Cide Hamete speaks ironically of the productive use to which he has put Avellaneda's sequel in this volume. In the line following, he lumps in the spurious continuation with the books of chivalry—all of them "false and foolish" in light of Cervantes' two novels.

[13] Vale: Latin, "Farewell".

Contemporary Criticism

What a Knight Can Teach Us About Perfect Happiness: A Thomistic Reading of Don Quixote

Michael J. McGrath
Georgia Southern University

When the country gentleman Alonso Quixano becomes the knight-errant Don Quixote, the transformation unleashes a spiritual journey that culminates with the deathbed scene in which he reevaluates his life and proclaims, "Blessed be Almighty God for the abundant goodness he has shown me! In truth his mercies are boundless, and the sins of men can neither cut them short nor hold them back."[1] While Don Quixote begins the novel in pursuit of the fame achieved by the knights he reads about in his books of chivalry, I propose that he discovers so much more: perfect happiness. Saint Thomas Aquinas (1225–1274) posits that perfect happiness is attainable when a person leads a good life, the foundation of which is the cultivation of the theological and cardinal virtues and adherence to natural and divine laws:

> Now among all others, the rational creature is subject to Divine providence in the most excellent way, in so far as it partakes of a share of providence, by being provident both for itself and for others. Wherefore it has a share of the Eternal Reason, whereby it has a natural inclination to its proper act and end: and this participation of the eternal law in the rational creature is called the natural law.[2]

When we consider the knight's decisions and actions through the prism of Thomistic ethics, with a focus on the theological and cardinal virtues, we discover that the knight's spiritual journey exemplifies the moral principles that we, the readers, can emulate to attain perfect happiness.

According to Saint Thomas Aquinas, the person who lives a good life develops virtues through moral behavior. A good life, therefore, is predicated as much on "becoming" as it is on "doing".[3] Aquinas' good life is measured by two forms of happiness: imperfect and perfect. Both forms are based on a relationship

[1] Miguel de Cervantes, *Don Quixote*, ed. Timothy McCallister, Ignatius Critical Editions, ed. Joseph Pearce (San Francisco: Ignatius Press, 2026), p. 845. All subsequent quotations of *Don Quixote* are from this edition and will be cited in the text.

[2] Saint Thomas Aquinas, *Summa Theologiae* I-II, q. 91, a. 2, trans. Fathers of the English Dominican Province, 2nd and rev. ed., 1920, revised and edited for New Advent by Kevin Knight, 2017, www.newadvent.org/summa/. Subsequent quotations of the *Summa Theologiae* are from this edition, cited as *ST*.

[3] Pat Flynn, "How to Live a Good Life: Lessons from Aquinas and Aristotle", *Chronicles of Strength* (website), accessed October 22, 2025, www.chroniclesofstrength.com.

with God. The degree of imperfect happiness is in proportion to knowledge of God; it is an intellectual endeavor. Perfect happiness consists of a vision of God that is a perception that transcends the senses (e.g., sight). It depends solely on the person and God, independent of anything else. Aquinas also discusses what happiness is not. Before we look at the theological and cardinal virtues that Don Quixote exemplifies, let us address those desires that the knight eschews: wealth, pleasure, fame, and power.

In the *Summa Theologiae*, Aquinas writes the following about wealth:

> It is impossible for man's happiness to consist in wealth. For wealth is twofold ... natural and artificial. Natural wealth is that which serves man as a remedy for his natural wants: such as food, drink, clothing, cars, dwellings, and such like, while artificial wealth is that which is not a direct help to nature, as money, but is invented by the art of man, for the convenience of exchange, and as a measure of things salable.[4]

Alonso Quixano, as a hidalgo who belongs to the lower nobility, possesses artificial wealth. In fact, he sells many acres of farmland to buy the same books of chivalry that will inspire him to become Don Quixote. By not placing an inordinate value on artificial wealth, Alonso Quixano is able to begin the journey that will culminate with perfect happiness. The books he buys are responsible for his madness, but they are also the catalyst for his spiritual evolution because they inspire him to fulfill Jesus' commandment to "love your neighbor as yourself."[5] While Alonso Quixano's intentions as Don Quixote may be misdirected, they are nevertheless selfless.

Aquinas extols the virtues of intellectual pleasures but not bodily pleasures: "If, however, intellectual spiritual pleasures be compared with sensible bodily pleasures, then, in themselves and absolutely speaking, spiritual pleasures are greater."[6] Alonso Quixano's life as Don Quixote is an intellectual pursuit based on the books of chivalry: "With his wits now being quite gone, he hit upon the strangest notion that ever madman in this world hit upon. He decided that it was right and proper, both for the increase of his own honor and for the service of his country, that he should make a knight-errant of himself, roaming the world over in full armor and on horseback in quest of adventures" (see p. 27). Don Quixote is not motivated by bodily pleasures such as wealth, food, and possessions, unlike his squire Sancho Panza, whom Don Quixote promises to make the governor of an island, providing him with wealth and power, if he accompanies the knight on his adventures.

Don Quixote aspires to be a knight as well known as the heroes of his books of chivalry, but he assigns a Christian dimension to fame that provides the reader with insight into his spiritual evolution:

> All these and a variety of other great exploits are, were, and will be the work of fame that mortals desire as a reward and portion of the immortality their famous

[4] *ST* I-II, q. 2, a.1.
[5] Matthew 22:39.
[6] *ST* I-II, q. 31, a. 5.

deeds deserve; though we Catholic Christians and knights-errant look more to that future glory that is everlasting in the ethereal regions of heaven than to the vanity of the fame that is to be acquired in this present transitory life—a fame that, however long it may last, must ultimately expire along with the world itself, which has its own appointed end. (See p. 467.)

When the reader considers the final scene of the novel in the context of these words, perhaps he would expect Alonso Quixano to make a confession and to receive the Body of Christ. The knight prioritizes spiritual good over earthly fame, a sentiment that is in concert with Aquinas: "Man's happiness cannot consist in human fame or glory. For glory consists 'in being well known and praised,' as Ambrose says. Now the thing known is related to human knowledge otherwise than to God's knowledge: for human knowledge is caused by the things known, whereas God's knowledge is the cause of the things known."[7] Sancho, on the other hand, a Catholic who refers to homilies he heard during Mass before he became Don Quixote's squire (see Part I, chap. 31, and Part II, chap. 20), does not want his friend and neighbor Alonso Quixano to die. The squire exhorts him to get out of bed to the point of accepting the blame for Don Quixote's defeat at the hands of the Knight of the White Moon (Samson Carrasco): "If you're dying from grief over having been defeated, put the blame on me. Say you were knocked down because I did a poor job saddling Rocinante. Besides, you must have seen in your books of chivalry that it's a common thing for knights to knock each other off their horses. The one who's conquered today will be conqueror tomorrow" (see p. 847). However, it is at this point in the novel that Alonso Quixano illustrates perfect happiness.

Don Quixote does not seek power over the characters he liberates from what he perceives to be injustices. His actions are based on natural and divine law, which Saint Thomas Aquinas defines in the context of divine intervention: "Now to move by reason and will is to command. Wherefore just as in virtue of the divinely established natural order the lower natural things need to be subject to the movement of the higher, so too in human affairs, in virtue of the order of natural and divine law, inferiors are bound to obey their superiors."[8] The knight's understanding of power is perhaps best illustrated in the episode of the galley slaves. In Part I, chapter 22, Don Quixote and Sancho encounter "some dozen men on foot strung together by the neck like beads on a great iron chain, and all with shackles on their hands" (see p. 160). Sancho informs the knight that the men are galley slaves; "on the king's orders, they go by force to the galleys" (see p. 160). After Don Quixote hears each man explain why he is a prisoner, the knight attacks the guards and sets the slaves free. Don Quixote appeals to natural and divine law as a justification for his actions, "as there will be no lack of others to serve the king under more favorable circumstances. For it seems to me a hard case to make slaves of those whom God and nature have made free.... There is a

[7] *ST* I-II, q. 2, a. 3. The Saint Ambrose quote is from Saint Augustine, *Contra Maxim. Arian*. II, 13.

[8] *ST* II-II, q. 104, a.1.

God in heaven who will not forget to punish the wicked or reward the good. It is not fitting that honest men should be the instruments of punishment to others, they being therein no way concerned" (see p. 166). Don Quixote's only attempt to exercise power over the freed prisoners is an order that they go to the city of El Toboso to regale Dulcinea with the adventure of how her knight freed the twelve men from captivity. Then, Don Quixote instructs the men to live their lives how they wish: "This done, you may go where you will, and good fortune attend you" (see p. 167).

Saint Thomas Aquinas predicates happiness on natural and supernatural principles, namely, the three theological virtues of faith, hope, and charity (love):

> Hence it is necessary for man to receive from God some additional principles, whereby he may be directed to supernatural happiness, even as he is directed to his connatural end, by means of his natural principles, albeit not without Divine assistance. Such like principles are called "theological virtues": first, because their object is God, inasmuch as they direct us aright to God: secondly, because they are infused in us by God alone: thirdly, because these virtues are not made known to us, save by Divine revelation, contained in Holy Writ.[9]

The theological virtues enable a person to live a life whose ultimate achievement is salvation. They are the product of habitual grace, which allows a person to have supernatural inclinations to do good. Don Quixote exercises the virtues of faith, hope, and charity because he believes his actions are right. As Alonso Quixano illustrates in the last episode of the novel, he realizes that his actions as a knight, while performed with benevolent intent, are misguided, yet they lead to his salvation.

The reader knows very little about Alonso Quixano's life before he becomes Don Quixote. The knight first manifests his faith and hope in God when he commands Juan Haldudo to pay Andrés and to release him: "Pay him at once without another word. If not, by the God that rules us I will make an end of you and annihilate you on the spot. Release him instantly" (see pp. 40–41). There are many episodes in which the knight, as a contemplative in action, lives his faith by uniting contemplation with action. For example, when a forlorn Sancho expresses his frustration about not yet becoming governor of an island, in Part II, chapter 3, Don Quixote reminds Sancho that God has a plan for him: "Leave it to God, Sancho,... for all will turn out well, perhaps better than you think. No leaf on the tree stirs but by God's will" (see p. 41).

As a contemplative in action, Don Quixote believes that he receives Christ through material reality. In Part I, the knight prepares the elixir of Fierabras, which he thinks will cure him of the injuries he receives after the officer of the Holy Brotherhood smashes an oil lamp on his head:

> Don Quixote took the ingredients, from which he made a compound—mixing them all and boiling them a good while until it seemed to him they had come to perfection. He then asked for a vial to pour it into, and as there was not one in the

[9] *ST* I-II, q. 62, a. 1.

> inn, he decided on putting it into a tin oil bottle or flask, which the innkeeper gave him without cost. Over the flask, he repeated more than eighty Pater Nosters and as many more Ave Marias, Salves, and Credos[10] accompanying each word with the sign of the cross by way of benediction. (See p. 121.)

Don Quixote's confection of the ingredients may be interpreted as reminiscent of the Eucharistic Prayer, which the priest prays during the process of transubstantiation that converts the bread and wine into the Body and Blood of Christ during the Mass. After calling the Holy Spirit down upon the bread and the wine, the priest makes the sign of the cross over each species. The Eucharistic implications of the episode mediate its irreverent tone because Don Quixote, who is not far removed from the influence of books of chivalry at this point in the novel, seeks a cure for his injuries that he believes will cure him as if it were the Body of Christ. Unfortunately for Don Quixote, and soon after Sancho, the elixir has the opposite effect, as both knight and squire become violently ill. The knight's physical constitution is no match for the elixir's sickening potency, but he demonstrates in this episode a desire to experience Christ's presence in everyday life. Don Quixote's ritualistic preparation of the elixir, while humorous, underscores the unitive process that takes place when the contemplative in action exteriorizes his spirituality. In another episode, Don Quixote advises Sancho to act in a virtuous manner before Sancho becomes the governor of the island of Barataria: "Remember, Sancho, if you make virtue your aim, and take pride in doing virtuous actions, you will have no cause to envy those who have princes and lords for fathers and grandfathers; for blood is an inheritance, but virtue an acquisition, and virtue has in itself alone a worth that blood does not possess" (see p. 665). Don Quixote's spiritual evolution becomes more evident when he and Sancho encounter the twelve peasants who transport the statues of Saint George, Saint Martin of Tours, Saint James, and Saint Paul for an altarpiece in their village. After noting Saint Paul's conversion, Don Quixote reflects on his life as a knight-errant and expresses hope that he will experience a similar transformation: "But if my Dulcinea del Toboso were to be released from hers, perhaps with mended fortunes and a mind restored to itself, I might direct my steps in a better path than I am following at present" (see p. 756).

Saint Thomas Aquinas asserts that charity (love) is the most efficacious of the three virtues: "But faith and hope attain God indeed in so far as we derive from Him the knowledge of truth or the acquisition of good, whereas charity attains God Himself that it may rest in Him, but not that something may accrue to us from Him. Hence charity is more excellent than faith or hope, and, consequently, than all the other virtues."[11] Acts of charity demonstrate a person's love for God and others because he desires what is good. Don Quixote, as a knight-errant, engages in many acts of charity that promote the common good and personify the Church's social thought on the dignity of the human person. The first act

[10] Foundational prayers of the Catholic faith: the Lord's Prayer (Pater Noster), Hail Mary (Ave Maria), Hail, Holy Queen (Salve Regina), and Apostles' Creed (Credo).

[11] *ST* II-II, q. 23, a. 6.

takes place when the knight encounters Juan Haldudo and Andrés (see Part I, chap. 4). After "rescuing" Andrés, Don Quixote extols his meritorious actions:

> Well may you this day call yourself fortunate above all on earth, O Dulcinea del Toboso, fairest of the fair! For it has fallen to your lot to hold subject and submissive to your full will and pleasure a knight so renowned as is and will be Don Quixote of La Mancha, who, as all the world knows, yesterday received the order of knighthood, and has today righted the greatest wrong and grievance that ever injustice conceived and cruelty perpetrated; who has today plucked the rod from the hand of yonder ruthless oppressor so wantonly lashing that tender child. (See p. 42.)

The social and relational nature of Don Quixote's adventures, which also include the Toledan merchants (see Part I, chap. 4), the Benedictine friars who accompany the Biscayan woman (see Part I, chap. 8), the armies of Alifanfarón and Pentapolín (see Part I, chap. 18), the adventure with the dead body (see Part I, chap. 19), the galley slaves (see Part I, chap. 22), Princess Micomicona (see Part I, chap. 30), the adventure with the penitents (see Part I, chap. 52), the destruction of the puppet theater (see Part II, chap. 26), and the enchanted boat (see Part II, chap. 29) remind the reader that a person's individual desires and aspirations are not independent of what is good for society because each person's actions affect others. Each time that Don Quixote commits to help characters whom he perceives are in danger, he practices acts of charity that illustrate his love for God and others.

Saint Thomas Aquinas defines the cardinal virtues in relation to their effect on reason:

> Accordingly the above four virtues may be considered in two ways. First, in respect of their common formal principles. In this way they are called principal, being general, as it were, in comparison with all the virtues: so that, for instance, any virtue that causes good in reason's act of consideration, may be called prudence; every virtue that causes the good of right and due in operation, be called justice; every virtue that curbs and represses the passions, be called temperance; and every virtue that strengthens the mind against any passions whatever, be called fortitude.[12]

Aquinas asserts that the cardinal virtues, unlike the theological virtues, which are infused in each person by God, can be attained through habit. Furthermore, the cardinal virtues, like the theological virtues, can be maintained through application.

Aquinas defines "prudence" by drawing a distinction between the cognitive and sensitive faculty:

> Now sight belongs not to the appetitive but to the cognitive faculty. Wherefore it is manifest that prudence belongs directly to the cognitive, and not to the sensitive faculty, because by the latter we know nothing but what is within reach and offers itself to the senses: while to obtain knowledge of the future from knowledge of the present or past, which pertains to prudence, belongs properly to the reason, because this is done by a process of comparison. It follows therefore that prudence, properly speaking, is in the reason.[13]

[12] *ST* I-II, q. 61, a. 3.
[13] *ST* II-II, q. 47, a. 1.

Aquinas further defines "prudence" as "an application of the will"[14] that is "concerned for the quest of truth".[15] Of course, as a madman, Don Quixote is not a paragon of prudence because his application of the virtue is misguided. Yet, the knight, in his mind, applies right reason to action for the common good. When Don Quixote and Sancho see the windmills, the knight is convinced that they are giants, and he calls them "cowards and vile beings" (see p. 61) as he attacks them. While Sancho and the reader know that the windmills are not giants, Don Quixote truly believes his actions are necessary. In his mind, he is doing what is right as he considers the situation and acts upon it. Shortly after the episode with the windmills, Don Quixote once again believes he applies right reason for the common good. The knight and his squire see two friars approaching them on camels. Each friar wears traveling spectacles and a sunshade (see p. 64) and carries a parasol. A separate traveling party, consisting of several men on horseback and two servants who escort a lady in a coach, is behind the friars. The knight informs Sancho the friars are enchanters, and the lady is a princess, whom the enchanters kidnapped. Don Quixote attacks one of the friars with the same determination with which he attacks the windmills. The result of this adventure is the knight engages in a fight with one of the squires who accompanies the coach. While Don Quixote's actions toward the windmills and the friars may not be prudent in nature, I suggest that if we consider that they are the result of involuntary ignorance, which Aquinas defines "as when a man, through stress of work or other occupations, neglects to acquire the knowledge which would restrain him from sin",[16] then we are able to conclude that the knight acts in a way that *he* believes is the truth and what is best for the common good.

Aquinas identifies two types of justice in the *Summa Theologiae*:

> This order is directed by commutative justice, which is concerned about the mutual dealings between two persons. On the second place there is the order of the whole towards the parts, to which corresponds the order of that which belongs to the community in relation to each single person. This order is directed by distributive justice, which distributes common goods proportionately.[17]

Miguel de Cervantes promotes both forms of justice throughout the novel. In Part I, Don Quixote, during his discourse on arms and letters, states that the goal of humane letters is "to establish distributive justice" and "give to every man that which is his" (see p. 306). In Part II, Don Quixote tells Lorenzo that a knight-errant "must be a jurist and must know the rules of justice, distributive and commutative" (see p. 524). The bandit Roque Guinart, also in Part II, bases how he and his men share in what they steal on distributive justice, dividing it "for the whole band so equitably and carefully, that in no case did he exceed or fall short of strict distributive justice" (see p. 776). In response, Sancho remarks: "From what I've seen here, justice is such a good thing that there is no doing without

[14] Ibid.
[15] *ST* II-II, q. 47, a. 2.
[16] *ST* I-II, q. 76, a. 3.
[17] *ST* II-II, q. 61, a. 1.

it, even among thieves" (see p. 776). It is reasonable to question Don Quixote's understanding of justice if we consider the harm he inflicts on other characters. According to Aquinas, however, an act may have two effects:

> Accordingly the act of self-defense may have two effects, one is the saving of one's life, the other is the slaying of the aggressor. Therefore this act, since one's intention is to save one's own life, is not unlawful, seeing that it is natural to everything to keep itself in "being," as far as possible.[18]

However, this principle of double effect may not be valid if the action is not in proportion with its end:

> And yet, though proceeding from a good intention, an act may be rendered unlawful, if it be out of proportion to the end. Wherefore if a man, in self-defense, uses more than necessary violence, it will be unlawful: whereas if he repel force with moderation his defense will be lawful.[19]

Don Quixote does not violate the argument of proportionate reason because his actions are in proportion to their end. He appeals to natural law as the basis for liberating Andrés and the galley slaves. He does not seek to punish either Juan Haldudo or the guards who accompany the galley slaves beyond what is necessary to free their "captives". Don Quixote's actions, while misguided, are not morally wrong because he believes they are performed in the service of the common good.

In response to the objection that temperance is not a virtue, Aquinas asserts the contrary: "Hence human virtue is that which inclines man to something in accordance with reason. Now temperance evidently inclines man to this, since its very name implies moderation or temperateness, which reason causes. Therefore temperance is a virtue."[20] Don Quixote exhibits temperance as the novel progresses; however, he does not early in Part I during his encounter with the priests who escort the body of a knight to Segovia for burial. Don Quixote insists that the priests explain what they are doing, but they refuse. The knight, offended by what he perceives is a lack of respect, becomes angry and grabs the bridle of a mule on which one of the priest travels. The mule, startled by the knight's actions, throws the priest to the ground and falls on him, breaking the priest's leg. When Don Quixote learns the nature of the priests' procession, he asks the priest to forgive him and to inform the other priests of his repentance for his actions. In subsequent episodes, Don Quixote's reactions are more measured. In Part II, when the knight sees that the Knight of the Mirrors is Samson Carrasco, he attributes the appearance to the enchanters that pursue him:

> It is all ... a scheme and plot of the malignant magicians that persecute me, who, foreseeing that I was to be victorious in the conflict, arranged that the vanquished knight should display the countenance of my friend the bachelor in order that the friendship I bear him should interpose to stay the edge of my sword and might of my arm and temper the just wrath of my heart; so that he who sought to take my life by fraud and falsehood should save his own. (See pp. 507–8.)

[18] *ST* II-II, q. 64, a. 7.
[19] Ibid.
[20] *ST* II, q. 141, a.1.

Later in Part II, Don Quixote once again displays temperance after the duke and duchess' chaplain insults the knight and Sancho:

> So, according to the laws of the accursed duel, I may have received offense but not insult, for neither women nor children can maintain it, nor can they wound, nor have they any way of standing their ground. It is just the same with those connected with religion; for these three sorts of persons are without arms offensive or defensive, and so—though naturally they are bound to defend themselves—they have no right to offend anybody. (See p. 608.)

In Don Quixote's encounters with the Knight of the Mirrors and the Duke and Duchess' chaplain, the knight exercises his cognitive power to control his appetitive power.

Aquinas defines "fortitude" as a special virtue, asserting that it "may be taken to denote firmness only in bearing and withstanding those things wherein it is most difficult to be firm, namely in certain grave dangers.... On this sense fortitude is reckoned a special virtue, because it has a special matter."[21] Don Quixote's display of fortitude is the result of an evolutionary process because he does not demonstrate this virtue completely until the end of the novel when he renounces his life as a knight-errant. However, as the episodes with the Knight of the Mirrors and the parish priest illustrate, Don Quixote's fortitude becomes more evident to the reader throughout Part II. The knight's desire to achieve eternal glory may be interpreted as the product of psychological egoism, but I suggest that it is a revelation that reflects a concern for his salvation. When Don Quixote renounces the books of chivalry and insists that he be called "Alonso Quixano the Good", he removes completely that hindrance of the will that Aquinas states a person can overcome by the virtue of fortitude:

> Now the human will is hindered in two ways from following the rectitude of reason.... Secondly, through the will being disinclined to follow that which is in accordance with reason, on account of some difficulty that presents itself. On order to remove this obstacle fortitude of the mind is requisite, whereby to resist the aforesaid difficulty even as a man, by fortitude of body, overcomes and removes bodily obstacles.[22]

The "difficulty that presents itself" for Alonso Quixano is the inordinate time he dedicates to reading the books of chivalry. However, each one of Don Quixote's adventures gradually removes the deleterious effects of the books of chivalry that distance Alonso Quixano from God. Fortitude, which according to Aquinas is a precept of the divine law that directs the mind to God, makes it possible for Alonso Quixano to be in communion with God as he prepares for his death.

In the *Nicomachean Ethics*, Aristotle compares a person's goals in life to two archers.[23] While both archers aim to hit a target, only one of the archers knows where it is. Aristotle asserts that most people are like the archer who does not

[21] *ST* II-II, q. 123, a. 2.

[22] *ST* II-II, q. 123, a. 1.

[23] Aristotle, *Nicomachean Ethics* I, 2, trans. Robert C. Bartlett and Susan D. Collins (University of Chicago Press, 2012), p. 2.

know the location of the target. Consequently, they spend their lives seeking one goal after another in search of elusive fulfillment. Alonso Quixano, as the knight Don Quixote, repeatedly experiences disillusionment as he seeks to imitate the knights from his books of chivalry, but at the same time, each adventure provides him with the opportunity to cultivate the theological and cardinal virtues. The application of these virtues demystifies the fabricated world of the books of chivalry and introduces Alonso Quixano to a life of reason and love that would not have been possible if he had not read these same books. In the last episode of the novel, Don Quixote, speaking as Alonso Quixano "the Good", renounces his knighthood and laments that he did not choose a different path in life:

> My reason is now free and clear, rid of the dark shadows of ignorance that my unhappy, constant study of those detestable books of chivalry cast over it. Now I see through their absurdities and deceptions. My only regret is that the destruction of my illusions has come so late that it leaves me no time to make some amends by reading other books that might be a light to my soul. (See p. 846.)

Not only does Alonso Quixano distance himself from his previous life, but he also embraces the life that awaits him. He requests to meet with a confessor because "a man must not trifle with his soul" (see p. 846). The knight Don Quixote teaches the country gentleman Alonso Quixano that perfect happiness, a vision of God that is a perception that transcends the senses, is attainable, and perhaps we, the readers, will learn the same lesson, regardless of how many metaphorical windmills we encounter throughout our lives.

Don Quixote and Sancho Panza: An Aristotelian Friendship of the Unqualified Good

Kathleen Sullivan
Christendom College

Don Quixote and Sancho Panza are a legendary duo: one, a self-proclaimed knight-errant striving to right all wrongs in a world devoid of chivalry and virtue; the other, a simple, sometimes greedy, peasant farmer eager to spout proverb-ridden speeches to any open ear. Although the tone of Miguel de Cervantes' novel reveals its satirical humor, the eventual friendship developed by Don Quixote and Sancho Panza rings true as an Aristotelian friendship aiming toward the good of each other, not simply toward some useful or pleasant end.

In Aristotle's investigation of the nature of friendship in the *Nicomachean Ethics*, he distinguishes among the friendship of utility, of pleasure, and of the unqualified good.[1] The friendship of the unqualified good contains all the goods, while the former two are limited to a certain good. Don Quixote and Sancho Panza's relationship progresses from a mere companionship to a friendship of utility, at times being a friendship of pleasure, and finally, develops to a friendship of the unqualified good, as defined by Aristotle.[2]

At the start of Cervantes' novel, Don Quixote and Sancho Panza are neighbors, mere acquaintances. After Don Quixote declares "that knights-errant were what the world stood most in need of and that in him was to be accomplished the revival of knight-errantry" (see p. 59), he decides to take on a squire. His neighbor Sancho Panza agrees to leave his wife and children in order to serve

[1] Aristotle, *Nicomachean Ethics* 1156a7, 15, 17, trans. Richard McKeon (Random House, 1941). All subsequent quotations of the *Nicomachean Ethics* are from this edition.

[2] As an interesting note, Cervantes mentions Aristotle in the first chapter. When Don Quixote struggles to understand the books of chivalry, Cervantes writes: "Over phrases of this sort, the poor gentleman's mind fell to pieces as he lay awake trying to understand them and untangle their meaning—what Aristotle himself could not have made out had he come to life again for that sole purpose" (Miguel de Cervantes, *Don Quixote*, ed. Timothy McCallister, Ignatius Critical Editions, ed. Joseph Pearce [San Francisco: Ignatius Press, 2026], p. 26; all subsequent quotations of *Don Quixote* are from this edition and will be cited in the text).

Although no specific mention of Aristotle's *Nicomachean Ethics* occurs, Cervantes' inclusion of the Philosopher as being just as perplexed serves as a touchpoint for this analysis of Don Quixote and Sancho's friendship, for although Cervantes writes that with "so much reading his brains dried up and he lost his wits" (see p. 26), Don Quixote's ability to make rational choices indicates that he is sane and thus capable of a virtuous friendship.

Don Quixote as squire. Their relationship develops from neighbors to master and servant. Sancho is awed by "such a fine master as your worship, who will know how to give me everything that suits me and that I can handle" (see p. 60). Even with the irony of Cervantes' characterization of Sancho as someone "with very little in the way of brains" (see p. 59), and Don Quixote as having "dried up" his brains with excess reading (see p. 26), readers note the wisdom of Sancho's words: a friend ought to will the good of the other. Indeed, Don Quixote promises Sancho the governorship of an island if Sancho serves him well, addressing him as "friend Sancho" (see p. 60). At this point, however, the relationship does not fall under any of Aristotle's three kinds despite Don Quixote's words, because the two men are of unequal rank. Don Quixote is Sancho's superior, and since a mark of friendship is equality,[3] the men must be equalized in some way.

According to Aristotle, a friendship is possible as long as the affection due to each man is proportionate according to his rank. The "better should be loved more than he loves ... for when the love is in proportion to the merit of the parties, then in a sense arises equality, which is certainly held to be characteristic of friendship."[4] Saint Thomas Aquinas comments on Aristotle's example of a friendship between a father and son to show how equality arises, stating that "when children show their parents what is due to those who generated them, and when parents show their children what is due to their offspring, there will exist between them a lasting and just or virtuous friendship."[5] Don Quixote is the means of Sancho's employment; consequently, Sancho shows him loyalty and obedience. Because Don Quixote promises to support and guide Sancho, equality between them arises, since each gives the other what is due to him; in this way, Don Quixote and Sancho Panza can cultivate a friendship. More than a companionship of necessity develops as they eat together, adventure together, and suffer together, for Aristotle claims, "there is nothing so characteristic of friends as living together."[6] Despite frequent complaints or grievances against each other at this stage in their journey, Don Quixote and Sancho Panza reveal marks of friendship, such as dependence and assistance.[7] Don Quixote depends daily on Sancho Panza for squirely assistance to perform his quest more ably than by himself.

To be friends and not simply companions, however, Don Quixote and Sancho must find each other to be a loveable good. According to Aristotle, this good can be of "a useful nature, of a pleasurable nature, or of an unqualified nature",[8] for a friendship entails a mutual recognition that each wills the other's good for a useful, pleasant, or virtuous reason.[9] Don Quixote sees the good his squire

[3] Aristotle, *Nicomachean Ethics* 1158b27.

[4] Ibid., 1158b24–27.

[5] Saint Thomas Aquinas, *Commentary on the Nicomachean Ethics* VIII, 7, 1629, trans. C. I. Litzinger, O.P. (Henry Regnery, 1964), https://isidore.co/aquinas/english/Ethics.htm. All subsequent quotations of the *Commentary on the Nicomachean Ethics* are from this edition.

[6] Ibid., 1157b19.

[7] Ibid., 1155a16.

[8] Ibid., 1155b18.

[9] Ibid., 1156a5.

gives him, as Sancho sees the good his master bestows on his own self. Most importantly, each man must be aware that the other wills his good. The love of an object incapable of recognizing love is not called friendship; for example, although Sancho Panza has a deep affection for his donkey and for the nag Rocinante, since an animal is not capable of returning that love in a rational manner, there is no friendship between man and animal, according to Aristotle's understanding. Moreover, if Don Quixote bestows good upon Sancho, without Sancho reciprocating any sort of good, Don Quixote would be called a benefactor, not a friend. Yet Sancho does return the good, in his dutiful care of his master, and consequently, there is a change in the one loved. This change results from the loved one reciprocally willing the good toward the one loving.

Between Don Quixote and Sancho, there is evidence that love is mutually reciprocated and that each does, in fact, will the other's good. Don Quixote takes pains to instruct Sancho on the ways of chivalry to assure Sancho of his protection: "You need not worry, my friend,... for I will deliver you out of the hands of the Chaldeans, much more out of those of the Brotherhood.... Greater secrets I mean to teach you and greater favors to bestow upon you" (see p. 76). Sancho, in turn, reveals his desire for Don Quixote's good, as seen in one example when he declares, "What I will venture to bet is that a more daring master than your worship I have never served in all the days of my life.... What I beg of your worship is that you get well, for a great deal of blood is flowing from that ear" (see p. 75). Taking care of each other not only in body but also in soul are signs that they will each other's good. Later in the novel, Sancho Panza does not hesitate to reveal his devotion to Don Quixote. He confides to Samson Carrasco, "I don't set up to be a fighting man, Señor Samson, but only the best and most loyal squire that ever served knight-errant; and if my master Don Quixote, in consideration of my many faithful services, is pleased to give me some island of the many his worship says we may stumble on in these parts, I will take it as a great favor" (see p. 447). He is ready to leave everything behind to be with his master, while the master is ready to leave everyone else behind except his squire. Since they are aware of their mutual goodwill toward each other, Don Quixote and Sancho Panza's relationship does contain all parts of Aristotle's general definition of friendship.

Yet even at this stage, Don Quixote and Sancho Panza are not friends of the unqualified good; rather, they are friends of utility. A friendship of utility develops because the friends love each other as a useful object. According to Aristotle, "Those who love each other for their utility do not love each other for themselves, but in virtue of some good which they can get from the other."[10] Saint Thomas Aquinas further explains this statement when he states that those "who do not love their friend for what he is in himself but for what is incidental to him ... [do not have a] friendship essentially, but incidentally."[11] Don Quixote knows from reading the books of chivalry that it is essential for a knight to have a squire; he does not love Sancho for what he is in himself, but

[10] Ibid., 1156a12.

[11] Aquinas, *Commentary on the Nicomachean Ethics* VIII, 3, 1566.

rather, he loves Sancho for being a squire. Don Quixote uses Sancho so that he can be a proper knight.

Sancho Panza, although he knows he owes Don Quixote his service, always keeps his promised reward of a governorship in mind. In fact, when Don Quixote fights a battle, Sancho, standing off watching, prays "to God in his heart that it might be his will to grant him the victory, that he might thereby win some island to make him governor of" (see p. 74). Aristotle states that friendship of utility often occurs between fellow travelers.[12] Each man finds many beneficial uses of the other as a travel companion. Thus, in the early days of Don Quixote's chivalric quest, he and Sancho Panza are friends of utility, as they each expect some use out of the other. At this point, each has not come to love the other for his own sake.

The friendship of pleasure is similar to that of utility. Like the previous friendship, the person is not loved for what he is, but rather for some other qualified good, namely, a pleasant good. Don Quixote finds enormous pleasure in reenacting the legends of knights-errant he read about in his books. He delights in having a squire so ready to admire his abilities. After his defeat of the Biscayan nobleman, he boasts, "But tell me, as you live, have you seen a more valiant knight than I in all the known world? Have you read in history of any who has or had more vigor in attacking, more spirit in persevering, more dexterity in wounding or skill in overthrowing?" (see p. 75). Sancho replies that he believes all that his master said; he, too, seeks pleasure from his friendship with Don Quixote. Remembering that he normally would be laboring away on his farm, Sancho finds it a novelty of journeying with a man with such an unusual quest. He relishes the thought of adventures Don Quixote has assured him that they will encounter. At moments, Sancho "never gave a thought to any of the promises his master had made him, nor did he count it as hardship but as recreation this going in quest of adventures, however dangerous they might be" (see p. 63). At these earlier times, then, Don Quixote and Sancho Panza's relationship can be classified as a friendship of pleasure.

The friendships of utility and of pleasure are imperfect; they are called friendships in virtue of a similarity to the true friendship of the unqualified good. Aristotle states that these friendships are incidental; for, "it is not as being the man he is that the loved person is loved, but as providing some good or pleasure."[13] The friend is not loved because of who he is, but rather, he is loved because of what he can do for the other. Both Don Quixote and Sancho Panza love each other for the use or pleasure gained from one another. And thus, such friendships "are easily dissolved … for if the one party is no longer pleasant or useful the other ceases to love him".[14] The friendship lasts only as long as each man is useful or pleasant to the other.

Yet, unexpectedly, Don Quixote and Sancho Panza persevere. They continue together, protecting and ministering to each other, fighting side by side, suffering

[12] Aristotle, *Nicomachean Ethics* 1155a21; 1156a30.

[13] Ibid., 1156a18–19.

[14] Ibid., 1156a20–21.

together, sharing meals, and keeping each other company day and night. Their relationship has, thus far, progressed from that of mere traveling companions, to friends according to Aristotle's general definition, to friends of utility, and even at times, to friends of pleasure. By the end of the novel, Don Quixote and Sancho Panza are able to progress further to a true friendship, defined by Aristotle as one between men who are good and resemble each other in virtue.[15] It is perfect in all respects since "in it, each gets from each in all respects the same as, or something like what, he gives; which is what ought to happen between friends."[16]

Don Quixote and Sancho Panza have knowledge of what it is to be virtuous and good. Both men know that a knight—indeed, any man—must be "adorned with all the virtues, theological and cardinal.... He must be faithful to God and to his lady. He must be pure in thought, decorous in words, generous in works, valiant in deeds, patient in suffering, compassionate toward the needy, and, lastly, an upholder of the truth though its defense should cost him his life" (see p. 524). This is the key for their friendship to move beyond use or pleasure: by acknowledging the spiritual reality of the world and conforming themselves to that truth of reality, not by seeking worldly fame as a knight or power as the governor of an island. Although Don Quixote and Sancho Panza are aware of the truth, they are both hampered by shortcomings that prevent them from consistently acting in accordance with virtue. Cervantes reveals, however, that despite their failings, the men have both the knowledge and the disposition of virtue, if not quite the habit.

When Don Quixote's fiery temper gets the better of him, for example, he repents and forgives. When Sancho exalts Princess Micomicona over Dulcinea, Don Quixote's wrath falls upon his squire in the form of blows and irate words: "Do you think, you scurvy peasant, that you will always be permitted to disrespect me, that you are to be always offending and I always pardoning?" (see p. 242). Yet soon enough, Don Quixote's anger does abate as does Sancho's indignation: "Sancho advanced hanging his head and begged his master's hand, which Don Quixote presented to him with dignity, giving him his blessing as soon as he had kissed it " (see p. 243). Such is one example of many in which Don Quixote flies into a rage, yet subsequently forgives and forgets, as exemplified when he tells Sancho a few pages later, "Friend Panza, let us forgive and forget our quarrels" (see p. 244). Don Quixote strives to achieve the ideals of the truly chivalric knights, getting back on track each time he strays.

Sancho Panza also possesses the disposition, although not yet the steadfast habit, of virtue. Despite his failings, his virtue shines forth in moments that matter, especially when he admits he would refuse the governorship if Don Quixote truly thinks he ought "for the mere black of the nail [smallest part] of my soul is more precious to me than my whole body.... And if there's any reason to think that because of my being a governor the devil will get hold of me, I'd rather go as Sancho to heaven than governor to hell" (see p. 672). Even with the satirical tone of Cervantes' novel, Sancho's words ring true. Don Quixote replies in

[15] Ibid., 1156b7.

[16] Ibid., 1156b34–35.

as genuine a manner: "I judge that you deserve to be governor of a thousand islands. You have good natural instincts, without which no knowledge is worth anything" (see p. 672). He reminds Sancho to commend himself to God and to set out with the clear intent of always doing right in every matter. Both men mutually will the good of the other in encouragement to conform themselves to the truth that man has an immortal soul that must avoid the devil in order to be in union with God eternally.

Don Quixote and Sancho display their ability to will the good of the other both in words and in deeds. They have a disposition for goodness and wish each other that same goodness. They share triumphs and failures, sorrows and joys together. In fact, Don Quixote claims earlier in the novel, "Being your lord and master, I am your head, and you are a part of me, since you are my servant. Therefore, any evil that affects or shall affect me should give you pain, and what affects you give pain to me" (see p. 435). Don Quixote and Sancho Panza, in their constant companionship and sharing of the good, most of all in their moral vision of the world, are able to surpass the imperfect forms of friendship and take part in the true one.

This true friendship is the most complete, because it has all the characteristics of the other two friendships as well as additional qualities. According to Aristotle, these additional qualities differentiate this friendship from the others: (1) it is not harmed by slander; (2) it is between men who are dear and trustworthy to each other; (3) it lacks nothing; (4) it endures.[17] The key characteristic of a true friendship is seeing the other as "another self".[18]

As for the first quality, they do not harm each other by slander. They defend each other's stories, as seen when Don Quixote promises to believe what Sancho saw on Clavileño if Sancho will believe what his master saw in the Cave of Montesinos (p. 662). Here, Don Quixote reveals that he knows of their exaggerations and yet values the friendship more than his fame among those listening to them. They model the second quality, being "dear and trustworthy", as seen when Sancho expresses his gratitude: "Master of mine, let it not be said of me, 'the bread eaten and the company dispersed.' ... Furthermore, I know and have learned, by many good words and deeds, your worship's desire to show me favor.... And so I offer again to serve your worship faithfully and loyally, as well and better than all the squires that served knights-errant in times past or present" (see p. 463). Sancho often goes beyond the normal duties of a squire, offering advice later in their journey, speaking to Don Quixote as an equal, and Don Quixote listens to him "more eager than ever to put his squire's scheme into execution" (see p. 392).

The third quality, that it lacks nothing, is seen in their understanding of each other. They have spent so much time together that affection remains even despite complaints toward the other. A friendship of utility may end because of complaints, but in a true friendship of the unqualified good, there is no offense at

[17] Ibid., 1156b11, 17, 24, 33; 1157a20–24.

[18] Ibid., 1166a30.

complaints, for as Aristotle asserts, "No one is offended by a man who loves him and does well by him."[19] Even when Don Quixote and Sancho Panza quarrel and misunderstand each other, they still are able to maintain a good-humored outlook. Don Quixote, for example, states, "Because I know you, Sancho, . . . I do not heed your words"; Sancho retorts, "Nor I your worship's" (see p. 560). This kind of familiarity without rancor reveals that they have grown to understand each other. Their bickering never reaches the boiling point at which they dissolve their friendship; rather, they continue together. No fight splits these two. Don Quixote and Sancho remain together seeking use, pleasure, and good from the other.

The final quality is that it endures. A friendship of utility or pleasure falls apart as soon as there is no longer mutual benefit to be gained. When it does end, there is no feeling of disappointment on either side because the use or pleasure involved disappears. On the other hand, a friendship of the unqualified good endures. After Don Quixote's defeat by the Knight of the White Moon, there is no longer a master-and-servant, or knight-and-squire relationship. This is confirmed by Don Quixote: "When I was a knight-errant, daring and valiant, I supported my achievements by hand and deed, and now that I am a humble squire I will make good my words by keeping the promise I have given. Forward then, Sancho my friend" (see p. 808). Don Quixote has promised to forswear knight-errantry, while Sancho Panza has, by this time, forsworn the governorship of the island. Neither one needs the other as they had done previously. There are no evident benefits to be gained from being in each other's company, and yet they remain together. In fact, Don Quixote suggests to Sancho that they emulate the "gallant shepherds who were trying to revive and imitate the pastoral Arcadia" and that he himself would be "the shepherd Quixótiz" and that Sancho would be "the shepherd Panzino" (see p. 814). When none of the causes that first formed their friendship remain, Don Quixote and Sancho Panza still opt to continue to be with each other. Aristotle states that "mutual love involves choice and choice springs from a state of character"[20] and that "loving seems to be the characteristic virtue of friends, so that it is only those in whom this is found in due measure that are lasting friends, and only their friendship endures."[21] In planning to be shepherds, each man will see the other as an equal, seeking the other's good as if for himself, for as Aristotle stated, in a true friendship each man sees the other as "another self".[22] Don Quixote and Sancho Panza's desire to be shepherds in Arcadia shows that they value each other's companionship and want to strive toward goodness together.

Since a true friendship endures, it ends only by external forces. When it is forced to end, much loss is felt by one or the other. For instance, Don Quixote's defeatist attitude on his deathbed leaves Sancho not knowing "what to say or do, so overcome was he with despair" (see p. 802). When Don Quixote stays in

[19] Ibid., 1162b8.
[20] Ibid., 1157b30–31.
[21] Ibid., 1159a35–36.
[22] Ibid., 1166a30.

bed, dejected, depressed, and in the worst of spirits, Sancho tries to console and comfort him. He even wants to take the blame for his master's defeat against the Knight of the White Moon, saying, "If you're dying from grief over having been defeated, put the blame on me. Say you were knocked down because I did a poor job saddling Rocinante" (see p. 847). When Don Quixote falls deathly ill at the end of the novel, Sancho remains at his bedside, and tears often burst from his swollen eyes (see p. 847).

Their friendship only ends because of external causes, namely, death. Don Quixote recognizes Sancho's loyalty and friendship and bequeaths him money in his will, and, true to Sancho's practical nature, Sancho appreciates this gift from his friend. Don Quixote also says he wishes he could make Sancho the ruler of a kingdom, because the "simplicity of his character and the fidelity of his conduct deserve no less" (see p. 847). Even at the end, Don Quixote wishes good to his friend. Sancho is devastated at his friend's death for his love goes beyond one of a servant for his master; it is the love of a friend.

Don Quixote and Sancho Panza develop from being neighborly acquaintances to companions, to friends of use and pleasure, into friends of the unqualified good. Don Quixote and Sancho Panza find all those goods in each other: the useful good, the pleasant good, and most importantly, the good in itself. Their quarrels, bickering, and other squabbles do not manage to deter their willingness to spend their days together. They stay side by side through the triumphs and the setbacks. Recalling their adventure in Part I, Don Quixote observes, "I took you from your cottage, when you know that I did not remain in my house. We sallied forth together" (see p. 435). Even in a satirical novel, Don Quixote and Sancho Panza's friendship by the end reigns as genuine, exemplifying how even misguided or flawed characters can seek the good of another in a friendship aiming toward virtue, enduring until it is dissolved by death.

The Sword and the Pen: Miguel de Cervantes Saavedra, the Chivalric Knight of Literature

Michael Dominic Taylor
Thomas More College of Liberal Arts

Miguel de Cervantes Saavedra lived a dark and troubled life—marked by disability, captivity, slavery, poverty, imprisonment, and professional frustrations—but it was not without its glories as well. The first of these was his participation, at the age of twenty-four, in that miraculous defeat of the Ottoman Empire at the Battle of Lepanto. The second, over the course of the next several decades, was becoming the author who would pen the two-part masterpiece *Don Quixote*, by all accounts the first of its kind and the best-selling novel of all time.[1] The third was dying in the grace of God in 1616, just three weeks after taking the habit of the Third Order of Saint Francis.[2]

Cervantes and his genius are celebrated in the elaborate 112-foot-tall monument in the center of Madrid's Plaza de España, built for the three hundredth anniversary of his death. This monument includes a massive stone carving of Cervantes himself, seated and looking out upon two larger-than-life brass figures of Don Quixote and Sancho, surrounded by fountains, and is crowned with a globe surrounded by allegorical figures of the five continents,[3] all reading his work. The monument is impressive in many ways and speaks to the reach and impact of Cervantes' work, but I wish to bring attention to some of its figures that are often overlooked. The artists have adorned the back of the monument with three more allegorical figures: Literature, highest and in the center, flanked by Military Valor on her left, and, to her right, Mysticism. These are well chosen, well depicted, and well *placed*: it was his left hand that was maimed at the Battle of Lepanto, and his right with which he penned his works and crossed himself innumerable times—before battle, while in captivity, and in his last hour. Notably, Mysticism is clad in a scapular of Our Lady of Mount Carmel, the signature sacramental of the Discalced Carmelites, who will become more important for us in a moment. Nevertheless, it is Lady Literature, clad like a

[1] This accomplishment would have a secondary effect that Cervantes should also be credited for: the complete destruction of the genre of banal "books of chivalry" that infected Don Quixote's imagination. Not a single work of this type, which had been the most popular by far, was produced after the publication of *Don Quixote*.

[2] Cervantes' death day was recorded in his local parish as April 23, though many historians insist that this be amended given the evidence that he had died the day before.

[3] Excluding Antarctica and counting the Americas as one.

noble princess, who captivated the mind and heart of our hero and whom he would defend with all his prowess.

This enormous and elaborate monument seems out of proportion with the humble tomb in which Cervantes is actually buried. According to his own will, his tomb can be found in the Convent of the Discalced Trinitarians, to whom he credited his rescue in 1580 from his five-year captivity in Algeria. History, always with its particular sense of irony, has situated the Trinitarian Convent on what, in 1844, became Lope de Vega Street, named for Cervantes' younger, more popular rival of the Spanish Golden Age.

Cervantes' other great literary contemporary was none other than William Shakespeare, whom the vagaries of history unite in the shared death date of April 23, 1616, the Feast of Saint George, who, according to Don Quixote, "was one of the best knights-errant that heaven's army ever owned."[4] What they also had in common was their Catholicism and a universal recognition of their genius, even among secular critics.[5] However, many modern accounts of these authors defend the thesis that their brilliance was in no way related to what they interpret as the mere trappings of Christianity, taken up as the occasion to demonstrate their personal prowess, or better yet, as a veiled disenchantment with or rejection of the faith. Some even go so far as to claim that Cervantes was a proto-Marxist who railed against the Catholic Church relentlessly, though between the lines of his works. These critics, unable to square their admiration for the undeniable genius of Cervantes and Shakespeare and their religious faith, seek to reinterpret their genius in a dualistic mode wherein form is only accidentally related to content, the latter being best understood by the readers themselves in whatever way is most meaningful to them.

In this brief commentary, I will argue that Cervantes was a believing Catholic and devotee of the Spanish mystics of his day, and explore what light this sheds on how we are to read *Don Quixote* and what Cervantes may wish us to learn from it. This will also lead us to consider more deeply Cervantes' status as a Catholic author fully engaged in the battle for *good, true, and beautiful* fiction and, indeed, one of its greatest defenders.

First, however, it is important to understand something of the literary and religious context of the time in which Cervantes lived. The printing press had

[4] Miguel de Cervantes, *Don Quixote*, ed. Timothy McCallister, Ignatius Critical Editions, ed. Joseph Pearce (San Francisco: Ignatius Press, 2026), p. 755. All subsequent quotations of *Don Quixote* are from this edition and will be cited in the text.

It seems that the coincidence of the shared date, however, was not temporal but symbolic, due to Protestant England's stubborn (170-year-long) resistance to the more accurate Gregorian calendar, adopted by Catholic and more scientific nations starting in 1582, which omitted ten calendar days and moved the start of a new year to January 1.

[5] For books on Shakespeare's Catholicism, see Richard Wilson, *Secret Shakespeare: Studies in Theatre, Religion and Resistance* (Manchester University Press, 2004); Clare Asquith, *Shadowplay: The Hidden Beliefs and Coded Politics of William Shakespeare* (PublicAffairs, 2005); and Joseph Pearce, *The Quest for Shakespeare: The Bard of Avon and the Church of Rome* (Ignatius Press, 2008).

been invented in 1440 and, as the technology progressed and societies became more affluent, reading would become wildly popular. New texts and new humanistic ideas would flow from the presses. European societies were not prepared for the challenges that the ready access to any one man's thoughts would bring, especially when his thought would challenge the moral and cultural authorities. Erasmus would promote the private reading of Scripture, and in the Greek rather than the traditional Latin Vulgate. Protestantism certainly took advantage of this new medium, not only to promote its own ideas but to detract from its enemies through the creation of what would become known as the Black Legend. The Church, for her part, did not formalize the system of ecclesial approval and prohibition of printed texts—the *imprimatur*, the *nihil obstat*, and the *Index Librorum Prohibitorum* (*The Index of Forbidden Books*)—until 1560, near the end of the Council of Trent. The Inquisition would spend a great deal of its time scrutinizing the many theological novelties of this era.

Meanwhile, in Cervantes' day, the most popular books were those of chivalric romance novels, fictional tales of knights and castles that over time became increasingly derivative and morally corrupt. At that time, fiction had not yet been established as a noble art—good and true and beautiful—for, in fact, fiction seemed solely to be produced for the purpose of idle entertainment and to turn a profit. Many secular and religious authorities would condemn fiction altogether, and not without cause, calling for readers to restrict themselves to the reading of true chronicles and histories of noble men and approved religious texts.

The debate raged on. Should fiction be done away with altogether, or be left relegated to the entertainment of the sordid masses? Or was literature to have a higher calling? Was there a place for it in high culture and the education of the youth? Providence would have it that, with the fall of Constantinople in 1453 at the hands of the Ottomans, many new Greek texts would make their way West with the refugees thereof. One of these texts was Aristotle's *Poetics*, which had been previously unknown in Europe. Italian authors seem to have been the first to discover its insights. Shortly thereafter, in 1596 in Madrid, Alonso López Pinciano published his *Philosophía antigua poética*, in which he put forth the lessons gleaned from Aristotle, defending the intellectual and moral value of fiction in the form of a dialogue of more than five hundred pages.

For Aristotle, fiction has cathartic qualities that "purge the soul" of emotion and expand the range of the audience's empathetic and ethical experience. Fiction is not "lying" but a natural desire of man he described as "mimesis", an imitation of reality that can present universal truths through the particulars of a story.[6] But in order to be *good* fiction, it must also make sense; it must be plausible within a fictional world that is coherent and integral, even if it contains

[6] In Part II, chapter 3, Cervantes has Samson Carrasco observe that "it is one thing to write as a poet, another to write as a historian. The poet may describe or sing things, not as they were, but as they ought to have been; but the historian has to write them down, not as they ought to have been, but as they were, without adding anything to the truth or taking anything from it" (see p. 440).

fantastical elements. Thus, the events in a plot must be explained as causally related, one to the other. It is this principle of verisimilitude that all "plot holes" and *Deus ex machina* endings violate.

Chivalric romances, though with a noble beginning in *Amadís of Gaul* (which Cervantes saves from the flames in Part I, chapter 6), had become more derivative and absurd, and yet they were all the more desired by the public (notably, Ignatius and Teresa of Ávila adored them, before their conversions). It could not be more clear that this exasperated Cervantes to such a degree that he declared them his mortal enemy and waged war on them through the figure of Don Quixote. Cervantes saw that these romances were bad literature, not only on a moral level but intellectually, and would fight for the unification of good morals and good literature on the whole as something both entertaining and instructional, understanding innately that these must not be separated.

Thus, much of *Don Quixote* is a parody of these novels, yet it would be a mistake to consider it *merely* parody. It is crucial to take note of the fact that within *Don Quixote* are included elements and commentary on *all* of the major literary forms and styles of the day: the picaresque novel,[7] the pastoral romance,[8] the Byzantine novel,[9] the Spanish *comedia*,[10] the Moorish novel (*novela morisca*),[11] and the Italian novella,[12] to name a few. Cervantes critiques all in turn, assailing their weaknesses, working for their improvement and generally critiquing the art of writing. Thus, we start to see how well it was that Literature was chosen as the central allegorical figure, hidden behind the glory of Cervantes' creations.

When it comes to *Military Valor*, it seems obvious that this is in reference to Cervantes' years as a soldier and his glorious presence at the Battle of Lepanto, about which he says in the prologue to Part II that it was "the grandest occasion that past or present has seen or the future can hope to see" (see p. 419). *Mysticism*, on the other hand, seems at first rather far removed from Cervantes and the silliness of *Don Quixote* and, thus, rather an odd choice. However, recent scholarship has revealed that there were good reasons for Cervantes to camouflage this connection, for not all of Cervantes' dearest sources and inspirations were approved of by the Inquisition at the time of his writing, which counted numerous future saints among those investigated, from Ignatius of Loyola to Teresa of Ávila and

[7] See, for example, all the events surrounding the life of Ginés de Pasamonte in Part I, chapter 22, and his transformation into "Master Pedro" in Part II, chapters 25–27, who further parodies the playwright Lope de Vega, as well as the actions of Roque Guinart in Part II, chapters 60–61.

[8] See, for example, the episode of Marcela and Grisóstomo in Part I, chapters 12–14, and Don Quixote's plan to become a shepherd in Part II, chapters 58–60.

[9] See, for example, the story of Cardenio, Luscinda, Dorotea, and Don Fernando in Part I, chapters 24–30, 42–46.

[10] See, for example, Master Pedro's puppet show (see Part II, chaps. 25–26) or the various theatrical episodes staged by the duke and duchess (see Part II, chaps. 30–57).

[11] See, for example, the captive's tale (see Part I, chaps. 39–41) or the episode of Ana Félix and Don Gaspar Gregorio in Part II, chapters 63 and 65.

[12] See, for example, *The Novel of the Imprudent Meddler* (see Part I, chaps. 33–35).

John of the Cross.[13] Cervantes had a deep regard for the Spanish mystics, starting with Fray Luis de León—the first to translate the Song of Songs into Spanish verse—whom he honored in *Galatea*: "Fray Luis de León it is I sing, Whom I love and adore, to whom I cling."[14] On the occasion of the beatification of Teresa of Ávila in 1614, Cervantes composed an ode in her honor, and it is reasonable to conjecture that the "Descent into the Cave of Montesinos" might have been influenced by her *Interior Castle*.

Yet it was John of the Cross (1542–1591) who was under particular threat of censure during the life of Cervantes, as his mystical and poetic works—which were circulated privately only among the monasteries and convents of the Discalced Carmelites—were unusual and largely misunderstood. Providentially, Cervantes' older sister was a member of just such a convent in their hometown of Alcalá de Henares, which John of the Cross would have visited frequently in the years following Cervantes' liberation from captivity in 1580. Even the first edition of John's writings, published in 1618, omits the *Spiritual Canticle* and shows other alterations in order to avoid suspicion. There is good reason to believe that the writings of the diminutive mystic, as well as news of his life and works, would have been sought after and found by Cervantes.

It is what occurred after John of the Cross' death, however, that will be most significant for this brief commentary. He died in 1591 at the Discalced Carmelite Monastery in Úbeda. Before his death, a noble widow by the name of Doña Ana de Peñalosa, who was under his spiritual direction, had arranged with the Vicar General of the Reform that—no matter where John of the Cross died—his body would be returned to Segovia, his native city, and be laid to rest in the monastery that he had founded there. However, the monastery in Úbeda was reluctant to give up the body of this new saint by popular acclaim, and the incorrupt state and sweet fragrance of his relics only heightened his fame, drawing pilgrims from all around. It is known that Cervantes himself was in Úbeda during the wheat harvest of 1592, doing the thankless work of requisitioning olive oil for the Spanish government. It is almost certain that he would have visited the saint with great devotion. The transfer of the body finally took place in secrecy in mid-1593. Traveling by night and avoiding main roads, Don Juan de Medina Ceballos oversaw the more than three-hundred-mile journey. Despite these efforts, the local citizens caught wind of their movements and confronted the group more than once. Nevertheless, they did arrive in Segovia eventually, where Saint John of the Cross is venerated to this day in the convent that bears his name.[15] We will come back to this story shortly, when we discuss Part I, chapter 19, but we must start from the beginning.

[13] See Luce López-Baralt, "Don Quixote and Saint John of the Cross's Spiritual Chivalry", *Religions* 12 (2021): 616.

[14] Miguel de Cervantes, *The Complete Works of Miguel de Cervantes Saavedra, Vol. II: Galatea*, ed. J Fitzmaurice-Kelly, trans. H. Oelsner and A.B. Welford (Gowans & Gray, 1903), p. 278.

[15] Though Pope Clement VIII ordered the body be returned to Úbeda, the convent of Saint John of the Cross' last days would eventually receive only a hand and a tibia.

Evidence for the influence of John of the Cross on Cervantes is hinted at from the outset of *Don Quixote*. Let us recall that "The Dark Night of the Soul" begins thus:

En una noche oscura,	On a dark night,
con ansias, en amores inflamada,	by flames of love possessed,
¡oh dichosa ventura!,	oh, blessed quest!,
salí sin ser notada	unnoticed I took flight
estando ya mi casa sosegada.	all my house now at rest.[16]

The spiritual significance of the lines is given by the author himself, so as not to be misinterpreted. It sings of the joyous trust, enflamed by love, that dispels any hesitance of the Christian soul from setting out, once the desires of the body have been calmed, onto the spiritual path of self-negation, where understanding does not reach. Don Quixote's very first sally in chapter 2 begins thus:

> Without giving notice of his intention to anyone and without anybody seeing him, one morning before daybreak (on one of the hottest days of the month of July) ... by the back gate of the yard [he] sallied forth upon the plain in the highest of contentment and delight at seeing with what ease he had made a beginning of his grand purpose. (See p. 30.)

The parallels are suggestive, but the similarities end immediately, as Don Quixote's joy turns to doubt, for "scarcely did he find himself upon the open plain when a terrible thought struck him, one all but enough to make him abandon the enterprise at the very outset. It occurred to him that he had not been dubbed a knight" (see p. 30).

The drama of Don Quixote's burning *desire* and absolute *incapacity* to be a true knight are the driving force of the entire work, the constant occasion for absurdity and humor, and the endearing quality that make him loveable despite his outrageous madness. Many who admire Cervantes' Catholicism would like to interpret Don Quixote simply as a holy fool, one who sees the spiritual reality of a fallen world and thus, to the world, only *seems* a fool. The crucial question, however, is, What is the root cause of Don Quixote's madness? Is it simply the case that the world has gone mad, or are things more complex? The stated cause of that madness, of course, was the obsessive, private reading of books of chivalry within a hermeneutic of literalism, and—it must be noted—a lack of sleep. Living in the decades following the Council of Trent, in the midst of the Catholic Reformation, Cervantes was well aware of the dangers of private interpretation and the deformities that it could spawn. But more importantly, what had happened to chivalry and the novels that purported to celebrate the knights that embodied this most noble of ideals? Cervantes' parody revealed how far both the modern world and the popular tales printed in books had strayed from anything of value.

In the very next chapter, Don Quixote has himself dubbed a knight in a ludicrous ceremony that maintains only the faintest resemblance to the authentic original. Arriving at an inn, which he believes to be a castle, he convinces the

16 My translation.

innkeeper to perform the ceremony and dub him a knight the following morning. As with many of the normal people Don Quixote interacts with, the innkeeper goes along with his madness if only to have a good laugh. However, nothing is as it should be. There is no chapel because it has been torn down in order to build a new one, so the ceremony must be held in the corral. There is no Bible, so the innkeeper's ledger is used instead. The only witnesses are two prostitutes and a boy with a candle. The words of the innkeeper during the dubbing are nothing but a mock prayer, mumbled in something resembling Latin. All in all, the effect of the entire scene is a tragic hilarity, as Don Quixote's errors are carried by Cervantes' superbly witty writing *ad absurdum*.

However, Don Quixote's sins will not go unpunished. Still at the beginning of the novel, in chapter 19, we hear of "the adventure that befell him with a dead body" in which Don Quixote attacks a group of priests whom he thinks are otherworldly demons as they transport a dead body through the night. On a very dark night, as the narrator notes, Sancho and his master witness a procession of a large group of mounted men bearing torches followed by a coffin and six more men mounted on mules, dressed in mourning. To Don Quixote, the body was no doubt that of a dead knight whom he alone could revenge. The entire situation cannot but conjure the memory of the solemn translation of the body of Saint John of the Cross, and Don Quixote's identification of the body as that of a knight is an assumption that is fitting for the particular brand of his madness but also deeply telling of Cervantes' own notion of spiritual chivalry that haunts the entire novel.

Don Quixote confronts the torchbearers and, when his inquiry into the nature of the situation is not met with the desired response, he proceeds to attack, injure, and disperse the party, who "all thought he was no man but a devil from hell" (see p. 137). In the madness, a seminarian named Alonso López is thrown from his mule and breaks his leg. Alonso explains that they are bringing the dead body from Baeza (a town conspicuously close to Úbeda), where the man "was interred" to Segovia, his native city (see p. 138). Upon hearing that he had died by a malignant fever (as had John of the Cross), Don Quixote abandons his desire for vengeance, helps Alonso back onto his mule, and sends him to the rest of his group, "of whom he begged pardon on his part for the wrong he could not help doing them" (see p. 139). As he is leaving, it is Sancho who adds that it is Don Quixote of La Mancha who begs their pardon, also known as "the Knight of the Woeful Countenance" (see p. 139).

When Don Quixote asks for an explanation for this title, Sancho says, "I've been looking at you for some time by the light of the torch that unfortunate fellow was carrying, and your worship truly does have of late the sorriest face I ever saw" (see p. 139). Shortly thereafter, Alonso López returns with the following announcement he "forgot to mention":

> Remember that you stand excommunicated for having laid violent hands on a holy thing: *Juxta illud, "si quis suadente diabolo," etc.* (See p. 139.)

López is quoting from the *Decretum Gratiani*, a medieval text of canon law, to which Don Quixote responds with casuistry, self-justification, and yet, the insistence that he is a good and faithful Catholic:

> I do not understand that Latin,... but I know well I did not lay hands, only this spear. Besides, I did not think I was committing an assault upon priests or things of the Church—which, faithful Christian and Catholic that I am, I respect and revere—but upon ghosts and specters of the other world. (See p. 139.)

Despite the plausibility of his words, Don Quixote's own countenance has already betrayed his defense, as if the light of the dead knight's torchbearer, in the midst of that dark night, revealed the truth of his tortured soul. The adventure with the dead body bears too many resemblances to that of the transfer of the body of Saint John of the Cross to be ignored.[17] In the closing lines of the chapter, Don Quixote expresses his desire to look at the body in the coffin to see if it "was nothing but bones" (see p. 140). Sancho convinces him not to, and we get a sense that Don Quixote was not yet prepared for what he might find: the incorrupt and sweet-smelling body of Saint John of the Cross.

One cannot but see a flicker of what must have been Cervantes' own sorrow in *Don Quixote*, that same sorrow the French novelist Leon Bloy described in *La Femme Pauvre*: "The only real sadness, the only real failure, the only great tragedy in life, is not to become a saint."

But why is Don Quixote the way he is? He is imitating a good and true calling: as he announced to the goatherds in Part I, chapter 11, "the order of knights-errant was instituted, to defend maidens, to protect widows, and to aid the orphans and the needy" (see p. 81). Again, in chapter 20, immediately after "the adventure with a dead body" (see chap. 19), Don Quixote reminds us that "by Heaven's will I have been born in this our iron age to restore to it the age of gold, or Golden Age, as it is called" (see p. 141). The Golden Age he refers to is the prelapsarian age, before sin took root in human society. And yet, everything Don Quixote knows of chivalry and knight-errantry he has learned from books that have, over time, become corrupted by authors who only wish to satisfy the worldly desires of the masses and the greed of booksellers. These books not only do not instruct in good morals but also fail to conform to the criteria of good literature. And so Don Quixote's madness is not in any way a condemnation of chivalry or even of knights-errant, whom later we discover include Saints George, Martin, James, and Paul.[18] No, his madness is precisely a condemnation of what Cervantes says (four times over in the preface alone) is his only aim: "the destruction of that ill-founded edifice of the books of chivalry, hated by some and praised by many more."

Here, however, it is worth mentioning another Spanish mystic with whom Cervantes was presumably very familiar: Saint Ignatius of Loyola. Ignatius had been a soldier who was famously fond of books of chivalry and requested some while he was convalescing after being injured at the siege of Pamplona. There were none in the house, and so he was given *The Life of Christ*, by Rudolph, the Carthusian, and another book called the *Flowers of the Saints*. Over time, by meditation on these holy books, he determined to imitate them as completely as possible: extreme penances, making a pilgrimage to the Holy Land, absolute poverty,

[17] This observation was first made by Martin Fernández Navarrete, *Vida de Miguel de Cervantes Saavedra* (Real Academia Española, 1819).

[18] See Part II, chap. 58.

and long vigils. This was all well known to Cervantes as Ignatius' *Autobiography* had been compiled by Father Luis Gonçalves and published in 1555.

If the story of Don Quixote sounds similar to that of Ignatius, we must recognize that it does so in form only but not in content. Don Quixote is no saint, and though we pity his errors and many drubbings, we long to see him pursue chivalry without the errors introduced by bad literature. Though there is no direct evidence for it, here I would like to suggest that it is at least helpful to think of Don Quixote as a *reverse imitation* of Saint Ignatius, a tragicomic cautionary tale of what would happen if you should permit the wrong kind of writing to absorb your mind—which is precisely what the majority of the public was doing at the time. This allows Cervantes to fill Don Quixote with the virtues and wisdom that make him loveable, while also portraying a man who is very much spiritually adrift, excommunicated, and, by the end of Part I, blindly attacking a Marian procession. Don Quixote is no holy fool, as much as he would like to be holy. And all the while, bad fiction remains the villain throughout, which the audience learns to reject just as much as Cervantes does.

We are given further insight into this existential drama that cuts through the uproarious chronicles of Don Quixote toward the start of Part II. In chapter 8, in a discussion about the honor and glory Don Quixote sought through his knight-errantry, Sancho suggests, "Let us set about becoming saints, and we will obtain more quickly the good fame we're striving after" (see p. 469). After citing the case of "two little barefoot friars" that had been "canonized and beatified" and the veneration they received, Sancho concludes, "It is better to be a humble little friar of no matter what order, than a valiant knight-errant" (see p. 469). To which Don Quixote replies, "All that is true ... but we cannot all be friars, and many are the ways by which God takes his own to heaven. Chivalry is a religion; there are sainted knights in glory" (see p. 469). The discussion ends with Sancho's observation that "the errants are many", and Don Quixote's response: "Many,... but few those who deserve the name of knights" (see p. 469).

The appellation "the Knight of the Woeful Countenance" will mark Don Quixote until Part II, chapter 17, in which Don Quixote insists on endeavoring to fight two lions who refuse to attack him, lying back down instead. Don Quixote is declared victorious and Sancho retitles his master "The Knight of the Lions" (see p. 520), surely a reference to one of the original Knights of the Round Table, *Yvain, the Knight of the Lion* (by Chrétien de Troyes, c. 1180), though it is also worth noting that Saint John of the Cross, in his commentary on stanza XX of his *Spiritual Canticle*, says, "Here the Son of God, the Bridegroom, leads the bride into the enjoyment of peace and tranquility ... in adjuring the lions, [he] restrains the violence and controls the fury of rage."[19] Perhaps we cannot know if Cervantes intended this reference as well, but there is no doubt that Don Quixote is a little less absurd after this adventure. Immediately afterward, we are informed in no uncertain terms that he has been set on an upward path—perhaps because he has now shown true courage before a danger not of his own

[19] Saint John of the Cross, *A Spiritual Canticle of the Soul and the Bridegroom Christ*, trans. David Lewis (Benzinger Brothers, 1909), pp. 156, 159.

imagining, perhaps due to the miraculous adjuring of the lions. Regardless, we are told: "All this time, Don Diego de Miranda had not spoken a word, being entirely taken up with observing and noting all that Don Quixote did and said. The opinion he formed was that Don Quixote was a sane man gone mad and a madman with a touch of sanity" (see p. 520). And, we might add, with sanity came sanctity. For while Don Quixote has no rosary in Part I, chapter 26, and must make one, by Part II, chapter 46, he has "a large rosary that he always carried with him" (see p. 687), a notable accoutrement, as no other knight-errant is recorded to have one. Other such improvements included no longer imagining inns to be castles (see Part II, chap. 59), recognizing that Providence, not Fortune, rules the lives of men, and that he was defeated by the Knight of the White Moon because he lacked prudence (see Part II, chap. 66).

However, Don Quixote would have to bear his excommunication from the time of the encounter with the relics of Saint John of the Cross in Part I, chapter 19, until the very end of the history, when he finally comes to his senses, makes his confession, receives the sacraments, and dies in grace.

Don Quixote is not merely a parody of chivalric romance novels, but a commentary on the meaning and place of the written word in the life of a culture and of a man. This is the genius of Cervantes, who sought to instruct, not by adding honey to the wormwood, but by trusting the reader to see through the many layers of playful parody, to understand his meaning, and to join in laughing at his jokes. Though he admired the Spanish mystics and surely had recourse to them in prayer and devotion, he was no Carmelite nor Jesuit. He knew that "we cannot all be friars, and many are the ways by which God takes his own to heaven" (see p. 469). In his final days, Cervantes would accept Sancho's advice in the form of the brown habit of *il Poverello*, but God had taken him by another way: through the honor of his past Military Valor and the Mysticism of his devotion to the seat of Lady Literature, who captivated Cervantes' heart. With pen and ink, he would defend her tirelessly. By seamlessly uniting good Catholic morality, sharp wit, and proper literary technique, Cervantes revealed the integral unity of truth, goodness, and beauty, creating a masterpiece, as if of one piece of marble, about which one will never be able to say enough. Thus, Cervantes also revealed that bad literature is not merely bad for lacking a necessary ingredient—whether it be verisimilitude, morality, or delightfulness—but more profoundly for even presuming that these necessary ingredients could ever be separated. "But now in this detestable age of ours" (see p. 81)—in this age of iron rather than of gold—this unity is lost on a world that would seek with Machiavelli to maintain the State at any moral cost, or with Milton to enjoy poetic mastery without attention to theological truth.[20] Cervantes fought for a better world and would forever change the profession in which there will always be many who are errant but few who deserve to be called knights.

[20] See, for example, Joseph Pearce, "Paradise Lost in a Nutshell", *Crisis Magazine*, January 15, 2022, https://crisismagazine.com/opinion/paradise-lost-in-a-nutshell.

Shakespeare, Cervantes, and the Romance of the Real

R. V. Young
North Carolina State University

There is no more arresting coincidence in literary history than the death of two of the world's greatest writers, William Shakespeare and Miguel de Cervantes Saavedra, on the same date, April 23, 1616. The coincidence is fitting because of the similarity in the depiction of the world attained by both men, who are equally credited with opening the way for modern literature, especially the novel, with its intimate engagement with "real life".

While both writers strive to represent reality, it is also true that human experience can only be manifest by means of ideas, which define in some measure what that experience is. Thus, the greatest literature of Western civilization both "imitates" our life and shapes our understanding of what it can be. While a full account of the complex engagement of either of these authors could hardly be managed in many volumes, a few examples from each can at least sketch their singular achievements in engaging both reality and romantic enchantment simultaneously.

Just past the midpoint of his landmark study, *Mimesis* (1946), Erich Auerbach offers consecutive chapters on Shakespearean drama and Cervantes' *Don Quixote*. The authors occupy a key place in Auerbach's argument that the growth of the West's unique literary realism is principally a matter of rejecting the hierarchy of stylistic and generic classifications characteristic of ancient classical poetry, which were, for a time, resuscitated by humanist critics and writers of the Renaissance, whose neoclassicism persisted into the seventeenth and early eighteenth centuries.[1] The aristocratic genres of epic and tragedy, according to this scheme, would deal with momentous events and heroic characters in a consistently lofty style. Commonplace occurrences and ordinary men and women would be confined to comedy, pastoral, and other lesser genres that eschew elevated diction and figures.

Shakespeare notoriously breaks all the "rules". He mingles clowns and kings in the same play, and his style ranges from sublime blank verse to coarse, often bawdy prose within the same scene. Hamlet speaks grandly to the splendid, though ominous, ghost of his father, but banters crudely with the grave digger. "To be or not to be" is followed within a few moments of stage time by "Get thee to a nunnery". As he slides in and out of madness, the aged Lear can speak

[1] Erich Auerbach, *Mimesis: The Representation of Reality in Western Literature*, trans. Willard R. Trask (Princeton University Press, 1953), pp. 312–58.

eloquent defiance to the divine powers that govern the world and subsequently mock Gloucester's blindness with cruel humor. One might argue that this tragedy's most heroic figure is the nameless servant who dies while trying to defend the helpless Gloucester and gives Cornwall a mortal wound—a bit of characterization quite out of keeping with the neoclassical norm—as is the prominent role of Lear's fool.

From this perspective, *Don Quixote* is even more manifestly a stage in the "disenchantment of the world", to borrow Max Weber's melancholy phrase. John Ormsby, who produced the most distinguished nineteenth-century English translation (1885), is at pains to disabuse his readers of the fantasies of romantic German theorizing:

> All were agreed, however, that the object he aimed at was not the books of chivalry. He said emphatically in the preface to the First Part and in the last sentences of the Second, that he had no other object in view than to discredit these books, and this, to advanced criticism, made it clear that his object must have been something else.[2]

Seeing the book as "a kind of allegory setting forth the eternal struggle between the ideal and the real, between the spirit of poetry and the spirit of prose", Ormsby continues, results in a monstrosity: "Perhaps German philosophy never evolved a more unlikely or ungainly camel out of the depths of its inner consciousness."[3]

In less than a century, however, this sturdy realist view of *Don Quixote*, which insists that Cervantes offers us a representation of reality itself rather than the ideal vision of romance, is challenged by the postmodern notion that literature also fails even to represent reality, because language can represent only itself, since "reality" is no more than representation in any case: "Magic, which used to permit the decoding of the world by discovering secret similarities beneath signs, now serves only to explain in a delirious manner why analogies always disappoint." Hence, the world is disenchanted with a vengeance: "What is written and things no longer resemble each other. Between them, Don Quixote wanders randomly."[4]

Much the same has occurred with Shakespeare. In the preface to his landmark edition of Shakespeare (1765), Samuel Johnson, whose neoclassical predilections were tempered by his solid common sense, praised Shakespeare for devising a unique moral realism:

> Shakespeare is, above all writers, at least above all modern writers, the poet of nature, the poet that holds up to his readers a faithful mirror of manners and of life. His characters are not modified by customs of particular places, unpracticed by the

[2] *Delphi Complete Works of Miguel de Cervantes* (Delphi Classics, 2015), location nos. 115399–408, Kindle.

[3] Ibid.

[4] Michel Foucault, *Les Mots et les Choses: Une Archéologie des Sciences Humaines* (Éditions Gallimard, 1966), p. 62: "La magie, qui permettait le déchiffrement du monde en découvrant les ressemblances secrètes sous les signes, ne sert plus qu'à expliquer sur le mode délirant pourquoi les analogies sont toujours déçues.... L'écriture et les choses ne se ressemblent plus. Entre elles, Don Quichotte erre à l'aventure."

> rest of the world; by the peculiarities of studies or professions which can operate but upon small numbers; or by the accidents of transient fashions or temporary opinions; they are the genuine progeny of common humanity, such as the world will always supply, and observation will always find.[5]

Postmodern criticism, however, problematizes the dramatic integrity of Shakespeare's characters. Discussing *The Tempest*, for instance, Lorrie Jerrell Leininger avers, "Caliban is made to concur in the accusation [of rape, because] Prospero needs Miranda as sexual bait, and then needs to protect her from the threat which is inescapable given his hierarchical world—slavery being the ultimate extension of the concept of hierarchy."[6] Shakespeare's characters not only do not fit the proper tragic mold; they seem to have an independent existence outside the play in which the playwright has somehow misrepresented them. Literature is thus consumed by the ideological preoccupations of the critic's perceptions of current reality.

But while the postmodern proposition that Cervantes and Shakespeare are unwitting participants in the deliquescence of literary representation of reality is altogether untenable, there is also something problematic about the notion that they are simply harbingers of the triumph of sturdy modern realism. Although the latter view is clear-headed and in some respects plausible, it hardly captures the experience of most readers and playgoers. Enchantment is as much on offer in the work of both authors as disenchantment. Most readers of *Don Quixote* do not approach it as they would, say, Émile Zola's *Thérèse Raquin*, and patrons of the theater are unlikely to confuse Shakespeare's dramas with those of either Samuel Becket or Henrik Ibsen.

William Dean Howells, the leading proponent of literary realism in nineteenth-century America, discovered *Don Quixote* as a boy:

> It was full of meaning that I could not grasp, and there were significances of the kind that literature unhappily abounds in, but they were lost upon my innocence. I did not know whether it was well written or not; I never thought about that; it was simply there in its vast entirety, its inexhaustible opulence, and I was rich in it beyond the dreams of avarice.[7]

He tells us that, as a boy, "I believe I carried the book about with me most of the time, so as not to lose any chance moment of reading it"; and, "when I was fifty, I took it up in the admirable new version of Ormsby, and found it so full of myself and my irrevocable past that I did not find it very gay." Nevertheless, "In what

[5] *Samuel Johnson on Shakespeare*, ed. W.K. Wimsatt, Jr. (Hill and Wang, 1960), p. 25.

[6] Lorrie Jerrell Leininger, "The Miranda Trap: Sexism and Racism in Shakespeare's *Tempest*", in *The Woman's Part: Feminist Criticism of Shakespeare*, ed. Carolyn Ruth Swift Lenz, Gayle Greene, and Carol Thomas Neely (University of Illinois Press, 1980), p. 289. For an account of other, equally bizarre contemporary approaches to Shakespeare, see R.V. Young, "Contemporary Theory and Shakespeare's Romances", in *Shakespeare's Last Plays: Essays in Literature and Politics*, ed. Stephen W. Smith and Travis Curtright (Lexington Books, 2002), pp. 217–38.

[7] William Dean Howells, *My Literary Passions* (Harper & Bros., 1895), p. 23.

formed the greatness of the book it seemed to me greater than ever."[8] It is difficult to imagine anyone feeling this way about *The Grapes of Wrath* or *Wolf Hall*.

By the same token, playgoers think of Shakespeare mostly in terms of delight, not hegemonic politics. His quality is intimated most succinctly by that cool neoclassicist, John Dryden, in his comparison of Shakespeare to his classically inclined contemporary, Ben Jonson:

> If I would compare him with Shakespeare, I must acknowledge him the more correct poet, but Shakespeare the greater wit. Shakespeare was the Homer, or father of our dramatic poets; Jonson was the Virgil, the pattern of elaborate writing; I admire him, but I love Shakespeare.[9]

If we recognize that "wit", in Dryden's lexicon, means something like what we mean by "imagination", then the force of the comparison is clear. No one loves *Volpone*, or, for that matter, *Hedda Gabler*, the way many men and women love *A Midsummer Night's Dream* or *The Tempest*.

In order to account for the unique place held by Shakespeare and Cervantes, both early influences on the development of *realism*, it is necessary to reconsider what is meant by the *real*. At its best, literature—drama, narrative, and the various forms of lyrical and satirical writing, whether in prose or verse—mediates between an objective world, existing independently of human perception or even awareness, and our conscious experience and imaginative apprehension of that world. Both are elements of *reality*, but we are perennially tempted to incline toward the one or the other, to regard either the ideal realm of our own minds or the concrete fact of the material universe as the exclusive domain of the real. The movement of literary fashion reflects this dichotomy, but Shakespeare and Cervantes transcend it.

Cervantes draws particular attention to the chivalric romances, those ravishing flights of untrammeled fancy, which had bedazzled Spanish readers for several generations by the time Don Quixote galloped across the Spanish plains on the back of his caparisoned nag, Rocinante. No less a figure than Saint Teresa of Ávila berates herself (and her mother) for a virtual addiction to chivalric romances, as if they were the soap operas of sixteenth-century Spain.[10] No doubt, there was some virtue in "discrediting" them. Still, no one would confuse *Don Quixote* with the gritty realism and searing cynicism of Fernando de Rojas' *La Celestina* (1499) or of the anonymous picaresque novel *Lazarillo de Tormes* (1554), which represent a sharply contrasting tradition during the century preceding Cervantes' great work.

Don Quixote creates a kind of "magic realism" *avant la lettre*. The achievement may perhaps be best understood by contrasting it with Cervantes' last,

[8] Ibid., pp. 23–26.

[9] John Dryden, *An Essay of Dramatic Poesy and Other Critical Writings*, ed. George Watson (J.M. Dent and Sons, 1962), I, p. 70.

[10] *Libro de la vida* 2.1, *Obras Completas de Santa Teresa de Jesús*, 2nd ed., ed. Éfren de la Madre de Dios, O.C.D., and Otger Steggink, O. Carm. (Biblioteca de Autores Cristianos, 1967), p. 30.

posthumous work, *Los trabajos de Persiles y Segismunda* (1617). The latter falls into the genre of the "Greek romance" or "Byzantine novel" of which the most prominent example is *An Ethiopian Tale* by Heliodorus, variously dated to the third or fourth century A.D., and widely influential in subsequent European literature. True to the genre, *The Travails of Persiles and Segismunda* features star-crossed lovers, hairbreadth escapes, and perilous wandering through fantastic and geographically varied settings. A modern analogue might resemble J.R.R. Tolkien's *The Lord of the Rings*.

But although Cervantes reportedly regarded *Persiles y Segismunda* as his crowning work,[11] I am aware of no ten-year-old boy in a later century who carried a copy with him at all times, as Howells carried *Don Quixote*, "so as not to lose any chance moment of reading it". The paradox of this great work of literary realism is, then, that it is more enchanting, more *romantic*, not only than the books of chivalry that Cervantes set out to mock, but also of his own effort at beguiling the reader with fantastic adventures, characters, and settings. Something analogous may be said of Shakespeare, who rarely devised his own plots, but rather lifted stories from hither and yon, turning material that ranged from ordinary historical chronicles to banal Italian novellas into fascinating dramas, in which the characters—their doings and their speech—take luminous shape in our imagination and yet seem compellingly *real*.

Cervantes and Shakespeare are thus the literary embodiments of the genius of Western civilization, which is both shrewdly critical and aspirational. To grasp, however faintly, their means of achieving this is to apprehend in some measure the transformation of lead into gold in a way never attained by alchemy.

Ormsby points out the incongruity that emerges immediately from the title of the novel, *Don Quixote de La Mancha*:

> It would be going too far to say that no one can thoroughly comprehend "Don Quixote" without having seen La Mancha, but undoubtedly even a glimpse of La Mancha will give an insight into the meaning of Cervantes such as no commentator can give. Of all the regions of Spain it is the last that would suggest the idea of romance. Of all the dull central plateau of the Peninsula it is the dullest tract.[12]

"To anyone who knew the country well", he continues, "the mere style and title of 'Don Quixote of la Mancha' gave the key to the author's meaning at once."[13]

But the actual effect of reading the book is to endow this dullest district of Spain—and its dullness is part of the story's design—with endless fascination for generations of readers. Just as the drab, utilitarian windmills of La Mancha become giants in the mind of Alonso Quixano, the somewhat down-at-the-heels country gentleman who has assumed the guise of Don Quixote, doughty knight-errant; even so, La Mancha becomes in the mind of the young William Dean Howells and countless others a magical landscape where the reader eagerly anticipates

[11] *Delphi Cervantes*, location no. 30753.

[12] Ibid., location nos. 115520–27.

[13] Ibid.

the next misadventure of our benighted knight. Don Quixote's "quest" is thus to discover in ordinary places among ordinary men and women a vein of meaning and purpose. Insofar as both readers and the other characters are compelled to go along with him, to enter into his chivalric fantasies, he succeeds in opening up a realm of imagination among the poor, dusty villages of La Mancha.

Ormsby is of course correct in rejecting the simplistic German scheme in which Don Quixote embodies the spirit of the ideal and Sancho Panza the spirit of the real, because both figures are a mingling of both tendencies—as are all human beings. This becomes clear, for example, when Don Quixote and Sancho fall in with a group of goatherds, who share their wineskins, roast goat, and acorns with the errant pair. Inspired by the acorns and the rural setting, Don Quixote delivers a lengthy, ornate paean to the innocence and contentment of the classical pagan Golden Age: "Happy the age, happy the time, to which the ancients gave the name of golden, not because in that fortunate age the gold so coveted in this our iron one was gained without toil, but because they that lived in it knew not the two words *mine* and *thine*!"[14]

The rustic, presumably illiterate goatherds understand Don Quixote's implicit praise of mythical "pastoral" life as little as they do his prior encomium of the adventurous life of the knight-errant. The "ingenious gentleman", who fails to notice the authentic generosity of the goatherds, seems to be as deluded by the sixteenth-century fashion of pastoral literature as by the chivalric romance.

But it turns out he is not alone. The next few chapters recount Don Quixote's involvement with a beautiful young heiress and a large number of mostly wealthy and well-educated young men who act out the literary conventions of a pastoral novel in the fields of La Mancha. Marcela, niece of an indulgent village priest, who is her guardian, flees to the countryside with a flock of sheep in order to escape the importunities of her numerous suitors, whom she suspects of desiring only her beauty. One of them, the recent university graduate Grisóstomo, pursues her, also in the guise of shepherd; and he is soon joined by the others, all of them proclaiming their ardor in pastoral verses nailed to trees. Eventually, Grisóstomo sickens and dies, blaming his fate on the cruel shepherdess (see pp. 99–100), who has refused to requite his love.

The culmination of this episode is the funeral of Grisóstomo, where all the other "shepherds" gather to extol his virtues, personal and poetic, and denounce the "murderess", who has killed him by rejection. Marcela disrupts this histrionic orgy of lamentation and sentimental poetry, however, by showing up and vigorously defending her right *not* to marry a man merely because he desires it so intensely. The condemnation of Marcela as guilty of the death of the scholar turned "shepherd" depends upon literalizing the tropes of pastoral poetry and Petrarchanism—even as Alonso Quixano in the guise of Don Quixote has attempted a literal realization of the conventions of the chivalric romance.

[14] Miguel de Cervantes, *Don Quixote*, ed. Timothy McCallister, Ignatius Critical Editions, ed. Joseph Pearce (San Francisco: Ignatius Press, 2026), p. 80. All subsequent quotations of *Don Quixote* are from this edition and will be cited in the text.

Hence readers, as well as the other characters, are brought up short by Don Quixote's stern defense of the lady's right to reject an unwanted suitor.

The surprise is that Don Quixote's deluded commitment to the kind of chivalry represented by romantic novels results in a demonstration of justice and prudence. When Marcela departs, having vowed to live free in modest seclusion, some of the bystanders, smitten with her beauty, "made as though they would follow her, heedless of the frank declaration they had heard" (see p. 103). Don Quixote, however, who saw "it a fitting occasion for the exercise of his chivalry in aid of distressed damsels,... laid his hand on the hilt of his sword" (see p. 103) and admonished everyone against pursuing Marcela. "Whether it was because of Don Quixote's threats or because Ambrosio told them to fulfil their duty to their good friend" (see p. 103), all the shepherds remained until the funeral was completed.

The effect is what Cleanth Brooks would call a structure of irony.[15] As happens throughout the novel, many of the more sophisticated characters who gather around the funeral of the lovelorn "shepherd" encourage Don Quixote in his literary madness for their own amusement; but the entire pastoral funeral, with its assumption that a man has died of a broken heart, that erotic desire is an uncontrollable force worthy of divine honors, is equally madness brought on by obsession with a literary and cultural fashion. As Cervantes' narrator slyly intimates, the effect of the knight's menaces is problematic; nevertheless, he is the only one to speak up in Marcela's defense. It is his chivalric delusions that effectively counter the Petrarchan pastoral delusions of sophisticated, presumably sane characters.

And this is how the novel repeatedly works: Don Quixote's obsessive fantasy serves not only to reveal the illusions of other characters, indeed of early modern Spanish society, but the absurd vagaries also bring to light in subtle fashion the genuine heroism and romance that lie hidden beneath the drab surface of ordinary life. The exposure of false romanticism thus recovers a realm of imagination within reality.

The best example is the Captive's Tale, which may be regarded as the culmination of Part I of *Don Quixote*, insofar as it offers the most poignant convergence of romantic fantasy and harsh reality. At an inn, which he persistently takes for a castle, Don Quixote joins a number of ladies and gentlemen as well as the barber and priest of his village. In order to trick the wandering knight into going home, they all conspire to convince him that he is journeying to free the kingdom of Princess Micomicona—actually Dorotea, one of the ladies in the company—from a fearful giant.

But while Don Quixote is preoccupied with his own mad world of chivalric fantasy, including an epic battle with a number of wineskins, quite remarkable—and romantic—events are taking place around him. The lovers Luscinda and Cardenio, who have been separated and persecuted by the selfish machinations

[15] Cleanth Brooks, "Irony as a Principle of Structure", in *Literary Opinion in America*, 3rd ed., ed. Morton Dauwen Zabel (Harper & Row, 1962), II, pp. 729–41.

of the dissolute nobleman, Fernando, are reunited; and Fernando, who has pursued them to the inn, confronted by Dorotea, whom he has seduced and abandoned, relents. He grants the two lovers their happiness and accepts Dorotea as his bride, when he is exhorted by the priest and the others to remember his duty as a Christian and a gentleman. It turns out that there truly are damsels in distress and wrongs that require redress; moreover, the inn, if not exactly a castle, is a place of enchantment for these four characters.

Into the midst of this emotional scene of reconciliation comes a Spanish soldier, accompanied by the young North African woman who has helped him escape captivity in her father's household in Algiers. This could hardly be a matter of mirth for Cervantes, who like the character in his novel, fought with the victorious Spanish forces at the Battle of Lepanto (the author's left arm was permanently maimed in this battle) and was taken prisoner by the Moors in a subsequent engagement. Unlike his fictional captive, Cervantes never succeeded in escaping, although he made several attempts—and was eventually ransomed.

Ormsby takes issue with Byron's charge, "Cervantes smiled Spain's chivalry away",[16] with an even more cynical assertion: "There was not chivalry for him to smile away. Spain's chivalry had been dead for more than a century.... What he did smile away was not chivalry but a degrading mockery of it."[17] Cervantes was, however, throughout his life proud of having participated in the Battle of Lepanto and rightly saw it as a great triumph for Christendom. The Ottoman Turkish Empire, by the middle of the sixteenth century, was a formidable power, threatening to clear the Mediterranean of European shipping. Odds-makers would have favored the Turks before the conflict was decided in 1571.

Once again, Cervantes' vision is conveyed through structural irony: Don Quixote's obsession with the absurd fantasies persists, while authentic romance unfolds around him, and a genuine hero strides into the "enchanted castle". Yet that is not the entire story; the aspiring knight-errant delivers in the midst of these arresting occurrences, of which he is hardly aware, an eloquent disquisition upon the much bruited question of the era, whether arms or arts was the superior undertaking.

One passage is especially powerful in the context of the arrival of the captured soldier, who has made such a daring escape:

> For tell me, sirs, if you have ever reflected upon it, by how much do those who have gained by war fall short of the number of those who have perished in it? No doubt you will reply that there can be no comparison, that the dead cannot be numbered, while the living who have been rewarded may be counted in the hundreds. (See p. 308.)

Don Quixote has repeatedly told Sancho Panza that knights-errant often win kingdoms and fortunes through the prowess of their swords and has consistently promised his squire that he will make him governor of an island. In a lucid interval,

[16] *Don Juan*, canto 13, stanza 11.
[17] *Delphi Cervantes*, location no. 115424.

he is aware of what true heroism is, and of what its reward is likely to be. His listeners at the inn, many of them gentlemen committed to arms, are astonished by the insight and prudence of the mad knight who is *errant* in so many ways.

The structure of irony is further complicated in Part II of the novel (1615) by Cervantes' frequent references to the First Part (1605): Don Quixote and Sancho, along with most of the other characters, are aware not only of Part I of Cervantes' work, but also of a spurious continuation (1614) ascribed to a certain Alonso Fernández de Avellaneda. Cervantes thus invents, early in the seventeenth century, the device of *metafiction*, which involves a reference within a work of fiction to its own fictional status. Long before the lucubrations of post-modernism, he found a way to take the reader into the novel by taking the novel into the "real world". The effect is to endow not only "realistic" fiction with an aura of equivocal romance, but also the real itself.

Eventually, in Part II of *Don Quixote*, Sancho does become governor of an "island"; like the other characters in the novel, readers are astonished by *his* insight and prudence, as he takes on a role that manifests much the same irony as that of his master with respect to the ambiguous tension between the romantic and the real. Sancho receives the rule of an "island" in the course of a lengthy sojourn by Don Quixote and his squire at the estate of a duke and duchess, who have read Part I of the novel. In order to continue enjoying the folly of the knight-errant and his squire, the duke and duchess subject the famous pair to a series of lengthy, elaborate, and basically malicious practical jokes, treating them both with elaborate deference and courtesy while still managing to subject them to various embarrassments through the collaboration of their servants.

Eventually the duke grants Sancho the governorship of one of his neighboring estates, which is not even near the coast, much less an island. Sancho, who has never seen the sea and will not until he and his master arrive in Barcelona near the end of Part II, is none the wiser. He thus appears to be as deluded as Don Quixote, and the duke and duchess take cruel relish in fostering the absurd delusions of both knight and squire.

As with the knight, however, Sancho's ignorant simplicity is qualified by genuinely admirable qualities. The denizens of the "island", all servants and retainers of the duke, make every effort to baffle and confound him by presenting a rapid succession of apparently insoluble legal cases; nevertheless, he acquits himself honorably by making prudent, equitable decisions based on practical common sense. "Sancho—foolish, boorish, and rotund as he was—held his own against them all" (see p. 704). As the duke's majordomo puts it, wondering at the illiterate Sancho's success as a ruler, "Every day we see something new in the world: mockeries become realities, and mockers find themselves mocked" (p. 705).

Shakespeare offers a similar interplay between fantasy and realism, between "mockeries" and "realities". *A Midsummer Night's Dream* (c. 1595) is an excellent example. The play is set in a fanciful medieval "Athens", surrounded by an English forest. As in Chaucer's *Knight's Tale*, Theseus is "Duke of Athens", but this altogether improbable transmogrification of the mythical Attic figure is the play's embodiment of hard-headed skepticism:

The lunatic, the lover, and the poet
Are of imagination all compact.
One sees more devils than vast hell can hold;
That is the madman. The lover, all as frantic,
Sees Helen's beauty in a brow of Egypt.
The poet's eye, in a fine frenzy rolling,
Doth glance from heaven to earth, from earth to heaven;
And as imagination bodies forth
Forms of things unknown, the poet's pen
Turns them into shapes, and gives to aery nothing
A local habitation and a name.[18]

Like Cervantes, Shakespeare is dealing in multiple ironies: the dismissal of poetry in Shakespeare's glorious blank verse is an obvious example, but there is also Theseus' ardent desire to consummate his upcoming wedding with the Amazon Hippolyta, whom he has won by defeating her in battle—which suggests that his eye has been very much beguiled by love. As for madness, it possesses all the characters in the play in the form of the famous English fairies.

Following the frothy, farcical business of the first four acts, act 5 consists of a thoroughly inept performance of a play within the play, *Pyramis and Thisbe*, based on Ovid's quasi-tragic tale of thwarted lovers who both end up committing suicide when their attempt to escape unrelenting parents goes awry. The play is put on by a group of Athenian tradesmen (a joiner, a weaver, a cobbler, and so on), and Shakespeare makes it as farcical as possible and displays the aristocratic newlyweds in the audience mocking the foolishness of the performance.

Thus, Shakespeare anticipates Cervantes' metafiction with metadrama: the audience has just witnessed the noble characters who deride the performance of the "mechanicals" acting out their own roles in Shakespeare's play with absurd ineptitude, and of course as members of Shakespeare's audience, we are implicitly invited to wonder how our "audience" regards our performance of the roles in our lives.

It is a moot point whether or to what extent Shakespeare or his contemporaneous audience "believed in" fairies, but Shakespearean drama most assuredly suggests that that there are realities in our world that transcend simple realism—much the same as Cervantes suggests that Don Quixote, foolishly seeking wonders in chivalric romance, fails to see how he and his squire are *really* romantic characters.

Like *Don Quixote*, *A Midsummer Night's Dream* is a comedy, but the kind of ironic vision that Cervantes and Shakespeare exhibit is not necessarily confined to comic writing. *Romeo and Juliet*, first staged about the same time as *A Midsummer Night's Dream*, also takes up the theme of "star-crossed lovers" and

[18] *A Midsummer Night's Dream*, in *The Riverside Shakespeare*, 2nd ed., ed. G. Blakemore Evans et al. (Houghton Mifflin, 1997), 5.1.276 (references are to act, scene, and line). All subsequent quotations of Shakespeare's works are from this edition and will be cited in the text.

ends tragically; but along the way it offers similarly complex and ambivalent images of love.

Shakespeare treats this theme with consummate subtlety in *Othello* (c. 1604), a mature tragedy that represents the playwright at the height of his powers. The dark-skinned Moor, mercenary general of the military forces of Venice, wins the heart of the fair Venetian lady Desdemona, to the horror of her father, with the charm of his words:

> She lov'd me for the dangers I had pass'd,
> And I lov'd her that she did pity them.
> This only is the witchcraft I have us'd.
> (1.3.167–69)

Othello is a thoroughly paradoxical character: a hardened veteran of the wars, who has spent his life in camps among soldiers and camp followers, with all that may imply; but he is also a chevalier of the imagination, whose storytelling turns his experience into a fable that enchants Desdemona.

But when Iago, a monster of malice and envy, succeeds in arousing jealousy by corrupting and dirtying Othello's imagination, then the dream of love becomes a nightmare. For Shakespeare, very often, tragedy is precisely a failure or perversion of imagination. Love is transformative, and a woman who is beloved truly transcends the coarse implication of Iago's reductive cynicism. "Realism" devoid of imagination, without the romance of the real, is ultimately false, and it is Othello's loss of his imaginative vision of his bride that ends in tragedy.

Even in those plays that generations of scholars have agreed to refer to as the "late romances", Shakespeare creates a complex interpenetration of the real with what seems mere fantasy. *The Tempest*, probably his last play, exemplifies the necessary recourse to what might be called the romantic or transformative imagination to get at all that is real in human experience. Without Prospero's magical powers—a figure for the poetic imagination—without the obscure reaches of human nature symbolized by the spirit Ariel and the fish-scaled monster Caliban, human life would be defined by the cynical calculations of Antonio and Sebastian, who plot against their king, regarding the power to dominate as everything.

The key to the meaning of the play is, then, that Prospero must renounce the seemingly limitless power of his magic. This magic is, to be sure, as much illusion as actual power to change the physical world: Prospero's magic unlike the black arts associated with Dr. Faustus, must not be used to alter reality, but rather to reveal it.[19] Like literature, it enhances our sense of who and what we are without allowing us to alter fundamentally our nature.

What makes *Don Quixote* and Shakespearean drama paradigmatic in the literature of the Western world is the uncanny ability of Cervantes and the great playwright to treat vulgar fantasy, such as the chivalric romances, with appropriate

[19] Cf. Jeffrey Hart, "Prospero and Faustus", *Boston University Studies in English* 2 (Winter 1956–1957): 197–206.

derision, while reminding generations of readers and audiences that the reality of human life is more rich, varied, and marvelous than we ordinarily acknowledge; that the real, the world we inhabit, is more romantic than anything we could make up for ourselves. As Hamlet observes, "There are more things in heaven and earth, Horatio, / Than are dreamt of in your philosophy" (2.1.166–67).

CONTRIBUTORS

Timothy McCallister is an Associate Professor of Spanish at Auburn University. His research centers on the intersection of religion and literature in early modern Spain. Figures of interest, in addition to Miguel de Cervantes, include Juan de Valdés and Garcilaso de la Vega. His current project is a book on Cervantes' providential worldview.

Michael J. McGrath is a Professor of Spanish at Georgia Southern University. His research focuses on early modern Spanish life and literature, with special emphasis on cultural studies, the *comedia*, and *Don Quixote*. He is the author of nearly seventy publications, including *Don Quixote and Catholicism: Rereading Cervantine Spirituality* (Purdue University Press, 2020), *The Art of the Game of Chess* (Catholic University of America Press, 2020), the first English translation of Ruy López's chess treatise *Libro de la invención liberal y arte del juego del ajedrez* (1561), and *A Primer of Pastoral Spanish* (Catholic University of America Press, 2022).

Joseph Pearce is the acclaimed author of numerous literary studies, including *Literary Converts* (Ignatius Press, 2006), *The Quest for Shakespeare* (Ignatius Press, 2008), and *Shakespeare on Love* (Ignatius Press, 2013), as well as popular biographies on Oscar Wilde, J. R. R. Tolkien, C. S. Lewis, G. K. Chesterton, and Aleksandr Solzhenitsyn. He is the series editor of the Ignatius Critical Editions.

Kathleen Sullivan is an Associate Professor of English Language and Literature at Christendom College in Front Royal, Virginia. She teaches Literature of Western Civilization courses for the underclassmen and offers courses in British and American Literature for upperclassmen. She has most recently published an article on Robert Frost's poetry, yet most of her writing and research is focused on Jane Austen and British novels of the nineteenth century.

Michael Dominic Taylor works as a Teaching Fellow and Dean of Students at the Thomas More College of Liberal Arts in Merrimack, New Hampshire. He has earned degrees from the United States, Italy, Spain, and Poland in biology and environmental studies, bioethics, and philosophy. In 2021, the Joseph Ratzinger Foundation (Vatican) and the Francisco de Vitoria University (Madrid) awarded him with the Expand Reason Prize for his book *The Foundations of Nature: Metaphysics of Gift for an Integral Ecological Ethic* (Cascade Books, 2020). Today he writes, speaks, and teaches on the humanities, metaphysics, bioethics, ecology, and the history of Spain.

R. V. Young is Professor Emeritus of English at North Carolina State University. He co-founded the *John Donne Journal* and for twenty-five years served as co-editor. Subsequently, he served as editor of the quarterly review *Modern Age*. He is the author of numerous articles and reviews, and his most recent book is *Shakespeare and the Idea of Western Civilization* (Catholic University of America Press, 2022). He is currently at work on the Ignatius Critical Edition of John Milton's *Paradise Lost*.